THE FOREST LORD COLLECTION

BY

STEVEN A. McKAY

This collection copyright ©2019

All rights reserved.

This book may not be reproduced in any form, in whole or in part, without written permission from the author.

CONTENTS

WOLF'S HEAD
THE WOLF AND THE RAVEN
RISE OF THE WOLF
BLOOD OF THE WOLF

Also by Steven A. McKay

The Forest Lord Novellas / Short Stories:

Knight of the Cross
Friar Tuck and the Christmas Devil
The Rescue and Other Tales
The Abbey of Death

Warrior Druid of Britain Chronicles

The Druid

Song of the Centurion

COMING SOON EXCLUSIVELY FROM AUDIBLE

Lucia

WOLF'S HEAD

Book 1 in *The Forest Lord* series

By Steven A. McKay

Copyright 2013 Steven A. McKay

All rights reserved. This book may not be reproduced in any form, in whole or in part, without written permission from the author.

For my daughter, Freya

With Love.

CHAPTER ONE

"Robin! Look out!"

The cry came from close behind him, and he dropped to the ground, rolling to his left and coming up in one fluid motion ready for the attack he knew would come.

"Hah. Nice move!" The man was laughing, but a meaty hand swung round viciously, aiming for Robin's neck.

He swayed backwards, feeling the massive fist of the miller brushing his shoulder, and, adrenaline coursing through his veins, lunged forward, arms outstretched. He caught the heavier, older man round the midriff, his momentum taking them both to the ground. Robin landed on top, his forearm pressing down on his opponent's windpipe.

"Yield, miller!"

The miller tried to laugh again, gasping as his round face turned purple. "You win…Get off, you daft bastard!"

Robin jumped up and spread his arms charismatically, grinning as he looked around at the cheering spectators.

"The winner of this bout: Robin Hood!" The adjudicator raised Robin's arm as the people of the village shouted and laughed in congratulations. The big miller, Thomas, smiled through gritted teeth, slapping his young opponent on the back, much harder than was needed. "You did well, lad. You've a natural gift for fighting. Maybe one day I'll test you properly. Better watch that temper though." He walked off, grimacing at his opponent, as the older village men mocked him cheerfully over his defeat.

Robert Hood, or Robin, as everyone knew him, was tall, and, even at just seventeen years old, had incredible upper body strength, with enormous arms and shoulder muscles thanks to his training with the longbow since childhood. His honest brown eyes and easy smile made him a popular character in the small village of Wakefield.

"You did it!" Robin's friend Much slapped him on the back, a broad smile on his open face. "I never thought you'd be able to beat my da, he's strong as an ox!"

It was a fine spring day, the trees just about filled out with their green covering again, and the May Games were well under way. Everyone in the village was dancing, singing, competing in something or other, or simply enjoying the ale and meat the local lord, Thomas, Earl of Lancaster, had provided. The sounds of revelry and smells of food cooking filled the air, as the few skinny local dogs that hadn't been eaten during the recent hard winters mooched around hoping to find some scraps on the ground.

Robin grasped Much's arm, laughing as he looked at his friend. "You're right; I never thought I'd beat him either! One good punch and he'd have had me; his arms are like tree trunks." He shook his head sheepishly. "I panicked when he almost got me; that's why I just threw myself on him."

Despite his modesty, Robin had the speed, agility and quick thinking to make him more than a match for most of the men in Wakefield.

"Aye, that was a wild move; my da wasn't expecting it. Don't think anyone was! Let's go an' get a drink." Much dragged Robin along and they headed for the ale sellers. "Look, the May Queen's coming."

Robin looked up eagerly; they both knew who would be Queen this year: Matilda, daughter of Henry the fletcher. Robin thought she must be the loveliest girl in all of England, and hoped, one day not too far off, to make her his wife. They had lain together occasionally over the past year, and promised themselves to each other, but Robin hadn't worked up the courage to ask her for her hand yet. For all his swagger he was still rather a shy young man, not entirely confident in himself.

Matilda appeared, walking slowly towards the village green, smiling happily. She wore a plain white dress which accentuated her slim figure, a garland of colourful spring flowers in her strawberry blonde hair, and, when her gaze rested on Robin for a second or two, he felt a small thrill run through him. She was followed by a great black bull, led by three Jacks-in-the-Green: village men in dark-brown cloaks, with ornate leaf masks covering their faces.

The Sword Dance began as the small procession reached the centre of the village. Swords were laid on the ground in a six-pointed star shape, then the villagers, Matilda included, laughed and whooped as they spun around the steel hexagram holding hands and swapping partners.

The bull was brought forward haltingly, as if knowing its fate, its hooves dragging in the damp spring grass, nostrils flaring and eyes bulging. It was an older beast, near the end of its life, but to most of the revellers it looked a magnificent animal.

As it reached the centre of the whirling Dance, a Jack-in-the-Green moved alongside and grasped the animal's great head, bringing a long knife out from underneath his cloak. The dancers slowed to a stop and watched in grim fascination as its neck was slashed open, the younger villagers gasping, wide eyed, as the blood flowed on to the grass below.

"Praise be to Herne!" The villagers cheered and clapped in appreciation as the great bull's life-force slowly ebbed away and it dropped ponderously to the grass with a gentle thud. Some of the blood was allowed to seep into the earth, in the spirit of the sacrifice, but one of the men soon placed a large wooden bowl under the incision to catch the valuable crimson liquid.

"That was a big bull eh?" Much shook his head admiringly. "Do you think it'll mean a good crop this year? Even my da struggled last year with the hard winter. You know what it was like, the whole village nearly starved."

Robin nodded, sharing his friend's hopes. His own family had gone short of food during many of the previous winters. He didn't want to feel the pain of a hunger-swollen belly again. The dying bull was the villagers' plea to God – any god: *In return for this mighty bull, let the year bring good weather for our crops.*

Although the people of Wakefield were Christian, the old gods and their ways had not been completely forgotten. While the Church didn't approve, it generally let the people get on with it, as long as they kept going to Mass.

With the black bull now dead, the crowd began to drift away to other amusements. An archery contest was about to start, and more people were dancing, as a travelling minstrel appeared and began cajoling the crowd to join in with his crude songs of love and lust, fighting and flatulence.

"Look, shooting. We'll win that!" Robin wandered through the crowd towards the archery competition, Much following in his wake.

Both young men, like most yeomen in England, had been practicing with bow and arrow since they were seven years old, and although it was illegal to hunt deer in the forest, Robin had found it necessary during the previous harsh winters to help feed his family. Bringing down unsuspecting game with a longbow had made Robin a crack shot.

Much usually had enough food to eat, being the son of the miller, but venison was always a welcome change from bread and pottage at the table in his house too, so he had become almost as good with a bow as Robin.

They would do well in the archery competition.

"Robin! Wouldn't you like to dance with me?" Matilda, the May Queen, came up behind Robin and grasped his hand. Her blue eyes flashed in the sun as she swirled away, somehow still grasping his hand. She pulled herself in close again, pressing her face, and her body, close to his. "Hmmm? Dance?"

Robin felt his face turn red as he gazed lustfully at the girl, and Much began to laugh. "He'd love to Lady May Queen, but the archery competition's just starting. He'll be back for that dance shortly!"

Matilda pouted suggestively at Robin as Much tried to drag him away. "You'd rather play with your longbow than dance with me? Lots of other men want to dance with the May Queen; I won't wait on you forever."

Robin grinned sheepishly, sensing the implied criticism in her words and, squeezing the girl's hand, promised he'd be back shortly.

The two young men swaggered off, Robin's eyes lingering on Matilda's lithe figure as she spun around into the dancing again. "Aye, she's got a nice arse, but forget about her until I've beaten you in the shooting." Much grinned, and pointed towards the wooden figures set up in the clearing, as Robin playfully smacked the back of his friend's head.

Today, he told himself. Today, I'll ask her to marry me, I've waited too long as it is . . .

Many of the local men had entered the archery contest, being well trained in the use of the longbow. Their lord expected those of able body to practise with the weapon, should he need a force of armed men in times of trouble, and, since carrying a sword was illegal for most villagers, the longbow was the main weapon for yeomen, villein and peasant alike.

As the contest progressed the number of competitors was whittled down until only the two friends and four other men remained, but as Much raised his bow for his next shot, there was a disturbance near the dancers in the centre of the village green, and the archers turned to look.

A loud voice could be heard, castigating everyone in the vicinity.

"What's going on?" asked Much, craning his neck to try and get a better view.

Robin, unlike his smaller friend, could see over most of the people in the crowd and shook his head darkly. "Looks like that prior from down south. Shouting about something. The bailiff's with him too."

Much glanced warily at Robin, knowing his friend had a great dislike for churchmen in general, and the wealthier ones in particular. Most of the villagers harboured resentment and bitterness towards the clergy – struggling to find bread to fill your family's bellies during a long, cold winter, while the prior paraded around the country wearing a small fortune in gold and silver jewellery tended to create ill feeling.

Robin had two younger sisters, Rebekah and Marjorie, but Rebekah, always the smallest of the smallest of the siblings, had been too weak from hunger to survive the harsh winter of 1315, some six years ago. Torrential rain had fallen on England constantly that year, ruining the harvest. The wheat that remained had to be dried out in ovens before it could be used, and even then it offered little nutrition when baked into bread. Many died of hunger, while travellers in the countryside were murdered by brigands desperate for the food they carried.

Wheat rose to eight times its normal price, while barley, peas, salt and other essential ingredients were also, suddenly, too expensive for most people.

Then the Scots came.

Buoyed by their success at the battle of Bannockburn, they raided deep into Yorkshire, stealing what little food the people of northern England had left, while King Edward II did nothing to help.

Robin had been only eleven then. He had seen people in his village eating horses and dogs – even heard whispered rumours of cannibalism – and he could still remember his little sister Rebekah's tiny seven year old body, wasted away – emaciated. And even though Rebekah's twin, Marjorie, had survived, she had never fully recovered her strength – her family were terrified she might go the same way as her sister if they suffered another famine like that of 1315.

The sight of an overweight, richly dressed churchman like this prior made Robin's blood boil.

"Come on; let's see what the fat bastard wants."

The pair headed over for a closer look, the archery contest forgotten.

The Prior of Lewes, John de Monte Martini, retinue in tow, was checking on those parishes he was responsible for, to make sure they were being run properly.

Today, it was Wakefield's turn.

The pleasant atmosphere of ten minutes earlier had gone, as the laughter and dancing died away under the clergyman's pious ranting, his small group of armoured guards glaring around at the villagers.

"Heathens! The lot of you!" the prior lambasted the people, forcing his way between them. "Animal sacrifice? Herne the Hunter? Green Men?" The clergyman snatched the mask made of oak leaves from the face of one of the men playing Jack-in-the-Green. The man glared back sullenly, but soon dropped his gaze to the floor. It didn't do to make an enemy of the church, and the man, Simon, a poor labourer, had no wish to get on the wrong side of the fat prior, especially with the bailiff there.

Although Wakefield was part of Thomas, Earl of Lancaster's manor holdings, his bailiff, Henry Boscastle, oversaw most of the daily business of the place. He knew everyone that lived there.

An angry voice shouted from the back of the crowd, "What's the problem, prior? We do this every year; it's just a bit of fun."

The churchman rounded in the direction of the voice, face flushing scarlet, as other villagers muttered in agreement. "I don't care what you do every year. My predecessors might not have minded this pagan…nonsense! But I do. I expected to find you people at mass today, yet when I arrive at the village chapel I find the doors bolted and my flock – that's you people – out here getting drunk on cheap ale and worshipping false gods." He didn't mention the fact that the local parish priest was nowhere to be found. In fact, Father Myrc had been enjoying a few drinks with the villagers and had run off back to All Hallows when he heard the prior was coming.

The village headman, Patrick Prudhomme, pushed his way to the front of the crowd and attempted to placate the irate prior.

"Forgive us, Father. These rites mean nothing. We're all good Christians in Wakefield, the bailiff will tell you that. This is just a bit of fun to celebrate the spring coming."

The bailiff looked as if he'd rather be drinking free ale and eating some of the great bull which was surreptitiously hauled away to the butchers. A sullen man at the best of times and not averse to abusing his position for money or other favours, Henry Boscastle was not a popular figure in Wakefield.

The prior was oblivious to all this, and carried on in an even louder voice, pushing his way further into the mass of revellers, moving further and further away from his hired guards, although the bailiff kept pace, thrusting people aside forcibly. "I don't care what this is. I expect you all to go home, now, and sleep off the drink you've all taken too much of!"

There were angry groans from the villagers, but no one felt brave enough to openly disagree with the prior, especially with the half-dozen mercenaries guarding him, although they looked fed-up with the whole situation. The prior wasn't paying them much and he was a terrible travelling companion.

Much shook his head in disgust, as Robin clenched his fists and fought to keep his temper under control.

The headman raised his hands sadly. "As the prior says, everyone, let's get this stuff cleared away, and make our way to our homes."

"You can all be at church tomorrow too," cried the clergyman, "making suitable offerings, in penance for your wickedness today!"

"Shove your offerings!" someone shouted, again, from the back of the crowd, well hidden in the sea of faces. Voices were raised in agreement, emboldened by their anonymity.

"Aye, shove them up your big fat arse!"

People laughed, but the atmosphere had turned dangerous, as the angry villagers, many of them half drunk, crowded threateningly around the prior and his retinue, rather than moving away as they'd been told.

The prior's mercenaries, although they couldn't see over the mob, realised things were getting dangerous and tried to form up around the clergyman but the villagers surged forward. The lightly armoured men, unwilling to draw their weapons in such a volatile situation, found themselves being shoved further and further away from their charge.

The prior's face turned white as the bailiff, sensing the crowd's hostility, and more reckless than the mercenaries, dragged his sword from its leather sheath and pointed it at anyone he thought looked a threat. "Get back, you bastards, or I'll take this to you."

Henry was an intimidating, commanding man, and the sight of his enraged face and drawn weapon calmed most of the crowd. "Go on, get back to your homes. Now!" he roared, kicking a retreating villager in the back, sending him sprawling. The man tried to get to his feet but found the bailiff's face against his, sword blade pressing against his neck. "Go home, before I open your neck," Henry growled, nostrils flaring with the promise of violence.

The man edged backwards on the ground, wide eyes fixed on the bailiff's sword, before he stumbled up and shoved his way into the mob, looking over his shoulder every few seconds to make sure Henry wasn't following him.

"Come on," Much said, looking on in disgust from their position near the back of the crowd. "No sense in hanging around here with all this going on. Let's go and get that drink from the alehouse – we never got one earlier."

Robin stood rooted to the spot though, staring over the other villagers' heads at the clergyman, as Much, oblivious to his friend's black mood, walked off in the opposite direction.

Just then, Matilda, the May Queen, head bowed, moved past the prior and bailiff. "You – idiot girl. Get that filth off you!" The prior grabbed Matilda's arm roughly and tore off the garland of flowers she was wearing in her hair, throwing it, and, inadvertently, Matilda, to the ground.

Before he knew what he was doing, Robin found himself, in a cold fury, striding towards the prior and the girl he'd loved since childhood.

While the prior's guards found themselves hemmed in by the baying throng, unable to move towards their master, the host of people seemed to part for Robin as he stormed towards the sneering clergyman.

"Keep your hands off her, you fat bastard . . . !"

The villagers still angrily crowding the village green stopped as one, open mouthed, staring in disbelief at the enraged young man striding through their ranks towards the prior.

Much, finally realising his friend was about to do something rash, pushed back into the crowd to try and restrain him, while Henry the bailiff, his sword back in its sheath, glared at the big yeoman, wondering if he'd imagined the outburst.

"What did you just say to me?" the prior demanded in shock, then, regaining his composure slightly, he stepped towards Robin and said quietly, "I'll have you in chains and thrown in jail for that."

"Robin, leave this, please, let's just do as the prior says." Matilda's voice was shaking with anger, but the fear in her eyes was clear as she climbed back to her feet and grasped Robin's wrist.

"Oh no, girl. You'll be going to the jail too." The prior moved even closer, dropping his voice again, so only Robin, Matilda and the bailiff could hear what he said next. "Maybe the sheriff's men will find some...use...for you there. Maybe I'll even come visit you myself to see you on your knees...begging the Lord's forgiveness."

Robin understood exactly what the prior was getting at. He knew many of the wealthier clergymen owned brothels in the big cities, and Prior John de Monte Martini was said to have a stake in several, even using their services himself regularly. The bailiff looked amused but didn't say a word, simply enjoying the entertainment, while Matilda regarded the clergyman in confusion.

"You piece of filth," Robin spat, shaking with nerves, but too angry to back away. "You touch her and I'll kill you."

The prior grimaced and ran a podgy hand along Matilda's arm, staring into her blue eyes. "Oh yes, after a few nights with nothing to eat I'm sure you'll be a lot more...open...to a humble prior like me. In fact, I'm sure I could find you employment in a local establishment, I own myself – the 'Maiden's Head' in Nottingham." He nodded towards Henry. "Take them into custody bailiff. My men will help, once they remove this mob." He glared around himself, trying to locate his guards, who were still too far away to know what was happening.

Henry, nodding his head with a grim smile, began to draw his sword again, shouting for assistance from the locals around him. No one seemed greatly inclined to help.

Robin heard nothing after that, as a roaring noise filled his ears and time seemed to slow to a crawl. His right fist shot forward, smashing into the prior's nose which exploded in a burst of scarlet. As the churchman fell backwards onto the ground the shocked bailiff finally dragged his sword out, but before he could use it, Robin kicked him brutally between the legs. With a scream of agony, Henry doubled over, and, as he dropped to his knees, sword forgotten, Robin grabbed the bailiff's head and smashed his knee into the man's face.

Henry collapsed, bloodied and senseless, beside the downed clergyman.

"You fucking...peasant!" the prior looked up, and screamed through hands clutching his ruined nose. "I'll see you hanged for this!"

Robin, adrenaline pumping, feeling utterly invincible, moved forward to finish off the clergyman, teeth bared in a wild grin, but the brawny miller, Thomas, Much's father, managed to grab him, pinning his arms to his side. "Stop this, you fool, calm that temper of yours! He means what he says. His guards will have you once they realise what's going on – you need to get away."

"He's right, you have to run!" Matilda pleaded, eyes flickering nervously between Robin and the crowd, half expecting a soldier to run her big friend through any second.

Thomas and Much, who had finally pushed his way through the throng, pulled Robin away from the cursing prior and unmoving bailiff. They moved in the opposite direction to the mercenaries, who only now understood something had happened to their master and were forcing their way aggressively through the villagers.

The people parted to let the miller and the younger men through – some folk even cheered and slapped Robin on the back as he passed by, happy to see the prior bloodied, and glad it wasn't them who would suffer punishment for it.

The crowd closed in protectively behind them, although not all the villagers were pleased by Robin's actions.

"You're an idiot, Hood!" The village headman Patrick appeared beside them as they hurried away. "Do you realise the trouble you've brought on yourself? And the village too? That prior isn't one to forget this – he'll make all our lives miserable now. Christ, you've probably killed the bailiff too! What the hell were you thinking?"

Robin shook his head, his anger fading as he started to realise the danger he was in. "He was saying things about Matilda, threatening her…I just exploded, Patrick."

"I don't know what he said, but you have to get away from here, fast. Get to your house and take whatever you need, the people will delay the mercenaries. Say your goodbyes; you won't be seeing anyone around here again for a while."

That finally hammered home to Robin what he'd done, and he wanted to puke. Or cry.

"Peace, Patrick, he's still young – hasn't learned to control his temper yet. Let's help him get away for now – he can worry about what he's done later." The miller grasped Robin's shoulder sympathetically. He may not have heard what the prior said, but he knew Robin. Knew he wasn't one to lie.

The headman nodded, shaking his head regretfully. "Get your stuff together, son. Good luck – you'll be needing it. Don't worry too much about your ma and da, or young Marjorie – the prior might be powerful, but the villagers won't let him take out his anger on an innocent family. He'll be off back down to Lewes soon anyway."

Robin's head whirled. None of this had crossed his mind when he'd exploded into violence at the prior's whispered promises. Could he have held himself in check if he'd realised the consequences of his actions? He honestly couldn't say.

It mattered little now. He let Much lead him home at a sprint, mind in turmoil. John and Martha, Robin's parents, were out somewhere, enjoying the day with Marjorie, oblivious, for now, to what their son had just done.

He hastily gathered his longbow, a loaf of bread, some dried fish and his cloak, and then dragged a box out from under his bed. In it was an old sword – not the finest steel in England, but it had been well maintained and had a decent edge to it. It had a threadbare leather scabbard, so he looped it around his belt and pushed half a dozen arrows in beside it.

Much, watching from the door for any signs of pursuit shook his head, eyes brimming with tears of frustration as he contemplated the life his friend would have from this day forward. Unless Robin was pardoned, which seemed impossible for a lowly yeoman with no money, he would need to live his life as an outlaw in the depths of Barnsdale Forest – a "wolf's head", as those outside the law were known. Deprived of all legal rights, any man could kill a wolf's head on sight, as if he were nothing but an animal.

Less than an animal, in fact. The king's Charter of the Forest made it illegal for commoners to hunt deer. But any man could hunt down a wolf. Or a wolf's head.

"Get going. Hide in the forest for a day or two until this all blows over. I'll leave you food and things at the old well. You know the place."

"Of course I do!" Robin tried to smile, although it came out as more of a grimace. "We used to spend hours there as children, playing."

"Aye," Much agreed sadly. "So we did – playing games, pretending to be mighty Saxon warriors killing the evil Norman invaders".

Now, though, real warriors would be hunting for his friend, with real steel.

The time for play was over.

"Shit!" Much gasped, eyes wide. "The soldiers are coming!"

Robin pushed past his friend out the door and saw four of the prior's men jogging through the village, looking for him.

"You there!" one of them roared, pointing his drawn sword towards the two young friends. "Hold!"

Much pressed himself against the door frame and raised his hands to show he wasn't a threat, and yelled at his friend to make for the forest.

The soldiers broke into a run, yelling for him to stop, as Robin sprinted off towards the outskirts of the village and the safety of the trees.

Three of the pursuers, older men in their forties, were blowing hard after a short distance, but, looking back over his shoulder, Robin could see one of the soldiers was keeping pace with him, his eyes fixed determinedly ahead on his quarry. This man didn't waste his breath shouting, and Robin felt the beginnings of panic building up inside him as he contemplated the possibility that he might have to make a stand.

He had never fought with a sword before – never even really practised with one. The bow was his weapon, like the rest of the young men in the village. But the man chasing him made his living with a blade in his hand. Robin knew he couldn't beat him, and the trees were still some way off.

Trying to push his body even harder, pulling in great lungfuls of air, he risked another glance behind and cursed in fear as he realised the soldier was gaining on him. He would not make it to the trees before the man's sword took him in the back.

With a sob of desperation, Robin spun round, facing his pursuer. The man's eyes widened in surprise as Robin hastily pulled an arrow from his belt, drew back his great longbow, and desperately let fly.

The shot was a poor one; Robin's whole body was quaking with the exertion of the run, and his arms felt leaden, but the arrow hammered home with a sickening damp thud into the soldier's thigh. The man spun backwards onto the ground with a scream of agony, his leg flailing behind him.

The remaining pursuers, some distance back, cried with outrage at the sight of their fallen comrade, as Robin shakily rose to his feet and stumbled off towards the forest, gasping with exertion, the downed soldier's cries of agony ringing in his ears.

CHAPTER TWO

True to his word, Much, helped by Matilda, had left food and blankets near the old disused well in the forest, close to the neighbouring village of Bichill.

Although Robin was hardly used to living life in luxury, it was a new and frightening hardship having to sleep outdoors, in the dark, lonely, night of the forest.

Much would have stayed by Robin's side, at least on some evenings, but he was fearful that the bailiff had paid some of the villagers to spy on his movements, in the hope of tracking down his outlawed friend.

The sheriff's men had arrived the day after Robin had attacked the churchman, but they hadn't been overly keen on searching the greenwood for a violent wolf's head. They knew the forest, which covered many square miles, harboured many outlaws, all of them more than willing to stick an arrow into a lawman's back.

The prior had been taken back down south to Lewes to recuperate – his incompetent mercenaries paid off by the furious clergyman. Henry the bailiff, almost recovered, but with badly swollen bollocks and a broken nose to match the prior's, had questioned Robin's parents on where their son might have gone to hide. While the bailiff liked an easy life, Robin Hood had utterly humiliated him before the people of Wakefield. He was eager to see the young man in a dungeon, or swinging from a rope. Or, even better, on the end of his sword.

The villagers, led by the headman, Patrick, had been polite, but un-cooperative with the hunt for Robin, and banded together to make sure no one suffered unduly over what had happened. The bailiff had been made to leave by the locals when it became clear his questions were upsetting an already distraught John and Martha Hood. And more violence had been threatened when the bailiff and his foresters had tried half-heartedly to take Matilda into custody.

Eventually, when it became clear information on Robin's whereabouts would not be forthcoming, the villagers were left in relative peace.

The bailiff and the prior might have been enraged over what had happened to them, but they knew it would do neither of them any good if they pushed the close-knit community of Wakefield too far. The Earl of Lancaster was an absentee landlord, leaving the running of Wakefield to his appointed steward and the bailiff, but he still expected the village to be productive. Civil unrest would not be looked upon kindly by the earl – the second most powerful man in England – as it often led to a drop in rents and the earl needed as much money as he could get, being locked, as he had been for years, in a power struggle with his cousin, King Edward II.

As a result, the bailiff reluctantly allowed the villagers to go about their lives as normal. He knew he would find some way to make them all pay, eventually.

Robin was not forgotten altogether by the authorities, though. Publicly declared an outlaw, it was made clear he would be arrested and likely hanged if he was ever captured. Assuming one of the foresters didn't get a chance to shoot him first.

Luckily for the young outlaw, spring was in full bloom when he found himself sleeping rough in the forest. The weather was warm, the days were long, and there was enough food to eat. With nothing to lose any more, Robin, sometimes joined by Much, hunted the king's deer and rabbit, fished, and collected those berries which grew at this time of year. The pair would regularly have too much for Robin to eat himself; so Much would take the extra back to Wakefield and share it among those families that needed it most.

But Robin knew he couldn't live like this forever. Summer would fade into autumn and that into winter. Life on the run, in a makeshift shelter in the forest, with food much scarcer, would not be as easy as it was just now.

"You're going to have to leave the area and try to find a life somewhere, away from the prior and the law." Much told him. "Hiding from the foresters is simple enough when you've thick trees to lose yourself in, but come winter there'll be no shelter here."

Robin stared into the crackling fire the pair were cooking a spitted brown trout on, his belly rumbling as the delicious smell filled the little clearing they were hiding in. At any other time, this would have been a wonderful late spring day – two young friends, surrounded by the lush green foliage of beech and oak, sunlight filtering softly through the leaves, violets and bluebells carpeting much of the ground, a small waterfall burbling quietly somewhere nearby, and a couple of fat fish to share between them.

"Robin?" Much prompted.

"I know," Robin sighed heavily. "It hasn't been a terrible life as an outlaw so far. But I need help."

"Help? You need to get away!"

Robin shook his head. "I can't just leave, Much. My family is here in Wakefield. You."

"Matilda?"

"Aye, Matilda," Robin agreed, softly, before his voice rose, becoming loud and angry. "Why should I be forced to leave my home because of that fat priest? He was out of order – just because he's rich he thinks he can do whatever he likes!" He jumped up and pulled the trout from its spit, biting off a great chunk viciously. "I was going to ask her to marry me . . ." he mumbled sadly, sitting back on the ground in dejection.

Much remained silent, letting his friend vent his emotions on the food for a while.

The sounds of insects, and birds singing merrily, filled the forest as the pair sat in thought.

Then a dry twig, a remnant from the previous autumn, cracked somewhere close to their right.

Robin sat bolt upright, his eyes seeking out his bow on the ground next to him. Much looked over at his friend, wide-eyed, questioning, frightened.

The sounds of men moving none too quietly through the undergrowth came to them, and Robin silently hefted his bow over his shoulder and grabbed his bag of arrows.

"Wait! You smell that? Fish cooking!" A voice, too close for comfort, reached them, as Robin stealthily gathered his blankets and tied them to his back, motioning Much to follow him as he moved into the trees in the opposite direction to the voice.

Suddenly, a man, his green and brown attire marking him as a forester, appeared through the foliage right next to Robin and the young man started back in shock. The undergrowth, most of it fresh and damp, had masked the sounds of the forester's approach, and Robin mentally kicked himself for his lack of woodcraft.

The forester roared a warning to his fellows in the bushes nearby and dropped a hand to his sword hilt, dragging the weapon from its sheath. Robin, startled, and frightened by the sounds of at least four or five other foresters converging on them, let his longbow slip down his arm and, grasping it two-handed, swung it as hard as he could into his opponent's face.

The man screamed, and fell on the forest floor, writhing in pain, his cries panicking Robin and Much even more.

"This way!" Robin gasped, grabbing his friend by the arm and dragging him into the deeper bushes, the sounds of pursuit close behind them.

The foresters must have stopped to check on their injured companion, as the two young men ran for a long time, as fast as they could through the trees, tripping over roots and low branches numerous times, before at last, utterly breathless, they collapsed on the hard brown soil beneath an ancient oak.

There was no elation at their escape. The adrenaline coursing through their veins gave them no pleasure as they sat, backs against the rough bark of the oak, throats and chests burning, dragging in great lungfuls of air, eyes darting around for signs of other pursuers.

"Shit!" Much sobbed, slamming his palm against the tree in frustration, knowing they had been literally seconds from death or at least capture. "Shit, Shit, Shit!" His head dropped and he hugged his knees. "How can you live like this?" he groaned. "Knowing those bastards can appear at any time and kill you? How can you even sleep at night for fear of one of them sneaking up and running his sword through you?"

Robin had no answer to his friend's questions, so he sat in silence, catching his breath, too exhausted to even manage a shrug of his huge shoulders.

After a while, their hearts stopped racing and the sense of immediate danger passed.

"You know," Robin grunted, "last week when I visited my family, my ma mentioned a group of outlaws who had been reported in the forest."

"Aye, I heard about them," Much replied. "But I heard they're a bloodthirsty lot too. Rapists and murderers."

Robin laughed bitterly, spreading his hands wide and looking around at the trees. "Bloodthirsty? They'd need to be – how the hell else would they survive, living their lives as outlaws in this godforsaken forest?"

Much looked away, understanding the point, but not liking where the conversation was heading.

"I can't do this on my own," Robin muttered. "I won't leave Yorkshire. I need to find people who can help me."

"But Robin, there's stories about these outlaws. Killing people for fun – killing children. Eating children . . . !" He shook his head in disbelief.

"Don't be bloody stupid!" Robin retorted angrily. "Who do you think's spreading those stories? The nobles! They don't want people to help the outlaws, so they spread ridiculous lies about them."

Much shrugged his shoulders. "You may be right, at least in part. But there's no smoke without fire. My da says the leader of this group's been an outlaw for years, and he's done a lot of bad things to a lot of people. Adam Bell, that's his name."

"I have no choice." Robin was almost pleading, hoping to gain some understanding from his oldest friend; hoping to gain some reassurance that this was, genuinely, the only option for him.

"How would you find this gang?"

Robin answered instantly, having thought this over repeatedly for the past three days. "They have to hunt, which means they need to buy arrows, right? Matilda's da is the fletcher in our village, so they probably get supplies from him sometimes. He might be able to send word that I want to join them."

The two friends sat for a while longer, still listening nervously for sounds of pursuing foresters, neither speaking as they contemplated how this idea of Robin's might turn out.

But the path was set. Robin travelled back to Wakefield with Much the next morning, to try and arrange a meeting with the band of outlaws.

* * *

"The king must be dealt with!" Thomas, Earl of Lancaster, slammed his palms on the hard stone bench in frustration, the noise echoing off the walls, and glared around at the other men in the chapter-house who were, mostly, nodding their heads in agreement at his proclamation.

The earl, a tall, slim man with thinning salt-and-pepper hair and heavy bags under his green eyes, had called an assembly in Pontefract priory, inviting many of the most powerful men in England to attend. In dribs and drabs they had arrived with their retainers and entered the imposing building hastily, as a heavy downpour drenched their fine clothes and a powerful gale whistled along the old stone corridors.

They were gathered in the chapter-house, a relatively cosy part of the building with a well-stoked fire burning brightly in a great hearth. Stone benches lined the elaborately carved walls, with columns and arcading all painted brightly, making the great octagonal room seem quite snug despite its high vaulted roof.

Thomas had paid the monks well to pile a table with Rhennish, Gascon and Spanish wines, and a selection of fine foods. The sight of expensive bread, fried herring, peacock and pork in breadcrumbs cheered the soaked magnates while they shrugged off their wet garments and tried to warm the damp from their bones. The wind and rain buffeted the spectacular stained-glass windows set high into the walls as the earl continued.

"Our tenants need help. There's no point in demanding taxes or grain from them when the crops have failed and they have no bread for themselves; nothing to sell to make money; and the constant threat of raids from the barbarians over the border!"

"Not to mention those damn Despensers!" Roger Mortimer, Baron of Wigmore shouted angrily. He, and some of the other Marcher lords who held lands around the Welsh borders, had travelled to this meeting after launching a devastating attack on castles belonging to the Despensers, who were loved by the king, but despised and feared, with good reason, by the other lords in the country.

Sir Richard-at-Lee listened, a slice of freshly baked, buttered *manchet* in his hand, as he gazed around appreciatively at the magnificent building, noticing with interest a grotesque, and disturbingly lifelike, leering satanic head carved into the wall far above the altar.

Sir Richard was the fifty-year old preceptor, or commander, of a modest estate in Kirklees, and had come to the gathering despite having misgivings. A knight of the Order of Hospitallers, with two fine sons, he was not too badly off under King Edward II. He knew throwing his lot in with the Earl of Lancaster and the lords from the Welsh Marches, could turn out to be a suicidal move.

Still, it was true that the king could be doing more to protect the north's interests, rather than allowing himself to be swayed by greedy, selfish and incompetent advisors such as the Despensers, which is why the proud Hospitaller had answered the earl's summons.

"The king sits in London demanding we tax our starving, impoverished tenants, but doing nothing to help while the Scots prepare again to ravage our lands!" The earl glared around at the magnates. "Stealing food from the peasants, killing our tenants – weakening *us*, gentlemen, for what are we without the income our tenants provide us?" He leaned back and crossed his arms over his chest, glaring round at the assembled nobles. "Meanwhile, the king is in the south, safe, while his greedy friends the Despensers fill his mind with poison . . . It cannot continue!"

There were grumbles of agreement again at that – the Despensers, both called Hugh, were determinedly ambitious and, with the support of the king, had managed to gain a great deal of power in the past few years. Many in England and Wales feared the Despensers ruthless greed, particularly the Marcher lords Humphrey de Bohun, the Earl of Hereford and Mortimer who had decided to take matters into their own hands, seizing castles and lands, including Newport, Glamorgan and Caerphilly, belonging to the Despensers.

Sir Richard helped himself to another cup of wine and looked around the chapter-house thoughtfully. Although there were a lot of powerful men in the room Richard wondered how many of them would back down if war was threatened by the king. Still, Edward would no doubt hear of this gathering and hopefully take it as a sign that he must do more for the northern and Marcher lords before things got that far.

"You have it right, Earl Thomas," Lord Furnival of Sheffield growled, chewing a baked spiced apple. "The king should be doing more to help those of us on his borders, as his noble father did."

A small, bald man with an immaculately trimmed moustache Sir Richard recognized as Multon of Gilsland, shouted in angry agreement from near the back of the room, his voice echoing across the distance. "His father, God rest his soul, was a real man – a real king. If he was still alive we'd have wiped out the threat from the Scots by now and be better off for it! I've been near enough ruined these past few years!"

The Earl of Lancaster kept his expression severe, but Richard guessed he was pleased by the glint in his eyes. Years of neglect by King Edward II had turned many of his subjects against him. The gathered magnates knew the time was coming when they might be forced to take steps to remove the weak monarch and make the country great again. With Thomas of Lancaster at the helm, of course,

Richard thought – he was the king's cousin after all, the wealthiest earl in the land, and hereditary steward of England, a title granted him years earlier by Edward himself. The big Hospitaller had no problem with that idea – the earl seemed a capable, if haughty man, who had tried repeatedly over the years to keep his cousin, the king, in check. Although Sir Richard was a Hospitaller – an Order which remained outwith petty local politics –he had come late in life to the order and, with two sons to provide an inheritance for, secretly retained ownership of lands adjoining his Hospitaller commandery in Kirklees.

The meeting carried on in similar fashion for a while longer, Richard and the other lords gladly eating and drinking their fill while airing a list of other grievances against the king such as his poor choice of advisors, his fondness for wine and his rumoured homosexual relations with former favourite Piers Gaveston, beheaded by Lancaster and his supporters almost ten years earlier.

Mostly, though, the Marchers demanded action against the Despensers, although the northern lords were more interested in knowing how Edward expected them to hold back the Scots should they attack again.

The Despensers greed and influence over the king was grave cause for concern amongst the noblemen throughout England, but to those in the north, such as Sir Richard, the threat of rampaging Scots was all too real, and seemed, at this stage, more immediate.

Eventually, a monk came in, head bowed, and silently lit the torches set around the walls, and Sir Richard realised it would be getting dark soon. He hoped the meeting would end before much longer, considering he had only travelled here today with his sergeant-at-arms, and the forests around these parts were thick with robbers and other outlaws. *Damn waste of good fighting men*, he thought, *someone could make a decent private army out of them.*

The Earl of Lancaster must have realised it was getting late too, as he stood and held his hands clasped before him until the gathered nobles noticed and fell silent.

"I'm glad to know we are all of the same mind, my lords," he smiled, meeting the gaze of those he knew held the most power and influence. "For now, though, I would counsel caution – we cannot afford to act recklessly, especially regarding the Despensers. Edward is still our king after all and he is very fond of those two." There were angry mutterings again; Richard was impressed at how well the earl was working his audience. "I, myself, will pledge to support the Baron of Wigmore and the other Marcher lords in their dispute with the Despensers, but I realise many of you gathered here do not agree with me on that point…yet." He glared at his audience, then shrugged his shoulder as if saddened by the magnates failure to make a stand against the king's favourites and, by extension, King Edward himself. "So, for now, I would simply ask you all to join me in swearing an oath to defend one another's lands against the Scots. If the king will not aid us, we must aid one another – we can't allow those savages to ravage our lands again."

Lancaster's plan was unanimously accepted, and Sir Richard knew the earl had made an important step. There was still some way to go though, before he had enough support to force the king to do anything about the Despensers.

"Very well, my friends," the earl smiled at everyone, meeting every eye. "I thank you for coming. Together – united! – we *will* repel any raids from north of the border." He spread his hands, looking around earnestly at the men he had gathered. "With your blessing, I will now write to bishop de Beaumont of Durham, bishop de Halton of Carlisle, and archbishop Melton of York, asking for their advice. If they are agreeable, I will invite them to meet with us on the 28th of June, one month from now. I hope to see you all there. Perhaps by then we may even be able to do something about the Despensers."

"Assuming the Marcher lords haven't already killed the bastards!" Multon of Gilsland shouted to laughs and cheers as the magnates pulled on their still damp cloaks and filed from the room, drunk with power and ambition as well as expensive imported wine.

The Earl of Lancaster had successfully enlisted the support of some of the most powerful men in northern England, if perhaps not as many, and not as unequivocally as he would have liked. Next, though, he would reach out to those nobles in the midlands and the south he felt would rally to his cause.

The earl grasped Sir Richard's hand as he filed from the room. They had met each other, in passing, various times over the years and had a mutual respect for each other.

"I'm glad you came," Thomas said. "We need men like you with us – good, patriotic men who only want the best for England. How are those boys of yours doing? Edward and Simon is that right?"

Richard was flattered that such a powerful man would remember his sons' names, and he nodded happily. "Doing well, my lord, Edward followed me and joined the Hospitallers in Rhodes. Simon, my youngest, he's off to a tournament in Wales as we speak – his first!"

The earl smiled and slapped the big knight on the arm. "I hope he does well. And I hope you'll come to the next meeting in a month's time. Too many landowners have been dispossessed recently, Sir Richard, as a result of the Despenser's and the king's actions. You and your son have as much to lose as any of us here."

The Hospitaller met the earl's eyes, wondering how the man knew about the lands he privately owned, but saw only honest concern there.

Still, a lot could happen in a month and he remained unsure whether Thomas and the Marcher lords would be able to sway the King to their cause, so he simply smiled and nodded as the earl moved on to say his farewells to the next departing magnate.

Sir Richard was impressed by the Earl of Lancaster. He would give the idea of attending the meeting at Sherburn-in-Elmet next month serious thought, as he knew the rest of the northern lords would.

Unknown to any of the assembled magnates though, Thomas, earl of Lancaster, steward of England, had sent a messenger seeking another alliance to an inconceivable place:

Scotland.

* * *

Joining Adam Bell's outlaw gang proved simpler than Robin had hoped. As Much and Robin learned, to their surprise, many of their fellow villagers often did business, covertly, with Adam Bell – selling him and his men food and other supplies.

Obviously, the outlaws had to get these things – arrows, clothing, ale, bread, rope etc, from somewhere. Robin just hadn't suspected that so many of their friends and neighbours helped outlaws. Either the bailiff also never knew, or he turned a blind eye to make his own life easier.

Matilda's father, Henry, repaired Adam Bell's men's old arrows, and sold them new ones when they needed them.

Henry had, a little reluctantly, asked Adam Bell to help Robin. Although the fletcher was content to do business with the outlaws, he too had heard the gruesome stories about Bell and his gang and, while not believing everything he'd been told, he knew the outlaw leader was a violent and uncompromising man. But, like Robin, Henry accepted the fact that the young man needed help and this was the only available source.

So Robin was introduced to Adam Bell; a tall, well built, yet strangely refined man, with thinning hair, intelligent green eyes, and a hooked nose. The outlaw leader was accompanied by two vicious-looking men, who, despite their size and hard demeanour, were strangely deferential to Bell.

"Don't think it's an easy life, boy," Bell growled at Robin, handing over a small bag of silver to Henry the fletcher, in return for a bundle of fresh arrows. "You pull your weight in my gang, and you do as I tell you, understand? No matter what."

Robin nodded nervously under Bell's glare, knowing this intense, forbidding man basically held the power of life and death over him. "I'm a good fighter, and I can shoot well. I won't be a burden to you."

Adam's two men grunted in amusement at that, but Robin ignored them, his face flushing. His temper had got him in enough trouble already.

They set off an hour later, after Bell had completed his business in the village, and Robin had said a final goodbye to his parents and Much. Matilda had met Robin on the village outskirts, safely hidden by thick trees and bushes, as Bell and his two men waited impatiently.

"I don't know when I'll be able to come back to see you," Robin had said, holding the young girl's hand earnestly. "I don't really know how Adam's group works. They travel around a lot, to keep ahead of the law."

"Why did this have to happen? Why couldn't that prior just leave us alone?" Matilda wiped angrily at her eyes. "God curse him, I hate that man!"

Robin hugged her close. "I know; me too. But the nobles and clergy do as they like, there's no one to stop them. I'll be back though. This'll all blow over, you'll see. And then…"

"Aye, then…what?" Matilda looked pointedly at Robin.

"Then I'll marry you of course!"

Matilda laughed gently. "Maybe. I've waited long enough for you to ask." She became suddenly earnest. "But I can't marry an outlaw, Robin. It'd be no life for us. When – if – we marry, you have to be a free man again."

Robin accepted this, knowing it was true, no matter how depressing. For all his talk of things "blowing over", he knew it would never happen. Outlaws *were* pardoned all the time in England, but it could take years, were it to occur at all. Matilda might be content to wait for now, but a girl in a village like Wakefield couldn't stay unwed for very long. Life was too hard in these times – family security was vital.

"I have to go," he told her, glancing round at the path into the forest as Adam Bell shouted at him to hurry up.

The couple shared a hurried kiss; their tongues exploring each other's mouths, before Matilda breathlessly pushed Robin away, giving his swollen manhood a playful squeeze through his trousers. "Come back to me when you're not an outlaw," she told him.

He gazed at her for a second, grinning, his body burning with desire, then, with a wave, hurried off to his new master.

Aye, you're the one for me, Robin, Matilda thought sadly as the young man ran off into the trees, tears filling her eyes again. *But I can't wait on you forever.*

CHAPTER THREE

There was a ringing crack as the quarterstaff rapped Robin's knuckles, and he yelped with the pain, almost dropping his own staff. Too late, he tried to raise it again, as his opponent continued his attacking move and thumped the weapon against Robin's shoulder, hurling him sideways into the shallow stream.

The outlaws cheered and laughed as the new young recruit splashed around, gasping in the water, before he managed to scramble back onto the grass again, cursing. He glared at his opponent, an older man called Matt Groves, all the while rubbing his bruised shoulder and blowing on his stinging fingers.

Life in Adam Bell's group was hard. There were sixteen men, not including Robin – all outlaws with nowhere else to go. The men trained nearly every day, with their great longbows, but also other weapons, such as swords, or as today, the quarterstaff.

It was a cool day, the forest filled with the sounds of loud bird song and the spring sun trying to break through fluffy white clouds in a light blue sky as the men sparred under trees filled with dark green new foliage.

"You're getting better, *boy*," Matt Groves nodded, his thinning blonde hair, arrow straight, bouncing in front of his cold eyes as he stared at the young outlaw. "You still fight like a fucking woman though."

Matt seemed to take some sadistic pleasure in besting Robin, perhaps trying to break his spirit, perhaps simply because Groves was a nasty bastard.

While he had been one of the toughest young men in his own village, these were hard, experienced fighting men Robin was with now. He regularly found himself lying on the forest floor, looking up at the trees with a throbbing shin bone, cracked ribs or aching kidneys, while the outlaw he'd been sparring with looked down at him gleefully.

"If you're finished your swim, Hood; how about catching us some breakfast?" Adam Bell tossed Robin a hunting bow, which he caught with a grimace as his painful knuckles tightened around it.

"An' don't be long, boy; I'm starving," Matt Groves smirked, lying down on the warm grass beside the other men.

Robin shook his head, his face red with embarrassment – at his defeat, and his being treated like a serf. But he held his tongue and strode from the camp into the thicker trees, promising himself he'd give Matt a good beating one day.

There was a vague hierarchy in the outlaw gang – Bell at the top, his most trusted men next, and everyone else around the bottom. As a newcomer, Robin found himself the lowest of the lot.

But his prowess with the bow, and resultant success hunting food the past few weeks had helped most of the men recognise him as a valuable asset.

Adam Bell himself rarely noticed Robin, nodding a greeting or barking an order at him occasionally, but never sharing more than a couple of words with him. Some of the other outlaws had begun to strike up friendships with Robin though, which made his new life less lonely and, in fact, the young man had started to accept his new life.

Suddenly spotting a family of grey hares relaxing in the sun near a clump of brambles he dropped onto one knee and silently fitted an arrow to the hunting bow, sticking another point first into the ground. He aimed at the largest of the little group and let fly. The other animals scattered instinctively as his arrow took the hare in the neck with a dull thump, but Robin smoothly pulled his second arrow from the ground and in a heartbeat had shot another. Smiling in satisfaction he collected the dead beasts and retrieved his arrows, his thoughts turning again to his new life as an outlaw.

A handful of merchants and well-off noblemen had passed through the forest since Robin had joined the gang, and Adam Bell had relieved them of their goods and purses. But Robin had not taken part in those robberies. Only a handful of men went along each time and Robin wasn't yet trusted enough to join in. Which suited him fine – he was quite content to stay in the background, out of harm's way.

Besides, many travellers hired bodyguards, and Robin didn't like the idea of using a sword against a man he didn't even know. Although he knew the day would come sooner rather than later, he was content to stick to sparring for as long as possible.

Sometimes Bell and his men would come back from those robberies with blood on their clothes, and wounds of their own. Robin would tell himself there was no other way – either the group got money somehow, or they would all die. Living off the land was only possible up to a point – his two hares wouldn't feed seventeen men for long. Money was still needed to buy clothes, salt, bread, arrows and other necessities from places like Wakefield and the other villages around Barnsdale.

He continued hunting for a while, catching a couple of blackbirds and a plump dove to go with his hares. They'd help make a tasty enough meal for the men tonight.

He made his way back to the camp, where one of the men had already filled their great iron pot with stream water and whatever vegetables they had lying around. Robin took out his knife and prepared the animals he'd caught. Skinning, gutting and plucking weren't his favourite jobs but no one offered to help, so he got on with it in silence.

When he was done, he added the meat to the pot and washed his bloodied hands in the stream. The other men were drinking ale round the fire, telling ghost stories, so Robin joined them, sitting near the edge of the group.

As the sun slowly started to set one of the other outlaws cheerfully handed him a wooden mug brimming with dark brown ale, which he accepted gratefully and, as the delicious meaty smell of the simmering soup filled the camp, Robin smiled in satisfaction.

It wasn't an ideal life, but it could be a hell of a lot worse.

* * *

"Morning, Hood," Adam Bell greeted him the next morning. It was a miserable, wet summer day, and Robin was planning on finding a nice big tree to shelter under where he could spend the day fishing. "We're going after a rich churchman today," his leader told him. "Get your weapons."

Robin was surprised, and found he was more than a little anxious. "You want me to come with you Adam?"

"That's right, lad. Your skill with a blade has improved a lot since you first joined us. It's time you put it to good use. There's a friar going down to visit the Prior of Lewes, and we know he's going to be carrying a fair bit of money. A friend of ours in Boroughbridge overheard the churchman talking in a tavern and passed word to us. He's probably hired a couple of guards to see him through the forest, but that'll be it. Move it now, get your gear."

Robin scrambled to obey. When it came to the military side of things, Adam Bell had an unmistakeable aura of command about him. Clearly he hadn't been a common outlaw all his life, but none of the other men trusted Robin enough yet to let him know what Bell's story was. Assuming they even knew it themselves.

He collected his longbow, along with the old sword he had brought from home, now with its edge nicely sharpened, and stuck a dozen arrows into his belt. He strapped on his gambeson as he ran to join the other men in the raiding party. This padded green fabric body armour was a gift from Bell, and, like his sword, had seen better days, but it came down to just above his knees and would turn many blows, short of a direct sword thrust. There was a patched hole in the back, from where such a thrust had killed the armour's previous owner. Robin tried not to think of that too much as he fastened it in place.

"Ah, you're coming with us today?" One of Adam Bell's most trusted men, John Little, slapped Robin on the back, almost knocking the younger man to his knees. John was a huge man, over six and a half feet tall, with the build of a wrestler, and a wild brown beard which made him look like a great bear, although at twenty four he wasn't much older than Robin. The outlaws jokingly called him Little John.

Robin liked the enormous man immensely, although he could be terrifying if enraged. Robin had rapped him painfully on the knuckles during a quarterstaff practice the previous week and had run off into the trees rather than stand up to the roaring giant. The other outlaws had found it hilarious, as had John when he calmed down and Robin returned sheepishly from his flight with a peace offering of a rabbit he'd shot for the big man's dinner.

"Feeling nervous?" John asked as the ten-strong group headed out of the camp to the main road through the forest, a spot just over a mile and a half away from their camp.

Robin swallowed, nodding gently. "I'll be fine though."

"I was shitting myself the first time I went out with Adam on a raid," the big man admitted. "Worried I'd freeze if any fighting started."

Robin was genuinely surprised – the thought of Little John being scared of anything seemed incredible.

John laughed, reading the look on Robin's face correctly. "Listen, my life may not be worth anything to the sheriff, but it means a lot to me! It doesn't matter how big you are if an arrow takes you in the back, or a soldier stabs you in the guts. There's no shame in being scared, lad, as long as you don't let it control you."

The conversation did Robin good, calming his nerves a little, but he knew he'd always be afraid of how he'd react in a real life-or-death fight until the day he proved to himself he could handle it. He still hoped today wouldn't be that day though– most of these robberies were simple, non-violent affairs. Bell's well-armed, hard men simply threatened whoever they'd targeted, and the money and goods were handed over. It would be suicide for a merchant or churchman, normally only accompanied by, at best, a handful of guards, to stand up to the well-drilled outlaws.

And yet it did happen from time to time, when they targeted someone as aggressive and proud as John or Bell himself. Robin hoped this friar they went to rob didn't have guards like Little John with him.

It didn't take long for the group to reach the chosen ambush point, and Bell began issuing orders. Robin was surprised again, when he realised Adam didn't just have the men hide behind trees until the target appeared, then jump out waving swords and demanding gold. On the contrary, Bell appeared to know this area of the forest well, and positioned the men in handily placed trees and bushes, encircling the vicinity. The road at this point narrowed, and both sides were fenced in – a rock wall on one side, and a dense grouping of bushes on the other. The only way out of the trap was ahead, or back the way the target had come, but the outlaws laid ropes before and after the ambush site, ready to be pulled up into position, effectively penning in the unfortunate friar and his party.

Bell had sent Robin off with Little John, to the young man's relief. If it did get violent, John was the best person to be with. They settled down to wait, taking up position in the thick summer undergrowth, at the rear of the ambush spot.

John took a piece of bread from his pocket, tearing half off for Robin. He began to chew contentedly, although his gaze never left the road.

"How can you eat at a time like this?" Robin wondered, looking at the bread he'd been handed.

John laughed gently. "Don't worry. We'll have plenty warning when the friar's near. D'you think Adam didn't bother sending out a scout?" He tore off another huge chunk of the thick loaf, his eyes twinkling with amusement. "Will Scaflock's gone on to see where the bastard is."

Robin grunted sheepishly, and tried his best to chew some of the bread, but his appetite was gone for now. He handed the food back to John and set an arrow to his bowstring, just in case. John laughed again, louder this time, shaking his head and chewing noisily.

Robin was relieved to find John had been right though, when, a short time later, there was a bird call from along the road and the big man got to his feet, grunting to Robin, "That's Will's signal. They're coming."

Robin stood up too, glad to find he wasn't as nervous as he'd feared he'd be. He was focused on the job at hand, without feeling too frightened.

Little John pulled an arrow from his belt, and the two outlaws stood ready, hidden by the thick tree they'd chosen as cover.

A while later they heard a horse-drawn cart creaking along the road and, as it slowly came into sight, Robin felt his pulse quicken as he realised this might not be as simple as he'd hoped.

The friar was riding a horse. In addition to the noisy cart, which carried a roughly made, but sturdy, wooden box, there were eight hard-looking riders. These men all wore gambesons like Robin's, for protection, with helmets in seemingly good repair, and long swords at their hips. Every one of them looked as dangerous as most of Adam Bell's men.

Robin looked a little nervously at John. The bearded giant looked back, shrugging his massive shoulders. "That friar must have something good in his box, to be travelling with all those guards."

As the party reached the ambush point, there was a piercing whistle from Adam Bell, hidden somewhere in the dense foliage, and the ropes at either end of the road were suddenly pulled taut, and tied to the trees, blocking the horsemen's path. Little John and the other outlaws raced forward silently to pen the friar's party in, although they stayed close by the thick tree trunks in case they needed cover. Robin followed, gripping his bow so tight he could feel it digging into his hands.

The friar sat back in his saddle, but didn't look particularly dismayed by the ambush. Robin was a little worried, though, to see the guards quietly and efficiently take up defensive positions encircling the cart.

The young outlaw looked quickly at Little John, but the big man just glared grimly at the guards. He'd clearly seen this all before, and Robin again felt himself relaxing a little. Adam Bell knew what he was doing. He must do, after all these years as a robber outlaw leader.

Just then, Bell himself walked into view, and stood facing the friar. He never looked once at the stony-faced guards who followed him with their eyes. Some of them had drawn short bows and held them aimed at Bell.

"Get those ropes out of the way. Before we cut you down." The friar's words were cool, his voice powerful and controlled, but Robin realised the churchman probably knew this was Adam Bell in front of him. And Bell's reputation was not a good one, when it came to how he treated churchmen who didn't co-operate.

The outlaw leader simply pointed to the cart. "We're taking that, friar. Those men" – he gestured to the eight soldiers –"can keep their weapons and continue along the way with you." He spread his feet and put one hand on his sword hilt, staring at the friar.

The clergyman shook his head. "There are nine of us. Get out of the way and nothing more need be said about this."

Adam Bell continued to stare impassively at the friar for another few seconds, before raising his hand and pointing at one of the soldiers. "Will!"

Bell jumped behind a tree as there was a snapping noise, and a thud. Robin was shocked to see the soldier Bell had single out thrown backwards off his horse, gasping and clawing wildly at the arrow that had hammered into his windpipe. Will Scaflock smoothly dropped his bow and pulled his sword from its scabbard, dropping into a fighting stance, an appalling animal grin on his wide face.

No one moved for a split second, until the shock passed, and the guards realised what had happened.

"Damn it, Scaflock!" John grunted, knowing Will could have easily incapacitated the guard with a shot to the arm or shoulder, rather than killing him.

"Dismount!" one of the soldiers shouted, realising they had no chance while on horseback, penned in as they were, and the rest followed, kneeling beside the cart, weapons drawn.

Adam Bell's voice could be heard from behind a tree. "There's eight of you now, friar!" He laughed coldly. "Now tell your men to drop their weapons and we'll just take that cart of yours." He stepped into view again, expertly drawing a beautifully forged sword.

Robin held his breath, as time seemed to stand still and the friar stared silently at Bell.

The stand-off was broken as the soldier who had ordered the dismount earlier decided he'd had enough. "Get the bastards!"

The seven remaining guards charged at the outlaws ringing them, and Robin found himself staring at a wiry, red-haired man, roaring wildly as he raised his sword to bring it down on the young outlaw's head.

Robin brought his own sword up, deflecting the powerful blow, as instinct and training took over and, leaning forward, he rammed a knee between his attacker's legs. The man fell to the floor groaning, as Little John's quarterstaff hammered down on the back of his head.

The two outlaws stepped over the unconscious man, looking for other targets, but it was a similar story all around. The friar's guards, hard as they may have been, were all down, injured or dead. Not one of the outlaws seemed to have taken a scratch.

Only the friar stood in the way of the cart now.

"Right, you fat, tonsured arsehole, get out of the way." Adam Bell strode forward, the outlaws close behind, ready to check the contents of the wagon. "I'm not really a religious man, but I'd rather not have to get too violent with a member of the clergy. I don't have a problem with it though, if you push me."

The friar was an overweight man, in the grey robes of the Franciscan order, with an open, honest-looking face. As Bell closed on the wagon, suddenly, from the folds of his robe, the friar produced a short wooden club, about a foot long, and, with blinding speed, blasted the breath from Bell's lungs with a thrust to the guts, and then battered him to the ground with a vicious blow to the temple.

Everyone froze in shock. Adam Bell lay unmoving on the forest floor, as the friar moved coolly into a fighting stance and, with a small smile, said, "All right then, boys. Who's next?"

The sheer violence and precision of the friar's attack seemed to hold the outlaws rooted to the spot, as they realised this was no normal churchman. Robin could just see Adam Bell's chest rising and falling gently, so, although he was still alive, he'd likely feel sick for a while when he came to. Robin was impressed with the friar's courage.

Little John must have felt the same respect for the hardy Franciscan, as he raised his great voice and ordered the outlaws to hold their positions. "That was good for a fat friar, but you know you can't fight us all."

"No?" The friar cocked an eyebrow. "Do you want to find out, my child?"

John burst out laughing at this show of bravado. "I'm sure you'd try too, father, but I don't want any more deaths today. Now put down the weapon and let us take what we came for. You can be on your way."

Will Scaflock was shaking his head impatiently during the exchange. "Come on John, what are we waiting for? I can stick an arrow in this fat bastard and we'll help ourselves. We need to get moving."

John rounded on Scaflock, his face red with anger. "Shut your fucking mouth Scarlet! You're always too quick at killing people. There was no need to shoot that guard in the throat, and there's no need to cut down this friar." He turned back to the churchman. "Now move it, you, we don't have all day and the longer this lasts the more likely he is to use you for target practice." He nodded at Will in disgust.

Will Scaflock was nominally Adam Bell's second in command, but in practice, the men followed Little John when Bell wasn't around. Scaflock was a bitter man, earning the nickname "Scarlet" amongst the outlaws as a result of his bloodthirsty temper and eagerness to use violence on anyone who got in his way. John, although a hard man, was well liked by the men, and his sheer physical presence was normally enough to cow even Will.

The friar glanced coldly at the muttering Scaflock and nodded his head in resignation. "All right, wolf's head. You win. Take your prize."

Robin let himself relax a little as the churchman dropped his club and went to check how his companions were.

A couple of the outlaws collected the ropes from the ambush site, some of the others rounded up the mercenaries horses to sell in the outlying villages, and Will Scaflock climbed nimbly into the driver's seat on the cart. John and Robin gingerly lifted Adam Bell, who was now groaning quietly, up behind Will, laying him out as comfortably as possible beside the big wooden chest.

The robbery had taken longer than Robin had realised, and, despite it being only late afternoon, the light was beginning to fail as the heavy grey rain clouds continued to hide the sun.

"It'll be too dark to check the cart properly tonight," Little John decided. "We'll search it tomorrow, once Adam's awake." With a gesture, he directed them back to camp with their prize, but he placed a big hand on Robin's arm as the other outlaws moved off.

"Wait with me for a bit, Robin," he rumbled. "I want to talk to this friar."

As the wagon, with its new, outlaw, escort moved off, John and Robin, still with weapons warily drawn, walked over to the clergyman.

"How are they?" John asked.

The friar shook his head sadly. "Eight men. Six of them dead. Two unconscious, although they should be all right." Robin was glad to see the red-haired man who had attacked him was one of the lucky ones still alive.

Little John shook his huge head. "I'm sorry about them, friar, I truly am."

The Franciscan grunted, glaring up at John. "Maybe you are, but I'm sure you won't be kept awake at night with your sorrow."

John didn't reply. The friar had it right. He didn't enjoy seeing men die, but an outlaw's life was a violent and dangerous one, and John had seen more than his share of death. He'd sleep just fine tonight, like the friar said.

"All right, Robin, let's be off." John turned with a farewell nod to the friar and began to follow the other outlaws.

"I'm coming with you."

Again, the churchman stopped John and Robin in their tracks. "What d'you mean?" Robin asked.

"I'm coming with you," the friar repeated, tucking his club back under his robe.

"Why the hell would you want to do that?" John burst out. "We're outlaws!"

The friar walked past the two men and followed the creaking cart. "You leave me no choice. I was taking that cart to the Prior of Lewes, John de Monte Martini. The prior hates me. I won't bore you with the details, but he'd use any excuse to make my life a misery. I can't turn up and tell him I was robbed and lost all his money. He'd blame me – have me locked up, the devil."

Little John was completely lost for words. Robin, genuinely liking the overweight clergyman, grinned. "He can fight, John, that's for sure. And I know myself what a bastard that prior is – it's his fault I'm even here. What harm would it do to let the friar come with us for now?"

The massive outlaw shook his head in disbelief, but with a shrug of his shoulders relented. "Very well, you can come with us. You better hope God and all his angels are smiling on you when Adam wakes up puking his guts out, though, and finds you sitting in our camp. He'll probably let Scaflock cut your balls off."

"Better men than him have tried," the friar laughed confidently, striding through the green undergrowth.

"Where did you learn to fight?" Robin wondered, hurrying after the portly clergyman, pushing branches and leaves out of the way as he went. "And what's your name?"

The friar's blue eyes glittered as he turned towards the young outlaw. "I wasn't always a man of the cloth, lad. And you can call me Tuck."

CHAPTER FOUR

"Ride!"

At the command the mounted men kicked their heels in, urging their horses forward, trying to build momentum behind the wooden lances couched under their arms.

The spectators – well-to-do men, women and children of Glamorgan – filled the benches of a wooden stand running the length of the lists. Cheering gleefully and clad in over-stated finery of wonderful colours each had their own favourite, often chosen for no better reason than the combatant's livery or place of origin.

The horses thundered down the field, sending great clumps of damp grass flying as they tried to gain as much momentum as possible.

Banners and flags of every hue were held aloft as the audience cheered and sang in support of their chosen combatant.

The blunted lance of one man hammered off the shield of his challenger and the crowd cheered at the victory. The two knights returned to their tents with nothing badly injured other than pride.

Taking the field that day in his first jousting tournament was Simon, youngest son of Sir Richard, Hospitaller Commander of Kirklees.

Simon was a big man, just twenty years old, with the same black hair and almond eyes as his father and his older brother Edward. He had never trained with a longbow or quarterstaff – as a young teenager, Simon had spent his time training on horseback, clad in chain or plate mail, and wielding a sword and shield.

Or a great lance, as he held now, looking nervously through the visor of his helmet down the lists at his opponent, Edmund Wytebelt, son of the wealthy Charles of Bodmin.

The lances were tipped with wooden blocks to make them less lethal, but Simon still felt a sense of trepidation as the sounds of the expectant crowd filled his ears.

A man stood in the middle of the list holding aloft a yellow flag, and, as he dropped his arm with a flourish, Simon gritted his teeth, raised his lance, and kicked his great white charger, Dionysus, forward.

His eyes narrowed, and the sound of the crowd faded so all he could hear in his helmet was his own gasping, excited breath, and the thunder of his horses hooves towards his adversary.

Edmund Wytebelt, clad in a livery of red and blue checks over his gleaming armour, the pure white belt that gave him his name tied gaily round his waist, filled Simon's vision and the young northerner, adrenaline coursing through him, grinned in anticipation, all his nerves and trepidation momentarily forgotten.

The spectators' cheers and whistles grew in volume, reaching fever pitch as the knights closed in on each other at a terrific speed, their horses' eyes bulging, teeth bared and legs blurring while the riders, armour clad and helmeted as they were, seemed weirdly motionless.

Driven along on his incredibly powerful equine projectile, Simon raised his lance and, fixing his eyes on his opponent, pointed the heavy wooden weapon at the target he visualised on Edmund Wytebelt's chest.

There was a tremendous bang, and the next thing Simon knew he was lying flat on his back, staring up at the wonderfully sunny sky through the small slit in his visor, stunned.

Slowly, it dawned on him he was still alive, although his head ached a little. And he was lying on the grass rather than sitting on his horse. *But at least I'm alive*, he thought, as he rolled onto his side with some difficulty, his armour being enormously heavy, and tried to see what was happening.

His squire, Alfred, a young boy of twelve from Kirklees, was already beside him, although he hadn't noticed the lad's approach.

"Where's Edmund?" Simon asked, still squinting through his visor and seeing his opponent's horse standing, rider-less, chewing the grass at the side of the tilting field contentedly.

Alfred helped the young knight remove his helmet and Simon noticed at once where his opponent was.

Like him, Edmund had been thrown from his mount onto the hard ground. Unlike him, Edmund had taken more than a glancing blow to the helmet.

"Is he alright?"

Alfred helped his master to his feet, the pair of them straining to lift the weakened and stunned armour-clad young man from the floor.

"Is he alright?" Simon repeated, louder this time, glaring at his squire.

"Not really, my lord." Alfred shook his head, looking around in consternation as armed soldiers converged on them. "He's dead. You killed him."

* * *

"Get up, boy. Hurry!"

Robin's eyes snapped open as a rough hand shook him awake. He had been on guard duty during the hours before sunrise and felt like he'd only just fallen asleep he was so tired.

"God's bollocks, what is it?"

Matt Groves gave him a sour look. "We're moving camp, get your things together, fast, and help us shift all our gear."

Looking around Robin could see the rest of the outlaws preparing to leave, and, panicking, he jumped to his feet and hastily strapped on his weapons. *What's happening? Have we been discovered?*

Matt walked off without any further explanation, but Little John wandered past just then, a huge pack of gear tied to his broad back.

"John! Why are we moving? Have we been found?"

John patted the younger man on the back with a reassuring smile. "Calm down, man, what's the panic?"

"Matt just woke me and told me to get my things, he never said why. I thought something bad had happened."

"Aye, well, he's just messing with your head again, lad," the giant grunted with a scowl in Matt's direction. "It's nothing to worry about – we move camp like this all the time. It makes it harder for the law to find us if we don't stay in the same place for too long."

Robin carried on stuffing his things inside his blanket and tied it shut before looping it around his shoulder. "No one mentioned we were going to be moving," he grumbled.

John laughed and led Robin towards the middle of the camp where the rest of the men were gathering. "Generally, none of us ever know when we'll be moving. Adam decides, but he doesn't tell anyone until the day he wants us to leave. Keeps the men on their toes, and means none of us know where we'll be from one week to the next if anyone gets captured."

"Adam?" Robin yawned and wiped grit from his eyes, feeling like he needed another couple of hours rest. "Last I saw him he was groaning and senseless on the back of that cart."

John grinned. His massive, hairy, face, which could be so incredibly intimidating when he was angry, looked almost childlike as his brown eyes sparkled at Robin good-naturedly. "He woke up during the night. Decided we'd been here long enough. He's probably expecting that box of Tuck's to be holding a lot of money. If it is, people will come looking for it, so – safer to move to a new camp."

Sure enough, Bell stood in the centre of their camp, directing the men and looking none the worse for Tuck's beating.

With a last look around to make sure nothing had been left behind, the men moved off to the east behind their leader.

* * *

As it turned out, the new camp site Adam had chosen wasn't that far from the old one – just an hour and a half's walk, the stolen cart groaning behind them the whole time. Within another hour and a half the outlaws had erected sturdy new shelters to sleep under, and found lookout points high in the trees to make sure no one stumbled upon them.

Setting up the iron cooking frame over a fresh fire-pit, Will had sent a couple of men to go and find some meat for the big pot.

The cart they had stolen from Tuck and his retinue contained many religious and historical texts, which Bell's men had no interest in, most of them being illiterate, but also in the cart was a very large sum of money.

Friar Tuck, whom Bell appeared to have forgiven for knocking him out, told the outlaws the money was to have been a gift to the prior, John de Monte Martini, from Archbishop Melton in York, ostensibly to help renovate the local churches, but Tuck guessed it would mostly be used by the prior on his personal ventures.

"Like his brothel?" Robin spat into the campfire, still seething weeks after the prior's threat to Matilda.

Tuck nodded gently. "Amongst other things I suppose, aye."

Matt Groves gave a crude laugh and rubbed his crotch suggestively. "I might just visit that brothel of his – it'd only be right. At least he'd get some of his money back."

The outlaws joined in the laughing and joking, although none of them would genuinely venture into the city on such a frivolous errand, especially Groves, one of the most wanted men in Adam Bell's group.

Robin was pleased at getting one over on the hated prior, but the men's talk had brought back memories of Matilda. He quietly slipped away from the camp, moving deep into the forest for some time alone with his thoughts.

* * *

Matilda's mother, Mary, slammed the wooden plate down on their table, making the girl jump and her father grumble irritably.

"You're sixteen now, girl. Well past time you were wed. Every other girl in the village your age has a husband, apart from that Clara."

"God have pity on the man that weds her," muttered Matilda's father. "Face like a cow's arse." He winked good-naturedly at his daughter, who stifled a laugh as he shovelled another spoonful of pottage into his mouth.

"Shut up, Henry! I'm being serious here." Mary took her own seat at the table and helped herself to a piece of bread, glaring at her husband.

"I don't want to wed any of the village boys, ma."

Through another mouthful of dinner, Henry asked, "What about that Richard lad, the one that we saw working in the fields today, arms like tree trunks?"

Matilda shook her head. "Ach, he's nice enough, but he's a big oaf. Remember, he set fire to his own house last year when he was drunk? The fire burned down two of his neighbour's houses as well before it was put out. Anyway, he's been with half the village girls already."

"Well, you better lower your standards, soon," her mother told her. "Or there'll be no young men left for you. You want to be a spinster all your life?"

"No, Ma I don't! I'll get married when I'm ready!" The girl took a sip of ale, wiping her mouth with the back of her hand. "If that prior hadn't…"

"For God's sake girl, you can't hang around here hoping Robin Hood comes back for you! Even if he does, he's an outlaw. You run off with him and you'll be an outlaw too. You know what the tithing would do to you if they caught up with you?"

Matilda knew only too well what would happen if she was declared an outlaw, she'd gone over this a thousand times in her head, since the day she kissed Robin goodbye.

"Drown you, that's what!" Mary finished the last of her meal and sat shaking her head at Matilda, but her voice softened as she carried on. "Forget Robin. He was a good boy, would have been a good husband too. But he's as good as dead now. Right, Henry?"

The big fletcher nodded reluctantly. "Your ma does have a good point, lass." Matilda dropped her eyes to the table, but Henry could see the tears glistening there. "Maybe Robin will be pardoned though," he smiled hopefully at his beloved daughter. "It happens often enough. If that prior dies or the parish is taken on by another clergyman . . . well, Robin might be able to come back to Wakefield then."

Matilda looked up at her father and broke into a bright smile that lifted his heart. Her mother told him to shut up again.

* * *

"You're coming with me, Hood." One of the older outlaws, a wiry, grey-haired man known as Harry Half-hand on account of having a hook instead of a left hand, grunted at Robin, with a grin. "Adam's heard there's some rich lady travelling to Pontefract with a big escort, so him and the rest of the lads are heading there. Me, you and Arthur here are heading for Watling Street to relieve a merchant of his – much lighter – purse."

Robin hastily shrugged on his gambeson in surprise as the main body of outlaws marched from their camp, Little John giving him a cheery wave in farewell.

"Just the three of us?"

"Aye," Harry nodded, scratching his ear with the blunt part of his hook. "It's an easy job. Merchant with a single guard, against the three of us."

Arthur laughed as he came over to join them. He was a stocky lad, not yet twenty, with greasy brown hair and most of his teeth missing. Robin liked him a lot – he always seemed to have a smile on his filthy face. "Aye, I'd rather be doing this than going after that lady. The boys are saying she's got a dozen guards with her! Fuck that!"

"Fuck that right enough," Harry Half-hand grinned in reply, and strode off towards Watling Street, which was the name for the great old Roman road that stretched from one end of England to the other.

The trio reached the main road before midday. Even though the sun hadn't yet reached its zenith, it was a scorching hot June day, and the outlaws were glad to find a sheltered spot to await their prey.

Still, Arthur had a short attention span and started to complain after a while. "How much longer are they going to be?" he grumbled. "I'm bloody roasting here."

"How long's a piece of string?" Harry growled to a blank look from the gap-toothed young outlaw. "If they left their lodgings near Ferrybridge at dawn they should be here any minute. So shut up and watch the road."

As he stopped speaking the sounds of a rider approaching reached them. "Robin, you watch the merchant. Arthur, you watch the guard on the far side of the road. I'll take the other guard, nearest me. All right?" The two young men nodded and Harry gestured Arthur to take up a position on the opposite side of the road. Robin was sent forward ten paces to hide in a dense clump of gorse, the plants' bright yellow flowers almost glowing in the bright sunshine.

Before long their target came into sight. Sure enough, there was one rider, a small, weasel-faced man, finely dressed in colourful clothes and flanked by a couple of broad young mercenaries on foot either side of him.

Robin took little notice of the little merchant, despite Harry's orders, dismissing him out of hand and concentrating on the guards who looked much more threatening.

Both were tall – almost as tall as Robin himself. They had decent quality light armour and weapons – one wore a sword, while the other had a wicked looking mace hanging at his side. The thought of such a brutal crushing weapon making contact with his head made Robin wince.

Harry Half-hand waited until the travellers were a few paces along the road in front of him then stepped from behind the big oak, his sword drawn and brandishing his hook menacingly, knowing the sight of it often made men nervous.

"Hold!" he commanded, as Arthur and Robin, longbows aimed at the group, stepped from their hiding places in front of the merchant's party.

The merchant looked shocked at the sight of the outlaws, the mercenaries just looked angry to have been ambushed so easily as they turned to face Harry.

"You two – drop the weapons," the outlaw ordered the guards. "Let's make this nice and easy. If any of you make a wrong move, my pals there" – he gestured towards the grim faced Robin and Arthur – "will put a nice thick arrow in your guts."

The merchant glared at Harry. "You want my purse, I assume, wolf's head?"

The outlaw grinned. "Aye that I do, so toss it over here and you can be on your way, and no one gets my hook in their face. You two" – he gestured at the two mercenaries. "Drop your weapons and move on. I promise you, we won't harm you and, let's be honest, you don't have many options anyway."

The guards looked at each other, and then the eldest shrugged and dropped his mace on the ground with a heavy thud. "They could have shot us already if they wanted us dead," he told his companion, who nodded agreement and dropped his own weapon.

As the two men walked warily off along the road, Harry nodded in satisfaction. "Now we just need your purse, merchant."

Arthur had kept his bow trained on the mercenaries as they moved further along the path. Robin could see the merchant had tears in his eyes and dismissed him as a weakling, training his bow again on the unarmed guardsmen who were, by now, a good thirty paces away.

"Here!" From the corner of his eye Robin saw the merchant reach into his belt for his purse and relaxed his aim. This had been even easier than he'd expected. Adam would be pleased with them…hopefully the others had been as lucky in their robbery of the rich lady in Pontefract.

Distracted, he saw Arthur's eyes grow wide in horror, and turned to look at Harry Half-hand.

The older man was lying in the dirt of the forest floor, blood bubbling from his mouth, a small dagger in his windpipe.

Still, Robin didn't see the merchant as a threat, his eyes searching the trees for the source of the dagger, until the horseman suddenly kicked his mount and bolted along the road towards the startled mercenaries.

Arthur loosed his arrow, the shaft, as thick as a man's thumb, slamming into the merchant's back just under his neck, throwing the rider onto the ground. The horse ran on for a few seconds before it came to a halt and stood, head bowed, oblivious or uninterested in its master's death.

"What the hell?" Robin cried, his bow still trained on the confused mercenaries who continued to back away along the trail. "What happened?" he demanded, looking at Arthur.

"You were supposed to be watching the merchant!" Arthur retorted. "Harry told you! The little bastard had a throwing dagger in his belt! He got Harry with it!"

The two guardsmen, desperate just to get away from this alive, had reached a turn in the road and suddenly sprinted away, much to Robin's relief.

"Oh shit," he gasped, rushing over to the downed outlaw. "He's dead!"

"Of course he's fucking dead!" Arthur shouted. "He's got a dagger in his throat – makes it hard to breathe! Come on."

The young man took the weapons from Harry's corpse then jogged over to the merchant he'd shot.

"Grab the horse," he told Robin, who, dazed, moved to do as he was told while Arthur used his dagger to cut the merchant's purse from his belt. "Right, let's go."

"What about Harry?" Robin asked.

"Unless you want to carry him – or dig him a grave" – Arthur growled – "leave him for the wildlife. And next time you're told to watch someone – bloody watch them!"

CHAPTER FIVE

"Robert the Bruce? Fuck off!"

"I'm telling you," Friar Tuck nodded his tonsured head solemnly, despite Will Scarlet's disbelieving laughter. "That's what people are saying: the earl of Lancaster has been seeking an alliance with the Scots."

It was a warm, humid night in the second week of June. The forest was pitch black and silent for miles around apart from the sounds of insects and laughing outlaws. Harry Half-hand's death was mostly forgotten by everyone except Robin already. Life was cheap when you were an outlaw.

Robin knew the man's death was his fault though – his lack of experience had made him focus on the two mercenaries, rather than seeing *everyone* as a threat, even the apparently harmless merchant. He wouldn't make the same mistake again.

The campfire blazed merrily in the middle of the small clearing, for light rather than heat, and Adam Bell shrugged his shoulders, looking at Tuck seriously.

"I wouldn't blame him if he's been talking to the Bruce."

Scarlet leaned forward on tree stump he was sitting on, his laughter replaced by indignation. "You wouldn't blame him? He's supposed to be defending our people from those bastard Scots, not forming alliances with them!"

Robin watched as Adam took a drink from his ale. He was surprised to see his leader glaring at Will – one of his most trusted confidants – with a look of utter disdain, but the expression only lasted a moment before it was replaced with a smooth smile, and no one else seemed to notice.

"Perhaps," Adam grunted, "the earl of Lancaster thought enlisting the aid of the Scots an acceptable price to pay in order to remove England's worthless King? Sometimes a leader has to work with people he knows are beneath him."

Robin was watching closely again as Bell's eyes lingered on Will scornfully, but Friar Tuck's booming voice drew everyone's eyes to him.

"That sounds like Prior de Monte Martini trusting me with his wagon," he laughed, "the good lord knows he saw me as being far beneath him."

"He was right an' all," Little John grinned.

Robin and the rest of the outlaws smiled at that as Tuck continued.

"I wonder what happened when those two guards got back down to Lewes and told the bastard his cart had been stolen."

* * *

After the raid on the prior's money cart the two surviving guards decided it might be safer if they returned to where they started their journey, in York, rather than going on , empty handed, to de Monte Martini away down in Lewes with the bad news. So, it took some time before news reached the prior of the theft. When he discovered it was Adam Bell and his gang who had stolen all his money he was enraged even further.

"Adam Bell! Bell has my money! Do you know how much money there was in that cart?" de Monte Martini roared at his bottler, Ralph, throwing the letter from York onto his desk. "Two hundred marks! That's how much!" He began pacing the chamber furiously, wringing his hands as he did so.

Ralph was astonished at the figure. Two hundred marks was a substantial amount of money, even by the prior's standards. He simply nodded dumbly, trying his best not to irritate the irate de Monte Martini.

Ever since the prior had been attacked by Robin, he had felt a burning, and thoroughly un-Christian desire, for revenge. It had taken weeks for his shattered nose to heal well enough for him to breathe properly, and even now, he knew he would bear the disfigurement for the rest of his life.

"Do you know what makes it worse, Ralph? When that bastard Robin Hood disappeared, the rumours in Wakefield said he had joined Adam Bell's gang. So that young piece of scum breaks my nose, then escapes justice and now he's sitting enjoying my money!" The prior picked up a silver goblet, which Ralph had just filled with wine for him, and smashed it against the wall. "Summon that bailiff from Wakefield! If he won't put in the effort to catch those outlaws on his own, maybe I should offer him a reward to do it!"

The bottler needed no more persuading to flee the room.

* * *

The weather grew even hotter as summer fully settled on Barnsdale, the trees and bushes becoming thick with foliage and flowers to hide in, and many ripe, juicy berries to eat.

Like the flora, Robin had also grown and matured during his weeks in the greenwood.

The time he spent every day, sparring with John, Will and the other men, and firing the great longbow at straw targets hung from trees had changed Robin in ways he had never foreseen. Physically, his body had become a hard, fighting machine: he had enormously powerful arms and shoulders from a young age, thanks to his practice with the bow, but now the rest of his body had filled out with muscle too, yet he retained the grace and speed he had always been blessed with. He could outfight, and outshoot, most of the other outlaws in practice now.

He had also taken to questioning Adam about military tactics. It was never mentioned explicitly, but Adam accepted that the outlaws knew he had been a soldier at some point in his past, and he was open to discussing the strategic aspects of it with any who had an interest. Until Robin had joined the group, only Will had really had the desire, or aptitude, to understand cavalry formations, use of terrain, siege warfare or any number of other martial topics. While Will had been a mercenary previously, so already had an idea of things like how to use higher ground, Robin had never thought about such things until he'd become an outlaw.

Adam took Will Scarlet aside one warm afternoon as the men were practising. Robin was sparring with Little John, both men using wooden swords, and Bell watched with interest.

"What do you make of our new recruit?"

Will looked in Robin's direction, as the young man expertly deflected a thrust from John and stepped inside the bigger man's guard with a "killing" blow of his own.

"He's improved a lot since he joined us a few weeks ago," Will shrugged. "But you could see from the day he first came here that he had something about him none of these other lads have."

Bell nodded agreement. "And yet, don't you find it remarkable just how *much* he's improved in such a short space of time?"

The sounds of Robin and John sparring ferociously, the grunting of exertion and the clicking and thumping of wood upon wood filled the air. Most of the other outlaws had stopped their own practising to watch, as the giant and the newcomer traded blow after blow, neither managing to land a clean strike for a long time.

"What are you getting at?" Will wondered. "You think he's not the innocent little villager he says he is?"

Bell crossed his arms, fascinated by the sparring match before them. "I don't know," he admitted. "His story checks out, as far as I can tell. And yet . . . give him a few months and he'll be a better swordsman, or archer, than anyone else in this group."

There was a loud cheer as Little John, tiring, suddenly dropped his practice sword and rushed forward, grinning madly, to grab Robin in a great bear hug.

"Yield!" the giant roared with breathless laughter, as his opponent's face turned crimson and he gasped in surrender.

"You alright, there, Hood?" Matt Groves cackled, looking around at the laughing outlaws. "Maybe we should start calling *you* Scarlet, instead of Will. Your face looks like it's about to explode!"

Robin collapsed onto the grass beside John, panting like a thirsty dog. "Fuck…off…Groves…!"

"Aye, fuck off Matt," Little John roared with a massive grin, slapping Robin on the back defensively. "You sour faced little twat."

Will looked at Adam with a small smile. "Who knows? Maybe he's King Arthur reincarnated and that's why he's got all this potential. I'll tell you something though: he's not just going to be a good fighter – he's going to be a leader one day too. The men have all taken to him like an old friend."

"All except Matt," Adam grunted, gesturing towards the surly Groves as the men lost interest and returned to their own sparring matches.

Will nodded agreement. "Aye . . . but Matt doesn't like *anyone*."

"Time I reminded them all who's in charge then, eh?" Bell grunted and walked over to Groves, taking his wooden sword from him and turning to face Robin who still lay on the ground catching his breath with a smile on his face.

Adam Bell never sparred with the other men, instead practising in private with Will or John. Robin assumed this was so no one could ever publicly best Adam, which would perhaps undermine his authority.

"Right, Robin, time I tested you myself. Grab your weapon, lad."

Robin looked up in surprise, before scrambling to his feet and lifting his heavy practice sword from the grass. He had started sparring with a wooden sword that was nearly double the weight of his steel sword. Will had shown him this trick, telling him the invading Roman legionaries used to train with similar weapons a thousand years ago. Once your body got used to using such a heavy sword in practice, fighting with a lighter steel sword in the heat of a real battle was much easier.

Not all of the outlaws practised with the heavy wooden swords though – Will and Adam were the only other two who bothered. Little John tended to stick to his enormous quarterstaff, young Gareth didn't have the strength, and Tuck simply said it was too much effort since he was a man of peace with a group of strong outlaws around to defend him in a fight.

Robin had struggled greatly with the heavy weapon at first, despite his thickly muscled arms, but Will assured him it would be worth it in the long run, so he persevered with it, suffering defeat after defeat in his bouts with the other men. Eventually, though, he became used to the heavy practice sword, wielding it almost as easily as he could one of normal weight.

As their leader walked into the practice area, rolling his shoulders and swinging his arms to warm the muscles up, the other men looked at each other in surprise. Of all the people Adam could have sparred with, they didn't expect him to pick Robin Hood – simply because they thought Robin might win.

Will shrugged as Little John threw him a questioning look, while Robin, also looking perplexed, moved across, set his feet in a defensive stance and prepared to take on his captain.

The young man knew that Adam was not using one of the heavier practice swords, as he was – Matt Groves never did. Robin was also out of breath and tired from his efforts of the past hour or so, while Bell was fresh. He realised Bell intended to send a message to the men here. At his expense.

A light rain started to fall as the two combatants began to circle one another, Bell making the odd feint or lunge to warm his muscles up, while Robin was content to move and watch, trying to get the measure of his opponent, enjoying the cooling shower after his exertions sparring with John.

Bell flicked his sword almost impossibly fast at Robin's midriff, but, in a blur, Robin parried the blow, reversed his weapon and aimed his own, blocked, attack at Bell's stomach and the two men fell apart, both breathing a little heavier.

Although Adam had watched his young recruit's progress, he found it disconcerting to finally come up against Robin's astonishingly fast reflexes. He had hoped to gain a significant advantage by using the lighter sword, but all it seemed to do was even things up somewhat.

Little John had often told Robin of Adam's skill as a swordsman. The big man had been in countless battles beside his leader, seeing at first hand how fast, agile, strong and utterly ruthless he was. But Robin could see the trepidation in Bell's eyes – his first attack had been easily rebuffed and it had shaken the man.

For a few minutes more they sparred, the anger growing in Adam's eyes as he realised he might not be able to beat the young yeoman.

Robin's adrenaline was pumping, as he fended off Bell's attacks, but he held himself in check. He felt like he could explode into a combination of moves his rival would have no defence against, but he knew beating the outlaw leader would be a huge mistake.

He wanted Adam to respect him, value him – teach him his skills.

He did not want Adam to fear him or feel Robin's presence undermined him.

His eyes took on a hunted, fearful look, as he wiped the rain from his forehead with his sleeve then, with a bellow, swung a wide blow at Bell's left side, but his right foot suddenly slipped on the wet grass. Bell easily warded off the half-completed swing and stepped forward to hammer his sword against his hapless opponent's ribs. Robin collapsed on the wet grass with a cry, his hand grasping feebly at his injured side – it felt like Bell had cracked a couple of his ribs.

The outlaws cheered, and Bell smiled at them triumphantly. Little John clapped him on the shoulder in congratulation as he walked past to kneel by Robin.

"You all right, lad? That sounded painful."

"It *was* painful!" Robin forced himself to his feet, still clutching his side, and looked at Bell. "You got me, Adam – too fast for me." He grimaced in pain, and moved out of the practice area, grasping a jug of ale someone thrust at him.

The other men began talking excitedly about the fight, recounting the best bits, embellishing things so it sounded like a much more exciting contest than it had actually been.

Adam came over and sat beside Robin. A mug of ale had been handed to him too. "That was a good fight, lad. I almost thought you were going to be too good for me there."

Robin took a huge pull of his ale, shaking his head with a grimace at the burning pain in his ribcage. "I've been practicing, and picked up a lot since I joined your group, but I knew I couldn't beat you – John's told me how tough you are in a fight."

Bell smiled graciously and took a drink himself. "Anything can happen in a fight Robin, the most important thing is to stay alert. I knew you'd make a mistake eventually – I just had to make the most of it when you did."

Robin downed the last of his ale and was thankful as the rest of the men gave up their training for the day and came over to congratulate Bell on his victory. The atmosphere had grown tense during the fight, the outlaws sensing trouble should it not go the right way. Now that Adam had won it was as if the tension had been released and the men felt like celebrating without even understanding why.

Bell himself truly believed he had bested Robin, as did Little John and the other outlaws. Only Will Scarlet looked thoughtfully at Robin, but his green eyes were unreadable, as always.

CHAPTER SIX

Matilda was in the forest, not far from the village, collecting wood for her father when she felt hands suddenly grab her around the waist. She gave a small cry and tried to elbow her attacker in the ribs desperately.

"Ow! It's me, Matilda, calm down!"

The hands lost their grip and Matilda spun round, panting. "Robin, what the hell are you doing?"

Suddenly, sneaking up on her didn't seem like such an amusing idea, and Robin raised his hands defensively. "Sorry. I was just playing."

Matilda's eyes blazed furiously and she set her fists on her hips. "Well it wasn't funny you bloody idiot. Everyone in the village has been wary since Mayday when you punched the prior – the bailiff keeps coming round hassling us. I thought you were one of his men."

Robin hadn't even thought of that, and he apologised again, taking the girl's hands in his own and drawing her into a hug.

"Fine. Don't ever do that again though." To emphasise her point, Matilda kneed him playfully in the bollocks, but smiled and hugged him tighter as he squealed. "How have you been? I've missed you; it's been weeks since I saw you."

They began to walk through the forest, hand in hand, and Robin told Matilda about his life with Adam Bell's men, assuring her the outlaws weren't all murderous rapists, and trying to convince her he was having a great time.

As the outlaws had begun to accept him, so came more responsibility and Robin had found himself leading small raiding parties as they targeted rich merchants travelling through the forests of Yorkshire. By the summer solstice, most of the outlaws had come to see Robin as third only to Adam Bell and Little John.

Although Will Scarlet had great experience, and the men trusted him, not many actually liked him as a result of his brooding, dark presence. Robin, on the other hand, was a pleasant companion, full of laughter and jokes. Granted, he could retreat into his own little, grim world on occasion, but so could all of the outlaws when they thought of their families, friends and lives left behind, often as the result of some lord's injustice.

Will seemed content to accept Robin's rise over his own social status, but Adam Bell was careful never to send the two men on a raid together.

Friar Tuck and some of the other men had gone off to Bichill for some supplies today; a warm morning, the sun high in the sky and only a gentle westerly breeze to stop the temperature becoming unbearable. The gang had plenty of food in their larder though, and nothing else to do, so Adam had allowed Robin to come to Wakefield to visit his family and friends.

"I miss you," he told Matilda. "I wish I could see you more. But if the bailiff's men are still coming round hunting for me, I'd be putting you in danger if anyone saw us together."

"Yes, yes, I know that," Matilda snapped, flashing him a wry smile. "My mother never tires of telling me about the dangers of Robin Hood. And she's right. It would be nice to see you more though." Her eyes glittered and she gave a laugh. "What about Much though? He's always sneaking around my da's fletching shop, asking if I've seen you."

Robin grinned. "I'll go an' see him later on. Adam said I could spend the day here as long as I was careful, so I visited my ma and da and Marjorie, then came to find you."

Matilda gave him a questioning look. "Adam Bell worries you might come to harm?"

Robin laughed. "Of course he does. He wouldn't want to lose one of his most deadly fighters would he?" Matilda's eyebrows arched and he continued, smiling ruefully, "Not really, he's just worried I might give them away if I'm caught."

Matilda returned his smile sardonically. "'Deadly fighter', eh? As modest as ever, then."

The two continued walking, simply enjoying each other's presence, as they realised they'd come close to the village again. The mill came into sight, and Robin nodded towards it. "Maybe we could see Much now. I'll stay here out of sight, if you could tell him to come over?"

"Or maybe we could do something more interesting, for a while?" Matilda moved in close, eyes wide, pressing her small breasts against him, and cupped his balls in her hand through his breeches.

Robin felt himself stiffen almost instantly, and he grinned, pulling the girl down onto the grass beside him.

They kissed passionately, hands frantically removing each other's clothes, until Matilda climbed on top of him and he gasped as he felt himself slide deep inside her.

Matilda arched her smooth back with a wanton smile, as Robin squeezed her breasts and thrust himself almost desperately into her. Stuck in a forest with a gang of ugly men for weeks, Robin had become more than a little frustrated, and now, with this beautiful girl grinding herself into him, he couldn't contain himself for long. With an explosive gasp of pleasure, he shot his seed inside her.

Matilda leaned down and they kissed gently for a little while, embracing happily.

"Enjoy that?" the girl asked with a grin.

"Enjoy it?" Robin laughed. "It was unbelievable! The bailiff could have turned up just then and I couldn't have stopped I was enjoying it so much."

Matilda laughed, rolling onto the grass to look contentedly up at the cloudless blue sky for a moment. "Shall we head to the mill and find Much?"

"Aye," Robin agreed, pulling his trousers back on. "Hopefully he's" –

A terrible scream of pain shattered the peaceful afternoon air and the lovers looked at each other in horror.

"It came from the mill!" the young outlaw cried, frantically buckling his sword back around his waist. "Wait here!" He sprinted off, still half naked, towards the bridge that led to Much's home.

* * *

Thomas the miller screamed again as the bailiff slammed the heavy wooden mallet down onto his hand. Much was held back by two of the bailiff's men, as he struggled to somehow help his father who was bound hand and foot to one of his own chairs.

Henry the bailiff addressed Much again. "If you don't tell me where Hood's hiding, boy, your father won't have any hands left to work this mill."

The bailiff knew the miller's wife had died ten years earlier, and, since the mill was set apart from the village, no one would hear the agonized cries and come to see what was happening.

Much, tears in his eyes as he watched his father writhe against his bonds in agony, shouted in frustration at the bailiff. "I don't know where Robin is, I haven't seen him in weeks, since he joined Adam Bell's gang! I swear it! Leave my da alone, please Henry!"

The bailiff scowled at Much's denial. After having his nose smashed, the prior had demanded Henry bring Robin Hood to justice, offering him a nice sum of money to make it happen, and this had seemed the ideal way to locate the young outlaw. But this bastard Much was no help at all. He raised the mallet again, but this time he cracked the miller on the side of the face with it.

"Stop it!" Much screamed again, arms and legs thrashing as he tried to reach his father. "I swear to you I don't know where Robin is, you need to look for Adam Bell!"

Henry had to accept Much really didn't know anything helpful. He would have given Hood up by now if he did. The bailiff dropped the mallet onto a table, and Much sobbed in relief, his father lying on the floor, bloodied and dazed, but alive at least.

"Well then, neither of you are any use to me, but I can't leave you around to cause trouble – can't have the people of Wakefield complaining about me to the earl can I? He listens to the peasants too much, that one. We'll have to make it look like outlaws broke in and killed you both…"

The bailiff drew his dagger from his belt and slammed the small blade straight into the groaning miller's heart. Leaving it there, he turned, slowly drew his sword from its fine leather sheath and rounded on the horrified Much with a wicked smile. "Your turn, boy."

The door to the mill burst open, almost torn off its hinges, as a great dark figure tore into the dimly lit room. Henry raised his sword instinctively, but the shadow man came in low, thrusting his own sword upwards into the bailiff's guts, tearing muscle and flesh as he pulled his blade free. The bailiff grabbed feebly at his torn body, and collapsed on the floor, blood pouring from his slack mouth, eyes staring helplessly up at his killer.

Much fell to his knees on the floor then too, gasping in shock and disbelief at what was happening in his home, as his captors released him so they could draw their own weapons against this unexpected attack. The two foresters moved apart and fell into a defensive stance, swords held ready to face the young man who stood with his head down, glaring menacingly at them, his massively muscled bare chest heaving with exertion, thick blood dripping from the end of his sword.

"There's two of us…" one of the men began, but Robin, moving impossibly fast, lunged forward and rammed the point of his sword under the man's face, right up through the top of his head.

As the second forester moved to engage him, Robin dragged his sword free and kicked viciously at the front of the next attacker's leg. The blow sent the man stumbling face first to the floor as his knee gave way and Robin rammed his blade into the man's side. As the forester hit the floor the young outlaw punched him in the back of the head with his left hand and, for a second, everything was still.

Matilda ran into the mill and stopped, holding a hand to her mouth, her eyes staring around in horror at the sight of the four dead men in the room.

Much began sobbing again, repeating the phrase, "Mary Mother of God," over and over, sometimes looking at his dead father, still impaled on the bailiff's dagger, sometimes looking at Robin in shocked disbelief.

"Much." Robin, starting to shake with shock himself as the adrenaline drained from his system, knelt down and placed a hand on his friend's shoulder. "You need to come with me. They're going to come back for you, with more men. The prior must have ordered this."

Much moved to sit by his dead father, sobbing uncontrollably, until Matilda came and put her arms around him.

"Robin's right," she whispered, tears of disbelief in her own eyes. "You have to leave. If the prior sent the bailiff here he won't let something like this go. He'll want to make sure you don't talk."

Much sat for a moment, then raised his head to glare at his childhood friend. "This is all your fault, none of this would have happened if you hadn't punched that fucking prior!"

Robin had no answer to his friend's accusing stare, so he stayed silent.

"Much, we don't have time for this now," Matilda told her friend gently. "Maybe it is Robin's fault, but more men will be coming looking for you now – the bailiff's dead! You have to go with Robin, or you'll be hanged for murder!"

Much nodded almost imperceptibly and, after a while, got slowly to his feet, his eyes never leaving his dead father's face. "Let me get my things, please . . ."

"Of course," Robin replied. "Take everything you can carry. Money, weapons, clothes, food. We can't come back here, ever. But hurry!"

As Much, dazed, moved to collect his things, Matilda faced Robin, confusion and disbelief plain on her lovely face. "You killed three men. I've never seen anything like it."

Robin sank to the floor, his hands shaking badly. "I know. Adam's men are good teachers. I've never killed anyone before. I just wanted to stop them from killing Much." His eyes filled with tears.

Matilda took his hand gently. "You did well Robin, you saved his life."

"Maybe." He looked over at the corpses of the men he'd killed, and hid his face in his hands. He felt like throwing up.

"I'm ready." Much came back into the room, his face bleak, and Robin stood up, wiping away his tears with his hand.

"Alright. Let's go and find Adam."

* * *

"My lords!" Sir John de Bek, a dark haired man of advancing years filled the room with his enormous baritone voice, calling the meeting to order. The gathered noblemen – barons, knights and bishops from all corners of the country, fell silent as every eye turned to de Bek, who appeared to be acting almost as a chancellor, as if this was some sort of unofficial northern 'parliament'.

"The Earl of Lancaster," Sir John continued, nodding towards the grim-faced earl at the head of the enormous wooden table, "has called us here to discuss a number of issues. Firstly: the issue of the Scots."

The magnates sat in silence as the earl's "chancellor" talked at some length of the threat from the Scots. "For years they have been raiding deep into our northern lands – it cannot be allowed to continue!" de Bek vowed passionately. "At the last meeting in May some of us signed a pact agreeing to defend each others' lands against the threat from Scotland. Now, the earl asks those of you who were not at that previous meeting to sign the same pact."

Sir William Deyncourt led a chorus of cheers in agreement and it was clear from the mood in the room there would be no problems with this proposal. There were some uneasy glances towards the Earl of Lancaster as rumours of his fraternizing with the Scots had been heard by everyone gathered there, but no one raised the issue. The earl was the one proposing an alliance against the Scots – why would he seek friendship with them at the same time? It seemed a ridiculous piece of gossip, probably put about by the royalists to damage Thomas's reputation.

De Bek nodded to himself in satisfaction. "Since we all seem happy enough with that, I shall move onto the next item on the agenda."

He glanced down at a sheet of parchment in front of him and read off it a list of grievances against the king, including unlawful banishments, unwise treaties signed with foreign nations and, most contentiously, the bad character of Edward's closest advisors: the Despensers.

Thomas of Lancaster watched the reactions of the gathered men as de Bek outlined the problems, noting with dismay that many of them – particularly Archbishop Melton of York, the most powerful of the prelates at the meeting – appeared uncomfortable at the accusations against the king.

He swore softly to himself – not only did he not seem to be getting the enthusiastic support he had hoped for, but some of the northern lords had failed to show up for the meeting. Sir Richard-at-Lee must have decided, like his order's Grand Prior, to side with the king, Lancaster thought, noticing the big Hospitaller's absence. It wasn't a major blow to the earl's plans: Sir Richard was only a minor noble, with small personal resources, wholly unlikely to sway the Hospitaller Order in England to stand against Edward.

Still, the more support Thomas could enlist the better, and the Crusader knight would have been an excellent man to have on-side when the fighting inevitably started. Damn him! What was wrong with these people that they wouldn't stand up against such a weak and ineffectual king?

As the magnates debated the idea of opposing the king and the Despensers the door to the room was suddenly thrown open and Sir Richard-at-Lee stormed in. The big knight was clad imposingly in a suit of chain mail, over which he wore the black mantle of his order, with its eight-pointed white cross emblazoned boldly on the chest. As he pulled off his gauntlets his grey-bearded face was scarlet with fury.

There was confusion around the table, as those men who didn't recognise the stern-faced knight panicked, wondering if the king's men had come to put a stop their 'northern parliament'.

"My lords!" Sir Richard, oblivious to the effect he'd had on the room, strode to the head of the table, nodding a greeting to the Earl of Lancaster who rose and tried to calm the nervous lords.

As it became clear the Hospitaller was not there to arrest them, the noblemen quietened down, wondering what was going on.

"My lords," Sir Richard began again, looking around the room, "some of you know me, and some of you don't. I am Sir Richard-at-Lee, Commander of Kirklees. I fought in the Holy Land and Rhodes as a knight of the Order of St John – the Hospitallers." He stood proudly before them, hands spread wide as the rage left his voice to be replaced by outraged disbelief. "Although I am a Hospitaller first and foremost, I have also been a loyal subject to King Edward, and his father before him – indeed, after the Earl of Lancaster's last meeting a month ago, I wasn't even sure I should come here to this one, for fear of displeasing the king."

There were quiet mutters of understanding at that, as many of the gathered lords had harboured similar thoughts, only turning up for this meeting as a courtesy to the wealthy earl who was, after all, Steward of England.

"However," Sir Richard went on, "in return for my loyalty, our monarch has allowed his – current – favourite, Hugh Despenser, to imprison my youngest son in Cardiff castle on a trumped up charge of murder!"

Sensing an opportunity, Lancaster roared indignantly, demanding to hear the facts of the furious Hospitaller's case against his hated enemy.

As it turned out, the father of the young knight Sir Richard's son had – accidentally – killed in the jousting tournament was a family friend of the younger Despenser. Richard's son, Simon, had been arrested and was now being held in custody by men acting in the name of the Despenser who, on hearing what had happened from his friend, Charles of Bodmin, had demanded bail monies from Sir Richard of one hundred pounds.

"How am I to pay that?" Richard demanded. "Hospitallers take a vow of poverty when they join the Order. I can't pay a ransom like that! Why is King Edward allowing this?"

Despite the knight's righteous anger, the king did not actually have anything directly to do with the imprisonment – Sir Richard just blamed him by extension of his favour for the Despensers.

"This is outrageous!" Sir John de Bek cried indignantly, while others, even the wealthiest, gasped in shock at the enormous bail demands and the room was thrown into a noisy babble again.

"This is exactly why we are here today, my friends," the Earl of Lancaster shouted as the clamour calmed at last. "Sir Richard-at-Lee isn't the first innocent man to feel the illegal force of the Despensers' royally-sanctioned greed, and, unless we stop pissing about here, he won't be the last either!" He walked around the table, meeting the eyes of those he knew were undecided whether to support him or not. "Will you sit by and allow another of the king's unworthy favourites to ruin our country? I warn you now – the Scots aren't the biggest threat our people face. The Despensers are!"

There were angry shouts of agreement, some of them from men who had been undecided at the start of the meeting, and Thomas walked back to stand next to Sir Richard-at-Lee, his eyes fierce. "I will stand beside the commander of Kirklees in the fight for justice against these leeches – will you?"

Sir John de Bek called the assembly to order and asked the clergymen to retire to the rector's house to consider what they would do, while the lay lords would deliberate where they were. It was another unusual move, copying parliamentary procedure and didn't go unnoticed by the magnates, some of which were impressed while others were somewhat outraged at what they saw as Lancaster's arrogance.

When the deliberations were over, the earl was again disappointed by the reluctance of the northern and western lords to agree to his proposals. Although many of the men who had attended the meeting pledged themselves to the destruction of the Despensers, many others – some of whom suspected the rumours of Thomas's overtures to the Scots may have some truth to them – refused to follow his lead.

The prelates, led by the Archbishop of York, agreed to aid Thomas as best they could against the threat of the Scots, but they decided to reserve judgement on John de Bek's accusations against the king until the next – official – parliament.

It was not a complete failure, the earl, mused as the gathering broke up and the men made their way home again. Yes, many of the most powerful lords would probably never go against the king, but some new friends had been made today and, he knew, the more support he could muster, the more likely it was the king would take heed of them.

Sir Richard-at-Lee nodded a distracted farewell to Thomas, and the earl pulled him gently aside.

"What will you do about your son?" he wondered, apparently genuine concern written on his long face.

Sir Richard sighed, his eyes heavy with stress and exhaustion. "The abbot of St Mary's in York has offered to loan me the money to pay Simon's bail. It's a massive amount, I fear I'll never be able to repay it but…I need to get my son out of jail then, hopefully once all this is sorted, Despenser will be forced to return the money. It's extortion, nothing more!"

The earl narrowed his eyes. Abbot Ness of St Mary's had not said a word during the meeting – Thomas knew the man was a staunch Royalist, and today had only reinforced that opinion.

"I have no need to know what terms you agreed to the abbot's loan under," Lancaster clapped the big knight on the shoulder. "You should be wary of him though – I fear you may be swapping one evil debt for another."

Sir Richard shrugged and rubbed at his eyes. "What's done is done," he muttered. "I must go now to free my son. I thank you for your words in there and, you can be sure, for what little it's worth – you will have my sword at your side against these bastard Despensers!"

CHAPTER SEVEN

The outlaws were happy to take Much into their group. He was good with the longbow, knew the forest well, and his outgoing nature made him popular with the men. Despite the reasons for his joining the gang, Robin was pleased his friend was with them. Although it had taken a few days grieving, Much had finally forgiven him for his father's murder – the bailiff had killed his da, not Robin. If he hadn't turned up when he had, Much would be dead now too – Robin had saved his life.
To Robin's great relief, then, they were still friends.
"What's the story with Adam?" Much asked one afternoon while they were out hunting together.
"I'm not sure," Robin admitted. "Everyone's heard of him – he's famous. But there's more to him that he never lets on. Even Little John doesn't really know the full story. But Adam's more than just a yeoman turned outlaw. He's been a soldier at some point."
Much nodded. "Aye, and he's been a leader of soldiers too. You can see it in his bearing. All the stories of Adam Bell say he's a common outlaw, but he's a nobleman, it's obvious."
Again, Robin just shrugged. Much was right – Adam Bell carried himself like a nobleman, fought like a soldier, and was a military tactician. They also knew the stories of Bell had been told around campfires since long before they were born, which should make the outlaw leader at the very least in his sixties. Yet the man looked not much more than forty five summers.
The pair were silent for a while, as they made their way through the trees searching for game.
"Do you think that's a French accent he's got?" Much looked at Robin curiously. "He doesn't talk much, but when he does, I could swear he's got a funny accent."
Robin laughed softly, always aware, even subconsciously, of the sounds of the forest and alert against disturbing the natural rhythm needlessly. "You think Adam Bell, the Saxon outlaw hero, is actually a French nobleman?" He shrugged. "Who knows? I just assumed it was a Scottish or Welsh accent he had." Truthfully, there were so many variations in local dialects throughout the whole of the country, there was no way for most people to tell where a stranger came from, unless widely travelled themselves.
Much didn't reply. The suggestion that Adam was a noble was clearly absurd. Yet both men couldn't help wondering what Bell's real story was.
"We'll ask Will about it," said Robin. "He's closest to Adam. If anyone knows the story, Will . . . will . . . ?"
He looked at Much in mock confusion, and they grinned at each other. Just then a rabbit ran across their path but within a moment both men had pulled and released their arrows.
"That's another one for the pot!" Much hooted, as both arrows thumped home in their target.

When they returned to camp, Much and Robin found most of the outlaws had already eaten, so they prepared their catch and added it to the big stew pot over the fire.
As they settled down to eat, there was an urgent whistle and, for a split second, everyone froze.
"On your feet!" Will Scaflock hissed to the outlaws, shouldering his bow. The rest followed his example. Robin dropped his bowl of food and hushed Much who had no idea what was going on.
"Someone's come close to our camp," Robin whispered to his friend. "Grab your bow, you might need it again." He hastily kicked the campfire out, covering it to prevent any smoke, and tightened his gambeson.
Will and Little John efficiently directed men to positions around the camp.

The outlaws were silent, and well hidden amongst the thick undergrowth, the fading daylight helping to make the small clearing less noticeable, although the smells of recent cooking would lead any hunters straight to their camp.

Slowly, the sounds of a dozen or so men moving stealthily through the forest carried to the hidden outlaws. Low voices could be heard conversing and some of the men – the sheriff of Nottingham and Yorkshire's soldiers by their uniforms – stepped cautiously into the clearing, swords drawn and shields held ready.

Again, there was another whistle and the outlaws let fly a volley of arrows. Three of the soldiers collapsed to the forest floor, while a fourth screamed and grabbed at the shaft sticking from his thigh.

"Attack!" The sound of Adam Bell's voice carried loudly through the evening air and the outlaws fell upon the remaining soldiers.

Much hung back in confusion, not being a part of the well-trained fighting unit, but he watched in frightened fascination as he saw his boyhood friend Robin moving with astonishing speed and efficiency to dispatch one of the sheriff's men. Much's eyes swept over the battle, which the outlaws were winning easily, and settled on Adam Bell.

Bell had engaged the soldier's leader, a tall nobleman, with dark hair and a small, neatly trimmed moustache.

Much could see the noble mouthing the word, "You?" a shocked look on his face as Bell thrust his sword directly at his groin, seeking a quick killing blow. The man parried desperately and shouted something in a strange language; akin to that spoken by the nobles he'd seen visiting Wakefield – French? Much wasn't surprised when Bell grunted something back, apparently in the same dialect.

The outlaws were finishing off the other soldiers, and Adam Bell didn't take long to find an opening in his opponent's defence, raking his sword across the man's throat and slamming an elbow into his side, knocking him to the ground. The soldier spat a final, defiant sentence at the outlaw leader and then choked, eyes bulging in pain, as Adam Bell thrust his sword into his chest.

Robin and the others were already taking the weapons and armour from the corpses of the soldiers, but Much glanced over and saw Tuck watching Adam Bell, a surprised look on his face, which he quickly masked as he met Much's gaze.

"Good work, lads!" shouted Adam Bell, wiping his sword clean on his dead opponent's clothes, and ramming it back into its scabbard. "Get 'em stripped of valuables and dumped. Much – see if you can find yourself some armour and a decent weapon on one of these corpses. Will – you and John with me. We've got a prisoner. Let's find out what these bastards wanted in our forest."

Normally the outlaws would simply dump the corpses of men they killed in the forest for scavengers to find. But since Tuck had joined their group, he had insisted they bury the dead, in accordance with Christian custom. Although the outlaws were all Christian, they didn't enjoy digging holes for people who had tried to kill them, but Tuck was insistent and his personality was such that the men found themselves complying with his wishes.

Tuck himself never lifted a spade, but stood at the side offering blessings, and promising the cursing gravediggers rewards in heaven for their piety.

By the time the sheriff's men had all been buried in very shallow graves, Adam Bell had finished interrogating the prisoner – a straggler, captured as he took a piss, by Bell himself. Adam had let the man go after questioning, to carry the news of the outlaw's triumph back to Nottingham. Every victory like this added to their legend.

"They were after you, Master Much." The outlaw leader took a long drink of ale from his cup as he spoke but it was Robin he fixed his gaze on. "And your big mate here. Seems the prior sent some men to Wakefield to question you and your family, and none of them came back."

Robin nodded. "That's right, you know that Adam, we told you what had happened."

Bell grunted. "You told me there had been a fight. The way that soldier told it, you single-handedly carved up the bailiff and two of his best fighting men. Problem is – you didn't kill all three of them like you thought. One of them lived long enough to be found, and he gave a description of you." He grinned and raised his cup high. "I doubt we've heard the last of this either – those weren't just foresters, they were the sheriff's own soldiers. You've got the prior *and* the sheriff pissed off now, lad!" The other men cheered and raised their own cups in salute to Robin.

The young outlaw smiled nervously, and took a pull of his own ale, but could take little satisfaction from his leader's apparent pride in him. He had killed another man in the fighting tonight, but it didn't feel noble, or mighty. What worried Robin was the fact that this time hadn't felt horribly wrong, as it had when he slaughtered the men attacking Much. Although he hadn't gained any pleasure from tonight's violence, neither did he feel like throwing up, as he had after he rescued his friend.

Killing was just something that had to be done. Robin was shocked as he realised he was desensitized to the brutality of the outlaw lifestyle already. He looked at Tuck and was surprised to find the friar gazing back knowingly.

The rest of the men settled down to drink and enjoy their night, knowing the soldiers would not return for at least another day or two, by which time they'd be long gone to another part of the massive Yorkshire forest.

Tuck came over and sat beside Robin, chewing noisily as he tore another chunk from the leg of roasted venison he carried.

"I thought monks were supposed to live a life of austerity, Brother Tuck." Robin was annoyed at the man for imposing himself on him, but regretted his words instantly, as he felt a genuine friendship for the clergyman.

Tuck just laughed loudly, and took a long drink from his wine cup. "As you may have noticed, Robin, I'm not exactly the most orthodox clergyman you'll meet. And I'm a friar, not a monk." He winked and patted his large stomach as he took another bite of his venison. "I am a man of God though – if you feel the need to confess any sins, or just to talk, I'm here for you my son." He squeezed Robin's wrist and the sincerity in his eyes gave the young outlaw some comfort. The men may have been forced to live as thieves and killers, but they were bound to each other by friendship.

"No confession, Tuck, thank you. I'm doing what I can to survive, like all of us. I just can't take pleasure in killing."

Tuck nodded. "That's good. When a man loses himself in blood lust, he becomes nothing more than an animal."

Robin glanced over at Will, and Tuck followed his gaze. "Don't be too quick to judge that one, Robin. Who knows what he's suffered in his life to make him embrace violence so readily? I see a loyal and, deep down, good man, in Will Scaflock."

Robin was surprised to hear the friar defending Will, but shrugged his shoulders. "Maybe you're right. He's a good man to have on your side anyway."

The two men sat quietly for a while, eating and drinking, and enjoying the banter and songs of the other outlaws round the fire. It was a cool, clear evening in the forest, and Robin felt the stress of recent days drain away until he felt as happy as he had since becoming an outlaw.

As the men finished a ribald song, Tuck crossed himself in mock disgust, and Much came over to sit beside them. He looked around to make sure no one else was listening and said to Tuck, "So, what did that soldier say to Adam?"

For the first time since joining them, Tuck looked uncomfortable. "What soldier?"

"The one he killed, the captain of the sheriff's soldiers. He shouted something at Adam in some funny language. French maybe? You can speak French can't you? You clergymen can speak all sorts of languages. That soldier looked like he knew Adam."

Friar Tuck sighed heavily, nodding. "Yes, I can speak French, Much. And yes, that's the language Adam was talking in."

Robin was just as curious as his friend now. "What did he say then?"

Making sure Bell was well out of earshot, Tuck looked at the two younger men grimly. "The captain knew Adam all right. But from where, I have no idea. Before he killed him, the nobleman told our leader he would burn in hell for his betrayal. Whatever that might have been, who knows? He called him 'Gurdon'. I assume that's his real name."

Much looked confused, but Robin was nodding his head. "This makes sense. Adam Bell should be older. In all the stories he was just a yeoman too, but this man leading us is obviously a trained soldier – a knight. This explains how he's got us all working together to fight like a unit: it's second nature to him to train and lead soldiers."

Tuck agreed, but Much still looked puzzled. "That may be so, Robin, but if he's really someone else, why's he going around the forest telling everyone he's Adam Bell? It doesn't make sense."

The rest of the outlaw band took up another loud song, ale and wine and the high of their victory over the soldiers tonight making them merry.

Tuck helped himself to another swig of his own wine and looked earnestly at Much. "It's brilliant, what Adam's done here. Think about it. If an outlawed noble –a knight – was to look for help in the villages around Yorkshire, what do you think the people would do? They'd be straight to the Sheriff. Bell, or *Gurdon*, wouldn't last a week without the help of the locals. But the people of Wakefield know who Adam Bell is. They've all heard the tales round campfires just like this one. He's a hero. People want to help a man like Adam Bell – it's one in the eye for the nobles."

"You're right." Robin nodded at Tuck. "But if this is all true, where's the real Adam Bell? And how did a knight or whatever he is, like…him-" he nodded towards Adam, "manage to get everyone to believe he was really a folk hero?"

Tuck had been thinking about the same questions ever since he heard the sheriff's soldier shouting out Gurdon's real name. "I can't tell you where the real Adam Bell is. For all I know he never existed except in folk tales. Have you ever seen Adam Bell?"

Robin and Much shook their heads.

"Do you even know what he was supposed to look like? How tall was he? Did he have a beard or clean shaven? Blue eyes or brown?"

Again, Robin and Much shook their heads. The tales of Adam Bell never went into details of his physical characteristics, only his amazing deeds.

"You see, then?" Tuck slapped his knee. "It's not so hard to pretend to be someone when no one knows what you're supposed to look like!" He smiled at the two friends and grabbed another piece of meat from his wooden bowl, wiping his chin with the sleeve of his robe as the juices dribbled down his chin. "Brilliant, it really is brilliant what he's done."

The three men sat quietly again for a while, letting the sounds of the outlaws' feasting wash over them, and wondering about what they'd learned.

"Where does this leave us?" Much asked quietly, staring into the fire.

"For now," said Robin, "nothing changes. We carry on as before. If Adam was really a knight at one point, he's lived in Barnsdale for the past few years as a wolf's head. He has a lot he can teach us – about warfare and surviving as outlaws. I don't know about you, but I mean to take whatever I can from his lessons."

CHAPTER EIGHT

A few weeks passed and things seemed to continue as normal for the outlaws. They had again moved their camp to another part of the forest, and things were quiet, but Robin knew the peace wouldn't last long. Prior de Monte Martini seemed to have given up on the idea of hiring someone to hunt down him and Adam Bell – it must have cost too much – especially if the hunter failed, as Henry had. Certainly, since Robin had killed the bailiff, there had been no sign anyone else had come into Barnsdale looking for him.

Unknown to the outlaws, though, the prior had sent a letter to the sheriff demanding he uphold the king's peace and bring the wolf's heads to justice. Which was why the soldiers had been in the forest looking for Adam's gang a fortnight earlier.

Now, Sir Henry de Faucumberg, Sheriff of Nottingham and Yorkshire couldn't let the destruction of his men go unpunished; it would send the wrong message to the people of Yorkshire. He'd try again to capture or kill the outlaws somehow. It was just a matter of time.

Robin was repairing a hole in the roof of the makeshift shelter he shared with Much when Little John approached him.

"You heard the news, yet?"

Robin put down the timber and iron nails he was using and shook his head, knowing, from the look on John's face, something unpleasant was coming.

"The sheriff's made you a wanted man."

Robin didn't understand. "We're already wanted men. We're outlaws!"

"Up until now, we've just been normal outlaws. Now the sheriff's put a price on your head."

Robin was stunned. "A price?"

John put a big hand on his friend's arm. "Anyone who helps the sheriff capture you gets twenty pounds. And if it's an outlaw that turns you in, they'll be pardoned too."

Robin's blood ran cold. This was a disaster. Twenty pounds was a huge sum of money for most people in England, and the promise of a pardon would be just as attractive to outlaws who wanted nothing more than to go home to their families and live a normal life again.

"Who told you all this?"

"I went to Locksley today to visit a friend," John told him. "The whole village is buzzing with the news, Robin. People aren't openly saying they'll turn you in – they know you're part of Adam Bell's group and are afraid of what he might do if he's crossed. But sooner or later someone will decide it's worth the risk." He leaned in close to Robin and, in a low voice, said, "You're going to have to watch your back even with some of these lads. Not all of them are as honourable as me and Tuck!" He smiled at that, and slapped Robin's back, but they both knew there was a grain of truth in what he said. Although Robin was a popular man in the outlaw band, some of the men might see this as a golden opportunity.

"I'll be careful. Thanks for warning me. I'd better have a word with Adam about this; he's not going to be too happy at the thought of all the trouble I've brought down on us. God, he might even tell me to leave."

Little John grunted. "Don't worry about that, Robin. Adam knows you've got friends here now. We'll have your back no matter what happens. We might be wolf's heads, but some of us are still good men."

They grasped arms, and Robin went off to look for Adam, casting wary glances at the rest of the men, paranoia settling over him already. *Mary, mother of God,* he vowed silently, *I will earn myself a pardon! I can't go on living like this – I will, somehow, be pardoned!*

He searched the entire camp, but couldn't find Adam Bell. While he was wandering around he bumped into Will Scarlet.

"Have you heard about the price on my head?" Robin asked, wondering how this violent, quick tempered man would view the sheriff's bounty.

"I've heard." Will grunted. "But you're one of us now, Robin. You're probably wondering about some of the lads here – wondering if they'll turn you over to the sheriff."

Robin tried to keep his face impassive as Will carried on. "Maybe one of them will, but I don't think so. You know the stories of what Adam does to traitors – he won't stand for it. If one of these men turned you in Adam would have the rest of us hunt him down. His life wouldn't be worth living, money and pardon or not. Don't you worry – I'll be having words with everyone, let 'em know this is a brotherhood. We stick together. You stood up to that prior, bust his nose – that makes you a good man to my mind."

Robin was struck by the sincerity in Will's eyes. Will Scarlet, a man Robin always stepped carefully around, was vowing to put his life on the line for him.

"Thank you. You don't know how much it means to me to know you men are there for me."

Will smiled grimly. "Well, I feel a bit responsible, to tell the truth."

"How so?" Robin asked in surprise.

"If I hadn't been teaching you how to use a sword so well for the past few months, you'd never have been able to kill the bailiff and his men!" He laughed and slapped Robin on the arm, pushing past him. "Come on, I'm going fishing, you might as well come too unless you've got anything better to do."

In the months Robin had been an outlaw, he had never had a real conversation with Will Scaflock. Maybe today he'd find out what made this man tick.

As the pair sat on the grass with their rods in the river, they shared a large skin of strong ale together. The drink seemed to make Will relax more than Robin had seen in all his time with the group.

"What's your story, Will?" he asked. "It's obvious you've been a soldier. It's even more obvious you hate our noble rulers. How did you end up a wolf's head?"

For a minute or so, Will sat in silence, staring out across the water, which sparkled like gold as a bright afternoon sun shone down from above.

Then, quietly, he began to speak.

"I was a soldier," said Will. "A mercenary. I fought in many battles, in many different countries. France, Germany, I even fought alongside the Hospitaller knights in the Holy Land. I was a good soldier. I loved the life, I loved the danger. I loved the fighting. I never loved the killing though, not then. Although I was paid well to fight, I picked my wars – I only fought for causes, and men, I felt were honourable."

"Then, when I was back at home in Nottingham for a while, I met a girl. Her name was Elaine. I'd never met a girl like her. She was beautiful, with long brown hair and dark eyes, and we could spend hours together, just talking. We never got tired of each other's company," he smiled, picturing his wife, then his customary frown fell on his face again.

Will couldn't stand the thought of being away fighting in another far off place, away from Elaine. So he took a job as a forester, in Sherwood, to be close to her. It wasn't as exciting as being a soldier, but Scaflock was happy, and, for the first time in his life, content.

"We eventually married," Will said with a grunt, casting his line into the sluggish river again. "We had a small house in Nottingham. Then we had three children: two boys, Matthew and David, and a little girl, Elizabeth. My little beautiful Beth..." he stared out at the water, his eyes dull, the expression on his face almost childlike as he thought again of his daughter.

After a while Will seemed to come out of his reverie and carried on. "But the boys were getting bigger, and Elaine kept saying we needed a bigger house. She was right, but being a forester didn't pay well enough for us to move to anywhere else."

Then Will had heard that one of the nobles living in Hathersage was looking for bodyguards, and went to see him. The man knew him – Scaflock had fought under him in Damascus a few years before. He offered Will a job, with a much higher wage than he was getting as a forester, so he jumped at the chance.

"Christ, how I wish I'd never met that man!" Will hissed. "Roger de Troyes, his name was. He probably wishes he'd never met me either now…" a dark smile lifted the corners of his lips for a moment before he continued his tale.

Everything had gone well for a few months. It became clear why the nobleman needed a bodyguard – he was forever getting drunk and treating people like filth. Will had to restrain people from killing him quite a few times.

"He was an unpleasant bastard, he really was," Will grumbled. "But me and my family had moved to a bigger house in Hathersage, away from the stinking tanner's workshops and filth of Nottingham, and I needed the money he was paying me to pay my rent. So I just got on with it. I had to.

"Then one day, me and de Troyes were back in Nottingham at a feast thrown by the sheriff. No, not the same one that's there now, this was a few years ago before de Faucumberg got the job. Anyway, de Troyes and some of the other guests were getting drunker by the minute, as I sat in a corner making sure no one tried to kill him if he got to be too much of a pain in the arse."

Again, Will paused, replaying the moments in his mind – the moments that changed his life forever, and turned Will Scaflock into Will Scarlet.

"I went off for a piss," he went on, "and when I came back to the hall, he was nowhere in sight. I found him in a side room, with a couple of others, taking it in turns with this young girl. But the girl wasn't willing; she was crying, and trying to get these so-called noblemen off her.

"I dragged them off – they were so drunk they just laughed – and sent them back out to the hall to pass out. The girl was in shock, but I didn't know what to do. I'd seen women raped before, but during wars, in the heat of battle, not like this. She was breaking her heart, so I tried to calm her, and gave her some money – I thought she was just a serving girl, see – and went back out to make sure my piece of shit employer behaved himself for the rest of the night."

Robin was appalled, but he wasn't naïve. He knew things like this happened all the time, up and down the country. "The nobles can do what they like," he muttered in disgust.

"Exactly," Will snarled angry agreement. "If a nobleman wants to hump a serving girl – he does. If anyone tries to stop him, they get killed, or outlawed, or…you know, Robin! You're lucky your girl Matilda wasn't stuck in some brothel by that bastard prior, 'cause he could do you know. He could.

"Anyway, I thought everything was sorted out. Things went on as usual for a couple of weeks. Then . . .''

Will had gone to Nottingham to buy a new dagger. He was only gone a matter of hours. But when he got home to Hathersage…

"I found Elaine." Will whispered, his head drooping, the fishing rod in his hand completely forgotten. "She was lying on the floor, holding onto my little boy Matthew. They'd both been stabbed, over and over again. My other son David, he had only a single wound in his side, but it was deep and long and his blood was everywhere…Our servants….everyone, everyone in my house had been butchered. Even our pet dog had had its back broken. My entire family, wiped out…

"I couldn't take it all in," he looked at Robin with a look of disbelief on his weather beaten face. "My mind just snapped. I couldn't bear to look at it, I had to get away. It was as if I left my body. I don't even know where I went for the next few hours. I just remember waking up in an alley, with some beggar trying to steal my fancy new dagger.

"After that, I had nothing left to live for. My whole life had been stolen from me. Even if the law were interested – which they wouldn't be – my family were gone. I had nothing. I've…*got*…nothing any more."

Will never knew who had murdered his family, but it seemed obvious he had been the main target and the murderers would still be after him. For that reason he slipped into his employer, Roger de

Troyes's, house when he finally came to his senses, to see if – with his money and connections – de Troyes could help find out who had done this.

"I didn't expect his reaction," Will growled. "He was terrified when he saw me, obviously thought I would be dead. Before I could say anything he blurted out the whole story."

The girl de Troyes and his friends had raped wasn't a serving girl after all. She was another – very powerful – nobleman's daughter. When her father found out his girl had been raped at the feast, he demanded to know the story from Roger de Troyes, since he recognised de Troyes from her description.

"De Troyes said it was me!" Will exploded, jumping to his feet and hurling the fishing rod onto the grass. He turned back to Robin, his fists clenched in rage. "That noble scum blamed me for the rape! I had *stopped* the bastards from brutalizing her any more, I'd tried to comfort her . . . yet her father had come to *my* house and butchered *my* family!"

In a fury Scaflock had drawn his dagger and, seeing his death coming, de Troyes begged forgiveness. "Said he was sorry for blaming me for the rape, offered to pay me fortunes to leave, and cried that he was my friend really." Will slumped back onto the grass beside Robin and held his head in his hands, tears coursing down his face. "Of course I killed him, then and there: slit his throat with my dagger. But it didn't really make me feel much better.

"I would have gone after the man whose daughter had been raped – the man who had killed my family. But in my blind rage I'd been too hasty: I'd killed de Troyes without even asking him who the man was. He might have blurted it out when he was confessing, but I couldn't remember if he had or not. If he did, it's never come back to me."

When he left de Troyes house, Will was covered in blood, wild eyed and crying to himself like a wounded beast. Of course people saw him, and knew his face – Hathersage being a small place.

He moved from place to place for a long time, but the memory of his butchered family would never let him find peace. Visions of the bloody murder scene woke him in the night and haunted his days.

"The only thing that keeps me going is my rage," Will said matter-of-factly. "My hatred for the real scum in our society: the rich and so-called *noble-* men. I'd take my own life and pray I'd meet my family in heaven, but I plan on killing as many of those fucking "noble" parasites as I can before God judges me."

Will sat in silence for a long time after he finished his tale, staring out at the river, the tears he had shed drying slowly in the warm breeze. Robin kept his peace, knowing there was nothing he could say that would make his brooding companion feel any less empty.

Eventually, Will reached for the ale skin again and took another long pull. He forced a bleak smile. "That's my story. I might not be the most sociable outlaw in Adam's band, but you know you'll always be able to count on me if there's any noblemen after your hide."

Robin returned the smile. "I hope you find some peace, Will."

Scarlet just grunted, but the pair recast their fishing lines and talk drifted to more mundane matters – the quality of the fish in the river and the warm weather they had enjoyed so far this year. Little John eventually joined them with a jug of ale of his own and the intense bond of camaraderie Robin had briefly shared with the taciturn Will passed – the young outlaw wondered if he'd ever feel such a bond of friendship with the man again.

Tuck's words had proved correct though, Robin mused. There were certainly hidden depths to Will Scarlet. His rage was understandable given the horrors he had suffered, but would his anger consume him in the end?

* * *

"Move aside!" Sir Richard, dressed in his most impressive Hospitaller armour roared at the two guardsmen, who shared a nervous glance at the sight of the two riders coming towards them.

Even their huge horses wore coats of mail covered with mantles of black and white, while the men themselves seemed to be dressed ready for battle.

"Stand aside!" the knight shouted again, removing his helmet to reveal his grey-bearded face. "My name is Sir Richard-at-Lee. Your lord" – his mouth twisted in disgust as he spat the word – "is expecting me. I bring the bail monies for my son who has been unlawfully imprisoned here!"

The two guards had been told someone might come to pay the bail for the young man from up north, so they nodded respectfully at the knights and stepped aside.

Sir Richard had travelled a few days earlier to St Mary's abbey in York, where he had collected the money Abbott Ness had promised to loan him. From there, he had come to Glamorgan as fast as possible; every minute his son was imprisoned felt like an hour to the fiercely protective big knight.

Richard and his sergeant – Stephen – pulled their swords from their scabbards and handed them over to the guards, who waved them through the gatehouse.

The steward of the castle had been warned of their approach, and he appeared now to greet them, a pair of stable boys rushing over to take their horses to be fed and watered. The Hospitallers lifted heavy saddlebags from their mounts and glared at the steward, a haughty, proud looking thin man of about forty years.

"You must be the commander of Kirklees," said the man, a heavy Welsh accent making him hard to understand, squinting in the bright late-afternoon sunshine. "I bid you welcome."

"Never mind that bollocks," Sir Richard cut the man off. "I'm here to pay your lord for the return of my son. Where is he?"

The steward looked irritated by the knight's rudeness. "My lord Despenser is away with the king. I am his steward here, I act in his name. As for your son, he has been well looked after. If you will follow me to the great hall, I have sent word for him to be brought to meet us there."

The castle, of motte-and-bailey design and built on the site of an old Roman fort, was hugely impressive, in comparison to Sir Richard's own rather modest fortress. It was manned by a large garrison, in response to trouble with the locals who disliked their Despenser lord, and the guards were a highly visible presence as the three men walked along the corridors to the great hall.

"Does your lord make a habit of extortion?" the big knight demanded.

The steward never turned as he continued walking, "Your son has been accused of murder, my lord. It is entirely your choice to pay the bail fee – you can leave him here until a judge arrives from the King's Bench and he can receive a fair trial, as the law demands."

"How long will that take?"

"Maybe a few months," the steward shrugged, pushing open the door to the hall which was empty apart from five guardsmen, armed with pikes. "Maybe much longer – who knows?" He turned and smiled. "These judges are very busy men."

Sir Richard wanted to punch the smug bastard, but he noticed his son, who looked sullen although healthy enough, standing by the long table in the centre of the enormous room. "Simon!" he cried, hurrying over, angered at the sight of the manacles on his son's wrists. "Get these damn things off him!"

"All in due time, all in due time." The steward sat in a chair on the other side of the table and opened a ledger, running a long finger down it until he found Simon's name, which took some time as the man seemed to suffer from poor eyesight. The steward never offered the visitors a seat as Richard embraced his son and they stood waiting together, facing the man as he read what was written on the parchment silently, his lips moving, nodding his head occasionally.

"I see, yes," he glanced up, squinting disapprovingly at Simon who growled at him. "A very serious matter this, your son apparently used a lance that hadn't been blunted, which is why his opponent was killed."

"That's a lie!" Simon shouted, shaking his head furiously as he looked at his father. "The lance was blunted, I remember it distinctly. It was an accident! It could just as easily have been me who was killed."

Sir Richard patted his son reassuringly on the arm as the steward continued. "That may be the case, my boy, and it could be the judge will agree with you, but the charge is so serious that your bail has been set by my lord Despenser at one hundred pounds."

The big Hospitaller snorted. "What you mean, you pompous little arsehole, is that the victim's father is a friend of your lord. Between them, they've decided to make my son and I suffer for what was nothing more than an unfortunate accident."

The steward shrugged and pressed his bleary eyes with his fingertips. "You have the money?"

Sir Richard nodded to his sergeant and they hefted the saddlebags onto the table. "It's all there, I counted it myself."

The steward smiled. "Of course, I trust you, a knight of God, but you understand my lord expects me to make sure. You can wait outside while I make sure the full amount is here." He waved dismissively to the door, ordering one of the guards to remove the manacles from Simon on the way out.

The three men stood in the dim hallway while the money was checked, Simon fidgeting nervously at the thought of walking away a free man again. At least until the trial.

"Where did you get all that money, father?" he wondered. "Our family isn't rich – you gave it all away when you became a Hospitaller. I've never seen so much silver."

"I borrowed it from an abbott," Sir Richard grunted. "Only Christ knows how I'll ever pay it back, but the main thing is to get you out of here. These bastards would let you rot in their jail for years." He stopped and fixed his son with a calm gaze. "You did have your lance blunted, didn't you?"

"I did!" Simon shouted, his voice echoing down the long stone corridor. "I swear it. I did nothing wrong. We tilted, I found myself lying on the grass, dazed, then Alfred ran over and told me I'd killed Wytebelt. It all happened so fast, I think the lance must have slid up and caught him in the face, breaking his neck. It had nothing to do with the lance being blunted or not, it was simply an accident."

Richard nodded. He knew Edmund Wytebelt had indeed died of a broken neck – when the squire, Alfred, travelled back to Kirklees with news of what had happened the boy said the dead man's head had been lying at a funny angle.

Hugh Despenser's greed was sickening – the Hospitaller knew he was as good as ruined, while Despenser sat somewhere laughing with the king, accumulating wealth illegally from good men like Sir Richard.

No wonder the Earl of Lancaster and the Marcher lords were determined to do something about the injustice that was rotting the very heart of the country. Well, Sir Richard would help any way he could.

"For now," he growled, looking at his son and his loyal sergeant, "we get the hell out of this castle and back up the road to Kirklees. Once we're safely away from here, we'll see what we can do about all this."

"I'll have to come back to stand trial, won't I?" Simon muttered fretfully.

His father never replied, but the look on his face suggested none of them would ever be coming back to this place.

The big door opened again and a page boy came out, handing a rolled up piece of parchment to Sir Richard: a receipt. "The steward says everything's in order," the lad told them in a reedy little voice. "You're free to go. He says you'll be summoned to attend a trial at some point, when you'll have to return."

The page showed them back to the courtyard and pointed to the stables. "You can retrieve your horses and leave, my lords."

Richard grunted a word of thanks and led the other two into the low building. Stephen breathed deeply and smiled – he loved horses, the smell of them brought back memories of his time with the Hospitallers in the Holy Land, and he was pleased to see his destrier had been well looked after.

The head groom saw them and came over, gesturing to the two big war-horses. "I had my boys rub 'em down and feed 'em before they were allowed to go and have their own meal," he smiled. "We take better care of our horses than we do people here."

"My thanks to you," Sir Richard nodded, tossing a small coin to the groom. "Saddle my son's horse, please and we'll be on our way."

The groom looked confused. "Your son's horse?"

"Dionysus," Simon replied, as if talking to a simpleton. He saw his own mount in a stall next to his father's and stepped over with a grin to greet the big animal which made a soft noise almost like a laugh as it spotted its master.

"No one said you were taking that one," the groom shook his head firmly. "You'll just have to get up behind your da," he told Simon. "Your horse belongs to my lord Despenser now."

Simon wasn't sure what to do, but his father was. "Stephen," he glanced at his sergeant. "Saddle Dionysus as quickly as possible please."

As the groom moved to stop him, Sir Richard grabbed the man round the throat and slammed his back, hard, into one of the wooden pillars supporting the roof. The whole building shook at the force and the man went limp as the burly knight slammed him into the pillar again. "Give me those!"

Simon grinned and lifted the stirrups his father had indicated from their hook on the wall next to him. The Hospitaller used them to bind the man's arms behind his back, and then tied another piece of leather round his mouth to stop him shouting.

"Get them outside," he ordered his two companions who led the three horses from the stable, into the courtyard, the setting sun casting long, menacing shadows from the surrounding towers onto the dusty ground.

Sir Richard dragged the semi-conscious groom into Dionysus's vacant stall and threw him onto the hay, locking the door. "Your lord Despenser has my hundred pounds of silver you little prick. If he needs something to ride, he can ride you."

He walked outside and jumped into his saddle. "Let's move!" he ordered, and, after collecting their weapons from the gatehouse, the three men rode as fast as possible out of Wales.

CHAPTER NINE

"Where the fuck is he?"

The night had worn on with no sign of their leader returning, and Robin was growing increasingly edgy.

"Probably found some willing young lass in one of the towns hereabouts," John grinned. "Don't worry yourself – we all like to have a night away from the camp now and again."

Robin accepted this with a grunt, but as it had grown dark that evening and Adam Bell hadn't returned to camp the young wolf's head felt a knot in his stomach for no reason he could put his finger on.

The outlaws had set guards, as usual, and the rest of the group relaxed around the fire. It was the middle of August and, although the weather was extremely hot during the days, on cloudless nights like this one it could get chilly.

"What if he's been captured?" Much asked. "He could lead the sheriff right to us."

"Aye, he could, lad. But we've got four lookouts posted in trees around the camp's perimeter. You'll be taking one of the watches yourself later on, right? If a load of heavily armed men try to sneak up on us in the pitch black, through the trees, I'm sure one of our guards will notice." Little John slapped Much on the back, grinning good naturedly. "Like I said – don't worry."

"Does he do this often? Disappear for days without telling anyone I mean?" Robin wondered.

John laughed at his friend's obvious concern. "Christ, if he knew you cared so much he could have just stayed here and shared his blanket with you instead of looking for an eager girl!"

Robin reddened, and John, not wanting to upset the young man, grew serious. "Relax. Adam knows how to take care of himself better than any of us, there's very little chance of him being captured."

The big man could see his reassurance hadn't quite worked yet. "Listen, if Adam's not back by mid-morning tomorrow, we'll talk about it then. Trust me" – he leaned forward earnestly, spilling much of his ale onto the grass – "there's nothing to worry about!"

John's confidence took some of the edge off the fears of the two younger men, and they began to relax and enjoy the ale and the biblical tales Tuck was telling round the fire. Adam's absence seemed to be somewhat liberating. Robin noted, with some surprise, that men who were normally quiet and shy were enjoying themselves immensely tonight, like children when their strict parents leave the room. The bright cooking fire threw flickering shadows on the trees around the camp as the men ate and drank their fill of roast venison and ale, singing and laughing late into the evening.

Much left to take his turn on guard duty, so Robin moved to sit on a log next to Will Scarlet, who seemed to still be lost in the melancholy brought on by his earlier tale.

"You alright?" Robin asked gently.

Will looked up in surprise at the big young man's sudden appearance next to him. "Christ, you can move like a ghost! I never heard you coming at all."

"Sorry," Robin replied sheepishly, feeling guilty for disturbing the tortured Scarlet. "I seem to be picking up the woodcraft skills you've all been teaching me."

Will forced a half smile then looked away, watching the rest of the men laughing and singing a short distance away. One of the men was playing a musical instrument and the others slapped their legs and stamped along with the rhythm.

"Aye, I'm fine," Will replied. "Why aren't you joining in with that lot?"

Robin shrugged. "Don't really feel like it. To be honest, I'm a bit nervous about Adam. He's been gone a while – where is he anyway?"

Will grunted. "No idea, he never told me. You'd be better asking John."

Robin leaned over and looked into Will's eyes. "Are you serious? You don't know where he is?"

"No," Scarlet replied irritably. "I just said so, didn't I? What's the big deal?"

Robin straightened, his hand moving reflexively to his sword, and he peered anxiously around at the dark trees surrounding the outlaws' camp. They seemed to take on a sinister, threatening look as the young man's imagination began to run away with itself and he forced himself to keep calm.

"I think we need to move camp, Will. Now."

Scarlet stood and faced Robin, a baffled and somewhat angry look on his face. "What the fuck are you on about? Move camp? In the middle of the night? When half the men are half drunk? Who put you in charge anyway?"

"It's not about who's in charge," Robin retorted. "You don't know where Adam is – well, neither does Little John, I asked him earlier. Don't you think that's worrying? Our leader goes off somewhere and doesn't tell either you or John where he's going or when he'll be back?"

Will listened and found himself agreeing with the younger outlaw – the fact John didn't know Adam's whereabouts was a surprise – but he was in no mood to have Robin ordering everyone around like he was in charge.

"Listen, Hood" – he growled, pointing a finger menacingly at the other man.

"What's the problem?" Little John had noticed the discussion and strode over from the campfire to stand between Will and Robin before things could get any more heated.

"He doesn't know where Adam is either," Robin replied, nodding at Scarlet. "I'm telling you, something's not right. If we don't move camp we're going to regret it."

Will snorted, but John looked at him seriously. "Hang on; maybe the boy's got a point. Adam always tells one of us where he's going if he thinks he might be away for a while."

"So, what then?" Scarlet demanded. "We all pack up our stuff and run off into the forest in the pitch black?"

"If Adam's been captured," John replied, "he can lead the law right to us. Aye, he can fight better than any of us, and he knows the forest like the back of his hand, but anyone can be taken by surprise."

"Adam wouldn't let himself get captured!" Will shouted. "You know him – he'd fight to the death before he let himself be taken. He's even crazier than me! I've had enough of this shit, John – I'm away to sleep."

As Scarlet stormed off, muttering to himself, Robin remembered the conversation he'd had with Much and Tuck a few days earlier and in a flash of inspiration things suddenly became clear.

"We have to move, John," he told the huge outlaw earnestly. "Adam hasn't been captured – he wants that pardon. He's going to lead the sheriff right here – and wipe us all out."

* * *

Two days earlier Adam Bell, or Gurdon, had left the outlaws' camp and made his way to Nottingham, where he had struck a deal with the sheriff.

He had shaved and dressed himself in his finest clothes once out of sight of the outlaws, and, on reaching the castle, had begged an audience with the sheriff, telling the guards he knew the location of the notorious murderer Robin Hood. The guards, after divesting him of his weapons, had ushered him in to see Sir Henry de Faucumberg, Sheriff of Nottingham and Yorkshire.

"Well, well! Adam Gurdon – my former bailiff in Stamford!" De Faucumberg's eyes opened wide in surprise when he saw his visitor. "I haven't had the pleasure of your company in years! Where have you been hiding? Along with the other wolf's heads in my forest? I seem to recall you disappeared when word got around you had been a Templar knight."

Gurdon inclined his head to the sheriff, who he had indeed known, years ago, before he was declared an outlaw. He had once saved de Faucumberg's life, yet despite that, Adam suspected the sheriff may have been the cause of his ruin . . .

"Things in Stamford went to shit once I left and the king split the manor in half, eh?" de Faucumberg grinned. "Those two fools that took over from me made a right arse of things. I heard they had you enforcing marriages the brides didn't agree to just to claim tax on the dowry!" The sheriff's face grew stony. "You imprisoned people on trumped-up charges just to extort bail money. You even let rapists off as long as they bribed you well enough . . . yes?"

Gurdon remained silent. The sheriff's accusations were true – de Faucumberg had been a decent lord in Stamford – fair and mostly honest – but when he had moved on the people of Stamford had become sick of their corrupt bailiff and the two new lords, Gilbert ad Pontem and John Chapman. The king was petitioned by some of the wealthier local residents, and, in order to convict the two lords, Gurdon gave evidence against them, in return for the charges against him being dropped.

Chapman and ad Pontem were imprisoned while Gurdon simply returned to his job as bailiff in Stamford, under the care of another new lord, Edward Le Rus.

"Well, speak up, man!" the sheriff cried. "Have you been living in the forests with those outlaws or not?"

Gurdon snapped out of his reverie and stammered a reply. "You're right, Sir Henry. Somehow," he emphasised the word and met de Faucumberg's eye looking for a reaction, but the sheriff remained impassive, "the people in Stamford found out I had been a Templar and I was forced to flee into the forests. I had to take up with the scum and dregs of society: it was the only way I could survive. I had to act like them, speak like them, dress like them – become just like them. After years of this…existence, I heard of your offer of pardon to any who turns in Robin Hood of Wakefield."

Many of his former brothers in the Templars had been arrested, imprisoned, tortured, and even killed after the Papal Bull of 1307. Although King Edward II had taken his time in carrying out Pope Clement's instructions to arrest all Templars, the monarch had eventually given in and, in late 1309 effectively ended the Order. Arrests, accusations of apostasy, torture…Hundreds, perhaps thousands, of Templars, had no choice but to become outlaws and seek refuge in the forests of England, Scotland, even Ireland.

"You know where that young savage Hood is hiding?" de Faucumberg asked, leaning forward and eyeing Gurdon thoughtfully.

"I do. What's more, in return for pardon and a chance to serve in your guard, I'll lead you straight to Hood *and* the rest of his gang. Seventeen outlaws, my lord, in one fell swoop."

The sheriff crossed his legs and stroked his chin in an almost theatrical manner, as he pondered the implications of Gurdon's proposal. While it was in his power to pardon the outlaw, he knew the disgraced former lords of Stamford Gilbert ad Pontem and John Chapman. When they had been imprisoned they had sent word to de Faucumberg offering to pay for any information he might have that would help them ruin Adam Gurdon. He had gladly told them Gurdon had once been a Templar knight – de Faucumberg had been disgusted by his former bailiff's behaviour in Stamford and it galled him to know the man was walking the streets a free man after ruining so many people's lives. Besides, ad Pontem and Chapman had paid him well for the information.

But they had been released from prison by now, de Faucumberg knew, and had been restored to positions of relative power and influence. They would not look too kindly on the man who pardoned Adam Gurdon.

Still, it was his duty as sheriff to uphold the king's law, no matter who it upset.

"This Robin Hood must be brought to justice," de Faucumberg stated firmly. "He killed a bailiff for God's sake. If you can deliver him and his friends to me it'll send a powerful signal to the rest of the outlaws around here. It might also shut up that nagging prior from Lewes. I'm sick of his whining letters." The sheriff shook his head in disgust. "You will have your pardon."

Gurdon smiled widely and thanked the sheriff with a bow. "You will not regret it, my lord."

De Faucumberg stared at him and nodded. "I hope not. Now, before you lead my men into the forest, you must meet Sir Ranulph de Craon. Normally, a man of your particular military skill would find employ as the captain of my guard. But Sir Ranulph already holds that position. You will serve under him."

A bearded, haughty-looking bear of a man stepped forward from behind the sheriff's chair and gazed at Gurdon, who felt a little dismayed as he realised he wouldn't be walking into quite as powerful a position as he had hoped.

"Of course, lord sheriff. I will serve in whatever capacity you deem fit."

"Good. De Craon will take you to the quartermaster and have you kitted out although you look surprisingly well fed for one who's been scratching an existence in the forest for years." The sheriff stared again straight at Adam, his eyes questioning. "How *do* you know so much about these outlaws anyway, Gurdon? While I can believe you had to live with those criminal scum, I *cannot* believe you allowed any of them to tell you what to do. In fact…now that I think on it, that particular area of the Yorkshire forest has been plagued by a particularly well-organised outlaw band for…well, years. About the same length of time as you were there, probably."

Gurdon opened his mouth to reply – he had expected questions like this and had concocted an elaborate story to explain how he had served under an English former noble called Adam Bell, but the sheriff raised his hand.

"Never mind. I've heard all about this Adam Bell, I expect you took orders from him."

Gurdon nodded in relief, sensing the danger pass.

"You do seem to match Adam Bell's description very closely though. You even share his Christian name…"

Sir Ranulph de Craon looked questioningly at de Faucumberg and placed a wary hand on his sword hilt, not sure where this was leading, but the sheriff gave a humourless laugh. "Ah well, that can be a story for another day, eh? Sir Ranulph, take our new sergeant and see he is kitted out. Then take thirty men into Barnsdale Forest and destroy Robin Hood and his friends."

"My lord." De Craon gave a shallow bow, and gestured Gurdon to follow him out of the hall.

"I take it you have a plan how to do this, Adam," de Faucumberg asked as the pair walked from the room. "I mean, without my men being wiped out by those blasted longbows the outlaws favour?"

Gurdon smiled grimly. "Don't worry Sir Henry. I know how the outlaws live. Thirty of your men will be more than enough to destroy these vermin once and for all."

* * *

"Wake up, Matt! Allan, get up! We have to move – everyone, up!"

Robin moved quickly around the outlaw's camp, shaking, shouting and gently kicking everyone awake.

Little John had finally, after talking to Friar Tuck and hearing what he had to say, agreed to lead the men to a new campsite – just in case Robin's theory was right. John had sought out Will to discuss it with him, but Scarlet was lying near the fire, curled under his blanket, staring at nothing, and simply waved the big man away with an angry growl when he tried to talk.

John knew they were safe during the night – only a fool would lead armed men into Barnsdale in the dark hunting outlaws, and Adam was no fool. So he had decided to let the men rest until first light, then they would pack up and be on their way.

The sun was only just beginning to crest the horizon so the outlaws had little light to see what they were doing under the thick foliage around their camp, and the thick morning dew lent the air a chilly atmosphere.

"I don't understand what the bloody hurry is." Matt Groves was in a foul mood, and didn't appreciate being told to get up and ready to move when no one had explained to him what was going on. "Has someone found us? Are there foresters about?"

"We'll explain it all once we're on the move," Robin replied, loud enough for the other men to hear, so he didn't have to keep repeating himself. "Just help us get all the gear together ready to go."

"Just because Adam ain't here, doesn't mean you're the leader now, Hood!" Groves spat, moving towards the young man "Don't you start ordering me about!"

Luckily Little John came to Robin's aid, grabbing Matt by the arm with a fierce look that warned of further argument. "Look, it doesn't matter right now why we're moving. Just get your stuff together and move. Or stay here if you like, maybe this is all a waste of time and we're leading you out of a nice comfortable campsite for nothing. Your choice, Matt, but the rest of us are going."

"You bought into it then," Will shook his head at Little John. "This is a wild goose chase."

"If you'd let me talk to you last night instead of having a tantrum you'd have heard what Robin – and Tuck – had to say," John retorted angrily. "If this is a waste of time, so be it. I'd rather waste a little time moving camp than hanging around and getting a forester's sword up my arse."

In an extreme emergency the outlaws could escape the camp in a few minutes, and fade away into the trees so anyone hunting them would have little chance of finding them. Robin was sure they had enough time to collect together all their belongings before Gurdon and the sheriff's men were upon them, so, although they were in a hurry, nothing was left behind and they were on the move within half an hour, with little trace left to show they had ever been there. Another half an hour later, the outlaw band had travelled a fair distance to the west, along the road to Kirklees, in the opposite direction to Nottingham, where Robin knew Adam Gurdon would come from.

"Right, Hood – that's us left our nice comfy camp behind us." Matt looked at Little John. "Where are we going? And what about Adam?"

"Adam is the reason we've had to leave the camp. He's betrayed us." Robin expected some extreme reaction to this news from the volatile Groves – anger, fury, threats of violence and vengeance maybe. He hadn't expected him to laugh.

"Adam's betrayed us? We left the camp because you say Adam's betrayed us? Why would he do that?"

Matt had stopped walking and, as his initial amused disbelief at Robin's claim wore off, he began to get annoyed again. The rest of the outlaws halted as well and every eye turned to Robin to hear what he had to say about their missing leader.

"He's betrayed us to the sheriff: to be pardoned. Where do you think he's been the past couple of days?"

"I don't believe I'm hearing this. Are you listening to this shit, John? You know Adam – he'd never betray us. And now this…boy, tells us Adam's turned us all in?" He looked back at Robin, "If Adam's not around any more, we'll be needing a new leader, eh? I expect you think that'll be you? If you think I'm taking orders from you…"

"Will you give it a rest for a fucking minute?" Little John rounded on Groves, his face like thunder. "Give Robin a chance to speak!"

For all Robin's leadership instincts, and Matt's accusations that he wanted to take control of the gang, Robin wasn't used to addressing all the outlaws at once. He felt his cheeks flush as he looked around at the people he had spent the last few months living and fighting alongside.

"I'm telling you, it's the truth, I'm sure of it. Adam Bell wasn't who he claimed to be. He was a disgraced knight or something, not some peasant folk hero."

Friar Tuck held up a hand as some of the men began to jeer and laugh at this. "He's right." His powerful orator's voice cut through the hubbub, and he told them all what he had heard when the sheriff's soldiers, with their Norman captain, had attacked their camp.

Will, who of all the outlaws had been closest to Adam Bell, couldn't or simply didn't want to, accept what he was hearing. "If you knew Bell was really some kind of noble why the hell didn't you tell the rest of us?" he shouted.

"Would you have believed us?" Tuck asked gently.

"No!" Will dropped his belongings on the forest floor and grabbed Robin's cloak, pinning him against a tree. "And I don't believe you now either! I've been part of this gang for three years and

Adam's done right by us all that time. I don't give a fuck what you have to say about him – he wouldn't betray us! We're brothers, we look after each other – Adam more than anyone."

It was true; Adam Bell had been a good enough leader. Not exactly a friend to any of the outlaws, not even Will. Bell had always seemed aloof – superior to everyone else. But he had kept them safe from the law and kept their bellies full even in the horrendously harsh winters of recent years, when so many people all over Europe had starved.

Adam may not have been well liked by the men of the gang, but he was highly respected and, perhaps more importantly, *trusted* by them. Many of them had seen how he reacted on the couple of occasions over the years when former members had tried to betray them to the law – Adam had hunted those turncoats down and killed them without mercy.

Bell had always appeared to live by a violent code of honour that made it so hard to believe he could betray them all to the very people they had been hiding from for so long.

Robin could see the outlaws would never accept what he was telling them – in fact, their disbelief would soon turn to distrust and his position within the group would become untenable. He had to prove what he said was true.

"Damn it! I wanted us to get as far away from him as possible, but if you insist on seeing for yourselves, fine. Let's make a temporary camp here, and then we can go and watch our great leader bringing his new friends to butcher us."

CHAPTER TEN

Adam Gurdon and Sir Ranulph de Craon had left Nottingham Castle at dawn that morning, with thirty men. All were mounted on warhorses, although these weren't armoured since they were purely for transportation to and from the forest, and would not be used in any fighting. The men themselves were all seasoned fighting men, clad in good quality chain mail which would keep them fairly manoeuvrable in the tight confines of Barnsdale Forest.

In a straight fight, twenty or so lightly armoured outlaws would stand little chance against such a force. And Gurdon expected this to be far from a straight fight – this was to be a massacre. Adam would take care of the lookouts at the outlaws' camp himself – he would know roughly where they would be, since he himself had organised the protocols for choosing the positions of such lookout posts. The lookouts themselves would not see any danger in the form of "Adam Bell" approaching, making it easy for the pardoned soldier to dispatch them.

It would then be a simple matter for the sheriff's men to walk into the unsuspecting outlaws' camp and massacre every one of them before they had a chance to fight back.

It was a straightforward plan, but one that seemed infallible. Gurdon was convinced it would work, and de Craon, while not overeager to commit to a possible rival's plan, was content to see how things went. Even if the outlaws sprung the trap, there seemed little danger to de Craon's men. They were simply too well armed, too well trained, and too battle-hardened. De Craon was also no fool, and understood the outlaws had probably been made leaderless with the defection of "Adam Bell".

"You were a Templar, Gurdon?"

It was still quite dark, the thick trees running along the side of the road blocking much of the slowly rising sun's light.

Adam, hunched over his horse, cloak wrapped around him to ward off the chill glanced warily over at his new captain. "I was. For years I fought the Saracens in Armenia and Syria. I decided to come home when we lost Tortosa – it was clear to me the order was dying."

De Craon growled angrily. "They were a fine Order – it was a disgrace what happened to them."

Adam grunted agreement but didn't particularly feel like discussing something that could still see him arrested.

"How did you come to meet the sheriff?"

"I saved his life," Gurdon replied. "I'd come home to Stamford and couldn't find a decent job. I was in the local alehouse when a fight broke out and a man attacked de Faucumberg with a dagger. I smashed a chair over the man's head. De Faucumberg offered me employment as his bailiff."

De Craon rode on in thoughtful silence for a while before turning to Gurdon again.

"You've lived with these fugitives for years. Yet here you are leading a force of men to destroy them. Did you form no friendships with any of these outlaws?"

Gurdon snorted. "Friendships? No. How could I ever empathise enough with a bunch of simple peasants to the extent I'd form friendships? We were simply too different, although I managed to play my part well enough to fool them into thinking I was just another yeoman fallen on hard times." He looked frankly at de Craon. "I formed no friendships, because I'm not the type. I'm too self-centred to have made many friends in my life, never mind any of those outlaw scum. I admit I did develop a grudging respect and admiration for some of them though."

The sun started to appear above the treetops, throwing soft shadows on the old Roman road behind the armoured horsemen, and, as birdsong and the almost hypnotic, rhythmic drumming of hooves filled the cool morning air, the forest seemed a wonderfully peaceful place.

"Tell me, then. Who of these wolf's heads impressed you?" De Craon seemed genuinely interested in Gurdon's opinion of the outlaws, perhaps planning ahead in case anything went wrong with the morning's work.

"There's a friar, he joined the group not long ago. An overweight, jolly-looking man, but he's incredibly strong, and can use a sword or quarterstaff almost as well as any man I've ever met. You should have a couple of your men take care of him as soon as possible – he could cause problems otherwise."

"Go on," de Craon prompted.

"My . . ." Gurdon looked hurriedly at Sir Ranulph, realising he had given away his role as leader of the outlaw band with one careless word. But the damage was done, and he understood de Craon probably knew all about his former role as Adam Bell anyway, so he carried on, ". . . the . . . second in command, was William Scaflock, or Will Scarlet as you probably know him. Although I was closer to him than any of the other outlaws, he would skin me alive if he knew I'd betrayed him. He's a good fighter, nothing particularly special normally, but he's filled with so much rage and hatred that I sometimes feared he would even turn on us, his companions, during the night. I believe his mind has snapped to some extent – he barely holds himself together. All he seems to live for is to kill nobles and any lawmen who might try to stop him. Of all the outlaws, you should take him down first, before he's aware of what's happening. There'll be no reasoning with him."

Sir Ranulph de Craon looked thoughtful as his horse picked its way around a fallen tree, glancing all around himself, constantly alert for danger, hand on his sword hilt. "What about this Robin Hood, the one we're here for? What's so special about him?"

Gurdon's horse carefully followed the route de Craon's horse had taken, scattering old, partially rotted orange and brown leaves left over from the previous autumn. Gurdon felt a shiver down his spine, yet couldn't have said why. He shrugged. "I'm not sure. He's young and seems guileless in his dealings with the rest of the men. To all appearances he's just another yeoman with a temper that got him into trouble. Certainly, that's how he sees himself. Yet . . ." Gurdon shrugged. "There's more to him, but I was never sure what. He can fight with a sword far better than the training we gave him warrants. He shoots with incredible accuracy, better than any man I've ever seen – and I've seen some master marksmen, believe me. He has instinctual knowledge of battlefield tactics, without knowing himself where his understanding comes from...And he has a sixth sense for approaching danger."

Sir Ranulph looked over sharply at Gurdon, who shrugged. "He's no soothsayer. Don't worry, he won't see our approach in his crystal ball, he just seemed to sometimes have an uncanny edge over his opponents." Gurdon paused, lost in thought for a few minutes. "Given a few years, Hood could become a fighter of unsurpassed skill, and a leader to match it. He almost beat me not too long ago . . ."

Gurdon's reputation as a swordsman had preceded him, and de Craon knew his new sergeant was utterly deadly with a blade, so the admission that such a young yeoman wolf's head had almost bested him was surprisingly honest.

"You know...." Gurdon turned with an almost comical look of genuine surprise towards de Craon, "when I think back to our sparring match, I begin to wonder if the boy let me win!" He shook his head and laughed, but the uncertainty was clear in his eyes.

Sir Ranulph grunted disagreeably. "You're not filling me with confidence that this will be an easy mission! A superhuman friar, a berserker, and what sounds like the best swordsman in the country, who has a sixth sense for approaching danger?"

Gurdon laughed, but he was supremely confident that the outlaws wouldn't expect this attack. Their destruction was a formality, and he mentally kicked himself for talking too frankly to this de Craon, a man he hoped to usurp sometime in the near future. Conversing with a nobleman again after so many years – one close to his own perceived station in life – had made him relax too much, he realised irritably.

"Well?" Sir Ranulph raised an eyebrow towards him.

"Well what?"

"Is there anyone else among this band of wolf's heads we should be aware of?"

"Only one." Gurdon lifted himself in his stirrups and raised a hand. The soldiers behind him slowed to a stop as they neared the outlying reaches of the outlaws' camp.

Gurdon's eyes flicked around the forest, searching for signs of danger, then, seeing nothing, he dropped down from his mount and nervously placed a hand on the hilt of his sword.

"The bear we called Little John."

* * *

"Ow!" John squealed, as he lay on the ground and inadvertently pressed his big elbow onto a little stone.

"Keep the fucking noise down, you big girl!" Scarlet hissed as they crawled beneath a thick stand of gorse, startling a red squirrel which loped off as it heard the giant outlaw's pained cursing.

The rest of the outlaws had stayed hidden at their new campsite while Robin had gone back with Will and Little John to see if his claims of Adam's betrayal were true. It would be much easier to hide from any soldiers if there were only three of them – seventeen men would make a lot more noise and be a lot more visible. The others hadn't been too happy at being left behind, but they knew it made sense.

The sun had almost crested the horizon and the waiting outlaws were getting restless when, finally, the sound of riders approaching reached them.

Their hiding place in the bushes was less than a mile from their now deserted old campsite and, as the soldiers came into view, with Adam Bell at their head, Will swore softly in rage, watching their former leader as he dropped smoothly to the ground.

His voice carried to the concealed outlaws, telling the sheriff's men to tie their horses to the trees off the road and to follow him on foot. Two men were ordered to stay behind and watch the horses.

Robin could clearly see the pain of betrayal written on Little John's honest face.

"That bastard," the giant growled. "I'll fucking kill him." He started to fit an arrow to his bow but Robin held him back, not wanting a chase from a party of well-armed soldiers led by a man who knew the forest at least as well as any of them.

Will stared numbly at the men below. "How do we know he's betrayed us? All I see is Adam and a group of soldiers. Maybe he's their prisoner."

Robin looked at Will in disbelief, while John, exasperated said, "Oh come on, Will! Do you see any chains on his ankles? He's even got his sword with him!"

"Who's that?" said Robin, pointing.

They all looked at the tall, very heavily built, but older man who was clearly in charge of the soldiers.

"Sir Ranulph de Craon," said John. "I remember seeing him with the sheriff once when I was in Bichill. He's never come after us personally before. He's the Sheriff's right-hand man and not a bad character from what I've heard. Well," he grunted, "as lawmen go."

Robin nodded thoughtfully. "At least the Sheriff didn't give Adam control of the soldiers. If there's one man we don't want in charge of hunting us down it's Adam. I can't see this fellow de Craon taking too kindly to being told what to do by a former outlaw. Hopefully they'll find our abandoned camp and Adam will be discredited. The Sheriff won't be too pleased when they go home empty handed."

Will began to move forward, following the line of soldiers. "We'll track them and see what happens when they realise we're not where they expect us to be. I still don't believe Adam's betrayed us all, even if he" – Will stabbed an angry finger towards Robin – "says so."

Robin nodded. "Fine, we'll follow."

"Well keep it quiet then," Little John murmured as he moved quietly after Will. "I'd rather not get into a fight with that lot."

* * *

"Right, men, fan out," Adam Gurdon ordered. "I want ten of you left, ten right and the remaining ten centre with me and Sir Ranulph, that way – "

"Gurdon!" De Craon's sharp tone brought everyone up short. "I'm in charge here, Gurdon, I'll decide how we proceed. You're only here to advise me, please don't forget that."

Adam flushed at the rebuke, knowing the soldiers were watching the exchange with amusement.

"Your pardon, my lord," he said, bowing slightly, in deference to the older man. "I'm so used to being in command of men I forgot myself."

"In command of a bunch of peasant outlaws, eh, *Adam Bell*?" De Craon snorted mirthlessly, making Gurdon flush again, anger burning in his brown eyes.

"Nonetheless," de Craon went on, oblivious to the Englishman's ire, "Gurdon's plan seems sound so" – he pointed with his sword – "you men, go left, you lot, right. The rest come with me and the wolf's head. When I blow the horn, we all move in and attack the camp. They'll hopefully all still be asleep and we'll have an easy morning's work."

As the soldiers moved to take up their new positions Sir Ranulph murmured to Adam, "I would have expected there to be sentries posted, Gurdon. Are you planning on taking care of them before they rouse the entire forest?"

The former outlaw leader looked uncomfortable. "I checked ahead earlier when your men stopped to water their horses. I never found any sentries where I expected them to be."

De Craon stared at him. "What do you think that means?"

Gurdon shrugged. "They must have relaxed their routine since I've not been there the past two days to organise them."

"Let's hope so, that should make our job even easier." De Craon ordered the party to begin moving forward carefully towards the site Adam Gurdon claimed was the outlaws' camp.

When he was sure the men flanking left and right must be in position the sun had only just begun to show itself, but the thick foliage in this part of the forest meant little light was cast on the target area. No one was visible, but the flickering shadows played tricks on the eyes.

The captain turned to his men. "It's all quiet in there, they must all be asleep. The lazy peasants haven't even set sentries so all we have to do is gut them while they sleep. Ready?"

The soldiers nodded, knowing what to do. Anyone unarmed was to be captured for a public trial, while those who resisted arrest were to be shown no quarter.

Gurdon slowly eased his sword from its leather scabbard as de Craon raised his hunting horn to his lips and blew one long blast.

With a roar, the soldiers charged into the clearing, weapons held ready before them. The two flanking parties charged at the same time until all of de Craon's men stood, staring around themselves into the gloom in confusion.

"There's no one here, Gurdon!" shouted the captain, turning on the former outlaw leader. His adrenaline was pumping and he was ready for a fight.

Gurdon looked around in consternation. "They must have moved camp."

"You said they would remain in this place for three days, you fool! This is only the second!" Sir Ranulph roared, shaking his sword in a fury.

Gurdon sheathed his own weapon and looked around at the deserted campsite, baffled. "I've no idea why they moved camp. They should have waited on me returning... I would suggest we are wary though...they may have set traps."

De Craon looked astonished. "Traps? Why would they do that? They never knew we were coming, did they? Men! Let's get back to Nottingham, this has been a waste of time. We're going to look like fools when this gets out, and you, Gurdon"- the angry soldier moved his horse in and shoved his face into Adam's – "will look the biggest fool of us all. I'll see the sheriff sends you back into these godforsaken woods where you belong!"

Gurdon's plans were coming to nothing. In despair he dragged his sword from its sheath again as de Craon turned his back on him. He was ruined anyway; it would make no difference if he rammed his blade into this arrogant bastard's spine. He might even be able to escape into the forest and find Will and the rest of the outlaws.

As the bitter thoughts spun around his head, something out of place, a noise perhaps, a tiny movement in the air, made Gurdon drop to the ground as de Craon spun round and stared at him in astonishment. A split second later a single arrow blasted through the leaves, passing through where Gurdon had been standing a fraction of a second earlier, and lodged itself in Sir Ranulph de Craon's throat.

Almost instantly, the sheriff's soldiers' training took over and one of them barked an order. The men formed a shield wall around their fallen captain, while Gurdon remained prone on the forest floor, eyes darting around him warily.

No more arrows came from the trees though, and after a few moments Adam rose to his feet. His calculating mind was inwardly cheering at this unexpected turn of events and he knew his situation had improved dramatically.

"You two: lift Sir Ranulph. The rest of you: tight formation round them. Let's move, back to our horses, and Nottingham!"

Gurdon's voice and bearing, so naturally used to command, was enough to still any doubts the soldiers might have had about following his orders. They were just glad to have someone with them who seemed to have an idea what to do.

The hunting party warily set off back home to Nottingham, empty-handed.

* * *

Robin, Little John and Will Scarlet had watched the soldiers bluster into their former campsite from a well-hidden vantage point. John had found the whole scene amusing, while Robin looked more apprehensive as he wondered what might happen next.

Will hadn't said a word since the so-called attack on the camp began. He simply stared coldly at Adam Gurdon, the leader who had betrayed them.

As de Craon had raged at Gurdon, the other two outlaws had exchanged smiles – this was the end for Adam Gurdon, surely. No matter what Adam said, the sheriff would take de Craon's advice and, at the very least, send Gurdon on his way. He would not be leading any more searches for them, and life for the outlaws could go back to normal. They had all known they probably wouldn't last long if Adam were to lead any sustained hunt for them on behalf of the sheriff. His knowledge of the forest, and their methods, combined with such well-drilled manpower, would make life extremely difficult for any outlaws.

Now, though, it seemed they were safe.

As relief washed over him, Robin heard the snap of a bowstring and watched in horror as the arrow missed Adam Gurdon and tore into the big captain.

"No," the young outlaw gasped in horror. "No!"

Little John turned on Will who was busy fitting another shaft to his bow. "Enough, Will! They'll be after us now, we have to move." The big man grabbed Will's shoulder and dragged him onto his feet. "Come on Robin, move!"

The three outlaws ran back into the forest, John leading them a circuitous route as they headed for the sanctuary of their new camp. They never noticed the sheriff's soldiers, now led by a pleased looking Adam Gurdon, had lost interest in them . . .

* * *

"How very fortunate for you . . ." The sheriff of Nottingham, Sir Henry de Faucumberg, poured himself another cup of wine and took a long pull as he looked knowingly at the recently returned Gurdon.

"My lord?" Adam looked innocently at the sheriff, who had failed to offer him any of the wine – an expensive French red.

"Don't be coy with me, man. The soldiers have told me de Craon was going to recommend I chase you from my castle with your tail between your legs. Apparently my now deceased captain thought you were a blundering fool. I expect I would have taken his advice: he was a very good judge of character."

The former outlaw leader held his tongue as the sheriff continued.

"He was a fine captain you know. The men liked him, probably because he tended to be rather soft on them. He was getting on in years and didn't have the same ruthless vigour for soldiering as he once had."

Seeing an opportunity, Gurdon spoke up. "I could see that, my lord. He was overly cautious as we tracked the outlaws, as if he couldn't really care less whether we caught them or not."

The sheriff nodded, tapping his fingers absently on the side of his cup. "You care a great deal though, eh, Adam?"

"I do, Sir Henry. They are vermin: scum without honour. They need to be purged from our lands."

The sheriff smiled coldly. "You were the leader of those vermin not so long ago, Gurdon – an outlaw just like them. In fact, you never did help us capture Robin Hood or any of the rest of them, as was our agreement when I pardoned you."

Adam looked away, knowing his life was once again in the hands of the sheriff.

"I don't understand why you feel quite so bitter towards your former comrades – perhaps they're a reminder of your own fall from grace. A reminder of when you had to steal to eat – to survive. A reminder of the fact that you were nothing." The sheriff leaned forward suddenly, his eyes hard. "You are still nothing, Gurdon, unless the king – or myself, as his representative in this – decides otherwise."

De Faucumberg seemed determined to humiliate him, to make sure he knew exactly who held all the power in their relationship. Yet, Gurdon noticed, his dressing down didn't come in front of an audience. The soldiers who had returned from the failed mission with him had all been dismissed. Hope flared in him again, as the sheriff drained his cup and rose from his ornately carved seat.

"You're on probation," said de Faucumberg, brushing past Gurdon as he headed for the door that led out of his great hall. As he reached it he turned and continued in a grim voice. "The Earl of Lancaster needs a bailiff in Wakefield, since Robin Hood killed the last one. I've been asked to find a replacement. Despite today's farce, you've proven yourself a capable man in the past, so I'm sending you to Wakefield. If you can do a good job as bailiff there until I find a suitable replacement, you will take over from de Craon as captain of my personal guard. I expect you to do at least as good a job as he was doing until today. Better! But first – bring me Robin Hood and the rest of those outlaws."

Gurdon breathed a sigh of relief, and nodded in agreement. "My word on it, Lord Sheriff!"

De Faucumberg stopped and looked back darkly as he left the room. "Adam, I warn you: do not mistreat the villagers in Wakefield. There's been enough unrest and nonsense there in the past few weeks. You treat the people fairly or you'll have me to answer to."

CHAPTER ELEVEN

For the next four weeks, as summer began to give way to autumn, and the green leaves turned to brown, red and orange, the outlaws moved their camp much more often than previously, as Adam Gurdon and his foresters tried to track them down.

The outlaws managed to stay one step ahead of their pursuers, but it was close on more than one occasion. Gurdon's knowledge of the forest, and of the outlaws' tactics, allowed the lawmen to get closer to capturing them than ever before.

Little John had, unofficially, taken over as leader of the group. Some amongst them felt resentment towards Robin, seeing him as the source of their present troubles.

"Life was never this hard until he joined us," Matt Groves muttered to Little John one evening, as the men sat drinking and telling tales round the campfire. "Adam would never have betrayed us to the law if it wasn't for Hood. Now we're hunted like dogs by the man that was our own leader just a few weeks ago!"

John understood the fear and frustration of Groves and the handful of others who felt the same way. When winter drew in the food would become scarcer. The thick foliage that the group was able to hide in had already started to fall from the trees and bushes, and the warm comfortable nights would very soon be replaced by harsh, biting snow, wind and ice.

If Gurdon and the Sheriff decided to continue their hunt for the outlaws during a hard winter, John knew his men wouldn't see the bluebells herald another spring.

Will Scarlet had also changed since Adam's betrayal. Always an intense, moody character, Will had become even more withdrawn and the other outlaws had begun to fear he might explode violently at any moment.

Little John, seeing him sitting alone by the river one chilly sunset, crouched down and, with a small smile, asked if he was alright.

"No, not really," Scarlet replied with a grimace, seemingly oblivious to the icy wind that was blowing across the water. "Me and Adam were never what you'd call mates, but I thought we respected each other. I can't believe he's betrayed us – betrayed me!" He had felt like there was little to live for after his family's destruction, but he had a place high in the outlaws' hierarchy with a leader who, apparently admired, trusted and respected him. That had kept Will going in the mornings, when it didn't seem worth it to get off the forest floor.

Now, Gurdon had become his persecutor – thrown his lot in with the hated nobles who hunted them like animals! And, like Matt Groves, Will seemed to think it was mostly down to Robin.

The young outlaw had hoped to share more quiet moments with Will, as they had that sunny day fishing by the riverbank, but Will barely spoke a word to anyone anymore.

John decided he had to speak to Robin, to see if they could find some solution to their problems, so he stood up, patting Will awkwardly on the shoulder and headed off to look for the young man from Wakefield.

He found him soon enough, working with Much to place animal skins over their small shelters to keep the worst of the autumn winds out.

"We can't go on like this, Robin," the bearded giant muttered without preamble. "Some of the men feel resentful about what's happened and Will acting like he has a death wish is putting everyone on edge. We have to do something."

Robin sighed, shrugging his shoulders resignedly and dropped the tatty old sheepskin he was holding. "I know. I seem to have brought nothing but bad luck since I joined you men. If we could find some way to reach Will – brighten his mood, give him something to live for – maybe everyone would feel better."

John nodded his massive head as Robin sat down next to him. "But what? Will's lost everything – his wife, children and now, even his pride. He trusted Adam."

"If we're to survive the winter, we need Will, you know that," Robin frowned. "Will has skills none of the rest of us have now Adam's gone. We need to help him."

"I know," the big bearded outlaw agreed. "I've spoken to people who knew Will years ago, before he became an outlaw. They all say he was a happy, friendly lad, but with a hint of steel in him. After everything he's been through, all that's left is the steel. His humanity's been torn out of him."

They sat in silence for a time, the drunken revelry of the other men doing nothing to lighten their mood, and then Robin pushed himself to his feet. "I'm going to try and help him. I'll take Allan with me in the morning; his experience should come in useful. We'll be gone no more than a few days, hopefully. Maybe with me out of sight for a bit some of the men might cheer up!"

Little John smiled mirthlessly. "What are you going to do?"

"Find Will's humanity."

* * *

Robin and Allan-a-Dale, a broad shouldered, confident young man who had been a minstrel before he was declared an outlaw gathered some food, money and concealed weapons about themselves before setting off.

"Where are we going, Robin?" Allan asked for the tenth time, having been given no answer yet from his grim-faced friend.

"Hathersage," came the reply, at last. "We need to see if we can find some information that might bring Will back from the purgatory he's living in."

Allan snorted, shaking his wiry brown hair gently. "Purgatory? Hell more like."

The two young men knew the way well enough to Hathersage, it was only about fifteen miles southwest from their camp, and they made good progress before the sun began to dip below the horizon, when they decided to make camp for the night.

After a short search of the area they found a suitable place, well off the main track and lit a fire to cook a little supper and take the chill from the air. Allan took first watch, Robin the second. With Bell's extra patrols hunting the outlaws, it didn't do to be unwary although the night passed without any trouble.

Robin's dreams were vivid during the night and he slept fitfully, but all he could remember on waking was a girl's face, unhappy and dejected.

They arrived at Hathersage just after midday. Neither of them had been into the village before, always waiting on the outskirts when the outlaws came to buy or trade for supplies, so there was little chance of their being recognized as wolf's heads. As strangers they would naturally be viewed with suspicion, but that was to be expected.

"Will told me he lived in a nice house near the mill; we should start around there, see if anyone has any information about what happened to his family."

Allan shrugged. "What is it you think we're going to find here? Will told you: his family were all killed. Everyone knows that."

Robin looked thoughtfully at the path ahead, trying to answer the question himself. It did seem like nothing more than a wild-goose chase, but he was hopeful something good would come from this trip to Hathersage.

"I honestly don't know what we'll find here, if anything," he admitted. "It can't hurt to ask around though."

The mill was easy to find, simply by following the river. The miller's wife was in the garden, tending to some carrots she was growing there, probably the last crop of the season and not a particularly good one judging from the occasional curses the woman was grunting.

"God give you good day, lady," Robin smiled, openly.

The miller's wife glanced up warily and returned the greeting before returning to her work.

"We're just looking for an old friend of ours, used to live around here. William Scaflock was his name. Do you know him?"

The miller's wife looked up again, a cautious look in her eyes. "He's been gone from here for a few years, boys. Upset some of the nobles and he suffered for it."

The outlaws feigned surprise at the news. "But he had a family – what happened to them?"

The woman clearly didn't feel too comfortable talking to two strangers, but her natural desire to gossip won out. "The soldiers killed them all. Although, when our men came to clear the mess that was left, they said there were only five bodies. Should have been six, but the little girl was missing."

Robin's eyes flared eagerly but he tried to act calm. "What happened to her?" he asked.

The woman leaned in closer, looking around as if someone hidden might be listening, which was absurd, given their open location. "No one knows for sure, but some of the villagers go to the manor house up on the hill to trade or do work for the lord, and some of them swear Scaflock's daughter is up there. A kitchen maid she is. So they say…I've been there to pay my rents, and for feasts, but I've never seen the girl myself."

Robin and Allan, although buoyed by the possibility that the little girl might still be alive, were outraged.

"You mean the local lord took an English girl and made her a slave?" Robin demanded.

The woman shrugged. "It's probably just a tale – some other girl that looks like Scaflock's daughter. I don't know, but if it is true, well, at least they never killed her like they did the rest of her family. Here, you two can do me a favour in return for all that information: take these two bags of flour to the baker in the village. Ask him about the girl when you're there – he's seen her, and he was a friend of Scaflock's."

The two young men grinned as they were loaded up by the helpful woman and set off to the baker's with a renewed sense of purpose.

* * *

The baker, Wilfred, took the delivery from Robin and Allan with a gruff word of thanks, inviting them into his shop and offering them a jug of ale each in return for their help. He joined them for it, his rosy red face, purpling nose and run-down premises suggesting he often took a break from work for an ale or two.

"Aye, Will was a friend," he admitted in reply to Robin's query. "We used to drink together sometimes when he wasn't off fighting Saracens or whoever."

Robin watched the baker's face closely as he asked about Will's daughter and what the miller's wife had said.

"Bah, that woman's tongue is too bloody loose, she needs to learn to keep her mouth shut. Talk like that can get people into trouble."

The ale had begun to warm the three men by now though, and Wilfred gazed thoughtfully at nothing until Robin tried again. "It's true though? The girl is at the manor house? She's a kitchen maid, or some kind of servant?"

The baker stared at Robin, then Allan, trying to decide how much he should trust these two dangerous-looking young men.

"I promise you, Wilfred, we are friends of Scaflock," said Robin gently. "He's in a bad way – he cares for nothing any more, other than revenge against the rich nobles. We'd like to help him. Give him something to live for again."

Wilfred took another long pull of his ale, and refilled his mug before fixing the two men with a stare and replying. "He's a wolf's head now, so I suppose you two are as well."

Robin and Allan shared an uncomfortable glance, well aware of the danger they could be placing themselves in by trusting in this gruff baker.

"I knew the girl well," said Wilfred. "She was a lively thing, full of energy and mischief. I see her at that manor house now and she's like a wraith. Never smiles, head always down – and what will happen to her when she's older? If it hasn't already?" An anguished look crossed his face, and he sipped his drink again, wiping his eyes angrily, as well as his mouth.

The outlaws grimaced at the implications of the baker's words, knowing they were true. Will's daughter had no life to look forward to if she stayed at the lord's house.

"What I don't understand . . ." the baker muttered, "why did Will never come back for the girl? I'd have expected him to come looking for revenge, same as he did with Roger de Troyes."

"He doesn't know Beth's alive," Robin replied. "He saw the rest of his family, brutally murdered, and he lost his mind with it – anyone would. Then, in a rage, he killed de Troyes before he found out who'd done it."

Wilfred shook his head. "Christ, poor Will. When you tell him it was Lord de Bray that destroyed his family and took his daughter…He'll get himself killed trying to fight his way into de Bray's manor house."

Allan grunted. "Robin has a better idea: you'll like this."

"We need your help, Wilfred"- Robin nodded, looking directly into the baker's eyes – "to get into that manor house, so we can take the girl. You'll be saving two lives – neither Will or Beth have any future if we don't do this."

The baker stared into his empty ale mug for long moments and then whispered, "I saw what those butchers did to that family. It was a massacre. I'll never, ever forget it. I don't know why they spared little Beth's life" – he looked up at Robin, a determined look on his face – "but if I can make some of this right for Will, I'll do whatever I can."

* * *

Matilda had stopped for a break from working at her father's fletching shop. The sun was high in the early afternoon sky and it was unseasonably warm today. She drew herself a cup of water from the well in the centre of the village and savoured its coolness as she tipped it into her mouth.

Just then, a man reeled from the alehouse, obviously worse for strong drink and the effects of the heat.

Matilda groaned inwardly as the drunk spotted her and began weaving his way over. Simon Woolemonger was an older man, nearly forty years old, and an unpleasant character even when sober. Rumours spoke of him informing on neighbours and generally causing trouble for the villagers.

"Hello, Matilda," he leered, sitting unsteadily beside her by the well, his eyes glassy. "Fancy a walk down by the riverside? It's nice at this time of the year with the leaves all orange and stuff."

Matilda was horrified at the thought of being alone with Woolemonger, but politely tried to hide her discomfort.

"No thank you, Simon. The recent warm weather has turned the Calder sluggish. I'm thinking it won't be too nice down there today." She stood up and replaced the wooden cup beside the well. "I better get back to work. God give you good day."

"Don't you want a man, girl? That fool Robin's not coming back for you and you'll be too old for anyone else soon." Simon leaned forward and ran his hand along Matilda's thigh, pressing it against her crotch. "Come on, girl; let's go down to the riverside where it's nice and quiet."

Matilda was so shocked she froze, but then her revulsion and outrage took over as she furiously slapped him hard on the side of his face. "Don't you ever touch me, you disgusting old sot! I'd sooner die than have your filthy hands on me!"

There were a handful of other villagers nearby and they stopped what they were doing to watch what was happening. Some shook their heads at the reeling Woolemonger, while others laughed and shouted insults at him. The drunk staggered to his feet, face flushing scarlet with both embarrassment and Matilda's slap. He burned with humiliation, but, even in his inebriated state he knew he couldn't physically attack Matilda in public – she was a popular girl in Wakefield.

"You think you're better than us, don't you, you little bitch?" His eyes bulged and he spat as he spoke. "Well, you'll pay for that. No woman hits me, you'll see…"

"You're worse than that new prior, Woolemonger, you dirty bastard!" someone howled, as the crowd laughed and jeered at the unpopular drunk again, and he staggered off shouting obscenities at the onlookers.

Matilda shook her head in disgust and walked back, shaking, to her father's shop. If only Robin were here, she thought, fools like Simon Woolemonger wouldn't dare bother me!

* * *

Wilfred the baker had a twice-weekly standing order from Lord de Bray's manor house, for bread and savoury pastries so he readied the delivery to be made the next day, telling Robin and Allan they could travel with him, disguised as travelling minstrels.

Allan, who had performed many times before falling foul of the law, had his gittern, a small stringed instrument, which he carried everywhere, while Robin had borrowed the baker's own citole, with its holly-leaf shaped body and short neck. Robin was a passable player, and he, along with the much more accomplished Allan, would often entertain the other outlaws at their camp. The inhabitants of the lord's manor house would undoubtedly be used to finer entertainment than a couple of scruffy-looking young men playing borrowed instruments, but Wilfred assured them the lord would be happy to hear music in his hall and that he would give them a meal and a night's shelter in return.

Somehow, they would have to persuade the girl, Beth, to hide in Wilfred's wagon before they left the manor house the next morning.

It was an absurdly simple plan, but, since the lord and his underlings were expecting no trouble, the outlaws hoped it would work well enough.

"What if we're discovered though, Wilfred?" Robin asked the baker, who shrugged.

"I'm almost fifty now, I'm an old man. My wife died fifteen years ago and we had no children. I spend my days making cakes and my nights drinking ale. If it comes to a fight I have little to lose. But, I'll tell you…I haven't felt this alive in years! A chance to stick it up those bastards, and help my old friend?" His big red face broke into a huge grin. "Come on lads, let's go make this delivery."

So they set off, Wilfred's cart fully laden with his boxes of bread and pastries along with some barrels of beer he'd offered to deliver for one of the village brewers. Barrels big enough for a small person to hide in…

Allan and Robin practised their minstrel act on the road to the manor house, and Wilfred declared himself impressed. They may not have found employment at King Edward's court, but they were good enough not to be kicked out of John de Bray's hall after their first tune.

It was an overcast day, and windy, orange leaves blowing off the trees all around them, but the three men were in good spirits, especially the old baker who saw the whole business as a noble adventure. He had fought in battles himself as a young man, but had thought that was all behind him. He had, in truth, hoped it was all behind him, having seen up close the horrors of war and its dire aftermath. But now, travelling with his bright, confident young outlaw companions, Wilfred felt more excited than he had in twenty years.

"I can see you lads are still young enough to feel like you're arrow-proof" – the baker smiled – "invincible almost." His face became deadly serious. "But you're not – if we're caught we'll be killed. Don't take this lightly, especially once you get a few ales down you in the lord's hall."

Robin nodded solemnly and whispered a prayer to the Blessed Virgin Mary as the manor house slowly came into sight.

While not as impressive as most of the other lords' residences in England, it was still an imposing and, to Robin and Allan, worrying sight. It looked more like a small castle than a house, despite the fact Lord John de Bray was only a minor noble, of Norman descent, who counted Hathersage as his only manor.

A three storey building, built from stone, with heavy oak doors and, Wilfred told them, an undercroft where the food and drink was stored. There were numerous windows, all with glass in them, and even a drawbridge, although the moat was empty of water. There was a single lightly armoured guard at the entrance, who knew the baker from his regular visits to the house.

"Morning, Wilfred!" shouted the guard, grinning broadly as the old cart rumbled up to the gatehouse. "You got any cakes on that cart for me?"

The baker smiled and reached into the cart, pulling out a large pork pie. "Here you go, Thomas. Just for you."

The guardsman's eyes lit up and he took a bite of the pie, glancing at Allan and Robin. "Who's these two, Wilfred?"

"I met them on the road, Thomas, travelling minstrels they are, on their way to London to make their fortune."

The guard laughed sardonically at that.

"I told them, Tom, wasting their time going to that dump -" the baker smiled – "but I thought Lord de Bray would probably be glad of a couple of minstrels to entertain his hall on a dreary autumn night."

Wilfred took out his dagger and handed it over to the guardsman. Robin and Allan did the same with their longbows and bags of arrows, although they both had blades concealed in their clothes.

The guard, Thomas, still cramming pork pie into his mouth gave the two young men a quick look, and, seeing no other obvious weapons, just the gittern and citole, he waved the cart on through, shouting his thanks again for the pie.

Wilfred waved merrily as they passed into the courtyard and the two outlaws breathed a sigh of relief. They were in.

The square courtyard was a large, busy place, with liveried servants rushing to and fro between the whitewashed buildings, carrying firewood, water and foodstuffs. The lord's coat of arms – a magnificent yellow peacock – was displayed on a scarlet flag that blew wildly in the strong wind.

Wilfred drove the cart over to the wide doorway that led to the undercroft and food stores. The three men climbed down and, under the baker's direction, began to unload the cart.

A groom appeared, the gatekeeper having alerted him to their presence.

"You two are minstrels? Well, I hope you're better than the last troop we had, lost control of their dancing bear, wrecked half the hall and three of their own performers before they cut the beast down."

Allan and Robin exchanged glances. "Well, we don't have any bears with us, sir, so unless people enjoy our playing so much they become bewitched, there shouldn't be any trouble." Allan winked at the bored-looking groom.

"Anyway," replied the man, "you're not hanging around here idle all day, you can earn your keep until dinner time by helping the baker unload his wagon."

The two young outlaws nodded obediently, and went back to helping Wilfred with his load.

Everything was going perfectly.

CHAPTER TWELVE

After Matilda's unpleasant experience with Simon Woolemonger, she had been relieved to have seen or heard nothing from him around the village for the next couple of days.

She had put the incident to the back of her mind, with the hope he had sobered up and forgotten what had happened or, with any luck, he'd gone down to the River Calder himself and fallen in.

Some of the villagers had teased her about it for a while, but interest had died down as other, fresher, pieces of gossip had come along.

Matilda and her parents were sitting down to breakfast just before dawn on the Wednesday morning, her mother, Mary, laughing at a story she'd heard about some local boy caught by the butcher trying to steal a leg of beef bigger than the lad himself.

Matilda's father was quiet. He'd been upset when he heard what had happened with Woolemonger and took the chance to tell Matilda, again, to give up waiting on Robin Hood and find herself a suitable husband.

Mary ladled pottage onto their plates from the steaming cauldron over the fire, and set a mug of weak home-brewed ale at each of their places. She had cooked their meal outside, since it was a chilly but nice, clear morning and cooking indoors in a little house such as theirs was an unpleasant smoky job. The family, like most of the villagers, rarely ate breakfast, but the pottage was close to being spoiled so Mary had insisted they eat it while they could – food was too precious to waste, especially with winter so close.

As the family began to eat, the noise of an excited commotion reached them, and they turned to see what was happening.

"Oh, Christ," Matilda's father muttered, earning a pious rebuke from his wife.

Coming towards them, through a throng of sleepy villagers, was the new bailiff, Adam Gurdon, mounted on an impressive-looking horse. More than twenty of his men were with him, most of them on foot. All were grim-faced, except Gurdon, who smiled as he caught sight of Matilda.

"What's he want, lass?" asked Henry. "Tell us now – if you've done something, so we can sort it out."

Matilda shook her head. "I haven't done anything, Da. I don't know why he's here."

As Gurdon and his men came to the Fletchers' gate, Matilda caught sight of a figure near the back of the clamouring villagers. Simon Woolemonger. Her heart gave a lurch and she felt the strength leave her legs as the drunkard grinned maliciously and gave her a wave.

"He's told them I was talking to Little John," Matilda mumbled through tight lips. "John came to the village a few days ago to buy supplies. You were out so I sold him some arrows. Simon must have seen us."

Her mother groaned, but her father put a reassuring hand on her shoulder and smiled. "Plenty people talk to John Little and no one arrests them. We'll sort this, don't fret." His smile turned to a grimace as he fixed his eyes on the leering Woolemonger. "And that little bastard will rue the day he crossed my family. If John doesn't do for him, I will!"

Adam dismounted expertly from his horse, handing the reins to one of his foresters, and let himself in through the gate. His men took up positions outside on the road behind their leader, who smiled again.

"Ah, this must be Matilda: I've heard so much about you. My old acquaintance, that notorious wolf's head, Robin Hood, was always telling me about you. You're even prettier than I imagined – no wonder you caught the prior's eye!"

The fletcher moved to stand in front of his daughter. "What do you want here at this time of day, bailiff? My girl's done nothing wrong – none of us have."

Gurdon's smile fell from his face and his eyes turned towards Matilda's father. "Hello, Henry. Still doing good trade selling arrows to outlaws?"

"Aye, and I supplied you with plenty when you were their leader, 'Bell'!"

Adam's face had turned red with rage at the fletcher's impudence and the foresters moved closer to the bailiff defensively, hands threateningly on the short cudgels they had tucked into their belts.

"No matter, Fletcher, I'm not here for you today," Gurdon growled, visibly restraining himself. "Perhaps another day. For now…" He looked at Matilda and raised his voice to carry over the watching villagers. "I am here to arrest Matilda Fletcher, for providing aid to the outlaw known as Little John. We have a witness, and you will come with me to Nottingham where you will await trial for this accusation."

"Witness?" Matilda spat. "You mean that filthy drunk Simon Woolemonger!"

Gurdon nodded. "You are aware of who saw you with the outlaw then. That seems a clear admission of guilt to me. Take her."

One of the foresters moved in and tied Matilda's hands. Her father could take no more and lunged towards the bailiff, who moved with lightning speed to deflect the fletcher's blow, tripping the big man as Matilda yelped in dismay. One of the foresters brought his cudgel down on Henry's head, and the fletcher lay still on the ground as Matilda tearfully struggled to free herself.

The villagers were outraged. Loud shouts of protest went up, but Gurdon vowed reprisals if anyone else raised their hands to stop them, and the angry shouts turned to angry muttering.

"Let's go," said the former outlaw, nodding his head in the direction of the main road, the rising sun casting long shadows on the ground, and the men, pushing Matilda in front of them, moved through the gate. They half helped, half pushed the girl up to sit on one of the horses. A burly forester climbed up behind her and grinned at her irate expression.

Matilda's mother, Mary, knelt beside her husband, who still breathed, but was out cold. She cradled his head lovingly, tears staining her cheeks. "Don't worry Matilda! We'll not let them harm you!" she shouted reassuringly, but in her heart she feared the worst.

Gurdon placed a foot in his mount's stirrup and jumped smoothly onto the beast. "Let it be known," he shouted, "Simon Woolemonger is a witness to a crime. If any of you people decide to harm him, you will be declared outlaws yourselves. And I will hunt you down, as I will hunt down Robin Hood and his men. Woolemonger is under the King's – and my – protection!"

With that, the foresters moved off onto the main road through the greenwood, heading to Nottingham with their prisoner.

Simon Woolemonger, with two friends of his, also known in the village as idlers, stood grinning around himself. He wore a fine new white cloak, no doubt paid for by Gurdon in return for his information about Matilda.

"Let's go get a drink, boys," he laughed. "I'm feeling flush today."

Adam Gurdon's reputation as "Adam Bell" was enough to stop any of the villagers raising a hand against Woolemonger, but the atmosphere was venomous.

Patrick, the village headman, came into the garden to talk to Mary and Henry, who was beginning to come around.

"We must get word to Little John and Robin, Patrick," groaned the fletcher. "They're the only ones that can help Matilda."

Patrick nodded reassuringly. "I'll send one of the local boys to take word to the outlaws, Henry. You take care of yourself and…when all this is over with, have no fear: that scum Woolemonger will be run out of the village!"

* * *

"I know this isn't what you want," Sir Richard-at-Lee told his son. "But there's no other choice."

"Rhodes, though!" Simon muttered. "It's so far away."

Richard nodded sadly. "I know, son. You'll be fine though, your brother will make sure you settle in, and the Hospitaller lifestyle will suit you. The weather in Cyprus is better than in England too!" He smiled encouragingly, but he was depressed at having to take this course of action just to avoid Despenser's 'justice'. They knew Sir Hugh would send his men from Cardiff castle with a summons to trial for Simon, and there would be no reasoning with those men. Richard also knew there was no chance his son would be found innocent of murdering that Wytebelt fellow – Despenser wouldn't give up his hundred pounds bail monies.

Simon would hang, Sir Richard would be ruined, and there would be nothing left for his firstborn, Edward, to inherit. It would mean the end for their family.

Although he loved both his sons equally, Richard felt more protective of Simon. The elder son, Edward, had always been tough – clearly cut out to be a knight from a very young age, always willing and able to take care of himself.

Simon on the other hand had been much less warlike – more interested in reading and riding his big horse Dionysus than fighting.

When Edward had left to join his father's Order in Cyprus, and his wife had died just a year later, Sir Richard became even more protective of his beloved youngest son.

So, the Hospitaller had decided, with a heavy heart, to send Simon overseas, to join his brother, Edward, and the Hospitallers at their base in Rhodes. Once his son was safely out of the country, far from the grasp of Hugh Despenser, Sir Richard and his sergeant would try to raise money to pay off the new debt to Abbott Ness of St Mary's by seeking loans from other local lords. And then they would help the Earl of Lancaster in any way they could in his struggle against the corruption that was bringing the country to the brink of civil war.

Things were looking up in that respect, as the king had recently agreed to exile the Despensers and issued pardons to the Earl of Lancaster and hundreds of his supporters. And yet, although they were supposed to be banished, the Despensers continued to exert great influence over the country, as Sir Richard was discovering now.

The Hospitaller and his son Simon, accompanied by the gruff sergeant-at-arms Stephen, had ridden out that morning for the docks at Hull, a journey of two days, where the young man could find passage to Cyprus. The letter of introduction his father had written, and his elder brother's presence on the island, would see Simon inducted as a Hospitaller sergeant-at-arms without any problems. It would be up to him how far he progressed in the Order from then on.

They wore no mantles, or identifying marks of any kind – their usual Hospitaller eight-pointed white cross against a black background would be a dead giveaway to any hostile pursuers.

Stephen had hung back on the road, to allow father and son time alone before their parting, but the loyal sergeant was alert for any sign of pursuers. He was disgusted at what had befallen his lord. A Hospitaller knight, basically robbed by their own king's best friend, and now forced to part from his own child, while looking over his shoulder like a common peasant chased by the tithing for stealing a loaf of bread!

Thankfully, it was a pleasant autumn day, with a gentle wind behind them, and the road was quiet, with few other travellers. Those they did meet moved deferentially aside, lowering their eyes at the sight of the three mounted and well-armed men.

They ate a small lunch of blackberries, boiled eggs and bread from their packs, eating while in the saddle to try and get to the port as soon as possible.

Sir Richard and Simon were sharing a joke together when Stephen suddenly hissed at them to be quiet, turning in his saddle to stare back along the road.

"What is it?"

Stephen grunted, his eyes still scanning the horizon. "Thought I heard a shout. Probably nothing. You two were making so much bloody noise laughing like little girls, makes it hard to hear anything else."

Simon grinned. "Christ, man, what did you eat for your lunch? Blackberries or lemons?"

"Ah fuck off"- the sergeant grumbled, then swung back suddenly to look behind them again, pulling his horse to a halt. This time there was no mistake, as the sight of half a dozen mounted men came into view, cantering over the horizon towards them.

"What d'you think?" Stephen wondered, glancing at his lord and fingering the handle of the mace he had brought along in case they did meet heavily armoured resistance. The crushing power of a mace was much more useful against plate mail than a sword. It looked like it may come in handy now.

"I don't know, they're too far away," Sir Richard replied, looking to his son in case his younger eyes could see any sign of markings or a livery that would identify the approaching riders but Simon shook his head.

"We're outnumbered so it makes sense not to hang around waiting to see if they're friend or foe," the Hospitaller decided. "Ride!"

They kicked their mounts and galloped off, noting with dismay the men behind them were keeping pace. "Shit, they must be after us," Simon cursed.

His father shouted in agreement. "We'll keep up this pace for a while – whoever it is back there must have been pushing their horses to have caught up with us even though we had a head start. They'll drop back before we do."

They rode hell-for-leather a while longer, then allowed their tired horses to slow. Sir Richard's words proved right, as their pursuers had fallen back and, despite the straight, flat section of road they were on, there was no sign of anyone behind them.

"At least we know the bastards are after us now," Stephen muttered. "All we have to do is keep ahead of them until we reach Hull."

Sir Richard rode in silence, wondering if his sergeant was right and they should just continue to the port as fast as possible, or try some different strategy to evade their pursuers. Set up an ambush? Pay some locals in the next village they passed to throw Despenser's men off the scent and in another direction?

He rejected the ideas – their followers must know their plan to get Simon on a ship out of the country, they wouldn't be easily diverted, and the idea of the three of them trying to ambush six mounted knights was an unappealing one.

Stephen was right. Their best bet was simply to reach Hull before Despensers men.

With a last glance over his shoulder, he spurred his horse again, giving a shout of encouragement. "Let's move!"

* * *

The day before Matilda was arrested Robin and Allan-a-Dale ate an exotic (by their standards) meal, in Lord John de Bray's great hall.

They had unloaded Wilfred's cart at a leisurely pace; then, despite the groom's earlier admonishment, they had spent a restful afternoon practising their minstrel's act and surreptitiously watching the house's inhabitants bustle about their business.

They had not seen the girl they prayed was Will's daughter, Beth, but Wilfred hoped if the hall was busy enough tonight the girl would be serving tables along with the older servants.

So, after eating a lavish dinner of salted beef, cabbage and bread, grudgingly served to them by a sullen page boy, Robin and Allan were full and content, although nervousness began to settle on them at the thought of their next few hours work.

They knew they would have to perform their music well, to avoid being thrown out of the manor house as beggars, but that was almost a minor worry. Now that they were actually here, and realised how many hands would be raised against them should their plan to kidnap Beth go awry, they began to feel a little fear knot their stomachs.

"Just try to relax," Robin told his grim-faced friend. "We'll play for these people, who'll all, no doubt, wake in the morning with thundering hangovers. They won't be in the mood to keep an eye on the minstrels from the night before – all we have to do then is bundle Beth aboard the cart and roll out the door."

"The *guards* won't all be drinking tonight, Robin. They'll be fresh enough in the morning and they're the ones I'm worried about!"

Robin laughed. "We'll deal with that if it happens. There won't be guards watching us load the cart tomorrow, and that will be the dangerous part."

Allan nodded, but his knuckles were white as he played his gittern. After a few minutes he stopped and said quietly, "What if the girl doesn't want to come with us?"

Robin sighed at his friend's continued black mood. "We're here now; we have to go through with this right? So stop worrying about it. We need to talk to the girl first and take it from there. For now, just concentrate on playing that gittern for a while so we can give these people something to dance to later on."

Wilfred had spent the afternoon talking to some of the other merchants and tradesmen who were delivering goods to the lord's house, but the big baker joined his outlaw friends now.

"It's to be a fine busy feast tonight, boys. They'll need every available servant to keep the food and drink flowing. You'll get your chance to talk to Beth then, I'm sure. Just don't make it too obvious, or we'll arouse suspicion – she's still just a wee girl, mind."

Eventually, the sun began to go down and pages scurried to light the torches set around the walls of the hall. The enormous room looked hugely impressive to the young outlaws, who had never seen such a big room before. There were fresh reeds on the floor, fine expensive tapestries depicting heroic scenes from history and mythology decorated the walls and the guttering orange flames from the torches cast long shadows over everything. It was a fine place for two minstrels to perform.

The more distinguished wealthy and noble visitors began to file in from their rooms, joining, although not mingling with, the lower classes like Wilfred and the rest who were lucky enough to be there that night enjoying the lord's hospitality.

The volume began to increase as the ale and wine was served, then finally, Lord John de Bray himself appeared, accompanied by his wife. She may have been a real beauty in her youth, but her severe features bore a look of such boredom and disdain for everything around her that she was now rather unpleasant to look at.

"My friends!" Lord de Bray, a fat, jowly man who looked as though he could probably still wield a sword well enough, clapped his hands and the room slowly fell silent. He smiled and spread his arms to encompass the two long tables where the nobles were sitting. He ignored completely the benches and small tables on the corners and around the walls of the great hall, where the commoners, including Robin and Allan, sat. These people were clearly of no interest to the portly lord, only being there out of necessity and etiquette.

"Please, enjoy the humble feast I have had prepared for you," he continued. "Drink your fill of the finest wines my cellar has to offer, imported from France and Italy. And," he smiled widely again as his noble guests cheered loudly at his promise of alcohol, "we are lucky enough to have entertainment this night. Some of you will know my own pet fool, Rahere. A more amusing man could not be found in all the courts of Europe!"

An old but painfully enthusiastic jester stood and bowed, exaggeratedly, somehow managing to break wind loudly as he bent, which brought more laughter from the already half-inebriated guests.

"We also happened upon these two strolling players," de Bray continued, as the jester sat back down on his chair which collapsed theatrically.

The lord waved into the shadows as Robin and Allan stood, giving smiles and waves around the room.

"They promise to keep us amused! And if they don't, well...we'll set the dogs on them, eh?"

The guests thumped their mugs on the tables at this, roaring and cheering loudly.

Lord de Bray smiled wickedly at the two "minstrels", who had started to feel even more nervous about their night's work. "Now! Let the feast begin, friends!"

* * *

Beth Scaflock had been just five years old when her family were cut down by Lord de Bray's soldiers. On finding the little girl hiding, terrified out of her wits in a cupboard, the lord had decided to take her home since his wife was always on at him to hire more servants for the kitchen. To all intents and purposes, Beth had become his property, for who could stop him, the Lord of Hathersage?

She had been given a pallet in the kitchen, in a tiny cupboard like the one she had hidden in while her family was murdered. She slept and spent most of the little free time she had in this tiny space, when she wasn't doing chores around the kitchen for the cook, a cold middle-aged woman called Joan.

Beth and Joan were the only two females who lived in the lord's household, apart from his own wife. Like the rest of the manor houses in England, the vast majority of residents were male. Joan had cut her hair short, like the boys, so most people never even noticed she was a little girl.

Beth was thankfully left alone for the most part. Lord de Bray had never taken any notice of her again and, once she had learned to do her kitchen duties quickly and efficiently, Joan had stopped beating her so often.

It was, though, a horrible existence for the now eight-year-old child. Although many of her memories of her previous life had begun to fade, she still sometimes cried herself to sleep when she thought of her mother cuddling her after she'd fallen, or playing with her brother and their pet dog, Sam. She would also cry when she thought of her doting father, Will.

Although Beth was too young, even now, to understand what a mercenary was, she knew her father could be a violent, terrifying man. Yet he never acted like that around her – he had always made time to play with her when he was home, and her memory of his smiling face, full of joy as they had climbed in trees together and ran through the little stream by their house with her on his back twisted her heart until she felt she would never get over it.

She had wished for a long time that her father would come and take her home from this terrible house. But he never had, and her tears had, mostly, dried up as the hopelessness of her existence had begun to crush her spirit.

Tonight, there was a feast, as there often was at the manor house. This night Lord de Bray was entertaining more guests than normal though, and Joan had told her to serve ale at the tables of the commoners.

The sounds of men and women laughing filtered through the kitchen door – a sound she never shared in any more.

She joined the serving boys, shoved to the back of the line, being by far the smallest, and waited humbly to carry drinks to the men in the shadowy corners of the hall.

"Here, you!" A tray was thrust towards her, loaded with wooden mugs of watered-down ale, and Beth took it without a word, turning with practised ease, and went out into the great hall, where the noise of revelry was almost overpowering, even at this early stage of the feast.

She took her tray into the farthest corner of the room and set it down on a table, as her arms were too small to hold it while handing out the drinks as the other servers could do.

She saw two young men, both holding musical instruments, watching her as she worked, so she carried her tray to them before they started roaring at her as everyone always did when thirsty for ale.

"Hello, lass," said one of the young men. "I'm Robin. This is my friend, Allan, and this is Wilfred, the baker from Hathersage; you've probably seen him before."

Beth dipped her eyes; she knew not to get into conversations with the people she served, or Joan would have words, or worse, with her, for wasting time.

"There you go, sirs," the girl said, eyes still downcast as she placed a mug of ale before each of their places.

"What's your name, girl? We've given you ours, it's only polite to tell us yours." The big man, Robin, smiled warmly as he lifted his mug and took a small sip.

"Elizabeth, sir. I must be on with my work now or I'll get in trouble."

The three men shared a glance, and the one who had spoken looked around the room warily before saying to the girl, "We're friends of your da, Beth. Carry on with your work as normal, but be sure to serve us later on." He winked at her and looked away towards the jester, Rahere, who was cavorting ridiculously around the Lord's Table to much amusement.

The little girl's heart skipped a beat and she felt too weak to lift her half full tray for a moment, but she sensed the need not to draw attention to herself or these two minstrels and their baker companion, so she pulled herself together, gave a small curtsey and moved on to the next table.

She emptied the tray, filled it with empty mugs and carried them back to the kitchen to be refilled. Her eyes flickered over the three men. The two minstrels seemed relaxed, practising their instruments, presumably in anticipation of performing at the feast tonight. The baker, who she had indeed seen before making deliveries to the kitchen, was happily stuffing his round face with sweetmeats and ale. His eyes turned and met hers, and a memory came rushing back to her, of her father, Will, and this baker, standing together in the local tavern drinking and laughing together as she played happily on the floor.

A lump filled her throat and she hurried through the door into the kitchen, the sounds of laughter chasing her as the jester cavorted around the room.

The jokes were ribald, childish, filthy and misogynistic, and Rahere's audience were in stitches at every fart and punch line. Often the punch line *was* a fart. Robin took it as a good sign when he saw one man, a noble too, fall right off his chair he was laughing so hard.

"The crowd are pretty drunk and in a good mood, Allan. We just need to sing a few songs as if we were back at the camp with our mates, and we'll be fine."

Allan nodded gloomily despite Robin's ever-present grin. In fairness, Allan had little to worry about, having performed professionally as a minstrel many times in his past. He could play tonight's planned repertoire in his sleep. Robin, who, as a youth, had spent much more time practising with the bow or a wooden sword, had more reason to worry about their forthcoming performance. But Robin had a natural flair and charisma that was ideally suited to the role of a minstrel. Allan took comfort from the thought and, as he finished his ale and the time to play approached he felt a calm resolve settle over him.

"That's better, Allan!" Robin laughed as he saw his friend finger a fast run on the strings of his instrument.

Allan smiled. He was actually looking forward to their "show" now. He loved to play for an audience, and this would make a fine story to tell the rest of the outlaws when they got back to camp.

Just then, Rahere, the jester, his act exhausted, gave a bow and, to hearty applause and cheering, walked off the floor, belching loudly in time with every step.

There was a short break then, for everyone to get another ale or wine, and to laugh about the funniest parts of Rahere's act. The steward caught Robin's eye and signalled the two minstrels to start their performance.

"This is it, Allan. A few songs, another ale, then back to camp in the morning with a surprise for Will."

"Good luck, lads!" Wilfred cheered, supping a fresh ale, and smiling blearily at them.

"Thanks, Wilf! Just you make sure you're able to drive that cart tomorrow eh? Take it easy on the drink!" Robin laughed, but his look was serious, and the baker nodded sheepishly, placing his mug back on the table.

The two outlaws walked confidently onto the middle of the floor, near the lord's own table, where the torches burned brightest, and began to play.

CHAPTER THIRTEEN

The other outlaws had gone on with their usual routine in the absence of Allan and Robin, until the young boy from Wakefield, sent by Patrick, the village headman, found them. Or rather, the outlaws found him, wandering around the forest shouting for Little John.

"What are you playing at, lad? You trying to get yourself arrested by the bailiff's men, for consorting with criminals?"

The boy started in shock as he suddenly realised he was surrounded by half a dozen burly outlaws. He had heard or seen no sign of them until John suddenly spoke, almost right in his ear.

"You have to help," he stammered. "Matilda's been arrested!"

Some of the outlaws knew, and liked, Matilda. Not just because she was Robin's girl, but they had met her when buying arrows from her father Henry, and her pretty smile won most men over. Even the stone-faced Will Scarlet.

"What are you babbling about, boy?" Will demanded. "Arrested by who? For what?"

"Aye, I saw her just a few days ago, she sold me some arrows," added Little John. "She never mentioned being in any trouble."

"That's the problem," said the boy, Andrew. "You were seen with Matilda, John, and Simon Woolemonger went an' told the new bailiff, Adam Gurdon, about it. He came and arrested her right from her own house. Battered the fletcher and warned everyone off going after Woolemonger."

The outlaws had heard about their former leader being appointed bailiff of Wakefield but they hadn't expected him to make a move like this.

"Who's this Woolemonger?" Will asked, still looking confused. "What's his problem?"

"He's one of the village drunks," Much replied in disgust. "Waste of bloody space, someone should have thrown him in the river years ago."

The boy nodded agreement. "The bailiff must have paid him for his information about Matilda; he's going around the village like he's the lord of the place, paying for his mates and him to drink themselves stupid."

"We've got to do something about this, John," said Will, to a chorus of agreement from the rest of the outlaws. Even Tuck nodded his head coldly.

"He's right, John," said the stocky Franciscan friar. "If we don't do something about this everyone will think they can get away with informing on the people who give us aid. Our supplies will dry up, no one will trade with us in case they have the foresters after them because someone like this Simon informed on them."

John nodded his huge head. "I know, lads. This time of year we'll be needing all the help we can get too." He looked at Andrew. "Simon Woolemonger needs to be taught a damn lesson. But we need to get Matilda back too, or that bastard Adam will use her as a tool to get at us. Do you know where he was taking her?"

Andrew nodded. "He told everyone he was taking her to Nottingham. He left a few hours ago."

"Were they on foot, boy?" Will asked.

"Some were, but the bailiff and a couple of others had horses. They put Matilda on one of them with a forester."

"Shit!" Will hissed. "How are we going to catch them on foot?"

There was silence for a few moments as everyone thought about the situation.

"The ford at Hampole Dyke?" Much wondered, half to himself. "If some are on horseback they'll have to stick to the main road. If we cut through the forest we should be able to head them off."

Will grunted unhappily. "We'll have to move some if we're to get there before them, Much."

The miller's son shrugged. "We better get a move on then!"

"Right. I'll take the men and we'll get Matilda back from Adam," said Will, moving to gather up his weapons. "I've a score to settle with the bastard, and this is my chance. You and Much can go pay this Simon a visit."

John was reluctant to let the volatile Will Scarlet take charge of something like this, with Matilda's life at stake, but he knew refusing Will's suggestion would only lead to an argument in front of the rest of the men. There was nothing for it but to agree.

"You mind and be careful then, Will. Don't just rush in waving your sword over your head like a maniac. We want Matilda to come out of this safely. Be as stealthy as possible."

Will simply grunted something about not being stupid, and moved off with the rest of the men to start the run to Hampole Dyke.

"I'll keep an eye on him, John," Tuck reassured his giant friend, as he stuffed a handful of arrows into the already straining cord he used as a belt round his grey friar's robe. "I won't let him put Matilda in any unnecessary danger."

Little John slapped the jovial clergyman on the arm and thanked him. "Come back here when you have her. Me and Much will be back by then anyway – sorting this informer won't take long. Hopefully Robin and Allan will be back by then too, wherever they are."

He grabbed his huge quarterstaff, a foot longer than most men's staffs; slung his similarly oversized longbow over one shoulder, and stuffed a piece of bread from his pack into his mouth. "Right, Andrew, lad!" he shouted, spitting crumbs at the boy. "Let's go sort this bastard!"

* * *

When Robin and Allan began their act the audience had taken little notice, but after a song or two most people were watching, with more than a few tapping their feet and humming the melodies to old favourites like "As I Lay upon a Night" and "Man in the Moon".

The pair had played a selection of upbeat, merry songs, mainly about girls, drinking and fighting, before slowing things down and performing "Alison", a ballad in a minor key.

Their voices worked well in harmony, with Allan taking the higher vocal and, as the last chord faded, the lord's hall erupted in loud applause, with more than a few of the women, and even some men, wiping a tear from their eyes.

The outlaws stood and enjoyed their moment, bowing to all, and grinning widely at each other.

The crowd reaction was almost certainly down to the free flowing alcohol and generally happy atmosphere in the hall that night, rather than any musical genius on the part of the two performers, but it hardly mattered. Their ruse had clearly worked. Even Lord de Bray handed them a few marks each with a grand flourish, and, as they returned to their seats in the shadowy corner of the room, well wishers thumped them on the back and praised their skill.

Robin laughed and smiled at the compliments, while the normally reserved Allan was on a high. It felt to him like this was one of the best performances of his life, and the grin stayed on his face for the next half an hour.

Then young Beth appeared at their places carrying two more ales for them, and the outlaws suddenly remembered the real purpose of their visit here.

"Beth," Robin began, but the girl cut him off, her face twisting.

"Why hasn't my da come looking for me?"

Both outlaws looked at the ground, embarrassed, feeling the little girl's obvious pain.

"Your da thought you were killed along with the rest of your family, lass," Robin told her, glancing around the room to make sure no one had noticed their conversation with the upset serving girl. No one seemed to be paying any attention.

"Listen to me. You have to pull yourself together. Don't attract any attention to us or yourself. We're going to get you out of here and take you back to Will."

The girl placed a mug in front of Allan. "How?"

"In the morning, we'll hide you in one of the baker's barrels, load it on his cart and take you straight out the gate. Will you be missed?"

Beth shook her head, her greasy brown hair falling around her dirty face. "The kitchen staff will be up early, but the housekeeper, Joan, will be up late drinking and won't be out her bed 'til later in the morning. If we leave early I won't be missed for a while."

Robin and Allan nodded and Wilf promised to have the cart loaded and ready to go not long after sunrise.

"Carry on as normal then, Beth," said Robin. "But be ready to leave in the morning. We won't have time to come and find you if you're not around."

A flicker of a smile came to the little girl's lips and a glimmer of hope flared in her eyes for the first time in months. "Thank you, sirs!" she whispered to them, and walked off to the next table to serve the rest of the mugs on her tray.

"A strong wee lass, Robin," Allan said approvingly.

"She's had to be, to survive what she's been through…" replied Robin, shaking his head at the thought of the hopelessness and fear Beth had suffered for the past three years.

Wilf laid a meaty hand on Robin's arm and locked eyes with him. "Tomorrow, we set this evil right."

* * *

Although the outlaw's camp was a fair distance away from Wakefield, it didn't take Little John, Much and the youngster, Andrew, long to reach the village outskirts.

"All right, lad, thanks for coming to get us. We'll sort this out now; you take word to Henry everything will be fine." He ruffled the boy's hair and handed him a small silver coin, which Andrew took with a grin and loped off towards the fletcher's house.

Much thought the best place to find Simon Woolemonger would be the local alehouse. This belonged to Alexander Gilbert and was literally more of a house than a tavern or inn.

The outlaws wandered up and peered in the side window. Sure enough, Woolemonger was inside, a mug of ale before him and two friends at the table with him. They were the only people drinking in the alehouse at that time.

The three were joking noisily as if they hadn't a care in the world, their drunken laughter filtering through the unglazed window loudly, while Gilbert threw them dark looks every so often.

There seemed little point in wasting time. John wanted to get back to camp as soon as possible in case Robin and Allan returned from wherever they'd gone and wondered where everyone was.

He pushed open the door and strode over to the table Woolemonger sat at. The three drinkers looked up indignantly.

"What do you want?" one asked, just before John's massive fist slammed into his nose, throwing him backwards off his chair in a spray of crimson. The man lay on the ground groaning.

The second of Woolemonger's friends fumbled at his belt, presumably for some weapon, but Much moved faster and kicked him hard in the face. The combination of excessive ale and the blow to the head was too much for the man, and he collapsed on the floor vomiting noisily. Much gave him another kick and leaned down to growl in his face. "Stay the fuck down, or we'll come back for you."Woolemonger knew many tales about Little John and, while his friends had instinctively tried to defend themselves against the outlaws, Woolemonger had simply frozen in fear as he recognised the giant.

"What do you want with me?" he squealed, eyes wide with fright.

John grabbed him by the throat and hauled him out the front door, where a crowd had gathered on hearing the commotion.

Woolemonger tried to free himself, flailing his legs wildly, but Little John punched him hard in the stomach, blasting the breath from the man, before throwing him into the road where he lay, crying and gasping.

There were cheers from the villagers, but John raised his hands for silence.

"You all know why I'm here," he said loudly. "This piece of shit here has been telling tales about me, to the bailiff. Everyone knows what we do to people who inform on us."

Woolemonger spluttered a denial, but John wasn't listening. He looked around the crowd slowly.

"People that cause me, and my outlaw brothers', trouble…regret it." With that he pulled his sword from its leather sheath and pointed it at the man on the ground.

"Wait!" Woolemonger cried. "I can help you. The bailiff knows you and your friends will try to rescue the girl. He's setting a trap for you!"

John and Much exchanged a worried glance at this, and the big outlaw lowered his sword a fraction.

"Where?"

"The ford at Hampole Dyke," whimpered the informer, clutching his guts in pain. "Adam expects an attack there, because the bridge has collapsed and it's an ideal place for an ambush when your friends are struggling through the ford. The bailiff's going to station his men all around the place and wipe the lot of you out. He won't even be there; he's going to continue on the road to Nottingham where he'll hand over the girl to one of Prior de Monte Martini's men at his brothel."

"The prior?" John demanded in confusion. "What's he got to do with it? I thought Adam was working for the sheriff?"

"The sheriff isn't interested in the girl; he just wants you outlaws dead or captured, this is nothing to do with him. The prior paid the bailiff to arrest the girl – she's to be put to work in the prior's brothel. Gurdon's expecting to make some money *and* wipe out your friends when they try to rescue the girl."

Matilda's father had pushed his way to the front of the crowd and he spat at Woolemonger now. "This is all your fault, you bastard! None of this would have happened if you'd kept your drunk nose out of it!"

Much grasped Little John's arm. "Finish this! We need to warn Will and the rest, now."

The big man nodded, a look of disgust on his normally jovial face. "The fletcher's right – this is all your fault." He leaned over and rammed his blade into the drunkard's heart, impaling the man on the ground. Woolemonger stiffened in shock, staring first at John, then down at the blade impaling him.

There were gasps of shock and fright from some of the villagers, many of whom knew Little John as a gentle giant. This was a side to him they had heard stories of but had never seen before. Some of the children in the crowd began to cry, and their mothers pulled them in close to comfort them.

"That's what happens to people who betray me or my friends!" John roared as he pulled the sword free, wiped it on Woolemonger's fancy new coat.

"I thank you all, who trade with us and sell us provisions. We'll always look after those who help us – but let this be an example. If anyone betrays us, we *will* hunt them down and kill them."

John knelt and used his dagger to cut the purse from Woolemonger's belt. He walked over to Patrick, the village headman, and handed the money to him. "The sot might have already drunk half of the payment he got from the bailiff, but use the rest of it for whatever the village needs."

Patrick nodded his thanks to John and Much, as Henry Fletcher clapped them on the back. "You two better get moving, and warn your mates. I don't want any more good men to die because of that scum. You can borrow a couple of our horses – they're no *destriers* but they'll get you where you need to go a lot quicker than on foot."

Much grimaced; he wasn't much of a rider, but there was nothing else for it. "He's right, John, it makes sense. And don't worry, Henry, we'll get Matilda back safely, I promise you."

Patrick gave a shout at one of the villagers and the man hurried off, returning a few minutes later leading two horses saddled and ready to go. "Don't be beating them," the man warned, handing the reins to Much and Little John with a glare. "Treat them right and they'll treat you right."

The fletcher smiled weakly at the outlaws as they warily eyed their mounts. "God go with you, lads. Help my wee girl."

They climbed awkwardly onto the palfreys and, with a nod of farewell, kicked them forwards through the crowd of villagers, many of whom shouted thanks up to them for dealing with the hated Woolemonger.

As they urged the horses into a run through the forest, John told Much they would head back to the camp first, in case Robin and Allan had returned. "We're going to need every man we can get if Adam's laid a trap at Hampole Dyke."

Much didn't reply as he gripped the reins fearfully, praying fervently they would be able to outwit Adam Gurdon.

Behind them in Wakefield the villagers buried Simon Woolemonger in an unmarked pauper's grave.

* * *

Morning came quickly for Robin and Allan-a-Dale. Wilfred the baker, despite vowing to drink little at the feast, was nursing a hangover, and was jumpy and irritable as a result.

The two outlaws were annoyed at Wilfred but could do nothing about it.

Having no previous experience of a morning in a lord's house, Robin and Allan had hoped the place would be quiet before dawn, but many servants were up early, quietly tidying things from the night before. They stepped over sleeping revellers, sometimes carefully, sometimes not so much, depending on whether the revellers had been nice to them during the previous evening's drunkenness.

More than a few were woken by a servant "accidentally" standing on them. Or kicking them in the bollocks, before dodging out of sight.

"This isn't going to be as simple as we'd hoped, Robin," Allan grumbled.

"None of these servants will be paying us any attention. Calm down," Robin muttered. "Come on, we'll start loading Wilfred's cart, and slip Beth on board once we're nearly done."

Wilfred had found a couple of ales left over from the feast, and declared himself ready for anything after swallowing them. The two young outlaws almost puked watching the old baker drinking the stale beer so early in the day, but it genuinely seemed to liven the man up, and the three moved into the kitchens to set about loading the wagon.

John de Bray's steward hurried over as he saw them approach. The irritating little man seemed to have spent the night in his bed rather than drinking and feasting, as he was bright and alert.

"You two. Minstrels!" he shouted. "I want that cart of his" – he jabbed a finger at Wilfred – "loaded up and gone within the next hour, got it?"

The outlaws nodded.

"Will do, sir!" Robin replied deferentially. "Our thanks to you for having us."

The steward grunted, somewhat mollified by Robin's servile attitude.

"By all accounts you were passably entertaining last night, but Lord de Bray wants his house cleared by mid-morning, so get a move on. And don't even think of lifting anything that doesn't belong to you. We have half a dozen guardsmen here who'll quickly sort you out. I know your type, and I'll be watching you like a hawk."

Allan's blood ran cold at the steward's vow, but neither outlaw replied, they simply nodded again and set about loading the cart.

As the wagon slowly filled up with the empty crates and barrels, it became clear they would never smuggle Beth on board without being spotted. There were too many people about, and the steward hovered around the place constantly.

"How the hell are we going to do this, Robin? That bastard steward checks up on us, and everyone else, every few minutes!"

"I know Allan," Robin hissed. "We're stuck unless we can get him out of the way. When you see Beth ask her if she can create a diversion. Time's running out."

But Beth never appeared. Wilfred overheard two of the serving girls talking, and it seemed Beth had been vomiting that morning and was lying terribly ill in her bed.

The three conspirators began to panic. This was the only chance they would ever get to rescue the little girl and take her back to her father, Will.

"Right, we have to get the steward out of the way and Beth, sick or not, into one of these barrels. Allan, you find the girl. Wilfred, carry on loading the wagon. I'll take care of the rest."

Allan groaned, while Wilfred looked queasy.

"Don't make a commotion, Robin," said the big baker, "or we're done for."

Robin nodded, his hand dropping reflexively to his waist, where his dagger was concealed.

"Let's go."

Allan-a-Dale wandered further into the kitchens, looking for open doors, trying to appear as innocent as possible. The place was busy, and everyone had jobs to attend to, so no one paid him any attention.

Robin went through the door the steward had taken a minute earlier. It led to a deserted hallway, with storerooms on each side and the courtyard at the far end.

The young outlaw moved slowly along the corridor, wondering where the steward was, when the man suddenly appeared at the far entrance.

Robin quickly asked for directions to the latrine.

"Latrine?" roared the steward. "It's not likely to be along here beside the food stores is it? You idiot, get back out there and finish loading that wagon. You can piss when you get on the road to London!"

The steward put his hand on Robin's arm to shove him back towards the kitchens, but the young outlaw grabbed the man's wrist and twisted it behind his back while slapping his other hand over the man's mouth to stifle any cry.

"Struggle, and I break your fucking arm," Robin whispered, pushing his captive into one of the unlit, fusty smelling storerooms. Warily looking to see no one had noticed them go in, he shoved the steward forward and shut the door behind them.

"If you shout or try to escape, you die." It was almost pitch black in the cool room, but as Robin drew out his knife the little sunlight that filtered under the doorway was enough to throw the wicked looking length of steel into sharp relief. "Trust me. Now, where does the girl, Beth, sleep?"

The steward looked bewildered, but his eyes flared angrily as he gave directions to the little girl's sleeping area.

"Thank you," said Robin, but the furious steward, outraged at being treated like this by a simple peasant, opened his mouth and roared for help.

Robin panicked and without thinking, rammed the point of his dagger into the steward's belly, more than once. Slowly, he lowered the dying man to the ground.

"I'm sorry. I truly am," the outlaw whispered in anguish, thankful for the darkness so he couldn't see the life draining from his victim's eyes. "But we need to escape and I can't have you raising the alarm."

He quickly wiped his blade with shaking hands and piled some sacks of fruit over the steward's corpse, then made his way back to Wilfred's wagon as fast as he could, thankful that no one seemed to have heard the steward's cry for help.

He was relieved to see Allan waiting for him, a small smile on his face as the servants hurried around the kitchen busily, the steward's absence obviously unnoticed.

"Got her!" Allan hissed. "She was pretending to be ill and watching out for us from her bedroll. Where's the steward?"

Robin looked miserably at his friend, feeling nauseous and guilty after murdering the nosy official, even though he knew it was the only way they could escape. "Dead. Is the girl on board?"

Allan nodded. They had hidden the girl in a barrel behind the wagon, where no one could see, and loaded it on along with the rest of the empty load.

"We're ready to go," Wilfred told them, his red face anxious. "All we have to do now is get past the guard at the gates before anyone raises the alarm."

The baker climbed onto the driver's seat and the two outlaws clambered up behind him. They lifted their instruments from the top of a crate where Allan had loaded them, and began to strum a simple tune – more to conceal their nerves than from any desire to play.

Wilfred gave a hoarse "Yah!" and cracked the reins over his two old oxen. As the wagon moved off with a lurch, Robin felt the bile rise in his throat and a cold sensation like pins and needles crawled up his hands and arms.

He put down his citole and prayed.

CHAPTER FOURTEEN

Hampole Dyke was miles away from the outlaws' camp. Will Scarlet knew the place well enough – they had robbed a few rich merchants and churchmen here over the past two years or so. It was the only place to cross the river for miles, but it was surrounded by trees on either side, so there was plenty of cover to spring an ambush.

When the outlaws came close to the ford they had seen no sign of Adam Gurdon or his foresters. Will assumed he and the other outlaws were in time, so he began formulating a plan to rescue Matilda.

Tuck gently pulled Will aside and asked if Adam knew the area.

"Aye he does, "Scarlet replied. "It was him that planned any robberies we did here – I scouted the land with him myself."

Tuck looked worried. "Don't you think he might be expecting us to ambush him right here then, Will?"

Scarlet looked thoughtful for a moment, but his lust for revenge lit his eyes like a fire and he swung away from the portly friar.

"He has no reason to expect us to be here. Why the hell would we be? He only just arrested Matilda a short while ago. Why would he think we even heard about it yet?"

Tuck shook his tonsured head in consternation. "You're underestimating Adam, Will. He's not a fool – you know that!"

Scarlet began sending the men to positions within the surrounding foliage, shouting over his shoulder at Tuck as he went. "No, he's not a fool – but he is a traitor, and we're going to get our revenge on the bastard today. Right lads?"

The men cheered, unaware of Tuck's misgivings, but as they began to move to their hiding places in the trees an arrow flashed through the dense undergrowth catching an outlaw in the chest, spinning him onto the ground, gasping and clutching feebly at the wooden shaft sticking out of him.

"Ambush!" Tuck cried, running for cover behind a fallen tree as more arrows whistled murderously through the air around them. "They've been waiting for us!"

* * *

It seemed to take the baker's old cart forever to reach the gatehouse, but it was the same young sentry on duty who had let them in the day before.

"Wilfred!" the guard grinned. "Those minstrels you found were all right last night; I fair enjoyed my evening off."

"Thank you, sir," Allan smiled, and Wilfred slipped the man an oatcake, glancing around and winking conspiratorially.

"Nothing too sweet or stodgy, Thomas, since you're no doubt nursing a hangover, same as me, eh?" the baker laughed ruefully. "No eating on duty, mind. I wouldn't want you getting into trouble with Lord de Bray."

The guard took the cake with a rueful smile and waved them through. "Hangover? Aye, that I have, Wilfred; too much of his lordship's watered-down ale!" He squinted up at Robin and Allan. "If you two are passing this way again, make sure you come and play for us, eh? We see too few entertainers these days." He handed their weapons back to them with a friendly nod.

The cart rumbled slowly over the entrance bridge and the outlaws waved merrily at Thomas as he surreptitiously bit into his oatcake.

They were out.

Now they just had to get far enough away from the place before the missing serving girl and dead steward were discovered.

"Even if they do find him," Allan murmured, leaning back as the cart rumbled onto the rough road, "they have no real reason to blame us. Same with Beth: why would they connect her disappearance with us?"

"They think we're heading for London anyway," Robin nodded, "not Barnsdale."

All three men began to feel a little safer, as the road brought them closer to the forest and freedom, at last, for the little girl hidden in a barrel on the cart behind them.

"You can come out now, Beth," Robin said as the groaning wagon was finally swallowed up by the thick trees, and he prised the lid off the cask with his dagger.

The little girl smiled shyly at him, blinking in the daylight, and stood up slowly, her legs stiff from hiding in such a cramped place.

"You're free, lass!" Robin gently lifted Beth out of the barrel and Allan whooped like a little boy, as Wilfred laughed and roared in delight. "We did it!"

A grin spread across Beth's grubby little face and she looked around, wide eyed, at the outside world she hadn't seen for so long.

"Now," she asked, eventually, "can I see my da?"

And she burst into tears.

* * *

Little John and Much headed back to the outlaws' camp as fast as possible, desperately hoping Robin and Allan-a-Dale would be there to help rescue their friends from Adam Gurdon's trap.

They were.

Once the road from Lord de Bray's manor house entered the forest Robin, Allan and Beth had thanked Wilfred and headed back towards Barnsdale, while the baker made his way home to Hathersage.

The girl had struggled to keep up with the fit, hardy young men so they had taken turns to carry her on their backs or shoulders. She laughed as she swatted aside branches, the happy sound making Robin think sadly of his own little sisters – Rebekah who passed away when she was much the same age as Beth, and Marjorie, at home in Wakefield. He missed them both, and his heart ached as he thought of them, but Beth's simple joy at being free was infectious and his mood soon lifted.

John and Much returned to the camp and dismounted noisily, tying the horses to the branch of a slim young beech tree before hurrying over to see Robin and Allan.

Robin grinned as he saw his two friends approaching and, holding Beth by the hands, he spun the squealing child round in a circle.

"Who's this?" John asked, glancing at Much who shrugged his shoulders in bafflement.

"This," Robin replied, still smiling, "is Elizabeth. Will's daughter!"

John looked at the beaming little girl, his eyes wide, and puffed his cheeks out in astonishment.

Robin finally realised something wasn't right as his eyes took in the deserted outlaws' camp and the two palfreys. "Where is everyone? What's happened?"

"Bad news," Much told his boyhood companion. "Adam's arrested Matilda" –

"What?" Robin roared, making Beth flinch back in fright to stand, wide-eyed, next to Allan who patted her arm reassuringly. "Why? Where's he taking her? I'll kill the bastard!"

Little John nodded, understanding his friend's outrage. "He's taking Matilda to Nottingham, but we have another problem: we know his men are going to ambush Will and the rest of the lads at Hampole Dyke while he takes another route to the city. We have to warn them."

Robin swore. "I have to go after Matilda!"

John shook his head firmly. "You can't, we need to help the others or they'll be butchered."

"You three go on and warn Will and the rest, then" – Robin started, but John cut him off with another shake of his wild brown hair.

"You can't take on Adam on your own, he'll have foresters with him; it'd be suicide. You have to come with us. We'll stop the ambush and then we can *all* go after Matilda."

Much placed a consoling hand on Robin's arm. "John's right. Adam doesn't know we've found out about his plan, so he won't be in any great hurry to get to Nottingham. We can catch him up once we help the others."

Robin cursed again, but he knew his friends spoke the truth. "Alright," he growled, "but we've walked all the way from Hathersage today. Me and Allan will take the horses if that's alright? Beth can climb up with me – we can't leave her here."

John grinned and rubbed his backside which ached even from the relatively short ride from Wakefield. "Aye, fair enough, my arse is killing me anyway."

The one thing in their favour was the fact Adam and his men would be expecting *all* the outlaws to blunder into their trap. If Robin and the others couldn't make it in time to stop the ambush, they might at least be able to help their friends fight their way out alive.

"If we can figure out exactly where they'll spring the ambush we can work our way to their rear and hit them one by one," Robin suggested.

John nodded thoughtfully as he kept pace with the trotting horses. "Aye, they won't have a clue how many of us there are behind them, so if we can take out a few of them the rest might panic."

Robin expected Adam's men would take up positions in the trees either side of Hampole Dyke and strike while the outlaws were crossing the water, out in the open with no cover and nowhere to run, where they could pick them off with their longbows.

"We'd be better splitting up" – he decided – "since we have the horses. Me and Allan can go on ahead and cross the river upstream at one of the other fords. We can work our way round behind the dyke and hit them from that side while you and Much come at the ones on this side of the water."

It was a good plan, and everyone was happy to go along with it, so Robin helped Beth climb off the horse and onto Little John's shoulders.

"How'd you like your new steed?" Robin smiled at the girl.

"Smellier than the horse," Allan grimaced. "Hairier too."

"Shut it you little prick"- John clapped a hand over his mouth as Beth burst out laughing. "Pardon my language, lass," he grinned sheepishly.

"Right, let's get a move on," Robin, impatient to get after Matilda, looked over at Allan, and they headed towards the river's edge where the horses could move faster. "See you in a while, lads!"

As Much and Little John neared the Hampole Dyke John lifted Beth down and hid her near a great old oak tree, telling her to wait there on their return.

"What if something happens to you?" the girl asked, her face screwing up anxiously, as if she were about to cry.

"Look at the size of me!" John replied, smiling reassuringly. "Do you think anyone's going to harm me?" He stood up, his massive frame towering over her, a fierce look on his face, and the girl giggled. "If no one comes for you before it starts to get dark," he laughed, ruffling her hair, "head towards the river and follow it downstream for half a mile. There's a cottage there. It's not too far and you'll be safe. Just tell them Little John sent you."

Beth nodded at the bearded giant uncertainly, and the two men set off towards the ford, only a few minutes jog away, moving silently through the undergrowth at the side of the path.

As they neared the river, the sound of men shouting filled the air and Much groaned. "Adam's men must have sprung their trap, we may be too late!"

"The noise will help us," John replied resolutely. "We can sneak up on the foresters without them hearing us coming. Let's split up. You go left, I'll take the right. No prisoners." He looked his companion in the eyes and hefted his quarterstaff grimly as Much nervously drew his sword, crossing himself for luck.

As they moved off in their separate directions Robin and Allan had worked their way across the river. After safely tying the horses and splitting up as John and Much had done, they were now creeping through the undergrowth looking for signs of Gurdon's foresters. The shouts from the battle were strangely muted and Robin wondered what was happening. Were Will and his men already dead? Had Adam Gurdon's ambush worked to such devastating effect that the outlaws had succumbed in so short a time?

He carried on through the trees, heart thumping nervously, towards the river.

As he got closer he realised Gurdon's foresters, lacking his expert leadership, must have attacked too soon, allowing Will, Tuck and the rest of the outlaws to find cover behind the old collapsed bridge. There was the ping of a longbow to his right, from under a big beech tree, its green summer foliage almost entirely lost, and he inched his way towards the noise. A forester, oblivious to the danger creeping up on him, was fitting another arrow to his string. Robin swiftly came up behind him, and thrust his sword powerfully into the man's back.

The forester fell with a cry of pain and disbelief, blood bubbling from his mouth, as Robin withdrew his blade and listened for signs of more foresters. He moved on again as he heard another bow being fired somewhere close to the left.

There were two men this time, standing side by side, and the young outlaw knew he would have to work fast.

Throwing caution to the wind he made straight for the pair, who were intent on Will Scarlet and the outlaws pinned down with seemingly no escape route. Robin could see Will, face red with rage and frustration, shouting obscenities about Adam Gurdon.

As he came up behind them, one of the foresters began to turn towards Robin, so he lunged forward, swinging his sword savagely into the man's neck, almost decapitating him.

"Attack! We're under attack!" the second man screamed, dropping his bow and fumbling for his sword, but he was too slow, and Robin much too fast.

The outlaw calmly stepped over the corpse of the man he had just killed and chopped his blade down into the arm of the shouting forester, feeling the bones crunch.

The man's shout changed from a warning to a scream of pain, until Robin slammed the pommel of his sword into his mouth, smashing teeth and bone. As the forester fell back, eyes wide in horror, Robin shoved his blade deep into the man's guts and disappeared into the trees again.

From some distance to the right another cry went up, swiftly silenced, then, a few moments later, another shout of alarm came from amongst the trees on the other side of the river. This lasted longer, a cry of terrible pain and slow death. John must have left someone half alive Robin realised, to spread fear among the foresters.

It was a brutal but effective tactic, as Gurdon's men began shouting to each other across the water, wondering what the hell was going on, and who was attacking them from within the trees.

"Will!" Robin roared towards the ford when there was a brief few moments of quiet. "It's Robin Hood! I've brought the rest of the men – we've circled the bastards! Prepare to leave your cover and attack; we'll smash them between us!"

By now, the outlying foresters had begun to panic and make their way from both sides of the river towards the clearing near the ford, giving up their hiding places, and cover, amongst the trees in order to find their captain who had positioned himself there to direct the ambush.

One forester came close to Robin so he quickly fitted an arrow to his longbow and fired it into the man's backside. His agonised roars of pain as he stumbled towards his companions only served to spread the alarm among the foresters even further.

Allan-a-Dale moved into view and Robin crept to join him.

"What now?" Allan wondered. "Looks like there's only about ten of them left, all shitting themselves."

Robin had no desire to cut down these men. The foresters weren't, for the most part, trained soldiers, just decent local men, who normally didn't find themselves caught up in a pitched battle with a squad of hardened outlaws.

"Will!" Robin shouted.

"Aye!" came the eager reply from the other side of the great fallen tree.

"Hold, for now!"

"What?" Scarlet was ready to unleash the fury that had built up inside him. He stood, grasping his sword, as Tuck tried to restrain him.

Little John jogged through the trees his eyes shining with adrenaline as he raised his enormous bow and fixed it on the frightened foresters who were milling about around the ford, clearly lacking any real concrete leadership, swords held out desperately before them. Much appeared like a ghost from the undergrowth and, aiming his own longbow, took up position beside his giant friend.

"You men! Adam Gurdon's foresters!" Robin roared. "Either we can cut you down like wheat during harvest, or you can throw down your weapons and live. I know the bailiff isn't with you. We have no quarrel with you."

The foresters, knowing they were utterly beaten, slowly began to put down their swords, as the one who appeared to be in charge, an overweight, balding middle-aged man, shouted in reply, "My name is Samuel. We surrender Hood. I only hope you men are as honourable as the villagers around here seem to think."

Robin nodded thankfully to himself. "Will! Tell the men to collect those weapons and make sure the foresters are subdued. Peacefully! We'll keep you covered until it's done."

Little John patted Robin on the back. "That was nicely done, lad. Those men are indebted to us now. Looks like we got here just in time."

As Friar Tuck and the rest of the outlaws moved onto the ford and began taking the dropped swords, staffs and longbows, Will Scarlet screamed in rage and flew towards the foresters.

"Where the fuck is that bastard Gurdon?"

The brawny forester, Samuel, seeing Will's intent, quickly retrieved his sword from the ground and started to rise, bringing the weapon up to defend himself.

The outlaws watched in horror as Will, moving too fast to stop himself, ran straight onto Samuel's blade.

"No!" Robin burst from the trees and raced forward to restrain the rest of the men. "No more killing!"

He looked forbiddingly into Samuel's eyes and the big man, a frightened look on his face, pulled the sword from Will's side. "Drop it, and you and your men can be on your way."

The forester nodded. He placed his bloodied sword back on the ground, beside the stricken Will Scarlet, who lay in the icy shallow water, eyes staring straight up at the cloudy afternoon sky.

"John, Tuck! Get Will out of the water! The rest of you, finish collecting those weapons. You foresters, sit on the bank, make no threatening moves and you have my word, no one else will raise a hand to you." He stared around at the men, eyes blazing, hand on his own sword hilt.

The power in the young man's voice was unmistakable, and everyone moved to follow his instructions.

"Will," Robin said gently, when Little John and Friar Tuck had lowered him onto the dry riverbank.

"I'm sorry, Hood. You knew my temper would kill me one day. I've lost so much in my life . . ." Will shuddered, grimacing in pain and clutching the wound in his side as a tear squeezed from between his eyelids. "All I have left is death and vengeance and . . . I won't even get my revenge on those bastards now: Adam and the bastard that took my family . . ." His eyes closed and he shook his head weakly.

Tuck knelt down and examined the wound in Will's side. "It's impossible to tell what damage has been done internally, but . . ." He looked up at Robin and shrugged his wide shoulders hopelessly.

Just then, the sound of running footsteps reached them, and little Beth burst into view through the sparse autumn foliage. She saw Robin and broke into a smile, making her way over to him, then her face crumpled as she saw Will, blood caking his side, his skin deathly pale. But his eyes fluttered open briefly, just as Beth screamed, "Daddy!"

* * *

Sir Richard-at-Lee and his two companions made good time, pushing their horses to their limits, and reaching Hull late in the afternoon the day after leaving Kirklees.

They paid for their mounts to be looked after in a stable near the town gatehouse and made their way to the harbour, which seemed loud and crowded after their journey on the near deserted road.

Shouting sailors loaded crates and barrels onto ships, fishmongers hawked their freshly caught wares from stinking stalls, blood and fish guts littered the ground in some areas making young Simon in particular feel like puking and prostitutes of all ages and nationalities showed their wares with varying degrees of enthusiasm.

Sir Richard asked a few questions and, eventually, a ship bound for Cyprus, the *la Maudelyn*, was located. They made their way aboard, meeting the captain on deck, and passage was booked for Simon. The captain told them, however, he still had much of his cargo to load, so they wouldn't be leaving until dawn the following day.

"My son has to leave tonight," the big Hospitaller told the sailor, a man similar to his own age, who shrugged and spread his hands wide.

"Sorry, my lord. I've told the men they can spend the night drinking and whoring in the town – there'd be a mutiny if I told them I'd changed my mind just so some rich boy could leave early."

Sir Richard laughed sardonically at the idea they were rich, given the debt he owed to Abbott Ness, but he pulled a small bag of silver from his pouch and emptied it on the table. "Tell your men they can drink and fuck in Cyprus. You leave tonight."

The captain glanced at the money. In truth, it wasn't all that much – the Hospitaller simply couldn't afford any more – but it was still a substantial amount and his men had already spent a few days in the town anyway, frittering away their pay. Besides, this big knight with the thick neck and bushy grey beard didn't look like a man to haggle with.

He smiled. "You have a deal, my lord. Once the ship is loaded, we'll leave. Take yourselves off to one of the local taverns – I can recommend the Dog and Duck, just a few yards that way – and come back in a couple of hours. We'll be ready to cast off by then."

Sir Richard grinned in relief and led his son and sergeant-at-arms back down the gangplank and onto the bustling street where they could see the gaudy green and gold sign for the Dog and Duck swinging in the autumn breeze.

"Come on," the Hospitaller shrugged. "We'll be out of sight in there at least."

"Aye," Stephen smiled as one of the prostitutes waggled her tongue at him suggestively. "And I've been choking for a drink all day!"

Simon grinned at his father's gloomy sergeant, a man he'd known almost all his life. "Who'd have thought it? All it takes to put a smile on your face is the thought of an ale and a saggy old pair of tits."

Sir Richard howled with laughter at that, as Stephen grimaced, and they made their way through the packed street to the inn.

"When you see your brother," Richard smiled at his son, "tell him I miss him, and I'm proud of him."

Simon nodded, pushing his way through the people thronging the docks.

"I'm proud of you both," Sir Richard continued. "You've been fine sons."

Despite the hour – it was almost sunset – the street was still heaving with people and, as they approached the door to the Dog and Duck with dry mouths, Simon suddenly stumbled, the people around him buffeting him as he fell forward.

Stephen grabbed his right arm and made to help him up, but the young man felt like a lead weight and, as Sir Richard grasped his other arm, Simon collapsed, face first onto the ground.

"What's wrong" – the Hospitaller demanded as he looked at his son and saw the red stains spreading over his back.

"Stephen!" he roared, trying to pull his sword from its scabbard. "He's been stabbed!"

The crowd, which had been pressing so close until then, suddenly parted, leaving the three men in a circle of their own as the burly knight drew his blade and held it defensively over his fallen son. Stephen had his own weapon drawn by now and the two men searched the mass of people for threats.

A man was pushing his way, forcibly through the people on the street and, when he looked back, Stephen gave a cry of rage and raced after him, waving his sword over his head to try and clear the way.

Sir Richard, fearing the worst as the small red wounds on his son's back had spread to form one great crimson stain, knelt down and grasped Simon by the shoulder, turning him over.

The young man's eyes were glazed, staring straight up, unseeing.

Lifeless.

Despenser's men had managed to catch up with them.

The commander of Kirklees screamed in despair. His beloved son was dead.

CHAPTER FIFTEEN

Friar Tuck bandaged Will's wound, but the outlaws knew it was hopeless.

Robin felt a great sense of helpless frustration. To have rescued Scarlet's daughter, only for the hot headed fool to impale himself on a sword in a moment of madness before he could be reunited . . .

Little Beth was inconsolable, having to be dragged off her father in despair, while Tuck tended to him.

"We need to move fast, Robin," Little John said to his young friend. "If we're to stop Gurdon locking Matilda away in some Nottingham dungeon, we have to catch up with him."

"What about Will, though?" Allan-a-Dale asked. "We can't just leave him here to die."

John expression was dark as he turned to Allan. "Will only has himself to blame for what's happened. He let his temper get the best of him and he's paid the price. We need to help Matilda while we still have the chance. If Adam gets her into the city she's as good as dead – we would never be able to rescue her from there. If we can catch them on the open road in time though…"

Beth had stopped crying by now, and she gazed at Robin forlornly. "Please help my da," she sniffed. "I have no one else."

Robin leaned down and clasped Beth's small hand in his own.

"I won't lie to you…your da took a terrible injury. It doesn't look good for him. But we won't leave him here. And whatever happens, lass, you won't be alone. We have friends and family in the all the villages around Yorkshire. We will find you a home, with good people."

He smiled reassuringly at Beth, and she nodded in return, but her eyes flickered to Will again, which brought a fresh bout of sobbing.

Robin patted her awkwardly on the arm and stood up. "Tuck. You, Allan and young Gareth there make a stretcher and carry Will back to our camp. Make him comfortable and…just do what you can for him Tuck."

The friar met Robin's eyes and both men knew what the young leader meant – Will would need the Last Rites before the day was out.

"Come on, Beth, help us find some straight branches to make a stretcher for your da," said Allan, leading the girl into the trees. Gareth, a fifteen-year-old outlaw from Wrangbrook, followed them, eyes roving across the ground searching for sturdy sticks.

Robin turned away sadly. "You foresters can be on your way, as I promised."

The captives stood up gratefully, relief plain on their face. Most of the outlaws around the great forests of England would not have been so merciful.

"Just remember this day," Robin told them, "should we ever find ourselves in a situation like this again, with the roles reversed."

The foresters nodded and moved gratefully off along the road towards Nottingham. Their big leader, Samuel, grasped Robin's hand firmly.

"I thank you for our freedom, Hood. If ever the day comes when I can aid you in return, know that I will do all I can for your men."

Robin clapped him on the arm, nodding, although he knew it was unlikely Samuel would find himself in charge of men often, after his rout at the hands of the outlaws. It was plain the middle-aged forester was no gifted leader of men. But he was another friend to the outlaws, and they needed every one they could get. Robin waved the grateful man off and checked his weapons were firmly secured.

"Make ready to move lads!" he roared at his men. "Adam must still be on the road to Nottingham. We might have time to catch up with him if we cut through the forest. He must only have a couple of men in his party now, so, as long as we move fast enough, we can stop the bastard and repay him for everything he's done."

"Let's move!" Little John's huge voice shook the trees, and the outlaws moved into the hidden pathways of the forest that they knew so well, yet which would have been invisible to any outsider.

Friar Tuck, Allan-a-Dale and Gareth quickly fashioned a crude but sturdy stretcher and eased Will onto it. Then they, along with Beth, struck off towards their camp.

"How do we know Gurdon is on the Great North Road?" Matt Groves demanded as the main party of outlaws hurried through the forest. They had collected the two horses and brought them along, in case Gurdon saw them coming and tried to get away, but no one was riding them just now. Robin wanted them as fresh as possible, should they be needed for a chase.

"I found out his plans from Henry Woolemonger, before I ran him through," Little John replied to Matt. "Adam's plan was to crush us at Hampole Dyke while he escaped unchallenged with Matilda."

"If it had worked he would have wiped us out in one blow," the teenager, Arthur, grunted. "Just as well you four came along when you did."

Little John nodded. "Aye. Now *we* have the element of surprise with us. The turncoat bastard thinks we're all dead. He'll be in no great hurry to deliver Matilda to the prior."

"That's my fear..." Robin admitted.

"What do you mean? Surely if they take their time it gives us more of a chance to catch them?" Much glanced over in surprise at his boyhood friend.

Robin stared ahead of him, face set in determination, as he picked up the pace, forcing the rest of the outlaws to speed up to avoid falling behind.

"Aye, Much, but Adam and his men...left alone with Matilda; in no great hurry...they might just decide to make a whore of her before the prior gets her into that brothel of his."

Adam Gurdon was a brutal man. Much expected he would enjoy using Matilda – whether she consented or not. Much had known the girl as long as Robin; she had been a good friend of his in Wakefield too.

"Come on lads," he shouted, pulling alongside Robin. "Time for the bastard to pay for his betrayal!"

* * *

"All right boys, let's take a rest and have something to eat." Adam Gurdon reined in his horse and his two companions followed suit gladly.

The late summer sun was still warm and the three lawmen were thirsty, as was Matilda who had been forced to endure a steady stream of inane and often filthy chatter from Gurdon and his men as they made their way along the well-worn road.

The bailiff dismounted smoothly and, none too gently, helped Matilda down.

"Sit." He pointed her towards a large boulder, on to which she gratefully slumped. The girl was not used to riding, and even after a short period on horseback her whole body, particularly her buttocks, felt stiff and sore.

Gurdon's two foresters made themselves comfortable on a rotten old log, and drank their fill from their ale skins, murmuring contentedly as they relaxed in the warm sun.

"I'd love to know how you managed to fool the outlaws into thinking you were Adam Bell," one of them suddenly asked the bailiff, shaking his head wonderingly.

Gurdon laughed and shrugged his shoulders, wiping wine from the side of his wet lips.

Almost everyone in England knew the folk tales about the outlaw Adam Bell, a Saxon hero, who hailed from the town of Inglewood. Bell, with his friends Adam Cloudesley and Clim of the Clough, had great adventures, outwitting the sheriffs and lords of whichever county the tale happened to be told in.

"What did Adam Bell look like, lad?" Gurdon asked the forester.

The man racked his brains for a while and looked to his grizzled companion for support, but neither of them could answer the question.

"Exactly," Gurdon smiled. "The stories don't say. All I had to do was find a small group of outlaws, tell them I was Adam Bell and, before long everyone believed it was true." He dropped his ale skin and pulled an apple from his pack, eyes sparkling merrily as he bit into it. "If he ever lived," Gurdon went on, spitting juicy flecks of fruit from his mouth, "Adam Bell and his mates must have died years ago. Who could say I wasn't him?"

The foresters nodded in admiration at their new bailiff's ingenuity.

"Here, girl." Gurdon, having half drained it, passed his own ale skin to Matilda. She took a sip, but found it was much more bitter, and stronger, than she was used to.

"You like that?" Gurdon watched her drink, his eyes roving across her body unashamedly.

Matilda squirmed under his gaze and handed the ale back to him defiantly. "No, I don't. It tastes like piss."

The three men laughed at that.

"I can see why young Hood covets you so much, girl," the bailiff told her, wiping the thick sheen of sweat from his forehead. "You've got a fine body on you, eh lads?"

The other two made lewd replies, grinning like young boys, but their eyes were humourless. Matilda felt a cold shiver run down her spine.

"You can forget about Hood," Adam continued, taking another drink of his ale. "He'll be dead by now. Him, and the rest of those fools I used to lead will have chased off after you, right into the ambush my men prepared at Hampole Dyke."

Matilda felt her blood turn to ice, but her captor continued, walking over to stand before her, triumphantly.

"Those idiots will walk right into a storm of arrows, and any that survive the first volley will be cut down where they stand by my foresters."

Matilda remained silent as Gurdon carried on, a self-satisfied smile playing around the corners of his mouth.

"There's no one left to help you, girl." He leaned down to look into her eyes, grinning savagely. "The prior will make sure you're tried, and found guilty of aiding the outlaws. Then…"

His hand moved slowly down to cup Matilda's left breast. "Then the prior will put that body of yours to work in his brothel – the 'Maiden's Head'. It's a nice place; you'll have a lot of fun there."

The two foresters grunted. "I'll be in to visit you a lot, girl," one of them promised, staring at her malevolently. Matilda felt the panic begin to build in her. Tears filled her eyes as Adam pulled her top down to expose her nipples, drawing more grunts and gasps from the two foresters.

She desperately wanted to fight the bailiff off, but her arms wouldn't respond as she screamed inside and tried to block out what was happening to her.

Gurdon leaned down further and roughly bit her breast, pushing her legs apart, and the girl felt a wave of black despair wash over her. She and Robin would never be together now.

She thought of all the good things in her life: her loving parents and her friends in Wakefield, her home. She went limp with grief as she thought of Robin, shot through and broken by the arrows of Adam Gurdon's men.

"There boys, she's starting to relax. She's a natural!" the bailiff laughed and stood up, undoing his trousers as Matilda watched numbly.

"Now, girl. Open that pretty mouth of yours…"

* * *

There was no time for anyone to plan or prepare. Robin had taken the lead, his men struggling to keep pace with him as he pushed himself on, tortured by visions of Adam abusing Matilda.

They were beside the river again, which followed the course of the road at this point, and the water gurgled noisily over a small waterfall, so neither party heard the other until Robin jogged around a small rise and almost ran into Gurdon, his breeches at his ankles, Matilda sitting in front of him and his two henchmen laughing gleefully. Their faces fell as they caught sight of the outlaw just two yards away, but the bailiff had his back turned, and neither of the foresters had ever seen Robin before, so they were slow to draw their weapons.

The young outlaw stopped dead in his tracks, frozen to the spot, as Matilda squirmed, tearfully trying to keep Gurdon's cock away from her mouth.

Then she saw Robin appearing like an avenging angel, and felt a surge of elation. He wasn't dead! As her lover's hand moved to his sword hilt, Matilda looked up at Adam Gurdon with a look of fierce triumph and opened her mouth.

Robin swiftly drew his blade and rammed it into the nearest forester's guts before the man realised what was happening. He dropped to his knees like a stone, and Robin savagely ripped the blade free, spilling the man's intestines onto the grass.

Too fast for the eye to follow, the outlaw spun completely around and hacked into the side of the second man's sword arm. The forester collapsed, bellowing, clutching at his near-severed limb.

When she'd seen Robin attacking, Matilda had taken Adam's manhood in her mouth…and bit down as hard as she could.

The bailiff screamed in agony as half his cock was completely severed, blood pumping thickly from the horrendous wound. Matilda spat it onto the grass in front of his disbelieving eyes.

"You fucking bitch!" he screamed in shock, feebly clasping his hands over his bleeding crotch, the shock at his mutilation rendering him oblivious to the fate of his two companions. "I'll kill you, I'll fucking kill you!"

His cries were cut off suddenly, as the point of a sword erupted out the front of his chest.

Robin leaned in behind his former mentor and whispered in his ear. "You won't be killing anyone. I'm going to take your carcass to Nottingham and leave you there for everyone to see."

He pulled his sword free with a wet, sucking, sound and kicked the sagging Gurdon sideways onto the grass, where he clutched at his terrible wounds, whimpering pitifully.

Matilda, adrenaline pounding in her veins, picked up Gurdon's severed penis, and rammed it into his weakly protesting mouth furiously.

"There, you can suck it yourself now, you evil bastard!" she shouted hysterically, forcing him to gag on it.

The second forester had tried to make a run for it, his sword arm almost hacked off by Robin, but Little John and the rest of the outlaws had caught up with him. They pushed him back into the clearing, crying like a child and clutching his arm in terror.

John took in the carnage before him, eyes wide in disbelief. "What do we do with this one, Robin?"

Hood turned, his face frozen in a grimace of rage, and calmly drove his sword into the man's belly.

"Leave those two animals," he said, pointing with his sword to the two foresters. "Gurdon we take with us."

No one argued, as Robin lifted Matilda to her feet and took her in his arms. She was shaking uncontrollably now, as the adrenaline faded and shock took its place.

"He said you were all dead," she sobbed.

Robin held her fiercely, his own hands starting to shake as he stroked her strawberry-blonde hair. "Aye, that was his plan, but we beat him Matilda. We're fine. And you're safe now."

They stood like that for a while, everyone silent in the face of the awful violence they'd just witnessed, before Little John spoke to two of the outlaws.

"Lift Adam. We should get moving."

Robin nodded. "Me and Much will take his body to Nottingham, and make sure Prior de Monte Martini and everyone else in the town finds out what happened to him. That'll send a message to anyone else that might decide to come hunting us."

It seemed an extreme gesture to Little John, but right now, in this mood, Robin was in charge, so the giant simply nodded his head and promised to take Matilda safely back to their camp with the rest of the men.

"We'll meet you back there when we're done," Robin said, his gaze still vacant, his sword still drawn, dripping blood onto the pale green grass.

"All right, we're done lads. At last. Let's get back to camp and celebrate!" John smiled half-heartedly, and some of the men cheered as they began the journey home.

Although they had beaten Adam and gained their revenge for his betrayal, most of the outlaws felt it was a hollow victory. They knew they would still be wolf's heads when they woke up the next day, and the day after that. No matter how many of their pursuers they killed, they would never be able to go back to their families and a normal life again.

Adam Gurdon's body was loaded onto his horse, while Robin and Much inexpertly mounted the two horses the foresters had been riding.

"Be careful, Robin," said Matilda, quietly.

He nodded. "We won't be long. Then tomorrow we'll take you home to your ma and da."

The girl's eyes filled with tears again and she forced a smile as Robin and Much rode off towards Nottingham, the bailiff's mutilated body strapped tightly to the horse he had ridden so proudly into Wakefield earlier that day.

* * *

Although Robin had told Tuck to take Will back to the outlaws' camp, the friar knew that was a death sentence for the wounded Scarlet. They only had rudimentary medical supplies at camp and, although Tuck was fairly certain Will would not survive no matter what aid he received, he felt it his duty – to Beth if nothing else – to seek out the best help possible.

Allan-a-Dale and the youngster Gareth, outlawed for stealing food from a chapel for his sick mother, carried Will's stretcher through the forest, with Tuck taking turns to relieve one of the other periodically.

"Obviously, this isn't leading to our camp, Tuck," Allan noted after a couple of miles. "Where are we going?"

"Kirklees Priory," Tuck replied, wiping sweat from his tonsured head with the sleeve of his grey robe. "The nuns there have a better chance of saving Will than we do. The convent has skilled surgeons, and medicines that will help him."

The friar felt guilty as Beth looked towards him, her face alive with hope. He had seen too many sword wounds over the years, and never had he seen a man survive one as grievous as that which Will had sustained.

He mouthed a silent prayer to St Francis, and gave the little girl's shoulder a reassuring squeeze.

"How much further?" Beth asked him.

"We'll reach there just after sunset, lass," Tuck replied. "Do you need a rest?"

Her small face grew determined and she straightened her shoulders. "No. Let's get there as fast as we can."

Tuck nodded and gave her an encouraging smile. It was obvious Will's daughter was struggling – she'd spent the past three years cooped up in a house. True, she had worked hard every day, but long distance travelling, indeed *any* travelling, other than between rooms in the manor house, hadn't been part of her routine. Tuck was glad she was still little – he knew she would need carried soon.

It was going to be a long hard journey to Kirklees Priory for them all.

* * *

It was sometime after the sun had set, and the constellation of the dragon looked down on the small party, when they finally reached Kirklees. Tuck had carried Beth through the dark forest for the last mile, her short legs and undernourished body having in the end given out. She had fallen asleep in his arms. Although he was a portly man, who ate and drank too much, the friar was as strong as an ox. Still, his arms ached terribly as they hammered on the door of the priory.

Allan-a-Dale and Gareth were as exhausted as Tuck. They were hard, fit lads, used to physical exertion and forced marches, but the fast pace they had set, along with the burden they carried, meant aching backs, arms and legs. They were glad when a young nun opened the great wooden door and invited them in once Tuck had explained – after a fashion – their predicament.

She had looked at Will, pale on the stretcher, then Beth, exhausted in the large friar's arms, and waved them inside, promising to fetch the abbess.

When the abbess came, she led them to a small room and bade them place Will on the bed there. Beth drowsily insisted on staying with her father, so the nuns brought her a blanket and the little girl fell asleep again in a chair by Will's bedside.

The men were shown to a sparsely furnished chamber with four beds and little else inside its grey stone walls. It was cool and, to men used to sleeping on the forest floor, hugely comfortable. They were brought a little bread and cheese each, with cool water to wash it down.

Allan and Gareth, having carried the stretcher for most of the way, ate their small meal gratefully and quickly fell asleep, completely drained.

Tuck sat a while in the small chapel, saying another prayer for Will's well being. The abbess came and questioned him there, about Will and how he came to be so horribly wounded, but she seemed to care little for the answers, or the truth of them. She knew very well they were probably not entirely true.

Tuck simply claimed bandits had attacked Will and his daughter in the forest, and he and his two friends had found them as they made their way along the road to Nottingham.

"You don't expect him to survive do you?" she asked.

Tuck shook his head sadly. "I'm surprised he isn't dead already, truth be told."

The abbess agreed. "We have cleaned the wound but I have no doubt he has internal damage which we cannot heal. What will happen to the girl when he dies? Where is her mother?"

"She told us her mother was dead, but she has an uncle in Wakefield. We will take here there when…if…her father dies."

The nun nodded. "I won't keep you any longer, you should get some rest yourself – you must be worn out. It was very good of you and your friends to carry them all this way…" She gave him a calculating look, and he burst out laughing.

"I expect a reward!" he smiled. "In *heaven*…Although, if you have any spare communion wine around, that would be pleasant indeed."

"You're pushing your luck, friar, you shouldn't even be in here," the nun snorted, surprising him with her knowledge. "It's against the Rule of your own Franciscan order: 'Brothers should not enter the convents of nuns.'"

She wandered off, shaking her head sternly but when Tuck returned to the chamber Allan and Gareth were asleep in he found a jug of poor quality, yet strong wine next to his own bed.

As he felt the bitter liquid begin to relax him, he mouthed another prayer: Mary, mother of our Lord, help Will, and little Beth, whatever happens during this night…

Then at last, he fell asleep.

* * *

Will Scaflock was dying. Indeed, he should have been dead already – *would* have been dead already if not for one thing.

In some dark, hidden corner of his subconscious mind Will knew he had heard his daughter's voice before he had blacked out at Hampole Dyke.

Before today he would have embraced death as a release at last from his tormented life, but now, his little girl's face filled his soul. His body would not give in to death so easily.

The nuns had known Will was dying, from the evil smell coming from his wound. They had cleaned it as best they could, and stitched it up with a healing poultice, but they knew that smell. They knew the little girl clutching the man's hand would, in a few hours, maybe less, be left without her father, despite their prayers.

Beth knew none of this. Her da looked quite peaceful lying in the bed. She was sure he would be fine: he was strong, a fierce warrior; nothing ever hurt her da!

Then he began to turn blue, and his hand started to feel cold and clammy, and Beth began to wail, fresh tears streaming from her brilliant blue eyes.

Consciously, Will Scaflock knew nothing of this. Yet, as his ruined body lay comatose within the great stone walls of the priory, he dreamt – a more vivid dream than he had ever had before.

His wife, Elaine, came to him. She looked as she had in life, but she carried a lantern which only served to light her dimly. All around her was darkness.

"You're a fool Will Scaflock!" she chided him with a smile. He had no strength to argue, and knew she was right anyway. "But you have a part to play in this yet. You mustn't give in to death just yet. Fight it, Will, fight it for Beth!"

His wife seemed to come closer to him and she placed her hand on his side. Without looking down, Will knew there was a terrible gaping hole in him, yet as Elaine touched the wound he felt something…a strength, or force, coursing through him.

He grinned as the power filled his soul and he raised his eyes to look at the woman he had loved since the day he had first met her.

But it wasn't Elaine looking back at him. As he watched, her face seemed to shift and change in the darkness, until another face Will knew was staring back at him: Robin Hood, his face set in stony determination, gazed into his eyes. Yet it wasn't quite the Robin he knew: the face was somehow older, somehow different, somehow more…commanding, Will thought.

By his bedside, two nuns had come running when Beth started screaming in despair, and they watched in wonder as Will's blue lips slowly began to turn red again, and his grey flesh became a healthy pink.

In his fever dream, Scaflock stared at 'Robin'. "Leave me alone, Hood. I've nothing to live for. I can go and be with my family, with Elaine. I want to die!"

His skin slowly turned blue again.

Beth had not noticed the change in him and continued to cry the whole time, heart broken. As she laid her head down against Will's face, her tears rolled onto his pale cheeks. "Daddy!" she cried. "Please don't leave me again!"

Will's body gave a spasm, and he gasped for air, his eyes snapping open in shock, seeing his daughter's little face for the first time in three years.

"Beth . . !" he breathed. Then his eyes closed again and his body went limp. But this time there was a smile on his lips and he only slept. His daughter *was* alive! And, for now, so was he.

CHAPTER SIXTEEN

"Bastard!" Sir Richard-at-Lee roared with anger, kicking his chair and sending it flying despite its weight.

Stephen grimaced but remained silent as his lord vented some of his frustration.

"This is all because 'Sir' Hugh Despenser, in his greed, wanted to extort some money from a decent man!" the Hospitaller shouted, the hurt he was feeling evident in his voice. "The bastard's supposed to be in exile, yet he continues to bring his black influence to us!"

After his son had been murdered, Sir Richard had brought his body back to Kirklees and buried him by the priory, his heart close to breaking with rage and despair. Stephen had been unable to catch the assailant in Hull, so they had no legal redress – not that it would have counted for much anyway. The Despensers appeared to be above the law, even in exile.

Sir Richard, in his grief, had wanted to ride to Cardiff and attack the castle with his own small garrison, but Stephen had stopped him. The Marcher lords would take care of Despenser – indeed, serious trouble was brewing for both the king and the Despensers, as Leeds castle had been besieged by Edward in the past few days, with the Marcher lords Mortimer and Hereford riding to the aid of their ally Lord Badlesmere against the king's forces.

The country was truly on the point of civil war as a result of the Despensers evil influence over the king.

Half an hour earlier, Sir Richard had gathered the staff in his castle at Kirklees and given them the bad news.

"I know, it's coming into winter – the worst time I could do this to you," he told them sadly. "But I have no money left to retain your services – my personal income will have to go towards my debt to Abbott Ness, until I can secure more loans to cover that debt."

His staff cried out in shock – how would they look after their families without a job? Food was almost too costly even with a regular wage coming in, what would they do now?

The Hospitaller could only spread his hands wide and beg their understanding.

To ruin so many lives, after his own son being murdered…it was too much.

* * *

Robin awoke with a gasp, drenched in sweat, his head pounding.

"What's wrong?" Matilda asked, sitting up beside him under their shared blanket.

Robin and Much had reached Nottingham in the afternoon. They had made sure Adam Gurdon's cock was firmly stuffed in his mouth, tying it there with a piece of torn linen so it couldn't fall out, then gave his horse a slap on the rump. It had raced off, through the gates of the town, chased by the surprised gate guards.

Robin knew everyone in Nottingham would have heard about the bailiff returning tied to his horse, mutilated and humiliated in death. The note Friar Tuck had written before they split up, they had pinned to Adam's body. It would serve as a warning to any who might think to come after them in future.

This is Adam Gurdon, Bailiff of Wakefield, formerly known as Adam Bell – traitor! it read. *This is what happens to lawmen in Barnsdale. The forest is ours!*

Although only a small handful of people would see the note, tongues would wag, and, in a big town like Nottingham, within a few days everyone in the place would know what it said.

Robin and Much had made their way back to the camp in the Yorkshire forest where John, Matilda, and the rest of the gang waited.

Tuck's party were, of course, nowhere to be seen, but one of the men, Arthur, the nineteen-year-old from Bichill, had noticed the stretcher-bearers' trail had changed direction on the path to camp and it was assumed the canny friar had decided to look for aid at Kirklees Priory.

Despite rescuing Matilda, and destroying their despised former leader, the mood in the outlaws' camp was somewhat sombre, since no one knew whether Will Scarlet lived or not. He may not have been the most pleasant of companions, but he was one of their own, and had saved many of their lives at one point or another.

Ale had been drunk, they sang a song or two, but no one really felt like enjoying themselves. Robin had led Matilda to his pallet when night fell, the camp fire burned low, and the outlaws, after setting the watch, had turned in.

Matilda shed tears of relief as she made love to Robin in the darkness. Will may have been mortally wounded, but Matilda had never met him. Robin though, *her Robin,* was here, and in her arms. For that, she cried and said silent prayers of thanks.

A short while later, she was surprised to hear sobbing coming from beside her. It was a moonless night, and the campfire had burned low, so she could hardly make out Robin's face in the shadows as he turned and buried his face in her shoulder.

"What's wrong?" Matilda whispered, shocked and a little frightened by Robin's unexpected show of emotion.

He didn't reply for a while, just held her tighter. "It's all too much," he wept. "I'm only seventeen, yet I'm practically leading a gang of outlaws. I've killed men; my mate Will's dying after being run through in front of his little girl; it's my fault Harry Half-hand's dead…and still, the law will be after us tomorrow. Just as they always will be."

His voice cracked and he buried his face deeper into Matilda's shoulder as she stroked his hair comfortingly. "It feels like the weight of the whole world is on me!"

They held each other tightly in the darkness. Matilda was lost for words so she simply whispered comforting noises as if to a frightened child, and eventually they fell back asleep.

Until Robin started awake, again, not long before dawn.

"It's Will," he gasped, sitting up wide-eyed. "Something's wrong. Seriously wrong."

Matilda put a hand on his shoulder, frightened by his tone.

Robin shook his head. He had dreamt of Will, he was trying to help him get better, but…Will didn't *want* to get better, and Robin had woken then, despairing for his friend. He looked at Matilda in the darkness, her face beautiful in the dim orange glow from the embers of the campfire, and forced a smile.

"What will be, will be. Let's go back to sleep."

When the dawn sun rose, Robin took Little John and set out for Kirklees Priory.

"The men will be brooding about Will," Robin had said to Matilda as they prepared to leave. "So we've told them to spend the day in combat training to take their minds off it. You can go pair off with Much – if you're going to be staying here with us for a while you need to learn how to defend yourself."

Matilda nodded. She had never been in a true physical fight in her life, not even as a child, but, since the foresters would be hunting her now, she had to learn how to live as an outlaw. And that meant fighting.

"Don't worry." Robin grasped her hands and gazed at her, the previous night's self-pity gone as fierce determination filled his eyes. "Somehow I'll get a pardon for us. For all of us. Adam managed it, we can too! I won't live like a hunted animal for the rest of my life, I swear it."

She forced a smile and Much handed her one of the lighter wooden practice swords with an encouraging grin. Robin gave her a last lingering kiss goodbye before he and John headed off towards the priory.

After only an hour or so they were met by Allan-a-Dale and Gareth, who Tuck had sent back to camp to take the news of Will's recovery to the rest of the outlaws.

"He lives, Robin!" Allan cried, a grin lighting up his handsome face.

"A miracle, truly!" put in young Gareth.

Robin and John looked at each other in disbelief.

"How?" John asked. "That wound he took was mortal, we could all see it!"

Allan shrugged, laughing. "I told you: a miracle. One minute he was dead, and little Beth was crying her heart out, the next his eyes opened and he spoke to her. Just for a moment, though. He's been sleeping ever since, but the nuns say his wound's clean and the smell from it's gone."

John shook his great head in wonder. "Aye, a miracle right enough. God be praised!"

Robin smiled, but felt Beth had been the one who had brought Will back from the dead, rather than the nuns' prayers.

"All right, you two head back to camp and let the others know. Me and John will go and see how he fares, and what Tuck would have us do next."

Allan and Gareth nodded, and whooped as John promised a proper celebration feast for them all tonight.

* * *

The great stone walls seemed to crowd in on Robin, as a pretty young nun led him and John to Will's sickroom in the priory.

The outlaws were used to the open skies and the leafy canopies of the greenwood, occasionally the low thatched roof of a village alehouse. These great high ceilings, tiled floors and cold, grey stone walls made both men nervous, but the nun had smiled happily at them when they had knocked on the door, asking after Will.

"Your friend has made a miraculous recovery," the girl said. "Truly God was at work in our priory last night!"

John smiled back, admiring the gentle curves of the young woman's body, which the dark habit couldn't hide. Robin nodded distractedly as the big man nudged him, smiling lecherously behind the nun's back.

Despite the girl's enthusiasm, both Robin and John were stunned to see Will sitting up in bed, wolfing down a large bowl of apple stew. He smiled sheepishly at them, and Beth leapt up from her chair to rush over and hug Robin's legs.

"He's all right! I knew he'd be all right!" she laughed happily.

"So I see, lass," Robin replied, ruffling her hair as he looked down at Will who finished off the last of his meal and closed his eyes, grimacing slightly as a shiver of pain ran through his side.

"I'm alive, but it still bloody hurts," he grunted.

"How's the wound?" Little John asked. "Allan said it had healed over – surely that's not true?"

"The nuns stitched it up, they say it's clean and will heal up nicely soon enough. As for it healing over, well, Allan's a bloody minstrel isn't he? He likes to exaggerate. Still…we all know I should have died yesterday, so I can't complain." He smiled weakly.

"You can't stay here for long," Robin told him. "Someone's bound to find out who you are and the sheriff's men will come for you. We need to get you back to the forest as soon as you're able to travel."

Will nodded. "What about Beth? The forests are no place for a child."

"I've spoken with Matilda about Beth," Robin replied. "She says her ma and da will be happy to take care of her. They'll have the extra space now, since Matilda will be living with us for a while…"

Will grinned in relief. "That sounds good my friend. And…" He lowered his eyes, as they filled with tears. "I don't know how to thank you and Allan for getting my little girl back for me." He pulled Beth to him and hugged her tightly. "I never believed she was still alive. I feel guilty now for never looking for her myself. I thought the soldiers had killed them all." His body shook as he sobbed gently, stroking his daughter's long brown hair. "I'm so sorry, Beth."

"Well, she's safe now," Robin replied awkwardly. "You two can start again."

"Aye," John laughed loudly. "And maybe now since you have something to live for you won't be so bloody miserable all the time?"

Everyone smiled at that.

"Aye, you're right. I know I've been hard to be around. But now, well, like you say I've got something – someone – to live for. Thanks to you Robin."

Friar Tuck wandered into the room, chewing a piece of black bread. His eyes lit up as he saw his friends. "Truly a miracle, lads," he cried, crumbs spilling from his mouth. "The Virgin Mary gave us our brother Will back – she must have a purpose for him here."

"Oh I have a purpose all right, Tuck." Will's smile turned to a steely glare. "I want to be up and about as soon as I can. Because once I'm better, I'm going after the bastard that took Beth from me!"

* * *

"The king must be dealt with!"

The magnates gathered by Thomas, Earl of Lancaster in another of his "parliaments" rumbled agreement at his assertion, although some looked uncomfortable at such a treasonous statement.

"The younger Despenser – with Edward's connivance – has embarked on a career of piracy!" Lancaster, his face red with anger, slammed a fist onto the long table before him. "The Despensers have been banished, yet the younger of them continues to act as he pleases, while the king does nothing. In fact, the king *aids* Despenser in his criminal activities!"

"At least his father has accepted his fate and gone abroad," Sir John de Bek growled.

"Many of us," Lancaster roared, "pledged ourselves when we last met in June to secure the destruction of the Despensers. Both of them. Yet the younger is allowed to live the life of a murderous pirate, waylaying many English merchant ships on the Channel, while I have heard strong rumours that the king has been in contact with him and plans to recall both father and son before the end of the year."

There were cries of outrage at this.

"Surely Edward would not be so foolish?" Sir Richard-at-Lee demanded in disbelief. "He knows the depth of feeling against the Despensers. If that piece of murdering filth ever sets foot in the country again I will hunt him down myself!"

"The king cares nothing for our feelings!" Lord Mowbray spat. "Do my lords forget the other…*favourites*…the king has kept over the years? The Despensers have manipulated him for years – and will continue to do so – just as Piers Gaveston did."

The Earl of Lancaster nodded in agreement. "My cousin is not fit to rule I'm afraid, gentlemen. When I was made Steward of England I naively thought I could influence him. I hoped to curb the influence of men like Gaveston and the Despensers, but Edward is blind to the faults of these…friends…of his."

Lord Clifford shook his head despairingly. "It grieves me greatly to say it, my lords, but I fear the time has come that we take matters into our own hands, before the king ruins us all, as he has recently ruined Lord Badlesmere."

There was a silence in the room at this pronouncement, as each of the assembled magnates contemplated the terrible fate of Badlesmere, who had sided with the Marchers against the king.

Edward's wife, Queen Isabella, had sought lodging for the night at Leeds Castle, of which, Badlesmere was constable. Although he was away at the time, his wife, Margaret, had refused the royal party access, going so far as to have her archers shoot down half a dozen of the queen's retainers. The king had, understandably, been incensed at this, and had laid siege to Leeds castle.

Some of the Marchers, including Mortimer and Hereford, had travelled to Lady Badlesmere's aid, they had arrived too late and the castle had fallen to the king.

Although Lord Badlesmere had not been captured, his wife, their children and other immediate family had been imprisoned in Dover Castle, while many of his supporters were hanged.

The king had shown a new side to his character: decisive, ruthless and merciless. His actions had shocked Sir Richard-at-Lee and most of the other lords gathered here at Pontefract who were used to seeing an indecisive, weak and inept Edward.

The Marchers, and the Earl of Lancaster, were particularly worried. If they did not act soon, the king's newfound sense of purpose would be the end of them.

Time was not on their side.

"The king has shown by his unlawful treatment of Lord Badlesmere, who has been found guilty without due legal process, that he will do as he pleases even to his most devoted subjects. He has gone insane with power – he has become a tyrant!"

Sir Richard noted a few frowns around the room, but the loud roars of outraged agreement from the Marchers and their friends filled the room.

"The time to act is almost upon us, gentlemen," Thomas stated. "Or any one of us will be the king's next target. Would you sit twiddling your thumbs while Edward strips you of your lands?" He glared at the men seated before him. "Will you wait, like lambs to the slaughter, hoping our beloved monarch and his friends will not imprison or even murder *your* children, as the king has done to Badlesmere, and Despenser did to Sir Richard-at-Lee?"

Again the Marchers shouted angry demands for action, and Sir Richard could tell Lancaster's speech was having the desired effect as many of the lords who had appeared undecided at the start of the meeting were now joining in with the cries of outrage.

The commander of Kirklees grinned savagely. He had paid the ransom to the younger Despenser and freed his son, but, despite that, his son was dead and Sir Richard was as good as ruined. His private estate was small; it didn't provide the sort of income he needed to repay his debt to the Abbott Ness. The situation enraged him and he had vowed to stand with the Earl of Lancaster against the Despensers and, by extension, the king.

He had lost almost everything anyway.

All he wanted now was revenge.

The meeting ended with most of the magnates signing a petition warning the king of their intent to defend themselves by force of arms, should his attitude not change.

It was all the justification King Edward needed to move, once and for all, against his rebellious lords.

There would be war.

CHAPTER SEVENTEEN

Divine assistance or not, Will was well enough to travel within a week and rejoined Robin and the other outlaws at their camp with grins all round.

The nuns at the priory had informed Archbishop Melton in York of their miracle patient, and he had travelled to Kirklees to see for himself. Will and Beth had sneaked out the evening before he was due to arrive. Will was not ungrateful for their help, but he knew the more people that saw him, and the more fuss made, the more likely someone would recognise him for the outlaw he was.

Little John had told him he was a fool for returning to the camp.

"What the hell are you talking about, you big oaf?" Will growled. "Where was I supposed to go?"

"You're a walking miracle!" John grinned, slapping him on the shoulder. "The priests would have made the King pardon you. You could have lived like a lord."

Will laughed. "Until the next miracle came along, and they lost interest in me. Then the sheriff would have come along and hanged me for a wolf's head."

Despite the fact he was able to travel, Will was still not fully healed, so, as summer finally gave way to autumn and the leaves that hid them so handily started to fall off the trees, there had been no more mention of hunting down Lord John de Bray for enslaving Beth. Robin was glad. He had hoped that the return of his daughter might have softened Will's outlook on life – dimmed his never-ending need to kill powerful noblemen.

While he understood the desire to avenge Beth's cruel imprisonment for so long, Robin still wished Scarlet would forget about it.

The little girl had settled in well with Matilda's parents, Henry and Mary. They were upset at their daughter having to take up with the outlaws of the greenwood, but looking after Beth tempered the blow. Considering what she had endured in her short life, Henry told them the girl was as bright as a button and Mary was pleased to have a willing helper around the house.

Since they had destroyed Adam Gurdon and his foresters no one else had made an effort to hunt them down. It would have been a happy time for the outlaws, if food wasn't so scarce. They managed to hunt just enough venison, rabbit, birds and fish to survive, buying milk, eggs, salt, bread and other foods when they were available from the surrounding Yorkshire villages for exorbitant prices. But, like Robin's family in Wakefield, people all over the country could barely get enough food to survive. It was a source of worry for many of the outlaws, who had family and friends living in the villages surrounding the forests of Barnsdale.

Robin had been accepted by all the men, if only grudgingly by Matt Groves, as their leader by now, despite his youth – he had just turned eighteen in October – and lack of experience. Little John, Friar Tuck and Will Scarlet were always available for advice, if and when he needed it.

"You know, things are going to get even harder than this?" John said one frosty morning as they skinned a pair of small rabbits they'd trapped.

"Harder?" Robin looked at his big mate in disbelief. "Are you taking the piss?"

"You joined us in the spring," John replied, peeling back the fur from one little animal's carcass. "You've been an outlaw only during the easy weather, when there's plenty of game and fruit to eat, plenty of rich travellers to rob and plenty of leaves on the trees to hide us. But it's coming into November now – winter. And it's been a shit year for growing food, as you know yourself."

Robin sighed in frustration. "I know. My little sister Marjorie's probably going to suffer. I've been trying my best to help my family with food and money but..." His voice tailed off and he stared at the trees disconsolately. "What can we do?"

Little John finished skinning his rabbit before he rinsed off his hands and knife in the swiftly flowing stream next to them, then he stood up and looked down at his young leader with a sly smile. "I know a certain local we might be able to rob – it'd please Will too."

Robin sat for a moment, wondering what John meant, then he realised. "You're having a laugh, right? Are you seriously saying we should attack John de Bray's manor house?"

John nodded his head vigorously, and walked over to sit facing Robin, his hazel eyes gleaming earnestly. "The people in Hathersage say de Bray's got a great pile of food stored away in that undercroft of his."

"What?" Robin demanded, his face twisted in fury. "He's hoarding food, while folk like my sister Marjorie are starving to fucking death?"

"So they say," John shrugged. "Smoked or salted meat and fish, pickled vegetables, dried fruit. It's perfect. Scarlet wants his revenge on the bastard – and we know the layout of the place thanks to you and Allan. Beth could probably help us plan it as well. She must have a good idea of the kitchens and undercroft. Think about it! How much money and food has that little prick got lying around in his fancy manor house? Winter clothes? Weapons? Armour? If we go in during midwinter, we'll come out with enough food and money to feed and clothe the whole of Yorkshire 'til next spring!"

Of all the manors in the surrounding areas, John de Bray's in Hathersage was one of the smallest. Some powerful English nobles, like Thomas of Lancaster or the Earl of Warenne counted scores of villages among their holdings, but John de Bray was Lord of Hathersage alone. De Bray was still a wealthy man though, and, as Robin knew from personal experience, his manor house wasn't that well defended.

It was an ideal target for a small gang of outlaws, especially if the wicked bastard had been hoarding food so he could stay fat while the villagers starved through the winter.

Robin was lost in thought, wondering if John's plan was feasible, when a shout came from near their camp.

"Robin! John!" Much appeared from the trees, eyes scanning the forest.

"What is it, Much?" Robin got to his feet, helping John up with him.

The miller's son hurried over to them, excitedly.

"Men – coming this way. Gareth spotted them. From his description, Tuck and Will say it sounds like Hospitallers."

Robin and John shared an uneasy glance as they all started back towards the camp. The Knights of St John – Hospitallers – were an immensely powerful and wealthy order of warrior monks who had grown even stronger with the demise of the Templars. A hostile force of Hospitallers would pose a huge threat to the outlaws.

"How many are there?" Robin demanded.

"Only two of them," Much replied. "Well armed and armoured though, and on big warhorses too."

"They can't be hunting us, then." Little John heaved a sigh of relief. "They must simply be travellers, passing through."

Robin nodded, winking at his giant friend. "*Rich* travellers…"

They reached the camp and found the rest of the outlaws waiting on them, already armed and ready to move.

As John and Robin strapped on their own light armour they, with Will and Tuck, discussed what to do.

"These aren't a couple of soft, fat priests," Will cautioned. "No offence, Tuck."

"None taken," laughed the friar.

"Looks like a Hospitaller knight and his sergeant," Will went on. "They'll be dangerous, and could be damn hard to bring down if they decide to fight."

The outlaws headed for the main road, where they would ambush the Hospitallers. They had chosen a heavily wooded area, which would hinder the mounted men greatly, should a fight break out.

"We'll have a handful of the men in plain sight, high up, with their bows ready and aimed at these Crusaders," Robin said. "The rest of you take up positions close to me, by the roadside. I'll talk to them, see if we can avoid any bloodshed."

Matilda was told to hang back with Much.

They reached the road at midday, and the sound of a distant church bell could be heard tolling mournfully in one of the surrounding villages.

Will and Little John ordered the outlaws into their positions, and they settled down to wait for the knight and his man-at-arms.

A short while later, the sound of heavy horses could be heard coming through the trees towards them. Harnesses jingled, the animals snorted softly and their great hooves made distinct thuds on the hard ground.

The riders were silent, and, as they came into sight, both men looked gloomy and downcast. They were indeed heavily armoured, with black tunics, and bore black shields with white crosses painted on them. Hospitallers right enough.

Robin let them come closer and, when they were around twenty yards away, he stepped out from behind the oak tree he had been hiding behind.

"Good day, sir knights!" he smiled, folding his arms across his chest, and leaning against the tree, his brown eyes glinting cheerfully.

The men pulled up their horses, and both moved their hands instinctively to their sword hilts, eyes scanning the woods around them.

Now that the outlaws could see them clearly, it was plain these two soldiers had fallen on hard times. Their armour and clothes were shabby, and their horses looked poorly fed.

"What do you want?" said the largest, and slightly better dressed, of the two knights, a thick-necked, grey-bearded, commanding looking man.

"To invite you to dinner," replied Robin.

The men looked at each other in bemusement, but both drew their swords, sensing the danger they were in.

Robin gestured up at the high verges on either side of the road. The knights looked and saw a dozen men pointing longbows directly at them.

Will Scarlet, Friar Tuck and the great figure of Little John emerged from the trees to the front and rear of the two mounted men.

"I ask again: what is it you want?" said the big Hospitaller. "I assume you mean to rob us. I can assure you we have no money, that's why we're even on this damn road. So you're wasting your time." Despite the overwhelming numbers arrayed against him and his sergeant he seemed fed-up, rather than frightened.

Robin smiled. "You take us for common outlaws, Sir Richard. We see few visitors in the forest, and simply wanted you to share dinner with us. You can tell us the tale of why you're in this damn forest."

The second Hospitaller growled. "They're only peasants, my lord. Let's just kill them and be on our way. Look." He pointed into the trees at Matilda. "They even have women fighting with them!"

Sir Richard-at-Lee looked again at the bowmen around him, and the other armed men on the road. He had dealt with highwaymen before. Generally, such men were poorly disciplined, poorly trained and poorly armed. They would normally shout and make insults at their victims, their bravado often masking their own fear.

These men were not like that. They stared at the Hospitallers in confident, and unnerving, silence. They had the look of well-trained soldiers. The bowmen, Sir Richard felt certain, could each put an arrow through even the Hospitallers' thick plate mail. If he were to take his sergeant's advice and attack these wolf's heads, he wasn't convinced they would be able to kill even one of them before they were cut down themselves.

"Put your sword away, Stephen," said the grey-bearded knight with a sigh, sheathing his own weapon. "It seems we shall dine with these men. We could do with a decent meal anyway."

* * *

Back at their camp, the outlaws relieved the Hospitallers of their weapons. The sergeant had protested, but, as Robin said with a wink, "You would surrender your weapons when you enter a lord's manor house, wouldn't you? Well, this" – and he spread his arms wide, to encompass the greenwood around them – "is *our* house."

The sergeant bristled at Robin's arrogance, while the outlaws laughed, and even Sir Richard smiled a little. He liked this exuberant young man with the pretty girl by his side. He reminded him of his murdered son.

He just hoped the wolf's heads' would allow them to leave their camp alive...

There was a big cauldron of pottage bubbling over their campfire. Whatever the outlaws had available that day had been tossed into the pot. The rabbits Robin and John had caught, some old cabbages that were turning to black and almost spoiled, a few leeks, some mouldy bread, even a couple of old apples.

It was simple fare, but better than many people enjoyed at this time of year, and Friar Tuck knew how to add a touch of salt, parsley or garlic so that it tasted much nicer than it should have.

Robin himself filled a couple of bowls and handed them to Sir Richard and his grimacing sergeant, Stephen, along with some dark barley and rye bread. He gave them ale as well, and accepted Richard's thanks with a grin, before sitting down and getting stuck into his own food.

"So," Robin began, shoving a slice of meat into his mouth, "you look like you've fallen on hard times." He chewed as he looked at the big Hospitaller. "What happened?"

Richard's sergeant put his bowl down angrily. "Sir Richard's business has fuck all to do with you, wolf's head."

The outlaws ignored the man, and Robin continued to eat, looking at Sir Richard, eyebrows raised curiously.

"Peace, Stephen. Finish your pottage," said the knight. His man swore, but picked up his bowl and began to eat again, the rage plain on his face.

"It's no secret," Richard-at-Lee went on, smiling sadly as he swallowed some of his ale. His face dropped again though, as he continued. "My son, God rest him, was in trouble, and, as a result, I owe a great deal of money to the abbot of St Mary's in York. I've just been visiting Lord John de Bray in Hathersage to ask him for a loan so I can repay the abbot, but de Bray laughed in my face. The bastard wants to buy some of my lands from the abbot, to increase his own manor. I should have known he wouldn't help me. My loss will be his gain."

Friar Tuck laughed humourlessly. "If you owe Abbot Ness money, you had better pray to Our Lord for help. That one will bleed you dry."

Sir Richard nodded grimly at the friar. "You have it right, brother. I mortgaged my lands to Ness so I could pay bail for my son, who killed a man – accidentally – in a jousting tournament. He was arrested purely to extort money from me. The abbot's demanding repayment now or he'll seize my lands and I'll lose everything. Of course, the church has strict laws against usury, but no one seems to care. Anyway...that's why I was passing through 'your' forest." He smiled sadly at Robin. "I've been to every lord within a hundred miles trying to borrow the money to repay my debt. That bastard abbot – or the king – must have warned them all not to help me. I haven't managed to raise so much as a shilling." His voice trailed off and he stared into the fire sadly. "Hugh Despenser had my son murdered. I'm paying a debt for nothing."

"You must have noble friends that could help you," Little John said, but the knight shook his head.

"The only one who could help me repay such a huge debt is the Earl of Lancaster, but he has troubles of his own just now – I haven't had the effrontery to approach him for money."

The outlaws had all heard of the earl – a noble lord who actually stood up for the poorest people in his manors. He had petitioned King Edward II for aid on behalf of his tenants whose crops had failed for the past couple of years. As lords went, the earl of Lancaster was a popular one with the lower classes, including the people of Wakefield. Robin had heard his mother and father talking well of the earl many times when he was growing up, as had Much and Matilda.

However, it was common knowledge in the villages around Barnsdale that the king had ignored the earl's petition and relations were strained between the two powerful men. Sir Richard also knew Lancaster needed all his coin to pay for the army he would need to stand against the king.

"What about your Order?" Tuck wondered. "The Hospitallers have more money than they know what to do with, especially these days, since the Templars were disbanded and much of their wealth was passed to you."

Sir Richard shook his head in consternation again. "You haven't been keeping up with things in the wider world, have you, friar? The English Prior of the Hospitallers – Thomas L'Archer – is a senile old fool. He's ruined us, financially, in this country. I'd have more luck making a pact with the devil!"

The men sat in silence for a moment, eating and drinking, before Matilda asked, "How much do you owe this abbot of St Mary's?"

"One hundred pounds," Sir Richard replied, to gasps and whistles from the outlaws.

"That's a lot of money," Will grunted sympathetically.

"State the fucking obvious," Stephen muttered sarcastically.

"Oh give it a rest," Sir Richard told his sergeant. "These men have fed us and been good hosts. Have some courtesy."

"Good hosts?" Stephen replied. "They'll be robbing us as soon as we're finished this food."

Robin looked at the man, then nodded to Much and the youngster Gareth.

"Search their packs."

"See!"

Sir Richard laughed. "Stephen, what are they going to steal from us? We have nothing!"

Much and Gareth went through the Hospitallers' packs, but turned up only a few small silver coins.

"They're telling the truth, Robin," said Much, after he counted it all. "There's only a few marks here."

The young outlaw leader finished off the last of his ale and smiled at the Hospitaller. "I think we may be able to help each other, Sir Richard-at-Lee."

The knight raised his eyes to the sky and, with a hopeful smile, made the sign of the cross.

* * *

After discussions with Richard and his sergeant, plans were made and preparations begun to rob Lord de Bray's manor house.

Sir Richard and Stephen had helped the outlaws draw up a more complete map of the building, as they had spent time in the areas reserved for noble guests. Along with what Robin and Allan were able to recall from their short time there, they had a fairly detailed plan of de Bray's house to work from.

Sir Richard would make another visit to the manor house, ostensibly to plead again for a loan from de Bray. He and Stephen would wait until the dead of night, and then open the gates for the outlaws to come in and ransack the place.

Will Scarlet was desperate to get moving.

"I'm going to skin that bastard de Bray alive, for what he did to me and my family," he said to Robin, after the other outlaws, and Sir Richard, had gone to sleep.

Robin shook his head.

"No you're not – not yet. If we kill him, the king and all the lords in England will come for us. We'll never survive the winter with so many people hunting us. We're simply going to steal his money and whatever supplies we can carry."

Will looked angrily at his young leader, but it was a sign of his new found respect for Robin that he didn't start a heated argument.

"You seem to know what you're doing." Scarlet sighed. "Rescuing Beth and saving us from Adam proved that. So I'll accept what you're saying for now. But I want revenge on that piece of shit. I *will* have it."

Robin laid a hand on his friend's arm. "You'll have it, Will. But we can't just murder him. That much is obvious. Murdering a lord would bring the king's attention on us. If we think we have it hard now, it would be ten times worse if we just wander in and kill de Bray."

Scarlet shrugged, but looked away in defeat – Robin was right, they had to think of the bigger picture. "I suppose not."

"It's almost Christmas," Robin said, with a sly smile.

"So what?"

"Lord de Bray relies on his tenants' good will and hard work to keep him as wealthy as he is. One of the things he does to keep those tenants loyal is to provide a Christmas feast for them."

Scarlet nodded, but still looked confused. "Aye, I know, I remember being at his Christmas feasts with my family. Before he murdered them…"

"How are the people of Hathersage going to react when they hear their Lord won't be providing their feast this Christmas? Many of them are almost starving as it is – the lord's Christmas meal might be the only chance of a filling meal they'll have all winter."

Will thought about that and smiled. "They'll be pissed off. De Bray won't be popular. It's not like he is anyway – everyone in the village knows he's an evil bastard."

Robin nodded with a sly smile. "We'll take all his food so he can't provide a feast, and all his money so he can't pay his guards. Then we'll stir up trouble in the village, and the people will turn against him. John de Bray will be ruined."

"He'll lose his lands!" Will laughed wickedly. "He'll find himself in a worse place than Sir Richard is in just now, but without us outlaws to help him."

Robin grinned back at Scarlet. "And *then*, when he's landless and penniless, and a nobody…"

Will's face became hard again. "Then, I can kill him."

"Aye, and afterwards we'll provide the villagers with some of the food we steal so they see us as heroes," Robin smiled.

Will glanced at his young companion thoughtfully. It would never have occurred to him to use the situation to impress the people of Hathersage. Clearly the young yeoman from Wakefield had picked up the skill of self-promotion from Adam Gurdon, along with so much of his military expertise.

"I'm glad you're on my side, Hood," he laughed. "You're a devious bastard."

CHAPTER EIGHTEEN

Two days later, in the middle of November, the outlaws gathered up their weapons, put on whatever armour they had cobbled together, and headed for Hathersage. Robin took Will Scaflock, Little John, Matt Groves, Allan-a-Dale, Much and four other men he felt were trustworthy – and skilled – enough to pull off such a dangerous raid. Matilda stayed at the camp with the rest of the men.

The Hospitaller knight Sir Richard, and his sergeant, Stephen, had gone on ahead and gained entry into Lord de Bray's manor house, to beg again for aid from the lord.

Robin had gone with Will Scarlet into Hathersage village to speak to Wilfred the baker, who was overjoyed to see his old friend again. The outlaws needed a wagon to remove de Bray's valuables and food, and Wilf's was as good as any, assuming they could get him to agree to their plan. Robin didn't see a problem in that, and sure enough, Wilf was more than happy to help out.

Little John and the rest of the outlaws had found a place near de Bray's house, well hidden amongst the trees, and far enough from the road that no unwary traveller would stumble across them.

There, they waited for night to fall. Some of the men played dice, some of them drank ale to bolster their nerve, although Little John made sure no one drank too much and still had their wits about them. Tonight called for balls and bravery, not drunken over-confidence.

"Right men," Robin said quietly, appearing with Will from the darkened road to Hathersage. "Gather round."

He pulled a rolled-up piece of parchment from his pack, and spread it out on an old tree stump.

"Wilfred the Baker has agreed to bring his cart along for us to fill with de Bray's stuff. And Sir Richard and Stephen helped us draw a map of the manor house. They've been in the guests' quarters. Me and Allan have also been here before, in the servants' areas. So, with all our knowledge combined, we have a pretty comprehensive plan of the place. It's not complete, obviously. There's parts of this manor house that none of us have ever seen – the upper floor, for example, where Lord de Bray's bed chamber is. But we know roughly how big the house is, and we know roughly how many guards there will be in the place at this time of year."

"How many?" Matt Groves asked.

"We doubt there will be any more than five armed guards," Robin replied. "We don't expect them to be hardened soldiers for the most part. If they have been soldiers, they're probably older men, past their prime."

The outlaws nodded.

"Don't think it's going to be a stroll along the Calder, though, lads," Will cautioned. "We have no idea where the guards might be stationed when we get into the place, and an old soldier can be as dangerous as a young one if he knows how to use his weapons. John de Bray's been a soldier too, so he can handle himself. Remember too, we're not going to be fighting in the open: we'll be inside. Be ready to use your daggers if there's no room to swing a sword."

"There are also more people in this place than just the guards," Robin continued. "The cook, the grooms, the servants in general might not take kindly to a bunch of dirty outlaws running riot in their lord's home. We need to incapacitate *everyone*, women and children included."

"That don't mean killing them!" Little John growled. "We take out the armed men first, but anyone that doesn't fight back we lock in one of the storerooms. If you look at the map, you can see where they are."

"The servants aren't likely to feel any great love for Lord de Bray," Robin said. "Some of them might even want to join with us to ransack the house. Don't let them. We can't have an unknown factor like that roaming around the place until we're finished. Like John says, lock them all away. They can get out afterwards."

"What if they fight back?" Groves wondered.

"Do what you have to do, Matt," Robin said. "Just remember these people aren't our enemies. If they fight back it's probably because they think you're there to slit their throats or rape them."

Robin knew the men he had picked would not slaughter the servants purely because of blood-lust. That was one of the reasons he had chosen these particular men. It was one less thing to have to worry about – if they went around killing their own people, the villagers around Yorkshire would soon turn against them.

"Right," the young leader grunted. "Everyone take a good long look at this map. Learn it as best you can. Any questions about it, ask *before* we go in. Then, if you need it, grab some sleep.

"Sir Richard will, all being well, take out the guard at the gatehouse sometime after midnight, and open the doors for us."

Will smiled wickedly. "Then all we have to do is take the place. And that bastard de Bray is mine."

* * *

"Get much sleep?"

The stocky red-haired guard, Gilbert, shook his head. "No, it's too bloody cold to sleep, even during the day, since his bloody lordship won't keep the fire banked. Miserable fucker."

Thomas grunted agreement and clapped his relief on the back sympathetically.

"All quiet out here?" asked the red-haired guardsman.

Thomas nodded. "Aye, fine. That Hospitaller, Sir Richard-at-Lee, turned up again, with his torn-faced sergeant. He must be fucking desperate to come here again looking for help from de Bray. The noble lord will laugh him out the door after watching him squirm a bit. I feel sorry for him – he seems a decent sort and his son was murdered not long ago."

Gilbert stamped his feet and blew on his hands with a bored expression. "All quiet in there too; everyone seems to be in their beds."

Thomas grunted. "Aye, I think I'll head to bed as well, after I grab some bread and cheese. I'm starving."

With that he wandered off indoors to seek warmth and his supper, as Gilbert yawned and rubbed his hands over the small brazier in the gatehouse.

It was midnight.

An hour later the guard, Gilbert, was asleep at his post.

* * *

"Ready?" Sir Richard-at-Lee rose from his bed and patted his ribs where he had concealed his dagger.

Stephen grunted assent and stood up with his companion.

They would need to move quickly and quietly through the house, so both men left off their plate mail, only wearing their gambesons for protection. They had, as was the custom, surrendered their swords at the gatehouse, but Stephen, like his lord, had concealed his dagger within his clothes. Besides, these were no common soldiers: Richard and his sergeant had fought alongside the elite Hospitaller and Templar knights during the Crusades. These two men were highly trained killers.

Robin and his outlaws could have stumbled upon no better allies.

"Let's go." Sir Richard quietly pulled open the door to their chamber and slipped out into the dimly lit hallway, followed silently by his grim-faced sergeant-at-arms.

When they had arrived back at de Bray's earlier in the evening, the fat lord had not been pleased to see them, although he had been courteous enough to allow them dinner – a thin, greasy, beef broth.

"You again, Hospitaller?" the lord grimaced, spilling his soup down his chins. "What d'you want this time? You'll be expecting me to put you up for the night eh, as well as feed you."

Richard-at-Lee knew his part well, though, and begged de Bray, again, for a loan to pay off his debts. "I'll be ruined, John," he wheedled. "Please, for the love of God, all I ask is fifty pounds. I'll repay you, with interest."

John de Bray snorted derisively. "Listen, you're never going to raise the money you owe the abbot, so you might as well give up now. I've been offered some of your lands for a very fair price too," he grinned wickedly as the big Hospitaller clenched his fists in silent rage. "Once the abbot legally takes full control of your holdings, he's promised to let me have some of them – the ones adjoining my lands, at Kirklees. I'll need a bailiff to take care of them though. Maybe you would think of applying for the position? You know the area after all."

De Bray burst out laughing at that.

"You're a filthy piece of dog shit," Sir Richard growled. "I should" –

"Enough of this!" roared de Bray. "Make no threats against me in my own manor house, Hospitaller. Especially when you're here expecting a bed for the night. Your Order demands that you surrender all your property to them when you join – yet you retained your old lands against those rules. You're lucky I'm not sending a messenger to your Grand Prior telling him of your corruption."

He waved a hand dismissively.

"Get out. You can take your soup with you. My steward will show you to your beds. Be grateful I'm not kicking you back out into the night."

Sir Richard and Stephen had stalked angrily from the room with their bowls of tepid broth.

Now, in the dead of night, the Hospitaller and his man were going to teach Lord de Bray a lesson in humility.

Voices came from the great hall. It sounded like a couple of men were having a late game of dice. Stephen and Sir Richard, who was gingerly carrying his bowl of cold soup with him, clung to the shadows as they crept along the hall silently. Their passing wasn't noticed by the gamers.

"Shouldn't we deal with them just now?" Stephen whispered.

Sir Richard shook his head. "Our priority is opening the gates for the outlaws. We can't get sidetracked."

They crept along the corridor, moving silently between the shadows cast by the few dim torches de Bray allowed to be lit at night.

Sir Richard held up a hand as they reached the front door. "This door creaks a little when opened, I noticed on the way in." He poured his bowl of greasy soup onto the hinges. "Be ready to move fast. If the guard is alert he'll have the whole place awake before we can silence him."

Stephen nodded and pulled his dagger out from the sheath hidden in his thick sock. Richard drew his own weapon and, as gently as he could, raised the wooden bar that held the doors locked.

He pushed it open a touch and the two men cringed, half expecting a creaking noise to betray them, despite the lubricating broth smearing the hinges, but there was no sound from the door, and no cry of alarm from the gatehouse.

Sir Richard slipped out in a crouch and edged towards the main door and the gently glowing light of the guardsman's brazier.

Stephen remained at the inner door, to prevent anyone locking them out and undoing the entire plan.

As the big Hospitaller crept towards the gatehouse the sound of gentle snoring reached him and he shook his head. Falling asleep while on duty was a heinous crime – one that could lead to the deaths of everyone you were supposed to be helping protect. Richard smiled grimly at his own good fortune though, as he peered into the gatehouse and saw the red-haired guard slumped against the wall, completely relaxed and oblivious to the doom that was coming for him.

Sir Richard hadn't expected the man to be asleep, and, as he slid towards the snoring figure, he wondered if he could simply tie him up rather than killing him. The Hospitaller must have made a sound then, though, or perhaps Gilbert the guard finally sensed something amiss, as his eyes flickered open wildly, and he gasped in shock at the sight of the armed man right in front of him.

Sir Richard's dagger slammed straight into the slim white throat of the young guard, crimson spraying wildly, and a low, tortured gurgling filled the small gatehouse.

Richard dropped the body on the floor, and wiped his dagger on Gilbert's sleeve. "God forgive me," he murmured sorrowfully, thinking of his own murdered son, then he quickly lifted the bar on the main doors and swung them wide open.

A moment later the outlaws, all ten of them, appeared like wraiths from the gloom of the night.

"Good work!" Little John, looking even more massive and terrifying in the darkness, clapped Sir Richard on the arm.

"Any trouble?" Robin wondered, as the party moved inside. They pulled the doors closed behind them, although they left them unbarred in case they needed to escape quickly.

Sir Richard shook his head. "One guard. Sleeping, the stupid bastard. I would have spared him, but he woke up and left me no choice. Stephen's inside watching for us." He moved back into the gatehouse as they passed, emerging a moment later with his and Stephen's surrendered swords.

"Let's find de Bray," he growled.

Will grabbed him by the arm. "You leave him alive, Hospitaller!" he warned. "Whatever that bastard's done to you is nothing – *nothing* – compared to the scores I've got to settle with him. We leave him alive – his time will come soon enough."

Richard, the shame of his earlier meeting with de Bray still burning in him, opened his mouth to argue, but the intensity in Will Scarlet's green eyes made him pause.

"Fair enough," he shrugged, eventually, before his wide face broke into an evil grin. "Let's go and clean the fucker out!"

Two of the outlaws remained at the gatehouse to prevent anyone escaping into the village and raising the hue and cry. The rest of the men split into three small groups – one group for each of the storeys in the manor house.

Sir Richard and Stephen tied linen round the lower part of their faces so no one would recognise them, and went with Robin and Little John to the upper level, where the lord and his family's quarters were.

Will Scarlet took Matt Groves and the brawny young lad from Bichill, Arthur, to the middle floor, while Friar Tuck, Much and Allan-a-Dale headed for the undercroft and the servant's area.

"Remember," Robin cautioned quietly. "The guards are probably skilled enough, and they'll be decently armoured, so be careful."

"Aye," Little John nodded. "And try not to kill any of the servants!"

The house appeared silent, and was only very dimly lit by the occasional flickering torch on the grey stone walls. To the outlaws, unused to being indoors, the place gave them an eerie feeling, and enhanced the sense of danger as they all moved into the building, weapons drawn, alert to any threats.

"No talking from here on," Sir Richard told John and Robin, automatically assuming command of his small group. The two outlaws were happy to accept his guidance – he did, after all, know a lot more about manor houses and, indeed, leadership of soldiers. They nodded in agreement and the two Hospitallers led the way silently upstairs.

As they reached the landing, Robin, the lightest on his feet of the four, placed a hand on Sir Richard's arm and moved past him into the long hallway from which the bedrooms led off. The other three waited as the young outlaw leader scouted ahead, taking note of the glow from the occasional guttering torch to make sure he remained hidden by the shadows.

"Huh?" a deep voice grunted in surprise and the sound of a man getting to his feet came to Robin as he passed a dim alcove. The outlaw spun back to his right and slammed the pommel of his dagger into the guard's face. The noise of bone and cartilage breaking seemed deafeningly loud, and the man gave a squeal as Robin moved in and battered the weapon against his temple, knocking him to the floor, blood beginning to cake his broken nose and face. Robin bent down and, taking out some rope, hurriedly tied the unconscious guard's hands and feet together.

He waited, breathlessly, half expecting someone to raise the alarm, but the hallway remained silent.

Robin moved quickly back to his waiting companions and motioned them forward.

"The guard won't bother us. Which room is de Bray's?"

Sir Richard pushed ahead and waved the others after him as he made his way to a door in the middle of the hallway. "You two," the knight whispered, "deal with de Bray and his wife. Me and Stephen will deal with anyone that comes out of these rooms. Since we're going to leave the bastard alive, it'd be best if he doesn't see me, right?"

Robin and John nodded as Richard extinguished all but one of the torches, making the hallway even more foreboding, but also harder for anyone to make out what was going on, should they stumble out of their room in alarm. Richard handed the final torch to Little John and moved off to the end of the hallway, while his sergeant took up a position at the opposite end of the hall.

John placed his hand on de Bray's chamber door and lifted the iron latch slowly, then pushed the door open. A horrendous creaking filled the hallway, and Robin hurried into the bedroom as John's torch flooded the room with a hellish orange glow.

Lord de Bray was a light sleeper and was half out of his luxurious bed when Robin's fist slammed into his face. He roared in surprise but the young outlaw continued his attack, using his elbows and knees to bring de Bray to the ground, whimpering.

Little John had followed his friend into the room and, as de Bray's sour-faced wife opened her mouth to scream, John placed a giant hand round her throat and squeezed gently, cutting off the sound. He shook his head in warning and she shrank back into her pillow, eyes bulging in terror at the enormous bearded man carrying a flaming torch into her bedroom.

Robin moved fast, quickly using the rope in his pack to tie and gag the lord and his wife. He and Little John looked out into the hallway to make sure Sir Richard and his sergeant had dealt with any other threats. All was well. The Hospitallers had quietly dealt with a couple of guests who had peered out of their doors to see what was happening.

Now they began to move into each room to tie up whoever they found.

"Help them," Robin growled to Little John, before he headed to the stairs and made his way to the middle floor.

Arthur stood nervously, fingering his dagger, but his eyes lit up when he saw Robin. The botched robbery with Harry Half-hand seemed a lifetime ago now – Robin had certainly learned a lot since then, Arthur realised.

"Everything all right?" Hood asked.

Arthur nodded. "Aye, fine. There was a guard, but Will took care of him. They're clearing the other rooms now."

Robin smiled encouragingly at the young man and squeezed his shoulder. "Good work! You keep guard here until Will and Matt are done. De Bray's tied up, the upper floor's clear. I'll check on the undercroft." He flashed a grin and moved quickly back to the stairwell.

As he headed down to the lower floor, Robin was dismayed to hear shouts and the clatter of weapons. They had expected the undercroft to be the easiest part of the building to subdue, it being occupied by servants. What the hell had gone wrong?

He burst through the door into the undercroft and was met with the sight of his men trying to hold off an attack by a gang of servants wielding kitchen utensils. Much and Allan-a-Dale, marshalled by a sweating Friar Tuck, were using their staffs desperately, backs to the wall, clearly trying not to hurt anyone.

Robin shook his head and drew his sword.

"Enough!" he roared, and moved into the room.

The servants warily stopped their attack, eyes moving to watch this new threat, while the three outlaws kept their staffs raised defensively.

"Your lord is tied up, with his wife, in their bed chamber," Robin shouted, glaring at the servants. "I'm Robin Hood. My men have taken the house; the upper floors are subdued. The only reason you people are still alive is the fact you're peasants and yeomen, like us, and we don't kill our own kind."

The outlaw leader pointed his sword at the biggest servant, a man almost as tall as Little John although nowhere near as brawny. "Now drop your fucking weapons and get into that storeroom there. All of you!"

The servants all looked to the big man leading them, unsure what to do. They'd all heard of Robin Hood. He was a murderer. Merciless, the stories said, he'd killed the bailiff of Wakefield and half a dozen of his men without blinking. Yet here he was being merciful. Was it a trick? The young man seemed earnest enough.

"What do we do, Harold?" one of the servants asked the big man Robin had addressed.

Harold, adrenaline rushing through him, saw glory beckoning. If he could stop these raiders, Lord de Bray would surely reward him. Maybe promote him to the position of steward. He raised the thick wooden broom handle he carried and flew towards Robin, a maniacal grin on his face. "Kill them!" he screamed, swinging the pole down towards the outlaw with terrible force.

Robin bent his knees and rolled to his left as the lanky servant flew past him, broom handle cracking off the stone floor and snapping in the middle.

The other servants remained undecided, as they stood watching the confrontation. Robin knew he had to finish it quickly, before the rest found their courage, or there would be a bloodbath down here.

He came up swinging his sword and felt it bite into the side of Harold's knee. A terrible scream filled the cold, dimly lit room, and the servants shrank back in horror.

Robin stepped forward, ready to smash the hilt of his sword into the servant's temple, but the big man on the ground was desperate and his snapped wooden pole shot out desperately, slicing deeply into Robin's thigh.

The young outlaw gave a cry of rage and, instinctively, brought his sword down on the tall servant's skull, cracking it wide open. Blood and brain matter spilled on the floor, as the watching servants cried out, and Robin dropped to one knee, his injured leg giving way beneath him.

"Fucking deal with them, Tuck!" he roared, squeezing the wound on his leg.

The big friar, with Much and Allan at his side, moved forward forbiddingly, shepherding the servants towards one of the store rooms. The servants were really frightened now – none of them had ever seen a man killed before, especially not so violently, and they moved willingly enough, most of them crying, or gagging at the sight of their broken comrade.

Tuck slammed the door shut, dropping the heavy latch into place once the prisoners were all safely inside, and hurried over to Robin. Much and Allan piled some heavy sacks of food against the door to stop anyone escaping for a while.

"Are you all right?" Tuck asked, checking the nasty wound on his leader's leg.

Robin grunted. "Aye, it's not that deep, but it hurts like hell. Help me up."

Much and Allan grasped an arm each and lifted Robin to his feet.

Tuck found a piece of linen used for cleaning dishes and tied it round Robin's thigh tightly. The friar had also found a few wineskins and he handed one to his young friend now.

"Right, check the storerooms for anything valuable," Robin ordered, taking a long pull of the strong wine. "And open the doors" – he grimaced, as the vinegary taste hit his throat – "so Wilfred can get his wagon in. It looks like we've had a successful night's work, lads!"

A muffled voice came from the locked storeroom where the servants were imprisoned. "You'd better get out of here, Hood! One of our men made a run for it when we saw your lot coming – he'll be in Hathersage soon, bringing the tithing up here after you!"

Robin swore colourfully. He had two men stationed at the gates to stop anyone escaping, so he knew any runaways wouldn't be getting through to raise the hue and cry, but he hoped his men had managed to subdue the servant without killing him.

"Damn it," he grunted as he moved back to the stairwell. "Let's move quickly now lads, before anyone else tries to be a hero."

He slowly climbed the stairs back up to the first floor, where Arthur was helping Will Scarlet and Matt Groves to pile valuables in the hall, ready to be carried downstairs to Wilfred's waiting wagon.

Robin nodded in satisfaction and made his way back up to the top floor. The pain in his wounded leg had lessened a little thanks to the tight bandage Tuck had applied, and the strong wine.

As he hobbled back towards Lord de Bray's bedroom he heard Little John's great baritone voice raised threateningly. Sir Richard-at-Lee and his sergeant, Stephen, were, like Will and Matt a floor beneath, collecting any valuables they could find in the hallway.

Robin limped into de Bray's room. The lord's wife was lying, bound hand and foot, on their bed. The fear had gone from her eyes and she looked at Robin contemptuously as he came through the door.

John had tied the lord's fat hands to the arms of a chair, and was questioning him angrily about the location of his money. Bruising was beginning to show on his face, where John had tried more forcibly to extract some information.

"What's happening?" Robin asked, quietly, in the silence between one of John's shouted questions.

The huge outlaw glared at his young friend in annoyance. "The bastard won't tell me where his money's stashed."

As he looked at the smug-faced noble, the knowledge of what this man had done to little Beth and her family filled Robin's mind. In a cold rage he drew his dagger and moved to stand in front of de Bray, who smiled dismally. "You won't harm me, I've -"

Robin placed his blade on de Bray's right pinkie and pressed down hard. Blood pulsed wetly and there was an almost imperceptible little thud as the severed digit landed on the lavishly carpeted floor. De Bray screamed like an animal, and thrashed against the chair.

Little John looked at Robin in surprise, then shrugged and punched de Bray in the guts again, silencing the roaring man.

"Don't fuck me about!" Robin shouted, pressing his face against the whimpering nobleman's. "That's nothing compared to what'll happen if I let Will Scaflock in here! Now – where's the money?"

De Bray struggled against his bonds, but his feet were also tied to the chair and his efforts simply wasted energy. His eyes bulged fearfully at the long-forgotten name of Scaflock, but he spat a mouthful of blood at Robin and muttered an oath in French.

Robin looked out into the hallway, and nodded in satisfaction as he saw Sir Richard and his sergeant had cleared all the valuables down to the undercroft. They were ready to leave – all they needed was the lord's money.

"Last chance," Robin told de Bray, as he stood over the bruised and bound Lord of Hathersage. "I don't have all night, and you won't have any fingers, or toes, or a cock, or a tongue, left, unless you tell us where the money is." The young outlaw placed his dagger over the remaining three fingers of de Bray's right hand, and pressed gently, drawing more blood from the fat digits.

"It's hidden over there!" de Bray screamed, his mouth foaming with fear. "Behind the wardrobe, there's a concealed door, the money's all in there!"

His wife mumbled, and tried to shout through her gag, but it was her husband she was raging at, furious at the fact he had given up their wealth to these outlaws.

"Oh shut up, you sour old bitch!" de Bray shouted back at her, which only made her grunt into the gag even more ferociously.

Little John laughed cheerfully over at Robin. "Young love, eh?"

He shoved the heavy oak wardrobe out of the way effortlessly. In the gloomy lighting there was no sign of any obvious hidden doorway, so he and Robin tapped on the wall systematically, looking for hollow spots.

It didn't take long to find the cupboard, and Robin prised it open with his dagger. Inside was a large pile of silver coins of all sizes.

Little John growled happily, like a great mastiff having his ears rubbed. "How much do you think's in there, Robin?"

The outlaw leader shrugged, and began scooping the cash into a sack. "We'll find out back in the greenwood when we count it."

De Bray and his wife had given up on their one-sided conversation, and stared furiously at the two outlaws.

"They don't look angry enough," Robin said, thoughtfully, rubbing his injured leg. "Search the room for more hidden compartments." He watched the nobleman closely, and was rewarded with a look of desperation as John began tapping the other walls in the room.

There was more still to be found here.

Before the night was out, they would effectively ruin this man. Robin would be sure of that before they made their way back to the forests of Barnsdale.

CHAPTER NINETEEN

"She's dying!"

John Hood shook his head in exasperation, waving a hand at his wife to silence her. "No, she's not, woman!" He stroked his daughter's pale forehead gently, as tears blurred his vision. "She'll be fine," he muttered.

They sat in their little house in Wakefield, smoky from the fire they had banked high to try and keep the winter chill from their poorly daughter Marjorie's bones.

A cauldron of pottage was cooking over the hearth, but it was a thin concoction – mostly water and oatmeal, with no vegetables and little nutritional value. John and Martha kept their strength up by eating lots of bread, but Marjorie had found it difficult to digest the solid food recently, so had been eating little but the watery broth her mother made.

Martha sobbed at the sight of her little girl – thin at the best of times, but now weak and bedridden as winter closed in and good, nutritious, food became ever scarcer. "She's ill, John. We haven't been feeding her well enough."

John nodded disconsolately. "Christ knows how Robin turned out so big and strong," he muttered, "while Rebekah and Marjorie have always been so weak."

"Robin!" Martha breathed, staring at her husband.

"What about him?"

"He can help! He might be able to find food from somewhere – buy it from one of the other villages! Steal it from someone!"

"Christ almighty, woman," John growled. "Now you want your son to steal food from starving people?"

"I never said from starving people," his wife retorted. "Some people must have more than they need. Maybe Robin can get fruit and vegetables from them."

They sat in silence then, lost in thought, watching their daughter breathing shallowly, and wondering if their outlaw son could help save his little sister's life.

* * *

The outlaws had piled Wilfred the baker's wagon high with all the money and food they found in Lord de Bray's house. John had discovered another two hidden compartments in the noble's bedroom and Robin felt fairly sure they had found everything there was to find. The livid, then pleading, reaction of the lord and his lady gave Robin confidence in the complete success of their evening's efforts.

Robin and his men had completely emptied the manor house of anything of value. If they could get the lot back to Sir Richard's castle in Kirklees de Bray would be ruined, and the Hospitaller would be able to pay off the grasping Abbot Ness of St. Mary's.

It had been a good night's work.

"All right, Will?" Robin grinned and slapped Scarlet on the back contentedly.

Will nodded, but didn't share Robin's smile. "This is all very good, Robin, we've done well here. But I won't be happy until that bastard is forced out of his house and ruined. Then I'll hunt him down and really make him pay for what he did to Beth and the rest of my family." Robin promised they'd exact their revenge on de Bray soon, and gave a shout for the wagon to get moving. The inhabitants of the house were all locked in storerooms or cupboards – the outlaws had only been forced to kill two of the guards. The rest, including Thomas, Robin was pleased to see, had thrown down their weapons and allowed themselves to be imprisoned.

The captives were left with enough food and water to last a couple of days until someone discovered them or they managed to break the doors down. By that time the outlaws would be safely away with their plunder.

De Bray and his wife were locked in their own bedroom, screaming at each other, which at least made Will crack a small, grim, smile.

As the cart trundled ponderously out through the gatehouse and onto the road towards Kirklees, Robin sent Matt Groves and Allan-a-Dale to scout the road ahead, just in case anyone tried to stop them. It was the middle of the night, though, and there should be no travellers around at this time.

Sure enough, they met no one during their nocturnal journey, and were safely inside Sir Richard's castle in Kirklees before daybreak.

The Hospitaller was looking forward to a good night's sleep before paying off his debt to the abbot...

* * *

Abbot Ness, seated on the misericord of St Mary's Abbey, took a sip of his wine, a very fine red imported from Gascony, and took another mouthful of his dinner. The majority of the monks were eating fish in the refectory, where meat eating was not allowed, but the abbot stuffed himself on beef, pork and bacon in the misericord every day except Wednesday, Friday and Saturday, assuming it wasn't Lent or Advent. Today, a Tuesday, the abbot was gorging himself on umbles, a great favourite of his: sheep entrails cooked in dark ale, with breadcrumbs and imported spices.

Outside, frost coated the stained glass windows and thick snow carpeted many parts of the country, but in the misericord of St Mary's a roaring fire filled the room with heat and light and Abbot Ness leaned back in his chair, grinning contentedly.

He was entertaining a guest, and was in a very good mood. Today was the deadline for Sir Richard-at-Lee to repay his debt to the abbot. If the Hospitaller knight did not show up with one hundred pounds of silver, the abbot would become the owner of much of the lands adjoining Kirklees. He had already agreed to sell most of it to Lord John de Bray, a neighbour of Richard-at-Lee.

His guest was Sir Henry de Faucumberg, High Sheriff of Nottingham and Yorkshire. The abbot needed a representative of King Edward's justice to make his seizure of Sir Richard's lands legal. Abbot Ness had wined and dined the sheriff all day to gain his good favour, and had given him a substantial bribe of twenty pounds to make sure he was on his side.

"Enjoying the wine, Henry?" Abbot Ness asked, swilling a mouthful of his own, eyes already red and bleary from too much of the stuff.

"Very much, abbot," De Faucumberg smiled, raising his silver goblet in salute to the Gascony's quality. "I've enjoyed your hospitality today." He placed the cup back on the table and looked seriously at the clergyman. "Don't mistake me though. I may have accepted your bribe"-

"It was merely a contribution from the church towards the running of the king's estates"- Abbot Ness replied hastily, trying to look shocked.

"As I say," the sheriff continued as though he hadn't heard the abbot, "I accepted your bribe. We're men of the world, you and I. We understand how things are done. If we can help each other out while profiting ourselves, it's all to the good. Please be aware though, I will help you only so long as what you're doing is entirely legal."

Ness nodded enthusiastically. "Legal. Of course – you can be certain of it! I hope this can be the first of many such visits, sheriff. I'm a very ambitious man, and it's always good to have someone like you onside."

De Faucumberg smiled, and spooned some of his meal into his mouth with a grunt of agreement as a freezing winter wind howled against the windows, the sound of whistling coming from various parts of the room as the draught forced its icy way in. "It's rumoured that this Sir Richard-at-Lee has been conspiring with the Earl of Lancaster to undermine the king," the sheriff went on, hunching his shoulders against the cold. "As you know, I'm the king's man, so if you can bring down the Hospitaller legally, you will find me helpful in future."

"Abbot," a young monk came quietly over the small round table where the abbot and his guest were eating. "The Hospitaller is here to see you."

Ness grinned. "At last, he's finally turned up. This will be fun."

The sheriff finished the last of his dinner and pushed the plate to one side. "You're sure he won't have your money?"

The abbot laughed wickedly. "Not a chance. He's been over the whole north of England trying to borrow money, but no one would help him. I made it known the Church wouldn't look kindly on anyone loaning money to the father of a murderer."

De Faucumberg smiled and picked at a bowl of grapes. He liked how the abbot thought, although he would know to be wary of him in future.

"Show him in, then, lad," Ness shouted at the young monk, who scurried off, to return a few seconds later with Sir Richard-at-Lee in tow. Stephen, his sergeant, had been told to wait outside.

The big Hospitaller was, as expected, poorly dressed, Abbot Ness noted with a smirk, eyeing the man up and down. His armour was dented, his clothes torn and mended numerous times, and he even looked dirty. Almost as if he was trying to look pitiful in the hope of rousing some Christian charity in the abbot. Ness almost burst out laughing at that thought, but restrained himself to a gleeful smile.

Sir Richard walked over to the small table and knelt humbly before the two nobles. His frayed leather scabbard got stuck under his legs, almost tripping him.

"Sir Richard," said the abbot, emphasising the epithet sarcastically. "You came, as agreed. Today is the deadline for repaying your debt to me."

"My lord abbot," Richard bowed his head in assent.

"Well? You have my money?" Ness leaned forward in his seat, rolling his extravagant wine goblet in his hands, the hugely expensive liquid spilling on the table almost obscenely.

Sir Richard shifted his weight to a slightly more comfortable position. The abbot had left him kneeling on the floor like a common servant, in a belittling breach of etiquette.

"My lord," Sir Richard began, addressing the two noblemen before him.

"Here it comes: the begging," Ness whispered theatrically to the sheriff, who nodded distastefully. The sight of a once proud warrior monk bowing and scraping on the cold stone floor disturbed de Faucumberg, even although he desired the ruin of a possible rebel.

The Hospitaller knight kept his eyes on the floor, ignoring the insulting treatment as he continued. "One hundred pounds is a huge amount of silver. You understand my son did not kill that man on purpose; he was wrongly accused. It was an accident."

"Not my concern," the abbot snapped. "The law set your son's bail at that amount, and I loaned it to you in good faith. Today you repay me, or I legally," he glanced at the sheriff, "seize your lands and property. It's clear to us you're a man living in poverty. You're dressed in the manner of a peasant – despite that once fine Hospitaller armour you insist on wearing."

Sir Richard's ears turned red, but he kept his face down until the churchman finished his tirade.

"Abbot Ness, you know I fought bravely in the Holy Land, in our Lord's service. Could I not repay some of my debt to you in your service, perhaps as a bailiff or steward?"

"The man's desperate." Sir Henry growled, feeling genuinely uncomfortable at what he was seeing.

The abbot roared with laughter, wine and crumbs spilling from his mouth unpleasantly, and the sheriff was almost tempted to walk out the room in disgust.

Abbot Ness wiped the spittle from his lips and, after a time, his face became hard again.

"Enough of this, nonsense, Hospitaller. Don't disgrace your knightly Order – or yourself – any further. Since you've barely a mark to your name, I'll call on my colleague here, the sheriff of Nottingham and Yorkshire, Sir Henry de Faucumberg -"

"'Henry of Hell,'" shouted Richard angrily, referencing the not entirely fair nickname the sheriff had earned for the rumoured treatment of prisoners in his dungeons. The knight raised his eyes at last to glare at his two tormentors.

"I will call on Sir Henry -of Hell – as you say," the abbot laughed loudly at that, as de Faucumberg glared back coldly, "to witness my seizure of your lands and estates."

"Fine," the sheriff growled, "let's get this over with." He finished his wine and refilled his goblet, hoping the alcohol would make this whole episode more palatable. Abbot Ness produced a small collection of legal documents from a leather bag beside his chair.

Sir Richard-at-Lee stared contemptuously at the drink sodden abbot seated before him. "You've kept me kneeling on your stone floor like a peasant-"

"You *are* a peasant, now!" the abbot sniggered, almost choking on another mouthful of wine at his joke.

Sir Richard stood up.

Despite his shabby armour and clothing, he was a powerfully built man with the unmistakeable bearing of a knight. He strode over and stood menacingly in front of the sturdy wooden table Abbot Ness and the sheriff sat at, glaring malevolently down at them, his dark eyes strangely triumphant.

The two seated men shrank back, as Sir Richard opened his lungs and roared, as if in the middle of a pitched battle somewhere in the Holy Land, "Stephen! Bring me the bag!"

His sergeant appeared on cue, carrying a clearly heavy sack, and handed it to his master, with an angry glance at Abbot Ness, who sat with a look of bewilderment on his flushed, round face.

Sir Richard took the bag and leaned forward to shove his face right up against the abbot's. "Here, you fucking leech. Your money!" and he upended the big sack onto the table. "The rest is outside in a locked chest. Your lackeys are counting it now."

The abbot and the sheriff stared open-mouthed as a great pile of silver coins of all sizes rained down onto the table, spilling onto the floor and into their laps as they instinctively grasped at them.

In total, the outlaws had managed to steal £160 in cash from Lord John de Bray's manor house, plus a quarter of that again in jewellery, weaponry, ornaments and other valuables. They also managed to carry off a sizeable amount of food which they traded or simply gifted away in the villages surrounding Barnsdale.

The Hospitaller and his sergeant were given the generous sum of £30 for their help in the robbery, while Robin Hood had agreed to lend Sir Richard the £100 he needed to repay his debt to Abbot Ness, to be repaid whenever the knight was able. The outlaws kept what remained of the spoils – still a considerable sum – in their communal fund to help see them through the winter.

Sir Richard was in the outlaws' debt, but he would no longer be in the abbot's.

"One hundred pounds!" the big Hospitaller growled. "Exactly what I owe you. If you'd been courteous and treated me with the respect due a Hospitaller knight, you might have been rewarded with more."

The abbot looked to Sir Henry de Faucumberg for support, but the sheriff of Nottingham had quietly pushed his chair away from Ness and sat apart as if none of this was any of his business, a small smile of approval playing around his lips. The abbot opened his mouth to say something, but Sir Richard slammed his hand down on the table with a huge thud, cutting him off.

"Shut your mouth, priest!"

He reached forward and lifted the scrolls Ness had laid on the table before him: the documents needed to legally take ownership of the Hospitaller's manor.

"My lands" – Richard tore the documents in half – "remain" – he ripped them again – "mine! Your sheriff of Yorkshire and Nottingham can witness *that*!"

Sir Richard leaned forward all of a sudden and grabbed hold of the abbot's robes, pulling him halfway across the table, so their faces almost touched. The big knight took the torn papers and shoved them into the face of the clergyman, grinning in satisfaction.

"And these scrolls – you can shove these up your arse!"

He pushed the abbot backwards onto his chair, but the wine had taken its toll and the churchman lost his balance, chair and torn scrolls skittering wildly, as he sprawled on the floor, his face white in shock.

Sir Henry de Faucumberg sat and enjoyed the show. He raised an eyebrow and smiled a wry farewell to Sir Richard as the Hospitaller and his sergeant stormed from the room, fists clenched.

For a while Abbot Ness simply lay on the floor: humiliated, frightened and embarrassed. Then, he began to wonder.

"Where?" he asked, almost to himself, as he grasped the arm of his chair and dragged himself into it. "Where did he get that money?"

The sheriff refilled his wine cup and waved his hand dismissively. "What does it matter? At least you have your money back."

CHAPTER TWENTY

For a while, things in the greenwood became quiet again, as the weather worsened and December began with thick, heavy snows, stopping all but the most determined traveller from passing through the outlaws' domain.

With the weather so bad, there was little chance of the law either hunting for them or stumbling upon their camp by chance. The bailiffs and foresters in the closest towns and villages had more pressing things to attend to than a wild-goose chase in an icy forest populated by dangerous wolf's heads.

So, Will Scarlet had led them through the frozen forest to a new campsite, previously chosen by the now dead Adam Gurdon. There were a couple of good-sized caves to store their small supplies of food and drink, or shelter in for a while if the weather got really bad, and thick trees all around against which they erected sturdy lean-tos, covered in thick hides stolen from merchants. The trees around here were mainly yew, with juniper and holly bushes also in thick clumps. So, unlike most of the trees familiar to the outlaws, such as the oak, beech, hazel or ash, they retained much of their foliage and provided excellent shelter even in the winter, dispersing the tell-tale smoke from campfires and forming a thick protective canopy against the snow, wind and freezing December rains.

Robin wondered if the evergreen trees and bushes in this part of the forest had been planted by a previous sheriff, to provide winter cover for the animals the king loved to hunt.

The outlaws had enough food and ale to survive, with plenty of money to buy more if they could find it in the local villages. Of the money left over from their raid on John de Bray's manor house, Robin kept most of it in the common fund, and split ten pounds fairly between the men, who used some of it to buy decent winter clothes and blankets.

Despite the cold, then, the small band of outlaws was comfortable. They spent the days training, and hunting the meagre game they managed to find. The nights were occupied by drinking ale round warm fires, laughing and telling tales, singing and playing dice. Some night's small groups would head off to one of the larger towns to visit the inns and brothels.

Robin was glad of this, otherwise the atmosphere around the camp could have become severely strained when Matilda joined them and began to share his bed each night. As it was, he knew some of the men muttered amongst themselves, asking why Robin should be allowed his woman around the camp when none of them had such a luxury.

As a result, Robin made sure Matilda was pushed hard during combat training. He had to show the men she was a useful member of their group, not a passenger.

Thankfully, the girl was a quick learner, and made up for her lack of strength with speed and enthusiasm. She could not pull the great longbows the men used – that took literally years of practice to build the strength required – but her accuracy with a smaller-sized hunting bow was such that the other outlaws appreciated her skill. She also learned how to use a smaller quarterstaff and the short sword Robin gave her well enough.

Matilda was no killing machine, like Will or Little John or Robin himself, and she was untried in battle, but she pushed herself to show everyone she was no giggling little girl just hanging around to share a bed with their young leader.

"Ow! In the name of Christ, lass!" Will yelped as her quarterstaff deftly deflected his, before she brought it up and cracked it against his chin. "That was sore!"

The men howled with laughter as Matilda held the tip of her staff threateningly at Scarlet's face. "That's what you get for under-estimating me," she smiled.

The gruff outlaw stooped to retrieve his dropped quarterstaff, his eyes remaining warily fixed on Matilda's weapon. "Aye, I won't be doing that again," he muttered irritably, but his eyes glittered with good humour.

Little John nudged Robin as they watched the sparring. "Your girl's fitted in well enough. I was worried she might not be much use – it wouldn't take a lot for Matt Groves to start complaining and maybe turn the men sour against her."

Robin nodded affectionately. "Aye. She can also cook a tastier rabbit stew than Tuck, which has helped keep even Matt happy enough."

During this time, Robin was genuinely happy. Like all the outlaws, he had a deep resentment of the system that had made him a social outcast – a wolf's head. But the camaraderie of his small group and the companionship of the girl he had loved since he was a boy made the onset of winter seem more pleasant than he would have expected.

One person in particular, though, frowned on Robin's relationship with Matilda.

"Are you going to marry that girl, or not?" Friar Tuck demanded one morning as the pair sat eating a small breakfast of bread and cheese washed down with ale.

Robin was surprised. As far as he was concerned, he and Matilda *were* married. They had shared a bed. They had even shared simple vows with each other in private one night in the darkness. What else was needed?

"We are married, Tuck," he replied, tearing into the end of his small dark loaf.

"Not in the eyes of the church, you're not," Tuck told him, disapprovingly. "Clandestine marriage is not recognised by Our Lord."

Robin shrugged. Hardly anyone bothered with a church ceremony when they wed, why should he, an outlaw, care about it? Matilda was his wife as far as he was concerned.

The friar knew Robin loved the young girl. More than most men loved their partners, certainly. Still, he was a religious man, and he wanted Robin and Matilda to have their union properly blessed.

Robin didn't really care, but he could see it was important to his friend, so he smiled at the friar and agreed to a formal ceremony.

Tuck grinned, his eyes gleaming happily, and the two men continued to eat their meal in companionable silence for a while.

"You know, Tuck…" Robin tailed off, not sure how to continue the conversation. Although he thought of Friar Tuck as a good friend, he never knew anything about the big clergyman. Not even his real name.

"Spit it out, lad!" Tuck demanded with a grin, knowing where this was going. The friar had expected this conversation ever since he had joined the outlaws, and was surprised it had taken so long for one of them to ask him about his past. It showed that they were all friends, who would put their lives on the line for each other, but would also allow one another their secrets.

"I don't understand why you joined us," Robin said, turning to look at the tonsured friar in puzzlement. "You had no need to, as far as I could see. Aye, we stole a lot of money from you and your friends, but…why would you join us? We killed most of the guards, I doubt the abbot would expect you to have fought us all off and brought back his money, so. . ?" Robin shook his head, eyes fixed on Tuck, hoping for an answer without explicitly asking for it.

Robin wanted to know Tuck's reasons for joining them because, like all of the other outlaws, he was curious. But Robin was also now the leader of the outlaw band, and Tuck's willingness to join them seemed curious to him. He had to clear it up, in his own mind if nothing else.

Why would a reasonably well off friar join a band of outlaws?

"I wasn't always a friar," the cheerful Franciscan told him. Neither had he always been called Tuck, which was simply a nickname for the way he wore his grey robes.

"My real name is – was – Robert Stafford, and, as a young man, I was part of a travelling jongleur group.

"The group included a variety of performers and entertainments. We had the lot: minstrels and fools, acrobats, bear baiting, cock fighting, and my own particular skill: wrestling."

There would be a large prize, dependant on the number of entrants, but generally around twenty shillings – more than a fortnight's wages to most people – offered to the winner of the wrestling competition. The local men would pay a fee to join in, and the last man standing would walk away with the money.

"I would spend the day mingling with the locals," Tuck set down his bread and moved his big, chubby fingers to and fro, mimicking a walking motion, "acting like one of them, and then I'd enter myself in the wrestling tournament."

He wasn't outlandishly tall, at a shade under six feet, or noticeably well muscled, being rather portly even back then. He was then, as now, a rather unassuming individual. He had no great charisma to draw people's attention. So his appearance never put people off entering the competition.

"What the locals never knew was that I'm much stronger than I look, and I trained long and hard as a wrestler," the friar went on, biting off a large chunk of cheese and swallowing some of his ale noisily. "I know how to use my body-weight, how to throw people, how to hurt them enough to stop them fighting back without damaging them. I was, generally, unbeatable, even with opponents much bigger than myself."

In nine towns out of ten, Stafford won the wrestling, his jongleur group made a fat profit since they never had to pay the prize to the winner, and no one was any the wiser.

"I enjoyed the life." Tuck smiled distantly. "It was easy enough – unless a town had some big hard bastard that managed to beat me – and I was well paid. I could eat and drink my fill after I'd taken care of business at each fair, and I never saw myself as a cheat. After all, if someone could beat me, they would win their twenty shillings: it was always paid out on the very few occasions it had happened."

It was, he thought, a fair fight, one-on-one, whether the entrants knew he was a ringer or not. That was important to him, because he was, essentially, a good man, with a strong moral code. He didn't like the idea of cheating people, so he frowned on some of the other members of his group, who used loaded dice, sleight of hand, and other unfair means of fleecing people out of their money.

For three years Robert Stafford travelled with his jongleur group, enjoying himself, until one afternoon, in the village of Elton, by the banks of the River Nene, he was discovered.

"It was inevitable, I suppose," Tuck sighed, his wide shoulders slumping. "I'm surprised I managed to avoid detection for so long. In Elton, though, I was spotted by a man I'd beaten a few weeks before in King's Ripton. The man realised what was going on and gathered a few of the locals together as my wrestling competition began."

A while later, after Robert had won as usual – beating a giant, red-faced, bald man in the final round – he took himself off to the local alehouse. Supposedly, the landlady had just brewed a vat, but Stafford could tell by the liberal addition of herbs and honey this was no fresh brew.

"Not that I cared much," he grinned sheepishly. "After a few mugs of it, cheap at just a shilling per gallon, I could have been handed a jug of piss and swallowed it gladly."

Robin laughed as the Franciscan took a long pull of his ale and belched in appreciation.

"I knew I'd had enough so I stumbled out the door and started making my way back to our camp. I remember weaving through a really dark part of the village, near the outskirts I think, then… I never knew what hit me," he shook his head with a wince. "I was too drunk. I just realised, suddenly, that I was lying flat on my face, in the road, with blows raining down on me from all sides."

Instinctively, he had curled himself into a ball to protect his head and stomach, too inebriated and bewildered to even think about trying to land a blow of his own.

"It went on for a long time," he winced, his breakfast forgotten as he recalled the pain and fear of that night. "Or at least it seemed to; maybe it was only a few seconds, I don't know. I was vaguely aware of voices shouting at one particular person to stop. It was the man from King's Ripton they were shouting at. He was actually crying with rage as he battered the shit out of me."

Eventually, the locals dragged him off, before they all had to face a murder charge, and the man, his fury almost spent, shrugged off the men holding him back.

"I finally managed to get it together enough to look up at him just as he spat in my face. He shouted at me, demanding to know if I remembered him." The friar looked at Robin with a sad smile. "I didn't even know what day of the week it was, never mind remember one face from the hundreds I'd seen that week. I couldn't answer, couldn't even shake my head, so I just stared at him as he screamed in my face about how I'd stolen his money in my rigged competition. Apparently he'd owed his lord the money and had been thrown out his house – along with his family – because I'd cheated it from him... He was about as pissed as me," Tuck sighed.Even in his intoxicated, and severely beaten, state, Tuck knew his attacker's logic was severely flawed, but he couldn't say anything to refute the man's tirade, so he simply closed his eyes and wished his rapidly purpling limbs and torso weren't beginning to hurt so badly.

The attackers faded away into the night then, thankfully, dragging the man from King's Ripton with them to stop him killing the prone wrestler, and Stafford passed out. Some of the minstrels, themselves returning to camp after a few ales, found their jovial wrestler unconscious on the road and carried him back to his pallet.

"When I woke in the morning my whole body ached terribly, but I was lucky," the friar smiled and shook his tonsured head ruefully, picking up his loaf again and swallowing a mouthful. "No bones were broken and my thick skull was intact, although I'm sure a number of my ribs had been cracked. One of the minstrels brought me more of the local ale with henbane in it, which alleviated the pain a bit."

The jongleur troupe moved on the next day, to Peterborough.

Stafford never wrestled for them again. He left them a few days later, when his bruises had healed somewhat and he was able to travel on his own again.

What the King's Ripton man had said to him had hurt Stafford deeper than any of the physical blows he had received that night.

"I knew it was a foolish case he'd made against me," the friar grunted. "The man had obviously frittered away all his money gambling, drinking and whatever else. I hadn't forced him to enter the wrestling competition with the last of his wages, he made that choice himself. I was just a convenient scapegoat for his miserable weaknesses."

Robert Stafford knew all this. He was no fool.

"Yet...there had been an element of truth to what the man had said," the clergyman admitted miserably. "Men entered the wrestling competition for fun, expecting to be up against untrained, regular men like themselves. They felt they had a fair chance of winning the prize.

"Would they have entered the competition if they had known how skilled I was? No, most of them probably wouldn't have done."

Stafford had never looked at it from their side before, and he realised now, he *had* cheated all those men out of their very hard-earned money. "It *hadn't* been a fair fight," he muttered, "when I'd beaten all those countless farmers, labourers, peasants and yeomen in the towns and villages. Not really."

No, no one had forced those men to enter the competition, but they had done so expecting a fair chance to win, and that had never been the case. How many of them had left their families without food to eat that night, or behind with their rent, because Stafford had tricked them out of their day's wages?

"The thoughts tormented me," he confessed to his young leader. "Aye, I enjoyed fighting, and winning... but I couldn't handle the idea that I had cheated honest men."

So he gathered his belongings, and the money he had saved over the past three years, and left the troupe.

His savings had been quite sizeable, and he was reasonably comfortable for a while. But his attempts to find suitable employment all failed – he was too used to an easy life, and couldn't bring himself to do back breaking labour in a field all day for just a shilling and a meal. Without any skills other than fighting, his options for employment were limited.

He had decided, without much enthusiasm, to become a mercenary. His martial skills were not limited to wrestling: he had also been trained to use a quarterstaff and a sword, and it seemed to be the only way to support himself, using the only real talent he had.

"It wasn't my ideal career," Tuck said. "But I thought I might be hired to guard some sweet noblewoman on her travels or something like that. You know" – he looked at Robin, his eyes twinkling – "protecting a beautiful young maid from blood-thirsty outlaws like you lot. That was my hope anyway – I hadn't taken vows of chastity at that point."

"Dirty old bastard," Robin muttered in reply, shaking his head with a grin as Tuck continued his tale.

"I spoke to a man in the Stag's Head, a seedy tavern in Cambridge, and my employment was arranged. I was to work as part of a small personal militia defending Thomas Clerk, a local merchant.

"I felt dirty agreeing to the job, but the pay was good. It seemed like money was the most important thing I needed to survive then," he said, shaking his head in disbelief. "My savings were almost spent and the wages being offered were much better than what I could get as a simple labourer."

Terms of employment settled, he left the tavern and made his way along the stinking road – known locally as "Shitbrook Street", for obvious reasons – back to his lodgings. The former wrestler wondered despondently where he would eventually end up in the world. Would he ever find something to bring meaning to his life? Or was he destined to flit from one menial, depressing, poorly paid job to another until he expired, too old, or drunk, to move, in a pile of human waste in a place like Shitbrook Street?

"Then I heard someone scream," Tuck said. "It was a man, as I found out, but it sounded like a frightened woman." He smiled at the memory, and then his face grew hard. "I'd taken to carrying a cudgel since my beating in Elton, and when I heard the cry again I knew I had to do something. I couldn't ignore it, like everyone else seemed to be doing."

Two dirty-looking robbers had a well-dressed monk, or priest – Stafford couldn't tell the difference back then, he simply knew it was some kind of clergyman – pinned against the wall of a house in the alley around the corner. One of the men had a hand on the priest's throat and was squeezing hard enough to stifle any more cries for aid, while his other hand waved a tarnished old dagger in the clergyman's face.

The other thief, seeing the priest safely restrained, knelt down and began to search the pack of another, younger, clergyman clad in grey robes, who lay on the ground, blood oozing thickly from a horrendous, and certainly fatal, wound to his forehead.

"I watched it all for a few moments. I had no idea what to do," Tuck told Robin with a shrug. "I had no love for religion or the Church, so I felt no pious duty to help the priest. He meant no more to me than any other man…But, I had no love for robbers either. What I was seeing in that filthy alley disgusted me."

As quietly as he could, he slipped into the alleyway, pulling out his cudgel, and crept towards the robber kneeling on the ground.

The thief never noticed his approach, so engrossed was he in his search of the fallen priest's belongings.

Stafford slammed his weapon down on the back of the man's head with a loud thump.

The thief crumpled to the ground, but the sound of the blow had alerted his accomplice who released the asphyxiating, blue-faced priest and spun, dagger held defensively before him, to face Stafford.

The robber glanced down at his fallen accomplice and, panicking, rushed at Stafford, waving his dagger around wildly, while the priest knelt on all fours amongst the human waste on the street, coughing and gasping as he tried to suck air in through his squashed larynx.

Robert's training took over as he dodged nimbly to the left, grasped his opponent's wrist in his right hand and squeezed, hard.

"I remember it like it happened just last week," the friar said. "For all my wrestling matches, this was the first true, life-or-death fight I'd been in, I'll never forget it."

The grimy dagger dropped to the ground with a dull metallic thud, as Stafford twisted the robber's arm until it was behind his back; then the big wrestler slammed the screaming man's face hard into the wall of the house.

Once, twice, three times, he battered the would-be thief into the solid timber, then he dropped the senseless man to the floor, face broken and bloody, and his arm twisted at a sickening angle underneath him.

"I went over to check on the priest, who was still coughing his guts up on the floor. When he got his breath back he looked at me as if I was Christ himself," the Franciscan crossed himself quickly, and carried on. "His eyes rose heavenwards, and he said to me: 'The Lord sent you to save me, my son!'

"I just shrugged and slid my cudgel back into my belt. I was more worried about friends of the robbers turning up than discussing if I was an angel sent from heaven, so I lifted the priest and carried him back to my own lodgings in Shitbrook Street."

As it turned out, the "priest" Stafford had rescued was actually John Salmon, the Bishop of Norwich. He and his murdered companion, a Franciscan friar, had taken a wrong turning on their way to a meeting with other clergymen and been accosted by the robbers.

The bishop genuinely seemed to think Stafford had been divinely sent to rescue him, and his enthusiasm for that belief was infectious.

Before long Stafford began to think maybe the man was right. After all, if almost any other man had chanced along as the robbery was in progress, things would not have turned out for the best, as most other men would have simply run off or else been slain by the robbers, wouldn't they?

"'Surely it wasn't coincidence that a man like you – that can fight like you – appeared at just the right time,'" the bishop told me, and, eventually, I realised he was right. God had sent me for a purpose. I'd been trying to find my way for months and now, it seemed like it was staring me in the face."

He smiled gently, nodding his head in pious contentment. "I never fulfilled the mercenary contract to defend the rich merchant Thomas Clerk.

"Bishop Salmon helped me and I became a Franciscan friar: took the grey robes, shaved my crown and devoted the rest of my life to God.

"I had, at last, found my true calling."

For the first time, perhaps ever in his life, he was happy and full of hope for the future.

"Of course, it wasn't to last," Tuck sighed, "which is why I'm here now. But that's a tale for another day."

* * *

Sir Richard-at-Lee smiled. He felt a small sense of peace again after the tortured few weeks since his son's murder.

Thanks to his short alliance with Robin Hood and the other wolf's heads in Barnsdale he had been saved from financial ruin.

It was the start of December and his castle had felt cold and lonely since he'd been forced to sack his staff a few weeks ago.

The door to the great hall opened as he was piling logs on the fire and he glanced over his shoulder, smiling as he saw the people coming in and the blaze began to build in the hearth, warming the room and casting a merry glow on the room.

"My friends," he smiled, rising and rubbing his cold hands as he walked over to meet the newcomers. "Welcome back!"

His former staff members smiled back uncertainly, wondering why they'd been summoned to their lord's castle again.

"Cheer up," Sir Richard told them, placing his hands on his hips and gazing at them. "You can thank Robin Hood and his friends for it – I know I'll be helping them any way I can from now on. I'm re-hiring every one of you."

As the men and women realised their lord was being serious, they raised a cheer of thanks to Sir Richard and Robin Hood.

Maybe winter wouldn't be quite so desperate after all.

CHAPTER TWENTY-ONE

In the first week of December, Friar Tuck performed a small wedding ceremony for Robin and Matilda under one of the giant oak trees in the forest not too far from their camp. The outlaws feasted and, with heated mugs of ale, sang and danced long into the cold winter night, a great fire burning merrily, bringing light and warmth to the revellers.

Robin was glad Tuck had talked him into the ceremony. It didn't mean much to him, despite the fact he considered himself a decent Christian, but he could see Matilda was happy to be properly wed in the eyes of the church.

Robin was no fool. He knew this was no life for a young couple. Matilda was already past the age where most young women had begun having children.

With things as they stood now, though, every one of the outlaws knew they could not lead a normal life. Robin was just happy to give Matilda whatever happiness he could, and the joyful look on her face when he had proposed the formal wedding ceremony had given him some comfort.

Their life together was not perfect, but at least they were together.

So life went on in the freezing forest of Barnsdale. The outlaws, wealthy from their attack on Sir John de Bray, had no need to rob as many unwary travellers, which Robin saw as a good thing. It allowed them to lie low, and gave the foresters no incentive to go out of their way hunting the outlaws.

Despite the period of quiet, though, the outlaws always kept lookouts posted around their camp. All through the day the men – and Matilda – would take turns, hidden high in the branches of whatever evergreen trees grew nearest to the forest pathways, to make sure no one sneaked up on them. There was no need to set a watch at night – no attacker would be foolish enough to stumble blindly around the pitch black woods in the middle of winter. Even so, Robin insisted on it – better safe than sorry, he thought.

The lookouts had proven a wise precaution. Several times foresters had almost stumbled upon the outlaws' camp, only to be seen by the lookouts and shepherded, with shouts and other noises, away in the opposite direction.

Two weeks before Christmas, Will Scarlet sat, comfortably nestled in the branches of a (rare for Barnsdale) Scots Pine, with a thick blanket wrapped around him. The outlaws had cut away enough branches to make an opening large enough for a man to fit, and hammered in wooden boards to make a small platform to rest on. Not quite comfortable, or large, enough to fall asleep in, but tolerable enough for a couple of hours at a time.

As always, he heard the people approaching long before he saw them. The sounds of fallen, dried-out twigs cracking, as inexperienced, or simply unwary, travellers walked on them, generally gave their presence away and allowed the lookouts time to prepare for their arrival.

Will grinned as the noisy party of wayfarers came into view along Watling Street, the main road from one end of the country to the other.

Clergymen. Two of them. Will's smile became thoughtful as he noted the number of armed guards escorting the two priests. Twelve mercenaries, grim and competent-looking, every one of them.

Twelve. That was good. No one would hire such a large band of soldiers to defend them unless they were carrying something valuable.

The priests had something worth stealing then, and the slow-moving horse drawn cart Scarlet could see in the centre of the party no doubt carried it.

Will gave the travellers time to pass, then he swung down from the tree silently.

He wasn't sure who got the biggest shock, as he landed on the forest floor with a soft thump: himself or the swarthy mercenary he landed in front of.

Instinctively, Will went for his dagger first. He could draw it quicker than his sword, and, at such close quarters, it would be more useful, especially if his surprised opponent reacted as he expected and tried to draw the unwieldy long sword at his side.

The mercenary didn't try to draw his sword. The mercenary captain was clearly competent enough to realise their best chance of surviving an ambush was to have as much warning as possible, so must have told his men to make raising the alarm their first priority on being attacked. Hence the scout that Will had, literally, stumbled upon, turned his back on the stocky outlaw and began to run back towards his companions, lungs sucking in air to roar a warning.

The mercenary never got the chance to warn his fellows. Being unused to wandering around in the deep forests of northern England, he didn't notice the thin but sturdy tree root underfoot which sent him sprawling on his face, his cry of alarm dashed from him instead as a low painful grunt.

Scarlet was upon him instantly, dropping both knees onto the man's back, thrusting his dagger into the side of the fallen mercenary's neck, killing him instantly.

The outlaw quickly rose to his feet, looking warily around for any more mercenaries, but the trees around him were silent.

He knelt and wiped his dagger clean on the fallen mercenary's gambeson, checking the corpse for valuables as he did so, then hastily, but silently, hurried back to camp, hoping none of the other lookouts were surprised by more of the mercenary group's outlying scouts.

A couple of the outlaws were away collecting food and other supplies from the village of Wooley, but thankfully the rest of the men were close to the camp, and they all gathered round the small fire when they heard Scarlet arrive, sounding the birdcall they all knew meant danger.

"What's happening, Will?" Robin demanded, seeing the excited grin on the lookout's face.

"Foresters?" Matilda asked, her hands tightening around the staff she had been using to spar with Much.

Will shook his head. "Better. A couple of priests, with a horse-drawn wagon, and around a dozen men escorting them through the forest."

Friar Tuck grunted. "That's a lot of men."

Matt Groves smiled thoughtfully, and said what everyone was thinking: "A lot of guards means a lot of money . . ."

The other lookouts came hurrying back into the campsite as the outlaws discussed what they should do. They also reported twelve guards, although none of them had noticed outlying scouts. Will mentioned the one he'd run into though, as he was worried there may be more.

"Hang on," Robin cautioned. "Twelve men, at least, possibly more, presumably well armed and well trained. That many guards could mean some of us getting killed. For what? We don't need the money. Why not just let them go?"

Will snorted derisively, his eyes twinkling. "You're getting soft, Robin, sitting around here all day drinking ale, eating venison and whispering poetry into your wife's ear."

There were whoops and sniggers of agreement at that, and Robin shrugged his shoulders good-naturedly. The men clearly needed to stretch their muscles after a few weeks of relative inactivity.

"Fine, we'll rob these priests if we must then. I just don't see much point in risking our lives when we have no need to."

Friar Tuck laid a brawny hand on his young leader's arm. "A good general never throws away his men needlessly, Robin, I think you're right."

"Aye, he *is* right," agreed Little John. "But I'm bored. Let's go kick these mercenaries' arses and steal all the priests' money."

Robin laughed along with the rest of the men, and shook his head, but the matter was settled.

In truth, the young outlaw was quite happy to rob the priests, but he didn't think he should lead his men on such a dangerous hold-up when they had so much money already tucked away for the winter. Why take a chance?

For all his charisma, and his skill with a sword and a bow, Robin was still very inexperienced as a commander. He was only just learning that men, particularly soldiers – which was basically what his outlaws were – soon get bored unless they have something to do. And a camp full of bored, testosterone-filled soldiers could quickly become a volatile place unless there was some focused outlet for their aggression.

"Right, everyone, grab your weapons, and your heaviest armour. You too Matilda, let's see if you can shoot a real target as well as you can a bag of grain hanging from a branch."

His young wife thumped Robin on the backside with her staff playfully then rushed to their shelter to pick up her sword and bow, sticking a handful of arrows into her belt as she fell in with the outlaws who were already moving off.

"We'll head them off on the ridge beside the pair of old oaks, eh?" Little John suggested.

Robin thought for a moment, but shook his head. "There's not enough cover there – the trees have all lost their leaves, and there's hardly a green bush to hide behind."

John pictured his suggested ambush point in his mind's eye, and realised Robin was right.

"What about the bent beech trees, a quarter of a mile further on from the pair of oaks?" rumbled Will Scarlet, who had fallen in beside the two men at the front of the column.

There was a momentary pause as John and Robin visualised the spot Will suggested, then both nodded approval.

"There's some juniper bushes to the west *and* east of there," Robin agreed. "And some holly dotted around as well that we can hide men behind."

"Aye, and it's a bit further off than the two oaks, so we'll have more time to prepare," Will said.

Robin clapped his two lieutenants on the shoulders with a confident grin and picked up the pace, wanting to gain as much time as he could to set up their ambush.

The spot selected by Will turned out to be ideal. One third of the men, led by Scarlet, were able to hide in the undergrowth to the east of the road, while another third, with Tuck at their head, huddled amongst a great patch of juniper on the other side of the track, just a little further ahead. The rest of the men, including Robin and Little John, concealed themselves behind some thick holly, its berries bright as blood against the frost and snow covering the rest of the forest.

Robin had got into the habit of taking Little John with him whenever they robbed people on the road. When Robin stepped out in front of the victims and demanded their valuables, he knew people would be less likely to try and fight their way out when they saw the near seven-foot-tall, bearded giant standing menacingly at his back.

And he had taken Matilda in his party this time too, simply so he could protect her if anything should go wrong. She had yet to face a combat situation, and Robin worried she might not handle it. Fighting a man desperate to kill you was quite different to the sparring Matilda was used to with the outlaws.

Once the men were all in position, they waited.

After half an hour the priests' party came along the road and Robin, with his huge friend behind him, roared at them to halt.

The hard-faced, and obviously competent, mercenaries had quickly drawn up into a circular formation, small shields held before them, forming an impressive barrier around the two clergymen and their wagon.

"Come on now," Robin said. "There's no need for any bloodshed. You men know we *will* be taking all your valuables whether you try and stop us or not."

"There's only a handful of them!" one of the priests shouted at his guards. "And one of them's just a woman! Kill them, and let's be on our way before more of the scum turn up."

The guards hesitated, eyes taking in the surrounding undergrowth. Robin watched as the mercenary captain noted the juniper and holly bushes the other outlaws were hidden in.

"Aye, we have you surrounded," Robin nodded. "The clergyman might think we're a bunch of village idiots, but you know that's not the case. If you fight, every one of you will die. All we want is the money, jewellery, that sort of thing, from the two priests. You men can keep whatever you have and be on your way."

"Kill him!" the priest screamed again, not liking where this situation was going at all. "You're being well paid to protect us, so earn your wages, fools!"

"Will! Tuck!" Robin shouted calmly, turning his back on the mercenaries and looking at the ground in apparent boredom. The rest of the outlaws appeared, arrows already fitted to their bowstrings.

The two priests began to pray.

"What's it to be then, lads?" Robin asked the mercenaries, still facing in the opposite direction. "You're outnumbered. We won't bother you any more if you leave right now. It's your choice."

As always, the rest of the outlaws remained unnervingly quiet, staring calmly at their intended targets.

The captain raised his shield before him a little higher, and shouted to his men, "Use your shields to block their arrows, then engage at will. Forward!"

Robin was surprised at the mercenaries' decision to fight, but he spun round with a shouted command, "Choose your target carefully, then fire!" and drew his sword. He saw Little John at his side, bringing his great quarterstaff up defensively in front of himself.

Matilda loosed her arrow but it embedded itself harmlessly in the shield of one of the guards, so she smoothly pulled another missile from her belt and had it aimed at the same man almost instantly, her hands surprisingly steady.

The majority of the outlaws saw their arrows embed themselves in shields, or bounce uselessly off onto the forest floor. Only three found their mark: one made its way right through the defensive circle and took a guard in the back; one ricocheted off a mercenary's helmet and pierced the man to his left through the neck; the third caught an unwary man straight in the face as he lowered his shield too early to see where he was going.

Some of the outlaws did as Matilda had done, quickly fitting another arrow to their longbow, as their companions moved defensively in front of them, swords drawn. The outlaws' second volley, rushed as it was, also managed to take out three mercenaries, as the guards panicked under fire and pressed their charge recklessly.

The remaining six guards now reached the waiting outlaws, and the close combat began.

Matilda was stunned at what she saw. The mercenaries, grim-faced, hard-looking men, attacked, but the outlaws outnumbered them and worked together like a brutal killing machine, their endless days of relentless training making them utterly unstoppable.

Little John engaged the guard captain, as Robin slipped past the man and stabbed him in the side. As the mercenary cried out, twisting away in pain, John's enormous staff swung upwards into his chin and lifted the man off the floor with a sickening crack, his neck broken.

The other outlaws worked in a similar fashion, one man defending while another pressed the attack from another direction.

In only a few seconds the mercenaries were all dead. Not a single outlaw had taken a scratch.

Matilda stared at the carnage before her then dropped to her knees sobbing. Robin tried to comfort her, but she shoved him roughly away, and, rising slowly, walked over to a boulder where she sat, tears streaming down her pale face, staring into the distance.

"Check the bodies for valuables," Robin ordered Matt Groves and Much, who set to their dark task efficiently.

"Are there any more guards with you?" Will roared, pointing his still bloody sword at the two priests, who were cowering in terror beside their wagon.

The churchmen looked blankly at him, but didn't reply.

"Answer me!" Will shouted, his face the bright red of his nickname.

The priests shook their heads.

"There better fucking not be," Scarlet growled. He turned and muttered to Allan-a-Dale next to him, "A handful of outlying scouts like the one I fell on could have really caused us bother."

Allan nodded agreement, his eyes warily scanning the forest, just in case the two priests were lying.

"Where were you going?" Robin demanded, as the outlaws gathered round their prey. "Everyone knows these woods belong to us. Why would you come through here in the middle of winter? What's so important?"

The elder priest, the one who had been extorting his guards to attack the outlaws, now sat silent, his face grey and slack.

The junior priest replied, his voice shaking with nerves. "We're on our way to Hathersage. To see Lord John de Bray."

"That bastard?" Will growled. "What you going to see him for?"

"We're from the Abbey of St Mary's. The abbot agreed to lend Lord de Bray some money after he was robbed in his own home by a gang of depraved outlaws."

"Hey! You watch who you're calling 'depraved'!" Little John cried with mock indignation, and the other outlaws roared with laughter.

"Well. This *is* a stroke of good fortune," Robin smiled thoughtfully. "I assume the money your abbot was sending to de Bray is in this chest here?" He nudged the great wooden box on the cart with the point of his sword.

The young priest looked away sullenly, without replying.

"Of course it is," Little John grunted, pulling himself onto the cart and smashing off the lock with a stone Allan-a-Dale passed up to him from the side of the path.

"How much is in there?" Will asked the priests.

Neither man replied, as Little John lifted the lid of the heavy box and hooted with delight.

The outlaws crowded round to see the great amount of silver held inside the chest.

"How much?" Will demanded again, grabbing the elder priest round the neck and hauling him to his feet.

"Two hundred pounds!" the clergyman shouted in fright. "The abbot is sending Lord de Bray two hundred pounds in silver!"

"Fuck me, we thought we were rich already," the teenager Gareth of Wrangbrook gasped, his eyes wide with shock. "What are we going to do with all that money?"

"Right now, we get it back to our camp," Robin replied decisively, sheathing his sword and motioning Little John to close the chest again. "Let's move. Allan, you can drive."

He looked at the priests. "You two can go," he told them.

"Go?" the elder replied. "What do you mean, 'go'? We have no escort thanks to you, and the road is teeming with wolf's heads!"

"Not my problem," Robin answered, dismissing the pair and heading off to check on Matilda.

"You!" the priest cried at Tuck as he walked past, joking with Gareth. "You're a Franciscan! How can you ally yourself with these brigands? Who are you? I'll see you excommunicated for this!"

Tuck shook his head pityingly at the priest. "Father, I have my own reasons for being part of this gang of outlaws, don't be too quick to judge me. Anyway, by the time you get back to St Mary's and your abbot chastises you for losing his two hundred pounds, well... *you* might wish you were still hiding out in this forest."

The two priests, pale and wan already, looked stricken as they realised Tuck was right. The abbot would be incensed with them when they returned. They stared at each other, eyes wide with fright.

Tuck shrugged his shoulders, told them how to reach the safety of the nearest village, and walked off.

The wagon groaned into life as Allan-a-Dale cracked the reins of the two carthorses, and the party headed back to their campsite.

Matilda, her initial shock and revulsion at the death and violence she had seen wearing off, allowed Robin to put an arm round her waist and the couple followed the creaking wagon along the hidden paths of Barnsdale forest in silence.

CHAPTER TWENTY-TWO

"The bastards have been killing, raping, pillaging our people for years – and you want us to parley with them?" Sir Richard-at-Lee glared at the Earl of Lancaster in disbelief, using his sleeve to wipe wine from his thick grey beard. "Are you mad?"

The earl raised a hand to placate the burly Hospitaller, shaking his head in consternation. "Think about it, Sir Richard! We are beset by foes from two sides – the Scots from the north and the Despensers from the south. Which threat is most immediate?"

Unlike the recent meetings where Sir Richard had met the powerful Earl of Lancaster, there was no one else present here today other than the two of them. The earl had arrived, unexpectedly, at Sir Richard's small castle an hour ago. Richard had told his steward to bring the earl and his small party in from the biting December winds before inviting Thomas into his hall where a great fire burned noisily and the table was set with mulled wine and sweetmeats.

The commander of Kirklees opened his mouth to reply, but Lancaster cut him off before he could begin. "Yes, I know what the Scots have done, they raided my lands too don't forget. But the king is moving against us now – will you stand and watch as he rides over me, as he and his toadies are about to ride over Mortimer, Hereford and the rest of the Marchers?"

Sir Richard shrugged uncomfortably. The Scots! How could they ally themselves to the hated old enemy?

"You do realise," Thomas continued, "that the Despensers banishment has been annulled by Archbishop Reynolds and the king's other cronies? The bastards will be back in England within the week!"

"What?" Richard hadn't heard this news. "Are you certain?"

"Yes, I'm certain. The king is ready to invite them home under his own personal protection. They laugh in our faces! And you were hoping the king would return the ransom money they extorted from you?" The earl laughed in disgust and Sir Richard felt his face flush in anger.

"Damn them! If this is true, my lord, I'm with you," the Hospitaller shouted before crossing himself and cursing. "I'd make parley with the Devil himself if it meant the destruction of that bastard Despenser."

"It's true, Sir Richard, believe me. And once the king has crushed the Marchers he'll be after the rest of us who oppose him. I've had copies of the petition we all signed at Doncaster sent to London to be circulated, so the people there can see for themselves what the king has brought on his head. I've also sent a messenger north to treat with Bruce and the Black Douglas."

"Robert the Bruce eh?" Sir Richard grunted with a tight smile. "Well, if anyone hates Edward it's the Bruce."

"You're with me then?"

The Hospitaller nodded. "Aye, I'm with you."

"Good." Lancaster smiled in relief. He had hoped to gather an army large enough to crush the king's, but his efforts so far had been much less successful than he'd expected. "Raise your men. We must be prepared when they come."

"I will," Sir Richard replied thoughtfully. "And…I might even be able to enlist the help of a few extra longbow-men too…"

* * *

Sir Henry de Faucumberg, Sheriff of Nottingham and Yorkshire, was enjoying the brisk morning air. It was almost Christmas, and the snow lay thickly on the fields around Nottingham, the frost on the trees a pretty winter replacement for leaves. He was hunting with his favourite peregrine falcon, although there wasn't much prey to be had. Still, his servants carried wine and sweetmeats for him to snack on, and it was such a fine day he couldn't help having a fine time.

"My lord..." one of his retainers muttered, glancing over his shoulder towards the city.

"What is it, man?" the sheriff replied irritably, looking in the direction indicated. "Who the hell's that?"

Stumbling towards him through the snow was a small party of clergymen. De Faucumberg eventually recognised the man leading them.

"The abbot of St Mary's. What's brought him out of his warm abbey to come and see me?" he wondered.

He called his falcon back, and placed its hood over its head just as the abbot, red faced and puffing, finally reached him.

"Sheriff!" the churchman gasped.

"Abbot Ness!" de Faucumberg replied with a wicked grin, enjoying the abbot's wheezing discomfort. "Catch your breath, man, catch your breath. What brings you all this way?"

"That bastard Robin Hood, that's what brings me here!" the abbot grunted breathlessly. "Why aren't you doing anything about him? He's already ruined one nobleman, and he's near ruined me as well, while you spend your time out here hunting instead of bringing that wolf's head and his men to justice!"

"Calm down, abbot," the sheriff replied, still grinning. "Come, this is no place to discuss business, let's head back to the castle, where it's nice and warm."

Ness nodded irritably, his face falling even further when he turned and realised he'd have to make the long trek back the way he had just come. De Faucumberg read the abbot's thoughts but was wise enough not to laugh out loud as he strode off towards his Nottingham stronghold, the clergyman struggling along behind him, face scarlet against the crisp white of the winter snow.

On their walk back to the castle the abbot tried to engage the sheriff in conversation but de Faucumberg hushed him with a raised hand. "Not out here, with my servants around us, my lord abbot," he cautioned. "Robin Hood and his men are quite the folk heroes in Nottingham these days. I don't want what we say getting back to him, as unlikely as it may seem. We'll talk in private."

Half an hour later the pair sat in comfortable chairs in a small room in the castle, a log fire burning merrily in the hearth and cups of gently warmed red wine held in numb fingers. The servants had been sent away, and a thick oak door, complete with trusted guardsman outside, would deter anyone foolish enough to try and eavesdrop.

"Really, Sir Henry," the abbot chided. "Don't you think you're taking all this a bit too far? I mean, even if Hood has become something of a hero to the lower classes of the city, I hardly think your own servants would be so stupid as to carry gossip to him."

The sheriff nodded, taking a small sip of his wine, and sighing in contentment as it slowly warmed his whole being. "You're most likely right, abbot, but I don't want something overheard in our conversation finding its way into a local tavern, then growing legs and finding its way to the ears of the wolf's head. Whatever we decide to do about him will have more chance of success if he isn't forewarned about our discussion."

Ness shrugged irritably before draining his cup and letting himself relax in his seat with a contented sigh. "What do you mean these fugitives have become folk heroes anyway? The leader's just an arrogant boy."

"You know how it goes with the peasants," de Faucumberg grunted. "Local nobody rises up and deals a blow against us, the hated upper-class persecutors, peasants rejoice. The problem is – this *boy* has inherited one of the best-trained outlaw gangs in England. Adam Gurdon was a Templar Knight before he was outlawed: a natural leader of men and highly versed in the arts of war. He forged his rag-tag band of criminal scum into a lethal fighting force, apparently able to move, and act, unseen within the forests of Yorkshire. Robin Hood has taken control of Gurdon's gang."

"Where's this Gurdon then?" the abbot demanded. "Have him hunt these people down."

"Good idea, abbot!" de Faucumberg replied sarcastically. "I already tried that. Gurdon was killed by Hood and sent back to Nottingham with his own cock in his mouth, while the foresters I sent with him were routed."

Ness shuddered and shook his head in disbelief. "Well, *something* must be done. He's cost me a lot of money – and land too, if the rumours are true."

"What rumours?"

"The money Sir Richard-at-Lee owed me, remember? The man somehow managed to find it, which stopped me gaining ownership of the man's lands? You were there when he repaid the loan! Well, apparently it was loaned to him by Robin Hood, who stole it from the Lord of Hathersage's own manor house. Sir Richard was implicated, but nothing can be proven."

"Ah yes, I heard about that." The sheriff nodded thoughtfully. "A gang of outlaws, apparently with some inside knowledge of the building, was able to empty the place of valuables. I have to say, if the Lord of Hathersage" – he cocked an eyebrow at the abbot, who muttered, "John de Bray," in response -"yes, if John de Bray, can't defend his own house against a gang of outlaws, well, he deserves to be ruined."

"Maybe so," snapped the abbot. "It's hardly my fault the man let Robin Hood steal all his money, though, is it? But it was me that lost out on a very nice manor when Richard-at-Lee was able to repay the money I'd loaned him."

The sheriff shrugged. "I still don't understand why you're so upset. What's happened since I last saw you?"

Abbot Ness refilled his cup from the large wine jug on the table before continuing. The sheriff noticed the man's hands were shaking with rage as he poured the expensive liquid into his cup.

"Lord de Bray, like Richard-at-Lee before him, asked me for a loan, as the outlaws had ruined him. The man had no money to pay for the upkeep of his manor and, with Christmas almost here, he knew he would also have to pay for a feast for his villagers. I kindly agreed to lend him the money-"

De Faucumberg spat a mouthful of wine across the room. "Oh, how noble of you, abbot!" he roared with glee. "Interest free, was it, this loan, like the one you gave to Sir Richard-at-Lee? I thought that sort of thing was against the Church's laws, yet this is the second time you've spoken to me about loaning people money!"

"Never you mind the terms of our agreement," Ness retorted indignantly. "The fact is I agreed to give the man the money. I was doing him a favour, regardless of anything else."

"Let me guess," the sheriff smirked, holding the abbot's eye. "You agreed to loan the man some money, with an exorbitant interest rate, and if he failed to repay you within say…three years…he would forfeit his manor to you. Am I close?"

"You may mock, de Faucumberg," the abbot replied patiently. "But the Church is not made out of money. I made Lord de Bray a loan – if he chose to pay a little extra as a donation to the Church, that would be perfectly legal, as you well know."

"Save your sermon for the pulpit, abbot," the sheriff grinned, spilling wine down the sides of his lips as the alcohol started to take effect. "You wanted to line your own pockets – I'm sure you weren't planning on sending any of this 'donation' to the Pope. Get to the point, man. You agreed to loan this fool some money, yes? So what's the problem?"

"The problem, *sheriff*," the abbot spat out the word with sarcasm equal to de Faucumberg's own, "is that Robin Hood and his gang of wolf's heads waylaid the men I sent to Hathersage with the money! While you mess about with your falcons, or sit in this castle with your finger up your arse, Robin Hood is spending my two hundred pounds!"

De Faucumberg had leaned forward in his chair angrily as the abbot delivered his rant, but he sat back, open-mouthed, when he heard the amount of money Hood and his men had made off with.

There was silence for a time, the two men brooding into their expensive wine.

"No wonder this boy has become a folk hero," the sheriff finally grunted. "He's the king of outlaws. The man's rich!"

"Exactly!" Ness roared. "And it's all my money!"

The sheriff didn't even bother retorting. He was too stunned at what he was hearing. The more he thought about it the more he knew something had to be done, whether it was the middle of winter or not. King Edward would eventually hear of this. Abbot Ness had probably already sent a messenger to London with his complaints.

The king would expect his servant, Sir Henry de Faucumberg, Sheriff of Nottingham and Yorkshire, to do something about this. Or His Grace would find a replacement for the sheriff, just as he had a couple of years before when de Faucumberg had been charged with extortion . . .

"What is it, exactly, you want, abbot?" de Faucumberg asked, all trace of humour gone. "I've only just got my job back, and I'd like to keep it this time."

"I want that bastard Hood hunted down like the animal he is – his men too!" the abbot ranted. "And I want my money returned to me!"

The sheriff sat deep in thought for a while, while the abbot continued to throw wine down his neck in a black rage.

"It's about time for dinner, my lord abbot," de Faucumberg finally said to his guest. "Let me think on this for a time. I'll come up with something."

In truth, the sheriff could see no way to track down such a well-trained gang of outlaws, in a forest they knew better than anyone, in the darkest depths of winter. It simply wasn't possible.

There was only one way Sir Henry de Faucumberg could think of to solve this problem...

* * *

The sun tried to force its way through the thick blanket of fog and snow shrouding Wakefield as the outlaws – Robin, Will, John, Matilda and Much, made their way through the uncharacteristically quiet streets. Frost lay thickly on window ledges, and the smell of wood smoke filled the air as the villagers tried to warm their homes with blazing fires.

The mist muffled the sounds of those people who were working – even the metallic sounds from the blacksmith's workshop seemed weirdly stunted as the man saw them and gave a small smile in greeting, the only person in the village sweating on such a cold day as his furnace continued to turn out horse shoes and arrow heads.

"Christ, the people look grim," Little John muttered, giving the blacksmith a wave in return.

"The people are starving," Will replied softly. He nodded towards the smith who had turned back to his anvil, his thick arms cording with muscle as he hammered a horse shoe into shape. "The big man's children are probably at home crying because their bellies are empty. You wouldn't be laughing either."

"Well their bellies will be filled today," Robin growled, dismayed at the sight of the people he'd grown up around suffering impotently, the effects of another poor harvest and spiralling food prices taking their toll on all but the wealthier people of England.

They trudged through the thick snow, their feet making dry crunching sounds, and every now and again one would slip as their sodden shoes lost grip on the hard-packed surface. John led a pair of docile horses, their harnesses jingling quietly but, apart from the occasional snort, they were nearly silent as the fully laden cart they pulled slid through the snow slowly, leaving deep tracks to mark their passage.

A small crowd began to form behind them, the villagers throwing on their thickest cloaks to brave the cold and see what was happening.

They arrived at the village green and stopped, John holding old apples up for the horses to eat as he grinned and stroked their manes, mumbling soft inanities to them. Robin couldn't help smiling at the sight of his giant friend – so terrifying when angered or in battle – yet so placid and gentle otherwise.

The young wolf's head blew on his hands and nimbly climbed on top of the wagon, careful not to lose his footing on the frost and dusting of snow that had covered it.

He waited as more villagers joined the chattering throng, smiling and waving as he saw his father, John, pushing his way through to the front of the villagers who deferentially moved aside, recognising him, then Robin raised his huge archer's arms.

"Friends!" he roared, looking around at the people with a smile. "How are you?"

"Fucking hungry!" someone shouted in reply and there were smiles and grim laughs at that.

Robin nodded as the crowd fell silent again, wondering what he would say. "I know your bellies are empty, while some of our 'betters' hoard food!"

There was a chorus of angry shouts at that.

"I won't waste time with a speech," Robin cried, shaking his head. "We've brought you a present, courtesy of Lord John de Bray of Hathersage." He leaned down and pulled off the blanket covering the wagon, making sure he tugged it hard as the frost had hardened it in place.

The wagon was filled with barrels and crates. "Smoked and salted fish and meat. Dried and honey preserved fruit. Vegetables in brine. Cheese!" Robin raised his voice, grinning as the gathered people started to chatter excitedly, their mouths watering, as he pointed at the containers on the cart.

"Henry!" he shouted towards the village headman who had also been allowed to push his way to the front of the gathering. "There's not enough here to see everyone through the winter with a belly like a priest," he paused to let the smiling people cheer at his joke, "but if you ration it, it will make life a lot easier – and tastier! – for everyone." He held his hands high in the air again as everyone cheered then, with a laugh, cried, "Enjoy!" and jumped to the snow beside the other outlaws.

The crowd surged forward as if they would ransack the wagon, but John, Much and Will Scarlet drew their swords menacingly and roared at them to get back, telling the people to be patient.

Henry organised a party of guards from the villagers to look after the wagon until the contents could be organised and doled out or stored, and the villagers began to chant. "Hood! Hood! Hood!"

The outlaws smiled happily, pleased at their day's work, and Robin felt a lump in his throat as the people he had grown up with chanted his name in grateful appreciation. His eyes welled up at the thought of these good people being so hungry that a wagon load of food would bring them so much happiness and he quickly pulled his proudly smiling father aside.

"Come on," he shouted over the chanting crowd. "Let's go home. I've got some things here special." He pulled a sack from the wagon over his shoulder and nodded to the other outlaws who waved or smiled in reply and moved off to carry out whatever tasks they had planned. Matilda, Will and Much hefted sacks of their own for friends and family, while John had arrows, bread, spices and other provisions to stock up on.

"How's Marjorie?" Robin asked his father as they left the happy crowd behind and headed for their own modest house a short way off.

John shook his head sadly. "She's weak," he admitted. "She always has been, ever since…" His voice tailed off. Even after all these years, the passing of his other daughter still hurt terribly – he thought of Rebekah every single day, wondering what she'd be like now, hating himself at times for not being able to provide food for his family, even though he knew it hadn't been his fault – no one had any food back then, it had been much worse than it was now. But the thought of Marjorie maybe going the same way – starving – devastated him.

Robin patted him on the back reassuringly. "She'll be fine. I've brought good food for her – food fit for a lord of Hathersage!"

They smiled and pushed on through the snow until they reached the family home and made their way inside gratefully, the cosy fire warming their exposed faces and hands.

Robin's mother smiled in surprise at the sight of her beloved son and gave him a tight hug as John began telling her about his performance on the wagon.

Marjorie lay in bed, which had been made up close to the fire. Robin was shocked at the sight of his little sister – always thin, but now she had nothing on her, skin stretched tightly over her small frame. He had learned how to act though – how to hide his emotions and appear tougher than he really was – during his time with the outlaws, and he smiled at the girl as if nothing was wrong.

"Look what I've got for you!" he grinned, dropping his heavy sack on the floor and pulling a jar of honeyed apples from it. "And that's not all!" He emptied the food onto the ground as his family laughed and gasped. "Here," Robin handed his sister a piece of cheese and her eyes lit up as she bit into it.

"It's wonderful!" she gasped, her hollow cheeks screwing up slightly at the bitter, but delicious taste.

Robin piled small pieces of food onto Marjorie's bed until his mother stopped him. "That's enough for now," she scolded. "Too much of this and she'll be sick or it'll run right through her – that won't do her any favours!"

Marjorie smiled at her mother's fussing, but they knew she was right, so most of the food was taken to be stored away in the darkest, coldest part of the house, in a hole in the ground. Normally it would be stored outside, where it was even colder and the food would last longer, but in these hard times even the best neighbours might steal another's provisions for their own family.

"You sit by the fire with your sister and da," Martha ordered imperiously.

Although Robin was by now used to telling men what to do, he still automatically followed his mother's hard stare and commanding tone, dropping with a smile into an old chair as his father poured him a mug of warm ale from a jug next to the fire.

"Now, I'll make us a nice meal from some of this salted pork you've brought," Martha nodded appreciatively, lifting some meat along with an apple and some spices. "And you can tell us how you managed to find all this food."

Robin took a long pull of his ale, grinning in satisfaction at his sister as the liquid warmed his belly and he began the tale of the raid on Lord John de Bray's manor house.

It was good to be home with his family, even if only for a short while.

CHAPTER TWENTY-THREE

It was dark in the greenwood. A cloudy night, so the temperature wasn't too low. The young outlaw leader and his wife were in their makeshift bed in the big cave the gang were using to sleep in during the coldest winter nights. Outside the cave the other outlaws were sitting round the great campfire enjoying a supper of venison they had caught that day. They were roasting cuts of the meat on arrows held by hand over the fire, drinking ale and telling ghost stories. Matilda had gone off to bed early, and, sensing her low mood, Robin had followed her into the dimly lit cave.

He lay down beside her on their pallet, and pulled their thick, cosy blankets over them both, cuddling her in tight, sharing their body heat in the bitter night.

"I can't live like this, Robin."

The young outlaw raised himself up on an elbow and shook his head at his wife, holding an arm out in despair, casting great twisted shadows on the walls in the dim light from the braziers they used to keep the cave from freezing during the nights.

"What are we to do, Matilda? We're both outlaws. We're lucky-"

"Lucky?" the girl cried. "How are we lucky? Hunted like animals, until the weather's too cold even for the foresters to come out in? The threat of arrest, imprisonment, death, always over us every day we wake up? And you call that 'lucky'?" Her voice, which had been rising in both pitch and volume tailed off into a strangled whisper, tears running down her cheeks.

Robin pulled her in close and they held each other tightly for a while.

"I miss my ma and da," Matilda sobbed.

"I know," Robin replied. "I miss my parents, too. And Will misses little Beth. But at least we all still have those people and we still see them when we visit Wakefield. Much'll never see his da again, after the bailiff killed him . . ."

Matilda didn't reply, so he forged on. "We *are* lucky. Most outlaws have no chance – either the law gets them or the weather or hunger does. We have a group of friends here to look after us, plenty of food, money, warm shelters and caves to sleep in…things could be a lot worse." He leaned away from her, his earnest face shadowed in the brazier's orange glow, and took her hands in his. "I know this isn't what you dreamed of when you thought of marriage but it'll get better one day, I swear it will."

His young wife wiped her face and smiled prettily. "At least we have each other," she said, squeezing his hands.

"Exactly!" Robin laughed and gave her a quick kiss, but his face fell as he saw her expression drop again.

"I just don't think I can live like this much longer," she told him. "I thought I was tough. I've seen my share of violence and cruelty – Christ, haven't we all? But that day we robbed the priests…the killing and violence…And I never even killed anyone! How will I feel when I do?"

Robin stayed silent. He was surprised at Matilda's despair though. He'd known her all his life. She had seen much death and hardship in Wakefield growing up. He knew she was a strong young woman and he'd expected her to deal with life in the greenwood a little better.

He looked closely at her, seeing the tears still streaming for her eyes. "What's really wrong, Matilda?" he asked gently.

The girl's face crumpled as she looked at him. "I'm so frightened Robin, I can't live in this forest forever… I'm pregnant."

Robin lay in stunned silence for a while, completely lost for words. He knew enough to understand Matilda was expecting a reaction though, so he gave her a grin and hugged her in close before she took his silence the wrong way.

She smiled through her tears and gently broke his embrace. "You're happy, then?"

"Of course, I am!" He smiled, but his face soon became solemn, and he nodded at his wife. "I understand why you're so worried now. The forest is no place to bring a baby into the world. Are you sure about it though? How can you tell, you don't look any bigger…"

"I know, Robin. You might not be able to see it, but women have ways of knowing. Here." She grasped his hand and pressed it against her right breast. "Feel it?"

He gave a gentle squeeze and nodded, before trying the other one. "They feel heavier," he said, pressing his body against his wife's without even thinking about it.

"Robin!" she laughed in mock indignation, pulling away from him and the slowly hardening bulge between his legs. "Not now!"

She had brightened considerably on sharing her secret, but Matilda grasped her husband's hand fretfully, and wondered what they were going to do.

"I don't know," Robin admitted. "But we'll think of something."

They smiled at each other and lay back, quietly, for a while, minds racing with thoughts of parenthood.

Eventually, the campfire burned low, the pork and apples, ale and ghost stories were done, and the rest of the outlaws came to bed. Only the sentries on the first watch – and a thoughtful Robin – remained awake in the freezing December forest.

* * *

"You're up at last, then!"

Henry de Faucumberg grimaced as the abbot's loud voice rang through the hall. He waved a dismissive hand at the smiling clergyman who seemed no worse the wear for the previous day's wine.

"You're in a good mood, Ness," the sheriff grunted, as he sat down for breakfast opposite his guest. "No hangover?" He reached for a piece of bread and forced down a mouthful, glaring at the abbot.

"Hangover?" The clergyman laughed. "I'm a devout Christian – all things in moderation. You should take a leaf from my book. Greed is a sin, especially when it comes to wine."

De Faucumberg leaned over and grabbed the cup from the abbot's hand. He took a sip and smirked at the furious abbot. "This is wine, you pious oaf. No wonder you're feeling so bright."

Ness snatched his cup back and took a mouthful. "Have you decided what to do about Robin Hood and his outlaw gang, yet?" he demanded, slamming down his cup and tearing off a great chunk of bread.

"I have." The sheriff, filling a cup with watered wine of his own, forced down a long pull and stuffed more of his bread into his wet mouth. "I don't see any way to hunt down the outlaws in the middle of winter." He held up a hand to silence the protesting abbot. "It's not possible, Ness, not with the men I have. I'd need an army to find and kill those outlaws, and, given what's been happening recently with the Earl of Lancaster and his friends, well – the king's not about to send me resources to waste on hunting down a handful of criminals, is he?"

"Are you just going to sit here stuffing your face then?" the abbot demanded, spitting crumbs on the table in front of himself in consternation.

"Yes, my lord abbot," de Faucumberg retorted, "at least for the next half an hour anyway, while I eat my breakfast. Although you seem to have eaten half the contents of my kitchen this morning already."

"Get to the point, sheriff! What are you going to do about the outlaws in Yorkshire?"

The weak wine de Faucumberg had forced down his gullet was beginning to take some effect, the warm glow rising through his body and into his brain. It made his plan seem slightly more palatable.

"Since we can't even find them, never mind kill them, here's what I suggest…."

* * *

"Matilda! Robin!"

Gareth of Wrangbrook was on lookout in a thick old yew tree when he heard the man shouting. The teenager leaned down for a better look and recognised the fletcher from Wakefield: Henry. Matilda's father.

Gareth knew better than to reveal himself – it might be a trap after all. So the youngster silently shinned down his tree and ran back to the camp to alert the rest of the men.

"You're sure it's Henry?" Robin asked when he had delivered his report.

"Aye, I've seen him before when I've gone to Wakefield for supplies. It was him for sure."

Robin rubbed his chin thoughtfully.

"Oh come on, Robin," Will Scarlet laughed. "Henry would hardly lead us into a trap would he? Not with his own daughter here. Stop being so cautious."

"Will's got a point," Little John agreed. "Let's go and see what the man wants."

Robin smiled at his friends, his brown eyes sparkling cheerfully. "Fair enough. But I want Arthur, Allan and Matt to flank us, and keep out of sight. Just in case. I'll go on ahead with Will and John. Gareth, you better get back to your lookout post."

Matilda grabbed Robin's arm. "I'm coming with you. He's my da!"

"He's mine too, now," Robin replied with a grin, as his wife slapped him hard on the shoulder.

"In the name of Christ, don't you two get enough of that in bed?" Scarlet grinned, bringing more laughs from the rest of the outlaws, and an outraged flush from Matilda.

"Very good, Will. Come on then," Robin laughed, pulling his wife to his side and leading the way in the direction they could now hear Henry calling from.

As they neared the fletcher, Robin became serious again, signalling the outlaws to a halt. The men took defensive positions without needing instruction, hiding behind trees and whatever other foliage was still available in the barren winter forest.

"Robin! Matilda! It's me, Henry!"

The fletcher stepped back in shock as Robin suddenly appeared in front of him without warning. "Hello, Henry," the outlaw leader smiled, his eyes warily scanning the forest behind their visitor.

"For fuck sake, lad, you nearly gave me a heart attack there!"

"Sorry about that, Henry," Robin replied, his hand on his sword hilt, still staring into the trees and undergrowth around them for signs of an ambush. "Are you alone?"

"Of course I am" – the fletcher began, then his face broke into a massive grin as Matilda, flanked by Little John and Will Scarlet, stepped out from behind a thick tree trunk and raced to her father for a hug.

"Da!" she cried, tears in her eyes. "Oh Da, I've missed you!"

Henry was oblivious to the outlaws watching as he cuddled his daughter fiercely, his own eyes wet. "I'm here now," he told her, his deep voice cracking with emotion. "And everything's going to be all right, like it used to be!"

Robin wanted to ask the fletcher more, but Little John intervened. "Not here, Robin. Even if the fletcher did come alone, that doesn't mean he hasn't been followed. We should get back to camp."

The young leader nodded in agreement with his giant friend and John waved everyone back towards their camp, the fletcher following them with his daughter.

Safely off the well-worn pathways through Barnsdale forest, the outlaws, lookouts back in their positions, settled down to hear why Henry had come looking for them.

"The sheriff is asking for a meeting with you Robin," the fletcher told his new son-in-law. "Word is the Abbot of St Mary's came to visit him, and complained about you stealing a lot of his money."

"So why's he want a meeting with us?" Will asked. "Is he expecting us to hand back the cash? Not likely."

"Aye, Will, he does want the money back." Henry raised a hand to silence the outlaws' laughter. "The sheriff has promised pardons for some of you in return for the abbot's money."

That silenced the gang, who looked at each other hopefully.

"*Some* of us, Henry?" Little John asked. "Who?"

The fletcher looked slightly flustered as he replied, "Well, just Matilda, really…" His voice tailed off in embarrassment, but he placed a protective arm around his daughter and met John's eyes defiantly.

"You must be mad, Fletcher!" stormed Matt Groves. "That money's ours now. There's no way we're giving it up just so your daughter can go back to her nice life while the rest of us struggle to stay alive in this fucking forest! You've got a cheek, you have!"

Some of the outlaws grunted their agreement of Groves's statement; others were unsure what to think.

When the noise had died down, everyone looked to Robin.

"Well, Robin?" Groves demanded. "You're our leader. Tell the fletcher to go back to Wakefield and let the sheriff know he can shove his pardon up his arse."

"Give it a rest, Matt." Robin looked over in surprise as Will stepped forward to speak.

"Henry's only trying to look after his daughter; you can't blame him for that. Any one of us would do the same in his place." The fletcher nodded approval as Scarlet continued. "We already had plenty of money to see us through the winter, from *Lord* John de Bray's house. It's not like we really need the rest of it. What can we do with it in the forest anyway? Climb around the trees in fine silks? Lie in the cave eating lark's tongues?"

"So you're saying we just give the abbot his money back?" Groves asked in disbelief.

"Aye, that's exactly what I'm saying," Will told the older man. "Being part of this gang isn't just about staying alive and stealing from people. It's about friendship and looking out for each other. Well, we have a chance to look out for Matilda. One day, maybe someone will do the same for you."

Matt shook his head angrily, clearly unconvinced by Will's logic, and stormed off into the trees.

"Robin?" the fletcher looked over to his son-in-law again. "What say you?"

Robin's heart had leapt into his mouth when Henry had mentioned a pardon for Matilda – it was the answer to their prayers!

"The thing I want more than anything," he replied, looking around at the men earnestly, "is for us all to be pardoned – to be free again. I think this is a start. One pardon is better than nothing and, like Will says, we don't need the money stuck here in the forests. Let Matilda go home, I say."

Matilda gently released herself from her father's embrace and came over to hold Robin's hands. "But we're married now," she whispered, tears in her eyes. "We should be together."

Robin smiled. "We will be, some day, I swear it. I don't know how, but one day we'll all be free men again. Then we can be together, like a proper married couple."

Little John gave a laugh. "All we have to do is keep stealing money from rich abbots and the sheriff will eventually have to pardon the lot of us!"

The outlaws cheered at that, and the fletcher began to relax, sensing his daughter's freedom becoming a reality.

"However," Robin raised his voice again, "we have plenty of silver, but that money isn't mine to do whatever I like with. Every one of us has a say in this. Like Will says: we're more than just a gang, we're friends as well. The abbot's chest held two hundred pounds. There's seventeen of us. That means we're each due a share of…" He looked over at Friar Tuck who screwed up his round face and thought for a few moments.

"About eleven pounds!"

"Eleven pounds each," Robin nodded. "Matilda's my wife, so I don't mind giving up that money to free her, but I can't tell anyone else to do the same. It's up to you."

At Friar Tuck's suggestion they all agreed on a vote by show of hands. It was carried unanimously, although a small handful of the men were reluctant at first. Robin told them he would personally repay their share of the money himself, even if it took him forever, but, eventually, the men agreed to hand back their own share of the abbot's money in return for Matilda's pardon.

All except Matt Groves, who seemed to have disappeared sometime after the fletcher's arrival.

"I don't know what to say," Matilda told the outlaws, humbled by their sacrifice for her.

"Well, don't say anything then, lass," Little John grinned. "You get off home to Wakefield with your da, and make the most of your freedom."

"Look out for my Beth, will you, until I can steal enough money to get my own pardon?" Will asked her with a grin.

"Of course I will," Matilda smiled. "I'll treat her like my own wee sister."

All the outlaws said their goodbyes to Matilda. Every one of them had grown fond of the girl, and would be sorry to see her go.

Especially Robin. He felt like he'd been kicked in the guts as it slowly sunk in that he'd be living apart from his new wife from now on.

"What now, Henry?" Little John asked the fletcher. "How do we go about this?"

Matilda's father told them the sheriff would be at the old stone bridge a mile outside Wooley two days from then, at midday. There, he would give Robin – or whomever the outlaws chose to send – the letter of pardon for Matilda, in exchange for the abbot's silver.

The outlaws were happy enough with this: Wooley wasn't far from their camp, only a few hours walk, and the chest with the money in it was sitting, intact, in the very back of their big cave. They still had the little cart and the two old horses to pull it, so everything should be fine.

"Right, that's sorted then," Robin nodded, "You won't be leaving for Wakefield until the morning though, Henry, will you?"

The fletcher looked at the sun, gauging the time, and shook his head. "No. To be honest, I was hoping you lads would let me spend the night here. The light won't last much longer and I don't want to get caught out here when the temperature starts to drop."

Robin nodded, "Of course you can stay the night with us. We'll have a feast to celebrate Matilda's pardon, if we have enough food stored away. I'm sure we've some ale around too."

Now that Matilda's fate had been decided, everyone felt buoyant, even the men who had originally been unsure about giving up such a huge amount of money to save her. They genuinely did like Matilda, and were pleased to know she would be free again. Their reticence had, Robin reflected, been completely understandable.

Eleven pounds! It was a huge sum of money – more than most workers in England would earn in their lifetime.

But, as Will had pointed out, what was the point in being rich if you couldn't enjoy it? Besides, they were all still quite wealthy from the money and valuables they'd taken from Lord John de Bray's house.

They may be outlaws, Robin thought proudly, but they're good men.

He put the issue of Matt Groves to the back of his mind and joined his friends in preparing the feast. If this was to be his second last night together with Matilda for a while, he was going to damn well enjoy it.

The ale was passed around, some salted meat was roasted and the outlaws, along with Henry, enjoyed a celebration. The snow fell in Barnsdale forest as they celebrated life round a roaring campfire – their life together as friends who looked out for each other; the life Matilda would have restored to her and, for Robin and his wife, the life that grew inside Matilda.

Outlaws they may have been, but they were happy and free together that night.

Matt Groves appeared a while later, shuffling into the dim light sullen as ever, but Robin took him aside and told him he could have his eleven pounds of silver. Matt brightened considerably after that and the party continued long into the winter night.

Robin and Matilda didn't make love that night. Matilda slapped his eager hands away when they went to bed. "Not with my da here!" she snapped. "He might see us!"

The cave was so dark, even with the braziers lit, that Robin thought there was little chance of the fletcher seeing them doing much, but he didn't protest. They fell asleep after a kiss and cuddle, holding tightly to each other.

* * *

Hushed voices woke him during the night; the anxious tones intruding on his subconscious until he opened his eyes and wondered who was still awake at this time of night.

Carefully, so as not to wake Matilda, he rose from the pallet and pulled a heavy sheepskin around his shoulders to keep off some of the cold. Pushing aside the animal skins covering the entrance to their cave he quietly made his way to the small, but merrily crackling campfire where Little John and Will Scarlet sat, deep in conversation.

Shivering, Robin blew on his hands and settled down on a log next to his companions. "What are you two doing out here? It's fucking freezing, even this close to the fire."

"We didn't want to wake everyone," John replied.

"We're worried about this deal with the sheriff," Will added, his face anxious in the flickering orange firelight. "You know he's not going to just hand over Matilda's pardon and let us all walk off, right?"

John nodded. "I've heard de Faucumberg is an honourable man, for a noble, but we're wolf's heads – there's nothing to stop him killing the lot of us and taking the silver."

The three men stared dully into the campfire, entranced by the hypnotic flickering flames and their problem.

"What can we do?" Robin finally dragged his gaze away and looked at his friends. "Try and hide the men in the trees, ready to fire if the sheriff double-crosses us?"

Will shook his head. "De Faucumberg will be expecting something like that – he'll bring more men than us and have them search the area before he even arrives. We're going to have to come up with something better than that."

"This is what we've been trying to figure out for the past hour," John agreed. "The sheriff's men have already had their arses handed to them by us more than once recently – they'll be well prepared for any tricks."

Again, silence descended on the camp, broken only by the gentle crackling of the fire, until a smile slowly spread across Robin's face and he softly clapped his hands together in satisfaction.

"Here's what we'll do…"

CHAPTER TWENTY-FOUR

"You're really going to pardon one of these outlaws?" Abbot Ness was furious at the idea. "It'd be better if you would just hunt them all down. You have enough soldiers."

Here we go again, thought Henry de Faucumberg. "I've already explained to you, it wouldn't matter if I had a thousand soldiers. Finding a handful of men in an area the size of Barnsdale Forest, in the winter, is like looking for a needle in a haystack."

"But there's nowhere for them to hide!" the abbot shouted indignantly. "Look!" He pointed at the trees as they rode past. "The leaves are all gone. Where can they hide in winter?"

"There are still some trees with their foliage, even in winter," the sheriff explained. "And apart from that, the snow and ice makes it almost impossible to travel within the forest."

"The outlaws seem to manage..." the abbot grumbled.

"Oh shut up, man!" de Faucumberg snapped. "You're getting your two hundred pounds back aren't you? Besides, do you think I'm about to let the outlaws just walk away?"

The abbot sat up straighter on his horse and looked at the sheriff conspiratorially. "What d'you mean?"

"I didn't bring forty soldiers along with me just to keep the peace. The outlaws have seventeen men, I've been told. Well, sixteen minus the girl. We outnumber them more than two to one. And I chose a meeting point that's out in the open, so the bastards can't swing away up into the trees like monkeys, the way they normally do."

Abbot Ness smiled wickedly, then his face fell. "You're putting my life in danger with this plan, de Faucumberg."

The sheriff grinned. "Hmm? Yes, I daresay I am. No matter, I'm sure God will watch over you."

They reached Wooley an hour before midday, so the sheriff told his men to eat lunch, but to remain alert.

It was a misty morning, with a white blanket of snow covering the ground and the sun a small dim circle hardly visible in the cloudy grey sky. De Faucumberg sat on a big boulder, eating a chunk of buttered bread. A robin landed beside him and he watched it contentedly until another appeared and they chased each other off.

"They're coming, my lord," one of his soldiers shouted, as the faint creak of a horse-drawn wagon reached them through the damp mist.

"Mount up!" the sheriff roared, his breath steaming. "Be alert!"

"What about me?" Abbot Ness asked plaintively.

"Get on your horse, man. Just wait beside me." The sheriff shook his head in disgust.

Eventually, through the mist, two horses appeared, pulling a small cart after them with a great wooden chest on it. As it came closer, three heavily armed figures came into view, beside the cart. More than a dozen shadowy figures followed a little way behind, shrouded in fog.

"Robin Hood, Will Scaflock and John Little, I presume?" the sheriff shouted into the chill, moist air, his voice barely carrying.

"Aye!" the one in the middle replied, with a confident grin. "Who the fuck are you?"

The three men laughed.

"Very amusing, Hood," the sheriff shouted in reply. "Where are the rest of your men?"

"Shagging your mum!" Little John shouted, his great voice somehow piercing the mist all around. Even the sheriff's own men laughed at that, although they tried to hide it when de Faucumberg glared at them.

"Where's my money?" Abbot Ness demanded, the thought of his two hundred pounds lending him courage.

"Right here," Robin replied, patting the chest on the cart. "All yours. Once we get the pardon for Matilda Fletcher of Wakefield." Technically, she was Matilda Hood now, but Robin saw no reason to mention that to his enemies.

"Check that chest!" de Faucumberg ordered some of the monks who had travelled with the abbot. "Make sure there's two hundred pounds in it."

"There's not. There's one hundred and eighty-nine pounds. I give you my word on that." Robin told the sheriff.

"Our agreement is for two hundred pounds, Hood".

"Yes, two hundred, wolf's head!" Abbot Ness shouted, spittle flecking his lips in anger.

Robin shrugged. "Take it or leave it. One of my men refused your deal, so we had to take his share out of your chest. Our friend – a friar – says two hundred pounds less eleven is one hundred and eighty-nine, so…that's what's in your box, abbot."

"That's not the deal!" Ness ranted, but the sheriff waved a hand at him.

"It's only eleven pounds, for God's sake man. Is it all there?"

One of the men he had ordered to check the chest nodded his head from atop the cart, his hands still digging through the huge mass of silver coins as his companions tried to count the total. "It looks like it, my lord sheriff!"

"Where's the girl's pardon?" Will growled.

"Pardon?" Henry de Faucumberg retorted in apparent confusion, one eyebrow raised. He waved his hands at his men. "Circle them!" he roared.

Little John and Will Scarlet drew their swords, both looking angrily at Robin.

"Come on then, you fuckers," Scarlet yelled, drawing his sword and holding it in front of himself defiantly.

Little John held his huge quarterstaff before himself confidently, but he looked at Robin questioningly. The sheriff's forty men outnumbered them almost two to one. "If your plan's going to work, it better happen soon," he growled, eyeing the sheriff's soldiers warily.

"You men are outlaws." The sheriff nodded towards them. "What made you think I would honour a bargain made with men such as yourselves, who are outside the law? I'm sorry to do this – for outlaws you seem like honourable enough men but I must see justice done," he shook his head as if genuinely sorrowful, but raised his voice and shouted to his men. "Advance! Kill them all."

De Faucumberg's men began to close in on the outlaws, who, regardless of the freezing air, were sweating freely.

"We're not getting out of this," John grunted bitterly. "But I'm going to do my best to make it to that bastard sheriff before I go down."

Robin, dismayed at the failure of his plans, murmured his assent. "On my word, then…"

"Hold!"

Despite the freezing mist, the powerful voice, full of authority, reached everyone in the clearing. No one moved, eyes straining warily to see who had shouted the command.

"Stand your men down, de Faucumberg!"

Robin heaved a huge sigh of relief and flashed a knowing grin at his tense friends as Sir Richard-at-Lee and his sergeant, Stephen, materialized through the haze, their black mantles and snow white crosses seeming almost ethereal in the cold light.

Another armoured noble rode beside Sir Richard, and, by the noises following them, they had brought a small army along.

The sheriff's face fell as he saw the newcomers approaching. He knew who Sir Richard and his noble companion were, as did Abbot Ness who cursed in surprise at the sight of the man he had sought to dispossess of his lands not so long before.

"Get your men back out of the road, de Faucumberg, now!" Sir Richard ordered.

The three outlaws heaved sighs of relief as the sheriff grudgingly waved his men back behind him.

"Sir Richard came then," Will smiled ruefully.

"Aye, and just in fucking time too," John laughed, starting to relax as the threat of imminent doom passed.

"You have a document, I believe?" Sir Richard demanded of the sheriff, who remained silent. "A pardon for the girl, Matilda of Wakefield?"

The sheriff still said nothing, even ignoring the confused and worried whispers of Abbot Ness.

"Well hand it over then, de Faucumberg!" Sir Richard roared. The soldiers behind him were plainly visible now, even through the thick mist. He had at least fifty men with him, all in chain or plate mail, including a dozen or so mounted knights.

In contrast, the sheriff's forty men had come lightly armoured, and on foot, to aid movement through the forest, since they had been expecting a possible fight with seventeen highly mobile outlaws through the greenwood.

A pitched battle in the clearing they found themselves in now would be a slaughter and the sheriff knew it. His precarious position became even more obvious as the rest of the outlaws, marshalled by Friar Tuck, moved closer to the clearing, the fog parting to reveal longbows trained on De Faucumberg's men. And him.

He reached into his saddlebag and lifted out a scroll.

"Here," he grunted, nudging his horse forward, then, when he was close enough, he tossed it at Robin's feet, his face scarlet with rage and humiliation.

"Let's see it, Robin," Sir Richard said, beckoning the outlaws to come towards him.

Little John and Will still had their weapons at the ready, and they followed their young leader as he moved towards the mounted Knight Hospitaller.

Richard unrolled the scroll and glanced over it. "Good, it's in order," he said, returning the document to Robin, warning him to keep it safe.

"Now you may go, de Faucumberg." The big knight waved a dismissive mailed hand at the raging sheriff.

Abbot Ness finally found his voice as he realised the sheriff was going to retreat. "What about my silver? That cart and its contents belong to St Mary's Abbey!" he cried, pointing desperately at his money. "That wolf's head stole it!"

"Get out of here, now, de Faucumberg, while you still can," Sir Richard said to the sheriff. "And take that grasping abbot with you before I remove the bastard's head – man of God or not."

Ness tried to protest but the sheriff knew he was beaten and roared at the abbot to forget it and follow as he turned back towards Nottingham.

"The king will hear of this, Hospitaller!" de Faucumberg shouted angrily over his shoulder.

For the first time Sir Richard's noble companion spoke, laughing coldly at the sheriff's retreating back. "King Edward will soon have more to worry about than your whining, de Faucumberg. Next time we meet, I won't let you run away with your tail between your legs. England has had enough of Edward, and his lackeys like you!"

The three outlaws looked at Sir Richard-at-Lee in surprise, expecting some reaction to his companion's treason. The knight sat stony-faced on his great warhorse though, watching the sheriff and his men disappear into the mist.

"You're Robin Hood, then," Sir Richard's noble companion turned his head with a smile, fixing the young outlaw leader with a commanding gaze. "I've heard a lot about you, lad."

Sir Richard laughed at the blank expression on Robin's face. "This is the Earl of Lancaster," the knight said to the outlaws. "We spoke of him when I first met you."

Robin, Will and John had no idea how to behave around an earl, so they did what seemed proper and dropped to one knee, heads bowed.

Sir Richard laughed again, but his words were indignant. "Get up you fools! You never knelt to me when we met. Quite the opposite!"

The three outlaws were not enjoying this at all. They had no idea why the Earl of Lancaster had helped save them from the sheriff.

Richard was amused to see the three tough men nervously scratching the backs of their necks and fidgeting like naughty children. "Relax, lads, you're in the company of friends now," he smiled reassuringly.

Robin warily got to his feet, John and Will following his lead, and looked at the earl, still somewhat overawed. "You wanted to meet us, my lord?"

Thomas, Earl of Lancaster jumped down from his horse and walked over to stand in front of the outlaws. "I did, Robin," he agreed, extending a hand which Robin shook. The man's grasp was firm, but his face was open and his eyes were smiling. "I've heard a lot about you, from Sir Richard here, and also from my tenants. You killed my bailiff in Wakefield – Henry."

Robin placed a hand on his sword hilt but the earl smiled reassuringly. "Don't worry, lad, you did me a favour. I never realised how much the villagers hated him – since I replaced him the people have been more productive, which is all a lord wants to hear from one of his holdings."

Richard-at-Lee had dismounted as well by now and gave the three outlaws friendly pats on the back, smiling the whole time.

"The earl has a proposition for you, boys," the Hospitaller told them. "Why don't we head for one of the nearby villages and we can discuss it?"

Robin shoved Matilda's pardon safely inside his cloak and shrugged. "Let's go then," he replied. "Wooley isn't far, and I could do with an ale or two after this afternoon."

"What about the money?" Little John wondered.

Robin was no fool. He knew Sir Richard was a friend, and the Earl of Lancaster – who was watching Robin intently from atop his horse – had come to help them as well for some reason. But near two hundred pounds was a lot of silver. Enough to strain any apparent friendship.

"Since the earl and Sir Richard saved our skins, why don't we give them half the money?" Robin decided, with a smile towards the two horsemen.

"I still owe you men £100 for the loan you gave me to pay off Abbott Ness," Sir Richard noted, raising an eyebrow at Robin's generosity.

"We can forget that," the young outlaw shrugged, laying a restraining hand on Will's arm as the fuming outlaw tried to protest. "We helped you, you've helped us, and we all," he glared at Scarlet, "come out of this much, much richer."

The noblemen broke into wide grins. Robin knew – from the way the earl had been gazing at him – if it had come down to it, the earl would have demanded all of the money. He had more than enough men to back up such a demand after all.

But Robin's offer was enough to placate the lord and everyone, even Will when he realised what had just happened, was happy with the idea.

Sir Richard and the earl each filled their men's horses' saddlebags with silver until there was roughly half of the original one hundred and eighty-nine pounds left in the chest.

"I'll take the cart back with the rest of the lads," Little John offered. "Scarlet has more experience dealing with nobles than I do – I'm just a simple village blacksmith!"

Robin nodded gratefully at his giant friend and handed him the document of pardon for Matilda. "If it comes to it, forget the money, John. Just make sure this letter gets safely back to Matilda."

The great bearded outlaw nodded solemnly and tucked the document inside his bearskin cloak.

"Ready, lads?" Sir Richard asked, wandering over and putting a brawny arm round the shoulders of Will and Robin.

"Aye," Robin laughed. "Let's go get a drink."

The young outlaw was in good spirits. His men still had near a hundred pounds of silver they didn't expect to have after today, they were still alive, and his pregnant wife was a free woman again. The day had worked out perfectly. The only thing that could make him happier, he thought with a wry smile, would be a pardon for him and the rest of his men.

CHAPTER TWENTY-FIVE

"A pardon? For all of us?" Robin gasped in disbelief.

The Earl of Lancaster nodded enthusiastically. "Yes, Robin. For you, and every one of your men."

Robin looked at Will, who shrugged his shoulders and took a drink of his ale.

A short time ago they had arrived in the small town of Wooley and found seats at a table in one of the local taverns, a neat looking place, with two hearths in the main room. The earl had sent most of his men home, but kept a handful of guards with him, in case of trouble. Those men waited discreetly by the front door. Well, as discreetly as was possible for half a dozen armoured men in a small-town inn with only a handful of tables in it.

Robin, Will, Sir Richard and the earl had a table of their own and, since it was only mid-afternoon, the inn was quiet, so they were fairly private.

Small fires were smouldering in the hearths when they walked in from the frozen winter streets, but a shout from Sir Richard had seen the landlord piling on a few logs. Soon enough the room was lit by a cosy orange glow from each end and the four men sat contentedly with their mugs of ale, feeling the warmth seeping into their bones, drying out the icy mists of Barnsdale forest.

"What do we have to do for this pardon?" Robin asked eventually, as the chill left his bones and the ale warmed his head enough to help him think straight.

The Earl of Lancaster drained his own mug and shouted for another round, fixing Robin with a stony gaze. "Join the rebellion," he said quietly.

Again, Robin and Will looked at each other, but neither man said anything.

"You know I asked the king to help my tenants after a few hard years?" Thomas asked. "Well, he promised aid, but never followed up on his promise. My tenants are struggling to stay alive – that means people like your family in Wakefield, Robin. The king expects me to pay him the same rents I paid when harvests were good, which would mean me squeezing more money from my tenants. Money they simply don't have. If I take any more rent from them they'll die, or have to become outlaws...No offence, lads," he smiled, draining his ale, "but we have enough outlaws in Barnsdale already."

Robin had no idea how to deal with the situation. Although he was the leader of the outlaws' gang, he was still only eighteen. He looked at the more worldly wise Will hopefully.

Scarlet shrugged his wide shoulders. "I'd say it's a good deal," he told his young friend. "What other options do we have? The king's a bastard, just like his da. He'll squeeze the people until they've nothing left to give, to pay for his wars against the Scots and the Welsh and whoever else."

"You think the earl's a better option than the king?" Robin asked, not caring that the earl was sitting at the table with them. He knew Will would be honest no matter who sat with them.

"Aye, he is," Scarlet replied. "I'm sure he's expecting to take a lot of money and lands out of this rebellion. Even take the throne for himself." He glanced at the earl but the man just stared back, giving nothing away. "From what the people say though, and since Sir Richard's backing him...well, I think he's probably a decent enough man who genuinely wants to help the people."

"Can his rebellion succeed?"

Will shrugged. "I've been stuck in the greenwood with you lot, I don't know how the balance of power lies. I don't see how it matters though."

Robin looked at his friend quizzically.

"You don't pick sides based on who'll win, do you?" Will grunted. "You choose the side that has the same goals and ideals as you do yourself."

Robin was out of his depth. He finished his ale and gladly accepted another from the landlord who was hovering around refilling each man's mug as it was emptied.

"I don't know you," the young outlaw said eventually, after some other small talk, "but I trust Richard and I think Will knows which way the wind's blowing so I'll join your rebellion, in return for a pardon once we win."

Richard-at-Lee hadn't said much so far, but he reached forward and clasped Robin's forearm now. "You're a strong man," the knight told him earnestly. "Exactly the kind of man we need to make England great again."

Robin felt his face flush red in embarrassment. He was no fool though.

"We'll join your rebellion, assuming every one of us is pardoned, but what about our wages? And the chain of command?"

"If you join our army you take orders like everyone else," the earl replied.

"That's fine," Will replied, understanding where Robin was going with his question. "But it would make sense to keep us – all sixteen of us – as one company. There's no sense in assigning new captains to a group of soldiers who already fight as a unit."

Thomas looked thoughtful but Sir Richard nodded at him and agreed with Will.

Robin grinned at Scarlet. "He's right, Sir Thomas, we fight best with our own chain of command. If we join your rebellion you should let us fight the way we know how. It's to your advantage."

The Earl of Lancaster wasn't too bothered whether the outlaws joined him or not, if he was honest. He was trying to gather the biggest army he could, and Sir Richard-at-Lee had told him Hood's men would be a good addition to his fighting force. But they were only sixteen men. As good as they supposedly were they weren't critical to his plans. He drained his ale and slammed a fist down on the table with a laugh.

"Fine! Whatever, Robin! You can lead your own men under Sir Richard's Hospitaller banner. And when we win: a pardon for the lot of you!"

Robin grinned and looked at Will for advice.

"Can't say fairer than that," Scarlet smiled, draining his own ale mug. "One more thing though…the Lord of Hathersage, John de Bray?"

"What about him?" the earl wondered, confused by Will's question.

"I ain't taking orders from that prick. Is he part of your rebellion?"

Sir Richard shook his head with a wolfish grin. "He was never one of us, you know that – he's a king's man. Besides, the bastard's been ruined, Will. He has no money left, his tenants have turned against him, and, as we speak, the king is sending a man to replace him as lord in Hathersage. He's nothing."

Robin clapped his friend on the back. "I told you we'd make him pay, Will."

Will drained his ale and set his mug on the table grimly. "Once we're done here, then, I have some business to deal with in Hathersage."

The earl had no idea what Will meant, but he didn't care either. He had to get moving, to try and add more men to his growing army.

He stood up, Sir Richard rising with him, hastily downing the last of his own ale.

"Take care of your business, then, lads." Thomas nodded to the outlaws. "Sort out whatever you have to sort, enjoy your Christmas. Then be ready to bring your men to Sir Richard's castle at Kirklees when we call on you in the next few weeks."

"After that," Richard smiled boldly, "all we have to do is destroy the king…"

CHAPTER TWENTY-SIX

"So – who feels like kicking King Edward's useless arse for him?" Robin demanded.

The outlaws cheered and raised their ale cups to the night sky jubilantly, the joyful sounds filling the forest. The young wolf's head had never seen the men so excited.

"I can't believe it," the youngster Gareth grasped his leader's shoulders happily. "I never thought I'd be a free man."

"Slow down," Robin laughed, tossing back a mouthful of ale. "We still have to defeat the king's army first!"

Gareth shrugged as if the task was trivial and, grinning widely, wandered off to join the rest of the men dancing and singing by the great campfire which had been banked high to stave off the bitter winter chill.

"You'd think we kill kings every other day," Robin shook his head ruefully, enjoying the outlaws' reaction to the earl's proposal, but fearing the raucous celebrations were premature.

"Let us have our fun," Friar Tuck advised. "No, it won't be easy to beat the king's soldiers. Quite possibly every one of us will die in the battle, even if the earl wins in the end." He shrugged. "But we finally have a goal – a purpose. Something to aim for, rather than just scratching an existence from one day to the next in this forest, hoping the law doesn't catch up with us."

Robin realised the friar was right. No wonder the men were so excited. "Alright then, Tuck, what are you waiting for? Let's see you dance!" With a whoop, he tossed his empty cup on the ground, grabbed the portly churchman by the wrists and dragged him round in a manic jig.

On Christmas day, the outlaws who had family or friends in nearby villages went to visit them. It had snowed sporadically for the past few days, and the roads were treacherous for unwary travellers. The law would not be out hunting for wolf's heads in such harsh weather, so the men made the most of it.

Little John went off smiling and whistling to Holderness to see his wife and son. Gareth went to see his poorly ma in Wrangbrook, and Arthur visited his parents in Bichill. Some of the outlaws, like Friar Tuck and Allan-a-Dale, were happy to stay at the camp, feasting, carolling, and playing drunken games like blind man's buff with each other. They had even gathered some ivy and holly, with many bright red berries, and decorated the cave with them.

Matilda had taken her pardon and, escorted by Robin, and Will, gone home to Wakefield, a free woman.

Robin had asked Much to come to the village with them, but, with his da murdered and a new miller living in the mill where he had grown up, Much had decided just to stay at the camp with Tuck and the others.

In Wakefield, Matilda's parents greeted her with joy, as little Beth wrapped herself around Scaflock's legs, screaming in delight.

The Fletchers' house, like the outlaws' camp, and all the other properties in the village, had been decorated with evergreen foliage, which stood out gaily against the frost and snow, and many villagers were singing carols.

Robin headed off to spend the day with his parents, and Scarlet, who had brought his own bedroll, stayed with the Fletchers, who gladly agreed to put him up for the evening.

Before they went to watch the mummers performing their festive play in the village green, Will took Beth for a walk down by the river, a huge grin on his face the entire time. He would never forget what Robin had done for him by rescuing his daughter and bringing happiness back into his life. She was a wonderful little girl, despite her harsh three years in de Bray's house, and Will knew his wife, Elaine, had been a fine mother. He wished she could see Beth now, but pushed the bleak thoughts out of his mind, and just concentrated on enjoying the day with his daughter.

Since it was Christmas he had brought her a gift – a little carved wooden dog on wheels, and they laughed and ran together through the snow, pulling it jerkily along behind them. Will's heart was light, and he offered a silent prayer to God for his good fortune.

Robin visited his family, taking them a ready cooked goose and some pickled vegetables for their Christmas dinner. He also handed his father a bag of silver to make sure they enjoyed the season without worrying about money.

Martha piled plates for them all, and they enjoyed a meal as a family for the first time since Robin had been outlawed seven months earlier. After the main course, a big mince pie was produced and Marjorie, who was looking much better since Robin had seen her last, was allowed first bite and told to make the traditional wish.

The big outlaw's heart swelled to see his little sister grinning as she bit into the tasty meat savoury, and he made a wish of his own, that Marjorie would enjoy many more happy, healthy Christmases.

Although she was stronger, his sister was still too poorly to go into the freezing afternoon to see the mummers with Will, Beth and the Fletchers, so the Hoods stayed home, happy in their own company, as the sounds of revelry filled the village outside.

As the light faded outside, making the already dim, smoky room seem even darker, they sat around the fire drinking warm ale and Robin told them of his intention to join the earl's planned rebellion. They knew King Edward would call the villagers to fight for him against the Earl of Lancaster's forces. Robin didn't want to find himself on a battlefield facing his own father.

"Don't worry about that, son," John told him. "If it comes to that, I'll join the same side as you. The earl has tried to be a decent lord to Wakefield, while the king continues to persecute men like you. There's no way I'll fight for a king whose unjust laws made my son live in the forest like an animal!"

Robin was cheered by his father's support, and the talk soon drifted to happier subjects, including his marriage to Matilda, which his parents were more than happy about. They talked long into the night, a well-banked log fire chasing the worst of the winter chill from the air, bathing the small room in a cosy orange glow.

John and Martha finally went upstairs to the little loft to sleep, kissing their son and daughter good night as they stretched out on their own straw pallets beside the fire which Robin now placed the stone cover over.

"He's a good lad," Martha whispered proudly to her husband as they climbed into bed and pulled the thick blankets over themselves. "A good man."

"Aye, he is," John agreed. "And maybe if the Earl of Lancaster can defeat that worthless bastard Edward…"

"Our boy can come home."

They hugged each other close and, full of hope, slept better that night than they had for months.

In the morning, Will and Robin said their farewells to their families, hopeful they would see them again soon, as free men. Still, even Will had tears in his eyes as he said goodbye to his little daughter, cuddling her fiercely and telling her how much he loved her.

Robin had embraced his parents and Marjorie, promising to visit more often, then went to the Fletcher's house to say goodbye to Matilda.

The two of them walked alone, thick cloaks round their shoulders as a light but icy wind whipped about the trees on the village outskirts.

"Did you tell your ma and da about…?" Robin wondered, placing a tender hand on his wife's belly.

Matilda shook her head. "No, not yet. I'll wait a couple more weeks until I'm showing more then I'll say to them. I don't know how they'll take it – they still think of me as their own wee girl. And, with you still being an outlaw…"

They walked a little longer, feeling melancholy at their parting.

Robin was overjoyed at Matilda being pardoned, and being able to live in Wakefield with her parents again, where she could raise their child in a normal environment.

He felt sad that he might not be able to enjoy being a proper father to the baby though. He'd never thought about having a child until now, but he wanted to do things right.

"I promise you, Matilda," he told her, grasping her hands and looking in her eyes earnestly. "I'll be here for you and our baby. I'll fight for the earl, and win my pardon. Then we'll be a proper family together!"

They held each other tightly, neither wanting to let go, but eventually they made their way back to Matilda's home, where Robin and Will bade everyone a last farewell, and headed into the forest to return to their camp.

The day before, Robin had visited the Wakefield headman, Patrick, and given him a bag of silver, as a Christmas gift to the village. Patrick had been shocked at the amount, but had promised to put it to good, and fair, use during the bad weather. He also told Robin he would make sure the villagers knew exactly who had given them the money.

Matilda, Marjorie and Beth would be well looked after by the people of Wakefield.

The two outlaws reached the camp by late afternoon, despite the thick snow, which slowed them and tired their legs.

"Scarlet!" Allan-a-Dale shouted as he saw his friends approaching. "Good news!"

"What's up, Allan?" Will wondered.

The minstrel hurried over, eager to share the news.

"Wilfred the baker sent word from Hathersage! The new lord there turned up yesterday with a dozen soldiers. John de Bray's been sent packing. Him and his wife were seen on the road south, struggling to get their horse and cart moving through the snow. Probably heading to London."

"Just the two of them?" Robin wondered.

"Aye," John nodded. "He's got no money to hire guards, has he?"

Will nodded grimly. "I'm going after him. Finally...finally, I'll have my revenge . . ."

Robin grasped him by the shoulder. "Do what you have to do. Take one of the horses."

They still had the two horses that had pulled Abbot Ness's cart of silver, so it would make the journey much quicker if Will took one of them to hunt his quarry.

"D'you want me to come with you?" Robin asked his grim friend. "Or one of the others? It'd be safer if you aren't alone, there's more outlaws than just us around these parts."

Scarlet thought for a moment; then he shook his head. "No, I have to do this alone."

In truth, he would have been happy for one of the other men to go with him for company but the fact was, he didn't know how he would react when he finally came face to face with the man who had murdered his family and made a slave of his infant daughter.

He believed he might butcher John de Bray, and possibly his wife too if she got in his way, and he didn't want any of his friends to be there to see it.

He saddled the youngest of the two horses and headed south without a word to the rest of the men.

When he returned to camp late that evening no one asked him what had happened, they simply welcomed him home warmly.

He accepted a mug of ale from Robin and gave his friend a melancholy nod of thanks.

It was done. Will Scaflock could, at last, move on – the darkness in his soul had finally been cleansed.

Robin never found out whether his friend had killed de Bray and his wife or let them go. The pain in Will's green eyes – the anguish Robin had there since the day he had met him – was gone at last.

Friar Tuck believed Will, a new man since rediscovering his daughter, had done the Christian thing and let de Bray go, while Matt Groves muttered to the outlaws of how he imagined Will had butchered both de Bray and his wife.

It didn't matter. Will Scarlet was, finally, Will Scaflock again.

For now.

* * *

"Fucking bastards!"

The servants cowered as de Faucumberg raged in his great hall in Nottingham castle, smashing things left, right and centre. These outbursts had been happening regularly, since the sheriff had returned from his humiliating meeting with Robin and the Earl of Lancaster.

"Bastards, the lot of them!" he screamed, face almost purple with rage. "Treat me like a fucking peasant?" He kicked over a chamber pot, piss spilling all over the floor. Even though he had made the mess himself, it only made him angrier as he screamed at his servants to clean it up.

"My lord . . . ?" The steward crept surreptitiously into the hall, trying to remain as anonymous as possible as the sheriff stormed around the room. "You have a visitor."

"Unless it's Richard-at-Lee or the Earl of Lancaster crawling on their knees begging my aid, you can kick them out! I'm in no mood for visitors!" de Faucumberg roared, before he eventually calmed down and, with a sullen grunt, dropped into the high backed chair at the end of the room.

"Well?" the sheriff roared at the cowering steward. "Show them in then!"

A tall, black armoured knight strode confidently into the great hall when the door was opened. He had dark eyes and walked as if he owned the castle.

The sheriff disliked him straight away.

"Who are you and what the hell do you want?" de Faucumberg demanded, as the man stood in front of him confidently, his big arms clasped behind his back.

"I'm here to hunt your outlaws, sheriff," the man replied, his face expressionless as he removed his helmet, revealing hair as black as his armour.

De Faucumberg snorted. "Oh are you? Well, I've been hunting those men for months – years some of them – and had no luck. I hope you can do better than I've managed. Who sent you? "

The stranger stood stock still, but his eyes moved to fix the sheriff in his gaze. "Everyone in the north of England has heard of these outlaws, and your failure to bring them to justice."

De Faucumberg's face became even angrier, as he glared at the stranger who had walked into his own castle and insulted him in front of his own people.

"You can hold your tongue, sir!" the sheriff snapped. "If you must criticise me, do it in private, not in front of my own men."

The big stranger remained silent, eyes fixed on an invisible point on the wall in front of himself.

"Who are you, anyway, and who sent you to save us all from the mighty Robin Hood and his men?" the sheriff demanded, spittle flecking his lips.

The knight moved forward, graceful despite his size, left hand resting gently on the pommel of his sword. He stood in front of de Faucumberg and looked boldly into the sheriff's eyes.

"King Edward himself has sent me, to destroy these outlaws that plague you. And I will destroy them, you can be sure of it."

He leaned down and placed his hands confidently on the table as he gazed at de Faucumberg. "You may have heard of me, lord sheriff. My name is Sir Guy of Gisbourne."

Historical Note

Writing historical fiction throws up some interesting challenges, and it's not always easy deciding how to overcome them.

During the time period covered in this series there was more than one sheriff in the north of England, where the action takes place. Some readers might have liked me to write the novel with 100% historical accuracy, and used the correct names for each different year. However, I decided to pick one man to fill the role of sheriff, who readers could get to know, and stick with him for the entirety of the series rather than introducing a different character for each book, who would flit in and out of the story, before readers could get to know them.

Sir Henry de Faucumberg was Sheriff of Nottingham and Yorkshire from 1318-1319 and again from 1323-1325 – around the time I've set *Wolf's Head* and its sequels. If Robin Hood did operate around the time of the Lancastrian revolt, as I think likely, de Faucumberg would have been a major thorn in his side for much of his life. De Faucumberg is also an interesting character in his own right, being charged on three separate occasions between 1313 and 1315, for theft and contempt of court, before somehow finding his way in life and being named sheriff shortly after in 1318.

He hunted down the Lancastrian rebels – the "Contrariants", was sheriff when the king visited the area in 1323 and, before being appointed sheriff, lived in Wakefield, just like Robin. He also held an estate in Holderness, where Little John originates.

Sir Henry de Faucumberg, with all these (coincidental?) connections to our other characters and places in *Wolf's Head* is the ideal candidate for our sheriff, I hope you will agree. Or at least see my point in choosing him for the position.

The next book in the series will see Robin, Will Scarlet, Little John *et al* dealing with the aftermath of Thomas, Earl of Lancaster's revolt. Sir Guy of Gisbourne will also pose a new threat to Robin and his friends – a hunter more deadly than Adam Bell/Gurdon ever was...?

I hope you'll join me to find out!

Steven A. McKay,
Glasgow,
December 26th, 2012

THE WOLF AND THE RAVEN

STEVEN A. McKAY

THE WOLF AND THE RAVEN

Book 2 in *The Forest Lord* series

By Steven A. McKay

Kindle version

Copyright 2014 Steven A. McKay

All rights reserved. This book may not be reproduced in any form,
in whole or in part, without written permission from the author.

For my son, Riley, and my daughter Lianna, with all of my love.

Acknowledgements

There are too many people I owe a debt of gratitude to, like all the lovely folk on social media who have shared my stuff, all the people who left nice reviews for *Wolfs Head* on Amazon and elsewhere, and those who helped me promote that book with interviews and blogs etc.

I'd also like to thank my beta-readers Bill Moore, Emma-Jayne Saanen, Pat Goodspeed, Neal Aplin, Luke Burns-McGruther, Paul Bennett, Robin Carter and Niall Hamilton, with special gratitude to Chris Verwijmeren for technical advice on the archery side of things.

To Gordon Doherty, author of the Legionary series of novels, for all his help and advice, particularly when I was working on *Wolf's Head* and Glyn Iliffe, author of The Adventures of Odysseus series for providing a glowing strapline for that first book – you guys rock.

To the people at Amazon, particularly the KDP team (you know who you are!), for making it possible to successfully publish my work when it had proved otherwise impossible and for continuing to support me on my self-publishing journey: thank you so much!

Thanks to my wife Yvonne, my children Freya, Riley and Lianna and my mum, Bernadette, who all support and inspire me every day in different ways.

And finally – thank you to YOU, the readers who bought *Wolf's Head* and now *The Wolf and The Raven*. Your support means everything, believe me.

Apologies if I've forgotten anyone – let me know and I'll list you in the next book!

CHAPTER ONE

England, 16th March 1322

"Loose!" Robin roared, hoping the soldiers he commanded would be able to hear him over the deafening sounds of the battle.

His men, fifteen in total, released their arrows, along with dozens of other longbow men in Thomas Plantaganet, the Earl of Lancaster's, army.

The missiles formed an ominous dark mass in the sky before hammering down, into the forces of King Edward II, led by Sir Andrew Harclay, 1st Earl of Carlisle. The king's men desperately tried to shelter behind their shields, but many of them were killed or horribly injured. Their commanders screamed at those still standing to hold firm, as the rebel forces advanced upon them.

Robin shuddered at the screams of dying men, the thunder of horse's hooves and the looks of terror on the faces of the men being driven on by the mounted nobles behind them. He had never seen anything as horrifying as a full scale battle before, and the hellish atmosphere shocked him.

He forced himself to concentrate, fitting another arrow to his bow and bellowing again. "Keep shooting; we have to allow the Earl's men a chance to reach the ford or we're finished here!"

It was true. The Earl of Lancaster's forces were badly outnumbered by the king's men. Sir Andrew had also managed to reach the river before the rebels which had allowed him to take full advantage of the surrounding terrain.

Positioning his knights and men-at-arms on the opposite end of the bridge, almost in a spear-wall, Harclay knew the Earl would have to try and break through as more of the king's forces were travelling to attack his rear.

It was becoming more and more obvious to Robin the battle was going badly. Lancaster was trying to lead his men, many of them wearing his livery of argent and azure, to a ford further upriver while his lieutenants, the Earl of Hereford, Humphrey de Bohun, and Roger de Clifford of Skipton, tried to storm the bridge. The king's longbow men were taking a terrible toll on Lancaster's men as they tried to reach the ford though, while Hereford had been killed by a pikeman hiding underneath the bridge. When Clifford was also wounded, the assault on the bridge threatened to grind to a complete standstill.

Robin and his men had been living as outlaws in the forests of Barnsdale a few months earlier, when the Earl of Lancaster had promised them all pardons if they joined his rebellion. It had been a simple choice for the outlaws. They could either continue to live like animals in the freezing winter, hunted by the foresters and sheriff's soldiers, or join a rebellion against the king whose unjust laws had driven them into the greenwood in the first place.

The weeks leading up to this point had been hectic for the outlaws, as the earl sent word summoning them to join his army besieging the royal stronghold of Tickhill Castle. From there the army had moved on to Burton-on Trent, setting fire to the town when they found out the king was coming after them, before heading for Dunstanburgh on the coast. They'd only managed a few miles before Harclay's men had caught up with them here at Boroughbridge.

For most of Robin's men this wasn't the first time they'd been a part of such a large, organized force; many of them had stood against the Scots or, like Will Scarlet, served as mercenaries, fighting in battles all across the world. In the past, though, they had joined up because they were either summoned to do so by their local lord, or were being well paid to fight for an employer.

Here, Robin and his friends felt like they were fighting for a cause that directly impacted on their own personal lives. Although none of them knew much about the wider political picture in England, they knew they wanted their freedom and the Earl of Lancaster promised that. It was widely known that the earl stood up for the lower classes living in his manors, while King Edward II spent more time playing around in boats or at sports than he did taking care of his people.

It was a simplistic view of the situation – black and white with no shades of grey in-between, although Robin had been outraged when the earl had set fire to Burton, and rumours of a treaty with the Scots had spread amongst the army, enraging many of them.

They were here now though, the rumours were nothing more than hearsay and no-one would convince Robin they weren't fighting for a just cause. They weren't just struggling to survive here, as they had been doing as outlaws for months or even years in some cases. They were trying to do some good, for themselves, yes, but also for their fellow countrymen.

As Robin had said to them all in a short, but rousing speech just before battle commenced: "We have a chance to actually *change* things here, lads. A chance to bring justice and some form of equality to the country. A chance to show the king we're not going to take his shit any more!"

The men had cheered their young leader's words and gone into the fight with pride and determination burning in their eyes,.

Robin grimaced as he let fly another arrow, knowing it would find its lethal mark in the closely packed line of soldiers on the other side of the river. A moment later he had pulled another from the ground at his feet and nocked it to his bowstring, the rock-hard shoulder muscles rolling as he drew back the great warbow and took aim again.

The earl had seemed confident in the success of the rebellion when Robin had agreed to join him, but it was going badly wrong. The king's men were happy to stand safely behind their spears as the rebels tried to force their way across the river, and, with such an advantage in numbers and terrain, Lancaster's forces would soon be crushed.

The air was heavy with the harsh sounds of blade on blade, screams of wounded men and horses and ragged, desperate war-cries.

"What do we do, now, Robin?" the giant known as Little John shouted at his friend, his great voice carrying effortlessly even through the din of battle.

Robin was torn. It was against his nature to run from a fight. But the battle was lost – he could see that. Once Harclay's forces had killed enough of the rebels the king's man would surely lead his vastly superior force over the bridge to destroy the rest of them. It would mean certain death for Robin, and the men who had placed their trust in him to lead them.

His heart swelled with pride as he glanced along the line at his friends, still shooting grimly into the enemy lines. Allan-a-Dale, Friar Tuck, Will Scaflock, his childhood friend Much…They were more than just outlaws; they were Robin's friends: blood brothers.

A great cry of victory went up from far to his left, and Little John, his great height giving him a better view of the battle, cursed. "The assault on the bridge has broken! It won't be long before the earl's men take it, and the bastards'll swarm over the bridge and circle us! We're done, Robin!"

The young leader looked around, trying to find their commander, the earl, but there was no sign of him. "Keep shooting, John!" Robin bellowed. "We're not finished yet!"

He knew they *were* done – he just hated the idea of running from the battle, possibly taking a sword in the back as they were charged down by the enemy cavalry. Even if they did make it to the trees a short distance away, what then? Back to a life hiding in the forest, not only an outlaw, but a rebel too. He tried to shoot faster, desperation fuelling his enormous arms, but fatigue was beginning to set in and the enemy numbers seemed to be as overwhelming as they had been when the battle started.

Once Harclay's men came across the bridge Robin's outlaws would have to draw their swords and, with trembling, aching, spent limbs, fight a foe enraged by the arrows that had been killing and maiming them and their comrades.

Robin could see his men were beginning to realise the same thing, as they began to glance nervously in his direction. He shouted in rage and continued to release arrow after arrow, each one sailing up almost majestically, before tearing down, viciously, into a target. Yet still the enemy stood, a vast host of men, as immovable as a castle wall.

Suddenly another cry rose from dozens of throats, this time to their left, where the earl's men had given up their attempt to reach the ford, and, as their allies began to run for it, Robin knew the battle was as good as finished. An image of his wife, Matilda, smiling, her belly swollen with the child growing inside her, flashed into his mind and tears of frustration blurred his vision.

He would not die here.

"Retreat!" he cried. "Head for the trees! Head for the fucking trees!"

Only those closest to him heard, as his tired voice cracked with the strain.

Little John filled his great lungs and repeated the command. The outlaws looked along the line to make sure they had understood the order, then, seeing Robin, sword drawn, gesturing towards the copse of beech trees behind them, began to run.

Many of the earl's men on either side of the fleeing outlaws shouted in dismay, telling them to hold their positions, but the outlaws ignored the cries.

Robin waited until his men were all moving towards the forest before he began to follow. He felt a terrible sense of guilt to be leaving the earl's men behind to face their fate, but he knew the battle was lost. He could see other groups of soldiers on all sides streaming back towards the forest in desperation now and knew he had ordered his friends to retreat at exactly the right time.

Another great cheer went up from the bridge as the king's men realised they were close to smashing their enemy and began to run across the bridge in pursuit, and Robin forced himself to move faster, his whole body aching, lungs burning.

From the corner of his eye he saw a mounted nobleman screaming in rage, trying to order the men to hold the line. It was Thomas, the Earl of Lancaster. He had his sword drawn and was hacking at his own retreating men in fury, desperately trying to stop the rout.

Robin was horrified at the sight of the earl attacking his own men, but the sound of pounding feet behind him told him King Edward's army were coming fast and he grimly pushed on towards the trees, knowing he would be cut down should he falter or stumble.

Ahead in the trees, he could see Little John and Much waving to him, willing him onwards, and mixed emotions struggled within him: anger at them, for not getting as far into the safety of the forest as possible, but also gratitude that they hadn't simply left him behind.

As he raced towards his friends in desperation, he could feel the ground tremble beneath him and he knew enemy cavalry were close behind. He couldn't risk a look back to see how close they were, for fear of stumbling, but he expected any second to feel a sword hammer into his spine.

He was more frightened than he had ever been in his life, and again, Matilda, and an image of a little boy, came into his mind as, sobbing, he bared his teeth and tried one last time to make his legs move faster.

The metallic taste of blood filled his mouth and he knew he must have bitten his tongue as the pounding of hooves came closer and an enemy knight charged through the grass behind him. He imagined the pursuer laughing in grim satisfaction at the unresisting target fleeing desperately towards the trees.

Much and John looked on in frustrated disbelief as Robin suddenly came to a halt and turned, sword held before him.

"Come on then, you bastard!" he shouted, spreading his legs and moving into a defensive stance.

The enemy horseman thundered towards him, almost fifteen hundred pounds of muscle and steel. In comparison Robin was closer to two hundred pounds and only lightly armoured. The gambeson he wore was the same beaten-up one his old captain, Adam Bell, had given him almost a year ago. He never wore a helmet or carried a shield, needing both hands free to shoot his enormous longbow.

Even if he somehow managed to land a blow on the knight, the sheer weight of attacking horse and man would destroy Robin's body.

He lost his sense of fear as the knight bore down on him, and time seemed to slow to a crawl. The horse's eyes bulged, its great nostrils flaring, as its rider swept his longsword back, perfectly timed for the killing blow, and Robin felt a feral growl escape from his throat, enraged at the oncoming doom, but determined to meet it head on.

From behind Robin an arrow tore through the air, somehow finding its way through the thin visor on the horseman's helmet, lodging in his brain and catapulting him backwards to land, arms and legs flailing, on the hard ground behind.

The charging horse, with no one to control it, veered to one side, away from the grateful outlaw, who stood rooted to the spot, thinking inanely of King Harold and how an arrow to the eye had killed him nearly three hundred years earlier, changing England forever.

Hands grabbed his arm and he came back to the present, as Little John dragged him into the trees, towards Much, who held his longbow, ready to cut down any other pursuers. Robin grinned towards his childhood friend in gratitude, and Much laughed in relief.

"We'll talk about how lucky that shot was later," John grunted. "Once we're safely away from here. Come on, let's move!"

CHAPTER TWO

"Now what?" Will Scaflock demanded. "We're back where we started!"

When Robin's men had run from the battle, although they were scattered, they had slowly made their way back, in ones and twos, to meet up again in Barnsdale, at a prearranged spot well-hidden from the main roads.

The king's men had chased and harried all the fleeing rebels but many of them, including all of Robin's gang, who were experienced woodsmen, had managed to escape into the forest, and safety. For now.

Matt Groves slammed his open palm against a tree in frustration. "We're not back where we started at all, Scarlet!" he shouted at Will. "Before this we were outlaws, hunted by foresters and, now and again, the sheriff's men. Now we're rebels – the king's own soldiers will be after us!" He pointed an accusing finger at Robin. "This is all your fault, Hood! You told us to join the rebellion, and we followed you! Now what? We're fucked!"

Robin sat on a frost-covered fallen tree and shook his head wearily. He was tired of Matt Groves and his complaining. The rest of the group shared a strong bond of friendship and mutual respect, but Groves had slowly become something of an outsider in their small band. The sheriff had offered to sell Robin's wife, Matilda, a pardon a few months earlier, but Matt had refused to part with any money. Every one of the other outlaws had been happy to help the girl and, thankfully, she had won her freedom eventually, but the incident still angered Robin.

"I never told anyone to join the rebellion," Robin retorted. "I decided to throw my lot in with the Earl of Lancaster and Sir Richard-at-Lee. The rest of you were free to do what you wanted."

"We all wanted to fight," Much nodded, agreeing with his big friend. "Not just for pardons, but to bring some sort of justice to the country. This was our one chance to make a difference – to help the common folk. To help our friends and families in places like Wakefield and Hathersage."

There were grunts of agreement at that, but Matt snorted, looking around at the rest of the men in disgust. "The common folk? You mean like the people at Burton where Lancaster burnt the place down about their ears?" He turned to glare at Robin again, barely drawing breath as he continued. "You're supposed to be our leader, Hood. We all trusted you to steer us right. You said it was a good idea – 'we'll all win pardons,' you said. Well, where's my fucking pardon then? And what about that king's man, Sir Guy of Gisbourne? That bastard has a hard-on for you and we're all going to suffer for it now!" As he ranted, his voice had grown steadily louder and he had moved slowly closer to Robin, so, his last, shouted words, were spat right in the young man's face.

Although Robin felt humiliated and angry, he also understood Matt's frustration. No, he hadn't told the men to join the Earl of Lancaster's rebellion but he had suggested it was a good idea. Robin was still a very young man, only eighteen, and his lack of experience often made him question his leadership skills. Deep down, he wondered if maybe Matt Groves was right, and it *was* all his fault.

Groves misread Robin's silence and downcast eyes, assuming his young leader was ignoring him. "Are you listening to me, you arrogant young prick?" he demanded, his hand shooting forward to grasp Robin round the neck.

Without realising what he was doing, Robin reacted instinctively. His left wrist flicked up and round, knocking Matt's hand past his shoulder, as his right fist shot out, slamming straight into Matt's nose with a crunch of bone and cartilage.

Groves fell back onto the frosty wet grass, his eyes wide in shock, but before he could react, Little John and Will pinned him to the ground.

"Just stay where you are, Matt," John grunted, as the fallen man struggled to rise, his face a mask of fury, blood trickling from his nostrils. The rest of the outlaws stood watching the confrontation in silence, wondering where it would lead.

Robin thought quickly. Although Matt Groves was not well liked amongst the outlaws, thanks to his sour nature and constant complaining, he *was* respected. All of the men had been in fights with Matt at their side, and many of them had been saved from the point of a forester's sword by his actions.

The young leader couldn't just tell Groves to leave their group; he had to deal with this situation properly, while retaining his authority in front of the men.

"Let him up," Robin muttered to Will and John, who warily let go of Matt's arms, the three of them climbing slowly to their feet, Groves wiping his upper lip and grimacing in disgust at the blood smeared on the back of his hand.

Robin looked around at the men, addressing them as one. "I'm going to head back to our last camp-site, and carry on as before. We have no other choice. Aye, it'll be hard – even harder than before the rebellion. But there's nothing else to do – so…I'm not ordering anyone to follow me. You're all big boys; you can make up your own minds. Barnsdale's a big place, with lots of trees to hide in, especially now as spring's on its way. I'm sure you can all find somewhere to try and keep out of the king's way. Anyone that wants to, though, is welcome to come with me." He looked into the eyes of the men, his face earnest. "I hope you all do."

Matt Groves hawked and spat a gob of blood onto the forest floor.

"You can do what you like," Robin glared at him. "For what it's worth, I'd be more than happy if you'd just fuck off. Go your own way, so we don't have to listen to your complaining all the time. But it's your choice: go where you will." He moved forward to stand in front of Groves and lowered his voice to a menacing growl, just loud enough for everyone else to hear. "If you ever try and lay a hand on me again though, old man, I'll rip your face off and nail it to a tree."

Matt held eye contact with the younger man for a moment then turned away with a sneer.

Robin collected his few belongings and moved off in the direction of Notton, not far from Wakefield, where the outlaws had spent the previous winter. It was as good a place as any to set up camp, he thought. He didn't look back as he made his way through the forest, but he muttered a quiet prayer to Mary Magdalene that his friends would all follow him.

Much caught up with him, clapping a big hand on his leader's back, sympathetically. "You all right?"

Robin shrugged. "Not really. Will's right – we're fucked. Back worse off than we were before Christmas. And not just us: the whole country." He shook his head angrily, the disappointment of being on the losing side in the rebellion threatening to overwhelm him. His hopes and dreams had gone up in smoke as he had shouted at his men to retreat from the battle of Boroughbridge. He had desperately wanted the pardon the Earl of Lancaster had promised him. His wife Matilda was carrying their unborn child and he wanted so much to be a part of the little one's life; a real father. A real husband.

That would be nigh on impossible living as a wolf's head in the forest. His rage boiled impotently inside him, and he almost hoped Matt Groves would attack him again so he could take his frustration out on the bastard.

He felt suddenly ashamed as he looked over at Much, a young man who had lost his home and his entire family and been left with nothing. At least Robin still had his parents and his wife in Wakefield, even if he couldn't be with them as often as he'd like. He put an arm around Much's shoulder and threw his old friend a grin. "We'll be all right – we just need to find some other way to earn a pardon now."

There was a sarcastic laugh from behind him at that, and he turned to see Will Scarlet following, his green eyes twinkling. Little John and Friar Tuck were a little way behind and, as he looked back along the trail Robin's heart soared as he realised his men had all decided to follow him.

He might not have his family beside him, but this gang of outlaws was a brotherhood. He grinned at them all and walked on with his head high.

Matt Groves traipsed along at the rear, shoving branches and foliage out of the way angrily, his face twisted in a scowl. It would be suicide to head into the forest on his own just now though, with the king's men still hunting the rebels, so he followed Robin and the others bitterly.

His nose ached, and the blood drying around his mouth cracked uncomfortably as it dried in the chilly morning breeze. Hood had beaten him today – humiliated him in front of these men he had known for years. But Matt Groves was a man that knew how to hold a grudge – he would find a way to pay the young arsehole back eventually.

He just had to be patient, and watch for his chance.

* * *

"Shut up, you scum!" Henricus Chapman, steward to the Sheriff of Nottingham and Yorkshire, roared at the people gathered in the great hall of the castle. "The king is at the gate! Make yourselves presentable, and keep your mouths shut!"

The sheriff, Sir Henry de Faucumberg, shook his head at his steward's harsh words, but his own nervousness at the impending royal visit stopped him from reprimanding the over-zealous official.

As a result of the failed rebellion many men from the surrounding villages who had thrown their lot in with the defeated Earl of Lancaster had either been killed or chased into the forests as outlaws. Now, their families – wives, children, brothers, parents – came to the sheriff pleading for mercy. Who would work the land if so many men were declared outlaws and hunted down? Who would support their children? More importantly to the sheriff and his noble peers, who would pay their rents?

De Faucumberg was prepared to grudgingly allow the hundreds of defeated rebels to return quietly to their homes. He was no philanthropist, but the local economy needed those men – not to mention the fact hunting them all down would be a major burden on his own military resources.

Now, though, one of his men had hurried to see him with news from one of Nottingham's gatehouses. King Edward II was at the gate, making his way to see the sheriff. It wasn't an entirely unexpected visit, but de Faucumberg had hoped for a little more notice than this.

He absent-mindedly smoothed imagined creases from his expensive robe, ran his hands over his short greying hair and breathed on his gold chain of office, working it to a nice shine with his sleeve. He looked up irritably as the newest addition to his staff strode confidently up to stand before him.

Sir Guy of Gisbourne had been sent by the king a few months earlier, to hunt the outlaws hiding in Barnsdale. Robin Hood in particular.

De Faucumberg had failed to catch Hood and his gang as they robbed a number of powerful nobles and clergymen during the last year. King Edward had grown impatient and, eventually, sent his own man to help. Gisbourne was an experienced bounty-hunter – ruthless, intelligent, and an expert forester to boot. The king expected him to soon take care of the notorious Hood and his gang, who were fast becoming folk heroes to the poor, downtrodden people of northern England.

Sir Henry de Faucumberg couldn't stand the sight of the tall, self assured Gisbourne. He had no choice but to work with him though, and, if the king's man managed to kill Hood and his men – well, good! One less wolf's head to worry about. Then the overly confident lanky big bastard could bugger off back to the king.

"Oh, get up here and sit beside me, Gisbourne," the sheriff groused. "The king will expect to see his bounty-hunter." De Faucumberg indicated the empty seat to his right, and Sir Guy stepped onto the raised dais before settling into the vacant chair with a grin at the sheriff.

De Faucumberg, nervous at the thought of meeting the king under these circumstances, suddenly leaned forward to glare into Gisbourne's surprised face.

"You watch what you say to the king," he whispered with a snarl. "Don't forget, he'll be gone in a day and you'll be left behind again…with me and my men."

There was a commotion near the doors as the steward hurried back into the great hall and lifted his powerful voice.

"His royal Highness, King Edward!"

"I'll be left behind with you?" Gisbourne quietly asked the sheriff, as the king and his retinue filed into the hall. "You're assuming you'll still be sheriff after I give my report to the king…"

De Faucumberg glared at Gisbourne, but the king's man grinned back, clearly enjoying the sheriff's discomfort.

King Edward cut an imposing figure as he strode to the front of the hall. Handsome and tall, even taller than Sir Guy, and much broader across the shoulders with long wavy fair hair that curled around his neck.

Gisbourne dropped to one knee, his head bowed respectfully as England's ruler approached them and De Faucumberg quickly followed suit.

"Highness, be welcome!" the sheriff intoned, eyes on the impeccably polished wooden floorboards.

"Yes, yes, very good, Sir Henry." King Edward swept past his kneeling subjects and took his seat, in the middle of the table, between the sheriff's and Guy of Gisbourne's chairs.

"Get up. I don't have time for this," the king shouted to the gathered people. He lifted the silver goblet of wine before him and drained it with a loud gasp of pleasure. A wide-eyed serving boy rushed over, jug in hand, to refill the cup, but the king waved him away irritably.

"Let me guess, de Faucumberg," Edward growled, as the sheriff took his seat and looked at the king. "These people are here hoping their men who took up arms against me will be pardoned."

De Faucumberg nodded. "Yes, my liege. It seems many local villagers joined the ill-fated rebellion. Without those men the economy will struggle."

The king nodded grimly. "I understand that. It's hard enough for these people to survive, yes?"

The sheriff nodded again, thankful that the king understood the issue so well.

"Then they should have thought of that before they rebelled against my rule!" King Edward suddenly slammed his hand on the table, his face red with anger. "You people!" He roared, glaring at the men and women gathered in the hall. "Get back to your villages, and make sure you pay your rents! When your children are starving, and your bellies are swollen with hunger again maybe your men will think twice about rebelling against their rightful king. Get out!"

De Faucumberg, his earlier thoughts of leniency to the villagers forgotten in the face of the king's rage, shouted at his guards. "You heard him! Get those people out of here, now!"

As the frightened men and women streamed out of the hall Edward leaned back and, brandishing his empty goblet, shouted for a refill.

"I understand your dilemma, de Faucumberg," the king told the sheriff, gazing up at the vaulted ceiling. "But I want these traitors hunted down and destroyed. Every last one of them." He held up a hand as the sheriff opened his mouth to protest. "You need soldiers, I know. I have them for you: another thirty men."

De Faucumberg let a small smile creep over his face at the thought of such an increase in his personal militia, and he glanced over at Sir Guy with a triumphant smirk.

"They will be under Sir Guy of Gisbourne's command."

The sheriff's face fell in disbelief as Edward continued. "You're tied up with your administrative duties in Nottingham and Yorkshire, Henry. Sir Guy will hunt down the rebels. I don't know why you look like someone's pissed in your wine – you've got it easy."

"Sir Henry is one of the best administrators I've ever worked with, Sire," Gisbourne told the king solemnly, as the sheriff listened in surprise. "I'm sure that, between us, we can hunt down these rebels while making sure the rents are paid on time." He glanced at de Faucumberg, eyebrows raised. "Eh, Sir Henry?"

The sheriff, a man who had known great power over a period of many years, felt lost under the steely eyes of the king and the smirking bounty-hunter. He nodded.

"Yes, my liege. We'll look after things for you. But…"

The king looked irritably at the sheriff. "But what?"

"Well, without their men…some of the local villages won't survive the winter."

The king shrugged his shoulders and emptied his goblet, wine running down the side of his mouth. "Fine," he said, wiping his chin neatly with a napkin. "Pardon the ones you see fit. Not the ringleaders though – not the knights and noblemen. Those you will kill or imprison until I can decide their fate, yes? And what about that outlaw I sent Gisbourne here for in the first place? Have you managed to catch him?"

De Faucumberg shook his head, not wanting to admit Robin Hood and his men had been spotted within the ranks of the Earl of Lancaster's army. "Not yet" –

"Fear not, sire," Sir Guy broke in, his earlier smile replaced with a determined scowl that chilled the sheriff to the bone. "The commoners see him as some legendary swordsman – a great hero like Arthur or Lancelot. I'll show them he's nothing more than a dirty peasant with ideas above his station. Count on it, my liege: I'll bring the wolf's head to justice, one way or another…"

"Good, that's all settled then," King Edward nodded contentedly, gesturing to the serving boy for another refill. "I'll leave you two to sort it out – I'm off to deal with my cousin the Earl of Lancaster in the morning. Now…where's your entertainment, de Faucumberg? I'm looking forward to a fine evening. The sheriff of Manchester has a minstrel who can fart a tune you know."

* * *

"That stinks, you dirty bastard!"

Will Scarlet grinned, as Little John covered his bearded face theatrically with his sleeve.

"Sorry," Will laughed. "I must've eaten too much of that cabbage yesterday. It's good for the digestion they say."

"In the name of God," John grunted with a scowl. "I thought it was hell on Earth fighting the king's men but your arse is deadlier than a blade in the guts."

Winter was retreating, so, as they settled back into their old camp near Notton the outlaws were able to sleep in the open again, under sturdy shelters, rather than crushed together in a cramped cave as they had been before joining the earl's army.

They clustered around the camp-fire, enjoying its warmth and light as glowing embers crackled into the night sky, drinking ale, playing dice, and singing songs.

So far they'd managed to avoid the king's soldiers, although they'd heard tales from the locals roundabout of other rebels being caught in the forest and hanged or worse. It was only a matter of time until they'd be forced to fight for their lives, Robin mused, as he sat, staring into the camp-fire and nursing a mug of ale.

He had sent a message to Wakefield, to let his family, and Will's daughter Beth, who also lived there, know they were all alive and well, although still outlaws.

"Any idea what we're going to do?" Friar Tuck sat down with a grunt next to the young leader, an ale in one hand and a leg of roast duck in the other.

Robin smiled at his portly friend, shrugging his shoulders in reply. "Not really. I can't see anything for us to do, other than what we've been doing all along: living here in the greenwood, robbing rich folk, counting on the good will of the villagers' hereabouts…and killing anyone who comes hunting for us." He shrugged again, despondently. "If you've got any advice, Tuck, I'd like to hear it."

The friar nodded, understanding Robin's frustration. "I don't have much to offer by way of advice," he replied. "But you should take heart from the fact these men followed you after the Battle of Boroughbridge, and still trust you to lead them."

Robin stayed silent, brooding as he gazed at the black silhouettes of the tall trees, like giant sentinels all around them.

"Men like John Little and Will Scaflock are no fools," the friar had a pleasant, persuasive voice and he carried on, fixing his young captain with a knowing look. "Either of them could lead their own gang of men, but they choose to follow *you*. Look, the rebellion wasn't meant to be – the earl burned Burton and he treated with the Scots." He waved away Robin's half-hearted protest. "The rumours were true, Lancaster could have crushed the Scots over the years but he always let them escape. Aye, he promised a lot and he probably would have been a better king for the likes of us than Edward ever will be but...maybe it'll turn out to be a blessing that we failed at Boroughbridge. I know it's hard to believe, with your wife carrying your child and you stuck out here with all of us, but... God will look after you. Never give up hope!"

Robin was taken aback by the vehemence in Tuck's voice.

"Trust me, lad: our Lord has a purpose for you. That much was clear to me from the day I met you. You have to believe in yourself the way these men believe in you." He spread his arms wide, encompassing the whole outlaw camp. "And they're going to need you now – that bastard Gisbourne will come for us soon..."

Robin shivered. When they'd been part of the earl's army he'd heard rumours about Sir Guy and the things he'd done. He looked across at Tuck and pushed the king's man from his mind, grinning back at the rosy-cheeked friar who drained the last of the ale in his cup and nodded towards the rest of the gang.

Despite their defeat in the battle against King Edward's forces, and their continuing status as outlaws, the men were enjoying themselves tonight. They laughed and sang around the camp-fire, seemingly without a care in the world. Every so often one of them would wave over to him, grinning and raising their mugs in salute.

Robin felt humbled by their friendship, and their faith in him as their leader.

His eyes grew moist and he looked away from Tuck, wiping the tears with his fingertips. *Never give up hope...*

The big friar stood up, and clapped his young leader on the back. "Come on, it's time you joined in."

With a smile of gratitude, Robin followed Tuck back to the fire, and found himself singing and dancing with the rest of the men, his cares, for a while, forgotten.

At the edge of the fire's orange glow, Matt Groves stood alone, watching the others enjoying themselves, his expression blacker than the starless sky overhead.

CHAPTER THREE

After Robin and the other outlaws had fled the battlefield at Boroughbridge, things had not gone well for the Earl of Lancaster's forces, or his Marcher allies. They had suffered horrendous casualties from the sustained assault of Andrew Harclay's longbow men and, in desperation, had managed to obtain an overnight truce but the majority of their remaining soldiers had deserted during the night.

The rebellion was over.

In the morning, the earl, along with his other captains, had surrendered to Harclay, who had them manacled and taken by boat to the earl's own castle in Pontefract.

Thomas had been locked in a cell with his ally, Roger Clifford, 2nd Lord of Skipton.

"What do you think Edward will do with us?" Clifford asked, gasping in pain from the terrible cut in the side he had suffered at Boroughbridge. Before imprisoning him, the king's men had poured wine on it to clean it, and roughly tied a strip of linen around his torso to stop the bleeding, but the deep wound was beginning to fester and become ever more painful.

Thomas shrugged, too weak from hunger and dehydration to offer a reply.

For three days they had languished in the freezing jail underneath the castle. The guards occasionally threw some mouldy bread in to them, and skins filled with cheap, vile tasting wine, but mostly they were left alone in the near total darkness. The cell stank, as they were forced to relieve themselves in the corners, but the mess inevitably spread. There weren't even any rushes to soak up the filth.

The earl sat contemplating the irony of being held captive in his own castle. If he'd known this was going to happen he'd have at least had the floors stocked with rushes! He almost smiled at the idea.

"Do you think he'll pardon us?" Clifford breathed, gazing at the ceiling which was filthy with years of damp and mould. "We're too powerful to be held prisoner for long, don't you think?"

Lancaster never even offered a shrug this time, his eyes glassy, as if lost in a daydream.

Both men stirred as the sound of heavy footsteps approached them. Would it be another guard to toss more scraps of food for them to scavenge off the shit-stained floor, like dogs again?

The massive door, close to four inches thick was flung open, the light from the torches their jailers carried momentarily blinding the captives.

"You. Up." It was one of the king's soldiers, a huge bear of a man with a small but distinctive scar on his upper lip which made him look even more daunting. He was flanked by two other men, not as tall as their captain, but with the enormous arms and shoulders of longbow men. All three wore the king's heraldic badge of three yellow lions on a red background, and they glared at the earl, watching as the disgraced nobleman weakly tried to stand.

"Help him."

The two shorter men moved into the cell, swearing at the stench, and grasped the wretched earl by the arms, dragging him to his feet effortlessly.

"Take him."

Thomas was half-dragged from the cell, his head spinning so badly he feared he might puke on his two 'helpers'.

"Where are you taking him?" Clifford whimpered, but the huge soldier simply slammed the door shut with a thump, throwing the miserable cell into darkness again and leaving the Lord of Skipton to his fate.

"What about me?" he shouted, his voice cracking as the burning pain in his side almost made him pass out.

As he was pulled along the draughty corridor the Earl of Lancaster felt sorry for Clifford. His wound was mortal, that much was obvious – the man would be dead in a couple of days even if the king did pardon him.

Thomas, on the other hand, would be fine once he had something to eat and drink. His mouth watered at the thought of a nice cut of roast pork and a mug of ale.

Obviously, the king – his cousin – would have to punish him somehow.

An exorbitant fine perhaps. Christ, maybe even exile. That would be terrible.

But the earl was of royal blood himself – the Steward of England and the second wealthiest man in the country after Edward himself. He had survived the king's wrath before, most notably when he had beheaded Edward's lover Piers Gaveston.

Yes, he felt pity for his ally Clifford, left to die in a piss-soaked, freezing jail cell, but at least Thomas would be all right.

He felt sure of it.

As he was taken into the great hall – his great hall! – Thomas's confidence faltered. The king sat at the table, with those loyal earls and other magnates that had supported him against the rebels. At Edward's right hand sat Hugh, the younger Despenser, with a look of malevolent triumph on his face. The Elder Despenser, along with other earls who had remained loyal to the king were also seated at the long table.

The two soldiers let their charge go at a nod from the scarred giant, and Thomas slumped embarrassingly, and painfully, onto the floorboards, too weak to lift his arms protectively as his face hit the ground.

He was offered no food or drink, and his manacles remained locked in place on his wrists and ankles, as the king himself stood to list the charges against him.

In his weakened state he could only crouch on the floor as Edward railed at him.

"You raised an army against me!"

After a while, Thomas couldn't concentrate on what was being said. His head was spinning and he longed to sleep, which seemed such a ridiculous idea that he burst out laughing.

His laughter stopped a moment later as the king sat down and Sir Henry Despenser stood to proclaim judgement. It took a few seconds, but even in his fragile state of mind the words shocked the earl.

"Thomas Plantaganet, Earl of Lancaster, Leicester and Derby, you have been found guilty of treason. You are hereby sentenced to death by being hanged, drawn and beheaded."

Exhausted and half mad, he looked up at his cousin, King Edward II with a wild stare.

Then, with tears streaking his filthy cheeks, he burst out laughing again.

* * *

"Robin!" The girl's eyes lit up as she saw her husband standing at the door, but, as she looked at him, they welled up with tears and the outlaw took her gently in his massive arms.

"I know, I know," he muttered. "The rebellion failed. I'm still a wolf's head. I'm so sorry."

They moved inside, locking the door behind them. It was before dawn and the village was mostly silent in the early spring gloom, but Robin didn't want anyone seeing him. He remembered only too well the trouble that had come to Wakefield last year as the law hunted for him and Matilda had been arrested herself as a result.

"Ah, it's you lad! We thought it was a cat scratching at the door so quietly before sunrise." The village fletcher, Henry, Matilda's father, smiled warmly at his son-in-law and moved across the small room to grasp him by the hand.

"It's good to see you," Mary, Matilda's mother added, reaching up to kiss Robin gently on the cheek. "We were worried...well, when we heard the king's men had beaten the earl's forces and were hunting you all down."

Robin nodded sadly. "We had no chance in the end. I ordered the lads to run before Harclay's men got close enough to catch us. It felt like a betrayal, running like that, but we were done for."

"You did the right thing," the fletcher said. "The Earl of Lancaster should have made more of a fight of it instead of throwing away so many lives needlessly. The villages hereabouts have lost a lot of fathers and sons. The good Lord knows what'll happen when the harvest's to be planted."

Robin waved a hand dismissing Henry's fears. "The king might be a fool, but I don't think he'll let the people starve just to teach a few peasants and yeomen a lesson. He's not that vindictive. He'll probably hang a few of the rebel leaders to make an example of them, but the earl is too wealthy for the king to do much."

"You think this will all just die down?" Matilda led Robin by the hand to the small table the family kept by the wall and bade him sit and eat some of the porridge she'd just ladled out for him.

"Will seems to think so," he replied, tucking into the warm food gratefully. "And Will understands these things a lot better than I ever will. We're going to be in even more danger than we were before for a while, though, until the king's men flush out the rest of the rebels. We'll be all right though," he smiled reassuringly at the worried look on Matilda's face. "We know how to hide in the forest, you know that. It's those other lads I feel sorry for."

"Hopefully you're right," Henry said, "and this dies down quickly, so things get back to normality, although it's been said this Guy of Gisbourne has been ordered to hunt you down" –

"Forget him," Robin broke in, not wanting Matilda to be alarmed by talk of the king's bounty hunter. "Me and the lads know how to look after ourselves in the forest."

The fletcher threw his tunic around his shoulders and nodded at Robin. "I hope so. Now, I have to get to work. It was good to see you, son."

"You too," the outlaw agreed warmly. "I won't come back around like this again, not for a while. I don't want to place you in any danger."

Mary gave the seated man another kiss on the cheek. "I have to nip out to get some things from the baker. You look after yourself, Robin."

Matilda's parents waved goodbye and left the young couple by themselves. Matilda looked almost shyly at her husband, who she hadn't seen for weeks, and he gazed back fondly, noting how she absent-mindedly stroked her swollen belly.

"How is...it?" he asked awkwardly, flushing slightly at the girl's laughter.

"'It' is fine. I can feel kicking now, especially at night. We've got a little fighter in here." She stood up and came over to stand beside her young husband, holding out her hand. "Come on, we should make the most of the time. I've missed you."

They made love, passionately but hurriedly, for fear of Matilda's mother returning, then Robin kissed the girl softly in farewell, rubbing his hand affectionately across her tummy.

"Do you have any names yet?"

Matilda smiled down at the bump. "I like Mary, if it's a wee girl."

Robin nodded. "That's perfect. Mary. I'll go with that." He eyed her belly and returned her grin, placing an arm affectionately around her shoulders. "What if it's a boy?"

The girl shrugged. "I'm not sure. I like Arthur. Or maybe Edward."

"Arthur, that sounds good," the outlaw replied. "But I'm not so keen on naming our child after a man that's sent a bounty-hunter to kill me."

"What about Adam then?" Matilda smiled impishly at him.

"That's even worse!"

They held each other in close again, smiling and imagining a future where they could both live freely, watching the life that was growing inside Matilda become a child and then an adult.

"I will visit again when I can," Robin told her, pulling away reluctantly, "but this new bounty-hunter of the king's might turn out to be another bastard like Adam Gurdon so I won't place you or the baby in any danger."

She smiled up at him and squeezed his buttocks playfully. "Don't make it too long," she warned. "Pregnant women have needs too, and I've been told they get even stronger urges as the baby grows."

"I'll think of you at night when I'm in the greenwood," he told her, his blue eyes drinking in the sight of her and committing it to memory.

"Get going, then," she giggled. "I love you."

"I love you too, both of you. And I still intend to keep the promise I made you last year: I *will* earn a pardon, somehow, and be a proper husband and father."

He hurried out into the street and, with a last, longing wave, disappeared into the shadows cast by the early morning sun.

Matilda sighed as she watched him go, missing him already. *At least I'm not alone*, she thought, holding her belly and giving thanks to God.

* * *

A week passed after what was being called the Battle of Boroughbridge, and the outlaws had settled comfortably back into their old routine. The soldiers hunting them had failed to find them. Although Sir Guy of Gisbourne was a hugely experienced bounty-hunter, he simply didn't know the forests of Yorkshire well enough yet. He had hired local guides, and was creating a detailed mental map of the area in his head, but Robin and his men were able to stay a step ahead of their pursuers easily enough.

Of course, Gisbourne wasn't just hunting Robin's gang now; he also had to find the dozens of defeated rebels who had taken refuge in the greenwood after Boroughbridge. Although those other rebels were diverting attention away from his own men, Robin had grave fears about the presence of so many lawless men roaming the region. While his gang tended to steal from the rich nobles and clergymen who passed their way, these other rebels were apparently happy enough to rob from anyone they could – peasants, yeomen and villeins, as well as those much better off. When Robin's men visited the outlying villages for supplies, they heard worse tales: rebels accused of carrying off livestock from poor families who might only own, and depend on, one or two sheep or hens; drunken men wandering through villages stealing from traders, and viciously assaulting any who complained; even accusations of rape and murder.

As a result, Robin and his friends found it difficult to get the supplies they relied on from the surrounding villages, as the locals became more defensive and began to arm themselves.

Unless the locals knew the outlaw well, they would be chased off with the promise of violence.

Of course, everyone in Yorkshire knew of Little John, thanks to his great height – near seven feet tall, and built like a bear with a shaggy brown beard to match – so he ended up having to collect the outlaws' supplies whenever they needed anything they couldn't catch or make themselves: butter, salted beef and pork, fruit, bread and eggs although those were scarce in winter.

"I'm fed up with this," John grumbled as he returned from Bichill one afternoon, dropping a pile of supplies on the ground by the camp fire. "I feel like a woman, doing everyone's shopping for them. The sooner the rest of the rebels are caught, the better!"

Will Scarlet gave a loud laugh and came over to stand in front of John, grinning. "Hark at her! I thought you enjoyed shopping." He tugged at the sleeve of the giant's worn old brown cloak. "You always put on your fanciest dress for it."

Little John lunged at Scarlet, but Will danced back out of reach, gesturing the big man to come ahead, while Robin and the rest of the men watched the entertainment with broad smiles.

"I'm glad you all find it so funny," Friar Tuck grunted, dropping a sack of loaves on the ground beside John's supplies. Tuck had gone to Bichill with John, but he was dismayed at the stories they'd heard there.

"These other outlaws have no respect for anyone. Someone should stop them."

"It's nothing to do with us," Robin replied, glancing up from his log by the fire, where he sat stirring a big cauldron of pottage.

The men muttered in agreement, but Tuck fixed his young leader with a glare. "Will you still be saying that when they rape someone in Wakefield?"

Robin shook his head, looking away from the clergyman. "What would you have us do, Tuck? We're outlaws ourselves. We can't go around Barnsdale hunting down other rebels. All we can do is hope we meet these men and they join up with us."

The men shouted agreement at that, but Tuck shook his head. "These men aren't like us. They're desperate – starving."

Matt Groves snorted. "Desperate? I've been an outlaw for years, friar! Men don't get much more desperate than me."

"What's that in your hand then, Matt?" the portly friar demanded, gesturing towards the gently steaming bowl of pottage in Groves' right hand. "All of us here have food, money, warm clothing and a loyal friend at our side to defend us if the foresters find us."

Matt waved a dismissive hand and turned his back on Tuck with a scowl.

"You might think you're desperate," Tuck stated, looking around at the other men, his eyes finally meeting Robin's. "But I fear we're going to find out all too soon what truly desperate men will do when they're trapped in these woods with nowhere to run."

* * *

Guy of Gisbourne had been tired and irritable before he and his men had, purely by chance, stumbled upon the group of rebels hiding in the forest.

They had been searching an area of Barnsdale where reports suggested some of the insurgents were camping. They were on foot, since horses were no use for moving between the dense undergrowth and, after much of the day walking and stumbling over fallen logs and trailing plants Gisbourne was about ready to call a halt to the search for the day.

Then his second-in-command, and friend of many years, Nicholas Barnwell, a bald man with a disconcerting gaze, had caught the sweet scent of wood smoke. He held up a hand, motioning for silence and sniffed the air again, as the unmistakable smell of roasting meat came to them. The soldiers remained silent, senses straining as they tried to glean whatever information they could about the unseen cook.

A faint laugh carried to them through the trees and Gisbourne nodded to his sergeant, motioning his men – twenty five of them – to make their way towards the source of the sounds and smells.

As they carefully moved forward the gentle murmur of a number of men in relaxed conversation could be heard and, when the soldiers came to a small clearing they could make out the tell-tale grey smoke from the camp-fire a little way ahead of them.

Sir Guy gestured to his men to encircle the camp and, with the efficiency and discipline of professional soldiers they moved to obey his silent order.

Although there was a good possibility these men cooking meat and laughing together were innocent travellers – merchants perhaps, or even wandering friars – Gisbourne was too experienced a bounty-hunter to take any chances.

He carried a small, neatly made crossbow, painted black, rather than a longbow. Generally, the crossbow was an inefficient, unwieldy weapon, mainly used by peasants or untrained soldiers. But Gisbourne's smaller weapon, which he'd had specially made by an Italian craftsman, with its stock made from hazel, a steel bow and a hemp string, was deadly at closer ranges.

He carried it on a leather strap slung over his right shoulder, but now he slipped it down into his hand, placed a bolt in it and cocked it by pulling the lever down.

He waited a few moments to let his men get into position, then as Nicholas nodded, judging enough time had passed to have the camp-site encircled, Gisbourne raised his arm.

"Move in," he growled, gesturing towards the rebels.

This close to the men by the fire it was impossible to remain undetected for long as twenty five lightly armoured men rushed forward between the trees, bursting through the undergrowth to stand, weapons drawn in a loose but impressive perimeter around the small clearing where the remains of an old sheep was slowly roasting over the little fire.

The surprised rebels, in a panic, scrambled to defend themselves. It was obvious they were no merchants or churchmen from their threadbare clothing and array of pitiful weaponry which they brandished threateningly at the silent soldiers surrounding them.

Gisbourne, his mouth watering at the sight and smell of the mutton skewered above the fire, held his crossbow by his side as his eyes took in the frightened faces of the men before him.

He was a tall man, although he wasn't powerfully built, being more wiry than massively muscled, but his clothing and bearing clearly marked him as the leader of the soldiers facing the rebels. With his short black hair and stubble, dark eyes and confident, relaxed stance, every one of the rebels felt their gaze drawn to him like iron filings to a dark magnet. Clad all in black, from head to toe, with a boiled leather cuirass moulded to show the shape of his chest, he knew he was an imposing figure and revelled in the sinister power he exuded.

"What do you want?" One of the rebels asked, his voice wavering. He was a broad shouldered young man, obviously an archer, although his bow was nowhere to be seen, probably discarded when he and his comrades fled from Boroughbridge. He hefted a cheap looking sword and tried his best to look menacing. "We've done nothing wrong."

Gisbourne wandered forward and, drawing his dagger with his left hand, cut a small piece of meat from the bottom of the skewered mutton. He lifted it to his lips and blew on the crisp meat gently to cool it, his eyes taking in the men before him, resting eventually on the man who had spoken. The leader, obviously.

"You've done nothing wrong, eh?" Gisbourne took the small slice of meat in his mouth and chewed slowly, a smile of pleasure lighting his dark features. "Where did you get this meat then?"

The rebel was ready for the question, stammering his reply almost before the question was asked. "We bought it from the butcher in Wooley, you can ask him."

Sir Guy finished the mouthful of mutton and placed his dagger back in its sheath in his boot. "You men are rebels. Outlaws," he stated, ignoring the cries of denial from the men before him as he continued. "And you have stolen this sheep from some local farmer."

The men again shouted their innocence, the fear plain on their faces. These were no hardy soldiers – they were armed mostly with pitchforks, blunt hatchets and hammers. Not one of them wore even light armour.

Every one of them looked terrified and desperate.

"Please, my lord," their young leader begged. "We're just peasants. We were forced to join the Earl of Lancaster's army!"

"Peasants you may be," Gisbourne replied disdainfully, "but your king seeks justice for your treason." He raised his crossbow. "Kill them," he ordered, as he squeezed the trigger and watched the wicked steel bolt hammer into the young rebel's chest, throwing the man stumbling backwards onto the grass where he lay, gasping and crying pitifully.

The soldiers moved in and engaged the panicked rebels who offered little resistance, the pitchforks proving no match for the sharpened steel Gisbourne's men wielded so mercilessly.

One of the outlaws flew straight for the black-clad bounty-hunter, screaming with rage as he pulled his axe – more suited to chopping wood than cleaving skulls – behind him, ready to bring it down on Gisbourne's head. "You shot my brother you bastard!"

Sir Guy dropped his crossbow on the ground and sidestepped the rebel's wild downward swing, pulling his sword smoothly from its scabbard as the youngster barrelled past. The polished silver steel stood out in stark contrast against Gisbourne's all black attire as, spinning nearly full circle, arm outstretched, he hammered the razor sharp blade into the axe-man's neck.

The young man, only just into his teens from the look of his beardless face, was thrown sideways to the ground, the great wound erupting in blood as he fell.

The fight was over within seconds, as Gisbourne's soldiers cut down the frightened peasants. The victorious soldiers searched the dead men for valuables but found nothing, as their dark leader took out his dagger and cheerfully helped himself to more slices of roast mutton.

"Dig in, lads," he grinned, gesturing at the dead rebels. "These boys have lost their appetite."

* * *

Late that afternoon, as Robin and his men sat around the fire talking quietly and eating their pottage the sounds of fighting could be heard, carried by the light westerly wind that ruffled the new green leaves in the trees.

"How close do you think that is?" Much wondered, hand dropping instinctively to his waist, although his sword lay on the ground beside him. He picked it up and fastened the belt reassuringly around himself. "Doesn't sound that far off."

Will shook his head. "It sounds closer because of the wind – we're in no danger, whatever it is that's happening."

The sounds of metal on metal and men shouting, or occasionally screaming, faded soon enough; the silence that replaced it feeling oppressive and eerie under the canopy of beech trees the outlaws were using as a camp.

"You think that was the sheriff's men and some of the other rebels?" Tuck asked no one in particular, lifting his thick blanket and wrapping it around his thick torso.

"Aye, no doubt," Little John nodded, his great voice jarring in the stillness. "Those rebels don't know how to use the forest like we do," he went on, quieter this time. "They've got no chance – the soldiers will eventually get them all."

"The soldiers will leave then," Will nodded, stretching out on the grass, watching the sky as the sun set. "We'll have less to worry about when that happens. Just the foresters and this bounty-hunter the king's sent after us."

"Guy of Gisbourne," Tuck agreed. "He's tied up chasing the rebels for now, but we'll have to be on our guard for him. They say he's like a shadow, just appears beside you when you least expect it."

"The Raven," Allan-a-Dale muttered. "Black as night and merciless too."

"Trust the minstrel to have something romantic to say!" Will snorted, drawing laughs from the others.

"Shut it, Scarlet," Allan grinned back good-naturedly. "I never came up with it; the people in Nottingham are calling him the Raven."

"They can call him whatever they like," Robin stood up, carrying his empty bowl over to the nearby stream to rinse it out. "We've been hunted by Adam Bell remember – a Knight Templar, who knew this forest inside out. And even he couldn't stop us," he shouted over his shoulder, kneeling to dip the wooden vessel in the clear waters.

The men began to relax again as night drew in, knowing the four lookouts they always had posted around their camp would alert them in plenty of time to any danger. The sounds of men fighting, and dying, so close by had unsettled most of them though.

Robin decided to move their camp again in the morning.

* * *

The young outlaw had chosen a spot near the village of Hathersage for their new base. Little John and Will told him of a good place they had used once before a couple of years earlier, when Adam

Bell had led them. On their way, they carefully scouted the area they had heard the sounds of battle coming from the previous afternoon.

Twelve men lay dead in and around a small clearing they had obviously been using as a camp-site. From the looks of it, they were all poor men – peasants. Their cheap clothes were threadbare, and their hands showed the tell-tale signs of years of hard labour. Only a couple carried swords, which were of inferior quality and as good as worthless or their killers would have taken them rather than leaving them discarded on the grass. The rest of the dead men had only the tools of their trade: pitchforks, hammers or axes.

"They never stood a chance," Tuck noted, moving among the corpses, closing their sightless eyes and muttering blessings. "A dozen poorly armed peasants against a force of well-drilled soldiers." He shook his head sorrowfully, gazing down at a boy no more than thirteen summers who had been almost decapitated. "May you find peace in heaven, my child."

As the outlaws travelled to their new camp-site, they brooded silently, the sight of the dead rebels dampening any thoughts of banter or good cheer.

They reached their new base not long after midday, and set about making the place secure. Most of the men had stayed here before and knew the lie of the land. Robin smiled with satisfaction as the outlaws erected their animal-skin shelters and renewed the lookout posts they had used during their previous stay.

Will caught his smile and nodded with a grin of his own. "They hardly need a leader this lot. They know how to look after themselves."

"Let's leave them to it then," Robin agreed. "I'm going into Hathersage for some supplies – you coming? It'll take the rest of the day to get there, so we'll stay the night in the inn. Have a few beers..."

Will's grin widened – not so long ago he would have never set foot in Hathersage for all the money in the world. He had lived there once, and – he believed – his whole family had been butchered there by the former lord of the manor. But Robin had returned his beloved little daughter, Beth – alive! – to him, and as a result Will's old scars were beginning to heal over. A trip into the village would suit him well enough and he'd be glad to share an ale with his friend Wilfred, the baker.

"Come on, then," Robin said, slapping him on the shoulder, "we'll take Tuck with us too."

* * *

As they neared Hathersage the sun was setting, casting long shadows along the path, and the three outlaws glanced at each other, wondering if they were imagining things. The sounds of men engaged in combat from the night before seemed to echo through the trees again, and they halted in their tracks, listening intently, hands tightening around their sword hilts.

It was unmistakable: there was fighting in Hathersage.

"Move!" Robin cried, racing towards the village.

His two older companions followed at a slightly slower pace, Will charging wildly after his leader, sword held high, and the overweight friar bringing up the rear breathlessly, gripping his stout quarterstaff grimly, muttering to himself. "I warned you about those rebels."

As Robin raced into the village's main street, he could see they were just in time. A small group of armed men, no more than a dozen at Robin's count, stood grinning wickedly, brandishing their weapons confidently. At their feet lay a hefty white clad figure, the crimson stain forming around his midriff suggesting he wouldn't be getting up again any time soon.

A crowd of frightened villagers faced off against the men, but only one of them – the blacksmith – was armed. He hefted his great hammer menacingly, thick blue veins bulging almost obscenely on his heavily muscled arms. The other village men looked bewildered, although more appeared, with one or two finally having the presence of mind to collect their longbows from their dwellings. Robin could see more of the locals darting off into the forest – mothers carrying children, older women trying their best to move quickly but glancing fearfully over their shoulders in case their doom should find them. Even some of the village men, unused to violence of this nature, were deserting the place until things calmed down.

Of those remaining, their faces were angry, but they lacked the confidence to tackle the gloating rebels, especially when one of their own lay dead on the street in front of them.

Robin slowed, dropping his cumbersome longbow on the ground, trying to catch his breath as he walked up to stand in front of the rebels, a little way apart from the villagers. "What's happening here?" he demanded, glaring at the men before him. They were a motley lot, most of them looking somewhat malnourished after their time hiding out in Barnsdale. One of them, an ugly looking bastard with a great scar on his cheek and only a couple of blackened teeth left, stared back arrogantly at the young outlaw.

"We just came here looking to buy supplies," the rebel smirked, spreading his hands wide innocently. "Then this fat old prick tries to stab one of my friends here."

The other rebels chorused agreement, but the village blacksmith roared indignantly. "Liar! You were stealing from the traders, and when you lifted Wilfred's loaves he tried to stop you. You murdered him!"

Robin's stomach lurched and his eyes dropped to the white figure on the ground. Blood had formed a thick pool around him, and now the young man recognised the murdered villager. It was his friend, Wilfred the baker, who had done so much in helping him and Allan-a-Dale rescue Will Scarlet's daughter from her enforced slavery just a few months before.

A low growl rose in his throat as he met the scarred leader's eyes, and without thinking, began to move towards the gang, who looked surprised but not particularly worried at the sight of a single swordsman coming at them.

"Fan out!" the rebel captain ordered with a toothless grin, bringing his dull-looking sword up before him defensively. "Looks like we'll have to do a bit more killing, before we can enjoy what this town has to offer."

CHAPTER FOUR

"How long can we hold out?"

The Hospitaller knight, Sir Richard-at-Lee, glanced over at his sergeant, Stephen, and shrugged his broad shoulders, although, clad in chain mail as he was, with the black mantle of his Order over it, the gesture was hardly noticeable. "A couple of weeks I'd say, if they don't break the door down."

"Not bloody likely," Stephen growled with a confident smile. He had good reason to feel secure inside Sir Richard's castle in Kirklees. A small moat surrounded the site and, although it was almost empty, once the drawbridge was up, it meant the main entrance was impossible to reach without some sort of platform.

Although they only had a dozen men with them, it was enough to hold off any attempts by the king's men gathered outside to erect such a platform before having to batter the main gate down with a ram.

The two men – hardened veterans from countless battles in their Order's service – looked down from the battlements at the men besieging them. Twenty part-time soldiers, at most, led by some minor royalist noble Sir Richard didn't recognise. They had turned up a day after the Hospitaller had led what remained of his followers from the defeat at the battle of Boroughbridge back home.

Such a small force had no chance of either penetrating the great front door, or scaling the walls, unless the Hospitaller and his men relaxed their guard. Which would not happen. Stephen would make damn sure of that.

It was a stand-off and, with enough food and drink stored within the castle to last them a fortnight at least, Sir Richard felt reasonably secure.

"The only way they're getting in here is if the king sends more men with siege engines," Stephen mused. "Otherwise, they'll have to starve us out."

"I can't see them hanging around out there for a couple of weeks," Sir Richard grunted, stroking his bushy grey beard thoughtfully. "Those men will have to return to their own villages. Besides, there must be easier targets for them to hunt scattered throughout Barnsdale forest."

"Like Robin Hood and his mates, assuming any of them survived the battle," his sergeant-at-arms replied. "They're going to have a hard time of it for a while with all these bastards chasing around the forest after rebels."

"Robin and his men know how to hide. They'll be fine. Christ knows what'll happen to us though." The Hospitaller sighed, feeling lower than he'd ever felt in his life. Not only was he a wanted man – a rebel – but his son had been murdered by someone acting for Sir Hugh Despenser not that long ago.

As Sir Richard stared out disconsolately over the spring countryside, the nobleman leading the king's men rode boldly forward, halting as he came close enough to converse with the big knight on the battlements without shouting at the top of his voice.

"Oh-ho!" Stephen nodded. "The king's lackey wants a word."

One of their men stationed on the battlements beside them fitted the string to his longbow and pulled an arrow from his belt. "You want me to take him down, my lord?"

"What?" Sir Richard, startled from his reverie, waved a hand. "No, Peter. Let the man say his piece."

The horseman gazed up at them. "My name is Sir Philip of Portsmouth. I assume you are Sir Richard-at-Lee, former Lord of Kirklees."

"I'm the preceptor of this commandery, yes," the Hospitaller replied.

"Former preceptor," the nobleman replied. "The king has declared your lands forfeit to the crown as a result of your recent treasonous actions against him."

He waited for a reaction, but Sir Richard remained silent. This news was no surprise after all.

"No doubt you feel very secure locked up in your little fortress," Sir Philip cried, waving a hand in disdain at the walls which had frustrated his attempts to arrest the Hospitaller and his men. "Well, your castle has bought you some time: I must take my men onwards, so you can relax for a while."

Stephen let out a tiny gasp of relief as the knight continued.

"Do not think this is the end of it though, Sir Richard! Your men might slink off back to their homes in the village as if none of this ever happened, but the king has vowed to make an example of those so-called noblemen – like yourself – who planned this rebellion. Eventually, more of his men will be back for you. Better armed, better prepared to take this pitiful castle down about your treacherous ears! Make the most of your freedom while it lasts, Hospitaller!"

With that, the horseman turned his mount and kicked his heels into its sides, spurring it into a canter back to his own men and out of range of the archers on the walls behind him.

"Wanker," Stephen muttered, drawing a smile from Sir Richard.

"We'll give them time to leave, just in case they change their minds," Sir Richard said. "Then you and the rest of the men," – he looked over at the archer, Peter, beside him – "can 'slink off' back to your homes."

The look of relief on Peter's face was plain, as he dared to hope he might see his family again, and go back to his normal life.

Sir Richard slapped the man on the back with a smile, told him to remain on watch and alert for now, and then led his loyal sergeant-at-arms down the stairs and into the great hall.

"That…wanker," he threw Stephen a sardonic smile as he filled a wooden goblet with wine, "thinks I'm going to sit here waiting for death, or else I'm going to try and make a run for it."

Stephen filled a mug of his own from a large jug of ale on the table beside the wine and raised an eyebrow. "So did I," he admitted. "What are we going to do then?"

Sir Richard took a sip of wine and wiped his mouth with the back of his hand, eyes blazing.

"I'm not done just yet," he vowed, "no matter what Sir Philip of Portsmouth might think! I may only be a minor noble, but I'm also a Hospitaller Knight…"

* * *

"Wilfred!" As Will came into the street behind Robin and recognised the baker lying dead on the ground, he screamed in rage and, at his young leader's side, tore into the rebels who shrank back from the berserk gleam in his eyes.

"Get them!" Scarface shouted, his voice wavering as he saw Friar Tuck barrelling into the street, brandishing his quarterstaff expertly. Suddenly it seemed this might not be such an easy fight after all, especially as the young man with the piercing gaze and the enormous archer's shoulders was coming straight for him.

Robin never slowed as the rebel swung his sword in a vicious arc; he parried the blow and swept the man's feet from under him with his foot. As the man went down, Robin rammed the point of his long sword into his throat, pulled it free and carried on, swinging the bloody weapon upwards into the armpit of another rebel, almost taking the screaming man's arm off.

In contrast to Robin's unnerving silence, Will was roaring the baker's name like a madman as he battered into the shocked rebels. When his blows were parried, he rammed his forehead into the defender's face, or kneed them in the groin, before finishing them with a sword thrust.

Realising they were done for, as the villagers, led by the blacksmith, finally found their courage and ran forward to join the fray, the remaining rebels, seven of them, simply turned and began running for the forest.

"You!" Robin roared at one of the local youngsters. "Throw me your bow!"

The outlaw caught the weapon and, whipping an arrow from his belt, sighted on one of the fleeing rebels, taking a fraction of a second to steady himself and visualise where he wanted the missile to strike.

With a feral scream the rebel dropped to the grass as the outlaw leader's arrow tore into his calf.

"Let the rest go!" Robin shouted. "They've had enough."

The villagers were happy to give up the chase, as the adrenaline began to leave their bloodstream. They had chased off the invaders – that was enough for them.

Friar Tuck finally managed to halt the enraged Scarlet, who walked back to the fallen baker, sobbing with rage as he turned the man onto his back and closed his eyes.

Robin looked away from his weeping comrade, not wanting to intrude on the naked show of emotion. And yet, Robin felt a great sorrow too. Wilfred was a good man – he had helped the outlaws. He had, in fact, given Will his life back.

"He didn't deserve to die like this," the blacksmith muttered sadly, wandering over to stand beside them. Meeting Robin's eye, he carried on. "That little adventure he had with you and your mate last year made him feel like a youngster again – gave him a real zest for life. When those bastards came here acting like they owned the place, Wilfred thought he could take them all on."

"You should be proud of him," Robert nodded. "And learn a lesson from this too. Next time your village comes under attack from a gang of wolf's heads, you all need to stand up to them!" He glared at the village men who dropped their eyes sheepishly. The big blacksmith simply hefted his hammer thoughtfully and muttered agreement.

"Chances are, those men will come back here looking for revenge – you better be prepared. So arm yourselves – properly."

Fifty paces away the rebel Robin had shot in the leg was groaning as he tried to drag himself away into the trees, before finally giving up and lying panting on the damp spring grass.

"Come on," Robin growled to Tuck and Scarlet. "Let's go and see what that bastard has to say for himself."

* * *

In humiliation akin to that of Christ, Thomas, the Earl of Lancaster, was forced to wear a torn old wreath made of cheap cloth and ride an old mule, with no bridle to steady himself properly, and led to the place of execution.

He had made his peace with God in the few short hours since his sentence was handed down but still, he was frightened as the worthless old mount carried him to his doom, the locals jeering loudly and pelting him with snowballs so that he almost fell onto the ground once or twice.

As they neared the platform he raised his voice, which seemed weak and thin after his days of ill-treatment, and cried out in anguish. "King of Heaven, have mercy on me, for the worthless king of England has shown me none!"

The men and women of York roared in outrage at that, thoroughly enjoying the whole spectacle, and rained more hard-packed snowballs on the defeated earl, who was dragged from the mule by two footmen, angrily trying to stop the missiles hitting them too, and thrown on his knees onto the wooden platform.

Silence descended on the place, except for the occasional sound of someone stamping their feet or rubbing their hands to try and warm themselves, breath steaming from everyone's mouths, noses running unchecked as every eye was fixed in fascination on the great earl's pitiful downfall.

The executioner, a lean man with a black hood over his head, strode forward and, raising his voice so it would carry to the furthest reaches of the crowd, grabbed Lancaster and dragged him around to face northwards.

"Turn to face your allies, the Scots. Traitor!" The executioner roared, to howls of hatred from the mass of spectators, "and receive your foul death!"

Although he had been sentenced to be hanged, drawn and quartered, the king had shown leniency and decided a simple beheading – as Thomas had done to Edward's friend, Piers Gaveston ten years earlier – would be enough.

It took three strokes of the great axe to completely sever the earl's head, and the thump as it dropped to the frost-bitten wooden platform was drowned out by the laughter and near-hysterical cheering as people who had previously supported Lancaster became lost in the spectacle and enjoyed the day's entertainment.

CHAPTER FIVE

The man screamed as Will stood on his calf beside the protruding arrow and pressed down with a snarl.
"You sack of shit. That was a good man you and your lot killed!"
Friar Tuck gently pulled the enraged Scarlet backwards and the grounded man gasped, squeezing both hands around his wound to try and dull some of the pain.
"I didn't kill the baker," he grimaced. "I didn't kill anyone."
Robin leaned down and opened the leather pouch on the man's belt. The rebel tried to slap the big outlaw's hands away but Robin cuffed him, hard, on the ear and emptied the contents of the man's purse onto the road.
"That's my money!" A heavy, red-faced older lady pushed her way to the front of the gathered villagers and spat at the thief as she knelt and scooped up the small silver coins. "I was selling ale – just made a fresh batch this morning – when that arsehole came into the house with his friends. Helped themselves to my ale and this one" – she glared down at the sullen man – "helped himself to my takings."
"Your ale tasted like piss," the man muttered, before crying out as Will booted him in the face.
"Shut your mouth or I'll rip that arrow right out of your leg!"
"Where are the rest of your friends camping?" Robin asked, crouching down on his haunches to look at the man, who opened his mouth to make a smart reply, then glanced at Will Scarlet and changed his mind, replying with a question of his own.
"Why should I tell you anything? You don't have the look of lawmen." His eyes took in the light armour and weaponry of the three outlaws and he gave a small humourless laugh. "You're probably rebels just like me and my mates."
A child's voice piped up from somewhere in the crowd of villagers. "He's Robin Hood, he brought us food at Christmas!"
The injured rebel spat on the ground in disgust as the other villagers shouted agreement. "You're a real hero," he smirked at Robin. "Good for you."
"Right, fuck this," Will leaned down and began to slowly pull Robin's arrow from the rebel's calf. Tuck crossed himself sadly as the man thrashed his shoulders and screamed in agony. "Where's your camp-site?" Scarlet roared, twisting the shaft of the arrow slightly to cause the man even more pain.
"A clearing!" The rebel's voice dropped to a tortured whimper as Will released the pressure on the arrow. "About half an hour's walk from here, to the north-east."
The three outlaws looked at each other, but none of them recognised the place the man had described. "We need more information than that," Will snarled, placing his hand back on the arrow, as blood oozed thickly from the wound. "Is it near the river? A waterfall? Any trees that look unusual?"
"A waterfall!" the man shouted, eyes wide at the sight of Scarlet's hand on the arrow. "Aye, there's a waterfall! Not a very big one, but we thought it would mask any sounds from our camp-site." He fell back with a sob.
Robin looked to Will again, who stood up, nodding. "I know where he's talking about. He's right – the sounds of the waterfall will hide the sound of them laughing about the people they've murdered. It'll also hide the sound of men approaching to wipe the lot of them out."
"How many of you are hiding out there?" Robin asked the man who was now beyond the point where he cared about resisting.
"Twenty-two."
"Who leads you?"
"Sir Richard Willysdon." His eyes flared again, momentarily, and he stared at Will. "You think you're a hard man, but old Dick'll show you. He's a wicked bastard. He'll eat you three alive." The

rebel grinned through gritted teeth, but shrank back with a whimper as Scarlet jerked his leg as if about to kick him again.

"All right, let's get the supplies we came for as quickly as possible," Robin replied. "Then we'll head back to camp and decide what to do about these rebels."

"What about this one?" Tuck gestured to the man on the ground, who had by now almost passed out from the pain in his leg.

"Not our problem," Robin shrugged, turning to the villagers. "He robbed your ale-seller and was part of a gang that murdered your baker. It's your place to dispense justice, not ours."

As the three outlaws moved away to buy their provisions and find a room for the night, the angry mob closed in behind them around the terrified rebel, who shouted for mercy.

By the time they left the inn to head back to their camp-site just before dawn the next day, the man was swinging gently by a rope hanging from a big oak tree at the roadside. His breeches were heavily stained at the front and back and crows were already gathering, watching from the branches of nearby trees until it was safe for them to move in and feast on the hanged man's soft flesh and eyeballs. Robin's arrow was still embedded in his bloody calf.

Tuck crossed himself again. "Christ, what a sight. The people of Hathersage don't waste any time, do they?"

Will shook his head. "Serves the bastard right," he growled. "And once we find his mates, they'll be wishing they'd died as quickly."

* * *

Wilfred the baker had been a good friend to the outlaws. Not only had he helped Robin and Allan-a-Dale rescue Will's daughter, Beth, from a life of slavery in Lord John de Bray's manor house, he had also helped them rob the same lord. They had piled his wagon high with cash, jewellery, tapestries, silk bed-clothes, silver cups and plates and a huge amount of hoarded food.

His murder at the hands of a gang of rebels had outraged Robin's men when they heard about it.

Robin, Tuck and Will had returned from Hathersage with their tale of the previous day's events, but by then the sun was beginning to set in the spring sky again so the outlaws spent a quiet night, their anger building at what these rebels were doing in the forest. Their forest.

As dawn broke the next morning, Allan-a-Dale and Will Scarlet woke the men, impatient to hunt down the rebels that had killed Wilfred.

"What about breakfast?" Little John wondered, his hair and beard comically tangled as he dragged his enormous frame from his straw pallet on the forest floor.

"Eat it on the way," Scarlet shouted, tossing the giant half a black loaf. "Get ready to move!"

A short time later Robin was leading the outlaws north-east, towards the waterfall the injured rebel had described. He called John and Will, his two most trusted advisers, to him as they made their way through the early spring undergrowth.

Although Much, his childhood friend from Wakefield, was the outlaw Robin had the closest bond with, he lacked the military skills and tactical knowledge of the terrain around Barnsdale that John and Will had. Robin sometimes felt a little guilty leaving his friend out, but he knew including Much in the planning of missions would be seen as favouritism and, being honest, the young outlaw leader knew his lifelong friend was best employed as a simple foot-soldier.

"What's the plan then?" Little John wondered. "Do we have one?"

"If they're camped where I think they are," Will replied, "they're hemmed in on two sides. The waterfall is a short way to their back, with another tributary feeding in behind their clearing, both feeding into the main course of the river which continues to the east."

"It shouldn't be hard to pin them down then," Robin nodded, trying to visualize the terrain Will was describing, although he didn't think he'd ever been there before.

"That's it then?" John rumbled. "We just come at them from two sides, knowing they've nowhere to escape? Doesn't seem like it leaves us much room for manoeuvre."

"Doesn't leave them much room for manoeuvre either," Will grinned. "That's the idea!"

John shook his great head, his long brown hair flailing. "There's sixteen of us, and there's about twenty of them, according to that lad you left hanging in Hathersage. Even if we surprise them, we're still outnumbered. We don't know anything about these men."

Robin and Will exchanged glances, realising their giant friend was right. In their rage and desire to avenge Wilfred's death they hadn't given much thought to this.

"We know their leader's called Sir Richard Willysdon – Old Dick," Will noted with a shrug. "And he's a right dodgy bastard. Apparently."

"What about the rest of them?" John asked, spreading his hands wide. "They could all be landless knights. We might be walking into the hardest fight we've ever had. I think we need a better plan."

The outlaw gang moved through the forest almost silently, their experienced eyes spotting dried twigs that might crack and give away their position, and using the available cover to remain hidden from anyone travelling on the main road.

Robin pondered the dilemma, knowing John spoke the truth. Although the dozen men they had found butchered near their camp had been poorly armed peasants, many of the defeated insurgents hiding in Barnsdale were knights or at least well armed mercenaries.

"All right then," he smiled. "How about this…"

* * *

Stephen had set off from Kirklees, early in the morning. It was raining hard, and thunder rumbled some distance off. Thankfully, the wind was behind him, so the driving rain stayed out of his face, but it wasn't long before his black surcoat was soaked through.

He wore his gambeson underneath his chain-mail, so he was warm enough, but as he became more sodden and uncomfortable he cursed the circumstances that had brought him to this point.

"Where would I go?" Sir Richard had asked Stephen the previous night as they sat by a brazier on the battlements, mugs of warmed wine in hand, gazing out at the lush countryside around them. "Aye, there's no one besieging us just now, and I could escape. But where would I go? Take passage back to the Order's base in Rhodes, to live a life of austerity as a lowly brother knight? I've had my time doing that – being given the commandery of the manor of Kirklees was my reward for many years of loyal service."

He would fight to hold onto it, rather than running with his tail between his legs.

"This is my mess," he clasped his faithful sergeant by the arm, fixing him with his steady gaze. "If you want to go, I'll release you from my service" –

"That's enough of that shit," Stephen had growled, cutting off his master with an angry gesture. "I've stuck by you for years. I've no more intention of buggering off back to Rhodes than you have. What do you want me to do?"

Sir Richard had written a letter and, dripping wax from a ruby-red candle onto the envelope, pressed his ring into it to mark it with his own personal Hospitaller seal, showing a man kneeling before a cross. He handed it to Stephen with instructions to take it straight to Clerkenwell, in London.

The Prior of the Hospitallers in England, Thomas L'Archer, had his headquarters in Clerkenwell. Although Sir Richard thought the prior had become an incompetent fool in his old age, he was still the most powerful Hospitaller in the country, with direct access to the king.

With the dissolution of the Templars just a few years earlier, the Hospitallers had grown greatly in power and influence. If anyone could help Sir Richard, it was Thomas L'Archer.

So, as dawn broke, Stephen had taken his master's letter, filled his horse's saddlebags with food and drink and the two old companions embraced one another as brothers rather than a master and his servant.

"It'll take me six, maybe seven days to reach Clerkenwell," Stephen had cautioned. "A round-trip of" –

"I know, I know," Sir Richard had nodded with a small smile. "Two weeks without you to look after me. It'll be hard, but I'll manage somehow."

"Aye, you can bloody laugh," Stephen retorted dourly. "Just watch yourself. There's probably a bounty for you. We're lucky the villagers like you, or they'd have handed you over to the law already, but that won't stop outsiders."

Richard waved a hand dismissively. "Don't worry about me – no one's coming over these walls uninvited. And, as you say, the villagers like me. I've always tried to do right by them. Travel as swiftly as you can though," he gazed at his sergeant earnestly. "Eventually someone will come and try to force their way in. And I can't sit here, cooped up like a falcon in its cage for ever."

The drawbridge was lowered, groaning loudly as the chains rotated on their axles, and, with a last grim nod, Stephen had kicked his mount forward and headed for the capital.

The Hospitaller sergeant was a hard soldier, who had spent much of his life fighting in wars. Not much frightened him: he had seen men, some of them his friends, butchered and mutilated beside him. He had decapitated, disembowelled and dismembered countless men in the name of Christ.

And yet, the thought of addressing the superiors of his order made him sick with nerves. It was so ridiculous he almost laughed.

He crouched down low against his palfrey as the rain hammered against his back and kicked the beast into a canter, hoping to cover as much distance as possible before the light failed and he had to make camp for the night.

His actions over the next few weeks would decide his fate and the fate of Sir Richard-at-Lee.

A sudden, massive rumble of thunder boomed overhead, making his horse skitter sideways nervously, its eyes bulging and he patted the beast reassuringly.

Two weeks for a gruff, uncouth sergeant-at-arms to travel to Clerkenwell and persuade a senile old prior to intervene with the king on his master's behalf.

Thunder cracked the sky overhead again and Stephen shook his head dismally at the impossible mission.

"We're fucking doomed."

* * *

"Logs? You want us to ride fucking logs down the river?" Will Scarlet burst out laughing at his young leader's suggestion.

"Aye!" Robin grinned at the rest of the outlaws as they walked through the forest. "We find a few logs, lash them together with this" – he patted a coiled length of rope he and some of the other men carried on their packs – "then split up. Some of us take these rebels from the west and some from the logs. You say there's a second tributary behind them. They won't expect anyone to attack them from there."

"So they're all going to stand watching us in front of them when we turn up through the trees shouting a challenge," Little John shook his head with a smile. "While some of us sail down the river at their backs and shoot them."

Scarlet laughed again, the type of laugh that was so genuine and uninhibited it was infectious, and many of the other men joined in with him.

"I don't see why it wouldn't work, though," Friar Tuck shrugged, wiping his shaved crown, sweating despite the chill air. "I'm not sailing on any half-arsed raft though, I'll stick to dry land."

"I'll go on the raft," Much volunteered. "My da used to take me fishing in a little boat on the Calder when I was younger." His face dropped at the thought of his father, murdered in front of him, in their own mill, less than a year ago. "I like the water," he finished quietly.

"I'll go on it an' all," an older outlaw, Peter Ordevill agreed. "I used to be a sailor and it sounds like the safest place to be in this mad plan."

Another older outlaw, James Baxter offered to take a place on the raft too as Robin nodded.

"All right, you three it is: we're going to need skilled archers on the water, to take out as many of the bastards as possible. The river's not flowing that fast just now, but even so, you won't have much time to get your shots off before you'll be past."

"And then we're three men down," Matt Groves grunted. "By the time those three get off this raft of yours, the fight'll be over, one way or the other, and we're outnumbered as it is, if they've really got twenty-odd men at this camp."

"Aye, but if Much and the others manage to take out even four or five of these rebels," Robin replied patiently, "it'll throw them into chaos. They won't know which way to turn."

"What if they don't take out four or five of them?" Gareth, the thin teenager from Wrangbrook wondered. "It'll be hard to aim from the water won't it?"

"Nah," Much shook his head. "The river will be calm. It shouldn't be much different from shooting the longbow at a moving target on land, as long as we have something to brace ourselves against."

They were nearing the rebel base now, as the sound of roaring water came to them, so they made sure to go well around the spot where Will expected the camp to be, and started to make their way upriver to find suitable logs for the raft.

"Will," Robin waved his friend over. "You go and scout out these rebels. Make sure they're really there. Try and see how many of them there are, weapons, armour and kill any lookouts" –

"I know what I'm looking for," Will broke in, raising an eyebrow indignantly. "I've been doing this for a lot longer than you, lad."

"Sorry," Robin smiled sheepishly. "We'll find the wood we need for the rafts while you're gone."

As Will disappeared into the undergrowth, surprisingly nimble for such a sturdy man, the rest of the outlaws walked on for a while then began to hunt for thick branches. They found plenty, torn from the trees in the previous winter's storms, and chose ones as flat as possible to make a smooth platform which Much, Peter and James could shoot from. A couple of men carried axes as their close-combat weapon of choice, rather than swords or maces, and they quickly cut the wood to similar lengths.

"Won't the rebels come and see what all the thumping is?" Much asked Robin as the fallen branches swiftly turned into somewhat similarly sized logs.

"Why would they?" his boyhood friend replied. "For a start they've made their camp beside a noisy waterfall, so they'll hardly hear this noise so far upriver. And even if they do hear it, so what? Why should they think it's a threat to them?"

Peter, the former sailor, proved to be an expert with ropes and knots and managed to lash the branches together, forming an odd-looking craft that would, hopefully, work.

"That abomination is never going to float," Matt Groves sniggered. "If one of you farts it'll sink. This is fucking madness."

"No it won't," Peter retorted, confident the hastily- built raft would float just fine on a calm and relatively sluggish river. He had directed the axe-men as they quickly cut the wood to form a flat base, a rudder and a tiller which he would be able to tie off, holding the "boat" on a relatively straight course for long enough to shoot their bows at the rebels. "It's big enough to stay steady while the three of us get off a few shots. That's all we need."

"Aye, well, you're welcome to it lads," Groves smirked. "I'd rather have my feet on something sturdier."

Will Scarlet reappeared, blowing slightly, but smiling wickedly.

"They're there all right," he reported, sitting down on a boulder to catch his breath. He gave the raft an approving grin and took a couple of sips from the ale skin at his waist before continuing. "I counted seventeen of them – some of them must be off at some village looking for supplies. Probably because we" – he nodded towards Tuck and Robin – "disturbed them yesterday, before they could take what they needed from Hathersage."

"Shit," Robin murmured, hoping the five missing rebels hadn't decided to head for Wakefield to find what they needed.

Little John could see his young captain was worried, and he clapped him gently on the back with a grin. "Don't worry – this won't take long. The numbers are almost even now."

"Terrain?" Robin wondered.

"As I described it to you before," Will replied. "They're camped right beside the river, which is to their east. To their north is a rock wall, which the waterfall comes down. It's not that all that high, but none of the rebels will be climbing up it once we attack; it's too steep for that. The lads here can get the raft around to the tributary if they head north-west for a short way and double back. West and south of the rebels it's all trees and bushes. It's a good hiding place to be honest – if that son of a whore in Hathersage hadn't told us where they were we'd never have found them."

"Sounds simple enough, then," Allan-a-Dale grunted, making sure his string was in its pouch ready to fit to his longbow.

"Aye, but take care, though," Will raised a cautionary hand as he took another swig from his ale skin, slowly catching his breath. "These aren't peasants like the ones we found butchered the other day. These men are all wearing light, and even pieces of heavy, armour. And, from what I saw, they all have good quality weapons. There's no pitchforks – it's all swords, maces and proper battle-axes."

Robin looked over at Much and the other two outlaws making ready to carry the raft round to the tributary on the other side of the rebels' camp. "You'll have to pick your targets well," he told them. "Leave the ones with the heavier armour, in case your arrows can't penetrate. Your shots might not have the same force they normally do shooting from this thing," he kicked at the hastily lashed together logs.

"Don't worry," Much nodded confidently, grasping his friend's hand with a grin. "We'll take out as many of them as possible."

"All right!" Robin shouted, looking around at his men with a determined gaze. "Let's get this thing into the water and make those bastards pay for killing Wilfred and God knows what else!"

The raft was sturdy, but light enough to be carried off to the north-west by Much, Peter and James without much trouble.

"Give us enough time to get into position back downstream," Robin told Much as the three men moved away with their burden. "Then cast off. We'll post a lookout to watch for you coming and distract the rebels just before you arrive at their backs."

"Good luck," Much smiled.

"You too. Try not to shoot any of our own lads..." Robin grinned back with a wave as he led the rest of the outlaws back through the foliage to the rebels' camp.

The waterfall grew louder the closer they came, and Robin took Will, Tuck and Little John aside.

"Me, John and Tuck will take the west side of their camp with half the men," he decided.

Tuck was no archer, so would be wasted in Will's section, while John, at almost seven feet tall, was so physically intimidating Robin always felt it was good to have him in open view.

"When we show ourselves to the rebels I'll talk to the leader and distract them," he said. "We'll set Gareth as lookout to signal us when he sees Much and the raft coming."

Gareth was a young lad from Wrangbrook, too thin to be an archer, or much of a fighter, but smart enough to be useful in other ways. Most of the outlaws looked on him as their little brother.

"You take some of the men to the south," Robin went on, looking at Will, "and when you see the signal, start shooting. Get as many of the bastards as you can before they know what's happening."

The more he thought it over, the more Scarlet liked Robin's mad plan. With his half of the remaining outlaws shooting at the scum that had killed his old friend Wilfred, and the three on the raft shooting at them as well, they should be able to take out at least ten or eleven of the seventeen rebels before they even knew what had happened.

Then Robin, John, Tuck and the rest of the men would engage them from the front and the fight would be over. It was devastatingly simple. Foolproof!

"For such a young lad," Will smiled, playfully slapping Robin on the back of the head, "you've got an old soldier's brain in there."

"Aye, it's a good plan," John agreed as they came near to the rebels' camp-site.

Will picked the five best archers from the remaining outlaws, including Matt Groves, and took them off to take up position to the south, while Robin gave Gareth his orders and sent him to the top of the waterfall with a strip of white linen from Tuck's medical pouch to wave when he spotted Much and the raft nearing their position.

As they waited, the image of the rebel peasants they had found killed that morning played on Robin's mind.

"Who is this Guy of Gisbourne?" he wondered. "The sheriff must think he's got the skills to catch us."

Little John and even Tuck, who had travelled extensively over the years, had never heard of Gisbourne until a few months earlier, when he had turned up leading the Sheriff of Nottingham and Yorkshire's men on sorties into Barnsdale. Still, none of the outlaws had even seen the man the locals had dubbed 'The Raven'.

"There!" Allan-a-Dale hissed, as young Gareth suddenly appeared on the waterfall above them, waving his long strip of bandage. "The raft's coming – time to move!"

Robin gestured to his men and they drew their swords, moving forward through the foliage towards the rebel camp which was only a few yards away.

"Do you think Gisbourne really dresses all in black?" Robin asked, shoving branches out of his way and making sure he stepped quietly from force of habit, although a cracking twig would go unnoticed with the raging waterfall so close.

"I hope he does," John growled from just behind. "Black will show up easy amongst the green leaves of the forest – we'll see him coming from a mile off."

Robin nodded silent agreement, then gasped in shock as half a dozen figures appeared, like wraiths, through the undergrowth to his left.

The roaring waterfall had masked the sounds of their approach, and, as he brought his sword up instinctively before him, his eyes were drawn to the man leading them.

A tall, slim man, dressed all in black.

The outlaws recognised him straight away.

"Gisbourne!"

CHAPTER SIX

"I wondered who that fool beside the waterfall was waving at," Sir Guy of Gisbourne smiled, resting his hand on the pommel of his sword as his eyes flickered across the armed men in front of him, assessing the situation.

The outlaws stood, frozen to the spot, looking to Robin for guidance.

"You obviously know my name," the black-clad bounty-hunter noted. "How about you give me yours?"

Robin's mind whirled. Gisbourne had a lot of men with him – maybe twenty, or even more; it was hard to tell given the density of the undergrowth here. He knew he had to act fast though, or the soldiers would encircle them.

Clearly their attack on the rebel's camp would have to wait for another time, assuming they somehow escaped from this with their lives, which didn't seem at all assured.

"No matter," Sir Guy shrugged, drawing his sword. "It's clear you are wolf's heads or rebels of some sort or another and, since I'm in Yorkshire specifically to clear your sort from the forest…" he waved his left hand in the air and pointed to Robin and the outlaws, opening his mouth again to issue the command to attack.

"We're bounty-hunters!" Robin shouted. "We're here to wipe out a gang of rebels who are hiding out beside the river, there." He nodded towards the river behind Gisbourne, who had halted his order to attack, and stood looking slightly confused. "Our man up there is signalling us to attack, we have more men coming down the river on a raft – we have to move now, or we'll miss the chance to surprise the rebels!"

It was possible these men were hunting rebels, as Gisbourne was. The king had employed many such man-hunters to clear out the Earl of Lancaster's supporters from Barnsdale and its environs. As he stood gazing at the young man he heard, sure enough, men's voices, raised in laughter, loud enough to be heard over the waterfall not far from there.

"I see," Gisbourne replied smoothly, a dark eyebrow raised questioningly. "Well, let us help you then. Lead the way to this rebel camp and we'll destroy them together."

There was nothing else for it. Robin nodded and made his way past Gisbourne, expecting the man's wicked looking blade to pierce his back at any moment.

Tuck and the rest followed behind, Little John hunching over to try and appear smaller.

"How the fuck do we get out of this?" Allan whispered to Robin.

The young leader looked at the four men with him. "No idea," he admitted. "Hopefully Will realises what's happening and takes out some of Gisbourne's men. Once the shooting starts, kill anyone that isn't one of our friends, then…either make a run for it, or try and jump in the river. There's no way we can beat that lot," he gestured with his thumb to the cluster of soldiers following behind them.

"Aye," Tuck groaned. "And Christ himself knows how the rebels will react when they see us coming…"

"They're no bounty-hunters," Nicholas growled to his captain, gesturing to the outlaws conversing in hushed tones in front of them. "A young man leading a Franciscan and a giant? It's Robin Hood and his men!"

"Well done," Gisbourne replied, fitting a quarrel to his crossbow as the outlaws led them through the trees. "But there's only five of them – so we let them lead us to the rest of their gang. And, if there really are rebels hiding out here, so much the better. This will be a very productive afternoon!"

It only took a few moments for Robin and the rest to reach the outskirts of the undergrowth at the edge of the rebel's camp. He turned to Gisbourne and gestured, wondering what the bounty-hunter wanted them to do?

The man simply shrugged with a relaxed smile, so Robin turned back and, trying to find a target through the foliage, raised his sword and, as the raft carrying Much and the other two slowly came into sight, shouted, "Attack!"

* * *

The Don was calm and the raft held steady as Much, Peter and James floated steadily downriver and the rebel camp came into sight.

The men were clustered around their camp-fire, drinking from wine-skins, laughing and joking together, oblivious to the bizarre sight on the water just yards behind them.

Much let out a relieved sigh. If there had been a lookout with a bow they'd have been easy targets but Will had done his job and removed any sentries. "Ready, lads?" he wondered, standing and fitting an arrow to his bowstring, his two companions following suit.

"Don't try anything fancy," Peter warned them. "The raft might be steady now, but we could hit a branch, or an underwater current at any time, so just take the easiest shot you can."

Much couldn't help grinning, the blood beginning to really pump in his veins, as Robin suddenly burst from the trees behind the rebels, sword raised, shouting something at the startled men.

Little John, Tuck, Paul Fuller and Allan-a-Dale appeared in loose formation behind their young leader, weapons ready, faces grim, as the shocked rebels leapt up from their seats by the camp-fire, scrabbling for their own weapons.

"Shoot!" Much shouted, loosing his arrow which flashed across the short distance and hammered into a rebel's back, sending the man stumbling forward onto the grass. Peter and James also let fly, their missiles finding targets too, and the three archers quickly nocked another arrow to their bowstrings.

The rebels were in chaos, as three of them were taken down by an attack from behind, then, from the side, more arrows battered them when Will Scarlet and his men joined in.

Sir Guy sauntered into view, his men slowly fanning out behind him, and the rebels, already panicked, completely lost any semblance of disciplined resistance, looking around for an escape rather than working together to hold off their attackers.

"Make for the raft!" Robin shouted at the outlaws beside him. "Fight your way through these idiots, and jump onto the raft before it's too far downstream!"

Tuck crossed himself, his eyes heavenward, and with John and Allan at his side, they tore into the rebels, not stopping to finish their targets off, just barrelling past to try and catch the raft before it sailed away.

Robin raced towards the trees where Will and the rest of their men were still concealed, gesturing towards Gisbourne and his soldiers, screaming as loud as he could. "Run for it! Run!" One of the rebels had been taking a piss in the bushes, and, seeing Robin coming towards him, lunged at the young man with his dagger.

Without even slowing, Robin swatted the short blade aside and battered the hilt of his sword into the man's face, feeling teeth crunch and warm blood on his knuckles as the rebel fell back and Robin continued his mad dash.

By now, Sir Guy realised Robin Hood's men might well escape. "Finish those men off, quickly!" he ordered his men, pointing his crossbow at the remaining rebels, none of whom were offering any real resistance as their original attackers seemed to be fleeing. "Then get after Hood and his gang!"

"What the hell's going on?" the rebel leader, Sir Richard Willysdon shouted, as the remainder of his dazed men stared about themselves, wide-eyed. "Get a grip of yourselves, damn you! Form a circle around me!"

Will Scarlet had seen Robin coming towards him, and the man wearing the exquisite black armour could only be Sir Guy of Gisbourne, so it didn't take him long to figure out things had gone drastically wrong. "Retreat!" he shouted, turning and waving his men back towards the south. "Lose yourselves in the trees; meet back at camp later on if we get separated!"

Robin pelted into the trees at their backs, with a glance over his shoulder.

Thankfully, Sir Guy's men were engaging the remaining rebels. By the time anyone came after him and the rest of his friends, they would hopefully be long gone, disappeared into the forest they knew so well.

Little John had managed to jump onto the raft, almost capsizing it with his enormous weight, while Allan-a-Dale had landed in the water just short of it. Much and Peter helped him climb on board, as John and James moved to the opposite side of the wavering craft, trying to displace the weight so it wouldn't flip over.

Although the river wasn't moving all that fast, Friar Tuck wasn't as fit as the other outlaws. His face was scarlet as he puffed along, trying to catch up with the raft, but it was slowly pulling away from him.

Robin halted his flight, crouching down amongst the bushes, praying that Tuck would make it, but his heart sank as the craft pulled away.

"Jump in!" the outlaw leader whispered to himself. "Jump in, Tuck! Let the current carry you to safety!"

To his shock, Tuck slowed to a stop, breathing heavily, watching in anguish as the raft with his friends on it sailed inexorably downstream.

"What's he doing?" John shouted, as the mismatched fight between the rebels and Gisbourne's men came to a conclusion and Gisbourne walked towards the breathless friar who dropped his sword on the riverbank and raised a hand in defeat. "Why won't he jump in?"

"He can't swim," Robin groaned as the realization dawned on him. "Ah shit. Now we'll have to rescue Tuck!"

Gisbourne's men killed the last of the rebels, but Nicholas ordered their leader, Sir Richard Willysdon, to be spared and tied up. From his expensive-looking armour and arrogant bearing the man was clearly a noble. The king would reward them well for bringing the man to him for a public trial.

The outlaws on the raft collapsed in frustration and exhaustion as the battle-fever left them and reality hit them. As it sailed out of sight around a bend in the river Robin prepared to head back to their camp again, where they could regroup and make a plan to help Tuck.

He watched as Sir Guy ambled over to the overweight churchman, the pair talking although Robin couldn't hear what was said.

"There's another one of them!" One of Gisbourne's soldiers spotted Robin and, pointing towards the hiding outlaw, led his fellows into the undergrowth.

As he turned to sprint off, Robin saw Gisbourne lift his finely-carved black crossbow and heard the sharp crack as the bolt was released.

"No!" he sobbed, but there was nothing he could do as the wicked bolt hammered into the jovial friar and his friend was hurled backwards into the river.

* * *

The forest was quiet that night.

The outlaws had made their way back to camp in dribs and drabs, exhausted and, in Allan's case, soaked through.

Astonishingly, only two of the group were missing. Will had led his group back and the volatile Scarlet now sat dejectedly on his own apart from the group, thinking of his old drinking partner Wilfred and the absent Franciscan friar.

Much and the rest of the men on the raft had let the current carry them back to Oughtibridge then made their way warily back to camp.

When he arrived back last of all, Robin had told them of Tuck's shooting, but young Gareth hadn't returned either. It seemed certain Gisbourne's men must have killed him.

"The bastard knew who we were the minute he saw us," Robin spat. "He probably sent a couple of his soldiers after Gareth while we were heading towards the rebels' camp."

"Poor lad," John shook his big head sorrowfully. "Couldn't pull a longbow, or wield a sword very well, but he was a fine companion with that daft toothless grin of his."

When Robin had shaken his pursuers he had searched along the riverbank for signs of Tuck's body, but it was pointless and he'd eventually headed home in despair.

As the light faded the men had cracked open a barrel of ale and were gloomily downing the dark liquid, huddling close to the camp-fire for it was a bitter cold evening again.

"He might yet be alive," John said, wandering over to Robin and clapping his young leader on the shoulder reassuringly. "Tuck's a hard man. It'd take a lot to kill him."

"He was shot with a crossbow and fell in the river. Since he couldn't swim, I'd say that's a lot to survive." His shoulders slumped. "It's my fault. I should have come up with a better plan. Or better yet, should never have led everyone to tackle the group of rebels in the first place."

"Don't start with the self-pity crap," John growled, glaring at his friend. "Your plan was a good one – you think differently to everyone else, that's how you come up with ideas that are so mad they work. It was sheer bad luck Gisbourne and his men turned up when they did."

The giant wolf's head could see his words hadn't worked. "Listen, Robin, those bastard rebels killed our friend Wilfred – a good man, who only wanted to defend his livelihood and stand up for what he knew was right. The men all wanted to avenge the baker, you didn't just decide that's what we were doing. Mourn Tuck if you have to, but don't sit around here feeling sorry for yourself with a face like someone took a shit in your pottage."

Robin felt his temper rise, his cheeks flushing at John's telling off, and he locked eyes with the big man – but then glanced away in shame, knowing he deserved the rebuke.

They sat drinking in silence for a while, but Robin felt the need for companionship that night.

"Why are you an outlaw, John?"

Robin had never wanted to pry into the other outlaws' histories unless they offered up the information themselves, but he had been curious about this ever since the day he had met the big man and now seemed as good a time as any to ask.

* * *

John Little had originally lived in the village of Holderness, where he had a wife, Amber, and a small son, also called John. He was a blacksmith by trade, with his own little shop at the front of their house. His father had been the village blacksmith before him, and taught John the skills required to forge a plough or shod a horse.

His life was simple, but pleasant, and his family and friends in the village made him happy while his work was interesting and he always tried to improve on the small weapons and implements he crafted.

"Then," said John, "one night – autumn it was – blowing a gale outside and pitch black, my wife came back from visiting her sister and started going on about the baker, knocking his wife and kids about their house. Nothing unusual. The baker was a drunk with a vicious temper – everyone in the place knew it. He'd been spoken to before by people around the village, including me, telling him he shouldn't act like that, not with little children around. He'd act all ashamed, blame the drink, promise not to do it again – then he'd stumble home from the alehouse and knock them about worse. There were even stories amongst the village women that he forced his eldest girl into his bed, but...They were just rumours. I don't know how anyone could have known anything like that was happening...

"I didn't like any of it," John muttered, his voice low, "but... What could I do?

"Anyway, this night my wife said it was worse. The baker was going crazy, had locked them in his house and was shouting about burning their house down with them all in it. The young ones were screaming and crying, and there wasn't a sound from his wife, which wasn't a good sign since you could usually hear her crying or shouting at him to stop.

"Well, I knew what the baker was like with a few ales in him: I thought he might well set alight to his house, and you know what it's like in a village like Holderness, especially on a windy night: one house starts to burn and it sets off the ones next to it until half the place is burning. And our house wasn't too far away from the bakers.

"So, I go along to his house and sure enough, there's a lot of noise coming from inside. I knock on the door and tell him to calm down and come out.

"'Fuck off, Little, this is none of your business!'" he shouts, probably called me an oaf or something like that too, pleasant fellow he was."

John gave Robin a sardonic look, and carried on as the young outlaw smiled silently, not wanting to disturb the big man's story.

"I tried to reason with him – the kids are frightened, they haven't done anything wrong, you've just had too much drink – that kind of thing, but he wasn't having it, just kept shouting. I could hear him hitting the children too, so I was getting angrier myself and, when I heard him breaking up furniture to set fire to the place I'd had enough."

John's mood as he told his story had been relatively light so far, his natural good humour shining through. Now though, his expression turned dark, as he remembered the rest of that night.

"I couldn't just stand there shouting like an idiot while I knew he was trying to burn his house down, so I kicked the door in. Didn't take much: one good kick and it went right in."

The giant turned his face away from Robin and his voice became even more strained as he went on. "The bastard had killed his wife. She was lying on the floor with her neck broke, you could tell straight away. I'd never seen someone with a broken neck before but her head looked weird, didn't seem to be on right, you know....And his kids were there – three of them he had. Three girls. Two of them, the little ones, were crying and huddling against each other in the corner, while he was...he was on top of his eldest...on the bed... His own daughter... His own daughter Robin, she was only eleven! And the worst of it was, she wasn't even struggling...it was like she was used to it, she just looked at me as I came through the door with a blank look in her eyes, like she wasn't even there, like she couldn't even see me."

Little John shook his head, the pain in his voice turning to fury as he carried on, his fists clenched.

"Well, he didn't take any notice of me coming through the door, he just carried on, his horrible white arse pumping up and down, so I came in and dragged him off her, threw him onto the floor. He went down, but only for a few seconds, then he came up, flying at me. Like I said, he was quite a big man and strong – I wasn't much of a fighter back then and...I was frightened, and shocked, by everything that was happening. So when he came at me in a rage I just punched him in the face as hard as I could."

The sun had gone down by now and, in the darkness, a cold breeze whispered through the leaves of the trees surrounding the camp. The rest of the men were a little way off, talking and joking around the camp-fire which glowed a bright orange as Robin looked at it, although it cast little light outside its own small circle. John hid his face in the shadows as he continued, but the dim light couldn't hide the hurt in his voice.

"He fell right over backwards – must have been knocked right out when I hit him. By that time some of the other village men had come along and they grabbed me, dragged me outside. Of course, I was shouting and struggling and . . . in all the noise and with the children crying and whatever, no one thought to check on the baker straight away . . ." John turned, his face wet with tears that glistened in the light from the camp-fire. "He'd fallen right into their hearth. Face first. The children saw him burn to death."

The big man's head dropped and he hugged his knees in an almost childlike way. "Those two little girls ran out the house screaming and crying and started hitting my legs, saying I'd killed their daddy, they hated me, I was this and that." His open, honest face took on a look of bewilderment. "Even after what he'd done, they still loved him, he was still their da… And I'd killed him. I was the Devil to them, even though the bastard had killed their ma, raped their older sister and I'd stopped him from burning their house down around them!"

The bailiff had come and arrested Little John. He had, after all, broken into another man's house and killed him. He couldn't deny it and it didn't seem to matter that he'd only been trying to stop the drunken fool of a baker burning down the village. The baker's eldest daughter hadn't said a word to anyone since the night her father died – her mind had gone, the villagers said, and so she'd been sent off to live with the nuns at the local priory.

The corrupt magistrate would have been lenient if John had any money, but, although his family managed well enough, they weren't rich.

So Little John had been sentenced to hang. He had escaped from the bailiff's men on the way to the gallows though, and taken refuge in the forest before Adam Bell's men had found him and taken him into their group.

"That was seven years ago now. My brothers have helped my wife and son, thank God, but, you know as well as anyone, I hardly ever get to see them, even after all this time."

He looked up at his young friend. "I miss them, Robin. I miss them every day. All I did was try and help." His huge shoulders shook, his head slumped forward and he heaved a sigh that was full of hurt. "There's no justice…"

Robin sat for a moment, then he grasped John's shoulder and squeezed, trying to do something reassuring, to offer some comfort.

As the genial big outlaw sat, depressed and hurting, Robin thought again of the missing – probably dead – Tuck and Gareth, and the young outlaw captain wished that he'd never asked to hear John's story after all.

* * *

When Gareth had seen the raft approaching he had begun to wave the strip of white linen madly, but his lofty vantage point gave him a good view of the landscape where Robin and the rest of his friends were.

He had seen the approach of the man in black and the soldiers, but couldn't think of any way to warn the outlaws. When he had seen Robin and the others apparently joining forces with the soldiers he had heaved a sigh of relief and looked at making his way back down to join them.

When the sounds of fighting reached him he realised there was no point in rushing to take part in the battle. He knew his limitations – knew he was much better as a scout or lookout than a fighter. His mother had struggled to feed him – and herself – when he was a child. The effects of malnutrition had remained with him as he had grown into early manhood. Although he had more than enough to eat nowadays, he still only ate sparingly and his frame remained slight as a result, unlike the rest of the outlaws.

Robin, John, Will and the rest were killing machines though, he thought. They could deal with things on the riverside without him and his sword.

He climbed back up to the top of the waterfall and looked down on the scene below.

"What the fuck?" he breathed in disbelief.

His friends were running from the battle.

As he watched a little longer, it became clear the black figure commanding the soldiers was no friend. The rebels were massacred, all except their leader who was struggling in the grip of a couple of soldiers, and Gareth's outlaw mates had all fled.

Apart from Tuck.

When the ominous black figure had shot the clergyman, Gareth had looked on in horror as his friend was thrown into the Don with a massive splash.

Without thinking about it, he ran as fast as he could to where the men had cut logs for the raft on the river bank earlier and hauled the thickest branch left over into the water, straddling it as the freezing water hit him and the current dragged the makeshift boat downstream.

The current was slow, so he kicked his legs to propel himself along faster, but it seemed to take an age before the rebel camp-site hove into view.

The soldiers were searching the dead rebels for weapons and other valuables. He could see the man in the fancy black leather cuirass talking to a bald man and, as he swept past, he took a great deep breath and ducked under the water so only his hands were visible grasping the log, offering a silent prayer to the Magdalene to make him invisible.

No one shot at him, and he came up for breath moments later, opening his eyes gingerly to get his bearings, hoping he was out of sight of the soldiers.

Although the river was moving slowly, the current had carried him well beyond the rebels' camp, so he pulled his torso onto the log, out of the freezing water, hoping the soft spring sun would dry him out before he became ill with the cold.

He continued to pray for help as the branch carried him along, his eyes scanning the water for anything that seemed out of place for signs of Friar Tuck. Although the clergyman had landed on his back, Gareth knew his head would sink beneath the surface before long – he had to find him, fast.

A dark mass came into view to his right and he dismissed it out of hand. The churchman was wearing grey, while the boulder he was looking at was black.

As the log swept by he realised the rock was actually Tuck in his sodden habit. The friar was face-down in the river, apparently snagged on something underwater.

With a desperate cry, Gareth kicked himself away from the safety of his log and swam against the current to reach Tuck.

His thin arms weren't suited to swimming, and, by the time he reached the friar, the youngster was almost exhausted. He knew his limbs would begin to cramp soon.

Sobbing with fatigue he threw himself at Tuck. His weight was enough to dislodge the unconscious friar from whatever was holding him in place and the pair began to move downstream with the current again.

Desperately kicking his legs, knowing he had to push them towards the riverbank or die, Gareth gritted his teeth and rolled the friar onto his back so his face was out of the water again.

Slowly, ever so slowly, he swam sideways until, at last, the water became shallow and, with a last agonized effort, the slim teenager propelled the limp friar onto dry land.

The young man simply lay on his side for a while, gasping from the exertion, and shivering uncontrollably from the cold. He knew he had to check on Tuck, but his tired body wouldn't co-operate until he rested a little.

"Move, you idiot!" he told himself, realising he was about to pass out.

Whimpering, he dragged himself on his hands and knees to Tuck and, making sure to avoid the crossbow bolt which was still in place, pressed on his chest, up and down, up and down. He had seen one of the villagers in Wrangbrook doing this when a childhood friend of his had fallen into the water when they were playing by the mill one day, years ago.

He had no idea what the purpose of the exercise was – it had done nothing for his friend, who had been blue when they took him from the water and had stayed blue – but it was the only thing he could think of doing to help the friar.

"Come on you bastard!" he sobbed, looking imploringly at the sky, past the limit of endurance. "God, help him!"

As the youngster collapsed, utterly spent, on the mud and stones of the riverbank, Tuck suddenly convulsed, water spurting from his mouth as if he was vomiting.

Gareth watched in disbelief as the friar curled up, gasping and coughing, looking at him through glassy unseeing eyes. With a final gasp, Tuck stopped moving and Gareth panicked again, but he could see his big friend's pale lips moving as he breathed heavily.

They were both alive. But they were far from help, Gisbourne's men were still in the area, they were both soaked to the skin in the cold spring air, and Tuck had been shot.

Gareth had saved them both, simply to die here on the riverbank.

* * *

Gareth woke, but the sunlight was bright, so he kept his eyes shut and pulled the blankets around him even tighter.

Then he remembered what had happened and sat up, fearful of what he might see.

He was lying on a crude bed of straw, beside the fire-pit in what looked like a peasant's house. There was a big pot of something cooking above the fire, porridge from the smell, which was making his mouth water. Beside it were his clothes, obviously hung there to dry out.

He realised he was naked under the blankets and felt his face flush in embarrassment.

No one else was in the room. Where was Tuck?

He scrambled up and threw on his clothes, happy to note his weapons – a dagger and a short sword – on the floor.

Where the hell was he? And how did he get there?

The sounds of a busy village came through the thin walls and he wondered what to do.

The door suddenly burst open and a man strode into the room, nodding as he saw the young man dressed and up.

"You're awake then, good." He pointed to the porridge. "Help yourself, lad, you must be starving."

Gareth's eyes cast about for a bowl, spotting one on a small table against the wall. There was a shallow wooden spoon with it, so he ladled some of the bubbling, creamy oats into the bowl and blew on it, so hungry he was tempted just to shovel some of it in even though he knew it would be burning hot.

"Where am I?" he asked, eyeing the man, who had sat in a chair by the fire. "How did I get here? And where's the friar I was with? Is he…is he all right?"

The man frowned. "He's alive, aye, but he's been unconscious since we brought him here to the village. He's at the barber's place. You're in Penyston." The man gestured to a stool. "Sit. Eat."

Gareth gratefully sat down and began to spoon some of the hot food into his mouth, hoping the local barber was skilled in medicine as well as trimming beards. It was rare to find a qualified physician – and certainly one wouldn't be working in a little village like this. Instead, small places like Penyston were served by surgeons or barbers who learned their trade by experience and from reading books – it wasn't at all unusual for a patient to die as a result of the barber's lack of medical knowledge, but there was usually no alternative in England's backwater villages.

"Me and a mate were fishing in the Don," the peasant said. "We saw you dragging the big Franciscan out of the water and came to help. It took us a little while to reach you, mind, since we were on the opposite bank. You were lucky, lad. You came ashore close to the village, so we were able to find a boat nearby and bring you and your friend back here before either of you got a killing chill."

"I owe you and your mate my life," Gareth nodded solemnly. "I'll reward you for it. You have my thanks."

The man raised an eyebrow at the thought of this skinny young man – probably a wolf's head – rewarding him in any meaningful way, but his manners stopped him from making any remark.

Finishing off the porridge gratefully, Gareth stood up, stretching his aching muscles. "Can I go see Tuck?"

Recognition flared in the man's eyes at the name and he stood up to show the young man out. "Aye, come on then, I'll take you. Don't tell anyone else in the village who the friar is. Or yourself either for that matter. No one needs to know. That way when the law come round looking for you and your gang no one will get into any trouble for helping you." He looked at Gareth with fear plainly written on his face. "All right?"

"Of course," the outlaw agreed. "I don't want to bring you or anyone else any bother. I'll check on Tu – I'll check on the friar then head back to our camp for help. Like I said, I'll reward you, and the friar will be taken away from your village before trouble comes."

The barber's place was a nice two-storey building, with the shop on the ground floor and the house above. It was of similar construction to the peasant's dwelling, but bigger and with nicer furnishings.

Gareth was shown in by the peasant, who didn't offer his name before making his way quickly back home with a nervous wave and a blessing.

The barber looked gravely at him when he brought him to see Friar Tuck, who lay on a wooden bed, the crossbow bolt in his chest removed and the wound heavily bandaged. Blood had seeped through the dressing, and the smell of alcohol was strong from the solution the barber had used to try and clean the wound.

"He was fortunate," the man told Gareth, gesturing to Tuck's light armour which lay on the floor beside the bed. "His gambeson took much of the force out of the bolt so it didn't go in too deeply. It's mostly a flesh wound." The barber looked questioningly at the young outlaw. "Unusual for a Franciscan to be wearing such a finely constructed piece of light armour under his habit," he mused.

Gareth pretended he hadn't heard that.

"If it's just a flesh wound, when will he wake up?"

The barber puffed out his cheeks and shrugged. "I have no idea. Maybe never – or, if he does, he might be unable to care for himself."

Seeing Gareth's shocked look, the man continued. "He almost drowned. And if the filth in the river water got into his wound it will become infected." He shook his head, looking down on the sleeping churchman pityingly. "However, he looks a strong man, and his skin is a healthy colour so he may wake up soon and be absolutely fine. I've prayed for him, there's not much else to do." His gaze moved to Gareth and he eyed him appraisingly. "What about you, lad? I've heard how you pulled the friar out of the river then collapsed yourself. You should be resting. Or is someone after you?"

"You're better not knowing anything about that," the outlaw replied. "As for me – I'm all right. Tired and sore, but otherwise fine. I need to get back to my friends so we can get the friar away from here."

The barber nodded and led Gareth back to the front door. "Wait a second," he called, hurrying into another room. When he returned he carried a small bottle. "Here, take some of this, it'll help the chill in your bones."

The young man took the cork from the bottle and sniffed. "God's bollocks," he gasped, recoiling from the overpowering smell. "What is it?"

"My own recipe. A concoction I distilled from wine after hearing about it from an Italian merchant," the barber smiled, used to the reaction. "I've added some herbs and such to it. Drink some – just a little at a time. I guarantee you'll feel much fitter after a few moments."

Gareth took a swig and cursed even more colourfully this time. It tasted vile and burned the back of his throat. The barber motioned him to drink more though, so, hoping the man wasn't poisoning him, the young outlaw forced down another few gulps then, thanking the man for his help and promising to return for the friar soon, he stumbled into the street.

A short time later, he was sprinting through the forest heading for Robin and the rest of the gang with a happy smile on his face, wondering how much of the barber's medicine he could carry when they returned to the village for Tuck.

CHAPTER SEVEN

"You're alive!" Little John grinned as Gareth trotted into their camp. The lookouts the outlaws always had posted around their base had seen the youngster coming and alerted the rest. They crowded around, clapping him on the back, happy to see him safe.

"Sit down," Robin laughed at the puffing lad, handing him an ale-skin which Gareth grasped gratefully.

"So, what happened? How did you get away?" Much demanded, the others shouting questions of their own.

Gareth caught his breath and took a long drink of ale, raising a hand to silence his curious friends.

"We don't have much time for questions," he said. "Tuck's alive."

There was uproar as everyone demanded the tale from the young outlaw.

"Let him speak, for God's sake!" Robin roared, silencing the men.

"He's in Penyston." Gareth continued. "I saw that bastard in the black armour shoot him into the river, so I jumped on a log and floated downstream until I found him, then I dragged him out of the water."

"Nicely done," Robin smiled as the men made appreciative noises. "You must be stronger than you look to have dragged the old friar onto dry land."

"I don't know where I found the strength," Gareth admitted. "I pressed on his chest until he spat out the water he'd swallowed, but then I passed out. When I woke up this morning I was in a bed in Penyston. Two fishermen from there had found us, and taken us to the village."

The outlaws were quiet as they pictured all this unfolding in their minds.

"Tuck's alive, you said," Little John grunted, scratching his thick beard. "How is he?"

Gareth shrugged. "The local barber removed the crossbow bolt from his chest and cleaned the wound up, but he's unconscious. He might never wake up."

"So we have to go and bring Tuck back here before anyone – like Gisbourne – discovers him." Gareth nodded and took another swig of ale as his leader went on. "If Tuck's discovered, the people of Penyston will suffer for helping a wolf's head."

Robin stood up. "Right. Who's coming with me to get him?"

Little John nodded. "I'll fetch the stretcher."

Much and Will volunteered to go as well. "Tuck carried me on a stretcher when I was wounded," Scarlet said, "the least I can do is return the favour."

Gareth finished the last of the ale in the skin and, wiping his mouth contentedly, stood beside Robin. "I'm coming too."

Matt Groves snorted with laughter. "No offence, boy, but you're too skinny to be much help carrying that fat churchman. And Penyston's a good few miles away – you must be worn out already."

Gareth was used to Groves's snide remarks, so he just ignored the man, addressing Robin again. "I have a debt to pay to the men who saved us. Just let me collect some of my money from my things" –

"Don't be daft," the young outlaw captain shook his head. "We'll repay them with money from the common fund. Those men didn't just help you, they helped Tuck too."

"Aye," John agreed. "Besides, if the villagers around here know we appreciate their help, they're more likely to keep offering it."

Robin nodded to Gareth, handing him a small key which he kept on a leather thong around his neck. "That's a good point. Go and take two pounds of silver from the common chest. We'll split it four ways: seven shillings each for the two fishermen and the barber, and the remainder for the village headman to buy everyone in the village some meat and ale as a thank you from us." He grinned at the thought. "They can throw a feast in our honour."

"And when we get back here with Tuck," John smiled. "We'll have a feast in young Gareth's honour. You're a hero, lad."

The teenager laughed, embarrassed but pleased at the praise. "I've found just the thing we can celebrate with too," he told them as they made their way through the forest to Penyston. "The barber has this amazing drink!"

The barber was happy to sell them some of his strange brew, although he warned them not to drink too much. "It's a lot more potent than ale," he told them as they lifted the stretcher with the unconscious Tuck on it, a man to each corner, Gareth following at the rear carrying a few skins filled with the powerful drink.

They didn't want to attract too much attention, so Robin had given the barber his seven shillings payment for taking care of the friar, and asked him to pass on the other seven shillings for the feast to the village headman. He gave the barber a stern look as he handed over the silver, making it clear without saying anything that they would find out one way or another if the man kept all the money for himself.

Gareth quickly ran to the house of the peasant that had brought him to the village and handed over their share of the money – more than a month's wages – to the astonished man, asking him to give half to his fisherman friend, then the youngster rejoined Robin and the rest and they made their way as fast as they could back through the trees to their camp.

Tuck looked peaceful enough lying on the stretcher, but the barber had told them again that the portly friar might never wake up.

As they jogged back to camp, trying not to jostle the stretcher too much, they breathed prayers to God, his saints, and the Magdalene to help their injured friend.

* * *

"So that was Guy of Gisbourne." John mused when they returned safely with Tuck to their camp in the woods near Notton, helping himself to a large chunk of venison from his wooden plate. "Impressive, eh?"

Robin nodded thoughtfully but Will snorted.

"Impressive? What was so impressive about him? He's a soft, skinny noble. Good Christ, you were almost three times the size of him John! The only thing impressive about him was that armour of his."

The rest of the outlaws around the camp-fire murmured agreement at that. Gisbourne's light black armour may have been ostentatious, but it was obviously functional and made its wearer stand out in a crowd. It was the kind of armour men coveted.

"You never spoke to him, Will," Robin said, gazing into the flames. "John's right – Gisbourne had something about him. Something more than just fancy clothes. He had a kind of hypnotic gaze – almost made you forget he was an enemy when he spoke to you. I could imagine men hesitating for just a fraction of a second when they looked into his eyes – just before they felt his knife in their guts."

"Aye," John agreed. "He had charisma; reminded me a bit of you." He nodded towards Robin, no trace of humour on his big honest face.

The young outlaw leader waved a dismissive hand, his face flushing slightly at the compliment from his giant friend.

Allan-a-Dale, gittern in his lap, strummed a cheery chord. "My money would be on Robin if the two of them ever get in a fight," he stated, eyes on the fingerboard as he traced a short melody. "That black armour looked nice, but it wouldn't stop one of you big lads if you were to ram the point of a sword into it."

"Who's taking bets on it?" Arthur, the stocky young man from Bichill shouted with a grin, raising his ale skin in the air, spilling much of it on the forest floor. "Anyone want to put money on it? Fight of the century!"

Allan laughed and stood up, hammering out a few repetitive, sinister-sounding notes on his instrument which he wore on a fine leather strap over his shoulder.

"The Wolf!"

He pointed theatrically at Robin, drawing loud cheers from the inebriated outlaws as he continued the ominously descending riff on his gittern.

"Versus…the Raven!"

The men played along, booing and laughing loudly as Allan mimicked a bird – cawing, and flapping his arms ridiculously around the camp.

No bets were placed on Sir Guy – the men had too much faith in their young captain's strength and skill with a sword to wager against him.

The evening wore on, the outlaws happy to have their friend Tuck back in the fold, even if he was still unconscious. At least the bastard Gisbourne and his cowardly crossbow hadn't managed to kill the merry Franciscan yet. For this night, he was still breathing, and the men celebrated their escape from the men hunting them like animals.

Robin looked over at the unconscious friar.

They had tried to make him as comfortable as possible, covering his grey robes with blankets and laying him out on a bed of straw under a shelter near the fire. Still, it was another cold night for all spring was on the way, with the threat of frost – maybe even snow – in the air. Robin resolved to have Tuck moved into the large cave before the men turned in for the night.

The outlaws – living a life where death was an ever-present threat – were right to enjoy the evening. They had escaped from the man sent to kill them, after all. And the scum that had murdered their friend Wilfred had been destroyed.

Things could have turned out much, much worse for them that day.

But, as the others danced and sang and downed their ale, and Gareth produced a bottle of the barber's 'medicine' with a wild grin, Robin sat thoughtfully on his own.

Gisbourne's men weren't like anything they'd faced before in the forest. They had clearly been well drilled by the king's bounty-hunter. The soldiers also outnumbered them, and were at least as well armed and armoured as the outlaws.

Robin took a long pull from his ale skin, tensing his huge bicep muscles as the bitter liquid warmed his belly. Aye, in a fair fight, one-on-one, he'd probably beat Sir Guy, he thought.

But he doubted Gisbourne was the type of man to fight fair, and, as he watched the rest of the men smiling and enjoying the evening, he realised he'd have to watch his back from closer to home. He wasn't the only one not joining in with the revelry: Matt Groves sat alone under a thick old beech tree, staring at him.

As their eyes met, Groves curled his lip derisively but looked away, draining his ale skin and wiping his wet mouth with a stained sleeve.

This has gone on too long, Robin realised. He hates me. Eventually he'll find the courage to slip a knife in my back...

The outlaw leader, half-drunk himself, glared at Groves, willing the man to react so he could finish it right there and then, but Matt never looked at him again.

As he glanced back down at his good friend Friar Tuck, unconscious, possibly never to wake up again, Robin decided.

These were *his* men now. They were loyal to him, despite his youth.

It was hard enough having men like Gisbourne and the sheriff, de Faucumberg, after them, without worrying about members of his own group.

He would talk to Little John and Will Scarlet in the morning. It was time they removed Matt Groves.

* * *

The loud crack of wooden practice swords clattering against each other filled the cold morning air.

Sir Guy of Gisbourne liked to be up at dawn to read from his bible then to practice his one-on-one combat skills with whoever was awake and not too hungover from the previous night's ale. Today, he sparred with a tall, but fat soldier. Gisbourne hadn't bothered to ask the man's name and, irritated by his opponent's lack of finesse, had given him quite a beating.

Since Thomas of Lancaster's failed rebellion, Sir Guy and his bounty-hunters had taken up temporary residence in the earl's former castle at Pontefract which was now in the hands of Sir Simon de Baldreston, although de Baldreston's seneschal, Sir John de Burton, looked after the day-to-day running of the place.

The majority of the escaped rebels – including Robin Hood and his men – had fled into the forests nearby so it was an ideal base; certainly it was closer than de Faucumberg's castle in Nottingham, so the sheriff had been quick to suggest Gisbourne seek Pontefract's hospitality for a while.

"Ow, fucking hell!" the fat soldier roared, dropping his practice sword from numb, scarlet fingers. "We're on the same side you know," he muttered, clasping the injured hand under his armpit with an angry glare at his black haired tormentor.

"You taking out your frustration on the peasants?" Gisbourne's sergeant Nicholas Barnwell, came into the courtyard carrying a mug of ale and half a loaf. The angry soldier stormed off, muttering under his breath, much to the amusement of Sir Guy.

"I don't know how oafs like him dare to call themselves 'soldiers'," he replied, tossing his own wooden practice sword noisily back onto the pile in a corner of the practice area. "No defence and too fat to attack without giving his opponent time to react. Good for nothing but arrow-fodder."

Barnwell laughed. "Nothing to do with you being pissed off at Hood's escape then?"

"Aye, that too," Gisbourne shrugged with a small smile. "That fat bastard's lucky I didn't use a real sword to spar with him." His face became serious again as he continued. "I can't believe we were so close to the man we've been sent here to kill. And his whole gang too!"

"Now you know why the king sent us here," Nicholas mumbled, mouth filled with crusty bread. "Hood and his men seem to live a charmed life."

Gisbourne nodded agreement. The stories the sheriff had told him about Hood, and his predecessor Adam Bell's, time in the forests of Barnsdale suggested it would be very hard, if not impossible, to catch this gang. They were well trained, well armed, had the support of the common people who seemed to love them, and their leaders had great tactical skill. Not to mention much better knowledge of the local terrain.

"Perhaps we need to try something different..." he mused.

"Fuck it." Nicholas turned away. "Stop fretting. There'll be another time to catch them. Come and have some breakfast with the men."

"You know I don't eat in the morning," Gisbourne replied. "You go back in; I'm going to finish my practice session. I want to be ready for Hood and his men the next time we meet."

As his sergeant wandered off, ale mug raised to his lips and waving the hard bread at his leader, Gisbourne drew his sword from its ornate black sheath and began to practice with it, flowing from one position to another with an economy of movement that was breathtaking to watch.

As he spun and twisted, his mind worked over the problem of Robin Hood and his men and, as he finished – his body moving astonishingly fast to end gracefully back in a defensive stance – a smile spread over his face. A passage from the Gospel of Matthew had come to mind.

Yes. He would find thirty pieces of silver and then they would try something different to catch this wolf's head...

* * *

"Exaudi nos, Domine sancte, Pater omnipotens, aeterne Deus: et mittere digneris sanctum Angelum tuum de caelis, qui custodiat, foveat, protegat, visitet atque defendat omnes habitantes in hoc habitaculo. Per Christum Dominum nostrum. Amen."

Allan finished the prayer, watching Tuck hopefully, but the friar remained unconscious. Maybe the minstrel had got the Latin wrong? He'd heard the prayer once, as a child, when his father had been dying, and memorized it.

"What did all that mean?" Much asked him.

"No idea," Allan admitted, to looks of amusement from Much and Robin who sat crouched on the forest floor beside the friar. "I heard it years ago, when my father was dying, and I memorized it. It seemed appropriate to say it now." He shrugged apologetically, but the two young men from Wakefield nodded encouragingly. Anything was worth a try after all.

Most of the outlaws were away from camp that morning, either hunting, fishing or gone off to local villages on errands. Robin, Much and the minstrel had stayed behind to watch over the camp, while a few of the others sparred and practiced with longbows close-by.

When Robin had woken up, hungover, he'd decided not to tell John and Will about his thoughts on Matt Groves the previous night after all. What had seemed like a good idea under the influence of ale now, in the cold light of morning, seemed extreme and unnecessary.

Matt would need to be dealt with somehow, but murdering him in cold blood just wasn't in Robin's character.

He shrugged and put Groves out of his mind for now then motioned towards Tuck.

"He told me how he came to be a Friar, but he never got around to telling me why he joined us. Seemed insane to me, leaving his safe life, to become a wolf's head. Something to do with that bastard prior, de Monte Martini."

Prior John de Monte Martini was the reason Robin had become an outlaw in the first place. The clergyman's threats towards Matilda at the previous May Day celebrations in Wakefield had led to Robin smashing the prior's nose and the young man being declared a wolf's head as a result.

Much nodded. "Aye, that's right, Tuck told a few of us the story one night when we were sitting by the camp-fire. You must have been on watch at the time or something."

"He did?" Robin leaned forward eagerly. "Go on then, let's hear it. I've been curious about it ever since we first met him."

Much waved a hand at Allan. "You tell it, you're the minstrel," he smiled. "You'll make it a better story than I would."

"Well," Allan began, making himself more comfortable on the log he sat on, "you know Tuck was a wrestler but gave it up when he was accused of cheating? And he saved the life of the Bishop of Norwich – what was his name again…?"

"Salmon," Much offered.

"Aye, John Salmon," Allan agreed. "Well, Tuck went off with the bishop and, with his help, Tuck became a Franciscan. Learned to read, learned Latin, studied the bible and so on."

Robin nodded. He knew all this already. "What did he do after that?"

"Well, the Franciscans knew about Tuck's previous life as a wrestler. They knew he could look after himself, so they used him to escort valuables around the place – money, religious relics, that sort of thing – against the threat of outlaws like ourselves."

"That's what he was doing when we robbed him," Much offered, remembering the day they had stopped the friar and his guards taking a chest full of silver through the forest. The outlaws had beaten the guards easily, but Tuck had shocked everyone when he brutally knocked out their previous leader, Adam Bell, using a cudgel hidden in his grey robes.

They all grinned at the memory and Allan carried on. "Aye, he would often travel to places with groups of mercenaries and he ended up in Lewes Priory one day. The prior asked him to travel to

France, to buy some religious relic or other." He furrowed his brow and looked over at Much. "What was it de Monte Martini wanted?"

"Some hair from Christ's beard," Much replied. "It had turned up in some French village – Eze I think Tuck called the place – and the prior thought it would look good in his collection."

Allan took up the story again. "That's right, the prior gave Tuck some crazy amount of money to go to France and buy this hair. Off he went on a ship with half a dozen guards and the silver. He didn't tell us much about the journey, other than to complain about having to walk up some huge mountain to reach the village! At least no one bothered them on the way. I suppose France isn't infested with wolf's heads and robbers like England." He smiled and continued. "Anyway, this Eze is, apparently, a small village, and the local priest was more than happy to sell the relic for such a huge sum of silver. Tuck and his men made their way back through France" –

"Sampling the best of the exotic local food and drink," Much laughed, nodding towards the unconscious friar's round belly, "at de Monte Martini's expense."

"I can imagine," Robin smiled. Tuck liked his food, there was no denying that. "I bet he enjoyed that journey."

"Until they returned to England," Allan nodded grimly. "When they got back to Lewes, Tuck paid off his guards and, taking Christ's hair, which was in a small, fancily decorated reliquary inside a plain wooden box, went to give it to the prior." He paused and met Robin's eyes. "Now, you know Tuck. You know he takes his faith very seriously."

Robin nodded. It was true. Although he was a man outside the law, the friar was still very much a man of God – more of a Christian than the likes of Prior de Monte Martini with his string of brothels would ever be, that was for sure.

"Well, as he sat outside the chapter house, waiting on the prior to see him, Tuck opened the little box for a last look at the hair. He hadn't looked at it since they'd bought it from the priest in France – Tuck thought it would be disrespectful to keep staring at it, so he'd stopped himself until then, but when he opened the wooden box, *Pater Noster* on his lips, for a final look at the relic..." Again, Allan paused dramatically.

"It was gone!" Much broke in to the minstrel's annoyance.

"Shut up!" Allan shouted with a glare. "I'm telling the story."

Robin and Much shared a laugh at their mate's indignation.

"The box was empty," Allan went on. "One of the mercenaries must have taken the reliquary when Tuck was sleeping off too much French wine one night. When the guards kept asking for a look at it, the daft bastard had told them no one would be opening the box until he handed it over to the prior."

Robin shook his head sadly, looking over at his unconscious big friend. "Always wants to see the good in people, does Tuck," he said. "Naïve old sod."

"Of course, the prior called him in then, and he had to tell him what had happened. It didn't go down too well."

"I see why Tuck wasn't too keen to go back to de Monte Martini when we robbed him," Robin muttered.

"Exactly," Allan replied. "The prior suspected Tuck might have stolen the relic himself, so he had him stripped naked and searched. Of course they didn't find it, and the local bailiff was called to hunt down the mercenaries. They found five of them, but one had left town as soon as they'd parted ways with Tuck, and the rest of them didn't know where he'd gone."

He shrugged. "No one ever found the relic, and de Monte Martini made Tuck's life miserable afterwards. When we robbed him on his way down to Lewes with the prior's silver, Tuck knew he would be blamed again and be thrown in jail or worse."

"So he joined us," Robin said, and the three men sat in thoughtful silence for a while.

It had been two days since they had brought Tuck back to camp, and he'd shown no signs of stirring, despite the prayers of the outlaws.

"There must be some religious relics in the churches around here," Robin mused.

"So what?"

"Well, I'm just thinking…if they're as powerful as the churchmen tell us…maybe one would help our prayers to wake Tuck?"

Allan and Much looked at each other. Why not? It must be worth a try.

"There's something – I don't remember what – in Brandesburton," the minstrel told them. "When Little John returns to camp, maybe he'll be able to tell us more; he knows that area well."

"I'm not keen on the idea of stealing something like this," Robin said, but then he smiled and shrugged his massive shoulders. "Maybe we can borrow it for a while though."

CHAPTER EIGHT

"The fat friar's as good as dead now," Matt Groves growled over his shoulder as he relieved himself against a tree.

"Always so cheerful, you," Paul, the former fuller from Nottingham replied with a scowl.

"I'm just being realistic." Groves did his breeches up and turned round with a shrug. "Keeping him alive's not doing him any favours. Someone should put him out his misery."

Paul and James, one of the men who had been on the raft with Much when Tuck was injured, had accompanied Groves to Darton that morning. They had come specifically to Darton because a local merchant was able to supply them with rope, something only port towns normally specialized in, but the two men had grown tired of Matt's incessant grousing.

"When we get back to camp, you can sort the friar out then," Paul muttered. "Can we bloody hurry up though?"

"What's the rush?" Groves wondered, lifting his pack from the grass and following the others.

Matt had managed to conclude his business quickly in the village, while Paul and James had been forced to take more time inspecting, and paying for, the rope that Little John had asked the merchant to obtain for them on a previous visit.

Matt had spent the time waiting on his companions in the local ale-house. He'd also bought a skin of the dark ale which he'd been sipping from as they made their way back to camp.

"Guy of Gisbourne has spies in all the villages about here, now," James noted. "I'd rather not hang about in case 'the Raven' hears we're around and comes hunting us. If you'd stop swilling that ale, and pissing it out, we'd make better time."

"The Raven!" Groves hooted, taking another mouthful of ale from the skin. "Fuck him and his fancy armour. He's a fool. Had us in his grasp and let us escape." He waved a hand dismissively. "Gisbourne's no threat."

"All the same, can we hurry up?" Paul retorted, utterly fed up with his half-drunk companion. "The sooner we get back the better."

"Wait!" James stopped, holding a hand up for silence, his eyes wide.

"Oh, what now?"

"Shut up, you prick!" James glared at Matt, his hand on his sword hilt, listening intently.

The unmistakeable thundering sound of horses close behind came to them.

All three were hardy fighters, but none was a leader. They gazed at each other in fear, wondering what to do.

"Run for it!"

Paul shouted and spun to make his way into the undergrowth but a horseman burst through the trees beside them as they ran, swinging his longsword into the back of the fuller's skull.

James tried to head towards the thicker foliage nearby, but another mounted soldier charged into view, his horse clipping the outlaw on the shoulder and sending him sprawling on the ground.

More riders appeared as he tried to rise, while Matt Groves stood, sword drawn, but with a blank look on his face.

Matt instantly recognised the black armoured man as he rode up, crossbow in his right hand while expertly guiding his mount with his left.

James sprinted towards a massive old oak, trying to find some cover, as, with a dull thud, Gisbourne released the trigger and his iron bolt hammered into the cold bark of the tree just beside his head.

"Damn! Surround him!" The black knight roared with a grimace, tossing his weapon to one of his men to reload and wheeling his horse around to face Matt Groves. "This one's not hiding anyway!"

Groves held his blade before him defensively. The ale he'd swallowed that day coursed through him, making him feel invincible, even though he could barely walk in a straight line.

"Come on then, Raven," the outlaw spat. "Get down from your horse and I'll shove my sword up your arse!"

Sir Guy raised his eyebrows in surprise, and then laughed. It was a genuine, happy laugh, and weirdly out-of-place in the present situation.

"Very well."

Groves spread his feet wide defensively, the ale focusing his mind solely on the man directly in front of him as Gisbourne dropped from his mount and faced up to him, sword in hand.

Matt Groves was no unskilled peasant. He had been a member of well-trained outlaw gangs for years, and that experience, combined with his natural aggression, made him a dangerous swordsman.

He grinned as the black-clad Gisbourne walked towards him, waving at his men to stand down.

"You're the Raven, eh?" Matt growled, swinging his sword in a vicious, controlled arc, testing his opponent's defences.

"That's me," Gisbourne grinned, parrying the blow and stepping in close to ram his boiled-leather gauntleted fist into the outlaw's nose.

Groves fell backwards onto the ground, stunned, blood streaming down his face as the bounty-hunter smiled down at him.

"Bastard!" The furious outlaw pushed himself to his feet, remembering Robin Hood breaking his nose not so long ago, and threw himself at Gisbourne, swinging his blade from side to side brutally, as if he was trying to smash his opponent's weapon by sheer brute force.

Sir Guy parried the onslaught for a few moments, then deftly stepped to the left and, as the outlaw fell slightly forward, the bounty-hunter slammed the pommel of his sword into Matt's chin, throwing him to the ground, bloodied and stunned.

"Don't get up," Gisbourne grinned, holding the point of his blade against Matt's throat. "I want to talk to you." He looked to the right as his men brought a silent, bloodied James out from behind the oak and dragged him over, throwing the wolf's head onto the forest floor beside Groves.

"Now there's two of you, and I only need one."

The outlaws glanced at each other wondering what was going to happen next as Gisbourne carried on.

"I need one of you to do something for me. A...favour, let's call it." He looked down at the two men lying on their backs and smiled. "Who'll do me a favour?"

For a few moments there was silence, and then James gave a short, forced laugh. "Fuck off, lawman. If you think we're going to betray Robin and our friends you can think again" –

The king's man swept forward and shoved the point of his sword deep into James' neck, so hard it came out the other side and stuck in the grass underneath. Steaming hot blood spilled onto the grass below as the outlaw died, his eyes and mouth opened wide in shock and pain.

Matt Groves watched his companion expire then looked up to meet the Raven's eyes.

"I'll do you a favour."

* * *

"St Peter's thumb?"

Little John nodded. "Aye, father, we need it."

The Priest of St Mary's in Brandesburton looked bemused at the strange request, but shook his head firmly. "I can't just give you one of our relics John, these things aren't bread, or fish, to be bartered. St Peter's thumb has been in the company of Christ himself. The people of our parish are proud to have it here – pilgrims come to pray before it."

"And pay you for the privilege," Will growled.

Father Nicholas de Nottingham, a small, completely bald man with intelligent eyes nodded defiantly at the glowering outlaw. "Aye, they give alms, what about it? Do you think our roof repairs itself when the January winds blow the slates off?"

"Doesn't God repair it for you?"

"He does, yes," the priest replied to a cynical-looking Scarlet. "God sent us the relic people pay to see didn't he?"

Robin laughed at de Nottingham's unassailable logic, and waved a hand for Will to give it a rest.

"Look, father, we need the relic. Our friend, Tuck, is badly injured. We hoped the relic might be able to heal him." He held up a hand as the priest opened his mouth to reply. "We appreciate St Peter's thumb brings your parish revenue. So, we'll buy it from you." He dropped some silver coins into the churchman's palm. "Three pounds. That should buy you a few roof slates."

Father Nicholas gasped at the money, his eyes wide.

Will had suggested they simply walk into the church and take the relic, but the other outlaws, more pious than Scarlet, had rejected the idea. Little John, who had lived in nearby Holderness, told them Father Nicholas was a good man – a local, not high-born, who had tried to do his best for the villagers while living frugally himself, unlike many of the other clergymen in England.

In John's opinion, the priest would spend the three pounds of silver wisely and fairly, for the benefit of the parish, rather than just buying himself jade rosary beads, new silk vestments and some imported French communion wine.

"You're good men," de Nottingham smiled. "Even that one," he nodded at Will, bringing laughs from Robin and Little John. "But" – he spread his hands, meeting Robin's gaze – "it's St Peter's thumb! St Peter himself, our first pope! I can't just sell a relic like that; it's beyond price."

The three outlaws looked at each other in frustration. None of them, not even Will, wanted to take the relic by force, not after speaking to the sincere priest. But time was running out for Friar Tuck and they didn't have time to hunt for another powerful relic.

"Where did you get it?" Robin wondered.

Father Nicholas looked uncomfortable. "It was a gift from Our Lord" –

"Be honest with us," Robin sat on one of the cold wooden pews, looking up at the churchman earnestly. "How did something like St Peter's thumb end up in a tiny parish church in the arse-end of nowhere?"

Father Nicholas had genuinely warmed to this young outlaw, with his open face – not at all like most of the other cut-throats infesting the greenwood – and found himself being more truthful than he would have expected when the three rough-looking wolf's heads had wandered into his church a short while earlier.

"A man – from London judging by his barely understandable accent – sold it to me for…well, that's not important. He said he'd been given it as a gift for rendering some service or other to a bishop."

"And you believed him?" Will laughed.

"No," the priest shook his head. "It was obvious he'd stolen it."

"Why did you buy it from him then?" John wondered, sitting down beside Robin, his massive legs barely fitting into the space.

"The reliquary is quite exceptionally crafted," de Nottingham replied. "And it was clear the fellow was desperate. He wasn't asking much at all for it, despite the obvious value of the thing. I believe he must have tried selling it in many different places, but been turned away – perhaps even chased by the local lawmen." He shrugged. "As you say, this is a small parish in the middle of nowhere. We have some other relics, but they were nothing in comparison to this. I took pity on the man, gave him his price and sent him on his way."

"What does a thousand-year-old thumb look like?" Will asked.

The priest shrugged again. "No idea, I've never been able to open the reliquary. It's locked, I don't have a key, and it's simply too precious to damage by forcing it open."

The outlaws looked at him in disbelief.

"You've never even seen it?" Robin demanded. "How do you know it's not just an empty box?"

Father Nicholas looked at the three friends with a small smile on his face.

"You're missing the point. It doesn't matter what's inside the box. I was told it was St Peter's thumb – so that's what I tell the pilgrims that come to see it. I've personally seen people with terrible afflictions touch the reliquary and become cured. It really doesn't matter what's in the box." He waved a hand dismissively. "Besides, as I said, the reliquary is so ostentatious, so obviously valuable, it stands to reason it holds *something* of great value."

"It might hold nothing at all!" Will hooted derisively.

"Then I bought a hugely expensive reliquary for a tiny sum, what's the problem?" the little priest demanded, glaring at Scarlet who looked away, abashed.

Robin stood up, the wooden pew creaking loudly in the cool silence.

"Father, we need" –

"Yes, yes, your friend is dying and so on," the churchman butted in. "So you've said." He moved towards Robin and looked up, meeting his eyes imperiously. "You're an honourable man, so I hear."

The young outlaw remained silent, not quite sure whether he was 'honourable' or not.

"So, I'll tell you what I'll do," de Nottingham continued, turning his back on the trio and disappearing behind the altar.

He reappeared a moment later, carrying the reliquary which was finely-decorated and, as the priest had said, obviously very valuable.

"Here," he thrust it towards Robin. "You can borrow it. But – whether your friend lives or dies – I expect you to return it to me."

"You're a good man, father," Will grinned.

"I told you he was," Little John agreed, slapping the clergyman on the shoulder gratefully.

Robin took the small box reverentially and gingerly placed it into a pocket under his gambeson, nodding his thanks to the priest.

"What do we do with it?" he asked. "I mean, how do we get it to heal Tuck?"

"Place it on his chest and pray. But" – he raised his hand in warning – "don't expect too much. It may be your friend's time has come. He might be beyond healing."

With glad smiles and words of thanks the three outlaws made their way to the big oak doors, promising to return the valuable relic as soon as they could.

As they stepped out into the sunlight, squinting as their eyes became accustomed to the brightness after the dim church, Robin turned and tossed the bag of silver to Father Nicholas who scrambled instinctively to catch it.

"Hey!" the priest shouted, running after them as the outlaws wandered off. "Don't forget I want the relic back – what's this money for?"

"Your roof," Robin grinned over his shoulder. "It won't repair itself when the slates blow off in January, will it?"

* * *

Stephen made good time on his journey to Clerkenwell, pushing his horse close to its limit in his desire to find aid for his master as soon as possible.

In truth, he wasn't sure exactly what he would find when he got there. It was many years since he had visited the place, and he doubted he would recognise any of the brothers residing there now.

Not far from his destination – no more than two or three hours – dark grey clouds suddenly filled the sky, blown by a bitter wind from the east, and the Hospitaller cursed in frustration as light flakes of snow began to fall.

He had hoped to reach the capital tonight, but knew it would be dangerous to continue his journey in the face of a gathering snowstorm.

With an angry sigh he turned his horse about and headed back the way he had come. He had passed through a small village – Finchley according to the signs – just a couple of miles earlier. He'd noticed a small but, from the outside at least, cosy looking inn where he would spend the night.

As his tired palfrey made its way along the road, Stephen felt his disappointment lift and he allowed himself a small smile at the thought of a roaring fire, a cosy bed and a few ales.

Aye, he had hoped to be within the sturdy stone walls of the Hospitaller headquarters tonight, but you couldn't argue with a snowstorm. Besides, he'd ridden hard and spent the previous six nights under cold blankets in a simple tent – he and his mount had earned a proper roof over their head tonight.

Tomorrow morning he'd ride into Clerkenwell and deliver Sir Richard's letter to the Prior.

* * *

"Where's the three that went off to Darton this morning?" Much wondered, stirring the big cauldron of pottage over the fire, sniffing at the contents with a small smile of pleasure. "It'll be dark soon."

"That's why it's so peaceful around here," Allan-a-Dale looked up from where he sat resting against a tree, a broad grin on his face. "That sour-faced bastard Matt's not here."

"Don't speak too soon." The skinny youngster, Gareth, jogged into camp. He was acting as one of the lookouts and, from his vantage point high in a thick old beech, had spotted Matt approaching. "Coming from the west, alone, no sign of Paul or James. And he's got blood on his face, looks like he's been in a fight."

"Everyone up!" Robin roared, running for his longbow and arrows, his stomach lurching in apprehension as the men followed his lead, hurriedly strapping on swords, bracers, helmets and whatever other weapons or armour they each favoured.

"What now?" John wondered. "Someone might be following him."

Robin nodded agreement. "Everyone find a place to hide. Those of you who can shoot a longbow, have them trained on the path to the west, where Matt'll appear. The rest of you, have your swords, axes or whatever ready. I'll wait here for him."

It was a measure of Robin's ever growing stature amongst the outlaws that no-one questioned his orders, the men melting away like wraiths into the dense green undergrowth, the sounds of insects and birds filling the air and lending the scene a serenity the young captain didn't feel inside.

It took a short while, but eventually Matt Groves walked into camp, looking at Robin warily.

"Where is everyone?"

"Where do you think?" Robin retorted, his eyes scanning the trees behind Groves uneasily. "We saw you coming."

Matt nodded in understanding, wandering over and lifting a wooden bowl from beside the fire which he ladled some of the pottage into.

"You can tell them to come out," he grunted through mouthfuls. "I haven't been followed, I managed to lose them." He met Robin's eyes, meat juice dribbling down his chin, but his look was unreadable. "The bastards got James and Paul though."

Robin cursed, his stomach lurching again at the thought of two of his friends not coming home to camp tonight.

"Who got them?" he demanded.

Matt placed the bowl of food on the ground, clutching his chest and scowled momentarily. "Gisbourne and his men," he replied. "Sly bastard rode us down. Shot James himself, while one of the riders stuck a blade in Paul. One of them tried to do the same to me – gave me a kick in the face the prick – but he knocked me down the side of the trail. Steep bit. I slid down a good fifteen feet, battered my chest off a bloody rock at the bottom." He grimaced again. "Still, I was lucky. Their horses wouldn't follow down after me, so I was able to get away before any of them bothered to dismount and chase me on foot."

He gulped down the rest of his pottage and lay back on the ground with a groan. Robin felt a pang of guilt. It was clear Groves was in genuine pain – the blood caking his face and the exhausted look on his seamed face weren't an act. The man had been hurt and made his way back to the safety of their camp, surely hoping for a better welcome than this.

"You're sure you weren't followed?"

"Nah," Groves muttered without lifting his head from the grass. "I don't think they were too interested in a chase – they'd killed the other two lads anyway. Bastards."

"You hurt anywhere else?" Robin asked, but he was met with silence and he realised Matt had fallen asleep.

Shaking his head, sick of the harsh life they were forced to lead, the young outlaw called for the men to return to camp, with the lookouts ordered to be extra vigilant throughout the night.

In the morning they would try and recover their fallen friends' bodies for a proper Christian burial.

Robin felt almost as tired as Matt. Their former leader, Adam Gurdon, had known the greenwood of Barnsdale better than anyone; he had been an ex-Templar knight, a man of considerable military skills. And yet, when Gurdon had betrayed them and tried to hunt the outlaws down he hadn't been able to kill even one of the group before Robin had rammed his sword through the turncoat's chest.

But Sir Guy of Gisbourne – a stranger to the area – had, in the space of a few days, managed to put Friar Tuck into a sleep he might never wake from and now he'd slaughtered two of their mates and promised to do the same to Robin.

No wonder the locals talked about this sinister black knight in hushed tones.

Little John, as he did so often, guessed what his young leader was thinking and walked over to slap him reassuringly on the arm.

"Have faith," the giant growled. "You'll see: things'll work out. A raven is no match for a wolf."

CHAPTER NINE

"I can't speak bloody Latin!"

"None of us can, this is a waste of time." Will nodded agreement with Allan-a-Dale, who had been tasked with holding the relic and praying for Friar Tuck's cure.

"Why do I have to do this anyway?" Allan demanded. "I'm not a priest. I only know the one Latin prayer, and it might be a prayer for crops to grow for all I know!"

"You know how to make a sermon though," John replied. "Always blabbering on about stuff. If you hadn't become a minstrel you'd have made a damn good bishop."

There was laughter at that which somewhat eased the tension in the air.

Although the men didn't visit church frequently – how could they? – they were all Christians. They all believed in the power of God and his saints. The presence of a true holy relic had them in awe, and the atmosphere as they gathered around their unconscious companion was both nervous and reverential.

Matt Groves had been typically condescending when the ornate reliquary had been produced by Robin, who told the men it couldn't be opened.

"Of course it can be opened," Matt had laughed mirthlessly. "Give it here, I'll open it."

"We can't damage it," Robin shook his head. "It's not ours. Father Nicholas was good enough to let us borrow it – we return it to him as he gave us it."

"Let's have a look," Peter, the old sailor held out his hand curiously. "I've seen lots of strange boxes. We used to carry all sorts of foreign cargo on the ships I worked on. Maybe I'll be able to see how the thing opens without breaking it."

Robin handed the reliquary over cautiously, but Peter took it as carefully as if he were handling a newborn babe.

Eyebrows lowered in concentration, the sailor turned the box this way and that hunting for some catch that might unlock the fancy little case, then he exhaled softly in defeat before giving it back to his leader with a puzzled frown.

"It doesn't need to be opened anyway," Robin said. "Father Nicholas told us he's seen people cured by the relic even inside its box and I trust him." He bent down and placed the box on Tuck's chest. It rose and fell slightly with the friar's shallow breathing and Little John ordered the men to get on their knees and pray for their friend.

"In nomine Patris," Allan had started before he had given up in frustration.

"Just repeat that prayer you said the other day. The Latin one. You don't have to pretend you're a real churchman." Robin nodded encouragingly at the embarrassed minstrel.

With a sigh, Allan bent his head again, the rest of the men following his lead and clasping their hands piously as he recited the prayer he'd memorized as a child. As he finished, the respectful looks the other men gave him encouraged him to continue.

"In the name of the Father, the Son and the Holy Ghost," he mumbled, before he glanced at Tuck and his voice grew in strength and confidence with the desire to see his friend well again. "We are gathered here to ask you, St Peter, to help our companion. He is a good man – a man of the cloth – who almost drowned and now can't be revived. By the power invested in this, your holy relic, we humbly pray you will cure our friend."

He couldn't think what else to say, so some of the outlaws muttered, "Amen," and Will whispered, "Is that it?"

"Just pray, for goodness' sake!" Little John hissed, and the men bowed their heads and closed their eyes again, silently sending their supplications to the venerable Saint.

Nothing happened. No flash of lightning, no angelic healing hands appeared to help Tuck.

"It'll work eventually," Robin told the men. "Have faith. We'll pray for him again tomorrow."

* * *

Matilda felt enormous.

Her ankles were swollen. Her back and legs ached, and her breasts were becoming so heavy she worried they'd hang like empty sacks when the baby finally arrived.

Her parents tried their best to help her through the pregnancy, but they had their work to do every day, as did she. What she needed was her husband beside her, to look after her and make her feel better about the changes her young body was going through.

What she didn't need was to be pawed at.

Robin had made his way through the forest to visit that morning, upset at the relic's failure to cure Friar Tuck, and knowing Henry and Mary would be out at the fletcher's shop so he could spend some time alone with his wife, despite her irritation the last time he'd seen her.

Matilda had let him into the house, overjoyed to see him, but she was beginning to wish he'd never turned up.

"Stop it!"

Robin flinched in surprise at the rebuke as he tried to caress Matilda's swollen breasts in the dimly lit room.

"They hurt," she glared at him.

He apologised with a bemused smile and cuddled her for a few moments, before the swelling in his trousers overcame his good sense and he tried to slip a hand between his pregnant wife's legs.

"Are you an idiot?" Matilda shouted, shoving the surprised outlaw away. "I told you: my body aches."

Robin looked at her in confusion and she almost felt sorry for him. He looked so young and innocent and was obviously too stupid to understand what was wrong.

"I'm sorry," he mumbled, his eyes downcast momentarily, before they rose and settled again on her swollen breast and she could actually see his erection swelling again underneath his trousers and knew exactly what he was thinking.

"I'm sick every morning. My feet ache. My legs ache. These" - she cupped her breasts, fury rising in her again as she saw Robin's eyes light up - "are breaking my back! And this baby is keeping me up all night, kicking and jumping around like a court jester!"

It was true. Matilda was exhausted. Her legs jerked when she tried to rest, and the baby rolled about inside her so distractingly she hadn't been able to fall into a proper sleep for days.

"I've never felt so tired in my whole life," she told him, glaring at him as if it was, somehow, his fault. "Sleeping rough in Barnsdale as a wolf's head was easy compared to this."

All she wanted was a cuddle and for Robin to spend a little time talking to her about what she was going through. But she could see from his expression he was only interested in sex.

He tried to hide it with a placating smile, but his eyes roved over her heavy breasts when he thought she wasn't looking and, when he cuddled her she could feel him pressing himself against her backside almost in desperation.

"Get off me!" she shouted, pushing him away. "Go back to your mates in the forest. Maybe one of them will let you stick it in them."

Again, the confused expression on his handsome face made her hesitate, but she was in no mood to deal with this.

"Go. Come back when you can be a proper husband."

Bemused and upset, Robin stormed out the fletcher's house without another word.

* * *

The inn at Finchley proved to be as cosy and inviting as Stephen had hoped.

By the time he reached the village the snow was falling heavily and the wind whistled about him, making him glad of his thick black surcoat, emblazoned with the white cross of his Order.

This far from the North he saw no reason to hide the fact he was a Hospitaller, so when the snow had started he'd taken the surcoat from his pack and gratefully put it on.

When he'd ridden into the village the locals had bowed their heads or smiled up at him respectfully. Everyone knew the Knights of St John. When Stephen had first joined the Order fifteen years ago he had been inordinately proud of the normal folks' respect for the military Orders. The Hospitallers and Teutonic Knights – even ex-Templars, if any were discovered – were generally held in great esteem by the common people of England.

After a decade and a half of travelling the world and fighting thankless battles, Stephen had grown apathetic to the views of strangers. The villagers saw a man wearing chain-mail and automatically assumed he was someone of power and significance; a man somehow worthy of respect for the horse he rode and the attire he wore. But Stephen had fought beside plenty of courageous, loyal, Godly men who'd been nothing more than simple yeomen, like the good men of this village.

He'd also known plenty of cruel, selfish and damn evil men who acted like the red, black or white cross emblazoned on their shield somehow absolved them from whatever immoral deeds they chose to be involved in.

Images of women raped, children brutally murdered and rows of worthy foes treated like cattle at the slaughterhouse by 'honourable' men in the name of Holy War filled his head and he cursed inwardly.

Aye, he had seen some terrible things before he came back to England as Sir Richard-at-Lee's sergeant-at-arms, but it didn't help to be maudlin.

Passing an old church dedicated to St Mary, he reached the inn – the Wheatsheaf from the crudely painted sign over the door – and, with long practised ease climbed from his mount, leading it towards the adjoining stable.

There were no stable-hands around, so Stephen found a vacant stall for the palfrey and made sure it was secure. He patted the beast on the neck fondly. "I'll send someone out to tend to you, lad," he muttered, feeling somewhat foolish. He'd never owned a pet as a boy, and always felt like an idiot talking to animals, but this horse – which he'd never even given a name – had served him well for years and, despite his reticence, there was a bond between them that the sergeant acknowledged.

With a backward glance at his mount, which seemed to be looking at him with an amused expression on its long face, he huddled into his surcoat and walked round to the front of the building.

The sound of music and song filled his ears as he pushed the sturdy door open, wandering gladly into the warmth and light cast by a well-banked fire on the far wall of the room. The rushes on the floor hadn't been changed in a while, so the stench of dung, urine and stale vomit permeated the air making the room smell worse than the stable, but it was to be expected in a place like this; Stephen knew he'd get used to it within a short while.

Locals nodded gaily to him as he made his way to the bar and waved the inn-keeper over.

"I'll have an ale – warmed if you please. And my horse needs tending to." He handed a coin to the man, who nodded pleasantly and shouted through a door at someone – the stable-boy presumably – to move his lazy arse and see to the gentleman's steed.

"There you are, my lord," the barkeep smiled, placing the mug of ale in front of Stephen. "There's a couple of pokers in the hearth – help yourself."

The sergeant lifted the mug with a nod of thanks and weaved his way through the crowded room to the fire. He lifted a poker from the flames and placed the red-hot tip into his ale, which hissed as it instantly warmed, and took a small sip, grinning in satisfaction as the mild heat filled his mouth and spread throughout his body. They brewed their ale strong in Finchley!

He made his way back to the bar, sipping his warm drink as he went. "I'm no lord," he told the inn-keeper. "I'm only a sergeant, but I do need a bed for the night."

"You're in luck," the man replied, with a broad smile. "I have a room for you: bed freshly made up, floor newly swept – you'll have the best night's sleep you've had in ages, I promise you."

The Hospitaller nodded. He'd heard it all before, in every inn in every town in Christendom and beyond.

"Aye, very good. I don't give a shit about the dust on the floor. I'll sleep like a babe as long as it's cheap."

The inn-keeper laughed good-naturedly and moved off to serve another customer. "A shilling for the night," he smiled over his shoulder. "I'll do you some pottage and a few ales too. Can't say fairer than that."

Stephen nodded and raised his mug in salute. "Good enough."

He took a long pull of the powerful warmed ale and looked around the room which was filled with dancing shadows cast by the cosy orange glow from the roaring fire in the hearth.

There were twenty or so villagers in the large room. Most of them were singing along with a man playing a battered old gittern. Stephen wondered how they could hear what the hell he was playing over the sound of their own tuneless voices, but they all seemed to be having a good time.

The sergeant's gaze roved across the people, seeing the usual types in a village of this sort: peasants; yeomen; a priest; a couple of hard-looking fellows that probably made a living guarding property somewhere nearby... and there was the loner, sitting by himself in a dark corner, nursing a mug. Stephen wondered what tragedy had befallen the man, whose eyes looked dead as he gazed at the table in front of him.

His eyes moved on and widened slightly as they came to rest on a beautiful red-headed girl, no more than twenty-five or twenty-six summers, seated at a table with an older man – her father, no doubt. She wore a tight fitting dress which did little to hide her ample bosom, even though it showed no bare skin at all.

Stephen found himself staring at her, admiring her figure and her clear, pale skin.

As if feeling his gaze, the girl suddenly looked straight at him and the Hospitaller flicked his eyes away in embarrassment.

He took another sip of his ale and looked over at the red-head again. She was staring at him, her full lips opened in a little smile, showing whiter teeth than Stephen had seen in a long time.

Christ, she was lovely!

He had fought in many battles, and killed many men. He had travelled the world, and seen sights most men would never see.

But he had only lain with one woman in his life, and even that single night's pleasure lay heavy on his soul, as it had been a betrayal of his Order's vow of chastity.

Vows meant little to some men. Priests, bishops, cardinals and, unbelievably to Stephen, some popes had lain with women – and men! – whenever they felt like it. Even the Hospitallers in England had been tainted by sexual scandals: the young preceptor at Buckland had been removed in disgrace after rumours of fornication with the nuns they shared a building with. The Prior of England, under instruction from his superiors in Rhodes, had eventually replaced the young preceptor with a much older man, hoping it would put an end to any more scandals.

Stephen took all his vows seriously. He had dedicated his life to the service of Christ and his Hospitaller master, Sir Richard. He had been terribly drunk the night he had slept with the lovely olive-skinned girl in Rhodes. In fact, he had been so drunk, he could barely remember what had happened, but he knew the alcohol had rendered him incapable of any legendary feats of lovemaking.

He felt guilty – dirty even, that he had broken his vows. But, deep down, it rankled even more because he couldn't remember much of it.

At least if he had a clear memory of an incredible night's loving with a dusky beauty the guilt and shame might be worth it!

Irritably, he turned away from the flame-haired girl and drained the last of his ale, shouting at the bar-keep to refill his mug.

Christ, that ale was strong, right enough!

His head swam slightly after just one mug and he knew he'd have to take it easy – and be in bed early – if he was to be off for Clerkenwell at dawn the following morning.

He sat watching the musician for a while, the ale and the warmth of the room seeping into his bones. He hadn't felt this relaxed in a long time and he savoured the feeling.

Another ale went down and he found himself tapping his foot in time with the music, although it would take an awful lot of alcohol to make the gruff Hospitaller join in with the raucous singing.

"May I sit with you, sir?"

Startled out of his comfortable reverie, Stephen looked around and was shocked to see the gorgeous red-head sitting down at his table.

There was no sign of her elderly male companion.

"Where's your father, girl?"

"He's had enough of Hobb's ale," she laughed, her green eyes sparkling as she nodded towards the busy inn-keeper. "He makes it too strong, and my da can only handle a few before he can barely stand up. So I sent him home, but I felt like staying and listening to the music for a while." She looked at the sergeant-at-arms somewhat sheepishly. "A girl can't be seen out on her own though can she? I'd be the talk of the village, sitting in an alehouse, drinking by myself."

Stephen raised his eyebrows. "But you won't be the talk of the place for sitting with a stranger?"

The girl smiled again, pushing her long red hair away from her face. "You're a Hospitaller. A man of God. I'm safe with you – I might as well be sitting with the pope himself."

She was really quite beautiful Stephen thought to himself, his eyes lingering on her smiling face.

"Aye, lass, I suppose so. Unless you mean Benedict."

Pope Benedict IX had, almost three hundred years earlier, been notorious for his sexual depravity – being accused of everything from homosexuality to rape and even murder – but the girl looked blankly at Stephen, clearly having no idea what he was on about.

"Never mind," he grunted, signalling Hobb to bring another couple of ales over. "You're safe with me, but it's been a long time since I sat drinking with a woman. You might find my conversation boring."

She grinned and leaned against him for a second, nudging him companionably with her shoulder. "Let's just listen to the music for a bit then, eh?"

The girl seemed totally oblivious to how attractive she was, or she wouldn't be acting so familiar with strange men, Stephen thought. He looked at her as she watched the minstrel, enjoying the sight of her perfectly rounded nose, full lips and trim figure.

She suddenly turned to him, catching him watching her, and smiled, curling her tongue onto her teeth, her green eyes shining, before turning her gaze back to the minstrel. From any other woman such a look would have been openly wanton, yet this girl appeared to be simply having fun, enjoying life to the full.

Silently, the Hospitaller swore to himself as he felt his loins tingle and his trousers begin to bulge.

The ale had gone to his head and he felt confused. A man of his age and experience should know better, but the presence of the stunning red-head was playing havoc with his emotions. He didn't know whether he was falling in love or just desperately wanted to lie with her, but, without even realising it, he stared at the girl, his eyes drinking in the sight of her as she moved slightly, almost dancing in her seat to the music.

Every now and again she would look at him and grin.

Before too long Stephen had lost track of the time, his mission forgotten, and he found himself singing and dancing with the girl, whose name he still never knew, amongst the other drunken revellers in the Wheatsheaf.

Eventually though, the powerful drink was too much for the Hospitaller and he sat down, his head spinning, nursing the dregs in his mug breathlessly.

"You're worse than my da!" The girl laughed, leaning against him and shouting in his ear over the music. He grinned blearily, enjoying the fleeting touch of her mouth and the feel of her breasts pressing gently on his arm.

He looked at her and she gazed back, her wide green eyes surprisingly alert.

"Come on, I'll help you to your room. You need to go to bed."

Even though he was by now well in his cups, Stephen somehow stopped himself from replying, *Aye, and I need you to come with me.*

His body ached to be closer to her though, as she helped him along the narrow hallway to his guest room.

He never wondered how she knew where his chamber was, and he never noticed the disapproving look Hobb threw the red-head as she escorted the Hospitaller out of the common room.

Stephen was drunk, and, for now, hopelessly besotted; his vow of chastity forgotten once again.

When she closed and bolted the door to his room behind them and, with another bright smile, kissed him, her tongue forcing its way into his mouth, the Hospitaller felt closer to heaven than he ever had killing men in the name of God.

CHAPTER TEN

Robin awoke feeling like he'd barely slept. He worked his neck from side to side with a grimace, hearing the tight muscles pop as he made his way to the stream by their camp to wash his face.

Two of his men – friends – had died yesterday. Tuck was in an unnaturally deep sleep, despite the holy relic. And he desperately missed his wife, Matilda, despite their falling out the last time he'd seen her.

He sighed as he knelt on the grass by the gently bubbling water next to the outlaws' camp-site and threw handfuls of the freezing liquid over his face. He wouldn't let the gloom take him again, he vowed, forcing himself to put his troubles to one side and just enjoy the sights and sounds of the hazy spring morning.

It promised to be a warm one, once the sun climbed high enough to burn away the clouds.

"God give you good morning!" Much wandered over to his friend's side and mimicked his actions, stooping to wash the grit from his eyes with the fresh water of the stream. "Ah, that feels good!" He grinned, wiping his face with his palms, but his own expression fell as he looked at Robin.

Since his father had been murdered by Wakefield's previous bailiff Much hadn't been the joyful young man Robin had known growing up in the village. It wasn't in his nature to channel his emotions into rage and violence, the way Will Scarlet had done for so long.

Instead, Much had drawn into himself, some days barely managing a smile.

Robin felt guilty as he saw the grin on his friend's face disappear.

"What are we like?" the young outlaw leader asked, forcing a laugh. "It wasn't us that were killed by Gisbourne yesterday – we shouldn't be so morose. Come on!"

He stood up, smiling, and dragged Much up with him by the arm.

"The men won't want to do much today after James and Paul were done in by that prick Gisbourne, but I don't want to hang around here feeling down all day. Fancy coming hunting with me? Or fishing?"

Much smiled in return. "Aye, that'd be good. Let's get our stuff and head out."

They made their way back to camp and gathered their weapons, along with food and some ale skins.

"Ho, Robin! Off hunting?"

The outlaw captain turned and, instinctively, felt his heart sink as he saw Matt Groves walking towards him. His annoyance turned to guilt though, as he remembered Matt's ordeal and fortunate escape of the day before, and knew he should have probably been nicer to the man than he'd been at the time.

"Aye, Matt!" he nodded, clapping the older man on the arm. "Me and Much don't fancy spending the day sitting about feeling sorry for ourselves so we're going to do some hunting and fishing."

Groves looked upset, which was most unlike him, and Robin knew the previous day's meeting with Gisbourne had taken its toll on the sullen outlaw.

"You want to come along with us?"

The words were those of a good leader. A man who wanted to do the best for his men. Yet, when they were out, Robin kicked himself. He couldn't fucking stand Matt Groves!

But Matt's face lit up, as if one of the girl's at Nottingham's *Maiden's Head* had offered him a freebie. "Aye, that'd be good! Give me a minute to get my longbow."

He hurried over to his bedroll, as Much rejoined Robin with a questioning frown. Robin simply shrugged and rolled his eyes.

They decided to head southwest, in the direction of Barnsley, hoping to bring down a young deer or at least a few rabbits, before spending some time by the bank of the River Dearne with their ale-skins.

Ah well, Robin mused as they made their way quietly through the undergrowth, the sun just beginning to appear through the clouds and fresh spring foliage. *Maybe me and Matt will be able to put aside our past differences and become friends today...*

Somehow it didn't seem likely, but they were on their way now.

* * *

When the bright sunlight coming through a gap in the curtains woke him Stephen cursed as he realised he'd overslept. His mouth felt dry and his head ached.

As the fog in his brain slowly started to lift and fragments of the previous evening returned to him, he desperately reached under the bed, hoping the innkeeper had place a chamber pot there.

Grasping the filthy metal vessel gratefully he dragged it out and dropped to his knees on the hard floorboards, vomiting copiously.

Spitting the last of the bitter bile from his mouth, gasping, he sat back down on the bed guiltily.

He'd been given an important mission to complete, yet here he was, dawn long since broken, wasting time, while Sir Richard fretted back in Kirklees.

There was no sign of the girl and, when he realised he was still fully clothed he sighed, both with relief and disappointment.

He hadn't broken his vow of chastity then – but she might have been worth it.

Shaking his head ruefully, he collected his belongings, intending to make his way downstairs, down another of those strong local ales and be on his way to Clerkenwell with all haste.

"Shit!" he cursed, as he finally noticed the coin-purse at his belt was gone. "She robbed me!"

He hadn't been carrying much money, but that wasn't the point. Furious and embarrassed at the realisation the girl had played him like a gittern he patted the pocket sewn inside his mantle and his blood ran cold.

She'd taken the letter.

He retched into the stinking chamber-pot again, his mind whirling. Maybe he'd put the letter somewhere last night?

Searching the small area frantically, he roared in frustration and hurried from the room.

It was a small inn, which was just as well, as Stephen couldn't remember making his way from the common-room to his chamber the previous night, but there was only the one narrow corridor leading to the main hall.

His weapons were thankfully still with him, and he placed his left hand on the pommel of his sword as he stormed into the bar, seeing the inn-keeper, Hobb, at one of the tables, eating a large breakfast of bread and cheese.

The man looked up with an obviously guilty expression, but he painted a smile on his round face as the Hospitaller stalked over to him.

"Morning, my lord! You'll be wanting some breakfast eh?" The stout man stood up and made to move towards the bar area. "An ale, perhaps?"

Stephen moved straight for him, grabbing the man by the throat and shoving him backwards until his spine was bent painfully over the bar.

"The girl. Where does she live?"

"The red-head you were with last night? I don't know where she lives!" the inn-keeper gasped in fright. "She's not a regular. I've only seen her in here a couple of times. Please, you're hurting me!"

"I've not even started yet, you lying sack of shit," the sergeant-at-arms growled. "You know who she is. She must have done this before to other guests of yours. Do you get a cut of whatever she steals, eh?" He squeezed Hobb's throat tighter and the man struggled to free himself, but Stephen was a powerful man who knew how to restrain someone.

"It's not like that!" the inn-keeper wheezed. "Please – her man's a maniac. They threatened to burn down my inn if I didn't let them rob people. The girl gets travellers drunk, steals their purse, and then pays me the room's rent for the night. I don't make anything out of it!"

The Hospitaller slowly released the pressure on the man's neck and let him sink to the ground, where he sat, desperately trying to suck in air.

Stephen walked behind the bar and lifted a mug, filling it from one of the ale casks. He downed it in seconds and refilled it, watching Hobb struggle upright onto the chair beside the table he'd been eating his bread and cheese at.

"Here," the Hospitaller placed the ale in front of the panting Hobb, who looked at him suspiciously, then gratefully sipped some of it to ease the burning in his throat.

"How long have they been doing this?"

Hobb lowered his head, clearly ashamed of his small part in the scam. "About two months. They're not from around here. Turned up out of the blue one day, but her man, Jacob, said he was a blacksmith. The village hadn't had a proper smith since old Simon died close to a year ago, so they were welcomed."

He sipped some more of the ale, flinching slightly as Stephen stood up, but the sergeant was simply going to get more ale for himself.

"What about her da?"

The inn-keeper looked puzzled for a moment, then shook his head. "The old man that was with her when you came in? That's not her da, just one of the locals. She sits with whoever she pleases and, to be honest, the old men are happy to have company like that for the evening."

Stephen swallowed his ale with a scowl, rubbing his pounding temples.

"I'm sorry," Hobb mumbled. "You didn't lose much money did you?"

"The money's not the problem. I was carrying a letter and she took it. That letter is, literally, a matter of life and death for my master. So, you can see why I need it back."

The inn-keeper's face paled as he understood what Stephen was saying.

"You can't just go demanding it back, they'll kill you! Then they'll kill me!"

Stephen glared at the cowering man. "They'll have a hard time killing me. As for you, you'd better speak to your village headman, because I *will* get that letter back. Tell me something – why haven't the locals run these bastards out of town?"

"Like I said, the village needs a smith. Besides, they only ever target travellers, not locals, and they never steal their clothes or weapons – generally the men wake up and are so ashamed of what's happened they go on their way without making a fuss."

Stephen checked his weapons and armour were all fitted securely, and drained the last of his ale, fixing Hobb with an icy stare.

"Well, this time they robbed the wrong man."

* * *

As the sun reached its zenith and the three outlaws had only managed to shoot a couple of small brown hares, Much muttered about a wasted morning.

"Ach, stop moaning," Robin laughed at his friend. "Maybe we'll have better luck fishing."

Matt snorted. "We can't go back to camp with nothing but a couple of hares and some fish to show for a day's work. The lads wouldn't let us live it down."

They walked on in gloomy silence for a while longer then Matt spoke quietly, his voice almost reverent. "When I was going to Darton with James and Paul the other day we saw the biggest stag I've ever seen. His horns were the size of a house! Herne himself didn't have horns like that."

Robin shrugged, liking the idea of relaxing by the riverbank with their ale skins better than chasing about the forest, but Much jumped on Matt's comment.

"Where did you see this stag?"

Matt's forehead creased in thought, then he pointed off to the east. "Around Wheatley Wood. Not too far from Darton itself. It saw us though, and buggered off into the trees before any of us could string our bows."

"Let's see if we can find it then. Wheatley Wood must be only a couple of miles from here."

Robin groaned. Walking such a distance, on the off-chance that they might be able to find this great stag, seemed a much poorer choice to him than fishing and drinking by the Dearne. Matt comparing the animal to Herne the Hunter also seemed a bad omen: Robin had become an outlaw at the previous year's May Day games in Wakefield when their new prior had taken offence to the villagers' celebration of pagan times. The churchman's venomous face came back to the young man, glaring around at the villagers.

"Heathens! The lot of you!" the prior had shouted. "Animal sacrifice? Herne the Hunter? Green Men?"

Robin had eventually broken the man's nose when he'd laid hands on Matilda.

The young wolf's head would prefer to forget Herne and his great horns.

But Much and Groves, curse him, had altered course and were now heading for Wheatley Wood. Robin grumpily fell into step behind them.

He knew it had been a bad idea to invite Matt along.

* * *

It wasn't Stephen's style to come up with some elaborate plan. That was the main reason why he'd never been promoted any higher than a sergeant-at-arms within the Hospitallers.

He didn't analyse situations in great detail – he was a doer, not a thinker.

So, while Sir Richard-at-Lee would have found some way to get the smith – Jacob – and his female accomplice on their own, somewhere out of sight, to avoid any trouble, Stephen simply followed Hobb's directions – and the sounds of metal on metal – to the smithy near the outskirts of the village.

There was no sign of the girl, but the bald man with the ginger moustache working the forge was enormous. Standing almost as tall as the outlaw from Barnsdale that people called Little John, the smith's upper body was bare except for a leather apron. Sweat glistened on his hard arm and chest muscles as he worked a set of bellows, and the Hospitaller knew he had to be wary of the big ox.

"You." Stephen strode up to the front of the workshop and fixed the smith with a calm gaze. He rested his left hand on the pommel of his sword, but made no threatening moves. "I don't have the time or inclination to talk about this with you. I want the letter your slut of a wife stole from me."

Jacob's eyes glanced at the villagers working and passing nearby. He didn't look at all frightened by the imposing sergeant-at-arms clad in chain mail in front of his shop, but Stephen guessed his unconscious look around at the locals betrayed his desire to avoid a scene in public. The blacksmith had a good thing going here, and clearly didn't want to jeopardise it.

The big man calmly wiped the sweat from his brow and walked around his forge, removing his apron as he went and tossing it onto his workbench.

Some of the locals had stopped to watch what was happening, muttering to each other with interest. They all knew, or had heard rumours, about the smith and his shameful wife, and the sight of this grizzled soldier coming to take the enormous Jacob to task was something no one wanted to miss. The couple were tolerated because the villagers needed nails made, weapons or tools mended and horses shod, but they weren't liked.

Especially the smith's red-haired wife. The local women hated her for her beauty and flirtatious manner, totally unbecoming in a Christian lady. They also hated her because they could see their husbands eyeing her lustfully every time she walked past.

As the smith walked out of his workshop, meaty hands raised placatingly towards the Hospitaller, a crowd of neighbouring women began to form, clustering in little groups to talk in low voices as they watched the scene with disapproving looks.

They were loving it, Stephen knew. Well, he'd give them something to enjoy if this big bastard didn't hand over the letter and his money.

"My lord" – the smith began as he came closer to the angry sergeant, but Stephen cut him off, pulling his sword from its leather sheath and pointing it towards Jacob's groin as the gossiping women squealed in obvious delight and children ran off to spread the word amongst the rest of the villagers.

"I'm not a lord, and I told you: I don't have time to talk about this. I want that letter back, or I'll" –

"You'll what?" Jacob laughed. "You wanted to share a bed with my wife, Helena, did you?" The crowd gasped in outrage at that, and the smith, apparently enjoying himself raised his voice over the muttering. "Aye, tried to get her drunk and took her back to his room to try and put his seed inside her, this so-called *soldier of God!*"

Stephen hadn't expected things to go like this, and he mentally kicked himself for not thinking things through before he barged in, sword drawn.

"Now he's angry because he got drunk and lost something, and he's turned up here to blame my good wife. Aye, she told me all about it this morning, Hospitaller! She fought you off and made her way home to me, while you must have passed out after all the ale you'd had. You're a disgrace to your Order!"

The men in the crowd muttered angrily, glaring at Stephen. This wasn't going well at all, he realised. The sorceress hadn't just bewitched him last night, she'd bewitched all the men of the village too, and now they were going to take the side of the lying smith!

He looked around warily, watching for signs of an attack, as the blacksmith gave him a smug look and some of the men began to move forward menacingly, no doubt to try and restrain him.

Oh fuck, the Hospitaller thought to himself as he hefted his sword defensively, glancing around to see where the first attack would come from. *This isn't going to go down too well with the Prior. Or Sir Richard.*

"You're a filthy liar, Jacob!"

Stephen's gaze flicked to the left, as an overweight woman shoved her way through the watching crowd, past the surprised men in front of her. She must have been a good-looking girl in her youth, Stephen thought, but she'd lost her figure through time and, no doubt, a few childbirths.

"Everyone in Finchley knows your wife's a whore!"

The smith's face was dark with rage, but he held his silence as more of the local women pushed past their men to stand by their portly leader.

"You tell him, Mary, it's time someone did!" one of the women bellowed, ordering her mortified husband to shut-up as she forced her way through the throng to stand by her neighbour.

"Your wife, Helena, gets travellers so drunk they can barely stand up," Mary shouted indignantly. "Flutters her long eyelashes at them, flashes her tits, and then steals their purses from them when she gets them alone."

The smith, almost foaming at the mouth, spotted Mary's husband in the crowd and shouted at him. "You better shut your wife's mouth, Alfred. I'll not hit a woman, but I've no problem breaking *your* face!"

Stephen found himself grinning as the crowd howled indignantly at the smith's loss of control. Things were definitely swinging back in his favour, he thought.

Jacob looked over at him, furiously, and tensed himself to move forward to attack the sergeant-at-arms, but Mary and her cronies, fuelled by their righteous anger, crowded in on the big smith, pointing their fingers and yelling, feeding on each other's outrage.

The Hospitaller slid his sword back into its sheath as he realised the danger to him had passed. The villagers – thanks to the petty jealousy of a few vocal women – were on his side.

He folded his arms, watching the scene unfold in front of him with satisfaction.

He was surprised a moment later to find himself face-down on the hard earth of the street, the back of his head exploding with pain.

* * *

By the time they reached Wheatley Wood Robin was sweating heavily. For some reason Matt had set a much brisker pace than seemed necessary, but, although he was their leader, Robin was still a proud young man, full of bravado, and didn't like to show any sign of discomfort so he simply matched Matt's hasty stride without complaint.

He was damned if he couldn't keep up with a man more than double his age.

"Christ, I'm sweating like a Templar on Friday the 13th," Much grunted. "Are we nearly there yet, Matt?"

Groves had been looking around constantly for the past while, his eyes looking for landmarks, and he nodded in satisfaction as they finally reached the main road through the forest. "Aye, this is the spot."

Robin wondered at the bright, almost manic stare in the older man's eyes, and then his blood ran cold as a number of armed men appeared from behind the foliage around them.

His eyes were drawn instinctively to the black-armoured, smiling man holding the crossbow. "Gisbourne..!"

"Well met, Hood." Sir Guy bowed with a flourish, never taking his eyes from England's most wanted wolf's head. "This time, I'm afraid you won't be escaping. Drop your weapons."

Much glared at Matt Groves, his face scarlet with rage. "You sold us out you arsehole!"

"Aye, I did," Matt retorted fiercely, turning from Much to fix Robin with an angry glare. "You've brought us nothing but trouble since you appeared, Hood. Lording it over the rest of us as if you were the king, or Hugh Despenser himself! Well, no more, you little prick! Sir Guy here will see you hung like the scum you are, and I get a pardon for my trouble."

"What about the rest of the men?" Much shouted. "How can you betray the men who've been like brothers to you for so long?"

Gisbourne cut in, shaking his head with a bored expression. "Matt here didn't tell us where the rest of your men are hiding. They're not important to me. The king demanded I bring him the head of Robin Hood, and now I have him." He waved his black crossbow towards Robin and Much. "Take them."

As Gisbourne's soldiers moved in Groves took a step back, smiling wickedly.

Much, totally enraged, felt the hurt and tension of the previous year exploding inside him. His right hand dropped to his belt and he whipped his sword from its simple leather sheath.

Time slowed to a crawl for Robin as his childhood friend's face twisted in a feral scowl, teeth bared and eyes bulging as he lunged forward, but Matt, still a dangerous man despite his middle-age, saw the attack coming.

Flicking his own sword out and around in time to deflect the blow, Groves rammed his forehead forward into Much's face, shattering the young man's nose.

Much stumbled backwards, reeling, and Robin heard the click as Gisbourne pulled the trigger on his crossbow. The bolt hammered into Much's chest just as Groves leaned forward, placing his body weight onto his right leg, and shoved the point of his sword into the miller's son's stomach.

Robin screamed. It wasn't a battle cry; it was a mournful sound, as he watched the young man who had been his friend throughout his whole life die in agony.

By the time Robin realised he should fight back, someone had come up behind him and battered the pommel of their sword into the base of his skull, throwing him to the ground, stunned.

The attacker dropped onto his spine, pressing him into the forest floor, as others grasped his arms and legs, holding him fast.

As the dark figure of Sir Guy of Gisbourne approached, Robin felt tears coursing down his face and he struggled to rise. To fight. To kill this bastard people called The *Raven*.

"Leave the dead one for the crows, and bind this one," Gisbourne growled, looking down at the young outlaw with a satisfied smile. "It seems we have a wolf's head to hang."

CHAPTER ELEVEN

For the second time that day, Stephen awoke with a throbbing head and a moan of pain.

His hand moved to the back of his skull and he felt, through the bandage someone had applied, a tender lump half the size of a hen's egg.

"You're lucky she never cracked your skull," someone told him, and he flicked his eyes to the dimly lit corner of the room. "If she'd found a bigger rock you wouldn't be here now. Crazy bitch."

It was the heavy woman from earlier – the loud one – Mary, was it? This must be her house, Stephen realised.

"Where are they?" he growled, swinging his legs over the side of the pallet he'd been lifted onto and getting to his feet somewhat unsteadily.

"Gone." Mary nodded in satisfaction, putting down the threadbare cloak she was mending and leaning forward so the dim light of the cooking fire illuminated her round features. "After that little slut hit you with the rock, we ran the pair of them out of town. The men weren't too happy at losing a blacksmith, but we couldn't have them here any more. They were wicked. Finchley's a God-fearing village, and they were turning the place into a den of sin!"

She filled a cup with ale and handed it to the Hospitaller but he waved it away. "I've had enough of the ale in this place," he muttered. "Do you have any water, lady?"

As she moved to fetch him a drink, he asked where Jacob and his wife had gone. "They have a hugely important letter from my lord," he told her. "I must get it back."

"You could try searching their house," Mary shrugged, pushing the mug of cool water into his hand. "They weren't given much time to collect their belongings – the villagers were in a right fury."

Aye, stirred up by you, Stephen thought to himself, imagining the scene.

"There's a good chance your letter will still be there."

He handed her back the empty cup with a word of thanks and asked her to point him towards the blacksmith's newly-vacated home, shading his eyes from the early afternoon sun as he went. He cursed as he noticed the positions of the shadows, realising he must have been unconscious for an hour or two. He couldn't afford to lose this time – Sir Richard was depending on him, in the name of Christ!

It only took a short time to reach the house, a small, single-storey wooden building with a poorly-thatched roof, where he found a man and a young boy of about nine years old.

"Ah, the good knight," the man smiled apologetically as Stephen walked across. "I'm the headman – Baldwin. This is my son, Geoffrey. I'm truly sorry for the terrible time you've had in our village" –

"Forget it," Stephen interjected. "It was my own fault. I'm here to search for a letter those two stole from me. May I?" He pushed his way inside, eyes scanning the single low room.

"You're welcome to look," Baldwin replied, "but me and the lad have already searched the place and put anything valuable aside for the village. We never saw any letter, did we?" He glanced at the boy, who agreed with his father in a small, high-pitched voice.

The house had few items of furniture, so it only took a few moments for Stephen to be sure his letter wasn't hidden anywhere. He swore colourfully, and the little boy grinned on hearing a new word to tell his friends.

"Which direction did they go?" the sergeant-at-arms asked, his patience now wearing very thin.

"They took the road south, brother knight," the headman pointed vaguely. "I heard the girl saying something about London. A place called Clarkson, or Clarking, I didn't really catch it right."

"Clerkenwell?" Stephen demanded in astonishment, and Baldwin nodded.

"Aye, that was it, I think. You know it?"

One of them must have been able to read. They were taking Sir Richard's letter to the Prior!

Why, though? What could they gain from it?

His blood ran cold as it dawned on him. They were going to make up some story about him – probably say he raped the girl, the blacksmith knocked him out and they found the letter on him. They'd be hoping for a reward.

Stephen knew exactly how believable that red-headed girl could be. The Prior would excommunicate him! And God knows what would happen to Sir Richard.

"I have to stop them!" he roared, racing back to the Wheatsheaf for his horse, calling over his shoulder at the bewildered headman. "Were they on foot?"

"No – they had a good looking palfrey. Just the one mind."

Only one mount between them, but a head-start of at least an hour.

There was no choice though – he *had* to stop them before they reached Clerkenwell!

* * *

Sir Richard took a long pull of his watered wine and gazed out over the battlements at the land around his stronghold.

Stephen had been gone a week – he should, hopefully, be on his way back home with good news from Prior L'Archer. The letter Sir Richard had sent virtually guaranteed the old man would do something to help the commander of Kirklees.

Sir Richard hated to resort to blackmail, but what other choice did he have? He'd kept the prior's secret for ten years, never telling anyone else about it. And he'd take it to his grave too, as long as L'Archer made himself useful and did something to help him.

He took another sip of the wine and heaved an irritated sigh.

"I'm bloody sick of sitting here in this castle by myself," he growled, standing up and striding purposefully down the stairs to the armoury.

The king's men had returned to the castle only once since Stephen had ridden out, and their last visit was four days ago. They had clearly given up on taking the Hospitaller.

Well, he'd had enough of eating tough salted meat and dried fruit. He lifted a hunting bow from its place on the wall, and stuck a few arrows into his belt. A nice young rabbit would make a fine stew with some of the pickled vegetables in his undercroft, which he made his way through now, carrying a torch to light his way.

Making his way past the barrels, sacks, bottles and jars of stored food to the far corner of the cool, dark room he placed the smoky torch in an iron holder on the wall and, rolling a heavy barrel out of the way, found the trapdoor, just big enough for one man to fit through.

A heavy bolt held it locked, so he undid it quickly and lifted the thick wooden door open. He kept the hinges greased with goose-fat so it opened silently and he lifted the torch again, using it to illuminate the pitch-black stairway underneath.

He grinned as he remembered when he first took over the commandery here in Kirklees and his bottler – a local man named Luke – had told him of the existence of this secret passageway out of the castle. At first he had planned on closing it off: filling the tunnel with rubble and sealing the entrances, but he had eventually decided against it. Yes, it compromised the castle's security somewhat – but it would take a battering ram to break through the doors and he knew from past experience an extra escape route might be useful one day.

He had never used it before – he'd never had to. But it was coming in handy now.

He couldn't have simply raised the great iron portcullis and walked out the huge oak front doors. With no way to seal the entrance behind him, and no retainers to guard the place, the king's men – or anyone else passing by – could have simply walked in and taken control of the castle without a fight.

He made his way along the damp, narrow corridor stooping as he went since the ceiling was only as high as his shoulders, until, after a short time, he reached an iron door – again, bolted from the inside.

He undid the crude, but sturdy, locks and pushed the door to, squinting as the bright sunlight flooded the little passageway and the sounds of birds and insects came to him on a gust of fresh air, which he sucked in greedily.

The doorway was well hidden behind a thick clump of gorse and juniper bushes and he shoved his way through the foliage, swatting branches out of the way with his hand and revelling in the sense of freedom.

The thought gave him pause, as he reflected on the fate that awaited him should the king's men capture him. Days, weeks, months in a tiny cell, with only rats and his own shit and piss to keep him company…

"Let them try!" he smiled grimly, touching a hand to the hilt of his sword instinctively, then, looking around and, spotting a pair of little brown hares lounging on the grass he pulled an arrow silently from his quiver and slid his bow into his left hand.

An hour or two, hunting in the sunshine, then he'd return to the castle, cook up a nice, fresh stew and finish the wine he'd started earlier. Only this time he'd not water it down. He might even have a go on the old citole he'd been trying to learn for the past six years.

Praise be to God, he thought. *This would be a good day!*

* * *

As he kicked his heels into his mount, forcing it into a near-gallop, Stephen was thankful he at least knew which direction his quarry must have taken.

South. Towards London and the Grand Prior.

He cursed himself repeatedly as the spring countryside passed, wondering how he could have been stupid enough to allow this to happen.

In truth, he was being too hard on himself. Although not an ugly man – quite the opposite in fact, with his battle-hardened physique and square jaw – he wasn't exactly the magnetic type. Women didn't usually show an interest in him and, despite his vow of celibacy it hurt him when his master, Sir Richard, with his easy smile and outgoing nature drew admiring glances and giggles from girls young enough to be his grand-daughter.

When Helena had shown an interest in him, Stephen had been flattered. And, given her simple beauty, love of life and apparent sincerity, the Hospitaller sergeant had been utterly smitten.

The strong ale hadn't helped matters either.

Still, he derided himself for a fool. She had played him expertly, like that Allan-a-Dale character in Barnsdale played his gittern.

He dug his heels into his mount with an angry cry, pushing it close to its limit, knowing he only had a very short time to catch up with his quarry.

As the afternoon wore on the sun moved slowly around in the sky until it was directly above and before him. The trees that lined the road cast dark shadows directly behind themselves as the outskirts of the capital city slowly came into sight and Stephen, squinting, growled in frustration.

He was almost there yet had seen nothing of the blacksmith and his wife.

The Hospitaller felt his stomach lurch in despair as he realised he had failed his master, and probably ruined his own status within the Order he'd served faithfully for the past fifteen years.

His horse was blowing hard and sweating after being pushed hard for so long, and, with a sob of rage and defeat, Stephen allowed the beast to slow to a walk.

What now?

He wondered if he should turn back. Without Sir Richard's letter, the prior had no reason to send aid to Kirklees. Carrying on to Clerkenwell was pointless.

His head had ached for the past couple of hours, and a feeling of nausea made him want to retch as he squinted at the road ahead, contemplating his failed mission, the sunlight almost blinding him even though it offered little warmth.

"Wait!"

His horse paid him no attention as it trotted along the slightly muddy road, its sides still heaving from the day's run.

Stephen's raised his right hand, shading his eyes from the sunlight as he tried to see ahead.

His sight wasn't what it had been as a younger man, and he blinked as his eyes watered from staring along the road into the harsh sun. Still, there was no mistake.

At the side of the road stood a horse and, as the Hospitaller urged his mount into a canter, the abandoned horse looked at them with a bored expression.

Could it be the blacksmith's own horse had gone lame?

Daring not to hope, Stephen pushed his own mount forward, until, finally, his heart soared in jubilation.

There, casting great shadows along the road in their wake jogged two figures: a huge man and a willowy woman.

The pair must have noticed his approach since they tried to move faster, but the city was still a distance away and the Hospitaller bore down on them like the tide at a full-moon.

He drew his sword and roared as he charged along the road after the fleeing couple, the relief at finally catching up with his prey making him smile in triumph.

The jubilant grin dropped from his face as Helena suddenly turned, her beautiful features cloaked in shadow but her mane of hair flaming from the sunlight directly behind her. She held a bow – not a longbow, but a smaller hunting bow – and, as the sergeant-at-arms bore down on them the girl loosed her arrow.

"No!" Stephen cried in outrage, not just because he saw his plans ruined, again, but for the sake of his faithful horse, which slowed to a halt, Helena's missile stuck deep in its steaming chest.

As its front legs gave way the Hospitaller could see the red-haired girl about to loose again, this time at him, and he hastily unhooked the shield he had strapped to his mount, bringing it up just in time as the next arrow lodged itself in the wood covering his face.

"You fucking bitch!" he screamed, hurling himself from his expiring horse before Helena could shoot again.

The girl shrank away from his fury but Stephen slammed the pommel of his sword into her face, feeling her teeth smash as she was thrown backwards onto the ground.

His eyes flicked to his right, expecting an attack from the blacksmith. Although the battle-fury was upon him, the Hospitaller was an experienced soldier. He knew how to fight multiple enemies – had done so on countless occasions at the side of Sir Richard in England and the with others of his Order in Rhodes.

Jacob, although be was built like a warhorse, had none of Stephen's skill or experience. As he saw his wife battered to the ground the blacksmith roared and swung his big hammer at Stephen as if he was forging a horseshoe.

It was an incredibly powerful blow. If it had connected it would have smashed right through the sergeant's light armour into his ribcage but the Hospitaller saw it coming even before Jacob had fully begun his swing and he stepped lightly to the side, bringing his sword round as the man stumbled past, and hammered the blade viciously into the blacksmith's spine.

There was surprisingly little blood for such a devastating blow, and Jacob only gave a quiet, high-pitched gasp of agony as he collapsed, face-first, onto the road, his great torso jerking spasmodically.

Helena struggled to her feet, her eyes wide with disbelief at the sight of her crippled husband but, as her bloodied face contorted with rage, ready to launch herself at the Hospitaller, Stephen stepped towards her and grasped her around the throat with a gauntleted hand, squeezing hard to choke off her shouts.

"Shut up!" he growled, grasping her right hand as it flailed among her skirts for a weapon. "You brought this on yourself, and I've no more time to fuck about with the pair of you."

She tried to spit in his face but Stephen squeezed tighter and the spittle ran down her own chin as her eyes bulged defiantly at him.

"The letter you took from me," he said. "I want it. Your man's already as good as dead so I can search him for it. But you're still alive," he pressed his face against hers, feeling a surge of shame as he did so, remembering how he had felt so drawn to this sweet-looking girl just a few hours before.

He dropped her to the ground where she lay on her back, panting and staring up at him murderously, but he'd learned his lesson not to underestimate her, and he placed the point of his sword against her breast.

"You won't fool me again. Now where's the letter, Helena?"

"Fuck off, monk."

She stretched flat on the grass and gazed at him, her legs slightly parted, panting with exhaustion and somehow still exuding an air of innocence despite her smashed teeth. But Stephen had taken enough of this.

He leaned down and battered his sword hilt against her temple, watching as her head slumped to the side and she slipped into unconsciousness.

The smith was dead, Stephen could see, as he glanced over at the man face-down in the dirt. He sighed in resignation and methodically began to search the girl's clothes for his missing letter. He felt the beginnings of panic again when he couldn't find it, before he hurried over to Jacob, turned the huge man onto his back and, with nervous fingers, almost tore the giant's clothes apart in his search for the precious parchment.

"God be praised!"

The sergeant-at-arms smiled and exhaled in relief as he pulled the document – now unsealed but otherwise intact – from a pocket in the blacksmith's leather apron.

His mission was saved. All he had to do now was deliver the letter to the Prior in Clerkenwell.

"Ah shit," he growled, looking over at his dead horse. "I'll have to walk the rest of the way."

* * *

Sir Richard had managed to bring down three decent-sized hares before deciding that was enough. When he'd picked the little carcasses clean he could come back through the secret tunnel and catch some more, so it seemed wasteful to shoot anything else.

At first he'd been wary; jumping at the slightest noise, fearful the king's men might sneak up on him, but, after an hour, with the spring sunshine filtering gently through the fresh green foliage and birds and insects going about their business peacefully after the short-lived snowfall yesterday, he started to relax and enjoy the freedom of being outside again.

How did Stephen fare? he wondered. Had his man made it to Clerkenwell safely? Richard knew his sergeant was a hardy fighter, so he was sure Stephen would have made it there safely.

Would the Prior send help though? This was the question that worried the veteran Hospitaller, but he shook the fears from his mind as he contemplated the letter he'd sent to his Order's headquarters.

Years ago – more than two decades ago in fact – before he became Grand Prior of England, Sir Thomas L'Archer had been Turcopolier in Cyprus, while Sir Richard had newly come to the Order, already a husband and father to two boys.

Richard knew, from entertaining travelling Hospitallers at his commandery in Kirklees recently, that L'Archer had become quite senile over the past few years. Indeed, the old man's administrative powers – once the stuff of legend – seemed to have utterly deserted him, and, as a result of the Prior's mismanagement the Order was practically bankrupt in England, despite their growth in the wake of the Templar's demise.

The Thomas L'Archer Sir Richard had known back in Rhodes had been a rather different character though. Far from being senile, he was as sharp as an arrowhead, with an easy smile and an outgoing, friendly way with the locals on the little island.

The sight of a young hart startled the knight from his idle reverie, but it spotted him before he could even think about nocking an arrow to his bow and disappeared silently back into the bushes.

Richard grinned at the sight of the beautiful animal, then he remembered the day he'd found Thomas L'Archer in a…compromising… position back in Cyprus, almost twenty years ago in 1304.

He'd felt like that frightened hart when he blundered into the room and seen the newly promoted Turcopolier, prostrate on the floor, apparently worshipping a stone head. The face was carved with a thick red beard and long hair and it bore a terrible expression which had chilled the new Hospitaller to the bone. He'd mumbled a stunned apology to his superior before closing the door and hurrying from the castle to try and make some sense of what he'd seen, and what he should do about it.

Richard had heard rumours of the rival Order, the Templars, worshipping idols and performing strange rituals, but he'd never expected to find one of his own brethren involved in anything so blasphemous. In the end, Sir Richard had done nothing. He'd never mentioned it to anyone, not even L'Archer, and the Turcopolier had never brought the subject up either.

He liked L'Archer and he was fearful the Order would be irreparably damaged, possibly even destroyed, if something like this became public. Besides, he wasn't even sure exactly what he'd witnessed, he told himself. So, Richard had held his silence on Cyprus, and later while stationed in Rhodes, and been glad of it a few years later when the Templars had been ruined as a result of similar accusations.

Thomas L'Archer was soon promoted even higher in the Order and Sir Richard had found his own fortunes improving as time went on, no doubt thanks to the influence of L'Archer who must have been quietly helping the younger knight in gratitude for his silence.

When L'Archer's close friend, William de Tothale, had been given the position of Grand Prior in England, Sir Richard had been offered the commandery at Kirklees, a place the new prior knew Richard had ties with, his family owning much of the surrounding lands.

Richard had never even considered blackmailing his superior for his own gain – it simply wasn't in his nature, he was far too honourable a man. And he had been rewarded for his silence.

But desperate times called for desperate measures. Without the help of the prior Sir Richard and his faithful sergeant-at-arms would be destitute, jailed, hanged even, while the king would seize the manor and all its lands from the Hospitallers.

That was why Sir Richard had, with a heavy heart, put in writing a threat to Thomas L'Archer: intervene with King Edward or I'll tell everyone your secret.

When Stephen delivered the letter to him, the prior would have no choice but to help. If the story got out the scandal would ruin him and irreparably damage the entire Order.

Sir Richard moved quietly through the trees, heading for the hidden entrance back into the castle, lost in thought. Yes, the prior would help, he was absolutely sure of it.

Or the Hospitallers might suffer the same fate as the Templars before them.

* * *

When Sir Philip of Portsmouth had ordered Edmond and Walter Tanner to remain close to Kirklees in case Sir Richard should try to escape the king's justice they had gladly agreed. Sir Philip was paying well enough, and all they had to do was sit around hiding in the trees close by the castle entrance where they could see who might go in or out. If Sir Richard set foot across the castle door, they were to ride to the village of Kirklees for help in capturing the Hospitaller. King Edward wanted to make a show of the noblemen who had rebelled against him.

Edmond and Walter were brothers and it was obvious to anyone who looked at them. Sons of the tanner in Kirklees and learning the trade themselves, Edmond was older and rather taller, but they shared the same thickset bodies, stumpy limbs and thin brown hair and beards. Walter wasn't the sharpest arrow in the quiver though, and, as children, Edmond had often been forced to defend his sibling from village bullies. Even now, when they went to the local alehouse Walter's dull wit seemed to antagonise drunk people. Fortunately they were both able to handle themselves when it came to it, which was why Sir Philip, when he'd heard of their fighting skills, had left only the pair of them to make sure Sir Richard didn't escape justice.

"Christ, who's that? Is that Sir Richard?"

Walter barely glanced up at his brother's surprised whisper.

"It is! Fuck me, how did he get out here? We've been watching the front door of that castle for days and it hasn't moved!"

"It moved when his sergeant came out," Walter replied innocently.

"Shutup!" Edmond hissed irritably. "You should have woken me up; it's not my fault he escaped!"

In truth, Edmond had slept late the morning Sir Richard's sergeant-at-arms had disappeared along the road to the south. Walter had seen the horseman leaving, but, since he'd been told to watch for Sir Richard, hadn't bothered to waken his hungover brother.

"Never mind him anyway; Sir Philip doesn't have to know about that. We've got more to worry about – look!"

Walter finally turned to follow his older brother's pointing finger and smiled as he saw the figure some way off, moving between the undergrowth, oblivious to their presence.

"Look, it's Sir Richard!"

Edmond grinned and slapped his slower brother on the back. "Aye, it is. And he's alone, with no idea we're here or he wouldn't be out. Hunting, from the look of the game he's carrying."

"We'd better hurry then," Walter muttered, standing up and moving in the direction of the village.

"Wait!" Edmond replied, waving his sibling back.

"We need to hurry," Walter whined. "Or he'll get away, and Sir Philip will be angry with us."

"Sir Philip will be bloody overjoyed when he sees us coming," Edmond grinned, fingering the hilt of his sword. His smile disappeared as he realised his brother didn't understand what he meant. "We'll catch the knight by ourselves! Come on, move quietly, and have your weapon ready."

He moved stealthily into the foliage and headed towards the unwary Hospitaller.

"Edmond, we can't!" Walter hurried behind fretfully, drawing his own poor quality sword silently from its worn old hide sheath. "He's a knight! He knows how to fight. We should go to the village and tell the men to catch him."

"We know how to fight too!" Edmond retorted. "He's alone, and hasn't seen us. We ambush him, take his weapons and lead him to Sir Philip. He'll reward us! Those arseholes in the village won't laugh at us then."

The pair flitted through the trees, making their way to a place Edmond knew would make a fine spot for their ambuscade.

Walter didn't like to argue with his sibling. He knew he wasn't as smart as Edmond, and he knew his big brother always tried to do what was best for them.

He set his jaw and gripped the hilt of his sword firmly. If Edmond said they could take the knight, that's what they were going to do.

They came to a large patch of juniper and Edmond motioned for Walter to hide at the back of it, where the little overgrown path came past. "Wait here. When you see Sir Richard coming, step out with your sword and order him to stop. I'll be over there." He pointed to the thick trunk of an old beech tree. "When you stop him, I'll come up behind and stick the point of my sword into his spine."

Walter grimaced. "Don't kill him, Ed, he's been a good lord to us."

Edmond shook his head and waved his brother behind the bush. "I won't, I'll just let him know he better surrender to us. Now, go!"

The knight was in no hurry, it seemed, and Edmond started to think he'd changed course or even returned to his castle by whichever means he'd exited it. Eventually, though, the sounds of heavy footfalls reached him and he tensed, looking over to make sure Walter couldn't be seen behind the thick branches.

As if he hadn't a care in the world, Sir Richard appeared, whistling gently to himself, and Edmond smiled, the blood coursing through his veins in nervous anticipation.

"Stop!" Walter, small and short of limb as he was, had an imposing glare at times, as if he might go completely, and violently, crazy. He brandished his sword at the stunned knight, who, for a moment wasn't sure how to react.

"Aye!" Edmond slipped out from behind the beech and pressed his sword against Sir Richard's back. "Stop."

The Hospitaller vaguely recognized the small man in front of him from the village. The tanner's son: a nice lad, if a little touched. "What do you men want?" he demanded. "You realize I could cut you both down in seconds if I choose?"

Walter looked nervously over his shoulder, as if he wanted to run away, but Edmond confidently pressed the point of his blade harder into the gambeson Sir Richard wore.

"Shut up. One move and I gut you like were planning on doing to those rabbits at your belt."

As he finished speaking, Edmond was surprised to find himself on the grass, his nose bloody and the point of a sword at his throat.

The Hospitaller had moved with incredible speed, drawing his blade as he spun through one hundred and eighty degrees and hammering the pommel into Edmond's face before the young villager could react. Edmond had under-estimated the knight, and yet, the knight had under-estimated Walter.

The little man had reacted instantly as he saw the attack on his beloved big brother, rushing forward and swinging his blade with terrible force at the veteran Crusader.

Sir Richard saw the attack just in time. He brought his own sword up, pushing Walter's weapon to the side and, instinctively, reversed his swing and dragged the blade across the inside of the man's thigh.

A killing cut.

It severed the artery, and as blood bubbled from the wound Walter collapsed on the grass in shock, staring at his brother, too surprised to even try to hold the wound shut.

Sir Richard watched the lad fall, horrified, as, unbidden, the memory of his own son's killing less than a year earlier flashed through his mind.

Then there was a scream – a scream of anguish like he'd never heard before, and the world went black.

CHAPTER TWELVE

"Wake up, you bastard!"

Sir Richard felt as if he was drowning, somehow trapped underwater, and his mind tried desperately to reach the surface again.

"Get up!"

He heard the voice again, clearer now, and he felt his arm being kicked roughly but he was too dazed to react.

As his eyes opened, he saw Edmond glaring down at him, his grubby face tracked with white streaks where tears had wiped away some of the grime.

The young man bent down and tried to haul the Hospitaller to his feet, but Sir Richard was too heavy, and, with an anguished sob, Edmond let him drop, aiming a half-hearted kick at his arm again, before sitting on the grass himself.

"You killed Walter."

The young man was staring straight ahead, seeing nothing, and Sir Richard knew he should strike the boy down while he had the chance, but he was too weak. The back of his head ached, and he realised Edmond must have given him a lump the size of an egg with the pommel of that cheap sword. He was lucky if his skull wasn't cracked.

Groaning, Sir Richard rolled onto all-fours and tried to sit up, retching as his fingers gently probed the back of his aching head. "You and your brother were taking me to my death – can you blame me for defending myself?"

Edmond didn't reply as his eyes turned to look at his brother's corpse which lay in patch of crimson grass and shook his head mournfully.

Sir Richard's fingers flexed tentatively as he noticed Edmond hadn't disarmed him – his sword lay beside him, within easy reach.

The younger man noticed the Hospitaller's body language and jumped back to his feet with a snarl, pointing his blade at Sir Richard's face. "Get up you old bastard, get up! You won't get away with murdering my little brother – I'm taking you to Sir Philip. I'm going to watch you hang!"

As Sir Richard shakily rose to his feet Edmond moved in and lifted the finely crafted Hospitaller sword, tossing his own inferior weapon into the bushes. He hefted the expensive weapon appreciatively, and placed it against the knight's cheek.

"I know you have a dagger about you somewhere – give me it."

Knowing it was pointless to deny the presence of his second blade, Sir Richard slowly removed the short dagger from the leather sheath on his belt and handed it to the volatile bounty-hunter who tucked it into the frayed old rope he wore as a belt himself.

"Right. Move."

Edmond gestured with his sword, east, in the direction of Pontefract, and Sir Richard groggily moved forward.

The younger man's eyes fixed again on the body of his brother and it was clear he didn't really know what to do. Should he leave Walter lying here, where foxes and crows would come to tear the eyeballs and flesh to pieces? What about the last rites?

With another tortured sob, Edmond punched Sir Richard in the small of the back, shouting at him to move as the old knight staggered forward in pain. There was nothing else to do – they couldn't bury Walter and there was no way to carry him.

"Get on with you, Hospitaller! I'll see you to Pontefract, then come back to take care of Walter." His voice broke as he finished and he kicked Sir Richard in the backside angrily.

They moved along the overgrown trail in silence, the knight slowly coming back to full consciousness, knowing his grieving captor would, eventually, let his guard down.

And then Sir Richard would get away. Because Edmond didn't know about the other little dagger concealed in his boot.

* * *

"He's awake!"

When he saw Friar Tuck's eyes flutter open, the grin on Little John's face was so wide it threatened to swallow his beard.

"Tuck's awake!" he shouted again as the rest of the men ran over to join him.

The friar groaned weakly as he tried to focus on the figures around him. "Gisbourne shot me," he muttered. "Then I drowned. I must have died twice…If this is heaven, there's a hell of a lot of ugly men up here."

The outlaws bellowed with laughter at the joke, not because it was very funny, but because they were all relieved and overjoyed to see the cheery clergyman back in the land of the living.

"What happened?" Tuck asked, as John knelt beside him.

"You're right, Gisbourne shot you and you fell in the River Don. But Gareth here jumped in and hauled you out. He's a hero!" John grabbed the young man by the arm and pulled him down beside them.

"Really? A skinny lad like you managed to pull a fat friar like me out of that?"

Gareth nodded, embarrassed again by the attention. "Not so fat now though, Tuck," he replied, eyeing the clergyman's shrunken waistline. "You've been unconscious for a few days."

Tuck nodded slightly. "I feel as weak as a newborn babe."

"Here." Allan-a-Dale hurried over carrying a bowl of venison stew, as John and Gareth helped Tuck sit up. Allan lifted the bowl to the friar's lips, feeding him small sips while John finished the story of his rescue and miraculous recovery.

"Praise be to St Peter," he whispered, closing his eyes with exhaustion as Allan wiped spilled stew from his face like a wet-nurse. "May I see this relic of his?"

"It's right here," John nodded, lifting the ornate little reliquary from the ground where he'd placed it as Tuck sat up to eat. "Been sitting on your chest for a while now. Looks like it works, just as Father Nicholas said it would."

As the giant outlaw lifted the box for Tuck to see, the friar's eyes narrowed for a moment as he studied the meticulous carvings and obviously superior workmanship.

"Christ our Lord," he breathed, and the men grunted agreement.

"Give it to me," Tuck gasped, opening his palm, his eyes fixed on the reliquary.

"Fancy eh?" Will grinned as Little John placed the box onto Tuck's hand. "Shame none of us could figure out how it opens" –

Scarlet stopped, open-mouthed, as the friar moved his fingers and the reliquary sprung open.

"Here, that's not St Peter's finger!" Will exclaimed.

"No, it's not," Tuck agreed, still staring at the relic. "It's hairs from Our Lord Christ's beard. I don't know how it ended up in Brandesburton, but this little box is the reason I'm an outlaw!"

* * *

"We're going to hang you, wolf's head."

Robin glared at Gisbourne's sergeant, Nicholas Barnwell, as the man threw him a malevolent gap-toothed grin. "Ever seen someone hang? I bet you have – you know what it does to you. You'll shit yourself like a babe, while everyone watches."

Robin held his peace. They had bound his hands behind his back and he was still in shock at the death of his childhood friend. That wasn't the only thing that kept him silent though.

He felt ashamed to admit it, but he *was* frightened. Barnwell was right – he had seen men and women hanged before. It was a humiliating and often slow death, if the hangman didn't lean on the person to ease their suffering.

Besides that, the face of Matilda haunted him. She carried his child. His life had come to nothing, and now Gisbourne would end it like he ended Much.

Yes, he was frightened. But he straightened his back and pushed out his chest, towering over the men leading him to the jail in Nottingham.

Barnwell noticed and threw him another spiteful grin.

"You won't feel so big when we get you to the castle, boy. Sir Guy will probably use you as a sparring partner before your trial. He'll tear you to shreds."

"Why don't I spar with you right now, you ugly old bastard?" Robin finally found his voice but his captor just laughed and rode ahead to join his captain at the front of the group, leaving Robin to be dragged along by a couple of footmen.

They didn't reach Nottingham until the next day and, when they arrived at the Cow Bar gatehouse a crowd was there to welcome them. Gisbourne had sent one of his men ahead to spread the word – the Raven had captured Robin Hood!

The news spread like wildfire. Robin and his men were heroes to the common people who hoped this rumour proved to be false. Hundreds of them had gathered at the gates, held back by the guardsmen who threw angry glances at Gisbourne as he rode into the city like a conquering hero, oblivious to the trouble that might arise from this.

Sir Henry de Faucumberg appeared, with a couple of dozen guards to the relief of the gatemen, although, if things really turned ugly they were still badly outnumbered. The sheriff nodded to Gisbourne as his party made their way into the city, but de Faucumberg walked past and entered the gatehouse, appearing moments later on the battlements, looking down on the gathered throng.

"People of Nottingham," he cried. "Hear me!"

His voice was mostly lost in the clamour, but some folk noticed the sheriff and pointed him out to those around them, until, eventually, an uneasy silence descended and the people waited to hear what he had to say.

"For months now, the forests around our city have been plagued by outlaws. By wolf's heads who rob, rape and murder innocent travellers – even men of God!" He hurried on before anyone could shout a smart reply. "Now, my men have captured the leader of those vicious felons – Robin Hood! Not only an outlaw, but a rebel as well: the King himself demanded I bring him to justice. And now…I have!"

He raised his hands in triumph, and the city guardsmen cheered half-heartedly. Gisbourne was furious at the sheriff taking the credit for capturing Hood, and he vowed to have words with de Faucumberg later on. For now though, as the crowd stood watching their sheriff to see if he would say anything else, Gisbourne waved his men on, towards the castle, moving to drag Robin along in their wake.

"Sir Guy!" the sheriff shouted down, beckoning the furious king's man to climb the stairs. "Bring the wolf's head up here, so the people can see him!"

The sight of the walls made Robin want to retch, and he felt panic welling up inside him as he was shoved inside the gatehouse and made to climb the stairs. He was used to the freedom of the greenwood – the thought of being encased in a gloomy stone prison, surrounded by walls like these – was almost too much for him to bear.

As they came up onto the battlements Barnwell saw Robin's hunted expression and read his thoughts. He caught the young man's eye and, with another malicious smile nodded a little way to the north, on the road to York.

Robin tried to spit at Gisbourne's grinning lackey, but his throat was dry and what little spittle he could produce dribbled embarrassingly down his own chin as he followed the man's gaze.

His stomach lurched and his tired legs almost gave way when he saw what Barnwell was looking at.

On a hill, dominating the skyline, stood an enormous wooden frame almost four metres tall. Two corpses could just be seen, hanging suspended from the sinister construction while tiny black specks – crows no doubt – wheeled in the sky overhead, taking turns to fly down and peck at the eyes and soft flesh of the dead felons. The sight of the structure was all the more ominous surrounded as it was by gently rolling fields and a couple of picturesque windmills.

The gallows.

"Take a good look, wolf's head," Barnwell grinned. "There lies your doom."

* * *

He was half-dragged, half-led down to the dungeon by a couple of the sheriff's men. Robin felt claustrophobic cooped up within the cold stone walls which grew even colder as they moved underground.

Criminals stared out at them through thick iron gates. Some shrank back as the guard's torch lit the gloom; others proclaimed their innocence, begging to be released. Robin's felt his heart wrench as one pitiful man sobbed unashamedly, asking to see his family again before he was hanged the next day.

The guards ignored the cries, leading the tired outlaw to his own cell which lay at the far end of the corridor. As he was shoved in, one of them battered the back of his head with his pole-arm. "That's for the good soldiers you and your mates have killed in Barnsdale, you piece of filth. Some of them were my friends."

Robin dropped to his knees, clutching his skull in agony as the gate was pulled shut and locked with a loud, final click. The guards left, taking the torch with them, and bolting the massive oak door at the end of the corridor at their backs, and complete darkness filled the freezing dungeon.

Stumbling into a corner, Robin sat with his back against the wall, his eyes trying unsuccessfully to adjust to the inky blackness, as the other prisoners cried out in anger, fear or madness.

His eyes welled up, but he angrily wiped them, not giving in to the self-pity that threatened to overwhelm him and he remembered Tuck's words from not so long ago: *"Never give up hope!"*

He clenched his fists and forced a smile into the oppressive darkness. It would take more than this to break Robin Hood.

It might have been minutes later, it might have been hours, Robin couldn't tell, but the door at the far end of the corridor creaked open and the dim orange glow from a smoky torch made its way along until it was outside his cell.

The outlaw stared at Gisbourne's sergeant, who had his usual wicked smile on his scarred face.

"Get up, Hood. Sir Guy feels like a little sparring practice before he has his supper."

Slowly, knowing he had no choice, Robin stood up and walked to the cell gate which was unlocked by the same guard who had battered his head earlier. "Supper eh? What are we having?"

Barnwell roared with laughter at that. "Good lad! Let's go then."

They made their way back up to the courtyard of the castle, where the captive drank in the fresh air and the early evening sunshine. He'd only been in his cell for a short time; he wondered how he would feel seeing the sky again if he was locked up for even longer next time.

"Ah, the famous wolf's head himself!"

Gisbourne stood, stripped to the waist despite the cold, his slim, yet wiry body heaving from exertion. He had been practising his combat moves, watched from a large open window by some of the giggling women of the castle.

"I've heard all sorts of stories about you, boy," Gisbourne said, lifting a pair of wooden swords and throwing one to Robin which he failed to catch. His face burned as the girls above laughed mockingly and he stooped to retrieve the weapon.

"They say you can fight three men at the same time and kill them all without breaking a sweat. They say you defeated a Templar and cut off his manhood. They say" – he fixed Robin with a piercing gaze and took up a defensive posture – "that you can't be beaten."

Robin smiled, spreading his hands wide. "The people exaggerate. How about a wager though – if I beat you, I go free?"

Gisbourne spat on the hard ground, angry at the outlaw's apparent self-confidence. "You won't beat me. Now...let's see for ourselves how well you fight."

Barnwell and the guardsman moved away, and Robin flexed his muscles which were stiff from his incarceration. The back of his head still ached – there was a lump the size of half a pigeon's egg there now – and he felt exhausted. Drained by Much's murder and his capture.

Gisbourne could see all this reflected in his young opponent's blue eyes now, and he darted forward aiming a blow at Robin's shoulder.

Instinctively, the outlaw brought up his own wooden sword and, with a crack that echoed around the stone walls surrounding the courtyard, the two blades met.

Gisbourne grinned and hooked his foot behind Robin's, dragging the younger man's leg out from under him.

The women screamed in delight as he crashed to the floor, the breath knocked out of him, and Gisbourne danced back gracefully.

"Get up, scum!" One of the women was louder than the rest, and her eyes flashed in delight at the promise of more violence.

Robin got to his feet and warded off another of Gisbourne's blows, this time using his own greater bulk to lean into the lawman's attack and force him stumbling backwards.

Wanting to finish this as soon as possible, the outlaw moved after his foe, raining blow after blow on him. Gisbourne somehow parried them all, and as Robin moved to take another swing the Raven unexpectedly jumped forward, smashing his forehead into Robin's face.

Again, the women cheered and hollered, almost in a frenzy as the outlaw collapsed on the ground, blood dripping from his broken nose. Gisbourne laughed and kicked Robin in the ribs.

"Take him away. It seems the tales of Robin Hood's fighting prowess have been wildly exaggerated."

As he was dragged by the arms back down to the dungeon, the mocking laughter and catcalls of the noblewomen ringing in his ears, Robin felt despair again, this time like an evil black wave that washed over him, filling his soul. Drowning him.

When he was thrown into his freezing cell again he curled into a ball and wept.

* * *

"Where's Robin anyway?"

It had taken a couple of days, but Tuck was just about able to sit up now and, as Will handed him another steaming bowl of spring vegetable soup, he asked the question all the outlaws had been asking.

"We don't know," Will admitted. "Him, Much and Matt went off a couple of days ago, hunting. We haven't seen any of them since."

Tuck's eyes grew wide. "You've looked for them surely?"

"Of course we have! The problem is, Robin said they weren't going far, then planned on finishing the day fishing and drinking. We've searched all around but can't find any trace and – well, Barnsdale's a big place. They could be anywhere."

Tuck tipped the rest of his soup into his mouth and sighed. "Funny they took Matt with them."

Will shrugged and explained how Matt had escaped from Sir Guy of Gisbourne while Paul and James hadn't been so lucky.

Tuck shook his head and tried to stand up, but his legs were still shaky and he slumped backwards onto the pallet, head spinning so badly he almost threw up.

"Where? Where did Gisbourne kill Paul and James?"

Will spread his hands wide, his eyebrows drawn in consternation. "I don't know – somewhere close to Darton. That's where they'd been visiting that day, trying to buy rope."

"You must send some of the lads to look close to Darton then!" Tuck gasped, exhausted even after his moment of exercise.

"John! Arthur! Come here!"

The two men hurried over at Will's shout, worried something was wrong with Tuck, but the friar explained his fears to them.

"Matt conveniently escapes from Gisbourne and his men," he breathed, resting his arm on his forehead, "then the next day he goes on a hunting trip with Robin? We all know they can't stand the sight of each other."

John and Will exchanged glances, understanding better than anyone that Robin had come close on a couple of occasions to casting Groves out of their group, or even killing the obnoxious older man. Arthur just looked baffled.

"None of you thought that odd?" Tuck demanded, incredulous.

"Well, no, not really." Little John looked at the ground, like a little boy being scolded by his father. "Matt seemed upset by what had happened to James and especially Paul – they were close in age. I thought Robin and Much just took him along with them because they felt sorry for him."

"Aye," Will agreed. "You know what Robin's like. Always tries to be the good leader – the better man. If Matt had asked me to go hunting with him I'd have told him to fuck off, but Robin's not like the rest of us."

Tuck recognised the truth of what they were saying, and he lay his head back down on the pallet, somewhat mollified.

"Well," he went on, his eyes closed as he fought the damnable exhaustion that had plagued his few waking moments for the past two days, "it seems to me, Matt was hired by Gisbourne to lead Robin into an ambush. It wouldn't have taken a lot for the bastard to betray Robin, would it? And the simplest place for them to take him would be wherever they'd met the previous day. So…"

He opened one eye and glared at the three outlaws. "What are you waiting for? Go and find Robin and Much!"

* * *

Will felt they were wasting valuable time travelling to Darton to hunt for their missing friends, but Little John knew there was no choice.

"We don't know if Tuck's idea is right," the giant outlaw grunted as they raced through the greenwood. "For all we know they were injured by a stag or something and are lying waiting for us to find them."

"A stag?" Will laughed in disbelief.

"Now you mention it, I heard Matt saying something about seeing a big stag on his way back from Darton, before Gisbourne caught them." Arthur nodded agreement as he pushed past a small clump of gorse, pollen from the bright yellow flowers staining his brown breeches.

"There you are," John nodded at Will. "We can't just go chasing off to Nottingham expecting to find Robin and Much have been captured and taken there. Not until we check out Tuck's guess about what happened."

"What will we do if they *have* been taken to the sheriff?" Arthur wondered.

Neither Little John or Will Scarlet could offer a reply. If Robin and Much had been taken to Nottingham they were as good as dead. It was as simple as that.

A few outlaws weren't enough to storm the castle, which sat on a hill inside the city walls, and mount a successful rescue.

Little John lengthened his already enormous stride, praying his friends were safe somewhere, while Will and Arthur fell silent, conserving their breath for running behind their big friend.

"Trust in Robin," John growled, his eyes fixed straight ahead as he ran. "A Raven is no match for a Wolf."

* * *

"It hurts!"

Matilda's mother, Mary, grasped her daughter's hand, and nodded sympathetically. "I know, but it'll all be worth it, I promise you."

Matilda's baby was going to be a handful, Mary could see. The child kicked her daughter relentlessly through the nights, so hard you could see the little feet pushing against Matilda's belly.

Mary didn't think the pain could be that bad, but she knew the constant movement inside you made it impossible to sleep properly and Matilda was exhausted now.

First had been the morning sickness, which had lasted for weeks, and now this. Matilda often told her parents she wished she'd never let Robin get her into this state, but they knew those feelings would pass once the babe was born.

Didn't all women feel the same during pregnancy, Mary wondered?

Still, for all her wisdom, Mary – and her husband, Henry – didn't know how to react when their daughter cursed Robin Hood. On hearing her anguished cries during the night they instinctively, inwardly, agreed with Matilda in wishing the wolf's head had picked another young girl from Wakefield to fall in love with. And yet, both Mary and Henry knew Robin was a good man who would like nothing better than to be here to comfort his pregnant wife.

"I'd have been better letting that bastard Woolemonger lie with me," Matilda grunted, doubling over on the bed. "At least he wasn't an outlaw!"

Mary glared at her husband, warning him not to respond to that. Simon Woolemonger had been killed by John Little the previous year after he'd tried to assault Matilda then informed on her to the old bailiff which had led to her being arrested. Woolemonger was scum, and Mary knew Matilda didn't mean what she was saying.

"Hush, child," she whispered to her daughter, gripping her hand tightly as Henry looked on, bewildered, as men always did when it came to situations like this. "Robin will be pardoned one day, and the three of you can be a family."

Matilda grimaced as the baby kicked again, hard, and Mary shook her head, wishing she could do more to ease her girl's pain. She knew Robin and Matilda were meant to be with each other and yet...sometimes, as a parent, she did wish her daughter hadn't fallen in love with a wolf's head.

He was probably having a great time hiding away in Barnsdale just now, she thought, looking down at Matilda's tired, pale features. He'd be drinking ale and singing songs with his friends while her daughter – his wife – tried to deal with the child growing inside her.

Men. They thought they knew about pain, but they had no idea!

CHAPTER THIRTEEN

"Even if they were ambushed and are lying injured or..." Arthur couldn't finish the sentence. "Well, they could be anywhere! We can't search the whole forest."

They'd almost reached Darton and had still seen no sign of Robin, Much or Matt.

John knew his young companion was right, but they had to keep looking.

"Why don't we go to the village and find someone with a good dog?" Will suggested, and the other two nodded agreement.

"Aye, good idea," John replied as they barrelled through a cluster of bracken that had grown right over the path. "A dog will" –

The three outlaws stopped in their tracks, staring in shock at the ground just a short distance ahead, then they broke into a run.

"It's Much!"

It was instantly obvious their friend was dead. If the terrible wound in his stomach wasn't enough, the crossbow bolt embedded deep in his chest and the blank stare in his eyes confirmed it.

"No!" Little John's anguished cry was swallowed by the trees as he knelt by the body, placing a big hand almost tenderly on the unmoving chest. "Not Much...he was a good lad – not like the rest of us!"

"That bastard, Gisbourne!" Will shouted, his eyes transfixed by the black crossbow bolt protruding from Much, voice cracking with anger and despair. "He's destroying us, one by one!"

Arthur stood at the side quietly, numb with shock, but his eyes scanned the thick trees and bushes around them.

"Where's Robin and Matt?" he mumbled.

Scarlet was lost in a world of his own, consumed by rage and grief, but John realised they could be in danger and he stood up, grabbing Will by the shoulders.

"They've taken Robin – probably to hang him. We have to take Much back to Wakefield and give him a proper burial."

"He's dead!" Will roared. "We can't do anything for him – we need to find that bastard Gisbourne and help Robin!"

John could feel Scarlet's anger as he held him by the shoulders, but he stared down, deep into Will's eyes in determination.

"They've taken Robin, probably to Nottingham for a show trial. We can't just chase after them – three of us! On foot! We take Much home, and then we talk to the rest of the lads and decide what to do."

Will glared up at the big bearded giant, but the sense of it finally penetrated his fury and he nodded, leaning down and lifting Much's arms. "Fine – one of you grab his legs then and let's move. Quickly now!"

They were all tired after their journey here, but their anger spurred them on as they made their way back towards their camp with their dead friend, taking turns to relieve one another – especially the much slighter Arthur.

"Don't despair lads," John growled, gazing at his two companions. "Robin is still alive, maybe in a dungeon somewhere, but still alive until they can make a show of him."

Arthur didn't reply, his whole body aching from carrying Much's corpse, but Will spat on the thick undergrowth beside them.

"I owe Robin for what he did, saving Beth," he muttered, to himself as much as anyone else, remembering the previous year when Robin and Allan-a-Dale had posed as minstrels to sneak into the manor house where his little daughter was being held as a servant and rescued her. "If he's in a dungeon, I'll kill myself trying to get him out. 'The Raven'," he spat the epithet in disgust, "better watch his fucking back! As soon as we've taken Much home, I'm going to Nottingham."

* * *

"How's your father?"

"Eh?" Edmond had been staring at the road ahead, but now he turned, casting a venomous look on his noble captive.

"Your father – the tanner?" Sir Richard asked again.

"None of your fucking business," Edmond spat. "You don't know him, so what do you care?"

"On the contrary," the Hospitaller replied. "Your father has been making harnesses for my horses for years. I remember you and your brother running around outside his shop as children…"

Edmond's eyes became damp again, but his throat tightened and, when he tried, he couldn't tell the knight to shut up.

"I am truly sorry for Walter." Sir Richard's voice was calm, and the sincerity in his words was obvious from his resigned tone and the look of sadness on his face. "My own boy was taken from me not long ago…I'm getting too old…seen too much death. I'm sick of it."

The tears spilled from Edmond's eyes at the thought of his beloved brother – who'd never had a real chance in life from the day he was born – lying dead and unburied miles back along the path as he shepherded their old lord to his death.

Edmond knew, deep down, his brother's blood was on *his* hands. He had been the one who wanted to capture Sir Richard, even though the Hospitaller had been a good lord to the people of Kirklees.

Edmond had been the one who'd wanted to make a name for himself by capturing a rebel.

As he thought of his brother's body lying cold and dead in the undergrowth he wondered if Sir Richard had been worth it, especially since their father had died not too long ago and Edmond was now all alone in the world.

"Shut up you bastard!" he screamed, kicking the knight in the back through his tears, almost sending the big man falling to the ground.

"You're going to hang!"

* * *

"What are we going to do?" Will Scarlet furiously repeated Allan-a-Dale's question. "I don't know what anyone else is doing, but I'm going to Nottingham to find Robin!"

"Peace, Will." Friar Tuck raised his hand, shaking his head in resignation. "This is no time to be haring off in a blind rage. We'll have to think about it."

"What is there to think about?" Will demanded. "We know Gisbourne's taken him to the castle and plans on hanging him. Sitting here planning isn't going to do anything – no plan in the world's going to make this easy."

Tuck made to reply, but Little John clapped a meaty hand on Scarlet's shoulder. "I agree with Will," he rumbled, bringing a look of surprise from the weak friar. "We don't have time to mess about, trying to think up a clever plan. Besides, Robin's the one for that, and he's not here."

Tuck closed his mouth and nodded for John to continue as the rest of the outlaws gathered round, wondering where this would lead.

"All we can do is be direct," the massive outlaw asserted. "We have to get into the castle, kill or otherwise incapacitate the guards, and somehow get out of the city with Robin."

"Is that all?" Allan snorted sarcastically. "Piece of piss."

"We can't all go," Gareth said. "They'd spot us straight away, especially you," he nodded at Little John. "Not many people in Nottingham are as big as you. Probably no one!"

"Maybe we could disguise him as a dancing bear," Allan grunted, nodding at John. "Wouldn't take much disguising."

No one laughed and Allan fell silent, embarrassed to have made the silly joke at such a stressful time.

"I'll go in myself," Will stood up, patting his weapons instinctively to make sure they were all in place. "One man has a better chance than all of us together. I'll find a way to get inside and free him."

"Wait." All eyes turned to Tuck again as he swung his legs off his pallet and shakily got to his feet. "I'm coming with you."

"Don't be bloody stupid," John shook his head in disbelief. "You're too weak. How will you be any use?"

"I'm not that weak," the friar retorted. "The journey south will build my muscles back up and I'll be able to help Will get into the city if nothing else. Remember, everyone – including the sheriff's men and Gisbourne – think I'm dead. And thanks to this" – he rubbed the short bushy beard that had grown on his face while he was unconscious – "they'll never recognise me anyway."

Will agreed. "He has a point, John."

"This is insane," the giant grumbled. "The only exercise you've had in the past few days is the odd wander around the camp. How are you going to walk to Nottingham? You might have lost some weight, but you're still too fat for Will to carry all the way there!"

"I'll go on ahead to Royston," Gareth volunteered. "I'll buy a horse and bring it back. You," he nodded at Tuck and Will, "can meet me on the way."

"Perfect," the friar smiled at the young lad appreciatively. "I can alternate between walking and riding. I've got my appetite back, so by the time we reach the city I'll be my old self again."

"All right then," Will began packing some food and drink for himself and Tuck. "Take five pounds from the common fund to pay for the horse and head off to Royston. We'll meet you on the road."

Gareth nodded and headed over to the big wooden chest where the outlaws stored their money as Tuck got himself ready for the journey.

"Here," Little John tossed his great quarterstaff to the friar. "You can use that to steady yourself until you get stronger."

"Thank you," Tuck replied with a grateful smile. "But it's much too big for me – it'd make me stand out and that's exactly what we have to avoid. I'll take my own staff."

Gareth gave a wave and raced off into the trees, his spindly limbs allowing him to move much faster than any of the other outlaws. Will and Tuck clasped arms with the rest of the men who wished them luck and promised to pray for the success of their mission.

John wished desperately he could go along with them, and he unashamedly grabbed Scarlet in a great bear-hug as they said their farewells.

"Be careful, Will. The most important thing is that you, Tuck and Robin make it back here alive. Don't go looking for revenge for Much. We can deal with that another day."

Will nodded at his big friend. "Don't worry, I'm not an idiot... If I get the chance though – I'll run that bastard Gisbourne through."

John smiled as Friar Tuck, swigging from his ale skin and cramming bread into his mouth in a ridiculous attempt to regain his former strength, shouted for Will to get moving.

"Just make sure you come back to us in one piece, Scarlet, you moaning faced bastard."

* * *

Gareth was true to his word, meeting Will and Tuck on the road to Nottingham with a tired-looking horse.

"Christ, we've got enough money – you could have got us something a bit stronger looking," Will grumbled, but Tuck laughed and patted the young man on the shoulder.

"You did well, lad. If we turned up at the city gates riding a great charger we'd stick out a mile." The smiling friar stood by the horse, stroking its mane gently. "This fellow will do us just fine, I'm sure."

Scarlet gave a grunt and they waved Gareth off as he hurried back through the trees to the campsite.

"Help me up." Tuck laid a hand on the saddle and gestured for his companion to give him a shove.

Once mounted, they set off at a faster pace than they'd been able to manage with the weakened Tuck on foot. All being well, they would reach Nottingham within a couple of days.

"Maybe I should have thought this through a bit better," Will muttered, a rueful smile on his round face. "The guards might recognise me at the gates, or in the city."

"My body might have lost some of its vigour while I was out of it," Tuck replied, reaching for the pack he carried and pulling something from it. "My mind, thankfully, still works fine. Here."

He threw the object at Will, who caught it and opened it out with a grin. It was a grey robe, the same as the one Tuck was wearing. "My spare clothes," the Franciscan nodded. "Try not to lose it or get too much blood on it."

"You're a genius, Tuck!" Will threw the robe on over his head and pulled the hood up, his face instantly becoming lost in shadow. It was an ideal disguise.

"True," the friar agreed with a nod. "I deserve something as a reward." Reaching into his pack again he pulled out some strips of salted beef and grunted in satisfaction as he began chewing.

"Aye," Will agreed grimly. "Reward yourself as much as you can – you're going to need your strength back when we try to get Robin out of the city..."

They made good time and reached Nottingham just before nightfall the next day, when the sun was low in the sky. The air was cold with a light rain and a gentle wind making it feel even cooler, while the fading light cast long shadows on the road behind the two travellers as they approached the city's northern gatehouse.

They had made good use of their time on the road, thinking of a back-story for Will. The former mercenary had fought in the Holy Land with French armies as well as English, and picked up a little of the foreign tongue there.

"You can pretend to be a visiting French friar," Tuck told him. "The guards won't be able to understand what you're saying anyway. And if you throw in the odd Latin phrase it'll fool them long enough for us to get past and into the city."

Will nodded. "We'll find an inn near the castle and see if the local gossips know anything about Robin."

"You two – halt!" A loud voice boomed at them from above and Tuck looked up to see the guard, while Will kept his head down and under his hood in case the setting sun showed his face too clearly.

"It's late. What do you want?"

"We're travelling friars, my son," Tuck shouted back in a voice almost as powerful as the guardsman's, and Scarlet smiled. It seemed his weak companion was indeed growing stronger after his recent ordeal. "We seek to spend the night in your city, before we set off on the morrow to Canterbury."

The sound of talking, muffled by the massive stone walls, filtered down to the travellers, before the city gate was slowly opened and another guard gestured them impatiently inside. He gave them a cursory look, and waved them through as Tuck grinned and Will made the sign of the cross while mumbling, "Gratias tibi ago," at the bored looking man.

It was as simple as that. The guard gave them a wave and ran up the stairs to where his fellows huddled around a brazier at the top of the gatehouse, and the two outlaws entered Nottingham.

Although it was getting late, people still bustled about the place, while children ran between them, screaming playfully, and mangy-looking dogs sniffed at the travellers hoping for a scrap or two.

Tuck asked a local man if there were any taverns near the castle and the pair set off in the direction the man pointed to obtain a room for the night before the weather got any worse.

"I hope they have some good thick beef stew," the friar smiled, rubbing his shrunken belly. "Can't beat some good red meat for building up your strength."

When they reached the inn – so close to the castle you could actually see its great bulk dominating the skyline from the front door – they made sure their palfrey was comfortable in the rickety old stable that was attached to the building and hurried inside gratefully.

Scarlet's stomach rumbled loudly at the thought of food and he pictured in his mind's eye a cosy inn with a roaring fire, beautiful serving-girls and barrels full of freshly brewed ale.

It wasn't to be.

"Ah, bollocks!" Will cursed quietly as the stench hit him and his eyes took in the sight of the *King and Castle* common room. Smoke from the fire filled the place, while the rushes on the floor hadn't been changed in days. He carefully avoided a stinking, dried up patch of vomit and followed Tuck to the bar, noting the toothless old barmaid – breasts hanging almost to her knees – with a rueful shake of his head.

Fuck it. At least the place had a roof.

CHAPTER FOURTEEN

"Ah, Gisbourne!" Sir Henry de Faucumberg grinned and slapped the king's bounty-hunter on the arm. The sheriff's eyes were slightly glassy and it was obvious he'd had a glass or three of wine. "Good job capturing the wolf's head – I'm certain the king will reward you handsomely. I'm hosting a feast tonight to celebrate Hood's incarceration and imminent doom. I trust you will be joining us?"

Gisbourne glowered at the sheriff, still unhappy at the man for stealing his thunder at the city gates. De Faucumberg had a point though – King Edward would reward him well for his work here, and he, along with his sergeant, Nicholas, could leave this place. It wasn't that Gisbourne particularly disliked Yorkshire or Nottingham, but now that the notorious outlaw was safely locked up, there was no challenge left here. The Raven was a man who liked to pit his wits, and his sword arm, against the best – against those criminals no one else could stop.

"Aye," he agreed, forcing himself to smile back at the sheriff. "We have much to celebrate. The outlaw will hang, the king will look upon us both with favour, and I can move on. I'm sure that will please you as much as it pleases me."

De Faucumberg looked confused. "Move on?"

"Indeed," Gisbourne nodded. "Robin Hood is no longer a threat to anyone. I was sent here to kill or capture him, and my job is done. As fine as your hospitality has been," he smirked as the sheriff frowned at the sarcastic tone, "the north of England is a boring place and I'll be glad to get back to London. Who knows where I'll end up next? Hopefully somewhere warm, with a little more culture, like the Languedoc maybe."

The sheriff shook his head, a smile of his own playing on his lips. "My good man, I don't think you understand the situation. The king sent you here to take care of Hood – but his gang are still out there. You will be going nowhere until the rest of them are hanging from the gallows outside the city."

Gisbourne snorted. "I caught the ringleader, de Faucumberg. I also killed the fat friar and at least two more of them. Surely you can capture the rest of the scum? I'm a bounty-hunter, not a damned forester."

The sheriff shrugged, enjoying the moment as Gisbourne grew increasingly angry. "I have the king's orders, Sir Guy – you are to remain here until the forests hereabouts are cleared of outlaws and rebels. It seems King Edward sees you as a forester, eh?"

The smug look on de Faucumberg's face enraged Gisbourne and he burned to smash his fist into the man's throat. With an effort he controlled himself and stalked stiffly away, the sheriff's snigger ringing in his ears.

Damn the man, and damn the king!

The sounds of revelry echoed along the stone corridors, blackening his mood even further, and before he even knew where he was going he found himself at the iron door to the dungeon.

"Bring the prisoner," he growled to one of the two guardsmen.

"Which one, my lord?"

"Which one d'you fucking think, you oaf? Hood!"

The man nodded, well used to his betters talking down to him, and hurried along the gloomy hallway to fetch the wolf's head.

Sir Guy of Gisbourne hadn't always been the ruthless, brooding bounty hunter he was now. As a young man he had been quite pleasant and well-liked around his home town. He had a stable family life as an only-child, his father being one of King Edward I's keepers of the peace while his doting mother looked after the household affairs. Young Guy had loved and respected both of his parents a great deal, particularly his mother who would tell him bedtime stories about King Arthur and the quest for the Holy Grail.

An able student, he'd done well in his schooling, while lacking the required interest in the subjects to ever truly excel. Still, with the help of his influential father, he had begun working as a hayward and was on his way to becoming a well-respected local official.

Life had suited him like that. He wasn't particularly ambitious back then and he had no destructive vices. He had a natural aptitude for fighting, but it had never interested him beyond childhood games with friends, pretending to be Sir Lancelot. Even the military training his father had paid an old mercenary to give him hadn't made him want to become a soldier.

Things had changed when he met Emma.

A stunning, fair-haired girl, she had come with her father – a well-off merchant – and her younger sister, to live in Gisbourne when Guy was seventeen and she a year younger.

The innocent teenage hayward had been smitten by her easy smile, playful nature and her infectious lust for life and the pair had been married just months after meeting for the first time at one of Guy's father's parties.

Unfortunately, Emma's playfulness wasn't confined to her relationship with her new husband, and her lust extended to more than just life.

Within six months, Guy and his wife's adultery were the talk of the village and the young man was crushed by it. The sneers, the mocking laughter when he walked past, the loss of respect of the workers he was in charge of...it had all been hard to bear, but not as hard to bear as the knowledge Emma didn't care for him the way he did for her.

He'd begged her to be faithful, to stop seeing other men behind his back, but still it continued.

His father and other men of the village had told him to beat some obedience into her – she was his woman and should be made to obey him, yet here she was making him a laughing stock!

But, to this day, Guy was never the type of man to physically assault a woman even when she was ruining his life as Emma was doing.

The situation had continued for almost two years, his wife becoming ever more brazen and unrepentant over her affairs while the villagers' view of Guy had moved from mockery to pity.

Then one night Emma had gone a step further than before and brought a man back to their house. Guy had walked in after his day's work and found her astride the man, a middle-aged local shopkeeper with a pot-belly.

That was the day Guy of Gisbourne finally snapped and his aptitude for violence became brutally apparent.

The case had never come to the bailiff's attention, thanks to his father's influence, although murdering a man who was fucking your wife in your own house was hardly a crime anyway.

From that day on though, Guy had become a different person.

It had felt good to deal out justice with his own hands. The respect he'd lost over the past two years had been won back in the space of a few short, bloody minutes. The village children no longer hooted at him when he walked past, and the men who had formerly looked at him with contempt now averted their eyes fearfully when he glared at them.

He'd thrown Emma out of their home although even now he was still legally wed to her, then he had sold the house and, with a letter of recommendation from his father, gone to London to find employment.

Starting as an assistant to one of the city bailiff's Guy had performed his duties with relish and eventually come to the attention of the king's own chamberlain who hired the brooding young man to work on behalf of Edward II himself.

Gisbourne shook his head ruefully as he thought back on it all now. Things could have been so different if Emma had just been a loving wife. They would have had children – lots of them – and, once he had saved enough money, lived in a big house by the River Ribble which was something he'd dreamt of since childhood. He'd always loved being close to water, particularly the Ribble where he'd spent many hours with friends as a child, fishing and sailing little wooden boats.

He would have been content.

As the notorious young wolf's head was led along the hallway towards him, Sir Guy's fingers tightened around his sword hilt and he pushed the old dreams from his mind. His life had turned out differently to how he would have chosen, but he was exceptionally good at his job. Good at bringing justice to those who flouted the law, like this boy Hood.

Well, Gisbourne was going to bring his own form of justice to the big bastard now.

Robin walked like a dead man as he was led along the dimly-lit stone corridor towards the bounty-hunter standing in the shadows.

"I'll take him from here," the king's man told the guard, who tried to object – his orders from the sheriff were to make sure Hood stayed locked safely away – but the furious, slightly insane, stare Gisbourne threw him turned the man's blood cold and he backed away, hands raised placatingly.

"Right, wolf's head. Move it. You know the way to the practice area. You're going to show me what you're made of, or in the name of Christ, you won't make it to the gallows alive."

The practice area was empty; the guards were all either at their posts or joining in with the feast which was now under way. The entire courtyard seemed eerily silent as Gisbourne and his captive walked out onto the grass and the bounty-hunter lifted a pair of wooden swords.

"I noticed the spark of hatred in your eyes when you saw me there, wolf's head. There's no one else here – if you're man enough, you can kill me and probably walk right out of the castle before anyone notices." He tossed a sword to Robin, who caught it and gazed at his tormentor.

Robin knew there was no chance of escape – the guards wouldn't allow him to walk past them when they saw him approaching the gatehouse, but there was a possibility of killing this black-clad bastard and the thought made the blood pound in his veins.

Gisbourne smiled as he saw the colour rise in the outlaw's face, and moved in to try a thrust, but Robin sidestepped and moved backwards, trying to work some strength into his muscles. He hadn't slept properly for days, and the cold, damp cell floor had made his whole body ache, not to mention the psychological torment he'd suffered recently.

Gisbourne aimed another blow at his opponent's side, which was again parried, but Robin was slow and before he knew it Gisbourne had reversed his strike and hammered the heavy wooden sword into Robin's ribcage.

Crying out in agony as he felt bones crack, the outlaw transferred the practice weapon to his left hand so he could clutch his injured side.

Gibourne was in no mood for mercy though, and attacked with a flurry of strokes which Robin desperately managed to parry until, inevitably, Gisbourne landed another blow, this time on Robin's thigh, deadening the limb.

Roaring in pain again, the young outlaw tried to move back, away from Sir Guy, in an attempt to buy some time for the pain from his injuries to hopefully lessen.

"You were supposed to be a test for me, peasant," Gisbourne spat in disgust. "But you're nothing. You fight like any other farmer. Will you be more of a challenge for me if you're angry? What if I tell you the king won't let me leave here until I've hanged every one of your band of friends?"

Robin, hoping to stall for as much time as possible, tried to laugh but the pain from his damaged ribs made him grimace. "Good luck with that. If Will doesn't kill you, Little John'll do it."

"The angry man and the giant," Gisbourne feinted left as he spoke and Robin, in his exhausted and injured state found it impossible to defend himself as the edge of the lawman's wooden sword cracked off his face and he fell to the ground, dazed and almost passing out from the blow. "I'll kill them both, just like I'm going to kill you. Fuck de Faucumberg and his show trial, I'm going to finish this now!"

By now, the celebration inside the castle was in full swing, and the joyful sounds of drunken revelry filled the courtyard. The young women who had cheered Gisbourne in his previous fight here had again come to the balcony and squealed delightedly at the sight of the outlaw being beaten so viciously.

As Robin unsteadily rose to his feet, the sheriff appeared on the balcony, shoving his way past the women to see what they were all watching. When he saw the state of his prisoner, and Gisbourne's body language, he ran back into the castle, roaring for the guards.

"Fight me!" Sir Guy shouted, punching the hilt of his sword into Robin's nose. Blood spurted onto his hand as the outlaw fell on his backside, grimacing up in pain and hatred at his persecutor.

"Fight back!" Oblivious to the fact Robin was almost unconscious and in no state to defend himself never mind retaliate, Gisbourne came in again, swinging his wooden blade down into his opponent's sword hand.

The pain was too much now and, mercifully, Robin's body began to shut down, a wave of blackness swamping him as his crazed attacker bore down on him, kicking and battering his unmoving body with the practice sword.

Even the drunk girls on the balcony above had stopped cheering now, as they realised they were witnessing a young man being brutally beaten to death.

The courtyard filled with the sound of stamping feet as Sheriff de Faucumberg and four guardsmen appeared, running towards Gisbourne. The bounty-hunter had to be wrestled to the ground and held down by the guards as the sheriff screamed in rage at him and shouted for a surgeon.

Eventually, Sir Guy came to his senses and the men let him up.

"What the hell are you doing, you fool?" de Faucumberg demanded. "This is my castle, and that is my prisoner! Have you lost your damn mind?"

Gisbourne took a deep breath and puffed out his cheeks, before closing his eyes and exhaling. As he looked into the sheriff's eyes it was clear the madness had left him, but he glanced at the ruined outlaw and shrugged.

"Whether you hang him or not makes no difference to me – King Edward wants him dead however it's done. Looks like your public hanging is off, sheriff."

The king's man calmly walked from the practice area, placed his wooden sword back in its basket along with the others, and strode into the castle out of sight.

"The man's a lunatic," de Faucumberg muttered, shaking his head in disbelief, before shouting over to the surgeon who had finally arrived. "If he's not dead already, do what you can for the wolf's head – he must survive until the weekend, so we can hang him."

* * *

Tuck and Will paid the landlord – a small, skinny man with a terrible red rash on his face – for a room. They weren't entirely sure yet if they'd need it: Will, as usual, wanted them to make their move as soon as possible.

"Don't be impatient," Tuck scolded him like a naughty child. "We should sit in here for a while and see if we can hear anything about Robin. He's a hero to most of the people in Nottingham; surely someone will be talking about him. We can't just wander around the castle walls at this time of the evening without attracting attention!"

Will knew the friar spoke sense, so they sat nursing two surprisingly fresh ales, pretending to chat but straining to hear other people's conversations.

Thankfully, Tuck was right – the sheriff's capture of Robin Hood was the talk of the place. The outlaws turned their attention to one particular pair of men seated at a table by the window, one of whom appeared to have a brother in the sheriff's guard.

"What's the word on Hood?" a dark-skinned fellow asked the man seated across from him.

"James says he was just coming off duty for the night when that scary bastard Sir Guy of Gisbourne came down to the dungeon looking for Hood. James thought he was looking for another sparring match."

"I thought he'd already beaten him the other day?"

The guard's brother put down his mug and messily wiped his mouth with the back of his hand. "Aye, so he did, Godfrey. He had a mad look in his eyes though, or so James said."

"What happened then?"

"Dunno – James left the castle. I'll tell you tomorrow when he comes back home!"

The men sat silently for a moment, then Godfrey muttered. "I hope Hood gave him a fucking hiding."

Tuck led Will over to the table the two men were sitting at and addressed them apologetically. "I'm sorry to disturb you, gentlemen," he began. "Would you mind if me and my brother friar share your table?" He gestured around at the busy inn. "All the tables are occupied."

The men moved along the bench with respectful nods of their heads, too inebriated to care much who sat with them. "Of course, father. Please, sit."

Tuck dropped onto the seat beside the guard's brother with a grin of thanks, while Will, hood still up lest anyone recognize him, grunted and gave a small wave of his hand.

"So, Robin Hood eh?" Tuck shook his head sorrowfully. "They say he's a wicked murderer. A blasphemer. A thief. And yet the people seem to love him."

The dark-skinned man called Godfrey leaned towards the friar earnestly. "The common people love him because he's one of us," he said. "Aye, Hood's a thief, but he steals from the rich lords and the likes of your bishops. He's done a lot of good for the villages around Yorkshire from what we hear. That's why the sheriff wanted him captured."

"What about his men though?" Tuck wondered, sipping from his ale. "Won't they try and rescue him?"

"No chance!" The guard's brother shook his head vigorously. "He's locked away in the dungeon. Those outlaws might be good at fighting in the forest, but there's no way into the castle; it's too heavily defended, even if they could get inside the city and through the castle gates. Mind you, tonight would be the time to try – the sheriff's throwing a banquet to celebrate Hood's capture at last."

Tuck shared a glance with Will, but let the men's talk move onto other things, while he paid the bar-keep to bring them more ale. It didn't take long for the locals to become quite drunk and the friar neatly steered the conversation back to the sheriff's prisoner.

"When do they plan on hanging the wolf's head?" he wondered.

"Two days," Godfrey replied sadly. "The sheriff wants as many people as possible to see it or he'd have done it by now. Bastard."

"Ach, to be fair," the second man shook his head. "Sir Henry's just doing his job. He's not the worst sheriff we've had in this city – not by a long shot. The outlaws undermined his authority, especially when they killed his man Gurdon last year."

Tuck saw Will's fingers clench convulsively around his mug – the outlaw had thought Adam Gurdon was his friend and it had hurt him deeply when the man had betrayed them. Thankfully, though, Scarlet remained silent and Simon growled at his friend.

"You're just saying that, Roger, because your brother's one of his guards and hoping to win a promotion. I bet you wouldn't think so highly of de Faucumberg if he found out about James sneaking out of the castle that time. The sheriff would have *him* hanged alongside the wicked wolf's head and you know it!"

"Shut up, you idiot," Roger retorted, glaring furiously at his companion. Although he was well in his cups, he didn't want gossip about his brother getting around the city.

Tuck roared with laughter, and patted Roger on the arm reassuringly. "Never fear, lad. We hear much worse things at confession every day – a friar knows how to keep a secret." He winked and drained the last of his ale, shouting to the landlord to bring another four mugs.

"It's true," Godfrey grinned at Tuck. "His brother's lady-friend was leaving to live in Scotland, but James was desperate for one last night of..." he remembered he was talking to clergymen and trailed off sheepishly. "Anyway, he couldn't get the night off, and he couldn't let anyone see him leaving or he'd be in trouble. So he climbed out the latrine on the east wall, then, before anyone noticed he was missing, he climbed back in the same way!"

Tuck's eyes were wide with disbelief as he listened to the tale, and Roger laughed, as the bar-keep placed the fresh ale on the table. "The worst of it is," Roger leaned over conspiratorially, making sure no one else was listening, "he was covered in shit and filth, so his girl wouldn't touch him!" The laughter left his eyes though and he became thoughtful. "He's a bloody fool. Just as well he made it back inside unseen or they'd have hanged him for leaving his post."

"Didn't his captain have anything to say about the smell?" Tuck asked.

Roger shrugged. "I think he managed to wash most of the crap off once he got back into the castle, or at least mask the worst of the smell."

Tuck grinned and, again, turned the conversation onto other things. It was late now, and, once they drained the last of their drinks, the friar and Scarlet bade their new friends goodnight and made their way up to the room the landlord had provided for them.

It had been a productive evening.

"I hope you don't mind me getting shit and filth all over your spare robe," Will grinned.

"Not as long as you wash it afterwards!"

CHAPTER FIFTEEN

"Do we really have to do this tonight?"

"You heard them," Will growled, making sure his weapons were all in place and ready under the grey Franciscan robe. "Half the castle will be roaring drunk tonight, while the minstrels and singing will drown out any unusual sounds. There'll also be more strangers than usual about the place; de Faucumberg will have invited all sorts of people for this. So, yes: we have to do this tonight."

Tuck shook his head. It made sense, but he'd hoped for at least one night in a real bed. "I'm too weak to go climbing up some latrine though; what will I do?"

Will laughed and poked the friar in the belly good-naturedly. "Even at your fittest you wouldn't have been able to climb a latrine, big man." He shrugged. "I don't know – come with me to find the place in case we run into anyone. You can do your clergyman thing until I deal with them. I'm going to need some light to find handholds too – you can help with that. Then, I suppose it'll be down to me. At least we know Robin's in the dungeon."

It was an insane plan; they would need God and all his saints on their side if it was to have any chance of success. "Just as well we have this," Tuck muttered, clenching the holy reliquary in his hand and offering a silent prayer to St Nicholas, patron saint of thieves, which seemed most appropriate.

"Let's move."

Their room was on the ground floor, so it was a simple matter to open the wooden shutters and climb out onto the street, even for the weakened Tuck. The city was shrouded in darkness, although a gibbous moon cast just enough light for them to move between the buildings. The castle was easy to spot, its great black bulk huge in the darkness, and many small points of yellow light shone from the windows and murder holes. It was an eerie sight and the outlaws felt the hairs on their necks stand up as a chill breeze blew along the slumbering street.

They headed for the east wall, moving silently up the hill that led to it, although Tuck struggled to keep up and was breathing heavily as they drew close to the castle. They had heard others out and about, but found it easy enough to remain unseen in the gloom and, before too long, stood by the massive wall of Nottingham Castle.

The latrine was simple enough to find – the stench was overpowering. Will had no doubt the mountain of shit that must accrue here every day would be used by some tradesman for something or other. They probably paid the sheriff for it too.

"Unbelievable," Tuck whispered. "A fortress, with walls almost as thick as I am tall, massive iron gates, defended by a garrison of hard men...and anyone that knows about it can climb in through the latrine!"

"I haven't done it yet," Will cautioned. "Besides, it's not that much of a security risk is it? You have to be inside the city walls to get here – so it's not that much use to an invading army. And who in their right mind wants to break into a castle, using a fucking *latrine* to do it? It's madness."

Tuck grinned, the moonlight reflecting off his yellow teeth. "Aye, you're not wrong there. Good luck with that."

There was a locked door barring the way into the building, but it was wooden and, thanks to the dampness of what it guarded, it was badly rotten. "The lock probably won't give, but the wood might," Will guessed, leaning down and aiming a kick at the bottom of the barrier, which splintered with a wet thud. Another blow took the bottom half of the door off and, after waiting a while to make sure no one came to investigate the noise, the companions crawled into the stinking toilet.

It was pitch black inside, so Tuck produced the torch he'd taken from their room in the *King and Castle* and rummaged in his pack for his flint and steel.

"Wait," Will hissed fearfully, guessing what the friar was doing. "I've heard stories about farts catching fire! You might blow the whole castle up if you light that torch in here!"

Tuck burst out laughing. He couldn't stop himself. The high-pitched sound rang out, bouncing off the steep stone walls, and he bent over, covering his mouth with his hand in an attempt to muffle the sound.

"What's so fucking funny?" Will demanded, trying to keep his voice low. He would have grabbed the friar if he could see him, but the darkness was total inside the fetid room, and he had to wait until the friar came to his senses.

Eventually Tuck wiped the tears from his face and lit the torch. As it flared into life he grinned at his furious companion. "The farts in here have long gone: out the door you kicked in. We're quite safe."

"Arsehole," Will growled, prompting another snigger from Tuck.

Thankfully, there was more than one opening in the wall to the latrine. Will only had to climb up one storey before he could make his way inside the castle proper.

The problem was the wall was covered in green slime and white mildew so thick and hairy it looked like it might get up and climb into the castle itself. Will threw a hand up to his mouth and gagged.

"Here." Tuck handed the ornate reliquary that held Christ's facial hair to his friend. "You're going to need this."

* * *

Matilda awoke in a sweat, tears streaking her cheeks in the darkness. The house was silent and she absent-mindedly stroked her swollen belly, the nightmare fresh and raw in her mind.

Robin had been in terrible danger, although she had woken up as the great black faceless figure had swept its sword down into his body. She shuddered and pulled the blanket tighter around her, telling herself it was just a dream.

She thought it must be her mind's way of reproaching her for the way she spoke to Robin the last time he'd visited, chasing him off as if she hated him. Which was, of course, nonsense – she loved him! – but the pained look on his face as he'd walked out the door had stayed with her and she wished she could see him to make friends again.

Sighing, she sent a silent message to him to let him know how she felt, hoping, somehow he would hear, or feel it, and closed her eyes to sleep again.

* * *

Climbing the wall of the latrine proved to be every bit as disgusting as Will had feared. Once he had looked at the hand holds, and fixed a mental image of the place in his mind, he told Tuck to extinguish the torch in case someone from the castle came in to relieve themselves and found the outlaws.

They had went back outside and found some old branches with as much foliage still attached as possible which Will used to scrape off whatever filth he could before attempting the climb. The mortar between the stones was old and loose and it was fairly easy for him to find good hand and footholds, but, by the time he was halfway to the opening he was drenched in sweat, not to mention the sticky grime that coated his hands.

He was almost at the top when he heard the creak of a door opening somewhere and he froze, pressing his body instinctively into the filth-encrusted wall, praying he'd be able to hold onto the wall.

The sounds of distant laughter and revelry filtered down through the latrine, and there was a dim glow which cast shadows on the walls, clearly from a torch in the room above.

The loud voices of two drunk men boomed off the stone walls, sharing inanities and laughing at nothing. Suddenly, for just a moment, there was silence, then Will almost screamed with fury as a stream of warm piss hit the top of his head and ran down the back of his neck.

Somehow, the outlaw closed his eyes and clung to his position in outraged silence, as the men above resumed their inebriated conversation and, at last, the stream of urine stopped.

The dim light, and the sound of their voices faded as the door closed behind them, and Scarlet cursed them and their children to the tenth generation. It took him a moment to clear his mind and begin his ascent again.

From the darkness below, Tuck's voice carried cheerfully up to him.

"At least they didn't need a shit."

* * *

"Do you know how far it is to Pontefract?"

Edmond glanced over at his captive and growled at him nastily. "No, but I know how to get there. We just have to follow the road to Wakefield then continue along and it'll lead us straight there. Then I'll see justice done."

Sir Richard plodded on for a while, then turned to look back at Edmond. "Pontefract is twenty miles from here. On foot, like this, it'll take us forever to get there."

The younger man's face fell, then he laughed nervously. "You're lying. Sir Philip wouldn't ask me to take you all that way."

"Sir Philip was probably expecting you to have a small group of men with you. Or horses. What happens at night, when you have to sleep? Or when you have to do the toilet?"

Edmond didn't reply as they walked along the little path, heading for the main road that would take them east, in the direction of Pontefract.

"I tell you truly, I wish your brother hadn't died. I was just defending myself, as is a man's right. You would have done the same thing in my position."

Still, Edmond remained silent, tears rolling down his cheeks as he pictured Walter's face in his mind. Poor Walter. His life had been hard, and his death even harder.

"Come, lad," Richard went on, looking up at the trees as if he was talking to God himself. "You'd be as well killing me now – there's no way you can hold me hostage for the length of this journey. Tell me what Sir Philip is paying you to capture me."

"It's not just about money, Hospitaller! I wanted to do something brave, and noble, and noteworthy. Something that would show those arseholes in Kirklees that Walter wasn't the useless idiot they made him out to be. The money is just a bonus."

The knight looked round at Edmond, taking in the stumpy body, large fish-like lips and short limbs. He guessed it wasn't just Walter that had been the butt of the villager's jokes.

A memory suddenly flared in Sir Richard's head. "Aren't you married? I'm sure I remember your father telling me his son was betrothed. He was very proud – as a father should be." His voice trailed off as he thought of his own son, killed before he could find a woman to share his life with.

"She died," Edmond snarled, his thick lips spraying saliva before him. "Same as my da!"

No wonder the man's so angry, Sir Richard thought, holding his peace for now. *He and his brother bullied for years, his wife dead, his parents dead, and now I've killed his only surviving kin...Christ above,* he prayed, *help me!*

As he mouthed his silent supplication, the weight of everything that had befallen him in recent months came down on his old shoulders and the Hospitaller knew what he had to do.

He stopped in his tracks and Edmond stopped too, leaning back into a defensive stance, the knight's sword held before him.

"Why are you stopping? Move on! Sir Philip never said I had to take you to him in one piece."

Richard raised a hand. "Calm down, lad. You can relax." He clasped his hands and gazed at his captor. "I'll travel with you to Pontefract Castle. I give you my word as a Knight of St. John, I won't try to escape. Whatever happens, I will allow you to take me, as your prisoner, to Sir Philip."

Edmond's eyes flickered from side to side warily, half-expecting men to burst from the trees to aid the Hospitaller. Surely this was some trick.

"Why?"

Sir Richard sighed, his bearded face falling, and suddenly Edmond noticed just how old the man was.

"My wife and my youngest son are dead. The king himself wants me hanged. I'm a disgraced rebel who's spent the last few weeks hiding like a frightened woman in a lonely castle." He smiled ruefully at his captor. "I have my eldest son – Edward – but he has his own life, far away in Rhodes...God has allowed me to fall into your hands, so...I will go to Pontefract with you, freely. You may sleep – or relieve yourself – when you must, without fearing I'll kill you or sneak off."

From the wary, and somewhat frightened expression on Edmond's face, it was obvious the young man had no idea what to make of this.

In truth, Sir Richard felt desperately sorry for the man. And guilty for taking his one sibling and friend from him. If he'd analyzed his own motives more honestly, the knight might not have made his promise to the tanner's son. But it seemed to him like this was a thing he could do to make Edmond's life better. He knew he couldn't hide out forever in Kirklees Castle – it would drive him mad before much longer, which was why he'd even been out in the open in the first place.

"I have your oath on this, Hospitaller? You're almost a priest right? Your oath, before Christ, has to be binding!"

Sir Richard nodded. "You have my oath."

"Thank God," Edmond grunted, dropping the sword onto the grass and pulling his breeches down about his thick thighs. "I've been desperate for a piss for ages."

The young villager continued to eye him suspiciously, warm urine splattering and steaming on the grass, and Sir Richard turned away, looking thoughtfully into the dense trees.

It felt like a weight had been lifted from his shoulders. He *would* go to Pontefract with Edmond. The young man would be well rewarded by Sir Philip, and be able to go back to Kirklees with a tale that would finally earn him the respect from the villagers that he so desperately craved.

Would the king hang him? Yes, Sir Richard knew he would. It would give Edward the perfect excuse to seize Kirklees – Hospitaller lands – permanently.

As Edmond pulled his trousers back up with a satisfied grunt, and stooped to retrieve the dropped sword, Sir Richard moved off along the overgrown trail again, casting another prayer skyward.

Lord, I place myself at your mercy. But it would be nice if my sergeant-at-arms turned up in time to save me from a humiliating death on the gallows!

* * *

When he finally made it to London Stephen was exhausted. He had pushed his body to the limit trying to make up for lost time and the fact he was now on foot. As he passed through Enfield he was able to buy a tired old palfrey, but by then he was close to collapse from the physical and mental pressure he had placed himself under.

When the Moorgate of London came into view he could have cried out in relief if he had the strength, but his elation soon left him as his eyes took in the sight of hundreds of people queueing to get into the city.

Making sure his shield was easily visible and the cross prominently displayed on his black surcoat, he led the palfrey off the road onto the verge and kicked it into a canter, racing past the patiently waiting queue. Most people, quickly spotting the Hospitaller livery and his arms and armour, kept their mouths shut, although one or two braver than the rest cursed him for skipping the line.

Stephen never even heard them, tired and focused as he was on entering the city at last. The crowd was a blur until he came closer to the gates and reined in his mount, roaring at the top of his voice for people to move and let him through.

Not everyone was quick to obey, and Stephen knew he was courting disaster as he rode the old horse directly into the queue of people, scattering them.

"Stand aside!" he shouted, trying to summon his most powerful parade-ground voice from protesting lungs. "Hospitaller on official business!"

Three men, wealthy merchants judging from their clothes and haughty manner, stood their ground, glaring at the sergeant-at-arms bearing down on them, but Stephen was in no mood to slow his progress now.

"Get out of the way you arseholes or I'll ride you into the ground!" To emphasise the point he pulled his sword free from its sheath and held it above his head.

The merchants, realising the crazed soldier wasn't slowing, scattered to the side of the road shouting curses at his back as he rode past them up to the gate.

The guards, used to seeing things like this all the time, stopped the Hospitaller to ask his business but quickly waved him on his way. Sometimes they would be rewarded with a coin or two when they fast-tracked someone in a hurry, but Stephen offered nothing. Despite that, the guards were glad to send the wild-eyed sergeant on his way before he caused any trouble.

He had a vague idea of where the Hospitaller headquarters were situated but it was a few years since he had last visited and his memory wasn't very clear. Stopping for a moment, he asked for directions and walked his horse through the streets in the direction indicated by the eager locals hoping – fruitlessly – for a small reward from the soldier.

It felt like an age before he finally reached the grand stone building that housed the Grand Prior of England's chapter of The Order of St John, and when he saw it, he felt his stomach lurch anxiously.

He shook his head with a rueful grin. He'd almost been killed numerous times in pitched battles with the Saracen, where it felt like hell had come to Earth and yet the thought of facing Prior L'Archer and possibly failing his master Sir Richard frightened him more than any fight he'd had since he was a raw young recruit.

Almost oblivious to the sights, smells and sounds around him, Stephen slowly dismounted, the muscles in his legs screaming in pain, and led his palfrey through the imposing archway that led into Clerkenwell Priory.

He was finally here, and, praise be to God, he still had Sir Richard's letter to the Grand Prior.

Let me be in time to help my master, Lord!

CHAPTER SIXTEEN

At last, panting and stinking, Will reached the top of the wall. The wooden bench that people sat on to relieve themselves pushed out of the way easily enough and the filthy outlaw scrambled into the room as quickly as possible.

Divesting himself of Tuck's sodden robe and feeling much cleaner for it, he hid the wet garment under the bench which he shoved back into position, then moved to the door, opening it a crack to make sure no one was around.

The corridor appeared to be empty, and as his eyes adjusted to the flickering light he took in the layout of the place. Closed doors led to what he supposed must be bedrooms, and a flight of stairs led up and down just outside of where he stood.

He crept down the stairway, hand on his sword hilt and shook his head. This was madness! He had no idea how to get to the dungeon, and chances were he'd be found if he just wandered about the place, but he didn't see what else he could do.

He reached another landing, on the ground floor he guessed, where the sound of the party was louder, but the steps stopped here so he slowly made his way along the corridor, praying no one was about. Again, closed doors led off to God-knew where and, thinking it wise to have a hiding place should someone appear, he listened at the first one he came to. It was impossible to know if anyone was inside over the noise of the feast which was obviously close-by.

Drawing his sword, he gritted his teeth and tried the handle. The heavy door opened easily and he moved inside, eyes flickering from side to side seeking any threats.

The place was empty and appeared to be a storeroom for bed clothes, curtains and other soft furnishings which were folded neatly or hung on rails. The fresh smell of lavender filled the air and the outlaw wished he could sleep on sheets like these every night. Exhaling softly, he decided to wait for a short time, to see if anyone would come past that might be able to lead him to the dungeon.

Leaving the door open a crack, he watched the corridor. Revellers passed every so often, obviously making their way to the latrine, or, in some cases, couples looking for somewhere private to get to know each other better. Thankfully they all continued along the corridor and up the stairwell – Will had no desire to kill innocent civilians should they stumble on his hiding place.

As another drunk middle-aged man stumbled past humming to himself, Will cursed and decided he'd wasted enough time; the feast wasn't going to last forever, and he hadn't even found Robin yet, never mind freed him.

He began to pull the door to the storeroom open, then quickly closed it again as two stocky men wearing the sheriff's livery appeared in the hall, making their way towards him. They carried pole-arms, but appeared lightly armoured, and Scarlet's mind whirled as he wondered what to do.

Hurriedly, he pushed the door shut and hid behind one of the great curtain rails close to the door then, trying to judge when the guards would be passing the room, he made a high-pitched squeal. Not a threatening sound, or too loud to be overly obvious he hoped.

Suddenly the door was pushed open, and Will heard the men wandering into the room.

"What was it?" one of them asked. "I never heard anything."

"Dunno," his companion replied. "Christ above, where's that smell of shit coming from?"

The voices moved in front of Will, going further into the room, and, steeling himself as they came near, he silently pushed through the curtains and plunged the tip of his sword into the side of the guard nearest him.

The man cried out as the outlaw pulled his bloody sword free, and, as he collapsed onto the floor his companion spun round, eyes wide with shock, before Will punched him in the guts with all his strength.

The door to the room was lying open, so he ran over and pushed it shut, then made his way back to the downed guards. The one he'd stabbed was no threat – he was already dead and Will nodded, knowing his thrust had been a good one. The second man had pushed himself back to his feet despite Scarlet's heavy blow, and now aimed a wild swing at the outlaw's head with his pole-arm.

Ducking just in time, Will launched himself at the guard and the pair fell back onto a pile of bedsheets, struggling for their lives. The man was strong and obviously well-trained in hand-to-hand combat, but Scarlet's massive upper-body strength was too much and, forcing the guard's hands down onto the sheets, the outlaw slammed his forehead into the man's nose, then, when he went limp, Scarlet leaned back and hammered another punch into the guard's stomach.

Vomit and bile filled the unfortunate man's mouth and his face turned red as he began to asphyxiate before Will pulled him onto his side, retching and spluttering as the foul liquid spilled out and his airway cleared.

Panting himself, Will sheathed his sword and drew his dagger, pressing it against the sobbing guard's neck.

"I already killed your pal," he growled, tossing the pole-arm away into the corner. "The only reason I didn't let you choke on your own puke is that I need information."

"Who are you?" the guard gasped. "What do you want?"

"I'm a friend of Robin Hood," Will replied. "I'm here to take him home. And you," he pressed the dagger against the man's neck, drawing blood, "are going to tell me how I find him."

"Fine! I'll tell you, just take that away."

Will released the pressure on the dagger, hopeful the man would be true to his word. He had no stomach for torture, but this guard *would* give him the information he wanted, one way or another.

The man lay still for a moment, trying to catch his breath, then, wiping the wet sick from his mouth and cheek, he leaned his head up from the dirty sheet and glared at Scarlet.

"I've no love for your leader – him and the rest of your gang have killed more than a few of my fellows. But I also have no love for that bastard Sir Guy of Gisbourne. He's made me spar with him twice now, and battered me black and blue both times. Sadistic, arrogant wanker he is. If you manage to free Hood, Gisbourne won't be quite the hero any more, and if you die trying, it'll fucking serve you right."

"How do I get into the dungeon then?" Will asked impatiently.

"Here, take my surcoat," the guard said, pulling the light blue garment with the sheriff's coat-of-arms emblazoned on the front over his head and tossing it weakly to the outlaw. "Hopefully it'll stop any of my mates challenging you. The stairs to the dungeon are at the far end of the corridor. There's a door, but Charlie on the floor there has the key. You'll have to get the key to Hood's cell from the jailer down in the dungeon though – Adam's the only person that carries the keys for the cells. Don't kill him like you did Charlie, will you?"

Will found the key on the dead man's belt and placed it in his pouch before turning back to face the guard.

"What are you going to do with me?"

Will shrugged. "I can't leave you to raise the alarm" –

"Don't kill me," the young man mumbled. "Please. I have two little boys, Matthew and Andrew, I...please..." His voice trailed off as he pictured his children and he held his head in his hands.

"Matthew and Andrew?" Will repeated, thinking back to the man in the inn. "Are you James?"

The guard looked up in surprise. "Aye, how did you know that?"

"I had a few ales with your brother earlier on. He told us about you climbing in and out of here through the latrine – that's why I stink of shit and piss. Never mind the rest," Will grunted, raising his hand to silence any more questions. "I don't have time. I also have no wish to kill you."

With his dagger he tore one of the sheets into strips and used it to bind the guard's hands and feet, then used another strip to gag him.

"I expect someone will come looking for you and your mate eventually. I just hope me and Robin are gone by then." He opened his pouch and took out some silver coins – probably six month's wages to the guardsman – and stuffed them into the small pocket sewn into the man's gambeson. "Look after your little boys."

With a wink, Scarlet stood and left the room, closing the door behind him.

* * *

"Don't think I trust you, or we're friends or anything like that, Hospitaller. Your warped sense of honour may be telling you to come to Pontefract with me, but you still murdered Walter and I'll watch you hang for it."

Sir Richard nodded at the young man's rant. They had been travelling for hours and he was tired and bored. Any attempt at conversation had been met with stony silence or threats of violence; sometimes Edmond would lash out physically as he just had, almost as if reminding himself of their roles.

"I didn't murder your brother: you two attacked *me*, remember. I saw two young men coming at me with naked blades – how would you have reacted?"

Edmond growled but didn't reply.

"You look a hardy fighter to me," Sir Richard went on, turning to eye his captor's powerful, if short, arms and a nose flattened from many brawls over the years. "I'm sure you'd have done the same as I did."

The tanner's son knew the knight had the right of it, and it gnawed at him to realise Walter had died because of him and his stupid plan. Two village boys overpowering a Hospitaller Knight, a man who had fought, and won, countless battles in the Holy Land! The idea seemed ridiculous now, and Edmond shook his head sorrowfully at his own hubris.

"Your mother died when you were young, didn't she?"

Edmond glared at Sir Richard, but the knight's face was open and sincere, with no trace of malice in it, and he muttered a reply. "She died giving birth to Walter."

"And your father?"

"He died two months ago. I took over his shop."

They walked on in silence for a while, the road wide and open at this point as the ancient Romans had paved it and the trees hadn't managed to reclaim the ground yet. Dark clouds filled the air and Sir Richard huddled into his cloak which wasn't a thick one since he hadn't been expecting this long journey when he'd left his castle.

"Did the villagers make things hard for Walter?"

Again, Edmond looked at his captive's face, trying to read the man's expression, but all he saw was apparently genuine interest. What harm would it do to talk to the knight? It might help ease his own guilt, if even a little.

"Walter was a nice person. The children his own age used to hit him because he was different to them – slower. But he never hit them back, he didn't really have it in his nature. He would come home and sit by the hearth crying. Da would tell him he had to stand up for himself, but he wouldn't, and that just made it worse."

The images came to his mind and he clenched his fists in anger at the cruelty of the boys. "Then one day he came in and his shoulder was out of place. The barber said it was..."

"Dislocated?" Sir Richard offered.

"Aye, that," Edmond agreed. "His face was pale and he screamed in agony when the barber put it back into place. Four of the children had..." his voice cracked in disgust, but he carried on through gritted teeth. "They had tied a noose around his neck and pulled him up onto a branch! The rope snapped and he'd landed on his shoulder – the boys had run off when Walter got his breath back and started screaming."

They walked on, the clouds growing ever more threatening, and Sir Richard let Edmond gather his thoughts for a while.

"How could children do something like that? So...evil? Walter was only eight! A little boy!"

The Hospitaller stared along the road, his own memory replaying images of cruelty and hatred perpetrated by men supposedly fighting for the glory of God.

"Did you" –

"Aye, I did!" Edmond replied. "I found out who had done it and I did the same thing to one of them, but his da told the headman and I was warned not to go after any more of the little bastards. To this day, whenever Walter and I would go to the inn for an ale after work, those boys – grown men by now – would snigger at him and make choking motions." The rage left him and he gazed at Sir Richard with wide, damp eyes. "All because Walter was born a little bit slow-witted."

The rain began to fall on them then, gently. "So you wanted to show the men of Kirklees that Walter was as much of a man as any of them by capturing one of the rebel leaders."

Edmond nodded, bringing the sword up threateningly as if just remembering where they were going. "Aye, but you ruined it; you, and this." He looked in disgust at the blade in his own hand.

Sir Richard held his peace and they plodded on, the rain becoming a torrent, ending any possibility of further conversation, but the old knight understood Edmond much better now. It was clear from his body language that he hadn't just wanted to prove Walter's worth to his peers – he had wanted to prove *himself*. With his stumpy little body and odd-looking facial features, Sir Richard knew the village bullies would have made Edmond's life a misery, almost as much as they had Walter's.

The rain coursed down his face and dripped from his grey beard but the Hospitaller felt too tired to wipe it away. So much hatred and pain in the world. At his age, after everything he'd seen and done in his long years, he would have hoped to be able to make sense of life. But he had no better understanding of the ways of men now than he did when he was Edmond's age.

He sighed and bowed his head to let the rain drip off onto the old Roman road. *These stones have been here for centuries, and nothing's changed: men still can't stop hurting and killing one another...*

* * *

Will forced himself to keep moving along the corridor as the door to the great hall opened and a figure came through. If it was another guard, Will would surely be recognised and that would be the end of his rescue attempt.

"You – where's the latrine?"

The man fixed Scarlet with a drunken glare and the outlaw let out a sigh of relief. Just another reveller, thank Christ.

"Up the stairs, and straight ahead, my lord," he replied deferentially, as the man staggered off without another word.

"Noble twat." Will hurried to the opposite end of the corridor, to the great door that stood closed, and fitted the key he'd taken from the dead guard into the lock. It turned easily and he moved through onto another stairwell, which led down into the dimly lit, and damp-smelling dungeon.

He left the door unlocked: no one would come down here by accident, even if they were drunk: it was obvious the stairwell led to the dungeon, and leaving it unlocked would speed their escape once he had Robin.

Voices came to him as he reached the bottom of the steps. Men shouted for water, or food, or freedom. One seemed to be singing a children's song and Will shook his head, knowing the prisoners would have been physically and mentally abused horribly down here where no-one could hear their tortured cries.

Well, that wasn't his problem – some of them probably deserved it anyway.

Setting his shoulders confidently, he strode up to the two guardsmen who sat at a table playing dice. They looked up curiously, but the sight of the light blue surcoat Will had put on stopped them from reacting immediately with alarm.

"What's up?" one of them asked, squinting up at him. Will had stood directly in front of a guttering torch, so the guards couldn't make out his face in the brightness behind him, and he made the most of the few extra seconds it bought him.

"Adam?" he asked.

"Aye, what is it?" the man demanded impatiently. "Why are you down" –

Scarlet hammered the point of the pole-arm he'd taken from the dead guard in the linen room into Adam's chest, hurling the man backwards into the wall, where he stood for a moment, before sinking slowly to his knees, a look of disbelief on his face.

Before the second guard could react, Will withdrew the pole-arm and brought the blunt end round in a ferocious sweep that sent the shocked man sprawling onto the floor. Reversing the weapon the outlaw plunged the bloody point through the groaning man's windpipe.

"Shit!" He cursed as he searched Adam's body for the keys to the cells. He hadn't wanted to kill the guards – if there had been just the one he would have overpowered him and locked him in his own cells. But it was too risky to try and beat two trained soldiers so there had been no other choice if he was to get Robin out of here alive. The guards had to die.

When he had exploded into violence, the sounds from the cells had stopped completely, and the eerie atmosphere closed in on him as he hastily made his way to the cell at the end of the stinking stone hallway.

The other prisoners pressed their faces against the iron gates, watching the man who had just murdered two of their hated jailers.

"Let us out of here," one of them shouted. "You have the keys, let us out!"

Will ignored them all as he reached the final cell and peered inside at the figure lying on the cold floor. "Robin!" he hissed, but the figure never moved.

The jailer's ring held a number of keys, all of similar shape and size, and he had to try half a dozen before the gate finally popped open with a harsh creak.

Warily, he made his way over to the prisoner lying on the ground, in case the man attacked him. "Robin," he muttered again, and this time was rewarded with a small groan from the prone figure.

By now, Will knew he'd found his friend – he recognised the clothes and the closely-cropped brown hair. Kneeling beside him, he laid a hand gently on Robin's arm and gave a gentle squeeze. "I've come to get you out of here," he told his young captain. "They're throwing a party upstairs to celebrate your capture, so I was able to climb inside. We have to move quickly though. Get up and let's go before we're discovered!"

The outlaw leader never moved, so Will carefully pushed him onto his back and gasped. Robin's eyes flickered open and his face split in an agonised grimace.

"I won't be climbing anywhere, Will."

"Holy Mother, what have they done to you?" The sight of Robin's blood-caked and terribly bruised face made Scarlet's blood run cold, and he guessed the rest of his friend's body was just as badly injured underneath his clothes.

"Gisbourne," Robin replied softly, obviously with great effort. His eyes filled with tears as he forced himself to continue. "The bastard killed Much!"

Will slumped onto the filthy stone floor and cradled Robin's head in his lap, feeling no shame as tears filled his own eyes at the sight of his broken friend.

"I know," he whispered. "We found him. I thought I'd be able to get inside here, we'd escape, and then we could hunt Gisbourne in the forest." He shook his head in frustrated rage. "I can't carry you out of here! I had to climb up the fucking latrine to get in, and it's the only way we'll be able to get back out!"

Robin shuddered as a wave of pain tore through his body and he gasped an apology to his would-be rescuer.

"Thank you for coming for me, Will. You're a true friend. But I can't even climb to my feet never mind climb down a wall. Leave me. You and John can lead the men. Take them away from Barnsdale – Gisbourne won't stop until he's killed every last one of us."

Scarlet hugged his friend's head as the tears of rage and sorrow rolled down his grime-encrusted face. He knew Robin was right: they couldn't just walk out of the castle past the guards at the gatehouse. It was over.

"Go!" Robin urged. "Before someone finds you!"

There was a sound from the end of the doorway above and Will growled like a rabid dog as he realised someone was coming down the stairs.

"Too late." He stood up and grasped his sword, gazing along the corridor. "Looks like we die here together, my friend."

CHAPTER SEVENTEEN

The rain had let up and thankfully the sun had broken through the patchy clouds, but it offered little heat and Sir Richard shivered in his sodden clothing.

Edmond was better off in his thick hooded cloak but he was huddled into it, clearly feeling the cold.

"We should stop and build a fire to dry ourselves and our clothes," Sir Richard said. "Unless you want us both to come down with a chill and be too sick to make it to Pontefract."

Edmond was lost in his thoughts and his head snapped up in surprise at the suggestion. "Aye," he agreed. "Fair enough. Night will be on us soon anyway. Let's hope we can find enough dry kindling to get a blaze going."

They moved off the road, Edmond watching his captive warily the whole time, sword still held ready even though his arm must have been very uncomfortable under the weight by now.

"Don't think about running" –

The Hospitaller waved him to silence and began hunting for firewood. A couple of old oaks grew near the roadside and they managed to find a few dry twigs and branches to build a small fire. "You get it going," Sir Richard suggested, as Edmond placed the little bundle in a pile. "I'll find more – we don't have enough there to dry us."

The thought of a warm blaze cheered Edmond as he set about constructing a small camp-fire and the big knight disappeared into the trees fringing the road. *Should I bring him back and keep him in sight?* He wondered. No, he had to trust the man's oath would hold – there was no way Edmond could watch him every moment of the day after all.

There was precious little dry kindling anywhere close to their makeshift camp, Sir Richard realised, widening his search irritably. He'd hoped to get a roaring fire going as soon as possible: the chill was seeping into his joints, making them ache, and he detested such pain for he knew it meant he was growing old. Christ, his own body-heat would have dried his soaking clothes twenty years ago! Now, he worried about catching his death if he didn't build a fire soon.

He shook his head ruefully, picking up what sticks he could find, discarding all but the driest.

Strangely, given his situation, he felt relaxed and somehow at peace. A captive on his way to what would very possibly turn out to be his death at the end of a rope, yet a comforting calm seemed to come over him as he searched for firewood and, as he looked around at the beauty of a spring forest coming into life again, he felt the joy of life for a while again and he smiled in appreciation.

The desperate scream of agony broke his train of thought, and he raced back towards the roadside, hand grasping for his missing sword.

* * *

"Can you stand?"

Will held the pole-arm he'd taken from the castle guard towards his injured friend, but Robin shook his head, clenching his teeth in pain. "I don't think so." He took the proffered weapon and with a super-human effort, managed to haul himself upright, but his vision blurred and he almost threw up as a wave of nausea swept over him.

"You'll do," Scarlet grunted appreciatively at Robin's display of willpower.

In truth, the young man had all but given up on life – he was physically and mentally utterly beaten. But the knowledge that Will had risked his own life to climb into this stronghold just to rescue him had given him back a little of his spirit.

Enough at least to face death like a warrior.

A man appeared, stopping momentarily to check on the two guards Will had dispatched, then, finding them dead, he stood and moved towards Robin's cell.

Will held his sword behind his back so it wouldn't gleam in the light of the torch that was being carried along the corridor towards them, while Robin clung to the thick wooden shaft of the pole-arm and prayed to the Magdalene to grant him the strength to wield it.

The torch-bearer moved straight along the passageway towards them, holding the light in his left hand and a quarterstaff in his right.

A cold sweat broke out on Will's back and neck; it was clear the man was coming straight for them, and felt confident enough in his own ability to take on whoever had killed two of the castle guards. It had to be Gisbourne himself.

Will could fight. He'd done so with distinction alongside the military Orders in the Holy Land after all. But he would be the first to admit his style was one of brute force, power and more often than not, sheer recklessness.

He knew he couldn't best Gisbourne. The only outlaw that could ever have beaten him was propped up on the stolen pole-arm next to him, gasping with the effort of holding himself upright.

Tensing himself, pulse thundering in his ears, Scarlet waited for Gisbourne to reach the cell door, determined to land the first blow; maybe he could take the bastard's hand off before he knew what was happening!

The king's man reached the cell and, with a roar, Scarlet threw himself at the cell gate, battering it open, but his target moved, stepping to one side and allowing the furious outlaw to barrel past.

"What the hell are you doing?"

Will faced his opponent in confusion as the torch was raised and he realised his mistake. It wasn't Sir Guy of Gisbourne that came hunting them after all.

"Tuck! How the hell did you get in here?"

The friar threw him a grin as he moved into the cell to check on Robin who still stood, swaying, as he clung onto his makeshift walking stick. "Walked in the front door. Much cleaner than climbing in through that latrine."

His eyes took in Robin's terrible injuries, but he too had served in the Holy Land, so he didn't allow his emotions to take control of him. They had no time to waste on questions or even rudimentary first-aid.

"We have to get out of here. Now," he said. "Where's that spare robe of mine you were wearing?"

"I left it in the latrine, under the bench," Will replied. "It stank, remember. Why?"

Tuck whispered a very un-Christian oath. "We might have been able to disguise Robin with it and leave the same way I came in. The guards weren't interested in looking at me too closely – I told them the sheriff had summoned me to preside over a wedding and I'd been late. They let me in without a fuss, despite the hour. They'd probably been drinking. But even so, there's no way they'll let me back out with Robin beside me."

"How high's that latrine?"

Will and the friar turned in surprise at Robin's question.

"Too high for you to climb in your state," Will replied sadly.

"How high?"

"The height of three or four men. Like I say, too high" –

"We need a rope then," their young leader mumbled through cracked lips. "You two should be able to lower me down, eh?"

Will thought about it for a second then nodded. "Aye, that'd work. We can make a rope out of the sheets in the room beside the latrine. I don't know how we'll get you along the hallway back there though. Anyone that sees you will know what's happening and raise the alarm. We can't fight our way out of here – Tuck's not much fitter than you, he's just woke up remember."

Tuck placed his torch into a sconce on the wall and shrugged out of his grey robe and pulled it over Robin's head, arranging the hood so it hid the young man's battered face. "Come on, let's get the hell out of here."

"Wait. Hold him," Will said to the friar, taking the pole arm from Robin's thick purple fingers and leaning it against the cell wall. He drew his sword again and carefully, but powerfully, hacked down on the shaft of the long wooden weapon, taking the steel blade off the end. He handed it back to Robin with shrug. "Looks a bit more like a clergyman's staff now."

The friar recovered his torch and then they walked as fast as possible back along the corridor, ignoring the pleas for help from the other prisoners, only stopping so Tuck could remove one of the dead guards' surcoats and put it on.

Two of the sheriff's men and a feeble old Franciscan friar... Maybe they'd get out of here alive after all...

They had to move slowly, with Tuck and Scarlet supporting Robin as they climbed the stairs back to the ground floor. If any of the other guardsmen had appeared it would have been the end for the outlaws, but somehow the friar's eyes retained their mischievous sparkle and Will's indomitable spirit saw him carry most of the weight of his injured leader.

"You'll have to walk from here," he said to Robin as they reached the top of the stairs and the door that led out onto the main corridor. "If we support you it'll look suspicious."

Robin sucked air in through his teeth and nodded in silent determination.

Will pulled the heavy door open and, all three of them praying silently, they moved into the hallway.

The sounds from the feast had grown louder as more wine and ale had been consumed – even through the doorway men's voices could be heard raised in jest or argument, while women laughed shrilly and the minstrels tried to be heard over the whole cacophony.

"Move!" The hallway was empty, so Will strode forward, grasping Robin by the upper arm, his eyes fixed on the final door on the right where he'd left the guard, James, bound and gagged, and where they'd find the sheets to make a rope for Robin to climb out of this place.

Tuck did his best to keep up and between them, he and Will practically carried their hooded friend for what seemed like an eternity, until they came to the door they were heading for and Will turned the handle to let them inside.

It refused to move.

"What's wrong?" Tuck demanded as Scarlet wiggled the latch and cursed.

"It's locked from inside," the infuriated outlaw replied, eyes flicking nervously along the hallway as he continued to try the handle. "The latch must have fallen when I left the room earlier!"

The sound of footsteps came to them then, and a man's voice, singing softly to himself, apparently drunk.

"Come on, Will!" Tuck hissed, but the door was locked and no amount of shaking was going to free it.

The singer – an obviously wealthy man from his expensive clothing – appeared from the stairwell to the latrine and cast an inebriated eye over them, an idiotic half-smile on his face. He nodded inanely at them as he moved past, and the outlaws felt a moment of relief.

The man stopped a few paces along the corridor and spun round unsteadily. "I know you!" he shouted, staring at Scarlet. "You're that" –

"Open the door, Will!" Tuck roared, and launched himself at the drunkard.

Robin was left to steady himself on his staff, as Will stood back and hammered kick after kick into the sturdy door while the friar landed a flurry of punches into the unfortunate nobleman who collapsed in a heap on the stone floor.

"Open it, now!" Friar Tuck glared at the red-faced, panting Scarlet and leaned down to drag the unconscious nobleman over to the doorway which, finally, burst open with a massive crash.

Robin limped into the room, as Will grabbed the right bicep of the unconscious party-goer and he and Tuck dragged the man inside.

They pushed the door shut behind them, just as a clamour of voices came to them from the feast. From the sound of it, at least half a dozen men had decided to go for a piss at the same time, and the outlaws shook their heads in relief.

"Just as well you got that door open," Tuck said to Will, who threw him a sour look as he finished with, "it took you long enough."

"Hurry," Robin muttered, slipping to the floor, his eyelids fluttering weakly.

"Right." Will nodded, taking in the sight of the guard, James, still safely bound on the floor, watching them intently. "We can use these." He grabbed a pile of neatly folded white sheets and hurriedly tied them together. "Four or five will be enough...are you going to have the strength to hold onto this as we lower you down?"

Robin watched his friend as if in a daze, and Will shook his head in frustration as he looked over at Friar Tuck. "I'll make it six so we can tie one around his waist. He's not going to be much help like that."

"What about him?" Tuck asked, nodding at the guardsman lying tied up on the floor. "He'll give us away. I'm pleased, but surprised, that you left him alive in the first place."

Will shrugged as he tied the sheets together. "We shared a few ales with his brother earlier tonight. He's the guard that climbed out the latrine to see his girl, remember?"

Tuck locked eyes with the bound guard whose expression was unreadable. He walked over to him as Will finished tying the last of the sheets together and leaned down, their eyes still fixed on each other's.

"Your brother seems a good man, and, from what he told us, so are you," the friar said. "So are we." He gazed earnestly at the man. "Look at what your Sir Guy of Gisbourne did to our friend. Robin Hood: a man who helped the poor to eat in winter! A man who steals from those who are obscenely wealthy to give to the likes of your brother. Gisbourne almost killed him, and Sir Henry de Faucumberg *will* hang him if he can."

Scarlet tied off the last of the sheets and bundled the lot together in his arms. "Don't give us away James, eh?"

The guard looked at Will, then at Tuck, and finally, nodded his head. Will smiled, praying the man would keep his promise.

"Let's get out of here."

* * *

Edmond, trusting the Hospitaller would return, had crafted a small fire and, exhausted by their long journey, sunk into a kind of a trance state once he'd managed to get a blaze going with his flint and steel. The camp-fire filled his vision and the heat drove the ache from his muscles as he gazed into the hypnotic dancing flame and pondered his life.

His brother was dead, but he still had the knight. Sir Philip would reward Edmond with silver once he turned over the Hospitaller – enough to expand his father's old tannery on the edge of town so he could continue to support himself.

The thought both comforted and sickened him. He would be able to make a comfortable living until he was elderly, which was all a man could ask for. But at the same time, he knew those bastards in Kirklees would continue to look down on him as if he was beneath them.

He felt old. Much older than he should have at his twenty-four years. He shook his head angrily. Once he built a bigger tannery he would be able to earn more money and he could find a new wife. The village men didn't care about looks when it came to marrying off their daughters, only status and, more importantly, money mattered.

He would have enough money to marry whoever he liked!

Then...then the men would respect him.

He slammed his fist onto the ground in frustration. He was as bad as them, trying to impress them, to be accepted for his wealth, as if their fucking opinion mattered.

For his entire life, Edmond had been confused, wanting to be accepted and respected, and resenting his brother for holding him back socially. The warm tears filled his eyes as he thought of Walter, innocent Walter, who simply wanted to be everyone's friend.

A cold rage filled him then, as the injustice of his whole life filled his head, and it was just as well, as a figure flew from the trees towards him, sword held high ready for a killing blow.

Edmond somehow managed to lift the sword he'd taken from Sir Richard and parried the attacker's blow awkwardly as he jumped to his feet. He felt his wrist twisting as the steel blades met with a deafening noise and pain lanced along the length of his arm, making him cry out.

He held the Hospitaller's sword before him, eyes flickering wildly, as two other men appeared either side of his attacker.

"What do you want?" Edmond demanded, his voice stronger than he'd expected, given the fear coursing through his veins at the odds stacked against him.

"Your fire," his original attacker grunted with a confident grin. "And any food you have – we're starving, see?" He patted his round belly which looked as if it had been filled with both food and ale often enough over the years, then his face became deadly serious. "And we'll have that fine blade."

Edmond's eyes moved between the three robbers and the anger built inside him again. People always treated him like a piece of shit! Even the dregs of society, like these toothless outlaws, would order him around as if he was nothing.

It didn't matter to Edmond then that the three men were well-armed and decently armoured, the rage was in him now and he didn't care if he lived or died.

All he wanted to do was kill these dirty, smug bastards.

Sweeping Sir Richard's sword up into the air, Edmond gave a hoarse war-cry and launched himself at the three robbers.

He would die here, but rather that than have anyone else treat him like filth.

* * *

When the hallway was quiet the three outlaws made their way out of the linen store and headed up the stairs to the latrine. Will went first, to deal with anyone that might get in their way, but there was no one there and they made it safely into the room.

Tuck had been forced to support his terribly beaten young leader up the steps, even though he himself was badly weakened from his own recent ordeal. By the time the pair reached Will, they were both breathing heavily and obviously struggling.

Will had shoved the wooden bench aside and retrieved the Franciscan robe, which he handed to Tuck as he hobbled into the room. "Stick it on. Aye, it stinks, but it'll keep the shit on the walls off you when you climb down."

"We can't all go down at once," the friar said, pulling the stained robe over his tonsured head. "Me and you will have to lower him down." He nodded at Robin who lay with his back against the wall, bruised face screwed up as the constant pain from his numerous injuries racked his body. "What if someone walks in? A guard?"

Will began tying the sheet around Robin's waist. "I'm dressed like one of them," he replied, patting the blue surcoat. "If anyone comes up the stairs we'll hear them and I'll tell 'em the latrine's busy. If it's a guard..." He shrugged. They'd deal with that if it happened.

"Come on, Robin," he knelt down and used his great arm and shoulder muscles to help the young man up. "You'll have to wake up a bit," he said, staring into his leader's eyes. "Otherwise you're going to end up lying in a pile of shit when you reach the bottom."

Robin gave a weak nod and glanced towards the opening as Will dropped the hacked-off pole-arm into the void.

"Right, let's do it."

Tuck and Will helped Robin over the edge of the wall, making sure they held the tied-together sheets firmly, and then they started to slowly lower him down to the ground.

They played the fabric out, hand over hand, their young friend doing just enough to keep himself from battering painfully off the grimy wall, then Will froze, his heart sinking as someone came into the room behind them. Turning, he heard the sound of a surprised breath being drawn before the man challenged them in a commanding voice.

"What the hell are you men doing in here?"

CHAPTER EIGHTEEN

Tuck didn't seem to hear the question, but Will's head spun round and he looked at the nobleman watching them in bemusement.

Concentrating as they were on lowering Robin down the stinking shaft, the friar and the ex-mercenary hadn't heard the tall man coming up the stairs. Will cursed inwardly as he took in the man's height – bigger than he and Tuck – and his apparently alert expression; this party-goer didn't seem to be anything like as drunk as the rest of the fools that had been stumbling around the castle for the past few hours.

Thankfully, the newcomer had taken in the guard's surcoat Will wore and, despite his curiosity, didn't seem too alarmed at what was going on.

"I dropped something down the latrine," Tuck smiled ruefully at the man. "My rosary beads. Archbishop Melton gave them to me," he added sadly. "This guard was kind enough to help me try and recover them without climbing in amongst all the...filth...down there."

As the man walked forward to look down the shaft where Tuck was gesturing, the two outlaws continued to play out the sheet until, thankfully, they felt the material go slack and knew Robin must have reached the bottom.

The big man peered down into the inky darkness just as Will released the sheet and brought his right fist up to hammer into the man's jaw, but, before he could collapse backwards onto the floor, Tuck grasped the back of his head and pushed him forwards, down the latrine shaft.

There was a wet thump as the stunned man landed face-first in the pile of shit below and Tuck couldn't suppress a shudder.

"He's unconscious," the friar said, looking over the edge, the light from the torches guttering in the room they stood in casting just enough orange light below.

"Or dead," Will growled in reply. "Get down there, in case he wakes up. Or drowns." He gestured to the sheet that still lay hanging down the shaft, tying it around the bench which he shoved against the wall as Tuck disappeared below.

Will stood, hand ready on the pommel of his sword, but no one else came into the latrine until the friar reached the bottom of the latrine wall.

He untied the white sheet and tossed it down the shaft so no one would see it and wonder at its purpose, then he carefully made his way over the ledge, his feet and hands finding the gaps in the mortar that he'd used to make his original ascent. He stretched up and pulled the mildew-encrusted bench over the opening behind him, casting the shaft into almost total darkness.

A man came in to the latrine to take a piss as the outlaw climbed slowly down into the void, but Will smiled thankfully as the warm liquid passed him some way to the side, splattering noisily onto the mound of waste beneath.

Below, Tuck's grasping fingers finally managed to find the torch they had left there earlier that night, and, as Will reached the bottom, the pitch flared into life and the outlaws shielded their eyes against the brightness Tuck's spark had ignited.

Robin sat near the door, his eyes closed as if in sleep, but Will could see the young man's chest rise and fall and he thanked Christ for it. That they had managed to get this far was a miracle, he thought.

The nobleman Tuck had shoved over the ledge hadn't fared so well, Will saw, taking in the sickening angle the man's right arm lay at in relation to his body. Clearly the bone was broken. They pushed him onto his side, hoping the faecal matter wouldn't infect the open wound where the snapped bone had torn through the skin.

"He'll live," Will growled, shaking his head contritely. "Unlike us if we're found. What do we do now, Tuck?"

Tuck looked at his friend in surprise. "I don't have a clue. I never expected us to get this far!"

Will shrugged his big shoulders. "We can't stay here; they'll rip the whole castle apart once they discover Robin missing and this one starts screaming," he nodded down at the unconscious noble. "We'll head back to the *King and Castle*. It's not far and our disguises should see us past any nosy guards. We can hide Robin in our room and pay to stay a couple more nights until we think about what to do next."

Tuck nodded uncertainly, his face pallid and sickly-looking in the torch's flickering glow. "What about that guard James? If he tells his brother what's happened tonight, word will spread and the sheriff will know where to come looking for us."

It was a gamble they had to take. There was no other choice. Even if Robin and Tuck had been fully fit, they couldn't have just climbed over the walls out of Nottingham, in the dead of night, without being spotted.

"Come on," Will replied, taking the torch from the friar and extinguishing it in the mound of human waste with a noisome stench that caught in their throats. "Let's head back to the inn. All we can do is pray God brings us luck. We're going to need it..."

* * *

Sir Richard was gasping for breath by the time he made it back to the camp-site, but he didn't have time to rest as his eyes took in the scene before him.

Edmond, blood covering his sword-arm, had been forced back against the thick trunk of an old beech, and desperately parried the attacks from two enraged men. A third man knelt on the ground behind them clutching his side which was also drenched in blood.

Awkwardly freeing the concealed dagger that was strapped to his calf, the big knight burst from the trees, surprising the attackers, and hammered the small blade into the nearest man's guts, forcing it up with all his strength and ripping it out with a wet sucking sound.

The man collapsed onto the grass, his eyes wide in shock and fear as his hands tried to cover the obviously mortal wound. Sir Richard kicked him in the face and grabbed the sword which fell from his limp fingers.

The remaining outlaw, terrified now, looked at the old knight, saw the feared Hospitaller cross on his black surcoat and decided to make a run for it. Before he could move though, Edmond swung his stolen sword in a high, wide arc and felt it bite into the side of the outlaw's skull, sending the man face-first onto the grass already dead.

Knowing the fight was over, Sir Richard placed his hands on his thighs and sucked in lungfuls of air.

Edmond, rage still burning in his veins, stalked towards his original attacker, who knelt, pale-faced, on the ground, blood seeping from the gash in his side that Edmond had inflicted on him.

"You win," the man growled, his face twisted bitterly. "Just let me" –

Sir Richard winced as Edmond hacked his sword down into the outlaw's shoulder, slicing halfway into the man's torso.

"Here," the tanner's son whispered, turning and throwing the sword onto the grass in front of the Hospitaller. "Have your sword back." Then he walked over to sit by the fire, staring into it in a daze as Sir Richard stooped to retrieve his weapon.

As the knight wiped the blade clean using one of the dead outlaws' cloaks, silent tears streamed down Edmond's face. It had been a hard couple of days.

Sir Richard searched the corpses, finding little of value other than some food and an ale-skin, then he dragged the bodies out of sight and hurried back to where he'd dropped the firewood he'd collected before the fight.

When he returned with arms full of kindling the sun had almost crested the horizon and it was rapidly growing dark. Edmond hadn't moved, so Sir Richard built up the fire and finally sat down beside the grieving young man.

Silently, he handed Edmond the ale-skin he'd found. "Drink. It will help settle your nerves."

Sir Richard leaned back on the grass, more tired than he'd felt in his life, but then he remembered Edmond had been hurt and, muscles protesting, pushed himself to his feet and moved over to the wounded man.

It was a long cut, which explained why there was so much blood on his arm, but it wasn't deep, thankfully. The Hospitaller moved into the trees where he'd dumped the bodies of the would-be robbers and returned with a blouson which he tore into strips and used to bind Edmond's arm.

The young man grunted his thanks, an odd look in his eyes, and Sir Richard shrugged. "Finish the last of that ale and eat a little of this." He handed over some of the food – cheese and bread – that he'd taken from the dead men. "Then get some sleep. I'll keep the fire banked and take first watch."

"Watch?"

The knight smiled. "Aye, lad, watch. Those three arseholes might have friends about here that'll come looking for them. You want to die in your sleep with a sword through your stomach?"

Edmond nodded, his expression now almost childlike. "I never thought of that."

Without another word, he ate the proffered food and finished the ale, then curled into a ball close to the fire and shut his eyes. Either he'd forgotten Sir Richard was supposed to be his captive, or he simply didn't care any more.

Or perhaps he trusts me now, the old man mused, and the thought made him smile.

He'd fought well, the lad. He had a natural talent for it. If Sir Richard hadn't been a wanted rebel he might have helped Edmond find a place as a sergeant-at-arms in the Hospitallers.

At that, his thoughts drifted and he wondered again where his own faithful sergeant was. Had Stephen even made it to London and the Order's headquarters, or had some evil befallen him on the road?

Sir Richard shook his head sadly. The way things were going for them recently, it wouldn't be that much of a shock if his friend had met his doom on the road to Clerkenwell.

Or if the Grand Prior has killed him to save a scandal...

* * *

"More ale, here, inn-keep!"

Will smiled and shook his head at the friar, who had finished two bowls of mutton stew with half a loaf of black bread and now sat patting his stomach in satisfaction.

After they had escaped from the castle they'd made their way, unhindered, back to the *King and Castle.* Although it was only a short distance, by the time they reached the inn, Robin had almost passed out from pain and exhaustion, and Tuck couldn't have walked any further.

Will had helped Tuck in through the window, then, between them, they hauled Robin in, before locking the wooden shutters behind them with relieved sighs.

The room had two beds, which were little more than flimsy wooden frames with dirty old straw mattresses placed on top, but it was just what Robin needed after lying on a cold stone floor for days. He fell into a deep, healing sleep as soon as his two friends helped him onto the bed, and Will had quietly but firmly told Tuck to take the other pallet while he collapsed into a rickety old chair, the only other piece of furniture in the room.

The next day, Will had woken feeling good, but dirty. The filth that had caked him as he climbed up and down the latrine had dried into his skin and the room stank worse than it had when they'd first arrived at the inn. Still, he grinned as he looked at his two sleeping companions. They'd done it! Rescued Robin from a heavily defended castle, right under the nose of the sheriff!

His grin faded as he realised they weren't in the clear yet, far from it. The guards would have discovered their prisoner was missing by now; the castle would be in uproar. Sir Henry de Faucumberg would be livid and Christ knew what Sir Guy of Gisbourne would do.

The sun had already risen and was streaming through the gaps in the window shutters, so Will got up and shook Tuck gently awake.

"Give me your robe, and whatever else is covered in shit," he ordered. "I'll get it all washed somewhere. You'll have to help me get Robin's stuff off him too – he won't be able to do it himself."

In the light of day, Robin's injuries made Will and Friar Tuck wince as they undressed him. The young outlaw's entire body seemed to be covered in red, purple, green and yellow bruises. His fingers were terribly swollen, as was one side of his face. Dried blood caked his nose and mouth.

Scarlet felt rage building inside him as he took in the sight of his friend so horribly beaten. That bastard Gisbourne would pay for this.

Eventually, Will had the dirtiest of their clothes clutched in his hands and he pulled Tuck's spare robe, stinking as it was, over his head. He would need it to make his way through the city without being recognised.

"I'll be back soon," he promised. "Keep the door locked."

With that, he'd opened the shutter on the window and waited until the street outside was empty, before jumping out. After obtaining directions from a local man, he hurried off towards the eastern part of the city, and the local wash-house, where he knew he would find women to wash his pile of clothes for a coin or two.

It was easy enough to have the garments, and himself, washed and he made his way into a deserted alley to take off the still-dirty grey robe he was wearing and pull on the wet, but freshly cleaned spare robe. Thankfully, the sun was high in the sky so he hoped that and his own body heat would soon dry the material before he caught a chill.

He took the final dirty robe to a different washer-woman and paid her to clean off the waste caked into it, slipping her an extra silver coin to silence her questions, then he made one last stop before heading back to the inn.

As he climbed in the window, freshly scrubbed and grinning in satisfaction at Tuck and Robin, there was a hammering on the room door.

"Open up, in the name of the sheriff!"

CHAPTER NINETEEN

He had been left to wait on an audience with the Grand Prior, and, although he had been made comfortable with meat and ale, Stephen sat picking at the dry skin on his fingertips wishing the prior would call on him.

"When's the last time you were here, brother?" one of the sergeants based in Clerkenwell asked him. He was a younger man called Henry, barely in his twenties, yet he had an impressive black moustache and a ready smile which even the grumpy older Hospitaller appreciated.

"Years." Stephen shrugged, sipping a little from the cup Henry had just refilled for him.

They sat in the impressive great hall, at one of the long benches pushed in against the cold grey wall. Occasionally, people would pass through the room, some of the knights or other brothers offering a greeting, while those here merely on business – cleaners or delivery boys – kept their eyes respectfully on the ground as their footsteps echoed softly off the stone walls.

"A word of warning," the young sergeant muttered, moving closer and glancing around conspiratorially. "The prior is not quite the man you remember..."

Stephen dipped his head in acknowledgement. The men stationed here in Clerkenwell knew who he was – sergeant-at-arms to the outlawed preceptor of Kirklees – and they'd guessed his mission here.

Stephen appreciated the gentle warning, and he prepared himself mentally for the sight of Prior L'Archer, a man who had run the English Order of St John into the ground so badly that they were almost penniless.

"His moods are changeable," Henry went on in a low voice, stroking one side of his moustache thoughtfully. "If you find him in a cranky state of mind, your mission, whatever it may be, has little chance of success. If, however, he is in one of his benign stupors, there is a good chance he will acquiesce to whatever you ask of him."

Stephen grimaced as he pulled a little piece of skin on his thumb too hard, drawing a spot of blood and he sucked the stinging wound as Henry continued.

"Unfortunately, he's not often in a benign mood, and it's almost impossible to make him see sense, which is why we're living here in near-poverty."

The older man smiled sardonically at the suggestion Henry and his fellows in Clerkenwell were living in anything like poverty and he guessed the young sergeant came from a wealthy family and was yet to see action, or any other kind of service to the order, anywhere other than here in London.

They sat in silence for a while as Stephen fretted at his fingers and tried not to finish his ale too fast. He wanted to have a clear head when the prior finally deigned to see him.

Eventually the door at the far end of the hall creaked open and a stocky, bald man waved a hand at Stephen. "The Grand Prior will see you now."

He shared a nod with Henry and followed the steward along an oppressively narrow corridor, fingering his master's letter nervously, his heart thudding in his chest as if he were about to go into battle.

I suppose I am, he thought. *The result of this meeting will mean life or death for Sir Richard. I'll have to be on my guard here as much as I have in any fight I've ever been in.*

The steward showed him into a surprisingly small, cosy room. A fire burned in the hearth and a large glazed window allowed the early-spring sunshine to light the room and the ancient-looking man seated in a high-backed chair behind the huge oak desk that dominated the room.

The Grand Prior was staring at something on his desk: financial records Stephen guessed. Finally he looked up and gazed at the sergeant-at-arms through watery eyes.

"You are Sir Richard-at-Lee's sergeant, are you not?"

"Yes, Father."

"How is your master? I hear he has been disgraced. His – *our* – castle in Kirklees is under siege by the king's forces; and he has brought our Order into disrepute with his selfish actions. Frankly," his rheumy eyes, which had been wandering around the room, flicked back to bore into Stephen's. "I'm surprised to see you here. It would be better for everyone if you and Richard had been killed in the rebellion. As if we didn't have enough to worry about. Yet...here you are. Why?"

The grizzled sergeant wanted to tell the Grand Prior his financial mismanagement had done more damage to their Order than anything Sir Richard might have done, but he swallowed his retort and framed his reply more carefully.

"Father, I believe you know my master from many years ago: you served and fought together in the conquest of Rhodes. You should know, then, that he would not have acted as he did for any selfish reasons. What he did, he did for the good of his tenants, and for England."

L'Archer leaned forward in his seat, his brows lowered angrily. "His tenants, and England, are not his priority! His loyalty is, or at least should have been, first and foremost, to the Hospitallers. We can ill afford to lose the rent monies Kirklees provided, meagre as they may have been. Who knows what the king will do with the lands now? I hear he has already seized control of them and, although they are still legally ours, Edward will be in no rush to return their control – or rents – to us."

He sat back again, his thin arms resting on the big chair which seemed to dwarf him, then went on.

"You're right. I served with Richard for a time in Rhodes, and before that in Cyprus." He paused as his thoughts drifted back through the years and he remembered being a younger man, rising rapidly through the ranks.

Stephen thought the prior had fallen asleep, he remained silent for so long, but, after a while the old man sighed and gently shook his head. "Richard always wanted to do the honourable thing. I remember one of the battles we were involved in not long after he joined the Order. We were fighting in Armenian Cilicia, helping the Mongols defend some little town I forget the name of, but we were well beaten by the Mamluks. They'd been in the desert for weeks, low on food and water, and when the town fell we pulled back and left the Mongols to it. The inhabitants of the town were slaughtered: men, women, children. Raped. Tortured for sport." His damp eyes met Stephen's. "You know what I mean: you've been in sieges yourself. When the town falls, the place becomes hell-on-earth."

The sergeant nodded with a grimace, knowing it was true.

"Sir Richard personally tried to save every one of those townspeople: running here and there, dragging men off women, protecting children, stamping out fires... Eventually a couple of our brothers managed to pull him away and we made our retreat...Maybe he did some good there, who knows? I doubt it. Such is the way of war."

He shrugged. "Richard, as you say, must have been acting in the interests of the people of Kirklees. But, as in that town in Cilicia, his efforts were misguided and pointless. If you're here to ask me to speak up on his behalf with King Edward, you've wasted your time, I'm afraid. Richard is a good man; a man whose sword I was glad to have by my side in the East. Indeed, your master is the perfect knight in many respects. But his idealistic sense of honour always held him back – he would have been promoted far higher than preceptor in some little English backwater had he not been so damn...chivalrous. I'm afraid Sir Richard must fight this battle by himself – he has overstepped the mark this time. The Hospitallers will not intervene on his behalf."

Stephen felt his heart sink as the prior went on, his hands raised placatingly.

"The king will, I am sure, not be seeking any sort of vengeance against you, though. You may remain here in Clerkenwell, until I can find a suitable posting for you. They are always looking for experienced sergeants in Rhodes, for example, and it would get you out of the country."

"I thank you for your offer," Stephen replied through gritted teeth. "But if the Order will not aid us, I shall take the Great North Road back to Kirklees and stand by Sir Richard's side."

The Grand Prior tutted in annoyance. "I am your superior, sergeant. I could have you stripped of your rank and court-martialled for insubordination." He waved his hand dismissively towards the door. "I must admit, though, I admire your loyalty. You and Richard must have made a formidable team. Be off then. Refresh yourself and your horse and ride back north to your doom."

Taking a breath, Stephen pulled Sir Richard's letter from his pocket and stepped up to the desk. "Before I leave, Father, I ask that you read this."

L'Archer eyed the envelope suspiciously, then, with a speed belying his withered appearance, snatched it from Stephen's hand.

"The seal's been broken."

Stephen felt his cheeks flush. "The letter was stolen on my way here by... thieves. By the time I found them, they had opened it, no doubt hoping it contained something they could use for financial gain."

With a grunt, L'Archer pulled the parchment from the tattered envelope and began to read, his wrinkled mouth forming the words quietly as he did so.

Stephen watched as the old man's face turned first scarlet, then chalk white, and the burly steward moved forward from the doorway, concerned, as was Stephen, that the prior might faint and fall off his chair.

"Leave us," L'Archer growled at the steward, halting the man in his tracks.

"Leave us!" he ordered again when the worried man failed to move back.

The steward threw Stephen a murderous glance but he moved past him and let himself out the door, and the sergeant-at-arms realised with some surprise that the old prior was, despite his recent disastrous incompetence, still held in great respect – affection even – by some of the Hospitallers in Clerkenwell.

As the door slammed shut, the prior glared at Stephen. "Have you read this?"

"No. I was ordered not to, and I did not."

"The two...thieves, you say stole the letter from you. Did they read it?"

"I believe so, Your Grace," he replied, then raised a hand to halt the furious prior's next question. "Have no fear, neither of them will be a problem. One of them is dead, the other..." He stopped himself from admitting one of the robbers was a woman. "The other I left with smashed teeth on the Great North Road, miles back, just south of Finchley. Even if they were to tell anyone what they read, no one would believe them" –

"When you leave here, and before you return to Kirklees, you will find this other person and make absolutely certain they will never talk about this letter. Do you understand me?"

Stephen hesitated. He was no assassin, to hunt someone down like a wild animal.

"Do you understand me?" the Grand Prior demanded, his eyes suddenly clear and hard as iron. "You do want me to help your master, don't you?"

The sergeant nodded. Assassin or no, he was a soldier, and he followed orders. "I understand."

"Good." L'Archer replaced the letter back in its envelope, his hands shaking, whether from age or fury Stephen couldn't tell. "Once you have taken care of the thief, you may return to your master and inform him I will move with all haste to secure for him a pardon from our king, Edward."

Stephen felt the corners of his mouth twitch, but he knew it would be a mistake to grin. "Thank you, Your Grace."

"Get out, sergeant. I hope never to see you or Sir Richard again. Go!"

Hastily, Stephen let himself out of the room, the anxious steward pushing past him to check on the frail prior who sat, ashen-faced, staring into the merry flames in the hearth.

He had told L'Archer the truth: he had not read the letter. He had no idea what Sir Richard might have written in it. Whatever it was, though, it had worked.

Now, all he had to do was make sure Helena didn't talk, and make it back to Kirklees in time to make sure his master wasn't captured by the king's men.

* * *

"Get under the bed!" Will hissed at Robin as the pounding on the door intensified, gesturing to Friar Tuck to help move the injured young man beneath the wooden frame.

"Here!" He tossed Tuck a robe before removing his own and pulling on a dry one that matched the one he'd given to the friar.

"Open up, Franciscan, before I break the door down!"

Tuck looked dazed, but Will nodded reassuringly and, with a last glance to make sure Robin was well out of sight, gestured at the friar to take the lead and pulled the door open.

Two soldiers wearing the light blue of the sheriff's castle guard stood at the door, swords drawn. They looked confused as they took in the men before them.

"Forgive me, my son," Tuck smiled, rubbing his eyes theatrically. "My brother and I had a long night. We were still asleep when you came knocking. How can we help you?"

"We're looking for two friars," the foremost guard replied, glaring into the room suspiciously.

"Then you have found us!" Tuck grinned, raising a hand towards Scarlet who kept his face hidden in the folds of his robe.

The guards looked at each other. "We're looking for Franciscans," the leader replied. "Franciscans wearing grey robes that are probably covered in sh – I mean excrement, brother."

Tuck's face dropped. "Ah, well then, you've come to the wrong place. We are of the Order of St Augustine. And our robes are, I hope, quite clean." He cocked his head and placed a hand on the guard's arm. "May we be of service? Or must it be Franciscans?"

"Come on, it's not them," the guard at the back sheathed his sword, and his companion followed suit, eyes roving around the little room in confusion.

"No, thank you, brother. The landlord told us he had a couple of Franciscans staying here. I'm sorry we bothered you."

Tuck smiled beatifically at the retreating guard. "God's blessing on you, my son. May you find what you are looking for one day."

He closed the door behind him and threw the small bolt into place again, then sat down shakily on his bed. The outlaws remained silent, praying the soldiers wouldn't talk to the landlord and return, but moments later they could hear the guards passing in the street outside, discussing where they should try next in their search for two grey-robed Franciscan monks.

"You're a genius, Will." Tuck blew out his cheeks in shocked relief. "Buying these black robes was the best idea you've ever had!"

Will smiled sheepishly. "I didn't do it on purpose. When I washed all our gear it was soaking wet – there was no way it'd be dry for ages, but I knew the landlord would be expecting to see us in his common room at some point today. We couldn't go along for dinner wearing wet robes when it's not rained all day. So I looked for some new ones to buy. It was sheer luck that the old woman selling these," he tugged at the fabric of his garment, "only had them in black."

Tuck laughed loudly and looked piously upwards. "You work in mysterious ways, Lord!"

"Get me off this fucking floor."

Will and the friar hastily dragged their friend out from the floorboards under the rickety bed, and helped him on top of the straw mattress."Thanks lads," Robin mumbled. "I was starting to panic trapped under there. Did one of you mention dinner?"

Between them, they decided Tuck and Will should head along to the common room and have a couple of ales, just to let everyone – especially the landlord – know they were still there.

"You rest for now," Tuck said to Robin, before he realised the young man was already asleep. Shaking his head with worry, the friar led the way out of the room and Will followed behind, pulling the door shut and praying no one would go into their room and find Robin.

"Two ales, please, my child." Tuck grinned at the serving girl as they walked into the common room. It was getting late and most people had eaten their evening meal, but they found an empty table with two chairs and sank into them contentedly.

"What's the food today?" Will grunted as the barmaid set the mugs of ale on the little table.

"Beef broth," the woman replied. "We have plenty of fresh bread to go with it too."

Will's mouth watered at the thought and he and Tuck ordered a serving each.

They sat drinking their ale, quite relaxed, as the food was being prepared for them.

"Ah, brothers!" They looked up and saw the landlord carrying their wooden bowls of steaming broth along with a full loaf of bread, all of which he set down on the table before them.

The man eyed them suspiciously. "I could have sworn you were in grey robes yesterday night when you came in," he said.

Tuck shook his tonsured head indignantly. "You should really be more observant, inn-keep," he growled, glaring at the man. "We are Austins, we wear black. The soldiers you sent after us today, thankfully had better eyesight than you." He tore off a piece of bread and dipped it into his bowl of broth. "Franciscans indeed!"

Will felt like he should say something too. "Franciscans? Us?" he muttered, stuffing broth-soaked bread into his mouth. "Bloody grey-robed wandering arseholes."

The landlord didn't know whether to laugh or be shocked, so Tuck laid a comforting hand on the man's wrist. "Don't mind brother William," he whispered. "He had a bad experience with some Franciscans a long time ago."

"Right. My apologies, brothers..." the man backed away, a bemused look on his face, as Tuck shovelled more bread into his mouth and smiled at him from gravy soaked lips. "If you need anything else, just give me a shout."

Tuck waved merrily as the landlord disappeared into the back. "Wandering arseholes, eh?"

Scarlet smirked, watery brown soup dripping down his chin, eyes sparkling. "No offence."

The pair finished their meal, which was delicious after their previous night's exertions, then they sat chatting for a while over another mug of ale. To anyone watching they would have looked like any other innocent travellers enjoying the hospitality of a cheap inn.

They called the landlord over again and paid to stay in their room for another two nights, which he was clearly pleased about.

"My friend here is very tired, and we must retire for the evening, though." The friar gestured at Will who nodded in his cowl as Tuck handed over the coins for the accommodation. "But I'm still ravenous – your broth was delicious!"

The inn-keeper smiled proudly. "My own recipe, brother friar," he replied. "I'll make you up another bowl, you can eat it in your room if you prefer. Just remember to bring back the bowl in the morning."

Tuck smiled. "You have my word on it. I'll take some more of that lovely warm bread too, if I may? And could you fill our ale-skins too?"

"Aye, no problem," the man laughed, the rash on his face flaring scarlet. "I'll bring it all over to you, good friar, and welcome."

A short time later they made their way back to the ground-floor room, laden with food and drink.

Robin managed some ale and most of the broth, but it hurt him too much to chew, so Tuck finished off the bread before the three of them settled down for the night.

It was still quite early, and the sounds of merry-making drifted along from the common room, but the outlaws had full bellies, plenty of ale, and were happy to simply relax and try to recover their strength.

They were safe for now. But they would have to escape from the city eventually.

* * *

The next day Will and Tuck spent some time wandering around the city, trying to pick up bits and pieces of gossip about the search for the escaped wolf's head.

Robin was unable to move from the bed, and seemed content to simply lie there anyway, his eyes vacant and listless. Tuck in particular worried about the young man's frame of mind, but the most important thing was for his battered and bruised body to regain some of its strength so they could try and escape into the forest again.

They left their injured companion at the inn, praying the landlord wouldn't get nosy and discover Robin hiding in the room.

It was a fine spring day and the pair made their way here and there along the bustling streets and busy little marketplaces, sampling the local food and eavesdropping on conversations about Robin's miraculous escape, while Tuck doled out blessings happily.

The feeling amongst the populace seemed to be overwhelmingly one of repressed excitement, even joy. The people loved to see authority's nose out of joint, even if they appreciated the fact Sir Henry de Faucumberg wasn't the worst sheriff they'd ever had. More than that though, the citizens were drawn to Robin – he really was a folk-hero to them. Will and Tuck already knew this, to some extent, but it was humbling, and inspiring, to hear people supporting them in hushed voices.

Not just the lower classes either: well-to-do merchants and tradesmen grinned at each other in the streets, wondering if each other had heard about the outlaw being spirited out of the castle while the sheriff and his guests partied.

When they returned to the *King and Castle* in the middle of the afternoon, they carried a loaf of bread, a wheel of cheese and skins full of beer which Will hid under his cassock while Tuck engaged the inn-keeper in conversation.

"It's lamb for dinner tonight," the friar smiled as Will let him into the room and threw the bolt on the door so no one else could wander in. "I'll soon be back to full strength at this rate."

Will grunted sarcastically. "Full strength? Fat bastard more like."

"How dare you?" Tuck replied in mock indignation. "Fat bastard or not, I'll still kick your arse, Scarlet."

Will rolled his eyes and sat on the bed beside Robin who was watching the exchange with a hint of a smile on his cracked lips.

"The sheriff's got all his men out looking for you," Will said, tearing off a chunk of the loaf and soaking it in beer before feeding it to Robin who gingerly rolled the food around with his tongue until it was soft enough to swallow without chewing. Then Will crumbled some of the cheese in his hand and held some of that to his friend's mouth as well.

It wasn't the nicest meal Robin had ever eaten, but it would build him up again. They couldn't afford to keep asking the landlord for extra helpings of dinner to take back to the room every night – the man would become suspicious. Assuming he wasn't already, after their change from Franciscans to Austins.

After he finished eating Robin fell asleep so Will and Tuck sat for a while talking, wondering how they would be able to get out of the city before someone found them.

It seemed an impossible task.

"Something will turn up," Tuck promised, standing up. "The Lord will provide, you wait and see. For now, the landlord will provide. Come on, let's go and have some of that lamb while Robin gets some sleep."

The common room was quiet as it was still quite early in the day, so the pair sat at the same table they'd occupied the night before and ordered two helpings of dinner along with mugs of ale.

The food, when the serving-girl brought it steaming from the kitchen was hearty if bland. There wasn't much lamb in it, but both of the outlaws finished their bowls and shouted for second helpings.

They were happily filling their bellies when two men joined them.

"God give you good day, brothers," one of the newcomers said, staring into Tuck's eyes.

It was Roger and his friend from the night before. Tuck cursed himself for not expecting the men to return to the inn – it was their local after all, of course they would turn up!

And if Roger had spoken to his brother, James, the guard at the castle, he would know exactly who they were.

The friar's hand instinctively curled around the dagger concealed under his cassock and his mind whirled. Even if he and Will escaped into the city, Robin lay, unable to move, in their room. This was the end of them!

"Relax, friar. We won't give you away."

Will had been so utterly absorbed in his lamb that he hadn't taken any notice of the two men sitting down at their table, but he looked up now, gravy streaming down his chin and his eyes widened.

"I swear it!" Roger whispered, knowing exactly how dangerous these two seemingly incongruous "friars" could be if provoked. "James told me you were kind to him. Well, as kind as you could be in the circumstances," he smiled lopsidedly at Scarlet. "We're on your side."

His friend, Godfrey, nodded earnestly. "You can trust us, lads. We wouldn't be here otherwise, would we? We'd have sent the law and claimed the reward the sheriff's offered."

It was a good point, and Will nodded before scooping another mouthful of meat into his mouth. "Is your brother all right?"

Roger nodded as the serving-girl brought two mugs of ale over for them with a near-toothless grin. "Aye, he's fine," he replied as the girl hurried off into the kitchen to fetch some food for the newcomers. "Bit sore, since you beat the shit out of him. But those coins you slipped him will help his injured pride heal nicely." He placed his mug on the table and wiped his lip with his sleeve. "He sends his thanks. That was a lot of money you gave him, when you could have just slit his throat."

"Why didn't you anyway?" Godfrey asked seriously. "Kill him I mean. Seems a bit risky leaving witnesses alive."

Tuck broke in before his friend could reply. "We're not murderers. We're good men, like you and Roger and James, just doing what we must to survive. It's as simple as that. We don't kill for pleasure, we do it only when there's no other option."

Will grunted agreement. "I took a chance, aye, maybe a stupid chance. But after what you told us about your brother I didn't want to leave those nephews of yours without a father." He gazed at the two men disconcertingly. "Make no mistake though: if someone is a threat to us, I'll not lose any sleep if I have to tear their windpipe open."

Roger and Godfrey looked away, feeling the force of Will's glare before he wiped the gravy from his chin and began spooning the last of his meal into his mouth.

"So?" Tuck sipped his ale. "Why *are* you here if not to give us away?"

The serving-girl burst through the door from the kitchen carrying a small loaf and two bowls of food for Roger and his companion and the table fell silent as she dropped off the meals and moved away to serve other customers.

"To help you." Roger tore off a chunk of bread and dipped it into his gravy before taking a bite and moaning gently in satisfaction.

"How can you help us?" Will wondered, shoving his own empty bowl into the centre of the table and leaning back against the wall. "The city's heaving with the sheriff's men. Your brother's just a regular guard, not a sergeant or captain."

Roger shrugged sheepishly. "It's true, James can't get involved. He wants you and Robin to escape, but he won't help. If he's found out..."

"We expected you would have a plan," Godfrey growled, with a somewhat accusatory stare. "You're the experts at this. We can help create a diversion or something while you two sneak Robin out of the city?"

Will thought for a moment then turned to look at Tuck. They nodded. It was as good a plan as any and, since they hadn't come up with any plan at all, there didn't seem to be much choice.

"All right, let's think about this then," the friar nodded, clasping his mug in his hands and staring at the table, trying to work things out in his head. "Robin can barely walk. He needs someone to support him, or even a stretcher to carry him out of the city."

Will muttered agreement. "That's the easy part. The hard part will be getting past the soldiers patrolling the streets and then making it through one of the gatehouses without the sheriff's guards recognizing us. And they're going to be ten times more vigilant than normal too, to make sure Robin Hood doesn't slip past them."

"We can carry Robin on a stretcher," Godfrey suggested, looking at his friend earnestly.

"Nah," Will scowled. "We can do that ourselves. It's a diversion we need."

"But what?" Tuck muttered, clasping his mug in his hands and staring thoughtfully into it's frothy depths as the rest of the inn's patrons bustled about the room, casting dark shadows on the walls against the flickering orange light from the hearth.

"No matter what diversion we come up with," Roger told them, "the gatehouse guards will never leave their posts. So you'll still have to fight your way past them one way or another."

Will drained his mug, a thoughtful look on his face. "They don't have to *leave* their post...they just have to be distracted long enough for us to get out..."

"Blowjobs."

Roger and Godfrey stared at Friar Tuck in shock and Will couldn't help roaring with laughter. He caught himself, not wanting to draw attention to their table, but no one in the place took any notice of another man in his cups enjoying himself.

"Blowjobs?"

"Aye, Roger." Tuck agreed, looking at the man as if he was simple. "There's no better way to distract a guard than a blowjob."

"You distracted many guards, Tuck?" Will asked innocently before the friar rammed an elbow into his friend's ribs, drawing a gasp of pain and a grin.

"Do you know any prostitutes?"

Roger nodded. "Aye, friar, a few."

"Good. Find some that still have most of their teeth and with tits that aren't dragging along the ground. We'll pay them handsomely to...distract the guards at the Cow Lane gatehouse while you two," he nodded at the men, "create a diversion that will take out the rest of the sheriff's men."

"Before we make our move though," Will broke in. "We need someone to take a message to Little John and the rest of the men."

* * *

"Will you look at that?" The young guard gazed down at the well-endowed middle-aged woman in the street below. "I wouldn't mind getting a grip of that."

"She's old enough to be your mother, Jupp, you dirty little bastard," his sergeant laughed as the lady looked up and smiled coyly before disappearing into the crowd. "Now get your eyes off the ladies, and watch who's going out the gate. The sheriff's offered a big reward to whoever catches Robin Hood or his conspirators trying to leave the city."

The pair were stationed on the north, or Cow Lane, gatehouse that afternoon and had a good view of the countryside around the city from their lofty vantage point. It was a fine spring day, and the sun shone brightly, casting a golden glow on the world around them.

Jupp's eyes roved across the city hopefully. "Hood's probably already gone."

"Not a chance," the sergeant, Gerbert, replied. "The city's been locked up tight since he escaped the castle. Everyone that's went out has been searched. He's still in here somewhere."

"I couldn't care less if he gets away," Jupp said. "He seems a good sort, from what I hear."

"Aye, well, you better keep that opinion to yourself, or the sheriff will throw you off of here himself. Now: watch the people!"

The sergeant pointed into the city, which heaved with morning business as merchants and travellers made their way in through their gatehouse and met the bustle of humanity that spent their day making money – or trying to – in Nottingham. As he turned away from Jupp, though, his eye caught a flicker of movement in the trees outside the city.

He placed his hands on the battlements and stared out, but he saw nothing moving now.

"Jupp! Here! You see anything over there?"

The young guard followed his superior's pointing finger, his forehead wrinkled in concentration.

Suddenly, a figure darted out from the foliage and ran parallel to the castle walls. Two more men followed, clad in brown clothing and crouching low to the ground.

"I see them," Gerbert growled as Jupp opened his mouth to speak. "They're making for the west gatehouse." He turned to look at his subordinate. "It's Hood's men, it has to be: they're here for him."

"What do we do?"

The sergeant stared out over the battlements, looking for more signs of movement, hoping to gauge the strength of the force coming for them.

"Raise the alarm," he replied. "Tell the sergeant to fortify the western wall. There's no way Hood's men can break in here now we know they're coming. Move it, lad!"

"How do you know it's Hood's gang?" Jupp gasped, fingering the pommel of his sword in excitement.

"Who else could it be? Besides, my eyesight isn't *that* bad; I could tell the man leading them was a giant. It has to be John Little. What the fuck are you waiting for? Go!"

CHAPTER TWENTY

Robin and Will were back at the inn, while Friar Tuck, in his Austin disguise, had ventured out into the city to watch for the guards' movements. When he saw a force of a dozen men making their way hastily to the city's western wall he knew it was time and hurried back to the *King and Castle*. They would get out of Nottingham now, or they wouldn't get out at all.

"Come on," he urged, as Will opened the door to their room and he bustled inside. "John and the rest must be here: the sheriff's men have reinforced the western gate."

They had asked Roger to take word to their friends in Barnsdale, outlining their plan to Little John. Now, they would find out if it would work.

The three outlaws, all dressed now in black robes, climbed out the window into the street, bringing curious stares from passers-by, but it was too late to worry about that now. They headed for the north gate, Tuck and Will supporting Robin as he limped along between them.

The sound of distant shouting reached them and they guessed John and the rest of the men had started their "siege" on the castle walls. Of course, the outlaws wouldn't be so stupid as to seriously attempt to force their way into the city, but it would, hopefully, provide enough of a diversion for the three trapped men to escape while the guardsmen were otherwise occupied. Hopefully Roger and Godfrey had arranged the prostitutes to make things a little easier.

Robin was so badly injured he became almost a dead-weight as they made their ponderous way towards the northern gatehouse and Tuck was sweating before they'd covered even half the distance.

The guards would realise soon enough that the outlaws outside the castle didn't have the numbers, or equipment to pose a real threat. Then the soldiers would drift back to their usual posts and the opportunity to make it out would be gone for the friar and his two friends.

"Come on, Tuck," Scarlet growled, raising Robin higher on his side to ease the friar's burden a little. "We have to move quicker."

They reached the stables where Tuck had, two days earlier, paid for two horses to be ready to leave that day and, offering smiling blessings to the stable-master – and another silver coin – they lifted Robin onto one, as Tuck climbed on behind him to make sure the wounded outlaw didn't slip off into the road.

Will vaulted onto his own palfrey, and, with a cheery wave from the happy stable-master, who pretended not to notice the swords sticking out from under the black cassocks, they made their way at a trot towards the gatehouse.

"We're moving too slow!" Will growled.

Tuck knew the ex-mercenary was right, but they couldn't whip their horses into a gallop through the crowded Nottingham streets without attracting attention from the guards who still patrolled the area.

They approached the north gate and Tuck's heart sank as half a dozen soldiers jogged past them. The one at the front, a younger man, shouted up at the sergeant gazing down from atop the battlements. "It was just a diversion – only a dozen or so of them! Gisbourne says Hood must have been hoping to sneak out while most of us were defending the western gate."

"Oh shit," Will muttered, looking over at his companions. "Now what do we do? Head back to the inn? How the hell are we ever going to make it out of here now?"

The sergeant on the wall grinned down at his subordinates as they reached the gatehouse and began making their way back inside. "A diversion eh? They'll have to do better than that then!"

Even if Robin wasn't almost crippled the three outlaws couldn't have fought their way through the garrison on the wall in front of them. "Come on, let's turn back, before they see us." Tuck jerked his head in the direction of the *King and Castle*, the blood pumping nervously through his veins as he realised they were probably going to die in this city now.

Suddenly, from the south, there was a huge roar and the distant sound of people screaming filled the air. Everyone around the northern gate froze in shock, wondering what had made such a noise.

Then, into the silence there came another, even louder, thundering crack and the outlaws' mounts skittered nervously, eyes bulging in fear as the breeze carried the unmistakable smell of burning to them.

The soldiers on the wall looked to their sergeant for guidance, but he was unsure himself.

Then, from the direction of the noise and smell, voices could be heard, raised in panic, and the fear spread like wildfire through the thronged citizens, who began to make their way to their homes, where they could lock their doors and hide from whatever was happening. Soon, words could be distinguished through the babble.

"Robin Hood's men! Robin Hood's men are attacking!"

Tuck and Will Scarlet looked at each other warily, wondering what the hell was going on.

Suddenly, one of the sheriff's personal guard appeared, shoving his way through the throng, his face black with soot, eyes startlingly white in contrast.

"You men!" he roared up at the soldiers on the gatehouse. "Hood's men are attacking the Chapel Bar gate! They've used fire to destroy some of the buildings. We're in danger of being overrun, come with me, now!"

The soldiers, finally offered some leadership, rushed to obey, running down the stairs in the gatehouse to follow the sheriff's man who had disappeared off to the west.

"That was Roger, he must have borrowed his brother's uniform!"

Tuck grinned as the guards raced past, swords drawn. "Aye! Come on, I don't know what's happening, but he's emptied the gatehouse for us!"

They spurred their horses forward, and Will jumped to the ground, heading for the great wooden beam that held the two massive gates locked shut. He put his hands underneath it and heaved.

"You, friar, get the fuck away from there!"

The area was almost empty, the bewildered locals having made themselves scarce, so the sound of descending footsteps carried clearly to Will as he gave an almighty grunt and forced the heavy wooden lock from its fixings.

The guard sergeant, Gerberd, burst out of the tower with his sword drawn and headed straight for Will.

To him, it looked like a party of three clergymen – one of them seriously ill – had decided to try and escape the apparent carnage inside the city. But, as he closed on the Austin that had unlocked the gate, something made Gerberd hesitate.

Perhaps it was the way the friar held himself, or maybe it was the steely eyes that gazed out at him from under the cowl. Whatever it was, Gerberd pulled up before he reached the gate and raised his sword before him.

He was just in time, as Scarlet threw aside his cassock and pulled his own sword silently from its leather and wood sheath.

The two blades met with a sharp metallic ring, and both men instinctively spread their feet wide defensively.

"How come you didn't go with the rest of your men?" Will asked, bringing his sword round in a blur. "Too scared?"

The guard halted the outlaw's attack, batting Scarlet's sword to the side and aiming a blow of his own which was also parried.

"No – too smart!" Gerberd gasped as the weapons met again with bone-crunching force. "There was no way anyone would have had time to get up here from Chapel Bar so soon after those noises. It was a setup. It's just a shame the rest of my men were too stupid to realise it."

The man was good with a sword, and Will, hampered by the ill-fitting black cassock was forced onto the back foot as Gerberd aimed blow after blow at him.

Suddenly the outlaw stepped on the hem of the ridiculous robe and stumbled into his opponent who reacted with glee, showing Scarlet backwards, sprawling onto the ground with the breath knocked out of him.

He raised his sword triumphantly and collapsed sideways as Tuck's quarterstaff hammered against the back of his skull with a horrendous crack.

"Get it open!" the friar shouted at Will, gesturing towards the gate.

Scarlet scrambled to his feet, shoving his sword back into its sheath and threw his weight against one of the sturdy gates which opened readily enough.

Tuck and Robin rode out as Will hauled himself onto his own horse and followed behind them.

Somehow they'd escaped from Nottingham, but, as he spurred his horse to catch up with his friends Will looked at Robin's limp form and wondered if their young leader would ever be the same again.

* * *

"What will they do to you? Hang you?"

Sir Richard nodded as they walked on towards Pontefract, his expression thoughtful. "No doubt. The king wanted bloody revenge against those who rebelled, and Sir Hugh Despenser – Edward's closest friend – is no friend of mine. There's little chance I will get out of this alive, but we'll see what fate God chooses for me."

Edmond looked at the big Hospitaller, admiring the man's stoicism and apparent courage in the face of a near-certain death sentence.

Truth was, Sir Richard, rather like his friend Robin Hood not that far away in Nottingham, had felt his spirit break. His love of life had gone and the desire to fight no longer drove him. It wasn't courage that led him to Pontefract; it was simple apathy.

Yet Edmond took in the knight's proud bearing and felt himself warming to the prisoner he was about to deliver up for judgement to the king's men.

They hadn't spoke much since the robbers had attacked, but a mutual respect had developed between them. Sir Richard, for his part, felt pity for Edmond and the lamentable fate life had dealt the man, but he didn't allow it to show in his eyes, knowing it would crush Edmond even more.

The young tanner's son from Kirklees, given time to replay the botched ambush that led to his little brother's death, had come to grudgingly accept that Sir Richard wasn't to blame for it. And the Hospitaller had saved Edmond's life when the outlaws had struck after all.

Sir Richard's noble grace and bearing, and savagery in battle, impressed Edmond greatly and he found himself wishing he didn't have to hand him over to the law. Still, the knight apparently felt they were following God's will, so...he might as well make the most of the situation: take the money and the respect he would gain from capturing such a high-profile rebel.

If it was God's will, who was Edmond to question it?

Sir Richard looked over and gave him a sad, yet somehow encouraging smile, and the young man sighed.

An hour later, Edmond saw the top of Pontefract Castle towering over the treetops in the near-distance, and pointed it out in a subdued voice.

"Where?" the Hospitaller replied, screwing up his eyes and cursing, but all he could see so far off was an indistinct blur. "My eyes aren't what they used to be, lad. I'll take your word for it. Just in time eh? My feet are aching."

"Will Sir Philip be there, do you think?"

Sir Richard had no idea. "I hope so," he replied. "The sooner we get this over with the better for everyone."

Take care of Stephen for me, Lord, he prayed, wondering again where his faithful sergeant-at-arms was and hoping that, since he obviously hadn't succeeded in procuring aid for Sir Richard from the

Grand Prior in time to help him, he might at least find some other place for himself within their Order.

Traffic on the road became a little heavier as they neared the castle.

Merchants and waggoners delivering food and drink eyed them curiously, wondering at the proud Hospitaller being shadowed by the nervous-looking commoner.

"Here." Sir Richard handed his sword to Edmond as they neared their destination. "You'll want to make it look more like I'm your captive. Stand up straight. Try to look like a man that bested a Hospitaller knight not some scared peasant that can't wipe his own arse."

The crisp commands were uttered in a friendly tone yet Edmond found himself almost involuntarily obeying the older man, his shoulders pushing back and a grim expression coming over his face as he brandished the knight's sword menacingly.

Sir Richard nodded and smiled encouragingly. "Let's go get your reward, and see what the king has in store for me."

They walked up to the castle gates, the two guards eyeing them suspiciously, but the Hospitaller had allowed his proud shoulders to slump and his face looked old and haggard as he gazed balefully at the soldiers, who visibly grew in confidence as they took in the strange pair coming towards them.

"State your business," the eldest of the two demanded, grasping his halberd threateningly, although he didn't seem sure who to address: the defeated looking yet expensively armoured knight, or the unattractive sword-wielding commoner who seemed to be in charge.

Edmond spoke up, his nerves making his voice hoarse. "I am here to see Sir Philip of Portsmouth. He tasked me with capturing one of the rebel lords. As you can see, I have the man." The young tanner pointed the sword at the knight's back. "Sir Richard-at-Lee."

The guards looked at each other, although they seemed unimpressed and Edmond found himself feeling irritated at that.

"Move on then," the guard waved the pair through the gates as a heavily laden wagon rattled up behind them. "The steward will show you where to take your prisoner until Sir Philip sees you."

They walked through the imposing entrance, into the courtyard, and Edmond felt his stomach lurch. This was it. They were inside. No going back: Sir Richard would be hung, and it was his fault, just like it was his fault Walter was dead.

What have I done?

The steward, a tall yet strangely effeminate man appeared, hurrying over to them. He was flanked by two stocky guardsmen who moved quickly to search Sir Richard, none too gently, for concealed weapons. They removed the dagger strapped to his calf then took up positions either side of him, satisfied that he posed no immediate threat but alert nonetheless.

"Come. Sir Philip has been informed of your presence."

Edmond didn't have time to think about what was happening now, as the steward, who recognised the captured Hospitaller from numerous previous visits there over the years, led them through a thick door and along a short corridor that fed out onto the castle's great hall.

The large room was deserted, as Edmond and his prisoner were made to stand before the massive main table which was laden with jugs of wine and ale.

A short time later the eastern door of the hall was thrown open and six men strode into the room.

Sir John de Burton, newly appointed seneschal of the castle, led the way, followed by Sir Philip of Portsmouth and four more soldiers, one of whom wore a different livery to the rest of the guards they'd seen so far. Sir Richard assumed the man was Sir Philip's own captain.

The two noblemen took seats behind the big table and, staring almost gleefully at the defeated Hospitaller, filled their cups from the jugs before them.

"So..." Sir Philip turned his gaze to Edmond, who bowed comically, having no idea how to behave in this situation. "You managed to capture him! I have to be honest, I never expected this. A knight of St John, captured by a common villager!"

"Not just me, my lord," Edmond told him. "My brother Walter too, although the Hospitaller killed him..."

"Yes, well, congratulations, young man. You and your brother have my thanks, and the king's too. You will be well rewarded, have no fear."

The nobleman nodded and one of the castle guards moved forward, gently taking Edmond by the arm and leading the surprised young tanner from the room.

The door was pulled shut by the soldier and Edmond was led back out to the gatehouse where the castle steward stood talking to a merchant.

"Ah, the hero of the day," the steward smiled. "You have performed a great service to England, and Sir Philip has given me this for you, with his thanks." He pressed a small bag into the young tanner's hand and gestured to the gatehouse. "You may return to your village and tell them all you single-handedly captured a Hospitaller knight."

"It wasn't single-handedly, my brother Walter" –

The steward nodded, still smiling condescendingly, and looked at the guard behind Edmond, who again took him by the arm and steered him off towards the castle exit.

Too dazed to protest, the young man found himself back outside the castle, looking at the heavy grey clouds that threatened to burst upon the land at any minute.

Clearly Sir Philip and Sir John's gratitude didn't extend to offering him a meal, a room, or even a pallet in the servant's quarters for the night. He pulled his cloak tighter around him, trying to cover the top of his neck where a draught always seemed to get in, and resigned himself to making the long journey back to Kirklees.

"Fucking arseholes," he muttered to himself. Still, he had his reward, and he found his spirits rising again as he moved along the road back home and grasped the little coin-purse. He emptied the money into his hand, imagining what he'd do with his new-found wealth.

The sky above him split asunder and torrential rain hammered down on him as he gazed at his reward for capturing Sir Richard-at-Lee.

He wasn't great at counting, but Edmond knew the silver he held added up to fifteen shillings. To a peasant this was a great sum of money. But he wasn't a peasant, he was a tradesman who owned his own shop now – a tanner. This was no more than he could earn himself in a few weeks!

The rain poured down his face, mingling with tears of rage and he collapsed onto his knees on the soaking road. His brother had died for this? He was hardly better off than he was yesterday! His dream of expanding his father's shop was crushed, his family was gone, and, he knew, the people of Kirklees would hold him in the same contempt they had for his entire life.

He raised his face to the sky and screamed in fury until his breath gave out and he held his head in his hands in despair.

CHAPTER TWENTY-ONE

Stephen had left Clerkenwell at dawn the morning after his meeting with the Grand Prior. L'Archer would have liked to have thrown him back onto the streets directly after their meeting, but a lifetime of offering hospitality had forced him to allow the sergeant-at-arms to spend a few hours in bed and be furnished with some provisions to see him back along the Great North Road.

Pushing his mount, although not too hard now since he'd carried out his mission, he had found the spot where he'd ridden down the blacksmith and his wife, but there was no sign of either. There may have been a shallow grave somewhere in the undergrowth beside the road, but Stephen didn't have the time, or need, to hunt for it. He had to find Helena before she showed Sir Richard's letter to the Grand Prior. Judging by L'Archer's reaction, the information could have disastrous consequences for both himself and possibly the Order as a whole.

With no clues to her whereabouts, Stephen decided the most likely place to find her was in the nearest village, Highgate. Chances were that some locals had stumbled upon the injured girl with her dead husband, and would take her back to their village for medical treatment. What man could resist that innocent face?

He removed his black surcoat with its distinctive white cross that marked him as a Hospitaller, in case Helena had told anyone about him and tried to stop him from finding her.

It proved a wise move, as, on approaching Highgate, a pair of young men passed him on their way to their labouring job at a nearby farm. Greeting them cheerily, and asking after news in their village, he feigned shock when they blurted out that a beautiful girl had been terribly wounded and her husband murdered by a rogue Hospitaller knight.

Little of interest ever happened in Highgate, which was a tiny little place, so the two young men were glad to tell Stephen everything that they'd heard, shaking their heads and asking what the world was coming to as if they really cared.

The sergeant let them speak, nodding and gasping in apparent outrage as the men talked and, eventually, they told him she'd been taken to the local inn, which also doubled as a barber's shop.

Waving goodbye to them, Stephen kicked his palfrey, its big blanket bearing the Hospitaller cross also removed earlier that morning, and rode straight into the village, eyes scanning the surroundings for any sign of the girl. The labourers had said she was terribly wounded and had been confined to bed by the surgeon, but Stephen knew Helena was more than capable of having him beaten to death by a mob of angry men if she turned on her considerable charm.

The village was small, and the inn stood out like a cow in a chicken coop, but Stephen knew it was foolhardy to just walk in the front door and ask to see the injured girl. Night was approaching anyway, so he left his horse hobbled to a tree in the thick woods outside the village and, when darkness descended, made his way back through the gloomy streets to the alehouse, which beckoned through the chill spring air to weary travellers seeking some meagre comfort and warmth.

It seemed unlikely that whoever had brought the injured girl here would have carried her, or made her walk, up the stairs to the upper storey, but, having no idea which room she might be in, Stephen had no choice but to find a way inside and try each one until he found her.

If anyone tried to stop him, he would have to remove them as silently as possible. He was a natural, and highly skilled, fighter but he couldn't take on an entire village at once.

Stealthily making his way to the rear of the building, where passers-by wouldn't be likely to discover him, he chose the first unlit window he came to and stood outside, straining his ears for signs of life inside. Hearing nothing, he pried open the crude lock with his dagger and hauled himself into the room, praying to St John that the girl would be here, in a deep sleep, so he could get the hell out of there quick, and back to his beleaguered master.

The two low beds were unoccupied though, so he moved quickly to the door and, satisfied the hallway outside was silent, he moved out and along to the room on the left. If he had to check every room, he would. There could only be half-a-dozen guest bedrooms in a small village inn at the most anyway, and, even if he startled someone, any shouts of alarm would hopefully be drowned out by the racket coming from the common room which sounded like it was heaving with merry locals tonight.

Helena wasn't in the next room, or the one after, and the Hospitaller began to feel tense and angry, beads of sweat running down his back and making his armpits uncomfortably sticky.

He moved onto the fourth room, on the opposite side of the corridor, now working his way back to the room he'd started in. He felt like the Angel of Death, knowing his heightened state would probably lead to him killing anyone should they stumble from the common room into this quiet hallway. He stopped for a moment, slowing his breathing and forcing himself to relax.

"Give me a simple fucking battle any day," he muttered to himself, knowing the knot in his stomach was down to the fact he was here to assassinate a woman, and a beautiful woman at that.

Had it been a big, hairy-arsed outlaw, or one of the countless Saracen soldiers he'd faced before he'd followed Sir Richard back home to England, he would have been as focused and calm as a cat stalking a blackbird.

Exhaling a huge breath, visualising his nervousness leaving his body along with the spent air, he pushed open the next bedroom door and slipped inside, trying to get his bearings in the unfamiliar surroundings. The previous three bedrooms, on the other side of the corridor, had all shared the same layout, with the bed in the far right corner from the door, but he couldn't be sure these rooms would be the same, so he stood peering into the gloom, senses straining for anything that would allow him to get his bearings.

"Who's there?"

The voice that came from the left was unmistakable, although quite different to how Stephen remembered it, no doubt because most of Helena's front teeth had been smashed out by him the last time they'd met.

Knowing the girl would likewise recognise him should he speak, he remained silent but moved quickly towards the direction the voice had come from, cursing inwardly at the almost total darkness which would make this even harder than it already was.

The shape of the bed came into view and he stretched out to where he hoped her throat would be, grasping his dagger grimly in his other hand, his legs weak at what he knew he must do.

Understanding her nocturnal visitor meant her no good, Helena suddenly screamed, the sound filling the little room, but giving away her position almost as well as if daylight had flooded the place.

The Hospitaller reached out and closed his hand around her neck, squeezing hard enough to strangle the desperate cry and, despite the suffocating darkness, their eyes met and recognition flared in Helena's horrified stare.

"Please..." she gasped. "Please...!"

The sounds of revelry from the common room carried on in the background, as they looked at each other, but Stephen hesitated, his sense of honour rebelling at what he was doing, and he released the pressure on the girl's throat, his dagger remaining by his side.

For what seemed like an age they gazed at each other, both breathing heavily. Then, Helena's lip curled in disgust and, with a smile of satisfaction she whispered. "You! Even in the dark you're revolting." She laughed gently at his weakness, despite his hand still being on her throat. "The last time we were alone in a room like this you thought I was going to let you fuck me." Her voice rose again, almost shouting, yet still Stephen couldn't move. "You ugly old bastard – no woman would let you touch them!"

His right hand rose and fell and his dagger hammered into her chest, four, five, six times, and he felt warm blood spurting from her mouth onto the hand that squeezed her smooth neck.

As he stood there, numb, not quite understanding what was happening, the door at the end of the hall opened. The sound of at least a dozen men laughing and drinking seemed to deafen him and he came back to his senses with a start.

"You all right in there, lass?"

The voice was a woman's, and the Hospitaller knew he didn't want to kill anyone else this night. Without thinking, he launched himself shoulder-first at the shutters on the window, feeling them burst open with a loud crack. He fell through the opening and landed on the muddy road outside, breathless.

Inside the room, the woman, whoever she was, had come in, a candle lighting her way, and a scream filled the night.

Stephen, panting like a dog, ran instinctively through the village towards the trees where he'd left his horse, the meagre light cast by the crescent moon aiding his desperate passage as men's voices added to the woman's scream, filling the gloom behind him.

Stumbling, the air seeming to burn in his lungs, he crashed through the undergrowth, eyes flashing left and right, searching for the old palfrey that was his only chance of escape.

Sobbing at what he'd done, he cried out in relief as a soft, frightened nicker came to him from close-by and he hastily untied the horse before dragging himself into the saddle and, heedless of the dangers of low branches or trailing roots, kicked the animal savagely into a canter through the trees and onto the main road, clinging to the reins in fright.

Christ! Forgive me!

* * *

Little John was pissed off, and confused too. Since they'd brought Robin back to their camp in Barnsdale their young leader hadn't been himself. It was perfectly understandable, given the beating he'd suffered at the hands of Sir Guy of Gisbourne, but John had expected his friend to come out of his depression after a couple of days at the most, when some of the physical pain had started to ease.

But he hadn't; he was as lethargic and disinterested as he'd been when they met him at Nottingham's gates and brought him home. John didn't know how to deal with it.

He'd seen men change before, of course. When bad things happened, a person's character was bound to change, especially if they weren't that mentally tough to begin with. John had seen Robin as an immensely strong young man though – inside and out.

It worried the giant outlaw greatly. Not only was his friend a shadow of his former self, but without Robin they lacked leadership. He and Will Scarlet were more than capable second-in-commands, but neither of them had the vision or charisma to see them safely through a summer which promised to be tougher than ever before, with Gisbourne and the rest of the king's bounty-hunters searching for them.

The mood in the camp had been affected too. They had lost a few men recently, and been betrayed by one of their own, but for all that, the audacious rescue of their popular leader from right under the nose of Gisbourne and the sheriff had cheered the outlaws greatly. The first night back in Barnsdale after their trip to Nottingham they had celebrated with meat and ale, singing and ghost-stories. The sense of camaraderie had never been stronger John thought.

It didn't last long though, as the days passed and Robin sat, melancholy and morose, ignoring the men even when some of them tried to snap him out of it. Allan-a-Dale had made jokes, Tuck had spoke of God and the Magdalene, while John himself had got angry with the young wolf's head. All to no avail.

John shook his head, embarrassed at his treatment of Robin, but he couldn't just stand around and watch while his friend sickened himself into an early grave.

Finally, this morning, tired of sitting about the camp, constantly on watch for Gisbourne and the sheriff's men coming looking for their stolen prize, John had decided to take the fight to them.

Most of the outlaws knew this part of the forest well, having camped here for weeks at a time on different occasions over the past few years.

If Gisbourne and his men came looking for them, rather than moving on, today the outlaws would strike back.

John and Allan-a-Dale had led some of the men – twelve of them in total – into the trees, armed and ready to let out their anger at the past few months' events.

"D'you think we'll get a fight?" Allan asked as they pushed their way through the trees on one of the almost invisible little pathways the outlaws knew so well.

John shrugged. "I don't know. I hope so, but...to be honest, I just wanted to get out of the camp and feel like I'm doing something worthwhile. The king's men have been coming into Barnsdale in small groups for weeks now and, with Robin escaping the city, there's a chance even more of them will come hunting us." He hefted his great quarterstaff and grinned wickedly at the minstrel. "The bastards think they have us on the run, beaten down and terrified. Most of the rebels that are hiding out around here probably are. We'll give the soldiers a fright though, if they turn up anywhere near here today."

It was mid-afternoon, the men fed-up and grumbling, before, at last, they saw the signs of a body of men passing through the trees around them. Freshly snapped branches, grass still bent against the forest floor, and damp patches of urine where a couple of men had relieved themselves against one of the mighty oaks that stood like giant sentinels all told John that someone was close.

Friend or foe, they would soon find out.

"They're heading west," the massive outlaw noted as the rest of the men gathered around him. "They've stuck to the obvious path, which suggests they don't know the area as well as we do. They might be bounty-hunters looking for us, or they might be other rebels who're trying to stay ahead of the law." He fixed half-a-dozen of the outlaws with a steely gaze and ordered them into the trees following the path to the left. Allan-a-Dale was tasked with commanding the group.

"The rest come with me, we'll take the right. Move fast, but do it silently and try to keep in sight of each other, all right Allan?"

The minstrel nodded self-assuredly.

"If I attack with my men," John went on, watching Allan earnestly, "wait until the bastards have engaged us, then hit them silently from behind."

The forces split and, like dark wraiths, disappeared into the undergrowth either side of the beaten path, making their way west towards their quarry.

It didn't take long before John heard the men in front of them. They were moving at a leisurely pace, making a fair bit of noise, and he cursed. Obviously Gisbourne wasn't leading these men, or they'd be acting in a much more professional manner.

They could still be dangerous though, so John waited until they caught up with the travellers before making any uninformed judgements on their competency or deadliness.

Reaching a point a small way ahead of the men blustering through the trees as if they hadn't a care in the world, John brought the outlaws to a halt and they peered through the early-summer foliage, watching the party of hard-looking men that came towards them.

It was the sheriff's men. They wore the light blue livery of the Nottingham Castle guardsmen, and the outlaws realised Sir Henry de Faucumberg had weakened his own garrison in order to send out as many men as possible to hunt the escaped Robin Hood.

As tough as they looked, the soldiers were clearly no woodsmen. They blustered through the foliage, cursing as branches slapped and swatted them, stumbling over concealed roots, obviously confident in their numbers and official status.

On the opposite side of the path, John's trained eye could see the stealthy movement of the rest of the outlaws as they moved into position and, with a shake of his head at the incompetence of their would-be captors, looked along the line at his own half-dozen men and, hefting his quarterstaff, gave a nod.

There were fifteen soldiers, and, to their credit, they fell into a tight defensive formation when the first of them to notice the attacking outlaws gave a shout of alarm. John's men made no war-cry as they hit the blue-liveried guardsmen. The didn't use their longbows, in case they hit their fellows on the other side of the path – instead they fell on the soldiers with their swords, while John parried their leader's own thrust and rammed the butt of his staff into the man's face.

The sheriff's men, panic in their eyes, fought back savagely, and were, for a while, able to hold their own. They might not have been skilled at moving through the forest quietly, but they knew how to wield their weapons, and their light armour was of a good quality. Despite John's enormous quarterstaff, and the skill of his six men, the soldiers began to win ground, pushing the outlaws back.

Then, just as it seemed things would go badly wrong, Allan-a-Dale led his party of outlaws into the fight, appearing from the thick trees like wood-spirits and hacking at the backs of the soldiers.

Panic spread quickly through the embattled men as half of them fell in the space of a few moments, and the remainder tried desperately to fight on two fronts.

The outlaws had trained for, and used in combat, this sort of manoeuvre countless times though. When one of the sheriff's men turned his head to counter an attack from behind, one of Little John's men plunged his sword into the soldier's back or side.

It didn't take long before the battle was almost finished, but one of the soldiers shouted, "Robin Hood! We're here to talk to Robin Hood!"

John heard the shouts and roared at the outlaws to stand down and move back. The battle had been so quick that none of the outlaws had become lost in a frenzy of bloodlust, as so often happened in war and the giant wolf's head was pleased as the men lowered their weapons and moved back breathlessly to let the sheriff's man speak.

Three guardsmen remained alive, all breathing heavily, but no fear showed in their eyes, just determination and anger, and John found himself respecting their courage.

There was a short period of quiet, as everyone regained their breath, then John pointed his staff at the guard who had been shouting.

"You. What is it you have to say to Robin Hood?"

The guardsman, a short, stocky fellow with a great dark beard, glared at John and spat into the grass.

"You'll be "little" John."

"How did you guess?"

"We're here with a message, from Sir Henry de Faucumberg, Sheriff of Nottingham and Yorkshire."

John waved a meaty hand at the man. "Go on then, I know who he is and we don't have all day. We've got more of your mates to hunt down and butcher."

The guard ignored the taunt, although his two fellows fidgeted and eyed the outlaws nervously.

"Sir Guy of Gisbourne will fight Robin Hood in a duel. To the death. If your mate wins, he will be pardoned."

"Fuck off," John growled. "We've heard a story like that before from de Faucumberg last winter, and he double-crossed us. We're not going down that road again."

The previous year, not long before Christmas, the sheriff had promised a pardon for Robin's wife, Matilda, but had set a trap to kill the entire outlaw gang when they turned up to make the deal. John knew their leader wasn't stupid enough to make the same mistake twice, even if he'd been fit enough to fight "the Raven".

"This won't be like that," the guard retorted. "Hood can name the time and place of the duel, and your men can escort Sir Guy to it if you like."

The rest of the outlaws laughed and shook their heads. "Do you think we were born yesterday?" Allan-a-Dale demanded. "What's to stop us just slipping a blade between your damn Raven's ribs once we have him?"

The guard shrugged. "If you do that, Hood doesn't get his pardon."

"And if Gisbourne wins?" John shouted. "Why would we let him go? What's to stop us from killing him then?"

The soldier cursed. "I'm just delivering the message I was told to deliver."

"Let's kill these pricks and get back to camp," Peter, one of the men who had been on the raft with Much not so long ago, growled. The others muttered their agreement. The sun would set soon and they all wanted to get back for some warm food and a few ales. They'd had their victory for today and it felt good – now they wanted to celebrate, not bandy words with de Faucumberg's flunkies.

"Sir Guy's captain, Nicholas Barnwell, will meet you to discuss the terms if you agree." The guard, understanding his time was rapidly running out, shouted at Little John, desperation beginning to creep into his voice which had, until then, been somewhat arrogant.

John waved his laughing men to silence. "Fine. I can't speak for Robin: he does that for himself. But I won't refuse any chance of a pardon for one of us, even if it hinges on some ridiculous "duel" like this. You can go. Get back to the sheriff and Gisbourne and tell them we'll talk to Robin about this."

The three surviving guardsmen heaved an audible sigh of relief and began to inch their way along the path.

"You're going the wrong way," Allan grinned, shaking his head in disbelief. "Nottingham's that way."

The men halted their progress and silently moved back in the direction the fighting-minstrel had indicated, eyes warily fixed on the outlaws.

"Tell them to send you back with the terms," John said to their leader.

"How will I find you?"

"Don't worry about that: we'll find you, boy. Now get moving."

The three, sensing the danger pass, turned and began to make their way at a trot along the path back to the city.

As they went, Allan-a-Dale took his longbow from his back, pulled the hemp bowstring from the little pouch where he stored it and nodded at Peter to do the same. Sliding an arrow from his belt he fitted it and, waiting on Peter to match him, took aim and shot into the soldier on the left's back, directly between the shoulder blades. Peter's shot took the rightmost guardsman in the lower back.

As the last surviving soldier turned, eyes wide with shock and fear at the sight of his fallen companions, Allan aimed another arrow at him and shouted, "Run you bastard!"

"Let's get back to camp," Little John grunted as the man sprinted into the trees in terror, shaking his head ruefully at the killings. "Maybe this'll be exactly what Robin needs."

CHAPTER TWENTY-TWO

He should have known better.

When he returned to Kirklees, sick at heart over his brother's death and his part in the capture of Sir Richard-at-Lee, Edmond had hoped to at least continue with his life as before.

The small reward Sir Philip had given him had been enough to provide a burial for his brother – whose corpse he'd carried back to the village from outside Sir Richard's castle by himself – and at least repair or upgrade some of his father's old tanning equipment.

He'd repainted the sign that hung above the shop-front to try and make things look a little nicer and had the local carpenter mend the vats they used to treat the animal skins.

But the loss of his brother played on his mind constantly. His life had been fairly unhappy so far, but he had never, until now, felt lonely, not even when his young wife had died. He'd never loved her, it had been a marriage of convenience for both bride and groom and he'd shed few tears when she'd succumbed to fever a few months into their marriage.

He had loved Walter though, and had felt he was needed in the world while his brother was around looking for someone to take care of him.

But now...he felt unloved and useless.

Working every day, enduring the same old stares from the other villagers – pity, distaste, amusement – only to go home to an empty house with nothing but local ale to brighten the gloom. For a little while at least, until the brew took effect and left him feeling even worse.

Anyone else would have been a hero! He'd captured one of the rebel leaders – a knight! – and been rewarded by the king's man. He had expected the people of Kirklees to look at him with respect in their eyes when he returned from Pontefract and began telling his customers what had happened.

Instead, the villagers had shunned him even worse than before. Sir Richard had been a good lord to them, and the people didn't like the fact the unpleasant-looking young tanner from the God-accursed family had somehow beaten the Hospitaller in combat then betrayed him to some faceless agent of the unpopular King Edward II.

The fact that most of the Kirklees men had been out with the bounty-hunters trying to capture their erstwhile lord didn't seem to make any difference.

He paused, threw a hide into the big vat of urine he used to strip his animal-skins of hair, and took a swallow from the ale-skin at his side. He hadn't been much of a drinker before, but had gradually started to rely on it to get him through the days. "Shit." He cursed as the last few drops spilled into his mouth, and a passer-by, already wrinkling his nose in disgust at the smell from Edmond's workshop, situated on the very outskirts of town because of the hellish stench, threw him an angry look.

"Damn you to hell," he shouted at the man who, knowing the tanner could use his fists as well as anyone in the village, ducked his head and hurried on his way, muttering under his breath.

Edmond pulled the cover over the vat of urine, wiped his hands on his apron, and locked his shop behind him.

If he didn't have any ale left, he'd have to go to the inn for some.

Kirklees had a proper inn, rather than just a house one of the villagers brewed ale in as in many other villages around the country.

Edmond shook his head angrily, as he realised it had been Sir Richard who had funded the building of the inn, after the people had petitioned him to build one for them.

He walked along the road, ignoring the hooted laughter and catcalls of children too young to work, but old enough to have learned their parents' prejudices.

The inn was, thankfully, quiet at this time of day. The people of Kirklees were all out working, so only the innkeeper, Fulk, and his sour-faced, skinny wife, Agnes, were in the building when he went inside.

Fulk nodded to him. The inn-keeper neither liked nor disliked Edmond who had become a good customer recently, with a little extra coin from his reward and the black mood of a man that wants to spend that coin trying to find solace at the bottom of a mug.

"God give you good day, tanner. You'll be lookin' for some ale, eh?"

Agnes snorted and muttered something to herself, but Edmond ignored her and dropped a silver penny onto the bar.

"Aye. Refill this for me." He handed the empty skin to Fulk who took it with a nod and moved to the barrels behind him.

Fulk's wife, who was moving around placing fresh rushes on the floor to replace the ones that had become sodden with ale and puke and god-knew what else over the recent days, continued to mutter to herself, shaking her head and tutting in his direction every so often.

Clearly, she wanted Edmond to hear her, as, when the young man didn't respond she moved closer and raised her voice slightly.

Although he still couldn't make out full sentences, certain words were hissed with extra venom and the tanner found himself growing even angrier.

As Fulk returned his ale-skin to him, Edmond removed the stopper and swallowed almost half of it. "Shut your whining mouth, woman," he growled, glaring at Agnes whose eyes went wide, surprised at being challenged.

Her mouth turned up at one corner in a half-smile though and she threw a small clump of reeds at his feet. "You drunk already, boy? Again?"

Like most drinkers, Edmond hated to be reminded of the fact he was in thrall to the stuff, and he felt his temper rising as he turned to Fulk. "You better shut your woman's mouth, before I shut it for her."

The inn-keeper, a man used to dealing with violence from drink-sodden customers, pointed a long finger at the tanner. "Don't you threaten my wife, you ugly bastard."

He moved around the counter to stand protectively beside his wife who smirked, enjoying the drama. She'd tell everyone all about this later on when the workers returned from the fields!

It was too much for Edmond. The grief, rage and guilt bubbled inside him and, like a poorly constructed tanning vat, his temper exploded.

He found himself with his hands around Fulk's throat, trying to squeeze the breath from him, but the inn-keeper had seen the attack coming and managed to ram his knee between Edmond's legs.

The pain was intense and the tanner responded with similar violence, kneeing, kicking, punching and trying to throttle the man who fought back desperately, knowing the crazed young tanner had lost control of himself.

Agnes tried to drag Edmond off her husband and the three of them, snarling and spitting, battered off the wall and the bar.

It started as a furious, loud fight, with the men grunting as they traded blows and the inn-keeper's wife screaming at Edmond, but after a while the room became almost silent as exhaustion overtook them and the sounds of fear and desperation became almost obscene as the two men lost themselves in the struggle.

Eventually, Edmond managed to get a hand on the back of Fulk's hair and, forcing the older man's head sideways, battered it against the wooden wall with a thump.

There was a high-pitched whimper from Agnes as Edmond smashed her husband's head against the wall again. And again, but this time there was a cracking sound and the fight left the three of them.

Edmond let go of the inn-keeper who had become, literally, a dead-weight, and the body slumped to the ground, followed by Agnes who stared in shock at her man's unmoving body.

In a daze, the young tanner walked to the front door and, without a backward glance, walked out into the village.

His hands and clothes were blood-stained and, as Agnes appeared at the inn door screaming murder, none of the villagers nearby wanted anything to do with him.

He passed unmolested along the street; even Godfrey, his brother's childhood tormentor, moved quietly back into the shadows at the sight of the bloody tanner.

Vaguely, the sound of the inn-keeper's wife screaming came to him as he walked out of the village and was swallowed up by the looming forest of Barnsdale.

* * *

Stephen knew something was wrong.

The Hospitaller had stopped at Cossebi for provisions as he made his way back to Kirklees. Cossebi was a small town, so the two men following him were easy to spot. In their chain-mail and carrying swords they stood out from the locals.

Idiots.

The problem was, Stephen had no idea who they were or who might have sent them. They couldn't have come from Highgate, to bring him to justice for killing the girl, surely? No, he doubted that: the girl wasn't important enough. The villagers would have banded together and hunted for him with their pitchforks and wood-axes, but they'd not have sent these two mercenaries after him, even if they could have afforded the price.

The king's men? Stephen was still a rebel after all.

He shook his head. The king had more important people to worry about than a lowly Hospitaller sergeant-at-arms.

The small marketplace only boasted a few stalls, and those were poorly stocked, but he wasn't a man of opulent tastes so there was enough here to keep him going until he made it home again.

"When did you bake this, lad?"

The youngster at the bakers stall shrugged his thin shoulders. "My da baked it this morning, my lord. All our stuff is newly made today, see?" He picked up the loaf nearest him, squeezing it to show how soft it was.

"Good. Give me that one then."

The boy handed over the fresh loaf with a sullen look. It was obvious most of the wares on show were at least a day old, more in some cases, and Stephen had taken the nicest, and freshest, loaf on the stall now.

The Hospitaller smiled and tossed a small coin to the boy who scrambled to catch it.

"That's for this too." Stephen lifted a small meat pie along with the loaf and walked away, biting into the savoury as if he hadn't a care in the world. As he swung his head from side to side, checking out the rest of the goods and produce for sale at the stalls, he saw the two burly men following him at a short distance.

He was in no mood to be hunted all the way back home, though, so he nonchalantly made his way towards the far outskirts of the market and the centre of town, to a deserted street with gutters so choked with shit and piss even the local dogs seemed to shun the place.

He slipped into an alley, placed his prized fresh loaf on the ground and waited for his pursuers to come past. He drew his sword and breathed deeply to try and offset the effects of the blood coursing nervously through him as the sound of fast-moving footsteps approached him.

As the men passed his hiding place, the sergeant dived out and battered the pommel of his sword against the temple of the man nearest him, who went flying sideways, unconscious, into the filth of the street.

The second man was fast though, and as he saw the attack coming in his peripheral vision, had whipped his own blade free from its sheath and brought it up defensively in front of him. His eyes took in his fallen companion and their quarry, standing before him with a murderous look on his face.

"Who are you?"

The man moved closer, his sword held expertly before him. "We come from Sir Hugh Despenser."

Stephen's blood ran cold at that, and he felt the hairs on his neck rise. Despenser? The man had murdered Sir Richard's youngest son, Stephen, and obviously held a grudge against the Lord of Kirklees.

The Hospitaller flicked his sword down and placed it against the Adam's apple of the man lying on the ground. "How did you know where I was?" he demanded.

Despenser's man smiled, confident that his size and skill would be enough to kill the Hospitaller once the talking was over. "Your own Order gave you up, fool. I don't know what you did to piss them off, but they sent word that you were heading north and were to be stopped."

Stephen's mind whirled and he guessed it had been the Prior's bald steward who had betrayed him. "Stopped?"

The man grinned again, rolling his shoulders and head to work out any kinks in his muscles. "Stopped, aye. Meaning killed."

The man on the ground groaned and rolled to his side, retching from the effects of the blow to the temple.

Stephen booted the prone figure as hard as he could in the face, then swept his sword round in an arc to block the attack from the big man in front of him.

"Is that your best, you ugly sack of shit?"

Despenser's man was more than competent with a sword and held his temper despite the Hospitaller's annoying smile.

They traded blows for a while, neither giving ground, content to play it out until an opening presented itself. Stephen's mind was working though, and the realisation that his own Order were actively seeking to make an end to him was a sickening thought.

"What about my master?" he asked, parrying another raking blow from the left.

His opponent laughed and pressed the attack again. "No idea, but my lord Despenser's probably got something good in store for him too."

Stephen slipped as he parried yet another crushing blow and felt as if the earth was swallowing him as he fell face-down on the hard road. Despenser's man saw his chance and stepped forward, kicking at the fallen Hospitaller's head.

Desperately, Stephen threw both his feet round in an arc, grunting as the move paid off and his attacker stumbled over his legs, falling onto the ground beside him.

Baring his teeth in rage, the Hospitaller straddled the man and slammed the pommel of his sword into his attacker's face. He was rewarded with the sound of bone and cartilage cracking as the man's nose broke and he fell backwards with a roar of agony.

Almost insane with rage now, Stephen threw himself like one of the old berserkers on top of Despenser's mercenary, hammering his fist repeatedly into the man's left cheek until it was a bloody mess.

He lay there, sucking air into his burning lungs for a while, before getting shakily to his feet. The second of his pursuers whimpered and Stephen shoved the tip of his sword deep into the man's throat.

His own Order had sent men to kill him. The king's closest companion, Sir Hugh Despenser, wanted his blood. And God knew what fate had befallen his master.

Shaking his head he picked up his loaf of bread and stumbled back through the marketplace towards his horse.

God's bollocks! Today wasn't a good day.

* * *

They came for him at dawn. Bleary eyed and sullen from the previous night's drinking in Pontefract Castle's great hall.

They'd been glad to tell him who they were and where he was going when he asked them.

Nottingham. His heart had sank at the news the sheriff was going to hang him. Sir Henry de Faucumberg hated him after he'd helped Robin Hood and his gang escape the sheriff's "justice" last year.

Now de Faucumberg would have his revenge by publicly hanging the disgraced lord of Kirklees.

Sir Richard was frightened, but more than that, he was angry that his life would be ended, in front of a baying mob, on de Faucumberg's orders. Despair washed over him, but only for a moment, then his faith galvanized him and he rode, shoulders back and head held high, from the castle, out onto the road towards Nottingham surrounded by a dozen of Despenser's men, all heavily armed and riding great warhorses while he trailed along beneath them on a sway-backed old palfrey.

The journey took up the whole day and was uneventful: Despenser's men were well-disciplined and bore him no ill-will. He was fed regularly and given ale – indeed, he could have drank himself into a stupor for all his captors cared. As long as he gave them no trouble and stayed on his horse, they were content.

The men ignored him when he tried to start a conversation on the road though, and, on reaching Nottingham, they handed him over to the sheriff's men as if he were a common criminal.

God, give me the strength to get through this, he prayed. When he'd decided to give himself up to the king's justice it had seemed like the noble, honourable, Christian thing to do. Yet now, imprisoned in de Faucumberg's dungeon beneath Nottingham Castle, Sir Richard wondered if he'd made a terrible mistake.

He was frightened. Scared to die. Not for his own sake, but, although Sir Hugh Despenser had murdered his youngest son, Simon, Sir Richard had another son in Rhodes and the tears streamed down his lined face at the thought he would never see his boy again.

Hadn't he been a good Christian? A good man?

Christ's words on the cross came to him and he bowed his head in despair. *Father! Why have you forsaken me?*

CHAPTER TWENTY-THREE

"I can't best Gisbourne, John. Even before he beat the shit out of me, I wasn't a match for him. And now...look at me!" Robin shook his bruised knuckles at his big friend. "The man's unbeatable, trust me. I'm not walking into a duel with him, it's madness."

Little John threw his hands in the air. "You have to get over this. You can't hide here forever."

"I'm not" –

"Three months ago you would have jumped at the chance to fight Gisbourne," John cut in, pointing at his young leader while the rest of the men looked on, unsure whose side they should be taking in this discussion. "You're the best swordsman of us all. If anyone can beat the bastard, it's you." He walked over to stand in front of Robin, towering over the younger man. "I know you lost hope when you were in jail. I know they tried to break your spirit. But this is your chance to prove to Gisbourne – and yourself – that you're" –

"What?" Robin demanded. "What am I? I'm a yeoman from Wakefield. Not even that any more: I'm a wolf's head. A nobody. What have I to prove to anyone?"

John's face turned red with anger and he grabbed his friend by the front of his gambeson and hauled him off the ground as if Robin were no more than a child.

"You're supposed to be our leader! You're a husband. You're about to be a father for Christ's sake! It's time you started acting like a man again, instead of sitting around here brooding about what the big bad Raven did to you."

Robin glared at the giant but made no effort to fight him off.

"See," John dropped him back to the floor, waving a hand dismissively. "You've no fight left in you. Maybe it's best you don't meet Gisbourne like this after all. Go sit by the fire again, with your ale, listening to Allan's songs, while the rest of us make sure the sheriff and king's men don't kill us all."

"What's going on?"

Will Scarlet strode into camp with two of the other men. They'd been visiting New Mylle on Dam that morning, buying provisions and gathering news from the locals.

"Ask our famous leader," John spat towards Robin, turning his back and storming off through the ranks of sympathetic men.

Will looked curiously at the bowed head of his young friend, but Robin moved away without explanation and sat down with a heavy sigh beside the little camp-fire.

"Robin won't take on Gisbourne," Gareth offered. "He doesn't think he can beat him, injured like he is."

Will walked over to stand on the opposite side of the fire and looked down at the brooding young man. "Well, here's some news that might get your fight back: the sheriff's captured Sir Richard-at-Lee. They're going to hang him on Saturday. Looks like they've found a nobleman to take your place on the gallows."

Robin's head snapped up and he met Will's stare in disbelief.

"Don't even think about trying to rescue him. Me and Tuck were lucky to get you out of there before. That was a miracle that won't be repeated. They'll have tripled the guard on the Hospitaller and sealed the city until he's swinging. De Faucumberg lost a fine prize when you escaped – he won't make the same mistake twice. Word is, the Despenser had a hand in his capture, so his men will probably be guarding Sir Richard too. He's as good as dead already."

Robin shut his eyes and bowed his head. How many more of his friends must die? Sir Richard had helped them when they needed it. He'd introduced them to the Earl of Lancaster and, if the rebellion had succeeded, they'd all be free men now thanks to the Hospitaller.

Things hadn't turned out like that though, and here they were. Condemned men, waiting to die. And Sir Richard-at-Lee would be next to go.

Never give up hope! Tuck's words rang in Robin's head again and he felt the rage of the past few weeks building up inside him.

Little John had returned to listen to Will's news, and Robin glanced up at him now, his eyes blazing. "What day is it?"

"June the 8th. Tuesday," the big man replied, with a confused look.

"When did Gisbourne want to meet me?"

"Next Monday."

"Two days after they're to hang the Hospitaller," Will noted.

"Fine." Robin stood up and made his way over to where the practice swords were stored, lifting the heavier one he always used. "Spar with me, John. I have a few days to get my fitness back if I'm going to beat the bastard. We might not be able to save Sir Richard, but maybe I can stop the Raven killing any more of us."

The gathered outlaws cheered as if they'd all been granted a pardon.

* * *

Stephen knew something was wrong when he rode into Kirklees on his way back to the castle and the locals paid him no heed.

As far as he knew, he was still a fugitive, wanted as a rebel by the king's men. So how come people were turning away from him as if they were embarrassed, rather than calling out the tithing to chase after him as he'd expected?

In the name of Christ, some of the villagers were even waving at him!

Whatever had happened, he clearly wasn't in any obvious danger. Which was a bad sign.

"How goes it, Justin?" The sergeant pulled his horse up and slid to the ground, addressing the local smith as he did so. "Any news?"

"News? You haven't heard?" The man looked at him in disbelief. "Where the hell have you been?"

"I've been away in London," Stephen replied.

Justin grunted in reply and eyed the Hospitaller as if he'd just returned from the moon. Like the vast majority of the villagers, the smith had never travelled anywhere outside Yorkshire. "Well," he grunted, swinging his heavy hammer down on the horseshoe he was working on, "Sir Richard's been taken. Two of the local lads – the tanner's boys – captured him. Your master managed to kill one of them but the other took him to Sir Philip of Portsmouth at Pontefract Castle."

Stephen felt numb. His fingers tingled weirdly, as if the blood had been cut off from them and he moved to sit on a huge old log the smith kept as a chair.

"The lad that captured him – Edmond – came back a while ago, but people were angry at him. He attacked big Fulk, the inn-keep, and disappeared. No one's seen him since."

"Angry at him?" Stephen looked up at the smith in confusion. "Why? I'd have thought he'd have been a hero."

Justin shrugged half-heartedly and went back to beating the horseshoe. "Because Sir Richard was a good lord to Kirklees, and Edmond handed him over to the law. People didn't like it, and they let him know it too." He smiled ingratiatingly at Stephen, as if the Hospitaller should be thankful for the villagers' loyalty.

"Bollocks," Stephen spat, getting to his feet again. "Me and my master were left alone in the castle when the king's men came looking for us. I didn't see you or any of the rest of them standing up for us then."

The smith opened his mouth to protest, his eyebrows lowered indignantly, but Stephen waved a hand to silence him and climbed back onto his horse.

"Forget it, I care nothing for the tanner's sons, or for the rest of you. Where's Sir Richard now? Still at Pontefract?"

"No. We heard he'd been moved to Nottingham. The sheriff's going to hang him after at the weekend. They'd captured Robin Hood, but he escaped, so de Faucumberg's making a big deal out of this to try and make up for it."

Despite his shock, Stephen smiled at the idea of Hood escaping the sheriff's clutches. The wolf's head led a charmed life, sure enough.

"Kirklees Castle has been taken over by the king's steward," the smith shouted as Stephen kicked his horse into a walk past the inn and back towards the main road. "Sir Simon de Baldreston. You'd best steer well clear! They might have forgotten you for now, but if you show up causing trouble anywhere they'll hang you too!"

The sergeant-at-arms waved a hand in reply and spurred the big palfrey into a trot. It had all been for nothing. He'd taken too long getting to Clerkenwell and now, even if the Prior had sent a letter to the king on Sir Richard's behalf, it was too late. His master was to be hanged for treason.

It was all Stephen's fault – he should never have allowed that girl to sidetrack him! All he could do now was ride to Nottingham to witness his master's death.

Christ and St John only knew what would become of him after that.

* * *

He had no trouble joining the crowd on Gallows Hill outside Nottingham. Why would he? A middle-aged man, of average height and build; just another visitor come to see the Hospitaller Knight swing.

Of course, he'd left his black surcoat with its give-away white cross back amongst the trees on the roadside, along with his chain-mail, his horse and even his sword. He wasn't here for a fight, and a weapon like that would only draw the guards' attention to him.

He lost himself in the surging mass of people. The atmosphere appeared to be one of celebration and a younger man might have felt sick at the glee these folk seemed to feel at the idea of watching a good knight die in such a horrible way.

Stephen had seen it too many times before to let it affect him visibly though. Of course, it surprised him, as it always did, that normal, everyday people – mothers with their excited children; whole families in some cases, from the youngest babe to the oldest doddering, cackling crone – could get so excited at another person's miserable death, before heading back to their homes to continue their lives as normal.

But he'd made a career – a life – from killing men, who was he to question humanity's baser instincts? Hadn't he just murdered a woman in her sick-bed?

The crowd washed him up like a piece of flotsam on the outskirts of the audience awaiting the hanging, so he discreetly but firmly pushed his way through the tightly-packed people, silencing anyone who tried to complain with a murderous glare, until he made it almost to the front. He positioned himself behind a small group of women so he could see over them straight to the sinister-looking wooden construction which would end his master's life before the day was out.

Small children pushed their way between the gathered people, offering meat pies and pastries; merchants hawked more exotic snacks like oranges, figs and dates; men and women discussed their favourite executions and how they imagined the Hospitaller would go to his death. Most of those around him thought Sir Richard would be stoic and proud to the end, but Stephen had to restrain himself from punching one drunken loud-mouth who claimed to know the former Lord of Kirklees was a coward.

Of course, there were more people to be hanged than just the knight. The sheriff wanted to make this a day the inhabitants of Nottingham would enjoy – a day that would make up for the loss of the wolf's head, Robin Hood. The people had been looking forward to that, which sickened Stephen – he knew the lower classes saw Hood as a freedom fighter and a hero. A man who outfought and outsmarted the bastard noblemen that bled the people dry.

And yet many of them had been disappointed to miss out on a day's entertainment when Hood's men had led him back to the safety of Barnsdale Forest and robbed them of a good hanging.

The sergeant-at-arms gazed around at the people and shook his head in a black rage. Fucking idiots. So starved of joy and excitement that the sight of a man convulsing as his last breath was stolen from him by a length of rope was a highlight of their week. So easily led, that even the ones who knew inside this was wrong would stand cheering and laughing until they were hoarse just so they could be like everyone else.

Idiots.

His eyes swept the crowd in disgust until he noticed a young man and a spark of recognition flared. He looked again, taking in the thin beard and flat nose, and his heart missed a beat. Edmond: the tanner's son. The bastard that had brought Sir Richard to his doom, standing here, waiting to see the knight die!

Fingering the dagger strapped to the outside of his thigh, Stephen began to force his way through the crowd towards the young man. A few people tried to stop him as he barged past but the sergeant had lost any sense of danger and he simply battered anyone that stood in his path out of the way, leaving a trail of confusion and pain in his wake.

The blood was hammering in his veins as he neared the tanner's son and, from the direction of the gallows he could hear a man's voice raised to address the people. Sliding the dagger free from its leather sheath, Stephen held it in his clenched fist, with the blade under his wrist, ready to slip it between Edmond's ribs.

The crowd suddenly cheered, as Sir Henry de Faucumberg, Sheriff of Nottingham and Yorkshire, raised a hand with a smile and the disgraced rebel knight, Sir Richard-at-Lee was led up the stairs onto the gallows.

Stephen knew what was going on now, and he wanted to look at his master to see how he was holding up, but, as he came within arm's reach of the tanner's son and prepared to plunge his blade into the man, he was shocked to see Edmond cry out in anguish and try to push his way towards the gallows.

Assuming he'd misheard the sheriff and it was some other man about to be hung, Stephen looked round and felt as if an arrow had pierced his heart. Sure enough, his master stood, head bowed, looking like an old, old man, rather than the proud knight his sergeant had left on the ramparts of Kirklees Castle just a few days before.

His eyes roved across the crowd again, searching for the tanner's son who was by now a couple of rows in front of him, shouting and crying, although the sergeant couldn't make out the words.

A couple of the sheriff's men were watching Edmond curiously. He was too far away to be a threat, yet, but they hefted their great pole-arms and Stephen knew they would skewer the tanner's son before he could get to the gallows and do whatever it was he was planning in his near-hysterical state.

With a curse, Stephen used his strength to force his way through the crowd towards Edmond who couldn't command the same level of respect – or fear – as the grim sergeant and, as a result, found his way to the gallows was a slow one.

"Boy!"

Edmond ignored the voice close behind him, and, with a snarl, tried to shrug off the hand that had grasped his shoulder like a vice.

"Boy!"

Turning, ready to fight whoever was trying to restrain him, Edmond stared at the man and knew instantly who he was. Images of Sir Richard walking through Kirklees past his father's shop came into his mind. The smiling knight with his thick beard – which had been turning to grey even when Edmond was just a teenager – chatting to the tradesmen and accompanied, always, by his scowling sergeant-at-arms. The same man who held him now, like a jailer, by the front of his cloak.

Edmond's face crumpled and fresh tears made tracks in the grime on his cheeks. "I'm sorry! I'm so sorry!"

The guards were still watching – more in amusement now than anything else, but Stephen knew they'd be quick to break a few heads to reach them if they felt anything was amiss so he met Edmond's eyes and grasped his shoulders firmly.

"Get a grip of yourself, boy, now. The sheriff's men are watching us. You keep this up and they're going to come for us."

The sergeant's commanding tone – so like Sir Richard's as Edmond remembered from their short journey together – surprised the tanner's son and he met the calm stare of the older man.

"I'm sorry," he repeated, this time in almost a whisper. "I never wanted this. I thought capturing Sir Richard would make everything right. It's made everything worse!"

"Forget it," Stephen growled, his eyes drawn to what was happening on the gallows behind the weeping Edmond.

While they'd been talking Sir Richard had been led to stand in front of the crowd and the sheriff now read out the charges laid against the Knight Hospitaller. The people booed and cheered, laughed and hooted, cursed and joked as the list was read out and de Faucumberg played the part of master of ceremonies to the full.

The bastard will be loving this, Stephen thought, watching the sheriff ham it up. Sir Richard and the Earl of Lancaster had made a fool of him the previous Christmas by rescuing Robin Hood and his men from the trap the sheriff had set for them. Now it was payback time for the sheriff.

"Keep your hands by your sides."

The voice came from directly behind them, startling both men.

They had been so engrossed in their conversation, and what was happening on the gallows, that they'd failed to notice the soldiers coming up through the crowd at their backs. Four of them, two armed with swords and two with pole-arms levelled directly at their midriffs.

Singly, Stephen knew he could have taken them or at least evaded them in the crowd. They didn't have the look of killers. They did have the confident look of competent guardsmen though; men used to violence and dealing with it.

There was no escape.

"Don't even think about it," he said quietly to Edmond, whose eyes were flicking between him and the guards as if uncertain what to do. "Even if you got away from this lot, you'd never get out of the city. So relax."

He made a show of patting the tanner's son on the back as if he was calming a child after a tantrum. These guardsmen had no idea who he was, and Edmond wasn't an outlaw, so Stephen hoped they'd be left in peace if the guards knew there was no threat to them.

Unfortunately, Robin Hood's recent escape had made the sheriff and his men jumpy. They weren't about to let anything similar happen again.

Stephen collapsed on the ground as the pommel of a sword cracked against the back of his head, and Edmond fell a moment later with a cry of rage.

"Stay down!" the sergeant-at-arms grunted through teeth gritted in pain, grasping the angry younger man by the arm.

The four soldiers moved in, ringing the two downed men and disarming them, while the crowd which had hemmed them in so tightly just moments earlier pulled well back in case they should suffer the same fate.

The sheriff's men, fully in control now, ordered the pair to their feet and shepherded them through the crowd, past the gallows and towards the castle.

A tall man, dressed all in exotic-looking black armour, watched as they passed and Stephen met his gaze, knowing it must be the man the people called The Raven: Sir Guy of Gisbourne. The king's hunting dog.

Gisbourne stood with a bald, hard-looking man by his side, and three of the sheriff's men behind him. As Stephen and Edmond were marched past them, one of the blue-liveried sheriff's soldiers swung his head to watch, staring at the sergeant with a bemused look on his face.

304

"That's the knight's man! The Hospitaller!"

Gisbourne and his bald companion turned to look at where the soldier was pointing. "Hold!" Sir Guy commanded, looking at the shouting guardsman. "Let's hear what this man has to say."

"I remember him from last year when we tried to ambush Robin Hood and his men," the man shouted as Stephen and Edmond were forced to stop moving. "He was with them, wearing the Hospitaller cross."

Stephen wished he hadn't left his sword back in the forest now, but he still had his dagger and its weight on his thigh was reassuring, although he knew it would not be enough to let him escape from this.

It was clear Gisbourne knew Stephen was a dangerous man, but his confidence was unmistakable as he moved around to stand directly in front of the sergeant.

"Is that true? "

"I'm Sir Richard's sergeant-at-arms, yes."

Gisbourne smiled, but it was a strange smile and Stephen wondered if the man was all there.

Nicholas Barnwell suddenly reached out towards the guard holding Edmond and took the tanner's confiscated sword from him. "This is a nice blade," Gisbourne's man whistled, noting the fine craftsmanship. "A Hospitaller knight's blade I'd say. I'd better hold onto this."

"Come to rescue your friend?" Sir Guy asked Stephen, who glared at Edmond, assuming the young tanner had stolen his master's old sword.

"No," Stephen shook his head sullenly. "I'm no fool. There's no way anyone could rescue my master from this. I came to pay my respects, that's all."

"And you?"

Edmond glared at the dark bounty-hunter. "I came to try and undo the evil that I've done. I should never have turned the good knight over to you lot."

Gisbourne laughed, and turned back to Stephen. "You are also a wanted man. A wolf's head. I will have you taken onto the gallows beside your master...you can die together."

Stephen looked impassively at the king's man, honestly not caring at that moment whether he lived or died. It seemed a foregone conclusion anyway.

"Where would you go if I release you?"

"To my Order's headquarters in London," Stephen shrugged, caught off-guard by the sudden change in the conversation and forgetting that the Hospitallers no longer required his services.

Gisbourne laughed. "Your Order? Why do you think your master is here? Your Prior's steward sent word to the sheriff saying Sir Richard was a traitor and should be hanged, along with you if you were caught. You see," he leered into Stephen's face, "you are an outcast. A rebel, wanted by the king, and disowned by your own Order. You are dead."

There was silence then, as the bounty-hunter smiled, fingering the black crossbow that hung from his shoulder and the two captives looked uncertainly at their supremely confident captor, wondering where this was all going.

"And yet...I need a messenger." Gisbourne spread his hands. "Another one I mean. My last one saw his friends shot in the back and that's made it hard for me to find another one. You," he nodded at Stephen, "are, according to the guard here, acquainted with Robin Hood."

"We've met."

"Good. Then his men won't shoot you before you can deliver my message. Are you listening?"

Stephen shrugged.

"I said, 'are you listening', monk?" Gisbourne's open hand slapped him a stinging crack across the face and the Hospitaller was shocked by the speed of the blow. He hadn't seen it until his head was rocking backwards from the force.

"Aye, I'm listening," he growled.

"Good. I sent word to Robin Hood a few days ago that I wanted to meet him in the forest on Monday. I've heard nothing since. He is, no doubt, hiding somewhere, like an old woman awaiting the grim reaper."

"Or maybe he's waiting until you ride through Barnsdale so he can stick an arrow in your throat."

"Maybe." Gisbourne shrugged. "I wouldn't be surprised. He couldn't beat me in a straight fight, so if he resorted to hiding in the trees and shooting me from a distance, well...like I say, I wouldn't be surprised."

Stephen said nothing to that. He didn't particularly like Hood or his men. They'd held him and Sir Richard up as they travelled through the forest last year. He'd wanted to attack them, even if there had only been the two of them against the outlaw's entire gang, but his master had ordered him to stand down. In the end they had, together, ruined one of the most corrupt noblemen in England, a man who had hoped to destroy Sir Richard and steal his lands.

So Stephen remained silent as Gisbourne insulted Hood.

"We know the general area of the forest where the outlaws are living," the Raven went on. "You will take my message to him." He spoke and Stephen listened, nodding as the enigmatic bounty-hunter finished telling him what to say to Robin.

"What about this one?" a soldier asked, shoving Edmond forward with the butt-end of his polearm.

Gisbourne waved a hand dismissively. "He's nothing. Look at him. He can go with the Hospitaller – sorry, I should say, *former* Hospitaller. Let them watch their friend hang first though."

The wicked laughter followed them as they were led back to the gallows by the soldiers.

"What now?" Edmond asked quietly.

"Now?" Stephen muttered. "Now we say a prayer as my master draws his last breath. And then we find Hood and watch him tear that bastard Gisbourne's head from his shoulders."

CHAPTER TWENTY-FOUR

"So he's changing his tactics," Robin nodded after he'd heard Stephen's message from Sir Guy of Gisbourne. The Raven's intelligence on the rough whereabouts of Hood's gang had been accurate, and the sergeant, with Edmond silently trailing him, had been spotted by Allan-a-Dale as they moved none too stealthily through the undergrowth that morning. Moments later the two men had found themselves surrounded by heavily armed outlaws who appeared, seemingly, from nowhere. Edmond had almost shit himself.

"Instead of threatening us with violence and killing our men," Robin went on, "he's trying to play on my pride in order to flush me out."

The Hospitaller nodded. It was true: many men would rather face death in a hopeless battle than be called a coward and have their reputation sullied. Gisbourne's message had simply demanded, again, that Hood meet him in a neutral location and fight one-on-one, like warriors, to the death. If Robin didn't show up, the whole country would know he wasn't the fearless legendary hero of so many folk-tales told in ale-houses all over the north of England.

"I don't really care, for myself, if people think I'm a coward," the outlaw leader said. "And, honestly, the idea of facing that bastard again does frighten me. But one of the reasons we've been able to endure life in the forest is because the people in the villages around here respect and even, to an extent, fear us. They know we'll reward them if they help us and they know we'll hunt them down if they betray us to the law. The legend that's grown up around us is an essential part of our survival – if the villagers think I'm a coward they'll begin to lose respect and life around here will become even more difficult."

He wasn't just thinking of himself, or the men. Matilda and the rest of his family in Wakefield were left in peace, partly because they were well-liked in the village, but also because the people there had seen what happened to any who betrayed Robin's friends. Little John had killed Simon Woolemonger the year before, after he'd told the former steward, Adam Gurdon, that Matilda had been helping the outlaws. The girl had been arrested and almost raped before they rescued her – and Woolemonger had paid the price, publicly, for crossing the outlaws.

News of that episode had travelled far and wide and had, so far, made anyone else with a big mouth too afraid to inform on the gang.

If Robin refused to face Gisbourne that fear and respect he commanded would be gone and, with his wife due to give birth to their first child, it was never more imperative that his family were left in peace.

"Where am I to meet him?"

"Dalton, to the south-west of here." Stephen described a small stone bridge not far from the village. "It's a short walk from Watling Street Gisbourne says."

Robin looked at Little John who nodded. "True enough. It's a small bridge, just wide enough for a cart to cross, with a lot of trees around either bank. If you fight him there, the rest of us can hide amongst the foliage. If he brings his men and betrays you like the sheriff tried last winter, we can shoot him down and escape back into Barnsdale."

"Presumably that's why he chose the spot," Robin mused. "So we know we can trust him. He'd have picked somewhere more open if he wanted to ambush us."

"You really think he's just going to turn up and fight you, alone? Without trying to capture or kill the rest of us?"

"I do, aye. I think he's a vain man, desperate to make a name for himself. We've become famous" –

"Notorious!" Will Scaflock grinned.

"Aye, that too," Robin smiled. "Everyone's heard of us now, and the daft tales of me being a giant, with eyes of fire, that can beat ten men single-handedly...Hunting us down isn't enough for Gisbourne. He wants the whole country to know the Raven defeated me, fairly, in single combat."

Stephen agreed. "He was more interested in fighting you than anything else," he told them. "By rights he really should have had me handed over to the sheriff, to hang beside my master. Two Hospitaller's on the gallows...de Faucumberg would have loved that. Yet Gisbourne decided to let me carry his message to you instead. The man's a maniac."

The outlaws bowed their heads in silence for a moment, still upset over the news Stephen had brought of Sir Richard-at-Lee's death.

"What if Gisbourne does beat you, though?" Little John wondered. "It'll demoralize the people."

"And make many of them more likely to turn the rest of us in if they get a chance," Friar Tuck muttered. "They'll see your death as the beginning of the end for us."

"He won't beat me," Robin growled, glaring round at the men. "He won't."

"If he does," Will shrugged. "I'll stick an arrow in him before he can enjoy his victory."

"No! If he beats me, you let him and his men go. If we hope to be treated honourably we must act the same way, or no one will ever trust us again. If I lose, I'd suggest you all move camp, maybe even move out of Yorkshire altogether."

The faces around him were grim, imagining the worst.

"What are we all worrying about?" John shouted, forcing a grin onto his big bearded face. "Robin's the best of all of us with a sword. If anyone can beat that bastard Gisbourne, it's him." He looked up at the sky, noting the sun's position. "And we'd better get a move on if we're to reach Dalton by mid-afternoon."

The men moved silently, thoughtfully, to gather their weapons and strap on whatever armour they owned, while John stood in front of his young leader and grasped him by the shoulders, staring into his eyes.

"You will beat Gisbourne," the giant told him. "You must, for all our sakes, and for your family. Remember: the wings of a raven are no match for the jaws of a wolf."

Robin met his friend's stare and nodded, but, in truth, his guts were turning themselves inside out at the thought of meeting the black-clad king's man again.

"What about you?" the outlaw captain asked, turning to the former Hospitaller sergeant. "I'm sorry about Sir Richard...he was a good man. I'm proud to have met him."

Stephen bowed his head, acknowledging Robin's comment but also hiding the pain in his eyes at the thought of his master's hanging. "Fuck knows. My order betrayed me, and I can't go back to Kirklees." He looked out at the trees surrounding them. "I suppose this is my home now, the trees of Barnsdale – I'm a wolf's head, just like you."

"Then you'll join us," Robin replied, making it a statement rather than a question. "A man of your knowledge and experience will be very welcome in our ranks."

The sergeant gave a small smile, relief plain on his pock-marked face. "Thank you, lad. I'd be honoured to serve under you, until I can clear my name with my Order." No matter what, Stephen would always think of himself as a Hospitaller.

"Let's move!" Little John's massive voice split the air, and he hefted his great quarterstaff south, in the direction of Dalton. As he passed he handed a sword, one of the outlaws' spares, to the weaponless Hospitaller who took it gratefully.

"What about him?" Stephen gestured to Edmond who had stood silently beside him since they'd been surrounded on the path by the outlaws, and now looked up sullenly at the famous young wolf's head, expecting to be turned away – or worse – once his part in Sir Richard's death became clear. It seemed his place in life was to forever be rejected.

Robin shrugged, pulling the laces tight on his gambeson and moving off after John and the rest of the men with a preoccupied look on his face.

"He can come with us, for now, if he wants," Little John shouted over his shoulder. "Once this is over we can hear his story and decide what's to be done. Get yourself a weapon from the pile of spares over there, lad. You didn't hear anything in Nottingham about the lads that helped Robin escape with Tuck and Will did you?"

Edmond and the gruff Hospitaller shook their heads and John shrugged, hoping that was good news. Roger and Godfrey had sent a messenger into the forest to let the outlaws know they'd started the fires in Nottingham and spread the word to panicked citizens which explained the unexpected diversion that had allowed Robin and his two friends to escape the city. John had sent a sizeable reward back to them with the messenger, but he worried the two men might have been found out by the authorities.

It seemed not though – Gisbourne and the sheriff would have surely made a big deal of their capture if their part in the famous wolf's head's escape had been discovered. Barnsdale would have been alive with the news if anything had befallen Roger and Godfrey.

"Come on, lads," John shouted, breaking into a jog. "Pick up the pace!"

Stephen, happy enough with the longsword Little John had given him, shoved it into the sheath at his side and, none too friendly – he was still unsure how to deal with the tanner's son – beckoned Edmond to follow.

Sir Richard's captor must be able to handle himself in a fight – he'd bested a Knight Hospitaller after all – and that might be useful in the next few hours. One way or another, Stephen thought, things would forever change for the outlaws today, and the more swords raised on Robin Hood's side the better.

They moved out, to Dalton. And Sir Guy of Gisbourne.

* * *

Andrew was a fast runner, and agile, despite his youth. He had been sent into Barnsdale once before, a year ago, to take news to Robin Hood and his men.

That time it had been bad news: Matilda, Robin's lover, had been arrested by Adam Gurdon.

This time he had better news, and he pumped his legs as fast as he could, ignoring the stitch in his side until it eased and he found the wolf's heads' camp, and Friar Tuck.

The outlaws had kept the horses the friar had used to escape from Nottingham with Robin and Will and it was just as well, as Tuck was the only person left on guard in the camp and young Andrew's news had to be carried to Robin as fast as possible.

"God's thanks to you, lad!" the friar roared, as he hauled himself onto the back of one of the palfreys. "Get back to Wakefield now. I'll take your news to Robin!"

The horse was fresh and Tuck had picked the strongest of them so he made good time. He knew exactly where the outlaws were going, having passed through Dalton with Will not so long ago on their way to rescue Robin.

"Christ, please let me be in time." he prayed, whipping the big horse furiously along the road. "Robin has to know!"

* * *

They were all there. Usually only a few of the men would go on a job, led by Robin himself or one of his two captains, Little John and Will Scaflock, but today, for this, everyone apart from Tuck had come and Robin was glad of it although he had no doubt Gisbourne would hold to his word and meet him one-on-one as promised.

When they reached the agreed meeting place Robin had stood on the bridge and looked around, taking in the surroundings, looking for anywhere he could use to his advantage during the fight. John was looking for direction in where to set-up the men in case the Raven didn't hold true to his word and the sheriff's men attacked, but the young wolf's head was off in a world of his own, visualising how the duel might pan out and Will eventually took charge, directing the outlaws to the trees on their side of the little brook that fed into the River Don, making sure they were all well hidden with a clear line of sight to the bridge.

They didn't have long to wait.

Sir Guy of Gisbourne arrived, accompanied by at least twenty soldiers, including his own bald-headed second-in-command, Nicholas Barnwell. He waved them to a halt long before he reached the stone bridge though, ordering them to take up positions along the bank, in plain view. They carried small, but sturdy, shields and Robin smiled. They were learning to fear the outlaws' arrows at last.

Barnwell tried to argue with his commander but Gisbourne sternly waved the man back to stand with his men. There was to be no interference – one of these two men would die today, and no one could stop it. Barnwell moved back, face as black as the thunderheads gathering overhead, and the Raven walked confidently forward onto the bridge, his left hand resting on the pommel of his sword.

"Your bruises are healing."

Robin gritted his teeth at the hated voice which brought back vivid memories of the terrible beating he'd suffered at this man's hands the last time they'd met in Nottingham. It wasn't his style to offer taunts though, so he remained silent, watching Gisbourne for the attack which would certainly come.

"I'm glad you decided to meet me. Killing you will make me famous. You're something of a hero to the peasants, you know. Although I can't see why. No offence, but you were no better a swordsman than a dozen other men I've fought and killed."

The boiled-leather cuirass, greaves and bracers Gisbourne wore shone like metal despite the clouds overhead, and, when he drew his sword and held it in a two-handed defensive stance, he looked like something from a fairy tale. Tall, grim and dark; death seemed to hover around him like a black cloak.

Robin felt it, the sense of dread this man somehow exuded, but he too knew the power of appearances, so he hid his fear and continued to stare steadily at his opponent, gently flexing the great muscles in his shoulders and rolling his head to release the tension in his neck.

"Not in the mood for talking?" Gisbourne smiled and Robin shuddered at it for it was a genuine smile of pleasure. There was no trace of fear or trepidation in this man's eyes – he obviously trusted implicitly in his ability to defeat the younger, stronger man.

In contrast, Robin felt like puking. Never before, in his entire life, had he felt such fear going into a battle. Bigger, faster and more agile than the boys in Wakefield, he'd grown up knowing he could deal with almost anyone that tried to stand against him. When he'd become an outlaw and joined up with the men he now led, he'd learned fast, and suffered many beatings on the way, until he knew he could best any of his men – even John – either unarmed or with sword in-hand.

So why did he feel like his intestines were about to worm their way out of his mouth? He stared into the hazelnut eyes of Sir Guy and breathed deeply, trying to marshall his thoughts.

Without thinking he drew his sword and brought it up across his body, parrying the thrust Gisbourne had suddenly thrown.

Christ, but the king's man was fast! Faster than anyone Robin had ever faced before.

Gisbourne threw a few more experimental blows, parried easily enough by the young man from Wakefield, but Robin knew this was just the beginning. He expected to be played with, as he had been in Nottingham, but this time he didn't intend to stand by while it happened. He'd been in shock from the death of his oldest friend when he'd been captured by this man previously and it had slowed him; made him a much easier target than he would normally have been. Now, Robin meant to exact revenge for Much, James, Paul and Sir Richard-at-Lee. And for the torture he'd suffered himself at the hands of this dark monster of a man.

Sir Guy of Gisbourne was a man who pushed himself mercilessly to be the best. He tried to eat well without being a glutton, paid a surgeon to bleed him regularly, and he drank little alcohol, knowing his body would suffer if he indulged too much. Once he'd left his life in Gisbourne and been employed by the king he had remembered the bedtime stories his mother had told and begun to see himself as Sir Lancelot – a charismatic, flawed genius that could best any man alive with a sword. Indeed, his whole persona had been moulded on those old tales of Camelot and the round table. His armour had been influenced by the mythical Black Knight, knowing the colour inspired a primal fear in even the most hardened of warriors. His mistrust of women came from his adulterous wife, Emma, and, of course, Guinevere who had betrayed her own husband, King Arthur.

Parsival's quest for the Holy Grail was, right here, embodied in Gisbourne's battle with Robin Hood, a man the stupid peasants had started comparing to the mythical Arthur!

There was no holy cup filled with some mythical figure's blood. Gisbourne knew it was a metaphor – a symbol that showed those with the wit to see it as the way to enlightenment and self-improvement. The way to become a god.

He grinned in fierce pleasure as he aimed an upward swing at Hood's midriff, feeling power and self-belief coursing through his veins like righteous fire. He became utterly lost within himself as he traded blows back and forth with the wolf's head on the old stone bridge which had seen better days but had been neglected in recent years by the local lord.

His movements flowed effortlessly and he revelled in the feeling of invincibility as the young outlaw parried his blows desperately, rarely giving anything back, yet somehow managing to remain untouched himself.

It was a fine battle, Gisbourne admitted to himself as he danced into another attacking position. But the wolf's head was only doing enough to survive; he wasn't skilful enough to pierce the Raven's defences, and so it would end soon.

He bared his teeth in a joyful smile and went on the attack again.

When Robin had first joined the outlaws he hadn't been much of a swordsman. He could use a longbow better than most people, thanks to his years of practice growing up, like all the other boys in Wakefield. And he could handle himself in unarmed combat thanks to his quick reflexes and powerful build. But he'd rarely taken out the old sword his father kept stored under his bed. When he'd begun sparring with the outlaws all those months ago he'd been beaten and bruised mercilessly until, eventually, he'd learned how to fight with a blade in his hand.

As their leader, he wanted the outlaws to look up to him as a true warrior despite his age. And they did. Because he was the best of them.

He knew he couldn't beat Gisbourne though. It was becoming increasingly obvious that the king's man had almost supernatural abilities. When Robin launched an attack, Gisbourne knew it was coming and was able to either move out the way or parry it, seemingly without much effort. In contrast, the bounty-hunter's moves were so fast, so fluid and so relentless that the wolf's head was desperately tired already, both mentally and physically.

He couldn't hear his friends behind him, but he could feel their nervous stares boring into him as they watched the hated enemy, the Raven, gain the upper hand.

On the opposite side of the river, from the corner of his eye, Robin could see Gisbourne's soldiers watching, although their lack of movement or sound as their leader battered him relentlessly suggested they held little affection for their charismatic leader. Only his second-in-command, Barnwell, seemed excited by the whole affair, shouting encouragement to his master and hopping excitedly, almost like a child, from foot to foot as each blow was thrown and parried.

It couldn't last forever, though. Robin was fast becoming exhausted and his parries were beginning to come slower, with less strength behind them, and he was throwing fewer and fewer shots of his own as time went on.

The young man tried to rally, picturing Matilda's face in his mind's eye, holding their unborn baby in her arms. He so desperately wanted to be a father to that little child, and, for a few moments, another surge of determination allowed him to force Gisbourne onto the back-foot. But it didn't last before he tired again, his arms feeling like they were encased in lead, and the grim king's man took control again, his wickedly sharp blade – so finely polished it almost glowed in the setting sunlight – moving so fluidly it seemed to be made from liquid steel.

Robin knew he was going to die here today.

* * *

Friar Tuck literally fell off the big palfrey as he came at last to the bridge and found his friends watching the fight between their leader and Sir Guy of Gisbourne.

"What are you doing here?" Little John demanded, trying to keep an eye on the one-to-one battle before him while dragging the big clergyman off the grass as if he was no heavier than a child. "You're supposed to be resting at the camp. And watching our stuff!"

"Never mind that," Tuck retorted. "I have news! Robin has a son!"

The outlaws, nervously watching the fight between their leader and the man known as the Raven, suddenly cried out as they heard the friar's news.

"A son!"

"Robin has a son!"

"Are you sure?" John demanded, glaring into Tuck's eyes. "Robin's suffered enough in the past few weeks without hearing something that'll turn out to be nonsense."

"I'm sure," Tuck nodded, trying to catch his breath and rubbing his elbow where he'd landed as he dropped from the horse in his haste. "A boy, born on the Ides of June. Tell him!"

Little John grinned. "If you're sure, I'll let him know." He hefted his great quarterstaff over his head and gave a deafening shout. "Lads! Let's tell him."

Filling his massive lungs, the giant outlaw opened his mouth and bellowed across to the bridge and the men locked in mortal combat there.

"Robin! You're a father now. Matilda's had a son!"

The men behind him joined in and added their joyful congratulations, roaring and shouting happily. "Matilda's had the baby!"

CHAPTER TWENTY-FIVE

He had a son!

Images of a smiling little boy racing through the forest and the streets of Wakefield filled Robin's mind as he knelt in the mud under another of the Raven's relentless attacks. A boy with fair hair, eyes shining, gazing up at him – his father – as they played together in the thick green summer foliage.

The outlaw rose unsteadily to his feet and parried the unrelenting blows from the wiry king's man, desperately trying to stay alive as attack after attack rained down on him.

And then it happened. A simple stumble was all it took, as a foot failed to find purchase on a damp patch of grass and the blade was coming down, slicing mercilessly through skin and flesh, before scraping agonizingly down through cheekbone and jaw.

It took Gisbourne a moment to realise what had happened, before he held his left hand up to his ruined face and screamed, an outpouring of fear, pain and rage.

All his years of training to be the best, and a damp patch of grass was his undoing.

Robin could hear his friends now – cheering and whooping in happy relief as he stepped back to catch his breath, sword held loosely in his hand as he watched Gisbourne struggle back to his feet, still clutching his cheek which was bleeding terribly now.

"You lucky bastard." The bounty-hunter mumbled as he moved back into a fighting stance, and Robin shivered as he saw Gisbourne's crazed eyes and the crimson stain that was leaking steadily between his fingers. "I'm not done yet, Hood. I still have enough left to beat you."

Robin threw his sword up again, stunned by the speed the injured Gisbourne hurled himself back into the fight, and again they traded blows. This time, though, Robin knew he had the upper hand. Gisbourne's depth-perception was off as he tried to hold his face together and he was struggling terribly to keep up with the speed they were moving at.

Again, Robin's sword raked across his enemy's face, this time diagonally upwards, from left to right, taking the side of Gisbourne's nostril off, narrowly missing the eye, and the bleeding man continued to fight on, tears of fury spilling from his eyes and spreading the blood even more shockingly down his face, but refusing to accept defeat at the hands of this outlawed yeoman.

Both men were tired now, locked in their own little world of pain and blood.

Gisbourne tried a powerful overhand cut but totally misjudged his opponent's position and the bright steel whistled harmlessly down, lodging point-first into the grass.

They had been moving backwards as Robin's superiority forced Gisbourne onto the back-foot and were now standing in front of the old stone bridge. The sound of rushing water was the only thing the young outlaw could hear as his hated enemy stood, beaten and unmoving, looking at him through his insane dark eyes.

"You murdered three of my friends. One of them I'd known all my life – he was a good man, and you gutted him in front of me."

Gisbourne stared, mouth open, drooling slightly, his entire face, neck and that beautiful black boiled-leather cuirass covered grotesquely in blood. He never replied – indeed he didn't seem to know where he was any more, and Robin kicked him in the stomach, so hard that Gisbourne was thrown backwards to lie on the bridge.

Still lost in a place where only he and his foe existed, Robin moved forward with a murderous glint in his eyes and raised his sword to plunge it down into Sir Guy's heart.

He hadn't noticed Gisbourne's men being urged forward into a charge by the bounty-hunter's sergeant Nicholas Barnwell though, or his own men running desperately to reach him before the soldiers did.

Barnwell reached the bridge before anyone else, sword in hand, and he screamed in fury as he swung it at Robin who only now noticed the bald man not five paces away from him.

An arrow sliced through the air, catching Barnwell in the left thigh and he spun to the side before another arrow hammered into his chest knocking him onto his backside. He sat on the bridge, a look of surprise on his face, gazing down at the missiles lodged in him.

Gisbourne's soldiers seemed to have little enthusiasm for a fight as they moved slowly towards the bridge, clearly not looking to engage the outlaws even though they outnumbered Robin and his men and Will Scarlet was shouting obscenities at them.

"Move!" Robin felt himself grabbed from behind by strong hands as Little John hauled him off the bridge, the rest of the outlaws holding drawn swords or longbows aimed at the soldiers on the opposite side of the river.

Moving backwards, still staring at the mutilated, bloody face of Sir Guy of Gisbourne, Robin Hood allowed himself to be led away into the trees by his enormous friend, their men forming a protective barrier behind them in case Gisbourne's soldiers decided to come after them.

Stephen suddenly ran past them onto the bridge and pried Sir Richard's sword from Barnwell's dead fingers before he moved back towards the trees with the rest of the men.

"You did it! You fucking did it!" John's bearded, open face was split by a wide grin and, despite his facial hair and great size, Robin marvelled at how childlike the man seemed at times.

"He slipped."

John dismissed that with a wave of his hand as Friar Tuck moved in beside them, helping the giant to support their tired leader as they disappeared back into the forest towards their camp.

"Whether he slipped or not – and I never saw it – you beat the bastard."

As they moved deeper into the trees the excitement and blood-lust wore off, the realisation of what happened began to sink in and Robin grinned. "I beat the bastard. I'm still alive!"

If they hadn't been so disciplined, the men would have sung for joy.

Robin had won!

"Come on!" he shouted, stumbling through the mud. "I have to visit my son!"

* * *

"Will you leave us then, Tuck?"

The outlaws had made it back to their camp safely, elated after their young leader's victory over their feared enemy, and now they sat celebrating their good fortune around the camp-fire.

It was a cold evening, but the cosily crackling flames cast a homely glow on the small clearing and generous amounts of ale and roast venison had warmed the men nicely.

Robin had ridden straight off to Wakefield to see his new son, accompanied by Will who wanted to see his own little daughter, Beth. Now, the rest of the men were enjoying themselves and Little John gazed across at the jovial friar, who sat looking at the valuable reliquary they'd borrowed from St Mary's in Brandesburton.

"What d'you mean?" Tuck asked, looking up in surprise. "Why would I leave?"

John pointed at the holy relic cradled in Tuck's palm. "If you were to take that to Prior de Monte Martini in Lewes, he'd welcome you back into the church with open arms."

Tuck sat for a moment, lost in thought. He hadn't even considered that idea, but John was right.

"I can't take it," he replied at last. "You promised to return it to Brandesburton."

John shrugged. "Aye, so we did, but it was stolen from the Prior so I don't think Father de Nottingham would mind too much if you returned it to its rightful owner."

It was probably true. Tuck turned away from his big friend and gazed thoughtfully into the fire. He loved these men – like brothers, some of them. But he wasn't as fit as the rest of the outlaws and his recent health problems had taken their toll on him, both physically and mentally. He didn't feel as comfortable sleeping rough in the forest as the others, especially when winter came.

Maybe God had sent him the relic, as a way to leave this life as a wolf's head...? If that was so, it would be sinful not to use it for the purpose the Lord had intended...

"What's to be done with him, then?" Allan-a-Dale shouted suddenly, standing up and pointing. Edmond looked up, his cheeks flushing as the outlaws turned to look at him.

"Can you fight, lad?" someone demanded.

The tanner nodded, but his eyes remained self-consciously on the grass and soft old leaves carpeting the forest floor and Tuck instantly felt sorry for the young man who muttered a reply.

"Aye, well enough."

"That's enough for us, then, eh?"

Most of the men, half-drunk by now and in a happy mood, cheered Allan's words, but as Tuck saw the beginnings of a smile tugging at the corners of Edmond's fleshy mouth another voice spoke up.

"Hold on." It was Stephen. He had taken his fill of the ale like the rest of them, but he was mourning the death of his master, and friend, Sir Richard, and clearly didn't feel so much like celebrating that night. He walked over to stand in front of Edmond, looking down at him with an unreadable expression on his pock-marked face. "It's time you told us what happened between you and Sir Richard, boy – you owe me an explanation. And it had better be good."

Tuck clenched his fist protectively around the priceless reliquary, refilled his wooden mug and settled back to listen as the tanner from Kirklees began to tell them his tale.

Edmond wasn't much of a story-teller but the emotion betrayed in his voice – the obvious pain and sense of loss as he told the band of outlaws his tale – made up for his lack of eloquence.

Even Stephen felt sorry for the young man by the end of it.

Little John stood up as the men quietly digested Edmond's words. "Enough of this, we're supposed to be celebrating! Allan!" He glared at the minstrel who jumped to his feet under the giant's murderous gaze. "Give us a tune."

As Allan expertly strummed his gittern and the sounds of a merry jig filled the camp the men were pleased to shake off the sorrowful atmosphere Edmond's story had weaved around the place. The glad sounds of singing and dance filled the shadowy forest and the celebratory mood was kindled again.

John made his way over to Edmond and sat down beside him with a nod. For a long time they sat together in silence, watching the others enjoying the music and ale.

"I'm truly sorry for what I did," Edmond finally said to the bearded giant, tears making clean tracks in the grime on his face. "I know Sir Richard was your friend."

Little John leaned over and grasped the tanner by the arm, staring into his eyes earnestly.

"Listen to me. Every one of us here has a sad tale to tell. We all wish our life had turned out differently. But we're here and we live this life as best we can. As wolf's heads, aye, but as friends and brothers too. Forget your past, forget all the shit that life's thrown at you – you're one of us now."

The giant grinned and moved away to join in with the celebrations.

Edmond sat watching the outlaws singing, dancing, drinking and laughing together, all grinning merrily at him as they passed in their revelry and he felt the tears spill from his eyes again, only this time his heart soared and he thanked God.

Finally, he knew he had found a place where he would be accepted for who he was.

* * *

"Where is he?" The door burst open and the people in the house shrank back, eyes searching instinctively for something to use as a weapon.

"Where's my son?"

"Robin, you bloody idiot! I nearly shit myself there – have you never heard of knocking before you open a door?"

The big outlaw muttered apologies to Matilda's father and the rest of the relieved people gathered in the Fletcher's house. His own parents were there, Martha and Thomas, with his little sister,

Marjorie who ran over to give him a cuddle, a big smile on her thin teenage face. Will's daughter, Beth, was there too and she followed Marjorie's lead, jumping into her grinning father's open arms as he followed Robin into the modest house.

Robin's eyes settled finally on the old chair by the hearth, where his wife sat cradling a small bundle in her arms.

Matilda's eyes sparkled joyfully as she looked down at the child then up at her beloved wolf's head. "Your son has your nose," she told him.

Grinning at his parents he moved past them and stooped to look down at his child, placing a big arm around his wife and cuddling her in close as he gazed at the little person they'd created together.

"You can hold him," Matilda smiled, offering the sleeping baby to him, but he shook his head and leaned back, almost defensively. "No, no, you hold him, I might drop him."

Mary snorted from behind him and shook her head at her daughter. "Get used to that. Men are all the same – think they're so strong they'll break their own baby, or so clumsy they'll drop it on its head."

Robin never even heard his mother-in-law, transfixed as he was by the sight of his beautiful tiny son. His own mother, Martha came over and hugged him proudly.

"Congratulations, daddy," she said.

"Thanks, grandma," he replied.

"Come on," Henry's big voice boomed out in the low room, "everyone sit by the table, there should be enough space for us all to fit somewhere." He gestured at the things his wife had laid out for them: meat, bread, cheese and ale. "Eat. Drink. Robin, you're looking, well...battered, truth be told. What the hell happened?"

The outlaw had taken a seat right next to Matilda and the child, and he looked up from them now, his face twisted in a grimace.

"Sir Guy of Gisbourne."

The room seemed to grow smaller and darker at the very mention of the Raven, but Robin poured himself a mug of ale and nodded confidently. "He murdered Much...and would have killed me too if it hadn't been for the sheriff pulling him off. We needn't fear him any more though. I've just taken half his face off."

There was an awkward silence for a few moments as the celebrating families didn't know how to react to Robin's news.

"Kicked his arse for him, right enough, never seen a fight like it in all my life," Will nodded cheerfully, trying, unsuccessfully to lighten the atmosphere. "But Robin beat him good. 'The Raven' will be dead by now, after what Robin did to him."

"Are you all right?" Martha's maternal instincts took over and she stared at her son, who would always be her own little boy, no matter how big he was now.

He forced a smile back onto his face and stuffed a chunk of bread into his mouth, pushing the image of Much's corpse to the back of his mind. "Aye, I'm fine! I beat the bastard and my wife and son are well. A man couldn't ask for any more."

"A pardon would be nice," Mary muttered sarcastically to laughs from the rest of the group.

"What are you going to call him?" Marjorie demanded, moving around the table, followed by Beth, to touch the baby's tiny hands and nose.

Robin looked at Matilda, remembering their conversation months ago. "Arthur," she nodded, and her husband grinned approval.

"Aye, Arthur. Much better than Edward or Adam."

The rest of the evening, what remained of it, passed quickly with much laughter and joy as the ale flowed and Robin and Matilda's parents – and Will too – told stories of their own children's younger years, warning the proud new mother and father what to expect from their own mischievous little one. The women, along with Marjorie and Beth, were happy to take the babe for cuddles whenever he woke up and didn't need Matilda to nurse him.

Eventually, knowing they all had to work early the next morning, the Hoods made their goodbyes and left for home, taking Will and Beth with them. Henry and Mary retired to their own bed, leaving Robin and Matilda to bond, alone together, with their child.

"Arthur," Matilda whispered. "It suits him. He's perfect."

"He is. Just like his mother." Robin's arms pulled them in close and the little family stood together, savouring the blessing God had bestowed upon them.

"I'm tired, let's go to bed."

As they lay beside each other, listening anxiously for the gentle sounds of their baby's breathing as all new parents do, Robin thanked God and the Magdalene for his beautiful son.

As he drifted off into a fitful sleep, though, he remembered growing up in this village with his best friend, Much, and wished the miller's son could have been here tonight to share their joy.

That bastard Matt Groves thinks he's safe, somewhere, but I'll find him one day, and I'll make him pay. As God is my witness, I will find him, and I will kill him for what he's done!

* * *

Things had worked out perfectly. He had a drink in one hand and some giggling whore's soft little tit in the other, with coin to afford quite a few more nights like this before he'd have to find a way to earn more. Gisbourne had paid him well for betraying Robin Hood and that other idiot from Wakefield so Matt had made his way east to Hull, which would be far enough away that he'd never run into any of his former outlaw 'friends' by accident.

He'd been a good sailor before turning to piracy and, as a result of that, ended up on the run from the law in Barnsdale. Here in Hull he knew he'd be able to find work on one of the many wool ships that plied their trade between England and Flanders.

He spilled ale down his chin and groaned loudly as the girl's hand finished its work. He lay on the stinking old pallet for a while, grinning, before tossing her a coin and ordering her out of the room.

Aye, things had worked out perfectly for him...

* * *

"He's dead, my lord sheriff."

Sir Henry de Faucumberg fixed the soldier with an angry stare. "I can see that, you idiot. What happened?"

"Robin Hood and his men."

The sheriff hadn't known Gisbourne was taking men off to fight a private duel with the wolf's head, and he shook his head angrily at what he saw in front of him now. Today should have been a day of celebration: they'd hung the Hospitaller and the king would be pleased at the news. Now this...! Gisbourne and Barnwell were the king's own men, sent here by the monarch personally, to deal with Robin Hood originally and, latterly, to help round-up the Contrariant rebels.

The thought of telling King Edward that Robin Hood still lived after all this made the sheriff's stomach flip over and the back of his throat tightened. He coughed, trying not to puke as he looked down at the corpse in front of him.

The sound of agonised screaming suddenly came through from the room next door, so loud that even the thick walls of the castle couldn't muffle it completely, and de Faucumberg sighed.

"At least it won't all be bad news I'll have to send the king."

"My lord?" the soldier asked in confusion.

"God be praised," de Faucumberg replied sarcastically, turning to leave the room. "Unlike his dead sergeant here, the surgeon tells me Sir Guy of Gisbourne will live, despite his terrible wounds. I expect he'll want revenge for what Hood's done to his face. If Gisbourne was a lunatic before, Christ only knows what he'll be like once he's fit again..."

Author's Note

Hopefully you enjoyed *The Wolf and The Raven* and, if you read the earlier story, *Wolf's Head,* you liked how the story and characters have developed. I have to be completely honest and say I didn't actually plan things to turn out like this though!

Originally, as you may know, I had wanted this series to be a trilogy. Too many authors find success with a character or formula and string it out until it becomes a shadow of its original self and I didn't want that to happen with my first foray into the world of writing.

However, when I sat down and started to work on this book the characters of Sir Richard and Stephen seemed to take over and, being the type of writer who plans very little and lets the people in the story dictate much of it, some of the things I wanted to do got overlooked here.

Little John for example, is someone I'd like to explore in more depth yet he ended up having little to do in this tale. Similarly, Matilda plays very little part, being pregnant as she is, and it would be nice to look at the role Robin's wife and family might play in the future.

So, if I was to make the next book the last in the series I would have to shoe-horn in a lot more than I'd be comfortable with.

For that reason, I'm now planning on adding an extra volume to the trilogy, making a total of four books – a tetralogy! Of course, who knows what the characters will do in the next one once I get started..? What I *can* tell you is that Little John will play a much greater part, as will hopefully Robin himself and, along the way, there may be a few more surprises.

Please stick around, and join me to find out what the future holds for our merry men and women!

Steven A. McKay,
18 March 2014

RISE OF THE WOLF

STEVEN A. McKAY

RISE OF THE WOLF

Book 3 in *The Forest Lord* series

By Steven A. McKay

Copyright 2015 Steven A. McKay

All rights reserved. This book may not be reproduced in any form, in whole or in part, without written permission from the author.

For my wife Yvonne,
and everything we've been through together.
Love you.

Acknowledgements

As always, lots of people have been a great help to me in writing this novel. Kathryn Warner, author and historian, provided me with invaluable information on King Edward II's movements in 1323. Her fantastic blog also provided much interesting information on the much-maligned king's character. He wasn't all bad despite what you may have read.

Archery expert Chris Verwijmeren, as always, proved invaluable when it came to both my cover design and technical details. The sections about fletching were made easier to write thanks to his help. I am greatly indebted to him for his time and patience.

My beta-readers gave much useful feedback when I was in the early stages of editing, so big thanks to them: Bill Moore, Bernadette McDade and Robin Carter.

Again, I have to thank the team at Amazon's KDP for their continued support and also the staff at Audible and ACX.

You, my readers, are the people that have most helped these books enjoy the success they have though, so cheers to everyone who's bought the books, left a review, joined in with me on Facebook or Twitter or at my website and generally been so kind and supportive to a humble lad from Scotland.

Now, sit back, and enjoy *Rise of the Wolf*.

Prologue

The two girls smiled at one another as they pushed their way through the sparse late-winter foliage and caught sight of the snares they'd set the day before. One of the traps had managed to catch a hare in mid-hop and its little brown body hung, dead and ready for the pot.

"Well done," Matilda said, clapping her younger friend on the back. "That was one of your snares – you set it at just the right height and now," she glanced down at her own empty hands, "we have at least something to contribute to dinner tonight."

They moved forward to collect their prize but, as they reached it, a man pushed his way through the trees from the right, startling them with his sudden appearance and his size. Although he was a tall man, he wore light green and brown foresters garb which had allowed him to remain undetected by the two villagers.

"I think we've found our hunters, lads."

As the man spoke, a satisfied smirk appearing on his lips, more men revealed themselves from amongst the branches and bushes of Barnsdale Forest.

Matilda mentally kicked herself – she'd lived with her husband, Robin Hood, and his men within this very greenwood not so long ago and had learned much in that time. "I should have seen them hiding there," she muttered to her companion.

Marjorie was Robin's younger sister, a thin girl of fifteen, and her face twisted in fear at the prospect of arrest at the foresters' hands. "What will they do with us?"

"Well, now, that'll be for the warden to decide," the tall man shrugged, overhearing her wavering voice. "But you only seem to have caught one tired-looking old hare. Probably just be a fine."

Marjorie relaxed a little at that; her family had money enough thanks to her infamous brother's exploits. She'd been worried about losing a hand or even worse.

The man stepped in close, inspecting the two girls. "Or perhaps we could come to some other arrangement and we'll just forget this ever happened?"

As he raised a hand to touch Matilda's face the young woman suddenly lashed out, ramming the point of her knee into the forester's groin, and giving him a shove so hard that he fell, gasping, onto the damp ground.

Marjorie cowered, mouth open, eyes wide as her sister-in-law produced a wicked looking knife from somewhere inside her tunic and held it defensively in front of herself, daring the other lawmen to come for her.

"Any of you touch me or the girl here and I'll rip your bollocks off! Wouldn't be the first time I've done that."

The downed forester pushed himself onto one knee, blowing hard, face scarlet with fury. "You bitch, there was no call for that. I'll make sure the warden deals with the pair of you harshly. Take them lads."

His comrades didn't seem in any rush to challenge the confident girl with the blade whose stance suggested knowledge of fighting techniques so he pulled himself up with a growl and drew his own weapon. "Fine, I'll deal with her myself you cowards."

"He's got a sword, Matilda."

"I can see that, don't worry. I've beaten Little John and Will Scarlet; I can take this whoreson too, no problem." Her words were spoken calmly, designed to soothe the younger girl, but Matilda's darting eyes betrayed her nervousness. She'd never beaten either of those famous outlaws, not really, but these foresters didn't know that.

One of the other men slowly circled his way around to stand a little way off to the side, looking intently at the girls before recognition flared in his eyes and he raised a hand just as his leader was about to strike.

"Wait."

"Wait?" The big forester hesitated, glaring irritably at his mate. "Wait for what? It's two girls in God's name, I'm sure I can handle them even if you lot want to stand there gaping like landed trout."

"That's Robin Hood's wife. I've seen her before."

"So?"

There was silence as the implications of harming or arresting these two girls from nearby Wakefield hit the tall lawman and he stepped back, thoughtfully, sword still raised but obviously not intending to use it any time soon.

The forester that had recognised Matilda shook his head. "If we were to bring in Hood or one of his gang, aye, we'd be well rewarded. But I fear the only thanks we'll get for arresting these two is a sword in the guts from the wolf's head."

The leader stood, hesitating, angry at being made to look like a craven but sharing his comrade's respect – and fear – of the notorious outlaw who always repaid those who crossed him or his friends with brutal, deadly violence.

"All right," he grunted, sheathing his sword and waving the girls away. "You can go but –" He smirked and reached out to grab the hare from the little wire noose "– we're having this."

Matilda nodded and grabbed Marjorie's arm, hauling her backwards into the bushes, happy enough to let the man have that one small victory. A single hare wasn't much of a price to pay for their freedom after all.

When they were hidden by the foliage they broke into a run.

Matilda's eyes sparkled, the excitement and joy at surviving the unexpected encounter coursing through her veins like fire.

Marjorie's face, though, was streaked with tears of humiliation.

CHAPTER ONE

WAKEFIELD, NORTHERN ENGLAND
MARCH 1323

"He's got me Will... gutted me like a fish. I'm done for..." Little John fell to the ground clutching his midriff, bearded face twisted in pain as he looked up in despair at his companion. "Avenge me..."

Will Scarlet cried out, racing over to his giant friend's side, weapon held aloft, ready to fend off any more blows.

Their attacker laughed and the outlaws shrank back, begging for mercy, their faces twisted in fear.

"Arthur! What are those two doing with you?" Matilda Hood strode into the neatly-tended garden with its bright daffodils and snowdrops and scooped up her smiling infant. The boy waved the tiny wooden sword gleefully, almost hitting his mother in the face. "That's enough of that game," she scolded John and Will who shrugged innocently and grinned at the baby when Matilda turned away. "Robin, will you tell these two? I don't want Arthur growing up to be a fighter."

Her young husband wandered over to his two friends, smiling and tugging gently on his nine month-old son's chubby cheek as he passed. "Aye, all right, I will."

Matilda carried their son back into the Fletcher's house where she still lived with her parents. In a perfect world she and Robin would have had a nice house of their own to live in but with her husband being an outlaw that was an impossible dream.

"Come on, let's go to the inn for a couple of ales," John suggested, seeing the troubled look on his nineteen year-old leader's face and wondering at its cause.

Will agreed readily but Robin glanced towards the door his wife had just disappeared through, provoking an amused grunt from Scarlet. "You need to ask the wife for permission to go down to the inn, lad? I wonder what the men would think of that."

Robin laughed along with his friends, cursing them, and, with a sheepish wave to Matilda who had appeared at the window with a knowing look, the three of them made their way along the road towards the local ale-house.

"Three ales, please, Alex," Will shouted to the fat, purple-nosed inn-keep, who waved merrily in response and moved to fill the wooden mugs as ordered.

The room was cold and dim, the early afternoon sunlight not really penetrating the windows which were half-shuttered to keep out some of the chill spring breeze. The outlaws pulled their thick cloaks up around their necks and sat in silence until Alex had placed their drinks on the rickety table and, after accepting a coin in payment from Robin, disappeared discreetly into the kitchen.

"What's on your mind, lad?" Little John asked Robin, drying the froth from his beard with a grimy sleeve.

The young wolf's head lifted his own ale and took a drink, shrugging as he did so. "I'm just worried we've had things too easy recently, and it probably won't last."

"It makes a nice change, having Gisbourne out of the way and the sheriff's men not making much of an effort to catch us," John nodded. "I know what you mean though."

"Aye," Will agreed. "Some of the lads seem to have forgotten the fact we're still outlaws and fair game for anyone that might decide to stick a knife in our guts. And that includes you." He pointed a thick, grubby finger at his leader with an earnest frown. "Playing happy families with Matilda and the little one."

"I know!" Robin raised a placatory hand as he took another sip from his mug. "I'm as bad as any of them. It's been an easy life the past few months since I beat Gisbourne but we all know someone's going to come hunting us sooner or later. We have to be ready for it."

Little John smiled, his open face almost childlike despite his great bushy beard. "What do you suggest? That we gather the men and go back to living in the forest? I'm not sure if they'll take too kindly to that idea."

Some of the outlaw band maintained their camp deep in the Barnsdale greenwood, where the communal funds were stored, but most of the men had taken to spending their time in whatever town or village held most attraction for them. Little John had gone back to Holderness where his family lived, only coming today to visit his two friends, Will and Robin, who spent days at a time here in Wakefield with their own kin.

The bounty hunter, Sir Guy of Gisbourne, who had come to Yorkshire on the king's orders specifically to hunt down Robin and his outlaws, had been mutilated and almost killed in one-on-one combat with the young wolf's head the previous year. Without his single-minded leadership and the onset of another hard winter, the sense of danger that hung over the outlaws for so long had dissipated, as had the iron discipline that had kept them alive up until now.

It had been a wonderful period for Robin, who'd been able to spend the days and nights with Matilda, watching his little baby son grow. He offered a silent prayer of thanks to God and the Magdalene for his good fortune before returning John's smile.

"No, I don't want to go back to living in Barnsdale until we need to."

"Good lad!" the giant boomed, raising his own mug to his lips. "I'll drink to that!"

"Aye, me too," Will Scarlet nodded. "Although you really need to do more combat training, Robin – you're starting to get a paunch."

"And jowls," John laughed. "You're spending too much time in bed with your wife and drinking ale" –

Suddenly the front door burst open and one of the local men rushed in from the bright sunshine outside, squinting as his eyes adjusted to the gloomy interior. Finally, he spotted Robin and the other two outlaws.

"Come quick, one of your lads is getting a hiding from the fuller!"

Cursing, drinks forgotten, the three friends leapt up and hurried after the man.

It didn't take long for them to hear the commotion just a few streets away. A voice was raised in anger, while a small crowd of villagers had gathered to watch the entertainment and were laughing and shouting encouragement to the stocky little fuller who was grappling with a thin youngster with a bloody nose.

"It's Gareth," John growled.

"Pissed no doubt," Will replied. "Again."

They pushed their way through the small crowd of onlookers until they were able to pull the fighting men apart. John held the fuller but the man was so enraged and filled with battle-fever that he kept swinging his fists, almost catching Robin before his giant friend hurled the small man onto the ground and held him there with a hand around his throat until he finally calmed down.

The skinny outlaw, Gareth, was also furious, but too dazed to even attempt fighting off Will who shoved him back and, with a menacing stare, ordered him to be silent. Gareth knew better than to cross Scarlet, so he stood, swaying slightly, glaring at the fuller who had bloodied his nose.

"What the hell's going on here?" Robin demanded, his eyes moving from the fuller to Gareth and back again.

"That little bastard was calling my wife an ugly old cow," the fuller, Hugh, spat and struggled to his feet as John moved back to let him rise. "Drunk again he is – in the middle of the day, when honest people should be out earning a living!"

Robin winced at the barb, hearing a small ripple of muttered agreement at the fuller's words from the gathered villagers.

"Are you saying we're not fucking honest?" the volatile Will Scarlet moved towards Hugh threateningly, but the little man was so angry he didn't back down.

"Aye, I am!" the fuller retorted, pushing his chest out and waving a fist at the outlaws. "We're all out working to earn our keep, while you lot saunter around the village like lords, throwing coin about like it was nothing. You've outstayed your welcome here!"

Robin grabbed Scarlet, holding him back to prevent him from really hurting Hugh as the onlookers crowded in on them.

Although the villagers weren't openly hostile, it was clear they were ready to support the fuller, despite everything Robin and the other outlaws had done for Wakefield over the past two years. It was galling, but the wolf's head had learned not to take things like this too personally.

Life was hard and people had short memories, especially when they saw others apparently having an easier time of it than themselves.

"Outstayed our welcome, you little prick?" Will shouted at the fuller, before rounding on the other locals. "You lot must have forgotten what we did for you during the winters. The food we gave you when your bellies were shrinking!"

Robin grasped Gareth by the arm and hauled him away, gesturing for Little John to bring Will before any more trouble could develop, although Scarlet's angry words had mollified the crowd somewhat. Even the fuller had given up his rant and now stood, grumbling and shaking his head as the outlaws headed back towards the alehouse.

"What's the matter with you, boy?" Robin demanded of Gareth as they reached the low building and made their way back inside, seating themselves at the table they'd left not so long ago.

"I'll have an ale!" Gareth shouted across to Alexander, but Robin waved a hand at the inn-keep, telling him not to bother.

"No you won't, you've had more than enough."

Despite his intoxication, Gareth knew it would be a mistake to argue with his young leader, angry and flanked as he was by his two loyal lieutenants.

"We've got an easy life here in Wakefield," Robin said. "But your drinking's causing ill-feeling amongst the villagers. What the hell's wrong with you?"

Until recently Gareth had barely touched strong drink. He'd been a tiny, malnourished child who had been outlawed and chased from his home in Wrangbrook for stealing food for his sickly mother when he was barely into his teens. Despite that, he had become a valued member of the outlaw band, even saving Friar Tuck from drowning a few months previously.

Since then though, it seemed, the seventeen year-old had taken more and more to drinking and, like many men, he was an unpleasant companion when inebriated.

"It was that shit he got from the barber in Penyston," Will said. "The grain drink the man made himself from some foreign recipe. Ever since the lad tasted it he's been a drunk."

Gareth looked balefully at them but held his peace as his friends spoke about him as if he wasn't there.

John shook his head sadly. "It's true. He got a taste for it and he's not been the same since."

Robin was in no mood to listen to excuses for their companion's behaviour, not when it jeopardised his own fine life here in Wakefield with Matilda and Arthur.

"I don't care what's wrong with him, he'd better get a fucking grip of himself soon or he's going back to live in the camp in the forest. We can't have the people turning against us."

John shrugged his massive shoulders. "Maybe we *should* all head back into Barnsdale..."

Will snorted angrily and Robin gazed despondently into his mug.

Aye, he'd enjoyed the last few months with his family, living practically a normal life, but Will Scarlet had also been able to spend the time with his little daughter Beth, while John had greatly enjoyed his days in Holderness with his wife Amber and son John who he'd hardly seen in the years since he'd been outlawed for accidentally killing a man who was raping his own daughter.

Heading back into the greenwood was going to be hard on all of them and Robin vowed to hold off on their return for as long as possible.

Again, the front door was thrown open, sunlight flooding the dim interior of the ale-house and Will groaned as he placed his wooden mug back on the table with a thump. "For fuck sake, what now?"

As before, the newcomer gazed around the room, his eyes unused to the dim interior, and Robin shouted across, recognising the burly figure of Patrick Prudhomme, the village headman. "You're looking for us, no doubt. What's the matter?"

"Robin!" Prudhomme hurried over to their table breathlessly, his eyes wide. "You lads better gather your things. Gisbourne's here."

CHAPTER TWO

"There they are – get 'em!"

"Shit." Robin turned at the shout and spotted at least half-a-dozen foresters coming towards them. John, Will and Gareth had followed him at a run to his house where he collected his weapons and said a hasty goodbye to his family, hand lingering tenderly on Arthur's chubby cheek, savouring the moment. Now, the four outlaws headed for the trees on the outskirts of the village with the lawmen hurtling along behind, shouting for them to stop in the name of the king.

"Split up," Robin ordered. "It'll make it harder for them to follow us. We'll meet back at the camp."

Without a word the others broke left and right, the foresters cursing at their backs, wondering which of them to follow. For some reason all of them chose to stay on Robin's trail; he could hear them barging through the undergrowth although, to be fair, they seemed to be better woodsmen than most of the oafs that came hunting the wolf's head.

The young man was supremely fit, but his strength lay mostly in his upper body – the shoulders and arms that he used to deadly effect with his longbow. There was a good chance at least one of his pursuers would be a faster runner than him and he never liked the idea of an enemy at his back.

He had his bow in his hand and, fiddling inside the pouch at his waist, produced the string which he placed over the end of the weapon. Hoping he had enough time, he came to a stop and stepped across the bow, using his limbs to bend the massive weapon enough to slip the other end of the string into place.

His suspicions had been correct; one of the chasing foresters was right behind him, indeed, would have been close enough to plunge the tip of his sword into Robin's back before much longer if the outlaw had continued on his previous course.

With practised ease he pulled an arrow from his belt, nocked it to the string, took aim, and let fly. The missile took the unfortunate lawman hard in the chest, throwing him backwards and killing him instantly.

Without waiting to find out how the other foresters took the death of their companion, Robin turned and, moving off at a different angle this time, plunged back into the forest as silently as possible.

It seemed to work. There were cries of dismay and anger from behind but, mercifully, they didn't seem to be coming any closer. After a while the wolf's head relaxed and slowed his pace, breathing heavily as the effects of the chase and his unwanted but necessary kill wore off.

He hoped the others had managed to evade capture. He also wondered where Sir Guy of Gisbourne was; there had been no sign of the Raven amongst the lawmen that had come after them.

As he pushed through the branches dark thoughts assailed him but, before he realised it, he had reached the outlaws' camp. Home, for now.

He hadn't noticed the soft footsteps that shadowed his own. Nor did he see, a little while later, the watching forester that headed back the way he'd just come after tracking the wolf's head.

Back, towards Wakefield, and Gisbourne.

* * *

"So you're leaving us after all, Tuck, and going back to that bastard prior?"

The portly friar nodded his tonsured head, a look of regret on his normally cheery face. "Aye, Allan," he replied. "Once the weather gets a bit better I'll make the journey down to Lewes and return the holy relic to de Martini."

Allan-a-Dale spat on the hard grass of their camp which was flattened by weeks of heavy footprints and little sunlight. The outlaws all knew about Prior John de Monte Martini, the man who had threatened to sell Robin's wife Matilda to a brothel he owned in Nottingham and been rewarded for his threat with a broken nose from the brawny young archer.

Robin had been forced to join the outlaw gang to evade the prior's justice after that. Then Tuck had come along, escorting a wagon full of de Martini's money which the outlaws had stolen, although Tuck had soundly beaten Adam Bell, the leader of the outlaws at that time.

Rather than returning to the prior empty handed, knowing his fate would be an unpleasant one, the friar had remained in Barnsdale with the outlaws.

That had all happened two years earlier though, and, when Tuck realised Robin had come into possession of a hugely expensive relic stolen years earlier from Prior de Martini the big friar knew he held the key to a pardon in his hand. Freedom again. A normal life, without the threat of death around every tree stump or innocently babbling stream.

"The relic isn't ours though," Allan said, poking a stick into the camp-fire, making the flames leap and dance a little higher in the cool spring air. "It might have belonged to de Martini once, a long time ago, but it seems like you can't just take it back to him. Robin borrowed it in good faith from Father de Nottingham in Brandesburton. He promised to return it to him months ago."

Tuck remained silent, knowing the minstrel's words were true. Their young leader had asked to borrow the relic from St Mary's in order to revive Tuck after he'd been shot by Sir Guy of Gisbourne and almost drowned. Father de Nottingham had let the wolf's head take the holy relic, fully expecting it would be returned at some point.

It had done its job – Tuck had come to after days in an unnatural deep sleep, but when he saw it, the friar realised it wasn't the thumb of St Peter as the priest at St Mary's thought. It was actually strands of hair from Christ's own beard, held securely in an exquisitely decorated little box only Tuck – who had learned the secret years ago when he had bought the thing in a French village – had been able to unlock.

"It was good of the priest to let Robin take it," Tuck agreed. "But it belongs to Prior de Martini, no matter what anyone thinks of the man." He shrugged. "I'll go to Brandesburton and explain things. Leave Father de Nottingham some money to pay for his troubles..."

His voice trailed off and his bright blue eyes remained fixed on the fire in front of them. In truth, Tuck couldn't stand the wealthy de Martini who abused his position to gather wealth in most un-Christian ways. But the friar was getting on – he was forty-five years old as far as he knew – and although it was spring now, the thought of spending another winter in the greenwood, which wasn't anything like as green once the frost and snow descended upon it, wasn't a pleasant one.

He loved these outlaws like brothers, or even sons in some cases, but he knew he couldn't live out the remainder of his days here. He had found his true purpose in life: to spread the word of God. It was a task he couldn't perform very well while stuck in a forest in Yorkshire.

"Yes," he sighed, "I'll take the relic back to Prior de Martini. The thing's worth an obscene amount of gold so he'll be overjoyed to have it in his hands at last. Although he's a nasty piece of work, I'm sure he'll appreciate what I've done for him and the church will take me back into its service." His eyes flicked up and he gazed at Allan earnestly. "You know I really did enjoy life as a friar, as boring as it probably seems to you."

Allan waved the suggestion away. "Men come in different shapes and sizes. We all have our own tastes and ideas of what's good and bad. If you enjoyed that life, who am I to judge you? And, if you want to go back to that..." He returned the clergyman's gaze, "I'll be sad to see you go, my friend. But you have to follow the path you believe God's laid out for you. So, for what it's worth" – he lifted his gittern from the ground beside him and strummed a bright chord with a smile – "you have my blessing."

"On your feet you lot!"

It was a sign of their recent easy life – their lack of immediate danger and the resulting relaxed attitude to posting lookouts – that three men had managed to burst into the outlaws' camp without anyone raising the alarm.

Now, Gareth, Will and Little John moved hurriedly amongst them, extorting the men who had remained here with Tuck and Allan to prepare for a possible attack.

"Gisbourne's on his feet again," John told them. "He came to Wakefield with his men looking for us."

"Lucky for you lot he didn't start by looking here first," Will groused. "No guards watching for approaching danger? You've all gone soft. Gisbourne would have torn through you like an arrow through dog shit."

"We're not the only ones that've gone soft," Tuck retorted, taking in Will's breathless state with a raised eyebrow. "You can hardly get the words out you're so winded after the short run. Didn't you say you'd only come from Wakefield? Or were you visiting a friend in some other village? In Scotland perhaps?"

"Fuck off, Tuck," Scarlet grinned, watching as the men strapped on weapons and hastily took up positions in the trees overhead, longbows strung and ready to shoot. "Just get off your fat arse and help us move the camp before that whoreson Gisbourne appears. He's not going to be in a good mood after Robin took half his face off at Dalton."

"Like he was ever in a good mood," Allan shouted over his shoulder while gathering his own arrows and stringing his longbow.

"Aye, well, trust me," Scarlet replied. "If you thought he was dangerous before, he'll be even worse now. Being mutilated tends to make people angry! Just ask John – the midwife pulled him out of his ma face-first and the giant's never forgiven her for giving him a face like a mastiff doing a shit."

"Where is Robin anyway?" Tuck wondered as the men laughed at Will's insult, concern creasing his face as he used his quarterstaff to lever himself onto his feet.

Little John waved a meaty hand. "He'll be along soon – we had a head start on the foresters. Robin's safe enough." He grimaced at the smirking Will. "Any more of that shit though, Scarlet, and you'll be the one with the deformed face."

Their leader did appear just then, his glance taking in the rest of the men, seeing his two grinning lieutenants and the now-sober Gareth, before he nodded in relief. "Everyone's here then, good."

"Were you followed?" Stephen, the former Hospitaller sergeant-at-arms asked, sword already drawn as he watched the trees for signs of movement.

Robin sat down, helping himself to a mug and filling it from the barrel beside the campfire.

"Nah. One of them was like a hare, would have easily overtaken me, but I took him down. The rest gave up after that."

Will let out a small sigh and dropped onto the log beside his young leader, gesturing for Robin to hand him one of the other empty mugs so he could wet his own throat.

John made his way to his pallet and lay down, stretching his great frame and yawning like some beast of the forest. "We should really move camp," he muttered, gazing up at the branches overhead.

Will drained his mug and wiped his mouth with a grubby sleeve before replying. "We'll be fine. Gisbourne wasn't even with those men, they were just foresters. And, if one of them's been taken out they'll have no stomach to come looking for us. They're not stupid."

Robin mulled it over for a while. He glanced up, noting the position of the sun which was mostly hidden by dark grey clouds and knew it would be dark in a couple of hours anyway. "Will's right, we can leave and find a new base in the morning." The men gave soft cheers – moving camp was always a time-consuming, irritating chore and they were glad to put it off, even for just a few hours – but Robin held up a hand, gazing around at them. "Be on guard though, just in case."

* * *

When the forester that had followed Robin to the outlaw camp returned to Wakefield he went directly to Sir Guy. The Raven was indeed in the village, as were two dozen of his men – not foresters but proper, hard soldiers.

"Did Hood see you?"

"No, my lord," the man shook his head, keeping his eyes down respectfully under the bounty hunter's sharp look. "I watched them for a bit, but they were relaxed. Must have thought they'd got away all right."

"They would have too, if it wasn't for your tracking skills. Well done man. Here." Gisbourne tossed a coin to the forester who caught it with a surprised grin.

"I couldn't just let the wolf's head get away, not after he shot my friend –"

"Indeed." Gisbourne turned away, the conversation at an end, and waved his men in close. "This man will lead us to the outlaws' camp. Once we're close, I will have the foresters fire a volley of arrows and then you men will rush them. You all carry shields and wear good armour. Some of you may die – these criminals we go to find are skilled longbowmen, after all. Attack swiftly and without mercy, though, and the element of surprise should carry us through." He spun around again, gesturing for the forester to lead the way.

They moved as silently as possible but, as they approached the camp the outlaws could be heard laughing and talking amongst themselves and Gisbourne smiled. The forester was right – the wolf's heads thought they were safe and it would be their downfall. At last.

The bounty hunter halted his men before they got too close, fearing sentries would spot their approach. He signalled to the five foresters that remained in his company and watched as they readied their longbows. The sun was setting by now and the outlaws' camp-fire cast a tell-tale orange glow that gave the archers something to aim for. He looked around at his swordsmen, making sure they were ready to move, then, exhaling a deep breath, swung his hand down in an arc.

The snapping of bowstrings being released seemed to echo all around the forest before there were thuds and sounds of panic from the camp-site ahead.

"Charge!"

Gisbourne wasn't entirely certain how many outlaws they faced but he knew his men outnumbered them. Confident of victory, he led his men into the clearing to begin the killing.

He was disappointed to see none of his foresters' arrows had hit their targets but it wasn't surprising since they'd been firing blind. The missiles had served their purpose, scattering the wolf's head and his lackeys and throwing them into disarray, ready for Sir Guy's swordsmen to bring death to them.

It seemed he would, finally, rid the world of the craven bastard that had taken his eye and half his nose when they had last met, blade-on-blade, outside Dalton months earlier.

The outlaws hadn't survived so long by being undisciplined or incompetent though. Gisbourne held back, knowing he couldn't fight as well as he had before the loss of his eye.

But he could see well enough, as the man people ironically called Little John took out two of the Raven's soldiers with a quarterstaff that was almost a tree trunk.

His vision was clear enough to watch, in brutal detail, as the Hospitaller that had joined the outlaws swung his blade into the neck of a second of his men while a raging berserker that must be Will Scarlet tore the guts out of another and carried on his savage assault without even pausing for breath.

And the king's bounty hunter watched in a black fury as Robin Hood himself parried a thrust before sweeping his assailant's legs from under him and hammered the tip of his sword between a gap in the man's armour.

All around it was the same story. The outlaws had been alert and on their guard and Gisbourne's men were dying as a result.

"Fall back." Gisbourne's voice came out as little more than a grunt and he had to try again before his soldiers heard him. "Fall back!"

The men were only too happy to follow the order, retreating warily, thankfully, as the outlaws let them go, back into the trees with half their number dead or dying on the floor of the outlaws' campsite.

"You win this day, Hood," Sir Guy growled, his words somehow carrying over the panting and mewling sounds that accompanied the end of such a bloody battle. "But I'm back on my feet and I'll not rest until I see you swinging from those gallows outside Nottingham. You and all your men."

Hood's men jeered and called insults, laughing at Gisbourne for retreating like a coward but, in truth, the Raven was glad to escape with his life – and all his body-parts – intact.

Clearly an open assault wasn't going to work. He should have known. He realised that now, as they finally left the outlaws' mocking laughter in the distance. Lawmen had come and gone over the years but not one of them had managed to destroy this particular band of wolf's heads by simply attacking them – even with superior numbers.

The greenwood was *their* territory.

Clearly a new tactic was needed if Gisbourne was to have his revenge.

* * *

"Get your stuff, and get the fuck off my ship you whinging bastard, before I have the crew throw you over the side."

The burly captain stood up from the table where he had been trying to study maps for his next journey to Norway, although he knew much of his time would be spent in Iceland and the thought of the freezing waters of the North was making him irritable. He was in no mood for this man's endless complaining.

"Nothing's ever enough for you is it, Groves? When you joined us I thought you'd be an asset to the crew with your experience, but all you've done is cause splits between the men and I'll have no more of it. Now, go."

Matt Groves twisted his lip in the scowl the captain had grown to detest and shrugged. "Fine. I never came to Hull to be a damn fisherman anyway. I'll find a ship sailing to Portugal or Flanders. At least it'll be warm and won't stink of fish."

The first mate and another stocky crewman came in then, wondering what the shouting was about.

"Show Matt here out, lads," the captain ordered them. "He's going to Portugal."

The first mate grinned. He couldn't stand the surly Groves who was continually undermining his authority with the men. "With pleasure, captain."

A short time later Matt stood on the dock, surrounded by the noise and bustle of sailors and merchants readying their cargoes for the next money-making trip. After he had betrayed Robin and the other young outlaw from Wakefield, Much, to Sir Guy of Gisbourne, Groves had headed east with a pocket full of silver and plans to make a new life as a sailor, which was a job he'd done long ago in his youth.

This was the third vessel he'd been forced to leave. His time living in Barnsdale as an outlaw, where he could do almost whatever he liked, had made it impossible for him to bow to authority or accept the rigid order on board a ship. His constant questioning and refusal to carry out menial tasks made him an unpleasant companion.

He hadn't been popular when he was part of the outlaw gang either, but at least there he could take himself off to a village for the night, or visit a brothel to work out his aggression. Aboard a ship the crew had no way to escape the man's relentless grumbling, and, although he never admitted to being an outlaw, it was obvious he was a very dangerous man, making his presence on the lonely sea an altogether unsettling and unpleasant one.

He growled and spat a thick gob of phlegm onto the dock in frustration. The reward Gisbourne had given him to turn Judas on Robin and Much was long gone and he was sick of these base-born fishermen treating him like he was a nobody.

He wouldn't bother looking for that ship to Portugal or Flanders, after all. No... he had a better idea...

CHAPTER THREE

"Calm down, girl! Anger might seem like a good motivator but when it comes to a fight, it's much better to be calm." Matilda shrugged, feeling slightly foolish as she lectured the girl in front of her. She was no killing machine, but she had trained with Robin and the outlaws so, when Marjorie asked her to pass on her knowledge she had reluctantly agreed. "When people are angry they don't think things through; they just act, regardless of the consequences. The best swordsmen – or women – hold their emotions in check." She flicked her lightweight wooden practice sword out and was pleased when her pupil saw it coming and managed to parry, breathlessly.

Marjorie had always been a weak, sickly girl, despite her older brother Robin's impressive physique. She'd suffered terribly in the famine of 1315, her then seven year-old body wasting away despite her parents' best efforts to find food for the family. Robin, eleven at the time, had just enough weight on him to survive the worst of the hunger pangs but Marjorie's twin sister, Rebekah, had died.

She'd always remember her sister, and how she looked when she'd succumbed to the dreadful hunger: skin and bones, even though her empty stomach was bloated and round as if she'd eaten like a queen for weeks. It was a cruel way for a little girl to die.

Marjorie had survived – just – but, despite all the wholesome food her mother and father had prepared for her over the years, she'd never managed to put much meat on her bones. Even now, when Robin was a famous outlaw and a wealthy man who brought lots of fruit and vegetables, meat and eggs for his family to feast on, his sister remained thin, bordering on being malnourished.

"Block!" Matilda aimed a thrust at Marjorie, who appeared lost in thought, but the girl managed to twist away from the practice-sword and aim a blow of her own, which was easily batted aside although Matilda smiled encouragingly.

After the foresters had almost arrested them for trapping that hare, Marjorie had been ashamed of her fear. Ashamed of how useless she'd been, leaving her sister-in-law to protect her while she stood passively, waiting for the men do whatever they would.

Then, when news had come of Sir Guy of Gisbourne's return to action and Robin had left to go back to the forest again Marjorie had been irritated by the reaction of the people of Wakefield. The majority of them, even the men – and Matilda too! – had grown fearful at the prospect of the brutal bounty-hunter's soldiers coming back into their comfortable lives.

Marjorie could understand her big brother being wary of Gisbourne and going out of his way to avoid the man but – Christ above – the villagers needed to stand up for themselves. Why were they all content to be pushed around?

Eventually she realised the people accepted their treatment because they were weak. Not as physically weak as she was, no – the blacksmith, for example, was a bear of a man, by God and he liked to tell folk off if they got in his way. But he was no soldier; had no military training even though he'd been called up to the armies of the local lord over the years and had even seen what could loosely be termed 'action'.

He'd never faced an enemy sword on sword, or watched his own arrow pierce the body of an on-rushing foe.

Even if he had, Marjorie knew, he'd still be scared of the black-armoured king's man that people called the Raven.

Yet what could she do? She was only an abnormally skinny fifteen-year-old. She'd never, no matter how she tried, be able to draw a hunting bow never mind one of the giant warbows Robin or Little John used.

Similar thoughts had assailed her for years, even before Robin had become an outlaw. Her frail body had always angered her, but she'd never believed she could do anything to overcome the weakness.

Then the foresters had terrified and humiliated her, and Robin had left again, leaving them all to look after themselves, and Marjorie had decided enough was enough. She couldn't count on anyone to look after her – not her parents, not the burly blacksmith, not even her charismatic wolf's head brother.

Matilda came at her again and, as before, Marjorie managed to twist to the side with a strangled cry, just evading the blow although the effort left her gasping and she could feel a pain in her side that was growing worse with every passing moment.

She'd had enough of being the village weakling; the girl the adults looked down upon from sad, pitying eyes when they passed. She wanted to be like Robin. Of course, she wasn't stupid – she knew she'd never be the muscle-bound bear of a man her brother was, but she desperately wanted to toughen herself up. To learn how to wield a sword, or perhaps a crossbow since a bow would always be beyond her. *Anything* that she could use to defend herself and those she loved from the likes of Gisbourne and that filthy bailiff who had wanted to rape Matilda two years ago.

Marjorie had never been told the full story about what had happened when Adam Gurdon had arrested Matilda, but she'd listened to the gossip and had formed a rough idea in her head which she suspected was pretty accurate.

She was impressed by what the people said Matilda had done to defend herself. Marjorie, at fifteen, had not been with a young man yet but many of the girls her age or even younger were already married and gossiped freely about it, so she had a good idea what a hard, blood-engorged spindle looked like. Knowing Matilda had managed to bite almost right through Adam Gurdon's manhood told her all she needed to know about her brother's wife: she was the perfect teacher.

So, here they were.

Matilda had, at first, refused outright to train Marjorie. Not only was the girl thin and sickly, but Matilda doubted her own ability to teach anyone the ways of combat. Besides, they had more than enough to occupy their time, since she herself assisted her father in crafting arrows and Marjorie helped her own mother around the house.

But the girl had been persistent and eventually Matilda acquiesced. She didn't think the training would last for long before her student grew tired and fed-up and they could go back to normal life.

"Ha!" Marjorie, who had seemed exhausted just a moment before, suddenly jumped forward, ramming the point of her own little practice sword into Matilda's ribs.

"Ow, you little bastard!"

Marjorie grinned and raised her sword defensively as her sister-in-law grasped her bruised side and glared balefully at her.

"You told me to thrust rather than swing the sword," the girl shrugged innocently. "I'm just following your orders."

Matilda gritted her teeth and suppressed a smile. Will Scaflock had shown her how to fight with a sword and he'd based much of his technique – so he said – on the old Roman way of combat. They'd used short-swords rather than the unwieldy long-swords that men favoured nowadays and those smaller bladed weapons were ideal for women, Will had said.

One of the things he'd taught her was how to thrust with the short-sword, directly at an opponent, before stepping quickly back into a defensive stance. Most people didn't expect it, since the common long-sword – never mind the axe or two-handed bastard sword – was too slow for such a manoeuvre. It simply wasn't done.

That was why Matilda had shown the move to Marjorie. The girl was a fast learner she realised, clutching at her burning, agonized ribs.

But no amount of training could make up for a weak body and Robin's young sibling was wheezing already, her sword by her side rather than held up defensively as Matilda had shown her.

The girl would never be a match for a good swordsman in a fair fight, Matilda knew.

But not all fights were fair...

She waited until Marjorie had come to check she wasn't injured then slashed her own practice-sword around and into the girl's calf.

"There's your next lesson," Matilda grinned as she stood, glaring down at her fallen young foe. "Never underestimate your enemy!"

* * *

After Gisbourne's failed attack, Robin had led the men to a new camp-site, on the other side of Wakefield. As ever, it was well hidden by the foliage and terrain, and close enough to a stream that they could collect fresh water for cooking and washing.

Friar Tuck had gathered his meagre possessions that morning and now he sat by the fire with the rest of the men, chewing a piece of bread. A few days earlier he had made the trip east to St Mary's church in Brandesburton where he'd met with Father Nicholas de Nottingham. The priest – 'rightful' owner of the holy relic Tuck was taking back to Lewes with him – had been peeved to be losing the artifact which he'd only loaned to Robin Hood. The friar had explained things to him, though, and donated a sizeable sum of money as compensation.

Father de Nottingham had been impressed by the likeable Franciscan, and thought he might be right in thinking God had returned the holy relic to him for a purpose so, eventually, had given Tuck his blessing to take the exquisite little box back to Prior de Martini.

A good man, de Nottingham. One the big friar would have liked to share a few ales with, but, with the rumours of Gisbourne being on the hunt again, he'd wanted to get safely back to camp as soon as possible. Maybe sometime in the future Tuck would get a chance to spend more time in Brandesburton with the priest. He'd like that...

Robin had tried to persuade Tuck to stay but he would have none of it.

"I must leave Robin, today. God has sent this relic as a sign. Maybe it was returned to me because I've to go back to Prior de Monte Martini and save his soul... I don't know. I *do* know my body can't take any more of this life though. I'm old" –

"You're not much older than me!" Stephen, the former Hospitaller sergeant-at-arms muttered. He'd not been with the outlaws for as long as the rest of the men, but, like all of them, he'd grown to like and value Tuck's calming presence around the camp.

"Maybe not in years," Tuck agreed, with a small sigh. "But I feel old in my bones."

Will Scarlet shared a look with Robin. The Franciscan had been trapped in Nottingham with them just a few months ago – not long after he'd been shot by Gisbourne and almost drowned in the Don too – and he'd seemed hale and hearty then. In the months since he'd regained most of the weight he'd lost back then and, looking at him now, it seemed like he could offer any of them a challenge in a fight.

Robin knew better than anyone how being close to death could alter a man's perception of the world, though. He had almost given up hope when Gisbourne had captured him, beaten him within an inch of his life, then thrown him in a cell under Nottingham Castle. Although the young wolf's head had come back stronger than ever, Tuck, with his advanced years, clearly felt the after-effects of his own ordeal more keenly than Robin did his.

"You're not even a Benedictine, like the prior and all them in Lewes," Peter Ordevill, the old sailor from Selby grunted. "You're a Franciscan. De Monte Martini won't let you – a greyfriar – live amongst his Black Monks will he?"

Tuck shrugged and got to his feet, ready, at last, to make a move. "I don't know. Before I joined you lads I didn't really have a settled home. I was sent from place to place, escorting important people and relics and money and the like. Lewes Priory was where I spent most of my time though – de Monte Martini needed my services a lot so it became the closest thing I had to a home, despite the fact I wasn't one of their order." He shrugged again, uncertainly. He really wasn't sure what would happen when he reached Lewes. He didn't think he'd be much use as a bodyguard for the Church's shipments any more, but he knew he had to placate Prior de Monte Martini or he would never be a free man again.

"This is pointless," Little John broke in, his rumbling voice filling the small clearing where they'd set up their new camp. "He's made up his mind." He strode over and grasped the surprised friar in a massive bear hug which made his face flush red, from the giant outlaw's strength and embarrassment at the unusual show of emotion. "You look after yourself," John warned. "That bastard prior is one for the watching. If you think you're just going to walk back into his monastery, hand him his relic and all will be forgiven you should think again. He's going to make life hard for you."

It was true of course, but the thought of being a free man again brought a smile to Tuck's lips.

He moved among the men, clasping hands and sharing smiles then, with a final wave of goodbye, he disappeared into the trees.

* * *

Edward of Caernarvon, King of England tapped his fingers on the arm of his high-backed wooden throne and sighed loudly, drawing looks of disapproval from his courtiers, although they were careful not to let the king see them.

Another day of politicking, in Knaresborough Castle that day, which his father had paid a small fortune to rebuild, and he was already bored even though it wasn't yet midday. He could think of lots of better things to be doing on a fine spring day; rowing, or horse-riding, or just listening to his minstrels playing music would be infinitely preferable to this nonsense.

But he had his duties to attend to, so here he was, stuck indoors again. Although he was the most powerful man in the country – and there was no question of that since he'd put down the Lancastrian revolt so successfully the previous year – he still couldn't do whatever he wanted, curse his luck.

He'd been crowned king at the age of twenty-three, when his father, also Edward, had died but his reign had not been a particularly good one, or so the people of England seemed to think. The Welsh appeared to have an affection for him, even now, but his English subjects didn't think much of his rule. He had tried his best but the simple fact was, he wasn't really interested in the things a good king was supposed to do.

He enjoyed the company of commoners, for example, which scandalized most of his nobles. He'd even learned how to shoe a horse along with thatching, hedging and ditching – all necessary tasks, to be sure, but not ones to be performed by a king! Even his much-admired physique was mostly thanks to his love of rowing and swimming which were, again, seen as scandalous pursuits for a royal to be so involved in.

The truth was, Edward enjoyed such rustic pastimes so much because he felt lonely at court. Lonely and bored. It wasn't easy being the king and something as simple and good as repairing the thatch on a cottage brought him a great sense of peace.

"Sire..?"

The petitioner before him, a minor noble from Harrogate, looked embarrassed to be, essentially, upbraiding the king for his inattentiveness but it was clear Edward was lost in his own little world and wasn't paying the slightest notice to what was being said.

"Yes, yes, carry on, my lord, I'm listening," the monarch lied, waving a hand and forcing himself to sit straighter as the man blabbered on about some bridges needing repairing. Why the king had to know about it Edward had no idea, but he watched the petitioner and tried to look as if he was listening.

It had been good to put down the Contrariants, especially his cousin the Earl of Lancaster. For years they had been trying to undermine him – they had even killed his first and greatest friend, Piers Gaveston. He sighed again, remembering the handsome, charming young man who he had loved yet everyone else seemed to hate. But he had avenged Piers's death when he'd crushed that rebellion and executed the ring-leaders and, now, at last, the country was at peace.

The petitioner finished speaking and bowed his head before looking expectantly at the king for his decision.

"You make a good case, sir," Edward nodded, a genuine smile creasing his bearded face, glad that the man was finished at last. "I agree with the points you make." He waved a hand towards his treasurer, Walter de Stapledon, Bishop of Exeter. "Your Grace, please see to it. We can't have bridges collapsing, can we? The country would grind to a halt."

The nobleman smiled, pleased to have been granted the funding he'd travelled to Knaresborough to ask for. It had been a stressful morning for him too – the king almost never saw anyone these days, leaving much of the country's administration up to his new favourite, Sir Hugh Despenser the younger. But Despenser, the king's chamberlain, was away in Wales at that time and so the monarch had decided he must see to business himself that day.

It was a mistake Edward rectified now, as he stood up and smiled around the room. "I think that's enough for one morning. I will retire to my chambers."

Without another word, and followed by the disapproving stares of his subjects, he strode out of the throne room. The morning was gone, but it was still warm outside; he'd spend the rest of the day with his friends on one of his boats on the River Nidd which ran right past the castle. Sir Hugh would join him soon enough – then *he* could take care of the country.

* * *

Henry de Faucumberg, High Sheriff of Nottingham and Yorkshire, was angry. That morning, one of Robin Hood's men had strutted into the city as if he owned the place and offered his services as a bounty hunter.

As far as the sheriff knew, the outlaw had never been pardoned so was still a fugitive. De Faucumberg had ordered his men to arrest the man as soon as he'd realised who the hell he was. Then Sir Guy of Gisbourne had intervened.

The black-armoured, one-eyed, king's man had stepped in to stop the sheriff's guards from throwing the outlaw into the dungeon. Although de Faucumberg was the most powerful man in Nottingham he knew King Edward II expected him to work together with Gisbourne to capture or kill Robin Hood and his men.

It was an uneasy relationship that had only got worse since Sir Guy's defeat – and mutilation – by Hood.

Before, the king's man had been arrogant and unfriendly but he'd obviously enjoyed life. He enjoyed sparring with the sheriff's guards, defeating every one and brutally injuring some of them in the process. His legendary skill with a blade had been the one thing he was most proud of. He rose early in the morning to practice, and spent any spare moments going through combinations and tactics in his head, revelling in the knowledge he was the best swordsman in England.

Then Robin Hood had beaten him. And not only that, the wolf's head had torn off half of his face, leaving him with only one eye and a scar that made him look like a monster.

It had been a fair fight and Gisbourne was winning easily enough – toying with his younger foe – but sometimes the best man doesn't win and, when Sir Guy had slipped on a muddy patch of grass Hood had made the most of his opportunity.

The king's bounty hunter – who had been sent north specifically to deal with the problem of Robin Hood and his outlaw gang – had been left incapacitated for months, his lust for life lessening with every day he was forced to spend confined to a sick bed, while his hatred for Hood grew like a cancer inside him.

The damned wolf's head hadn't just bested Gisbourne though, his men had killed the bounty hunter's second-in-command, Nicholas Barnwell. The man had been the closest thing Gisbourne had to a friend – they'd worked together bringing outlaws to justice for the best part of three years and had shared much together in that time. Barnwell's death was a real blow to the Raven.

Although Gisbourne excelled at leading men in combat, he wasn't much good at dealing with the normal day-to-day problems and personal issues that affected any group of men, being aloof, arrogant and clearly considering himself superior to everyone beneath him. Barnwell had been a good go-between, with his earthy, sometimes sadistic humour endearing him to the men who saw him as "one of them", with no airs or graces.

Gisbourne knew he had to find someone to take Barnwell's place but none of the men in his current command were suitable, being mostly loyal to the sheriff, Henry de Faucumberg, or the king himself.

After his recent failed assault on Hood's camp Gisbourne also knew he'd need to try a different tactic to catch the outlaws. Perhaps find someone who knew where the wolf's head's camp-sites were. Someone who knew the secret, hidden trails in the forests. Someone, in short, that knew exactly where and how Hood's men lived.

It seemed divine providence then, when Matt Groves appeared in the city, looking for employment.

Sir Guy didn't know much about the man, having only met him on a couple of occasions – breaking his nose the first time – but he knew Groves had spent a long time as part of Hood's gang and, more importantly, hated the young wolf's head with a vengeance. His knowledge of Barnsdale Forest would be invaluable too, so, when the sheriff had wanted to hang the man, Gisbourne had stepped in to save him, offering the grizzled outlaw the position as his own sergeant.

"You remind me of my previous second-in-command," Sir Guy had told Groves as de Faucumberg shook his head in disgust and waved them from his great hall. "He was a sour-faced, weather-beaten bastard too."

A rare smile cracked the corners of Matt's lips at that. "You won't regret this, my lord," he vowed. "I know Yorkshire like the back of my hand. Hood never listened to me when I offered advice – thought he knew best, or asked Little John or Scarlet what to do instead. Arseholes, the lot of them. You can count on me, though, I won't let you down, in God's name, I swear it. You took a chance on me when no-one else would and I mean to repay you for it."

Gisbourne didn't like the fawning tone in the man's voice or the angry, darting eyes when he spoke but it was done now, the outlaw was his new sergeant. Whether he was useful or not remained to be seen. If he helped him kill Robin Hood – perfect. If he turned out to be a liability though, he would kill Groves himself without a second thought.

Praise be to God, it was good to be back in the hunt.

* * *

Robin sat nursing a mug of ale, gazing into the fire wistfully, thinking back to the day they had first met the now departed Friar Tuck. So much had changed since then and yet here he was, still a wolf's head hiding from the law.

Allan came over to sit with his brooding young leader. "I don't know for sure," he began thoughtfully, "but I think Matt Groves was riding with Gisbourne in Pontefract when I was there earlier today."

Robin's sat up, his eyes flaring and the minstrel held up a hand defensively, almost feeling the force or his friend's hatred like a physical blow. "I'm not sure if it was him or not! I was in a hurry to get the hell out of there before they found me so I didn't take the time to look too closely. It looked a lot like him though."

Without realising it, Robin's hand fell to the sword hilt at his waist and he snorted furiously. "It wouldn't surprise me if he's taken up with that bastard Gisbourne. Bitter old prick would love nothing more than seeing me hanged."

Allan nodded, then his eyes widened in surprise as Robin continued.

"This is the best news I've heard for a while. Aye, I hope it *was* Matt you saw," he said, in response to the look on Allan's face. "It means I don't have to go looking for the bastard – he'll come straight to me, and then..."

CHAPTER FOUR

April came, filling the trees with thick green leaves and the rains slowed, allowing the ground in the forest to dry out and become less treacherous. The sounds of nature reawakening after the chill of winter filled the air, as insects began to build their nests in dark, hidden places and many of the animals and birds that populated the undergrowth gave birth to their little ones.

"Here, listen to this!" Young Gareth hurried into camp one afternoon, red-faced and puffing, apparently from excitement more than exertion. He was followed by the Hospitaller sergeant, Stephen, who looked bored and irritated by his younger companion. The unlikely pair had been visiting the village of Tretone that morning to collect supplies.

"What's up?" Little John wondered, raising an eyebrow at Stephen who gave a disgusted wave and sauntered to the big cooking pot over the camp-fire to help himself to some of the thin soup bubbling away inside as the other outlaws who were around came across to hear Gareth's news.

"The sheriff's holding a tournament in a couple of weeks."

Silence greeted his pronouncement and the Hospitaller snorted with laughter as he spooned some of the hot food into his mouth.

"So what?" Allan-a-Dale asked. "What's that got to do with us?"

"There's to be games and prizes and stuff," Gareth replied, smiling as he moved over next to Stephen and lifted a bowl of his own which he filled with the – mostly cabbage – soup.

"Are you pissed again, boy?" Will Scarlet demanded.

"No, I'm not!" Gareth retorted, the watery broth dribbling down his chin as he glared at Will indignantly. "There's going to be an archery competition, and the prize is a silver arrow. An arrow made from solid silver."

There were gasps and whistles of appreciation from the men as the value of such a prize sunk in.

"That's impressive," Robin agreed, shrugging his enormous shoulders. "But why are you so excited? None of us are going to be winning the arrow."

"Why not?" Gareth replied, looking at Robin as he continued to eat. "You could win." He glanced over at John. "Or you." His eyes moved around the outlaws who listened to him in bemused silence. "You're all deadly with a longbow, you could beat anyone in England. Christ knows you spend enough time practising."

"You seem to be forgetting one thing," Scarlet growled. "We're fucking outlaws. The moment any one of us sets foot in Nottingham we'll be arrested and hanged. Particularly me or Robin, since some of the guards know what we look like and, as for him..." he pointed at Little John. "He stands out a bit, don't you think? Being the size of a fucking bear and all."

John laughed merrily and clapped Gareth good-naturedly on the back. "Ah, the innocence – and stupidity – of youth."

"Aye," Stephen muttered. "And if you think that silver arrow is going to be anything more than a normal wooden shaft with some paint on it, you're more than stupid."

The men began to drift off, back to whatever tasks they'd been involved in before the Hospitaller and his teenage companion had returned, laughing at the preposterousness of Gareth's suggestion.

Allan-a-Dale remained by the fire with Robin, strumming his gittern and thoughtfully eyeing the longbow which lay on the grass by his side.

"Maybe it's not such a bad idea of the lad's after all."

"Eh?" Allan was only half-listening, absorbed in the music as he was. "What idea?"

"The arrow," Robin muttered, plucking strands of grass from between his legs thoughtfully. "I'd have a good chance of winning the competition *if* I could hide my identity. Think how much money that arrow would be worth." He looked up, eyes shining. "Enough to buy us all pardons. All of us. We'd be free at last."

Allan nodded slowly. "That's true. But you'd be recognised as soon as the first guard saw you. Every lawman in the north of England knows what you look like by now and, you know yourself – this whole thing is probably a trap specifically to catch you."

Robin sighed. "Aye, you're right, of course. But..." he tossed the little strands of grass he'd been fiddling with into the air angrily. "I promised you men pardons but I don't see how I can ever fulfil the vow."

He fell into silence again for a time, but was soon startled from his reverie by the sound of another of the outlaws crashing through the undergrowth into camp. This time it was Arthur, the powerfully-built lad from Bichill who waved the rest of the men across, his near-toothless mouth split in a cheery grin.

"Keep it down," Allan hissed angrily. "You should know better than to come charging through the trees like a hunted boar."

Arthur waved a hand irritably and addressed Robin who had come over, brown eyes gleaming with interest.

"Two Franciscan friars on the road to Nottingham. No guards."

"If they've no guards they probably have nothing worth stealing," Little John grumbled.

Robin nodded, but the men murmured together, knowing travellers were often the best way to find out news from the wider country, even if they carried light purses hardly worth removing.

"Let's invite them to dinner," Robin laughed, strapping on his sword-belt and collecting his great war-bow. "It would be rude to let them pass without offering our hospitality."

He waved to Arthur to lead the way and followed the lad. "Make sure there's enough stew for our visitors," the young leader smiled to Edmond who nodded and waved farewell.

It didn't take long to find the two friars. Although it was a dry day, there had been rain in the night and it made the remnants of the previous autumn's leaves slick, slowing the travellers' progress to the city.

"Hail, and well met," Robin stepped into the road from behind a twisted old birch tree, raising a hand in greeting and smiling at the two friars who stopped in surprise, their faces registering fear and dismay at the sudden appearance of the large young warrior who greeted them.

"God give you good day, my child," the elder of the two churchmen replied, his eyes searching the undergrowth for signs of anyone else. His shoulders slumped as he caught sight of Arthur, hand gripping the hilt of the sword he wore. Clearly these men were outlaws. "We have nothing of value –"

"We're no robbers," Robin broke in, shaking his head and moving forward to stand before the friars, his gaze steady, searching for any signs that the men might try and offer some resistance. "I'm Robin Hood," he went on, noting the older friar's involuntary step backwards as he recognized the name of the infamous wolf's head. "This is our forest."

The friar opened his mouth to deny Robin's claim to the land but the young outlaw carried on, giving him no chance to speak. "We merely wanted to invite you to dinner. You look like you could do with some food."

The younger friar – no more than fourteen summers at the most – certainly appeared to be in need of a hot meal, being almost skeletally thin. He either hadn't heard of Robin Hood or simply found the idea of food so appealing that it was worth a trip into the lair of a gang of violent criminals. He glanced up at his older man, his eyes hopeful.

"I think not, although we thank you *in the name of Christ* for your generous offer. We are simply in too much of a hurry to be sidetracked."

The man made to move along the path, gesturing for his young companion to follow.

"I insist."

Robin placed himself directly in front of them and the smile fell from his lips, hand dropping to his sword hilt as Arthur stepped into the road behind the churchmen.

"Our camp is this way. Follow me."

"No, wolf's head!" The friar stood his ground, even stamping his foot like a petulant child. "We won't follow –"

"What food do you have?"

Robin turned at the younger friar's voice, meeting his hopeful gaze with a reassuring smile.

"We have cabbage soup, and our cook has just started making a big pot of venison stew," he replied, watching the skinny youngster's mouth working as saliva formed unbidden and the grumble of his empty stomach seemed to echo back from the sparse spring foliage around them.

"Hubert, get back here, boy. The abbot shall hear of this, you little bastard!"

The novice ignored his superior, following Robin as he set off along the trail again, and Arthur shoved the older friar in the back with a curt, "Move it, priest, or I'll knock you out and carry you."

It didn't take them long to reach the outlaw's camp and they were all glad to return, the grousing friar barely stopping for breath the whole way as he lambasted Robin and Arthur, promising them eternal torture and a place in hell beside the great tyrants of history.

"Two bowls of stew for our guests," Robin shouted over to Edmond. "Make the lad's bowl a big one." He grinned at the young page and bade him sit, which the lad did gladly, looking around at the other outlaws with interest rather than the fear his elder displayed so obviously.

"Be at ease." Robin laughed at the friar as Edmond handed him a steaming bowl and a crust of black bread. "We mean you no harm. You've surely heard of me and the rest of these men; you know we don't murder for pleasure. Be at ease," he repeated. "In the morning you can be on your way with a full belly and a tale to tell your brother friars."

The sun moved into the west and slowly fell, leaving only the crackling camp-fire to cast light on the outlaws and their two guests. The younger of the pair, Hubert, proved to be a friendly boy, who told them they were travelling to Nottingham for the tournament the sheriff was holding in a few weeks. Their abbot had sent them north to the city from Gloucester Greyfriars to bring the word of God to the great number of people who would surely be congregating there to watch or take part in the tourney.

The promise of a near-priceless silver arrow as a prize had sent ripples of excitement all around the north of England and Custos William de Bromley wanted to make sure the masses gathering in Nottingham would dip into their pockets and contribute alms for his church's upkeep.

The older friar, Brother Walter, refused to engage in conversation with the men. He shrank back from any of the outlaws if they came near to him, as if they were flea-ridden dogs or lepers and shouted at Hubert to hold his peace as the youngster spoke with Robin and the men, imparting what news he had from Gloucester and beyond. Still, Walter managed to eat two bowls of Edmond's venison stew and more than his share of ale before falling asleep with his back against a tree stump close to the fire.

"He says it's a sin to eat too much," Hubert grumbled, glaring over at his sleeping superior. "But whenever we stop at an inn he eats enough for a horse while only paying for a small bowl of porridge for me." He sighed. "I suppose this is God's way of teaching me humility before I become a proper friar."

Will Scarlet shook his head in annoyance. "Well, lad, you can eat as much as you like tonight. Eat until you throw up if you want."

Hubert smiled and took the piece of bread Will held out to him with a grateful nod.

When they awoke in the morning, Brother Walter was glad to see most of the outlaws were absent – gone off hunting or fishing or, more likely he thought with a scowl, *robbing* people.

Robin came over to him and helped him up. Young Hubert was already awake and mopping up the last of a bowl of porridge with another piece of bread.

"Here," the outlaw captain handed some of the steaming breakfast to the sour-faced friar. "Eat up, and you can be off."

"As easy as that?" Walter shovelled the porridge into his mouth with his hand, licking oats from his fingers as he looked warily at Robin, as if he expected the big man to skewer him any second.

"As easy as that," Robin agreed, watching the friar devour the meal with a twinkle in his eye. "Once you pay us for your bed and board."

Walter spat in fury and a mouthful of food dribbled down his chin.

"Whatever's in your purse will be enough to cover your debt I'm sure."

Before the outraged Franciscan could react the outlaw stepped in close and, with a knife that seemed to appear in his hand from thin air, sliced through the leather thong that held his purse onto his belt.

Moving back to sit by the fire Robin tossed the purse up and down, feeling the weight with a satisfied nod. "Yes, this'll be just enough I'm sure. I trust you enjoyed your stay here in Barnsdale?"

"You heathen scum –"

Little John and Allan-a-Dale appeared behind the protesting friar and shepherded him from the camp, back towards the main road, screaming for God to rain hell-fire and brimstone on the wolf's head.

Robin, grinning wickedly, clasped young Hubert by the shoulder and pressed the coin purse into the youngster's hand surreptitiously. "There you go lad, keep that hidden under your cassock and buy yourself a pie whenever you get a chance. You best be off or Brother Walter will tell the Custos on you."

Laughing, the skinny page made the sign of the cross, blessing the wolf's head, before stuffing the remainder of a loaf into his mouth and running into the trees after his elder.

* * *

"You really think this will work?" Gisbourne placed his black crossbow on the table beside him and rubbed irritably at his ruined eye-socket. Most people would have worn an eye-patch but the bounty hunter understood the power of appearances and liked to seem as menacing as possible. The sight of his weeping scar was enough to frighten most people.

Matt Groves nodded confidently. "Aye, I do. Hood himself isn't reckless, or stupid, enough to fall for it. But one of the gang members will want to win that silver arrow and they'll enter the competition. Then it's just a matter of capturing the fool and waiting for Hood to come and rescue them. The loyalty he shows to the men is admirable. And stupid."

Gisbourne grunted non-committally. It seemed a hopeful plan to him, but, even with Groves's knowledge of the outlaws and their habits, they'd not managed to come close to finding the wolf's head and his followers in the past few weeks. If Matt's idea flushed them out into the open it would certainly make things a sight easier. Going back into the dense undergrowth of Barnsdale didn't appeal to Gisbourne – his depth perception, and, as a result, his fighting ability, had been hopelessly damaged with the loss of his eye. So, he now had to rely on strategy and cunning more than simple brute force if he was going to kill the wolf's head and his followers.

Besides, Groves's suggestion that Hood was too smart to fall for their ruse was something the bounty hunter questioned. He had a good idea how the wolf's head's mind worked. The man was proud, and he wanted the people to love and respect him. That was why he'd turned up to fight Gisbourne one-on-one on the bridge at Dalton, even though he must have known he had next to no chance of winning the duel. Yes, his reputation meant the world to Robin Hood, and winning a silver arrow from his hated enemies would truly make him a legend. Could he pass up such an opportunity?

Maybe the young archer would turn up in person to enter the tournament after all. Only time would tell.

Sheriff de Faucumberg had, surprisingly, been quite open to the idea of a tournament with a silver arrow as the prize for the best archer when the bounty hunter had approached him in the great hall. Gisbourne had expected he'd have to persuade, argue or even fall back on the king's name to get the man to agree to Groves's plan, but de Faucumberg was almost as sick of the outlaws plaguing his jurisdiction as Gisbourne was. Anything that might get rid of them once and for all was worth a try. God knew, they'd tried everything else in the past few years, without much success.

"Yes, it seems like a reasonable idea. We can simply paint a normal arrow with silver paint; no one will be able to tell from a distance," de Faucumberg had suggested, rolling up parchments on the great oak table that separated him from the Raven and taking a sip from the silver goblet by his right hand.

Gisbourne had been adamant though. "Out of the question, sheriff. People are going to come and see it before the tournament – they'll be able to tell immediately if we just paint a normal, wooden arrow. No, we must have the local smith make us the real thing if we're to entice the wolf's head into coming here for it."

"And where are we going to find the silver to make this precious missile?" de Faucumberg wondered.

Gisbourne had laughed mirthlessly. "Come, now, sheriff. There's more than enough coin from taxes in your coffers to make something as small as an arrow. Melt some of it down. We're going to have a city full of soldiers on the lookout for Hood and his men, there's no chance they'll be able to ever get the arrow out of the city, so it's not like you'll be risking your silver."

The sheriff snorted angrily. "We had a locked city full of soldiers looking for the bastard just a few months ago, yet he managed to escape from the dungeon and walk right out through the gates. I wouldn't be so confident if I were you."

Gisbourne waved a hand dismissively but de Faucumberg carried on.

"Besides, what if none of the outlaws turn up? Or, say they do turn up, but someone else wins the competition? What then?"

"We give them a small bag of silver and send them on their fucking way!" Gisbourne barked, shaking his head. "You're the king's representative here, you wield more power than you seem to realise. Use it, man."

De Faucumberg took the rebuke with a frown, realising the bounty hunter was right. Hood and his outlaws had been allowed to do as they pleased in his forests for too long. Maybe it was time to play a little dirty.

"Fine," he agreed. "Take just enough silver to make your arrow. But you better make damn sure you and your men guard it with your lives, because if you don't... your lives won't be worth the dog shit I stepped in this morning, Gisbourne, trust me."

The Raven threw the sheriff a smug grin, the scar tissue that had healed around his missing eye wrinkling horribly as he raised a hand in mocking salute and strode from the room with a laugh, his black boot-heels echoing as he went. "I trust you, de Faucumberg. It's time you placed some trust in me. The wolf's head is as good as dead."

CHAPTER FIVE

Robin had ordered the men to move camp again on hearing Allan's news that Matt Groves might have taken up with the feared Gisbourne. Matt knew all of their usual camp-sites, having been a member of the outlaw gang for longer than most of them and Robin didn't want to make it easy for the turncoat to lead their doom straight to them.

Their usual hiding places had been chosen years ago by Adam Bell who, as an ex-Templar knight, had a great understanding and knowledge of how to use terrain to his advantage, be it to hide his own men or to mount attacks on others. But they needed to find completely new places to hide in now. Thankfully, Robin, although he didn't have the martial training of a knight, had an instinctive understanding of the forest and how to use it properly.

As ever, Will Scarlet and Little John helped advise their young leader when he found a spot, making sure they had easy access to a little stream for fresh water, while being well hidden amongst the thick foliage of beech, oak trees and lower level bushes, ferns, or long grass. It was not too far from the road between Penysale and Penyston and seemed ideal as there was a local market held close by every Tuesday which would allow the outlaws to collect supplies without having to travel too far afield. The stall-holders and patrons would also, no doubt, be a good source of information on rumours of Gisbourne's whereabouts.

"We should have stopped using those old camping grounds long ago, when Robin killed Adam," Little John murmured, lying back contentedly on a brown patch of grass in the middle of their new home. "It feels good to be somewhere different. Even if we're still not in soft beds, with a nice pair of tits to cuddle into."

It was an overcast, muggy, spring afternoon, with heavy black clouds covering the sky that threatened to burst and soak the land at any time, but the men had a cosy fire going and the new camp-site gave them a sense of security and safety. The thick trees which encircled them felt more homely than any grey castle wall ever could.

Robin laughed wistfully at his huge friend's words, appreciating the blunt language and pleasing imagery it conjured. "True, big man, true."

"True, perhaps," Will interjected. "But the men – including me, I admit - wouldn't have taken kindly to Robin ordering us to give up our old haunts back then. It's a mark of the respect we all have for you now, lad, that you can get us to follow you somewhere new without a shouting match."

Not so long ago Robin would have blushed crimson at the praise from the hugely experienced Will, a man who had fought as a mercenary in the Holy Land and seen much death and horror in his thirty-seven years. Now, the outlaw captain simply accepted Will's words with a grateful nod.

"Pah, I would have followed him if he'd suggested it," John snorted, his mouth twitching mischievously. "You lot just like an argument. Bunch of sour-faced lack-wits."

Allan-a-Dale and some of the other long-term outlaws bristled at that, shooting insults back at the bearded giant, while the newcomers like Stephen and Edmond, the fish-lipped former tanner from Kirklees, grinned and hoisted their ale mugs aloft in a cheer, enjoying the banter.

Robin threw John a thankful smile, knowing his friend, despite the humour, spoke the truth. Before he became their leader, the men hadn't completely trusted Robin. John had taken his side right from the start though and the young man would never forget that loyalty.

"Dinner's ready!" Edmond shouted, taking a last sip of his ale before swapping the wooden mug for a ladle. "Come and get it, lads."

Edmond had found it hard at first to settle amongst the close-knit outlaws, who were more like a military order than a random collection of violent criminals. The lads had been welcoming but a lifetime of being bullied and abused by his peers had made it hard for the tanner to lower his defences and build friendships. Men like Robin and Little John had gone out of their way to make the young man, with his thin beard, stumpy limbs and thickset body, feel like one of them.

More than any of them, though, Friar Tuck had helped Edmond come to terms with the fact he had captured Stephen's master, Sir Richard-at-Lee, and led him to his death on the gallows in Nottingham. Although he had now begun to feel at ease with the outlaws, the tanner felt Tuck's absence from their group keenly.

"How do you think the friar fares?" he wondered as the men settled down happily to eat the stew he'd made for them. "Will the Prior take him in again?"

"Ach, he'll be fine," Will waved his spoon confidently. "Tuck knows how to look after himself."

"I hope you're right," Allan-a-Dale replied, wincing as the hot food scalded the roof of his mouth.

"I wish he was still here," Edmond mumbled, eyes downcast, chewing on a hunk of bread that he'd dipped into his stew.

The comment was met with silence, the rest of the men agreeing whole-heartedly with it.

"I wish he was still here too," John growled, after spooning some of the food into his mouth. "Tuck could make much tastier stew than this piss-water you've cooked up for us."

Everyone laughed, even Edmond, glad to avert the melancholy that was so easy to fall into living out here in the forest as a wolf's head.

"He'll be fine," Robin said authoritatively. "Honestly, have no fears for Tuck. He used to earn his living as a wrestler; he can take care of himself."

Talk turned to other things as the stew – rather more appetising than John had suggested – filled their hungry bellies and a new cask of freshly-brewed Penysale beer was broached. Robin felt instinctively that he was right: Tuck would be fine. The portly friar could fight like a Templar, yes, but he also had a likeable charisma that often acted better than any heater shield or buckler.

The outlaw leader stood and made his way over to the big cooking pot to help himself to more food, smiling in thanks as Edmond grabbed his mug for a refill. Aye, Friar Tuck would be fine.

He wondered how his family fared, though.

* * *

It had been a while since Marjorie and Matilda had been able to spend some time training together. They both had chores to do at home and at work helping their parents in their own occupations.

That morning had dawned cool and misty, but Marjorie knew that the sun, once it was fully up, would burn the haze away and it would be a fine afternoon, perfect for sparring.

"Can we finish our jobs as soon as possible today," she asked Martha, her mother. "I'd like to go fishing later on, if it's nice."

Martha smiled. She was very close to her daughter, especially since Robin wasn't around much any more. "Of course, that sounds like a good idea. Let's get it all done and make the most of any sunshine – God knows we haven't had much of it lately. Here." She handed the girl an old basket. "Fetch some fresh rushes for the floor. Try and cut some sweet flowers too – they make the place smell nice."

Marjorie grabbed the basket and a knife from the table and hurried off.

It was still early but the men were already off ploughing the fields or mending the fences that penned in their livestock.

She waved cheerily to one of the neighbours, a pleasant old woman with small eyes that the children called Hogface, and shooed a barking dog that ran along after her for a time hoping for scraps.

She reached Ings Beck, breathlessly startling a kingfisher which took flight, then brought out the knife to collect the long green rushes that grew in abundance there. The blade was fine and sharp and it didn't take her long to fill the basket. As she made her way back home she kept an eye out for wildflowers or herbs which she plucked and tossed into the basket.

Her favourite was lavender, and she knew where some grew not too far off, but she wanted to finish her chores so made do with the daisies and buttercups that were so readily available along the road. They might not have strong, sweet odours, but at least their colour would brighten the room.

Her mother had swept the dirty old rushes out by the time she returned so, together, they spread the fresh ones on the floor of the house, smiling contentedly at one another when they were done.

"Your da will be happy when he gets home," Martha nodded. "Now. Since it's going to be such a nice day, according to you, we should wash the bedding and towels so they get a chance to dry off in the sun. Come on."

Not long after midday the pair had finished the laundry, eaten a small meal of salted ham, bread and ale, and it was indeed fine and sunny.

"All right, you've been a good help this morning," Martha grinned. "Off you go and catch us some fish then. Be back in time that we can have it ready for dinner. I'll feed the chickens then sit outside and do some spinning."

When her mother went out the door Marjorie collected her fishing pole.

"I'll catch us a big one," she shouted, waving as she hurried off towards the fletcher's workshop.

Matilda was busy, surrounded by baskets of swan's feathers and wooden arrow shafts, but she gladly agreed to take a break for a time.

Recently, Marjorie had been working on her own with the wooden sword, just going through different moves that Matilda had shown her, both defensive and offensive. She'd also been trying to eat more and even managed to do a few exercises to strengthen her muscles every day. She wasn't able to run for long, but she had been sprinting over short distances and, although she had no way to be sure, she believed that her speed had improved.

As a result of all her hard work she really thought she had grown stronger not just physically, but mentally too. She felt *good* when she was exercising, which had come as a real surprise. Yes, it was hard, and her lungs would burn for a long time afterwards while her muscles ached from all the new stresses and strains, but somehow she felt happy when she was training.

She was still slimmer than almost any of the other village girls, but as they walked to the little shaded clearing where they practised together Matilda noticed a distinct change in the younger girl's carriage. She held herself erect, her chin up and her shoulders back, where before she'd had a hunched, downtrodden look about her. Matilda smiled, pleased at her charge's new-found swagger and made a mental note not to damage Marjorie's confidence by beating her too easily today.

They reached the clearing, glad no-one was around since they didn't really want people to know what they were doing. Their fellow villagers would probably laugh at them – women weren't supposed to be soldiers.

"All right, ready?"

Marjorie nodded and they did a few limbering up exercises to get their muscles warm before Matilda produced their practice swords from the bundle she'd brought from home. For now the swords were all they had to work with; Marjorie couldn't draw a hunting bow and, although she desperately wanted a crossbow she had no way of getting one. Her big brother would, no doubt, have brought her one if she'd asked him but, for now, she didn't want even Robin to know what she was doing. He loved her dearly, she knew that, but he'd not look kindly on the idea of her learning how to fight in case she got hurt. Besides, where would she hide such a weapon from her parents?

"Ha!" Matilda noticed her student apparently lost in thought and lunged forward, ready to rap the girl on the knuckles to teach her to stay alert, but, surprisingly, the blow whistled through empty air. Marjorie had seen her opponent's muscles tense, a tell-tale sign of imminent attack, and had danced back before the wooden sword could catch her.

Matilda found herself on the back-foot instantly, as Marjorie tried to turn defence into an attack of her own. Their swords met with a sharp crack and they held them there, teeth gritted, until the older girl's strength won out and Marjorie had to draw back, panting, and angry at her puny muscles.

"What's wrong?" Matilda asked, seeing the fury burning from her sister-in-law's eyes and thinking she'd done something to hurt the girl. "Are you alright?"

"No, I'm not, and I never will be, will I?"

The practice sword was thrown to the ground in disgust and Marjorie sank onto the grass beside it a moment later, her knees drawn up to her small chest. She looked like a child, despite her fifteen years and pity filled Matilda who began to move forward, to cuddle the girl, reassure her.

Then she stopped herself, pulled her hand back. Marjorie wanted to learn how to fight didn't she? Self-pity wasn't something that should be encouraged; it wasn't the way to engender a winning mentality in a soldier.

"Oh, poor you," Matilda spat, glaring down at the surprised girl. "Little Marjorie, the runt of the litter, never able to eat more than a morsel of bread and half a cup of beer. Always destined to be the weakest girl in Wakefield. What a shame for you."

Sarcasm dripped from her words and Marjorie's eyes flared, but still she didn't get back to her feet. "What would you know?" she started, but Matilda broke in, not allowing the girl to launch into a self-pitying monologue.

"What would I know? I know that you were a twin. Rebekah wasn't strong enough to survive the famine. But *you* were. God saw fit to spare you for some reason, and now, at the first hint of hardship you're ready to throw away your sword and just give in?" She could see that her mention of Rebekah had struck right to Marjorie's heart but before the girl could react, Matilda carried on. "You're good with the sword – you clearly have the skill for it running through your blood. Blood which you share with Robin Hood, the legendary archer and swordsman." She held up a hand to halt any objections. "Aye, I know you haven't been blessed with his shoulder muscles or the stamina that lets him run from one village to another without stopping, but so what? Should we all just give up because we're not as strong as someone else? Get up. Now!"

Matilda held out her hand imperiously and dragged Marjorie to her feet. The girl was still angry but her dressing down had left her cowed and ashamed at her petulant behaviour.

"Look at you. In the few weeks that we've been training your posture's improved, your appetite's growing and your skill with the sword gets more impressive every day. Not so long ago you wouldn't have spotted my first blow coming – you'd have been left with rapped knuckles and an angry curse on your lips." Matilda stepped in close and grasped her student by the shoulder. "Aye, it's harder for you because of what happened to you as an infant. But you have to face your body's limitations and either work with them or break them down." She released the girl and stepped back, sword raised. "So, what's it to be? Are you going to pick up your weapon and continue sparring, or are you going back to the village to live the rest of your life as a whining cur?"

For a second Matilda seriously feared she'd gone too far with her verbal assault and Marjorie would feel too humiliated to do anything other than walk away. But the girl had an inner strength and Matilda smiled in satisfaction as she lifted the fallen sword and set her feet to stare into her mentor's eyes.

"You're right," she admitted. "I can't give up now. But I'm going to make you pay for your words."

The young girl charged forward, launching a blistering attack and Matilda genuinely had to use all her skill and speed to defend herself. It didn't last very long, as the attacker's stamina again failed her and they separated, Marjorie breathing heavily and, as before, looking frustrated by her weakness. This time, though, she didn't throw away her sword, didn't thrust out a petulant lower lip, she just stood in a defensive stance, watching her opponent circling, prepared to fend off any thrust or swipe that might come her way.

They sparred for a while longer then Marjorie held up a hand, bending over to try and catch her breath.

"Enough!" she wheezed. "I promised my ma a fish for the table. You get back to your work; I'll try and get one for you too."

Matilda grinned, feeling like an important bridge had been crossed that day. Maybe Marjorie had the temperament to be a decent swordswoman after all.

CHAPTER SIX

"Quiet this morning," Robin yawned, rubbing sleep from his eyes with his fingers. "Where's Allan?"

The minstrel's voice was often the first thing the outlaws heard each day, as he went about getting ready for the day whistling a tune or singing, depending on how hungover he and the rest of the men were. Today though, there was silence around the camp, broken only by the back-and-forth tweeting of a pair of blackbirds hidden in the trees overhead.

"Dunno," Little John grunted, shoving a lump of bread into his mouth, crumbs already lacing his unkempt brown beard. "Must have gone off hunting or something. I haven't seen him."

"Gone off?" Robin helped himself to some of the ale from the barrel they'd broached the previous night and sat on one of the fallen logs next to John and a couple of the other early risers. "That's not like him."

The giant shrugged, but Will Scarlet had learned from bitter experience not to ignore Robin when he made an observation about one of their men acting out of character. He stood up and moved around the camp, counting heads.

"Gareth's not here either," he reported, returning to the rest of the men and grabbing some of the loaf John had almost devoured already. "Where d'you think they've gone without telling anyone?"

"Maybe they did tell someone," Stephen suggested. "You'll need to ask the rest when they wake up." He took a sip of his ale, not being overly fond of the brew this close to dawn. "You think something's up?"

Robin shook his head with a confidence he didn't really feel. "No, Allan's a big boy. I just don't like it when anyone leaves the camp without letting one of us know."

"Allan might be able to handle himself," Will growled. "But Gareth can't, and if he's been on the drink again he could stir up a lot of mischief we could do without."

Robin momentarily held his palms up in resignation. "We've no reason to think anything's amiss yet," he told them. "They've probably just gone off hunting as John says."

"Aye," the big man nodded. "Gareth might be a skinny wee bastard, but even he can set a rabbit trap well enough. Give it till lunchtime; they'll be back with something nice for Edmond's pot later on."

Robin smiled but he remembered the look on Allan's face when they'd talked the day before about the value of the silver arrow. He prayed the minstrel hadn't decided to try and win them all the pardons they craved...

* * *

"Why did you want to come anyway," Allan-a-Dale asked his companion, who shrugged and looked away evasively.

"I'm fed up with the forest, feel like seeing the big city for a change," Gareth replied, fingering the coin-purse he carried hidden under his gambeson.

"Hoping to find some of that grain drink you got from the barber in Penyston, eh?"

"Nah," the younger outlaw shook his head nonchalantly. "Can't handle that stuff, I'll stick to ale. At least I don't get cramps in my guts with ale." He grinned over at the minstrel but Allan saw through the protestations.

Gareth wasn't much of a travelling companion, and he wouldn't even be entering the tournament since he was too weak to draw a longbow or wield a sword very well, but Allan hadn't wanted to head into Nottingham by himself so he was glad when Gareth had offered to come along to keep him company.

"What d'you think Robin'll do when he finds out where we've gone?"

Allan had wondered that himself, but he wasn't sure of the answer. "Either he'll go crazy that we've not followed his orders to stay in the camp, or he'll accept that we're all our own men and can do what we want."

Gareth didn't reply as they hurried along the road towards Nottingham.

"He'll cheer up when he sees the silver arrow I've won, though. Then we can sell it and win pardons for us all!"

The two men grinned at that. It wasn't such a fanciful idea – Allan was an excellent shot, his skills honed to a fine point by the hours of practice Robin insisted the fighters in the group performed each week. He had a very good chance of winning, should they be allowed to enter the competition without anyone realising they were wolf's heads. That didn't seem too big of a threat: neither had been to Nottingham any time recently so the guards wouldn't recognise them and both were unremarkable looking so they could lose themselves in the crowds.

Gareth might have wanted to head into the city to look for strong alcohol, but Allan was looking forward to performing in front of a crowd again. It had been nearly two years since he and Robin had entertained Lord John de Bray's guests in the great hall of Hathersage manor house. He missed the excitement, the nervous tension, that feeling of uncertainty that even the most experienced of minstrels felt when they put themselves in front of an audience. Shooting in the archery competition, before what would surely be a huge gathering of locals, would be much like playing the gittern for a hall full of rowdy nobles.

He smiled and revelled in the warm spring breeze as they walked.

This was going to be fun.

* * *

Tuck had ridden at a leisurely pace when he left the outlaw's camp, not being in any great hurry to return to Lewes like the prodigal son the prior had never expected to see again...

The friar was no fool. He knew de Monte Martini wouldn't look kindly on him when he showed his face there again. Not only had he 'lost' the prior's priceless artefact years earlier, but he'd then allowed outlaws to steal his superior's cart full of money and, to add insult to injury, Tuck had *joined* the outlaw gang who had gone on to further humiliate de Monte Martini when he and the Sheriff of Nottingham had tried to capture them.

The kindly clergyman grinned. Ah, but it had felt good to get one over on the nasty prior, it truly had. The smile fell from his fleshy lips, though, as he contemplated the welcome de Monte Martini would have for him when he appeared unexpectedly in Lewes. The fact that he was returning the lost relic – something the prior had paid an obscene amount of money for – would, he hoped, mollify the senior churchman and allow him to stay with the Benedictines at least until the Church found some other place for him, within his own order perhaps.

At the very least, Tuck hoped he'd *survive* the reunion.

"Hey, priest! Get off the fucking horse, now."

The harsh voice jolted Tuck back in his saddle and his hand strayed instinctively to the heavy cudgel he habitually carried within the folds of his grey cassock.

He pulled gently on the palfrey's reins, bringing it to a halt, his eyes scanning the area as he calmly assessed the situation. He'd gone along with Robin and the others often enough on robberies just like this to have a good idea of how things worked, so he knew urging his mount into a gallop would probably result in an arrow in the back.

He remained in the saddle, waiting for the would-be thieves to show themselves. Moments later, three men appeared from the thick foliage on either side of the road, while at least one other man coughed from behind him, letting the friar know he was covered on all sides.

"I told you to get off the fucking horse!" the man in the middle of the trio on the road ahead spat. He was a small man, bearded and dirty looking, with a slight build while the two that flanked him were much larger. Tuck had met men like this outlaw before – the maniacal gleam in his dark eyes suggested what he lacked in physical stature was made up for in violent lunacy.

Although his comrades were much bigger, they deferred to the little dark man. Tuck knew he had to be very careful if he didn't want to lose the coin-purse he carried inside his habit. Or his life. He dismounted, making a show of his clumsiness and clutching his back as if he was in great pain from riding.

"What can I do for you, my son?" he asked, smiling deferentially at the little man. "A blessing? Do you seek –"

"Enough, priest," the robber growled, sidling over and standing to look up at the palfrey whose ears were back as it sensed something was wrong. "We need no blessings in Sherwood. What we need is silver and gold. And food. And judging by the belly you're carrying around on you, you've got enough of everything to share with me and my companions here." He raised the sword he carried, unusually, in his left hand, brandishing it menacingly, and Tuck noticed the man was missing more than one finger from his right hand. Punishment for being caught stealing before perhaps, although that method of justice had – mostly – been done away with years earlier.

Dangerous, but hopefully stupid.

The friar looked back across his shoulder to see a tall young man holding a longbow with an arrow already nocked. His hands were steady, but the expression on his face was one of distaste. Not at the clergyman, no... the big man's eyes flicked to his leader for a moment and Tuck knew the youngster wasn't happy to be here doing this.

"Aye, he's got you covered, old man," the robber leader grinned, showing a mouthful of surprisingly complete teeth. "And the rest of us'll split you wide open – priest or not – if you don't hand over what you've got. Including that nice horse."

There was little point denying he was carrying money, Tuck thought. The robbers would know he'd need coin to pay for food and board as he travelled.

"Will you let me be on my way if I give you what I have?" he asked in a trembling voice, moving towards the small man and fumbling in his cassock. As he reached the robber, he smiled, remembering a similar scene a couple of years earlier when he'd first met Robin and the men.

"Here you go, have the lot!"

The two robbers further back on the road stood in stunned silence for a moment as their leader collapsed in front of them. Tuck had whipped the cudgel concealed in his robes up and into the jaw of the robber, then, as the man stumbled backwards, the friar brought it around in a tight arc into the side of the man's neck, sending him flying across the road, senseless.

Before anyone could react, Tuck turned and jumped forward, ramming the cudgel into the man on the left's face, feeling teeth crunch as his target reeled back and landed on his backside with a furious howl of pain.

By now it was obvious this was no normal priest and the final swordsman struck out with the battered old blade he carried, a killing blow aimed right at the clergyman's neck.

Tuck had been fast when he was young, but now... he twisted sideways, lashing out with his own weapon which hit the back of his opponent's skull with a shocking crack, sending the robber crashing to the hard earth of the road. The friar let out a breath of relief as he realised his flesh was unbroken – the oaf's blade had only slightly torn his cassock.

He made sure the three downed robbers were incapacitated then glanced back to the bowman and was relieved to see the youngster staring at the scene before him, mouth open in surprise, bowstring not even drawn taut. Still with one eye on the archer, Tuck moved over to the man with the wounded mouth and kicked out at the side of his head, hard enough to send the man reeling.

"What's your name, son?"

The young man watched the friar return to his horse and grasp the saddle, longbow still held low at his side.

"James."

"And where are you from?"

"Horbury."

Tuck shook his head with a frown.

"I can tell just from looking into your eyes that you're not like these men. You don't have the violence burning inside you that they do, especially the little one." He glanced at the unconscious robber leader and crossed himself before turning his gaze back to the young archer. "He's got the devil inside him, that one. You'd do well to get away from him now, before he leads you into trouble you can't escape."

James removed the nocked arrow from his bowstring and stuck it back into his belt with a grunt of agreement.

Tuck nodded in appreciation.

"The Lord's blessing on you for not shooting me. Perhaps one day I'll be able to repay your mercy." The friar grasped the pommel of his horse's saddle, placed his right foot into the stirrup and, with a grunt, hauled himself ungracefully onto the palfrey which danced nervously beneath him. "Take yourself home to Horbury. Stop robbing people with these men but, if ever the law are after you and you have nowhere to turn – seek out Robin Hood. Tell him Friar Tuck sent you."

James's eyes widened. "I knew you weren't just some fat clergyman."

"That's where you're wrong," Tuck replied with a smile, kicking his heels into the horse which trotted back towards the road. "I'm on my way back to Lewes exactly because I *am* just a fat clergyman."

CHAPTER SEVEN

Allan and Gareth were nervous as they approached the Carter Gate into Nottingham. They'd met some other travellers on the road – a bald little merchant who rode a fine-looking horse, with his two bodyguards – and joined their party. Now they all stood in the short yet slow-moving queue waiting to enter the city. The guards were checking everyone who sought entry and the outlaws could both feel the sweat trickling down from their armpits despite the chill afternoon air.

"You lot, move up!"

The merchant took the lead, smiling at the gatekeepers as he submitted to a perfunctory search for concealed swords; citizens as well as visitors being banned from carrying them during this period. Gareth and Allan only had daggers with them, which they were allowed to keep, but the merchants two bodyguards were made to hand over their long-swords, for safe-keeping until they left the city. There was much cursing and huffing at this which Allan understood. Although the blades the mercenaries wielded were poor quality they marked them as men of a certain class and a soldier felt as good as bollock naked without his sword.

"What you all here for?" one of the guardsmen asked, his voice betraying the boredom he felt at this repetitive task.

"These men are my bodyguards," the little merchant replied in a surprisingly powerful voice, waving a hand at his henchmen. "I'm selling fine gemstones. Here, take a look" –

The guard waved the merchant away with a scowl as the man opened his coat to display his wares.

"What about you two?"

"I'm here to enter the tourney." Allan brandished his longbow to illustrate his point. "That silver arrow the sheriff's offering as a prize is as good as mine." He winked at the guardsman confidently. "Seriously, mate, get your money on me."

"Aye, I'll be sure and do that," the guard nodded with a disinterested frown. "I'm sure you'll be able to beat that French archer that's been practising in the town centre for the past week." He glared at Gareth, taking in the young man's skinny arms and red-rimmed eyes. "What about you, boy? You ain't here for the silver arrow are you? You don't have the shoulders of your mate here. You don't look strong enough to peel the hose off one of the whores at the Maidenshead, never mind shoot a longbow."

The merchant roared with laughter at the guard's simple joke while his bodyguards grinned at the outlaw, daring him to make a smart reply to the old guard.

"I'm just here to watch the tourney," Gareth grunted, his face flushing scarlet in embarrassment. His lack of stature made him feel inadequate every day, especially living with a gang of outlaws who were, to a man, built like the trees they used to conceal their camp-sites. "So you can fuck off," he added angrily, but under his breath so the guard wouldn't hear.

"Wait! That one – hold him there. I know him."

A voice carried to them from the tower doorway behind the guards and Allan shared a worried glance with Gareth. The merchant surreptitiously inched away from them as another blue-liveried guard pushed past his fellows and stared at Allan.

"I know you."

* * *

Matilda wiped her brow and reached for the cup of fresh water her mother had brought her a short time ago. Her young student, Marjorie, had visited earlier on, asking if they could go hunting again but Matilda was too busy. Her father had been commissioned by a wealthy merchant in Sheffield to make a large batch of arrows. Not just any arrows though – these were to be the finest: birch fletched with eagle feathers.

Henry had managed to procure some, but eagles weren't common so he'd told Matilda to use sparrowhawk and peregrine falcon feathers as well. The merchant would just have to make do.

The young woman had helped her mother tidy the house in the morning and now sat outside in the sun, sorting the feathers into piles – left wing or right. Little Arthur was playing with some discarded, poor-quality feathers and he'd occasionally sing to himself or shout random noises which brought a big smile to Matilda's face. The boy's sweet voice certainly made chores more enjoyable.

Once she'd separated a batch of the feathers she shaped them then glued and bound them onto poplar shafts her father had already prepared. It was simple enough work but required nimble fingers and concentration. Thankfully her infant son was well-behaved and only rarely tried to wander off when he thought his ma wasn't watching.

This was her usual day, although, normally, she'd be using goose feathers and working much faster. Every now and again, though, her father would pick up an order from some nobleman who wanted fancy feathers or exotic woods for his shafts and production would slow. Her fingers ached after a day's work, even now when she'd been doing it for years, but it brought a decent wage and could be done inside in the winter months.

It wasn't a bad way to make a coin, not at all. Especially in this fine weather. Still...

She would have liked to go hunting with Marjorie, even just for a short time to break up the monotony of her work, but the merchant had ordered a large number of arrows and they had to be completed quickly or he'd pay them less.

It would do the younger girl good to catch a few hares on her own anyway. Assuming foresters didn't catch her again...

"Get down from there, right now!"

Arthur turned round guiltily, halfway up the stone wall that separated the Fletcher's from the field next to them.

"Now!"

The little boy slowly dropped back to the ground and ran to her, laughing, and she couldn't help joining in even though she knew she should scold him and beat him like all the other young mothers in the village did with their children.

She put down the shaft she was working on and stood to scoop up her squealing son, spinning him round and hooting herself before dropping onto the grass, gasping.

"Never caught anything. Not one bloody hare."

Marjorie walked into the garden and slumped onto the stool Matilda had just vacated.

"Off you go, little boy," Matilda grinned, kissing Arthur on the cheek and shooing him off towards the house. "Go and play with the wooden soldiers daddy brought you from the market in Barnsley. No more climbing or I'll smack your arse."

She watched him toddle off, then sat down on the ground next to Marjorie, lifting her unfinished shaft and starting work on it again.

"I set those snares days ago. Should have caught *something* by now."

"Maybe the hares are too smart for us now," Matilda shrugged. "I wouldn't worry about it."

"No, you wouldn't worry about it, because you always catch something." Marjorie growled, staring at her sister-in-law as if it was her fault she hadn't been able to catch anything for her family's dinner pot. She sighed, again.

Matilda could see Arthur inside the house, trying to climb the ladder that led to her parent's bed and, exasperated, she jumped to her feet. "Get down from there, right now," she shouted, flailing her hand angrily. "Down. Now!" She suddenly rounded on Marjorie.

"Look, you're no good at hunting. Tough. I'm trying to work here, while making sure my son doesn't break his neck at the same time. Why don't you go and make yourself useful instead of trying to be your brother?"

She regretted her angry words instantly, as tears welled up in Marjorie's eyes and the girl stood, knocking the stool onto the floor, before running off without a word. There was no time to chase her though.

"Arthur, get *down* from there right now!"

* * *

"Everything all right?" the gate guard demanded, glaring at the newcomer. "We've got a queue a mile long here, Thomas."

"Just trying to remember where I've seen this man. Let the others move on."

The merchant waved them farewell, a look of relief plain on his face as the queue began to move into the city again. From the corner of his eye, Allan could see Gareth's head swivel as if searching for the fastest escape route and a cold bead of sweat dripped slowly down his back, making him shiver.

Allan's clasped his hands, preparing to grab the dagger he carried hidden in his belt. They would not escape when the guard realised who he was; the crowd was too thick and the guards too many. The burly archer wouldn't go down without a fight, though.

At last the guard's eyes flared in recognition and he grabbed his older companion's arm roughly.

"I remember now! He's a minstrel. You played for us in Hathersage – Lord de Bray's manor house."

Allan's face creased in a huge grin and he moved his hand away from the hidden blade to pat his gittern case, relief flooding through him.

Thomas smiled at the other guard who looked irritated rather than impressed as he continued checking any visitors who looked like they might be coming into his city to cause trouble.

"Him and his mate – they looked like soldiers but played and sang like minstrels. It was a fine night." He glanced at Gareth then looked back at Allan. "After Lord de Bray was ruined I left to take up a job here in Nottingham. Strange business it was..." His voice trailed off as he remembered his former employer's downfall which had, unbeknown to Thomas, been brought about by Robin Hood and his men. "Anyway," he went on, face brightening again. "What brings you here? You and your little mate going to play music for Sir Henry?"

"Nah, I'm here to enter the tourney. I'm almost as good with the longbow as I am with the gittern. The sheriff might as well give me that silver arrow right now."

Thomas grinned then looked back over his shoulder at the guardhouse. "Well, good luck, lad. It was good seeing you again. I better get back to my post or the sergeant will kick my arse." He clapped Allan on the arm then turned away. "If you're bored and looking to earn an extra coin or two, make your way to the Cotter's Rest. That's where most of us guards go for a drink when our shifts are done. The landlord, Fat Robert, will put you up in return for a few songs. Farewell!"

At last the old gate-guard gestured impatiently for them to move on through the gates and Allan blew a long breath of relief as they left the gatehouse behind.

"My lord," a young lad of no more than fourteen years grinned at them from behind a stall stacked with oatcakes and loaves. "Freshly baked. Finest in the city, I swear it."

Allan produced a coin and tossed it to the boy, lifting a couple of the oatcakes from the display and handing one to Gareth as he bit into his own, crumbs spilling down his gambeson.

"We need a place to stay," the minstrel mumbled, eyeing the savoury snack in appreciation. "Somewhere far away from the Cotter's Rest."

The boy nodded and winked knowingly. "Want to avoid the law eh? I don't blame you – when they've had a skinful they cause more trouble than anyone." He pointed to the east side of the city and gave them directions to The Ship – an establishment he assured them was one of the best in the whole city.

Allan handed him another coin in thanks and the outlaws moved off into the crowd again.

They'd taken some money from their own funds back at the camp-site; not enough to draw attention to themselves should guards like the ones at the gate take an interest in them, but enough to pay for food, ale and lodging for a while. Maybe enough even for a visit to the fabled Maidenshead – Prior John De Monte Martini's own establishment – or one of the other brothels in the city, Allan mused, grinning to himself at the ease of their passage into Nottingham.

They moved from one inn to another, checking the quality of the accommodation and sampling the ale in each one. Although they were, to all intents and purposes, simple peasants – yeomen at best – they were rich men by the standards of most of Nottingham's populace, thanks to the success they'd enjoyed as part of Robin Hood's gang. Although they couldn't flaunt their wealth without drawing unwelcome attention to themselves in the potentially hostile city, they *could* afford to pay for some half-decent lodgings for the few days they expected to spend there.

"I like this place," Gareth smiled, his bony fingers curled around a wooden cup of cheap wine when they eventually reached The Ship and found a table to share. It was a pleasant enough place, with fresh rushes on the floor and a newly painted sign above the door which suggested the landlord took pride in his establishment.

Allan eyed his young companion sceptically. "You mean you like the drink they're serving up."

Gareth was past caring whether Allan knew about his taste for strong drink or not. "Aye, I do," he nodded, "it's not the barber's grain drink, but it's better than that piss-water you all drink. Ale. Pfft. This stuff," he held his cup aloft with a crooked smile, "is all right."

Allan paid the inn-keep the three shillings he demanded for a few nights room and board the next time the man passed their table, wondering if he'd made a wise decision coming here with Gareth. None of the other outlaws had shown any interest in taking part in the tourney, which had surprised the minstrel who knew better than anyone how good they were with longbows, long-swords or quarterstaffs. He'd expected some of them would want to test themselves against the best men the Sheriff's tournament would attract, but no... they were all content to sit around that God-forsaken forest, day after day, eating rabbit stew and talking about a time when they'd be free men again.

Well, Allan mused, Robin was right. Once he had the silver arrow he'd be able to sell it and bribe some powerful nobleman to grant them all pardons.

"More wine," Gareth demanded with a grin as he gazed at the buxom serving wench who came to clear their empty cups. "Bring me more, my beauty."

The girl looked amused as she carried the empties away and Allan sighed. Maybe it would have been better to be lonely than bringing this young sot along after all.

It'd be an early night for them both tonight, even if he had to drag Gareth away from the bar by his hair.

* * *

In the morning Allan asked the inn-keeper if he knew anything about the upcoming tournament.

"Aye," the red-faced man replied, nodding. "They seek to sort the wheat from the chaff. Anyone that wants to enter an event has to go to the castle to prove their skill in qualifying heats. What're you doing?" He took in Allan's wide shoulders and nodded. "Archery, eh?"

"Aye," the minstrel replied. "I'm not bad with a blade as well, but I don't think I could match the best in the shire. Shooting a longbow though..."

"A match for Robin Hood himself, eh?" the inn-keep smirked, one eyebrow raised almost mockingly. He'd heard these tales before countless times, and learned to take them all with a healthy pinch of salt.

Allan was just glad Gareth, who stood at his side, hadn't been drinking yet that morning. No doubt the youngster, if he'd been inebriated, would have told the barman all about their friend Robin.

"Aye," the minstrel returned the man's condescending smile. "I'd say I can match the famous wolf's head. But he won't be entering this tournament will he? Not if he's got any sense – the law would be all over him. So I reckon I've as good a chance as any of winning the silver arrow."

"Sure you have," the man shrugged in boredom. "If you want to enter, you'd better get yourself to the castle. If you're as good as you think you are, they'll let you enter the tournament." He moved away to continue cleaning up the worst of the mess from the previous evening's revelry, leaving his two guests to their conversation.

Gareth had decided to stay at the inn, rather than going to the qualifying heats. "All those soldiers? Someone might recognise me," he said. "Besides, I'm shit with a bow, I'll just get in the way. I'll hang around the inn. Might even take a walk about the town."

"Someone might recognise you," Allan growled sarcastically, fixing the younger man with a stern look.

"I'll keep my head down," Gareth replied, pulling the hood on his cloak up over his head to show how well he could hide in its dark shadows.

Allan moved to stand right in front of his companion and gazed at him. "I'm not joking," he said. "Don't sit around here drinking all day, mouthing off to anyone that'll listen. You'll get us both in trouble, and if you say enough, you'll bring hell down on Robin, Will, John and all the rest of our friends."

Gareth shook his head angrily. "I won't even be drinking," he muttered.

"I'll be back soon enough. There's no doubt I'll qualify for the tourney. After that I'll head straight back here. We can get a drink then, all right?" Allan patted the youngster on the arm reassuringly. "And don't go showing off your coin either, unless you want some thief to take it from you."

Lifting his longbow and checking the little pack he carried on his belt to make sure the hemp string was safely inside, Allan gave a last nod to Gareth and left The Ship to make his way to the qualifying rounds at Nottingham Castle.

* * *

Sure enough, Allan qualified for the archery section of the sheriff's tournament without any problems.

Getting into the castle was easy enough, although the guards did look closely at every entrant's face before granting them access to the courtyard where the heats were being held. The minstrel knew Robin would have been recognised immediately by the guards under such scrutiny – his description would have been well known to the soldiers and a fat purse would be the reward for any who spotted the notorious outlaw so despised by Sir Guy of Gisbourne.

Allan, on the other hand, was known to few of the lawmen although, in his younger days he had performed as a minstrel in many places and secretly hoped someone or other would shout, "You! You're that fine gittern player," just as the gate-guard had done.

It would certainly be preferable to being recognised for the outlaw that he was, but no-one gave him a second glance as he made his way to take part in the qualifying rounds.

The castle was, of course, home to a variety of equipment used in the training of soldiers, and it was all seeing action that morning as Allan walked to the big targets that would separate the skilled archers from the talentless.

The wolf's head was surprised at the number of entrants; the courtyard was full of them, all hoping to win the magnificent silver arrow that the sheriff had, perhaps foolishly, placed on display atop the battlements so the competitors could all see what they were striving for.

"Christ, that thing looks heavy," the middle-aged man in line next to Allan muttered, glancing at the minstrel with wide-eyes. "We'd never have to work another day in our lives if we won that."

Allan smiled. In all honesty, he was already a fairly rich man, as were all the members of Robin Hood's gang. The gold and silver coin they'd taken from the obscenely wealthy nobles and clergymen travelling through Yorkshire over the past couple of years had made them all financially secure. Set for life, they were.

It was just unfortunate they were all outlaws so could never enjoy the fruits such wealth might bring.

That arrow, though... It must have been worth a fortune, Allan guessed. Truly, such an amount of silver... It could be melted down or small slivers could be shaved off to barter with and there'd be enough to truly set a man up for life – even an outlaw like him. He could make his way to France, bribing lawmen and officials along the way to allow him safe passage. Then he'd build a house somewhere in Normandy or Brittany, buy the fanciest gittern he could find, and settle down to a life of wine, women and song, safely away from Gisbourne or the sheriff or anyone else. He'd have to learn to speak their language but...

"You lot! Move up!"

The sergeant's bellowed command startled Allan from his pleasant reverie and he moved forward with about twenty other entrants to take aim at the big targets lined up in front of them.

"Good luck!"

Allan grinned at the man next to him as they fitted their bowstrings, pulled arrows from their belts and took aim, ready for the burly sergeant's order to shoot, which seemed to take forever as the soldier peered along the line of bowmen, looking for any sign of obvious weakness in their stance. Finally, he stepped back, satisfied and roared, his shout reverberating off the great stone walls.

"Loose!"

Three times the archers shot, before the sergeant checked the targets and then informed them who'd qualified and who hadn't.

Allan knew this exercise was merely to weed out those who were truly unskilled, so he made sure to hit the centre of the target with only two of his shots, although he surely could have managed all three, as the distance to it was quite short and the target itself rather large.

Still, a few of the men in his qualifying group failed to hit the centre even once, and one competitor failed to strike the big round board at all, his missiles clattering harmlessly into the wall behind the target pitifully and sending some of the idly spectating guardsmen running, with angry curses spilling from their mouths.

"The next heat will be in two days!" The sergeant shouted, addressing Allan and the rest of the men who had successfully qualified. The man pointed at another soldier seated at a table close-by. "Collect a token from the clerk there, and make sure you bring it when you return or you won't be granted entry. Now get out of the fucking way, so the next lot can take their turn."

Thirteen remained from the original group of twenty and, as they all cheerfully made their way to collect their qualifying tokens Allan could see no threat from any of them. None had performed spectacularly, although one man did manage to hit the red circle in the centre of the target with each of his three shots. He was an older man though, and his arms would surely weaken and give out during the tournament itself. No, Allan didn't think any of the men from his qualifying group posed a threat to him.

Then again, some of them might be hiding their true ability just as he was...

Grinning, he collected the wooden token that would grant him entry back into the castle in two days and, with a cheery wave to the next row of nervous qualifiers, made his way out the castle and through the bustling streets to The Ship, hoping he wouldn't find Gareth in his cups telling the entire common room about his adventures with Robin Hood and Little John.

He heaved a small sigh of relief when he made it back to his room in the inn and found Gareth there, mending some of his clothes with a bone needle and some thread. His face was a little flushed, suggesting that he'd spent a few coins on wine that afternoon but he was by no means drunk.

"How did you get on?" the young man asked, eyes lighting up as his companion strode into their sparsely furnished room. "Did you beat everyone?"

Allan shook his head and slumped onto the flea-ridden bed, stretching out happily. "Nah, I got through to the next round, but if I'd been too good it might have drawn attention to me. I only want to do enough to get through the qualifiers and into the tournament itself. Then I'll show them what a lowly wolf's head can do."

Gareth jumped up and pulled on his worn old leather boots. "Come on, don't go to sleep, it's still early. I've been on my own all day, I'm bored. Let's go and get that drink you talked about this morning, and some of the inn-keep's food that I can smell cooking up."

There *was* a very meaty aroma wafting through the inn, Allan had to admit, and his stomach rumbled loudly as if in response to Gareth's request.

"Alright, let's go," he agreed, standing up and straightening his brown jacket. "But no mentioning Robin."

Their night was a pleasant one, and Gareth behaved himself well enough. The inn-keeper brought them bowls of beef stew with vegetables which was excellent if a little short on meat. Then they had a few ales, listened to some of the locals singing and eventually retired to their room.

Robin had been worried about nothing, Allan thought. Even if he didn't win the tournament, and the silver arrow, this was going to be an enjoyable few days. Who could possibly recognise him or Gareth in a city full of strange faces?

CHAPTER EIGHT

The next round of qualifying in the castle courtyard was a little harder than the first one, with the very worst of the entrants now gone and only those competent with the longbow left. Some of them were very good, Allan noted, as he stood waiting to take his own turn, watching the other competitors firing arrow after arrow into the worse-for-wear targets which hadn't been replaced or repaired in the past few days.

Three times Allan and his group shot, with three arrows each time, and the scores were tallied by the same sergeant that decided who progressed on the outlaw's earlier visit to the castle.

Allan made sure to hit the red-painted centre section on six of his nine shots. The other three he aimed close but hit just outside the middle. It was enough to see him through to the tournament itself, without drawing any unwanted attention from the guards or, indeed, the other competitors.

He enjoyed the afternoon's shooting, relishing the chance to stretch his great shoulder muscles, and he made mental notes of the best of the other archers, so he'd know who to watch out for when the tourney started for real in a few days.

Then he strolled back to The Ship with a swagger, pleased with how things were going and catching the eye of a group of young girls who were washing clothes on the banks of the River Leen. Their giggles and whispers as they watched him pass made him smile – he hadn't enjoyed female attention like that in such a long time.

Exiled to the greenwood as he was, living with only hard, hairy-arsed men for company, could be a lonely existence at times and he vowed to pass along this road again tomorrow, only next time he'd stop to drink from the well. Maybe even strike up a conversation with one or two of the pretty girls...

His thoughts came back to reality as he reached The Ship and remembered Gareth.

Again, he prayed the young man wasn't drunk but, as before he needn't have worried. Gareth was in the common room of the inn, and he had a mug of wine before him, but he was sitting alone quietly, observing a couple of the locals singing for the rest of the patrons.

"You made it through?" the skinny youngster demanded when he caught sight of his broad-shouldered mate coming towards him.

"Of course!" Allan grinned, gesturing to the serving girl to bring him an ale and settling his bulk into the wooden chair to watch the singers. "No problem. I'm in the tournament for real." He handed over a small coin, nodding his thanks before taking a long pull of the freshly brewed ale. "And I'm sure I've got a good chance." He wiped froth from his upper lip absent-mindedly, engrossed in the surprisingly good rendition of "Man in the Moon" that the two locals were belting out.

It was a song that brought back fond memories for Allan, who had performed that very tune with Robin a couple of years ago when they'd passed themselves off as travelling minstrels to gain access to a rich nobleman's house. They'd impressed Lord John de Bray's guests that night, before rescuing Will Scarlet's daughter Beth from a life of slavery the next morning.

The minstrel lifted his mug to his lips and drained the lot in one go, the glow from the alcohol and the happy memories spreading throughout his body almost instantly and he grinned to the serving girl, waving his empty mug for a refill.

As the singers finished their song Allan turned and fixed Gareth with a stony glare. "I feel like having a few ales here tonight to celebrate getting into the tourney but I'm warning you – keep silent about who we are, where we came from and who we know. You understand?"

Gareth gave a sullen nod and fiddled with his mug like a naughty child.

"I mean it, lad," Allan continued. "We can have a good time here this evening, but if you so much as mention Robin I'll fucking knock you out. Your tongue loosens when you've had a few drinks and it could get us all killed so..."

"Alright!" the younger outlaw shouted, slamming his mug onto the table angrily. "I'm not an idiot." He met Allan's eyes but continued in a much quieter voice as people turned to see what the commotion was about. "I won't say a word about anything. Alright?"

The minstrel felt guilty for upsetting his companion. "Good lad," he smiled, gripping Gareth's wrist. "Get yourself another cup of wine, then, and we'll order some food. Tonight we celebrate!"

* * *

Afternoon gave way to evening and The Ship began to fill up as Gareth and Allan enjoyed the drinks, the food and the banter. The minstrel watched his younger friend like a hawk in case Gareth mentioned Robin or the fact they were outlaws but the evening went smoothly and, as darkness drew in outside, the inn-keeper banked the fire in the old stone hearth and the low-ceilinged room was filled with light, laughter and music.

As they joined in with the rest of the inn's patrons on yet another sing-along Gareth shouted into his friend's ear.

"You brought your gittern, didn't you? Go and get it. We'll give this lot a tune to remember!"

Allan shook his head. "We can't draw attention to ourselves," he shouted back, cupping his hands against Gareth's ear to be heard over the raucous singing.

The wine and ale flowed as time wore on and the two outlaws had the best time they'd had in months. Their bellies were full of the inn-keeper's tasty stew, they had plenty of alcohol to drink and the locals had welcomed them warmly into their company. There were even some good-looking older ladies throwing them suggestive glances.

They were having so much fun, and the drink was flowing freely. Too freely. As always, tongues were loosened...

"Aye, I'm Robin Hood's right-hand man. We're like brothers!"

The woman fluttered her eye-lashes and smiled at the story, not really taking it in. The singing was loud and the man beside her was too drunk to be believed, but he had a purse full of coin and she planned on making the most of it tonight.

"I'm telling you," he went on, seeing the blank look on her face. "We've had lots of adventures. I'm only here in the city for this tournament. Keep it to yourself, but..." He leaned in close and tried to whisper in her ear, although in his inebriated state it came out as a bellow. "I'm an outlaw!"

Thankfully the music drowned out the confession. His companion heard him though.

"What are you doing? You'll get us both jailed!"

Allan shook his head with a snort. "Shut up, Gareth," he slurred. "No one's listening. Why don't you go an' get my gittern from our room?" The big outlaw stood up, a broad, drunken smile on his face. "I'll show these people how a true minstrel performs."

"Fucking sit down!" Gareth grabbed Allan's arm and hauled him back into his seat, looking around nervously to see if anyone had heard the confession.

Reality hit the minstrel, even through the alcoholic haze, and he grinned sheepishly, lifting his mug ostensibly to take another drink but in reality to try and hide from what he'd just done.

He looked blearily around the room but all he could see were happy revellers enjoying the singing. The ladies that had been sitting beside them shared irritated glances and wandered off into the crowd to try and find some other, less inebriated, drinkers to take advantage of.

"Ah, fuck 'em," Allan waved a hand after them, staring at Gareth who shook his head in return.

"You've got a cheek talking about me," the younger man hissed. "You're the one that's going to get us into trouble with your shouting about Robin Hood."

No one was taking the slightest bit of notice of them as far as Allan could tell. He shrugged, smirking like a naughty boy and drained the last of the ale in his mug.

"I'll get us another," he mumbled, fumbling in his pouch for coins.

"No you bloody won't," Gareth retorted. "You've had plenty. Just sit there and watch the singers until I finish my wine. Then we're going back to the room so you can sleep it off." He shook his head again in irritation. "And you were worried about *me* acting like an arsehole..."

* * *

Friar Tuck smiled at the bald old Benedictine monk that opened the large wooden door to the priory. "God be with you, brother."

The man's rheumy eyes glared at him for a moment, taking in Tuck's grey cassock that marked him as a member of the Franciscans.

"What d'you want?"

Tuck laughed; a genuine, happy sound, filled with affection and pleasure to be in a familiar place with a familiar face. "It's me, you old sod. Robert!"

He gave his real name, Tuck being merely a nickname shared by many friars on account of the way they sometimes wore their cassocks, with the material tucked between their legs for freedom of movement.

The gate-keeper narrowed his eyes in confusion, leaning out of the doorway to gaze at the man before him. "Robert? Is it you, truly? I remember you having a lot more meat on your bones."

The door was hauled open by a second, much younger Benedictine, and Tuck moved forward to grasp the older fellow's arms. "It's me right enough, Edwin," he grinned. "I lost some weight recently – nearly died, in truth – but the good Lord saw fit to return me to life, and to you too now." He nodded towards the second, younger monk, who returned the gesture.

"Well met, Osferth."

Finally, the old gatekeeper smiled and squeezed Tuck's arms happily. "It is you! Oh, Robert, it's good to see you again, the place has been quiet without you around. Come in, come in!"

They moved inside and Osferth shoved the heavy door closed, drawing the great iron bolt into place. They were safe enough these days, but old tales of marauding Vikings had left their mark on many clergymen who were happy to make themselves as secure as possible behind their thick stone walls and stout doors.

"I'll leave you to it," the younger monk said as he turned and made his way along the corridor. "I have chores to do."

"It's good to see you, Robert," the old man repeated, paying no heed to the departing Osferth. "But... why have you returned?"

Tuck shook his head. "I know the prior –"

"You *don't* know," Edwin interjected. "The man hates you. In the name of Christ, Robert, he'll have your balls for dinner when he sees you've returned. What possessed you to come back here? His hatred for you has barely dulled in the time you've been gone."

Tuck nodded and clasped his hands within the folds of his voluminous grey cassock. "I have my reasons," he replied. "Hopefully what I bring to the prior will go some way to restoring me in his favour."

Edwin snorted, an incredulous look on his face. "I'll give you one last chance, Robert. The brothers here all miss you, as do I, even if you're not one of us. But I'd rather you left than suffer de Monte Martini's wrath. Go now – back to your outlaw friends – and I'll not tell a soul you were here." He grasped Tuck by the forearm and stared into his eyes earnestly. "Go, my friend."

Tuck had expected Prior de Monte Martini to hate him after everything that had happened. De Monte Martini was a vindictive, petty man who liked to throw his weight around at the best of times but Tuck had done much to earn the man's hatred, even if he didn't deserve it. He had done his best to protect the prior's belongings – it hadn't been his fault they'd been stolen. Twice...

He smiled, trying to appear more confident than he felt.

"It'll be fine, Edwin. Prior de Monte Martini will be glad to see me, trust me."

The gatekeeper shook his head sadly, a heavy sigh escaping from his thin old lips. "If you say so, old friend, if you say so. Let me take you to him then."

He turned and hobbled off along the chilly corridor which seemed to press in on Tuck who had become so used to the open spaces and bright, natural beauty of Barnsdale Forest.

They passed one or two of the brethren who looked across in astonishment as they went by, and the prior's bottler, Ralph, who gaped open-mouthed then hurried back down to his cellar, before Edwin stopped in front of another great door made of dark, varnished oak and gave Tuck a final look.

"If you're sure about this, Robert, I'll tell the prior you've returned." He shook his head, again, at Tuck's firm nod and grasped the cast-iron handle. "If you insist, then. May God be with you."

* * *

"Oh, fuck."

It was a sign of Allan-a-Dale's advanced inebriation that he never even raised his head from the table at Gareth's muttered oath.

"Wake up!"

The skinny young outlaw grabbed his big friend's arm and shook him until Allan looked up with bloodshot eyes. "We've got trouble. Probably because of your big mouth." He nodded towards the bar and the minstrel looked around to see one of the city's guardsmen in conversation with the innkeeper. Three more soldiers followed their leader, all clad in light armour covered by the blue surcoat the sheriff's men wore as their uniform. Behind them stood two grey-robed friars: Brother Walter, smiling nastily while his charge, the oblate Hubert, looked around unhappily.

"Oh fuck," Gareth repeated, the panic evident in his voice. "The guards are coming over. What do we do?"

"Sing them a song?" Allan smiled, watching the oncoming soldiers who threaded their way through the inn's patrons, most of whom moved aside to clear a path although some of them stood their ground and stared sullenly at the lawmen pushing past.

"You." The guard sergeant stopped behind Allan's chair and glared down at them, his hand resting on the pommel of his sword.

"Sit, my lord!" Gareth grinned nervously. "What can we do for you?"

"We were given a tip from someone that saw you in the street earlier today," the soldier replied. "He says you're Robin Hood's men." The sergeant shrugged, as if sick of hearing these tales that inevitably turned out to be nothing. "I don't care if you are or not, but you're coming to the castle with us –"

Before he could finish his sentence Allan stood up and rammed the back of his head into the guard's face, sending the man reeling, nose shattered and bleeding before he collapsed onto the filthy rush-covered floor in a daze.

The remaining three guardsmen, used to dealing with rowdy drunkards, moved in to restrain their leader's broad-shouldered assailant, but, belying his inebriation, Allan side-stepped the first man's grasp and hammered a meaty fist into his opponent's cheek, sending the man sprawling into another table, drinks and outraged patrons scattering all about the place as screams of fright and roars of anger filled the air.

"I told you I was one of Robin Hood's men!" The minstrel shouted towards the middle-aged lady he'd been trying to seduce earlier. "You didn't believe me but –"

He was cut-off mid-sentence as the two remaining guards came at him. One rammed a wooden cudgel into his midriff and, before he could even bend over in deflated agony, the other tackled him to the ground and began to rain blows down on his head.

As the two guards battered his friend senseless, Gareth – bloodshot eyes wide in fear – fell to his hands and knees and pushed his way between the legs of the rest of the drinkers who stood watching the confrontation with glee.

"That's enough," the guard sergeant mumbled, pulling his men away and holding his broken nose gingerly. He aimed a final kick at Allan who lay, battered and unresisting amongst the vomit-and-ale-soaked rushes on the floor, before looking around the place in anger.

"Where's the other one?" he shouted. "This one's mate. Where is he? Tell me, now!"

The inn's patrons looked about the room innocently. Like drinkers everywhere they had no intention of helping the law capture one of their own, even if they didn't know who the fugitive was, or what he was supposed to have done to warrant arrest by the local militia. Many of them had been in the tavern all day and had shared a laugh and a joke with the thin young man who'd said he came from the nearby village of Wrangbrook.

The front door closed quietly behind him as Gareth slipped out and sprinted into the shadows, praying desperately that the furious soldiers hadn't beaten his friend to death.

Now what was he supposed to do? He was no fighter, he couldn't batter his way through the guards manning the gatehouse, and he was no charismatic charmer that could simply talk his way out of the situation either.

Christ above, he thought fearfully, *how do I get out of this one with my hide intact?*

CHAPTER NINE

In the end, Gareth's lack of charisma and nondescript appearance proved to be his salvation. He was able to join the steady flow of people leaving the city, having made his way hastily to the Chapel Bar gate before any alarms were raised and he simply walked right out as if he was a member of a noisy family who didn't even notice he'd latched onto their party.

The guards didn't give him a second glance, and, for once in his life he was glad to be such an unremarkable fellow.

He knew his luck might run out though, when the sheriff's men circulated his description. It was possible someone at the gate would realise he'd passed through not long ago and the chase would be on. One of Robin Hood's gang was a prize the soldiers would spare no effort to claim.

With a glance over his shoulder he sucked in a lungful of air and broke into a run again, leaving the main road and shoving his way past bushes and low-hanging branches, his eyes able to pick out a way through the foliage thanks to the many months he'd spent living in the greenwood with the outlaws.

After a while he relaxed his pace, chest heaving and throat burning, the sweet smells of spring filling his nostrils as he hawked and spat out a thick glob of phlegm. Even if the law did come after him, they'd never manage to catch him now, he was sure.

When he ran, gasping, into the clearing the outlaws were using as a camp-site the men that were there turned in surprise at his sudden appearance. If enemies were to try and sneak up on them the lookouts that were posted day and night should alert them to their approach, but Gareth knew exactly where he was going and had managed to get past the sentries and to the camp without the alarm being raised.

"It's Gareth!"

Little John appeared from his camouflaged shelter at the cry, a pair of worn brown trousers in one hand and a bone needle in the other. "Where the fuck have you been, lad? And where's Allan?"

More of the gang started to appear, anxious to hear the young man's news.

"Taken," he gasped, bending to place his hands on his thighs, gasping for breath.

"I knew this would happen," Robin shouted, pointing in anger at Gareth who winced at the force of his leader's ire. "You should never have gone off without saying anything to the rest of us. I assume you went to Nottingham for the tourney and the sheriff's men took him?"

"It wasn't my idea, it was Allan's," Gareth protested, his voice high and reedy, like a scolded child trying to shift the blame to a naughty playmate. "That friar you robbed, Brother Walter – he must have seen us going into the inn and told the guards. I was lucky to escape. Allan took a hell of a beating..."

"Ah, bollocks," Robin slumped heavily to the ground, staring at the dead embers of the previous night's cooking fire, his expression unreadable.

Allan was one of the men Robin was closest to in the group. They had become firm friends when, together, they'd rescued Will Scarlet's daughter from her enforced servitude in Hathersage. They had been blood brothers ever since. The idea of the cheerful minstrel being imprisoned in the city jail made him feel physically sick; he'd been captured and held there himself the previous year. It had been a horrible time that had almost broken the outlaw leader's spirit.

He hated to think what an experience like that would do to his friend. And he knew the sheriff would take no chances with his captive this time around; there would be no repeat of Friar Tuck and Will Scarlet's daring rescue of Robin the previous summer. Allan had no chance of escape.

"What d'you think'll happen to him?" Gareth asked.

Will gave a snort. "What do *you* think? They'll hang him as part of the tournament, won't they? More entertainment for the crowd."

"Never mind that," Little John rumbled. "The question is: what are we going to do about it?"

Robin didn't answer and neither did anyone else. They knew there was nothing they could do to help Allan.

"He's as good as dead..." the Hospitaller sergeant, Stephen, muttered ruefully, shaking his head. "Good lad too." He crossed himself and glared at Gareth, silently accusing the youngster for the minstrel's predicament.

"It's not my fault – he was going anyway. I just went along to see how he got on, so you can stop giving me dirty looks you old prick –"

"Enough!" Robin roared, jumping to his feet angrily. "It's done. There's no point in the rest of us falling out."

The men sat in silence for a while before Little John also stood up and moved back into his crude shelter before reappearing with his enormous longbow and quarterstaff, both of which were a foot longer than any normal ones.

"I know we can't storm the castle," the giant said to Robin as the rest of the men looked on in surprise. "And I know we can't sneak in through the latrine like Will and Tuck did. But I can't just sit around here waiting on news of Allan's hanging to reach us. I'm going to the city."

Robin shook his head in disbelief. "You can't – the guards will shoot you on sight. You stick out like a nun in a brothel for fuck sake!"

John shook his great bearded head. "I'm not going on a suicide mission. I just want to go and see if I can hear what the local gossip is. The travellers coming out of the city might be able to tell us what's happening."

He looked around at the rest of the men. "I know it's pointless, but it's better than sitting here doing nothing. I'm going."

It was a futile gesture but Robin understood his big friend's feelings.

"Fine," he nodded after a moment's thought. "Let me gather my own weapons and some food. I'll come with you. We'll go to Penyston and buy a couple of horses for the journey first, though. Might come in handy." He was rewarded with a grateful look from John before he turned to Will Scarlet. "You look after things here while we're away, all right?"

Will shrugged in resignation. "Might be an idea for us to move to a new camp," he said. "Just in case they –" he broke off, not wanting to voice his fears for their captured friend. "Just in case Allan tells them where we are."

Robin agreed. "Good point. Why don't you lead the men back to the old camp near Selby? You know, the one we were used for a short time last year? Seems as good a place as any. We haven't camped there for a while. There's no reason Allan would even think of telling the sheriff we were hiding out there again. And Groves doesn't know anything about it since he'd left us by the time we were camping there."

Robin collected his weapons while everyone else moved to gather their things for the move. They'd done this so many times over the years that it was second-nature to them – like a well-rehearsed scene from a play.

Before he left with John, Robin took Stephen aside.

"Will's calmed down a lot in the past year or so," he told the Hospitaller. "But he's still prone to moments of madness if his temper gets up. He's the obvious person to lead you all when me and John aren't around, but he needs someone to make sure he doesn't react in anger if there's trouble. Someone to keep a cool head."

Stephen nodded. "I'll keep an eye on him," he promised. "I never wanted to be a leader myself – I've always been happy to be a sergeant. But even Sir Richard needed someone to tell him to calm down at times." He smiled wistfully, the memories of his former master, hanged a few months before by the sheriff, coming back to him in a rush. "You and John go to Nottingham and see if you can stop Allan suffering the same fate as my master did. Don't worry about us, we'll be fine."

Robin grasped the Hospitaller's arm in farewell before shouting goodbye to the rest of the men and haring off into the undergrowth.

"God be with you," Stephen mouthed, with a final, hopeful wave to the two departing outlaws.

* * *

"You? In God's name, I can't believe it. You dare show your fat face around here again? After what you've done?"

Prior John de Monte Martini raged at Tuck, obviously forgetting the flabby shape of his own lined red visage in the astonishment of the friar's unexpected return as Edwin, job done, backed from the room and closed the door gladly behind himself.

Tuck stood, head bowed, as de Martini continued his tirade for a while longer, listing the friar's transgressions against him, punctuating his verbal stabs with a fist that he slammed every so often onto the table that separated them.

"Eh? You Franciscan bastard. I should have had you excommunicated. How dare you show yourself in my priory again, as if nothing had happened?"

Tuck spread his hands wide, not seeking forgiveness, but time to explain his side of the story.

"Go on then, man," the prior gesticulated towards him. "Let's hear it. Let's hear why I shouldn't have you burned at the stake like the heretic – nay, *wolf's head* – that you are."

Tuck nodded into the expectant silence and placed a hand into the folds of his cassock before drawing out the little ornate reliquary that he'd obtained from St. Mary's in Brandesburton. He was rewarded with a small spark of interest that flared in de Monte Martini's eyes.

"I have it."

The prior stared hungrily at the reliquary, knowing it was somehow significant and knowing too that he coveted it. But the man had never seen it before, the friar remembered. It had been stolen from Tuck years ago by one of his own mercenaries, before he had a chance to give it to de Monte Martini.

"The relic you sent me to Eze in France to collect. The one that was purloined from me just as I'd returned here."

It took only a moment for the prior to recall exactly what the former wrestler was talking about. He had given Tuck a huge sum of money to buy the artifact; its loss wasn't something a man as driven by worldly wealth as de Monte Martini could ever forget.

"Christ's beard!" He stood up, fingers grasping the edge of the table spasmodically. "You have it? Truly?" His voice dropped and he looked at the little box in Tuck's hand longingly before his tone hardened again. "How?"

The prior knew Tuck had been living amongst the outlaws in Barnsdale so the friar saw no reason to hide the facts of his story; besides, he didn't want to lie on holy ground to his superior. Even if the man *was* a wicked bastard that cared more for coin than he did for God.

When he finished his tale the prior simply stared at the reliquary hungrily before demanding the friar hand it over to him.

Tuck did so, then allowed the sweating, flushed prior to struggle for a while before he leaned forward and flicked the hidden switch that popped the box open and revealed the sandy-coloured hairs inside.

Christ's beard.

Both men held their breath and gazed in awe at the sight before them. They beheld a part of their saviour's own body; something that had miraculously healed Tuck when he had been thrown into an unnatural deathly sleep by the crossbow bolt of Sir Guy of Gisbourne and the icy-cold waters of the Don. Something cut reverentially from Christ's face when he'd been taken down from the cross, before his resurrection and ascension to heaven days later.

Tuck wondered, as he always did on looking inside the reliquary, why the hair wasn't darker as he'd have expected, coming from a Judean as it supposedly did, but... who was he to question God's holy relic?

"It's incredible." Prior de Monte Martini breathed in excitement and Tuck could almost see the gold coins flashing in the man's eyes as he contemplated how much money this sacred object was worth. Fortunes, no doubt. More than he'd given Tuck to pay for it years earlier for sure. Relics like this only ever appreciated in value.

And here was this wolf's head, outcast from the prior's own service, returning to the fold like the Prodigal Son and handing it to him to do with as he pleased.

He clasped his hands and offered a prayer of thanks, eyes raised skywards, a grin on his jowly face.

"Truly, God works in mysterious ways, Brother Stafford. Welcome back to Lewes."

Tuck smiled in relief, glad that his gift had pleased de Monte Martini but knowing the prior wasn't likely to just allow him to settle into an easy life amongst the Benedictines here.

Although de Monte Martini's face glowed with pleasure as he waved Tuck out of the room the friar couldn't miss the sadistic spark that still burned in the man's eyes when he watched him depart.

Still, it was a start. He was back in the Church again, no longer an outcast, with good men he called brothers even if they were from a different order. Not the type of brothers he'd spent the last few months with, like Will Scaflock, John Little and Robert Hood of Wakefield but his brothers just the same; brothers in God's service. Edwin the gatekeeper and Ralph the bottler and all the other acquaintances he'd missed during his time in Barnsdale.

He was looking forward to spending his days praying, reading the bible, tending the vegetable garden that lay inside the priory walls and having a pallet and a roof over his head every night even in the harshest of weathers. Thick stone walls were much better than trees for keeping the ice-cold winds of winter at bay.

It was no life of luxury in the priory, for sure, but it was a sight more comfortable than sleeping rough on the frozen earth of the forest, when the leaves had blown from the trees and the icy rains and bitter gusts battered the greenwood as it did every single year without fail.

Aye, he was glad to be back in Lewes, even if he would badly miss his friends in Barnsdale. He just hoped the prior wouldn't make his life *too* miserable.

* * *

"You think you could take me, minstrel?"

Allan stood, watching Sir Guy of Gisbourne warily, wondering what was happening but knowing whatever it was wouldn't be pleasant.

"Eh? A man with one eye? Look at you." The Raven had appeared almost silently inside Allan's gloomy cell and now moved to grasp the minstrel's great arms firmly. "Strong. Younger than I am. Angry."

Allan remained silent, warily watching his despised enemy but not wanting to bring any more trouble down upon himself. Robin's stories of his time in this very dungeon last year had been sickening, and the minstrel knew the bounty-hunter could turn violent at any moment if provoked.

"What do you want?" he asked, trying to keep Gisbourne in sight as the man continued to walk slowly around the cell, losing himself in the shadows where the light from the softly guttering torch he'd placed in the sconce on the wall didn't quite reach.

"I want to prove myself. Your friend hurt me badly not so long ago, and I'll never be the swordsman I was before Hood took my eye. I may never be able to shoot my crossbow very accurately either." His hand caressed the stock of the weapon. "I was very fond of this crossbow too – it got me out of trouble more than once. Almost killed your friar companion too."

Still he kept circling Allan, as if his feet were bewitched and he couldn't stop them moving.

"So what is it you want from me?"

"I want you to fight me, wolf's head. It's as simple as that."

It had to be a trick. Allan wanted to grin and tell the king's man he'd be glad to beat the shit out of him but he knew Gisbourne was no fool and, despite the loss of an eye, was probably still deadly. He held his tongue and at last the black-armoured Raven stopped walking and glared at him.

They were about the same height, although the lawman was slimmer – wiry where Allan was broad-shouldered and brawny, so their eyes met across the dank cell although the smoke from the torch made the minstrel blink and Gisbourne nodded.

"I'm not supposed to be down in the dungeon – the sheriff's worried I'll try and carve you up like I did to Hood when he was here. But I don't have any intention of doing that. Your leader was, supposedly, a worthy opponent for me. The best swordsman in all England, people said of him. They were wrong – I was the best. But I had to prove it by facing Hood, blade in hand, one-on-one. I had the chance to do that when we captured him and brought him here."

He shook his head. "I had him then – he was no match for me, despite what the ballads said about his skill. The sheriff stopped me from killing him but I proved I was the better swordsman." He stepped in close again. "This isn't about that. I simply want to prove that I can still win a fight with a man that genuinely wants to murder me. Sparring with the guards here is pointless – they're frightened of hurting me, even when *I* hurt *them*."

He moved back and looked out into the corridor, nodding to someone out of sight – presumably a guard – then turned back to face Allan.

"I have no real desire to kill you. De Faucumberg wants to hang you as part of the tourney's entertainment and who am I to deny the crowd their fun? No, I simply want to best you, man-to-man. No weapons other than those the good Lord gave us."

Allan clenched his fists, mind whirling.

"If you win, you go free. You have my word. The guard outside has his orders to see you escorted safely to the Carter Gate. I'm afraid you'll have to climb a rope down into the latrine, just as your friends did not so long ago. Most unpleasant, but better than dying, no? The door to the outside has been replaced since Hood's escape through it, but the guard has the key to it."

He began to swing his arms and stretch the muscles in his legs. "It's dark outside, you won't be spotted if you and your escort keep to the shadows."

Allan didn't know how to respond. He still felt it had to be a trick but, as he stood looking at the door a blow suddenly rocked his head back and he stumbled, cursing and lifting his arms to ward off any more attacks.

"You have no choice, really," Gisbourne growled, dancing from side to side and keeping out of Allan's reach. "Fight me or stand and be pounded into a bloody mess."

He darted forward again but the outlaw flinched to the side, bringing up an arm in time to deflect the punch.

"You swear in God's name I'll be set free if I win?"

"In the name of God, the Christ and all his saints, I swear it," Gisbourne replied, aiming another blow at the big longbowman who, again, managed to evade it easily enough.

Freedom was his. All he had to do was deal with this one-eyed bastard and he'd be in Barnsdale by the following evening. Of course, he'd been stuck down here for days with very little food or drink and he'd barely slept but...

He bared his lips in a feral grin and, as his opponent drew near once more, threw a haymaker of his own which just missed its target. "You have a deal, Gisbourne, you whoreson. I'm going to make you pay for all the shit you've done to us. You might not want to kill me, but I'll gladly crush the breath from you with my bare hands."

The cell was only dimly lit and small too. Gisbourne had to be mad if he thought he could best the powerful wolf's head in here.

But he is *mad,* Allan thought. *I need to finish this and get the fuck out of here.*

Knowing the Raven was faster than him, he charged straight forward, hoping to crush the man against the wall where he could use his superior strength to hold Gisbourne in place and rain blows down on him.

As he began to move, though, he tripped over the lawman's foot and bright stars burst upon his vision as a punch landed on his cheek. Then another, as his attacker switched fists.

"I'll make up a good song about this, once I'm back in the forest," Allan growled, raising his arms as Sir Guy stepped back and they faced off again. "I'll make sure everyone knows how easy it was to beat you, and how you shit your breeches when I throttled the life from you."

He aimed a kick but Gisbourne caught it and jerked, throwing him off balance before battering his own foot into the minstrel's knee, dropping Allan to the floor with a shocked cry.

It hadn't done any real damage but the Raven followed it up with another boot, this time to his downed opponent's face.

Even with only one eye Gisbourne was fast. Allan hauled himself upright, flailing his muscular arms to avert any more attacks.

"I'm getting used to it now," the bounty-hunter smiled, to himself more than Allan. "I thought I'd never be able to fight well without both my eyes but..."

He crouched as the outlaw roared and charged towards him, aiming a left uppercut that rocked Allan again although this time he did manage to grab hold of his tormentor.

Furiously, and with a sense of real fear beginning to set in, the minstrel put all of his weight into his knee, ramming it into Gisbourne's midriff. The blow hit home and he tried again, repeatedly, using both hands to try and keep his target in one place.

The Raven was as agile as a cat, though, and managed, after the first hit had knocked most of the wind from him, to keep his body away from the follow-up strikes before, finally, he twisted out of Allan's grip and poked a finger into his eye.

Dizzy from the blows he'd taken and the effects of his captivity, Allan knew he couldn't afford to give ground so, squinting desperately, he tried to regain his hold on Gisbourne, kicking his legs out in the hope of catching the bastard a sore one.

Suddenly, he felt an excruciating pain that started between his legs and quickly seemed to grow to fill his whole being.

Gisbourne grinned at him as he mercilessly tightened his grip on Allan's testicles, then he smashed his head forward and watched in triumph as the wolf's head fell to the floor making pitiful noises.

"Looks like you won't be going free today after all, minstrel."

With a laugh, the Raven strode breathlessly from the room. As the lock clicked inexorably back into place it was all Allan could do to roar, "Bastard!" before he leaned his head back on the ground and prayed for the pain between his legs to subside.

CHAPTER TEN

The outlaws back in the camp near Selby carried on as normal while Robin and Little John were away. Will Scaflock naturally assumed command, being the obvious man for the job. Before Robin had joined them Will had been their previous leader's second-in-command. The men all respected him and even feared him a little, although the volcanic temper that had given him the nickname 'Scarlet' was, mostly, gone nowadays.

Still, for all that, to some of the outlaws their young leader's absence seemed something of a holiday for them; a time to relax and let down their guard a little, despite Will's watchful eye. It wasn't as if Robin was ever hard or unfair on the men – he was more like a friend than a commander to them all but, as ever when the person in authority goes away for a time, things became just a little more open than usual.

One person who took advantage of the more relaxed atmosphere was young Gareth. Of course, he was his own man and could do whatever he liked pretty much, but he didn't like to drink too heavily around Robin. His captain's disappointed gaze always made him feel ashamed and, as a result, he tended to keep his drinking to a more manageable level, so he wasn't stumbling around camp walking into the fire or tumbling into the nearby River Ouse.

But, with Robin and John away to God-knew-where and for who-knew how long, Gareth became more open in his inebriation.

Will tried to warn the lad about it, but the steely glare from the ex-mercenary wasn't as effective as the pitying look Robin gave him whenever he was obviously too drunk. Will simply didn't care as much as Robin.

It was with some exasperation, then, that Scarlet found the skinny youngster by the riverside on his own one evening, a half-empty ale-skin by his side and tears streaking his grubby face.

"What's the matter with you, lad?" Will's voice was gruff although he was trying his best to sound friendly. He really couldn't be bothered with other people's problems – he had enough bad memories of his own to deal with after all.

Gareth didn't even look up, just placed the ale-skin to his lips and took another long pull, careful not spill a drop as the older outlaw dropped down onto the grass next to him.

"You're going to kill yourself if you don't watch your drinking. That's up to you," Will shrugged. "You're a big boy now, you can do what you like to yourself."

Gareth turned his damp eyes to look at Scarlet, sensing the 'but' before it came.

"But you keep this up and you'll do something stupid one day, and bring trouble down on all of us."

They sat in silence for a while, Gareth not too far gone to accept the rebuke without getting angry. He knew Will spoke the truth anyway, it was pointless disagreeing. He didn't *want* to drink every day; he just couldn't help it any more. Since he'd acquired a taste for the grain drink the barber in Penyston had given him he'd found solace in the cosy fugue that alcohol produced.

Recently his need had grown even worse.

"My ma's died."

Will looked at the younger man in surprise. Gareth hadn't visited his home in Wrangbrook for weeks as far as he knew. The lad must have kept his bereavement to himself all that time. No wonder he'd been drinking more than ever – his mother was the only family Gareth had left. Now he had no-one.

"She had a shit life," the young outlaw muttered distantly. "My da died when I was only about six or seven, I can hardly remember him. She always talked about him; they really do seem to have been good together, not like some folk in Wrangbrook. Or anywhere else for that matter, I suppose. She missed him badly although I think she was happy that I was around. Just as I was happy to have her." His voice tailed off and a sob shook his thin frame.

"She had a job working in the fields in the summertime and did odd-jobs around the village in the winter months – mending clothes, brewing ale, things like that. We were all right, although we never had much to eat."

Will watched Gareth speak but remained silent as he took in the spindly arms and legs the boy had been cursed with as a result of that childhood malnutrition.

"Then, one day when she was carrying a cask of ale to the inn she tripped and broke her arm. I mean, really broke it... the bone came right out through her skin, it was terrible." He shook his head sadly. "We didn't have a surgeon in Wrangbrook, just the barber. He did his best but he didn't know much about injuries like that. My ma's arm knit together twisted and she couldn't work properly with it any more. She was in constant pain. I was about twelve then. I did my best to find work to put food on the table for us but, well... I'm not much good at physical labour. We had to survive on handouts from other villagers."

He met Will's gaze, anger flaring in his tear-filled eyes. "It was humiliating! The people were kind and tried to help us but... it was so humiliating."

"Is that why you stole the food from the chapel?" Will asked softly, knowing some of the lad's story although he'd never heard it in as much detail before.

Gareth nodded. "When I was fourteen I started stealing food whenever the neighbours hadn't given us enough to fill our bellies for the day. I could have just asked them, they would have given us more I expect, they were good people, but it was too embarrassing. So I would lift a loaf from the baker's shop or a pie from the butcher's. I was always careful and never got caught." He stopped and stared thoughtfully at the dark waters of the Ouse. "Perhaps the baker and the butcher knew what I was doing and turned a blind eye."

Will thought that likely, since Gareth, despite his small stature, was never that light on his feet or particularly nimble, but he held his peace, not wanting to hurt the lad's feelings.

"We had a visitor one day – some important priest or bishop or something like that. There was a big fuss in the village and everyone came out to watch this churchman ride into the place like he was the king or something. I used to be very pious and I'd already been to the church that morning to say my prayers. The church was only a small building with one main room, so I could see the priest laying out a table with all sorts of fancy foods: roast chicken, fresh bread, apples, eggs. I didn't even know what some of the stuff was – I'd never seen it before."

Will's stomach rumbled and he cursed it silently but Gareth didn't seem to hear the gastric growling. "I sneaked back in when everyone was out welcoming the bishop and shoved some of the food inside my pouch. I didn't take any of the really fancy stuff, just things that I thought wouldn't be missed as much. Bread and eggs and the like. There was someone in the shadows though, one of the local men. He was praying silently at the back of the building and he saw me take the food. He shouted at me and chased me out the door straight into the mob."

Will could imagine the scene in his mind's eye. It would be nice to think the villagers would have shown the poor boy some compassion but it didn't always work like that, especially when a bishop was around.

"I don't know what they were going to do to me. I tried to tell them I needed the food because my ma was poorly but the churchman was shouting and stuff, like they do, and I was frightened. I managed to break through the crowd – some of them, I'm sure, moved aside to let me pass – and I ran into the forest where I eventually found you lot."

Will remembered the day. The lad was even skinnier than he was now, having been hiding out in Barnsdale for over a week before the outlaws had come across him.

And now his mother was dead and he was all alone in the world.

They remained seated in silence for a time before Will got to his feet and extended a hand to help Gareth up.

"Come on, let's go back to camp. I know it feels like you don't have much to live for and it's all too easy to lose yourself at the bottom of that ale-skin but you're not alone. We're here for you, all of us. You're our brother, lad, never forget it."

They made their way back to the rest of the men and Gareth lay on his pallet by the fire, falling asleep almost straight away.

Will sighed and shook his head. The lad's life had been a hard one, that was certain. But so had all of the outlaws – they had to deal with it, and so would young Gareth.

Will wasn't sure the boy had the strength; he just prayed the rest of them didn't go down along with him.

* * *

He'd known it wouldn't be easy when he returned to the priory, but Tuck hadn't expected it'd be so hard to take as it was turning out.

Prior de Monte Martini made sure Tuck was given the worst chores around the place – chores that would normally be done by new, young novices, not a veteran like himself who had just returned a priceless relic to the craven bastard.

Being made to clean out the latrine was the worst, the portly friar thought, as he shovelled a large pile of shit through the opening that would take it outside and down the slope, preventing the waste from building up too much. He grinned in spite of the stench as he remembered Will Scaflock climbing the wall of a similar latrine not so long ago when they'd rescued Robin from his imprisonment in Nottingham.

The smile dropped from his face soon enough though, the smell pervading even the dampened rag he'd tied around his mouth and nose to try and hold the evil vapours at bay and he gagged again, shaking his head, eyes watering.

There was a noise from above and, with a curse, he jumped back just in time as another turd dropped into the rancid pile.

Eventually he'd shifted most of the detritus and gladly left the latrine, wiping sweat from his tonsured brow and tearing the rag from his face irritably as he closed the heavy door behind him to try and block out the worst of the fumes.

If de Monte Martini thought he could break him by giving him the worst chores in the priory he could think again. Tuck was a man of the cloth and his place was in God's service. He'd been forced to leave his rightful place once before... it'd take more than a latrine full of shit to push him out again.

He tore off the filthy leather boots the friars used when they had to clean out the latrine and left them by the door, pulling on his own worn out sandals with a sigh of relief.

He'd earned a rest.

He began to make his way to the priory's larder where he hoped the bottler, Ralph, would share a cup or two of ale and some bread with him. As he walked he smiled and breathed deeply, imagining the smell of the freshly baked loaf that awaited him. It would be a lot nicer than the stench from the mound of faeces he'd just been shovelling.

"Go and tell him to sweep the leaves from the front path now," Prior de Monte Martini told his dean, Henry of Elmstow, as they stood watching Tuck from the opposite end of the corridor.

"But it's pouring with rain –"

"I know!" The prior smiled. "Blowing a gale too. Good enough for the bastard." He waved a hand irritably at the old dean who scurried off to give Tuck the bad news.

De Monte Martini hadn't forgotten the trouble Robin Hood had caused him. He still couldn't breathe properly after the wolf's head had smashed his nose all those months ago in Wakefield. And on top of that was the vast sum of money the despicable outlaw and his friends had stolen from the prior when they'd ambushed the cart full of silver that Tuck had been supposed to escort to Lewes not long afterwards.

Yes, he'd make Tuck's life a misery for a while, make him wish he'd never returned to Lewes. Then, when he was close to breaking, de Monte Martini would find some way of using the man. Perhaps he'd relent, and make a show of forgiving the friar.

The fat idiot would be so glad to escape his life of drudgery he'd tell the prior everything he knew about Robin Hood and his men. Then de Monte Martini would pass the information on to Sir Guy of Gisbourne.

The wolf's head had, so far, got away with breaking his nose and stealing his money, but God had been kind enough to deliver one of Hood's best friends into his grasp. He meant to use the good Lord's gift to destroy the outlaws once and for all.

And, if his little ruse to win Tuck's confidence didn't work, there were other ways to make someone divulge information...

For now, though, he'd just sit back and enjoy watching Robert Stafford shovelling shit and sweeping leaves in the pissing rain. There'd be plenty of time to make the friar's life even more painful soon enough.

* * *

"I need a favour."

Robin and Little John had stopped in the village of Mansfield for some provisions, but also because John had a friend that lived there. They sat in a small dimly-lit dwelling now, the shutter pulled over as protection against the cold night chill as much as against prying eyes, and the householder tossed another log into the fire, causing the small blaze to spit and crackle merrily.

"Anything," the man replied. "I owe you my life, or at least my hand, friend."

Three years earlier John and some of the other outlaws had been out hunting and stumbled upon some foresters who had arrested this fellow, Luke, a butcher, who'd been caught poaching. Although the penalties for such a crime weren't as severe as they'd been two-hundred years ago, when transgressors might be sewn into deer-skins and hunted to death by packs of dogs, Luke had still faced a hefty fine or even the loss of his hand.

But the outlaws had chased off the lawmen and set Luke free. He'd returned to his home here in Mansfield, promising to repay his debt if ever John had need of him.

"We'd like you to go into the city and find out what's happening to one of our friends – a minstrel, name of Allan-a-Dale. I'm not asking you to place yourself in any danger or to make yourself conspicuous; just go to the inn Allan was staying at – The Ship it's called – and see if you can learn anything about his fate."

Luke nodded and placed mugs of ale before John and Robin with a small, nervous smile. "Of course," he agreed. "I'll ride out in the morning. With God's blessing I'll return in the evening with good news. In the meantime, drink, make yourselves at home and tell me about your adventures in the greenwood."

Luke was as good as his word. He owned an old, but still healthy, horse which he normally used to pull his cart, and so he made the journey to Nottingham and back much quicker than he could have done on foot.

"How did you get on?" John demanded as Luke came into the little house. The giant and his young leader had remained cooped up inside all day, for fear of being spotted and reported by some local busy-body. Apart from the danger to themselves, they had no desire to bring trouble to the butcher.

"Good and bad news," Luke reported, pouring himself a drink and draining it with a gasp before splashing some tepid water from a big bowl onto his face to wash the grime and sweat of the road off. "Your mate's being held in the castle dungeon right enough. The sheriff plans to hang him."

John groaned but Robin spread his hands and glared at the butcher. "What's the good news then?" he demanded.

"Ah, well, the sheriff has sent messengers to London to see the king. He wants the king's permission to hang your friend, you see, so... I don't know if you plan on trying to rescue him or what but you have at least some time to try it before the friars return with the king's seal."

"Wait," Robin sat down opposite Luke. "Why would de Faucumberg need the king's permission to hang an outlaw?"

"I don't know, but that's the rumour." Luke shrugged.

"What about these friars," John demanded. "What've they got to do with it?"

"The sheriff asked the two Franciscan friars that informed on your mate if they'd go to the king and they agreed. They must be on the road right now."

John gripped Robin's shoulder. "That old bastard Walter. It wasn't enough for him to see Allan captured, he's going to make sure he hangs too."

Luke stood and helped himself to another mug of his ale with a sigh of exhaustion. "Well, lads. You can bed down here again –"

"No." Robin moved to gather his things, gesturing John do the same. "We're leaving right now. If De Faucumberg needs the king's seal to hang Allan he'll want it as soon as possible, so he'll have provided the Franciscans with horses. We don't have time to waste – we need to catch them and find out what's going on. Something doesn't add up."

A short time later Luke waved as the grim outlaws kicked their mounts into a canter along the road to Nottingham, the sound startlingly loud in the dark, silent village, like Gabriel's hounds or the Wild Hunt.

"I wouldn't want to be those friars when that pair catch up to them," the butcher muttered before he made his way back inside, shoved the bolt across the door and, with a shiver, tossed another log onto the hearth.

* * *

"I think we should get moving," Hubert said to Brother Walter as they dressed in the sparsely furnished but comfortable enough room they'd paid for in the inn.

The older friar waved a hand irritably at the young novice and took his time as he pulled on his worn old sandals, cursing the calluses and corns that beset him and wondering why clergymen were never allowed to wear socks. His head was pounding from the ale he'd consumed the previous evening and all he wanted to do was go back to sleep for a while.

No chance of that with Hubert around though.

"The sheriff said we should take his news to the king as fast as possible. If he finds out we've been tarrying he'll be angry."

Again Walter waved a hand in annoyance, this time spitting an oath at the youngster as well. It was true, Sir Henry de Faucumberg had asked the Franciscans to travel to London with all haste, even giving them a purse filled with silver coins to pay for their expenses. When Brother Walter had told the sheriff of their run-in with Robin Hood de Faucumberg had given the friar even more money to hire a couple of mercenaries to deter any other would-be robbers on the road.

Walter had every intention of travelling to the king but he saw nothing wrong in enjoying the sheriff's money on the way there. He also saw no point in racing to London as if the devil himself were after them. The outlaw – Allan-a-Dale – wasn't going anywhere.

The Franciscan made himself ready and muttered for Hubert to follow him as he left the room. The mercenaries he'd hired in Nottingham were waiting outside their door, bright and eager to earn their fee.

"We've already broken our fast," one of them said. "If you would like to get on your way?"

"In the name of Christ, you're as bad as this one," Walter groused, gesturing at Hubert who flinched back from his elder's ire. "All right, let's get some bread and cheese – and ale! – from the inn-keep and we'll be on our way."

The road was quiet when they eventually set out on the next leg of their journey to the capital, a hard, driving rain beating down on them as they huddled into their cassocks and prayed for clear skies. Walter knew Hubert was right about the sheriff being angry if they didn't get to their destination in good time so he kicked his heels into his mount and his three companions followed suit to keep up.

They moved at a stead pace through the sheeting downpour, but not too fast for fear of one of their horses slipping on the wet road. A lame nag was no use to anyone.

"God's bollocks, priest," one of the mercenaries, Philip, shouted over the sound of the drumming rain after they'd been riding for a while. "Can you and your boy not ask the Lord to stop the rain for a bit? I'm soaked to the skin – we'll all end up with a fever if we don't get dried out soon."

Brother Walter didn't like the blasphemous nature of the man's words but he agreed with the sentiment. Besides, it would be a good excuse to stop at the next village where he could warm himself by the fire of the local inn with an ale or three.

As he opened his mouth to tell the mercenary as much Hubert shouted happily. "It's stopping. Look, there's even a rainbow on the horizon!"

"Praise be to God," Walter muttered through gritted teeth, glancing up and seeing the clouds beginning to thin as the sun tried to force its way between their heavy grey bulk.

"Indeed!" Hubert agreed, oblivious to his elder's annoyance at missing out on another chance to spend Sheriff de Faucumberg's silver. "God sends us clear skies for our journey."

"That ain't the only thing he's sending us," Philip growled, turning to look back along the road behind them. "Look. Riders. And they don't look like they're filled with the love of Christ."

CHAPTER ELEVEN

Robin knew Brother Walter had recognized them as they approached, from the fearful look on the man's lined face. The friar reined in his horse, knowing they couldn't escape, and shouted at the two mercenaries to draw their weapons and defend them.

Swiftly, the two hired soldiers did so, hauling their mounts around to face the oncoming threat and setting themselves to ward off whatever attack was imminent. However, the sight of the heavily built men riding towards them, particularly Little John with his quarterstaff that seemed almost as long as a knight's lance, made the mercenaries baulk.

"Who the fuck are these two?" Philip demanded of the friars. "You never said anyone was after you. Look at the size of that one, he's a fucking giant."

His companion, Edwin, a stocky, ginger-haired man of advancing years nodded silent agreement but the pair were honourable men and they'd been paid good coin to do a job. They raised their swords, ready to defend the churchmen as the two riders approached, grim-faced, the threat of violence emanating from them like a wave.

"Hold!" Philip commanded as the two men came closer, their intent obvious as they glared murderously at Brother Walter.

Robin and Little John hauled on their mounts' reins, bringing the beasts to a halt just outside the reach of the mercenaries' blades and the bigger of the two glared at them from beneath his shaggy brown fringe.

"You know who I am?" he demanded, simply.

There was only one giant in the north of England that everyone told tales of.

Philip swallowed, eyeing the enormous staff that was aimed in his direction. "John Little?"

"That's him," Robin growled. "We have no quarrel with you two. But we want a word with that one there," he pointed his blade at Brother Walter. "So you can either stand and be cut down or you can fuck off. Either way, that friar is ours."

For a moment there was silence as Philip tried to take in what was happening. He'd been paid to protect the friars, and, although the two men facing him were notorious killers, the mercenary took pride in his job.

He glanced across at his companion, Edwin, and knew there would be no help from there. The man was gazing, awestruck, at the celebrated outlaws.

Philip looked at the younger Franciscan and shook his head sorrowfully. In truth, the mercenary cared little for the older clergyman, but Hubert seemed a decent enough young lad.

"Have no fear for the novice," Robin said, watching the mercenary's eyes and guessing what was going through the man's head. "We only want to speak to the older friar – Hubert can be on his way if he wants." The wolf's head jerked his head back along the road, indicating the direction the page and the mercenaries should go if they wanted to stay alive. "Move it, the three of you." His demeanour was calm, but young Hubert was shocked at the violent intent that flared in the big outlaw's eyes.

When Robin Hood had 'invited' them to dinner not so long ago the wolf's head had been good-natured and affable, even in the face of Brother Walter's incessant grousing. But now, Hood wore a mask of barely controlled rage.

"You go," Hubert nodded to the mercenaries who, although surprised at the command from the youngster, gladly followed his order and, with respectful nods towards the legendary outlaws, kicked their steeds along the road to Nottingham without a backward glance.

"I'll stay here with Brother Walter," Hubert finished in a small voice, feeling inside his pouch for the weight of the purse Robin had given him at their last meeting. That purse told him Hood wasn't a wicked man, and the young novice felt a duty to help his elder, even if the friar was a moaning, selfish old sot.

As the mercenaries rode off Little John walked his horse forward and poked his great oaken quarterstaff into Walter's midriff, sending the friar flying, to land with a heavy thump in the grass by the side of the road, where he lay cursing and crying like a smacked child.

The rain came back on then, mirroring the tears that sprang from Brother Walter's eyes as he lay, face-down on the ground, expecting a sword thrust to send him into God's arms in heaven at any moment.

Robin dismounted and moved to grasp the prone churchman by the scruff of the neck, hauling him up and glaring into his moist eyes.

Hubert moved to try and protect his elder but Little John was beside him and held him back, shaking his head slightly.

"You gave our mate Allan over to the sheriff," Robin said, his voice rising as he shoved Walter backwards until his shoulders hammered painfully against the trunk of a young silver birch. "You've condemned him to die! And for what?"

"Your friend is a wolf's head," the friar managed to reply, his anger enough to overcome his fear. "As are you, and your pet bear." He spat in John's direction. "May God strike the pair of you down where you stand."

"Where are you going?" Robin demanded, ignoring the jibe. "What did the sheriff ask you to do?"

"I don't know what you mean," Walter replied. "We're returning to Gloucester Greyfriars. When you stole our money we couldn't afford to stay in the city." He fixed Robin with an indignant glare but the young outlaw was in no mood for the friar's lies.

"I asked you where you were going," Robin asked again, cuffing the friar hard across the face and allowing the dazed man to sag to the ground, mewling like an injured cat. "And until you tell us, what remains of your miserable life is going to be filled with pain."

"Stop it!" Hubert pulled away from Little John and brushed past Robin to kneel beside the elder Franciscan, placing a hand reassuringly on Walter's arm. "We're going to the king," the youngster admitted, looking up at the outlaws as the rain streamed down from his thick brown hair into his wide eyes. "The sheriff gave us a letter to take to him."

"What letter?" Little John rumbled, his voice seeming like distant thunder to the sodden young page. "What does it say?"

Hubert shrugged. "The sheriff seeks the king's permission to hang your friend. We're to return with the royal seal."

Robin looked across at his huge friend, not quite believing the youngster's story. Why would de Faucumberg need to ask Edward's permission to hang a common outlaw? It made no sense – as the king's representative in Nottingham and Yorkshire the sheriff had power enough to mete out justice to the likes of Allan-a-Dale.

There had to be more to this letter than Hubert knew.

"Give it to me," Robin demanded, gesturing to Walter. "The letter – give it to me now."

For a moment the friar lay on the soaking grass, a murderous look on his face as he gazed up at the wolf's head, then, nostrils flaring, he grasped Hubert's arm and hauled himself to his feet before reaching inside his cassock.

"Come and get it if you want it."

Before either of the outlaws could react, Brother Walter had pulled out not the letter but a small knife, and pressed it against his novice's throat. "If either of you come any closer I'll kill this little sinner," the friar grated, holding Hubert's arm tightly.

John spat in disgust onto the ground. "Call yourself a man of God? You make me sick. That lad has more of the Holy Spirit in his little finger than you have in your black soul, damn you."

Walter was backing away towards his horse which had wandered from the road and found a thick patch of grass where it stood grazing, uninterested in what was going on behind it.

"You'll not get away from us," Robin vowed. "Give us the letter now or we'll take it from your dead fingers."

Walter shook his head. "I may not be the fastest rider on God's green Earth, but the next village isn't far. I'll be able to make it there before you – the people won't allow two criminals to murder a clergyman."

Robin cursed inwardly. The little prick was right. Yet he knew there was something important in that letter; something that might be the key to more than just helping Allan avoid the gallows.

There was little he or John could do it seemed. Young Hubert's face betrayed confusion and fear, as his companion's blade pressed against his windpipe and they slowly but surely inched their way back towards the big palfrey that still ignored their approach.

Allan was their friend, yes, but they wouldn't endanger the innocent young novice; Robin wasn't sure if the fear-crazed friar would actually harm Hubert but he couldn't take a chance with the boy's life.

The rain, already heavy, suddenly became a hammering torrent and Robin pulled his hood up to keep the deluge from running into his eyes as it bounced off the ground, forming deep brown puddles in a matter of moments.

The Franciscan finally reached his mount and, with a victorious smile, lifted his left hand to take the horse's bridle. As he did so, the palfrey stepped to the side nervously and Walter's foot slipped in the mud.

Robin and John watched in disbelief as a thin red line appeared on young Hubert's neck, stretching from one side to the other. The older friar regained his balance and, not even realising what he'd done, shouted triumphantly and dragged himself atop the palfrey, leaving go of the young boy as he did so.

He kicked his heels into the horse and galloped away with a laugh while the torrential rain turned the wound in Hubert's neck into a grotesque river of crimson and the youngster slumped face first into the grass.

"He's already dead!" Robin screamed as his shocked friend made to help the novice. "Leave him – we need to stop the friar before he reaches Quernendon."

They pulled themselves gracelessly into their saddles – neither was much of a rider – and, with a last, helpless look at the pitiful, soaking corpse in the grass beside them, chased after Brother Walter.

* * *

The cell was cold, despite the time of year, and the floor was sodden with piss and God knew what other filth. The sunlight didn't reach down here under Nottingham Castle but the rats and insects did and, after his beating from Gisbourne, Allan felt like he was going crazy. The smell wasn't an issue any more; he'd grown used to that, which was surprising given how hellish it was. No, the disgusting little sounds of rats and mice and – he shuddered – whatever else was down there with him, *crawling* about the walls and floors of his cell tortured him. He was a minstrel – he wanted to hear the open chords of a gittern, the perfectly tuned strings of a fine citole or the sweet singing voice of a young girl.

"Let me out you bastards!"

Allan groaned and dropped his head into his knees at the crude, echoing shout from one of his fellow prisoners somewhere along the gloomy corridor. If it wasn't dark slithering and scratchings it was half-mad rants from the other poor unfortunates that were imprisoned in the inky blackness alongside him. And now, the ever-present fear that Gibourne might return for round two...

Ah, well, at least he had a cell to himself. Praise God for small mercies.

"In here, dickhead."

The iron-strapped door swung open and Allan shrank back against the wall, drawing his legs up against him, eyes burning in the light of the torch that was carried by one of the sheriff's guardsmen.

An old, old man was pushed into the cramped room, falling to his knees with a whimper, and the door was slammed shut again, the lock clicking into place with the finality of a tomb.

The minstrel said nothing, just stared, unseeing, at the dark spot where his new cell-mate had been deposited. The man breathed heavily but there wasn't enough light to make him out and Allan sighed.

"Stay away from me."

The newcomer shrieked and Allan could hear him scrabbling away on his hands and feet into the far corner.

"Please, don't hurt me."

"Relax, old one. We're all in the same boat down here. Our time will come soon enough."

The harsh breathing softened eventually and Allan, starved for company asked the man's name.

"Edward," came the reply and Allan smiled in the darkness.

"Pleased to meet you, Edward. Shame it wasn't in happier circumstances."

The old man grunted self-pityingly. "You?"

"Allan-a-Dale."

There was another grunt, although this one was more like laughter. "Funny name." The prisoner must have realised laughing at someone down here wasn't a good idea, as he hastily added, "No offence, mind."

"None taken," Allan replied in a voice that suggested the exact opposite. "You might have heard the name before?"

There was silence from the opposite end of the cell and Allan sighed. Everyone knew Robin Hood and Little John and Will Scarlet, thanks in part to Allan's own songs. Yet few knew of the minstrel himself.

"What you down here for?" the old man wondered, his voice growing stronger, more confident as time passed and his companion hadn't stove his head in. "They caught me stealing a sheep. Bloody shepherd claimed he saw me having relations with it but he's a damn liar. I just wanted to eat the woolly bastard, not hump it."

Allan sat in silence for a long while wondering what in the name of Christ the guards had put in his cell with him then, eventually, he shrugged. He was bored, and an audience was an audience.

"I'm a minstrel," he began, his voice rising and seeming to fill the little cell with its power.

"Alright, no need to shout," his new cell-mate grumbled. "I'm only over here."

"I'm also one of Robin Hood's men," Allan went on, in an imperious voice, angry at the man's interruption. It seemed to do the trick – the old sheep... thief, held his peace after an almost imperceptible indrawn breath and the minstrel nodded into the dark in satisfaction before continuing.

"I've always been a musician – I was born to it. My mother and father were part of a big troop that travelled all around the country performing for lords and ladies. Sometimes they even went to France although I must admit I've never been there myself." He coughed, the foetid air clogging his lungs, then went on with his tale.

"We made a decent living and it was a fine life. Better than toiling in the fields that's for sure. I had an older brother, Simon and we'd often perform together, just the two of us, both playing the gittern. We worked out how to play different harmonies and things, you've never heard anything like it before. People loved it."

"How'd you end up in this shit-hole then, if you were so good?" the old man demanded.

"We played in Hull one night, at the lord's manor house. We went down well; everyone loved us. But the lord, I forget his name now... Christ I remember what he looked like though, lanky prick. Wish I could have five moments alone with him... Anyway," Allan growled, remembering where he was, "the lord tried to underpay us. He only gave my father half the agreed fee and, well, our troop didn't take it too well."

Allan sighed heavily, remembering that morning almost as if it had been a week rather than over a decade ago.

"A fight started and the lord was badly injured. My brother and I were in the thick of it – I think it might even have been me that stabbed the nobleman but everything was happening too fast. It was all a blur. We were well outnumbered by the guards though, so we forced our way out of the manor house, the women and children jumping into our wagons and riding them off as fast as they could. We made our way along the road to the next town, pissed off that we'd been underpaid but, God's bollocks, our blood was up from the fight – we'd shown that fucking lord not to mistreat us."

"Did they follow you?"

"Aye," Allan nodded. "Some of them did. The more vicious of them; the ones that couldn't accept defeat at the hands of some minstrel band..." His voice trailed off and there was silence for a time, unbroken even by the skittering of rats. "There wasn't enough of them to stop us and mount a proper attack so they just hit us once from the rear and rode off, shouting and laughing. Me and my brother were riding rearguard – I did my best to fight them off but Simon... he was cut down like wheat under a farmer's scythe."

A prisoner's maniacal laugh echoed along the corridor incongruously and Allan, finally giving in to the fear and stress that had been slowly crushing him ever since Gisbourne's beating, sobbed loudly, burying his face in his legs again.

"My mother and father never forgave me for not saving Simon," he whispered, wiping his eyes with the backs of his hands. "I was only thirteen and he was a grown man but Simon had been their favourite. I could play gittern but I couldn't sing in harmony with the rest of them very well whereas he could do it all. I think my ma wished it had been me that had died... I ended up heading off on my own. Tried to live lawfully but, you know how it is."

The old man slapped something crawling up his calf, feeling it crunch under his palm. He knew Allan's tale was done and wondered what to say after such a depressing story. Finally he cleared his throat and asked the only question he could think of.

"We're going to die here aren't we?"

"Aye," Allan laughed through his tears. "I believe we are."

* * *

The friar wasn't a skilled rider, that much was obvious as the two outlaws chased after him. Yet neither were they, and it was hard going as they urged their tired mounts on through the torrential rain, desperately hoping they'd catch Brother Walter before he reached the safety of Quernendon, a small market town with, undoubtedly, a large tithing to enforce the law...

The sun, already well hidden by the dark grey thunder-heads, had now begun to set and the countryside was a blur of lengthening shadows as the riders neared the town.

"We won't catch him in time," Little John roared over the drumming of hooves and rain.

Robin could see John was right, but he kept his head down, close to his palfrey's neck, and willed the beast onwards, cursing his lack of riding experience. He had his longbow and half-a-dozen arrows tucked into his belt but knew he'd fall off the galloping horse if he tried to use them. They couldn't let the Franciscan escape though – whatever was in the sheriff's letter was vitally important. They *had* to take it from the fleeing clergyman.

Not only that, the wolf's head despaired as he thought of young Hubert, lying dead in the grass, his throat slit like an animal sacrificed to some crazed pagan god. He'd be blamed for it, Robin knew. When tales were told of this day, the minstrels would assume he, the notorious outlaw Robin Hood, had killed the novice.

After all, who would believe the pious friar had torn the young boy's throat open accidentally?

Sometimes a dark reputation was a handy thing to have, but the idea of people seeing him as a murderer of the friendly young novice made Robin seethe and he kicked his heels into his mount's side, willing the big animal onwards.

"We don't know the people in that town," John shouted, waving a big hand forward. "We're not going to catch the little prick in time, and he'll have the law on us once he blurts out his story. We should turn back now."

"No!" Robin replied, his voice whipped away by the wind that tore at them as they flew along the road. "Not until he enters the town. I won't give up."

They continued, gaining on the friar who would occasionally turn in his saddle to look back at them, his face an angry mask as he lashed his feet into his own mount's heaving, steaming, sides, but he was almost there. Almost at the safety of Quernendon.

The town lay beyond a swollen river and Brother Walter laughed wildly as he spotted the bridge that would take him to safety. Then his joy turned to dismay as the pounding hooves of his mount carried him towards the stone structure and he cried out a most unholy curse.

The bridge had collapsed.

The horse raced on towards the damaged structure, the friar unable to decide what he should do. To stop meant certain death at the hands of the pursuing outlaws. Yet the river looked much too wide for his horse to jump across, even if he knew how to make the palfrey perform the feat.

"Christ protect me," he murmured, looking skyward as he kicked his heels in again and gritted his teeth in terror, knowing he had to make it to the other side of the swollen river if he was to survive.

His horse had better sense than Brother Walter though. It dug its shod hooves into the slippery wet ground and slowed to a sharp stop, so abruptly that the Franciscan was thrown forward to land face first in the grass at the edge of the raging water as his pursuers charged up behind him with triumphant howls.

"Where's the letter?" Robin shouted, dropping to the ground and running over to grasp the stunned churchman by the throat. "Give it to me or, so help me God, I'll strip you naked and search your clothes for it."

The friar knew there was no point defying the furious wolf's head now. He pulled the sheriff's letter from its hiding place inside his grey habit, handing it over shakily, his eyes wide with fear.

"You know you killed Hubert?" Robin demanded, shaking the friar viciously. "He's lying dead, face-down in the dirt a mile back along the road. Your knife opened his neck, you evil sack of shit."

The clergyman, already trembling from fear, and the damp that the rains had brought, shook his head in disbelief. He was a moaning, cranky old bastard, he knew that himself, but he was no murderer. He was a man of god, a friar, there was no way he'd ever take the life of another human, even that irritating young novice he'd been saddled with.

"You're lying," he shouted, almost hysterically, the rain running down his face and mingling with the tears of terror that spilled from his red-rimmed eyes. "*You* killed young Hubert, and now seek to lay the blame on me. As if anyone will believe that, you murdering wolf's head."

Robin punched the friar hard in the face, sending the man flying as he broke de Faucumberg's seal and tore open the letter.

Little John dismounted and grabbed Walter by the belt as he tried to scrabble away, sobbing, into the undergrowth by the river's bank. Robin was engrossed in the letter.

The young man had been taught how to read a little by Friar Tuck, but it took him a long time to make any sense of the sheriff's words, and Walter struggled against the giant's implacable hold as the wolf's head read and re-read the parchment in disbelief.

"Well?" John demanded, shaking water from his hair like a great, sodden hound. "What does it say?"

Robin looked up at him with a small smile. "We need to go to London to see the king," he replied. "If it says what I think it does, he has to read this."

John grunted and shook the friar again. "What about him?"

"If we let him go he'll give us away –"

"I won't! I swear in the name of God and all his angels. I won't!"

Robin shook his head sadly, thinking of the Hubert – a mere child – lying dead by the roadside and fixed Brother Walter with a hard stare.

"Take his clothes and valuables so no-one will know who he is. Then throw him in the river."

CHAPTER TWELVE

Although Robin couldn't read all that well, especially the Latin that the sheriff's letter to the king was written in, he was able to make out a few words; enough to make him think the document could be incredibly important to him and his friends.

After they'd stripped the friar of his robe, brass pectoral cross and the coin purse de Faucumberg had given him, Little John had thrown the screaming man into the raging torrent of the River Soar. "If you're so close to our Lord he'll fish you out, or send one of his saints to do it," the giant roared as the skinny white figure was carried away by the swiftly moving waters. "Somehow," he growled to himself as the figure, and its cries of terror, receded into the distance, "I doubt God will be much interested in you."

They made their way back to young Hubert's pitiful corpse and, with heavy hearts, stripped him too of his clothes and valuables before carrying his body back to the river and tossing him into the churning waters. They watched in silence, heads bowed in prayer, as the boy's pale, lifeless cadaver was washed away.

"We'll stop at the town," Robin said, climbing back onto his horse which looked fed-up as the rain streamed down its long face. "Dry out, get some food and, maybe, buy ourselves Franciscan friar's outfits since these ones are too small..."

John mounted his own palfrey, throwing his leader a look of disbelief. "You think the two of us will pass for friars? We're much bigger than any of the pious bastards I've ever seen. No-one will believe it."

Robin shrugged, kicking his mount into an easy canter back onto the road south. "A lot of old soldiers – sick of the death and killing and looking to atone for the things they've done in their lives – become monks or friars. Just because we haven't seen anyone as big as us doesn't mean much. Neither of us is very well-travelled."

John shook his great head like a hound, rain spraying off him. "Maybe," he conceded. "Perhaps Will or Tuck could tell us more if they were here."

They made good time, only stopping for a short while to burn the incriminating Francscican cassocks, and reached Quernendon by early evening. The rain had stopped and the spring sun had even made an appearance, drying the worst of the damp from their clothes although it was sinking into the horizon as they rode past the lone gate-guard and into the town.

"No riding in the streets," the guard, a middle-aged man with a head cleanly shaven, shouted at them, nodding in satisfaction as the two men dismounted with apologetic waves.

"We seek an inn," Robin said to the man.

"Mercenaries are you?"

The outlaw nodded, noting the older man's look of appraisal. "Aye, on our way south to seek work for one of the lords in the big city."

"Used to be a sell-sword myself, in my younger days," the guard replied. "Before I met my wife..." He shook his head with a rueful smile. "But you lads don't want to hear about my troubles, you look like you could do with a few ales and a warm fire." He pointed along the street to the west of the town. "Follow the road there, not far along it you'll find the Hermit's Arms. Stupid name, I know, but the landlord's wife brews a fine ale and there's a stable for your mounts."

The outlaws waved their gratitude and Robin tossed the man a silver coin for his trouble which the guard caught and bit into before grinning and turning back to watch the gate.

The Hermit's Arms proved to be a goodly-sized establishment with two stories and, as the guard had promised, a well-appointed stable where they left their palfreys in the care of a young lad no more than ten years old. Another small coin was enough for the boy to promise he'd take special care of the horses as Robin followed John into the inviting common room of the inn.

A serving girl warmed a couple of ales for them using the pokers that sat by the fire for the purpose, took payment for a room and promised to bring them some of the stew they could smell cooking.

The pair then spent an enjoyable night in the tavern. It was hard to believe, but Robin realised this was the first extended period of time the two friends had ever really shared on their own together.

In the past two years they had often fished by the River Calder, sat by the camp-fire sharing stories and robbed rich merchants in each other's company but there had always been one or more of the other outlaw gang somewhere nearby, and the threat of capture or death at the hands of the law hanging over them.

They felt safe here in the inn though.

The ale was indeed good, the fire cosy and bright, and the companions enjoyed a fine evening before making their way to the room they'd paid for. Once there they collapsed, exhausted, on the crude but comfortable beds and forgot about their troubles for a time.

In the morning, they downed some more of the landlord's ale to take the edge off their hangovers and left, with a wave to the man and his wife, who furnished them with bread and hard-boiled eggs for their breakfast.

The inn-keeper had pointed them in the direction of the nearest tailor with a puzzled look on his face, but he knew better than to ask questions of guests. Sometimes it was safer not to know certain things...

The outfitter was, like the inn-keeper, surprised when the two enormous, hard-looking men had walked into his shop and asked to buy the biggest grey cassocks he sold.

"Are they for," the man eyed them suspiciously, "yourselves?"

"Aye, they are," Little John nodded. Despite his great size, the giant had an open, honest face and his smile could disarm almost anyone. "We're heading to Manchester to visit a friend of ours. He heard a rumour we'd become friars so we thought we'd turn up dressed in cassocks to see the look on his face." He laughed, the infectious sound filling the small premises. "Can you imagine? Us? Franciscans? It's hilarious!"

The man smiled, not entirely convinced by the story, but the younger of the two men pulled a purse from his belt and opened it to fish out some coins. Clearly these two men – soldiers from the look of them – had earned enough money to throw it away on something as frivolous as a jest. And who was he to care who he sold his wares to? Their silver was good as any man's.

Sizing up Little John the tailor nodded and slipped into the back of the shop where he could be heard rummaging around for a short while. Eventually, he returned with two massive dark grey cassocks, shaking them out and holding them high up to show their length.

"They look ideal," Robin nodded approvingly. "We weren't sure if you'd have any big enough to fit us."

The man held one against John's great frame with a practised eye, murmuring to himself. "Oh, yes," he said. "Clergymen come in all shapes and sizes, they're not all thin old men. That being said," he looked up at John again, "I've never seen one as tall as you. But then, I've never seen *anyone* as tall as you; I'm afraid this will be rather short. You realise that, to complete the disguise, you'll have to shave your heads?"

John threw Robin a venomous look at the idea of wearing the clergyman's hairstyle but his young leader simply shrugged and grinned. The tailor was right – they'd need to lose their unruly thick hair.

They paid for the garments, promising to tell the tailor how their trick worked if they were ever back in Quernendon again before collecting their horses from the Hermit's Arms and riding south again.

To London. And the king.

* * *

"Get that filth cleared, you two!" The dean hooted at Tuck who had, again, been sent to clear out the latrines with his companion for the morning; Osferth, the monk that had helped Edwin open the door when he'd first returned to the priory.

The big friar ignored the mocking laughter from the prior's right-hand man, using his shovel to throw the human waste out of the building and down into the ditch far below, wishing Henry of Elmstow was lying suffocating underneath the mound of shit.

Not only had the former outlaw been made to do the filthiest, most menial tasks since his return to Lewes, but he'd also been told to take his meals – reduced in size under de Monte Martini's orders no doubt – with the novices, and the Benedictine monks had clearly been told not to converse with him. That was the worst penance; he didn't mind shovelling shit, or sitting with the youngsters, or even having less to eat than he was used to... no, it was the lack of companionship that really got to him. He was a sociable fellow and some of the brothers here had been friends of his before he'd joined Robin Hood's gang.

At least today he had someone to share the work with. Brother Osferth must have annoyed the prior too, to be given a task like this, although the younger man hadn't said a word to him since they'd started work that morning.

With a grunt that was half a sigh Tuck threw out another spadeful of watery, stinking muck and resolved not to let the prior grind him down. God had placed de Monte Martini's missing holy relic in Tuck's hand for a purpose he believed; he was meant to return here for some reason.

He'd just have to ignore the harsh treatment and pray the prior got bored with tormenting him soon.

As he worked he contemplated the idea of returning north to rejoin Robin and the rest of his outlaw friends but he rejected the notion sadly. His body was past it – the illness he'd suffered the previous summer after Sir Guy of Gisbourne had shot and nearly drowned him had taken its toll. Although he'd put some weight back on over the months, he now *felt* old; his bones ached. It was a hard thing to accept but it was true. The noisome fumes in the latrine made it difficult for him to breathe too, even through the damp rag, and he'd recently developed a racking cough that occasionally saw him bent double with the force of it.

His days of living in the greenwood were over; that chapter of his life was done. He knew when he returned here that the prior – an unpleasant man at the best of times but with a grudge against Tuck to boot – would make his life hard. It appeared the prior's steward had also made it his personal task to mete out Tuck's penance.

He mouthed silent prayers to God, sweating freely from the hard work in the confined, foetid space and asked for the Lord's strength and guidance.

Or at least a few days rest from shovelling human waste...

* * *

Marjorie avoided Matilda after their falling out. Any time the older girl tried to talk to her, to set things right, Marjorie would ignore her and leave to collect berries, or firewood, or flowers to decorate the house. Anything to get away from her sister-in-law.

It couldn't go on forever though. Matilda came into the Hood's house one morning when Martha and John were out, closing the door behind her and blocking it with her body.

"I'm sorry, Marjorie. Truly, I am. You have no idea how stressful it is trying to finish your work on time while watching an infant that has no sense of danger."

Marjorie glared at her, but said nothing.

"Look, you have to stop trying to be something you're not. Accept yourself for who you really are. Aye, you're no good at hunting – so what? Not many local girls are. Why should you be any different?"

Marjorie sighed and sat down in one of the chairs beside the trestle table the family used to eat their meals at. It was a fine table, well-made, and the family folded it away every evening to save space in the small dwelling.

"I have to be good at something," the girl said. "Everyone is good at something."

Matilda sat down next to her, relieved to have finally broken the barrier between them.

"You're young yet. I know, I'm not all that much older than you, and when I was your age I wasn't sure what I wanted to do with myself either. The thing is, life has a habit of leading you wherever it is you need to go – wherever you're needed."

Marjorie looked unconvinced as Matilda forged on.

"You're not a hunter, and you'll never be the greatest sword-fighter in England, right. But neither will I. Look at you – the training you've been doing has toughened you up – put meat on your bones. It will come in handy one day, just wait and see."

They sat in silence for a time but it wasn't an awkward silence. Their old friendship was back, and Marjorie was glad of it.

"I have to get back," Matilda said, standing up and smiling at her young companion. "We still haven't completed that order for the merchant. My da keeps finding loose fletchings and making me redo them. Feels like my fingers will be nothing but bloody bones by the time we get the order all done."

She opened the door, sunlight streaming into the gloomy house. "Come over to mine later – Arthur's been asking after you."

Marjorie smiled and promised she would visit sometime, but, when the door had closed again and she was left by herself she stared, unseeing, into space, wondering where her life was going.

She was only young but she felt very old. She'd seen so much in her short life and it got to her sometimes. She had to admit, though – training with Matilda had made her stronger in every way. She liked the feeling; enjoyed the sense of purpose the exercises gave her.

"Time to get back to work."

She stood up, feeling not quite as if she'd found her true calling but realising life would go on whether she wallowed in self-pity or chose to get out and make the most of things.

Matilda was right – life would find a use for her eventually.

CHAPTER THIRTEEN

The journey south took Robin and Little John the next three days but they enjoyed the ride despite its ultimate purpose. Spring was in full bloom so the fields were green with barley and rye, the grass and foliage that blanketed the countryside was thick and lush and the sun cast a warm light on the countryside meaning the night they camped out was fairly comfortable.

"Aye, England truly is a green and beautiful land," Robin said, watching the unhurried passage of a large black and orange butterfly with a contented smile.

"It is," John agreed. "When it's not pissing down or some ugly forester's trying to smash your teeth into the back of your skull."

"I've never been this far south before. In fact, before I was outlawed I don't think I'd ever even left Yorkshire."

John nodded. It wasn't uncommon for people to spend their whole lives within their own county – there wasn't any need for a peasant or yeoman to travel to a city and, even if they wanted to, the price of an inn was enough to discourage most.

"I've been here before," Little John said, looking around thoughtfully. "At least, I seem to have a memory of some of the landmarks we've passed today. My family travelled to the capital once, when I was very young, on a pilgrimage. My grandmother was ill, and the priest in St Michael's suggested we come away down to pray for her in St Paul's Cathedral. I don't remember much about it to be honest."

Robin was impressed that his friend had travelled so far in his life. "Did your prayers work? Did your grandmother recover from her illness?"

"No. She died a week later." The giant shook his head ruefully then his smile returned. "Waste of bloody time that pilgrimage."

It was unusual for John to mention his family, even now that they'd been friends for a couple of years, and Robin wanted to take the opportunity to find out something of the big man's past.

"Did you never travel with Amber and wee John?"

"Nah. My wife was a maid for one of the merchants in Hathersage – still is, in fact. She couldn't just take weeks off to travel to no good purpose." John's eyes stared fixedly on the road ahead as thoughts of his wife and son came to him. He sighed heavily. "I have more than enough money now that I could travel anywhere I like. Even Rome, or one of those other famous old places the minstrels sing about. I bet John would have a great time climbing those big monuments – you remember the ones Allan goes on about? The colloso... collosem or something I think one's called." His hand disappeared inside the grey cassock and touched the cheap amulet he wore on a thong around his neck that had been a gift from Amber long ago. "I have all the money to do what I want with my family and no chance to do it."

"You will," Robin assured him, meeting the giant's eyes. "I promise you. Somehow we'll win a pardon and you can take your family to Rome."

John grinned and looked back at the road ahead. "Ach, my wife would be just as happy travelling to Sheffield to visit her sister. Speaking of which, how's young Marjorie? Not so young now I suppose, she'll be nearly a woman eh?"

"Aye," Robin said, thinking fondly of his younger sibling. "She's well enough, although she'll never be as sturdy as my ma, or even Matilda. I expect my da will be looking for a husband for her soon enough – hopefully whoever it is looks after her. They'd fucking better or else..."

The pair fell into a somewhat maudlin silence as their thoughts lingered on loved ones far away and their mounts carried them towards the city. The light began to fail before they could get there though, so, as the sun slowly set and the road became treacherous for their mounts, they chose to spend the night in another small town, not that far from the capital's walls.

Before entering the place they found a small stream and, using their eating knives, shaved one another's heads in the same way Friar Tuck did, with the crown bald and the back, front and sides left as they were.

"You look like a right fucking oaf," John giggled, squinting at his friend in the dim light while running a hand over his own scalp and looking down at the bloodstained fingers ruefully.

Robin laughed. "Aye, I bet I do," he agreed, trying vainly to see his reflection in the stream before cupping some of the chill waters and using it to wash the crimson from the pores of his own head. "But at least we look more like friars now. Wait, you're not finished, you need to shave that beard of yours."

"My beard? I've been growing this for years."

Robin grinned. "Can't be a friar with a beard."

When they were finished even their friends wouldn't have recognised them straight away and, in Little John's case, maybe not at all.

They made their way into the town and, since they had coin enough to pay for decent lodgings were able to spend a comfortable evening in the local inn's common room. There was plenty of meat and ale to fill their bellies, but the overnight delay irritated the pair as they wanted to reach the king as soon as possible.

What they would do when they came face to face with England's monarch they weren't quite sure yet. Would they even make it in to see the king, or would they be recognised as outlaws and cut down before they even made it past the first guardsmen? Even if they did convince the guards that they were clergymen would they be able to fool the king too? Or would they be found out as soon as they opened their uneducated mouths?

Only time would tell but Robin was confident, as always. All would be well...

They were up before dawn the next day, even before the cockerel – which the landlord had promised was a perfect time-keeper – had crowed to signal the sun's ascent into the eastern sky. After bothering the inn-keep for some bread and cheese to break their fast they set off at a brisk pace, only stopping to hide their bulky weapons in a thick clump of bushes a little way off the road – they wanted to look like clergymen, not soldiers after all. Then, remounting they pushed their horses hard and reached the capital city's gates while it was still morning.

London.

Both outlaws had the hoods drawn up on the grey cloaks that they wore in what they hoped was the Franciscan style and, along with the pectoral crosses they'd taken from Hubert and Walter to hang around their necks, they looked like nothing more than normal – if extremely well-built – friars to the gate guards who watched them pass without a word of challenge.

"We should visit the Franciscan... church or priory or whatever the hell they call it," Little John murmured as they walked their mounts through the unbelievably crowded streets of London. "It's what real friars would do."

Robin snorted making his horse glare back at him with a bulging eye. "We're not real friars, even if we have spent so many months living with Tuck," he said, pulling on his palfrey's bridle. "We wouldn't know how to act like them and the Franciscans would see through our disguise in a moment. No, our best bet is to head straight for the royal palace and seek an audience with the king. We can deliver our letter and be on our way again before the day's out."

Little John smiled although Robin could see the stress of their situation written all over the giant's newly-shaven face. "Aye, straight back to Nottingham to free Allan without a hitch. Piece of piss."

The companions had never seen so many people gathered in one place: foreign merchants dressed in brightly coloured clothes chattered to one another in strange languages; carts laden with eggs and cheese rattled past; workers drove noisy sheep along the road to market and street vendors hailed them continually, with cries of "Hot peascods," and "Sheep's feet, come an' get 'em." Their mouths watered at the sight of the laden trays but they were in too much of a hurry to stop.

They had no idea of the layout of the city or how to get to Westminster Palace but there were enough people to ask directions, and, once they grew nearer, the imposing bulk of the place stood high above any other building in the vicinity.

Although their initial plan had been to find someone to read Sir Henry de Faucumberg's letter to the king that they'd taken from Brother Walter, in the end Robin had decided against it. Showing the parchment to anyone else would surely draw unwanted attention to them – no real friar or monk would ask a layman to read a letter for them. Especially a letter about the capture of a member of the notorious Robin Hood's band.

Robin felt sure that he'd picked up the gist of the document himself anyway, and he wasn't about to place their lives in danger just to fill in the few Latin blanks that he couldn't make sense of.

"So tell me, then." John grumbled as they neared the royal palace. "What you think the letter says. You've been keeping it a secret this whole time."

Robin looked around in wonder at the enormous stone walls and imposing architecture that surrounded them and threw his big mate a happy grin, his teeth flashing from beneath the cassock's hood.

"I believe the sheriff is telling the king that he's captured Allan, but, if I have it right, he's also complaining about Sir Guy of Gisbourne's treatment of the people of Yorkshire."

John whistled quietly. He hadn't expected de Faucumberg to speak out against the king's own bounty hunter. "I have to admit," he said, "the sheriff comes across as a decent man. Even if he did double-cross us the other winter. And Gisbourne has been even more of prick lately... What d'you think the king'll do?"

Robin shrugged. "What do I know about the workings of royalty? Hopefully the king will listen to his sheriff and call Gisbourne back here before sending him overseas or to Scotland or, well, anywhere other than Barnsdale."

"I take it you have a plan, or at least some idea of what to say once we're in front of the king?" John asked, raising a bushy eyebrow questioningly. "What about the letter's broken seal? How will you explain that?"

Robin shrugged again and laughed. They'd reached the palace and nerves grasped his insides but he pushed them aside, knowing he had to appear outwardly calm or the king's guardsmen would see through their outrageous disguise. "Don't worry, of course I have a plan – don't I always?"

"Aye, always," John agreed, lowering his voice as they approached the gates. "Most of the time they're crazy and suicidal though. I hope this time you have something a bit better because if the king doesn't believe our story, there'll be no escape."

The huge, cold, grey walls loomed high above them, staggering them with their sheer size and Robin felt a lump of bile forming in his throat. He coughed to try and clear it but it stuck, lodged there and he wished they'd stopped at a tavern for a few ales before coming here. At least if he was drunk he wouldn't feel so frightened.

But it was too late for that. They'd reached the great wooden gates to the palace and there was no going back.

The guard captain looked them up and down, taking in their great size and the grey habits they wore with a look of interest on his face before nodding respectfully.

"State your business with the king, brother friars."

Robin took a deep breath, not even noticing the uncomfortable phlegm had disappeared as an icy calm came over him and he began to tell the guard their tale.

* * *

"Bugger this, and bugger the prior."

Tuck smiled at Brother Osferth, his companion for the morning – again – and nodded sad agreement, glad that the fellow was feeling more talkative today. "Aye, God forgive me, but I'm beginning to wish I'd never come back here." He lifted another armful of logs which Osferth was splitting with an old axe and stacked them with the rest of the pile they'd been working on since dawn.

While the rest of the monks had been making their way to the early morning service of Lauds Prior de Monte Martini's dean, Henry, had waved Tuck and Osferth aside and told them the prior needed firewood chopped as there were important visitors coming from London that day. It was obviously nonsense; Tuck had seen the vast stores of fuel that were piled up by the priory's east wall, so even if there *were* visitors they didn't need any more wood for the hearth in the chapter-house but he hadn't bothered arguing with the dean.

Osferth, on the other hand, complained loudly and angrily about missing his morning devotions. The dean simply shrugged and told them it was the prior's orders and they'd better get on with it if they didn't want to miss their dinner as well.

A sharp crack filled the air as the younger monk hefted the axe again before wiping the sheen of sweat from his brow and sitting down on the pile of uncut logs with a heavy, angry sigh.

Osferth was in his mid-twenties, although he looked much younger, and had an open, pleasant face which fitted his personality perfectly. The other monks in Lewes Priory liked the man, but he had a problem taking orders and it had led de Monte Martini to mark him down as a troublemaker.

"God works in mysterious ways," he replied to Tuck, who grunted non-committally. "We all heard about you joining those outlaws up north. Never thought I'd see you here again but... God must have led you back here for a purpose."

Tuck allowed himself to slump down on the grass beside Osferth, a hacking cough bursting from his lips as he did so. "What purpose?" he growled. "To cut logs? To shovel filth from the latrines? To listen to the babbling of novices?" He coughed again, bending over until his head was almost on the ground before wiping his mouth and glaring up at his companion. "To eat even less than I did as a wolf's head in the snow shrouded forests of Yorkshire? Is that my purpose?" He shook his tonsured head irritably. "God be praised then, I've found my true calling."

Osferth smiled before standing up and lifting the blunt axe again. "Someone should really sharpen this bloody thing," he muttered before he placed another piece of timber on the block and brought the weapon down on it, splitting it neatly in two. "At least you're not with the outlaws any more. Once the sheriff knows where they are he'll make short work of them. This might be a harder work than we'd like but it's better than being killed."

Tuck hauled himself to his feet with a grunt, clutching at the sharp pain in his chest where Sir Guy of Gisbourne's crossbow bolt had almost ended his life the previous summer. "The sheriff's been after Robin and the lads for a long time now – years!" He smiled. "They know how to stay one step ahead of de Faucumberg and his men."

Osferth continued chopping wood in a mechanical fashion, occasionally wiping his brow or blowing a curse from dry lips. "Aye, maybe," he finally agreed. "But the prior's information will let the lawmen finally catch up with Hood."

Tuck's head spun round and he almost dropped the pile of wood he was placing neatly amongst the rest of the pile. "What information?"

The axeman's eyes flicked up at the note of surprise in Tuck's voice and he held the implement still for a moment. "You know – the location of Hood's camp."

Tuck dropped the firewood onto the ground and moved across to stand before Osferth, his eyes blazing. "What are you talking about?" he demanded. "De Monte Martini doesn't know where they are. How could he?"

Osferth stepped back, unnerved by the threat of violence that he saw reflected in Tuck's normally jovial features. "I don't know how he found out the location of their camp, but he did. He sent one of the brothers north to Nottingham just the other day, to tell the sheriff. Did you not know?"

Tuck sagged back onto the stone wall that surrounded the priory, his mind whirling. He hadn't heard anything about this, probably because he'd been made to take his meals with the novices and the other friars had been warned against talking to him by the prior.

"Hood and his men are probably all dead by now," Osferth grunted, swinging the axe to split another log. "I'm sorry," he said, as he placed another, fresh piece of wood onto the block and stepped back to half that one too. "I know you were close to some of them."

Tuck suddenly lunged forward and grabbed the Benedictine's right arm in a grip that shocked the younger man with its strength. "When? When did the messenger leave for Nottingham?"

The axeman shook his head. "I don't remember. A day or two ago I think. Brother Cedric it was. One of the –"

"– Younger men." Tuck finished for him. "Aye, I know who Cedric is."

The big friar leant against the wall and closed his eyes, his mind racing. What was he to do? His friends might be dead already. And yet... What was his life now? To be used and abused by de Monte Martini, a greedy, grasping man not worthy of the title of prior? Surely this wasn't God's plan for him.

No, it was a sign!

Tuck saw it clearly now. He'd known as soon as he'd set eyes on the long-lost holy relic back in Yorkshire with the outlaws that it had been given to him for a reason. He'd been stoic in the face of the prior's harsh treatment but he'd been unable to fathom the divine purpose in it all. Why would God send him back here simply to be treated like a serf?

Now it was clear. He'd been brought here to save Robin and his friends, not that damned prior.

"Brother Cedric only has a couple of days start," he said, turning to meet Osferth's gaze. "I can still reach Nottingham before him." He pushed himself off the wall and, firewood forgotten, hurried past his surprised companion, a fiery gleam lighting his eyes from within. He knew what his purpose was now, and chopping firewood or shovelling shit was not part of it.

"Wait. Wait!"

Tuck waved a hand irritably as Osferth chased after him.

"Stop, Robert!" The younger man shouted behind him. "Let me come with you."

That halted Tuck, although only for a moment. "You can't come with me," he retorted, shaking his head as he hurried back into the priory and along the gloomy corridor to his cell. "I'll be returning to a life as a wolf's head – an outlaw. A criminal that any man can cut down with church and state's blessing!"

Osferth caught up to him and fell into step by his side, a boyish grin on his face.

"So you say," he laughed. "But I'm no outlaw; I can go where I like and I'm coming too. It has to be better than this."

Tuck hurried along the corridor shaking his head. Osferth seemed touched but this was a step too far even for him. "You can't just leave your life here; what about your vows? Besides, the prior will send word to every Benedictine in the country about what we've done."

Osferth kept pace beside the older man for a moment then cocked an eyebrow at the older man in bemusement. "What we've done?"

"Aye," Tuck grinned. "That ungodly womaniser doesn't deserve to keep the relic I returned to him. With the Lord's grace I'm going to steal it and take it back to Brandesburton, where it belongs."

* * *

Another tiresome day listening to men prattle on about minor matters that, to them, seemed like grand problems but ultimately left King Edward II bored and irritated and watching the shadows lengthen as the sun moved across the sky outside, wishing it would move faster so he could get out and see his friends.

Sir Hugh Despenser the younger was his friend, and, as the king's chamberlain, had accompanied him on this trip to Westminster Palace. He was glad his closest friend and adviser was there; although they had put down the rebellion a year earlier, things had not been as peaceful as the king would have wished. The Scots had continued to be a problem and even Sir Andrew Harclay, who'd led Edward's forces so effectively against the Contrariants at the Battle of Boroughbridge, had taken it upon himself to treat with the Bruce. The king had ordered Harclay arrested and taken to London where he was executed for his treasonous actions. Thankfully, the Scots had, provisionally, agreed to a truce which had been thrashed out mostly by Sir Hugh himself and would hopefully sign it within the next few weeks.

For the first time in his reign, King Edward could rule without the threat of war in the north hanging over him. But the defection of Harclay rankled badly and Edward felt a black depression come upon him every time he thought of his formerly loyal general.

He was a lonely king, and he smiled at the younger Despenser, glad he was there with him. His wife, Queen Isabella, hated Sir Hugh, but Edward cared little for that – they hadn't shared the marital bed for months and had never been particularly close anyway, despite their four children. When the rebels had forced the king to exile Despenser two years earlier Edward had continued to support his friend financially and, as soon as possible, allowed Sir Hugh to return and reclaim his lands, titles, and position as his closest adviser.

Like Piers Gaveston before him, the younger Despenser was loved by Edward but their friendship didn't sit well with the people of England. Damn them all to hell, a king needed someone that he could trust, why couldn't they accept that? It wasn't as if his confidante and adviser was incompetent – on the contrary, both Hugh and his father, also called Hugh, were capable and ambitious men who had proven their worth to the crown, even in the face of the murderous hostility of the rebel magnates.

Still, there didn't seem to be much Sir Hugh could do about the seemingly endless line of irritating petitioners that waited outside the grand chamber. Edward would just need to get on with things until he and his friend could move on to more interesting pursuits.

"You look in ill humour, sire," Sir Hugh noted, a small smile playing on his thin lips.

"Do you blame me? This is interminable."

"Well, I think you'll enjoy receiving at least a couple of your visitors today." The chamberlain grinned and gestured at the line of petitioners who stood queueing to meet the king. Behind a small, balding man in ridiculously extravagant clothing stood two of the biggest friars the king had ever seen.

"They bring word from Sir Henry de Faucumberg, Sheriff of Nottingham and Yorkshire." Sir Hugh muttered.

Edward watched the clergymen as the bald man was announced and approached the throne, his eyes taking in their impressive physiques which even the shapeless grey cassocks couldn't hide. Sir Hugh was right, these two promised to be much more interesting than the usual mumbling, nervous nobles he had to deal with. Like the little fop that knelt before him now.

Edward sighed. He'd have to deal with this one before he could find out who the huge friars were. He forced what he hoped was a reassuring smile onto his handsome face and gestured at the supplicant before him. "Rise and state your case, my good man."

CHAPTER FOURTEEN

The audience room was astonishing. If Robin and John had been impressed by the architecture and sheer grandeur of the capital city before, they were left open-mouthed by the sight of the king's reception chamber.

There was, of course, a high-backed throne, although it wasn't as large or as ornate as Robin expected. It looked rather comfortable in fact, and the wolf's head supposed it had to be, if the king was going to spend extended periods in it dealing with his courtiers.

The walls were lavishly decorated with paintings and tapestries shot through with gold and silver which caught any light and shone beautifully. There were weapons – ceremonial of course although they would doubtless prove as deadly as any other if wielded in anger – displayed in stands in the corners of the room and even the table the king and his advisers sat behind looked as if it had been hewn from one great living piece of oak, with gargoyles and religious motifs carved delicately into the legs and corners.

In short, the room was stunning.

The two outlaws, hunched and hooded in their grey robes, waited in line behind those others who had come to petition the monarch. A wealthy merchant complaining about the activities of pirates in the waters off the coast of Cornwall; a bailiff from Derbyshire pleading for help with a gang of violent outlaws that were plaguing the area; a group of farmers from Lincolnshire demanding something be done about their lord who took too much grain from them in tax and a variety of others, all seeking the king's aid.

Edward looked utterly bored by the whole thing, only occasionally sitting up in his finely carved chair to listen intently when someone's story caught his interest. For the most part he played with the cuffs of his embroidered sleeves and seemed on the point of falling fast asleep. His advisers at least seemed interested; one man with a neatly-trimmed beard sat at the king's right hand, smiling and raising his eyebrows in consternation whenever a petitioner appeared to be upset, but it was clear nothing of any real importance was happening at court that day.

The petitioners took their turn to state their case and, depending on the outcome, passed Robin and John either grinning in triumph or muttering about the king's inattention. John fidgeted nervously as they waited their turn, but Robin stood stock still, taking in everything that was going on to make sure he knew how to address England's most powerful man.

"Pull your hoods down, brothers," a footman hissed in annoyance at the two would-be Franciscans as their time to address the throne approached. "You can't meet the king with your faces hidden."

Robin swivelled his head to meet Little John's wide eyes and the pair pulled back the cowls, revealing their tonsured heads. The footman that had reprimanded them took an involuntary step backwards, the sight of the young, hard faces giving the huge friars a somewhat sinister, threatening look. Had he been manning the gates when this pair had arrived he would have turned them away, but it was too late for that. The man in the line before them, a magistrate from Norwich seeking authority from Edward to seize the lands of a troublesome local baron, stated his case successfully and was waved away, smiling like a sailor in a whorehouse.

It was time to meet the king.

The footman stepped back, warily watching the two massive, grey robed, friars who approached the throne and knelt respectfully.

"You are Franciscans?" The greybeard on the king's left asked politely, his eyes taking in the unusual sight before him as Robin and John nodded. "State your names, and your business here today."

"Brother Hubert –"

"– and Brother Walter," Robin broke in, finishing the introduction and rising at a gesture from the old adviser at the king's side. "From Gloucester Greyfriars." He made the sign of the cross but kept his head bowed rather than meeting Edward's stare and fished inside the grey cassock to retrieve Sir Henry de Faucumberg's letter. The competent, professional-looking soldiers behind the king moved forward, pole-arms raised threateningly as the tall young friar with his enormous archer's shoulders put a hand inside his robe, but Robin produced the rolled-up parchment with a small smile and the guards relaxed.

A servant hurried forward to take the proffered letter and moved to kneel before the king, head down and hand outstretched. Edward, eyes still fixed on the two enormous clergymen before him took the rolled up parchment and finally looked down at it with a frown.

"We bring word from Sir Henry de Faucumberg, sire," Robin said, pleased to hear his voice ring out strong and true despite the nerves that gripped his insides. He could feel the sweat pooling uncomfortably under his armpits and he sensed Little John tensing beside him, ready to fight for his life should the king query the fact the letter's seal had been broken.

"This," Edward growled, looking up and meeting Robin's gaze, "is from the Sheriff of Nottingham and Yorkshire?"

"Aye, lord king, it is. He tasked us with delivering it into your hands. I can only apologise – we encountered some... trouble, on the way here. A pair of craven outlaws tried to rob us. They broke the seal on the letter although, needless to say they couldn't even read." He smiled slightly, confidently. "Brother Hubert and I managed to take back the letter and... chase them off."

The atmosphere in the hall had become strangely tense and Robin prayed silently that it was simply because he and John were much bigger than most other clergymen.

King Edward placed the parchment on the table in front of him without unrolling it and walked around to stand before them.

The outlaws tried to remain calm. This was new: the king hadn't moved out of his comfortable throne all day until now yet here he was, striding over to look into Little John's eyes.

"Stand up straight." As Edward spoke the guards moved in close, weapons held ready should either of the big friars seek to attack the monarch.

Little John's eyes flicked uncertainly towards Robin but he knew better than to refuse a command from England's ruler so he pushed his shoulders back and raised himself to his full height of almost seven feet.

There were gasps from the guards and from the petitioners lined up behind them as they took in the great size of the man – the friar – before them.

King Edward, though, grinned and stepped in closer, to stand so near to the giant outlaw that John could smell the delicate flower-scent that the king daubed on himself each morning.

"You're a big lad," Edward smiled approvingly, using his hand to mark his own height against Little John. The king wasn't a small man by any means – in fact he was just as tall as Robin, who watched the bizarre interchange with one eyebrow raised in surprise – but he only came up to John's neck. "How tall are you?"

John shrugged. "I don't know, sire. I've never measured myself."

The king grinned appreciatively and turned his eyes on Robin. "Friars, eh? I'm sure you did chase off those outlaws," he said, his voice full of wonder. "Excellent!" He returned to his throne and sat down, still smiling happily as he lifted the letter from Sir Henry de Faucumberg again. "I've never seen friars as big as you two before but I suppose you were soldiers at one time before renouncing the warrior's way of life and taking service with Christ. Good. I'd wager any more outlaws in my forests will think twice before they try and rob the pair of you once word gets around!"

Robin let out a nervous breath as the king tore open the rolled-up parchment without inspecting the seal too closely and began to read.

He grunted as he read before, at last, he snorted with laughter and handed the letter to the greybeard by his side.

"How did you two come to be de Faucumberg's messengers? And who is this Allan-a-Dale? What do you know of him?"

The king grilled Robin for a long time, the tall young 'friar' responding to the questions apparently truthfully and thoroughly entertaining the monarch with the tale even as the other petitioners lined up behind them muttered in annoyance at the delay in stating their own cases.

When he reached the end of his story the king looked at Robin thoughtfully, his eyes moving to Little John who tried to stand still but couldn't help fidgeting every now and again like a child apprentice under his master's harsh gaze.

"Do you know what the rest of de Faucumberg's letter says?" the monarch finally asked.

The outlaws shook their heads and Robin replied. "No, lord."

Edward grunted. "No, I don't suppose you would, would you?" He looked at the counsellor at his right hand who shrugged and shook his head, not sure what the king wanted to hear from him.

"The sheriff wants me to recall Sir Guy of Gisbourne. Apparently my bounty hunter has become something of a liability. And a violent one at that." The king threw the parchment onto the table irritably. "De Faucumberg needs a kick up the arse. You two will return to Nottingham with my reply, yes?"

"Of course, sire," Robin nodded deferentially. "We were to return there to continue our mission anyway. It would be our pleasure – nay, our *honour,* to carry your word back to the sheriff."

Edward smiled and muttered, "God be praised," before turning to face his steward who sat taking notes at a small table in the left-hand corner of the huge hall. "Make sure the good brothers are rewarded for their service to the crown," he told the man. "A donation to – where did you say you were from? Yes, Gloucester. Send a donation of fifty pounds to Custos de Bromley on my behalf. In the meantime, take a letter to Sir Henry in Nottingham."

Robin and John bowed their heads gratefully to the king for the donation to 'their' friary as the monarch dictated his reply to the sheriff before the steward placed the parchment in an envelope, dripped a great red candle onto it and Edward pressed his ring into the soft wax.

"Sire," Robin took the letter with a respectful bow. "We will gladly carry this to Sir Henry but... I fear he may not like your reply and..."

The king met the young man's eyes and nodded in understanding. "And he will blame you two. I see." He waved over to the steward again. "Write another letter for the brothers to carry – one that makes it very clear they are under my protection and should be treated with all the respect loyal subjects of mine deserve. Now..." England's ruler smiled at Robin and John. "You two have livened up these dull proceedings and I thank you for it, but you may go. Return to Nottingham and my sheriff. I pray we meet again some day for I've enjoyed your company. Do you row?"

The question was directed at Little John who shook his head. "No, sire, I much prefer dry land."

"That's a pity," the king sighed, pressing his ring again into the wax of the letter of protection his steward had written out for them and looking at the huge man in the grey Franciscan robe appreciatively again. "You would have made a fine addition to my team."

He waved them away with a smile and the pair walked from the room as fast as they could, trying not to appear too relieved to have survived the royal meeting.

"That went well," Little John murmured as they passed the two pikemen guarding the hall doors.

"Aye," Robin agreed, pulling the hood on his cassock back over his head as they made their way towards the spring sunshine that struggled to light the chilly stone corridor. "Now we just need to deliver these letters to the sheriff and pray to God he believes they're genuine. We might not get rid of Gisbourne but at least I managed to persuade the king that Allan wasn't as bad as the sheriff's letter made out... "

* * *

The black-armoured bounty hunter had always made the villagers around Yorkshire nervous, ever since he'd first appeared in the area to work on the king's behalf the previous year. But after he'd suffered the terrible injuries to his face at the hands of Robin Hood he'd become even more frightening and the locals all over Yorkshire now dreaded a visit from Gisbourne and his men.

Patrick Prudhomme, headman of the village of Wakefield, repressed a shudder as the soldiers, at least a dozen of them, walked past him. Even Gisbourne's new sergeant, Matt Groves, a man Patrick knew well enough from his time as an outlaw seeking supplies from the villagers, had a vicious manner about him. Still, even he lacked the air of unpredictable madness that now appeared to surround Gisbourne like a great dark cloud.

Patrick steeled himself, wishing someone else would take over the role of headman, and hurried into the street after the visitors.

"My lord!" he shouted, striding along to reach the front of the small group. "My lord, I bid you welcome to our humble village, it's been a while since you last graced us with your presence."

Sir Guy stopped and turned his remaining good eye on the fidgeting headman with a sneer. The sight of the lean man's ruined face was enough to send small children screaming and, truth be told, Patrick would have liked to join them at that moment, but he stood his ground and returned Gisbourne's malevolent stare.

"Ah, Prudhomme isn't it? Yes, I know of you, although you were nowhere to be found the last time I visited, when Robin Hood and his friends killed several of my men. Robin Hood of *Wakefield* –" The slight emphasis Gisbourne placed on his village's name brought out a cold sweat on Patrick's skin "– also struck me last year, when I was unable to defend myself and, as you can see," he tapped his missing eye. "Ruined my good looks."

The bounty hunter swung away and began to walk along the muddy street again, his soldiers, and the anxious headman, following in his wake although one of Sir Guy's men, at an almost imperceptible signal from the wiry man, made his way back along the road they'd just come along.

"I'm fully recovered now," Gisbourne continued without looking at Patrick. "But, as you can probably imagine – especially after the last time I was in your little village – I'm even more determined to bring that outlaw scum to justice."

The words were spoken softly but Patrick's mind whirled, wondering exactly what the disfigured man-hunter was going to do. He'd heard the rumours from other villages roundabout ever since Robin's band had defeated the lawmen; rumours of Gisbourne and his men's brutality and merciless persecution of those the king's man suspected of giving aid to Hood and his gang.

Before, Gisbourne had been kept on a fairly tight leash by Sheriff de Faucumberg who'd ordered the bounty hunter not to harm the villagers in his pursuit of the wolf's head. But recently the sheriff's authority had not been enough to rein in the man people called The Raven. He was the king's man after all – sent there by Edward himself to do whatever he could to bring down Robin Hood and his gang.

The people of Yorkshire were terrified of the black-clad soldier, but no-one would stand up to him.

"Have you seen Hood lately?" Gisbourne asked the puffing headman who hurried along, trying to keep pace with the tall soldiers. He might as well have been asking after the weather for all the apparent emotion in his voice, but Patrick, a surprisingly perceptive man, knew better. The Raven wasn't just a master swordsman and a wicked bastard; he was also an actor – a showman. You could never take Gisbourne at face value, for everything he did was calculated, and intended to create the atmosphere of fearful competence that he revelled in.

"No, my lord," Patrick replied truthfully. It had been weeks since Robin had left Matilda and their young son, Arthur, to return to life in the forest. "The outlaws must have moved their camp somewhere far to the east, for we've not seen hide nor hair of any of them for a long time now."

Gisbourne turned to look into the headman's eyes momentarily, apparently trying to measure whether he was being truthful or not before, satisfied, the Raven looked away again, continuing his walk towards the Fletcher's house.

Patrick cursed inwardly when he realised their destination. This was bad. Not that many months before another lawman – Adam Gurdon – had come to the village hunting for Robin Hood and had caused more than a little trouble at the Fletcher's house.

"My lord –" he began again but Gisbourne waved a gauntleted hand irritably.

"Shut up, Patrick, you're becoming annoying."

The headman closed his mouth, his lips pressed tightly together in a bloodless line as he fretted over what was to come. He was pleased to see many of the other villagers beginning to gather behind them and he tried to relax.

When the previous bailiff, Gurdon, had come to Wakefield and arrested Matilda, knocking her father, Henry the fletcher, out cold when he tried to intervene, the locals had been outraged. Robin Hood and his men had managed to rescue the girl though, and afterwards the people of Wakefield had complained bitterly to their then lord – Thomas Plantagenet, the Earl of Lancaster – who told Sheriff Henry de Faucumberg in no uncertain terms to leave the villagers alone in future.

To his credit, the sheriff had never sanctioned the arrest of Matilda Fletcher; indeed he'd known nothing about it at the time and, since then, he'd tried to make sure Gisbourne and the other lawmen in the county left the innocent people of Wakefield pretty much to themselves.

Although Sir Guy's reputation was as fearsome as his appearance, he only had a handful of soldiers with him and, Patrick noticed, many of the villagers carried the tools of their trade: hammers, axes, pitchforks... they could all be lethal weapons in the hands of an angry mob.

There would be no repeat of last year's débâcle, the headman vowed. If the bloody bounty hunter wanted violence the good people of Wakefield would give it to him.

"God's blood!"

Henry's curse carried along the street as the crowd approached the fletcher's workshop and Patrick, trying to act braver than he felt, shoved his way past the soldiers to stand beside Matilda's red-faced father who was finishing arrows with beautiful snow-white fletchings taken from a swan.

"You'll be Hood's father-in-law." The black knight made it a statement rather than a question and the fletcher simply stood, his fists clenched, glaring at the Raven and his companions and snorting in disgust when he saw Matt Groves, another former outlaw who had come to him looking for supplies not so many months ago.

"Another poacher turned forester," Henry spat at Groves's feet. "Just like Adam before you, and you remember what happened to him."

Matt's face burned scarlet with fury and he took a step towards the glowering man but Gisbourne placed a hand on his sergeant's arm and held him in place.

"I've heard the story about Adam Gurdon and his untimely end," Gisbourne nodded. "I've also heard about your daughter and her part in it. Good teeth, I hear..."

Matt sniggered at that although the bounty hunter hadn't been making a joke and the erstwhile member of Robin's gang moved around to stand behind the Fletcher and his daughter.

"I'm not here to arrest anyone," Gisbourne went on, to audible sighs of relief from the watching villagers. "I'm simply here looking for information on the outlaws' whereabouts. The king is tired, you see – as am I – of this gang being allowed to wander around Barnsdale as if they owned the forest."

He turned and addressed the crowd. "Robin Hood and his entire gang are not only outlaws; they're rebels too. They took part in an armed uprising against your king. They also killed a number of my men when we tried to arrest them recently. And that," he turned back to the look at the fletcher, "is something that cannot be ignored."

The villagers muttered nervously amongst themselves, sensing life was about to get a lot harder for every one of them if this Raven didn't get what he wanted.

Still, the simple fact was, no-one in Wakefield knew where Hood or his men were hiding out these days. Patrick had told the truth: none of the outlaws had been to their village since the day Sir Guy's men chased them into the greenwood weeks earlier.

Gisbourne absorbed the silence, his irritation rising and finally beginning to show in his demeanour as he turned his single hazelnut eye on Matilda who stood her ground defiantly despite the presence of Matt Groves, breathing noisily through his nose, close – too close – behind her.

"Lady, I have no interest in arresting you. I have no doubt it would draw out the wolf's head, but without any evidence of wrong-doing on your part I, legally, have no reason to take you into custody. The sheriff would be most annoyed if I were to go around arresting all and sundry simply because I felt like it." He smiled at her and, although it appeared genuine, the expression made her legs feel weak and the fletcher glanced at her in concern but before he could move to steady his daughter Matt Groves grasped her from behind.

It might have been said Groves was trying to help the girl; to stop her from fainting. But, although he did catch her from collapsing onto the grass, his hands came right around the front of her body and roughly squeezed her breasts as he leered into her eyes which met his in fury rather than fear. This wasn't the first time a man had touched her without consent and her blood rose at the filthy lawman's intrusion.

Suddenly, Groves's hands fell away as Henry Fletcher smashed his right fist into the side of the one-time outlaw's face, sending the man crashing sideways. Henry followed up the first blow with another, again to the side of Matt's face, and the unfortunate lawman dropped to the ground like a sack of grain.

The rest of the soldiers moved to draw their swords, and the villagers cried out, moving forward threateningly, but Sir Guy raised a hand imperiously and roared, "Enough!" in a surprisingly powerful voice.

Everyone, even the enraged fletcher, stopped in their tracks to look at the king's man.

"Bastard." Groves spat into the silence, shaking his head blearily and grasping his bruised cheek which he knew would hurt like hell for the next day or so – might even be cracked or broken. "You have your excuse," he grunted at his leader. "Arrest the big bastard for assaulting a lawman."

Henry shouted in outrage and his fellow villagers joined in, their voices clamouring for justice but, again, Sir Guy raised a hand and shook his head for quiet.

"You're newly come to my service," the Raven said to Matt reasonably. "So this can be a lesson for you: I don't disrespect women, and I don't allow my men to do it either. You laid your hands on the lady Matilda and her father rewarded you handsomely for it." He spoke to Robin's wife respectfully. "My apologies, lady."

Matilda bobbed her head in surprise, not entirely sure the whole encounter was real or some strange waking dream, but the bounty hunter continued, turning this time to address Patrick again, although his voice carried to everyone in the village.

"I came here today to give you people fair warning: from now on I expect you to send word whenever you hear news of Hood and his gang. I will return periodically if no messenger from your village is forthcoming and, each time I'm forced to return an... accident will befall Wakefield. I am a lawman, so I must uphold the law and that means I can't arrest any of you without reason – but that doesn't mean God won't strike your homes and workplaces with his righteous anger."

He suddenly glanced over Patrick's shoulder and pointed. "See there. The good Lord has heard my words and sent his wrath down upon you."

The headman looked around and his eyes widened in fear.

"Fire!" someone in the crowd shouted. "Fire!"

Although there were other buildings blocking the line of sight, Patrick knew it was his house that was burning, and he remembered the soldier that had left the Raven's party when they'd first arrived in the village. He threw a murderous glance at the smiling Gisbourne before running towards the curling black smoke that marked every villagers nightmare. Unchecked it would spread quickly between the wooden houses, the sparks and embers jumping between the dry walls and thatched roofs and, quite possibly, destroying half the village before it could be brought under control.

Everyone except the Fletcher and his daughter raced to gather water from the great butts they kept filled from the waters of Balne Beck to extinguish the fire in the centre of the village.

"Make sure you and your townsfolk heed my words," Sir Guy said to Henry who pulled Matilda in close beside him defensively although the soldiers were turning to leave, Matt Groves still glaring balefully at the fletcher. "No more will the people of Yorkshire harbour outlaws. I *will* bring the king's justice to Hood; in the name of God I swear it."

With that, Gisbourne walked back along the street, his men trailing at his back like a pack of faithful hunting dogs. The fletcher and his daughter watched him go, fear making an icy pit in their guts.

"What are we going to do?" Matilda whispered.

But Henry had no answer for her.

CHAPTER FIFTEEN

"Fire!"

The cries rang out in the cool night air and, as the monks blearily hauled themselves out of bed and understood what was being said, panic quickly set in.

It hadn't been Tuck's preferred way to get Prior de Monte Martini out of his bedchamber; he'd tried simply climbing up some handily placed ivy to his superior's window first, but the accursed plant had torn itself free from the wall under Tuck's weight and he'd found himself on his backside with a none-too-Christian oath on his lips.

So, unknowingly echoing Sir Guy of Gisbourne's arson back in Wakefield, Tuck had asked Osferth to go and set alight to one of the small wooden outbuildings within the grounds. It was far enough away that the friars would be able to douse the conflagration before it spread and became truly dangerous, while being just close enough to the main priory building that the sight of the flames licking skyward would be sure to cause havoc, if only for a short time, until the water buckets could be fetched and do their job.

Tuck stood concealed in the shadows outside the prior's private chamber, listening to the muffled shouts from outside. They were punctuated now by crashing sounds, as of timbers collapsing and the burly former outlaw shook his head irritably. Clearly Osferth had set a larger fire than he'd been asked. Tuck should have guessed as much when he'd seen the gleam in the younger man's eyes as he'd crept off to gather a tinderbox and some kindling.

The man's a pyromaniac, Tuck thought just as footsteps came hurrying along the high-ceilinged corridor and he pressed himself further back against the wall so the flickering orange glow coming through the few windows wouldn't reveal his hiding place.

It was Ralph, the prior's bottler, who ran to the sturdy door and pounded his fist on it. "Wake up, father! There's a fire! Fire!"

Still, there was no sound of movement from within the chamber and Ralph began to hammer on the door again, stepping back hastily when it was pulled open and the angry red face of de Monte Martini loomed into the dimly lit hallway.

"Yes, yes, I heard you. St. Peter himself must have heard you at the gates of Heaven, by God. Let me gather –"

"No time, father!" The bottler waved his hands in the air and practically hopped on one foot, causing Tuck to stifle a laugh in his hiding place. "Your safety is more important than any worldly possessions. Come, we must go now – everyone else is outside helping fight the blaze."

De Monte Martini stared at the nervously flapping man and shook his head in disgust before sighing heavily and shrugging his shoulders. He stepped into the hall and used a key to lock the big door then allowed himself to be led away to the nearest safe exit.

As soon as the pair turned the first corner Tuck took a deep breath and charged at the door which gave way much easier than he'd expected it to and he stumbled to a halt, breathing heavily, his eyes taking in the surroundings, searching for the little reliquary that he'd come to know so well.

The prior, of course, didn't clean his own chambers. Lower brothers of the order changed de Monte Martini's bedclothes, dusted his furniture, swept the floor and performed all the other menial tasks to keep the room in good order. The prior had been careful never to allow Tuck into the chamber, not trusting the former outlaw within his own, personal, quarters, but Osferth had sometimes carried out the cleaning chores in the large room.

"It's a fancy place," he'd told Tuck earlier that evening. "There's expensive rugs on the floors, fine tapestries depicting scenes from Christ's life on the walls, and on his chests of drawers he displays all the really fine relics he's collected over the years. That one you're looking for will be there, I'm sure, although I've not been in there since you came back so can't say for sure."

Tuck had been disgusted to learn the prior hoarded religious artefacts to display in his own chamber, for his own private delight. Now, as the friar stood looking around the room his disgust turned to anger.

There was a fortune in holy trinkets dotted about the place, some with fine engraved gold information plates underneath them that were probably valuable enough to be called treasures in their own right.

A towel Christ had used to dry his face; a fine silver cup that had apparently belonged to St Stephen; a glass vial of the Virgin Mary's breast milk; a little jar with some of the clay Adam had been fashioned from; thorns from the crown the Romans had forced onto the Lord's head before he made his final journey to Golgotha...

It was obscene. These spiritual marvels should be available for all to venerate. Who knew how many sick people could be cured by the touch of one or other of these? Yet here they sat, hidden from the world, so de Monte Martini could bask in their glory himself. It was, truly, a despicable sin.

Finally, his roving eyes came to rest on the one particular relic he sought and he hastily grabbed it, shoving the artifact into the pocket sewn inside his grey cassock before turning to leave.

And stopping dead in his tracks.

Prior John de Monte Martini stood, mouth open in shock, glaring at him murderously. "I knew you were wicked," he hissed. "I should have handed you over to the law when you came crawling back here. You must have been right at home with those filthy outlaws, you devil."

Tuck had no idea what to do. If it had been anyone else, he'd have simply knocked them out of his path but... despite the fact de Monte Martini was hardly a beacon of piety, the man was, still, a prior and, in theory, much closer to God than Tuck.

The prior's eyes flicked behind Tuck and noticed the empty space where the ornate reliquary should be. "Ah, so that's it," he smirked triumphantly. "We can add the sin of theft to your long list of crimes."

As the man opened his mouth to shout for help Tuck thought of the hoarded relics and the prior's all-encompassing greed. He thought of the brothels de Monte Martini owned. And he thought of Robin Hood and the rest of his friends whose location the prior's own messenger would, any day now, hand over to the one-eyed bounty hunter known as The Raven.

Before any sound could escape his superior's lips, Tuck balled a meaty fist and punched him on the nose, knocking him backwards into the door-frame which he slid down, to sit on the floor clutching his bloodied face. It had been a heavy blow, with many years of pent-up frustration behind it, and the prior sat, too dazed to move or even say anything. It wasn't the first time he'd suffered a broken nose: that young whoreson Hood had done the same thing to him two years earlier, an action that had, unbeknown to any of them at the time, set all these events in motion.

Unlike Robin though, Tuck had no desire to continue the assault. Indeed, he'd shocked himself by lashing out at de Monte Martini, and he knew now there was no turning back from the path he'd set himself upon. The law would be after him, the prior would see to that, and he'd hang like Sir Richard-at-Lee had – another enemy of de Monte Martini – the previous summer.

With a final glance at the dazed prior Tuck hurried from the room, picked up his quarterstaff and small pack that he'd left in the shadows and left Lewes Priory for the last time.

* * *

Sixty miles north of Lewes where Tuck and his new travelling companion, Osferth, were hastily making their escape from the outraged Prior de Monte Martini, Robin and Little John had just left London. They retrieved their concealed weapons from the thick foliage outside the city then headed back onto the road to Nottingham with the invaluable letter from the king to Sheriff de Faucumberg.

"He seemed a good lad," John said, and had to repeat himself when his words were lost behind their cantering horses as the pair tried to get home as quickly as possible.

"Who?" Robin shouted, looking over in puzzlement before turning his eyes back to the road ahead, the muscles in his thighs burning already as he gripped his palfrey too tightly for fear of falling off. He would never be much of a horseman he thought, trying to relax a little.

"The king! He seemed like a nice enough sort. I'd like to share a few ales with him, I bet he'd be a fine drinking companion."

Robin grinned at his friend's idea, imagining Edward spending a night by their campfire in Barnsdale with the grumbling Will Scarlet and the Hospitaller sergeant, Stephen, not to mention Allan-a-Dale and his ribald songs.

He pulled his horse's bridle gently to the side to slow it without hurting its mouth then let the beast continue at a walk which was much less painful on the young man's inner thighs. John noticed Robin's change of pace and checked his own mount, taking up position beside his friend.

"D'you think Allan's all right?"

John puffed up his cheeks and exhaled softly, brow furrowed. "No idea. You know better than me what it's like in Nottingham's dungeon. The sheriff didn't hang him straight away though, so hopefully that's a good sign."

Robin didn't answer. It wasn't the sheriff he was worried about, it was Sir Guy of Gisbourne...

"Imagine if he'd not been caught and had actually won that silver arrow," John said, watching his leader's sombre introspection. "How much do you think it's worth?"

Robin glanced across at the big man and smiled. "God knows – enough to buy us all pardons though. I suspect that's why Allan went into the city on that fool's errand in the first place. We spoke about it the night before he and Gareth left." He stopped short of blaming himself out loud for the whole mess, knowing John would just get irritated with him. Still, if he hadn't suggested the idea...

"Cheer up," John growled. "God works in mysterious ways, as Tuck was always telling us. We might still find the money to bribe some rich gentleman. After all, who would have believed a couple of outlaws would see and do everything that we have?"

It *had* been a strange time for the young outlaw leader. He'd been expecting to follow in his father's footsteps as a forester until that fateful Mayday in 1321 when his world had been turned arse-over-elbow and he'd found himself, lonely and frightened, in the forest with only a rudimentary knowledge of how to use his da's old sword and the longbow he'd spent years mastering but had never used in anger.

Now, here he was, on his way back from the most incredible city he'd ever seen or ever would see, after meeting the king himself!

John was right too – Edward did seem like a good sort. A man to drink with, indeed. Perhaps that was the trouble. Rather than spending evenings in village taverns with individual commoners like blacksmiths, as he notoriously had in Uxbridge, the monarch might have been better trying to do more for that whole underclass in general over the years by lowering taxes and holding back the marauding Scots as his father had.

"If he ever comes into our forest," Robin said, grinning, "we'll... *invite* him to dinner, as we did with Sir Richard."

The grin slowly left his face as he remembered their fallen comrade. The big Hospitaller knight had been a good friend to the outlaws but, like so many others in his life – not least his childhood friend Much – was now dead and, hopefully, buried, although it was probably more likely the knight's body had been left to rot on the gallows that stood so threateningly by the road outside Nottingham's walls.

Robin pictured his son, Arthur, and his spirits rose again. People lived and they died, it was the way of things. All he could do was continue to do his best for those who depended on him – not only his little son, but the other outlaws who looked to him for leadership as they struggled just to survive and stay one step ahead of Sir Guy of Gisbourne and the foresters that scoured Barnsdale for poachers and rebels and other criminals like them.

He kicked his heels into his mount and drove it ahead of John's horse, gritting his teeth in determination. Aye, he'd make sure they all stayed out of Gisbourne's grasp and he would, somehow, see all his friends pardoned: free men.

But first, they had to get Allan-a-Dale out of Nottingham's jail, and, despite their letter from the king, it wasn't going to be easy...

* * *

"What's that you've got there, Tuck? Is that a sword?" The youth hooted derisively and Marjorie felt her face flush in embarrassment as her tormentor's companions giggled along with their leader.

She'd been lost in thought as she made her way to another all-too-rare sparring session with Matilda. Sir Guy of Gisbourne's recent visit to Wakefield and his subsequent burning of Patrick Prudhomme's house had outraged the girl. All the people of the village just stood by while the so-called Raven came along, threatened them all, then set alight to their headman's own home. If she'd been strong enough she'd have stood up to the crooked lawmen she thought, and it had given her even more desire to build her strength and skills.

She hadn't noticed the three younger girls loitering near the outskirts of the village until one of them had shouted at her.

Marjorie's practice sword had been safely tucked inside her skirts as she walked through the village but, at the worst moment, had worked itself free of its restraint and fallen between her legs to land on the ground with a small thump.

Of course, Helen, one of the village bullies, had been standing with her companions just as Marjorie passed and she'd spotted the training weapon when it dropped onto the sun-baked road.

Helen's mother had died three years earlier, leaving her with only her labourer father to take care of her. He was a decent man who did his best for his daughter but his work meant he was away from home for long hours every day and Helen had started to become something of a problem child despite the fact that, at 13, she was almost an adult and was expected to look after the household now that her mother was gone.

Marjorie ignored the shouts from the girls who, although they were all four or five years younger than her, were somewhat bigger, physically. She bent to retrieve the dropped practice sword, trying to shove it back inside her clothing before anyone else saw it then continued on her way towards the clearing in the woods where Matilda waited to start their training session.

"Hey, Tuck, I'm talking to you, you fat bastard!"

Marjorie gritted her teeth at Helen's sarcastic taunt, clenching her fists and wishing with all her heart she had her big brother's muscular frame. But she was used to people commenting on her diminutive stature so she walked on, trying to remain calm as Matilda had taught her.

It was no good; she heard the sound of running footsteps behind her and turned to face them, right hand clasping the wooden practice sword that she still held concealed within her woollen tunic.

"Fuck off, you little arseholes," she growled, drawing her eyebrows down in the fiercest glare she could manage. "I'm busy."

Her pursuers stopped short at that, looking at each other in disbelief before bursting into laughter.

"'Little'?" Helen demanded. "Who are you calling 'little', Tuck? We're all bigger than you, you skinny bastard." The girl moved forward to take up a position directly in front of Marjorie who stood her ground despite being outnumbered. "Or maybe you were comparing us to 'Little' John?" She laughed and looked at her two friends. "Aye, that would make sense. I'm the giant wolf's head and you're the big, fat fucking priest that's good for nothing but eating and praying. Fatty." The girl poked her finger maliciously towards Marjorie's flat belly as she ground out the final insult.

A couple of months earlier Robin's sister would have felt the tip of that finger pressing against her stomach painfully, humiliatingly, and she'd have just accepted it. The big always bested the small and weak after all – it was the way of the world.

But Marjorie had been practising with the wooden sword for weeks now. She'd run for miles to build up her stamina, and she'd forced more food down her neck than she'd eaten the entire year before so, although she was still thin, her muscles had become a little bigger and more defined than they'd ever been and she knew how to take a blow thanks to the sparring with her sister-in-law Matilda.

"Fuck off, Helen, you craven bastard. And don't call me 'Tuck'. You look more like him than I do."

There was a moment of shocked silence then Helen's two friends burst into near-hysterical laughter. No-one ever spoke back to their leader like that. This promised to be a hugely entertaining morning.

Marjorie expected to be called more names. Expected the verbal onslaught to grow to a crescendo before anyone got angry enough to throw a punch, but she was wrong.

Helen's hand, balled into a fist like any experienced soldier's, came towards her face like a battering ram and Marjorie was only just able to avoid what would have been a thunderous and no-doubt incapacitating punch.

Without even thinking, Robin's sister lifted her right knee up to her waist and, leaning back for more leverage, hammered her foot into Helen's ribs, sending the bigger, older girl flying into the grass where she lay clutching her side.

Marjorie wasn't finished yet, though – her blood was up and she knew she had to teach her tormentors a lesson or they'd never stop hassling her.

She turned to face the biggest of the remaining two girls – a tall lass with near-flawless skin and high cheekbones – who stood open mouthed, gazing at the downed Helen.

"You want some too?"

The girls backed away although their pride made sure they looked angry rather than frightened by the show of naked aggression and their leader's defeat. The fact they moved away was enough to bolster Marjorie's confidence though, and she raised her left fist threateningly before remembering she had the practice sword tucked inside her belt under her dress.

"Come on then," she growled, pulling the wooden weapon out and brandishing it menacingly. "Let's see how hard you are now."

The pair glanced at each other then, without a word, ran off into the village, leaving their fallen comrade behind without a backward glance.

By now Helen had recovered and, grasping her side with an enraged expression on her round face, got to her feet and stared at Marjorie, eyes brimming with tears of rage and pain.

"You'll be sorry you did that. I'll get you for it you bitch, in God's name I will."

Marjorie slapped the girl on the side of the leg with the sword. Not hard enough to do any real damage but with enough venom that Helen squealed in agony, grasping her stinging limb with both hands, the tears now spilling freely down her cheeks as Marjorie stepped forward and looked down on her, the rounded tip of the sword pointing at her face.

"No you won't. If you try to hassle me again, I'll break your leg with my sword. And if any of your little lackeys cause me any trouble I'll have a word with my brother and ask him to pay your da a visit. How d'you think your da would like that? If Robin and Little John and Will Scarlet were to turn up at his door?"

Helen remained silent but it was obvious Marjorie's words had hit home, hard. Everyone in the village knew what Little John had done the last time someone had messed with Robin Hood's family. The giant wolf's head had turned up and beat the hell out of Henry Woolemonger before impaling the man on the end of his sword. The outlaws weren't men to cross.

Helen's face twisted and she turned away to hide it, gasping an apology at the same time.

Marjorie felt like a giant – never in her whole life had such a sense of power coursed through her veins. It was incredible.

Without another word she straightened and walked off towards the trees and the clearing where Matilda waited to begin their sparring session. She listened warily as she went, just in case Helen's anger and humiliation drove her to seek retribution for her defeat but the girl never moved and, eventually, Marjorie pushed her way into the trees and, with a small sigh of relief, lost herself within the dense foliage.

Eventually, a broad grin spread across her gaunt face and she chuckled to herself. She'd never been in a real fight in her life before but, in the name of God, she'd enjoyed it. Enjoyed the great feeling of strength and power that had filled her as she'd glared down upon her beaten tormentor and seen the fear in the girl's moist eyes.

As she pushed the leaves and branches aside, though, the feeling of excitement left her and, strangely, was replaced by shame.

Helen had lost her mother not that long ago; it must have been difficult for the girl to lose a parent and, on top of that grief, to have all the household responsibilities thrown upon her young shoulders. Was it any wonder she sought to strike out? To take her rage at life's injustice out upon anyone that happened to walk past?

Marjorie shook her head and sighed again. She'd been right to defend herself but perhaps she'd gone too far and the fact she'd felt so alive when she'd hit the younger girl made her feel disgusted at herself.

Aye, it had been good to teach Helen a lesson and now, hopefully, she'd be left alone. But, in future, Marjorie would need to watch her temper or she'd end up in trouble, just as her older brother had when he'd attacked that prior two years ago.

CHAPTER SIXTEEN

Osferth proved to be an entertaining travel companion. Full of nervous energy and always ready to burst into one of his favourite hymns, Tuck was glad to have him along on his return to Yorkshire. For some reason the man didn't seem to care that he'd left his life – and vows – behind in Lewes.

After he'd punched de Monte Martini Tuck had made his way out of the priory and met up with the waiting Osferth not far from the walls. When the friar had returned to Lewes he'd ostensibly turned over any valuables he carried to the priory's treasurer, but the wily former wrestler had hidden the gold and silver he'd earned while part of Robin Hood's gang. It was a lot of money and he had no intention of relinquishing it into the fat, grasping hands of the prior who would, doubtless, spend it on finery to adorn his already treasure laden private chamber.

They used some of the small coins in Cooksbridge to buy a pair of horses and pushed them close to their limits now. Not only did they have to escape any pursuers the prior might send after them, but Tuck also prayed they'd be in time to warn Robin and the rest of his friends that their location had been found out and passed to Sir Guy of Gisbourne. The man that sold them the mounts had asked where they were going and eyed their cassocks with interest but Tuck had batted the questions aside, only telling the merchant they were headed north on church business.

Osferth had a thatch of straw-coloured hair and was as skinny as one of the rakes they used in the priory to gather fallen autumn leaves. The man could probably have run all the way to Wakefield with a grin on his slightly simple-looking face, Tuck thought, but he himself had found it hard even just to match Osferth's pace on the way to Cooksbridge.

Tuck's days of wandering around the countryside were done. He wondered how he'd survive now that he was a wolf's head again, for surely Prior de Monte Martini would have the law after his blood harder than ever. It was a worry...

But it was a worry for another day – right now they had to make their way north as quickly as possible and warn Robin if it wasn't already too late.

That morning, as the sun was high in the sky and the morning haze had burned away the mist leaving the country for miles around visible they passed what looked like a merchant riding on his wagon full of goods accompanied by a pair of grizzled guards on foot at the side and Osferth, grinning and apparently full of the joy of God's gift of life, began to sing, loudly and surprisingly melodiously, "All Creatures of our God and King". The hymn, incongruous in such a setting, brought only bemused looks from the mercenaries who fingered their sword hilts, wondering if the crazed Benedictine monk might prove to be a threat.

"Hush, Osferth," Tuck growled once they'd left the suspicious travellers behind. "You're going to leave a trail for our pursuers to follow as if we'd left arrows scratched into the road behind us. We're trying to be as invisible as possible and your loud singing only serves to draw attention to us."

"Sorry." Osferth smiled sheepishly. He had a powerful voice that belied his spare frame and he enjoyed nothing more than filling his lungs and belting out his love of God's creation. "I'll try to be invisible – like a shadow in the dark." He pulled the hood on his cassock over his thatch of straw-coloured hair and Tuck shook his head ruefully.

Osferth didn't seem to be quite 'all there', and Tuck wondered how the man would survive on his own in the world, but at least their flight was proving to be a memorable one.

"What's your story?" the portly friar asked, turning to look at his companion. "How did you become a Benedictine?"

Osferth shrugged and smiled but remained silent as they rode on.

He was a good Benedictine. In fact, in the eyes of his superiors he was almost the perfect monk, being docile, slightly slow and ready to believe whatever he was told without asking awkward questions. Despite the fact he occasionally lit fires and acted like a petulant child he was much less trouble than some of the more intelligent monks who continually demanded answers and fomented trouble amongst their brothers. The odd room pile of junk being found in flames was much less hassle than tough questions about the council of Nicea.

Life as a Benedictine suited Osferth well, although he hadn't become a monk by choice. His father had been a magistrate from Brighton, a minor noble with a considerable fortune and large estates to his name. He'd become caught up in a lawsuit between two of Sussex's most notorious – and wealthy – smugglers though, and the losing party had taken his revenge on Osferth's father, killing him and appropriating his entire estate, apparently by legal means.

Osferth had only been a youngster at the time and the course of his life had changed drastically as a result of his father's murder. His mother, already a fragile, weak woman, had left, disappearing one night never to be seen by the confused boy ever again. His only surviving kin, an uncle, had been unwilling and financially unable to take Osferth in so he'd been sent to the priory in nearby Lewes to become a novice.

The lad might have been the son of a well-liked and successful magistrate but he hadn't inherited any of his father's razor-sharp intellect or charisma so, although he had no interest in religion he'd gone along with his uncle's wishes and joined the Benedictines.

He knew he wasn't smart anyway; knew he couldn't have survived very well on his own, so he'd been relieved when Prior de Monte Martini had accepted him into their brotherhood. He'd been grateful ever since, even if he was poorly treated as a result of his slowness.

At least he had a roof over his head and decent food in his belly; more than his dead father had for sure.

Sometimes he heard a little voice inside telling him to do things but he'd never spoken to anyone about it. God was talking directly to him, just as He had done with Moses on Mount Sinai, or Elijah, who had heard the voice of God and been taken up into the sky by His mighty whirlwind. One day Osferth knew he too would be taken up to Heaven by God in such a fashion.

The fires the voices told him to start always created chaos and consternation within the priory. Once he'd burnt down much of the east wing with many of his brothers lucky to escape the smoke and flames but he was only doing God's work. The monks had feasted on beer and fish that day and needed to be reminded of the fragility of their own existence, not to mention God's dominion over their gluttonous, fat bodies.

Osferth's fire had cleansed the priory and, he was sure, had shown his brothers the error of their ways. They'd not feasted for two weeks after the conflagration and every one of them – except the prior and his dean obviously – had been forced to help with the restoration work.

Fire was good. It cleansed sins both corporeal and spiritual but it was just a means to an end for Osferth. He didn't love the flames and the heady, aromatic smoke they produced for themselves; fire was simply a tool to do God's work. And that was what he had been put on Earth to do, using whatever was at hand.

Friar Tuck was a good man and a good friend to Osferth but he kept bad company.

Like the outlaws in Barnsdale.

They weren't part of God's plan. Something would have to be done about them, and Osferth was the monk to do it.

* * *

The tournament had gone well, Sir Henry de Faucumberg thought, smiling to himself as he watched another wrestling match. The audience – pleasingly large in number – cheered and roared in delight as the two combatants traded blows, grunted curses and threw each other around the grass, sweat dripping from their well-muscled torsos. Occasionally the bout spilled out of the roped-off area and into the crowd, but that only brought even louder shouts of encouragement, especially from the women.

Yes, it had been a successful tournament so far and the local traders would be doing brisk business; making money to bring in more taxes. Now all he needed was that letter from the king giving him permission to hang the wolf's head Allan-a-Dale and, more importantly, send the increasingly erratic Sir Guy of Gisbourne back to London with his new toady Matt Groves. Christ above, what a waste of skin that man was, de Faucumberg mused, glancing over to his right where Gisbourne stood watching the wrestling match with Groves at his side like an eager puppy.

"God's bollocks, sit down, Gisbourne, you're making me nervous standing there," the sheriff growled, waving a hand to the seat next to him but the bounty hunter ignored the gesture. Only The Raven would prefer to stand on such a warm day, his pitch black armour oiled to perfection and his hand resting menacingly on the pommel of his sword as if he feared a peasant uprising at any moment.

Sir Henry muttered an oath and turned back to the wrestlers irritably, helping himself to another cup of wine from the table before him.

"My lord!" A soldier clad in the blue livery of de Faucumberg's own garrison, rather than one of the men under Gisbourne's command, breathlessly pushed his way through the throng of people and, puffing hard, whispered into the sheriff's ear.

The messenger was rewarded with a grin that split Sir Henry's face from ear to ear and, as Sir Guy walked across to find out what was going on the sheriff hurriedly whispered his instructions to the soldier and waved him off back to his post at the Hun Gate.

"You look inordinately pleased with yourself," Gisbourne said, finally sitting in the sturdy wooden chair next to de Faucumberg and gazing at the sheriff while Matt Groves moved over to stand protectively behind his captain.

"The king sends word. The friars I dispatched to London have returned."

Gisbourne nodded, a smile playing around his lips. "Good news, then. The tournament will really come to life with a good hanging on Gallows Hill. Matt!" He turned his head to the side and beckoned the former outlaw over. "Fetch the minstrel from the dungeon –"

"You'll do no such thing!" de Faucumberg shouted, glaring at Groves who returned the look impudently, as if he knew his master Sir Guy was untouchable to the sheriff. "I'll read what the king has to say first, and then *I* will decide when to hang the outlaw. This is my city, Gisbourne, and my soldiers are in charge of the prisoner so you," he looked again at Groves, his lip curled in disgust, "can crawl back under your stone, you horrible bastard."

Groves's face turned crimson with rage but Sir Guy simply grinned at the sheriff's outburst. "Stand down, Matt, we'll wait and see what the king has to say about it. We are merely guests here after all." He helped himself to a small piece of roasted venison from the platter on the table and, still smiling, turned his attention back to the tournament.

By now the wrestling heats had been completed, the winners had their arms raised and all the competitors bowed to the sheriff before dispersing. Servants hurried to clear away the ropes that had marked the grappling ring and yet more servants carried archery targets onto the grass.

"Looks like the next event is archery," Matt Groves said, much to the amusement of Sir Guy who laughed even more when he saw the venomous look on the sheriff's face.

"You don't say?" de Faucumberg growled sarcastically. "Look, I invited you to sit with me, Gisbourne, but we don't need... that, here as well. He should be swinging from the gallows beside the minstrel anyway, not standing here at my table. You!" he barked, glowering at the erstwhile wolf's head. "Fuck off."

Groves looked like he might lose his temper and actually attack the sheriff whose personal guardsmen stepped in close and hefted their halberds threateningly.

"Go, Matt," Gisbourne waved without turning to look at his second-in-command. "Take yourself off to one of the taverns before the archery begins. I'll see you later."

Groves nodded to his captain and shoved his way past de Faucumberg's men, snarling at them like a petulant child.

"I thought your old sergeant was a blood-thirsty bastard," de Faucumberg told the bounty hunter with a shake of his head. "But at least Barnwell was a good soldier and had a modicum of intelligence. That wolf's head is nothing but an angry fool."

Gisbourne helped himself to another piece of venison which was perfectly cooked – moist and tender – and shrugged disinterestedly. "He is. But he hates Robin Hood even more than I do and he knows how the wolf's heads work. He'll lead us to them eventually, I'm sure. And if he doesn't, well..." He winked his good eye at the sheriff who had to suppress a shudder. "You can hang him if you like then."

The targets were in place by now and the crowd, which had thinned during the intermission, started to return, ale-skins refilled and meat pies or other savoury delights in hand, their obvious pleasure in this taking away some of de Faucumberg's annoyance. He tried to be a good sheriff to the people of Yorkshire and Nottingham, he truly did, and keeping the people entertained and well-fed and watered was the best way to avoid civil unrest while keeping the traders and merchants that paid so much to his treasury in taxes happy.

As the first of the longbowmen began to show off their skills de Faucumberg waited, occasionally glancing over his shoulder. Gisbourne watched him from the corner of his eye. It was obvious there was more to the king's letter than simple authorization to hang the outlaw minstrel. Like there had even been any need to petition the king for permission in the first place.

Clearly something else was going on, and Gisbourne watched the sheriff's sly smile warily.

"Oh, very good! Well done that man!" de Faucumberg raised his cup in salute to one of the archers who'd managed to hit the centre of the target, before, again, his glance turned to his rear. This time, though, he sat up in his chair and Gisbourne also swung around to watch the arrival of the Franciscan friars who had been sent south to the capital and King Edward II.

"What the hell is this?" the bounty hunter muttered, hand grasping his sword as he looked to the sheriff for his reaction to the newcomers approaching the table. The archery contest continued; the participants, and the crowd, oblivious to what was going on above them. "Those are no friars."

The two men in grey cassocks came towards them, the hoods on the garments pulled up to hide their faces in shadow but the great size of both, and one in particular who towered over everyone nearby marked them as a potential threat and Sir Guy got to his feet, sword instantly appearing in his hand from its exquisitely crafted black wood and leather sheath.

The sheriff's own blue-liveried guards, jumpy and nervous as a result of Matt Groves's dressing down and now Gisbourne's reaction to the two friars, crowded around de Faucumberg defensively but the clergymen continued their slow approach until they stood before the table, heads still bowed and faces hidden by their hoods.

"You're the messengers from the king?" de Faucumberg asked, standing to meet them, and was rewarded by the hood on the smaller – yet still massive – man bobbing up and down. "You seem to have grown since I last saw you," the sheriff noted drily. "Take those hoods off. Slowly, now."

The friars hesitated for a moment before first one, then the other, threw their head's back and their faces were revealed.

The sheriff took an involuntary step backwards, while Gisbourne whispered in shock: "You...!"

The guards now had their halberds pointed straight at Robin and Little John who watched the sheriff's eyes stray downwards to the parchment the notorious wolf's head held in his hands.

"We bring word from the king."

For long moments no one spoke, they simply stared in disbelief at the two infamous outlaws who had so brazenly walked into the city before Gisbourne finally broke the spell.

"Kill them!"

CHAPTER SEVENTEEN

"Hold!" The sheriff was a man well used to command and his voice reflected that fact as it rang out over the sounds of the crowd. He was pleased to note that none of his own men had followed Gisbourne's command to attack the two wolf's heads, but they had moved in even closer to make sure the big men wouldn't be a threat.

The king's bounty hunter found his path to Hood blocked by blue-liveried guardsmen and he spat in disgust at de Faucumberg's refusal to cut the hated outlaw down where he stood, apparently unarmed and completely in their power.

"You're Hood, and you're the big impudent bastard that made a joke about my mother the last time we met, yes?"

Robin shook his head but Little John couldn't stop a smile from appearing on his still cleanly-shaven face. "Aye, lord sheriff, that was me," he agreed. "Sorry about that." His cheeky grin marked the apology as insincere but the sheriff just grunted irritably.

"I assume there's a good reason you've walked into my city, and my presence, dressed as friars?"

"As I said, we bring word from King Edward." Robin held out the rolled up parchment, slowly so as not to provoke a nervous thrust from any of the halberd-wielding guards.

De Faucumberg nodded to one of the soldiers to bring him the scroll and, as he was given it he inspected the wax seal closely. It certainly appeared to be Edward's royal seal. "How did you come to be in possession of this? And what happened to the two real friars that I sent to London? Or do I not want to know the answer to that?"

Robin shrugged. "They decided the journey was too far and too dangerous. We went in their stead."

Gisbourne laughed in disbelief and the sheriff raised a questioning eyebrow himself at that idea before he broke the wax seal and, sitting back down on his great seat, unrolled the letter from the king and began to read.

"Are you taking this seriously?" Sir Guy demanded into the silence. "Why haven't you had these two criminals – dangerous criminals," he pointed to his ruined face furiously, "chained like the animals they are?"

The sheriff ignored him as he read but it was obvious whatever was in the king's letter did not please him. Robin and John knew de Faucumberg would be angry at Edward's refusal to recall his erratic bounty hunter but it was when the letter moved onto Allan-a-Dale that the seated nobleman jumped up and roared in disbelief.

"The king wants me to release the wolf's head? What is this nonsense?" He re-read the entire letter in a state of rising fury and shock before turning to glare at the two big outlaws. "This is your doing isn't it, you bastards? You spun Edward some tale and he believed it." He shook his head and sighed, throwing the letter onto the table in resignation. "You really do seem to be touched by God, Hood, I'll say that for you."

"What are you talking about de Faucumberg?" Gisbourne demanded, shoving his way past the guards to reach for the letter which the sheriff retrieved before the king's man could read it. Couldn't have him knowing the sheriff was trying to get rid of him, could they? That would make things even more unpleasant than they already were...

"It seems we've been outwitted by the wolf's head again," de Faucumberg replied, still glaring at the young outlaw who always seemed to be one step ahead of their efforts to capture or kill him. "I can only guess that these two – in their disguise as holy men – gave the king some fabricated story about the minstrel's innocence and, as a result, Edward has ordered me to release him."

Gisbourne snorted. "How can you be sure that letter's from the king? It must be a forgery."

The sheriff shook his head. "Oh it's genuine, no doubt about it – the seal was real and I recognise his scribe's handwriting."

"Fine, the minstrel can go free. He's nothing anyway. It's *that* young prick that we really want and I assume the king says nothing about us letting him go as well." He pointed his sword at Robin and smiled. "You probably thought you were doing the noble thing coming here to free your friend, but you're going to suffer for it now. I've waited a long time to repay you for taking my eye."

"I have one more letter from the king, my lord."

The wolf's head produced another scroll from within the grey friar's cassock and proffered it to the sheriff whose guard passed it to him.

Again, the seal was inspected before being broken and the parchment unrolled and slowly read by de Faucumberg who could only shake his head, a small smile of defeat twitching at the corners of his mouth. "Hood thought you'd say something like that, Sir Guy, and had the king – who appears to have taken rather a liking to our outlaws here – write another letter of protection. This time for the pair of them."

Now he did pass the scroll to Gisbourne who read it in silence, rage colouring his face as he realised all three of Hood's gang were simply going to walk right out of the city gates and back to their camp in Barnsdale and there was absolutely nothing he could do about it.

There was a grudging respect in the sheriff's eyes as he looked up at Robin and issued the command to one of his guards to bring Allan-a-Dale from his cell in the dungeon along with all his possessions. "It's a shame you're on the other side of the law," he told the young man. "I could find a use for someone like you in my garrison. Oh well," he shrugged again and settled back down into his chair, grasping his wine cup with a twinkle in his eye. "You've beaten us again this day and, no doubt, your minstrel friend will come up with some song all about it that will enhance your legendary status among the common people even more." He emptied the cup and refilled it from a large jug. "Make the most of your victory, wolf's head, because we *will* catch you one day. He'll make damn sure of it."

He raised a finger from his cup and pointed at Sir Guy who still stood, sword drawn, looking as if he might still at any moment attack the two outlaws, despite the king's order of protection.

"And, as for the king... when he finds out you deceived him, well, I doubt he'll be too pleased."

Robin wasn't so sure. "We'll see, lord sheriff. We'll see. Ned told us he'd be coming north again soon to see things were being run properly and said he hoped to meet us again. We got on well with him didn't we, John? He even asked if we'd like to join his rowing team."

Gisbourne growled at Robin's use of a diminutive nickname for their monarch. "Aye, well, the king always did enjoy spending time with the lower end of the social scale. I'm not surprised he liked your company."

"Shut it, Gisbourne, you ugly twat," John replied with a grin. "No one cares what you think."

De Faucumberg hid his smile behind his cup and was relieved to see his guard returning, at last, with the captured minstrel in tow. "Here he is," he said, waving towards them as they approached and everyone except the fuming Raven turned to watch.

Allan, face caked with dried blood and dirt, looked confused when he spotted his two friends shorn and dressed as friars but he held his peace, not wanting to upset whatever game it was they were playing with the sheriff and Gisbourne.

"You're free to go," de Faucumberg said, waving his hand to encompass all three of the outlaws. "My men will escort you to the city gates safely. Gisbourne, you will remain here so you don't do anything rash that'll bring the king's wrath down upon me for disobeying his orders."

"Disobeying his orders? You really think the king wants you to let Robin Hood and two of his men walk free, just like that, as a result of this deception they've perpetrated? Robin Hood, the man the king sent me here specifically to deal with?"

"No, quite possibly not," the sheriff agreed. "But I am the king's servant and, as such, I am expected to carry out his orders without question, unfortunately. His letters state very clearly that these three are to be sent on their way and so that is what will happen. We will just need to recapture them another day."

Although de Faucumberg was dismayed to be letting the three outlaws walk free, it cheered him and somewhat softened the blow to see the rage that filled Gisbourne. It felt very good to see the bounty hunter taken down a peg or two again, even if it was at the hands of the wolf's head.

Robin could also see the black rage that twisted Sir Guy's face and threatened to overwhelm the king's man, so he slowly began to move backwards, away from the sheriff's high table, gesturing John and Allan to follow his lead.

"You alright?" he asked the minstrel, eyeing him with concern.

"Aye," Allan grunted with a smile. "Nothing damaged other than my pride."

As they neared the competitors in the archery tournament Robin hissed a curse as he spotted the one man in the world that he hated even more than Gisbourne: "Matt Groves."

The young outlaw captain spat the name like the vilest oath when he saw Groves appearing through the crowd, half-a-dozen of Gisbourne's own men – all in the simple brown and green clothing of foresters – in tow. "That filthy piece of shit's brought men to kill us, no matter what the sheriff's commanded."

Gisbourne had noticed Robin's angry gaze and he turned to see his second-in-command nearing. His thoughts whirled as he debated whether to go against de Faucumberg's orders; it might mean fighting the sheriff's soldiers, if they decided to try and stop him.

But he did despise the lowly yeoman from Wakefield who had so painfully taken half his face the previous year. "Good work, Matt," the king's man shouted. "We're not letting those criminals just walk out of Nottingham. Cut them down!"

De Faucumberg was practically foaming at the mouth, enraged that Groves had returned after he'd been told in no uncertain terms to leave, and not only that, the sullen-faced prick had brought soldiers to defy him.

"Stop them," he roared at his own men who outnumbered Gisbourne's small Groves-led force, but the soldiers moved slowly, not really sure what the hell was going on and reluctant to get involved in whatever power-struggle was being played out by the two noblemen. The sheriff might be their commander, but it was a brave man who defied the Raven, especially recently, when he'd become even more erratic and volatile than ever.

The outlaws were unarmed, and they looked uncertainly at each other as Gisbourne's men came for them, swords drawn and obviously prepared to use lethal force – there would be no mercy from them, that much was clear, and the blue-liveried sheriff's men, although they were moving now to head-off the newcomers, wouldn't reach them in time.

All of this was going on unnoticed by most of the large crowd who stood engrossed in the archery competition. The longbowmen were also oblivious to what was happening at their backs but as Robin and his hastily retreating companions came close to them one stocky man with a shock of red hair turned, surprised to see two friars and a filthy-looking peasant about to be cut down by a group of foresters.

"May I?"

The archer stood, open-mouthed in confusion but handed over his great warbow and the broadhead arrow he had been ready to loose and Robin smiled his thanks.

"God bless you, my son," he grunted before nocking the arrow to the hemp string and rolling his enormous shoulders, smiling at the oncoming Groves. "Hold, Matt, or I'll take your fucking head right off."

Their pursuers stopped dead in their tracks and the former outlaw's face turned pale with the realisation Hood held his life in his hands.

"You've seen what an arrow like this can do to a man," Robin shouted although he hardly needed to as the cheering, chattering crowd that had been so absorbed in the tourney spotted the friar taking the longbow and now fell silent to watch the even more entertaining drama unfold in front of them. "The iron tip will penetrate right through that ugly face of yours and out the back of your skull," Robin continued, buying time until the sheriff's soldiers finally reached Gisbourne's men and blocked them off, ready to stop their progress should they try to move again. "Your head will explode like an old apple, and it'll make me happy to know I've avenged Much's death at your hands, you evil scum."

Robin raised the bow a fraction, ready to draw and aim it right at Matt but his gaze moved to the sheriff who stood watching the confrontation stony-faced. "I don't think Sir Henry would allow me to walk free if I was to kill you though. It'll have to be another day."

Knowing they were safe, Robin suddenly turned, drew the string taut, sighted instinctively and loosed his arrow towards one of the big straw targets.

The spectators held their breath for a moment longer as they looked to see where the shot had landed before a young boy, his eyesight sharper than most in the crowd, muttered in a high-pitched voice, "Holy mother of God!"

Little John and Allan-a-Dale both turned to fix their leader with shocked smiles and the noise of the people rose to a deafening clamour.

"A bullseye! He hit a bullseye!"

"Not just a bullseye – he's split it! He's split the other arrow right down the middle!"

"It's a miracle!"

"How the fuck did you do that?" Little John grabbed Robin's arm and stared at him in awed disbelief. "I've never seen anything like it in my life; I didn't even think it was possible to make a shot like that. And you did it without even setting yourself properly, you just turned and let fly. How?"

Robin just smiled enigmatically as if this had been his plan all along. "Allan, you know how to work a crowd. Get them to start a chant – we're going to get that silver arrow and win our pardons after all. John – lift me up, quick, onto your shoulders."

The spectators crowded in around them while Groves and Gisbourne's men were shepherded away by the sheriff's soldiers. De Faucumberg himself stood watching, wondering what to make of the day so far.

Yes, he'd lost the chance to execute one of Robin Hood's gang, and on top of that he'd been forced to let Hood himself, along with his giant right-hand man, walk free. But Gisbourne, and now his vile little toady Groves, had been sorely humiliated and that shot the young man had made... it was the stuff of legend. People would tell stories and sing songs about the sheriff's tournament for months once the minstrels got word of what had happened here...

De Faucumberg looked at Allan-a-Dale, wondering what song the man would concoct, and he noticed the minstrel was chanting something already, leading the people who had by now hoisted Hood onto their shoulders.

The crowd swelled even further as the news of what had happened spread throughout the city and the chant slowly grew in volume until the sheriff could pick out the words and, slowly, his mood turned black.

"Silver arrow... Silver arrow... Silver arrow..!"

It was Gisbourne's turn to grin, and the bounty hunter laughed at the sheriff's consternation. "Not so fucking cheerful now, are you?"

CHAPTER EIGHTEEN

"I promise you, you'll like Robin," Tuck smiled at Osferth, the affection he felt for the outlaw leader plain on his jowly face. "Everyone likes Robin. Well, apart from Gisbourne. And the sheriff. And Adam Bell. And Matt Groves..." His face broke into a wide grin and he waved his hands happily. "Everyone else likes him though."

Osferth had noticed a major transformation in the friar since they'd left Lewes behind them and headed farther north. While he'd always seemed confident and competent and hid his emotions fairly well, Tuck had been subdued and plainly unhappy when he was cooped up inside St Mary's. Now, though, it was as if the man had grown ten years younger physically, and thirty years had dropped from his mental age, so he grinned and hummed hymns like a spry novice. Clearly the thought of joining up with his outlaw friends was pleasing to the aging Tuck.

The journey wasn't as swift as it might have been – Osferth may have been somewhat touched but his devotion to Christ couldn't be questioned. He insisted on saying prayers eight times a day, from Lauds at five in the morning to Compline in the evening and everything in between – just as they'd have done had they still been in the priory. Tuck fidgeted irritably every time they dallied with the worship but he felt guilty to have drawn his younger companion into this adventure and, as a result, he bit his tongue and joined in with the Pater Nosters, Ave Maria and Credo.

In truth, Tuck was somewhat taken aback by just how devout Osferth really was. Someone like him should have been at home in St Mary's and yet, here he was, tagging along with the former-wrestler having been more than happy to give up his life as a clergyman. True, Prior de Martini had been hard on Osferth, but still, people like him often saw that as a trial sent by God, or penance for some unknown sin.

It certainly made the journey more pleasant, if rather slower, having the man along. Flight from the authorities could be a frightening, lonely experience and Tuck was glad to have Osferth with him to keep his mind from their potential troubles.

"I've never been this far north," Osferth said, looking about him, eyes wide as if the land thereabouts was somehow different to Sussex where he'd spent all of his thirty-odd years. "I feel like Joseph of Arimathea, travelling north to strange new lands, carrying the word of God and Christ to any who'd listen." He smiled and Tuck smiled back, happy to be with such a delightfully strange travelling companion.

"I have a feeling Prior de Martini doesn't see us in the same light."

"Maybe not, Robert, maybe not," Osferth shrugged. "But God works in mysterious ways. Who knows what the prior is thinking right now? We're all tools of the Almighty after all – even Prior de Martini."

"That bastard's a tool of Satan," Tuck grunted, touching a hand to the crucifix he wore around his neck to avert any evil that might be drawn to them by the Dark One's name. "I thought that was why you'd come with me."

"It is," Osferth agreed, nodding vigorously. "I couldn't stay in the priory any longer – De Martini isn't fit to be in charge of our brothers. So... tell me about the giant: Little John."

The abrupt change in the conversation threw Tuck, but he'd come to expect odd behaviour from his companion, whose thoughts seemed to flit from one place to another like a sparrow seeking a mouldy crust. And Osferth was just as innocent as one of the little birds, even if he did appear to have something of a dark streak hidden just beneath the surface. Tuck wondered what they would do with the strange, child-like monk when they finally reached Barnsdale and found the outlaws.

But they would cross that bridge when they came to it. For now, Osferth had asked about Little John and there was nothing Tuck liked better than telling tales about the exploits of his old friends.

"Huge he is. Massive! Biggest man you've ever seen in your life."

Osferth listened, eyes shining with interest as their mounts carried them north, and Tuck knew he'd chosen the right path. God was leading him home.

* * *

"I can't give him the arrow, in the name of Christ. It's worth a fortune. We had it made from solid silver, remember?"

"I don't think you've got much choice," the grinning Gisbourne said, nodding his head towards the huge crowd that had gathered and was continuing to swell as the chant increased in volume. "The people have decided Hood's the winner of your tourney."

"Silver arrow! Silver arrow!"

"Fuck the people," de Faucumberg shouted, eyes blazing and spittle flecking his neatly-trimmed grey beard. "We're to let three notorious outlaws walk free, taking my silver arrow with them? How will I pay the taxes to the king without the silver in that arrow? This is your fault, Gisbourne, you fucking oaf. You had the clever idea to offer a real silver arrow and now look where it's got us."

Sir Guy shrugged, the smirk ever-present on his ruined face now. "It was a quite remarkable shot, you must admit – certainly worthy of winning the arrow. And it *is,* as you noted yourself not long ago, King Edward's orders that the wolf's heads should be allowed to walk free."

As they spoke, de Faucumberg realised a new chant had begun and now vied with the first for dominance. The sheriff groaned as the cries of "Robin Hood! Robin Hood!" filled the air and Allan-a-Dale clapped his hands encouragingly with the people that stood closest to them.

This was a disaster; another little story at his expense to add to the burgeoning legend that surrounded this young outlaw from Wakefield and his gang.

"Silence!" de Faucumberg roared, holding his hands aloft and looking murderously at the noisy mob before him. "Silence!" He beckoned to one of his soldiers and whispered in his ear. "Go to the castle and bring reinforcements, enough to quell any rioting here."

The crowd had stopped their chants, eager to hear their sheriff's words. They had no idea the silver arrow had simply been a ruse designed to lure Robin Hood to Nottingham. No idea that any eventual winner was never supposed to be allowed to keep the magnificent, and insanely expensive, piece.

"Good people of Nottingham, and visitors to our fine city," the sheriff began, forcing a benevolent smile onto his face, "you are right: before us stands the famous outlaw, Robin Hood, with two of his friends."

"That's Little John that is," someone piped up from within the crowd, and his assertion was met with agreement from all around. "Aye, must be – look at the size of the bastard, he's huge!"

John smiled a little shyly, his face turning red from the attention, not to mention the not-inconsiderable weight of Robin atop his shoulders, but de Faucumberg carried on, drawing all eyes back to himself.

"Hood has made a remarkable shot using a borrowed longbow –"

"Miraculous!"

"Never seen anything like it!"

"Yes, an excellent shot," the sheriff nodded, smiling in agreement. "And, as a reward, I will allow Hood and his two friends to go free, although I *should* place them in chains and throw them into the castle jail to await justice."

The crowd began to grumble and mutter and the sheriff again raised his hands. "The tournament is not over yet; it would not be fair to award the silver arrow to someone that wasn't even a listed competitor and, as such, is not entitled to any prize."

The sheriff watched the crowd, as did Gisbourne beside him and it seemed the speech had done its work. The words were reasonable and fair and the people seemed happy enough to accept it.

Then the two noblemen spotted Allan-a-Dale saying something to the red-haired archer that Hood had taken the longbow from. The man nodded thoughtfully at whatever the wolf's head was telling him then he looked up from beneath the flaming curls and shouted towards the raised table.

"None of us will ever beat that shot, my lord sheriff. It was a once-in-a-lifetime effort. I forfeit any claim to the silver arrow for I'll never best that man's skill, aye, even if I lived 'til I were a hundred years old!"

Some of the other archers nodded and shouted agreement, giving up any claim to the great prize and, again, the troublemaking minstrel started the chanting.

"Silver arrow! Silver arrow! Robin Hood! Robin Hood!"

"Worthless bastard," de Faucumerg muttered, looking murderously at the clapping minstrel. "I should have hanged him the first day we had him in custody. Silence!" Again, he raised his hands and waited on the noise to abate before he spoke once more into the calm.

"I will not turn over the prize to an outlaw. It is enough that he's being given his freedom this day although, mark this well, Hood: Sir Guy and his men, along with my own garrison, will still be doing everything in our power to put an end to you and your criminal gang."

"You can bet your life on it," Gisbourne spat, pointing the tip of his elegant sword at the outlaws. "I won't rest until you're dead, you scum."

"Give Hood the arrow you swindler," someone shouted from the safe anonymity of the mob and many others cried out in angry agreement.

"Give him it or we'll burn the city to the ground!"

There were cheers at that shout and de Faucumberg noticed Allan-a-Dale had disappeared into the crowd. No doubt it was the minstrel who was trying to stoke the ire of the people and, unfortunately, it seemed to be working, as cries of "burn it!" began to ring out from various sections of the gathering.

From far to the rear of the mob there was a crashing sound as one of the vendor's stalls was tipped over and smoke slowly curled upwards from it, forming a greasy smear in the afternoon sky.

"Burn it to the ground!"

Another stall crashed over and some of the people began to howl and laugh making the sheriff realise his extra soldiers, who were now jogging into view, were not going to be able to contain this without a great deal of bloodshed. De Faucumberg was not the type of sheriff to deal with civil unrest with displays of brutality and killing, but that arrow... it was worth a fortune! He'd have to make up the missing tax monies from his own purse if he handed it over to the damned wolf's head.

"Whatever you're planning," Gisbourne barked, interrupting the sheriff's whirling thoughts, "you better get on with it. Either give Hood the arrow or set your men to cracking heads. That lot are about to erupt."

True enough, more and more of the people were joining in with the chants now, not just for the arrow and the outlaw, but, as they visibly steeled themselves for the inevitable outpouring of rage and destruction that accompanied any riot, many of them were taking up the cries of, "burn it!"

"Oh for Christ's sake. Alright!" De Faucumberg turned and waved a hand angrily towards the heavily guarded table that displayed the wondrous arrow. "Bring it to me, man, now."

The soldier that had been addressed hurried to obey, not relishing the idea of wading in amongst his own townsfolk with the halberd he wielded, simply to save the sheriff some money. He lifted the arrow, which was surprisingly heavy thanks to the high quality of the silver that had been used to construct it, and brought it over to his lord and commander.

"Come and get it, wolf's head," the sheriff shouted, shaking the arrow in the air furiously as the people, who had been readying themselves to go on a rampage now switched their mood and began to cheer and hoot in delight at their apparent victory over the nobles.

"Let me down," Robin said and John slowly bent his knees so his passenger could slide onto the ground. "Here, cover me."

He handed the giant the longbow, noting with satisfaction that Allan had also managed to procure one of the weapons from somewhere, then, making his way through the grinning crowd, he walked up the small flight of steps to the high table.

Sheriff de Faucumberg dropped the heavy silver trophy into the outlaw's open palms and Robin turned, a wide grin forming on his honest face as he raised the arrow skywards and was rewarded with a deafening cheer.

"Thank you, my lord sheriff," the young wolf's head winked over his shoulder as he danced past the impotent guards, down the steps and back towards his friends. When he reached them he looked at John and gestured for the giant to hand the longbow back to its red-haired owner. "Now, give me a boost."

John cupped his hands and Robin stepped into them, rising in the air so the entire crowd could see him. "This is a fine prize, my friends," he shouted, "and worth a fortune!" The people cheered and clapped, assuring him he deserved it for his fine shot. "But my companions and I have no use for wealth and finery in the greenwood. All we need are arrows, and food and friendship, and ale!"

"Lots of ale!" Little John roared agreement and everyone cheered again, thoroughly enjoying themselves.

"We'll take the sheriff's silver prize back to Barnsdale and cut slivers from it which we'll distribute amongst those most needy in the towns and villages hereabouts. God bless you all!"

The people went crazy, chanting Robin's name and patting the three outlaws on the back as they headed towards the city gates and freedom.

Sir Henry and Gisbourne watched them go, faces tight with rage and defeat.

"Look at the smug bastard, he has them eating out of his hand," the bounty hunter spat.

"This is your fault," de Faucumberg repeated his earlier accusation, turning to include Matt Groves who had reappeared behind his captain, Sir Guy. "You and that vermin. Not only was it your idea to offer the silver arrow as a prize, but it was your lackey's attempt to kill Hood that made the outlaw grab the longbow. If you'd have just let him leave like I ordered, Hood would never have made that unbelievable shot and I wouldn't be hundreds of pounds out of pocket!"

Groves opened his mouth to say something but the sheriff rounded on him viciously, eyes flaring, enraged like Gisbourne had never seen him before. "Get out of my sight, you arsehole! In fact, get the fuck out of my city. If I ever see you again I'll repeal your pardon and see you on the gibbet. And as for you," de Faucumberg glared at Sir Guy. "You can go with him. I don't want to see your face in Nottingham until you've destroyed Hood and his gang and returned that silver arrow to me."

* * *

"So you were a sailor, eh?"

Matt Groves nodded and took a long pull of the cheap ale that had been served to them in Horbury. When the sheriff threw them out of Nottingham, Sir Guy had taken Matt and the rest of his men north to begin their hunt for Robin Hood and his gang anew. The soldiers erected makeshift shelters outside the village while Gisbourne and Groves had come into the small village to rent a room for the night. If the place had been big enough all the men could have paid for their own rooms but the little inn only boasted four guest rooms and all were cramped, or 'cosy' as the landlord described them.

Now, the bounty hunter and his second-in-command sat in the inn's common room by a blazing fire which crackled and spit every so often apparently in protestation at the poor quality damp wood that was being burned. Still, it gave off enough warmth and light to make the room comfortable and the ale that Matt had heated with a poker was also helping him relax after their enforced journey. Gisbourne, a man who always liked to be in total control of himself, was drinking the weaker ale that the landlord gave to his children.

"Aye, I've been a sailor. Twice." Matt said. "It was my first real job when I was about fourteen, then when I left Hood's gang and the money you'd given me for betraying them ran out I took a berth on a ship sailing from Hull to Bergen, in Norway." He took another sip, relishing the warm feeling that was spreading quickly outwards from his belly, and grimaced at his captain. "I'm not much of a sailor to be honest. Or much of an outlaw either come to think of it. I hate being stuck in a small space with a load of other men."

Gisbourne hid a small smile behind his hand, imagining how unpleasant Matt's company would be if one were stuck aboard a ship with him for weeks on end.

"Well, at least now you're free to come and go as you please," the king's man said but Matt shook his head with a scowl.

"Not really. We'll need to kill that arsehole Hood. I don't want to be looking over my shoulder for the rest of my life, wondering when he'll come for revenge because I killed his mate."

Groves had led Robin and his childhood friend, Much, the son of the miller from Wakefield, into a trap set by Gisbourne the previous year. Much had been shot by the Raven then run through by Matt himself and both men knew Hood would never forget that day.

"We'll find him, never fear," Gisbourne promised. "We just need to put even more pressure on the villagers who give aid to the outlaws. Eventually someone will decide enough is enough and see us as a worse threat than Hood or his men. Once we know the location of their camp we'll get them."

"I wouldn't be so sure," Matt replied gloomily. "Lawmen have known where we were hiding in the past but we still always managed to escape. They'll have lookouts posted and, apart from that, they're all hardy fighters. As you know yourself..." His voice trailed off as Gisbourne reached up unconsciously to touch his ruined eye and glared at him.

"Once we find their location," the Raven promised, "I'll send word back to Nottingham and ask – no, demand – that de Faucumberg sends us enough of his soldiers to make certain we can surround the outlaws' camp and outnumber them more than three to one before we even begin any attack. Trust me – I've learned a few lessons since I've been sparring with Hood. He's no military genius, he's just some peasant that's had a lucky streak." He sipped the weak ale and wiped his mouth neatly. "Well, his luck won't hold forever. I can feel it; the end of my long chase is coming."

Matt smiled, strangely pleased by the crazed look that filled his captain's eyes. He knew why Hood and the rest of them had never been captured yet: it was because the people hunting them – Gisbourne and the previous bailiff Adam Gurdon before that – had played it safe. Neither of them had wanted to upset the commoners too much – Sheriff de Faucumberg had specifically warned both lawmen to tread lightly and not cause any unrest among the locals.

When Adam Gurdon had taken the law into his own hands and falsely arrested Hood's sweetheart Matilda there had been disastrous consequences for the bailiff and, ever since, the sheriff had made sure the villagers were mostly left alone.

It was a ridiculous policy, Groves thought. How could they be expected to catch the outlaws while the locals provided them with supplies and pretended not to know their whereabouts when the law turned up looking for answers? No, if Matt had been in charge, Hood would have been strung up a long time ago. Squeeze the villagers so hard that they'd be desperate to do anything that restored peace to their lives, even if that mean turning over the now-legendary wolf's head, Robin Hood.

Up until now Gisbourne's orders from the sheriff, and his own strange code of honour, had meant the people of Wakefield, Hathersage, Penyston, and all the other little towns and villages, had been allowed to live their lives unmolested by the men hunting Hood. But recently there had been a little spark of insanity in Sir Guy's eye and Matt had done his best to fan that spark into a raging balefire.

"The people around here were always happy to help us," Matt said, watching his leader's face. "They knew you and your men wouldn't harm them. They used to laugh about it. 'The Raven,' they'd say to us, 'not much of a fucking raven that can't use his beak or talons.'"

Gisbourne was no fool and he had an inkling Groves was also somewhat smarter – or at least more devious – than people assumed. He suspected his new second-in-command was goading him, pushing him to take more forceful action in their hunt for the accursed outlaw. But, in truth, Gisbourne needed little goading. Ever since Hood had humiliated him, and sliced off half his face, the Raven had been nursing a growing hatred for the young man which had only grown fiercer in recent weeks.

It was indeed time to use harsher measures to deal with Hood and his men once and for all. If that meant bringing violence to the villages that lay dotted around the forest of Barnsdale, so be it. Burning Patrick Prudhomme's house would just be the beginning.

"How did you end up a sailor then?" Sir Guy asked, changing the subject abruptly. "I thought you were born in Sheffield. That's not exactly a port town."

Matt sat back, mug resting on his paunch, and stretched his legs out towards the fire, chair creaking in protest as he settled his considerable bulk comfortably.

"Aye, I'm a Sheffield man originally but I left there when I was old enough to grow my first beard. My mother died of fever when I was a lad, so it was just me, my da, and my big brother Philip."

Matt's voice trailed off and he sat, gazing into the dancing flames for a long time, until Gisbourne thought the man must have fallen asleep. "Philip was more of a father to me than my da," he eventually muttered, eyes still fixed on the hearth. "He was four years older than me, and my best mate. We used to go fishing together all the time; Philip was a fine fisherman. We'd always come home with something for the pot. It was never good enough for da, though..."

Gisbourne sighed and shifted in his seat, beginning to regret asking to hear this story. It was not going to be a barrel of laughs...

"My father was a carpenter," Matt went on, oblivious. "It was a decent job and we never had a leaky roof or draughts coming in through holes in the door at night, no – my da was fine and handy. But Philip and I never really felt comfortable in the house." He looked up at Sir Guy and nodded towards the bounty-hunter's mug. "I admire you for sticking to that weak, watered-down ale, even if it does taste like piss. This stuff," he hefted his own mug of strong ale ruefully, "is the devil's own brew. It's the source of all evil in this world."

Ignoring his own platitude, Matt took a long drink, gasping with pleasure as he leaned forward and slammed the empty wooden mug onto the table. "More, inn-keep!"

As the landlord hurried to obey, Groves stuck a poker in the fire to warm before crossing his hands in his lap and continuing his tale.

"I like a drink, I have to be honest, I do. Nothing better in the world than a few mugs of ale and a nice pair of tits to get your hands on, eh?" He grinned at his captain but Gisbourne only nodded politely, thinking of lots of things he'd enjoy more than either of those.

"Well, my da liked a drink as well, even more than I do. It was all the bastard lived for." The smile fell from Matt's face and his usual sour expression returned. "You'd think he'd have wanted to spend time with us – his boys. See us growing up into men. But no, the useless sot would take himself straight to the local alehouse as soon as he finished work and had his pay in his purse. Then, when the place shut for the night, or he got himself thrown out, he'd come home and..."

Again his voice trailed off and the inn-keeper hurried over to hand him another mug brimming with ale. He lifted the hot poker from the fire and placed the bright tip into the liquid which hissed and steamed in protest.

"Philip got it the worst, probably because he was bigger, and he had more of a mouth on him than I did. I don't know why my da was always angry when he came home – maybe my mother's death had done something to his head. Or maybe the drink made him like that. Some people get happy when they have a few ales – they sing songs and dance about like idiots. My da always seemed to get pissed off when he had a few though..."

A small smile flickered on his face. "Aye, Philip would give as good as he got, with his words. But it would just make da even angrier, then he'd take off his belt, or use his bare hands. I must have been about six or seven when this was going on, so my brother would have been only ten or eleven. A boy, nothing more than a boy. My da was a big man too. I remember his hands were huge and always covered in hard, flaky skin that would crack and bleed in the winter. Served the bastard right."

Gisbourne had no idea any of this had happened in his new sergeant's past, but it didn't surprise him in the least. His head nodded and he forced himself to sit up straighter to avoid drifting off into a comfortable sleep as Matt went on.

"I took a beating a few times, aye... got a few black eyes and my ears..." He rubbed the side of his head and Gisbourne noticed for the first time that, underneath Matt's poker-straight dirty-blonde hair, his ears were huge; thick and puffy in a way that looked almost obscene to the king's man who suppressed a shudder and hid his distaste by sipping his weak drink.

"But Philip took the worst of it. He grew big and strong and eventually, one night when my da came home drunk and tried to use his fists, Philip was too fast."

Matt's eyes lit-up gleefully, remembering that night, re-living it as if it were only yesterday. "Smashed da's nose he did. Blood everywhere!" His voice dropped and he looked down at the floor. "I was terrified," he admitted. "I thought my da would kill him." There was another sigh and another long pause as Matt took a drink of the warm ale, letting the bitter liquid seep into his belly as he watched the flames flicker and dance in the hearth before them.

"So what happened?" Gisbourne demanded, interested in spite of himself. "Did your father kill him?"

Matt shrugged. "I don't know. I've never seen Philip since that night." He looked up and met his captain's eyes. "I ran away out the house and slept under a bush. Didn't come back until the next morning. When I got there my da was out at work as usual and there was no sign of my brother."

"Did you not ask your father what'd happened?"

"Aye, I did, once, when he'd not been paid and couldn't afford to spend the whole night in the alehouse." Matt shook his head in consternation. "He said he'd no idea where Philip had gone and I believe he spoke the truth. I think he was so damn drunk that night that whatever happened was wiped from his memory. Wouldn't be the first time that's happened to someone – God's bollocks, it's happened to me more than once." He grinned, as if proud of himself. "I've no idea whether Philip was killed by my da and dumped in the river or... maybe my big brother ran off same as me, only he never came back in the morning like I did..."

Gisbourne wasn't surprised to see tears in Matt's eyes. The man was quite drunk, which seemed rather ironic to the bounty-hunter given the gist of Matt's story.

"None of this explains how you ended up a sailor," the king's man said, waving towards the inn-keeper for a refill of his own. Although the ale he drank had been watered-down, it was still just enough to get a man like Gisbourne – who drank alcohol infrequently – comfortably numb.

Matt's head was nodding as sleep threatened to overtake him but his whole body seemed to jerk awake again at his captain's words and he looked blearily at Sir Guy, as if wondering who the man was.

Eventually, with another deep draught of ale, he continued the story, the landlord watching surreptitiously from behind the bar.

"I've never seen Philip since that night," he repeated morosely. "For the next few years my da took out his frustrations on me. I'd lie awake in bed dreading him coming home. I don't know... it seems like he beat the shit out of me near enough every night but it can't really have been that often. And he normally used his belt rather than his fists which hurt like hell but at least it didn't break bones. Still have the scars on my legs though; don't expect they'll ever go away."

A log cracked and split loudly, causing Matt to jump and take another sip of ale. "Anyway, I eventually grew big enough that I could look after myself. My da must have known he'd have a fight on his hands if he continued to beat me once I was full-grown and it stopped." He looked over at Sir Guy, his eyes surprisingly lucid for the moment. "I'd not forgotten what had happened with my big brother though; I missed him and I wondered how our lives might have turned out if we'd had a sober father instead of a sot. Anyway – the resentment built up inside me over the years... it wasn't a happy household ours, not by a long way."

"What happened?"

The flare of lucidity dimmed in Matt's eyes as he retreated back into himself again, the firelight casting a ruddy glow on his dour face. "My da came home one night, in a foul mood. He must have lost money at dice or something; whatever it was, he came in shouting and hauled me out the bed before trying to throttle me for not clearing away my dinner plate or some stupid thing." His voice became hard and his eyes blazed as he remembered that night.

"For the first time in my life, I defended myself. I wasn't a little boy any more, I was almost the same size as I am now. I hit him. And I hit him again, and again. When he fell on the floor, covering his head in his hands – just like I'd done as a child – it made me mad." He growled in satisfaction. "I beat him senseless – there was blood all over the room – then I took what money he had on him, or hidden in the strongbox under our bed, along with his dagger and what little food there was in the house. And I left. I've never been back."

Gisbourne was getting tired himself by now, his head beginning to slump onto his chest, but the story was obviously nearing its conclusion and he wanted to hear it.

"You found a job on some ship then?"

"Eventually," Matt agreed. "Although I had to scratch a living for a few months – stealing money and food just to survive. Sleeping rough in various towns, trying to avoid the guards... Then I came to Hull and, by luck or by chance, got caught trying to steal the purse from a sailor. Older man, from some freezing country away up to the north – Norway or that. He saw I was starving and desperate and was kind enough to get his captain to find a place on their ship for me. I sailed with them for nearly two years, learned my trade and then moved from ship to ship wherever the work took me... Got fed up with it eventually though, it was a hard life."

Gisbourne gestured impatiently for him to continue.

"Got into a fight in a tavern in Coatham one day. Arsehole tried to cheat me at dice and I stabbed him with my dagger. The same dagger I took from my da." His hand patted his hip, feeling the reassuring bulk of the weapon safely tucked away. "I had to escape from the law, so it was back to hiding and moving from town to town, making a living where I could. I did a lot of bad things then."

He shrugged as if he'd only done what was necessary.

"Wound up in Barnsdale and found Adam Bell and his gang. They took me in and looked after me. Had some good times with Adam until that whoreson Robin Hood turned up and took over the place." He tried to empty the remainder of his drink into his mouth but most of it spilled down his chin and into his tunic although he didn't seem to notice. Blearily, he got to his feet and shouted for the inn-keeper to show him to the room they'd paid for.

As the man half-led, half-carried Matt along the gloomy corridor the former-outlaw mumbled to himself. "Bastard Hood. I'll see him dead one day, I swear it!"

CHAPTER NINETEEN

"They're home!" Young Gareth ran into camp, eyes shining and a huge grin on his narrow face. "They're back!"

"Who's back?" Stephen, the former Hospitaller sergeant-at-arms demanded, buckling on his sword-belt which he'd grabbed from beside his pallet as soon as he heard the skinny youngster from Wrangbrook tearing through the slowly thickening spring foliage towards them. The rest of the men that were around the camp that day followed his lead, grabbing weapons and strapping on whatever armour they owned, ready for whatever danger approached.

"Robin and John," Gareth shouted, barely panting despite his mad dash from his lookout post high in a Scots pine. "Although they're dressed like friars," he reported, a puzzled look on his face. "Even got their heads shaved like friars. Never seen John without his beard."

Will Scarlet kicked earth over the camp-fire to extinguish it and placed a wooden board on top to disperse the tell-tale smoke over a wider area so it wouldn't give away their position so obviously. He ran forward to stare at Gareth, hope flaring within him.

"Friars? Have you been on the drink again?" he demanded. "Are you sure it's Robin and John and not someone else? Like Gisbourne?"

Gareth shook his head, angry at Will's suggestion he was too drunk to know what some of his best friends looked like. "It's them Scarlet, and I think Allan's with them. I've not drank any more than the rest of you this morning. You were pretty legless yourself last night too, so don't act as if you're better than me you sour-faced c–"

"Enough of this," Stephen growled, stepping between the two men before Scarlet could do anything. "Maybe it's them, and maybe it's not. The fact they're heading this way suggests they know where our camp is, so I'm inclined to believe it *is* them. It was Robin himself that suggested we come here to Selby after all. You," he nodded at Gareth. "Good work warning us of their approach, lad, whoever it turns out to be – at least we'll meet them with sword in hand rather than lying on our backs on the grass. Now get back to your post in case anyone else is behind them." He patted the young man on his shoulder encouragingly and was rewarded with a steely nod of gratitude before Gareth sprinted off into the trees again.

Will looked somewhat sheepish at the Hospitaller's command of the situation since he'd done nothing other than irritate the lookout. He nodded his thanks to Stephen then turned and addressed the men. "Archers, take your positions in the trees. The rest of you get behind me in a semi-circle with your weapons drawn. Whoever these men are, they'll not find us sitting on our arses – we'll be ready for whatever they're bringing us."

A nervous silence came over the men but no-one appeared. The birds continued to sing and forage amongst the previous year's fallen leaves, but as the men watched the trees in the direction Gareth had said the travellers were coming from there was no sign of anyone approaching.

Will, string fitted to his longbow, fingered the goose-feathers of his arrow and, as time dragged by he cursed to himself, wishing something would happen.

"Where are they?" The voice belonged to Arthur, the stocky young man with hardly any teeth left despite his tender years, but Will couldn't see him to offer an angry rebuke, resorting instead to a furious hiss he hoped would discourage any further lack of discipline from the men.

At last, just as the sun reached its highest point in the sky, casting a wan yellow glow on the greenery that surrounded them, voices filtered through the trees towards them and Will nocked the arrow to his bowstring, happy in the knowledge the rest of the men would also be preparing themselves for whatever happened next. Or *who*ever...

"God be praised, it *is* them," Edmond said as Little John's great booming voice echoed around the forest and Robin's unmistakeable laugh followed.

"Shut your fucking mouth and keep your weapon at the ready!" Scarlet commanded in a low voice, his face flushing crimson, and Edmond nodded guiltily.

Then, as if they hadn't a care in the world, Robin, John and Allan-a-Dale wandered, grinning, into the clearing and looked around at the vast array of weaponry that met them.

"Lads, is that any way to welcome us home?" Robin laughed, and Will, forgetting his own demand for discipline, ran forward to embrace his friends.

* * *

Surprisingly, Helen didn't come after Marjorie to avenge her humiliation at the older girl's hands. In fact, Helen and her friends gave Robin's sister a wide berth whenever their paths happened to cross.

Marjorie felt – perhaps stupidly – guilty about what she'd done to the girl. Yes, she might have deserved to be taken down a peg or two, but the pained look on her face when Marjorie had kicked her to the ground still played on her mind. She felt some empathy with the girl; harsh bereavement was a common factor in both their young lives and it affected people in different ways.

Before her mother died Helen had been quite a popular girl and, although she'd tossed the odd insult Marjorie's way, well, so had almost every other girl in the village – it was just what children did and, although it had been hurtful, Marjorie knew now that it had all helped make her who she was. It had all strengthened her and was now contributing to her drive to break out of the role of weakling that seemed to have been assigned to her by God and everyone in Wakefield. Even her parents who doted on her.

Eventually, she'd had enough of the sullen looks and crossed the dusty street one morning when she'd spotted Helen walking on her own, on some errand or other.

"Wait."

"What do you want? We've left you alone, just like you wanted." Helen's bottom lip thrust out and her fists clenched, as if preparing for another physical altercation and Marjorie spoke fast to reassure the girl.

"Look, I'm sorry I hit you. You were being horrible and when you got into my face I just wanted to defend myself and keep you away from me. Truly, I'm sorry. I should have just ignored you."

Helen looked at her warily, hands still balled into fists, not really sure how to react. She knew herself she'd deserved to be beaten; she'd been mean to the other girl for no reason. Yet here was the lass she'd been tormenting, apologising for standing up to her.

Marjorie smiled, apparently sincerely, and Helen looked ashamed. She was bigger than this girl, which was one reason why she'd picked on her. Smaller people were usually easy targets; didn't normally fight back.

"No, *I'm* sorry," she said. "Everyone knows why you're small. I was being a bitch and I got what I deserved. If someone spoke to me like that I'd have beaten them bloody and... well, you had that wooden sword so I was glad you let me go." Her eyes dropped to Marjorie's midriff, looking to see if the practice weapon was concealed again and this was all just the prelude to a thrashing.

"I've got it, aye," Marjorie smiled in reply to the unspoken question. "I carry it with me all the time now, so it becomes second nature."

Helen stiffened almost imperceptibly as the girl pulled out the weapon; short, with many nicks in the dull edge but sturdy and dangerous looking. Her eyes widened at the freshly oiled wood which Marjorie was obviously proud of.

"Could... could you teach me how to use one?"

Marjorie hesitated. Fighting was *her* thing. She didn't want to let another girl – especially one already bigger than her despite being four years her junior – share it with her. Then she remembered something Matilda had told her, a piece of wisdom that apparently originated with Will Scaflock: "If you truly want to master something, teach it."

From then on, Marjorie had a new sparring partner for those times Matilda was busy with little Arthur or with her work in the fletcher's. She and Helen became friends, finding they had much in common other than the fact they'd both suffered painful losses. The younger girl came to look up to Marjorie, impressed by her natural skill with the wooden sword and her dedication to improve herself despite the limitations of her body. Soon, other local girls were joining in with the sparring and training sessions. None took it as seriously as Marjorie, but all seemed to enjoy it and all seemed happy to look to her for instruction.

Marjorie found herself happier than she'd ever been in all her fifteen years on God's earth. She was close to her parents and enjoyed spending time with Matilda and Arthur as the baby grew and learned to walk properly and speak a few words. The way he pronounced her name always made her smile: "Mahjy." Proud Auntie Mahjy. She also progressed with her training – helping Helen and the girls was really paying off for her. She'd never be able to stand up to someone as big, or as skilled as, for example, Little John or Allan-a-Dale, but most men weren't like that. None of the villagers were as big as her brother and his companions, or as deadly with sword and longbow – those men were exceptional because they *had* to be to survive as outlaws.

Marjorie felt, somewhat naively, that she could hold her own if some village boy – like the miller's son who'd been giving her lecherous looks for weeks – had tried to molest her.

She felt good when she woke in the mornings now, and walked with a straight-backed swagger that people had started to notice and comment upon.

John and Martha Hood, of course, had seen the change in their previously skinny, quiet daughter and had pried the truth from Matilda. They'd agreed to turn a blind eye, despite the antinomian nature of Marjorie's new pursuit, since the change in her was so plainly for the better.

Matilda watched as her sister-in-law grew into a confident young woman and prayed to God her eager student would never need to put her fighting skills to use for real.

Behind her smile, though, Marjorie still felt like something was missing.

* * *

"Let's stop here for the night," Osferth suggested as a small village appeared on the horizon. "We've made good time today and it'll be dark soon. I don't know about you but I'd rather sleep in a bed than on the damp grass again. My neck still aches from last night's 'sleep'." He grimaced and bent his head from side to side as if to demonstrate his pain. "I'm not used to sleeping outdoors like you."

Tuck nodded. "Fair enough. We're nearly in Yorkshire anyway. Should reach Horbury by tomorrow if we're on the road early enough. I know some people there who might be able to tell us where Robin and the boys are camping. Hopefully the sheriff hasn't caught them yet."

They rode into the village – Bryneford according to the almost-illegible sign – which was little more than a handful of houses and a little wooden building that doubled as both church and the local priest's dwelling. There wasn't even an inn but one of the locals, a man named Philip, had a spare room in his house as a result of some disease that had visited the place a few weeks earlier and he allowed the two clergymen to stay with him in return for some small coins.

The villager had some ale which he shared with the clergymen and they made idle chatter to pass the time as night fell. Tuck seemed to grow drowsy very quickly although Osferth's eyes remained alert despite appearing to consume just as much of the drink as the older man.

"Come on, we'll get you into the bed," Osferth smiled, helping Tuck off the bench that ran along one side of the villager's house. "I'll stay up with Philip here for a while longer; I'm enjoying sampling all these local ales on our adventure. Makes a nice change from the same old piss-water we got back in the priory."

The villager gave them a candle which he'd lit from the big fire in the centre of the room and Osferth helped his friend into the little room with its pair of straw mattresses. Philip assured them he'd burned the old beds to get rid of any dangerous fluids or vapours since the previous occupants – Philip's teenage sons – had gone to their final resting place. Without his boys to help him on the small plot of land he farmed the villager had to find some other source of income so, with no inn in the little place, it seemed a decent idea to offer his spare room to any travellers in return for a few coins.

"I haven't had any 'guests' yet, other than you two," he'd told them when they first arrived. "So the mattresses will be nice and plump for you."

And indeed they were, heavy and comfortable, even if it seemed something of an intrusion to be sleeping in a bed that belonged to a dead boy not so long ago. Still, within a few moments Tuck was sound asleep and snoring loud enough to shake the rafters until Osferth rolled him onto his front, quieting the rumbling only marginally, and left the room with a somewhat nervous backward glance.

"Another?" Philip looked up as the monk returned, the big ale pot hovering above Osferth's empty mug.

"Not right now. May I borrow this candle?"

Philip looked puzzled but nodded agreement. "It's not windy so it should stay alight for a while but... where are you going at this time of the night?"

"I need to speak with the priest. Will he be at home?"

"Father Martin? Aye, he should be in the church. Young man he is, but he never really goes anywhere outside of the village. I suppose he might be visiting someone but..." He shrugged as if to say that was unlikely and Osferth thanked him before opening the front door.

"I won't be long. My companion will not awaken while I'm away."

"Eh? How d'you know that?" Philip wondered, but Osferth had already shut the door and was gone.

CHAPTER TWENTY

Tuck woke in the morning, surprised to have slept such a deep, dreamless sleep in the recently deceased villagers' bedroom. He couldn't remember waking at all during the night which was unusual for him as he often had to get up to empty his bladder in the small hours. And yet, despite his unbroken slumber, his head ached just behind his eyes and his mouth was dry.

"God above," he mumbled as he rose and stretched the kinks from his back. "How much of that ale did I drink last night?"

Osferth, who was already up and looking fresh, simply smiled and tossed a water-skin to his companion who pulled out the stopper and sucked down the cool liquid greedily.

"What time is it?"

"Sun's just coming up," Osferth replied, pointing to a small chest in the corner upon which lay a bowl of tepid water. "Philip must have left that there for us."

Tuck used the liquid to rinse the sleep from his eyes before drying himself off with his sleeve. "All right, we better get moving then. We want to get to Dodworth as soon as we can. The longer we tarry the more chance there is that my friends will be captured." He threw his pack over his shoulder and lifted his great quarterstaff. "We can break our fast on the road, come on."

Philip wasn't about and the travellers assumed he must have gone off to work, trusting them not to steal anything from the house. Tuck looked around and wondered what they could steal even if they were so inclined; there was little of any value in the small dwelling which seemed to exude an air of sadness still, or maybe that was just the friar's imagination.

"Let's go." He opened the door and moved outside. Their horses were in a small stable adjoining the church and, as Osferth got the mounts ready Tuck decided it would be polite to give God's greetings to the local priest before they left.

He knocked on the door but no-one answered and a villager shouted across to him. "Father Martin's not in. He was up before dawn and borrowed my horse to run some errand. I've no idea where he's gone though."

"No matter," Tuck smiled with a wave of thanks to the man. "It's not important. God give you good day."

They climbed onto their mounts and resumed the journey north, with dark glances at a sky that was filled with looming thunderheads.

"Come on, Horbury isn't far," Tuck shouted, kicking his heels into the old palfrey. "Let's reach it before we get a soaking."

* * *

James had tried, he really had, but there just wasn't any honest work available for him in Horbury. He wasn't an outlaw himself, for he hadn't been caught doing anything illegal, but the locals knew he kept company with thieves and wolf's heads and, as a result he couldn't even get a job labouring in the fields or on the site of the building works at the new brewery that was being built just outside the town.

How was he supposed to live an honest life if no-one would give him the chance to support himself?

His meeting with the portly friar just weeks earlier had truly had a profound effect on him and he'd vowed to stop his robbing ways before he was either declared an outlaw or killed by a forester's arrow. Christ, Sir Guy of Gisbourne and his men were staying in the town; the close proximity of the feared bounty hunter should have been enough reason for James to live within the law.

And yet, here he was, hiding under a bush, hood up as the rain had come on with a vengeance, flanked by two of the men the friar had bested so violently. The third member of their gang hadn't been so lucky – Tuck's blow had cracked his skull and he'd died the next day. Not that any of the rest cared much – none of them were close friends, simply acquaintances and the threat of violent death was an ever-present threat when you earned a living stealing from people.

Now they sat and watched the road for unwary travellers with coin to spare and little chance of fighting off the robbers.

James scowled. If people wouldn't trust him enough to employ him, what choice did he have but to live like this? He needed to put food on his table didn't he? It was just as well his wife had died young, before she could give him a child. He could barely even fill his own belly never mind anyone else's.

There was movement on the road and he sat up straighter, squinting through the torrential rain to try and make out who approached.

"Someone's coming," Mark, their short leader growled, his voice hopeful. "Perhaps this one'll have more about him than that last bastard."

They'd stopped a young merchant a short time before, travelling alone, and it soon became apparent why he hadn't felt the need to hire mercenaries to guard him on the dangerous northern road: he had little money on him and his 'wares' consisted of a pack filled with strange smelling ointments and liquids in glass bottles. The man had tried to explain to them what they were – some kind of medicines apparently – but Mark had silenced him with a brutal punch to the side of the face before taking his purse and sending the sobbing man on his way in disgust.

"Medicines for fuck sake. What good's that to us?"

James didn't reply, he was staring at the road as their potential targets approached at a fair pace, their mounts' hooves covering the distance to their position in good time.

Suddenly Mark gave a small, gleeful hoot and turned to his friends happily. "It's the friar, he's back."

"So it is." Ivo, the man whose teeth Tuck had broken muttered agreement, his hand pressing unconsciously on his lips, feeling the empty spaces left by the friar's cudgel. "Good. This time we'll be prepared for him. We'll see how *he* likes losing a few teeth."

"And his balls too," Mark spat the words viciously, still furious to have been beaten – humiliated – by a man of the cloth. "James, get an arrow ready. You can let his mate in the black robe ride on, but take out the greyfriar's horse. Once the prick's on the ground me and Ivo will take care of the rest."

James hadn't told his cohorts what had happened between himself and the friar when they had tried to rob the man before. How could he? They were already angry that he hadn't skewered the bastard when he had the chance; there was no way he could tell them he'd had a nice, friendly chat with the clergyman. Instead, he'd claimed to have been hit in the guts by the cudgel which he said the friar had thrown at him. Once he'd been on the ground, gasping for breath, he said, the friar had retrieved the weapon and raced off on his horse.

It was a feeble story and his cohorts had given him suspicious looks as he told it, but they had no reason to suspect he was lying. Little did they know Friar Tuck had made a friend of James that day and now, here was Mark demanding the young archer shoot the clergyman's horse...

"No."

The robbers swivelled their heads to glare at James who returned their looks with eyes as steely as their own.

"Do you not realise who he is?"

"I don't give a fuck who he is," Ivo spat. "He's going to pay for what he did to us."

Mark pointed his dagger angrily at James. "Just you get an arrow ready, dickhead, or it'll be *your* balls I'll be slicing off with this."

"Are you stupid?" James retorted more confidently than he felt in the face of his violent companions' ire. "How many friars have you heard about around here that can fight as well as he does? That's Friar Tuck. Robin Hood's mate."

Mark and Ivo were too angry to back down and their hated target was nearing their position rapidly, the horses close enough now that the spray thrown up from their hooves was visible.

"Shoot him now," Mark ordered, his eyes blazing in anger. Never before had James stood up to him or refused to do as he was told by the older, if smaller man. "Shoot him you arsehole, before he escapes or so help me God I'll cut your fucking eyes out."

James shrank back from his leader, knowing the man was just deranged enough to carry out his threat. He looked towards the road and realized he only had moments to take his shot before Tuck would be past and safely out of range.

"Shoot him!" Ivo shouted, the rain slicking the long black hair against his angry face.

James took a deep breath, his stomach contorting as if filled with a dozen live larks like one of the extravagant pies the wealthy supposedly ate, and raised his longbow with the arrow already nocked and ready to loose.

"Holy Mary, mother of God, protect me," he prayed and aimed along the shaft of the big missile, pointing the iron broadhead not at the mounted clergymen, but towards his own robber-companions.

Stepping backwards, slowly and carefully he held his aim steady as he distanced himself from the shocked – and utterly furious – Mark and Ivo who stared at him vengefully.

"I knew that story you told us about him throwing his cudgel at you was bollocks," Mark grated.

"I'm not shooting his horse just so you two can kill him. The man spared all of our lives the first time we tried to rob him, when he could just as easily have slit our throats. Hell, he'd have been given a *reward* for killing us; but still he let us go." He held his bow steady in his left hand while he quickly leaned down and grabbed his small pack of food with the right, throwing its strap across his shoulder before drawing the bowstring taut again and resuming his slow, backward movement. "Besides, he's a man of God for fuck sake. You don't kill a man of God!"

"I'll fucking kill *you,* you whoreson," Mark roared, his face scarlet, and Ivo screamed his own murderous oath.

"And on top of all that," James continued, shouting himself now, "he's one of Robin Hood's gang. If they found out we'd killed him they'd come hunting for us. You want Little John coming after you? 'Cause I don't."

He was a fair distance away from them now and, with a sigh of relief lowered the longbow, fitted the arrow back inside his belt and, curses filling the air behind him, broke into a loping run towards Horbury. Mark and Ivo were both well-known outlaws and wouldn't come into the town after him, especially not with Guy of Gisbourne lodging in the Swan as he was.

Aye, the Swan, James thought as his long stride carried him north. *That's the safest place to be just now. Mark will never dare to follow me there.*

He'd use his share of the money they'd stolen from the medicine-seller to pay for a room, then decide what to do next in the morning.

It had been a foolhardy move to cross the two outlaws but... by God it had felt good!

* * *

Tuck and Osferth made fine time but were not quite fast enough to outrun the oncoming clouds which overtook them and spilled their chilly contents on the travellers when they were still some distance from Horbury.

They cantered past the three robbers hiding in the undergrowth at the side of the road, oblivious to the danger that was so close and, by the time they reached the town and found sanctuary from the downpour in an inn, the clergymen were both drenched.

"In God's name, it's Tuck." The landlord smiled in surprise when he spotted the dripping friar who shook the water from his tonsured head like a great dog.

"Aye, Andrew, it's me – don't just stand there grinning like a lack-wit, man. Warmed ale for my companion and I!"

The inn-keep hurried to do as he was told, bustling over a moment later with two gently steaming mugs, the smile still on his face as he looked down at the seated clergymen.

"I heard you'd left Robin Hood's gang and gone back down south; didn't expect you'd be back here again, but it's good to see you, father."

Tuck sipped his ale and wiped the remaining dampness from his forehead with a big hand before returning the landlord's smile. "I did leave Robin and the rest of the lads," he said. "But I need to find them again, and quickly. Do you have any word of their whereabouts?"

It was before noon and, apart from the three of them, the place was empty at that time of day, but a loose tongue could be fatal and the man's eyes settled on Osferth.

Tuck waved a hand reassuringly. "Have no fear, this is my friend, one of the Benedictines from Lewes: you may talk freely in front of him."

Still, the inn-keeper seemed inordinately nervous, his eyes casting about his own inn to make sure no-one was hiding in the shadows and he leaned in close to address the friar in hushed tones.

"I haven't seen any of your companions around here in a long time, but word is Will Scarlet and some Hospitaller were in Selby buying supplies a few days back. Maybe they have a camp near there?" He shrugged but remained bent over beside them. "You'd know better than me."

Tuck looked thoughtful. Maybe Robin did have a hideout somewhere close to Selby but they'd never camped there when Tuck was with them. Still, the friar hadn't been with them as long as most of the others and it was possible there were camps the outlaws knew of but Tuck had never visited himself.

"One other thing, Brother," the landlord continued, his eyes again darting nervously around the shadows.

"For God's sake, Andrew, spit it out. There's no one here other than us – it's *your* inn, you must know that yourself!"

The man looked somewhat embarrassed and gave a nervous smile before continuing. "You're right, of course, but it does no harm to be careful when the likes of Sir Guy of Gisbourne are about. Aye," he nodded in response to Tuck's anxious expression. "The Raven has taken lodgings just up the road in the Swan. Apparently the sheriff ran him out of Nottingham when Robin took the silver arrow."

Tuck held up his hands to stop the inn-keeper's words, a baffled look on his round face. "Wait, hold on man. I've been down in Lewes remember, I have no idea what you're talking about. Fetch Osferth and I another ale – get one for yourself too – and join us. Tell us the whole story. In fact," he groped inside his cassock for a moment before pulling out a couple of small silver coins and placing them on the table. "If that bastard Gisbourne's about we'd better not be seen. We'll take a room – a decent one, mind. We'll head for Selby in the morning and hope the rumours you heard prove correct. In the meantime – where's that ale? Let's hear about Robin and the silver arrow."

With freshly-filled mugs before them, Andrew told Tuck and Osferth what had happened when Robin and Little John had gone to the city to rescue the minstrel Allan-a-Dale. The tale bore little relation to what had actually happened, having grown in the telling as it travelled from mouth to mouth on its way to Horbury via any number of storytellers, each of whom had embellished the events of that day.

When the landlord finished, a broad smile on his face at the sheriff's humbling by the bold outlaw hero, Tuck couldn't help but return a broad grin of his own. He knew the tale had been exaggerated, but at the core of the thing seemed to be the fact his young friend Robin had won a near-priceless silver arrow from Sir Henry de Faucumberg while he and Little John had saved Allan from a certain hanging.

It sounded like the sort of legendary feat that seemed to happen when Robin was around. No doubt the minstrels – Allan especially – would be expanding the tale even further until every man, woman and child in England knew what had happened in Nottingham.

It was late afternoon by now and the men of the town were starting to filter in through the doors, looking for warm ale to chase the damp from their aching joints so Andrew stood up, cheeks flushed from the four mugs of ale he'd downed while chatting with the two clergymen, and excused himself to deal with his new customers.

"I assume your wife is slaving away in the kitchen," Tuck called after him, sniffing the air as the pleasant aroma of meat and vegetables roasting wafted through from the back of the building. "Send us out a couple of bowls of whatever that is she's cooking up in there."

The meal – beef and ale stew with chunks of fresh bread – proved to be both tasty and filling and Tuck settled back happily in his chair to let the food digest.

"Maybe it's not such a good idea to sit around here all night," Osferth said, watching nervously as the front door swung open again and another pair of labourers came in looking for meat and drink. "If that bounty hunter's about, I mean. The Raven did the inn-keep call him? He knows you doesn't he? No point in getting caught before you have a chance to warn your friends is there?"

Tuck nodded ruefully. "Aye, you have a point. From the sounds of it the news of Robin's whereabouts haven't reached Gisbourne yet or he'd not be hanging around here. So we still have some time, praise be to Our Lord. Aye," he slapped the table decisively. "You're right, we should keep out of sight. Let me go for a piss then we'll retire to our room for the evening. We can get a good night's sleep and be up early on the morrow."

The burly friar got unsteadily to his feet and waved to Andrew who stood behind the wooden bar serving another patron. "Night! We'll be up at dawn – have some bread and cheese ready for us to take will you? Oh, and refill our drinks," he grinned, waving blearily towards a random pair of empty mugs. "We'll drink 'em in our room."

With a final wave the friars lifted the freshly refilled mugs and stumbled from the common room. Stopping only to relieve themselves at the latrine they made their way back to the lodgings Andrew had allocated to them for the night and Tuck slipped the bolt across the door with a satisfied sigh.

Ah, he'd always enjoyed travelling. Couldn't beat a night in a comfortable, cosy inn, with plenty of food, drink and good company – it was one of life's greatest pleasures.

He lay down on the bed and sipped at the mug he'd carried along the darkened corridor from the common room, savouring the delicious taste. Funny how even the vilest local ale tasted like Heaven's own nectar after seven or eight mugs he thought.

Osferth watched, his own mug resting untouched on a chest of drawers – the only piece of furniture in the room other than the two narrow beds, as Tuck's eyelids drooped and, after a short time, the big tonsured head fell forward on to his chest. The mug fell from limp fingers onto the floor, spilling the watery brown liquid on the grimy floorboards and a snore erupted from the friar's open mouth.

Osferth was glad it didn't take much dwale to send his companion into a deep sleep. Too heavy a dose of the stuff could be fatal and the younger monk liked his portly companion. He'd mixed the strange concoction – made from a variety of ingredients including henbane, vinegar and lettuce – with Tuck's ale whenever he needed the friar to take a long, unbroken nap. Like now.

The snoring filled the little room and Osferth smiled down at the slumbering form affectionately as he opened the door just wide enough to slip out into the hallway.

"Sleep tight, brother," he whispered, before losing himself in the shadows. "I'll be back just as soon as I've met the Raven."

CHAPTER TWENTY-ONE

James was lucky – the landlord of the Swan had one room remaining, a tiny cramped affair which seemed more like a storeroom than a place to spend a night but there was a pallet on the floor in which the young man could lie down if he kept his legs bent.

It was good enough for James who simply wanted a place to keep out of the reach of his erstwhile, murderous colleagues and the Swan, with its resident Raven, was perfect. Mark and Ivo, outlaws both, would never dare to set foot in the place, even if they knew their hated quarry was staying there for the night.

He had the silver they'd taken from the merchant and he decided to use it to enjoy his evening so he found a seat in the large common room as close to the fire as he could manage, although the place was busy and the benches nearest to the hearth were prime locations for cold and weary patrons.

He bought a mug of ale from the bald, bearded landlord and sipped at it contentedly. The king's bounty hunter was in the corner with his sergeant, much nearer to the fire than James. The man stood out like a fox in a henhouse; confidence and an air of barely repressed violence emanated from his black-clad figure and James was glad he'd decided to give up robbing folk with Mark and Ivo. The thought of the tall, wiry Raven hunting him down made him shiver.

A number of locals, clearly friends, sat together at a long table singing songs and telling jokes and James watched from the corner of his eye, enjoying the silly banter and ribald verse that was being belted out.

The bounty-hunter didn't seem to mind the drunken revelry but his companion, a dour-faced middle-aged man occasionally threw the noisy group an irritated glare and James suspected that hard looking lawman was more likely to be the source of trouble than any of the cheerful locals.

Another song ended and James finished his ale, smacking his lips in satisfaction and feeling in his coin-purse to see if he had enough for many more. *Plenty yet*, he said to himself and made his way to the bar, asking the man seated next to him to save his seat for him.

"Another of these, please, inn-keep."

The landlord held up a hand distractedly and James noticed the man was talking to a clergyman of some kind; a thin man in a black robe or cassock With a start, James realised it was Friar Tuck's travelling companion who'd ridden past him and the other thieves that afternoon. James scanned the room, fearful that Tuck might be there too and recognize him; he'd been friendly enough but still, the friar might give him away to Sir Guy.

The landlord was pointing at the sinister-looking bounty-hunter and, as Osferth apologetically shoved his way through the crowd of drinkers towards the lawman's corner seat James shook his head. Of course Tuck wouldn't give him away to Sir Guy – quite the opposite in fact, since the friar was, or had been, a member of Robin Hood's gang. It was common knowledge that Gisbourne and Hood's men were mortal enemies, there were even songs about it.

As Osferth leaned down and spoke into Sir Guy's ear James knew something was amiss. The barman handed him a fresh ale, taking a little coin in return, and the young man surreptitiously pushed his way through the patrons towards the fire.

He was curious and wondered why a companion of Tuck's would be sneaking into the Swan to talk privately with the king's man. As he went, muttering apologies to those he was gently moving aside, he made a show of blowing on his hands as if the warm, cosy hearth was what drew him nearer.

Gisbourne's sergeant watched his captain converse with the monk, a crooked smile on his face and, unnoticed by the trio, James stood with his back to them, straining to catch what was being said.

"How will we know where you're going?" Gisbourne was saying. "If we follow too closely the fat friar might hear us and lead us off in the wrong direction. Or the outlaws' lookouts will spot us and raise the alarm before we can silence them."

"I'll leave a trail for you to follow," the monk replied, smiling. "I'll carve a small cross on a tree whenever I can – all you'll have to do is look out for them to know the way. Tuck seems to think the camp will be about a mile north-east of the village."

"And you're sure the friar doesn't suspect you?"

"Aye, he's no fool," Gisbourne's sergeant put in. "A fat, pious prick, sure, but no fool."

Osferth shook his head but looked angry at the crude epithet the man had given Tuck. "No, he doesn't suspect anything. Why would he? I'm not acting nervously or anything like that which could give me away. I'm doing God's work and saving his soul." He glared at Sir Guy's right-hand man. "Tuck is a good man, whatever you think of him. He trusts me."

The bounty-hunter waved a dismissive hand in Matt's direction. "Ignore him brother – he thinks everyone's a prick. Well, that's it settled then: in the morning you and the friar will head for Selby. Me and Matt here will follow and look out for your carvings on the tree trunks. All being well, we'll discover Hood's camp and can prepare an overwhelming assault which will wipe out the wolf's head and his gang once and for all."

"You won't hurt Tuck, though," the monk said, looking straight into Sir Guy's eyes. Clearly the Benedictine wasn't overawed or frightened of the big bounty-hunter which made James wonder if the man was all right in the head.

"Fear not for your friend," Gisbourne said, then his hand dropped and he clasped the monk's wrist painfully. "If you lead us right in this I'm sure your prior back in Lewes will reward you with a promotion or whatever it is you desire, but..." A dagger seemed to appear from nowhere, its flawless blade glinting in the firelight as Gisbourne placed it under the monk's chin. "If you double-cross us or think to lead us into a trap, well, let's just say Christ and all the saints of heaven won't be able to stop the pain and suffering I'll inflict upon you."

The monk pulled his wrist back, looking annoyed rather than scared by the Raven's violent vow. "Just remember not to hurt Tuck."

The conversation obviously neared a conclusion so James slowly squeezed back through the milling drinkers and retook his bench with a smile of thanks to his neighbour who gave a small wave in recognition and returned to his own conversation with the local on his other side.

What did it mean? James's mind whirled as he watched the thin monk leave the inn. Was Tuck really going to lead soldiers to Robin Hood's camp? He should warn the friar, he thought, but... how could he? Why would the man even believe him, a common thief?

Where did they say Hood's camp was? Selby, wasn't it? James knew the way to that village. Suddenly it was clear to him what he had to do. He couldn't find a job in the town anyway and he'd burnt his bridges with Mark too so there was little reason to hang around here.

No, he'd head for Selby and warn Robin Hood himself. With any luck the tales of the wolf's head's fairness and generosity hadn't been exaggerated too much and he'd be grateful to James for saving them... might even be a nice fat reward in it since the outlaws were famously wealthy from robbing rich merchants and churchmen.

His mind made up, and feeling better about his prospects than he had in months, James downed the last dregs in his mug and followed the departed monk into the chill night.

* * *

He knew he was taking a chance, what with Gisbourne being after his blood even harder than before, but Robin missed his family and so he'd travelled to Wakefield with Will Scarlet that morning, which was where he heard the news.

"The king is coming," Matilda said, rearranging her clothes after a hurried but satisfying session of love-making.

Robin stared up at the wooden rafters for a moment, wondering if he'd heard his wife correctly before he sat up and stared at her, admiring her lithe figure as she buttoned the front of her tunic. "What?"

"The king's coming," she repeated. "He's visiting places around here to check they're being run correctly or something. Checking the sheriffs and the like are sending him as much tax as they're supposed to I expect."

"And he's coming here? To Wakefield?"

Matilda shrugged and sat on the bed next to him, a contented smile on her lips. God she'd missed Robin, it had felt good to feel his muscular body next to hers again. "Well, maybe not to Wakefield, but to Yorkshire. Maybe he'll pass through here on his way to one of the bigger towns or cities, who knows?" She fixed him with a hard glare. "Don't you even *think* about trying to rob him."

The big outlaw laughed and leaned forward, pulling his wife back down on top of him. "I'm not insane," he grinned. "Even if Edward is a personal acquaintance of mine, I doubt his guards would stand back while me and the lads stole his money."

"Get off," Matilda laughed in reply, pushing Robin's grasping hands away and standing back up. "Come on, little Arthur will be wanting something to eat. I've got some cheese he likes – you can share it too if you like."

A shadow passed over his face as he wondered how sensible it was to hang around in the village for too long but he pushed his fears aside and nodded. "Aye, it'd be nice to have a meal with my family again. I hope there's some of your ma's ale too. She knows how to brew, Mary, I'll say that for her."

"Yes, there's ale, and cheese, and bread too. Might even be some salted pork. My ma's out working a lot of the time now, though – I've started brewing the ale since I'm about the house with Arthur all day."

Although Robin's extended family, which included his own parents and sister as well as Matilda's mother and father, were well off thanks to Robin's success as a robber, the women were still expected to do their fair share of the chores, be it brewing ale, washing or mending clothes or cooking hearty meals.

The wolf's head clasped his wife's hand and squeezed. "That's good to hear, you were already the best wife in the world and now... you're making me ale. A man couldn't ask for more."

Without thinking the girl muttered something about him not being an outlaw and living at home with them, and she regretted the words as soon as they tumbled from her mouth, but Robin chose to pretend he hadn't heard her and they walked into the main room of the house still holding hands.

"There you are, you were in there for ages. What were you doing?" Robin's younger sister Marjorie asked innocently, her eyes taking in the unkempt hair and clothes of her brother and sister-in-law.

Matilda flushed crimson but Robin just raised an eyebrow and pointedly ignored the question. At her age Marjorie knew fine well what had been going on in the bed room - she'd be getting married herself soon enough he thought, wondering again if his father had found a husband for her yet.

"How was he?" Matilda asked, scooping her infant son out of Marjorie's arms, grinning and touching her nose to the boy's who squealed in delight, bringing a smile to Robin's face too.

Marjorie spent much of her time at the Fletcher's now, helping Matilda with chores and taking care of Arthur if his mother needed to do something. The girl had looked after him for the short time Robin and Matilda had been... busy.

"He was fine. Sat on the floor and played with his little animals." Marjorie waved to the finely carved little wooden toys – cows, sheep and pigs – that Robin had bought for his son in Barnsley when the big market was on.

"Oh, he loves those," Matilda said. "He sits and plays with them all day."

Robin was inordinately pleased to know his gift had brought his little boy so much pleasure but his gaze turned to his sister and he hid the frown that threatened to appear as he took in her diminutive stature. Despite Robin making sure his family always had enough money to buy nutritious food, his little sister's drawn face always made his heart heavy.

"How have you been?" He sat at the table, facing her, and smiled in gratitude as Matilda placed a wooden platter with bread, cheese and meat down in front of them. "Here," he said, handing a large slice of cheese to his sister who took it gladly.

"Fine," she said, shrugging as if his question was unimportant. "Did you know the king's coming?"

Robin allowed the shift in conversation to pass, not wanting to upset his sister. He hardly got to see her these days and the last thing he wanted to do was make her unhappy. So he simply nodded and smiled although he had to admit, as he watched her from the corner of his eye, she appeared to finally be putting a little weight on, God be praised.

"Aye, Matilda told me. He asked me to join his rowing team, you know. Well, it was John he asked, but he meant me too, I'm sure."

Marjorie rolled her eyes theatrically. He'd already told her earlier that day all about his meeting with King Edward, and Matilda groaned in the background.

"Yes, you already told us you met the king," his wife laughed. "Lucky him, eh?"

Marjorie sniggered and Robin grinned despite their teasing. It felt so good to be home again, to spend even a little time with the people he loved. Most men took a meal with their family completely for granted but, for Robin, it was a time to be treasured. He finished his meal then plucked Arthur from Matilda's arms and sat the boy on the floor where the two of them played with the wooden animals for a long time. His son was a beautiful little boy, always smiling, with a mischievous glint in his big blue eyes and Robin had great fun making the small toys moo, baa and snort as Arthur giggled and clapped delightedly.

Eventually though, Robin sighed as the shadows lengthened and he realised he'd have to head back into the greenwood before it grew dark and too treacherous to travel through the hidden paths and byways he knew so well in the daylight.

With a final hug for Arthur and Matilda, who surreptitiously squeezed him between the legs when she thought Marjorie wasn't looking, the young outlaw said his goodbyes – exhorting his sister to make sure she ate lots of meat and vegetables – and hurried off along the street and into the trees.

He shouldn't complain – he had a lot of money and a wonderful family which was a lot more than some people. His childhood friend Much, for example, whose father was murdered by Adam Gurdon, the previous bailiff, before Matt Groves and Sir Guy of Gisbourne had killed him too. Poor Much. At least Robin was still alive.

With each new day in the forest, though, he grew ever more bitter at the life fate had given him, but at least now he had the silver arrow.

He hadn't told Matilda but he'd already urged his men to put the word out – if any nobleman wanted the immensely valuable arrow they could have it, as long as they'd sign pardons for Robin and all his friends in return.

If Thomas, the former Earl of Lancaster, hadn't been executed by the king the previous year Robin knew he and his men would already be free. Thomas had the power to do as he pleased, pretty much, and he had been a friend to the outlaws. He'd have gladly taken the arrow off their hands and enjoyed rubbing Sir Henry's nose in it too.

The man was dead though and Robin wasn't sure who else would be powerful enough to go against the Sheriff of Nottingham and Yorkshire. De Faucumberg must be desperate for the return of the arrow after all – if some local lord was to take it from Robin in exchange for pardons the sheriff would surely not let the matter pass without a fight.

Perhaps one of the Despenser's would take the bait? Someone like that had power enough that they wouldn't need to worry about de Faucumberg's ire.

If not though, Robin had decided he use the wealth he'd already amassed to take Matilda and Arthur somewhere far away – Scotland or France perhaps – where they could start a new, free, life together.

Whatever happened, he wouldn't see another winter living rough in Barnsdale,. *By God and the Magdalene*, he vowed, *I* will *be free!*

CHAPTER TWENTY-TWO

Although James travelled light, carrying nothing but his longbow and some arrows, he was still exhausted by the time the sun started to show its face above the horizon.

He had no horse, so to beat Friar Tuck and his turncoat companion to Robin Hood's camp he'd had to travel through the night which, thankfully had been clear, with a gibbous moon overhead to shed at least some light on the road. If it had been cloudy or moonless it would have been impossible for him to make it to Selby – a trek of some thirty miles – in the dark. He simply didn't know the area well enough.

It had been a lonely, eerie journey and he'd ended up leaving the string fitted to his longbow with an arrow ready to draw from his belt at a moment's notice. The nocturnal sounds of owls and other animals, and the sight of shadowed trees almost seeming to sway of their own accord in the windless air made the young man's nerves frayed and stretched close to breaking. Twice he'd halted, breathing silently despite his fear, and aimed his weapon towards the foliage that crowded close.

He'd not seen whatever had spooked him on those occasions – presumably a fox or an owl – but he was glad when it began to grow light. The sinister forest had sapped his mental strength while the fast pace he'd been forced to set had made his body utterly fatigued. He hadn't slept that night either, of course, which no doubt played a part in the anxiety that assailed him through all that hellish flight.

Finally, as the day dawned and the chilly morning dew began to evaporate into the spring air, James wondered what the hell he was doing. Although he'd been in Selby before, he had no knowledge whatsoever of the land outside the village. It all looked much the same to him – trees and bushes interlaced with well-worn hunters paths and little-known, hidden tracks that only the most knowledgeable of locals could even find never mind traverse with any speed.

He began to feel rather foolish as his eyes scanned the apparently unchanging foliage all around him. How in God's name was he going to find Hood and his companions before the treacherous monk led the king's man straight to them? Well, James had come this far, he couldn't just turn back now. He had nowhere else to go anyway – Mark would cut his balls off if he went back to Horbury any time soon.

Some time after dawn but before noon he heaved a sigh of relief as his eyes picked out the gently-spiralling smoke from a number of fires. Some of it grey, denoting simple domestic, wood-burning hearths, and some of it dark and greasy, suggesting industrial processes of some kind. A village then, with perhaps a blacksmith working the bellows in his forge for a day spent repairing broken cartwheels or hammering new horseshoes into shape.

At least he'd be able to make sure he'd followed the stars correctly and hadn't travelled thirty miles in completely the wrong direction. And, God willing, those fires came from his destination: Selby.

"About a mile north-east of the village, the monk had said," James muttered to himself, steeling himself for that final section of his journey. "The outlaws are bound to have lookouts. All I need to do is find the general area and make enough noise that they come to see what's going on." *Or shoot me...*

He wondered if he should bypass the village altogether, rather than risk attracting any attention. Sir Guy of Gisbourne was due along after all and it would be safer for James if no-one could pass on his description. But James wasn't an outlaw – he had no reason to hide from anyone and, as long as he didn't ask after Hood or the rest of the notorious gang there was no reason for anyone to connect him with them. Besides, the River Ouse wound through Selby and the easiest way to reach the opposite bank would undoubtedly be the main road with its bridge near the centre of the village.

And his legs did ache, as did his parched throat. It hadn't been the most sensible or well-thought-out plan he'd come up with back in the Swan. He really should have bought some bread and a skin of water or wine from the landlord but, in his haste to make it to Selby before Tuck and his friend, James simply hadn't thought.

"Hail, friend, where can I buy a mug of ale?"

The local – a carpenter judging by the hard, calloused hands that carried a pile of wooden planks and the leather bag at his waist presumably containing iron nails – nodded a gruff, "God give you good day, stranger," and waved the young traveller towards one of the small houses. No comfortable tavern in Selby then, but that didn't matter as long as the inhabitants of the little single-storey dwelling had some cool ale to spare and a bench where he could rest for a short while.

Nervously, he glanced over his shoulder, eyes scanning the road behind for signs of the two mounted clergymen, but he could see no-one. This would have to be a short rest though, or his trip would have been for naught.

"Can I help you, son?"

James smiled at the older woman who addressed him as he knocked and pushed open the door. "Aye, lady, you may. An ale, please? And a chance to take the load off my feet for a short while."

The woman must have been tall in her youth but age had curved her back and she stooped now, although her eyes were still bright and sharp as she looked James up and down, taking in the broad shoulders and great longbow he carried.

"Sit down, then," she nodded and shoved a rough, filthy-looking old curtain aside as she went into a different room, returning momentarily with a brimming mug which she handed to the bowman. "Expecting trouble?"

Somewhat shiftily James glanced at the woman as he swallowed a long gulp of the pale liquid. "No. What makes you ask that?"

"String's still on your bow."

He smiled sheepishly, took another sip of the ale which had been spiced with cinnamon, no doubt to hide the fact it wasn't particularly fresh, then stood up. Placing his left leg through the string and using his right leg to brace the bow he pulled gently backwards on the top of the great weapon to release the tension and slipped the string off before folding it neatly into his pouch.

"That'll be a farthing for the ale," the woman nodded. "The bench is free. You want another drink, or is whoever's chasing you too close behind?"

James couldn't help spluttering into the mug and he regretted coming into the damn alehouse with its shrewd proprietor. "No-one's chasing me," he said, trying unsuccessfully not to look guilty.

The woman simply shrugged, irritated that her customer wasn't going to give her some interesting gossip to share with the other women but pleased to see, by the big young man's nervous reaction, that she'd read the situation right. "Please yourself. Don't get many people coming into the place on foot this early in the day, though. You must have travelled through the night and no-one does that without good reason. You want another ale then, or not? Or maybe something else?"

James looked at her blankly, not understanding what the woman meant and she laughed, her eyes sparkling at his innocence. "My man's out in the far cornfields and won't return until near dark." She undid the laces of her bodice to reveal the top of her breasts and gazed wantonly at him.

He stared back, shocked at her brazen attempt to seduce him and felt his cheeks burn red in embarrassment. "I'll have another ale, lady," he agreed, "but that's all, thank you."

"Suit yourself," she nodded, looking down at his trousers and he hastily covered the bulge that had unexpectedly – given the fact she was old enough to be his mother – appeared there.

Flustered, he lowered his eyes to stare into the ale mug and, with a gleeful cackle the woman went into the back and brought another drink for the bemused young man who was relieved to see she'd covered herself up again.

"Where are you heading for?" the woman asked seriously. "It's not safe to travel around these parts on your own."

Glad at the change in the conversation James shrugged. "I spoke the truth: no one is chasing me. Indeed, no-one even knows I'm here. And I'm no outlaw, despite what you may think." He drained the mug and wiped his lips. "But I am in a hurry. I carry news that... well, it's a matter of life and death that I deliver my message before..." He trailed off, unwilling to tell this stranger any more about his business and, in fact, surprised to have told her as much as he had.

"Well, God grant you luck, wherever you're going," she told him as he stood and made his way out the front door after handing her a couple of coins. "And if your travels bring you back this way, be sure and come to see me. I have no problem with outlaws – my own son's one, for his sins."

James turned back at that, his eyes wide at the muttered revelation. "Your son?"

For the first time the woman looked flustered herself and she stepped back into her house. "Aye, my son," she admitted. "But I have no idea where he is, if you're a lawman. Is that why you're in such a hurry?" Her previous confidence and mastery of the situation had evaporated now and James stared at her, wondering what he should say or do.

He turned to glance back over his shoulder at the main road again and his blood ran cold. Two small, mounted, figures could be seen in the distance and James knew it was the clergymen. Friar Tuck would be known in this village – someone would tell him how to find Hood's camp and that would be the end of it all.

"Your son," he repeated, turning back to the nervous woman. "Tell me truthfully: is he one of Robin Hood's men?" He shook his head to stop the denial before it could escape her lips. "Listen to me, I am no lawman! The law *is* behind me though – Sir Guy of Gisbourne himself is on his way to butcher Hood and his gang unless someone warns them. For your son's sake, you have to trust me."

The woman stared at James but she had no reason to believe what he said. She tried to close the front door but the big bowman pressed his foot inside and blocked it open. "Wait! I've travelled all through the night to warn your son and his friends of the danger they face and now those two horsemen on the road there are about to overtake me and lead the Raven right to them. You must tell me how to find the outlaws, please!"

The sincerity in his voice touched the ale-seller but still doubts assailed her. "What is it to you if my son dies? Or Robin Hood? You say you're not an outlaw yourself so why would you go to all this trouble to help men who *are* wolf's heads?"

James sighed, exasperated at the delay which brought Tuck and the other monk ever closer. "It's a long story but... one of Robin's men spared my life when he might have killed me – indeed, would have been justified in doing so. I feel like I owe it to him to help him and his friends." He shrugged and gazed directly into the woman's fearful eyes. "And, on top of that – I'm not an outlaw but I might as well be. No-one will give me a job and I have no prospects. I thought maybe Robin Hood could use another good longbowman..."

The whole tale sounded ridiculous even to his own ears but, finally, sensing the truth of his words, the woman opened her door wide again and gestured him hurriedly inside.

"Swear in the name of Christ and all his saints that you mean my son no harm," she demanded, then, when James did so she gave him directions – as best she could, having never actually visited the place herself – to the outlaws' camp in the forest. "My boy told me how to find him if I ever needed him, although those directions won't bring you right out in the middle of their camp-site. Robin Hood is no fool, that's why they've been able to stay one step ahead of the sheriff and the foresters and Gisbourne for so long. But, if you go where I told you one of the gang members will find you. It'll be up to you to convince them not to kill you after that."

She moved over to the door and peered out, muttering to herself as she saw how close the horsemen were now.

"Go," she hissed. "Go. They're nearly here and no doubt this will be the first place they head for, looking for something to wet their dry throats, just as you did."

James stood and looked out into the street, relieved to see no-one was watching their furtive conversation as the woman clutched his arm in a surprisingly painful grip, digging her nails in and glaring at him.

"You better have been telling me the truth, boy, or Robin will come looking for you. Now... go and save my Peter!"

* * *

Since returning to the greenwood after Gisbourne's men had chased them out of Wakefield Robin had insisted the members of his band get back into the habit of training, hard, almost every day. Archery, hand-to-hand combat, and sparring with wooden practice swords or quarterstaffs made the men fit both physically and mentally. The young outlaw captain was proud of them and knew most of them felt more like soldiers than they ever had before.

He watched, a pleased smile on his face, as Little John held the fish-lipped tanner, Edmond, at bay with his giant staff. Although John looked comfortable, Robin could tell that the giant wasn't having as easy a time of it as he had when Edmond had first joined them. Aye, the tanner had been a hardy enough fighter, but he'd lacked true skill or finesse and relied more on brute force and aggression, which was all well and good, but useless when you came up against someone like Sir Guy of Gisbourne.

The addition too of the outcast Hospitaller sergeant-at-arms, Stephen, had given the men some new techniques to learn. The bluff Yorkshireman had been trained by the very best – knights of the cross – and he was able to show even the likes of Will Scaflock and Robin, who were both absolutely lethal with a blade, a few new tricks.

Little John suddenly stepped back, a look of surprise on his face as Edmond feinted to the left before reversing his momentum and ramming the point of his quarterstaff forward, almost hammering the breath from John. The giant was just able evade the blow but he grinned appreciatively at the gurning tanner and Robin moved away, happy in the knowledge his men were ready for almost anything Gisbourne could throw at them.

"How are they getting on?" He stepped up to stand next to Stephen who watched dispassionately as Gareth wrestled with another recent recruit, Piers, a twenty-two year old clerk from Nottingham who'd been caught fiddling his master's accounts and escaped into Barnsdale where Allan-a-Dale found him before the law could.

Stephen muttered something Robin couldn't catch but he was sure it wasn't anything pleasant. There was an angry cry as Gareth was tripped by the newcomer, who pinned him until he conceded the bout and Piers jumped up, breathing hard but smiling broadly over at the Hospitaller and Stephen nodded encouragingly, despite his stony expression.

"Well done, lad," Stephen said to Gareth though. "You're learning. Keep up the hard work. It might not feel like it's worth it but trust me, even taking a beating can be worthwhile. Rest a little then get yourself a practice sword; I'll spar with you for a bit" He cracked a rare, if small, smile and waved the young man away to take some refreshment and catch his breath again.

"He'll never be a fighter," Stephen muttered to Robin, watching as Gareth shuffled off, holding his back like an old man. "He's just not made for it."

Robin remained silent for a while. The young man was a valued member of the gang but he wasn't really much use for anything other than as a lookout or a messenger. His youth – he was still only eighteen after all – and skinny frame, meant he was a good, fast runner over long distances but... with the amount of ale the lad had started drinking recently he'd begun to thicken around the midriff and simply wasn't as fit as he should be.

Although they couldn't afford passengers in their group, Gareth's place would always be safe – by rescuing Friar Tuck from the freezing waters of the Don the previous year, saving the clergyman's life in the process, Gareth would always be looked upon gratefully by the men who had all counted Tuck as a great friend.

And yet, Gareth had to watch as the likes of Edmond, and now Piers, joined the group and surpassed him easily when it came to fighting and hunting and general usefulness about the camp. Held back by a body that had never recovered completely from the effects of malnutrition in childhood, Gareth would never be as valued a member of the gang as someone like the old Hospitaller or even Arthur, the stocky, toothless young man from Bichill.

Robin was sure all of that explained Gareth's excessive drinking over the past few months but... it wasn't up to him what the man drank, or how much. As long as it didn't cause them any harm, or bring danger upon them, Gareth could do what he wanted, just like all of them.

"What about the rest of them?" Robin asked, looking around at the other men training. "How would they fare if, say, a similar number of Hospitaller sergeants were to attack us?"

Stephen took a deep breath and exhaled slowly, looking at each man and calculating their potential in such a confrontation. He nodded at last. "Aye, they'd do alright. I'm not saying they'd win," he qualified his optimistic assessment, "but they'd hold their own, I'm sure."

Robin grinned. "Good. There's not much chance we'll be attacked by such a force, but if we're strong enough for that, we should have little to fear from the likes of the sheriff's soldiers or even Gisbourne's better-trained men." He clapped the sergeant-at-arms on the back gratefully. "You've been a fine addition to our group, Stephen, I'm glad to have you here."

Stephen returned the smile, happy to be appreciated, but his eyes were hard as he contemplated the circumstances that had brought him there. Betrayed by his own Order after a life of faithful service... it still rankled and always would, he knew.

Suddenly there was a whistle from the undergrowth to the south-west and the two men shared a wide-eyed glance for just a moment before racing to collect their weapons. "To arms!" Robin roared, buckling on his sword-belt and bending his bow between his legs to fit the hemp string to it. "Get your weapons."

They all knew what such a whistle meant – one of the lookouts was approaching with news of possible danger. Judging from the direction the sound had come from, it was Allan-a-Dale who made his way hurriedly towards the camp and Robin wondered what was afoot. *Let it be Gisbourne*, he prayed, *with just a few men so we can take him out once and for all.*

It couldn't be the king's man, though, Robin knew that was just wishful thinking. The outlaws had a simple but effective system: one whistle meant someone unknown was nearby but not, from appearances, much of a threat. Still, it was always good to be prepared so Robin continued to berate the men in hushed tones for not moving fast enough while Little John and Will marshalled them all into pre-determined places hidden within the foliage or, in some cases, up in the branches of the trees which now wore their almost full summer greenery and – after some judicious pruning – afforded a decent place to conceal a few longbowmen.

Robin himself stood alone, in the centre of the camp waiting to hear from the lookout, but his bow was in his left hand, ready just in case, as Allan jogged into camp, his eyes looking about the small clearing, glad to find everyone in position thanks to his warning.

"What's up?"

"A single traveller, a man, ran into the trees just west of my position," the lookout reported. "He was blowing hard – looked fit to drop so someone must be after him. He's got a longbow, and looks sturdy enough to be able to use it."

"Recognize him?"

Allan shook his head. "Never seen him before. He was looking about him though, even up into the trees, as if he knew I – or someone at least – was up there watching."

Robin raised his voice so the hidden men could hear him clearly. "Any ideas anyone? A single bowman coming from the direction of Selby? Possibly knows we're camped about here? Piers?"

The clerk from Nottingham had come to them in similar fashion, although it had been purely by accident Allan had found him that day and brought him back to Robin and the rest. Maybe this was someone looking to do the same?

"Nothing to do with me," Piers shouted back, his surprisingly deep voice carrying easily from where he crouched behind a holly bush. "I told my family I was going to hide in the forest but I didn't even know myself whereabouts. No-one could have followed my trail all this time later."

"I watched for signs of anyone following him," Allan said, before Robin could even ask. "Couldn't see anyone, but I'm sure he was fleeing from something."

"Or *to* something...." Robin mused. "Right," decisively, "Allan, swap places with Gareth. Gareth, you head back to the lookout post and watch for signs of this lad's pursuers; we don't want to find ourselves discovered by an army."

Gareth nodded and ran to collect his belongings – short sword, a hunk of bread and a skin of ale which he furtively concealed inside his cloak before hurrying off to take up his post.

"Stephen, Scarlet – you two want to come with me?" Robin asked.

It was essentially an order from the outlaw captain, but he held his friends in such high regard that he often framed his orders as questions rather than statements. Of course, Will and the Hospitaller gladly came forward to go with him to find this interloper in their forest.

"Hold your positions," he told the rest of the men. "John, you know what to do."

There was a shouted, "Aye," from the big man who followed it with a, "good luck!" as the three outlaws headed into the trees stealthily, weapons at the ready, curious to see who this exhausted archer might be.

* * *

There was a knock at the door and it opened, letting in the orange glow of sunset.

"Matilda, nice to see you, lass." John Hood smiled and gestured at one of the empty chairs. "Come and join us," he said. "We're playing draughts."

Robin's wife shook her head, looking down at the checkered board to see Martha was beating John quite soundly. "I just came to see if you fancied going for a walk."

Marjorie looked up. "Nah. Don't really feel like it tonight." She slumped in her seat, staring at the game board as if she was planning her tactics to defeat the eventual winner.

"Go on," Martha muttered to her daughter although her eyes never left the little wooden game pieces. "It'll do you good to get some fresh air."

"I've already had a walk today," the girl said, meeting Matilda's eyes with a knowing look. "My legs are tired."

"Oh. Fair enough then. I'll get off home and get back to sorting those feathers. My da got another order from a merchant in another town," she explained to John who was listening intently. "Apparently our good work on the 'eagle' feather arrows has got around – we've got enough work to last us well into winter. Farewell then."

She turned to go but Martha finally looked up then, her eyes damp from the smoke and gloom inside the house. "Wait a moment," she said then turned to address her fifteen year-old daughter.

"What's wrong with you now?"

Marjorie shrugged and Martha wanted nothing more than to reach out and take the girl into her arms. It would be a mistake to do so she knew, so she remained seated and crossed her hands on the table before her.

"You've been brooding for days now. Are you with child?"

Marjorie looked up, shocked, and shook her head. "No, for sure I'm not. What d'you mean asking me that?"

"I'll just be off then," Matilda muttered, making a grab for the door latch, but Martha glared at her.

"You can just wait there. You're bound up in all this and it's time we had it out."

"Had what out?"

"We know you've been learning to fight," Martha replied. "Don't we?"

John nodded, the expression on his face making it clear he would like to be elsewhere right then.

"And we know you've been out hunting. Apparently you've been doing well, at the fighting at least. Isn't that right?"

Matilda nodded. "She's got the same natural skill as her brother. One of you two must have it in your blood."

"How do you know about it?" Marjorie demanded. "It was supposed to be a secret."

"We're not stupid, lass," her father smiled. "It was obvious you were doing something when you started eating more and putting some weight on. We're proud of you. Happy that you've found something worthwhile to do."

Marjorie returned the smile fondly but her face dropped.

"Spit it out then," Martha said. "What's wrong?"

The girl didn't reply for a while, as she gathered her thoughts and tried to make sense of her own emotions before even attempting to put things into words her parents would understand.

As if reading her mind Martha laid a hand on hers and nodded. "We'll understand, trust me. You're not the first young girl to wonder what her purpose in life is and you won't be the last."

Finally, she spoke.

"Aye, Matilda's been teaching me how to use a sword. I've even started showing the other girls the things I've learned. It's been fun."

"But?" John prodded, gently.

"But..." Marjorie met her father's gaze, disappointment etched in her eyes. "They're all stronger than me. I'm supposed to be their teacher, but the bigger girls could beat me easy, if they wanted to. None of them have – they're all being nice to me. But they could if they felt like it." She leaned back in her chair, letting her arms flop to her side. "As for hunting... pfft, don't even mention that. I couldn't catch a hare if it was lying dead on the grass. It'd somehow slip through my fingers and escape."

She sighed heavily. "I'm just not very good at anything. I've tried my best – I've put everything into sparring with Matilda but... I'm useless."

"You're *not* –"

Martha laid a hand on her husband's and squeezed, silencing him.

"You're not," he repeated, leaning back himself and looking sadly at his girl who was still little despite her years.

"Look, lass, what is it you think you're going to do with your life?" Martha refilled an empty mug from the jug of ale that sat on the table between them and passed it to her daughter, gesturing the still standing Matilda to help herself to some of the cool liquid. "You think you're going to join the lord's army and go to fight the Scots? No? Well, you plan on joining the foresters? Even though there's not a single woman amongst them? No? Well, what then?"

Marjorie sat in sullen silence, hating the eyes of her family upon her but hating it even more that she genuinely couldn't answer her mother's questions. She really didn't have any idea what she wanted to do with her life but she knew she would never be a soldier or a forester. Even if she *had* been stronger and fitter – women simply didn't do these things!

"What are you saying?" she demanded, meeting Martha's stare angrily. "That I've been wasting my time these past few weeks and months? That I should just give up and go back to doing nothing? Being nothing?"

"No!" Martha growled, clenching her fist and bringing it down on the table, making everyone, even Matilda jump. "No. I'm saying you need to accept who you are: a girl. A woman. And there's nothing wrong with that. Is there?" She cocked an eyebrow at her husband who raised his hands defensively.

"No, nothing," he replied. "Nothing at all – women are great. I think I'll go and milk the cow." He got his feet and hastily made his way out the front door.

"See?"

Marjorie smiled at her mother's triumphant look. "Who milks cows at sunset?"

"He knows his place, just as we all do," Martha told her. "And he knows who's the real head of this household." She smiled again and grasped her daughter's hand, looking over at Matilda to include her in her words too.

"You've been trying to learn all these skills and that's good; you've learned a lot from it, I can see that. But, first and foremost, you're a young woman. Your place is here in the home, with me for now and, when you're older, with your own children in your own house."

She lifted her right hand to silence any objections. "There's no shame in being a woman, lass. Just the opposite. There'd be no men in this world if it wasn't for the likes of us, right Matilda?"

Robin's wife nodded happily. "That's true," she agreed.

Still, Marjorie looked unconvinced.

"Look, Marjorie, Robin and his mates might live an exciting life but where do you think they'd rather be? Every one of them? They'd rather be at home with their families – with their women. Not out there, being chased around the greenwood by the likes of the Raven and his men."

"I know she speaks truly," Matilda chipped in. "Robin's told me as much himself many times. It might look like an exciting life they lead but... it eats him up inside. All he wants is to be with Arthur and I..."

The three women sat in silence for a time before Marjorie eventually spoke.

"So you're saying I should just accept my lot and be a good wife and mother?"

"Is there anything more important – or as rewarding – in the whole damn world, lass?"

Matilda nodded, thinking of her own beautiful little son. "Your ma's right. I've lived as an outlaw – as a fighter. I'd rather be at home making arrows for my da and shouting at Arthur to get away from the cooking pot before he scalds himself."

"Truly," Martha fixed her daughter with a piercing stare. "Women make the world go round. And you're as fine a girl as there's ever been."

Marjorie looked at her sister-in-law then back to her mother and stood up to embrace Martha, her eyes moist.

She knew now why she'd been so unhappy recently – she'd been trying to live a life that wasn't hers.

Still, she'd be the woman *she* wanted to be, not what everyone expected her to be...

CHAPTER TWENTY-THREE

James felt like he was about to pass out. His legs, particularly his thighs, ached terribly and it was an effort to keep lifting his feet as he pushed his way through the brambles and irritatingly lush foliage of the greenwood, insects, and wind-borne dandelion seeds, and god-knew-what-else flying into his eyes and gasping mouth as he went.

It was a shock, then, to realise a hooded man – and a big one at that – was standing silently in front of him, watching. The apparition wore a sword at his side and held a longbow, although neither weapon was raised threateningly.

James stopped, and let his head drop, resting his hands on his legs as his chest heaved and he tried to regain his breath without much success. Finally he managed to gasp, "In the name of Christ, I hope you're one of Robin Hood's men."

In his peripheral vision James noticed just a flicker of movement, first on the left and then on the right and he saw two more men flanking him. One was a grim-looking soldier with unblinking green eyes, while the other wore chain mail covered by a red surcoat emblazoned with the cross of some religious order, although the young man had no idea which one.

"I can do you one better than that," the biggest of the three said, smiling and appearing as relaxed as if he'd just met an old friend.

James returned the smile somewhat ruefully – he was a big man himself and he had his longbow but in the state he was in he was hardly a threat to these hard-looking lads. "Are you Hood?"

"I am. This is Will Scarlet and our friendly Hospitaller, Stephen. Now that the introductions are out of the way, let's make this quick since you're obviously running away from someone and I don't want to find a force of soldiers appearing at your back. What's your story?"

"You're right, I am running from someone but..." He stopped, wondering how to explain himself without the whole thing sounding insane but it seemed to be impossible.

"Spit it out, man!" The one Hood had introduced as Will Scarlet growled impatiently and James hurried to tell his tale. He was here now, he'd found Hood – if the man didn't believe him after all these miles, well...

"I don't know how much time you have, but Sir Guy of Gisbourne is coming for you, and he's bringing enough men to wipe you all out."

He expected disbelieving laughs or some other reaction from the men but they just stood, watching and waiting for him to continue.

"Your friend Friar Tuck is on his way here right now. He can't be far behind me and he's got a friend with him – a monk. Tuck doesn't know it, but his companion is working with Sir Guy. I don't know why; I saw the pair meeting in the Swan back in Horbury and tried to overhear their words as best I could but I only managed to catch some of it."

The outlaw leader glanced at his two companions who looked unsure of James's story before he turned round and beckoned the man to follow. "Come, you can tell us the rest as we head back to our camp."

The other two outlaws fell in behind James, who sighed in relief and began to move, trying to pick out the near-invisible trail Robin was striding along.

"If this is some trick, you'll find my blade in your back, my lad," Will Scarlet growled into his ear but James didn't reply, trying to save what remained of his stamina for the journey to the outlaw camp and praying fervently that it wasn't far.

"How did you know where we were?" The grizzled Hospitaller asked.

"I heard Tuck's mate telling Sir Guy you were camped somewhere near Selby, so I travelled there and, when I stopped at the ale-house to rest, the woman there told me her son, Peter, was one of your gang. I told her my story and she gave me rough directions how to find you."

"Is that all she gave you?" Scarlet demanded, laughing suggestively and James flushed as red as the outlaw's name. Peter Ordevill's mother had tried it on with all of the outlaws at one time or another, much to her son's chagrin.

"Their plan is for Tuck to come along and be found by your men, just as I was," James continued, trying to ignore the burning in his cheeks. "The monk with him will leave a trail for Sir Guy to follow, straight to your camp. And then..."

"And then we die," Robin said, to a grunt of agreement from the young archer behind him.

They lapsed into silence then, and, shortly, the foliage gave way and they walked into a clearing.

"John!" Robin shouted, summoning his giant lieutenant from the undergrowth. "The rest of you, stay hidden for now. We're still not sure what we face yet." He turned to James and pointed towards the fire. "There's ale and meat there. Help yourself and rest while we discuss this. Even if Tuck's right behind you, Gisbourne can't be too close – he'll have to keep a safe distance so our lookouts don't spot him and ruin his plan."

"Tuck?" Little John asked, baffled. "Gisbourne? What the fuck's going on? If the Raven's nearby shouldn't we be getting the hell out of here? He must have –"

Robin held up a hand to stop the flow of words. "Listen, and I'll explain what's happening, then we can decide what to do."

* * *

"They must be nearby," Tuck said, in reply to Osferth's grumbling about his sore feet and how much longer until they found the outlaws. They'd been advised to leave their mounts in the village by the residents of Selby, since the outlaws' nearby camp-site was hidden in a thick section of forest and both men were now thoroughly fed up with their walk.

"In fact," Tuck smiled encouragingly, "their lookout's probably spotted us already and ran to warn Robin and the lads of our approach. I'm sure they'll be along to see us any time now."

"You're not wrong there, father." A voice, seeming to come from directly overhead, startled both of them, Osferth almost dropping to his knees in fright but Tuck chuckled, recognizing the voice as that of Allan-a-Dale.

When Gareth had taken up Allan's recently vacated lookout spot, he'd been pleasantly surprised to see their old friend and mentor Friar Tuck appear with some other monk in tow. He'd sprinted back to camp as fast as he could to give the men the good news, only to find they were expecting the friar. He and the minstrel had then headed back, again, towards the lookout spot, Allan explaining things to his companion as they went, before he climbed a tree about halfway along the only obvious path the approaching clergymen could take. Gareth continued on, taking a circuitous route through the undergrowth back to the his lookout post high in the great oak tree with orders to stay and watch for Sir Guy of Gisbourne's inevitable approach.

Now, not far from the outlaws' camp-site, the minstrel jumped down and Tuck grabbed him in a great bear-hug, the joy at seeing one of his friends evident on his ruddy face. Osferth nodded a greeting of his own which was returned by the burly outlaw before the man stood back and looked Tuck up and down.

"You look... well, just the same as when you left us, really," he said. "Maybe a bit thinner again. You're not quite the big, pot-bellied friar I remember from that first meeting."

"Aye, well, Prior de Monte Martini didn't feed me as well as I'd have liked, the bastard. Still, I'm sure you've got plenty of meat and bread – and ale – at your camp. So, are you planning on standing there, gaping like a trout all day, or are you going to lead my companion and I to sustenance? It's almost dinner time. And this is Osferth, by the way; a friend of mine from Lewes. He didn't like the prior much either."

Allan glanced at Osferth and a look flashed across his handsome features but it passed almost instantly and Tuck was unable to read it.

"You'll never change will you?" The outlaw smiled, before turning to lead the two travellers into the undergrowth. "Can't do anything unless your stomach's filled. Come on then, stay close."

Allan glanced back to make sure he was being followed by the pair and, from the corner of his eye, he noticed Osferth, a small blade in his hand, marking the trunk of the tree nearest to him.

"Gareth saw you coming," the minstrel said, turning quickly to face the front again. "Edmond's got the pot bubbling away nicely you'll be pleased to hear. The men'll be glad to see you; we've missed you, old man."

Tuck smiled. "I missed all of you too, Allan. I had to go back to Lewes though, and I'm glad I did. God had a purpose for me, which is why I'm back around Barnsdale again. For good this time, I hope."

"Well, save your breath for now, you can tell us all about it when we get back. Come on," he began to quicken his pace. "It's not far, but I'm starving myself so let's hurry."

Tuck was glad when, soon enough, they came into the clearing where his outlaw friends were camped. The exercise had left him puffing hard and he had a painful stitch, but the sight of a grinning Robin, flanked by the bear-like figure of Little John and the stocky Will Scarlet made him forget his discomfort and he hardly slowed as he skipped past the fire with its attendant cooking pot and gripped arms with the outlaws.

"I've never been so happy to see a priest in all my life," Will joked, shoving himself away from Tuck's embrace, a broad smile on his face. "It's good to see you again, you old bastard."

The rest of the men seemed to materialize from the trees like ghosts, greeting Tuck happily, but he was surprised when the vast majority of the outlaws all faded back into the undergrowth after their hasty welcome. His feeling of unease only increased when he spotted a man – not one of the gang – sitting on a log beside the fire, nursing a mug of ale and watching him from wary eyes.

"You..." The friar racked his brain for a moment, trying to recall where he knew the young man from, before he nodded in recognition. "James, isn't it? The archer who spared my life when his friends would gladly have robbed and killed me."

"You spared their lives too," James replied, not mentioning the fact that one of the men had died later from the whack in the skull the friar had given him. No need to place that burden on the good friar's soul...

Tuck shrugged, as if to say the brigands had been nothing but a minor irritation, to be swatted aside like insects. "What brings you here?" He turned then to address Robin before James could reply. "What's going on anyway? Why are the men concealed, as if expecting something?"

"Ask your friend."

Tuck looked at Osferth, who still stood at the edge of the camp, in confusion. "What? What are you talking about, Robin? Will someone please tell me what in God's name is happening here?"

Osferth's eyes had widened and his hand had fallen inside his cassock as if grasping for a weapon.

"Your mate is working with Gisbourne. He's been marking the trees along the way here so the Raven can bring his soldiers and wipe every last one of us out, once and for all."

Tuck laughed and sat down beside James, helping himself to a slice of salted beef from the wooden trencher in the man's lap. "Osferth's been with me on the entire road here from Lewes, he hasn't left my side. How could he be helping Gisbourne? Why would he do that anyway?"

"It's true, father," James said quietly, looking at the forest floor sadly. "I'm sorry, but I was in Horbury at the same time as you were. Your companion came to the inn I was staying at – the Swan – and met Sir Guy there. I overheard their conversation." He looked up to meet Tuck's irritated gaze. "You helped me even though my companions and I had tried to rob you. That means a lot to a man like me so... when I knew that little rat bastard was going to betray you I came here to try and stop it happening."

Tuck tossed his half-eaten slice of meat back onto the plate and rose to his feet, watching Osferth, who stood silently and serenely, as if he was simply back at the priory listening to evening mass.

"Well? Is it true?"

Osferth nodded. "It is, but fear not: the soldiers will not harm you."

"What?" Tuck shouted in disbelief. "Fear not?"

"Sir Guy is coming to do God's work, just as I have done. These murderers – *sinners* – will know justice, and the world will be a better place for it, but Sir Guy knows not to harm either of us. Once this is all over we shall return to Lewes where Prior de Monte Martini will reward us."

Tuck stared in astonishment at the man he'd thought was slightly unbalanced but this... it was unbelievable. "Are you insane, Osferth?" he demanded. "I punched the prior in the face. I stole his precious relic. You set half the bloody priory on fire, man! If we go back to Lewes we'll be excommunicated and strung up. That's assuming we survive this nightmare you've brought down upon us." He strode across and grabbed Osferth by the scruff of the neck, almost lifting the slight monk from his feet. "The prior *hates* me. Why would he want Gisbourne to spare my life? Of all these men here I'm the one he'd like to see dead the most! Are you really so naïve?"

Osferth shook his head in denial of Tuck's words.

It was clear the Benedictine was lost in some fantasy where everything would turn out well for them, as God intended.

Friar Tuck released him with a shake of his head and turned to glare at Robin. "Well, what the hell are we still here for? If Gisbourne's coming shouldn't we be on our way?" He spoke again to Osferth, spitting the words out furiously through gritted teeth. "How many men does he have at his command?"

"I've no idea. At least enough to outnumber these evil-doers. I told him to send for reinforcements when I first sent word to him back in that little village... Bryneford, wasn't it? Where we slept in that local's house because they didn't even have an inn. I had the priest there ride to Nottingham to tell Sir Guy where we were heading and what our plans were."

"You've been in contact with him since away back then?" Tuck roared, again grabbing his turncoat companion by the front of his cassock. "How? You never left my sight the whole way here."

"Gwale. The prior gave me it before we left."

Tuck's face froze for a second as the full reality of the situation finally hit him. De Monte Martini had planned this whole thing. Osferth befriending him; the tale about the prior knowing the location of Robin's camp; everything... "That's why I slept like a babe those times, yet woke up feeling as if I'd drank an entire barrel of ale by myself. You little shit!" He released Osferth and hammered his fist into the man's mouth, hurling him backwards where he lay sprawled on the bark and moss, a look of shock and disbelief on his face.

"You're supposed to be my friend," the young monk said through split lips, his eyes filling with tears. "I've come here to save your soul. Why did you hit me?"

Tuck suddenly felt, unbelievably given the circumstances, like he'd just kicked a playful puppy, and he swung back to Robin, his face a mask of fury and confusion.

"Well? What are we waiting for? We all know the whole story now, all about how I was such a fool and led the Raven right to you. Shouldn't we be off before he gets here and kills us all?"

Robin nodded to Little John and Will who gave Tuck a last apologetic look, unhappy to have been witness to their portly friend's humiliation, before they too slipped into the trees and out of sight.

"What about you, friend?" Robin asked James who swallowed the last of the ale in his mug and stood up, grasping his longbow. "You better get off if you don't want to be part of what happens next. Here..." he fumbled inside his gambeson before pulling out a small purse and tossing it the young archer. "For your trouble. Thank you for coming to warn us. There's enough in there to see you right."

James nodded gratefully but didn't look inside the purse, just held it in his hand as he returned the outlaw captain's gaze. "Seems to me you could do with another longbowman at your side this day. If you'll have me."

Robin shrugged. Time was running out, Gisbourne would be upon them any time. He didn't know anything about James's life, or why he had come here and now offered to stand with them but it was true – another archer would certainly be useful.

"You're more than welcome to stay," he nodded. "Keep beside me so you don't get in the way. You must be exhausted after walking all through the night."

Tuck shook his head in consternation at Robin's words. "You're talking as if you're not planning on escaping. What madness has come over you all?"

In reply Robin hefted his longbow, bending it back to slip the string onto it. "We're done running, Tuck." He pulled an arrow from his belt and nocked it to the string, raising the weapon as he continued. "For the past two years I've been running. Moving camp every time Gisbourne, or Adam Bell, or the sheriff or whoever got too close. No more." He pulled back the string to his ear as Tuck watched, eyes widening when he realised what Robin was about to do. "No more running."

He released the arrow and watched dispassionately as it thudded home in Osferth's heart.

"Now we fight."

* * *

Sir Guy of Gisbourne reined in his big warhorse and looked warily from side to side, turning his head to do so since his missing left eye hampered his vision on that side. "What about their lookouts?" He lifted his leg over the saddle and slid easily to the ground to gaze into the thick trees that lay about a mile before them. "If they spot us coming there's little point in this – they'll simply run off and we'll be back where we started."

Matt Groves nodded grimly. "Don't worry about that. Wait here, and look for my signal."

Gisbourne watched as his sergeant kicked his heels into his mount and galloped off, not along the main road but to the left, through the long grass on the heath that ran parallel to the forest in front of them.

Matt had looked at that forest and knew exactly where a lookout would hide – he'd been an outlaw himself for years hadn't he? He could read the land as well as any of Hood's gang. One tree in particular stood out, even at this distance, for its height and the fact that its branches didn't grow so densely together as those surrounding it. A man could sit comfortably in a tree like that, he knew, with a fine view of the surrounding terrain.

He had to be sure the lookout didn't spot him so he rode for a while until the contours of the land and the sparse foliage dotted around the heath would mask his approach, then he turned his mount and galloped straight forward, towards the forest.

When he reached the thick line of trees he slid to the ground and tied his horse to a sturdy branch, the animal's chest heaving from the exertion but happy to rest and crop the rich grass that grew there. "Wait here, boy," Matt muttered, patting the horse affectionately. "This won't take long."

He moved along the edge of the forest quickly, back towards the tall Scots pine tree he'd marked as being the most likely lookout post, wondering as he went which of the outlaws might be concealed there.

"I hope it's that prick Hood himself," he muttered, although he knew that was unlikely. Robin didn't take many lookout duties since, being the leader, he was needed in the main camp in the event of any danger being sighted but still, there was a possibility he was in the branches of that big tree and if he was... Matt clasped the hilt of his dagger and gritted his teeth, praying to God it *would* be the enemy he so despised hidden in the foliage ahead.

At last the tree came into sight not far ahead, and Groves slowed his pace, stalking through the undergrowth almost silently, his eyes searching for any signs of movement in the branches overhead until, at last, he reached the gnarled, aged trunk and pressed himself against it, listening intently.

He nodded in satisfaction as he spotted the iron nails that had been hammered into the bark to form makeshift steps for someone to climb up. This *was* the tree the outlaws used as a lookout post, now all he had to do was deal with whoever was concealed above...

CHAPTER TWENTY-FOUR

"We ready to move then?" Sir Guy demanded as Matt Groves returned, his horse's chest heaving with exertion since its rider had pushed hard to make it back to his captain as fast as possible.

"Aye, we can move. The lookout won't be a problem, you can count on that."

He had a strange sardonic smile on his seamed face that Gisbourne found repulsive and he wondered what the man had done to the lookout. Probably tortured him before throwing him out of the tree or worse...

"I'll take your word for it," Gisbourne grunted and turned to face his men, thirty-five well-armed and highly-trained soldiers, addressing them in a low but authoritative voice. "Listen to me. This isn't your usual gang of outlaws – these men are not some undisciplined peasants carrying sickles and pitchforks. They are not old greybeards, or untested youngsters. Robin Hood was skilled enough to hold his own against me." Gisbourne could not accept he'd been defeated; it had been a freak accident that had been his downfall, he knew, not any greater skill on the part of the wolf's head. He touched his empty eye-socket thoughtfully before continuing. "His men train hard and many of them have experience in wars, either here or abroad. Although they don't expect us, they will react as soon as we attack – I know this for a fact, as do any of you who were with me when we attacked their camp near Wakefield not so very long ago. So be ready for them. Our victory is certain, but whether you personally live or die this day will count on you being prepared for whatever is thrown at you."

He stared around at them for a few heartbeats, measuring their resolve, before looking away, apparently satisfied at what he saw reflected in the soldiers' eyes. "Let's move. Be as silent as possible. And one more thing." As he pushed his mount into a gallop he shouted venomously over his shoulder. "Leave no-one alive. No-one!"

* * *

Tuck stood next to Robin and Little John, holding his quarterstaff tightly, lips pressed together grimly, still shocked by the day's events. Betrayed by his pious friend, who still lay, staring at him from dead eyes, under the beech where he'd been skewered by the outlaw leader's wicked broadhead arrow.

"I don't understand why you feel the need to take on Gisbourne and his men. They'll outnumber you – us," he corrected himself, realizing he was as much a part of this as any of them now, "probably two-to-one, and it won't be wet-behind-the-ears foresters this time; it'll be hard mercenaries."

"And they think they'll catch us completely by surprise," Robin replied, eyes still fixed on the hidden pathway he expected Gareth to appear along at any moment. "They'll get the shock of their lives. We've never had an opportunity like this before, Tuck. Never. We can wipe that bastard Raven off the face of the earth, along with his right-hand man, Groves." His voice trailed off as he pictured Matt's hated face, remembered how the turncoat had murdered their friend Much. "The king and the sheriff will hopefully give up persecuting us when they understand it's not worth the price they have to pay. The lives they'll lose if they continue to hunt us."

Tuck looked at him sceptically. It didn't seem very likely to him that the sheriff would just allow a gang of outlaws to live peacefully in his forest, especially if they were to kill out so many of his own men. Still, it was true that Gisbourne had been a terrible danger to them ever since he'd arrived in Yorkshire the previous year.

"He's grown even more brutal since you've been away in Lewes," Robin continued. "Taken to burning down peoples' homes and threatening them with worse unless the villagers start to inform on us. It won't be long before the people reach breaking point and give us up." He took his eyes from the path momentarily to gaze earnestly at the friar. "We won't be able to survive if that happens. This is our chance to put an end to him. We're living our lives in fear – what's the point in that? If we're so frightened of death, we might as well be dead!" He shook his head and looked back into the foliage again, white knuckles betraying his tension at the continued lack of action. "Where the fuck is Gareth? Surely Gisbourne's on his way by now."

Suddenly there was a small crack from the trees to the side, as of a dried-out twig snapping beneath a person's foot and Robin felt his blood run cold.

"They're here!"

* * *

Matt Groves knew better than anyone how deadly some of the outlaws were. He'd spent years living and fighting beside the likes of Little John and Will Scarlet and even newcomers to the gang like the Hospitaller sergeant-at-arms were well-versed in the arts of war. Matt had seen that for himself when, together with the sergeant and his master Sir Richard-at-Lee, the outlaws had robbed the manor house of Lord John de Bray less than two years ago.

The element of surprise that Sir Guy's men expected to enjoy here today would, though, be enough, along with their greater numbers, to rout the outlaws, Matt was certain. So when Gisbourne signalled their attack and the combined force of Sheriff de Faucumberg's and the Raven's own men moved in to begin the attack the former wolf's head had been somewhat surprised to hear his erstwhile young leader shouting "they're here," as if he'd been expecting them.

As a result, Matt had held himself back when the rest of the soldiers charged wildly into the clearing behind their black-clad, one-eyed leader. He wanted nothing more than to feel his blade bite into the skull of that bastard Hood, but he sensed something was amiss and the attack might not go quite to plan.

The scale of the rout – the brutality of it – probably shouldn't have been a shock to him, given Hood's lucky escapes in the past, but Groves really hadn't expected this today. The arrows flew from the trees, enormous lengths of ash or poplar, fletched with swan or goose-feathers and tipped with vicious iron heads that could blast right through a man's face or ribcage and out the other side with ease. Now the Raven's soldiers – the men Matt had been living and working with for the past few weeks – were dying in front of him and he was too horrified to help them.

He knew the outlaws' lookout hadn't given away the approach of Gisbourne's men, so how...? Then he spotted the monk, lying cold and dead on the forest floor, an arrow embedded deep in his chest and he cursed, misreading the situation. "Friar Tuck must have known all along, the fat bastard. We weren't springing a trap at all – Hood was the one leading *us* into an ambuscade of his own devising!"

The soldiers' numbers had been drastically reduced as a result of the first few volleys of the outlaws' arrows. Men lay unmoving or screaming in agony on the ground until another missile flew from the undergrowth to silence the pitiful, hellish cries, and Gisbourne's remaining men raced for cover behind the nearest trees, cursing loudly, eyes flickering all around as they searched for leadership which didn't appear to be forthcoming.

"Where the fuck are you?" Matt breathed, crouching low and searching for the Raven. He couldn't see him, or hear his voice in the bedlam that had erupted inside the previously calm forest. "Those arseholes must have killed him. Shit!"

He stared out from behind his leafy hiding place, watching as the outlaws decided their longbows were now ineffective and so appeared from the undergrowth like diabolical wraiths, long-swords drawn and held expertly before them as they moved with terrible efficiency to engage what remained of Gisbourne's great force of men.

He watched as the men Gisbourne had asked him to lead were cut down in front of his eyes. Their numbers were down to only a dozen or so now, although about half of those were giving a good account of themselves as the outlaws engaged them.

Little John was, as ever, wielding his massive quarterstaff, taking on two of the sheriff's blue-liveried men by himself. The staff moved in a blur, knocking the soldiers' blades to the side before first one man collapsed from a horrendous blow to the face, then the second was winded by a thrust to the guts. John appeared to be lost in the battle-fever though, and Matt glared through the leaves as the giant brought his weapon hammering down into his two downed enemies repeatedly until, chests smashed to a bloody ruined mess, the huge wolf's head looked up, crazed eyes searching for someone else to kill.

It was a similar, if slightly less brutal, scene all around the clearing. The soldiers' morale had been crushed by the death of so many of their comrades in that first wicked hail of arrows, and Robin Hood's men had spent so many hours training together that they fought as if they had some strange connection to one another's thoughts.

Matt sucked in a breath hopefully as he saw one of Sir Guy's men raise his sword for a killing blow behind Hood himself who hadn't noticed the man as he stepped out from behind a tree. The soldier's eyes blazed with a black fury as he lunged to skewer the wolf's head's liver and Matt grinned, but the minstrel, Allan-a-Dale, somehow appeared from nowhere, his sword hammering down and sending Gisbourne's man flying forward almost comically onto his face. There was no laughter though, as Hood spun and rammed his own sword-point into the downed man's temple. Even Matt grimaced at the resultant mess.

He watched as Will Scarlet and the snarling Hospitaller, still clad in his Order's impressive armour, fought side-by-side, hacking their way through their enemies with terrible efficiency, long-swords tearing flesh as if it was no more than the leafy green foliage that surrounded them so tightly.

It was painfully obvious to Matt that he was on the losing side. His leader had disappeared within the roiling, violent maelstrom of the outlaws' camp, no doubt impaled by an aggressor's blade, while the rest of the men they'd brought into Barnsdale – trained soldiers every one – were being ruthlessly cut down in front of him. There was no reason for him to die too.

He let go of the yew branch he was hiding behind and turned, sword in hand and still in a crouching position, to make his way back towards the safety of the main road.

A gasp, loud enough to be heard even over the battle that was winding down behind him, stopped him in his tracks and he raised his well-worn blade to face whoever was nearby.

It was the minstrel.

Matt had got along well enough with Allan. The outgoing younger man was essentially a show-off who always wanted to be the centre of attention, but he was a fine swordsman and an even better archer. Matt didn't like the fact the minstrel had been so close to his hated enemy Hood, but he appreciated the man's martial skill and had many happy half-drunken memories of sing-alongs to Allan's campfire performances.

"You!"

The near-whisper was almost a curse, and Matt found himself transfixed by Allan's hateful, venomous glare.

The two men, former comrades-in-arms, watched one another warily, mutual respect holding them in check despite the killing that was still going on behind them.

"You betrayed us," Allan growled, his hate-filled yet somehow baffled gaze boring into Matt like a drill. "You were one of us! And after everything we went through... you still betrayed us." He shook his head in wonderment at Matt's duplicity and his mouth twisted in disgust.

That look was enough. Groves had been viewed with distrust and even hatred for most of his life and the sight of a former companion eyeing him with such venom was enough to send him over the edge.

His blade licked out, catching the stunned minstrel on the side of the neck and a bead of crimson appeared as straight as an arrow on Allan's pale complexion. The scarlet line slowly turned into a dripping, gaping wound and the minstrel swayed, staring open-mouthed at his former comrade before he dropped unsteadily onto one knee, eyes still fixed on Matt in shocked disbelief.

"You filthy old..." Allan's left hand came up, flapping weakly at the bloody abrasion in his neck and he squeezed the skin together as best he could with one hand while brandishing his long-sword desperately in the other. Fear showed in his eyes though, and he tried to raise his voice, to berate Matt, but it was clear he was trying to attract attention to his plight.

Groves wasn't the sort of man to miss an opportunity. His eyes flared and he raised his blade high overhead, looking around for signs of oncoming attack but none of the minstrel's outlaw companions appeared to be close-by so he gritted his teeth and brought his weapon down as hard as he could.

Allan screamed as he saw the blow approach.

It was a pitiful, horrid sound, that made the combatants nearby stare in fear, almost forgetting their own dire peril, and his wide young eyes turned in disbelief to stare at the horrific gaping wound that had severed his right arm almost completely from his torso.

"I always thought you were one of the better ones," Matt grunted sadly, but he knew his side was losing and he'd become lost in the battle-fever that affected even the best of men. The point of his sword speared forward, directly into Allan's windpipe, silencing the minstrel's voice forever and the former-outlaw dragged his blade free, tearing skin and flesh apart in a bloody spray.

"Over there," a voice shouted and Matt knew he had to get away before the victorious outlaws found him and saw what he'd done to their friend. He broke into a run, forcing his way through the undergrowth as fast as he could, not even sure which direction he was going, but understanding the need to put as much distance between himself and his pursuers as he could.

He knew how to travel quickly through the densely packed forest, having done it for many years in the not-so-distant past, and it was just as well, he thought, smiling wickedly to himself as a cry of pure grief filled the trees. He knew that voice; Robin Hood had found his brutalized, dead minstrel pal. The smile on Matt's seamed face turned into a grin. Maybe he had lost today, but at least that prick Hood hadn't had it all his own way. The wolf's head still had to find his mate Gareth too...

He burst into a small clearing and allowed himself to stop and catch his breath. He wasn't a young man any more and, although he was fairly fit, he'd not done much training since joining Gisbourne's crew other than the occasional spar with his one-eyed leader, and his flight had tired him more than he wanted to admit to himself. He rested his hands on his thighs and sucked in lungfuls of air, the heaving in his chest eventually subsiding until, at last, he raised his head, still smiling, and spat a great glob of green phlegm into the old brown leaves underfoot. He noted the position of the sun and, since he had a fair idea what time it was, could work out which direction it was to Nottingham.

The sheriff might hate his guts, but someone had to tell de Faucumberg what had happened to all the soldiers he'd sent to deal with the notorious outlaws. He glanced back over his shoulder but there were no sounds of pursuit, just an almost even more unnerving silence and he turned slightly to the left to forge a path through the forest in the direction of the city.

He wondered what he'd do now, with his comfortable position as the Raven's second-in-command apparently finished. He wouldn't go back to a sailor's life again and, although he was a free man he didn't have any money; he'd blown it all on drink and whores. But Sir Henry was now short a dozen men in his garrison, so perhaps he could find employment there, with the sheriff.

Despite the overwhelming defeat his side had suffered that day, Groves felt strangely optimistic as he jogged towards Nottingham. Hood's gang were still at large after all, and who better to lead the chase now than one of their ex-members with his detailed knowledge of their habits, routines and local suppliers? Yes, the sheriff didn't like him very much, but perhaps he could persuade the arrogant, stuck-up arsehole to let him lead the search for Hood from now on.

The self-satisfied smile never left his face all the long road back to the city.

* * *

Somewhere in the dark recesses of his mind Robin knew he should control himself; his men were watching him and they needed leadership not a display of raw, naked emotion. But at that moment, when he saw his friend Allan-a-Dale lying, cold and bloody and dead, on the soft spring grass the young outlaw captain sank to his knees and held his head in his hands.

A tortured cry tore from his throat and tears filled his eyes, grief and a terrible rage warring within him and even Little John stood back respectfully and wary of disturbing his leader, lost as he was in his emotions.

Robin remembered that night when he and Allan had performed in the manor house, singing for the lords and ladies to much applause, before saving Will's daughter from her own hellish life the next morning. He remembered all the times the outlaws had sat around the campfire on a freezing night, with nothing but ale, Allan's music and one another's company to chase away the gloom. And he remembered just a few weeks ago, when he and John had rescued the minstrel from Nottingham. It had all turned out so nicely that day, as if God himself had been watching over them, but now...

Finally, the reality of their situation brought Robin back to his senses and, still looking down at his fallen companion, he growled, "Did we get them all?"

Will Scarlet shook his head. He, along with a couple of the other men, had checked the dead and wounded. "For our part," he said, "we only lost..." he stared at Allan's lifeless form, unwilling to say his comrade's name. "As for the enemy; who can say? We don't know for sure how many of them were in their party. We didn't get all of them though – whoever did that to Allan must have escaped into the trees. And... he's not the only one that's escaped..."

Robin sat for a moment, still unable to think straight, then he looked up, understanding flaring in his eyes. "Gisbourne?"

"Aye."

"We've looked but his body's not here," Stephen muttered confirmation.

Robin got to his feet slowly, his mind whirling. If they hadn't managed to kill the Raven, all this had been for naught. Gisbourne would simply return to Nottingham for reinforcements – perhaps the garrison would be too stretched and he'd need to wait on the king sending him more men, but, eventually they would come and then their hated enemy would return in a fury, again and again, until every last one of the outlaws lay rotting in the ground like Much and Harry Half-Hand and Wilfred and Sir Richard-at-Lee and...

"Allan died for nothing then. All of these men here today died for nothing."

"It gets worse." Little John hunched his great shoulders unconsciously, as he often did when talking to someone so he could look them in the eyes without appearing intimidating. "There's no sign of that arsehole Matt either."

Robin just stared in silence at the giant.

"We should deal with the survivors," the Hospitaller sergeant growled, breaking the spell that seemed to hold the entire forest in its grip and the men nodded, the agonized grunts and cries of badly injured men finally filtering through their shock at Allan's brutal demise.

"Stephen's right," Robin admitted, making a conscious effort to pull himself together, at least until all this was dealt with. "And we should try and find out where the fuck Gareth got to. That little prick should have warned us of Gisbourne's approach; if he's got drunk and fallen asleep while on watch I'll tear off his balls and feed them to him."

"I'll go," the newcomer, Piers, offered. "I know where the lookout post is and I'm a fast runner." In truth, the fight had appalled him – he'd never in his whole life witnessed so much blood and death, and the pitiful sounds coming from their maimed enemies were playing on his already frayed nerves. Even going off alone into the forest seemed better than staying around the camp right then.

Robin nodded, seeing the shock in their new recruit's face and knowing it would do the young man good to spend a little time alone. The memory of his own first battle as an outlaw was still fresh in Robin's mind – it seemed a lifetime ago, so much had happened since, and he'd become battle-hardened in the intervening time, but it was only... Christ above, it was only two years ago.

Piers hastened off through the undergrowth, trying to appear stoic and offering his captain a wave of salute as he went, while Robin moved back towards their camp to see who was still alive and what could, or should, be done with them.

Although Gisbourne's men were enemies, they were simply soldiers following their orders. The wolf's head felt no malice towards them for their actions, just a bitter sadness that so many men had to die to serve the purposes of their 'betters'. With the escape of Matt Groves and Sir Guy of Gisbourne Robin's battle-fury had left him and a gaping, maudlin hole remained.

Friar Tuck was already moving amongst the wounded, trying to help those most grievously harmed first. Stephen too had a decent knowledge of rudimentary healing skills and he tended to those Tuck couldn't get to quickly enough.

Of Gisbourne's force of approximately thirty-five men, twenty-two lay dead, sprawled on the ground or even slumped awkwardly over logs or lying cradled within the branches of some bush or other. Six were wounded, at least three of them mortally despite Tuck and Stephen's efforts. The rest of the soldiers were unaccounted for – presumably they'd decided to leave their comrades to their fate and had escaped into the trees along with their black-attired, one-eyed leader and his second-in-command, Groves.

Robin didn't know whether to curse the escapees for abandoning their companions or to be glad that at least some men would be able to return home to their families that night. It was all so damn senseless.

"What do we do now?" Little John asked, spreading his arms wide like some enormous bird-of-prey. "They know where we are."

"Aye, we should move camp again," Arthur agreed running a hand through his thick brown hair. "This place isn't safe any more."

Robin shook his head and filled a mug with ale from a cask on the wagon close to the fire before dropping onto one of the big logs they'd been using as seats for the past few weeks. "They won't return tonight. Or tomorrow for that matter. We have time yet." He felt weary. Drained. And not just from his part in the fight. Being the leader might seem glamorous to some but it placed a huge amount of stress on his shoulders and, although he was getting better at dealing with it all, times like this still took their toll on him.

John nodded, happy to accept Robin's decision and, along with a couple of the men who, like him, didn't feel like resting, moved off to find a spot to dig a grave for Allan-a-Dale.

What they would do with the near two-dozen enemy corpses John didn't know and, right then, didn't care. Robin wasn't the only one bone-weary and struggling to deal with the aftermath of the battle. Will and Stephen might have seen dead bodies piled up and blood saturating the ground when they'd fought in great armies overseas, but most of the men had never been a part of so much death.

Would the mood in the camp be different if Groves and Gisbourne had been killed? Would the men be celebrating, rather than moving silently around the place almost gingerly, as if they half-expected the sky to fall on them at any moment? The atmosphere was beyond eerie and only made worse by the fact one of the mortally wounded soldiers had begun to scream as the pain became unbearable. The tanner, Edmond, eyes wide and hands shaking, crammed a strip of linen into the man's mouth to muffle the horrible sound.

No-one even tried to stop him.

CHAPTER TWENTY-FIVE

Piers reached the lookout post in a short time, his youthful legs and loping stride carrying him through the undergrowth at a relentless pace as he tried to forget what he'd witnessed back at the camp. He'd seen death before, of course – who hadn't? But it had been *normal* death: his grandmother limp and ashen-faced in her bed one morning; his pet dog, murdered by a drunken sailor during the night; a vagrant, frozen to death the previous winter in one of Nottingham's side-streets when Piers had been making his way to work in the clerk's offices.

But to be attacked by so many soldiers, and to watch them being brutally cut down like chaff under a labourer's sickle... He shuddered and took a deep breath, glancing around himself, eyes searching the thick new-season foliage for hidden dangers but he saw nothing and looked up, spotting the cleverly concealed wooden platform the outlaws had built into the tree near the very top.

"Gareth," he hissed, trying again when there was no sign of movement from above, or even a sound of recognition. Perhaps the youngster *had* allowed himself to get drunk and fallen asleep as Robin suggested. Piers whacked the trunk of the tree – a venerable old Scots Pine – and tried shouting on Gareth again, louder this time.

Still no response from above.

A sense of foreboding came over him and he knew he'd have to climb the tree. He supposed if Gisbourne's men had somehow found the lookout post there would be blood or other signs of a struggle – Gareth wasn't much of a fighter but he had spirit and wouldn't just sit there while someone killed him. As he began the ascent, using the handily placed iron nails, Piers glanced down into the surrounding foliage, hoping desperately not to see Gareth's corpse there, thrown by some assailant.

A slight movement from beneath a juniper bush caught his eye but it was just a blackbird, foraging for worms, and he continued his ascent, trying to move as silently as possible, fearing what he might find on the rapidly nearing platform although he told himself it was more than likely empty.

Gareth must have decided he'd had enough of this life and buggered off, Piers surmised, finally grasping the platform and hauling himself up onto it.

He shrank back involuntarily, almost falling out of the tree, a horrified gasp escaping from his lips. "No!"

Gareth hadn't buggered off, he was still there. But the suggestion that he'd taken alcohol to his post appeared to be correct for an empty wine-skin lay by his side, flat and clearly drained. Rather like the empty shell that used to be Gareth's young body.

There wasn't a scratch on him but Gareth lay on his back, as if he'd fallen asleep after consuming all his wine. Dried vomit coated the man's mouth and neck though, suggesting he'd puked but been so drunk he hadn't even woken up. Piers wondered inanely whether Gareth had died from suffocation or drowning, as if the distinction somehow mattered.

The newcomer to the outlaw gang sat for a long time, just staring at his dead comrade, hoping to see some signs of life but it was futile and eventually the shock passed and allowed Piers to climb unsteadily back down to the ground, taking his time as his limbs were shaky and his head seemed to spin. When he finally reached the forest floor he made the sign of the cross, feeling somewhat silly and self-conscious but knowing he should offer some sign of respect for poor Gareth's departed soul, then without a backward glance, loped off into the trees to tell the rest of the men the bad news. As he ran his mind whirled; after a relatively pleasant few weeks as an outlaw living in the trees of Barnsdale things didn't seem quite so straightforward.

Holy Mary, mother of God! What have I let myself in for?

* * *

Twenty-three dead men in their camp. Their *home*! Robin sipped his ale, staring into the fire numbly. This wasn't his home, how could it be when his wife and little son were miles away in –

"Wakefield."

The voice carried to Robin through the still air and his eyes flicked up to see who had spoken. He didn't recognize the strangely accented voice and he knew it hadn't come from one of his own men. He jumped to his feet, and hurried across to the wounded prisoners that Tuck was still tending to.

"Who said that?" he demanded, glaring at the men.

One of them raised a hand weakly and Robin knelt beside him, offering him the ale cup he'd carried over without even realising it. "Here, lad, drink."

The soldier, probably not even out of his teens from the look of his unlined and beardless face, gratefully accepted the cup and gulped down its contents greedily.

"What about Wakefield?" Robin asked softly. He'd noted the great gaping hole in the man's side where the chain mail had been penetrated by a sword thrust and knew it wouldn't be too long before he expired.

The soldier gritted his teeth as a wave of nausea flooded through him and Robin watched impatiently, a sense of foreboding beginning to creep over him.

"Sir Guy... I heard him, just before he slipped into the trees and left us to die, the bastard." He sobbed, his hand fluttering weakly about the bloody gash in his side as the pain began to worsen.

"Rest easy, soldier." Robin forced a reassuring smile onto his face and held a comforting hand gently on the man's arm. "You're going to be all right. The good friar here will see to it."

The man shook his head, fear and resignation plain in his eyes as he met the wolf's head's gaze. "I'll be dead within the hour. Before that. But I can't go to my grave with more deaths on my conscience."

"Speak." Robin nodded, feeling guilt and sorrow for the man's agony but needing to know what the hell Gisbourne had said.

"Promise me you'll perform the last rites for me, brother," he gasped, before sighing in relief at Tuck's nod then gritting his teeth again. "When Sir Guy saw your lot's arrows coming out of the trees like some hellish rain he must have known he'd lost the battle before we'd even aimed a blow of our own. I heard him cursing to himself before he –"

Robin hissed at him as the light began to fade from his eyes and his fingers gripped hard on the soldier's wrist. "He what?"

"He said... if he couldn't kill you he was going to Wakefield. To kill your family instead."

Robin felt as if his blood had turned to ice but, before he had time to react, another voice burst in.

"He's dead too! Gareth's dead!"

There was an angry chorus from the stunned outlaws who crowded back into the centre of the camp to shoot questions at the overwhelmed Piers. Little John did his best to hold the men back so the young clerk could tell them what had happened, while Robin just stood, unable to move, mind reeling.

"Did Gisbourne's men get him too?" John demanded once he'd silenced the men and Piers had managed to get his breath back after the run.

"No. You were right," he glanced over at Robin who simply stared back uncomprehendingly. "He'd drank at least one full skin of wine then... he must have passed out and threw up while flat on his back." Piers shrugged, his face twisted in anguish. "He's dead," he finished simply.

No-one knew what to say. To rant about Gareth's stupidity seemed crass and disrespectful at a time like this, even if it was the first thing that came into most of the outlaws' minds.

"Fuck!" Little John finally broke the silence, his single shouted oath enough to sum up the feelings of every man in the camp.

"Looks like we'll have to dig another grave beside Allan's," Stephen muttered, collapsing wearily onto a log and picking at the skin on his fingers.

The men stood, or sat, for a long time in silence. It was a bad day and, mentally, if not physically, they were just about broken.

Suddenly Robin shook his head, and wide-eyed, he ran over to Little John, pointing at Will as he went. Their day wasn't over yet.

"That bastard Gisbourne's gone to Wakefield to kill Matilda and my son. I have to go after him, and he's got a head start. Will you two come with me?"

His two lieutenants nodded in unison.

"Of course we will," John rumbled.

"But we'll never be able to catch up with him now," Will fretted. "As you say, he's ages ahead of us."

Robin pointed at the wounded soldiers who were watching the outlaws with interest, despite their own predicament. "Those men came here on horseback. We need to find their mounts. It'll mean starting off in the wrong direction but it's the only way we'll be able to reach Wakefield in time." He knelt by the captured men. "Where are your horses?"

The soldiers, although wounded and even dying, were pleased to have been treated with respect by Hood's men since they'd been defeated.

"You've treated us fairly," one of them mumbled. "While our own leader pissed off and left us to die." He spat, a mixture of saliva and blood which he looked at balefully before continuing. "The horses are a little way to the west of your lookout post. Just follow the line of trees, you can't miss them. Poor beasts, they've been tied up there all day."

Robin, John and Will still wore their weapons and armour and Robin only tarried to grab his longbow and an ale-skin before giving his orders to the rest of the men.

"Stephen, you're in charge. As I say, I doubt there's much chance of any more attackers coming here within the next few days but be on your guard. Some of the soldiers we chased off might still be lurking nearby."

The Hospitaller nodded grimly. "Don't worry about us, lad, be on your way. God go with you."

Despite their exhaustion the three friends broke into a run and headed off into the trees to find the horses.

"Pray for us," Robin shouted over his shoulder.

* * *

A huge stretch of Ermine St, the main road connecting York and London amongst other places, was currently occupied by the great entourage that accompanied King Edward II on his travels around the country. He had spent much of the year visiting many of the towns and cities under his dominion, and planned to continue on until at least winter.

Travelling with him were an enormous number of people. From clerks and chaplains to cooks and bakers, and following behind them all came a goodly number of prostitutes and other undesirables who saw to the... *needs*, of the royal household which also included Edward's own personal bodyguard of twenty-odd archers and even more sergeants-at-arms.

It was late afternoon and they'd come from York with their destination being Castleford just a short distance south-east of Leeds, where they'd stop for the night. The king mostly enjoyed these journeys, often whipping his horse into a gallop and laughing at the freedom he felt as the great beast carried him off, away from the hangers-on and toadies that followed him everywhere.

Of course, his guards would keep him in sight at all times so he was never in any real danger – it would be an utterly insane criminal that tried to hold-up a royal party of such a size – but to Edward it was a wonderful release from the tedium of everyday politics, in-fighting and manoeuvering that seemed to occupy most of his time.

It had been a while since the king had treated himself and his mount to a mad dash into a field or along a minor road and he was beginning to get restless. The sun would remain high overhead for a while yet and it was swelteringly hot as a result, which was the only reason he'd held himself in check as his aides continually tried to engage him in trivia and matters of court which he really couldn't be bothered with.

"Boy!" Edward turned his head to look over his shoulder and gestured to one of the servants that remained near to him at all times. The lad's mount was laden with a wine-skin which he emptied into a silver, beautifully decorated chalice as he rode up to take his place respectfully behind the monarch. The wine, an extortionately expensive Malmsey from Italy, was warm, which rather spoiled the delicate taste, but it was refreshing nevertheless and Edward swallowed it quickly, wiping his handsome face with a big hand before tossing the near-priceless cup back to the boy whose eyes opened wide, terrified in case he should fumble the catch and damage it.

Edward looked back to the road, unaware of the terror he'd instilled in the poor page and gazed along the road into the distance, taking in the lush green, rolling hills, colourful fields with their various crops growing, blue, near-cloudless sky and watched as the heat made ripples on the horizon. Ah, it was terribly hot, but by God, England – *his* England – was a glorious land!

His eyesight was good and since he'd taken up position right at the very front of the great procession he was able to see for miles around. He caught a slight movement in his peripheral vision and turned to the left to get a better look, squinting against the sun's glare.

"Horsemen."

The captain of his guard kicked his horse forward to trot by the king's side, watching for himself as the shapes in the distance came closer, resolving eventually into three distinct figures, brown cloaks billowing behind them as they galloped towards the main road across a field.

The captain gestured to his men to draw their weapons and move into defensive positions all around the lengthy procession while he stayed by his master's side, hand ready on the pommel of his sword. The horsemen didn't appear to be coming in their direction – indeed they seemed oblivious to the king's presence on the road – but they had the look of soldiers about them and the captain wanted to be ready should they prove to herald a much larger force of possibly hostile men.

It wasn't that long since the Lancastrian revolt after all, and up here in the north the commoners saw the Earl of Lancaster as some sort of fallen hero. It made sense to prepare for attack, even if it was rather unlikely.

They continued to move forward, plodding at the interminable pace that irked the king but that such a large number of people necessitated and the three riders became ever clearer. Their paths wouldn't cross, not quite, but it would be close.

Behind the king, Sheriff de Faucumberg – who'd been ordered to travel from Nottingham and accompany the royal party for a week or so – watched the riders with a growing sense of unease. Something about them seemed familiar and he unconsciously moved his own mount forward, close to the king, to try and get a better view.

At last, one of the riders, the one at the head of the small triangle, became aware of the presence of the long procession of people and carts on the road to the north of them and he turned to look, just as they reached the small drystone wall that kept the sheep from straying out of the field.

The king screwed his face up even further, staring at the rider before them, who just returned the stare blankly, almost as if the man still hadn't registered their presence or perhaps didn't care.

"I know those men."

"Robin Hood!"

Recognition flared at the same time for both king and sheriff and, as Edward heard de Faucumberg muttering the name of the notorious outlaw he turned with a quizzical expression.

"Robin Hood? With the two friars?"

The sheriff looked baffled momentarily, until he remembered the whole blasted episode with the silver arrow and understood what his king was talking about.

"No, my liege, those are no friars. They passed themselves off as such to you, but they are, in actual fact, Hood himself, with his two companions, John Little and, I believe, Will Scaflock, popularly known as Scarlet."

The galloping riders slowed as they reached the small stone wall, betraying their inexperience on horseback as they tentatively coaxed the big palfreys across the minor impediment. Without another glance in the king's direction they rode into the trees on the other side of the road and disappeared from sight.

The king watched them go, an unreadable expression on his face, before he turned back to the sheriff.

"Clearly they're in a hurry. Too much of a hurry to use the road. What town lies yonder?"

De Faucumberg gazed into the trees, picturing the local area in his mind's-eye before replying. "Castleford," he shrugged. "Where we're headed ourselves."

"Anything else?"

Again, the sheriff thought for a moment, trying to access a mental map of the whole region before he nodded thoughtfully.

"Wakefield is basically on the same line from here as Castleford, sire. Wakefield is Hood's home, or was, before he became a wolf's head."

"Interesting." Edward continued to lead his people forward for a few moments, still staring into the undergrowth that had swallowed up the outlaws. Finally he turned to his captain.

"Bring half-a-dozen men and follow us," he swung back to de Faucumberg. "Sheriff – lead the way to Wakefield." He touched the hilt of his own great long-sword, grinning as he felt its reassuring bulk. "I'd very much like to see what's got my friar friends in such a state that they barely even register the presence of the royal household on the road next to them. Lead on, man, lead on!"

Sir Henry de Faucumberg, stunned as he was, knew better than to argue with a command from the king and he kicked his heels into his mount, urging it into a gallop and through the small gap in the trees which had recently claimed Hood and his companions.

King Edward II, monarch of all England, whooped like an excited child and followed, politics and all the other tedious nonsense he was forced to endure completely forgotten.

CHAPTER TWENTY-SIX

Sir Guy of Gisbourne wasn't in his right mind; he hadn't been for a long time now. Ever since that piece of filth Robin Hood had carved open his face. That was when it had begun. The defeat had done more than just wound him physically – his pride had suffered and he'd found himself having dark thoughts the like of which he'd never had before.
Self-doubt had begun to gnaw at him like a rat on a corpse.
Every time he thought of the wolf's head living on, enjoying a reputation not only as some legendary outlaw but, now, as the man who'd bested *him*, the king's own bounty hunter...
When Matt Groves had joined his group things had become much worse. Gisbourne might have known his new second-in-command was purposefully trying to stoke Gisbourne's hatred but it didn't matter – the black emotion had grown and grown until it became all-encompassing. When Hood and his giant mate had managed to free the minstrel from Nottingham it had felt like a physical blow to the king's man. After the sheriff had driven him out of the city and he'd managed to get some time alone, away from his men, he had actually vomited. The stress and fury inside him at Hood's charmed existence – while he himself was being made to seem like a bumbling oaf – had overcome him and it had been shocking to a man who prided himself on his rigid self-control.
He glanced up at the sky to check the sun's position overhead and make sure he was heading in the right direction. He'd have run all through the night if he could but exhaustion finally swamped him and it was probably just as well as travelling in the darkness was a sure way to suffer an injury by running into a tree branch or planting a foot in a dip in the ground and breaking an ankle or worse. So he'd found a small clearing and built a fire to keep inquisitive animals away, although it was cold and dead by the time he woke up before sunrise the following morning and his body ached terribly from the few hours sleep he'd had.
Some part of him knew he was acting irrationally and was planning to do something that went totally against his character, but he pushed his conscience to one side and upped his pace. He no longer cared about morals, honour, or appearances; all he wanted to do was bring pain down on Robin Hood, just as the despised wolf's head had done to him.
Life hadn't been good to him, he reflected. He'd never wanted to be a bounty-hunter, or even a soldier, but his wife, who he loved dearly, had cheated on him numerous times, prompting him to leave his home. Even then, under that sort of strain and knowing he was the talk of the village, he'd still never hit his wife. Striking a woman was something weak men did; men with little moral fibre and no self-control. It was a coward's response to a situation.
And yet here he was, on his way to murder not only a woman, but a child too. The thought didn't shock him or prompt any sort of emotional reaction at all – he felt numb and as if he was no longer in charge of his own body. Killing Hood's family was the only option open to Gisbourne now that the wolf's head had destroyed his soldiers again.
He wasn't going to Wakefield to indulge some sadistic fantasy – it was merely something he had to do to punish the outlaw leader. Gisbourne knew he wasn't half the swordsman he'd been before Hood had taken his eye, so there would be no wasting time once he reached the town.
He knew where to go; knew where the Fletcher's house was and once he'd completed his task, he'd head back to Nottingham. Or maybe London. Or France?
His mind seemed to spin frantically with ideas and emotions yet, paradoxically, he found himself in a serene sort of trance-like state as his soft black leather boots covered the miles and drew him ever closer to Wakefield.
Eventually, the smoke that rose from the hearths in the little town became visible over the tree-tops and Gisbourne's hand dropped to his sword hilt. He still carried the deadly little crossbow with its hazel stock and steel bow that he'd had custom made in Italy but he didn't even carry ammunition for it these days – his depth perception had been ruined when he'd lost his eye and he simply couldn't

hit the target with the projectile weapon no matter how much he practised with it. Still, it *looked* lethal, and impressed the peasants, which was why he still bore it.

No, he wouldn't be using the soft option when it came time to despatch Matilda Hood and her offspring. He would look them in the eye as he told them why they had to die and then he'd send them into God's arms on the end of his treasured longsword.

As Wakefield came nearer Gisbourne concealed himself in the trees that fringed the southern end of the village. The house that Matilda Hood shared with her parents was located quite close to the edge of town and it would be easier for the king's man to find his prey if he avoided walking through the streets for as long as possible.

He moved quietly, although he was no woodsman like Hood or one of his gang, and if anyone had been nearby they would surely have heard his approach. But the townsfolk were busy going about their daily work and no one suspected the danger that lurked so close-by. The air was filled with the sounds of that work – a hammer ringing brightly on an anvil; peasants singing as they tended the fields not too far off; women laughing and gossiping as they washed clothes in one of the streams that fed into the Calder...

It was a pleasant, sunny day like any other and Gisbourne felt a pang of jealousy at the simple, uncomplicated lives these commoners led. They were born, lived unremarkable little lives no-one outside of the town cared about, and then they died, forgotten and lost in the mists of time. And yet... they were happy, or at least they seemed to be happy enough as the king's bounty hunter watched from his hiding place.

Perhaps those peasants would never know what it felt like to be blessed with a rare and remarkable talent like Gisbourne's skill with a blade but they had their families and their inexorable routines, and he watched, wishing he had a life like that, and he hated them for it.

Finally he reached a spot near the street that the Fletchers' house was on but he stopped, wondering how to proceed.

He couldn't simply walk into the town without people noticing him, and perhaps attempting to impede what he'd come to do. Although his reputation would likely be enough to stop anyone from accosting him unprovoked, without any of his guards to back him up the locals might become violent when he found Hood's wife and drew his sword.

Then, as he knelt on the soft, damp grass, pondering his next move, he offered a silent prayer of thanks to God as he spotted two girls and a small, toddling figure coming out of a house and turning to walk in his direction, broad smiles on their faces.

Hood's wife and infant son.

God was clearly on his side.

This would be easier than he'd hoped.

* * *

"Was that the fucking king?" Will Scarlet shouted in disbelief as their horses ploughed into the undergrowth, picking their way through the trees with an uncanny grace that Little John, who'd hardly ever ridden, found astonishing.

"Aye," the giant replied, also raising his voice to be heard over the drumming of hooves, jingling of harnesses and wind in their ears. "The king, and the sheriff too from the looks of it. Christ only knows what they made of us three riding across their path without so much as a 'Your Highness'."

"What if they follow us?" Will shouted, more to himself than John or Robin. "If de Faucumberg recognised us, and tells the king who we are... the royal guards will come looking for us."

John remained silent and Robin wasn't even listening to his companions, being too focused on making it to Wakefield as quickly as possible. They too had been forced to rest when the sun set and the night had almost sent the young wolf's head over the edge with worry before they were able to continue their pursuit.

He'd met King Edward's eyes as they passed the royal party, just for a fleeting moment, before they managed to coax their mounts over the low stone wall and into the undergrowth, but he felt sure there'd been a spark of recognition in the monarch's eyes.

Ultimately, it made no difference whether the king and his soldiers came after them; Robin had to stop Gisbourne before he could harm Matilda or Arthur, and his two friends were willing to put their own lives on the line to support their young leader. Even if it meant fighting the King of England himself.

Wakefield came into sight as they burst out of the foliage and found themselves racing through a field of barley which was being tended by a number of peasants. The farmers fell back instinctively at the sight of the heavily armed and armoured grim-faced horsemen charging towards the town.

One man, braver than the rest, shouted what was possibly a greeting at them and Little John waved a big hand, nodding reassuringly towards the farmer who took in the size of the rider before his eyes travelled across Will and Robin pulling away at the front of the equine triangle.

The man grinned, glad to see the outlaws who always brought food or money to the people of Wakefield but his expression wavered as the riders charged past without slowing, silent and grim, and clearly engaged on some errand that promised to end only in violence and death.

The man hefted his sickle and ran towards the village himself, shouting for his fellow workers to come too. Robin Hood and his men were friends – whatever they were doing, they would have support of the people of Wakefield.

The outlaws thundered into the village's main street, eyes scanning the area for either Matilda or Gisbourne, but all they could see were bemused locals who stared back, wondering what in God's name was happening.

"We'll split up," Robin said, rounding on his companions. "Gisbourne is still dangerous but with one eye missing he can't possibly be the swordsman he was; any one of us should be able to handle him alone if need be, and we'll cover much more ground if we go in separate directions. John, you head for the well in the centre of the village. Scarlet, you find Patrick, the headman, tell him to gather the tithing – the more men we have searching for Gisbourne the better."

Will opened his mouth to argue – to say he was heading for the Fletchers' himself, since his own daughter Beth lived there too, but he knew Robin's plan made sense. There was no point in the two of them going to the same place when Gisbourne could be anywhere in or around the village. Besides, there had been no threat made towards Beth – Scarlet doubted the king's man even knew about the girl. The danger was all centred on his captain's family, so Will simply nodded in grim agreement.

Robin looked around, eyes darting from shadow to shadow trying to find his hated enemy. "I'll head for the Fletchers' and pray to the Magdalene that Matilda and Arthur are safe there. Go! And take care – he might not be England's greatest swordsman any more, but he's still deadly."

He kicked his heels into his palfrey's sides and held on desperately, cursing his inexperience as the horse almost threw him back into the road, but he managed to hold on and soon spotted the simple two-storey house that belonged to Henry Fletcher and was also home to Matilda and Arthur, as well as Will's daughter.

As he reached the building he looked further along the road and his heart leapt in his chest as he spotted the familiar gait of his wife, accompanied by a smaller girl he recognised her as his sister Marjorie. They were walking away from him, following the tiny figure of Arthur, his son.

Praise be to God, they were safe!

Still warily scanning the houses on either side of the street he dismounted and began to walk towards his family, hand resting on the pommel of his sword. Before he could shout on them to wait, though, a black-armoured figure appeared from the dense foliage at the end of the street and ran forward, long-sword in hand, the naked blade glinting wickedly in the sunshine.

A cry of despair tore from Robin's throat and he broke into a sprint, dragging his own blade free from its leather scabbard, but he was much too far away to reach Arthur before the Raven would.

His long legs ate up the distance between them, and Robin watched in amazement as his skinny, malnourished little sister Marjorie, obviously spotting the approaching danger, began to move herself. She shouted in alarm at the toddler ahead of her who turned, eyes wide in surprise, soft face twisted in a grimace of fear and confusion at the terror in Marjorie's voice.

Behind him, though, the one-eyed bounty hunter came on, black as night and just as inexorable, and Robin screamed a challenge at him, to fight one-on-one, man-to-man, as they'd done before on the outskirts of Dalton not so many months ago.

The Raven looked up from the small figure in the road in front of him, seeing Hood coming towards them but too far away yet to be a threat and he roared in triumph, completely lost in the madness that had overcome his life-long iron discipline.

Gisbourne raised his exquisite oiled blade and, single eye blazing, targeted the child standing in the dusty road before him.

Matilda screamed, as did her husband who charged along the road towards their son knowing deep down that he had no chance of reaching Arthur in time to save him.

But Marjorie – skinny, withered Marjorie – had also run forward when she'd seen the danger approaching. The toddler stood, bewildered and terrified, in the centre of the road as his aunt pumped her legs harder than she'd ever done in her entire life, then a cry tore from Arthur's lips as the girl knocked him sideways, hard, away from the oncoming sword of Sir Guy of Gisbourne.

The infant was sent crashing to the ground at the side of Gisbourne's feet, howling, and again, Robin was astonished as Marjorie pulled a short wooden practice sword from beneath her skirts and used it to desperately batter the Raven's sword hand away to the side.

It was enough to buy Robin time to finally reach Marjorie and, as he did so he lunged at Gisbourne, trying to skewer his son's would-be murderer, but the king's man dodged to the side and the wolf's head's thrust missed its target.

Knowing he couldn't survive a fight with the burly outlaw Gisbourne reached out and grasped the arm of the young girl who had thwarted his mission. He was much too strong for her, although she tried desperately to break free, even sinking her teeth into the Raven's hand but he simply slapped her, hard across the head and she went limp in his arms.

"Stand down, Hood."

Robin froze, staring in horror at the crazed, one-eyed madman that held his sister's life in his hands. Matilda came up behind him, shouting on Arthur as he got to his feet unsteadily and, tears streaming down his face, toddled hurriedly towards his mother who lifted him with a sob of her own and cuddled him in protectively.

Gisbourne glared at the despised wolf's head, both of them breathing heavily as they eyed one another with murderous loathing. The king's man had no idea who this girl he held hostage was – if he'd known she was Hood's sister he'd have surely killed her right then. As it was, she'd be a useful bargaining tool that might see him escape from what had become a hopeless situation.

"Drop your sword, Hood, or I kill this little bitch. Her life's in your hands." He squeezed his arm around Marjorie's throat until she started to turn blue and her attempts to break free stopped as she went limp.

Robin's mind whirled madly as he tried to take control of the situation but he could see no way out.

Suddenly the sound of pounding hooves came towards them and Gisbourne's wild eye widened in disbelief as he saw the newcomers behind Hood, although he never let go of Marjorie who appeared to be unconscious now.

"Robin!" From the street to the side even more voices approached and the outlaw captain saw Little John and Will Scarlet approaching in his peripheral vision.

"You men, drop your weapons."

Robin heard the voice and recognized it: King Edward II. He'd managed to follow them here after all. But the wolf's head ignored the king – he wasn't about to let the Raven murder his sister.

"Gisbourne!" Sheriff Henry de Faucumberg's furious voice filled the street now as he slid off the back of his mount with practised ease and walked imperiously towards the man he'd been saddled with for more than a year. "You heard your king. Let the girl go and drop your weapon."

Gisbourne remained silent, as if in shock at the sight of his liege-lord appearing so unexpectedly in this backwater village so far from London.

"I said drop the sword, you lunatic!"

De Faucumberg reached out, a look of disgust on his face, and grabbed Sir Guy's wrist.

Little John and Will hurried over to stand close to Robin, and Matilda turned to hand the frightened Arthur to the giant outlaw. The child went readily enough, despite the stressful situation, recognising the two men and knowing they'd keep him safe.

The king watched everything, bemused, wondering what the hell was going on and why his own bounty hunter was threatening a skinny local girl.

A crowd began to gather, eyes flicking in turn from the bizarre sight of a heavily guarded nobleman they assumed must be their king, here, in *their* village, and the crazed Raven whose face twisted now in a fury as the sheriff's fingers wrapped around his arm.

Gisbourne had never liked the sheriff and now he saw an opportunity to teach the bastard a lesson. He let go of Marjorie who slumped forward onto the road and lay still as her erstwhile captor turned his attention to Sir Henry de Faucumberg.

The sheriff cried out and desperately tried to jump backwards as Gisbourne's long-sword licked out. It was a solid strike but de Faucumberg's chain mail was in good repair and stopped the wicked blade from slicing completely through his ribs although he stumbled as he dodged, and fell over to land on his back on the road, blood oozing from his wound.

"Hold!" King Edward's voice held an unmistakeable note of command that everyone in the crowd recognised. Apart from Gisbourne.

He ignored his master's command and, with a feral growl, pulled his blade back to deliver a killing blow to the fallen sheriff.

Robin wasn't near enough to block the strike and he wasn't even sure if he wanted to. It was the Sheriff of Nottingham and Yorkshire – the man who'd been trying to hunt him and the rest of the outlaws down like animals these past two years and more.

"No!" De Faucumberg was no coward. He'd fought in battles against the Scots, and for the king against the Contrariants. He'd faced death before, but the sight of the insane Gisbourne's sleek oiled blade coming towards him brought the involuntary, instinctive cry from his lips and he looked up helplessly as his doom approached.

A sharp crack came from behind Robin and there was a collective gasp from the gathered crowd, King Edward II included, as an arrow tore through the air and hit Gisbourne in the shoulder, halting his forward momentum and dropping him to one knee.

All eyes turned to see Matilda, hunting bow in hand which she'd snatched from one of the watching villagers, already hurrying to nock another arrow to its string so she could stop the scarred bounty hunter that had come to kill her and her infant son.

The missile had pierced his black leather breastplate and Gisbourne knew he was done. Even if he survived this, the king would never trust him again – he'd be out of a job and outcast, while Hood and his family were still alive. Ignoring the arrow, with its beautiful white goose-feather fletchings, that was embedded in his shoulder, he stared at the sheriff who still lay on his back on the ground, watching him fearfully.

Matilda was nervous and dropped her next arrow, losing vital moments as Gisbourne once more moved to skewer the prone sheriff.

Again, though, he was thwarted.

Marjorie had gone limp and apparently passed out when the Raven had begun to choke her, but she'd been been aware of what was happening when he dropped her on the road, and she'd played dead, catching her breath and watching events unfold from hooded eyes.

Now the girl gritted her teeth, furious at this bastard Gisbourne, and, from her position in the road, spun sideways and slammed the point of her wooden sword into the Raven's leg, directly behind his right knee.

It was a good strike, if lacking somewhat in power, and was just enough to make Gisbourne stumble. He reflexively dug the point of his own sword into the ground and used the weapon to steady himself so he didn't fall again, but Robin had spotted his sister as she began to move and guessed what she would do.

The big wolf's head was ready, and attacked just as Gisbourne regained his feet and lunged at the sheriff.

Their swords met with a ringing crack that filled the air and de Faucumberg tried to crawl away on his hands and knees as Hood batted his opponent's blade to the side then leaned in close to headbutt Gisbourne.

The king's man screamed in rage and despair as his cheekbone broke and he fell back, flailing his arms, trying desperately to keep his footing so he could defend himself but, again, there was a snap and another arrow flew through the air to hammer into Gisbourne's breastplate, just a finger's-width away from the other one.

"Hush, lad, look at your ma go." Little John grinned at Matilda in appreciation, and cuddled the still-whimpering Arthur against him as the bounty-hunter finally went down.

It was over.

"Stand down! Stand down I say!" King Edward's voice rang out again, filling the air with its authority and everyone stood still, the audience holding their breath and the combatants breathing heavily, as every eye turned to see what their ruler would do.

"No!"

Gisbourne's time was up and he knew it. Ignoring the king's command he pushed himself back to his feet and charged again at the nearest target: Robin.

The Raven came at him, eyes blazing in an insane fury and Robin found himself moving impossibly fast, his own elegant long-sword snaking out to deflect Gisbourne's desperate thrust then, dancing to the side and reversing his blade faster than the eye could follow, he slammed it into the Raven's spine with sickening force.

Gisbourne, crying out pitifully, was thrown forward to land face-down in the road, sword clattering onto the ground, his body sprawled awkwardly on top of the whimpering sheriff who was by now too weak to even try and move the weight that had landed on top of him.

Gisbourne still wasn't done, though, despite the two arrows in his shoulder and the obvious agony that blazed from his remaining eye. He looked a hellish sight, crazed and blood-caked, teeth gritted as he tried desperately to raise his fist for one final, desperate, hopeless punch at the sheriff.

Robin kicked the bounty-hunter in the side of the head, rolling him off the fallen de Faucumberg and placed the point of his sword on Gisbourne's throat before standing over him to gaze down into his eye.

"You killed my best friend," the wolf's head growled, before he pressed down, placing his whole considerable weight onto the blade which tore right through Gisbourne's neck and stuck fast in the ground underneath, the dry earth quickly becoming saturated with blood.

Robin let go of the weapon and it stood in the air, like a steel grave marker. "That was for Much."

Everyone in the village was silent then, even the king. All that could be heard was Arthur's gentle sobs and de Faucumberg's rattling, laboured breath.

"Someone help the sheriff, for God's sake," the king ordered, eyes casting about for a surgeon or barber. "Come on, where's your headman? Who's in charge here?"

Patrick Prudhomme stepped forward, eyes fearful to be in such close proximity to the king himself, especially after what had just happened.

"That's me, my lord... liege. Pardon my manners. I'll make sure the good sheriff is taken care of." He looked into the crowd and shouted at some of the bigger men to help him carry de Faucumberg to the nearest house where he could at least rest on a straw mattress instead of the hard-packed earth of the road. As they went he also shouted at one of the locals, a man who owned a horse, to ride for aid to Pontefract, which was the nearest town with a decent surgeon.

The king glanced around at the large crowd that had gathered to watch the afternoon's events. He thought about ordering them back to work then shrugged to himself. Let them enjoy the entertainment. He dismounted and waved at the captain of his guards.

"Take the wolf's heads into custody."

Will drew his sword and took up a defensive stance, while Little John handed Arthur back to Matilda and hefted his own great quarterstaff.

Robin, his sword still dripping blood, moved to stand beside his two friends and the three outlaws looked at each other grimly. They could hold their own against anyone, but the armoured men approaching them now were the king's own bodyguard – the very best swordsmen in the country, and they outnumbered the outlaws.

"No, please!" Matilda screamed, grabbing hold of Marjorie who made as if to run to her big brother's side. "Robin, don't fight them – there are too many." She turned to look at the king as Arthur started to sob again, rocking his little head back and forward, hitting it against her collarbone and slapping his ears with his hands in consternation. "Sire..."

"Peace." The king waved a hand imperiously, irritated now that the excitement was over. "Your husband is an outlaw – an enemy of the crown and he's just killed my own bounty hunter. But, he saved the life of my sheriff so... I'm arresting him, and his friends, for now. We'll see what's to be done with them later."

Robin sighed heavily and, not wanting his son to watch him die like a dog in the street, put up his hands in surrender and nodded at Will and John to throw down their weapons and submit.

John looked into the king's eyes and felt somewhat reassured by the amused glint he saw there. He dropped his staff into the road with a loud clatter and raised his own great arms.

Will looked furious, his face as red as his nickname and it was obvious he was wondering whether to stand and fight on his own, despite the overwhelming odds. In the end, reason triumphed over rage – his own daughter Beth was in the watching crowd after all – and he tossed his sword down, glaring at the king's guards, as if challenging them to try and best him even unarmed.

"Good," Edward nodded and clapped his hands in satisfaction before addressing the captain of his guards. "Bind them and have the headman gather the tithing to escort them to Nottingham. Assuming Sir Henry survives he can deal with them on his return home. Now..." he rubbed his stomach and smiled. "I'm hungry. Where's the nearest inn?"

CHAPTER TWENTY-SEVEN

It took almost a week for the sheriff to recover from Gisbourne's near-fatal strike. Six days that Robin, Will and Little John spent locked in a cell in Nottingham castle while de Faucumberg, who had been carried safely there by the men of Wakefield, lay in bed as his wound healed. They were held in a room on the ground floor rather than the dungeon, for which Robin was thankful, given his terrible ordeal there the previous year when Gisbourne had captured him and his spirit had almost been crushed. There was even a window to the outside, small and barred as it was, which at least let some sunlight and fresh air in and brought a small measure of cheer to the captives.

When the guards brought them sustenance – just watered-down ale and bread, with perhaps an occasional lump of hard cheese to share – the outlaws tried to get them to talk; to tell them what was happening with the king and the sheriff and Wakefield.

Most of the guards remained silent, not from hatred, but because it didn't do to get close to prisoners. They might be hanged the next day after all, or, worse, be set free and use the jailer's words against him somehow as had been known to happen in the past.

Finally, on their sixth morning in captivity the soldier that brought them a grubby wooden platter with two loaves and an ale-skin on it, replied to their questions.

"The king's gone; moved on to Faxfleet from what I hear." The guard was a short middle-aged man, with a large belly and a red nose, but he had laughter-lines by his eyes and a pleasant demeanour. "One of your friends is in the dungeon though; lad called Matt Groves?"

The outlaws shared a glance and Robin felt his heart race at the despised name but he kept his face calm. Groves wasn't important right now.

"What about the sheriff? Does he live?"

"Aye, he lives, although he's grumpier than I've ever known him. He'll be wanting to see you later on from what I've been told. Reminds me of Sir Guy after you slashed his face apart." The man grinned as if he was talking about the fine weather lately. "Of course, the sheriff's all right, whereas Sir Guy was a fucking arsehole. Enjoy your lunch boys."

"Wait," Robin made to grasp the guard's arm but stopped himself, realising the man might see it as disrespectful. "What about our friends? Have you heard anything about them?"

"You mean your gang?" The guard turned back to look at the wolf's head but simply shrugged. "Not heard a thing I'm afraid, lad." All of a sudden his eyes narrowed and he glared at Will and John who returned the look with puzzled expressions. The guard's hand fell to his waist, apparently searching for the reassuring presence of his sword-hilt but, of course, he didn't have the weapon with him. Guards didn't carry swords into cells in case the prisoners managed to take it off them and went on a rampage.

"You expecting them to come for you again, like they did the last time you were imprisoned here?" The man shuffled backwards to the door, his expression grim, the pleasant smile gone. "Don't even think about it." He stepped out through the door and the guard waiting outside slammed it shut and slid the heavy bolts into place. "Don't even think about it you bastards!"

The guards' footsteps faded away along the corridor and Robin looked at his two companions in astonishment before all three burst into laughter at the soldier's sudden change in demeanour.

"They haven't forgotten you coming up the latrine wall to rescue me," Robin smiled at Will who grimaced, remembering the shit and filth he'd had to climb through to get inside the castle and free his young leader.

John stuffed a piece of bread the size of Robin's fist into his gaping mouth and mumbled as he chewed. "Shame no-one's going to come over the wall and get us out this time."

Their thoughts turned inevitably to Allan and the mood became maudlin as they remembered him, cold and dead, back in Barnsdale. The meagre meal was finished in silence after that and then the companions settled down on the wooden floor to await the sheriff's visit. Perhaps now that de Faucumberg was back on his feet they'd learn the date of their execution...

"What d'you think's going to happen to us?" Robin asked, eyes downcast, voice low.

John shrugged, stoic and apparently not worried about their situation. "He'll probably hang me for that joke about the men shagging his mum when we first met him," he said, smiling at the memory. "We *are* notorious outlaws after all – we always knew it might come to this one day. But you, Robin – you saved the sheriff's life. Gisbourne would have killed the bastard if it wasn't for you and Matilda."

"Aye, and Marjorie too, the girl did well," Scarlet agreed. "The sheriff owes you and your family."

"Maybe," Robin nodded. "But it might not be up to him. The king may have already told him what he was to do with us."

"No point worrying about it." John spread his palms wide and sat down to lean against the wall, his long legs drawn up against his chest. "We'll find out soon enough."

The shadows moved around their little cell as the sun wheeled in the sky overhead and it was close to midday when finally they heard more footsteps approaching, and the heavy bolts on the door were drawn back. It was a different guard who walked into the room this time, a tall man, competent and hard-looking, accompanied by half-a-dozen other soldiers.

"Follow me." The leader looked at them dispassionately, no trace of any emotion showing in his green eyes. The outlaws shuffled after him, the manacles that had been placed on their hands and feet when they'd first been placed in the cell not allowing them to move faster than a slow walk.

They were led along the corridor, through a great oak-panelled door that looked as if it could withstand a battering ram, and into another corridor, this one sumptuously decorated, with large windows that let in the afternoon sunshine. At last, their legs sore from walking in such an unusual manner, the outlaws stopped outside another sturdy door and the guardsman rapped on it with a gauntleted fist.

It opened from the inside, swinging inwards with just the merest hint of a sound, and Robin and his friends were ushered into the room which was apparently the castle's great hall. Sir Henry de Faucumberg, High Sheriff of Nottingham and Yorkshire sat on a high-backed, exquisitely carved, wooden chair which itself sat on a raised platform with more chairs on either side and a long table in front.

Only the sheriff sat at the table though, his skin pale and wan. He had a comfortable, expensive-looking robe on, which covered any trace of the wound Gisbourne had inflicted, and the heavy gold chain of office was around his neck. To the side, an elderly clerk sat at a desk with paper and pen.

Robin felt a knot of fear in his stomach. It was clear the sheriff had called them here to make their fate official. The sound of the big door closing behind them made him even more uncomfortable but he kept it from showing on his face. He glanced sideways to his comrades and felt a surge of pride at their apparent lack of fear or nervousness; both men gazed unblinkingly at the sheriff who looked back but didn't hold their eyes for long before he spoke.

"I'll make this quick. My wound is healing well enough but it requires constant cleaning and I have many other duties to attend to." He took a deep breath and lifted the goblet of wine on the table for a sip before continuing.

"You men are wolf's heads. For at least the past two years my men have been attempting to arrest the members of your gang with little success. You have robbed travellers on the road, including high-ranking members of the clergy. You have killed many of my own soldiers. You even joined the Earl of Lancaster in his ill-fated rebellion against the king. And the three of you, from what I understand, are the leaders of your little gang. In short, gentlemen, you are probably the most wanted men in my entire jurisdiction. The king himself sent that bastard Gisbourne here to try and bring you to justice." He shook his head in disgust and muttered to himself more than anyone else. "That didn't turn out so well, did it?"

The clerk in the corner stopped writing at that part and the sheriff gave him a small smile before he went on.

"The punishment for just one of those many heinous crimes is death by hanging. Your friend Sir Richard-at-Lee has already received justice in such a fashion." He gave a small groan and took another pull of his wine, this time almost draining the cup, perhaps hoping the effects of the alcohol would dull the pain from his wound. "What am I to do with you?"

The outlaws watched the sheriff in silence. He had a reputation for being a fair man; they could only hope he would deal with them mercifully now.

"You found the king in a particularly good mood," the sheriff went on. "He was bored and the little episode in Wakefield – and the chase to find you – pleased him." He shrugged in exasperation. "The king values physical prowess highly and he enjoyed the... fight with Gisbourne. When he ate lunch in Wakefield he had some of the locals, including the headman, dine with him – they informed him of Gisbourne's recent excesses; burning down houses and whatnot so, although Sir Guy was the king's own man, our highness thought justice had been served by his death. He also remembered the pair of you," he nodded to Robin and Little John, "from your visit to London. Anyone else would be angered by your deception but again, the king found it all most amusing. So," he waved a hand, "he told me to deal with you as I saw fit but to be merciful."

"What does that mean?" Will growled. "A life sentence in your dungeon rather than a public hanging?"

De Faucumberg smiled. "Perhaps," he began, but Robin cut in before the man could say any more.

"We have your silver arrow."

The sheriff looked at him, mouth open since he'd been just about to speak again. He closed it, lips pressed together in a thin line. "I remember. How could I forget?"

"We have no need of it," Robin said. "I'll bring it back to you this very day." He held up a hand as the sheriff leaned forward in his chair eagerly, the thought of his missing wealth being returned to his near-bare coffers making his eyes sparkle.

"In return I want a pardon."

De Faucumberg nodded impatiently, but again Robin broke in before the nobleman could speak.

"For *all of us*."

There was silence then, a silence that seemed to last for a long, long time as the sheriff gazed at the wolf's head and his troublesome companions.

Robin glanced sidelong at Will, noting the man's aggressive stance. Even without a weapon the volatile Scarlet was ready to attack the blue-liveried soldiers.

Little John's face was unreadable.

Even the sheriff's guards looked unsure how this would play out; Robin could see more than one of them fidgeting nervously and he picked one to go for first should De Faucumberg order an attack.

"Fine. You win." The sheriff glared at his clerk. "Write pardons for these two," he waved a hand irritably at Will and John. "Scaflock and Little, I believe, yes? Yes." The clerk quickly but neatly filled in two small pieces of parchment then took them to de Faucumberg who lifted his own pen and signed the bottom of each.

"Here," he growled, holding them out towards the outlaws.

"What about Robin?" Will demanded, not moving towards the proffered document. "Where's his pardon? He saved your life."

"Your loyalty is, truly, a pleasure to see," de Faucumberg smiled, apparently sincerely. "But I have other business to attend to with him so... if you would so kind as to take these bloody pardons from me and stop asking questions you can be on your way back to your homes."

John and Will looked at Robin and he grinned encouragingly. "Go on, what are you waiting for? This is what we've wanted – freedom! Don't worry about me, I'll see you soon. We still have his silver arrow don't we?"

The two outlaws walked forward and, still unsure of themselves, gingerly took the parchments from the sheriff, who nodded and ordered his guards to show them out.

"Our weapons?" Will wondered.

"Yes, yes, return their weapons to them," the sheriff grunted in exasperation. "Now get out will you? I wanted to get this over with quickly."

They followed the guard from the room, the door was closed over again, and Robin felt another pang of fear. Yes, de Faucumberg had proved himself to be – mostly – an honourable man, who'd tried to rein in the increasingly violent tendencies of the Raven, but Robin hadn't forgotten the time when the sheriff had double-crossed them. Only the timely intervention of Sir Richard-at-Lee and the Earl of Lancaster's soldiers had saved Robin and his friends that day, or the sheriff would have cut them down like animals.

So, although Sir Henry de Faucumberg appeared to be rather more honourable than many of his noble peers, the wolf's head didn't quite believe he could trust the man unquestioningly. After all, capturing Robin Hood and hanging him was always what the sheriff had wanted – it was the perfect way to send a message to any other would-be thieves and outlaws.

De Faucumberg beckoned him forward, to stand right in front of the table, and Robin wished he had his sword with him.

"You've led my men and I – not to mention Gisbourne – a merry dance these past couple of years, Hood. You appear to lead a charmed life or, perhaps I do you a disservice and you're really as skilled a leader as you are an archer. I suspect the truth lies somewhere in the middle and that makes you a formidable enemy."

Robin remained silent but he felt beads of sweat trickle down uncomfortably from under his armpits as the sheriff stared at him.

"But you saved my life and I am grateful so... I would like to offer you a position within my own household."

The wolf's head simply gazed up at de Faucumberg, knowing he must have imagined the man's words.

"As I say, you have proven your leadership abilities. I don't think any of my men have anything but respect for you in that regard, whatever they may feel for you personally. You and your fellows have killed rather a lot of them after all."

"Only in self-defence – what choice did we have –"

Sir Henry raised a hand. "There's no need to go into that right now. Perhaps once I'm fully healed we can discuss that sort of thing in more depth but for now... as I say I have other duties to carry out and the dressing of my wound takes up much of my time so...? What say you, Hood? I believe you have no official experience commanding men – you don't know the way things work in a castle garrison and that sort of thing, so I can't offer you the position of my personal captain just like that. However, I will find you a job that suits your exceptional capabilities. Who knows, I might even be able to find a place for others of your group. I lost a few men in that last, ill-fated, assault Gisbourne led on your camp, although I believe some of them still live, thanks to you."

That brought Robin back to Earth. *Others of your group*. Where were Stephen and Edmond and the rest of the men?

"What about the pardons for the other members of my gang?"

The clerk in the corner of the room rummaged amongst another pile of papers and lifted some in the air, showing them to the wolf's head.

"Those are blank." The sheriff said. "Once I have their names I can fill them in and your men will be pardoned. All of them." He raised a finger and looked seriously at Robin. "I only demand my silver arrow in return. Fair enough?"

The reality finally hit him and Robin crouched down, weeping in disbelief and happiness and sadness for all his friends who'd died before they could see this day. He didn't care what the sheriff or the clerk or the guardsmen thought of him, he was overcome by emotion and for long moments he simply stared at the stone floor, tears streaming down his face.

They'd done it. At last, they had finally earned their pardons, they would be free!

"Thank you, my lord." He rose, drawing himself up to his full impressive height and looked at the sheriff without bothering to wipe his tear-streaked face. "I would like to speak with my wife before I accept the offer of a position in your household. Before that, though, I have one more boon to ask..."

* * *

Matt Groves wished he'd never come back to Nottingham. He should have known how it would turn out. The fact the sheriff hated him didn't seem to matter though; he'd hoped de Faucumberg would have been so desperate for able-bodied, hard fighting men that he'd see Matt as a decent addition to his garrison.

But it hadn't turned out like that. When he'd made it back to the city from Selby the sheriff had been away with the king, so he'd made himself at home in one of the local taverns until the sheriff returned, spending what little coin he had left in his purse on a room and board for a few nights, hoping de Faucumberg wouldn't be gone too long.

When word had got around that the sheriff was back in the castle – and grievously wounded – Matt had made his way there to offer his good-wishes and support to the stricken nobleman.

Unfortunately for him, de Faucumberg had been well enough to recognise him and, in a near-delirious fury, had ordered his guards to imprison Matt until he was well enough to deal with Gisbourne's pet outlaw.

He'd languished in this shit-encrusted, vermin-infested cell for days now, with only black mouldy bread and tepid water for sustenance and he was thoroughly sick of it.

There was a noise from the end of the corridor which Matt recognised as the main entrance to the block of cells being opened and he held his breath, listening as footsteps approached. They stopped outside his cell and he got to his feet, stretching his muscles and plastering a smile on his face as the door swung open, hoping to see the sheriff or one of his lackeys come to free him at last.

One of the castle guards held a torch which burned brightly, blinding Groves momentarily as he squinted into the gloom at the two figures there, and then he found himself lying on the cold stone floor, amongst the shit and piss, his head spinning and his face aching.

"Get up you fucking arsehole." A low, gravelly voice came to him and he raised his hands defensively but they were batted aside and someone grabbed his short hair, pulling hard until he scrambled to his feet.

When he reached an upright position again fury rose in him and he swept his right arm out in an arc, trying to land a blow on the shadowy figure that now held him by the throat.

His attempt was weak though, and he fell backwards again, his teeth rattling as another blow landed on his face. He heard a crack as the punch landed and a searing pain blurred his vision. He fell backwards into the wall, knowing his cheek had been broken. He felt weak from his captivity over the past few days but, outraged at being struck, he roared, raising his arms and running forward towards the shadowman that tormented him.

Again, a closed fist hit him, this time in the solar-plexus, and he collapsed, retching onto the already filthy cell floor. He brought up the water and slimy half-digested bread that he'd eaten earlier on, burning tears streaming from his eyes, but he forced himself to stand up once more and raised his fists to block any more attacks.

"Do you know who I am?" he found himself shouting desperately. "I'm one of Robin Hood's men. Have you never heard how he looks after his men? He'll come for you when he hears about this, you bastard!"

His attacker halted his advance and Matt took heart. "Aye, that's right, dickhead. We look after each other in Robin Hood's gang."

He saw the next blow coming but was, again, too slow to dodge or even block it and a thunderous right hook landed on his face with a crunch of bone and cartilage and he fell backwards into the wall, blood pooling from his ruined nose.

"You look after each other?" The voice was low and filled with pure hate. "Then why did you betray Much?"

In the near-darkness Matt saw his attacker's foot coming towards him but before he could raise a hand he felt the crushing blow and he dropped, dazed and winded, onto the ground again. He didn't try to get up now; finally, he'd recognised that voice.

Robin Hood leaned down and glared into his eyes, the cowl he wore making him look distinctly sinister and wicked in the wan torchlight. "Get up and fight me like a man you old cunt. I've waited a long time for this; since I first joined the outlaws in fact. Remember? You almost broke my fingers the first time we sparred and then you knocked me into the river. Let's see how hard you are then, Groves. Let's see you break my fucking fingers now."

He heard Hood's ragged breathing as the big wolf's head glared down at him.

"We found Allan's body after the battle. Did you kill him too?"

For a moment Groves thought about denying it, but he knew he was done for anyway. At least this would be one final barb to throw at his former leader.

"Aye, I did. He just stood there, gaping at me like a fish. It was so easy for me to skewer the stupid-looking dullard. He cried like a girl when he sank onto the grass at my feet."

His words had the desired effect – Robin rocked back, eyes wet and filled with loathing for the man before him.

"Finish it then," Matt growled through split, bloody lips, unnerved by his attacker's glaring silence. "Or are you still too much of a fucking woman?"

He expected Hood to rain more blows down on him but none came and he lay on his back, sucking in lungfuls of air, his entire body numb.

For a long time nothing happened. The torch the guard outside in the corridor held cast flickering orange light on the walls and Hood's breath continued to come in laboured gasps while Matt just lay on the ground, almost passing out more than once.

Then, when he'd regained his breath, the wolf's head bent down and looked directly into Matt's eyes.

"I don't need to finish it, Matt. Justice will be served, have no fear. Your master Gisbourne is dead – aye, killed by me, my wife and my little sister – and your crimes will not go unpunished. I'm the sheriff's man now... and soon enough I'll see you on gallows hill, swinging by the neck for what you did to my friends."

CHAPTER TWENTY-EIGHT

It was a rather different Robin that returned to the outlaws' camp near Selby a day later, accompanied by Will and Little John. The smile was back on his handsome face and, apart from severe bruising around his knuckles he appeared to be in good health.

Of course, the lookouts had spotted the men approaching and sent word to the main camp where Stephen had gathered the men and ordered them to battle-readiness. It might have been their leader and his two lieutenants heading towards them but who knew what came at their back? It could very well be a trick of the sheriff's devising. So the former Hospitaller, careful as ever, had the men armed and ready for anything when he heard of Hood's return.

"Not the friendliest welcome I've ever had." Robin grinned at the sergeant-at-arms who met him, grim-faced, as he strode into the camp. "But it's good to see you have the men at the ready." He clasped Stephen's arm, grinning broadly and the man relaxed visibly, although he didn't return the grin; that wasn't his way.

"Are we safe?"

"Aye," Robin nodded, laughing as Little John came up behind him and barged past, grabbing the shocked Stephen in a massive bear-hug that he struggled vainly to break free from.

When he was back on his feet and before he had the time to berate the giant, Will Scarlet grabbed also him and pulled him into a friendly embrace, slapping him on the back and laughing loudly. "Well met, Hospitaller. Well met."

Robin could tell Stephen was inwardly pleased at the show of friendship, but the sergeant shoved Will away and glared at the three of them. "I take it we're not in any immediate danger? The sheriff's men aren't on their way to rout us?"

"No, they're not," Robin shook his head, still smiling and raising his voice so the rest of the men, still hidden in the foliage, could hear. "You can come out – we have news!"

They feasted that night, after freeing the sheriff's captured soldiers to return to their homes. Little John and Will had brought fresh black loaves and a pig from the kitchen in Nottingham Castle and, with that and the late spring vegetables stored in the outlaws' larder, Tuck made a wonderful thick stew which the men washed down with large amounts of ale and even some wine the sheriff's bottler had gifted to them before they'd left to return to their friends.

When Robin produced the papers that confirmed every man's pardon there had been disbelief and then deafening cheers that split the night like thunder and the young outlaw captain had cheered as loud as any of them. It was a momentous occasion. Even Stephen managed a grin, although things would be more complicated for him, since some of the Hospitallers had tried to kill him and, as far as he knew he was still outcast from the Order.

The rest of the men though, they were – at long last – free. Their young leader had often promised to win them freedom somehow and, well, now it seemed he had. It was incredible.

And yet the celebrations were tinged with more than a hint of sadness.

They wanted to return to their families, of course, but every man there now realised they'd possibly never see their companions again. They'd go back to their homes and, hopefully, take back the lives that had been stolen from them when they'd become wolf's heads, but most of them lived in different villages. Sure, they might pay one another the odd visit when they could but... it wouldn't be the same as spending long nights under the stars, with a roaring campfire, bread and meat and beer and brotherhood and music.

Music.

Robin had taken more than his own fill of ale and, although he felt a great joy in his heart to have finally – finally! – won a pardon, the lack of singing in the camp was obvious and it made him think of Allan-a-Dale.

The rest of the men didn't seem to share his melancholy, Robin noted thankfully. They ate and drank and told stories and talked about what they'd do when they returned home as rich men; the outlaws had lots of stolen gold and silver in the communal chest after all and it would make life very comfortable for each of them now.

"Cheer up – you're a free man. They all are!"

Robin looked up at the voice and smiled as he saw Friar Tuck.

"Aye, free at last," he agreed, patting the log beside him and sipping his ale as the friar sat down. "But at what cost...?"

They watched the other men for a while, drunk already, most of them. They had no need for lookouts any more, being free men, so the celebration of liberty was in full swing. Even the Hospitaller was half-pissed and deep in animated, but still friendly – so far – conversation with young Edmond the tanner.

Tuck, although he loved to eat and drink, never allowed himself to take so much that he lost control of his senses – Osferth's slipping dwale into his ale excepted. He'd learned his lesson when he was younger and now, although he still enjoyed a skinful, always stopped before he became too drunk to walk in a straight line.

Robin generally did the same – a good trait in a leader, Tuck thought.

Sometimes, though, it didn't hurt to let yourself go...

"Here." The friar handed a wine-skin to his captain. "Drink. Lose yourself for a while."

Robin took the drink but simply held it, unopened, in his lap as they watched the rest of the men. They'd finally begun to strike up a song or two, although they sorely lacked direction and a sweet, skilled, *tuneful* voice to lead them.

He pulled out the stopper and took a long pull, the wine burning in his chest pleasantly and he lifted the skin again, swallowing almost half the contents in one draught.

"You've lost a lot in the past couple of years," Tuck stated, his voice soft yet still audible over the carousing and Robin barely nodded in reply.

"Perhaps more than any of us," the friar continued. "The men that have died: Wilfred, Sir Richard, Allan... they were all our friends but... you also lost your childhood friend Much. It hurts, doesn't it?"

Robin nodded and took another drink from the wine-skin. "Harry Half-Hand died because of me," he muttered, remembering an event from when he'd first become an outlaw and, inexperienced, hadn't followed orders. "But all those who've died since are on my conscience too, since I was supposed to be their leader. I was supposed to keep them safe but I didn't. All dead. They should be celebrating their freedom like the rest of us tonight."

Tuck said nothing for a while, knowing Robin – despite his silence – wasn't finished yet.

"They're going to hang Matt."

"And you'll be there to see it," the friar replied.

"Aye, I'll be there," Robin growled. "I want to see that bastard die in agony, pissing and shitting himself as he goes."

Tuck nodded. "I understand. I too want to see justice for Much and Allan. But..."

Robin glanced at the friar. "But what?"

"Look at them," Tuck said, smiling and waving a hand at the happy former outlaws before them.

Robin shrugged, the wine already making his head foggy. "What about them?"

"They're happy. They are finally free." The clergyman grasped Robin's arm in a powerful grip. "You should be happy. You can watch Arthur grow up and be with Matilda."

"Are you saying I should forget Matt Groves?" Robin demanded. "Even if I could – the rest of the men won't. They all want to come to Nottingham with me to see the bastard hang. And so they should, after what he's done."

Tuck shook his head, the flushed cheeks of his young friend betraying an unusual level of inebriation and he knew he had to step lightly.

"No, I'm not suggesting you forget – or forgive – Matt. I think we should *all* go to his hanging."

Robin eyed the friar suspiciously. The expected sermon wasn't going quite as he'd expected.

"It would be wrong to celebrate his death," Tuck said. "But... I see no harm in celebrating a new beginning."

Although he was becoming bleary-eyed from both lack of sleep and strong wine Robin understood the friar's point. It made perfect sense – a celebration of life in death... After all, hadn't this whole journey started in the same way, in that Mayday celebration of two years earlier?

"You're a genius, Tuck," the young man grinned. "But, in all the joy at our freedom we've forgotten you, haven't we? The sheriff's pardons are secular and no doubt won't be honoured by Prior de Monte Martini, the little red-faced prick. Where will you go now?" He stood up, shaking his head somewhat blearily and held out a hand to his portly friend who grasped it to lever himself up from the fallen log.

"Don't worry about me," Tuck smiled. "Just enjoy the night. You're free!"

Robin gripped him by the shoulder and they walked towards the centre of camp where the other men had started a raucous sing-along. "So are you," he said. "And I think I know where you can hide from Prior de Martini, at least for a while. You said you brought the relic back from Lewes didn't you..?"

For the first time ever the group celebrated long and loud and without fear of imprisonment or death, their joyful voices splitting the night air and carrying on the wind across the Ouse even to Selby, where the villagers looked fearfully across the fields and wondered what demons were abroad that night.

They were *free!*

* * *

The next day those who wished it travelled to Nottingham with Robin. They passed through Wakefield again, where Robin spoke to Patrick and told him Much's killer was going to be hanged should any of the villagers wish to come with them to see justice done.

Of course, the vast majority of the local people couldn't just take days off work and Much's family were all dead so, in the end, only Patrick travelled with them, along with Will Scarlet's daughter, Beth and, of course, Marjorie.

Robin's sister's dream of owning a crossbow had finally come true – she carried the sleek black Italian-made weapon that had belonged to Gisbourne although, when he asked her how she'd managed to steal it from the Raven's corpse she just shrugged and smiled. The girls she'd been training had all been hugely impressed by her part in the fight with the infamous bounty hunter, as, indeed had all of the adults in Wakefield. Robin too was extremely proud of his sister, grown into a strong, vibrant young woman.

"You fought well," he told her as they walked.

"Aye," she nodded, pleased at the praise, and at her new-found status in the village. "Just goes to show – women aren't only good for cooking and mending clothes."

"Oh, I already knew that," Robin laughed. "The wife never lets me forget it."

For a time they walked together in silence, then Marjorie grinned up at him.

"You know, for a while I wanted to be like you. But now... I'm happy just to be me."

Robin returned her smile although he had no idea of her long journey over the past few months. Still, he could see by the way she carried herself that she'd truly come of age and was at peace with the world.

That was all anyone could ask for in life.

Matilda also came on their journey south, of course, and brought little Arthur with her. She wasn't sure about the idea of the boy seeing someone die on the gallows, Robin knew, but he felt that it was something their son should witness. Life was hard, and it often had a way of repaying in kind those who treated others badly.

Arthur should see Much's murderer pay for his crimes.

Will brought Beth simply because he'd missed her terribly all throughout his years as a wolf's head and wanted to spend as much time with her as possible now he was a free man.

Not all of the outlaws had decided to go to Nottingham for the hanging though; some of them still couldn't believe the sheriff had granted them their freedom and didn't want to take a chance walking into the city where de Faucumberg could imprison or kill them if he decided to double-cross them. Others were so overjoyed at their pardons that they couldn't wait to see their families again and restart their lives with the welcome fortune they'd managed to gather as part of Robin's gang.

The likes of Edmond and Stephen had no warm welcome or loving family awaiting them in their home-towns so they went along with the others because there was nothing better to do, although neither man had any particular, personal hatred for Matt, having joined the outlaws after the dour man had left and gone to join the Raven.

It was a merry party, then, that made their way along the main road to the big city. They'd brought plenty of fresh meat, eggs, fish, cheese, bread and, of course, ale for the trip, all bought that day in Wakefield because they understood they'd have to spend more than one night camping out as they were all on foot. It wasn't an issue though – Robin knew the sheriff didn't plan on hanging Groves for a couple of days and it would be fun to spend time with friends and family, out in the open for once, without having to skulk in the trees as wolf's heads, fearful of discovery and capture or death.

That journey was the happiest time of Robin's entire life.

The weather wasn't great, raining quite heavily for much of the trip, but that gave Robin a chance to lift his little son who was still not two years-old and carry him in his strong arms, snuggled in under a waterproof sheep-skin that kept the worst of the weather off the pair of them.

Beth ran on ahead, laughing and skipping in the rain, splashing in the puddles that collected in the divots and pot-holes that liberally dotted the ancient Roman road, while Will, half-heartedly, demanded that she keep dry or catch a chill.

Everyone was, understandably, in high spirits and, when the thunder-heads passed and night began to fall they were glad to stop and set up camp in a clearing not far from the main road, surrounded by beech, yew and oak trees which felt just like home to the men who'd spent most of the recent years of their lives in just such a place.

Once a fire had been kindled and the smells of meat and fish cooking on spits above it filled the air, everyone felt truly blessed by God. And that was before they'd even broached the cask of newly-brewed ale portly Aexander Gilbert, landlord of Wakefield's tavern, had given them for the trip south.

It was the best meal Robin had ever eaten. Matilda sat on the grass beside him, laughing and cuddling into him as the travellers told ghost stories and bickered good-naturedly among themselves while Arthur sat on his knee, taking little pieces of cooked meat from his plate and chewing it contentedly, laughing in a wonderfully endearing way whenever he thought someone was being silly.

The young archer looked around at his friends and lifted his ale mug in silent thanks to the Magdalene who he'd prayed to ever since he'd become an outlaw. She too had been seen as an outcast, looked down on by the authorities, and so she'd seemed like the ideal patron for a wolf's head. He grinned as Will aimed a ferocious verbal barb at Little John whose mouth dropped open in dismay, the expression looking hilarious on the giant's face which bore a thick brown beard again.

He truly was blessed to have friends like these – the Magdalene had watched over him well these past two years.

"It's getting late." His wife's words broke into his comfortable reverie and he glanced at her, eyes sparkling in the orange firelight. "Let's bed down for the night. Arthur is about ready to go over anyway..."

She smiled, flicking her tongue over her teeth impishly and Robin felt a small thrill run through him.

"Good idea," he replied, standing up, cradling the dozing toddler in his left arm and using his other hand to help Matilda up.

There were ribald comments shouted after them – which they pointedly ignored – as they found a spot to sleep in for the night that was just far enough from the fire to hide them from watching eyes yet close enough to offer protection against any hungry animals, although wolves hadn't been seen in northern England for decades.

Arthur was soon asleep and, as they made love under the stars Robin allowed himself to become lost in the moment. They climaxed at the same time, holding each other tightly and stifling their joyful gasps as the happy feast carried on behind them.

After all the heartache and betrayal and death of the past two years, Robin was finally at peace.

It felt good to be alive.

CHAPTER TWENTY-NINE

"Time to die."

Robin stood in the cell that held Matt Groves, wearing the blue livery of Sheriff de Faucumberg although he retained his own weapons and leather gambeson – the same one with the patched up hole that he'd been given when he'd first joined the outlaws.

Although he wasn't due to become one of the sheriff's staff for another week – he'd specifically asked for that time so he could spend it with his family back in Wakefield – he wanted to be here for this, so, with de Faucumberg's blessing, he'd borrowed one of the guard's uniforms and, along with a couple of burly soldiers almost as big as he was, he walked into Matt's cell to take him to the gallows that stood outside the city walls.

The sight of hanged criminals on the road into Nottingham was supposed to scare potential law-breakers onto the straight and narrow path of the lawful but Robin didn't think it really worked. Certainly, it had never stopped him from robbing rich clergymen. Still, it was as good a place for justice as any other.

"Get up, Groves." He looked down dispassionately at his former gang-member who returned his gaze from wide, frightened eyes. Matt didn't want to die.

Robin shrugged and turned to the soldiers behind him. "Lift him."

The guardsmen moved to drag Matt up from the floor. He struggled but the bigger of the two soldiers punched him full in the mouth with a gauntleted fist and it was enough to make the prisoner more pliable. One of them squeezed his cheeks and the other poured a bitter, acrid liquid into his mouth. Unwatered wine, to stop the prisoner from causing trouble on the way to their destination.

They led him – half walking and half dragging – out of the grim, dank cell and along the corridor behind their new superior officer.

When they reached the courtyard there was a wagon with a wooden cage and the guards dragged the wild-eyed Groves up a ramp and threw him into it, their hard, threatening stares enough to stop him trying to escape or even protest at the humiliating captivity.

Penned like an animal on its way to the Shambles for slaughter.

Robin mounted a warhorse which wore simple barding in the same blue with red piping livery as he wore himself and nodded at the cart driver. "Move on – to Gallows Hill."

The wagon rumbled out of the castle grounds and into the city, heading north-east towards the carter gate. The cobbled streets weren't lined with cheering people as they would have been for a high profile hanging – most of them had never heard of Matt Groves – but there were still plenty of citizens around, either with nothing better to do than watch the prisoner's last, lonely journey or simply because they wanted to see a criminal meeting well-deserved justice.

Life was cheap for the lower-classes in Nottingham; the locals were just glad it was someone else being taken off to hang while they and their families lived another day.

Robin rode at the side of the slow-moving wagon. He was still no great horseman but was starting to become more comfortable when mounted; he no longer felt his thighs burning after a short distance and didn't expect his horse to turn and bite him whenever he offered it direction.

Matt tried to talk to him; to plead with him for his freedom, or at least for a lesser sentence than the death penalty. It was out of Robin's hands – the sheriff was the law in Nottingham, even if he had granted Robin more than one favour lately – but he had no desire to help the sour-faced, hateful old bastard Groves anyway. So he ignored the man, now desperately trying to recall times when he and Robin had shared moments of friendship back in Barnsdale.

Those moments were almost non-existent though. The only time Robin had felt like Matt was becoming close to him had been an act; a ruse to draw him and Much into the forests where, ultimately, Sir Guy and his men had ambushed them. Much had died that day, with the Raven's crossbow bolt in his chest and Matt's sword in his stomach.

Robin held his peace grimly as the wagon trundled on through the streets and out the Carter Gate into the open countryside where Gallows Hill could be seen in the near-distance.

He felt calm and almost emotionless. Even the memories of Much or Allan's bloodied bodies weren't enough to shake him on that sombre journey.

It didn't take very long to reach the place of execution. The gallows stood on the summit of Mansfield Road, close to a rickety old windmill. When the horses were reined in and the cart drew to a halt Matt became silent at the sight of the sinister wooden structure that stood a short distance away.

The gallows had been built with huge, thick timbers and its simple design spoke of cold, merciless efficiency. Matt had seen many such constructions in his life; indeed he'd witnessed them being put to use on a number of occasions. He'd always enjoyed the sight of a man being hanged, especially when the executioner wasn't very good at his job and had to swing on the victim's legs or even climb onto their shoulders to finish the job.

His arms and legs tingled with pins-and-needles and he couldn't stand when the pair of burly guardsmen dismounted and came to take him up the stairs to the platform. They knew their jobs though, and had seen this reaction before when men became so terrified that their limbs wouldn't work, so they unlocked the cage door and simply dragged him, feet-first, out of the cart, hauling him upright before his head cracked off the road below.

Robin watched dispassionately as his despised enemy stood shakily, eyes fixed on the gallows. The guards gave him a moment to regain his equilibrium then, grasping an arm each, hauled Groves up the stairs and onto the platform which was badly discoloured despite the cleaning it received after every execution. Some stains could never be washed off, no matter how much water and lye soap was used.

Looking out over the crowd that had gathered for the day's grisly entertainment Robin spotted Matilda with Marjorie, John, Will and the rest of their friends clustered around, watching in silence as the prisoner was made to stand, head bowed to hide his fear, beneath the crossbar of the gallows, just in front of the noose which swayed almost imperceptibly in the warm westerly breeze.

Robin almost wished he hadn't asked the sheriff if he could preside over this now that he saw the size of the audience; of course he had become accustomed to addressing the men in his gang, but those were his friends and weren't that great in number. There must have been at least a hundred people – strangers – gathered there that day though. People with no personal axe to grind with Groves but also with no work to go to for whatever reason, so they'd used their free time to come along and watch another criminal get his comeuppance.

Still, Robin had never been particularly shy, except around Matilda when they'd been younger, so he dismounted, handing the reins of his horse to a nearby guard with orders to return the beast to the castle stables. Then he climbed the steps up to the gallows and stood at the front of the raised platform where he gazed out at the crowd silently. Eventually, the people noticed the blue-liveried soldier and realised the show was about to begin. The clamour of happy, excited voices dropped until, at last, there was silence. Some unfortunate gossips failed to notice the quiet and were shouted down, red-faced and abashed at the dozens of angry eyes boring into them.

Robin took a deep breath, cleared his throat and, with a small smile towards his wife who returned the look encouragingly, addressed the gathering.

"This is Matthew Groves of Sheffield: convicted thief, murderer and rebel. By the authority of our King Edward, second of that name, and his representative Sir Henry de Faucumberg the High Sheriff of Nottingham and Yorkshire, the criminal is sentenced to be hanged by the neck until death doth ensue."

Robin watched as the wide-eyed prisoner was readied for his doom then turned back momentarily to look at his friends and family. Will glared up at Groves as if he wanted to kill the man with his bare hands; Little John's steely eyes glistened and Robin wondered what was going through the giant's head; Friar Tuck made the sign of the cross and his lips moved in sad, silent prayer.

Matilda's expression was the one that hit him the hardest though – she was watching Matt almost as murderously as Will and Robin nodded to her in understanding. Much had grown up with her in Wakefield too after all.

He was glad little Arthur was nowhere to be seen. Aye, he'd wanted his son to be there to see justice done but now the time was upon them... it didn't seem right to make such a small child watch a man die. He wondered where the boy was, then recognised the back of his sister Marjorie's head moving away through the crowd, his son's small blonde head by her shoulder and another diminutive figure – Beth Scaflock – by their side.

The young-folk had no desire to see the execution.

Robin gazed around at the excited mob, cheerfully awaiting the sight of a man they didn't even know suffering a humiliating, painful death and he sighed heavily.

Such was the nature of man. It was why they were here today, after all.

He turned to look at his former outlaw companion whose glassy eyes focused on him, lip curling into a sneer of sheer hatred as Robin stood directly in front of him, hand raised.

"I'll see you in hell, Groves," he growled. "Say hello to Gisbourne and Adam Gurdon for me. I'll be along eventually with my sword and longbow to make eternity fucking miserable for you all."

His hand dropped and the hangman kicked the stool out from under Matt's feet.

Robin let out a long breath that he hadn't even realised he'd been holding in.

It was over.

Adam Gurdon/Bell. Sir Guy of Gisbourne. Matt Groves. All dead now. Only the bastard Prior John de Monte Martini still lived but he was an old, old man and would be dead within a year or two if Tuck's judgement was right, while Robin and his men and their families were free and had, God willing, many long happy years ahead of them.

Leaving Groves's corpse to swing Robin jumped down from the gallows and pushed his way through the cheering, hooting crowd to take Matilda in his great arms.

"I made you a promise," he told her. "To win a pardon, one way or another, so we could be a proper family. Well – now we can be a proper family."

They embraced, tears of both joy and sadness in their eyes and then, without a backward glance, the big yeoman led his wife away to find Arthur and Marjorie and all their friends.

For now, their adventure was over. They were free at last.

It was time to live.

TO BE CONTINUED...

Author's Note

I had to make some tough decisions when writing this, the penultimate book in my Forest Lord series. Allan-a-Dale being killed off was probably the hardest, being a character I really enjoyed writing, but outlaw life was dangerous and even the good die young...

The final scenes were also hard. In my original draft Matt Groves suffered a long, drawn-out and quite gruesome hanging. One of my first beta-readers suggested it was too much so I toned it down. Even at that my editor said it was too much. I felt it had to be in there in some way, though. Matt's been a big part of the series after all, so... hopefully I managed to strike a decent balance.

The first three books in this series have covered a period of only two years. The next, and final, book in this cycle will, necessarily cover a much longer time period. I always wanted to stick closely to the original Robin Hood ballads while throwing in little twists and ideas of my own and I plan to continue in that vein for the last Forest Lord novel. He's not an outlaw any more, but will he and his companions finally find the peace they've desired for so long?

I don't know, honestly, I haven't even begun to plan out the story! You'll just have to wait and see...

In the meantime I'm working on another novella, similar to Knight of the Cross. This one will star Friar Tuck, takes place in Christmas 1323 not long after the events in *Rise of the Wolf,* and will be published in December 2015.

After that... who knows?

Thank you all for joining me on this amazing journey. I never in my wildest dreams imagined so many of you would read and enjoy my books.

You rule!

BLOOD OF THE WOLF

STEVEN A. McKAY

BLOOD OF THE WOLF

by
Steven A. McKay

Copyright 2016 Steven A. McKay
All rights reserved. This book may not be reproduced in any form,
in whole or in part, without written permission from the author.

For my Grandma, who always wanted to see a book of mine in the library.
I hope I made you proud.

Acknowledgements

First and foremost I'd like to thank all my readers. Your incredible support has been the greatest encouragement any writer could ask for.

Thanks must go, as usual, to all my beta readers, particularly Robin Carter who actually sowed the seed that grew into the plot of this book, and Nicky Galliers who helped me hone the early drafts with her fantastic knowledge. Similar thanks go to Bernadette McDade, Blair Hodgkinson and William Moore for flagging up early errors and great moral support. My editor Richenda deserves huge praise for helping me take my books to a higher level.

My son inspired me every day with his wonderful, wild nature, and my daughter is always a big help, even taking some great PR photos of me in my study. Not bad for an eight year-old!

Since this is the final book in this series I'll also thank my cover designers More Visual, for creating such great art and helping me find a wider audience than I could have imagined, and Nick Ellsworth for bringing the audio versions of my books to life so entertainingly.

I've been blessed to have you all around. Thank you.

CHAPTER ONE

Dewsbury, England.

1326AD, Summer

Little John didn't expect the attack on his leader. It came as a shock and, cursing inwardly, he knew he should have learned by now not to judge someone on how they looked.

Still, the little landlord's punch was weak and, although it hit Robert Hood – commonly known as Robin – flush on the side of the face, the lawman barely seemed to register the blow. He instinctively lashed out, ramming the flat of his palm into the landlord's cheek, sending him flying sideways into a table, drinks flying and patrons roaring in anger at their spilled ale.

"Watch what you're doing there man, for fuck sake!" one shouted, but closed his mouth and looked the other way when he noticed Little John's glare fixing on him.

"Up, you."

Robin leaned down and hauled the landlord to his feet effortlessly, the muscles in his huge archer's arms bulging. "Since you won't discuss this reasonably we'll have to go somewhere more private." He practically lifted the man off the floor and headed towards the room behind the bar, John following at the back. The half dozen men drinking in the Boar's Head grumbled to one another, watching the lawmen with distaste.

"Fucking arseholes. Weren't so happy to treat us like this when they were outlaws themsel—"

"What's that?" Little John spun, leaning down to meet the seated drinker's eyes. "Did I hear you saying something?"

The man who'd spoken shook his head nervously and John nodded in satisfaction just before a stool shattered into his back. He dropped to the ground as splinters flew all about him and the sodden rushes he landed on.

"Get the bastards!"

The landlord grinned when he saw the altercation but his enjoyment didn't last for very long, as Robin punched him right on the bridge of the nose, hurling him into the wall. He slid down, legs gone, and sat on the floor holding his face.

Little John had three men on top of him, all raining punches down on his head and body, while another three tried to aim kicks between their comrades, thankfully without much success. The fallen giant struggled to throw the attackers off, shaking the rafters with his frustrated roar.

The villagers' senses were dulled by alcohol so their blows were mostly ineffectual but John knew the ale, and force of numbers, would also make the men more likely to try and use deadly force. He strained his great body, teeth gritted, face scarlet as he attempted to stand up, but a foot caught him in the ear and he collapsed with a cry, trying to raise his arms over his head.

Abruptly, one man's weight disappeared, then another, and the giant bellowed like an enraged bull, throwing the final assailant off as he shoved his way back to his feet and looked about the room, ready to destroy the next person that came near him.

Robin stood, panting, watching the villagers who could still move stumble out the front door. He held a cudgel in his hand and two of John's attackers lay on the vomit-encrusted alehouse floor. One groaned, rubbing the back of his head, while the other was unconscious.

The three who had been standing aiming kicks at John backed away, palms held out in apology as the huge man threw his shoulders back, his head almost touching the ceiling. He stared balefully at them.

The landlord tried to follow as they turned and sprinted for the open door, jostling one another in their haste, but Robin was too fast and grabbed the man by the collar, dragging him back and throwing him onto the ground where he lay, panting and wide-eyed.

"You're a damn crook, Hood," he gasped. "You're supposed to be one of us."

Robin shook his head and spat. "You haven't paid your rent, Martin. I'm just doing my job. Now – pay up or I'll throw you out on the street and find a new landlord."

"You can't do that," the man shrieked. "What about my family? This is our home!"

"Pay your rent then," Robin said. "Like everyone else in the town. I've already given you extra time but you're messing me about and it ends here."

The landlord looked across at John pleadingly. "How can you just stand there and let him do this?"

"Your mates just about broke my back there," the huge bear of a man replied, although he looked at his leader uncomfortably. He hadn't expected to be collecting money from poor folk when Robin accepted the position as Sheriff Henry de Faucumberg's enforcer and then asked John to be his second-in-command. "We all have to pay our rent," he finished lamely.

For a few moments the landlord just lay there propped up on his arms, glaring, as though he would murder them with his eyes.

"Come on," John said, not unkindly, as he reached down and grasped the man under the armpit, raising him to his feet just as Robin had done a short time ago. "If you don't have it all just pay whatever you can. That's all right, eh?" He looked at Robin who shook his head.

"He's had enough time to gather the money, John." He looked back to the landlord. "Do you have it or not?"

"No." The reply was barely a whisper.

Robin strode forward and dragged Martin away from Little John who watched in bemusement while his friend opened the inn door and shoved the landlord out into the street.

"I'm evicting you then. I'll place your belongings in the barn, there, at the side of the building. Think yourself lucky I'm not arresting you."

He slammed the door in the shocked man's face and turned back to John.

"Come on, we have to gather his stuff and secure the place before it's too dark to travel. I want to get home to Matilda and Arthur!" He grinned at the thought of his family waiting on him back home in Wakefield.

Little John eyed Robin as he strode past towards the stairs to the upper level with a determined look on his handsome face. Didn't he care about the fact he'd just made another family homeless for the sake of a few coins?

He knew the bailiff was simply doing his job and they were following the letter of the law but...

In the name of Christ, it didn't seem right somehow.

When they'd been pardoned by Sir Henry de Faucumberg three years ago, Robin was given command of a few of the sheriff's soldiers but guard duty didn't suit the former outlaw at all. So, after a few months of that he'd been made captain of de Faucumberg's guard but, again, there was too much standing around Nottingham castle – away from his family – for Robin's liking. After that he was made temporary bailiff of one of the towns near Wakefield, which was fine, but then the regular officer returned from illness. For the past year Robin, with John who'd been at his side for all those years, was employed as a sort of roving bailiff. He retained the title, and salary, but instead of being tied to one place he went all around Nottingham and Yorkshire, collecting unpaid rents and fines and generally bringing low-level law to the people.

"Hurry up!"

Robin's shout broke his lieutenant's reverie and, with a heavy sigh, John climbed the stairs to help shift all the evicted landlord's possessions outside.

Thankfully, there wasn't much to collect. The landlord was married but there were no children – thank God, John thought – so it didn't take very long to gather the few items of clothing, bedding, a tired-looking old sword hidden under the sleeping pallet, and various other small items.

"Good work," Robin nodded, tossing an armful of his own into the blanket before John pulled the corners together and hefted the lot over a shoulder. "Let's go."

They clumped down the stairs and the young bailiff glanced back over his shoulder as they neared the bottom. "I'll give the man a coin so he can find somewhere for him and his wife to stay for a night or two. They won't be out on the streets."

John raised an eyebrow but only grunted in reply. It was better than nothing, he supposed, but the whole thing still seemed wrong. The fact he himself was the one carrying all the landlord's belongings outside meant he couldn't really upbraid Robin; he was just as much at fault as his friend. And they *were* merely doing their job.

If they didn't do it, someone else would, he knew, and they'd probably be even bigger bastards than he or Hood.

"Here's your stuff," the massive lawman rumbled as they made their way outside to face the sullen evictee. "Check it's all there if you like." He looked away uncomfortably, just glad the man's wife wasn't around. This was bad enough without another furious woman screaming at him in the street. "Nice sword," he added, somehow hoping the compliment would make up for what was happening to the man, but the words were hollow. It was a shit sword and they both knew it.

"Sorry, Martin," Robin said, standing and looking down directly into the landlord's eyes. "I'll need the keys from you too." The bailiff appeared quite at ease with the situation and John wished he had the same composure and sense of self-belief as the younger man. Robin always seemed to believe what he was doing was right and did it with total conviction.

The inn-keeper put hand inside his tunic and drew out a small bunch of keys which he tossed to Robin with bad grace.

"Here," Hood said, catching the keys in one hand and offering some coins to Martin with his other. "Take this and find a room and a meal for you and your woman." He pressed the money into Martin's hand and then spread his arms wide. "If you can find the rent money within the next couple of days and get it to Earl Warenne's steward, he might let you move back in."

"Doubt it," the evicted landlord spat. "He's probably got a new tenant already lined up."

"Don't mention it," Robin retorted sarcastically and John wondered if his friend really expected the man to thank him for the small monetary gift when he'd just been made homeless.

Maybe he did – the bailiff had changed quite a bit in the past three years.

"Right. I'm away home," Robin said, walking across to the stable at the side of the inn and climbing into his horse's saddle. "You coming with me? I'm sure Arthur and Matilda would be glad to see you."

John shook his head. "Tell them I said 'hello', but I want to see my own wife and son so I'm off to Holderness. I'll meet you in Wakefield in a couple of days and we'll see what Sir Henry has lined up for us next, eh?"

"All right. Take care on the road!"

They waved to one another and rode off eagerly towards their homes.

Martin stood forlornly outside his old inn, wondering how he'd explain this to his wife and wishing he had the balls to burn the damn place to the ground.

CHAPTER TWO

As promised, John rode into Wakefield two days later, the summer sun shining high overhead as he reached Robin's house.

The bailiff was in the garden with his infant son, Arthur. They didn't seem to be playing any structured game as such, just running around on the well-tended grass whooping and shouting but the little boy was loving every second of it. The huge grin on Robin's face suggested he was having fun too.

John watched somewhat wistfully. His own son, also named John, was thirteen now and almost a man. The big lawman missed the days when he could play such innocent, nonsensical games with his own boy. Still, his visit to Holderness had been enjoyable. His wife, Amber, was always glad to welcome him home with a fine meal before they went out to the alehouse together and danced to the music played regularly by a couple of farmers who fancied themselves as minstrels.

Amber was the perfect companion, John thought. She rarely complained about anything and, after John's long years living in the greenwood as a wolf's head, she'd been overjoyed to finally have him back living in their home when the sheriff granted Robin's men pardons.

"Uncle John!"

Arthur spotted the bearded figure on horseback watching their game and sprinted for the gate, his little arms and legs working furiously as his father watched with a fond smile.

The massive lawman slid somewhat clumsily from his horse and grabbed the boy under the arms, tossing him high into the air. Arthur squealed in delight and terror, laughing as John caught him and hugged him close.

"Hello, you little rascal!"

Matilda appeared at the door to the house and waved.

"I'll pour you some ale," she said, and disappeared back inside as John came through the open gate, placed the excited child back onto the grass and grasped forearms with his captain.

"Well met," Robin smiled. "Come on inside and have a drink. I haven't heard from the sheriff about our next job so we've got some time to relax and do nothing."

The interior of the Hoods' house was cool after the blazing sun that had been John's companion on the road that morning and the ale that Matilda poured for them was most refreshing.

Robin's wife joined them at the table as they chatted idly and drank and ate gooseberries which Matilda grew in the garden, knowing her husband liked their sweet sourness.

"Come on outside, John," Robin finally said with an appreciative nod to his wife for their repast, pushing his stool back from the table. "I better check on Arthur – he's gone quiet and that's often a sign he's up to mischief."

The two men went outside, squinting in the sunlight and Robin was happy to see Arthur sitting quite innocently on the grass watching a line of ants hard at work.

Just then the sound of thundering hooves came to them and the lawmen instinctively grasped their sword hilts, eyes searching along the road in the direction of the noise.

The rider soon came in sight – a man in the familiar blue livery of the sheriff's guards.

"Well met, Thomas," John boomed, as the rider reached them and brought his mount to a noisy halt.

"God give you good day, big man." The soldier grinned in return before turning his attention to Robin. "Sir Henry requests your presence, bailiff."

"What, now? I was just telling John that we'd earned a few days rest."

"Now I'm afraid, aye," Thomas confirmed. "Well, I say now, but I'm sure I have time for a drink or two, and my horse to have a rest before we set off."

Matilda peered out at them, shaking her head.

"What is this? Am I to feed all of Barnsdale today? Those gooseberry bushes only yield a small harvest you know." She smiled at Thomas and beckoned the men inside again. "Come on, I'll see what's left. You can tie your horse to the fence there. Arthur!"

The little boy glanced across, covering his eyes with a small hand to try and stop the sun getting in his eyes. "What?"

"Come and get some oats. You can feed Thomas's horse."

When they were seated and the messenger had slaked his thirst with a long drink of ale he leaned back on the stool and looked at Robin and John seriously. "There's trouble in Holmfirth and de Faucumberg wants the pair of you to deal with it."

"What sort of trouble?" Robin wondered, lifting another plump fruit from the trencher in front of them.

"Whole place has been bewitched!" Thomas replied, eyes wide. He made the sign of the cross and nodded emphatically. "It's true. Satan himself's taken control of the village."

Robin turned to meet John's gaze but his friend simply frowned in puzzlement. Stranger things had happened; demons and devils were real weren't they? There was no reason to doubt the story although the idea of facing a village full of evil spirits sent a shiver down the bailiff's back and he felt for the reassuring hilt of his sword.

At least it would be a change from evicting poor people…

"All right then," Robin said decisively. "Your horse looks rested enough to me Thomas – my boy's fed him most of our oats from the looks of it. Come on, John – mount up."

"Hang on a minute," the giant replied, shaking his head fearfully as his captain walked back out into the sunshine. "Are you sure about this? We're lawmen, not priests."

"That's exactly why we'll head for the church first," Robin nodded grimly. "Come on."

"The church? Hold on –" Thomas shouted, trailing in the bailiff's wake as they left the house and Robin went to fetch his mount from the small stable that abutted his dwelling.

"If Holmfirth has been taken over by the Devil we're going to need someone qualified to fight him off, aren't we? That means we go to St Mary's before making our way down to Nottingham for Sir Henry's orders. Don't worry, I'm sure you'll get another ale or two when we're there."

"But why the church?" Thomas asked as he hopped nimbly back onto his horse. "Who's going to help us there?"

Robin kicked his own mount into a walk and rode past the sheriff's messenger with a grin, Little John following at his back.

"Who do you think? Friar Tuck of course!"

When Robin had first been pardoned three years ago he found it hard to adjust to life as a normal man on the right side of the law again. He and his friends had spent so long as outlaws that he'd begun to wonder if he'd ever be free, so, when the sheriff granted him a pardon it was like a gift from God.

It was true, a huge number of people in England were declared outlaws at one time or another in their lives, only to be allowed back into society later, and some of those were criminals of the very worst kind. And yet men like Will Scaflock and John Little had been wolf's heads for years without any sign of redemption and, although Robin was gifted with a great sense of self-belief, it had, at times, seemed as though he was doomed to live in the greenwood until some forester or bounty hunter finally put an end to him.

The sheriff's pardon gave him a new life though, and he knew he should show his gratitude for such good fortune in some tangible way.

He was a wealthy man, having stolen huge sums of money from many noblemen during his time as a wolf's head, and the old parish church of St Mary's in Wakefield had seen better days. It was an easy decision for Robin to pay for, and oversee, the renovation of the place, while also extending it with a section dedicated to that other redeemed sinner, his patron, Mary Magdalene.

Not only had Robin worked with a mason from Nottingham – an acquaintance of the clerk, Piers, one of the later recruits to his gang – to come up with the simple design of that new section, but he'd helped the labourers and stonemasons in any way he could to rebuild the modest, yet attractive, place of worship for his fellow villagers.

Built close to the waters of Ings Beck, which had always seemed a friend to Robin, the renovated church looked much the same as Father Myrc's original church, with its long, low section and a tower at the western end. The new extension made it all a little bigger though, and the fresh new stone transported from the quarry at Sheffield for that part looked wonderful; clean and unspoiled, perfectly symbolising Robin's new start in life.

It brought the former wolf's head a deep satisfaction when the building was completed and Father Myrc said his first ever mass there on Christmas Day two winters ago.

Robin was sure the new church would be a wonderful place for the people of Wakefield to celebrate their weddings, baptisms and the passing of loved ones. And, when Tuck needed a home, Father Myrc had gladly agreed to take the jovial friar in.

St Mary's was where Robin, John and Thomas found their old friend now and recruited him into their band of exorcists bound for Holmfirth on the sheriff's errand. It didn't take much to persuade the portly friar, who – although he enjoyed living in Wakefield, assisting Father Myrc and ministering to the villagers – rather missed the excitement of his time in Hood's notorious outlaw band.

"I've heard of this happening before," the tonsured clergyman mused after he'd ushered them into the manse and, to Thomas's delight, produced ale and bread. "Bad business for everyone – the folk that are possessed can't be reasoned with, while those who manage to avoid Satan's black touch find they're outcast in their own insane village."

The burly friar set his mug down and wiped his mouth with a grey sleeve. "We should do something about this as soon as possible, Robin."

The bailiff met Tuck's eyes and nodded agreement. "We're leaving right now, my friend. You'll come then?"

"Of course! Unless you plan on taking your blade to everyone in Holmfirth – and I know you better than that – you're going to need God's help. I'll ask Father Myrc to accompany us as well. There's bound to be a ringleader. Hopefully we can bring him – or her – to their senses and everyone else will fall into line." He shrugged, having no prior, personal, experience of exorcising an entire village. "Who knows? I'd suggest we carry quarterstaffs with us just in case the villagers *can't* be reasoned with."

Little John grunted and patted his own massive staff which lay propped against the table they were sitting at. "Any of those demon-spawn come near me and they'll be getting this in the damn teeth."

Thomas laughed and Robin shook his head with a weary smile, but Friar Tuck glared at the giant lawman.

"Defend yourselves, of course. But remember, these people are bewitched – they're not in their right mind. They need help, not violence."

John's head bowed and he hid behind his mug which he emptied slowly, mollified by the friar's scolding. He always felt like a naughty boy when Tuck gave him that look.

Thomas leaned back in his chair and made to spit a glob of phlegm onto the floor before he remembered where he was and swallowed it again with a grimace.

"Do you think you'll be able to cast out the devil or...whatever it is that's taken over the place?" He jerked a thumb over his shoulder. "Back in Nottingham I remember dealing with a man that'd been possessed by some demon. The priests couldn't do anything – in fact, he killed one of them and tore another's face open with his bare teeth. We had to kill him in the end – it was the only way to stop him." He sipped his ale thoughtfully. "I don't fancy dealing with a whole village as mad as that."

The four men sat in silence, nursing their drinks and imagining how things might go when they reached Holmfirth.

Hopefully the tales of the villagers' possession had been greatly exaggerated and all would be well...but Robin fingered his sword-hilt, knowing a quarterstaff might not be enough to deal with whatever they came up against.

"All right, lads, we better get on the road. We have to go south to Nottingham first for the sheriff's orders and, I assume, collect some of his men to back us up. Let's move!"

* * *

"In the name of the Holy Spirit, I command thee –"

"For fuck sake, Tuck, move!"

Little John's staff snaked out and the butt caught the man on the side of the head, toppling him to the ground in a daze before his grasping, dirt-encrusted hands could reach the friar's throat.

"I don't think there was any need for that," Tuck muttered, dismounting and kneeling to place his bible onto the fallen villager's chest, glaring balefully up at his huge saviour.

"You're welcome." John grinned in reply, kicking his horse into a walk beside Robin and Thomas, the rest of the sheriff's soldiers following at their backs nervously while Tuck and Father Myrc attempted to exorcise the would-be attacker.

The five travellers had made their way south from Wakefield and met with the sheriff in Nottingham where he'd given Robin his orders over a fine meal and tried to explain the situation in Holmfirth a little. After a night's sleep Sir Henry sent twenty of his guards off with them before dawn broke and promised to pray for the success of their mission.

"Try not to break too many heads," he shouted to John with a raised eyebrow as the horses clattered from the castle courtyard. "Those villagers are all taxpayers and the king needs every penny he can get right now, what with Queen Isabella and her troublemakers."

They had reached Holmfirth the next morning. It was, to Robin's eye, an inhospitable place with its rolling hills and steep roads. A heavy mist collected in the lower parts of land and, as they approached the place each one of them grasped their staffs – or their bible in Father Myrc's case – nervously.

A village in the middle of the week – even before the sun climbed above the horizon – should greet travellers with certain sounds and smells: a blacksmith's hammer striking the anvil, children's playful shouts, dogs barking, or the welcoming scent of a baker's fresh loaves rising in his oven. But there was none of that.

The only sounds they heard as they neared Holmfirth was the cawing of crows and the occasional scream or laugh, totally incongruous and infinitely sinister in the heavy, oppressive fog.

There were no smells of cooking; even the stink of piss was mostly absent as they passed the tanner's on the outskirts of the place which lay silent and seemingly unoccupied.

Father Myrc started to pray loudly but his voice only seemed to make things even more otherworldly, swallowed in the mist as it was, and Robin was glad to finally ride into the village which was surrounded by hills.

His relief faded when half-a-dozen men and women streamed out of the first two houses flanking the dirt road that ran the full length of the place.

Robin had never seen anyone behaving like those people. Each of them wore a crazed look – wide-eyed and wild-haired, their mouths ringed red with sores, apparently from licking their lips repeatedly which they did as they capered out into the street to greet the five riders and the accompanying soldiers.

"In the name of the Holy Spirit –" Tuck began again, but one of the older village women turned her back, lifted her skirts and showed her bare backside to him.

"Fuck off!" she cackled, gleefully.

The riders winced at the unpleasant sight, although Little John gave a snigger and Tuck glared at him reproachfully.

"In the name of the Holy Spirit, I command thee to leave these people and return whence thou came!"

Father Myrc's strong voice was swallowed by the fog as he pointed a large crucifix at the dancing lunatics who shrank back, apparently in fear at the sight of the cross, and ran off into the village, screaming and crying like scolded toddlers.

"In the name of God," Robin breathed, eyes scanning every section of the street, "these people truly are possessed by demons. I'd thought it would all turn out to be a storm in an ale mug; didn't expect to see – or hear – that."

"What are we going to do about it?" John muttered, hefting his staff. "We can't just go through the place cracking heads, can we?"

His leader shrugged and spurred his mount forward, guiding it towards the centre of the village. "If that's what it comes to," he said. "Come on, let's try and find the headman, or whoever's in charge around here. They may have lost their sanity, but even madmen follow some of the rules of society – there's bound to be a leader who can help us put a stop to this insanity."

As they trotted along the main street faces appeared in doorways and from behind shuttered windows. There were more strange noises – screams and laughter and shouted, blasphemous profanities accompanied by thuds and thumps as of axes chopping into wood.

No-one else came out to challenge them, though. Not until they reached the village green.

"Looks like we've found our leader," Little John said, gazing through the fog at the shocking scene before them, while the two clergymen came up behind and gasped in horror.

The grass in front of them – site of so many Mayday, midsummer and St Crispin's Day celebrations over the years – now played host to a gallows. It was a crude structure but that, and the blanket of chill mist, only added to its loathsomeness. The corpse hanging by the neck from it didn't help either. Not just any man, this was a clergyman; the local parish priest no doubt.

Father Myrc crossed himself and visibly shrank back in his saddle while Tuck muttered an un-Christian oath. Before Robin could tell him to wait, he'd dismounted and was walking towards the grim construction and the people that occupied the platform.

"Let's move." Robin climbed down from his own palfrey and John followed although he grumbled as he did so, not being quite as lithe as his friend. "You men," he waved an arm at the blue-liveried soldiers. "Fan out behind us. Be prepared for attacks from any side but use your staffs unless it's absolutely necessary to kill."

As he hurried to catch up with the irate friar, Robin took in the strange sight before them.

Standing on the filthy boards of the gallows were two men and a bent old woman, while directly behind the hanged priest sat a stocky middle-aged man with short, dirty blonde hair. His seat appeared to be a poor representation of a throne – it had a high back, and was topped off by gargoyles that were probably torn from the nearby church. Robin wondered inanely what stopped the gurning stone monsters from falling off the pitiful throne since they looked far too heavy and precarious to balance as well as they appeared to.

"In the name of Christ our Lord and Saviour –" Tuck shouted, hefting his quarterstaff menacingly, but the man seated on the gallows chopped his hand down angrily.

"Speak not that name here, cleric, or suffer the fate of your brother there." Without moving his head he rolled his eyes up to look at the hanged man and grinned.

Robin hesitated for a moment, something – some memory – flaring in the back of his mind at the sight of the apparently possessed villager's expression. It seemed strangely familiar…

"Pah!" Tuck reached the gallows and started to pull himself up, his face a mask of outraged fury.

"Hold, Tuck," Robin called, hurrying to catch him as Little John and Thomas stopped, feet spread wide and staffs held out defensively, ready for whatever might transpire next.

Without warning the withered old woman on the platform screamed in laughter and fell to her knees, pressing her face close to Tuck's. Never before had Robin seen anyone that looked as much like a witch as this apparition with her blackened teeth – stumps mostly – and numerous warts on her skin.

Yet the friar stood his ground and met her gaze as she shouted at him.

"Your Christ has been banished from Holmfirth. Now, my lord Satan rules in his stead!"

Robin heard the soldiers behind him draw shocked breaths and knew more than one grasped their sword hilts, despite his order for there to be no bloodshed.

Tuck was made of stern stuff, though. "Get out of my way, woman," he grunted, reaching out to grasp the kneeling woman by the hair and dragging her bodily from the raised platform onto the sodden grass at his feet. She tried to fight him off, scratching and clawing and biting, but he held her down and Father Myrc ran forward to help.

Robin turned his gaze back to the villager on the ridiculous throne, taking in the thinning, straight blonde hair and the disdainful curled lip before the man got to his feet with a bellow.

"Get them! I command you, in the name of our dark lord and master – kill them all!"

The lawman's heart sank as the sound of crazed screaming filled the air on all sides – coming not only from the throats of men and women, but children's voices also seemed to join in with the hellish chorus. He whirled, staring into the fog, knuckles white on his staff, desperately trying to see where the first attackers would hit them.

"Should I go after him?" Little John shouted, nodding at the man on the gallows who, with his remaining two companions was climbing down from the other side of the platform to make his escape.

Robin shook his head, his eyes widening as the villagers' army of the damned appeared through the fog, racing towards his small force of men.

"Leave them! I think you're going to be needed here for now..."

CHAPTER THREE

Gasping in desperation, Robin dropped his left shoulder, narrowly avoiding the meat cleaver that was about to carve his shoulder wide open. At the same time he rammed his staff into another assailant's midriff then swung the weapon back around to catch the first attacker's legs, sweeping them out from under him. The man dropped his cleaver with a roar before he was silenced by a brutal blow to the forehead. Without stopping, Robin twisted and cracked his quarterstaff into the second, winded man's temple, felling him like a rotten tree.

The young bailiff blew out a long breath and spread his legs in a defensive stance, looking around, searching for another threat in the pitiful army that faced them.

His soldiers were targeting the fit young men first, and, once they were beaten down, it was a simple enough matter to hold off the women and children who – despite their Satanic madness – were cowed by the sight of Little John's massive bulk tearing through their ranks like a righteous whirlwind. Some of the villagers, however, wielded daggers or chipped axes normally used for chopping firewood, and more than one of the sheriff's men were hurt before they could take down their attackers.

The sound of running footsteps approached to his rear and Robin turned to see a woman with a dull but deadly knife coming for him, a murderous look in her eyes. He raised his left hand as she lunged and grasped her fist, twisting hard so her whole body snapped back as if struck by lightning. The knife dropped to the ground, as did the woman and, loathe to assault her, he shouted on Father Myrc. The priest hurried over and sat on her chest, loudly intoning a passage from the bible as Robin stood.

He saw a tall, thin man with a wispy beard charge at Tuck, and winced as the Friar lifted his arm straight up and hammered it right into his attacker's neck, slamming the unfortunate man to the ground, dazed and choking.

The battle, inevitably, didn't last long, though. The villagers – enraged and insane as they were – had no chance against the staffs and superior training of Robin, John and the sheriff's soldiers.

There were many injuries. Some of the locals were unlucky and didn't recover from the blows they received, while half-a-dozen of the possessed men were so lost in their madness that there was no reasoning with them. They bit and clawed, howling like wolves as they did their best to murder the lawmen who retaliated with brutal yet restrained efficiency. Finally the fog had burned away in the afternoon sun and, at last, the village green lay strewn with unconscious or dead villagers.

Friar Tuck and Father Myrc moved amongst the survivors, offering blessings – or exorcisms in the more severe cases – in the name of Christ, and it was enough to restore sanity to Holmfirth. The madness seemed to have lifted now that their ringleader had vacated his 'throne' and those who could walk made their way sheepishly back to their homes to reflect on the whole bizarre experience, Father Myrc exhorting them loudly to be at mass the following morning to seek forgiveness from God.

Robin ordered Thomas to stay behind with the rest of the soldiers so they could restore order to the village while he, Little John and Tuck would report back to Sir Henry. The village headman – an old fellow with skin like parchment – was arrested and bound. The bailiff attempted to question him over the madness, in particular the priest's murder, but it was a waste of time, since the man, like the rest of his fellow villagers, was in a state of shock. So they decided to take him with them to Nottingham and the sheriff.

Father Myrc offered to stay on in place of the hanged clergyman for a while, until he was sure the devil had truly been cast out, and Tuck promised to look after the church in Wakefield until the priest returned home. Father Myrc would also see to his murdered brother's funeral and he moved off now, shouting for someone, anyone, to cut the pitiful body down.

None of the sheriff's guardsmen had been killed, although a few were quite badly injured.

The mission was a success, and Robin should have been pleased. Little John certainly was – the grin on his bearded face looked wide enough to swallow a wheel of cheese – but Robin couldn't get the man on the throne, the ringleader, out of his head. There was something unpleasantly familiar about him, but, for now, the young lawman was unable to put his finger on it.

Ah well, he was sure it would come to him eventually, he mused, as they rode out of Holmfirth along the road back to Nottingham. They'd have to hunt the man down and arrest him after all, before the maniac could cause any more trouble.

* * *

"Wine?"

Robin nodded and Sheriff de Faucumberg filled a mug himself before handing it over to the young man who'd become something of a friend these past few months. He told people Robin was his "mastiff", who he could let off the leash whenever anyone around his jurisdiction was being troublesome, and the former wolf's head would dutifully deal with the issue quickly, effectively and sometimes brutally.

"So you managed to restore the people of Holmfirth to sanity," de Faucumberg said, sipping his own wine, a fragrant red which had just been delivered to his bottler that morning. "Without too much bloodshed I trust?"

He raised an eyebrow and Robin, who'd waved John and Tuck off at an inn in the city an hour earlier, nodded. "Aye, have no fears on that score. I know you don't like the people to be treated unfairly so I made sure the men were as gentle as possible. All is well again, although, unfortunately the ringleader managed to escape, along with two others. We caught one of them – a local – but the others got away. The leader looked strangely familiar to me; came to Holmfirth from out of town apparently, not long ago and somehow managed to get the superstitious villagers to do his bidding. Shame he escaped." He raised his cup and sipped the liquid, grimacing; he didn't have a taste for the expensive stuff the way the sheriff did. "I'll catch the bastard one day, though. I'll not forget that face, you can count on it."

"Strange business all around," de Faucumberg sighed. "A whole village possessed. How can that happen?"

Robin shrugged and lifted a small piece of cheese from the trencher in the middle of the table which was piled with fresh foods. "According to the headman their parish priest probably caused the whole thing," he said, popping the food into his mouth with relish. "Apparently the clergyman – a newcomer to the place – was forever warning against demons and devils and seeing witchcraft in the most innocent of situations. The whole place was on edge as a result and...you know how it is: any emotion can be contagious. One person thinks the devil's taken control of them and it frightens someone else who starts to see bad omens in the blood that was in the shit they did that morning, or the fact their cow gave them a funny look when they milked it, or anything else that seems out of the ordinary. Before you know it some poor bastard – the priest in this case – becomes a scapegoat for all the pent up fear and, once they've given in to the madness the people feel free to do whatever they please."

De Faucumberg gazed at his young charge thoughtfully. "Very perceptive," he grunted at last. "You're not just good with a longbow are you?"

"That's why you like having me about," Robin grinned, draining the last of his wine. "Five years ago, Sir Henry, if you'd told me we'd be sitting here – drinking mates – chatting about the ills of the world, I'd have laughed and thought *you* possessed by a devil."

They sat in companionable silence for a time, eating and drinking their fill, before the sheriff stood up and called for a servant to take away the cups and plates.

"Where to next?" he asked, as his man quickly and efficiently cleared the table, head bowed the whole time as he left the room almost like a ghost.

"Back up the road to Mirfield," Robin replied, also getting to his feet and pulling on his green cloak. "A baker there has an unpaid fine which the local bailiff has been unable to extract from the man so..."

The sheriff looked at him seriously.

"Do you enjoy this job?"

Robin shrugged. "Aye, I suppose I do. It's interesting travelling around the county, even if it can be unpleasant putting people out their homes and the like. Someone has to uphold the law though, eh?"

"Indeed." De Faucumberg waved the big lawman farewell but he stood, lost in thought, for a long time after Robin had gone.

* * *

His relationship with the Sheriff of Nottingham and Yorkshire may have blossomed surprisingly over the years he'd spent in the man's service, but right now, it was the situation with his own wife that worried Robin.

"I'm sick of this," Matilda stated, flatly, her voice barely betraying any emotion. As if she really meant what she said; she'd truly had enough.

"Sick of what?" Robin demanded, feeling his temper rise as it always did when these discussions started. "Sick of our nice house? Sick of the fine clothes you and our son wear? Sick of me being at home rather than being stuck in the damn forest living the life of an outlaw?"

"You're never here any more," the girl said. Some of the anger went out of her face, which was still unlined and, Robin thought, as pretty as ever. "Keep the money and the clothes and you might as well still be a wolf's head. You're out doing Sir Henry's bidding all the time. I miss you. Arthur misses you."

She glanced over at the little bed next to theirs, where the four year-old boy was sleeping and smiled. The lad had a room of his own but Matilda liked him near her all the time, especially when Robin was away working in other towns and villages.

"We don't need money; we've got plenty from your days as the fabled outlaw the minstrels all sing tales about. You could do anything you want, here, in Wakefield, with your friends and family."

"Like what?" he demanded. "Be a blacksmith? Or a farmer? Or a baker? That's not any life for me." His voice trailed off. "I wish it was, but..."

"Where are you going now?" Matilda growled, as he turned his back and pulled his green cloak around his shoulders. "It's late."

"I'm going to the alehouse to see Tuck and John. I'll not be out too long – I've got an early start in the morning –"

"So you're going out drinking with your mates as if you were still a daft boy? Then pissing off to some other town as soon as it's light, leaving me and Arthur behind as usual?" She stepped in close and glared up into his eyes. "I'm not living like this, Robin. In the name of God I deserve better."

He shook his head and pulled away from her, stepping out into the cool night and slamming the door closed, shaking his head, a lump in his throat born of sadness and confusion as he gazed out at the village wondering what to do.

All of a sudden the door was thrown open behind him and he braced himself.

"Did you have to be so loud you selfish bastard?" Matilda hissed out into the gloom. "No thought for your sleeping child, it's always about you and what you want."

Robin waved a hand angrily, dismissively, and muttered an oath before he made his way along the street towards the local alehouse. He could feel his wife's stare burning into him every step of the way until he turned a corner and his shoulders slumped visibly as he walked.

It had been like this for a few months now. They'd been trying to have another baby for a long time but for some reason Matilda had never, thus far, managed to conceive again. They'd prayed and made offerings at St Mary's, and Tuck had even performed a blessing on them but all to no avail. Arthur remained an only child.

In truth, Robin was quite content with the situation – he loved his son so much and they had so much fun together, despite Matilda's harsh words, that he wasn't desperate for another crying babe in the house just now.

But Matilda took it hard, he knew. She never said much about it, so he wasn't sure whether she blamed herself, or Robin, or even God for her barrenness, but he'd noticed her mood becoming darker and darker until it seemed he could do nothing right these days.

No wonder he was happy travelling so much.

Aye, Matilda was right. He *did* enjoy his job and it was extremely important to him. For long enough he'd been a wolf's head – an outcast, and a man anyone, even the lowest beggar, could strike down with impunity. But the sheriff had given him a position that held real power – he didn't mind admitting to himself that he enjoyed the respect he saw in people's eyes when they knew he was a lawman. Yes, respect and even fear.

Of course, he'd had that when he'd been an outlaw too – the people loved him and his men after all. But now he had all that *and* he was a free man, dealing out justice to those who deserved it and able to enjoy the money and status his position afforded him.

He couldn't do that when he'd been living rough under a fucking tree in the pissing rain in Barnsdale, could he?

The alehouse door gave way to his gentle push and the sounds of men laughing filled the air. He sighed heavily and made his way inside to join his friends.

Things would work out he thought – they always did.

CHAPTER FOUR

"What are we going to do now then?" Eoin asked, his low voice betraying the hint of an Irish accent.

Philip was a big man at a shade under six feet tall, and powerfully-built too, but he was dwarfed by his companion, who looked at him now, ready to follow wherever his friend said they should go.

"Dunno," Philip shrugged in reply. "Shame those lawmen turned up in Holmfirth and put an end to our fun. We were living like kings there." He laughed and slapped Eoin on the arm good-naturedly, resuming their walk towards the village of Flockton where they hoped to buy some supplies. "I suppose now we're outlaws we should find some more of our kind to join up with. My brother was in a gang around here, or so I heard a few years ago. We could try and find him."

"How?"

Philip shrugged again. "Ask in the villages hereabouts."

Eoin nodded. He was happy to go along with whatever his friend suggested.

He'd met Philip in a tavern one night, a little over three years ago. Eoin's great size had, as it so often did, drawn attention and he'd been attacked for no good reason by three drunken idiots. They were unskilled but armed with knives and things would have gone badly for the big man had Philip not taken it upon himself to take Eoin's side.

Three corpses later the fight was done and witnesses were quick to tell the bailiff the three drunks had been killed lawfully, in self-defence.

Ever since then the two men had been friends, although Eoin was sometimes disturbed by Philip's tendency to violence at the slightest provocation. Especially since the older man was so good at it.

But Eoin was loyal and felt he owed Philip for saving his life so the pair remained close no matter what.

They hadn't planned on making the people of Holmfirth go mad. It all started when they'd tried to find work labouring for the blacksmith who they were told had just been awarded a big contract to craft weapons for the local lord. The man had been happy to hire them at first, but after a few days began to grow frightened of Philip's somewhat unhinged nature. He soon came to believe his new worker was possessed by the devil and Philip had played along, for fun, ordering the blacksmith first to pay them double the agreed wages, then to allow him to sleep with the terrified man's wife.

Somehow, the blacksmith's fear was transmitted throughout the village and Philip, revelling in his satanic role, milked the whole insane situation for all he could. The women slept with him, the men paid him homage in food and coin and it was all harmless enough until the priest tried to step in and put an end to things.

Hanging the man had been the villagers' idea, so far were they gone in their madness. Eoin wanted no part of the brutal business, but Philip encouraged it, knowing the priest's murder would only make the peoples' bond to him even stronger.

If the sheriff's men hadn't turned up they'd still be living as nobles in Holmfirth right now, rather than hiding like animals in the forest, hoping to find someone they could steal a crust of bread and a jug of ale from.

"Hold!"

The cry was high-pitched but filled with aggression.

With the promise of violence.

Philip stopped dead in his tracks, eyes scanning the foliage all around them.

"Who said that?" Eoin rumbled. "Show yourself."

A small man stepped out from behind the massive trunk of an old yew tree, longsword in hand. He was clean shaven with dark eyes, and appeared to be quite filthy. And yet, when he grimaced at them, Philip was surprised by the fellow's full set of almost white teeth.

"You two look like you can handle yourself," the small man noted. "So I won't get any closer." He laughed unpleasantly. "Take my word for it though, if you don't do as I say my mates will fill you with arrows so quick you'll die looking like a pair of giant fucking hedgehogs. Drop your weapons and throw your purses over here. Quick now. Those hares strung around your neck too."

Eoin glanced down at Philip, who simply nodded and slipped his coin-purse – which was as good as empty – from his belt and tossed it onto the ground in front of the robber. Eoin followed suit, although his purse really *was* empty, and so light it flopped sadly to the ground only a short distance away from him.

"Oh for fuck sake," the little robber spat in disgust. "Is that it? You two were hardly worth it." He held up a hand and, with an air of bored resignation, spoke to the trees.

"Shoot the big one first. I'll deal with the other one myself."

Philip dropped instantly, and swung his leg around, tripping Eoin just as an arrow tore through the air where they'd been standing.

He pushed himself back up onto one knee and drew his dagger.

"Get that ugly bastard," he growled.

The thief brought his sword back, ready to charge, but Philip swept up a short, stout branch from the forest floor and threw it at his face. The man parried it just in time but the manoeuvre left him off balance, and the huge weight of Eoin barrelled viciously into him. They fell onto the ground with a thud that Philip imagined he could feel as well as hear.

"Hold him down," he shouted to Eoin. "By the neck!"

He turned and addressed the trees and bushes all around them, a grin splitting his face as if this was a great game.

"You out there – you can shoot us, but my big friend there will snap your leader's neck before he dies. Or, you can come out and we can talk."

Eoin wasn't just holding the downed robber; outraged at the attack, his hands were squeezing inexorably on the man's throat.

"All right, all right!"

A man no older than forty, longbow in hand but with – in stark contrast to his downed friend – no front teeth at all, slipped out from his hiding place to their rear. "Leave him be, let him up. We didn't plan on killing you, I was aiming for the big man's leg –"

"Then you'd have taken our money and left us as good as dead in the middle of the forest?" Philip finished the sentence sarcastically. "Well, as you can see..." he retrieved the coin-purses he and Eoin had dropped and emptied them into his hand. "We haven't got any fucking money. Did have, but we left it behind in Holmfirth when the law chased us out."

Eoin had let the small robber up by now and they stood glaring at one another now: the giant and the purple-faced, breathless thief.

Philip gazed across at the little man, sizing him up, and came to the conclusion he'd rather go toe-to-toe with Eoin.

The dark-eyed robber had a maniacal gleam in his eye that was deeply disturbing; reminded him of himself, truth be told. They'd need to be careful around this one although...if they could get him on their side...

"Come," he smiled, walking forward and grasping the little robber's hand. "We're all outlaws together aren't we? You must be as hungry as we are."

He reached up and pulled the hares on the string around his shoulders over his head with a grin. "Let's eat."

It was a cool night but the fire brought a comforting warmth and light to the otherwise pitch-black forest.

The hares had been finished earlier – skinned, gutted and spitted they'd made a fine, if small, stew for four hungry men, and the smell of their bodies roasting still seemed to permeate the air.

"What's your story then?" the small robber asked, picking at a stubborn piece of gristle in his fine teeth. "You wolf's heads like us?"

Philip snorted humourlessly. "Aye, I reckon we are now. Had some trouble in the last village we were in and a clergyman found himself on his way to meet God sooner than he'd expected."

He upended his wineskin and took a short draught of the strong liquid.

"What about you boys? Just the two of you eh? I expected more when you ambushed us." He jerked his chin at the little man who was so clearly the leader of the outlaws. "What's your name? I'm Philip and my big mate here is Eoin."

The man eyed him for a moment, apparently wondering if he could be trusted. Finally, eyes locked on Philip's, he replied. "Mark of Horbury. I've been living in and around Barnsdale for the best part of seven years. The law have probably forgotten all about me but I like it out here, where I don't have to work like some beast of the field. Out here I just take what I need from anyone that comes along the road."

Philip whistled softly. "Seven years eh? That's a long time to evade the foresters."

Mark smiled, still staring disconcertingly at Philip who looked back unperturbed. "Not just foresters. After the Lancastrian revolt the king's men were all over the forest like flies on a tasty turd. And, since Robin Hood was living around here at the time, the man known as the Raven – Sir Guy of Gisbourne – was always a threat." He laughed shortly. "Until Hood tore him a new one, that is. Things have been a bit quieter around here since then."

Philip and Eoin had both spent the last decade or more down south, around London, until recently so, although the tales of Hood and the Raven had reached them, they'd not placed much stock in the fanciful stories.

"Last I heard my younger brother was an outlaw somewhere around here. You know of him?"

Mark shook his head when Philip named his brother. "Never heard of him, friend. There's a lot of us around here."

Philip smiled. "No matter, I've not seen him in years anyway, probably wouldn't even recognise him if I met him. If there's so many of you," he went on, "why don't you all band together? Surely it'd be safer than roaming around in pairs."

Mark looked into the crackling fire they'd roasted the hares over, his eyes shining orange in the glow. "Who'd be the leader in a big group like that?" he wondered, before returning his stare to Philip. "I don't like taking orders. I like *giving* orders. But so do lots of men, especially wolf's heads. Nah," he grinned and stood to leave the firelight to relieve himself. "We're happy as we are, ain't we Ivo?"

His toothless companion grunted assent over the sound of his leader's piss splashing onto the forest floor but Philip thought Ivo's response lacked enthusiasm and the acorn of an idea began to grow in his head.

Still, it would be better if they didn't need to kill Mark...the little lunatic would be a good man to have on their side. Assuming he could be controlled.

Philip would have to take things slowly; win these men over, before they could move onto bigger things.

If he was to live as an outlaw, he may as well do it in style.

"You being hunted?" Mark asked, settling back onto his log by the camp-fire. "From that village, where was it? Holmfirth, aye. The law searching for you, d'you think? Should me and Ivo be on our way in the morning in case your trail leads them right to us?"

Eoin shook his great head. "Nah. They had their hands full when we left, didn't they?" He grinned over at his friend and Philip returned the look with twinkling eyes.

"Aye. The villagers attacked them just as we decided to run for it. Although," the mirth left his eyes and he turned thoughtful. "I doubt those fools lasted long against the two lawmen. Big lads they were – one was a fucking giant, biggest man I've ever seen. He was even bigger than Eoin."

Mark was gazing into the fire again, apparently lost in its hypnotic flickering, but his eyes snapped up now and he spat an oath. "Little John. And, no doubt, his captain: Robin Hood himself."

Philip shrugged. "Aye, could have been. I never thought about it until now but, aye, all the stories I heard about them said Little John was bigger than any other man. I assumed it was a joke; a play on his name. And he was taking orders from another hard-looking man with the broad shoulders of a longbowman so...aye, you could be right."

"Fucking traitors." Mark growled, his hand falling to his dagger apparently of its own accord, instinctively, as if the little man wished he could take it then and there to the lawmen. "They were wolf's heads like us. Just like us. Worse if some of the stories I've heard about them are true. Hood sliced the fingers off a nobleman in his own manor house, you know? Aye, and they murdered countless churchmen too before they killed the king's bounty hunter. Yet what do they get?"

He glared at Philip and Eoin, who shuffled his feet nervously under the smaller man's crazed stare.

"A pardon and places on the sheriff's own staff, that's what. And now they ride around northern England dispensing justice."

"They hunt outlaws?"

Mark shook his head. "Not like us. They just collect taxes and stuff like that. It's only a matter of time though." He picked up a small twig and broke it into pieces before tossing the fragments absent-mindedly into the fire. "Like I said, there's a lot of thieves and cut-throats hiding in the forest and, since Gisbourne's death, there's been no-one leading any real effort to hunt us down. It won't last forever and who better to send after a forest full of outlaws than the most famous wolf's head of all?"

All the more reason to bring the gangs together into one large, powerful group then, Philip thought, but kept the idea to himself.

"How would you like a couple of extra members of your band, Mark? We know how to fight, you've seen that for yourself."

The outlaw sized them up before nodding and smiling. "Fair enough. Just make sure you do as I say and we'll all get along fine."

Philip grinned his thanks and raised his wineskin to Eoin in salute. "Looks like we've got a new home for a while, big man."

It wasn't much, but it was a start.

* * *

There was a storm during the night and Robin slept fitfully. The ale he'd shared with his friends didn't help, but the sound of the wind battering their home always made him fretful; he knew there'd be things needing repaired in the morning.

Matilda hadn't said a word to him when he returned from the tavern. She'd pretended to be asleep and Robin had been glad at that. No more arguing.

Arthur was fast asleep beside her but the little boy shifted around in the bed a lot during the night and every movement brought Robin awake again – he'd always be a light sleeper after his time living as an outlaw in the forest.

As a result of all this he woke in the morning with a dry mouth and an aching head, wishing he didn't need to travel to Mirfield that day on a job.

Matilda got up and made a small breakfast of black bread softened in ale for Arthur, who fed himself the sodden chunks greedily before growing bored and sending the remainder flying around the floor and mashing it into the table with a determined grin.

Matilda scolded the boy but said not a word to her husband, who dressed himself and gratefully downed the cup of water that she'd left out on the table for him.

"I have to go to a job in Mirfield."

No reply.

"It shouldn't take me too long; might be back by early afternoon. Maybe we could ask my ma and da to watch Arthur and we could go for a walk with some cheese and ale? We haven't done that in a while."

"Didn't you get enough ale last night?" The words were spat through gritted teeth and Robin shook his head in anger, lifting his weapons and throwing his light cloak around his shoulders. He kissed Arthur on the cheek and bid him a loving farewell but Matilda's voice harried him out the door as he left, barely listening to her words.

Sometimes he wondered if he'd be better off living in the forest again.

The common room in the alehouse was empty that early in the morning, but Alexander Gilbert, the landlord, appeared when he heard Robin coming in the front door.

"I'll have an ale, please, Alex," the big lawman grunted, somewhat embarrassed to be drinking at that time but knowing the stuff would cure the hangover that threatened to ruin his morning. "Where's John? I'd expected him to be up and ready and emptying your wife's kitchen of its contents."

The landlord shook his head as he handed the mug over and pocketed the proffered coin. "Haven't seen him, lad. Must still be asleep."

Robin quickly quaffed the ale. It wasn't like the giant to oversleep. All the men who'd been outlaws with him were in the habit of waking early, ready for whatever – or whoever – the day brought to them.

"I'll check on him."

Alexander waved him towards the hallway. "He's in the second room along there."

Robin drew his dagger as he walked silently along the gloomy corridor which was short and had no windows. He stopped at the door and placed his head against it, listening intently.

A groan came from the other side and Robin quickly wiped the sweat from his palm before gripping the dagger again. He softly pressed down on the latch, then rammed his shoulder into the wood, rolling onto the ground and coming up on one knee inside the little room with his blade held out before him.

"What the fuck are you doing you madman?"

The guest room had a window which was un-shuttered to let in fresh air and the early morning sun. John's face looked green in the pale light and Robin got to his feet with a crooked smile.

"Hangover eh? I was worried someone was in here killing you."

The huge man's beard was damp and flecked with bits of regurgitated food and he retched over the chamber pot pitifully, although nothing came up, which was just as well as it was already close to overflowing.

"Not a hangover," John muttered, rolling back onto the pallet and holding a hand over his eyes. "Had plenty of them in my time – this is something else. I've not stopped shitting and puking for hours."

Robin's smile dropped away and, without even thinking, he lifted the stinking pot from the floor, emptying the contents out the window into the grass outside. "You want me to fetch the barber from Pontefract?"

"Nah, I think the worst of it's over. It's all out now. I hope." He lifted a hand away from one eye and peered up at his friend. "Thanks for emptying that, you're a true friend. I've shit my breeches too – you fancy taking them to the Calder and rinsing them out for me? Or asking Matilda to –"

"Fuck off," Robin broke in with a horrified glare. "My friendship has limits. You can wash them out yourself when you get up. You won't be coming with me to Mirfield today in that state, eh? Oh well, can't be helped, I suppose." He placed the chamber pot back onto the floor beside John's recumbent figure and patted him on the arm. "I'll tell Alex to send you some bread and ale."

John looked queasy at the idea but grunted his thanks nonetheless. "Tell him no more of that stew he fed me last night, though. That's probably what's given me the shits." He retched again, but only a wet, awful smelling, belch came out and Robin shuddered.

"Aye, all right, I'll tell him. See you when I return."

He passed the message to the landlord and made his way back to his house where he stood for a moment, wondering if he should go inside to bid farewell to his family again, but decided against it. He mounted his horse and trotted along the main road towards Mirfield.

His job that day was to collect monies owed to the sheriff from a baker. The man had been fined – the second time that year – for selling underweight bread, and had made a couple of payments in good time, but there had been no word and no money from him in three weeks. Sir Henry had told Robin to find out what the problem was, and to add an extra ten shillings onto the fine as a penalty for late payment.

It wasn't a job that Robin expected he'd need Little John's quarterstaff to back him up on, but the big man's company made these journeys more pleasurable. And there was always the threat of robbery or worse from the ubiquitous gangs of wolf's heads that dotted Barnsdale and the rest of the surrounding forests.

The idea of making the trip on his own also meant he'd have time to dwell on his problems with Matilda., which wasn't a pleasant thought.

He sighed as he reached the outskirts of the village and resolved to push his mount hard so he could complete the job as soon as possible.

"Where's John?"

Robin glanced to the right at the voice, the smile returning to his face as he saw Tuck outside St Mary's, collecting broken roof tiles which must have been dislodged in the night by the storm. Indeed, the whole of the small churchyard was a mess of debris and one of the young trees that had been planted when Robin was a child lay on its side, roots completely torn from the earth. Father Myrc, who had just that day returned from Holmfirth, was visible at the far corner of the building, a brush in his hand as he tried to clear shards of slate and other detritus from the pathway.

"He's not well – dose of the shits from the looks of it." Robin waved a hand at the look of concern that creased Tuck's usually jovial features. "Don't fret, I think he's over the worst of it but he's not up to travelling with me to Mirfield so I'm on the way there by myself."

For a moment, the friar's eyes scanned the devastation the wind had wreaked and Robin could almost see the thoughts flitting through his head. Tuck was a great friend, a great warrior, and a great man to share a few ales with but...he wasn't the greatest worker in the world.

"Why don't I come with you, then? Yes, I'd better come along – can't have you travelling that road by yourself. There's outlaws all over the place and they'd like nothing better than to claim a lawman's head. Especially the fabled Robin Hood. Give me a minute!"

Robin grinned and nodded as the burly friar hurried into the church, reappearing moments later with his staff and a pack filled, no doubt, with food and drink to keep them going on their ride. He spoke to Father Mryc for a time before he disappeared again, this time to the rear of the church where the stables were located.

"Right then." Tuck was a fine horseman and he expertly guided his rouncy past the windblown debris in the churchyard and onto the road beside Robin. "Let's be off."

Father Myrc watched them go, arm in the air in farewell, a weary but fond smile on his face before he returned to his sweeping.

CHAPTER FIVE

"Afternoon, Harry." Robin lifted one of the meat pies from the counter in the baker's shop and bit into it, nodding appreciatively as the juices filled his mouth. "Freshly baked, eh? Very nice."

The baker, a bald man with a grizzled beard and thin lips, glared at him as Tuck hung back near the door, watching with interest. He'd never really spoken to Robin in any detail about his new line of employment, and this was the first time he'd ever seen his former captain doing a job for the sheriff.

"That'll be a penny," Harry muttered, holding his hand out, his stare never leaving the young bailiff's face.

Robin reached into his pocket and tossed the coin over to the man, who fished it from the air expertly.

"Your turn now." Robin pulled some papers from his pocket and stared at them for a moment. He wasn't a great reader but, eventually, he went on. "You haven't paid off your fine, Harry, as you know. I'm here to collect it."

A customer walked into the little shop then, seeing Robin, backed out and hurried off to find sustenance elsewhere.

"How am I supposed to get the money together when you're chasing away my customers?" the baker demanded, voice rising an octave in frustration. "No, I don't have the cash. I only have half." His voice dropped again but his eyebrows went up and he spread his hands wide. "Give me another week, eh? I'll have it by then, I swear it. Those loaves might have been a little underweight but they were best quality! I'd rather make a good small loaf than a worthless heavy one."

Robin continued chewing the pie and then wiped the grease from his lips with a sleeve. "I don't think I can give you any more time, Harry. The sheriff was pretty insistent and you've had weeks already..."

He trailed off but looked expectantly at the baker who returned his stare for a moment, clearly wondering what he should do next and Tuck felt a wave of pity wash over him for the man. Harry didn't have the look of a sot or waster – he simply looked like a villager who was struggling to make ends meet. His merchandise was tasty and of a high quality, judging by Robin's reaction to the meat pie, and the price asked for it. The man was clearly a fine baker but not much of a businessman. Perhaps if he used cheaper ingredients and charged a little less for his wares he'd not need to resort to making underweight loaves and would, as a result, make a better living in these hard times.

Some craftsmen took their art too seriously to do it in what they saw as a half-arsed way though and now Harry, who made pies and savouries fit for noblemen, was suffering because his only customers were the poor peasants and yeomen of Mirfield.

"Like I say, I only have half the remaining fine," the baker mumbled, shoulders slumped. "What if I give you ten shillings for yourself, and you give me another week to collect the full amount?"

Robin nodded, lowering his voice conspiratorially.

"I'll take that for now then, just between you and me. I'll fob the sheriff off for another week, all right? Don't tell anyone, though – I don't want people to know I'm a soft touch."

Tuck felt a coldness sweep through him at what he was witnessing. He watched as the baker disappeared into a tiny room in the rear of the shop and returned moments later with a handful of coins. He held them out to Robin who took them with a smile.

"Thanks Harry," the sheriff's man muttered, tucking the money into his purse. "I'll tell the Sir Henry you're doing your best and deserve a little extra time. How does that sound?"

The baker's eyes flicked from Robin to Tuck, back in the shadows, and Tuck felt the man's despair almost like a kick in the stomach. But Harry simple lowered his head and, in a voice that was barely audible replied, "That sounds fine, my lord. Thank you, I'm very grateful for your kindness."

"Excellent!" Robin slapped his big hand on the counter and grinned. "I'm glad we sorted this, Harry. I'll be back next week to collect the full amount, I'm sure you'll have it all by then. I hate throwing men out of their businesses." He turned and nodded to Tuck who eyed the baker sadly then walked out into the street.

"That pie was tasty," Robin said over his shoulder as he followed the friar outside. "You should really charge more for them – maybe you'd not be in debt if you did!"

Tuck made his way over to his mount and untied it from the tethering post before dragging himself into the saddle with some difficulty. Robin looked up at him in surprise.

"What's your hurry?" he demanded. "Don't you want to stop awhile in the tavern for a couple of drinks and some food? The *Wayfarer's Arms* has some great ale, I've been there a few times recently. Prices are fair too."

Tuck grunted and kicked his horse into a walk without waiting for his companion to follow. "I need to get back to Wakefield and help Father Myrc tidy up after the storm. You head off to the *Wayfarer's,* and I'll see you later."

Robin stood, open-mouthed, for a moment. Since when did Tuck refuse a meal?

"Wait," he shouted, freeing his own palfrey from its tether and vaulting nimbly into the saddle. "Wait," he repeated, urging the horse into a canter. "What the hell's the matter with you?"

There was no reply and Tuck simply stared at the road ahead as his young friend caught up with him and grabbed hold of the friar's reins.

"What's going on? You've never been in a hurry to sweep leaves in your life, especially not when there's freshly-brewed ale on offer. What's the problem here?"

Tuck turned, at last, to glare at Robin, who let go of the other man's reins.

"What's the problem? You took a bribe from that poor baker."

Robin smiled in disbelief. "So? I did him a favour. If I hadn't given him extra time to gather his rent I'd have had to throw him out onto the street. He'd have lost his livelihood." He raised his arms in supplication. "Isn't this better? You're a man of the world; I assumed you'd understand or I'd never have brought you along."

Tuck pointed a meaty finger at him angrily. "Man of the world? Pah. Will he have your rent next week, when you return?"

Robin shrugged. "I hope –"

"No, he won't. You know it as well as I. He'd done his best to gather half the money and you took ten shillings of that for your own pocket? He had little enough chance of paying his debt off as it was but you've made it impossible. Why, Robin?"

The anger had left Tuck, to be replaced now with disappointment.

"You were a wolf's head yourself. You used to talk about society's injustice and how you wished you could make things fairer – better – for men like Harry. And now, here you are..."

Robin kicked his mount into a walk and muttered something about just upholding the law and trying to be fair. Tuck followed, pulling his horse away from what seemed to be a particularly tasty piece of grass.

"No wonder Little John felt sick at the prospect of coming here with you today. I feel like going for a bath in the Calder myself after seeing you in action –"

Robin rounded on him, face scarlet, horse's head dragged rudely back as he brought it to a halt.

"I uphold the law, Tuck. That's my job. I'm not a wolf's head any more." He seemed to wilt under Tuck's stony gaze though, and urged his mount forward again, its heavy hooves thudding gently on the soft earth as they left Mirfield and joined the main road again.

"How many men have you thrown out of their homes or businesses?" Tuck asked softly.

Robin shrugged before replying moments later. "A dozen? Two dozen? I don't keep count." His eyes swivelled to look at Tuck. "I never put anyone out without the law on my side. It's not my fault they didn't pay their debts."

Tuck couldn't believe his friend – the fabled Wolf's Head of so many ballads – was talking like this. "When you took up with de Faucumberg I assumed you'd become a bounty hunter for him. Hunting down rapists and murderers. Not throwing honest bakers out onto the street!"

"The man sold underweight loaves," Robin countered. "He's as much a criminal in the eyes of the law as any rapist."

"Listen to yourself," Tuck muttered, shaking his head. "That man making his tasty meat pies is as bad as a rapist or a murderer?"

"In the eyes of the law," Robin said. "They're all lawbreakers –"

"Peace." Tuck turned back to the road and his horse gathered speed again. Robin didn't bother trying to catch up this time and the friar was glad of it.

Truth be told, Robin had acted just as everyone would have expected when he was first tasked with collecting fines and overdue taxes. He'd gone easy on people and even, in some cases, felt so sorry for them that he'd quietly paid off their debts using his own money. But word had soon got around that he was a soft touch and folk started to take advantage. It took him a while to realise it and it had hurt when he did – were people really so selfish that they'd exploit any opportunity to line their own pockets at the expense of someone trying to do right by them?

So he'd had to grow a thick skin and deal with everyone the same way. Aye, he took the occasional bribe, but so what? Every other bailiff he knew would take much more in bribes than he ever did and leave the people with no chance of ever making up their debts.

Robin wasn't heartless, but he liked to believe he'd grown wise and if folk owed money, they'd have to pay, it was as simple as that. He didn't enjoy that part of the job though, it was true and now, seeing the look of disappointment on the friar's face, it irritated and even, deep down, shamed him.

The journey back to Wakefield seemed to take forever but, at last, the trees parted and St Mary's steeple came into sight. As he dismounted, Tuck stood and watched Robin's mount carry him towards the village.

"Ask yourself if your work is worth it, Robin," Tuck called. "Is it worth giving up all your former principles? Is it worth losing your family?"

Robin had told them about the recent, growing, troubles with his wife when the companions had been in the alehouse the previous evening and now Tuck thought he understood why Matilda felt as she did.

The friar raised his eyes to heaven and prayed his young friend would find his way, before it was too late.

* * *

The next few days were not really memorable for Robin. Matilda was polite if distant towards him, but Arthur continued to grow and develop although the lad was something of a firebrand and often got into trouble with the other local children, adding even more stress to his parents' relationship.

Tuck avoided him which was hurtful, but the young man was too stubborn to try to talk the friar round and Little John stayed by his side so he never felt too lonely while he continued to travel around the villages of Nottingham and Yorkshire dispensing the sheriff's justice.

Tuck's words in Mirfield played on his mind, though. Maybe the money and power had gone to his head, for he *had* become basically a tax collector. Yes, the people he evicted had been given fair time to repay their debts but...the friar was right – this wasn't what Robin wanted to do with his life. If he was going to be a lawman he wanted to take down truly wicked men, not humble villagers fallen on hard times.

He knew John didn't enjoy their work either, but the giant was too loyal to his best friend to make much of a fuss. Robin had no doubt he would eventually get fed up with it though, and then what? Would he lose John's friendship as he seemed to have lost Tuck's?

And Matilda...

She'd given up haranguing him over his work, but she'd also given up sharing his bed. They'd talk about Arthur, or other family matters whenever Robin was home, but that was the extent of their relationship and it shocked him to realise he was glad.

Not glad that they'd drifted apart, just relieved not to have her complaining all the time.

Their son had fallen asleep early that night – his eyes rolling in his head as Matilda tried to get him to eat the vegetable soup she'd made for dinner and Robin decided to go out to the alehouse again. He didn't like being alone with his wife any more – it was awkward, as she tutted or huffed to herself whenever he did anything – so he'd taken himself off without a word.

Tuck was there but he simply nodded a half-hearted greeting to his one-time captain and Robin scanned the room, hoping John would be there. He wasn't, of course, so he joined a couple of other locals he'd grown up with. Good men who had a lot of respect for Robin, but, as he nursed his second ale he found himself completely outside their good-natured conversation.

The men spoke of their wives, their work, the mildness of the summer that year and any number of other mundane topics which the former wolf's head felt bored and even mildly irritated by, and he found himself drifting off into his own thoughts as he gazed into his ale mug.

Times when Matilda had spoken harshly to him filled his memory. Things she'd said during their many arguments about him being a terrible husband and father…

He hated her, he thought. He'd be better off without her.

A sigh escaped his lips and he sipped his ale, oblivious to the roars of ribald laughter from the men beside him sharing some inane joke.

No, he didn't hate his wife – he loved her as much as he ever had. He just wanted things to go back to normal between them, so they could enjoy their life with Arthur as they'd always wanted.

He'd been too stubborn – too selfish, he admitted – to see it before, and it had taken wise old Friar Tuck to finally get through to him, but now he knew what he should do.

In the morning he'd ride to Nottingham and ask Sir Henry to find him a different job. Even if it was simply as one of the sergeants in his guard.

Matilda would be pleased and all Robin's troubles would be over.

With a grin on his handsome face the big lawman drained the last of his and ale stood up, smiling a farewell to his companions. He even managed to catch Tuck's eye and smiled broadly at his erstwhile friend as he paid one last visit to the landlord before heading home to bed.

The friar would appreciate the free ale Robin had paid for, there was no doubt about that. It was the least he could do since the portly clergyman had doubtless saved his marriage.

As he strode towards the door with a glad heart a small man bustled up to him, an angry look on his round, weather-beaten face.

"Hood! Hood, here!"

The little man waved angrily at him as he approached through the crowd of drinkers and Robin recognised him as one of the village carpenters, although for the life of him he couldn't remember the fellow's name.

"Well met, my friend," the bailiff smiled, nodding a greeting, but the carpenter glared at him in return and stood before him, blocking his way to the door.

"Don't give me that bollocks. Do you know who I am?"

"Aye. You're…" he trailed off into an embarrassing silence, as everyone in the place noticed the confrontation and stopped their own conversations to watch the excitement.

"I'm a cousin of Martin Black, you know? The landlord of the Boar's Head in Dewsbury."

Robin felt the eyes of everyone in the place on him as he remembered the man he'd evicted not that long ago.

"Aye, I remember him. What about it?"

Without even being conscious of it he'd straightened up and let his hand fall to the sword that he wore at his waist but the angry man before him was unimpressed.

"I thought you'd like to know," the carpenter's voice rang out over the expectant silence, "that Martin's wife just died of fever. They'd been forced to sleep outdoors after you evicted them and that heavy rain we had last week got into her body and killed her."

Robin didn't say anything and neither did anyone else for a time. At last the furious carpenter stepped in even closer to the bailiff and pointed a finger up at his face.

"I hope you're fucking proud of yourself."

For a while Robin simply stood looking at the man. What could he say? Eventually he muttered an apology and pushed past the carpenter as half the village watched, to make his way out into the night and home, walking as if there was a heavy weight on his shoulders.

* * *

"I'd like to speak to you about the work you've got me and John doing," Robin started but Sir Henry broke in distractedly as he watched the cloudless sky.

"I'm glad you visited me today, because I wanted to speak to you too. I have a new job for you and the giant to undertake, if you think you're able." He adjusted the leather gauntlet on his right arm and shouted some encouragement to an older member of the hunting party before turning back to Robin. "I think it will be perfect for you. Come."

It was a fine day – the sky was sunny but not cloudless and a cool breeze stopped it from being oppressive. A perfect day for the sheriff to indulge in one of his favourite hobbies with some friends and a few retainers: falconry.

Robin followed, gazing at Sir Henry as they followed the bird in the sky overhead, hoping his superior wasn't going to send him to collect more rents from some merchant. He hadn't told Matilda what he planned before he travelled down here but his mind was made up, no matter what the sheriff said.

"Have you heard of the outlaws in Barnsdale recently?" De Faucumberg asked, surprising Robin completely.

"Not in particular. I mean, aye, I've heard of them, there's always outlaws about the place. Any traveller knows to be wary when using the roads around here."

"You haven't heard of – or noticed – any increase in their activities in recent weeks then?"

Robin thought a moment then shook his head. "No. Should I have?"

The sheriff made a fist with his left, ungloved hand, gleeful as he noticed a pair of wood pigeons that his falcon was lining itself up to attack.

"Your gang was something of a rarity," he said over his shoulder, eyes still on the sky. "Around two dozen men united under one leader. Go on, my beauty. Watch this Robin – it's incredible. In a dive, the falcon is the fastest bird in the world you know?"

The party stopped as the bird of prey dropped out of the sky like a stone, aiming for one of the two pigeons. It hammered into the target and a handful of feathers exploded as the falcon carried its prize away, pecking downwards once with its powerful beak and killing the unfortunate pigeon before carrying it down to the ground.

"Yes! That's another one for the pot."

De Faucumberg glanced at the servants but they were already heading towards the falcon's landing site.

"I hope they hurry up. There's been times I've had birds take their kill away up into the trees, gorge themselves, then fall asleep high up in the branches. You can't get them down for hours!"

He laughed as if he'd just told a hysterical joke then, noticing Robin's bemused expression, forced himself to carry on with the previous line of conversation.

"Most gangs of cut-throats and robbers are small in number and tend not to cause too much trouble before they try to steal from the wrong person and find themselves dead in a ditch somewhere. Apart from you – and your predecessor Adam Bell before you of course – there's been no-one I can think of who's managed to unite any significant number of lawless men into one cohesive whole."

"Fulk Fitzwarine?" Robin suggested.

"That was a hundred years ago," de Faucumberg waved his gloved hand dismissively. "I'm talking about recently."

The sheriff's huntsman had reached the falcon by now and managed to coax it away from its kill with a morsel of raw meat. Sir Henry whistled and the falcon swooped towards them, making Robin flinch involuntarily but the graceful, majestic bird landed perfectly on the sheriff's hand and accepted another bloody titbit in reward for its obedience.

"It seems we have a new Robin Hood," de Faucumberg said as he expertly hooded the falcon to keep it calm, the grin on his face at his pet's success belying the dread import of his words. "Someone is uniting the outlaws of Barnsdale again, and he doesn't have the morals you – or even Adam Bell – had."

"What do you mean?"

"Reports from villages nearby suggest at least three smaller outlaw gangs have joined forces. This larger group have robbed half-a-dozen parties making their way through the forest. Only one person survived – a young girl who must have been extremely fit, for she was able to outrun her pursuers and make it to safety. Which is just as well...God knows what the wolf's heads might have done to her."

"I can guess," Robin growled. "What about the other people they robbed?"

The sheriff handed his falcon over to the head huntsman and waved the man away before turning and making his way across the field towards the city gates as he undid the laces on the bulky glove.

"Merchants and clergymen but also a couple of simple folk going from one village to another on errands. As I say, the outlaws killed them all. The girl who escaped was sure one man was in charge."

"Description?"

De Faucumberg shrugged. "She was terrified and looking to make her escape before they had their way with her so she wasn't the most observant witness. All she could say was the fellow was big – about your size I suppose, with straw coloured hair. He smiled the whole time too, which she found unnerving, given the situation."

Robin's mind filled with the image of the man who'd orchestrated the madness in Holmfirth. The description fitted but...well, it could also describe a thousand men dotted around the north of England.

"So what do we do?"

The sheriff stopped in his tracks and spread his arms wide. "What in God's name do you think I brought you here for? You and your giant friend will need to find these outlaws and bring them in. It should be more interesting than collecting rents from folk, eh? If a tad more dangerous...But you're used to that. You and John are the best men for this with your knowledge of the forest and how to survive out there."

Robin nodded and followed de Faucumberg who'd moved off again, his stride long as he headed for some cool wine and fresh bread.

"I'll need more men," he said. "The two of us can't take on a whole force of outlaws by ourselves."

"Yes, yes, I know that. You know my garrison by now. Select a dozen of them – clear it with their captain first mind you – then get after these bastards." He glared over his shoulder at the young lawman. "I thought all this nonsense was behind me once I'd dealt with your lot. I can't be doing with it all over again, so destroy these scum as fast as possible."

Robin's face broke into a small smile as he trailed after the sheriff. This was ideal. He was finally going to do a job that was worthwhile. Matilda would be happy!

CHAPTER SIX

Mark had been surprised to find their new companions were even more uncompromising than he was himself. Well, the leader, Philip, was at least. The giant, Eoin, simply did as he was told, even when you could see in his eyes that he didn't really want to.

He followed orders though, no matter what, and that told Mark that Philip was a man to keep an eye on. A man not to turn your back on…

When they'd first joined forces, just the four of them, they robbed a young couple who'd been unfortunate enough to walk too close to the new gang's camp.

The pair looked no more than fifteen years old, and carried little of value which irritated Mark, who hated wasting his time for nothing. He punched the young lad a few times, broke his nose and knocked out a couple of teeth, then told Ivo and the other three to let the couple go on their way.

But his new companion, Philip, had surprised him.

Pulling his dagger from its sheath the newcomer to Barnsdale had slammed it into the youngster's back half-a-dozen times, his face bland in its murderous concentration.

Even Eoin looked stunned, while Mark and Ivo exchanged shocked glances. They had no problems with killing the folk they robbed, but only if their targets fought back. Murder was a sure way to bring the full force of the law down on you.

The girl was too stunned, and terrified, to attempt any escape then. She simply crumpled onto the soft grass beside her dead young friend, a high keening escaping her lips.

"Go and see if you can catch us a hare or two for dinner," Philip said to Eoin, who looked up from the bloody corpse, eyes wide in surprise and confusion.

"Off you go, big man," Philip smiled. "My belly's rumbling and I'm sure our new mates are hungry too. Aren't you?"

Eoin didn't reply but his mouth worked soundlessly, as if he wanted to say something but couldn't find a way to articulate it.

The girl's howls had dropped to a low sobbing by now, her face hidden against the neck of her dead friend and, when Eoin's eyes fixed upon her again Philip repeated, harshly, "Go and catch us something for dinner. Now."

Mark watched the giant outlaw as he struggled within himself, but, eventually, the big man nodded and lumbered off into the trees.

The crying girl was oblivious to what was going on, and Philip waited a few moments until the sounds of undergrowth being brushed aside faded away, then he grinned at Mark and undid the laces of his hose.

"Hold her down. I'm not going after you two dirty bastards have had a turn."

The girl wasn't Mark's type. She was too young, too skinny, and her face was covered in tears and snot. But he hadn't emptied his balls in weeks so, once Philip was finished, he'd taken his own turn. By the time Ivo had spilt his seed inside her her anguished cries had dropped to no more than a whimper.

And then Philip had told him to shut her up.

"She's no threat," Mark shrugged, leaving go of her wrists as Ivo stood up, a satisfied smile filling his toothless mouth. "We can let her be on her way."

Philip's ever-present smile disappeared just as the sun started to dip beneath the horizon, the shadows giving his face an ethereal, unpleasant look as he stared directly at the smaller man.

"She knows what we look like. Kill her."

Ivo glanced over at Mark, a worried expression on his seamed face.

"I'm not killing her," the little outlaw shook his head. "We've had her way with her, you've stabbed her young man to death, and she's not a threat to us." He placed a hand on the hilt of his dagger and spread his legs. "Men are one thing, but I won't kill a young lass."

The girl's tear-streaked face was expressionless as she watched the exchange. Her spirit had been broken by her ordeal but her eyes widened as she saw Philip shrug, draw his sword and step forward to slide the point deep into her belly.

Mark knew better than to react to the agonized scream that tore through the forest then. He had no wish to show any sign of weakness to this man he'd chosen to join up with. Ivo, too, remained silent but his jaw clenched as he watched the girl's blood spill from the gaping wound onto the rich green grass of the forest floor.

"I don't know how you managed to survive this long," Philip growled, the smile slowly returning to his face as he withdrew the blade and wiped the bloodied tip clean on the girl's clothing before pointing it in their direction. "You're soft." He spoke to both of them but his eyes stayed fixed on Mark who bristled at the insult but didn't know how to reply.

"I'm away back to the camp; it's getting cold and Eoin will be along with something for the pot soon, no doubt. At least I know I can count on him."

He spat that final barb then made his way through the foliage to their camp-site as if he hadn't a care in the world, leaving Mark and Ivo to stand in his wake, wondering what the hell they'd got themselves into.

The girl was in obvious agony although she seemed unable to make a sound by now, and Mark knew she'd die a long, lingering death. He wondered if that had been Philip's intent and the thought made him shudder.

And yet her eyes seemed to accuse *him*, as if it had been *he,* Mark, who'd run her through with his blade!

He couldn't stand her agonized glare any longer so he followed Philip into the bushes, back to camp, Ivo trailing at his heels as the young girl's gasps faded into the forest behind them.

Mark was silent as they walked, stunned by the brutality of their new companion. No good would come of this he was sure – the law would hear of it and come looking for them.

He sighed as the darkness drew in, battering foliage aside as he walked. Why did bad things always happen to *him*?

That had all taken place a few weeks ago, and since then their gang had grown, as Philip welcomed anyone they found living in the forest into their ranks without question.

The hierarchy, to Mark's fury, had slowly become clear: Philip was the leader now, at the top of the pile, with the lumbering form of Eoin to back him up, while everyone else – including Mark and Ivo – were simply there to do as they were told.

The little wolf's head would have left and gone back to his old haunts around Horbury, but he had a strange sense that staying with Philip would lead to interesting opportunities to make money. If nothing came of it, he thought, he'd simply knife the smirking bastard in the back and usurp his position.

"What are you thinking about?"

The familiar voice broke in on his reverie and Mark glanced up guiltily, wondering how the hell Philip had managed to creep up on him so quietly.

"Nothing," he muttered, and knew Philip could see through the lie.

But his new leader simply smiled down at him. "Well then, since you're not busy, why don't you and Ivo go and see if you can catch us something for dinner? I'm sick of bread and mouldy cheese." He gestured to a tree nearby, against which two fishing poles were resting. "Trout would make a nice change for everyone, don't you think?"

Mark bristled, enraged at the fact this strange newcomer to the area was giving him orders, but the smile never left Philip's face and Mark knew instinctively it would be a terrible mistake to challenge him now. Too many of the recent recruits to their group supported him, for some unfathomable reason. And there was still the threat of Eoin, who sat close-by, smiling stupidly as a couple of men – southerners from their accent – sang a ribald rhyme.

"Aye, good idea," Mark returned Philip's smile and rose nimbly to his feet. "I'm sick of bread and cheese myself. I'll take Ivo – and a skin of ale! – with me."

"Excellent. Just be careful you don't fall in."

With a humourless laugh, Philip moved away and joined in with the southerner's rhyme, leaving Mark to glare at him, wondering how he knew the words to their song.

"Ivo! Come on, we're going fishing."

For now he'd take orders, and see how things turned out.

* * *

Matilda groaned in pleasure.

"Shh, you'll wake Arthur," Robin whispered, and she returned his smile contentedly.

He'd returned from Nottingham that afternoon in a good mood, and his manner reminded her so much of the young man she'd fallen in love with that she'd found herself thawing towards him.

They'd shared a meal of fish with bread and ale before Robin brought out a toy he'd bought in the big city for Arthur. It was a carved wooden knight, complete with horse and lance. The little figurines had fired the lad's imagination and he'd spent the evening chasing his laughing father about the house.

When the little boy had finally fallen asleep they finished the last of the recent batch of ale Matilda had brewed then Robin asked how her day had been. When she complained, mostly in jest, about how hard it was to help her father fletch arrows while Arthur was being wild Robin surprised her by offering to massage her back.

Now she lay on their bed – which was a fine one since they were no peasants – on her stomach, while Robin straddled her legs and used his strong hands to knead the knots and tension from her shoulder blades.

She turned her head to the side and looked up at him from one eye. "That's nice. You should do this more often."

His hands moved down to the small of her back, still gently squeezing and her legs jerked at the almost ticklish sensation that shot wonderfully through her body.

"Oh, yes, that feels good..."

He continued for a while, just kneading the flesh and muscles of his wife's back before he moved down to her thighs and, inevitably, her buttocks, which were firm and lean like the rest of her. She knew there would be an ever increasing bulge in his hose and it made her grin like a naughty teenager.

"What's come over you anyway?" she asked in a low, contented voice. "You've barely spoken to me for days and now this?"

For a time he didn't reply, just continued to massage her body, every so often surreptitiously squeezing her backside before moving back to her thighs or shoulders.

"I'm fed up with us arguing all the time," he said, at last. "I dread coming home to you every day. I know –" he stopped her harsh reply before she could open her mouth "– it's as much my fault as it is yours. Maybe mostly mine," he finished, somewhat sheepishly, no doubt in response to the fact she hadn't raised her lowered eyebrows yet.

"So this is your solution?" Matilda rolled onto her back beneath him and met his gaze. "Ply me with drink and give me a rub-down?"

Her smock had fallen open when she turned over and Robin's hands, seemingly of their own volition, moved up to grasp her breasts softly. His fingers squeezed lovingly and, again, she felt a tingle course through her body.

It had been so long since they'd made love.

"You'll be glad to hear I've got a new job," he mumbled, bending to kiss her neck. "I won't be going from village to village collecting taxes any more."

"That's good," she smiled, putting her feet around him and pressing them down on his backside so she could feel him against her. "I'm glad."

He pressed his mouth against hers, kissing her again, and she forced her tongue into his mouth, now as desperate as he was to end their recent chastity.

"There's a new gang of outlaws in Barnsdale," he whispered, finally squeezing himself between Matilda's legs. "John and I are going to hunt them down."

Matilda felt as if someone had walked into the room and thrown a bucket of ice water into her face.

She stiffened but, for a few moments Robin didn't notice, as he continued thrusting into her unresponsive body.

"You're what?"

He spasmed and went limp, then, finally raised his head and, in the flickering orange glow from the fire in the hearth, looked at her in surprise.

"We're going after these outlaws," he said, his hand still caressing Matilda's nipple, but he sensed the change in the mood and his already softening manhood slipped out of her as he leaned back on one arm and watched her, his face a mask of confusion. "They're robbing people and raping women. They're scum," he finished, his words trailing off.

"So you've gone from harassing poor men and women to chasing after supposed murderers and rapists? And you think I'll be glad to hear it?" She sat up but kept her voice low – controlled – so she'd not wake their sleeping son who lay in the bed beside them.

Robin simply stared at her. The puzzlement evident in his eyes might, at one time, have elicited pity in her – a loving sympathy at his manly stupidity.

Now it just made her angry.

"Do you not remember where you were a few short years ago? Where we both were?"

"But –"

"But nothing," she hissed, slapping a hand onto her naked thigh. "Why would you accept this job? I assume it was Sir Henry's idea?"

He nodded, but the softness had started to leave his expression as his own anger bubbled to the surface.

"Why wouldn't I go after a gang of rapists for fuck sake? Who better to hunt them down than me and John, who know the forest so well? Or do you think we should just let them go around killing people? What's the problem here? Why do you have to complain about everything I do?"

"Keep your voice down," Matilda growled, glancing over at the sleeping Arthur who snuffled and rolled slightly at his father's enraged tone. "We were both outlaws not that long ago. Didn't de Faucumberg and Sir Guy of Gisbourne and all the other nobles around here spread rumours about us being brutal murderers? Didn't they say Will was a rapist? That you yourself had defiled a clergyman in an ungodly way?"

Robin waved his hand dismissively but Matilda carried on, shaking her head as if her husband was an imbecile. "That's what they do: they *lie*. So people like you won't help the outlaws."

"I know Sir Henry well now," Robin retorted, shaking his head. "He's not making this story up. Those men are committing crimes against normal people. Crimes none of my men would ever have contemplated. Well, maybe Matt Groves," he ended, doubtfully, and Matilda jumped on the admission.

"So maybe these new outlaws have some sick bastard like Matt in their group. Are you going to punish them all for his crimes? Would that have been fair if Gisbourne had cut *your* face apart because Matt had raped some woman or young Gareth had stabbed some merchant? Are you going to destroy these men when you don't know a thing about them? When chances are they're just normal men fallen on hard times, *like you were?*"

They'd moved as far apart from each other as they could, and Matilda wrapped the bedclothes around herself while Robin sat, still naked, muscles taut, the low firelight glinting in his brown eyes.

"They're *not* like us," he said, finally, softly. "You know what we were like. We were good men."

"Who robbed priests and bishops and killed boys and ate children." She shook her head at his naivety. "Who knows where the reality ends and the stories begin? Yes, *we* do," she stopped his reply with a curt gesture, "but the people of Nottingham don't. The people of Hathersage don't. Or the folk in Penyston. All they know is what they hear from the minstrels, and most of the time those bastards are singing songs in order to please the nobles, so they'll toss them a coin or two." She lifted her legs around off the bed and placed her feet onto the rushes on the floor.

Robin, in contrast to his wife's movement, lay down and pulled the blanket over himself roughly, almost sending Matilda flying. He turned his back on her.

"So John and I will hunt them down and find out the truth," he said, his voice low, harsh and distant. He blew out the candle that flickered softly on the shelf next to him, sending angry, racing shadows across the still dimly fire-lit room. "Good night."

For a short while Matilda simply sat, deep in thought, before she lay back down and tried to get some sleep. The fire burned itself out and the room around her became dim, but, beside her, a low, contented snoring escaped Robin's lips.

She gritted her teeth and vowed never to speak to him again, as tears spilled from her eyes.

She didn't even know why she was crying.

CHAPTER SEVEN

"You lot ready?" Robin shouted irritably at the sheriff's men who'd accompanied him back to Wakefield and spent an uncomfortable night on the floor of the alehouse while he'd gone home to Matilda.

They looked tired and sore from their night's rest, but even so Robin wished he'd stayed with them instead of with his wife.

"Aye, we're ready, sir," one of the soldiers replied, hauling himself onto his mount's back with a grunt. "Lead the way."

Robin nodded and turned to Little John. "We still agreed Ossete is the best place to start looking for the outlaws?"

The two men had discussed a plan of action when they'd left the sheriff and journeyed home, and it seemed sensible to begin their investigation in the last place the outlaws had been reported.

"As good a place as any," John said. "Although you know as well as I do, they've probably moved their camp since that last report. It was over a week ago after all; they'd have to be mad to hang around there since the girl escaped to tell what they'd done."

"All right then, let's go."

He kicked his heels and led the way east, grim-faced, as John and the rest of the men followed.

They rode in silence for a time, pushing their mounts hard along the road which was well-maintained and allowed them to make good time. As the sun reached its zenith, though, John moved alongside his captain and shouted over the wind rushing past them.

"What's wrong?"

Robin jerked in surprise, not noticing John beside him until the big man spoke, then he turned his attention back to the road.

"Just some things Matilda said last night." He rode on for a while and John remained silent.

"We were outlaws ourselves not so long ago," he continued, at last. "Just like these men. Are we going to ride into their camp and cut them down without even hearing their side of the story? What if they're all innocent – or at least good – men fallen on hard times? Just as we were."

They'd slowed their horses' pace to make conversing easier but, even so, the countryside seemed to whip past as they neared the little village of Ossete which was by now visible on the horizon.

"I don't remember ever raping anyone," John said.

"Maybe these men didn't either. Maybe the stories have been exaggerated – just as they were when people told tales about us."

For a while John didn't reply, but they were almost at their destination and he was clearly confused.

"So what are you saying? We just let them go about their business? Why are we even here then?"

"I'm just saying we should give these outlaws time to state their case." He raised himself in his stirrups and turned to look at the soldiers following close behind. "You hear that? No-one looses an arrow until I say so. I want to find out what the leader of these men has to say."

"Assuming we even find them," John growled, not expecting his words to be heard.

"We'll find them," Robin vowed. "I'll make sure of it."

They rode into Ossete, villagers scattering at their approach as they spotted the blue livery worn by the sheriff's soldiers, although both John and Robin wore their own brown cloaks as they always did.

A visit from Sir Henry de Faucumberg's men could only mean trouble.

Robin dismounted and told his men to wait on the outskirts of the place. So many horses riding through the cramped confines of Ossete wasn't a good idea.

"Come on," he waved to John. "The alehouse will be the best place to start, I'll wager. Men living rough in the forest need arrows and food but the most important thing is their drink."

Both lawmen knew the layout of the village well enough; they'd been there a number of times over the years, both as outlaws and, in more recent months on the sheriff's business. The alehouse was, as its name suggested, no more than a single-storey dwelling, although slightly larger than most of the others in the area.

One old man sat outside on a rickety bench, mug in hand and a contented smile on his face as the warm breeze blew through his thinning grey hair.

Robin looked at John and shrugged. Might as well start their search right here.

"Well met, friend," he smiled down at the seated villager. "Enjoying the sunshine, eh? Can't beat a warm day and a mug of ale."

The elderly man raised his mug and grinned, revealing a mouth completely devoid of teeth. "You got that right, lad," he gurned. "Get yourselves a drink and join me."

Robin shook his head. "We can't stay long, but I'll stand you an ale if you can help us. You heard of the gang of outlaws hiding out around here?"

The man might have been old but his eyes were still bright and clear and he met Robin's gaze with a shake of his head. "Seen them about, aye, but I don't know anything about them."

"Who did you see?" Robin asked. "Can you describe them for us? These men are extremely dangerous – rapists and murderers. Not the type you'd welcome into the village if you knew what they were about."

The man shrugged and took a long pull of his ale. "I care nothing for the business of outlaws. I might have stood up to them when I was younger and had a family but they're all dead now. The world passes me by as I sit here with my drink and that's the way I like it." He looked back up at Robin. "If these men are as dangerous as you say they are, they'd kill me if I told you anything about them. But I don't know anything anyway lads, sorry."

Robin sighed, knowing this was going to be the story they heard from the vast majority of people they questioned here. Without bribing or torturing people there wasn't much he could do to squeeze information from the nervous locals.

Without another word Robin pulled open the door to the alehouse and led John inside, where the landlord looked up and forced a smile onto his face at the sight of his two huge, dangerous-looking customers.

"Ale?" the man asked. "Freshly brewed yesterday."

"Aye," John rumbled. "My throat's as dry as the soles of a Saracen's shoes."

The landlord thought about that for a moment, trying to work out the apparent joke, then, giving up, poured two mugs for them.

"I'll cut straight to the point," Robin said, after he'd taken a drink. "We need to find the outlaws that were last reported around here. You must have seen them. I know how it works since I was a wolf's head myself for long enough; they'll have been in here looking to buy a large quantity of ale."

He watched the landlord for any reaction to his words and, from the man's darting eyes it was obvious the outlaws *had* visited him.

"If you know how it works," the man finally said, softly, "you'll know they threatened to come back and burn my place down if I spoke to the law about them."

Robin nodded. Threats had been a tactic he'd never really had to use as a wolf's head, because he'd joined an established and well-respected – feared – gang. Everyone around the north of the country knew them. But these newcomers had to protect themselves somehow, and violence was their most obvious, and effective, tool.

"Hopefully they won't be around much longer to burn anyone's place down," Robin said. "Can you give us anything? Descriptions? Any idea of where they might be based? Or is there anyone else in the village who might be able to offer us more information? Your headman maybe?"

The landlord shrugged. "I can't tell you anything other than they left the village by the south road, so their camp is probably in that general direction."

"Narrows it down a bit," Robin nodded, ignoring the sarcastic grunt from John who held out his mug to the landlord, hoping for a refill.

"Thanks for your time then." Robin reached out and grabbed the refilled mug before John could take it from the landlord. "I want you with a clear head, in case we do stumble across those outlaws," he smiled, and without another word walked out through the door, back into the blazing sunshine.

"Here, old one."

The man on the bench grinned and took the mug from Robin's hand, nodding his thanks as the two lawmen started off, heading along the road to see the headman.

"Be careful, lads."

They stopped, turning back to look at the elderly villager who was wiping froth from his seamed mouth and chin.

"One of those outlaws is almost as big as you." He gestured with the mug towards John and turned away to stare at the scene in front of him, as children played and women walked past carrying soaking wet clothes they'd been washing in the stream.

A man almost as big as Little John. It had to be the second man who'd escaped from them at Holmfirth; they were on the right track then. Robin waved his thanks for the little crumb of information, and resumed the walk to the headman's house.

The headman proved no more helpful than the landlord, offering provisions for their search but no useful information. Robin couldn't tell if the man was too scared to tell what he knew, or if he really didn't have anything to tell them. Yes, he said, a large force of men had visited their village two or three times recently but they'd behaved themselves and spent money which the locals were happy enough to take. Where their camp might be he had no idea, but they always rode to the south, just as the landlord at the alehouse had attested.

The sun was still high in the sky as they made their way back to their mounts and the rest of the men so Robin decided they might as well head along the main road in the direction of Netherton. Perhaps the outlaws would have left some trace of their presence along the way.

"Or maybe they'll just cut us down as we ride," John groused, his usual good humour sorely tested by their dangerous hunt.

"Maybe," Robin agreed. "But with fourteen well armed and armoured soldiers in our party it'll be a foolhardy outlaw leader that orders an attack on us."

"You would have."

Robin had to smile at that. "Aye, perhaps I would. But I wasn't followed by a rabble, was I? I was blessed with men like you, Will and Stephen to back me up. I'm hoping these outlaws we're after have no such men in their ranks."

John grunted thoughtfully. "Let's hope so." Then, lowering his voice and shaking his big bearded head, "I wish we had Will and the Hospitaller with us now. These lads are all right but I'd be happier with our friends beside us."

Robin shrugged. Will Scarlet was living in Wakefield as a simple farmer with his daughter Beth, while Stephen, the Hospitaller sergeant, had, the last they'd heard, taken a job as a bodyguard to a wealthy merchant in Leeds. Ever since his own Order made him outcast he'd been unable to settle for long and, chances were, he'd moved on from that town already.

They rode in contemplative silence for a time, eyes scanning the foliage that skirted the mostly well-maintained road, thinking back to their adventures as outlaws themselves.

"Maybe we should have brought fewer men with us." John muttered, eyes casting about the dense foliage that fringed the old road. "This group of wolf's heads can't be much more than a dozen men – you really think they'll attack us?"

The question didn't need an answer and Robin remained silent. John was probably right but until they had a better idea of the size and organisation of the outlaw gang he didn't want to take any chances. Aye, just the two of them riding through the forest would probably guarantee the outlaws would show themselves but it could also be suicidal.

He wanted to stop these men but not die in the process.

* * *

"I know those two."

Mark followed Philip's nod, gently shifting a branch to the side to get a better view of the travellers. He shook his head and allowed the thick leaves to hide him again.

"So do I. Robin Hood and John Little."

"That's the bastards that chased us out of Holmfirth," Philip said.

"And now they've come to chase us out of Barnsdale."

"I don't think so. Not this time. Come on, let's get the rest of the men."

It had only been a couple of weeks since Mark and Ivo joined forces with Philip and Eoin, but even in that short space of time they'd managed to recruit more than half-a-dozen other outlaws to their cause. Men that were living in the greenwood around Horbury and shared the same suppliers as Mark heard the call and answered it. Word spread fast when it was known there was a new gang looking for members. Of course, any newcomers had to believe they were joining a group that could make their lot better than it was – make them richer in other words. And Philip's strange charisma, combined with Mark's well-known ferocity, convinced those new recruits.

So far, they'd only robbed a handful of poor, basically defenceless travellers. Now, Philip apparently saw a chance to put their gang members to good use and hurried off back towards their nearby camp-site.

Mark followed as fast as he could without making any noise that would alert the lawmen to their presence. Surely Philip didn't plan on ambushing Robin Hood? Even Philip wasn't that mad.

Was he?

CHAPTER EIGHT

Robin spotted the man in the road ahead before anyone else, and he instinctively pulled his hunting bow from its place on his horse's saddle and took the string from its little pouch.

"Hold," he muttered, bringing his mount to a stop and raising a hand. "There's someone on the road. Might be nothing but we better be prepared." He turned and gestured to Thomas. "You and those three – dismount and flank me and John. Have an arrow nocked." He slipped out of his own saddle, straddling his bow to string it, and John followed his lead.

"The rest of you stay on your horses but keep twenty paces back from us. And draw your swords and shields. Watch the trees as well as the road behind and in front – if the outlaws have an ambuscade prepared they'll hit us from every side."

He turned to John with a small smile. "Ready, big man?"

"Aye, let's go and see what this prick wants."

One of the sheriff's men took their mounts, along with the other archers', and tethered them to trees nearby.

"Glad I wore my helmet and this," Robin said, pulling back his cloak and patting the chain mail he'd donned that morning in place of his usual, battered old gambeson.

John laughed. "That won't stop an arrow if it hits properly. You'd be as well bollock naked."

"Thanks for that insight," Robin growled, raising an eyebrow irritably. "I feel much better about meeting this fellow now."

John's words certainly had an element of truth to them but Robin knew his giant friend had also chosen to wear a coat of mail under his brown tunic that day. They'd need any advantage they could get when it came to facing these outlaws, of that he was certain.

"Christ above, it's him right enough – that bastard from Holmfirth. The one that hanged the priest."

John squinted – his eyesight wasn't as good as his younger leader's – before nodding agreement. "Aye, looks like it. On his own too. I think it's safe to say we're about to be attacked."

Robin was stunned at the outlaw's confidence. Surely he hadn't managed to rally much more than a dozen men, and those surely just the usual untrained rabble that lived rough in the forest. Yet there the man stood, blocking their way, a little smile on his seamed face and again Robin felt a pang of familiarity.

"Are we just going to walk into his trap?" John hissed. "There's probably longbowmen hiding in the trees ready to pick us off."

Robin took in the terrain and mentally kicked himself. The outlaw had chosen his spot well.

Ahead, where the man stood, the road narrowed, and a massive fallen log provided cover should the outlaw find himself attacked by Robin's archers. To the sides the foliage was thick and John was undoubtedly correct in suggesting bowmen were concealed there.

Robin again lifted a hand and brought his party to a halt, wondering how best to proceed. The sensible thing to do would be turn around and avoid the outlaw altogether until they could meet the man in a better position. But Robin didn't feel like running away – he wanted to talk to this man and find out his story, although, knowing it was the murdering scum from Holmfirth told him pretty much everything he needed to know.

Still, he couldn't lead John and the sheriff's men into such an obvious trap.

"Dismount, all of you." He was glad to see the soldiers instantly follow his order. They were a formidable-looking bunch in their armour and blue surcoats, weapons at the ready, and he nodded in satisfaction. "You three," he swept his hand around to encompass the men on the right. "Head into the trees and clear out whoever you find there. Keep your shields up, don't be complacent and stop moving forward when I do." He gestured again, this time to the men on the far left. "You three take the other side and clear that." If there *were* bowmen hidden in the foliage they'd find it much harder hitting Robin's men if they came through the trees rather than out in the open road. "The rest of you, form a line in front of me and John. Hold your shields up, aye, like that. Good."

Only Thomas and his archers were left now and they took up positions flanking Robin and John as the whole party again started forward, towards the solitary outlaw who watched the whole thing with that strange smile on his lips.

"Very impressive." The wolf's head nodded and waved a greeting at Robin. "We meet again. Only this time I have the upper hand."

"Is that right?" Robin replied, listening intently for any signs of conflict in the trees either side of the road. "I don't think so. Your little band of rapists is outnumbered. Who are you?"

The man placed a foot on the fallen log and spread his arms wide. "Depends who you ask. The people of Holmfirth would probably tell you I'm Satan himself, or maybe one of his demons. But most people call me Philip."

Robin nodded grimly. "Well, Philip, we've heard reports of you and your mates raping and murdering travellers. Is that true?"

The outlaw shrugged expansively, his every move apparently calculated to be as infuriating a possible for the lawmen who couldn't believe the man's confidence.

"Bastard reminds me of you," John grunted. "Full of himself."

"He's a fucking arsehole," Thomas broke in. "Why don't we just fill him with iron? Me and the lads could hit him from here, easy."

Robin ignored their comments, the nagging feeling that he knew this man from somewhere else playing on his mind as he wondered what to do next.

"I know who you are," Philip said. "The famous Robin Hood. You're my inspiration." He cackled at that but it was a deeply unpleasant sound; not at all contagious. "I'm going to lead my merry men all around Yorkshire taking what I want and there's not a fucking thing the law – that's you – can do about it. My gang is growing every day and pretty soon I'll have an army."

Robin shook his head and returned Philip's smile. "An army of scum. The dregs of society." The smile fell from his face to be replaced by a furious glare. "You and your gang are *nothing* like me. My men were hard, trained soldiers. Mercenaries who'd fought in the Holy Land. Hospitaller sergeants-at-arms that had fought side-by-side with Templar knights. Warriors! We were able to evade capture because we knew how to hide in the forest but also how to fight better than the men that came after us. You and your rabble are a pathetic collection of criminals, and I'll not rest until every last one of you is swinging from the gallows outside the gates of Nottingham."

Philip simply stared at him, the smile undiminished. Eventually, Robin looked away, breaking the man's gaze and cursing himself for it, but it seemed like the crazed outlaw was in some trance.

"Damn it, I'm sure I know him from somewhere," he muttered to John, who nodded slowly.

"Aye, I get the same feeling." He stared at the wolf's head for a moment then shrugged. "Kind of looks like Matt Groves doesn't he?"

A chill flowed through Robin as he realised John was right. The thinning dirty-blonde hair, the eyes, the timbre of his voice...He thought back, searching his memory for times he'd actually shared a conversation with Groves, but the two men had never got on. After leaving their gang Matt had killed Robin's childhood friend Much and then become Sir Guy of Gisbourne's lieutenant. He'd finally murdered their minstrel friend Allan-a-Dale before being captured by the sheriff.

It had been a satisfying day when Robin watched the bastard hang.

"Matt had a brother," John continued, oblivious to his friend's musings. "I remember him telling a tale about his childhood once. His da beat them bloody one day and his big brother fought back then disappeared or something. I don't remember the whole story – Tuck would know better than me – but maybe that's him."

"Philip," Robin shouted. "You have a brother? Matt?"

For the first time the outlaw's smile faded and his face became hard, but only for a moment before he regained control and the smirk returned. "I don't think so," he replied. "Why d'you ask?"

"Matt Groves was a member of my gang."

Philip's expression was frozen, immobile.

"He was a sour-faced prick." Little John growled and was rewarded by a momentary scowl from the outlaw leader.

"Aye, he was a prick alright," Robin agreed with a grim nod. "Until I killed him. He died, shitting and pissing in his breeches on the gallows, as I stood and watched with a smile on my face."

There was almost-complete silence for a short while, as everyone held their breath waiting to see what would happen next.

"You talk of warriors," Philip shouted, eventually, as if the last few moments of conversation had never happened. "Is that what you've got with you today? I don't think so." He made a gesture and from the trees on each side of the road came the unmistakable snap of longbows being released, followed by thuds and screams and howls of pain.

"Kill him!" Robin brought his own bow up and loosed his arrow at the outlaw leader. John and the others beside him also let fly but Philip had already ducked beneath the great fallen tree trunk and was gone.

"What now?" Thomas shouted, as the sounds of men fighting amongst the trees fell away and was replaced by an eerie, foreboding silence.

"Fall back," Robin grunted, watching the foliage warily. "Get back to our horses."

"What about the rest of the men?" Thomas demanded, shooting an arrow blindly into the trees where Philip had disappeared and pulling another from his belt, ready to loose again.

"If they manage to defeat the outlaws they'll show themselves and all will be well. But if they've been beaten...I don't want to be standing here in the open, do you?"

Thomas shook his head as they retreated, obviously torn at the thought of leaving his companions behind in the forest. "Shouldn't we try and help them?"

"If we go into those trees we're dead men," John roared. "Now shut the fuck up and fall back like you've been ordered!"

They had just reached their tethered mounts, who watched their return skittishly, spooked by the sounds of dying and stench of sweat and fear that came from their riders, when the cry came from the foliage to their left.

"Loose!"

"Shields up!" Robin cried, dropping his longbow on the ground and wrenching the heater shield from his mount's saddle, raising it over his head and trying to make his great muscular body as small as possible.

Arrows hammered into their shields and the ground around them, some striking the horses, some striking men. Screams of pain and fear filled the air, equine and human, Robin couldn't tell which was more horrific.

"Retreat! Fall back into the trees!"

The remaining men untied the surviving horses and hurriedly led them into the trees. Robin and Thomas helped a soldier whose foot had been pinned to the forest floor by a broadhead, pulling the arrow free from the earth and lifting him bodily into the foliage, whimpering in agony. John helped another injured man to the relative safety of the trees just as another volley of arrows filled the air.

Again, the lawmen raised their shields desperately, hopefully, over their heads but this time they had the forest around them and most of the missiles thudded into the bark of the beech and oak trees that ringed them. Another two horses, still in the open road, were hit, and their pitiful screams worked on the soldiers' nerves like a blunt knife sawing at a piece of gristle.

"We can't stay here like this," John gasped, his eyes wide. "Waiting to be skewered. We should attack."

Robin nodded agreement and opened his mouth to give the order but, before he could, Philip's voice – high-pitched and near-hysterical – came to them.

"You'll regret crossing me, Hood. Matt was my little brother and I *will* avenge him! You and your friends – all of them – will pay. I swear it! Already men flock to our banner. Men that hate you! Isn't that right Martin?"

"Aye."

From the trees to the right a shout rang out and Robin shared a look with John, both men recognising the evicted landlord's voice instantly.

"You took my livelihood and sentenced my wife to death, Hood, you bastard. I'll see you suffer for it though – our gang grows by the day!"

"These men aren't like you, Martin," Robin returned, shaking his head sadly as he looked uselessly into the thick trees. "They're rapists, murderers...Men with no honour who'll stab you in the back as soon as look at you. Give it up now, all of you, or I swear, everyone of you will die: By the sword; with an arrow in you; or by hanging in front of a baying mob that laughs as you shit your fucking breeches!"

His voice had risen in power and fury as he went on but the pronouncement was met with silence.

For a long time, there wasn't a sound other than the occasional whimper of pain from an injured man or horse – it was as if even the forest animals and insects held their breath and waited to see what would happen next.

"I think they've gone." Thomas mumbled. "We should get the fuck away from here quick in case they come back to finish us."

"What about the men that went into the trees?" someone asked.

"They're dead," Robin sighed. "We can't go looking for them, it'd be suicide with our depleted numbers. We have to move."

They hurriedly helped the injured men to mount while Thomas, a man with great experience of horses, put the injured animals out of their misery. It seemed to take an age before they were finally ready but, at last, the surviving members of the sheriff's party – eight men, including Robin and John – kicked their heels into their mounts and galloped back to the safety of Ossete.

CHAPTER NINE

"Oh, Christ above." Sir Henry de Faucumberg groaned and hid his face in his hands as Robin and Little John watched him, embarrassed. "You lost all those men to a bunch of outlaws?" He groaned once more. "It's happening again." He glared at Robin who met his eyes but felt the sheriff's anguish and looked away, abashed. "Another bunch of maniacs running riot in my forest and, apparently, there's little I can do about it."

He had half stood up when Robin told him of their losses but now he slumped back into his chair and laid his hands on the table. He stared at nothing for a while, apparently marshalling his thoughts, then, at last, straightened and spread his hands wide, palms up, almost begging.

"What in God's name are we going to do about these bastards?"

As they journeyed back to Nottingham with the remainder of their force Robin and John had discussed this problem. Clearly the sheriff's men weren't up to the job of hunting down such a ruthless, and ever-growing, gang of outlaws. Maybe, given time to train, time to learn the ways of the forest, the guardsmen would be adequate, but they didn't have time. The longer this went on the bigger Philip's group would get and, as their numbers swelled, so would their confidence. And their brutality.

Robin also had other things on his mind: they'd taken a detour to Wakefield on the way here and, when he'd gone home to gather fresh clothing and supplies, he'd discovered his wife and son were gone. Matilda had left and taken Arthur with her, to live with her parents, Henry and Mary, at the fletcher's workshop. She'd finally suffered enough.

He hadn't been in the mood for another argument and, deep down, he was hurt and even frightened by Matilda's actions, so he'd gathered John and the men and hurried to Nottingham without even visiting the fletcher's.

Robin cleared his throat, now, not at all sure how Sir Henry would view the plan he and John had devised on the road south.

"We would like your permission to recruit some of our old friends."

The sheriff looked at them thoughtfully. "What's wrong with my men?"

"Nothing," John said quickly, glancing at his young leader, who nodded agreement, not wanting to cause any offence by casting aspersions on Sir Henry's soldiers.

"They're good lads. Hardy fighters."

"But?"

"They haven't a damn clue how to move silently in the forest." Robin stated, bluntly. "They don't understand how to read the signs in the foliage when a man's hidden there. Or to pick up on the little changes in the atmosphere when danger approaches through the undergrowth."

"They're city boys," John finished. "No offence to them, but they don't have the experience we need to catch this lot."

"So take the foresters instead of my own guards."

Robin shook his head while John snorted, trying to stifle a laugh.

"The foresters have more wood craft, aye, but they don't have the fighting skills we need. These outlaws are ruthless, as we've already seen. And the man leading them is, in my opinion, a lunatic. Trust me," he leaned down and looked at the sheriff steadily. "We need men that know the forest and can also fight like Templars."

"Our friends," John nodded.

"I'm sure they'll do it for a modest wage," Robin finished and the sheriff looked at him thoughtfully for a few moments.

"Fine, you've convinced me," de Faucumberg eventually sighed. "But even if you can persuade them to join you in this, there won't be enough of you will there?"

"No, but we can make up the numbers from your garrison. We'll pick out the best of your men – the ones that grew up in the villages hereabouts rather than within Nottingham's walls. With the likes of Will Scarlet and the Hospitaller, Stephen, we'll have enough to stop the outlaws before they can grow too powerful to contain."

De Faucumberg shuddered at the thought. "Pray to God you're right," he grunted. "For the king won't be best pleased to hear about another band of cut-throats roaming the greenwood. This could spell the end for me as sheriff. And," he pointed at them in turn, "that means the end of your employment too."

Robin doubted that prospect was particularly worrying for Little John; he wasn't even sure how he felt about it himself but...whatever happened, he knew they must stop Philip and his men.

The sheriff stood up and pulled the laces of his tunic in around his neck as though he was cold despite the summer sun streaming in through the window.

"I have other business to attend to today," he told them. "Take yourselves off to the barracks and choose more men. Take twenty. Along with your friends that should be enough, no?"

Robin looked at John, who shrugged. "Aye, that'll do, although we won't take them with us just now, they'd just get in the way. We still have to find the outlaws' camp first. Once we do, and are in a position to make an assault on it – I'll send word for your soldiers to join us. All right, my lord?"

"Good enough. Keep me informed. We must not let this get out of hand. Even if I have to" – he shook his head with a sigh – "petition King Edward for more men. That would be better than the outlaws growing to an unstoppable size. And that's possible," he warned. "We must stop this *now*."

The former wolf's heads bowed as the sheriff showed them out into the corridor, promising to let him know how things progressed in their hunt, then they headed towards the barracks which was located near the centre of the western wall.

"He's not a bad sort, is he?" John asked, quietly, the stone walls and high ceilings of the castle interior making him feel almost as if he was in a church.

"No," Robin replied. "He's as honourable a man as any, as I've come to learn over the past couple of years. But he'll do whatever it takes to win, in the end. He was an outlaw himself once, after all."

John stopped in his tracks, the clatter of his weapons echoing along the stone hallway. "Eh?"

"Aye, he was a wolf's head too, he told me the story a few days ago, didn't I tell you? No? Listen then, I'll tell you as we walk."

* * *

Henry de Faucumberg was born in Sheffield, earlier than the midwife had expected and, as a result, was a tiny babe. His loving parents had prayed to God that their second son – they'd already been favoured with a beautiful toddler, John, two years earlier – would survive.

God apparently heard their prayers, as little Henry was blessed with a hearty appetite; his mother's milk and, later, the fine meat, fish and vegetables that the de Faucumbergs' were able to afford, had seen him grow into a sturdy child.

He and his older brother were full of mischief, enjoying practical jokes which were often dangerous, like the time they balanced a metal bucket half-filled with iron nails on top of a door. Their French tutor, Jacques, had been knocked out cold when he'd sprung the trap and the heavy container with its sharp contents landed on the crown of his bald head.

Their father, Richard, had punished them with a severe beating for that trick, but they'd laughed about the joke for years afterwards, counting their thrashings worth it.

In general though, Henry, was a smart, intelligent boy who behaved himself and enjoyed learning about the world around him. John, on the other hand, only seemed to become more mischievous and wild as he grew into adolescence, until one afternoon he'd 'borrowed' a horse from one of their neighbour's stables and been thrown from the saddle, splitting his forehead open on a rock as he landed.

The lad had never been the same after the accident. Henry tried his best to remain close to his older brother but eventually grew frustrated at the change in John who seemed to have turned back into a four-year-old again, even if he had the body of someone ten years older.

Henry's mother, Diana, spent most of her time with John after the accident but his father, realising his first-born would never be the powerful magnate he'd always hoped, turned his full attention on young Henry.

While his brother was allowed to play with the old toys of their childhood, Henry was forced to study languages, history and philosophy, along with martial arts like sword-fighting although he was never as good at the physical side, excelling instead at his book learning, which he mostly enjoyed.

"When I was fifteen," he'd said to Robin, as the pair sat with drinks in the sheriff's study one evening after the bailiff had completed another job, "my father found me a position as steward to a hugely wealthy old merchant. The man was an importer of fancy goods from all around the world and I began to truly learn my trade: how to keep accounts, skimming just enough so the king's tax collector wouldn't notice; how to organise a workforce; how to foresee and prepare for problems in advance. In short, I learned how to be a successful businessman."

De Faucumberg shook his head, a small nostalgic smile on his lips. "That merchant made me work for my pay but those were good times. I owe much to that man, even if I did curse him as a slave-driver at the time."

His face fell and he raised his goblet to his lips, staring out the glazed window at the gently swaying trees outside.

For a long time he said nothing and Robin cleared his throat, breaking the man's reverie. "Then you became sheriff?"

"Oh, goodness me, no," de Faucumberg shook his head, replacing the goblet on the table and leaning back in his chair almost defensively. "Not for a long time after that. I was arrested first –"

Robin almost choked on his wine. "Arrested? You?"

"Indeed," the sheriff affirmed. "I too was a wolf's head for a time." He smiled again, but sadly this time. "As I say, my employer was a very hard task-master, pushing me mercilessly to earn ever more money for his coffers. It got too much one day and, when my shift was finished, I followed some of the labourers to a nearby tavern on the way home. They liked me well enough, as I was always fair with them and even managed to pay them a bonus once, without the old man knowing, so they were happy enough to invite me into their company."

"Were you a drinker?" Robin wondered. The sheriff often seemed to have a cup of wine in his hand since Robin had been in his employ, but he found it hard to imagine a teenage de Faucumberg joining a group of low-class labourers in some seedy tavern for a night's debauchery.

"Oh no. I'd been drunk once before that but the experience was so unpleasant that I'd decided never to make a habit of it. But that day, well, I was exhausted and I felt like my head would explode with one of the contracts my employer was asking me to negotiate with a Spanish fellow. Looking back on it now I realise the old man was taking advantage of me – I was much too young and inexperienced to have that sort of weight on my shoulders. But the old bastard was shrewd; getting an apprentice like me to run so much of his business was cheaper than hiring someone else."

He waved a hand good-naturedly. "I'm glad for it now anyway – it was a truly valuable period in my life but...well, it didn't feel like it that particular day. So I went to the tavern and, in my youthful bravado, tried to match the labourers drink-for-drink."

Robin grinned. "Ouch."

"Quite," de Faucumberg grunted. "By the time I staggered out the door I could barely remember my own name. It was a longer walk home than it was back to the merchant's premises so I, foolishly, decided to return to the shop. It was a cold night and, even in my inebriated state, I knew I'd want a fire to heat my office, where I planned to sleep on the floor. I also knew there was precious little fuel left for the hearth so...I decided to just take some from a store beside a house I was passing."

He shrugged. "I would have paid for the wood but...it didn't seem like a good idea to go knocking on the householder's door at that time of the night, pissed out of my mind, offering to buy some fuel. So I just grabbed some logs and made off along the street, giggling like a mischievous child no doubt. Unfortunately for me," he heaved a gusty sigh and met Robin's eyes, "I was spotted and, in the morning the bailiff came and arrested me."

Robin shook his head in disbelief; he'd never suspected this side of the sheriff's past. Still, he thought, sipping his drink, a skinful of wine could make *any* man act like an arsehole. He'd learned that more times than he could count while living as an outlaw with his friends in the greenwood.

"What happened to you then?"

"They fined me," de Faucumberg replied. "Not a lot. I didn't mind losing the money at all. But my employer saw the whole thing as a scandal – sent me packing, back to my father who wasn't too pleased I can tell you."

"At least you didn't end up in jail, or in the forest," Robin muttered. "As a peasant, with no way of paying the fine, would have."

The sheriff nodded agreement. "You're right of course. That's one reason why I try to treat people of all classes the same."

That was mostly true, Robin conceded. De Faucumberg was as fair a nobleman as he'd ever come across which was why he accepted a place in the sheriff's service when he and his men were pardoned.

"How the hell did you end up in such a high office then, with that crime on your record?"

"Money," the sheriff said, simply. "My father knew I'd been good at running the merchant's business empire so he took me on himself. I continued to learn the ways of business – of politics if you like – and I also began to meet powerful, important people. I built up a network of contacts – of noblemen who liked and trusted me, who valued my judgement on matters of importance. That all came in very useful but, ultimately, as I say, it was money that greased the wheels."

He stood, stretching his arms above his head and rolling his head slowly from side to side, grunting as he did so. "Been sitting too long," he murmured to himself, then continued, louder again. "When my parents died their estate should have passed to the eldest son: my brother, John. But my father had changed his will and, apart from some monies set aside for John's care, everything came to me."

He smirked. "Strangely enough, once I was a wealthy man in my own right, lots of those powerful men I'd become acquainted with wanted to ingratiate themselves with me. My star was in the ascendancy. Word reached the king of my astute business mind and he offered me the position as Sheriff of Yorkshire which I gladly accepted."

Robin stood himself and joined de Faucumberg at the window. "And you proved yourself capable so he gave you Nottingham too."

"Yes. I'm one of only two men to have ever been sheriff of both counties you know." His eyes sparkled with pride and Robin smiled, thinking again how ridiculous this whole situation would have seemed to him four or five years earlier when he was an outlaw.

Now he actually thought of Sir Henry as a friend.

"I'd started to fear Edward might have stripped me of my position here after the Despenser's rebellion," the sheriff said, his eyes following a tabby cat as it stalked across the grass beneath the window. "When you and your bloody friends were causing so much trouble and that mad bastard Sir Guy of Gisbourne couldn't catch you."

"It turned out well enough for us all in the end," Robin shrugged.

"Not for Gisbourne it didn't," the sheriff grunted with a snort of laughter, hand reaching up subconsciously to touch the faded scar beneath his tunic. The bounty hunter had, in a fit of insanity brought on by his total failure to bring Robin and his friends to justice, tried to kill de Faucumberg. He would have succeeded too, if Robin, aided by Matilda and his sister Marjorie, hadn't stopped him.

The two men stood in companionable silence for a time, sipping their drinks, lost in their own memories.

Eventually the sheriff belched and wiped his mouth with a hand. "We've both seen what it's like on the other side of the law. We can sympathise with how hard the system can be. But I can't allow this new outlaw gang to become as powerful as yours did, Robert."

There was steel in his voice and Robin took his meaning. It was up to him to stop Philip and his men, and he had to do it fast.

Before Barnsdale became a bloodbath.

CHAPTER TEN

Eoin bent his great frame and looked at Philip sympathetically. "You all right?" His friend had been in a strange, silent mood for days; ever since they'd attacked Robin Hood and his soldiers now that he came to think of it.

It wasn't that unusual for Philip to withdraw into himself – it happened every so often and Eoin had grown used to it. But normally he'd come out of it after a few hours, so this time was different and the big outlaw was genuinely worried for his leader's welfare.

"Aye." The word was ground out between clenched teeth, but Eoin heaved a sigh of relief to finally hear his friend's voice.

The rest of the outlaws – already wary of their new leader – had given him a wide berth once he'd retreated into his fugue state and Eoin didn't blame them. Clearly something was gnawing at the man's mind and Eoin knew better than anyone how that could lead to trouble. Brutal, bloody trouble, for anyone that annoyed Philip.

Eoin wasn't afraid of his friend though – he was much bigger and stronger than him after all. Aye, Philip was vicious and would stick a dagger in a man's back as soon as his guts but Eoin knew his mate wouldn't do that to him. They'd been through too much; they respected and even liked one another.

So while Philip was brooding in their camp Eoin brought him food and drink and even spoke to him, not the least bit put off when his conversational attempts met with blank silence.

He smiled now, happy that his perseverance had paid off.

"I'm all right. But that bastard Hood won't be. Did you hear what he said?"

Eoin nodded and sighed softly although he knew better than to lay a sympathetic hand on his friend's shoulder as he instinctively wanted to do. "I did. I'm sorry."

"He killed my brother. D'you know when I last saw Matt?" He stopped, counting on his fingers before giving up. "I haven't seen him since I was just grown into a man. My da tried to beat me but I was too fast for him and I ended up kicking the shit out of him, while Matt watched and cried. He was only a little boy. But I had to leave – I couldn't stay there after that and I hated my da anyway." He slammed his clenched fist onto the ground before drawing his knees up against his chest again, the anger apparently gone. "I always planned on going back to take care of Matt – make sure my da didn't hurt him or anything but...I never got around to it for years. When I eventually did go back our house had a new family living in it. They didn't know anything about Matt or my da."

Tears rolled down his face and Eoin, without thinking, edged back a pace. This was a side of his friend that he'd never seen before.

"Years went past and word eventually reached me that my brother was part of an outlaw gang in Barnsdale Forest. I really thought we'd finally meet again when you and I turned up here."

The tears in his eyes had dried by now, to be replaced by a fire that made Eoin even more nervous.

"Those arseholes killed Matt. Robin Hood, Little John...All of them." He sat for a moment longer then pushed himself to his feet, hand resting on the pommel of his longsword. "Well my brother will have his revenge – we're going to make his killers pay."

"What about the rest of our men?" Eoin asked, waving a huge hand to encompass their camp and the more than a dozen outlaws gathered there.

Philip's smile returned to his face at last. "They'll help. No-one will be able to stop us."

* * *

Will Scaflock was busy. He was busy and he was angry.

"Fucking storm," he growled to himself as he lifted a plank of wood and battered a nail into it, the muscles on his big arms cording, as he fixed it to the new fence post he'd been forced to sink following the previous night's gale force winds.

It was a mild morning, with a few grey clouds that covered the sun every so often, but the fence that penned his few sheep in was blown over and he was out repairing it now. He furiously hammered in the iron nails as if he they'd kicked him in the bollocks. He had better things to be doing that morning than mending a fence he'd put up not six months earlier.

"Bastard storm," he reiterated, thumping home the final nail and stepping back to check his work was sound. The fence wasn't the neatest, with posts at different heights and spars sloping this way and that, but it would hold a few sheep. Until the next storm at least, he thought ruefully.

"You Will Scarlet?"

He'd been aware of the three men approaching for a while. They made no attempt to hide in the foliage or mask their heavy footfalls, and their confident bearing – coupled with the swords each one carried at their side – alerted Will to the possibility that they weren't here simply to ask for directions to the nearest alehouse. He was glad his thirteen year-old daughter, Beth, was away that morning collecting supplies from Wakefield and visiting her friends there.

"No."

His reply threw the man, who was tall but incredibly thin. He glanced sideways at his two companions.

"You're not Will Scarlet?"

Will turned his back and walked along his mended fence towards them, shaking the posts to make sure they were sturdy enough.

"No."

The questioner looked confused, but one of his companions, an older fellow – probably in his mid-fifties Will guessed, but still brawny looking – drew his sword and pointed it at him.

"Aye you are. The villagers told us where to find you, and there can't be anyone else around here that fits your description."

Will turned and smiled sardonically at the man. "What description would that be?"

"Average height, stocky build, green eyes and an angry, *ugly* fucking face."

Will stepped forward, close to the older fellow, still smiling, the weight of the hammer reassuring in his hand which had started to sweat as the excitement of impending battle began to course through his veins.

"Do I look angry to you?" he whispered.

"You're going to look dead in a bit," the first, tall, newcomer muttered, drawing his own sword and moving in as the third man followed his lead.

Will was almost forty years old now, and his body was beginning to show it. Gone was the rock-hard, flat stomach and slim waist he'd had when he was a wolf's head, to be replaced by a burgeoning beer-belly and a slightly receding hairline. But, underneath the new layer of fat, his muscles were still hard – kept in shape by the work he did on his farm, like mending fences and shearing sheep, which was always a horrendous task for him, although probably insanely comical for anyone watching his clumsy efforts.

Before the older man knew what was happening, Will brought the head of his hammer straight up and into his jaw. The whole force of his brawny arm was behind the strike and Will was pleased to hear the crack of bone breaking as the grey-haired man's jaw snapped and he fell back onto the ground, making a pitiful whining noise and glaring up at the former outlaw from pain-filled eyes.

"My name," Will growled, turning to face the two remaining men, "is Will *Scaflock*."

He launched himself at the tall, thin man who'd drawn back his sword and swung it now in a low arc, but Will was too fast. He barrelled into his opponent, shoulder hitting him in the chest and sending the man flying back onto his back on the grass.

Will ducked, just in time as the final assailant's sword swung around, through the space his head had just occupied, then he battered the head of the hammer into the side of the man's knee.

He was rewarded with a scream and, again, the crunch of bone shattering. Just to make sure, Scaflock jumped across the grass like a spider and brought his hammer down once more, this time right in the middle of the fallen man's forehead.

The screaming stopped instantly and Will stood up.

The smile was gone from his face.

"*Now* I'm angry," he said, glaring at the two still-conscious but downed attackers.

The men glanced at each other, and then the taller one shouted, "Get him!"

Before he could even stand up Will's hammer came down on the top of his head, so hard it sent pain lancing through Scaflock's arm, but he couldn't waste time rubbing the jarred limb, as the final, older assailant lunged, broken jaw making his mouth hang open obscenely, but the edge of his sword sliced across Will's side, slicing his tunic and drawing a line of blood on his white flesh.

Dropping flat onto the grass, Will kicked out as hard as he could, his foot dragging the grey-haired man's legs out from beneath him and, as he fell with a tortured cry, Scaflock dropped his hammer and threw himself forward, hands grasping the man's throat and squeezing, squeezing, until the would-be assassin passed out.

Will collapsed onto the wet grass, breathing heavily, his arms aching and the blood that oozed from the wound in his side now beginning to congeal uncomfortably on the top of his breeches.

Still, it was over and he'd won.

"Oh, fuck off." He pushed himself onto his elbows as the sound of horses approaching came to him, the thought of having to fight again almost too much to take and he smiled, in spite of the situation, knowing he'd have enjoyed this much more ten years ago.

Roaring in determination he lunged across the ground and picked up his dropped hammer, then pushed himself back to a standing position to face the riders who he knew he'd never be able to fight off. Not with just a hammer and not in the state he was in.

But he'd have a fucking good go.

"Looks like we're just in time."

"Aye, and the outlaws picked the wrong man to target first."

Will stared, trying to focus on the riders but he must have lost more blood than he realised as his head swam and he found it impossible to fix his gaze on the mounted men. Still, he raised the hammer, ready to go out fighting.

Then, at last, his brain caught up and, as he recognised the voices he sagged, sobbing in glad relief.

It was his old friends, Robin Hood and Little John.

"You're a bit late," he growled, then collapsed onto the grass.

CHAPTER ELEVEN

Will's wound was a minor one and John soon had it cleaned and wrapped in a fresh piece of linen he'd found in his friend's nearby cottage. He suspected Will's collapse was due to exhaustion rather than blood loss – the ex-mercenary was so driven, so determined to make a go of his farm, that he put every drop of effort he could into it. The excitement of the fight had been too much John thought.

Certainly, there wasn't a great deal of blood on the torn tunic.

But he knew it would do no good to tell his old companion he'd collapsed from simple tiredness, so when Will came to and complained about his wound the giant lawman grunted agreement and tried to sound sympathetic.

While John tended to their downed friend, Robin knelt by the surviving assassin whose lower face had already started to swell alarmingly.

"Wake up. Wake up you arsehole."

Slapping and kicking the unconscious man didn't have much effect but a bucket filled with rainwater soon had him gasping and mewling like a sodden cat.

"Who are you?"

The man grunted an obscenity at Robin and it sounded more terrible thanks to the smashed jaw, but the young lawman was in no mood to waste time.

"I asked who you are," he shouted, slapping the fallen man in the face, and was rewarded with a loud groan of agony. He brought his hand back for another blow but the man, eyes wide in rage and fear, recoiled in the mud and raised his hand.

He grunted his name but Robin couldn't make it out.

"Why are you here, trying to kill my friend?"

Again, the man grunted something and it took a few moments for Robin to make sense of the sounds.

He was a member of Philip's gang. An outlaw. As Robin had known all along, but he needed the confession. As a member of the sheriff's staff, and a lawman, he needed to be able to prove the man's guilt.

He pushed himself up to a standing position as he heard John and Will approach.

"He's one of the outlaws right enough, John. Looks like the bastards failed with their first attack on our old friends, thanks be to the Magdalene. We got here in time."

Will snorted at that, but Robin just grinned.

"What's that? What are you mumbling dickhead?" Little John bent his great frame and glared into the outlaw's eyes as the man tried to say something. "You're not the only ones?"

The words were repeated and, as before, it took Robin a short while to figure out the grunts and make words out of them.

"They're not the only ones sent to kill our old gang," he finally spat, glancing at Will and John worriedly. "Another group of them went after someone else nearby."

The outlaw sagged back, glad he'd manage to impart his final, barbed message. He tried to smile at them but winced in pain as his mouth opened, and, whining pitifully, his head fell onto the grass.

Robin stared at the man, mind whirling.

"What do we do?" John asked, looking to his leader for guidance. The giant was a formidable fighter and a loyal companion but he always bowed to his younger friend when it came to their next move.

Robin nodded towards the downed outlaw who was breathing heavily and making even more noise as the shock wore off and the real agony of his horrendous injury began to take hold.

"You said the rest of your mates had gone after a man."

The outlaw watched Robin but didn't reply.

"Was it a clergyman?"

The injured outlaw's blank look told Robin all he needed to know.

"It's not Tuck they've gone after then." He moved the point of his sword up to the man's eye and rested it on his cheek. "I'm done fucking about with you. Where have they gone?"

"I don't know his name," the outlaw gurned, his voice rising in pitch as he felt the blade press against the soft tissue of his eyeball. "A tanner. In Kirk'ees!"

"Edmond," John and Will said in unison. It had to be.

When Robin's gang were pardoned by the sheriff Edmond had gone back to his home village of Kirklees and used some of his share of their stolen money to rebuild his old tannery. He'd even, despite his strange fish-lipped face and bulky body, found himself a wife and, as far as Robin could tell when he'd last been in the village, the couple were happy enough.

Edmond was a decent fighter who could take care of himself well enough, but he was no mercenary – no professional soldier like Scarlet had been.

"Come on then," Will shouted, striding towards the door of his cottage to collect his weapons and light armour. "Maybe we can still be in time to stop the bastards."

"What about this one," John said to Robin as Will disappeared inside his dwelling. "We can't just leave him here. You want me to tie him up?"

The outlaw glared at them malevolently and tried to spit in Robin's direction but his injury meant the spittle simply trickled down his own chin and he grunted a curse instead.

"Aye, we better do that. Can't just kill him now we're lawmen ourselves. Grab that rope there – we'll leave him here for the headman, Patrick, to deal with."

They finished binding the man's arms and legs together and Robin glared at him, tugging hard on a knot which drew a squeal of agony.

"You and your mad leader should have listened to the songs people sing about me and my friends. No one crosses us. No one."

Will appeared in his doorway then, armed and armoured and already heading for the horse that stood, watching them balefully from the small stable attached to the house.

"Why didn't you just kill the bastard?" Scarlet wondered.

"I'm a bailiff now," Robin replied, climbing into his saddle with a last backwards glance at the bloodied and bound prisoner. "I have to follow the law."

Will smirked and shook his head. "You've gone soft you mean."

Robin shrugged and smiled.

"We'll see. To Kirklees!"

* * *

Matilda had been happy when Robin announced his plan to pay for an extension to St Mary's to her. They weren't short of money – far from it, actually – thanks to the riches he and his friends had stolen as outlaws. Much of those spoils originally belonged to wealthy clergymen like Abott Ness and Prior de Monte Martini, so it only seemed fair for the bailiff to spend some of it on good works for the church.

There was no harm in supporting the clergy whenever possible, Matilda believed – surely it could only be good for one's soul?

The young woman regularly visited the newly built section of the church to pray. Mostly for one thing.

Tonight was no different, as, once Arthur had fallen asleep she'd asked her parents if they would keep an eye on their grandson for a short while. They were always happy to oblige and now Matilda knelt in the gloom of St Mary's, the only light a few candles and the last vestiges of sunset. It was a dry evening and the cool interior of the church helped her relax so she soon lost herself in her prayers.

"Lord," she mouthed, her head bowed. "I know You have reasons for everything You do and I'm grateful for our beautiful son, but why have You never granted me a second child? A brother or sister for Arthur to play with. So many of the other women have had four, five, six children, yet Robin and I just the one."

She sighed softly, thinking of those other mothers, knowing that, although they may have given birth to lots of children, many of them didn't survive past the first year. Like poor Agnes Reeve, who'd had three babies before she was eighteen, all of which had died within a week of their births, leaving the girl utterly bereft, a sad shell of her former self.

At least Matilda hadn't suffered such agony but she still felt as if something was wrong with her since she'd never even been able to conceive again after Arthur was born. Had she done something to make God angry with her? She couldn't think of any reason He might have to punish her in such a way but what other explanation could there be?

Her eyes became wet as she thought of Robin, who'd never berated her for not bearing him more children. He'd never blamed her for it – quite the opposite in fact, as he regularly thanked her for giving him Arthur, who he doted on.

And yet she'd made his life miserable for months now, because of the way she felt inside herself. Well, perhaps not entirely that – her husband was far from perfect but…

The tears spilled down her face but she wiped them hurriedly away and drew herself up, refusing to give into the gloom. She knew from experience that it did no good and would only make her feel even worse.

"Please, God," she closed her eyes and pictured her blonde-haired smiling son and felt her spirits rise again. "Grant us another child."

She remained kneeling for a few moments longer, reciting the *Pater Noster* then got to her feet, wiped away the last of her tears so her parents wouldn't know she'd been weeping, then walked slowly back to their house, wishing Robin might be there and everything between them back to normal.

How could she ever become pregnant, after all, if her husband was never there to share her bed?

* * *

The smoke – black, greasy smoke, of things other than wood burning – told them they were probably too late.

They'd pushed their horses hard and made the journey to Kirklees by early afternoon, even with a hasty stop in Wakefield to make sure Beth didn't return to the farm before Patrick Prudhomme could send men to clear the two corpses and arrest the surviving, bound outlaw.

Now, they approached Kirklees from the east, so had to pass through the main village to reach the tannery, yet the locals didn't seem too concerned about the fire. Edmond, although he'd been a decent companion Robin thought, had never been popular in his home town. Growing up he'd been bullied, as had his brother, simply because they were a little bit different to everyone else, in looks and in how they'd been brought up.

It surprised Robin when he found out Edmond had gone back there after their pardon, but perhaps the tanner just couldn't see anywhere else as home.

Still, the locals' inherent dislike and mistrust of him – made even worse when he'd almost killed the inn-keeper in a fight – clearly hadn't lessened in the years since he'd returned from life as an outlaw. If anyone else's property had been on fire the whole place would be rushing to fetch buckets of water.

But the tannery, with its stinking vats of urine, was located a short distance away from the main body of the village and there was little chance of the fire spreading before it burned itself out.

"Are you people blind?" Robin roared as they whipped along the main street. "The tannery is burning – fetch water and help in the name of God!"

The people gave him sullen looks but they knew who he was and they respected – even feared –

him. They moved to gather buckets but without any urgency. As far as they were concerned, Robin knew, the village would be better off without the stench of piss and the brooding, fish-lipped tanner.

"Maybe we should go in carefully," John shouted to his companions. "In case the outlaws are still there."

Robin thought about it but, before he could give the order one way or the other, Scarlet shouted, "I hope the bastards *are* still there!"

With a war-cry he pulled his sword free from its simple scabbard as his horse led the way to the tannery.

There seemed to be no-one around; no-one was outside the buildings at least, so Will slid from his mount and waited the few moments it took the others to catch up.

"Stay alert," Robin growled as he and John slipped from their saddles and the three of them headed towards the door of the workshop.

The roof at the rear of the building collapsed suddenly and a welter of flame and sparks and blackened embers roared up into the air, halting Robin in his tracks. He turned, eyes scouring the area.

"There's not going to be anyone in there," he said. "No-one still alive anyway – the place is about to cave in on itself." He nodded towards the house which was also on fire, but it hadn't quite taken hold yet. "You two check the house. The outlaws have gone, I think we can be sure of that, but Edmond or his wife might be in there."

John and Will moved unquestioningly over to the house, the bearded giant battering his shoulder against the door which came right off its hinges as he stumbled inside, Scarlet close at his heels as they disappeared from view.

Taking a deep breath, Robin pulled his tunic up, then he kicked open the workshop door, peering inside through the flames and the smoke which was almost unbearable already.

Edmond lay on the floor.

"Bastards. Bastards!"

Robin reeled back, away from the awful, searing heat and bent his head. They hadn't just killed the tanner, they'd tortured him too. Why, the lawman couldn't say; maybe just because Philip Groves was even more sadistic and hateful than his brother. The blood caking Edmond's battered face, and the stumps where his fingers used to be told their own story though.

Their old friend had not died well. Again, Robin vowed to bring Groves and his men to justice. Brutal, terrible justice.

The sounds of coughing came from the house and he turned to watch Will stumbling out of the house, followed by John who carried a female figure in his great arms.

They all moved away from the burning tannery, back, far enough that the heat and smoke didn't reach them. At last some of the villagers appeared with buckets filled with water and fought to control the blaze without much success.

Not that it mattered much now.

"Edmond?" Will asked, still hacking from the smoke he'd inhaled inside the house. "You find him?"

"He's dead. The scum tortured him then left his body to burn." His voice was hard but he had tears of rage and sorrow in his brown eyes. "What about her?"

Little John had placed Edmond's wife on the grass and he looked up sadly. The woman was breathing but for how long…?

Robin came over and knelt beside her. She was a small thing although she seemed to share some of the facial characteristics of Edmond and the lawman felt a lump in his throat at the demise of the perfectly-suited young couple who had been just embarking on their life together.

"You're safe now," he said to her, softly, reassuringly. "We're old friends of your man's."

"You're too late," she mumbled through bruised lips. "Five of them. Their leader raped me then…" she sobbed, "he made his men rape me too. All of them!"

"What the fuck is wrong with this brother of Matt's?" John hissed. "He's a worse enemy than Gisbourne or Adam Gurdon ever were."

The girl spoke again, her words almost too soft for Robin to hear and he bent his ear to her lips, gesturing irritably for John to be silent.

"They made Edmond tell them all the names of his – your – old gang members, and where he thought they lived." She stopped and more tears streaked her soot-blackened face. "He wouldn't tell them but that bastard with the filthy blonde hair started hitting him and cutting him."

With a soft sigh she finished and her whole body went limp as the smoke she'd breathed in finally killed her.

For long moments the three friends remained silent, oblivious to the flames and smoke and shouts of the fire-fighters.

They were all hard men; they'd all seen and done things that would live with them for the rest of their lives but...the violence and sheer wickedness here shocked them. To have such ruthless outlaws operating in their own home county was a sobering, fearful thought.

"What now?"

Robin shook himself from his reverie and shrugged without looking up at John. "We'd better find the rest of our friends before Groves and his men do or," he stared down at Edmond's dead, brutalised wife, "we'll have to deal with more of this."

One of the great vats filled with urine burst as the flames weakened the sides and the resultant flood ran handily downhill across some of the burning buildings. After that it didn't take long for the villagers to get the conflagration under control.

As Robin, John and Will walked back to their horses they discussed where they should head next.

"The nearest person I can think of is Stephen," Robin mused once he'd hauled himself up into the saddle. "He's working as a bodyguard for a merchant in Leeds, I believe, still hoping to be taken back in by the Hospitallers, which isn't likely to happen until the Grand Prior dies. You two make your way there and tell him what's going on. Persuade him to join us. The sheriff will pay a decent wage, don't worry about that." He hadn't even mentioned this to Will until now, just assuming his old lieutenant would return to their gang without any fuss; even if it was on the right side of the law this time.

"Where are you going?" Scarlet asked, accepting his position as one of de Faucumberg's – one of Robin's – men readily enough. He'd missed all this! Mending fences and collecting shit from cattle wasn't much of a life for a man like him.

"I'll head back to Wakefield and get Tuck," Robin replied. "He's likely to be high on Groves's list of targets. We know he doesn't think much of clergymen after all..."

Little John pulled on his reins and turned his horse in the direction of Leeds with a nod. "Matilda?"

"Aye," Robin replied. "I'll make sure she's safe. I'll pay some of the harder local men to guard them." He looked at Will. "I'll make sure Beth stays with them too, have no fears."

Scarlet grunted his thanks then he and John waved a salute and kicked their heels into their mounts' sides, cantering off to find Stephen, while Robin took the eastern road, back home to Wakefield, wondering what in God's name they'd have to do to stop this new outlaw leader and his twisted vengeance.

He shuddered.

It seemed as if Matt Groves was laughing at him from hell itself.

Would Friar Tuck be the next to die at the hands of Matt's insane brother, Philip?

Robin kicked his heels in, hard, and urged his palfrey along the road with little care for his own safety.

Not Tuck.

Please God, not Tuck!

CHAPTER TWELVE

"What now?" Eoin wondered, tearing a chunk of pork from the bone in his hand, the greasy juices spilling down his chin but the expression on his big face was that of a contented child, as the taste filled his mouth.

"Now we rest," Philip replied loudly, so the rest of the men could hear. "And enjoy the fruits of our labours." He raised his own plate of food in one hand, a pot of ale in the other and his followers cheered loudly, grins on their faces. The tannery in Kirklees had boasted a surprisingly well-stocked larder which they'd plundered eagerly.

After they murdered the tanner and raped his wife they ran off and waited a couple of miles to the south-west, to meet up with their three comrades who'd gone to Wakefield to deal with the farmer known as Will Scarlet. When the trio failed to appear the outlaws continued on their way south, across the River Calder and into the thick trees at Brackenhall, a tiny village not far from Huddersfield. They'd set up camp and were now relaxing, their missing companions forgotten already. It was a clear, moonless night, and a multitude of stars gazed back at Philip as he enjoyed his meat and stared into the dark.

"But what about the rest of Robin Hood's friends?" Eoin continued. "Are we not going after them now?"

Philip chewed thoughtfully for a while, gazing into the camp fire which was sending greasy black cooking smoke into the air. They should probably be more careful about giving away their position he mused, then discarded the idea. They were a dozen hard men – killers – and it was dark in Barnsdale. No-one would be sneaking up on them just now, so they could relax, eat and drink and, as he'd said, enjoy themselves.

"We're still going to kill all of Hood's old gang," he nodded, eyeing his plate then selecting a tasty piece which he popped into his mouth with that ever-present smile. "But there's no rush. We've sent a message to him; he'll be shitting his breeches now, wondering who we'll go after next. And, in the meantime, we'll look to recruit more wolf's heads to our cause, until we become truly unstoppable."

"Or too much of a nuisance," Eoin grunted, "and the king sends an army after us."

Philip raised an eyebrow, surprised at his friend's perceptive observation, then shrugged and washed down a piece of gristle with some of his ale. "We won't let it get that far. We'll grow until we're big enough to defend ourselves against the foresters and the sheriff's men, and we'll take whatever we want from the villages hereabouts before moving on to another county and starting all over again. In the meantime," he tossed the last of his meal – mostly bones and fat he'd spat back onto the wooden platter – into the bushes behind him and got to his feet, "we'll pick off Robin Hood's friends one by one."

Mark had been listening to their conversation and he stood up now to follow Philip, who took himself a short way into the trees to empty his bladder. His new leader glanced at him as he undid his breeches and released a warm stream of piss with a sigh of relief.

"All right, Mark?" the outlaw captain smirked. "Did you just follow me into the bushes to see my cock?"

The smaller man's eyes blazed but he held his peace, as Philip knew he would.

"Nah, I needed a piss myself. And I have a suggestion for who we could go after next."

"Really?"

"Aye," Mark replied, pulling up his own breeches and facing his mad leader. "An old friend of mine, name of James. He used to be one of my men. I have a score to settle with the bastard, and you'll be interested to know that he's the reason Hood and his friends are still alive today. He took word that Sir Guy of Gisbourne was about to ambush them and that allowed Hood to turn the tables on the bounty hunter. If it wasn't for James your brother would still be alive and that fat Friar Tuck would be dead. I ordered James to shoot the clergyman and the prick turned on me. He struts around Horbury like he owns the place now, telling anyone that'll listen what a fucking hero he is."

Philip stared at him, for just a moment too long, until he could see Mark's hand nervously reaching down towards the dagger in his belt, then he smiled broadly.

"Horbury, eh? He sounds like the perfect target for us. Good idea. We'll let things die down for a bit then go after this friend of yours."

Philip moved past, heading back to the camp-fire, and wiped his piss-dribbled hands on Mark's arms with a grin that was stark in the flickering light.

He knew the short man with the perfect teeth hated him, and would have liked nothing better than to murder and supplant him, but he also knew Mark feared him and his giant friend Eoin. He'd intimidate the intense little fool and make a mockery of him until he either snapped or, more likely, fell under Philip's sway.

Either way, the outlaw leader knew Mark would have to be dealt with eventually.

Until that day came, though, his brutal nature and skill with a blade would come in handy. Especially when they went after this fellow James.

* * *

When Robin returned to his home village he urged his mount along the main street, oblivious to the angry cries of pedestrians sent spilling sideways as they avoided his charge. At last he came to the church, heaving a sigh of relief when he spotted Tuck outside, comfortably seated on a bench, enjoying a mug of ale and the wonderful orange sunset.

The friar looked up at the thunder of approaching hooves, his hand falling instinctively to his waist, where Robin knew he still carried his trusty club.

"What brings you here?" Tuck asked, bushy eyebrows raised. The two men hadn't spoken since their disagreement weeks ago, although the friar still wondered why his former leader had paid for a drink in the alehouse that last time they'd both been in there.

"Trouble," Robin half-shouted, reining in the horse and sliding almost-expertly to the ground, although his foot slipped just a little as he landed and he cursed inwardly. He'd never be a natural rider, even if he wasn't as bad as Little John.

Tuck pursed his lips and made a "pfft" sound. "When is it ever anything else?" He got to his feet though, ready to face whatever it was that Robin was fleeing. Or chasing.

"Real trouble this time, my friend. Edmond's dead. His wife too."

Tuck's mouth formed a silent, horrified "O", then his eyebrows drew down and he glared at Robin. "Is this your fault?"

"What? No! Well, I suppose, in a way –"

"You and your extortion," Tuck broke in, face red with fury. "I knew it would bring trouble – knew you'd pick on the wrong person to blackmail – but Edmond? What did he have to do with it? Did you get him involved? Or was it him you were trying to fleece?"

Robin shook his head in confusion, lost in the friar's relentless stream of recriminations before he finally understood what was happening.

"No, it's nothing to do with any of that, Tuck. Enough!" He raised his palms and shouted almost directly in his portly friend's face. "Enough. Sit back down and let me explain, for fuck sake."

"Watch your language," Tuck warned. "This is holy ground." But he did sit down, much to Robin's relief.

For long moments they sat in silence, absorbing the terrible fact of their companion's death. Poor Edmond – his life had been a hard one but he'd found a place with Robin's gang. He'd been a valued member of their fellowship and things looked bright when he returned to his tannery and found himself a wife, but fate had never been good to the fish-lipped man and now…

The image of his mutilated corpse, blackened and blistered obscenely, filled Robin's memory and the lawman wondered if he'd ever be able to forget it.

Tears sprang to his eyes and Tuck, finally calming down after the initial shock of the bleak news, laid a hand on his wrist and gripped it tightly, reassuringly.

"Tell me, lad."

"It was Groves." He saw the baffled look on Tuck's face and nodded. "Aye, you heard me right. Matt's come back to haunt us – his brother is leading a new gang of outlaws hiding out in Barnsdale."

The clergyman leaned back on the old bench and let his head sag backwards, stretching the muscles in his neck. His eyes closed, then, finally, he turned his gaze back on Robin. "I remember Matt talking about a brother, but he hadn't seen him since childhood. How in God's name does he come to be around these parts all these years later and what does he have to do with Edmond's death?"

The sun had by now dipped beneath the eastern horizon and without its rays the evening air turned chilly.

"Come inside and tell me," Tuck grunted, standing up and heading for the church door. "I need a drink, and so do you from the looks of it."

Robin smiled gratefully then, spotting a couple of young boys passing the church grounds he whistled and gestured them over. "Take my horse home for me, will you lads? Make sure he's rubbed down and fed, if you can. Here." He tossed them a small coin each, which they took with wide eyes and toothy grins and then headed over to the palfrey, which was grazing on the grass over an ancient grave.

Then he followed the friar inside and told him the whole story.

"What will you do?"

Robin stared into the small fire in the manse's hearth, lips pressed tightly shut, the fingertips on his right hand incessantly rubbing against each other. He'd been asking himself the same question ever since he'd left the blackened tannery but he still wasn't sure of the answer.

He shrugged, almost spilling the watered-down ale he'd asked for. He was too weary to drink much that night, he needed a clear head.

"The sheriff had already given me permission to gather the men together again so the fact this bastard Groves plans on killing us all just means it's even more urgent. I wasn't sure if they'd all want to come back to a life of prowling the forests of Yorkshire but, well, I don't see that there's much of a choice for them now. And that includes you."

Tuck snorted and leaned back, away from him, a look of surprise on his round, jowly face.

"Are you joking? I can't rejoin you."

"Why not? You can still handle yourself. And it's too dangerous to stay here – Groves and his lackeys will come for you soon enough and even you won't be able to withstand their numbers."

The friar shook his tonsured head almost sadly. "I was too old and worn-out to be a member of your gang three years ago – remember, I returned to Lewes Priory for that very reason – and I've been in the wars since then too. I was badly injured that Christmas I spent in Brandesburton, you recall I told you about it?"

Robin grunted; Tuck had regaled him with that tale on at least a dozen occasions when they'd shared a drink in the past couple of years. The churchman had shown him the fleshy pink scars on his side and leg though, and he understood the truth of the situation: approaching his fiftieth year on God's Earth, Friar Tuck's time as a bounty hunter was long past.

Yet he could still be useful, Robin was sure of that…

They finished their drinks and embraced, their shared grief for Edmond and the threat of danger drawing them together again.

"Look, I know you're struggling with things just now. Your work, and family troubles and probably all the bad memories you've gathered over the years are weighing you down too. But you've come through harder times before. Stay true to yourself and remember: *hope*."

Robin nodded and a smile appeared on his tired face. He'd almost forgotten that word.

The two friends said farewell and then the young lawman, feeling six inches taller now, made his way to the fletcher's house. Matilda might not love him any more, but he had to make certain she and Arthur would be safe, whatever happened in the coming weeks.

He had to make sure *everyone* in Wakefield was aware of the situation. They'd need to arrange a local militia, ready to defend the village at a moment's notice should the wolf's heads decide to attack the place everyone knew Robin called home.

At least he had the ideal man to lead that defence. He just hoped the rest of the villagers would be up to the task.

At last, eyes drooping from sheer exhaustion – both mental and physical – he tapped on the fletcher's great, stout door and, smiling gratefully, was welcomed inside by the stern faced Henry.

"It's good to see you," Matilda's father said, his voice, and expression, neutral. "Bit late to be visiting though, isn't it?"

Robin could see his wife sleeping on the old pallet that had been hers as she'd grown up in this house, little Arthur snuggled under the thin blanket beside her, and he felt a pang of loneliness, wishing he was lying there next to them.

"It's a long story, Henry," he sighed. "And I'm too tired to tell it all again this night. Please, though, bar the door and have your axe next to you as you sleep. If it's all right with you, I'll sleep on the floor." He raised a hand to cut the worried fletcher off before the big man could begin questioning him. "There's no immediate danger, I'm certain, and I'll explain all in the morning, but...better to be prepared, just in case."

He could feel his eyelids drooping as he spoke and knew his father-in-law must have noticed it as well as he, thankfully, gave in and bade Robin find a place on the floor to sleep. He even threw an old blanket out from the chest in the small room he and Matilda's mother slept in.

As soon as he lay down on the hard floor next to his sleeping son – blanket pulled up, head resting on his bundled cloak – a contented smile touched his lips and he fell asleep.

CHAPTER THIRTEEN

"Who are you two ugly whoresons?"

Little John roared with laughter at the insult, but Will's brows, predictably, lowered into a menacing frown and a low growl rose in his throat.

"Your worst fucking nightmare, son," Scarlet retorted, facing up to the man who was about the same build but slightly taller and slightly uglier, with a nose that had obviously been broken more than once and a head shaved right in, leaving only stubble. "Now get out of the way or my big friend here will bite your bollocks off."

The grin left John's face, to be replaced by a look of surprise.

"I'm not eating anyone's balls, Scarlet. If you want to start a fight with this lad that's your business." He spat, then grinned mischievously. "You've got sharper teeth than me anyway."

The hired thug looked confused. Normally when he insulted people they lowered their heads and tried not to annoy him; he had no idea how to react to the banter between these two travellers who'd suddenly arrived, unannounced in his master's tavern.

"Is that the ritual insults done? Can we move on now and act like men instead of children?"

A new voice came to John and Will and a figure appeared from a side door, an irritated look on his face at their intrusion. He was an unremarkable man of average height and build, close-cropped brown hair and beard that were starting to show flecks of grey, and fine clothing. But his eyes were keen and intelligent and showed no signs of anxiety. This was a man of ruthless efficiency – Scarlet knew the type, having dealt with similar men many times over the years when he was employed as a mercenary or a bodyguard. There was no need to antagonise him, that wasn't what they were here for at all.

"What do you want in my establishment? From the looks of you" – the man curled his lip very slightly, conveying his distaste but not too overtly – "you aren't just here for a drink and some female company."

"We're just looking for a friend of ours," Little John said. "Man called Stephen. About this big," he raised a hand and held it level against his chest. "Pock-marked skin. We heard he was working for you, here – assuming you're Godwin Laweles."

John and Will had reached Leeds not long ago and asked some of the locals if they knew where Stephen was working. They'd known it was *somewhere* in this town but where, and for whom, they had to find out.

Thankfully, the former Hospitaller sergeant-at-arms stood out, thanks to his bearing and general air of competence. The men he shared bodyguard duties with were nothing like him the locals said, pointing them in the direction of *The Pewter Pot* – a tavern-cum-brothel owned by Godwin Laweles, the wealthiest, and most ruthless, merchant in Leeds – with warnings not to cause any trouble.

Laweles didn't take kindly to it apparently.

"And who are you?" he asked, not confirming or denying his identity. Three other men followed him through the side-door and they slowly moved to circle John and Will, with the first, shaven-headed guard directly behind them. Will could almost feel the violence emanating from that one in particular.

"We're friends of his," Will said, the hairs on the back of his neck tingling – it was a real effort not to throw his head back into the face of the thug behind him. "Can you just let Stephen know Will Scarlet and Little John are here to talk to him? It's important."

Clearly the man's bodyguards had heard of the former outlaws, as their eyes moved warily to their leader to see how he'd react to this revelation. Everyone in England had heard of these two. And everyone knew they weren't men to get into a fight with.

Godwin Laweles wasn't a man to show any nervousness though, and Will was impressed with his calm, confident bearing even when his own guards were unconsciously moving ever so slightly backwards, away from him and John.

"I don't give a fuck who you are, I'll –" the shaven-headed man behind them began but his employer glared at him, waving a hand to silence him.

The tension in the room was palpable. Will did his best to look bored, and a glance to his left told him Little John was doing the same. John probably *was* genuinely bored, Scarlet thought, envying the big man his relaxed temperament.

"Stephen!" Laweles raised his voice, which was surprisingly powerful, slicing through the air like an arrow although his eyes never moved from Will. He'd clearly marked the smaller of his visitors as the most dangerous which might have been true and it might not, but Will knew his giant friend would have noticed the same thing and be ready to take advantage of it should the need arise. "You have visitors."

There was silence for a while and Laweles showed signs of impatience, leaning his weight from his left to his right foot and letting out a soft sigh, before he opened his mouth to call on the Hospitaller again.

Muffled shouts reached them, filling the gloomy interior of the tavern, and Will's hand fell to his sword hilt instinctively, even though, if it came to a fight, he'd use the long knife hidden inside his tunic rather than the unwieldy longsword which would be useless in such cramped confines.

Laweles's guards didn't appear at all perturbed by the shouting though, and Will looked up at John who shrugged. Apparently this was a regular occurrence.

The voice grew louder, coming towards them from a corridor on the right of the main room, and a second, answering voice – high pitched and angry – could be heard now.

Suddenly the door from that hallway burst open and a man stumbled through, red-faced, furious, and still trying to tie the laces on his breeches back up.

A strong hand grabbed the scruff of the man's neck again and Stephen appeared with an expression of disgust.

"I don't want to see you in here again you arsehole," he shouted, pressing his pock-marked face up to the frightened man's ear. "I told you before – you don't get violent with the girls. Now get the fuck out of here." He slapped the man a ringing blow across the back of his head and watched as he stumbled out of the front door, clutching his skull and whining in pain.

An irritated sigh escaped Stephen's lips before he turned at last to his employer and, none too respectfully, shrugged. "I was busy when you called on me." He hadn't yet noticed his two old friends standing in the shadows.

"So I see," Laweles retorted, his lips a thin, furious line. "I already told you more than once that the punters can do what they want to the girls, as long as they pay and as long as they don't permanently mark them. Yet there you are throwing another wealthy man out into –"

"John! Will!" Stephen finally spotted the two men in his peripheral vision and turned to greet them, completely ignoring his employer's angry rebuke. "It's good to see you, my friends. What are you doing here in Leeds?"

"Come for you," John replied, a smile on his own bearded face, although it dropped away as he went on. "There's trouble brewing, Stephen. We're all in danger, including you."

"Aye," Will agreed. "You need to come with us. Back to the greenwood once again."

Stephen shook his head but before he could say another word, to demand the whole story, Laweles broke in.

"You're not going anywhere. I didn't become a rich man by letting my employees leave whenever they felt like it." He strode across and pointed a finger at Stephen. "You signed a contract. You're *my* man now. If you want to leave my employ you'll have to buy out your contract. And that won't be cheap."

Will raised an eyebrow and looked at John who laughed out loud. Stephen shook his head.

"I didn't sign any contract – I told you I couldn't write, remember? All I did was make an illegible mark on your piece of paper."

"That's still legally binding," Laweles retorted, then softened his tone a little. "Look, to be perfectly honest, you're a shit employee. Your strict moral code is bad for business in a place like this so...I'll be glad to let you go with the two wolf's heads."

"I'm no wolf's head," John growled. "I'm a lawman, one of the sheriff's own men."

"Yes, yes, so you are." Laweles waved a hand over his shoulder irritably, watching Stephen for his response.

"I'll tell you what," the Hospitaller smiled. "I'm leaving, now, and you can keep the wages you owe me."

Laweles's eyes narrowed. "I don't owe you any money – you were all paid this morning."

Stephen shrugged. "Oh well, then. Let's go boys, it'll be good to get back to the open forest after being stuck here for so long."

"Stop them!"

Godwin Laweles wasn't the type to let his assets walk out on him without a fight, but Will was shocked when the man's fist hit him a glancing strike on the side of the face. Scarlet had seen the blow coming and moved just in time, thankfully, or he might have suffered a broken nose. The foppish little business owner appeared gaunt but he must have had strong, wiry muscles hidden under his fine clothing, as his punch had been quite a powerful one.

Will turned, following Laweles as his momentum made him overbalance, and slammed his elbow into the back of the businessman's skull, dropping him like a stone to the floor.

Thankfully, John expected the shaven-headed man behind them to react quickly at the order to fight. The giant lawman brought his hand up just as the bodyguard made to charge at Will, grabbing his testicles in a vice-like grip and squeezing. When the guard had begun falling to his knees John rammed his left fist into his nose then, with the other hand still squeezing brutally, flipped the tortured man up and onto a table, where he rolled onto his side and curled into a ball, whimpering like a kicked dog.

The remaining three guards hadn't moved and, as he straightened up, Will could see why. Stephen held a dagger in his hand and was staring at them, almost daring them to attack. None did. They'd worked with him for only a short time, but every one of them – hard as they were – feared him.

Without another word, the three friends made their way out the front door.

The old gang was coming together again.

Stephen grinned as the warm sunlight hit his face. It was good to be free again!

CHAPTER FOURTEEN

Wakefield was in uproar. Or, more accurately, the people gathered in St Mary's were in uproar.

Robin stood at the altar, flanked by Friar Tuck on his right and the flustered village headman, Patrick Prudhomme on his left.

"Calm yourselves," Patrick was shouting, arms raised, flapping his hands up and down in what might have been a comical way if the situation hadn't been so serious. "Let Hood speak."

"You're the sheriff's man now," one local – a large, middle-aged man Robin recognised as a labourer – shouted, slightly louder than the rest of the folk, drawing most of the attention his way as a result. "If this band of rapists and killers is coming to pillage Wakefield why isn't de Faucumberg sending soldiers to protect us?"

"Aye," a portly, ruddy cheeked woman agreed in a shrill voice. "He has a standing army – he can afford to send a few of his men here to make sure this gang don't murder us in our beds."

The voices were raised again, unanimously in agreement with their two compatriots and Patrick shook his head in defeat, stepping back to take a seat beside Father Myrc who smiled in sympathetic understanding.

"Settle down you people. Now!"

Robin flinched as Tuck's powerful orator's voice boomed in his ear and he gave the friar a withering glance.

It worked though; the people, gathered in the house of God after all, took in the sight of the impatient clergyman and the shouting dropped to a mutter which, eventually, as Tuck's gaze sought out the offenders, faded into a nervy silence.

"That's better. Robin?" The friar gestured with his palms towards the lectern, a simple, undecorated wooden construction, and his younger friend nodded in gratitude, stepping forward to take up the proffered position.

"Thank you." He looked around, nodding at those he knew well, and noting with pride the respect he saw reflected in all the villagers' eyes. "As Patrick says, we have reason to believe this gang of outlaws may come here. In fact, some of them already visited" – he held up his hands before the nervous muttering at that revelation could turn into a rabble again – "but, unfortunately for them, they chose to attack Will Scaflock."

He grinned and the people laughed and cheered as they guessed the outcome of that meeting.

"So they are three men less thanks to Will, but they are growing all the time as more landless men come out of the woodwork and join up with them. From what we can gather their leader is...charismatic. He has a way of getting people to do his bidding."

"Sounds like a certain other wolf's head I remember," Alexander Gilbert, landlord of the tavern, shouted, but Robin didn't smile at the intended compliment.

"Make no mistake," he replied, his eyes sweeping the room, "this man is nothing – *nothing* – like me. He's already caused havoc in Holmfirth, even murdering their priest, and now he's spreading fear around the countryside."

"So where's the sheriff's men to guard us then, until the wolf's head can be brought down?" The portly woman repeated her question to a chorus of "aye"s.

"Sir Henry doesn't have enough men to send to every village and town the outlaws have threatened. It's as simple as that." Robin hadn't told the people the real reason for the threat to their village – he knew the people would resent Matilda and the rest of his family if they knew the outlaws were targeting them to get revenge on Robin. "We don't know when they'll come, or even if they will for certain. We're just working from rumours. The simple fact is: you will have to defend the village yourselves."

There were some nervous grumbles at that, but not many wanted to show themselves up as cowards, especially the men.

"You can all shoot a longbow," Robin stated, encouragingly. "We all started practising as children didn't we? So set up lookout posts on the roads approaching the village and arm the guards with longbows and hunting horns. Then there's others of you, like John Cobble," he pointed to a brawny middle-aged man with a flat nose, "who fought against the Scots when they raided a few years back. You can use a sword can't you John? Aye, and you've seen action so you won't run like a girl if you're under attack."

"Hey!"

The lawman's eyes flicked to the corner of the room and his face melted in a smile. "Of course, some of the women can fight just as well as the men, eh Marjorie?"

"Good lass," someone cheered, and there was scattered applause as the villagers, growing in confidence, remembered Robin's sister taking on Sir Guy of Gisbourne three years earlier and surviving. The sleek black crossbow she could often be seen practising with on the village green was testament to that, since she'd taken it from the Raven's corpse after her brother had finished the madman off.

"What about you, Henry?" Robin addressed his father-in-law. "You're not going to stand by and watch if some piece of filth comes here looking for trouble are you?" The fletcher's face flushed scarlet as dozens of pairs of eyes fixed on him, but Robin carried on, drawing the looks back his way. "Of course you won't – the last time someone came here threatening your daughter it was Matt Groves, Gisbourne's captain. And you belted him so hard in the face you almost broke his jaw from what I heard!"

Henry grinned and brandished his fist in the air as cheering broke out again. Matilda stood next to her father, little Arthur beside her, and she smiled proudly.

She'd barely spoken to Robin when she woke that morning to find him sleeping next to them. Robin had broken his fast with the Fletcher's, telling them what was happening and why he'd turned up at their door so late.

The lawman enjoyed sharing a meal with Arthur, helping the little boy eat slices of buttered bread and fresh cow's milk, and he'd found a new sense of determination to bring Philip Groves to justice as the family had filled their bellies before another day earning an honest living.

Wakefield wouldn't be an easy target for the bastards Robin vowed, while also mouthing silent prayers to God and the Magdalene to protect the village.

As he stood there, moving out now from behind the lectern to take up a position in the centre of the altar, Matilda still wouldn't meet his eyes but he didn't feel too downcast. His speech was working – the villagers had forgotten their initial, panicked reaction to the threatening news Patrick had delivered, to be replaced with a grim, and even somewhat excited, determination to meet violence with violence.

Still, though, many of the people looked nervous and unsure. They knew Robin would be leaving soon to lead his men in the hunt for the outlaws, leaving them leaderless. With the best will in the world, an army, even one as enthusiastic as the likes of the cobbler and the fletcher, needed someone to guide it.

And Robin knew the perfect man for the job.

"Friar Tuck here will be in charge of organising the defences." He gestured at his old friend whose head snapped around in surprise, mouth dropping open to protest, but Robin continued, giving the clergyman no time to protest.

"Tuck might be a man of God, but he's one of the hardest men I've ever met. And I've met a few," he grinned, glad to see the expression mirrored on many of the locals' faces as they shared his little joke. "You all remember Adam Gurdon, right?" Everyone did. A former knight who pretended to be the celebrated folk hero Adam Bell, he'd been the leader of Little John and Will Scarlet's outlaw gang when Robin first joined them. Eventually Gurdon had shown his true colours, betraying the gang to the sheriff in return for a pardon and being rewarded with the position of bailiff.

Adam Gurdon had been a Templar – a tough man and as skilled in combat as they came.

"Well," Robin went on, "I remember the first day I ever met Tuck. He stood toe to toe with Adam Gurdon and battered the man senseless with nothing more than a club." He allowed the audience time to look at the friar before finishing his endorsement. "Battered Gurdon in the guts before the bastard – sorry Father Myrc," a sheepish grin towards the stern-faced priest – "before he could react, then knocked him out cold with a blow to the back of the skull. Like that," he mimicked Tuck's moves, "it was over in a heartbeat. Never seen anything like it in my life."

Of course, the good people of Wakefield knew Tuck, and they knew he was no fool. Most of them hadn't really heard about this side of him though, and there was a new-found respect in their eyes as they contemplated the clergyman Robin Hood was nominating as the man to lead the defence of their village.

Father Myrc shook his head disapprovingly and Tuck had the grace to look somewhat sheepish, even if his eyes were dancing mischievously.

He hadn't always been a man of the cloth – as a young man he'd been an extremely accomplished wrestler, and even fought as a sell-sword for a time, before God sent him to rescue the Bishop of Norwich from robbers, twenty-five years or so earlier.

He'd become a friar after that but the church had used his considerable martial skills to guard their property and money as it moved around from county to county and even country to country.

Aye, Hood had chosen their captain well. A fearless fighter with God on his side – all he needed was someone to support Tuck in the task and help organize things since it would be too much for one man.

He wasn't sure who to ask though, despite going over options in his head for much of that morning.

"You'll need help Tuck," a voice piped up, and all eyes turned to gaze at the speaker who pushed through the crowd towards the front of the room. "Someone that knows how to train and how to fight and has experience of combat."

The hushed room became a babble of noise as everyone tried to talk at once but Robin was too surprised to call for order as the volunteer reached the lectern and stared at him defiantly.

"Marjorie's not the only woman in the village that knows how to fight," Matilda said to him then stepped up to stand before the people as she went on. "I stuck Gisbourne with a couple of arrows myself that day and I lived in the greenwood with Robin and Tuck and John and Will Scarlet and the rest of them, learning their ways."

The villagers watched her uncertainly and then her father broke the silence.

"You can't do this, lass," he rumbled, holding little Arthur in his arms where Matilda had placed him before moving through the crowd. "We'll need lots of arrows for our longbowmen so you'll be needed to fletch them with me."

Matilda shook her head irritably and chopped her hand through the air. "There won't be any need for arrows if we don't organise the defences properly, da. Tuck can't do it all by himself," she reiterated, "and I defy any of you – *any of you* – to stand here and tell me to my face that you can do a better job than me. My husband and I didn't just talk about making babies and what I was going to make him for his dinner of an evening over the years. I know how to fight and I know how to organise."

A couple of men near the back of the gathering raised their voice – more against the suggestion a woman should tell them how to defend the village rather than any opposition against Matilda personally – and Robin expected their dissension to spread rapidly and put an end to his wife's claim.

When he thought about it, her idea actually seemed a good one. She *was* a strong woman and more than a match for the majority of men in Wakefield with a short sword. If Queen Isabella could lead men, why couldn't Matilda?

Before he could lend his support to her plan, Friar Tuck's powerful voice rolled out over the room and, again, attention focused on the clergyman.

"I see nothing to argue about here," he said. "No-one else offered their services and, as Matilda

Hood says, she's more than up to the job. I can vouch for her myself."

"As can I," Robin broke in, feeling his wife's eyes upon him but not wanting to return the look, fearing what he might see there.

Their influence was enough to silence any more arguments. None there wanted to stand up against the dangerous friar and unpredictable bailiff. Besides, what more could Wakefield ask for? Most of the villages around Yorkshire would be hard pressed to find such a strong war-leader and quick-witted lieutenant.

The heads in the crowd slowly began to nod in acceptance and that was that.

His job was done, Robin knew. To say any more would be over-egging the pudding. The people were confident enough now; they'd follow Tuck and Matilda's advice by setting up lookout points and patrols day and night. It would be enough, he was sure. Certainly he felt better about leaving his family behind to try and bring down Groves and his disciples...Still, he felt a tightness in his throat and wished...

His heart lifted as Matilda met his gaze and there was pride and gratitude in her eyes. He'd rallied her fellow villagers – not to mention her da, whom she doted on – and voiced his support for her. And he was her husband still.

That one look brought him hope that things would all turn out well, eventually, and he slipped out the side door of the nave unnoticed to make his own preparations for the coming fight.

Fight?

No.

This was going to be a war!

* * *

Will suggested it might be a good idea for the three reunited companions not to spend the night in Leeds, what with the slighted brothel-owner and his men probably looking to teach them a lesson or two.

"I don't want to wake up with some hired thug's dagger in my guts," Scarlet opined, climbing atop his courser, as John did the same. "But it'll be dark soon so we'd best get a ways along the road and find somewhere to camp for the night, before it's too treacherous for the horses." He glanced at Stephen who looked back up at him. "Where's your mount?"

"Haven't got one," the Hospitaller replied, spreading his hands out defensively. "I never go anywhere these days. What the fuck would I keep a horse for?"

Behind them, the brothel's doors opened and Godwin Laweles walked out, his men at his back, nursing their wounds and glaring murderously at them.

"Aye, you'd better ride out of here, you whoresons," Laweles called. "You might think you're big men with big reputations but nobody comes into my place and beats up my men."

"Come on," Little John growled, eyeing the businessman and his thugs warily. "They'll grow a pair of balls between them soon enough and then we'll really have to fight. Let's get out of here. Where's the nearest stables?"

"There's one attached to the inn, about half a mile down the street there," Stephen replied as they moved off in the direction he indicated with a flick of his head. "Not sure if there'll be anyone around at this time of the day though."

"The stable boy will be about," Will said, his eyes never once leaving Laweles, who hadn't moved from his position outside the brothel. "We'll find you a mount, never fear. Even if we have to steal it. As John says, those pricks with your former employer will grow in confidence once we're out of sight and that's when the swords and the longbows come out. Let's move."

They rounded the corner, out of sight of *The Pewter Pot*, and Will kicked his heels into the courser's sides. "You two stay together and catch me up. I'll go on ahead and find Stephen something to ride."

"Aren't we going in the wrong direction for that?" John grinned, winking at the Hospitaller. "The brothel's back that way."

Will ignored the giant's poor joke and cantered off along the road on his errand.

Stephen had slightly misjudged the distance to the stables, or else Will had passed the one his friend was talking about, as it was more like a mile along the road before he spotted the big tavern with its attendant stable.

Light was spilling from the open windows into the red of the sunset that was beginning to bathe the town, and the sounds of drunken revelry filled the street. Will was glad he didn't have to live next to the place, the neighbours would never get much sleep.

Ignoring the main building he rode straight to the stable and reined in his horse, hopping out of the saddle and tying the reins round the tethering post before hurrying into the low building with its stench of animal breath and dung.

"Ho!" he shouted, eyes scanning the gloomy interior. "Anyone about?"

A young boy about eleven years-old appeared like a ghost from one of the stalls where he'd presumably been grooming the beast – a tired looking old packhorse – within. Wide-eyed and somewhat nervous, the lad peered at Scarlet but didn't come too close.

"I need a horse, boy. Your master got any for sale?"

"N-no, my lord," the youngster stammered and Will stifled a laugh at the idea he was a nobleman. The boy's master must tell him to talk to customers like that to try and please them; make them more open to being fleeced. "All these belong to travellers staying at the inn."

Will, grim-faced, walked along the row of stalls, eyeing each of the animals stabled there. There were four, including the old nag the boy had been grooming, and only one, a chestnut-brown palfrey, looked up to much.

Sighing theatrically, he reached into his pouch and drew out two coins. He nodded to the sleek palfrey and told the boy to saddle it.

"But, my lord, that's Strawberry, it's –"

The lad began to back away, probably ready to make a run for it out the back door and in to the landlord but Will had anticipated the movement and grasped his arm, not painfully but with enough iron in the grip to let the boy know trying to escape wasn't a wise move.

"Here." Scarlet handed the smallest of the coins in his hand to the boy, whose already wide eyes almost popped out of their sockets. It wasn't a huge amount but, to the stable-hand it probably amounted to a month's wages.

"Saddle the horse," he repeated to the boy. "This one," the second coin was held in the air and the sun's dying red light glinted off it, "is for its owner. This is probably double what the thing is worth so I don't think the owner will have a problem with the trade, am I right?"

The lad gulped and tore his eyes from the coin to meet Will's gaze. "Yes, my lord, you are. That's..."

"A lot of money, I know. And you better make fucking sure the money gets to Strawberry's owner, boy or I'll come back and tie your arms to the pillar here" – he slapped the post that held up the roof – "and your legs to the horse" – he pointed at the palfrey, whose long face seemed to take on a malevolent cast in the rosy light – "then I'll ride off. You understand me?"

The boy looked frightened at the mental image of his body being torn apart, but also affronted at the suggestion he'd shave some of the coin off for himself. He could tell this was a man who wasn't to be fooled with though, so he nodded and, when Will released his arm, hurried to saddle the horse that had been picked out.

"Good lad," Will smiled when the reins were handed to him. "God grant you a good evening."

"And to you, my lord," the stable-hand muttered, the small coin he'd been given for his services in his hand and a cheery smile on his face.

Will liked the look of the brown palfrey so much that he decided to keep her for himself. He tied the reins of the two horses together before hauling himself up into Strawberry's saddle.

"Go and pay the horse's owner that coin, boy," he shouted over his shoulder and, without a backward glance, cantered back along the surprisingly quiet road in the direction he'd come from.

He spotted the figures of his friends in the distance, unmistakable given John's great size and grinned as he rode up to them.

"In the name of God, Stephen, you've let yourself go working in that whorehouse," he laughed, taking in the ruddy cheeks and breathlessness of the Hospitaller. "A gentle half-mile run and you look fit to drop."

"Fuck off," Stephen retorted, untying his new mount's reins from Strawberry's harness and, with an effort, dragged himself up into the saddle, teeth bared as he sucked in air. "That was more than half a mile."

Laughing, Will led them out of the town onto the main road, eyeing the horizon.

"We should have just enough to time to cover a couple of miles back towards Wakefield," he judged. "Then we'll find somewhere amongst the trees to camp. I doubt Laweles's lads will follow us but...better safe than sorry."

"Pfft," Stephen pursed his lips and made a disgusted sound as they urged the horses into a fast walk, single file. "I'm not the only one that's changed, Scarlet. A few years ago you'd have wanted to set up an ambush for that lot. Now you're talking about hiding from them. You probably won't even let us light a fire in case they sneak up and kick your arse."

John laughed loudly, watching Will for the expected sour reaction, but it seemed Scarlet really had mellowed, as he simply smiled and ignored the taunt which was, after all, tongue-in-cheek.

"What you got for my supper anyway?" the Hospitaller asked, eyeing John and Will's saddlebags. "Something nice I hope."

"Oh aye," John replied airily. "We've got a pottage of stewed pheasant, followed by roast kid and plums in wine."

Will burst out laughing but Stephen scowled.

"Bit rich for my taste, thanks all the same. I'll be glad with a bit of black bread and a skin of ale."

"Plenty of those too," John grinned as they rode on, mouths watering at the thought of even such a frugal meal.

A short time later, and with occasional glances over their shoulders for signs of pursuit which never materialised, John pointed to a spot off to the right. His experienced woodsman's eyes had noticed an overgrown trail leading into what was deceptively sparse foliage at that point.

"That must lead to something," the giant lawman mused, nodding towards the hidden track. "Maybe a clearing."

Will shrugged. "It's as good a place to stop as any we've seen so far, and the light's almost gone."

They dismounted and led their mounts through the bushes into the trees which grew thicker a dozen paces away from the main road. They didn't have to walk much further before John's guess proved correct and they came to a clearing.

Someone had camped here in the past, as stones formed a fire-pit, although the lack of embers or half-consumed firewood suggested it hadn't seen a flame in months or more.

"Perfect," Will smiled, tethering Strawberry to a nearby tree. "Get the ale out lads!"

"Are we lighting a fire?" John wondered, peering into the darkness to see if there was much kindling on the ground. "Or do you think there's a real possibility those arseholes will come looking for us? It doesn't seem very likely to me."

They both eyed Stephen who, ever the soldier, was pacing the perimeter of their camp-site, picking at the skin on his fingers, searching for places any possible attack might come from, and trying to gauge how hidden their position really was from the main road.

"What d'you think?" Will asked the Hospitaller. "They were your workmates. Are they stupid – or vengeful – enough to come after us?" It didn't seem probable but Will had no intention of dying in the forest at the hands of some louts who spent their days throwing drunks out of a whorehouse. Not after he'd survived for so long in the greenwood even when the likes of Sir Guy of Gisbourne sought to kill him.

Stephen shook his head. "I doubt it. They were hard enough, and some of them were vicious with it but...they kept their distance from me and I suspect they'll be even more wary of tackling you two." He threw them a withering look. "Right pair of bastards you two, everyone in England knows that."

"That's us," John agreed, opening his breeches and emptying his bladder noisily into the bushes on the edge of the camp. "Complete bastards."

"Nah, they'll have forgotten all about us by now," Stephen smiled. "But if we're going to be getting back to living rough in the forest like this, I'd say it'd not be a bad idea to set a watch. Just in case."

Will groaned at the thought but nodded agreement, brightening as he did so. "Aye, fair enough. It's early yet though, and getting chilly now the sun's gone down – let's build that fire and get comfy with some meat and ale!"

"Good idea," John said, moving to find some kindling. "And while we rest for the evening, maybe Stephen can tell me how he came to be a Hospitaller in the first place. I don't think we ever did find out. You can take first watch, Will. Better get some sleep so you're fresh for it..."

"Aye, fair enough," Scarlet agreed and disappeared into the gloom outside the camp-fire's radiance. "I'll have a nap. Keep the noise down, and wake me when you two want to turn in."

CHAPTER FIFTEEN

After a few ales and a frugal supper of bread and dried meat Stephen and Little John settled down for the night and the Hospitaller began his tale. Much to the John's surprise, Stephen said he'd spent his childhood learning to be a stonemason in the nearby town of Halifax.

"Aye, my father was a great artisan," the sergeant-at-arms nodded, supping a small mug of ale, eyes sparkling at the looks on the others' face as he started his tale, "and he took me under his wing."

"I can't see you having the patience to carve stone," Little John said. "You'd be a much better labourer. No offence."

Stephen almost managed a smile at that. "None taken. As it turns out you were right – I usually ended up just carting the blocks around and helping the labourers, much to my da's irritation, but..." He gave a shrug as if that explained everything.

"Some men like to spend time making things pretty, while others just like to get the job done and go home without any messing about," John mused, and the Hospitaller seemed to like that description of his qualities.

"Aye, that's about right. So I didn't learn much about the finer arts of stone masonry, but my body grew hard and strong from the work. One day some Hospitallers came to the town – we were working on the church, replacing a wall and fitting some new windows, I remember it as if it were only yesterday – and they were after some recruits to go to Rhodes where they were trying to set up a new base. I joined them."

"Didn't your da try to stop you?" John wondered, picking a piece of gristle from between his teeth.

Stephen shook his head. "We were never very close, as his work took him away from home a lot. Not much work for a stonemason unless he was able to travel to the towns and cities roundabout so I never saw him all that much growing up. I was closer to my ma but her and my father both agreed I'd be better off learning my trade with the knights, since I'd never be a mason. And they were both God-fearing people who saw this as my chance to earn passage into Heaven."

"God help us all," John snorted. "Your cheery face in Heaven? Sounds more like Hell."

Stephen made a gesture with his hand that was so rude it might preclude his entry to paradise after all, then continued.

"I spent a few years in Rhodes, learning how to fight like a soldier. How to be a killer," he growled, looking pointedly at the giant who raised his hands in a mock defensive motion.

"We had to clear the Turks – Saracens – off the island before we could colonise it properly, and there were pirates controlling the waters all around. So I was taught how to fight on land and from the deck of a ship."

"And that's where you met Sir Richard?"

"Aye," Stephen agreed. "I was sergeant to another knight. A Frenchman named Sir Jean de Pagnac. He was killed though, in a tunnel beneath a little village..." His voice trailed off and he stared thoughtfully into the flickering firelight before shuddering and shaking his head as if to clear away some frightful vision. "Sir Richard's sergeant was killed in action that night too, so the Grand Master decided to put us together and pack us back home to Kirklees."

"A tunnel?" John demanded. "What the hell were you doing in a tunnel under a village?"

Stephen simply shook his head and refused to be drawn on the subject, his expression dark enough that John didn't push the issue.

"Where's Rhodes anyway?" the big man asked instead, changing the subject.

The strange atmosphere that had settled on their gloomy camp-site lifted as Stephen burst into laughter at his friend's lack of geographical knowledge.

"What? What the fuck's so funny about that?" John demanded, face flushing in the darkness, but that just made the other man laugh even harder.

"Keep your voice down," Stephen whispered gleefully, gesturing at the shadowy bundle on the forest floor. "You'll wake Scarlet."

Stephen finally replied to the original question when his mirth had lessened.

"Rhodes takes weeks of travel by a fast ship, and it's worth it, for it's always summer there. But Sir Richard and I came back to England and lived at the Hospitaller Preceptory in Kirklees for a few years. Good years." His voice trailed away, a wistful note creeping in as it became lost in the night and he idly picked at the dry skin on his thumb. "And then we met you boys and everything turned to shit."

"That's a lovely story, Stephen." An unseen man hissed at them from the darkness and the Hospitaller jumped to his feet, drawing his sword free from its sheath and moving back-to-back with Little John who'd grabbed his quarterstaff and stood now, face grim in the soft orange glow from the firelight, searching for the hidden speaker.

"I recognise that voice," Stephen growled, teeth pulled back like a wolf. "Edwin Baker. One of Laweles's men. Come on then, and let my sword taste your blood you ugly bastard!"

"Enough of the talk." A second voice spoke from the other side of their camp-site, and then a third grunted agreement from another direction, confirming what Stephen had suspected all along: they were surrounded. Probably by at least five or six of his erstwhile colleagues.

Odds of two to one didn't look good.

The man who'd spoken first stepped from the shadows into the light, a smile on his face, as if he knew the odds were stacked in their favour and he was going to enjoy repaying the fabled former-outlaws for the beating they'd handed out back in the *The Pewter Pot*.

"Why don't you just lay down your weapons there, lads," he said, with a smirk, "and we'll let you live. We'll take all your coin, weapons and clothes but you'll be free to return to your homes. Even if you will be naked." He barked a small laugh then nodded in disgust at Will Scarlet's bedroll. "Look at that – your mate's so ale-soaked he hasn't even realised you're under attack. I expected more from an ex-Hospitaller sergeant like you Stephen. You need to teach your friends some military discipline."

John looked down at the bedroll and filling his great lungs with air, roared, "Will!"

As Laweles's guards moved in to begin their one-sided assault there was a scream of pain from the deep shadows to the left. The air reverberated with the sound, which told of sheer agony, before it was cut off by the thud of metal striking bone. It was followed, eerily, by a grunt of sadistic laughter.

The attackers reeled in confusion and the leader's eyes narrowed, as he finally understood what was happening. He opened his mouth to urge his men on.

"It's a trick! The other one isn't lying on the ground drunk, he's –"

His words were cut-off as the end of Little John's staff - almost the trunk of a young oak tree – smashed into his mouth, sending him crashing back onto the ground where he lay, mewling and clutching at his ruined teeth.

"Fucking come on then, you arseholes!" John roared into the night, his shaggy brown hair and beard, and the feral, battle-fevered look on his face making him appear like some terrifying beast of the fields.

The thugs from Leeds, knowing there was an assassin hiding somewhere within the trees next to them, decided to move into the light and engage John and their former colleague, Stephen. At least they presented a target the men could actually *see*.

There was another outraged roar of pain from a different section of the encircling trees and Stephen knew that was one more assailant they needn't worry about. He had to concentrate now though, as two of Laweles's men came at him. One was armed with a sword, but the other, a small, black bearded man, only carried a long, heavy club.

Targeting that one first, Stephen swung his sword in a shallow arc towards him, and the man reacted as expected, blocking the attack with his club. The weight of the wooden weapon dropped his arm though, and, as he tried to recover, too slowly, the Hospitaller plunged the tip of his longsword into the bearded assailant's guts.

Tearing the blade free in a smooth, practised motion, he desperately raised it and deflected the second attacker's sword thrust, which would surely have torn his neck and throat wide open.

He dropped onto his haunches and plunged his sword upwards, deep into the man's belly, unfolding his knees as it went in and sawing it back and forward as he rose again to his full height. He paused for an instant to watch the light flee from the man's eyes but then, remembering they were still in a fight, turned to scan the camp.

John's sleeve was ripped apart and he sported a long gash which oozed blood as he traded blows with the final thug that remained in the fight. Another attacker lay unmoving at the giant's feet but the wound in his forearm was clearly hampering his use of the quarterstaff. Left to finish itself naturally, the fight wouldn't go well for the big man but, with a deafening war-cry, Will burst out of the darkness.

Stephen watched in relief as the tip of Scarlet's sword exploded out of Laweles's man's gambeson in a spray of blood.

The blade was slowly pulled back and, huffing to catch his breath, Will bent and wiped off the blood on the fallen man's tunic.

The three friends looked at each other, all breathing hard but still alive, and they grinned like children that had just won a game of Hoodman's Blind.

"That was good," Scarlet grunted, replacing his sword in its leather and wood sheath.

"Just like old times," John agreed.

"Aye," Stephen finished. "But we still have to deal with that one."

He pointed his still bloody longsword at the thugs' leader, who yet lived, although with much fewer teeth than when the fight started. The man pulled himself onto his hands and knees but his head remained bowed towards the grass. He was obviously still reeling from the force of John's quarterstaff.

The fight was done and the battle-joy had left the three victors, who moved now to stand over of their final would-be killer.

"What do we do with him?" Stephen asked, before he kicked the man in the ribs just to make sure he didn't try anything.

"We could send him back to *The Pewter Pot* with a warning to Laweles not to fuck with us again?" John suggested, eyeing the man as he retched from the force of the Hospitaller's boot.

Will thought for a moment then shook his head. "Nah, I think we've already sent that message by killing all his men. But I'm bloody exhausted and I don't fancy sleeping with that prick still around, waiting for a chance to gut me."

The man turned his head, a look of hatred which quickly turned to disbelief as Scarlet's sword took him in the back.

"I'd just cleaned that too," Will muttered irritably as he dragged the blade along the dead man's breeches, which simply smeared the blood. Too tired to care, he sheathed the weapon and, with a shrug, moved back to his bedroll.

Removing the rolled up cloaks they'd stuffed in it to make it appear occupied, he lay down – for real this time – and closed his eyes with a yawn.

"It's your watch Stephen. Wake me when it's my turn."

CHAPTER SIXTEEN

Their next step, Robin decided, was to warn their former friends about Philip Groves's murderous intentions while offering advice to the towns and villages all around Nottingham and Yorkshire about defending themselves against the outlaws.

Not many of their old gang survived now: Arthur, the toothless, greasy haired lad from Bichill; Piers, a fine swordsman who had joined them not that long before their pardons; Peter Ordevill, a sailor who they knew was living in Selby; and James, the bowman who had never actually been a member of their gang but who'd saved all their lives when he warned them of an imminent attack by the Raven, Sir Guy of Gisbourne.

Robin, Little John, Will and Stephen started in Selby, where they found Peter Ordevill attempting to run a boatyard with little success. He was glad to leave the struggling business in the care of a neighbour and rejoin his old friends who he'd missed very much in the three years since they'd parted ways.

Next they moved on to Horbury and discovered James down on his luck and near-destitute. Robin had rewarded him with a fair sum of money for his part in their survival when Gisbourne had come hunting them but the bowman had struggled to find employment since then and, as a result, spent almost all his money. Like Piers, he was more than happy to join Hood's band of bounty hunters.

Finally it was Bichill, where they were reunited with the short but powerfully built Arthur. In his mid-twenties now, he'd been a quiet but dependable member of their old gang and, since their pardon he'd went back to his home village and used his wealth to open an alehouse.

Unlike Ordevill and James, however, he'd married and had two children and refused to rejoin Robin and the others.

"You're putting your family in danger if you *don't* come with us," Will told him. "This outlaw, Philip, is coming after all of us. He knows who we are and, if he doesn't already, he'll eventually find out where we all live. Including you."

"So I should leave my wife unprotected?"

Arthur had matured in the years since Robin had last met him. He'd grown into an impressive man, with a proud bearing and a canny look about him, despite missing most of his teeth.

"She must have other family in the village," Will pointed out. "Send her to stay with them until we get this sorted."

"How long is that going to take?" Arthur grumbled. "I have a business to run here."

"We'll have a better chance of hunting the bastards down if we have as many of our old gang back together again as possible," Robin said reasonably. "We could do with your help and, as Will says, if you stay here you're just going to bring Philip and his men down on the place."

Still Arthur refused, and Robin could understand why. Bichill was a smaller place than Wakefield, with fewer able men and no seasoned warrior like Tuck to marshal the defences in the event of an assault.

"I'll tell you what," Robin said, after some thought. "We have to go to Nottingham to find Piers – you join us again, and your family can come to the city with us. I'll have the sheriff find somewhere for them to stay until this blows over."

Arthur mulled the suggestion over, knowing his wife, Mariam wouldn't like it, but also knowing Nottingham's walls would keep his loved ones safe.

"What choice do I have?" he sighed at last. "Can't just carry on hoping these bastard outlaws forget about me. Mariam will want her mother to come too though – she lives with us since her own husband died two years ago." As he glanced at each of his old friends in turn his face brightened and he grinned. "Ah, but I suppose it'll be good to be back in the greenwood, and free for a while again!"

As he'd done in Wakefield, Selby, Horbury and the other places they'd visited in the recent weeks,

Robin had Bichill's headman, Johannes – an old, old man with flaking skin and tired, red eyes – call a meeting, where they told the locals of the possible threat and what they should do to protect themselves against Philip's cut-throats.

Unsurprisingly, the people were frightened and demanded aid from Robin as the sheriff's representative, but he promised them nothing and advised them to set up defences, even simple ones, to put their minds at ease.

Then, paying for a cart and two horses to pull it – the whole party, including Mariam, her mother, and the two infants – made their way as fast as they could to Nottingham.

It was a surprisingly pleasant journey for Robin, as he entertained Arthur's children – a boy and a girl – and put thoughts of his troubles to the back of his mind for a while.

The roads were in good condition thanks to the late summer weather so the cart made good time and the travellers made it to Nottingham without incident, rolling in through the Chapel Bar gate and through the busy streets towards the castle.

"Will – you and Stephen go and see if you can find Piers. He was a clerk of some sort before he came to us, and his family were wealthy so it shouldn't be too hard to find someone who knows him."

"Easy for you to say," Will retorted. "It'll be like looking for a needle in a box of fucking needles."

"Aye," Stephen agreed, and Robin couldn't help laughing at the pair of them, with their sour faces.

"Piers de Toothill. There's not going to be very many people with a name like that in Nottingham. Start at the tax collector's place up the road there. We'll meet up in there later on, all right?" He gestured to a tavern, *The Blue Boar*, that was only fifty paces away, down a side street.

With a disgruntled wave Will wandered off towards the heart of the city, Stephen at his back looking as if he was about to go into battle.

"Moaning bastards," Peter Ordevill laughed.

"Aye, but they'll find Piers in no time," Robin nodded, confident in his friends' resourcefulness. "As for you two," he brought out his purse and handed over a substantial weight of coins. "Go and get provisions for the hunt, along with whatever weapons you might be needing."

James still had his faithful longbow but Peter needed both a sword and a bow since he'd kept neither when he bought his boatyard. The pair wandered off, soon becoming lost in the noisy, bustling traffic of the city, and Robin turned back to John.

"Right, let's go and see Sir Henry and find out what's to be done with Arthur's family."

As it turned out, the sheriff wasn't in the city that day – he'd been called to London by the king who was apparently trying to reassure himself of as much support as possible with the recent threats from France of invasion by his own wife, Isabella, and her – alleged – lover, Mortimer of Wigmore.

The sheriff's steward, William-atte-Burn, knew Robin well enough though, and he promised to see personally to the lodgings of Mariam and the little ones somewhere not too far from the castle, where the city watch would be able to keep an eye on them.

Before heading back down to the courtyard Robin and John made their way to the barracks to find Thomas, the sheriff's messenger. The young lawman still wanted to keep their group's numbers quite low for now, but he knew Thomas would be a good addition to their small band. The man had been a forester for years before the sheriff had promoted him – his skills would be useful, without a doubt.

Like the sheriff, though, Thomas wasn't around.

"He's on guard duty at the Hun gate," the quartermaster dismissed them with a bored expression. "The regular guard came down with a severe case of the shits so messenger boy got drafted in to take his place. Won't be off duty until this evening."

It was only early afternoon.

"We need to wait on Will and Stephen anyway," John shrugged, a small smile tugging at his mouth. "Might as well head for that tavern."

"Aye, good idea. Ask Thomas to come to *The Blue Boar* as soon as he comes back with his unit then, will you, friend?"

The quartermaster looked irritated and remained silent, until Robin realised the man was expecting a coin in return for passing on the message.

Rather than arguing with him – Robin was one of Sir Henry's personal staff after all, so far outranked this fat sergeant – he fished in his purse for the smallest coin he could find and tossed it at the man. "Don't forget to pass on the message or it won't be a coin you get next time, it'll be my boot up your fucking arse."

"Is that right?"

To both Robin and Little John's surprise the quartermaster got to his feet and glared at them, his hand on his sword hilt. "Jumped up young prick, coming into my barracks telling me what to do? You fucking arsehole, I'll –"

He never had the chance to say what it was he planned on doing, as Robin vaulted the counter that separated them in a heartbeat and, using both his hands, grabbed the sergeant by the neck and threw him backwards, against the wall. Teeth bared, his enormous shoulders bulged as he lifted the portly man off the floor.

"You'll what?" Robin growled, the quartermaster's face turning a deep shade of purple.

The man tried to hammer his fists into Robin's muscular arms but it did no good – his elevated position gave him no leverage and his face contorted as he began to lose consciousness.

"Enough, Robin."

Little John's amused yet insistent voice broke through the young bailiff's rage and, slowly, he released the pressure on the sergeant's neck, lowering the man gently to the floor although he didn't let go completely.

"You fucking tell Thomas we were here, and where he can find us, you fat bastard, or I'll take your face off next time."

He finally let go of the man, who fell, gasping and coughing loudly onto the floor of the chamber, too winded to reply.

Robin glared at the fallen quartermaster for a while, until John told him it was time to move and the fury that had built up inside him dissipated, like a smoke in the wind, and he wondered what had come over him. Aye, he was hot tempered at times – that's what had seen him become an outlaw in the first place after all – but he was normally able to control it nowadays. Throttling the sergeant was out of character for him.

At the back of his mind he knew it was the fear and stress of his disintegrating relationship with Matilda that had caused it, but he wouldn't admit it, not for a heartbeat.

He jumped back over the counter to stand by John. "Come on," he grunted, only slightly out of breath. "Let's find that tavern."

He never looked back at the quartermaster as they left the castle and walked back into the bright sunshine, but the man's eyes watched them go, burning with a murderous rage.

"That wasn't the best idea," John told him, shaking his big bearded head in – mostly – mock indignation. "You never know when you'll need a quartermaster."

Robin ignored him and, by the time they made it back out to the courtyard the cart – along with Mariam, her mother and children and all their belongings – was gone, leaving a somewhat forlorn Arthur lounging against a wall, squinting against the bright noon sunshine.

"Everything sorted already? That was quick."

"Aye," Arthur nodded to Robin's query. "A couple of servants came out not long after you'd gone in and took them to the house. It's not far – I followed to make sure they were all right and to say goodbye. There's a weaver's shop next to it. Mariam and her ma will work there until this is finished."

"Perfect," John boomed. "And no doubt the little ones will find their own amusements in a big city like this."

"Speaking of amusements," Robin grinned, eyes sparkling. "We'd better head for *The Blue Boar* and wait on Will and the Hospitaller returning with Piers."

* * *

Philip and Eoin had woken the men that morning with kicks and shouts, exhorting them to get up and arm themselves.

They were going hunting.

It was a damp day, with a mist of rain in the air that might clear up or might turn into a thunderstorm but the men rose excitedly, glad to have a purpose at last, after their days sitting around doing nothing but drink, eat and brag about their exploits.

Mark felt a nervous knot in the pit of his stomach – surely they were finally going to head for Horbury and that bastard turncoat James. At last he'd get his revenge. He grinned at Ivo who returned the look, but on his face it was much less appealing, since Friar Tuck had smashed most of his front teeth out years earlier when they'd tried to rob and kill the hardy clergyman.

"James is mine, when we find him," Mark growled, his eyes flaring, but Ivo simply shrugged.

"As long as I get to sink a few ales and empty my bollocks in some pretty lass, you're welcome to him."

The gang had moved camp more than once in the past few weeks, covering dozens of miles in every direction, as Philip knew the law – particularly Robin Hood and his men – would be searching for them. For the past couple of days they'd hidden in a clearing not far from the village of Mirfield. The spot was well hidden by trees and a little stream passed close by, providing them with fresh water for drinking and cooking, while they had plenty of meat, eggs and bread, purloined from a village on their way past.

But Mark knew the men would get bored just hanging around the forest – they needed something to stimulate them or else they'd bicker amongst themselves and, once the ale barrels were broached, bickering could soon turn to violence. He knew Philip understood it too and was undoubtedly the reason for their little outing today.

Buckling on his gambeson, which he'd spent the previous night patching up since it was tatty after long years of wear and abuse, Mark nodded to Philip when the outlaw captain passed nearby.

"We heading for Horbury then?"

Philip stopped and looked at him, the infuriating, ubiquitous smile tugging at the corners of his mouth.

"No. Brighouse."

Mark's face fell. The village of Brighouse was just as distant from their camp-site as Horbury was, but, as far as he knew, none of the men Philip wanted to hunt down lived there.

"What? Why the fuck are we going there?" he demanded. "You said we'd be going after that bastard James. I've been waiting years to pay him back for what he did!"

Eoin suddenly appeared at Philip's back, as if from nowhere, his great bulk filling Mark's vision.

"Do I have to explain every decision I make to you?" Philip asked, his voice low but his eyes hooded and dangerous.

"Well –" Mark began but he trailed off as Philip spoke over him,

"The foresters, the sheriff's men, Robin Hood...they all know by now that we're hunting for Hood's old gang members. They expect us to attack the villages where those men are living."

The rest of the outlaw band – their numbers swelled again to seventeen by now, even with the losses they'd suffered at the hands of Will Scaflock in Wakefield – gathered around to hear what their leader was saying.

"Do you really want me to lead the men to Horbury, Mark? When the villagers – and your friend James who, by your own admission is a crack shot with a longbow – will be watching for us? Are you really as stupid as you look?"

The men sniggered at that. Mark wasn't particularly unpopular or disliked, but the ever-growing group were not close and never would be. Philip was gathering to him men who were, by their nature, aloof, unfriendly and solitary. Men who didn't form friendships easily but would follow orders even when those orders would seem repugnant or downright wicked to most people.

More than one man had tried to join them recently only to disappear a few days later, when it had become clear he wasn't as brutal or unhinged as the rest of them. The last was a thirteen year-old from Grange Moor. He'd been full of bravado, despite his obvious nervousness upon meeting the gang of wolf's heads. Chased from his small village for stealing food from a baker's shop, the boy cried himself to sleep for two nights, even calling out for his mother as he slept. And then, on the third morning, he'd been gone.

No one asked, but Mark knew Philip had killed him. Their leader had no room in his gang for deadwood,

Ivo still stood beside him now, and Mark was grateful for his old companion's presence but, if it came to it, he suspected even Ivo wouldn't stand up to Philip or Eoin on his behalf.

"You see," Philip said, spreading his hands wide. "This is why I'm the leader and you're not. You'd have the men throw themselves into danger just to settle an old, meaningless score with a man you've not seen in years. Madness."

He scowled at Mark and shook his head dismissively, turning to address the others instead.

"Eventually I will hunt down and kill every last one of Hood's friends. On that I swore to God. But that task can wait! There's no point in us walking into danger when there's so many other, softer targets dotted all around the country for us to visit."

The wolf's head jerked his head at a young man who'd joined them only a fortnight earlier, yet had managed to get into fist fights with three of the other men thanks to his hot temper and inability to hold his ale. "Joseph – what say you? Would you like to travel to Horbury to hunt down Mark's old acquaintance? Knowing the law will probably be patrolling the area? Or would you rather we head for Brighouse – a small village with only a few dozen inhabitants that will present an easy target?"

The youngster smiled, inordinately proud to have been singled out by their captain, and Mark's heart sank. These idiots had fallen completely under Philip's sway.

"Brighouse!" Joseph shouted, jerking his fists and grinning like an excited hound. "I don't want to die on some lawman's sword – I want to stick *my* sword in some girl in Brighouse. That sword, there, I mean, not my real blade..." He trailed off, pointing between his legs sheepishly.

Instead of shaking his head in disgust at the irritating youngster, as Mark would have done, Philip stretched his mouth wide open, stuck out his tongue and waggled it suggestively, grabbing his own crotch and squeezing it at the same time.

The men roared in appreciation, even Ivo, much to Mark's chagrin.

"Come on then," Philip shouted, leading the way through the undergrowth towards the westward road. "Let's get to Brighouse and find some wenches to sheath our swords in! Mark can head for Horbury to meet his boyfriend if he likes."

Mark watched, stony-faced and forgotten, while the men moved off, laughing and joking and sharing tales of their previous sexual exploits. The sun, at last, poked out from between the clouds and bathed the land in a pleasant orange glow, as if blessing the gang's mission.

As they moved off, though, Mark was surprised to see Eoin looking back at him, a worried expression on his young face, and a tiny sliver of hope touched his heart.

The big man was protective of Philip and clearly felt a great deal of loyalty to his older friend who'd saved his life, but Mark knew Eoin wasn't the wicked, immoral bastard the rest of them were. The giant followed orders but, when they were looting and raping he never joined in with the worst of the violence; he hid his face behind a stony mask of indifference then made himself scarce while the others were enjoying themselves.

And here they were, off to attack a village, and Eoin's backward, worried glance, spoke volumes about the way things were going.

CHAPTER SEVENTEEN

"Oh, shit. Fuck me, they're coming. They're really coming!"

Luke-atte-Water glanced across at his companion, Blase, and, seeing the fear as plain as day on the younger man's face, jumped to his feet to have a look along the road.

Blase Cottar, a forester of just eighteen years, was right – Robin Hood's warning when he'd passed through a few days earlier seemed to be a timely one, as at least a dozen hard-looking men were striding purposefully along the heavily rutted path towards their village.

"Run," Luke commanded, clambering down from the tree they'd employed as a look-out post, his throat constricting, breath almost gone from him before he'd even reached the ground as fear filled his veins like a cask of strong ale. "Run!" he repeated needlessly, breaking into a breathless sprint as his wide-eyed companion thumped down on the hard earth and followed him away from the main road and into the safety of the trees.

He prayed to God that the approaching outlaws – for what else could they be, but the scum the lawmen had warned them about? – hadn't seen them. They weren't that far from the village but Luke wasn't that fast a runner, with his short stumpy legs and pot belly and he dreaded the thought of some nimble wolf's head overtaking them and...well, he carried a long knife but it would be much better to face these invaders from behind his warbow at a distance of a hundred paces or so.

There was a cry from behind him.

Blase.

For a heartbeat – just a heartbeat! – Luke continued running, his fear spurring him on, but the thought of leaving his fellow villager behind stopped him and he turned, drawing the blade from his belt and steadying himself for the attacker that had taken Blase down.

The assailant turned out to be a large divot in the grass, which had tripped the panicked young man as he fled.

Almost laughing in hysterical relief, Luke stamped back the few paces and grasped his downed companion by the arm, hauling with all his fear-given strength to help the forester back up.

They were almost at Brighouse and there were no signs of pursuit. They were safe.

Until the outlaws arrived in the village at any rate...

"To arms, to arms!"

The cry tore from Blase's throat as they raced into the village and Luke joined in when he was able to draw enough breath to do so.

Some of the people simply gaped at them like surprised fish but Robin Hood's warning had taken root in the majority of the locals' minds, and women ran to gather up their children as men hurried to gather the longbows and piles of arrows that lay stacked against the buildings in preparation for this day.

The headman, Gregor – a bear of a man with a bald, freckled head and flame-red beard – stormed out of his house and, in a deafening voice, repeated the lookouts' call to arms.

Luke watched in fascination as the people ran here and there, almost as if the whole thing had been practised and perfected. Children were escorted hurriedly to the church, the only stone building in the entire village, by their mothers, some of whom carried weapons and looked as if they could use them well enough if called upon.

The men, even youngsters and greybeards, took up positions hidden inside their houses or behind hedges and walls. The vast majority held longbows, which they were obliged to practise with every Sunday by law, but some, like Gregor, who strode into the centre of the road to meet the approaching outlaws, carried axes, swords and even spears.

Luke glanced around, noting the fear and nervousness that filled almost every face, and his heart sank.

These men that were walking calmly towards their little village were killers. He'd heard the stories of their brutal, callous exploits and it made his blood run cold to know he'd be facing such a force within the space of just a few more heartbeats and with only his fellow villagers to stand against them.

It was hopeless.

He would make a run for it, he decided. He had no children and his wife was forever nagging at him, why should he lay down his life? He was only twenty-six years old!

Christ help me, he prayed, but a look at Blase filled him with shame.

The younger man was plainly even more terrified than Luke. The outlaws had finally appeared on the horizon and their loud voices – they made no attempt to hide their approach, so filled were they with bravado – carried along the silent, deserted main road. A small wet patch appeared on Blase's breeches and Luke, surprising even himself, felt a rage welling up inside him.

Who were these outlaws, to come to Brighouse, frightening good people like Blase who had never hurt anyone in their lives?

His own momentary thrill of fear forgotten, Luke reached down and pulled an arrow from the earth at his feet, nocking it to his bowstring and raising the weapon in grim, icy determination.

The wolf's heads wouldn't find this village the easy target they expected, Luke vowed, and he hoped that all the other good men of Brighouse would be feeling the same way right now, their fear replaced with outrage.

"Halt, travellers," Gregor shouted, as the oncoming men came close enough to address, and Luke spotted a couple of villagers pushing into the trees flanking the road, to take up positions behind the outlaws.

The defensive strategy was devised by Robin Hood and his companions, Luke knew. Gregor had fought in battles before but he had no real experience as a war leader.

Now they would find out if the plans were sound.

The outlaws stopped at the headman's challenge, sharing amused glances with one another, although Luke noted the man at the front of their line. That one had a smile on his face, but his eyes were hard and remained fixed on Gregor, boring into the bald man.

"What kind of welcome is this for weary travellers looking to spend a few coins in your village?" The hard-eyed outlaw shouted, spreading his hands out wide before jerking his head backwards to the enormous man that stood directly behind him, almost like a bodyguard.

"My friend here's hungry and it takes a lot to fill his belly. Your baker will be a wealthy man by the time we leave, as will the rest of your merchants and ale-sellers."

"Especially your ale-seller," one of the newcomers shouted happily, to a chorus of "aye"s from the rest of the motley crowd who were, it seemed, dying of thirst.

"There's no welcome here for the likes of you," Gregor returned, evenly, the axe held in his hands almost reverently and Luke suddenly knew his headman could use the vicious weapon; indeed, *had* used it not so many years before. The way he carried it spoke of past brutality that Luke had never guessed at and it gave the bowman an added jolt of courage.

He sighted along his arrow, aiming the anchor-shaped point directly at the outlaw captain but not yet drawing the hemp string taut.

"Now, turn around and take yourselves back the way you came," Gregor continued. "We were warned you bastards might turn up and we're ready for you."

The outlaw leader's smile faltered momentarily and, again, Luke felt his confidence grow. That had surely been a flicker of self-doubt and surprise – the wolf's head wasn't the unflappable, immortal monster everyone had pictured in their rampant imaginations when they'd heard Hood recounting the devil's exploits. He was simply a man, albeit a man with a giant at his back…

The outlaws had fanned out by now, spreading themselves wide to make themselves less of a target, but even Luke, with no previous battle experience, could tell that they were a disjointed, uncoordinated group. He wondered how they'd managed to evade capture for so long and shuddered when he surmised it must be because their skill at killing outweighed their lack of cohesion.

And yet, here they stood, with their infamous leader – a wanted rapist, murderer and enemy of God – presenting a perfect target for Luke's broadhead arrow.

He had to take the shot. He had to!

This was his chance to *be* someone – for his name to go down in history.

The wolf's head would die.

Gregor was repeating his demand that the outlaws leave the village as Luke slowly drew back his bowstring. Time seemed to stop completely for him and the outlaw captain's face grew to fill his vision until he fancied he could even see the crow's feet by the man's eyes.

He drew the string taut and inhaled a long, steady breath, utterly calm, all trace of his earlier terror gone.

The sharp, violent snap of an arrow being released filled the village.

And then all hell broke loose.

CHAPTER EIGHTEEN

Philip watched in surprise as the arrow tore past his face by quite some distance and, from the sound of it, buried itself deep in a tree trunk.

"The bastards are shooting at us," he muttered, turning, one eyebrow raised, to look up at Eoin.

The giant's eyes narrowed as another arrow sailed past them at an almost leisurely pace – clearly these villagers were no crack shots – then he lumbered forward, placing himself in front of Philip and using his bulk to shepherd his friend backwards, into the safety of the trees, like some great mother hen.

"The bastards," Philip repeated, shocked at the organised resistance they'd met. This had never happened before when they'd visited a village and he cursed Robin Hood once again. The man was a thorn in his side that he'd need to remove sooner rather than later. "Attack them," he ordered, waving his hand forward distractedly. "Show these peasants what happens when people stand up to us."

His men needed no further encouragement.

The bald headman had retreated behind a building when the shooting started. His furious voice could be heard castigating the man that had loosed the first, wayward arrow – both for starting a fight that might have been avoided and, more importantly, missing the target.

The arrows continued to slam into the trees though, and the outlaws waited, judging the best moment to charge, before, at last, half a dozen of them sprinted towards the village screaming unintelligible war cries.

Philip watched as an arrow – probably more by luck rather than any skill – hammered into one of his men, spinning the unfortunate backwards, howling in rage and pain and effectively out of the battle.

The other five of his followers made it to the village and were met by a similar number of locals, led by the headman with his war axe.

Fascinated now by the melee, Philip stared, rapt, as the big bald man brought his weapon down on the head of an attacker, then used his foot to brace himself as he tried to free the blade which had become trapped in the dead outlaw's skull.

He wasn't fast enough though, and an attacker whacked the blade of his sword against the headman's torso. The blow was a powerful one and it sent the headman reeling backwards although the ill-fitting mail shirt he wore absorbed most of the force so no blood was drawn.

Philip's eyes flickered on to the next of his men and he cursed inwardly as a villager, face scarlet and terrified, landed a lucky blow with his crude hammer, smashing the wolf's head's eye socket into a bloody mess.

His gaze moved on again and this time the view was more pleasing.

Mark's toothless mate, Ivo, was competent – skilled even – with his sword, and he skewered one of the villagers before drawing the crimson blade free and moving to hack at the next in the defensive line.

Mark himself was at the far left side of the attackers' formation and he was a little ball of fury, hacking and slashing with silent venom, although his blows were being batted aside competently enough by his opponent, a similarly sized man with enormous, hairy forearms and a blade so rusty Philip was shocked it hadn't shattered upon the first parry.

There was no way the outlaws could win this battle though – there were still at least two dozen archers hiding in the buildings, too frightened to come out and join in with the hand-to-hand combat, but they'd be able to fill the invaders with arrows eventually.

"Fuck it."

Philip spat in disgust and turned to walk away, back along the road to their camp a few miles away.

"Where are you going?" Eoin asked, his eyes flicking between the fight and his departing friend.

"We're getting nowhere here. Tell the men to follow."

Eoin stood for a few heartbeats, mouth open, confusion plain on his face. Then he roared for the men to retreat.

"Cover them!" he shouted at the archers next to him. "Make sure they get away."

The remaining outlaws – Mark, Ivo and one other – finished their opponents, although they had a hard time of it, with Mark needing to come to Ivo's aid before, at last, the three of them moved backwards, dead villagers at their feet and bloody blades held up, defensively, before them.

The villagers let them go, although there were a few more arrows loosed at their retreating backs. None of the missiles struck an outlaw and, as the beaten men drew out of range of the longbowmen the sounds of laughing and cheering could be heard.

The people of Brighouse had won, and their joy – pride too – filled the ears of the disgusted, retreating wolf's heads.

"Beaten by a bunch of farmers and peasants," one surly youngster spat as the outlaws turned the corner and the trees hid the site of their capitulation. He wiped the sweat from his filthy forehead before stopping to quickly remove the string from his bow. The other archers followed his lead, packing their own strings away into little pouches before they all hurried to catch up with Eoin and the others.

Philip could be seen some way in the distance, striding along purposefully, and Mark wondered what was going through their unhinged leader's mind.

Eoin was shouting along the road. "Wait on us!" but Philip ignored them.

Mark knew how the man's mind worked and he suspected their defeat would be avenged in some brutal fashion. They would need to send a warning to the whole of Yorkshire – if they allowed the people of Brighouse to attack and even kill some of their number then there'd be nothing to stop everyone else in the north of England trying the same.

Philip was only walking and now Eoin broke into a jog, covering the distance between them in a few heartbeats. Mark wanted to hear what they said so he slapped Ivo on the arm and increased his own pace. "Come on, let's catch them up. I want to know what mad scheme that bastard will come up with for us next."

Ivo grunted but matched Mark's fast walk, rubbing his side where one of the villagers had managed to land a blow with some blunt weapon. The wrong end of a hatchet or maybe a hammer – it had probably cracked a rib or two.

Most of the outlaws hadn't bothered trying to catch their leader. In the black mood Philip was in, they knew it would be safer to remain a healthy distance away. So Mark and Ivo were able to hear the conversation as Eoin finally drew up beside his friend and, almost endearingly, try to comfort him.

"It's fine," the giant shrugged, a rueful smile on his face as he turned to look at Philip. "So they beat us – they had lookouts posted to warn them when we appeared. We'll learn from this and it won't happen again."

Philip remained silent as they walked, the only sounds the outlaws' many booted feet tramping along on the old road and the warning screeches of a pair of magpies hidden somewhere in the foliage overhead which had clearly identified their approach as a threat.

At last Philip laid a hand on Eoin's wrist and squeezed. It was a fatherly gesture and surprised Mark, who wondered if their mad leader did actually have a more pleasant, caring side to him.

"You're right," Groves agreed. "We will learn from this. Next time we visit a village for supplies we'll go in smaller numbers, rather than as an invading force. We need things like arrows and eggs and salt and ale and so on so we'll just need to behave like every other traveller for a while."

Eoin grinned, so obviously happy that Philip's mood had lifted that Mark envied their friendship. Aye, he and Ivo had been companions for years but, if it came to it, he'd have no hesitation in leaving the toothless man behind if it meant saving his own hide. And he expected Ivo would feel the same way about him.

Loyalty was a rare and precious commodity in these dark times.

"What will we do now then?" Eoin asked, his gait relaxing as the tension and excitement of the battle left him and the relative safety of the forest swallowed them up again. "Shouldn't we get off the road? In case there's foresters or Robin Hood's men about. Don't want to make an easy target for them, do we?"

Philip waved a hand dismissively.

"Fuck Robin Hood, his mischief has already seen our numbers cut today. No, we stay on the road until we find some travellers."

Mark felt his stomach tighten into a knot and Eoin looked confused.

"To rob them?" the big man wondered.

"To send a message," Philip growled, and the smile that never seemed to leave his seamed face was gone.

"Christ help whoever we run into next on this road," Mark muttered.

"It'll take more than Christ to help them," Ivo said, nodding his head to draw his companion's eyes along the road.

Heading straight for them was a young woman, an elderly couple riding a rickety ox-drawn wagon, and, running along beside them, two small boys squealing playfully as they whacked at one another with sticks.

"You'd best head off back to the camp," Philip said without bothering to look at Eoin. "Start a fire and heat up the big pot of pottage we left there, eh? The rest of us will be along in a while."

* * *

Robin felt sick to his stomach. Never in all his life had he felt like this before. Even when he'd been captured by Sir Guy of Gisbourne, beaten mercilessly and thrown in Nottingham Castle's dungeon he'd not felt as upset as he did now.

Will Scarlet looked ashen faced, his lips a tight, bloodless, line, and he was a man who'd seen all manner of brutality as a mercenary fighting overseas alongside the Templars and Hospitallers.

"Who found them?" the coroner, Edwin of Mansfield, asked. He was the only man that appeared unmoved by the scene before them and Robin didn't envy him his job if it made him desensitised to such cruelty.

"Forester from Brighouse," Robin replied. "Came out hunting and chanced upon them. Poor lad will never be the same again, I'm sure."

The coroner grunted and moved on to look at the next body.

"The forester raised the alarm and messengers took word to the other towns and villages close-by until, eventually, we heard about it. Presumably news reached you and the bailiff there via the same route." Robin nodded towards a surly, fat man, Dunstan de Boer, the bailiff of nearby Halifax, which was also where the coroner hailed from. Brighouse was part of their jurisdiction.

"Aye, no doubt," Edwin agreed distractedly, examining the wounds in the corpse he was bent over.

Robin and his men had been in Barnsley when the news of the terrible crime reached them but, despite riding to the scene as fast as possible, the coroner and bailiff had been the first officials to arrive and begin the investigation.

"There's nothing to investigate here," de Boer spat in disgust as he came over, eyeing the bloody scene before them and handed a piece of parchment to Robin. "Here. It's all your fault apparently."

"My fault?" Robin demanded in disbelief, snatching the parchment from the sour-faced bailiff.

"Aye," the man agreed. "Read it."

Friar Tuck had taught Robin how to read a little when they'd been wolf's heads together in the forest and, since Robin's elevation to polite society, he'd grown more confident in his skills so it wasn't a difficult task for him to understand the neat letters that had been scratched into the parchment in – disturbingly – what appeared to be blood. No doubt from one of these poor victims.

"What does it say?" Little John demanded, crowding in to peer over his captain's shoulder even though he himself couldn't read more than a word or two.

Robin scanned the writing, forming the words with his mouth silently. Then he re-read it, before he met his giant friend's eyes and shrugged.

"It's from that bastard Groves, but we knew this was his work anyway. He says this is what happens when people attack his men."

"Attack his men?" Will Scarlet demanded, gesturing at the lifeless bodies in the grass around them. "These people wouldn't have attacked a gang of outlaws, what the fuck is he on about?"

"You haven't heard?" de Boer asked then carried on when he was met with blank looks. "The outlaws tried to get into Brighouse." He glared at Robin. "Your little motivational speech – just like the one you gave in Halifax – bolstered the men of the village into setting up lookouts and a local militia just in case they were attacked."

"Good on them," Will growled, to agreement from the rest of Robin's listening men.

"Aye, perhaps," the bailiff nodded. "But it seems this fellow Groves was a little upset at the fact a bunch of peasants attacked his men. And this–" he nodded towards the body the coroner was currently kneeling beside "– is the result. Carnage."

"How the fuck is that Robin's fault?" Scarlet demanded, pushing forward and pressing his finger into the fat bailiff's chest. "Would you suggest the people of Yorkshire just lie down and let these lunatics wash over them like a tide of blood and steel?"

De Boer stumbled backwards, fear written all over his flushed face and held up his hands. "No, well, that's not what I meant, really..."

"Peace, Will," Robin said sadly. "Maybe he's right."

"Oh, you have a word with him John, he's in one of those moods of his." Scarlet shook his head in exasperation and stalked away, along the road towards Brighouse. "I'm going to get a drink. Any of you lads fancy joining me?" He threw Dunstan de Boer a final, venomous glance. "I've got a bad taste I need to wash from my mouth."

"Aye, on you go," Robin waved at the others. "No need for you to all hang around here. John, Stephen and I will catch up with you shortly. Don't finish all the ale! Will – have a word with the headman before you start drinking. See what he can tell you."

"What the hell are we going to do about these bastards," John muttered, to no-one in particular and the coroner looked up, momentarily stopping his prodding at the wound in the old man's side.

"My advice would be to catch them and hand them over to sheriff as soon as possible," the man said, bluntly.

"Easier said than done," Stephen retorted, annoyed.

The coroner returned to his examination and the three friends stood, Dunstan de Boer beside them, staring down at the death that lay before them.

Robin's heart ached for the two little boys, not very much older than his own beautiful son, who had been stabbed repeatedly by, the coroner had told them, daggers rather than a longer bladed weapon. The young lawman's imagination worked of its own accord, and he saw Philip Groves, pretending to be friendly, calling over the children. Befriending them, then, when they were smiling and relaxed, his dagger had done its work.

Robin had no idea if that's what had really happened but the vision wouldn't leave him and he felt dizzy for a moment. Horror and disgust that a man could do such a thing to little children.

Still, at least the brothers – which they surely were, red-haired and green-eyed as they were, in matching little outfits – had died quickly.

The old man too had seemingly died from just a single sword thrust through the heart, probably trying to protect the others.

It was a different story for the women though.

The younger one – no doubt the boys' mother – had been stripped and raped.

He glanced across at the older woman. Even she had been raped, despite the fact she was at least in her sixties. Her toothless mouth hung open in death and again Robin's imagination, unbidden and unwanted, supplied possible explanations for what had been done to her before she too was silenced forever by a slash across the neck.

"We have to find these monsters," he whispered, eyes drawn back, inexorably, to look at the murdered children. He saw Arthur lying there and forced himself to turn away before he went mad from the horror.

"How?" John demanded. "You know as well as any of us how hard it is to find men in a forest the size of Barnsdale. We evaded the law for years, even when there were huge parties of soldiers and foresters out looking for us after the rebellion."

Stephen concurred. "We'd need a thousand men to cover the land closely enough to flush them out and capture them. It's hopeless."

Robin stood in thought for a time, silent and grim. Eventually he shouted to the bailiff, de Boer, who had moved off to direct his foresters in covering and transporting the corpses to Brighouse for a Christian burial.

"You said a forester discovered the bodies?"

De Boer nodded. "Aye. Young man of about eighteen years, I don't think he'd ever seen anything like it."

"Take me to him. Maybe there's a way we can locate these murdering bastards after all."

CHAPTER NINETEEN

Sir Henry de Faucumberg read the letter from the king and felt a cold shiver run down his back as the words sank in.

This was what he'd feared for so long although he never truly thought the day would come: Edward was removing him from his post.

Well, not completely – he would still be the Sheriff of Yorkshire, but he was to lose Nottinghamshire. He had overseen both counties for a number of years now and, he believed, managed to do a fine job in the face of such trials as the Marcher rebellion in 1321 and the resulting lawlessness that followed. Robin Hood's outlaws hadn't been the only landless men infesting the forests during that time, yet he, de Faucumberg had managed to, mostly, bring things under control.

Until recently.

The king had been informed of the new band of wolf's heads spreading terror in Barnsdale and, if reports were true, in Sherwood as well now. It seemed Edward wanted Sir Henry to relocate north, to Yorkshire, while someone else – he had no idea who, the letter didn't say – would be assuming his duties, and his castle, in Nottingham.

The messenger who delivered the sealed scroll to him stood silently, head bowed, on the other side of dark oak desk, awaiting further orders.

"You may leave me," de Faucumberg said, nodding his thanks for the fellow's successful mission.

"I've to take your reply to the king –"

"Yes, I'm aware of that," the sheriff snapped, then his voice softened. It wasn't this man's fault he was being replaced after all. "Go and get yourself some refreshment. Ale, meat, whatever...I'll have my reply ready for you when you return."

The messenger couldn't help grinning as he bowed and hastily made his way from the room. De Faucumberg knew many barons and noblemen treated such men as if they were no better than animals and the poor lad was probably expecting he'd have to return to the king in London without a chance to do much more than take a piss and change his horse.

As the messenger disappeared though the doorway, the sheriff's steward, William-atte-Burn, peered into the room.

"Would you like anything, my lord?" he asked.

"Aye, bring me a jug of wine. The good stuff."

When the door closed again the sheriff sighed, rubbed a hand across his face, and sat in his high-backed chair, staring up at the ceiling, trying to marshal his thoughts. It was a fine day outside, and the sunlight spilled into his room catching myriad motes of dust in its bright glow, although the stone walls never warmed much, even at this time of year, so he felt pleasantly cool. The sounds of the bustling city not so far off, beneath Castle Rock, seemed to fade away as he contemplated his new orders.

Why would King Edward remove him from the prestigious position as Sheriff of Nottingham, with its attendant castle and welcome salary? Sir Henry had been loyal to the king, even when so many in these parts spoke openly of sedition and he knew the monarch appreciated that loyalty. Or at least he always believed so.

He felt anger build inside him: anger at the king for rewarding his years of service with this kick in the teeth; anger at those damned rebels, led by Thomas, Earl of Lancaster, whom the peasants seemed to revere now as if he'd been a saint; and anger at Robin Hood.

Hood, as an outlaw, had been a thorn in his side for a long time, de Faucumberg fumed, leading his merry band of bastards about the countryside, robbing powerful clergymen and even joining the ill-fated rebellion. Yet, when he'd been pardoned, the sheriff had rewarded the young man with a place on his staff and given him the job of rooting out this new robber-king of Barnsdale, a task

Hood simply hadn't been up to so far.

The latch was lifted with a dull click and his steward came in carrying a tray laden with a jug of wine, one brass goblet and a selection of sweetmeats.

The sheriff felt his mouth begin to water at the little delicacies and he sighed, forcing a smile onto his lips. "Thank you, William. You've been a good servant to me."

The steward had been in de Faucumberg's service for the better part of five years, working his way up from his first position as bottler. He knew the sheriff quite well by this time and met his lord's eyes now.

"You look...flustered, Sir Henry," the man said tactfully. "Did the messenger bring bad news?"

"Of a sort, yes."

"May I help?"

The anger had gone from the sheriff by now. He was being hard on Robin – when a gang of criminals chose to hide out in the great forests of northern England there was precious little the law could do to find them and bring them to justice. He understood that better than anyone. He also knew that, if anyone could track down this Philip Groves and his men, it would be Hood.

His anger at the king had also begun to dissipate as he tried to make sense of his apparent demotion.

"Pull up a chair," he said to William, lifting the jug and filling the goblet with the precious red liquid and passing it to the surprised steward who had shared a drink with the sheriff before, but never the good stuff!

"My lord –"

De Faucumberg waved away the protestation before it could leave the man's mouth and leaned back in his chair, strawberry tart in hand and a thoughtful look on his bearded face.

"The king has removed me from my position as sheriff here in Nottingham." He held up a hand to, again, silence the steward before he could speak and continued. "I'm to move to Yorkshire, using Pontefract Castle as my base. Presumably the seneschal there – Sir John de Burton – has already been informed of all this and it won't be a shock to him when I turn up with my entourage."

"Why?" William seemed to have forgotten the expensive wine in his goblet, so surprised was he at the news.

"That's what I'm trying to figure out. When first I read Edward's letter I assumed it was punishment for something. These new outlaws plaguing the countryside perhaps. God knows – as does the king – we've had more than our fair share of murdering, landless men in the forests around here over the years."

"That can hardly be blamed on you, though." William remembered his drink and tipped it back, letting not a single drop spill down his chin or around his lips.

De Faucumberg nodded agreement. "The king is beset with problems," he said, almost to himself, as he worked through the ideas that were presenting themselves to them. "Queen Isabella – damn her – has spent her time in France trying to raise an army. It won't be long before she arrives back on these shores with that idiot Mortimer of Wigmore and tries to usurp the throne. The king is doing his best to repair the coastal defences and fortifications in London but...why punish me? Does Edward not think me loyal enough? Does he fear I might join Isabella when she finally invades?"

De Faucumberg leaned forward to pour himself some wine, remembered he'd given the only goblet to William and sat back again with another strawberry tart.

"Perhaps the king isn't punishing you? Perhaps this is a reward for your loyalty to him over the years."

The sheriff gazed at his steward thoughtfully, finally catching William's meaning. "He's sending me north to be further away from whatever trouble might be coming..."

The idea made sense. Isabella and her supporters would not look favourably on those – like the Despensers and Sir Henry – who had been loyal to King Edward. By sending him further up north, to Pontefract, perhaps the sheriff would avoid the invaders' scrutiny when they seized power. Their attention would mostly be focused on London and the lands of the Despensers in the south.

And Isabella would take the crown for her son, de Faucumberg expected, eventually. This was one uprising too far – the king was too unpopular to remain in power thanks to those despised Despensers. The queen hated Hugh Despenser even more than most people; rumours suggested the man had actually raped her which would certainly explain her hatred of him, but Sir Henry had no idea about any of that.

"What do we do now then?" the steward asked, refilling his goblet, making the most of his master's generous mood.

"Make ready to move my household to Yorkshire. Have my possessions stowed on carts, tell my wife and children to prepare and make damn sure we take enough soldiers to deter those cursed outlaws from robbing us on the road!"

He stood up, a smile on his face and reached for the half-drained wine jug in salute. "Cheers William," he said, raising the whole jug to his lips, and spilling much of it into his grey beard as he tipped it into his mouth. "And God save the King."

He'd always liked Pontefract.

* * *

"You're the forester that discovered the murdered travellers on the road to the village, is that right? Blase Cottar?"

The Bailiff of Halifax had brought them to the church hall in Brighouse, a single storey timber building, with a couple of rickety tables on the floor and benches running along the walls, although the men had all chosen to remain standing. Somehow it didn't seem right to sit down for this discussion. He'd then commanded the headman, Gregor, to summon Blase to the hall.

The young man nodded, his glance flicking from the local bailiff to the larger figure of Robin Hood and the even more massive Little John. "Aye, it was me," he agreed in a husky voice. "Never seen anything like it and I hope never to again. I'll have nightmares about the lady's...well, you know what I mean." His nostrils flared and he went on, angrily. "What are you going to do about it, bailiff? We need more men to hunt down these bastards. Outlaws like that...they're worse than animals. I thought we'd chased them off but..."

De Boer looked annoyed at the forester's impertinent questioning but Robin interposed himself between the two men.

"We're doing all we can, Blase," Robin said, his voice low. Placating. He understood how the local felt – those murdered people hailed from the forester's own village. He'd probably grown up with the woman and seen the children playing innocently around the place every day. The sight of their bodies would have been a terrible shock. "But, as a forester yourself, you must know how hard it is to track even a large group of men in the greenwood, if they know how to use the terrain and foliage to their advantage."

The young man's shoulders slumped, but only for a moment, before his spirit returned. Robin liked this lad, and he liked him even more when he spoke again.

"I'd like to join you in the search for them. I'll not be able to sleep at night until the whoresons are brought to justice and the people around here are safe again."

"Good man," Little John rumbled from behind Robin's shoulder. "You're exactly the type we need if we're going to catch Groves's gang."

"Surely one more man isn't going to make a difference?" de Boer broke in, an irritated expression on his round face. "Especially one as young and inexperienced as this fellow."

Robin expected the forester would be much more useful in a fight than the haughty bailiff but he held his peace, knowing he might need de Boer's co-operation in the future.

"You're right," he said, raising a hand to stave off Blase's angry retort. "One man wouldn't make much difference, *if* we just wanted him to join us as we look for the wolf's head. But I have another idea," he looked directly into the young forester's eyes. "How would you feel about joining the outlaws? I mean," he clarified, seeing the confusion on Blase's face, "infiltrate their group. Become one of them."

De Boer said nothing to that. He knew very well such a mission could well turn out to be suicidal. If Groves or any of his men recognised the forester, or somehow found out his real identity...what had been done to the poor lady on the road would probably look like a pleasant experience in comparison to Blase's fate...

The lad ran a hand through his unkempt brown hair and said nothing for a time, lost in thought.

"I know we're asking a lot of you. You will be paid a salary from the sheriff's own purse, though," Robin said, but Blase waved him to silence.

"I'll do it." He set his jaw and dropped a hand to the dagger that was tucked inside his belt. "If this is the only way we're going to catch those animals, I'll do it."

"Good man," Robin repeated John's earlier sentiment, grinning at the forester who managed a tight, nervous smile in return.

Even Dunstan de Boer echoed Robin's words and clapped Blase on the back awkwardly.

"It would be better if there was someone else to go with him," Little John said. "It'll look more believable if two men turn up looking to join Groves's gang. One wouldn't last that long on his own in the forest before the law caught him or other, less friendly outlaws. Two on the other hand – two could survive forever, taking turns as lookouts and watching one another's backs when they visited villages for necessary supplies."

It was a good point, Robin conceded, but finding another man to take on this deadly task would surely be impossible. He knew his own men – John, Will, Stephen, or any of the others – would do it, but they'd be recognised too easily. Robin Hood's gang had been known by almost everyone in the towns and villages around here.

"My friend Antony might do it."

The three lawmen looked at Blase hopefully.

"He's a good fighter, bit bigger than me too. And he could talk himself out of any trouble as you know bailiff." He gave a boyish, lop-sided grin which only grew bigger at de Boer's irritable grunt. "He'd be perfect, if I can get him to agree." He turned back to Robin. "How much will we be getting paid? That might make things easier."

"Ha, go and find him, Blase, we'll discuss your wages once he's here." The smile left his face and he grasped the forester's arms, just hard enough to get his point across. "Don't mention any of this to him though. Leave that to us. And do not tell another soul about it either. Your own safety depends on it, you understand?"

The slim young man returned Robin's grim look, nodded once then, released from the lawman's grip, turned and hurried out into the street to look for his friend.

"Tell us frankly, bailiff: what's this mate of his, Antony, like? You clearly have some knowledge of him."

"Aye," de Boer growled. "Cocky bastard. Troublemaker. He's got a smart mouth on him, as the lad said. He'll fit right in with a band of outlaws." His face softened just a little then. "To be fair, both he and Blase aren't wicked men. They like a drink, as do most young lads in Brighouse, and sometimes it gets them into trouble. But there's no evil in them. I hope we're not sending them into the wolf's lair simply to be torn to pieces."

Robin and John exchanged uncomfortable glances at the bailiff's maudlin words, but what other choice did they have? They could waste months – years even! – trying to stop Groves, while he and his followers robbed and raped their way around the entire county.

If, on the other hand, they had men of their own inside the wolf's head's camp...a trap could be laid and the hunt brought to an end much, much quicker.

No, Robin mused, Blase Cottar had stumbled upon the bloody remains of that family for a reason. God had lit the fires of vengeance in the forester's belly and now they would harness that flame.

A servant left a jug of wine and another of ale on one of the tables by the wall and, as they waited, John walked over and poured drinks for the three of them: wine for de Boer, ale for Robin and himself.

They stood in silence, lounging against the wooden walls of the hall, sipping from their cups and thinking about the terrible crime that had been committed just outside sleepy Brighouse.

It wasn't long before the door opened again and Blase came in, followed by a gangly youth with a straggly brown beard and a gap-toothed grin. He was very similar to Blase, although a little taller. The two could easily pass for brothers.

Antony was friendly and confident, although his enthusiasm as he greeted the two famous lawmen seemed somewhat forced, and Robin guessed the lad probably tried too hard to ingratiate himself with people.

It wasn't to his own, personal liking, but perhaps such fawning reverence would suit Philip Groves's egotistical mindset. Robin prayed that would be the case, and the outlaw leader wouldn't question the two young men too closely when they tried to join his gang.

"What do we do if the bastards want to rob and murder more people?" Antony asked when the situation had been explained to him, voicing the biggest concern Robin himself had.

"Hopefully you won't be with them long enough for that to be a problem," Little John said, placing his empty ale-mug back on the table with a hollow thump. "They're sure to lay low for a time – they'll be well aware of the manhunt that's going on for them after what they did here in Brighouse. So..."

"Once you're in with them," Robin continued, taking up where his giant friend trailed off, "all you have to do is tell them you're going fishing, or hunting, one day, then head for the nearest village and have someone carry news of their camp's location to us."

"You'll have to be vigilant," John cautioned, arching his back to stretch muscles that were beginning to ache from standing indoors for so long, oblivious to how intimidating he looked. "When word comes to us we won't waste time heading for the wolf's heads' camp and mounting an attack. Be ready for it when it comes, so you don't get in the way and take a friend's sword in the guts."

"Get in the way?" Antony spat. He'd heard all about what the outlaws had done to the Brighouse family and he, like Blase, had been friendly with the young mother. He was as ready as his friend to bring justice to the perpetrators. "We won't get in your way. We'll be hiding in the shadows, ready to plunge our blades into those murdering dog's backs."

Blase licked his lips but nodded. "Aye, we'll support you from inside the camp. What d'you want us to do if we can take their leader out ourselves? Should we take the chance? Or does the king need him alive to be made an example of on the gallows?"

Dunstan de Boer answered before Robin could come to a decision, telling them it was imperative to capture Groves alive.

"He must be made to pay, publicly, for his crimes," the bailiff said flatly. "After what he's done the people will demand their place at his execution. The king has more to worry about than this right now, but the law requires a hanging for Groves's actions. Now..." He walked across to place his own, drained, cup onto the table and nodded to Robin. "I must be on my way or it'll be too dark to travel back to Halifax. God give you good day. And please – catch these criminals. There's no place for such filth in my jurisdiction."

John pursed his lips and gave a little, disgusted snort once the bailiff left and closed the door behind him. "That was a dig at us you know," he said to Robin. "Arsehole of a man."

"He is that," Antony laughed, and Blase joined in, nodding.

"He's also stupid if he thinks I'll ask you men to put yourselves – or this mission – in jeopardy by trying to arrest Groves in his own camp, surrounded by his own followers. No," Robin chopped a hand across in the air, as if slicing an outlaw's head off. "If you get the chance to kill Groves, take it. If we could get him out of the way I'm convinced the rest of his gang will splinter and disband. He's the glue holding them all together."

"But the king –"

"The king's not here, lads," John butted in. "And he won't give a shit if we hang these outlaws or gut them in a fight. All he wants is the forest cleared of outlaws. So don't try to be heroes."

"Any more than you already are," Robin said, smiling grimly. "You know how dangerous this is going to be? And the probable outcome."

Neither of the Brighouse men replied to that, they simply stood, stony-faced, possibly imagining their fate should they be outed as spies.

"How much are we getting paid?" Antony said at last, his smile returning, and Robin wondered if the young man was able to eat anything other than broth, so many of his teeth were missing. "I've got a few gambling debts to be cleared off."

Robin made them an offer and wasn't surprised when, with gasps of disbelief, they said they'd leave that very day to try and find their way into the outlaws' gang. To be honest, the money wasn't all that much, but it was a whole year's wages to the two young foresters who'd have taken on this job for much less, in the outraged mood they were in at the murders on their own doorstep.

"Please," Robin pleaded with them. "Be careful. You know better than anyone, Blase, what these people are capable of. Stick to your cover story and do *not* allow each other to become drunk. Ale will loosen your tongues and leave you vulnerable. You can drink as much as you like when we've destroyed the bastards."

"What *is* our cover story?" Blase wondered. "You have any ideas?"

Robin had been planning that since they'd made their way towards the village after examining the murder scene.

"Aye," he replied. "We keep it simple. The pair of you are foresters from Brighouse. I don't see any point changing that, because you know it and the fewer lies you have to tell the less chance there is you'll be caught out. So...you're from Brighouse, but you're shit foresters because you take bribes to let people go when you catch them up to no good and you hate the bailiff, de Boer, always undermining his authority. You were caught yourselves, by a farmer, two weeks ago, when you tried to steal one of his sheep, and chased out of the village by an angry mob. The people hereabouts didn't like you anyway, because you were always drinking and starting fights, right?" They nodded, rapt, and the big lawman continued. "You've been sleeping rough in the greenwood ever since, and robbed a few travellers, spending the money you've managed to steal from them on bread, eggs, cheese and so on in Brackenhall, where no-one recognises you. And you've been using your bows –" again he stopped and looked at them hopefully "–you can both shoot a longbow can't you? As foresters I'd hope so. Yes? Good. Well, you've been using your bows to hunt deer and so on. Your crime was a small one so no-one's been putting much effort into the search or you. Until today, when the massacred family was discovered – although you don't know about that – and the forest's been crawling with foresters, the sheriff's soldiers, and Robin Hood's men ever since. Are you taking all this in?"

Blase nodded silently and his friend shrugged non-committally. It was a lot to remember Robin admitted to himself, hoping the tall youngster would make the effort to get all of the cover story clear with Blase before they met Groves and his gang. If he didn't they'd both be dead.

"So you ran away from Brighouse, and, since you'd heard rumours about the big group of wolf's heads near Mirfield that were looking for new recruits you headed there to try and join them. You knew you wouldn't survive long on your own, with all the lawmen scouring the greenwood. How does that all sound? Does it make sense? Aye? Good." He emptied the last dregs of ale in his cup into his mouth and belched. "I suppose that's all then."

"How do we find them though?" Antony asked after a time. "We could spend months wandering blindly around Barnsdale and never stumble across their camp."

"As I said, we've had reports from friends of ours and we believe they're based somewhere near Mirfield. I'm sure the outlaws will find you once you get anywhere near their camp-site. They'll have lookouts posted all around their perimeter – as much to detect the law as to find new recruits. Remember, Groves *wants* new men – he wants to lead an army. So it shouldn't be too hard to get inside their camp."

"Staying there very long will be another matter," John warned. "Like Robin says: be careful, and look for the first opportunity to carry word of your location to the headman in Mirfield. We'll hide outside the village and tell him to pass your message to us when he has it, then you go back to Groves so they don't notice you're missing."

"Good luck." Robin clasped Blase's arm before moving on to Antony. "Go and gather some food and your weapons. Then say your farewells to your families, but *do not tell them where you're going*. And go over your cover story as you prepare to leave – your lives depend on it so you'll need to get it right. I'll send word to the sheriff to send us the soldiers he promised, so we're ready to make our attack as soon as we hear from you."

"What about our money?" Antony said, waving away John's confused look. "I know we can't take it with us just now but I'd like to know my family won't go short if we don't come back..." His voice trailed off a little, as the realisation of their situation finally sunk in.

"Rest easy, friend," Robin nodded reassuringly. "I'll leave your money with the headman. Gregor isn't it? I'll leave it with him. If anything happens to you, he'll make sure your families receive it. Otherwise, you can collect it once we wipe out Groves and his men for good, and then have the best drinking session of your lives."

"You can buy us one too," John grinned and the mood in the room seemed to lift again before the young foresters opened the door and left the church hall.

Behind them, Robin and Little John stood in silent contemplation for a time, praying to Almighty God and the Magdalene for Blase and Antony's safe return, and the success of the mission.

But both lawmen knew they'd probably just sent the Brighouse foresters to a violent death.

CHAPTER TWENTY

Henry of Elmstow, dean of Lewes Priory, was an elderly man with a deeply lined face and wild grey eyebrows. Like many older people, he was cranky and had little patience for the stupidity of youngsters.

It didn't help that Prior John de Monte Martini was also an irritable old man with a temper and both of them seemed to take pleasure in being vicious and nasty towards the young novices who'd been chosen to accompany them on their visit to Wakefield this summer.

"You boy," the dean shouted at Conrad, a young red-haired, freckle-faced lad of only thirteen, "bring more wine for the prior, and hurry up."

The boy sprinted over to the rumbling, covered wagon, which carried not only the dean and the prior, but also, in a compartment in the back, the stores of wine and food which were for the high-ranking clergymens' own personal use. The dean tossed the empty skin at him and he fumbled it, earning an exasperated sigh from his superior, before he scooped it up and refilled it from a stoppered jug.

Without a word, the boy handed it over to the prior deferentially. The elderly man never said a word of thanks and the dean waved him away with a sour expression on his seamed face.

Conrad stood, head bowed, for a few moments as the wagon was carried along the road by two big horses, and then he fell back into line behind it, along with the other novices and the mercenaries who'd been hired to guard the party on their journey north.

The red-haired youngster came from a wealthy family – his father owned a successful fishing business in Hastings – but, being the third son, his parents had sent him off to Lewes to become one of the Black Monks. A Benedictine.

Fate was cruel, Conrad thought – his eldest brother was a partner in their father's business, while the other joined the Hospitallers and was away somewhere learning to become a sergeant-at-arms or a knight or some other noble – exciting! – thing. And here he was...

"How many more days do we have to journey?" A voice broke in, shattering his thoughts and he turned to look irritably at the speaker who finished his query without noticing Conrad's angry glance. "My feet are killing me."

"We've only just left Oxford, there's still days of walking to go yet," the freckled young man replied. "So your feet better get used to it. Unless you want to ask those two for a lift on their wagon."

He nodded towards the groaning cart that they were following like rats after a piper he'd heard about from his widely-travelled father.

The other novice's eyes widened and he shook his head at Conrad's suggestion. "I'll just try and keep up."

"Ach, you'll soon get used to it. My feet hurt too at first but the blisters went away. Now it's my thighs that burn at the end of the day but I'm sure that'll pass too."

"It's my back that aches," another, older novice asserted, overhearing the conversation, and Conrad smiled sympathetically, turning away and focusing on the road ahead.

"Do you think there'll be any trouble when we get to Wakefield," the boy next to him asked.

"What do you mean, Gervase? Why would there be trouble?"

"You must have heard about the prior's run-in a few years ago when he made this same journey to check up on the running of Wakefield. When Robin Hood attacked him?"

Conrad's head snapped around at the mention of the infamous wolf's head. Here was a tale that needed to be heard.

"I don't know what you're talking about," he said. "Tell me!"

Gervase grinned and nudged the older boy on his other side. "Reynard told me about it. He went last year and heard the villagers talking about it. It's a famous tale in Wakefield – the people there hate Prior de Monte Martini."

Conrad grunted, understanding their feelings. The old man was arrogant and mean and if he'd done something to annoy Robin Hood…

"Tell me what happened then," he demanded, keeping his voice low for fear of their superiors in the wagon overhearing their conversation. He knew such a conversation would be rewarded with the prior's harsh version of penance which often meant self-flagellation rather than simply reciting a few *Pater Noster*s.

Reynard was an excitable lad, which made him a good companion, but even he knew to speak in hushed tones, so Conrad moved to walk closer beside him, leaning his head in to listen as the other boy told him all about de Monte Martini's visit to Wakefield five-or-so years earlier. How the prior had allegedly said something horrible to a local girl and been rewarded for it by having his nose broken by Robin Hood. That event was what had made the fabled Hood into an outlaw, for he'd been forced to run away and hide in the forest or the prior would have seen him hanged.

To the novices who weren't particularly fond of their scowling prior, the story was exciting and amusing. There'd been lots of times when they'd have loved to smack the old bastard in the face and this tale was almost as good.

"Is that why we've got so many mercenaries with us?" Conrad wondered, eyes casting about at the hard-looking armoured men who surrounded them, both on horseback and on foot. There were around a dozen of them and the flame-haired novice simply assumed the prior's wagon carried money or some other valuables which would account for such a large armed escort. But now… "If he fears the wolf's head no wonder he wanted so many guards!"

Reynard broke in, shaking his head with a superior air, as if, at fourteen, his extra year made him so much more knowledgeable and experienced than Conrad or Gervase. "Nah, the mercenaries are just a precaution because there's always outlaws ready to rob travellers. Robin Hood isn't a wolf's head any more. He was pardoned, didn't you know that?"

The younger novices were too interested to feel irritated by Reynard's patronising tone and, as the morning and the miles passed, sore feet and adventures in far-off lands were forgotten, replaced with tales of Robin Hood and his loyal men.

Conrad was looking forward to reaching Wakefield now. He hoped the pardoned wolf's head would be there. Meeting a famous outlaw would be a dream come true!

* * *

"What d'you mean, you've never heard of me? I'm a famous outlaw."

Philip grinned but his expression wasn't mirrored on the face of Prior John de Monte Martini, who scowled, clenching and unclenching his fists although Blase couldn't tell whether that was from fear or rage. Probably both.

"Philip Groves? My brother Matt was one of that bastard Robin Hood's men. No doubt you've heard of *him*..." The wolf's head spat onto a clump of bracken, the thick saliva dripping down unpleasantly from one blooming yellow branch to another. "But you can't be from around these parts if you haven't heard of me. Everyone knows me in Yorkshire. Me and my lads here."

He gestured to those of his men who were visible, ringing the Prior's party and there was a gleeful cheer from many throats as the robbers hailed their leader's salute. Blase and Antony joined in with the shouting, not wanting to appear out of place.

It had been simpler than they'd feared to join Groves's band. The outlaw captain was trying to attract as many people as possible to his metaphorical banner, so almost anyone that looked like they could wield a sword was welcomed into their group after only some cursory questioning.

The Brighouse pair spent four hours travelling to Mirfield then, from there wandered for three days around the forest close to where some of the locals in the alehouse told them the outlaws had been heard, singing drunkenly or screaming, as if fights amongst them were common. Blase hadn't asked them why no-one had sent word to the sheriff about the gang's whereabouts – it was clear to him. If the law turned up and were unsuccessful in hunting down Groves's men – which was probable – the people of Mirfield would suffer; their informing would be suspected and acted upon by the ruthless wolf's head and the village would end up a smoking ruin.

They'd wandered the greenwood, hunting as they went, even lighting a camp-fire on the first two nights, and made no attempt to conceal themselves or be silent. They were stopped in their tracks on the third day by the giant, Eoin, and four other dirty, scowling men.

Antony had done most of the talking. His boyish smile contrasted with the steel evident behind his gaze and the outlaws seemed to take to the tall young man immediately. Blase was accepted as Antony's companion and, once they'd told Eoin their story about being hounded out of Brighouse by lawmen searching for someone else they were in.

Especially since they carried a brace of hares and even a small deer which was unfortunate enough to cross Blase's path just as he'd been about to unstring his longbow.

Meat was always welcome in Groves's camp.

"It's just a shame you don't have a barrel of ale with you as well," Eoin smiled, clapping them both on the back as they'd headed towards the wolf's heads' base a short distance away in a location that had clearly been well-chosen for its defensive properties.

That had been two days earlier, and Blase had spent the time well, making a mental map of the whole, squalid camp and its surrounding area, while Antony drank and bantered with their new 'friends', drawing attention away from his friend's surreptitious reconnoitring.

He noted the small but steep rock face that backed onto the location from the north, meaning a sneak attack from that direction was improbable; he measured the distance along the thick, near-impenetrable trees that fringed the southern and south-eastern edges of the area that would impede any attacks either on foot or from longbows; he scouted along the river which ran to the east, finding no fords nearby; and he memorised the location of the gap in the foliage which was, essentially, the only way to gain easy access into the camp.

The place was well chosen, Blase thought, although he wasn't a military tactician and he didn't have the experience Robin and his men did when it came to reading terrain. So he stored his observations in his head, praying he'd have a chance – soon – to pass them onto the bailiff. Hood, or one of his friends, would doubtless be able to find some holes in the seemingly impenetrable defences.

Before they had a chance to slip off that morning without it being too obvious a lookout turned up and told Groves there was a party of men approaching with a large covered wagon drawn by horses.

"Looks like clergymen," the lookout reported. "Some high-up fucker will be in the cart drinking wine and eating sweetmeats. There's a few young novices trailing along at the back looking miserable and a handful of mercenaries but they won't be a problem if we surprise them."

A group of travellers like that meant two things to Groves and his men: money and sport.

Blase's heart had sunk like a stone when the seemingly ever-smiling wolf's head ordered everyone to gather their weapons and make ready to ambush the clergyman's cart. The young Brighouse man had just been glad that no women were reported to be in the travelling party – he had no desire to see another raped and bloodied corpse adorning the Yorkshire grass.

But now that the outlaws had waylaid the travellers Blase wasn't so sure the lack of females in their company would mean less unpleasantness. The novices, fresh-faced and cleanly scrubbed in comparison to the hairy-arsed wolf's heads, seemed to be just as attractive to some of the men as any pretty girl, judging by the comments Blase could hear his new companions making.

He glanced at Antony who shared his pensive frown as one of the clergymen in the cart – the eldest of the two within – shouted at Groves.

"Yes, the prior knows very well who Robin Hood is – and God will judge that sinner at the Gates of Heaven one day. But it is you, sir, who don't know who you're dealing with." The skinny old man lifted a foot out of the cart, almost entangling the limb in silk curtains, and placed it on the road before returning to his diatribe. "This is Prior John de Monte Martini – one of the most powerful and influential men in all of England."

The prior must have realised that news wouldn't help their situation at all and he slapped the back of his companion's head, hard, the noise of the blow ringing throughout the clearing in which the outlaws had sprung their trap.

"Shut up, Henry," the churchman muttered, dragging his dean back, fully, into the wagon. Blase saw the novices at the back smirking and he guessed the dean – and no doubt the prior too – weren't much loved by the youngsters. He hoped they'd still be smirking by the time this was all finished.

De Monte Martini was also an elderly man, as became apparent when he struggled out of the cart and stood as straight-backed and haughty as he could manage in front of the watching outlaws, breath rasping in his throat even after such a small exertion.

"What's the meaning of this?" the prior demanded, not addressing Philip Groves but rather his own mercenaries who stood, weapons drawn but unused as they sized up the situation. "I paid you to defend us, not to allow scum like this to try and rob us. What are you waiting for?"

The mercenary leader, a man almost as tall as Eoin and even harder looking, with a scar right across his jawline, shrugged his broad shoulders. "There's more of them than there is us," he said, reasonably. "And they have their bows trained on us."

Groves threw back his head and laughed at that. "I like you," the wolf's head told the guard. "Why don't you and your men join us? We're making a lot of money robbing arseholes like your prior there. We can always use more men, isn't that right, Antony?" He beckoned to the Brighouse man, who somewhat sheepishly walked across the damp grass to stand beside Groves.

"This young man and his friend only came to use a couple of days ago, because they'd heard how well I reward my followers. Here." He pulled out a purse that positively bulged with coins, reached inside and used his thumb to flick one first to Antony, then another to the mercenary. Both were snatched from the air as their targets spotted their colour: silver.

"In God's name," Prior de Monte Martini shouted, striding forward to slap his mercenary on the head as he'd done with the dean. He had to reach up though, and the guard simply sidestepped the blow before it landed. "Defend us, or face Christ's wrath!"

Groves laughed again and shouted some blasphemy which Blase couldn't quite make out, but the prior's shocked face told him all he needed to know.

The outlaw turned his attention back to the mercenary, whose men had slowly been edging their way closer to him, preparing for the worst.

"Last chance, friend. Join us, or join them," he nodded at the dean and the prior, "in their God's arms."

Antony had followed the mercenaries lead and shuffled his way back to his friend's side, knowing this stand-off wasn't going to last much longer.

"What the fuck do we do?"

Blase didn't reply to his companion's whisper. How could he? If they joined the prior's forces they'd give themselves away and, more worryingly, would be dead, since the outlaws outnumbered their opponents. But they couldn't attack the mercenaries could they?

They were innocent men, just trying to earn enough money to put a crust on their tables.

In the end, the choice was taken out of their hands.

"Ah, fuck 'em, they had their chance," Groves roared, to his men as a whole. "Kill the guards and do what you will with the novices, but I want the prior alive."

The mercenaries had been hired by the dean and he'd chosen cleverly. This particular group had a well-earned reputation for their loyalty and professionalism, which was reflected in their fee, at almost double what most other sell-swords demanded.

As Groves shouted his orders the guard captain lunged forward, plunging his sword into the stomach of the nearest target.

Antony.

The Brighouse youngster didn't even try to defend himself, so swift was his attacker's move, and Blase, shocked, stumbled backwards, away from the bloody blade that had taken his friend's life and now wavered in the air, ready for more victims.

He tried to regain his equilibrium, bodies surging past him as the outlaws, howling with joy at the prospect of a fight, loosed their longbows and threw themselves at the surviving mercenaries who clumped together in a tight formation.

The first wolf's head to reach the defensive formation fell as he, seemingly with no regard for his own life, tried to run right through the sword points that faced him. Blase watched in morbid fascination as another outlaw, howling some weird battle-cry, did the same, ending his life on the tip of a mercenary's blade.

What insanity was this?

Not all of the outlaws were crazed though. The rest engaged the defenders, falling into a steady, almost rhythmic battle, with cries of pain, or anger, seeming to engulf the entire world as Blase looked on, too frightened to move.

He stared in surprise as some of the outlaws ignored the fighting and ran straight past towards the novices. Surely they posed no threat?

He turned back towards the battle which was almost over already. Only the mercenary captain still stood, and he was beset on all sides. He'd managed to kill at least three of his opponents but it was futile, as a myriad small slashes and cuts pierced his torso and legs before, at last, the proud man dropped onto the grass where he was hacked to bloody pieces by whooping outlaws.

Still, Blase stood rooted to the spot. Sickened, terrified and bewildered, with no idea what to do. He'd thought finding the murdered family on the road outside Brighouse had been bad, but actually witnessing the brave mercenary captain chopped apart like a piece of beef turned his brain to pottage. Nothing could be worse, he thought, until a pitiful cry came from the ground behind the battle and his eyes were drawn there, almost against his will.

"No," he breathed, his voice nothing more than a sob.

At last, his legs decided to work again and he ran, into the trees, tears streaming down his face, hands pressed against his ears as he tried to block out the screams of the novices.

CHAPTER TWENTY-ONE

"Calm down, lad, for fuck sake, it can't have been that bad."
Will Scarlet glared at the sobbing Blase as the young man tried, haltingly, to relate his tale and provide Robin's men with the information they needed to find Groves's gang.
"Easy, Will," Little John growled. "He's not much more than a boy and this is the second atrocity he's seen in a short space of time. Let him gather himself."
Robin nodded agreement and Scarlet raised his hands, in apology or exasperation the lawman couldn't tell.
"Here," he said, handing Blase a mug of strong ale. "Get this down you, it'll help with the shock."
The Brighouse man took the drink from Robin with shaking hands, spilling much of it over the sides and into the rushes on the alehouse floor, but he managed to upend it and drained the contents almost in one go. He spluttered and coughed, head down but raised his arm aloft, gesturing the mug for a refill and Robin called on the landlord to bring more ale.
Robin's party had been camping not far outside Mirfield for the past two days, and they'd made the headman, Jacques, well aware of their presence. When Blase ran into town he'd been spotted straight away and Jacques himself had run to the bailiff's camp-site to apprise him of the situation and lead the men back to the hysterical forester.
Eventually, the drink took effect and the young man's shaking subsided although he still looked like someone had walked across his grave. He finished describing what he'd seen happen to the clergymen's party, confirming that it was, certainly, Prior John de Monte Martini who'd been in the wagon. Robin knew it wasn't Christian, but he felt a secret glee at the idea of that bastard finally meeting his end. The old man had caused him so much trouble, it was only natural to feel some satisfaction at his demise. Still, he mused, it wasn't the rest of the prior's party's fault – Groves and his men had to be stopped and the defiled novices avenged, it was as simple as that.
"All right, first of all: are you able to take us to the outlaws' camp?"
Blase looked terrified at the idea but he knew it would be impossible to direct the lawmen there just by describing the way. He nodded, taking another pull from his mug, which Robin pushed away, not wanting the lad to be too inebriated to help them.
"Let's go then. If Groves noted your absence he might guess where you've gone and move their camp."
The bailiff patted his sword hilt unconsciously and nodded towards the doorway which Will and John moved through and began issuing orders to Arthur, James, Peter, Piers and the rest of the men.
Robin had sent a messenger from Brighouse to Nottingham days ago, when Blase and Antony first headed off to try and join the outlaws. Sir Henry de Faucumberg hadn't left Nottingham to take up residence in Pontefract yet, thankfully, so, when he received the message from Robin he despatched the bailiff's hand-picked soldiers to Mirfield; all except Thomas, who remained with the sheriff.
Nineteen men should be enough, along with Hood's friends.
Blase sighed heavily and glanced forlornly at the ale mug but Robin gently helped the younger man up by grasping his arm then guided him outside. He tossed a few coins onto their table and waved to the landlord who grunted his thanks as the big lawman made his way out, into the sunshine. A squall had hit the countryside a short while ago so Robin was happy at the dispersal of the clouds and the warm air that now made the puddles steam gently.
"Ready, lad? Good. Take us to Groves's camp then."
They left the horses behind knowing they'd be of little use in the dense greenwood, and, as they walked, the young spy told the lawmen about his observations of the outlaws' base: its location and surrounding terrain; defences; number and quality of defenders; and his own thoughts on how best to assault the place.

"How high is that cliff you mentioned?" Will asked after Blase had finished. "The height of three men?" He grunted. "I'd say we can send a few men to climb down there then. We've got ropes and the scum won't be expecting an attack from there, even when they see us coming from the other directions."

"And the river can be crossed," John mused. "Not by me though, I'm a shit swimmer."

"You swim fine," Stephen growled. "You just don't want to get wet."

"That too," the giant grinned. "I had a bath in the spring."

"Aye, we know," Will spat in mock disgust. "Smelly big bastard."

Robin laughed along with the others, happy that the mood hadn't grown maudlin or fearful amongst the men. "Peter, you find two or three volunteers from the sheriff's men who're strong swimmers and show them what they've to do."

Peter Ordevill lowered his eyebrows at the idea. "How come I always have to be the one getting fucking soaked?"

"Because you were a sailor," Robin grinned. "Stands to reason you must love being in the water."

"I don't think you understand how ships work," Peter grumbled but he fell back in the formation to find the men he'd need as Robin looked at Blase again.

"You said the outlaws are in awe of Groves but they're not disciplined, from what you saw at least?"

"That's right," Blase confirmed. "They do what he tells them, but they didn't act like a military unit. I mean, like the way I'd expect an army to act," he mumbled, face flushing, knowing his lack of experience in these matters must be obvious to everyone there. "When we practise with our longbows on a Sunday, Gregor makes us act like soldiers. We have a job, and a place, and we stick to them. But the outlaws just seemed to mill about doing whatever they wanted. Complacent. I suppose they think their camp won't be discovered and, if it is, the lookouts they've got posted will warn them in time." He shrugged. "If we manage to get there without being spotted your men will have the advantage, thanks to your discipline and experience."

Blase was fairly sure Groves only posted two, possibly, three lookouts, all to the south west, which was where the path led to their camp-site. He'd taken his own turn there on one of the nights but had not seen or heard of anyone travelling in other directions to be lookouts.

Their plans were well set long before they arrived on the outskirts of the outlaw camp and Robin was quietly confident today would mean the end for Groves. At last. He wasn't counting his chickens before they hatched though; he knew from bitter experience things like this didn't always work smoothly.

"Blase, you lead Will close to the position you know there should be a lookout. He'll deal with it. Then run back and get us when the road is clear."

As the pair headed off like phantoms into the undergrowth Robin gestured Peter and the two volunteer swimmers forward and told them to be on their way. They were to swim the river and conceal themselves in the trees that Blase said fringed the outlaw base on the eastern side, attacking with their longbows as soon as they heard Robin blow his hunting horn. That was a new tool for the lawman, who'd never used it when he'd been a wolf's head himself since their best defence had been not giving away their location.

Now, though, it would come in handy.

He sent Stephen and Arthur off with another two men – and ropes – to head west then come round on the northern side of the camp's location. They'd climb down and, like the swimmers, await the signal before attacking with bow and sword.

This felt good to Robin. He'd missed the days of leading his men as a fighting force and now, despite the possibility of death in the coming battle, his spirits were higher than they'd been for a long time. He re-checked the straps on his gambeson were snug, his chain mail vest had no obvious holes, and he unfurled his bowstring from its pouch on his sword-belt, stringing his warbow with it. His men – those who were archers – followed his lead.

He was ready and, from the grim expressions on the rest of the mens' faces, they were too.

Blase appeared, breathing heavily but Robin was impressed by how close the forester got to them before his presence was noted.

"The lookout's dead," he reported. "I shouted up to him, saying it was my turn, and when he came down Will..."

Robin didn't need a picture painted, he knew how efficient Will was as an assassin.

"This is it then, lads," he called, not shouting but making his voice loud enough to address the remaining men that were with him. "They must still be in their camp or there wouldn't have been a lookout. We're probably going to be outnumbered, unless some of the wolf's heads have gone off to a nearby village for supplies. But it'll make no difference. They won't be expecting us, and their resolve will crumble when we attack them from all sides." He grinned. "This is where we finally put an end to Philip Groves's reign of terror."

And I end that cursed family for good, he thought.

They began to walk, following Blase, who looked terrified, along the overgrown path, until they met up with Will. He'd disposed of the dead lookout's body somewhere out of sight and he fell into step on Robin's left side – Little John was on their captain's right, as usual – as the party headed for the outlaw camp.

"We're almost there," the forester whispered, and Robin gave a nod of acknowledgement before waving him the back of their party, alongside James and Piers who were bringing up the rear. Blase was no soldier and would only get in the way once the fighting started at the front.

Robin felt the blood begin to pump faster in his veins and he slid an arrow from his belt, nocking it to his bowstring as he walked.

This was it.

Killing time.

There was a fire burning in the camp ahead as Robin and his men approached. The trees were thick all around and the smoke was dissipated by their leaves but it could still be glimpsed and the smell was unmistakable. As was the smell of food cooking.

Little John's stomach rumbled and Robin cocked an eyebrow at the giant, receiving a sheepish frown in return.

Not a word was spoken as they walked stealthily through the gap in the foliage that Blase assured them led directly into the outlaws' camp. Every one of them looked warily about, ready for the attack which would surely come once they were spotted.

Being watchful wasn't always enough, though.

Just ahead of them the forest gave way to a clearing, just as Blase had described. Half-a-dozen men sat around the fire, mending torn clothes, eating roast meat from wooden trenchers and conversing quietly but in a relaxed manner. One man stood a little off to the side, apparently cleaning his longbow.

There was a sudden snap as that wolf's head spotted them and, incredibly quickly, grabbed an arrow from a pile on the ground next to him, nocked it to his bow and released the deadly missile at them. As he shouted the alarm, his arrow hit one of the sheriff's blue-liveried soldiers just behind and to the left of Robin.

"Fuck. Take cover!" the lawman spat, crouching behind a worryingly slim young beech, while raising the hunting horn to his lips and blowing. He was rewarded with the sound of a war-cry from the east, followed a few heartbeats later by the easily-recognisable sound of Stephen, roaring some prayer to Almighty God as he led his men into the attack from the north.

The sheriff's man wasn't dead, only injured, as the arrow had caught him in the shoulder, but time wasn't on their side. The soldier would have to suffer unaided or they'd lose the momentum. He wondered where the rest of Groves's men were, but they'd have to wait until his men defeated those in the clearing. He filled his lungs and roared.

"Attack!"

The outlaws were thrown into disarray, disoriented completely as they were beset on three sides by armed men.

The one with the longbow managed to aim a second arrow at them and, again, his aim was true but not deadly as it slammed into another of the sheriff's soldiers, taking the screaming man in the arm this time and throwing him onto the ground which was muddy and churned from many footprints.

Stephen came up behind the archer before the man could loose again, hacking downwards into the outlaw's shoulder, sending a great gout of blood into the air and almost severing the arm completely.

The remaining outlaws weren't as brave as their now-dead comrade. Two more died where they stood, shocked by the lawmens' appearance, not even defending themselves, before Robin shouted at his men to stand down. Clearly the battle was over, for now, and he wanted to question the survivors.

He praised Stephen's group, and the sodden trio who'd swam the river for their fine work, then turned back to the rest of the men.

"John, James, Arthur – disarm them and bind their hands behind their backs. The rest of you, remain alert! We don't know where Groves and the rest of his vermin are so be ready for them."

"They're gone," an outlaw blurted, eyes fearful, clearly hoping to ingratiate himself with Robin by providing information. "Philip took the rest of the men to find a new camp to the north. He was worried our –" he looked nervous as he realised what he was saying and corrected himself as he continued, "*their* raid on the old prior's travelling party would bring the law down on us."

"Shut your mouth, Alf," another of the outlaws shouted. "You fucking turncoat bastard!"

Little John rammed his fist into the man's solar plexus, dropping him onto his knees, breath blasted from him, before he pitched forward flat onto his face.

"Carry on," Robin growled at the talkative wolf's head. "Why are you lot still here?"

"Philip wants to set up as many friendly camps as possible, all over England, so his gang has a safe haven to go to whenever they need it. We were supposed to lie low here and take care of the camp-site until they needed to come back and use it again."

Little John met Robin's gaze and shook his head. "You have to admire Groves's ambition."

"Fucking arsehole's stretching his forces too thin, though," Will noted. "We can pick little groups like this apart no problem, like we just did here. He'd be better keeping all his men together."

"How many are left in Groves's main party?"

The outlaw shrugged. "Probably about twenty-five or thirty. I don't know, I'm not good at counting."

"There's about fifty, at least," the man John had punched gasped from the ground, defiantly. "That's why we can afford to break up into smaller groups – we still have enough men to take you bastards on when the time's right."

"There's nowhere near fifty," Blase said, coming forward to stand beside Robin. "Sure, some of them weren't in the camp when Antony and I were here, so there's no way to be certain of their numbers but it can't be as many as fifty."

"He's right," Stephen agreed, gesturing around the clearing. "This place isn't big enough to hold that many men."

"Shouldn't we find the rest of their lookouts?" Piers asked, brushing his hair back from his handsome face somewhat nervously.

Robin waved dismissively. "We'd never find them and they've probably heard the fight. They'll be long gone, either to catch up with Groves or just to try and find somewhere to become anonymous. I think we're safe from an attack by a couple of lookouts. That being said," he nodded at John to lift the winded wolf's head. "It would be folly to tarry here longer than necessary. That one could be lying about Groves heading north. We'll go back to Pontefract with these whoresons – the sheriff can decide what's to be done with 'em."

"We were new recruits, we didn't have anything to do with any robberies or that," the outlaw called Alf opined. "Isn't that right, lads?"

"You're a lying sack of shit," Blase shouted, rushing forward to press his face against the older man's face, his patience and restraint finally worn through. "I saw you using your knife to tear the clothes off one of those novices." He spun to address Robin. "We should just string the bastards up right here and now. They were all part of it."

Will laughed humourlessly. "It'd save us guarding the three of them all the way back to Pontefract," he said. "I like the lad's idea."

Robin shook his head. "We're representatives of the law now, we have to uphold it. As much as I agree these men deserve a long, painful death – assuming they *were* party to what Blase told us about – it's not our place to decide that. Come on. We'll go and see where de Monte Martini's party was attacked, just in case there's any survivors."

Again, the belligerent wolf's head broke in, grinning. "I doubt it. If any *were* left alive, they'll be wishing they hadn't been."

Little John swept the man's legs away and, as he collapsed onto his face again, the giant pressed his hand into the back of the outlaw's head, forcing his face into the mud so he couldn't breathe.

"One more word from you, sunshine, and I don't care what Robin says, I'll fucking suffocate you in the dirt. All right?"

He held the man for a while longer before dragging him back to his feet. His face was completely brown, apart from his eyes and the pink of his tongue as he tried to drag gusts of air into his lungs. On another, less bleak day, it would have been a hilarious sight.

The outlaw never opened his mouth again as they searched for the remains of the prior's wagon and its attendants, which Alf guided them to.

There was silence all around when they finally found the site. A silence full of sorrow, pity, horror and rage that Groves's gang were continuing to carry out such brutal crimes.

As expected, there were no survivors. The novices had all been murdered, while the guards were hacked apart with such savagery that even Stephen narrowed his eyes at the sight of the mutilated corpses.

The money and valuables had, obviously, all been stripped from the wagon. The horses that had drawn it were perhaps spared, as there was no sign of them. No doubt they were carrying some of the wolf's heads northwards at that very moment.

An elderly man, spindle-legged and pot-bellied, had also been killed. Run through by a sword by the looks of the single wound in his belly.

"That's not de Monte Martini," Robin muttered, somewhat disappointed. "Probably his dean or something. Search the area – see if you can find the prior."

His men moved to obey the order, fanning out for quite some distance into the trees in case the prior's body had been carried away from the main site, or perhaps he'd run off and been hacked down.

But there was no sign of the elderly clergyman and Robin's heart sank. Groves had escaped again, and another atrocity committed, but for some reason de Monte Martini's disappearance worried him more than anything else.

"What happened to the prior?"

Alf shook his head and the puzzled look on his face told its own story. "I don't know. I wasn't paying attention to..."

"You mean you were too busy brutalising one of those young boys," Robin spat, "to notice anything else?"

The outlaw remained silent, eyes downcast.

"What about you two? Where's the prior's body?"

The man that John had assaulted looked as though the belligerence was beaten out of him by now so he didn't reply and neither did the final surviving wolf's head who just shrugged when the lawman glared at him.

"Come on, there's nothing else to be found here," Robin sighed, at last. "We'll get our horses from Mirfield and tell them to send a party to bury the dead. Make haste, it'll start to get dark soon."

He walked quickly along the path, back to the main road, despite the tiredness that was beginning to spread through his limbs.

"Groves will have to wait for another day. Again!"

* * *

The journey back to Pontefract was a slow one, much to Robin's irritation.

His men had their horses, but they now had Blase and the three prisoners in their party. Blase refused to ride behind anyone, saying the rocking motion made him ill, and the captured outlaws seemed too volatile to force into the saddle with anyone else.

So the four men were forced to walk.

The wolf's heads were tethered to Robin and Little John's mounts, with Blase jogging along at the rear of the long procession, puffing and blowing. He couldn't go home to Brighouse yet, as Robin knew Sheriff de Faucumberg would want to question him – wring every bit of information he could get about Groves from him.

So they made poor time and, to make matters worse, the weather turned. It had been sunny and hot for weeks but now the rain pelted them as they plodded along the westward road, their cloaks sodden and the water dripping in rivulets from the horses' long faces.

"Fuck this," Robin huffed when they were still hours away from their destination and the road had become mostly mud. The sun was beginning to set and thunder seemed to rumble far off to the south. "We'll stop here for the night. Make camp!"

His experienced eyes had noted the thick trees which would shelter them and provide support for the treated animal skins his men all carried in their packs to use as roofs for make-shift shelters when needed. As he dismounted, a sudden memory came to him of this place, or perhaps just one very much like it. A memory of his friend Much, smiling as they shared a joke together and it brought a lump to his throat.

He stood for a moment, wondering again what the point of his life – *anyone's life* – was, but the men's bustle eventually brought him back to reality and he started moving again.

It didn't take too long for them to tie the water-proof hides to the trunks and branches of the alder and beech trees beside the road, forming a rudimentary little circular village around the camp-fire which had its own roof to stop the downpour from extinguishing it.

The rain dripped down from the lush green leaves above, drumming on the animal skins rhythmically, as Peter Ordevill and Arthur set up the spit and began to cook some of the meat they'd found at the outlaws' camp. The smell of wood smoke and roast pork filled the damp air and the atmosphere was fine, especially when Little John broached a cask of ale, also taken from the wolf's heads' camp-site.

As darkness descended the fire crackled and spat, casting a homely orange glow around the place, and the incessant rain only served to make their dry shelters seem even cosier.

The three outlaws were made to lie on their sides, bound hand and foot under one of the poorer quality animal skins. They were mostly dry, and Robin made sure they were given enough to drink and small portions of food: tough dried meat from their own supplies, not the succulent roast pork that Peter was turning on the spit over the fire.

As usual, they set a watch, with either Robin, Will, John or Stephen being awake for each turn, accompanied by a couple of the other men. Before they retired for the night, though, they drank ale, ate their fill, told stories and sang songs.

The thunder they'd heard earlier had come closer, bringing even heavier rain with it, along with lightning which sheeted above them gloriously. The men, drunk and glorying in the freedom they felt out there in the greenwood, roared their songs ever louder, grinning and dancing with one another as if it was Mayday.

Some of the sheriff's soldiers, younger men, started arm-wrestling with one another, which led onto wrestling matches in the rain. Robin and his old, experienced, friends watched the entertainment with knowing smiles, laughing at the mud-coated, drink-fuelled younger men.

Of course, it didn't take much ale before Will decided to show de Faucumberg's men how a real man wrestled and he waded in, throwing bodies this way and that, roaring with laughter until a fist caught him, accidentally, in the eye, and he dropped like a stone.

Some of the others continued to sing raucously as Scarlet rubbed at his face, checking his fingertips to see if there was any blood from his injury but, even if there was, the mud that coated his face and hands would have hidden it anyway. That didn't stop him roaring with outrage and launching himself at the poor lad that had dealt the stinging blow.

Little John, alert as ever despite the massive quantity of ale he'd supped from the cask, jumped between Will and his victim and the whole thing turned into a sprawling, wet mess of limbs and anger.

Robin, Stephen and everyone else too sensible to get involved watched in the firelight as the filthy combatants rolled about the forest floor, storm raging overhead, filling the air with cracks, booms and unfettered, joyful laughter.

No, they hadn't killed or even captured Philip Groves that day, and the vast majority of his gang had escaped them. But out here, far from the villages and towns they called home, Robin's men revelled for a time in the unsullied freedom of the greenwood, enjoying the camaraderie only the aftermath of a battle could bring.

"What are we going to do about Groves?"

Robin, seated on an old moss and lichen encrusted log, spread his hands at Stephen's question. "We'll ask the sheriff for more men when we finally reach Pontefract." He upended his mug and downed its contents before wiping his mouth and sighing happily. "Groves can't hold his gang together forever – they're bound to get sick of us constantly after them, with no reward other than the spoils of the occasional robbery."

Stephen grunted, his mouth almost breaking into a smile as Will tripped Little John, sending the giant face-first into the mud again, the sheriff's young soldiers crowding around, trying to make the most of John's temporary defeat to pile onto Scarlet.

Robin looked on, the red flickering firelight making his unshaven features appear grim and almost hellish to Stephen's devout Christian eye. "We'll stop them, don't worry about that. But for now..."

The lawman stood, only a little unsteadily, and gazed down at the Hospitaller sergeant. "I'm going to sleep. Wake me when it's time for my watch. And don't let them kill one another, eh?"

CHAPTER TWENTY-TWO

Blase slept not at all, even when the men had all finished drinking and settled down for the night. He'd taken first watch, at sundown, along with one of the sheriff's guards, and Arthur. When they were relieved, both of those had then grabbed ale skins and joined in with the other men's revelry but Blase wasn't in the mood for drink

For a long time he simply lay in the darkness with his eyes shut, but the atrocities he'd witnessed during the ambush of the clergymen seemed to play out again, over and over, in his mind's eye. He wondered if he'd ever be able to forget those scenes; it didn't feel like it.

The sounds of camp – men snoring softly, cooling logs and embers in the almost-extinguished fire cracking, and the breeze whispering softly through the leaves all around them – should have made him drowsy but it was no good. From his position he could see the sleeping form of the wolf's head, Alf, who, although bound hand and foot, lay on his side, eyes closed, mouth open, breathing rhythmically.

The bastard had no conscience! How could a man sleep so contentedly, knowing the terror, agony and humiliation he'd brought on innocent young novices just a short time before? It beggared belief.

Truly, some men in the world were simply evil, Blase thought, clenching his fists as the outlaw let out a little snuffle before rolling over onto his other side, as if turning his back on the watching Brighouse man.

Disgustedly, Blase screwed his eyes shut and tried to concentrate on the sounds of the forest in an attempt to quiet his bleak thoughts. A long time passed and he grew ever more awake and frustrated, as he knew it would be dawn soon and he'd need to travel the next day, exhausted. Robin and his men wouldn't allow him to lag either.

He stared at the sleeping outlaw who'd turned in his sleep again so his face was visible. The man must have been enjoying a dream, as a little smile twitched at the corners of his mouth, just visible in the slight orange glow from the low camp-fire.

Blase watched, anger mounting, as Alf chuckled.

Furiously, but as stealthily as he could manage, Blase crawled across the ground like a great spider. He glanced around to make sure no-one was watching – Will Scarlet was on watch along with two of Sheriff de Faucumberg's men, but they were all looking outwards, away from the camp-site.

He reached Alf and drew his dagger soundlessly from its leather sheath, bringing it up to the outlaw's windpipe. It would be so easy to just draw it, hard, across the skin.

Too easy for the sodomite.

Blase wanted the man to know how he was dying, and why.

He clasped his free hand around Alf's mouth and squeezed. The wolf's head's eyes opened instantly, the whites seeming almost as if they were glowing, contrasting as they did with the gloom all around and Blase pressed his mouth to the groggy man's ear, warning him against making a sound. He pressed the blade against Alf's throat to emphasise the seriousness of his threat.

"Having a nice dream were you?" Blase growled. "Reliving what you did to that poor boy before you and your mates killed him?"

The outlaw stared at him fearfully, knowing he was utterly defenceless.

"Robin Hood might want you to face the king's justice, as the law says. But we both know justice can be bought, and men who should be hanged sometimes are allowed to go free because they have wealthy friends or because they offer to perform some other service to those sitting in judgement."

He was breathing heavily and his palms were slick with sweat. He'd come across here with the intention of executing the wolf's head but now, he wasn't sure he could do it. To take an unarmed, bound man's life was much harder than he'd expected, especially since Blase had never killed anyone before.

If Alf simply lay there quietly, Blase knew he'd lose his nerve – the righteous anger he'd felt while watching the sleeping outlaw was dissipating already and the fear of being caught by one of the lawmen was growing with every heartbeat.

Alf misread his young attacker's expression though, and, assuming he was about to be murdered, jerked his head back and tried to cry out for help.

Blase's reactions were fast though and he was able to clamp his hand back over the outlaw's mouth just as the cry came out. At the same time nervous, terrified excitement coursed through his veins and, without thinking, he slashed his dagger brutally across Alf's neck, opening a great, gaping wound which spurted blood up and across his arms and chest.

Releasing his captive, Blase looked around desperately, knowing the three watchmen must have heard the wolf's head's frightened cry before he'd been able to silence the bastard.

Incredibly, the sheriff's two men were nowhere to be seen – presumably they were patrolling somewhere to make sure they didn't fall asleep – while Will Scarlet remained seated on a log with his back to the bloodstained Blase.

He turned back and sighed with relief and horror, seeing the outlaw was already dead.

Hurriedly, he crawled back to his bedroll where he found his travelling cloak and drew it around himself. There was no way he'd be able slip away and wash the blood from himself until morning; the best he could do was cover it up.

He pulled his blanket up and, shaking badly as shock began to set in, spent some time weeping silently before, mercifully, sleep somehow stole over him.

* * *

Of course, Will Scarlet *had* heard Blase attacking the outlaw. The experienced mercenary had been fully aware of every movement the Brighouse man made as he crept clumsily around the camp-fire in the direction of Alf and his bound, dozing companions.

Rather than raising the alarm, or calling out to the young man, Will had quietly ordered the oblivious sheriff's men who were sharing the watch with him to take a walk around the camp's perimeter, ostensibly to make sure all was well.

Scarlet was curious to see what Blase planned to do. He was sure the young forester didn't have the balls or the brutal nature needed to kill the defenceless outlaw, but there was no harm in letting the lad land a few punches to try and make himself feel better about what he'd witnessed.

It was, then, something of a shock to Will when he heard Alf's cry cut-off before it was fully formed. There'd been no obvious sound of violence – no thump as a fist hit flesh; no crack as bone met bone. Just a shout of fear which ended in silence before Blase, panting heavily, crept back to his blanket and sobbed like a child.

Despite the darkness, Will had witnessed the whole thing, and what he hadn't seen with his eyes, his mind had filled in the blanks.

As the sun started to light up the sky that morning the men came awake and the crime was discovered, sending a ripple of shock around the entire group, uncomfortable at the idea of a man being murdered beside them as they slept.

The two remaining prisoners shouted for justice, demanding the killer be found and made to pay. It was one thing to be tied up and taken to jail, but quite another to see your partner-in-crime brutally murdered on the grass next to you. They made so much noise that Piers eventually punched one of them in the mouth and feinted at the other. Both fell into a sullen silence after that, but they weren't the only ones outraged at the crime.

"Did you see nothing?" Robin demanded, his arms spread wide as he glared into Scarlet's eyes. "How could you miss a man being murdered just yards away from you? Were you sleeping? Or drunk?"

Will's eyebrows lowered dangerously at the suggestion he'd been derelict in his duty. Sleeping while on watch was a heinous crime.

"You know me better than that," he growled. "Me and the sheriff's lads were awake and alert the whole time. Whoever killed the wolf's head must have been as silent as one of those Assassins the Crusaders feared so much." He shrugged. "Fuck him. He deserved to die anyway."

Robin clenched his fists and gritted his teeth at his old friend's flippancy. The truth was, he *did* know Scarlet well enough to know the man would never fall asleep on watch. He also doubted the outlaw had died as silently as suggested, and that could only mean one of two things: either Will had seen who carried out the brutal murder; or Will had been the killer himself.

The bailiff discarded the latter idea almost instantly. There was no sign of blood on Scarlet, and the terrible, gaping laceration that ended Alf's life must have sent a shower of crimson onto his killer's hands and arms at least.

Robin was relieved that his friend hadn't murdered a defenceless man, but disappointed that he'd lie to protect the murderer.

Sadly, he swung away from Will and raised his voice to address the camp in general.

"Everybody up. I'm going to check you all myself. The killer will have bloodstains on him so you shouldn't be hard to find."

Without needing to be asked Little John fell into step beside his captain as they moved around the men, and Robin was glad of the giant's presence, as always. He felt stupid inspecting his own men, especially those he'd known for years like Arthur, and it helped to have John beside him to share the burden.

The inspection didn't take long.

Blase, pale and fidgeting, turned away when Robin met his eyes and, when the bailiff looked down the dried blood was obvious on the Brighouse man's hands, since he'd not had time to rinse it off in the stream that ran beside their camp.

Robin turned his head towards Will, but Scarlet just shrugged and returned his gaze with a stony expression.

"Did you do it yourself, Blase? Or did you have helpers?"

To his surprise, the young man replied in a strong voice, full of conviction.

"I did it myself. Only wanted to teach him a lesson – give him a little taste of the pain he'd inflicted on those novices. But he tried to shout for help and..." He shook his head defiantly. "The bastard deserved to die."

There were murmurs of agreement from many of the others and Robin could tell from Little John's expression the big man felt the same way.

What could he do? The other prisoners cried out again, demanding the killer's arrest.

Before Robin was able to make up his mind Will stormed across to stand next to Blase protectively.

"What are you going to do then? Arrest the lad?"

"I'm a lawman now," Robin muttered. "I can't just let this go. He slit a defenceless man's throat for fuck sake!"

Scarlet waved his leader's words away, mouth twisted derisively. "So we've one less prisoner to guard on the road to Pontefract. Good."

The rest of the men, taking confidence from Will's defiant words, were louder in their agreement now.

Again, before Robin had a chance to speak, his volatile old friend continued.

"Are you forgetting the time you chopped the fingers off Lord John de Bray when we robbed him?"

"That was for what he did to your daughter, Scarlet," Robin retorted, growing angry himself now.

"Aye, and what Blase did to that wolf's head was for the boy the whoreson raped. Four years ago you'd never have batted an eye at justice being served like this. Let it go."

The bailiff looked around at the men, knowing this was a crucial decision he had to make. Yes, Alf was an outlaw so, in theory, outside the law. But the man had been in their custody, and tied up. He was sure that made Blase a murderer. Whether it did or not wasn't his decision to make though – that was up to the sheriff, surely.

Yet it was obvious he would lose the support of the men – apart from John perhaps – if he arrested Blase and took him to Pontefract as a prisoner.

Ever since Friar Tuck had taken him to task for the way he treated debtors, Robin had tried to uphold the law as fairly as possible; to do things by the book. And that meant treating everyone as equals – even a rapist and a terrified young forester who'd seen too much death and depravity in recent days.

But they still had to catch Philip Groves, and to do that, Robin needed the support of these men.

Shaking his head in anger, Robin jerked his head in the direction of Brighouse.

"Go. Back to your home, out of my sight."

There were cheers at that, and Blase sagged visibly from relief. Only Will didn't join in with the celebrations. He stared at Robin for a moment then turned his back on the bailiff.

Scarlet hadn't changed much in the years since they'd been free men, but Robin had.

Not for the first time he wondered if things were better when they'd all lived in the greenwood together, outcast and outlawed, but brothers in arms. Then an image of his son playing in the garden outside their home came to him, and he felt terribly homesick, wishing he could just take his family and leave all this behind forever.

"Mount up," he shouted hoarsely, pushing the feeling away. "I want to get to Pontefract today, if we can. And if anyone ever asks, Alf attacked us when we first arrested him and was killed in self-defence."

Will Scarlet glowered at the surviving prisoners and pointed at them. "Understand, you two? Keep your mouths shut about it, or you'll meet the same fate as your friend."

It had begun to rain again but only a drizzle that tailed off after a short time, and the road to their destination was in decent repair so the high towers of Pontefract Castle soon came into view.

Robin nodded in satisfaction, looking forward to a decent meal, some cool ale and discussing their next move with the sheriff. He wondered absent-mindedly if Sir Henry had settled into his new stronghold which had once belonged to Thomas, Earl of Lancaster. The sheriff, as a staunch royalist, had been an enemy to the earl, who was beheaded outside the castle after the ill-fated rebellion. Again, it struck Robin how much things had changed for him: he'd been on the Earl of Lancaster's side during the rebellion, fighting against the sheriff and the king, yet here he was a few years later, heading to a meeting with Sir Henry, a man he called friend as well as employer.

Was his life better now? It was certainly different...

"Someone approaches," Little John said, eyeing the road ahead and the small dust cloud that marked a lone rider moving at some speed towards them.

"Looks like a comrade of mine," noted one of the sheriff's men. "Whoever he is, he's wearing a blue surcoat like the ones we usually wear."

Force of long habit made some of Robin's friends grasp the hilts of their swords or draw bowstrings from their storage pouches but the bailiff had already recognised the rapidly closing horse with its distinctive white flash on its chest.

"It's Thomas, he's spotted us," he said loudly. "And by the way he's pushing his mount I'd say he's on some urgent mission to a nearby village."

The blue-liveried rider drew closer, his steed's hooves a blur and Robin felt the first prickle of unease.

"He's pushing the horse too hard to be heading to one of the surrounding villages," Will growled, drawing his sword which prompted some of the others to follow suit. "Either he's being chased –"

"Or he's coming for us," Stephen finished, pulling his own blade free from its sheath and spinning it in his hand expertly, face set, ready for whatever Thomas's hasty approach might herald.

The rider shouted something, but his voice was blown away by the wind until, at last, he came close enough to be heard.

"Hold, Robin! Go no further if you value your life!"

"What's going on, Thomas?" the bailiff demanded, eyes flashing at the unexpected threat from a man he'd come to know well in recent times. "Has something happened to Sir Henry? Is Pontefract under siege?"

The sheriff's messenger pulled hard on his horse's reins, bringing the sweating beast to an expert stop just before them, its great sides heaving, eyes wide.

"Worse," he broke in. "You've been declared an outlaw!"

CHAPTER TWENTY-THREE

It wasn't all violence and robbing – most of the time Philip's outlaw band enjoyed relaxing in their forest camp, just as Robin Hood's men had done not so many years earlier. Unlike Robin's men, Philip's followers didn't train with sword or bow very often, but they did share a love of drink and song and, if it ended up in a disagreement, so much the better.

Mark sat with Ivo on one such evening of revelry, drinks in hand, watching as some of the other recent recruits arm-wrestled for silver coins. The atmosphere was light and good-natured so far and Ivo nudged his friend with a leer.

"You should have a go. Those idiots will look at your size and underestimate you. I'll put some bets on and we'll win a nice little haul."

Mark watched as the giant, Eoin, dispatched another young contender with ease, his great tree trunk arm bulging with muscle, and Ivo's suggestion seemed a good one. Mark knew there was more to the contest than simple brute strength – technique and a little mind-games could bring a smaller man victory over a much larger opponent.

Still, Eoin, cheered on the whole time by a tipsy Philip, was a formidable foe. Only one of the outlaws ever came close to beating the giant but even that lad had folded eventually. The betting would be good for anyone willing to go against Eoin.

"All right," Mark smiled, showing his fine white teeth in the gloom. "I'll have a go. Don't bet all our money though – I probably won't be able to beat that big bastard and we don't want to be left with nothing to show for the past few weeks."

Ivo cackled and even slapped a hand on his thigh like an exuberant child as he stood and made his way over to talk to the rest of the onlookers who were watching Eoin attempt to beat two men at once. This bout was purely for amusement but the cheers were louder than ever as it seemed like the massive wolf's head might actually win. Slowly, though, one of the men began to shift Eoin's left arm, and, unbalanced by the unusual position, beads of sweat stood out on his forehead and a vein near his temple looked like it might pop, it bulged so obscenely.

Mark saw Ivo begin his haggling with the spectators, their eyes turning to look over at the challenger with the fine teeth and slightly manic stare. More than a few of them feared the little man, but apparently none believed he had any chance of defeating Eoin who, at last, succumbed to his two opponents and sat now, grinning and rubbing his arms as Philip filled a mug from a cask of ale and handed it to his old companion.

"You ready for another one?" Ivo asked, walking across and clapping Eoin on the shoulder with a wide smile. "Think you can beat my mate Mark?"

The big wolf's head looked across in surprise, fixing Mark with what seemed to be a surprisingly astute gaze before he shrugged and drained his ale.

"Aye, why not," he smiled, wiping his mouth with a grubby sleeve. "But this is the last. I want to sit and listen to some singing and drink myself senseless after this."

He stood up as Mark approached the log that was being used as a table and stretched his arms up above his head and around in a wide circle, groaning loudly as the muscles expanded. It made him appear even more enormous than usual and the outlaws who'd taken Ivo's bet on Mark smiled at the show of power. Surely their money was safe – Mark might seem something of a lunatic but he was much too small to defeat Eoin, the popular champion.

The pair seated themselves on smaller logs and eyed one another across the 'table', attempting to gain some psychological advantage before the competition had even begun.

"You sure about this?" Groves called, the ever-present smile wider than ever. "Eoin's double your size and already proven his strength. We don't want you getting hurt."

Mark took off his tunic which he'd been wearing since sundown as the air had cooled, despite the season. Now the flickering firelight cast shadows over his bare arms, revealing the hollows and swells of hard muscles in his biceps. For a small man, he was quite powerfully-built, but Eoin flexed an arm, the great bicep bulging to almost the size of Mark's head.

The men murmured in appreciation and anticipation of winning Ivo's foolishly wagered money and Mark shrugged as if he knew he'd no chance of winning.

"Let's do it, then," he smiled, placing his elbow on the fallen tree trunk and offering his hand to the giant.

Eoin nodded and set down his own arm, grasping Mark's hand gently and staring hard into the smaller outlaw's eyes.

The burly wolf's head, for all his bulk, wasn't as menacing as Philip Groves or Mark himself – both of whom wouldn't hesitate to stab a man in the back if it meant a few silver coins – but Eoin's gaze held a steely determination that somewhat surprised Mark. He'd expected the jovial giant to be too tired and ale-content to take this final bout of the night very seriously, but the man's stare suggested otherwise.

Perhaps this wasn't such a good idea after all…

"Ready?" Groves demanded, coming closer to look in turn at each competitor who nodded assent without taking their eyes from one another. "Go!"

There were calls of "Come on, Eoin," and other encouragement from the onlookers. None of them bore Mark any malice as far as he knew, but Philip's lieutenant was popular thanks to his easy smile and affable nature – the fact the men all had money riding on his victory helped cement their loyalty.

Neither man gave way for a time, eyes, and arms, locked in position until, at last, Eoin's greater weight began to tell and his hand very slowly shifted Mark's round, towards the smooth bark.

"You've got him!" someone cried to roars of agreement but, somehow, Mark locked his arm in place, halting the downwards movement. He didn't say a word, but a small smile tugged at the corners of his mouth as Eoin, flagging after so many earlier bouts, saw his own arm begin to twitch under the stress.

"Is that it?" Mark asked, allowing himself to smile fully now as he saw the sweat again forming on his foe's face, one bead even rolling down into Eoin's eye. The salty perspiration irritated the big man, and he blinked, but couldn't afford to lift a hand to wipe it properly for fear of disturbing the equilibrium.

More shouts of encouragement were raised, less cheerfully this time, but Mark noticed Groves didn't join in. His brooding presence could be felt though, even if Mark didn't take his eyes away from the giant's.

At last, to ever more desperate cries, Eoin's stamina waned and the smaller man began to gain the upper hand. Sensing victory, Mark pressed home his advantage, not wanting to allow his opponent a chance to rally. With a grunt, he put all his strength into one more push and steadily, inexorably, Eoin's arm fell sideways, downwards, until the back of his hand was pressed into the bark and Mark let go, standing up with a whoop of triumph, his perfect teeth shining in the darkness.

Only Ivo joined in with the victor's cheer, although, to their credit, the rest of the men, even the vanquished Eoin, congratulated the little wolf's head on his shock win.

"Any more of that ale?" the giant asked Philip, grinning despite his defeat and again rubbing his exhausted limbs.

Groves handed over another mug, threw Mark an unreadable expression, then stalked away to sit with the rest of the men who'd decided to follow Eoin's earlier suggestion and start a song or two, as Ivo moved amongst them collecting his winnings with a hideous smile.

The two combatants were left pretty much on their own, for the first time since they'd met on the road outside Flockton.

They sat, sipping their drinks, recovering after what had been, after all, an extremely draining contest. The men's song started and, although it wasn't the most musical effort, it was boisterous and loud and soon had all in the camp tapping their feet, singing along or even capering drunkenly like courtly minstrels.

Slightly apart from the main body of revellers, Mark decided to take the opportunity to find out a bit more about the giant who was Groves's right-hand man; the information might come in useful one day but if not, it would while away the evening since Ivo had joined in with the dancers, celebrating his new-found wealth.

"That was a hard match. Reckon I only beat you because you were exhausted."

Eoin looked sideways at the smaller wolf's head and shrugged non-committally. "Probably, but you seemed to have a way of stopping me just as I thought I had you. You'll have to teach me that trick sometime."

Mark laughed but shook his head. "Oh no, I can't give away my secrets – don't have your size so I have to make the most of any advantage I can get, eh?"

Eoin smiled and stood up, slowly, groaning as he did so. "You need a refill?"

"Aye, that'd be good."

The big outlaw returned moments later with two brimming mugs, handed one to Mark and lowered himself back down onto his log. They sipped at their ales, slower now, knowing their limits and wanting to retain some semblance of control. They were wanted after all, and, although there was little chance of any force of lawmen coming to attack them at this time of night, it wasn't prudent to become too inebriated.

Of course, not all of their fellows agreed.

"Look at the state of that arsehole," Mark said, shaking his head in disgust as he watched a man throwing up all over himself then rolling onto his back and mewling pitifully, complaining that the forest was spinning. "If Hood and the sheriff's men were to find us now he'd die in the dirt, covered in his own puke without even knowing he'd been skewered."

Eoin grunted agreement but didn't reply, his foot tapping in time to the men's song. It was a different one now, faster than the first tune they'd belted out and all the more raucous for it.

A few heartbeats passed then Mark said, "So how did you end up here, a wolf's head hiding out in the greenwood? A man of your size would have been a great mercenary. Ever try it?"

Eoin didn't seem to hear at first, lost in the song as he was, but at last he realised he'd been asked something and turned, startled and wide-eyed to look at Mark.

"What? No...I was never a mercenary. I've never been trained how to fight like a proper soldier, with a sword and shield and stuff. Never even learned to use a longbow."

Mark had already guessed the giant was no archer – he was a bear of a man but didn't have the freakishly large shoulders or left arm that bowmen always developed.

"But I know how to handle myself, so I did work sometimes as a bodyguard for merchants or the like. Don't have any desire to go killing people that don't deserve it though, so heading off on a crusade or that never interested me."

The smaller outlaw wasn't entirely sure but he didn't think anyone from England had gone off crusading for decades. He held his peace however and watched Eoin, waiting for him to continue his tale.

The song finished, the big man sipped his drink, and then he turned a bleary eye on Mark.

"You want to hear my story then?"

"I'm an Irishman, really," Eoin said, and Mark thought the man looked proud of his place of birth, although he couldn't think why; one place was as bad as another as far as he was concerned. "I lived in a village called Clondalkin until I was ten," the giant continued, oblivious to his audience's indifference. "With my ma, da and three sisters."

"Four women in one house?" Mark smirked. "That must have been a pain in the arse eh? One's bad enough."

Eoin didn't return the smile; if anything he looked downcast at the memory of his family. "No, I loved them all – they were good sisters; looked out for me when I was too small to do it myself. But there was no work in Clondalkin for my da – he'd trained as a stonemason but no-one was looking for churches or the like to be built. So he decided to take a ship to England because he'd heard they were always building palaces and monasteries and shit like that over here. He took me with him so I could learn his trade, although once he found a job we were to send word to my ma and the others and they'd come and live with us here."

He sipped his ale, staring into the middle-distance thoughtfully and Mark waited, not wanting to disturb him.

"I've never seen them since," the big wolf's head eventually continued and again lapsed into a maudlin silence. This time, Mark had to prompt him to continue or they'd have sat all night without ever reaching the conclusion of the tale.

"What happened?"

Another sip of ale. "My da fell overboard on the journey here."

"Fell overboard? Was he drunk?"

"No, my da could handle more ale than anyone I've ever known. I never once saw him drunk although he liked his ale as well as any man." He spat into the grass. "But that's what the captain of the ship told me when I woke up the next morning and found my da's sleeping pallet empty."

"How can a man just fall over the side of a ship?" Mark wondered. He'd only sailed a couple of times and been ill on both occasions. "Maybe he was seasick and lost his balance when he was puking. Or a big wave caught him."

"The sea was calm that night, and my da'd been on enough boats that he wasn't bothered by seasickness. No," he clenched his great fists. "I always believed one of the sailors pushed him over the side. Why, I don't know – maybe they got into a fight over a game of dice or something. I never did find out, but the captain was a good man and promised to take me back to Ireland on their return trip, even though we'd only paid for the journey over. Must have felt sorry for me when I started crying."

Mark blew a long breath. "Just as well; England's no place for a little lad all on his own. You'd have been fucked. Literally, probably."

Eoin threw him a stern glare and Mark shut his mouth, trying to hide behind his ale mug as he took another pull.

"Anyway, I helped them unload the ship when they got here. Liverpool I think we docked. We must have stayed a night or two so the men could visit the taverns and whorehouses but we sailed back home soon enough and the captain – a small, older man called McGinty – found a merchant that was heading for my village and I hitched a lift on his cart. When we got there though..." His face was bleak in the wan firelight and Mark fancied he could see tears glistening in the big outlaw's eyes. "My ma and sisters were gone, along with the rest of the people."

"Gone? Where to?"

"Who knows?" Eoin mumbled. "Someone had attacked the place. Chased or killed the people and burnt down most of the houses."

"What did you do?" Mark asked, finding himself more interested than he'd expected when the story first began.

"What could I do? The merchant went onto the next village along the road to sell his wares then he took me back to the docks. The only person that had shown me any kindness was the captain of the ship. I went back and asked him to give me a job on board. Cleaning, labouring, lookout – anything at all. I had no home, no family that I knew of and was still just a boy."

His voice trailed off and Mark knew self-pity was almost overwhelming the giant – the bitter memories and the ale combining to make the world seem an even more unfair shithole than it was normally.

Without speaking, the little wolf's head moved to take Eoin's cup from his unresisting fingers and refilled it, along with his own, from another cask someone had just broached, handing it back with a sympathetic smile before returning to his seat on the log.

"Did the captain agree to it? Take you on I mean."

"Aye. He'd seen my da, who was almost as big as me from what I can remember, so McGinty must have known I'd be a useful hand eventually. And there was plenty of work for a boy to do on board a ship – jobs the men hated." He shrugged. "But it was better than begging in the streets somewhere."

"How the hell did you end up here then? Surely life as a sailor was better than this?"

Eoin's face turned wistful, which was vast improvement over the man's previous sour expression Mark thought.

"Aye, life on the ocean was fine, for a time. It got old eventually, but for the first two years or so I enjoyed it well enough. At least, as well as any youngster who'd just lost his entire family in the space of only a few weeks. I scrubbed the decks, helped prepare meals for the men, darned and waterproofed their clothes, pitched in when it was time for repairs after any storms had damaged the mast or hull...All sorts of jobs. And we didn't just go between Liverpool and Dublin either – I saw places like Bristol and, a few times, France – although only for a short time before we had to cast off again. No, you're right: it wasn't a bad life."

"Why'd you leave then?"

The giant's bleak expression returned, and this time something else blazed in his eyes. Anger, Mark thought. Murderous anger.

"I'd grown in my time aboard the ship. I wasn't as big as I am now, but I was about the size of most men. Bigger than you." His mouth twitched in an attempt at a smile before he went on grimly. "I think the sailors sometimes forgot who I was – how I'd come to be on board their ship I mean – when they were drinking. I wasn't the little boy any more. One night I was below decks with some of them, sitting out a squall. They were bantering as men do," he looked across at the outlaws around the camp-fire who were still telling tales and singing, if not quite as boisterously as before. "I didn't drink very much then – I'd learned my limits even at that age – but I'd had a few swigs of wine or whatever foul tasting shit they were tossing back, I forget now. It's not important." He halted, as if he knew he'd been rambling and wanted to catch his breath. "There was a man – tall, with a black beard he kept trimmed in some stupid style. He didn't seem to realise I was there, started going on about how he'd got into an argument with a traveller from Ireland once, and 'accidentally' shoved the man overboard."

"Your da!" Mark burst out, rather drunk by now, and fully engrossed in the story.

Eoin shrugged and shook his head. "Someone must have nudged him, for he glanced over at me and, when he'd realised who I was, he changed the subject, and so did the rest of the men."

"It must have been your da," Mark repeated his assertion. "Is that why you left? Because you couldn't bring yourself to share a ship with the bastard?"

Again, Eoin shook his head, and his eyes came up to meet Mark's.

"I left because the captain made me. The man that had been boasting about killing the traveller was the captain's brother."

Mark sat for a moment then, not following, asked, "So?"

"He wasn't happy when the bastard disappeared overboard during the night. The men told him I'd overheard their conversation and he thought I'd pushed him over to avenge my da."

"Did you?"

"You're fucking right I did," Eoin growled through gritted teeth. "I waited until the deck was empty and he went out for a piss, then I sneaked up behind him, lifted him by the feet and shoved him right across into the sea. His scream of fear was swept away in the wind – not a soul noticed he was missing until the next day."

He raised his head to look up at the starless, cloudy sky and thought back to that night. "We were on our way back from Sweden at the time. He died in the Norwegian Sea. It was fucking freezing. I hope he lasted a long time before the water, or cold, finally took him."

"Good for you," Mark said, but the giant ignored the hollow words.

"The captain couldn't be sure if I'd killed his brother or not or I'm sure he'd have shoved me into the ocean too. But he didn't. He never spoke to me again, then, when we made it back to Liverpool again with our cargo his mate threw me off the ship."

Some of the outlaws were beginning to fall asleep and Mark rubbed at his eyes tiredly. He wanted to hear the rest of Eoin's tale though.

"What did you do in Liverpool? You were still just a boy weren't you?"

"I found some other orphans and fell in with them. Stole food, robbed people, just lived on my wits for a while but I'd started to really grow by then, so I was almost the size I am now. One of the local gang leaders noticed me and took me in with him. He thought I'd be a good man to do his dirty work but to be honest I was never very good at hurting people just because some bastard told me to." His voice trailed off and he glanced across at Groves who seemed to have nodded off while sitting upright. "I'm much better at it now though."

He stood up, grunting with the effort, and disappeared into the trees where the sound of splashing on dried leaves carried to Mark and he decided he needed to relieve himself too.

"How did you meet up with Philip then?"

Eoin turned and looked blearily at him, shaking his manhood with a small slapping sound that Mark did his best not to hear. "Eh? Oh...I was in a tavern one night. Someone must have recognised me or maybe they just didn't like my face – attacked me with fists and chairs. Philip was there and he saw it all. Jumped into help me and it's well he did for one of the bastards was about to stick me with his dagger."

Mark did his breeches back up and the pair of unlikely companions returned to the log that had played host to their arm-wrestling match hours earlier.

"Philip saved you?"

"Aye. And I've been indebted to him ever since. I'm not much of a leader, or a thinker."

Mark held his peace at that.

"So I was happy to follow Philip wherever he led. And we've done alright over the years. Look at us now." He grinned but there was a tinge of sadness in his eyes, Mark fancied. "Anyway, I'm done. Time I was asleep." He waved a hand and moved away to his bedroll which was beside his old friend and leader.

As he watched him go, Mark glanced up at Groves and noticed the man wasn't asleep at all – he was wide awake and staring at him with an unreadable expression. A shiver ran down his spine and he turned away hurriedly to find his own blanket.

* * *

Sir Henry de Faucumberg rubbed at his eyes with his fingertips and blew out a long sigh. The past couple of days hadn't been good ones.

Pontefract Castle was a fine new residence. Once described by King Edward I as "the key to the north", it boasted a number of towers – the King's and Queen's Towers being particularly impressive – all connected by sturdy walls with a huge keep crowning the whole pile.

Sir Henry's wife liked the place, although he himself found it strange when pilgrims would come to visit Thomas, Earl of Lancaster's tomb, which was just outside the castle walls. The executed rebel had become almost a saint to some of the people in Yorkshire which seemed absurd to the sheriff who'd known the earl and hadn't thought him very saintly at all.

He was glad enough to still be in a job, and a position of power though. Sheriff of Yorkshire, with temporary stewardship of Pontefract Castle, was far better than nothing and, judging by the news that came from the south, it was probably better to be as far from the capital as possible. Queen Isabella and her followers were gathering strength in France, and sure to mount their invasion within months.

The only really pressing problem Sir Henry had to deal with was the blasted outlaw, Philip Groves, and his murderous gang. But the sheriff had confidence in Robin Hood – the bailiff would use his skills to bring the outlaw down soon enough and then, hopefully, life would be nice and simple.

And then, two days ago, Prior John de Monte Martini had appeared out of nowhere in the great hall, shrieking like a madman, face black and blue.

Sir Henry bore no love for the greedy prior. He well remembered the proud Hospitaller Knight Sir Richard-at-Lee throwing a bag of money at the clergyman and humiliating him rather amusingly, which was no worse than the arrogant peacock deserved. He also knew the unscrupulous man owned a number of brothels which didn't seem at all right for a man of the cloth, so the sight of his battered face brought the sheriff a measure of satisfaction.

Until the prior began to speak.

The sheriff stared ahead, into the empty hall, as the scene played itself out again in his memory.

"De Faucumberg," de Monte Martini shouted, catching sight of the sheriff as he was helped into the great, high ceilinged room by two of the guards. "What do you here? Why aren't you in Nottingham?" The prior waved a hand feebly, dismissing any reply. "Never mind, it hardly matters. Will someone bring me a chair? And some wine, in God's name? Is this how you receive a guest of my standing?"

The sheriff waved a hand and William hurried away through one of the alcoves, returning a moment later with a high-backed chair which he helped the prior collapse into. Another servant followed a short time later with a goblet of wine and a platter of sweetmeats. De Monte Martini drained the wine and gestured irritably at the servant to refill it while he stuffed the savoury food into his mouth as if he hadn't eaten for days.

Sir Henry sat in silence, patiently waiting for the man to finish his meal, wondering as he watched what might have befallen the wealthy clergyman.

"Outlaws." The prior glanced up from the platter momentarily to spit the word out, as if it were a pip from one of the grapes he'd just devoured, then he looked down again to search for his next mouthful.

"Outlaws," the sheriff repeated. "They did that to your face? Where's the rest of your party?"

"Dead!" De Monte Martini cried out again with an outraged look. He tried to stand up but didn't have the strength and slumped back heavily in his chair, sipping wine with a faraway look. "The wolf's head and his friends killed them all and," he looked up to glare at the sheriff again, "it wasn't an easy death he gave them. Some – the younger novices – were even raped. It was...like I'd descended into Hell. Why is it when I visit my estates in this part of the country the lawless scum are allowed to brutalise me?"

De Faucumberg was too shocked to reply for a time. Groves's men were worse than a plague.

"My condolences, father," he finally managed to say. "We've been troubled by these outlaws for a while but I swear to you, on my honour, I'll see them brought to justice for their crimes against you and your retinue. Could you describe the men? Their leader?"

"I know very well who their leader was," the prior grunted, sneering at the sheriff's words. "And I can describe his men too, they held me captive, beating and torturing me, before letting me go; I assume they thought I'd be too weak to make it to safety, but God gave me wings. One was an angry, vicious man, while another was a lumbering giant."

Sir Henry nodded at the description. The 'angry, vicious' man could be anyone, but the giant was clearly Groves's right-hand man, Eoin. It was De Monte Martini's next words that shocked him to his core though.

"And the man leading them? Aye I knew him well… it was Robin Hood!"

The hall was fairly busy that afternoon as the sheriff had been dealing with a number of petty criminals and petitioners looking to gain his aid for one reason or another. Now, the people gathered there – who'd remained in the hall when the bruised prior had been shown in, sensing the intrigue that was sure to follow – began to gossip loudly.

"Robin Hood?"

"The bailiff's men did that to a clergyman?"

The vast majority of the voices were disbelieving but Sir Henry heard one woman muttering to her daughter, "Once a wolf's head, always a wolf's head." He knew there would be plenty of other people, especially those who didn't know Robin personally, who'd believe him capable of these heinous crimes.

It wouldn't be the first time a lawman had abused his position after all…

For his part, the sheriff didn't trust de Monte Martini's tale. Yes, the man appeared earnest, and clearly *someone* had assaulted him, but Sir Henry had grown to know Robin fairly well over the past few months and years. Something like this wasn't in his character. Even if it was, Little John wouldn't stand by and watch youngsters being molested. The whole idea was ridiculous.

He stared down from his own, raised, seat and met the prior's gaze. Their eyes locked for a heartbeat before de Monte Martini raised his voice, loud enough so everyone in the hall could hear him.

"Well? What say you, Sheriff de Faucumberg? Are you just going to sit there, or are you going to do something about the wolf's head and his murderous companions?"

What could he do? Everyone in the county knew the tale of Robin Hood punching Prior de Monte Martini in the face during the Mayday games – it was legendary. If Sir Henry denied the prior's charge he'd be calling the powerful nobleman a liar to his face, in front of dozens of witnesses. And, knowing the wily old bastard as he did, the sheriff suspected de Monte Martini would already have made a sizeable donation to Queen Isabella's supporters. If she was successful in deposing the king and placing her son on the throne, as seemed inevitable, Sir Henry didn't want her to have any reason to doubt his loyalty.

Crossing Prior de Monte Martini would ensure the usurper wouldn't see Sir Henry very favourably – the man's influence truly was that far-reaching.

There was nothing else to do.

"I hereby declare Robin Hood, and all those currently in his party, to be outlaws. Sir Roger?"

There were gasps from the onlookers as the sheriff beckoned the captain of his guards.

"Sir Roger, I task you with arresting Hood and his men. Take a dozen men. Start by heading to Hood's last known position, in Mirfield."

The sheriff hoped Robin was long gone from there and wanted to buy the bailiff a little more time to hear about this farce and make himself scarce.

He shared a knowing look with his captain as the powerfully-built man left the room. Sir Roger knew, and liked, Hood; he'd not shirk from his duty if he and his men came across the newly-outlawed bailiff, but the sheriff knew his captain would do all he could to avoid any such confrontation.

Prior de Monte Martini shouted his own advice though. "Wolf's Heads are fair game for any man or woman. No need to arrest them, Sir Roger. Just kill them and save everyone any more trouble. Hood has a strange way of escaping imprisonment, as Sir Henry knows full well…"

The captain nodded non-committally and strode from the room but the hall had become a mass of voices and even a few angry shouts from those who knew Robin and his friends. The sheriff ignored the hubbub and gestured to his steward, William, again.

"See the prior is given comfortable lodgings for the night, suitable to his station, and have someone tend to any wounds he may have. New clothing and so on…"

The steward hurried to carry out his orders and de Faucumberg stood up, shouting to the nearest guardsman to clear the hall. Business was over for now.

As the great room emptied he noticed the slim figure of Thomas who was apparently on guard duty himself that day. He caught the eye of the man – taking care to make sure de Monte Martini, who was slowly shuffling out of the hall by the eastern door aided by the steward – didn't notice.

"My lord?"

Sir Henry took in the sight of the messenger and was satisfied at what he saw. Thomas was always clean shaven, his hair trimmed neatly, and his blue surcoat free of stains or rips. The man was reliable and trustworthy, a good soldier, and his appearance was testament to the fact.

It was just as well, for Sir Henry needed a loyal man right now.

"You know as well as I do that Robin didn't attack that little shit's entourage."

Thomas nodded, a sour look on his face, but held his tongue.

"Sir Roger will head west to Mirfield, but we both know the bailiff's most likely already completed his mission there and will be heading back here to report, unless he's went off somewhere else chasing Groves's gang. I want you to watch the roads approaching the city to the north east. They should return any day, unless bad luck sees them run straight into Sir Roger; I'm sure he'll try to keep out of their way but he's had his orders to arrest Robin so… God knows how that might work out." He ran a hand across his face irritably. "Assuming that doesn't happen, when you see Robin's party returning ride out and warn them off, all right?"

"Where should they go?"

The sheriff shook his head. "I don't know, but if they come here the prior will demand their heads. I'd rather avoid that scenario if possible since I simply don't have the political clout to stand against him. It would turn into a bloodbath." He grasped Thomas by the arms and looked at him. "De Monte Martini won't be around for long, I'm sure. He'll head back down to Lewes and this will all blow over. Until then, Robin and his friends will simply have to stay out of the way."

The messenger had hurried off to complete his mission and now Sir Henry came back to the present with a start.

It had been two days since Sir Roger rode to Mirfield, ostensibly to arrest or kill Hood and his men. Two days that the prior had spent haunting the castle like a spiteful wraith, drinking the sheriff's best wines and eating his own weight in meat while continually asking him if he'd managed to find the wolf's head.

Sir Henry felt a sense of anger building inside him but he repressed it, knowing it would do no good to get into an argument with the man.

Damn de Monte Martini and his wicked lies. Why protect Groves by blaming his crimes on someone else? What possible motive could he have for this?

CHAPTER TWENTY-FOUR

"Revenge," Robin muttered in disgust. "Pure and simple. That's why de Monte Martini's accused us of robbing him when he knows fine well it was Groves's gang. Christ above, the two of them must have planned this."

Will Scarlet nodded agreement. "The prick hasn't been able to forgive us for stealing all his money, or you for giving him a sore face. Not very Christian of him is it?"

No-one laughed at the joke. Instead they looked warily back towards the road, although it was barely visible from where they'd decided to hide themselves. An old grove of beautifully lush beech trees would provide good cover, surrounded as it was on the ground by juniper and bracken should anyone come hunting them from Pontefract.

When Thomas brought them the news that they were outlaws once again it had been an awkward few moments, as the sheriff's soldiers who were in the party looked warily at Robin and his friends, wondering what the hell might happen next. Would the companions turn on them, fearing the sheriff's men might do the same now that their legal status was, at best, ambiguous?

Before nerves could get the better of anyone Robin had told the blue-liveried guardsmen to head back to Pontefract on their own. It was highly unlikely they'd have been implicated in any crime by the Prior, so they were told to filter slowly back into the castle – with their give-away surcoats removed and concealed inside their packs until they were safely inside the stronghold again.

"Sir Henry's been forced into this," Robin told them. "You all know he's an honourable man. He won't see any of you punished just for being a part of this, but let's make sure his hand isn't forced again, eh? If you head back to the castle one by one it'll attract a lot less attention than if you all turn up at once in full uniform. You go back with them Thomas, with my thanks for your warning."

The messenger nodded grimly.

"What about you lads?" one of the soldiers asked. "Seems unfair that you've been falsely accused. Maybe we can speak with the sheriff, tell him what the real story is?"

Will snorted. "Unfair? Unfair he calls it. Fuck me, that's an understatement if ever there was one."

Robin waved him to silence irritably. He knew Scarlet was merely trying to lighten the mood but this wasn't the time for it.

"I'm sure he knows exactly what's happened, but thank you for your offer." He smiled and thrust out a hand to the guardsman. "You're all good men. Once the Prior's gone off back down south and this passes I'll look forward to your company again."

The soldier shook his hand grimly, obviously angry at the injustice of the situation but accepting the reality: he was merely an insignificant piece on a political gaming board. The truth didn't count when it came to an accusation by someone as influential as a rich, corrupt prior.

When the sheriff's men headed along the road back to Pontefract with Thomas that morning they left behind a small, and rather downcast, group of friends.

"You think the prior will head back to Lewes soon then?" Peter Ordevill wondered, idly picking dirt from under his fingernails with a dagger.

Robin laughed mirthlessly. "I have no idea. I wouldn't put it past the bastard to hang around up here just so he can make sure Sir Henry puts plenty of resources into our capture."

James shook his head. "I don't know this prior personally but..." he trailed off in confusion. "It seems a bit far fetched to me. Groves murdered his acolytes. Surely he'd want to see the outlaws pay for that crime? Not to mention the fact Groves could have demanded a hefty ransom for the prior. It doesn't make any sense to me."

"If you knew de Monte Martini, you'd understand," John replied sadly. "He might be a churchman but he's the devil incarnate. Ask Friar Tuck the next time you see him."

Robin agreed with his old friend. "Aye, it might seem strange but it's clear that's what's happened.

Groves must have offered to spare de Monte Martini's life – and given up any ransom – on condition the clergyman accused us of his crimes. They both win from it – the prior kept his life while the law comes after the one man they both desperately want to see dead: me!"

"And us," Stephen muttered ruefully.

"Don't forget Groves must have stolen a hefty amount of money from the prior's wagon so might have been less inclined to look for a ransom when he had a chance to take us down instead."

"You're such good friends with the sheriff now," Will broke in. "Will he really tell his men to bring us in and hang us if they do?"

Robin didn't reply. He didn't know the answer to that question himself. Yes, he believed Sir Henry was a good man, who wanted to do the right thing. But he also knew their so-called friendship would count for little if the sheriff was ordered to hang them by whoever was running the country at the time. And he couldn't blame him – why should de Faucumberg throw everything away by refusing to dispense 'justice'? It would do no good anyway – if Robin's friends were captured and the sheriff refused to execute them, someone else would take his place and see the job done.

The outlawed bailiff had no intention of putting his unlikely friend in that position; they'd have to deal with this problem themselves...

The eight of them – Robin, John, Will, Stephen, Arthur, Peter, James and Piers – sat in gloomy silence for a time, each wondering what would become of their families and the new lives they'd managed to carve out for themselves since they'd been pardoned three years ago. A gentle breeze played through the big leaves in the beech trees, bringing welcome relief from the heat which was quite intense, even here in the shade.

At any other time the men would have thought this a glorious summer's day and cracked open a cask of ale but today...Robin looked around at his friends' faces and felt as though he was at a funeral.

He still hadn't decided what their next move should be. In the short term they had to get away from Pontefract in case any patrols stumbled upon them. But where should they go? He desperately wanted to head for Wakefield. Home. He could explain what had happened to Matilda and the two of them could gather their money and take Arthur north, to Scotland. They had enough money to live well, without any of this hassle.

His eyes strayed to his friends again, though, and he knew the idea of a retreat to Scotland was nothing more than a fantasy. He couldn't leave these men to their fate, even assuming Matilda would agree to take their son and go with him, and that seemed highly unlikely. No, he was their leader – he'd simply have to find a way out of this ludicrous situation.

* * *

Sir Henry de Faucumberg had spent the morning working on the monthly accounts in his chambers, trying to avoid the prior. The sheriff had a horrible suspicion the old clergyman would hang around in Pontefract for weeks, just to make sure the hunt for Robin Hood didn't let up.

The one time he'd ventured outside to enjoy the sunshine for a few moments he noticed one of his guards – out of uniform for some reason – heading along the passage that led to the prior's quarters, where the elderly man was supposed to be recuperating in bed. De Faucumberg felt sure the guard was one of the party Robin had taken to try and arrest Philip Groves and he'd been glad to see his men returning in secret. Clever, and doubtless Hood's idea.

Why the man had been walking towards de Monte Martini's chamber he had no idea but he'd hoped it was to throttle the troublemaking old bastard.

With a sigh, he made the sign of the cross and silently begged God's forgiveness for his vindictive thoughts before turning weary eyes back to the pile of ledgers before him. He hated being cooped up in this little room on such a fine day – he should have been out hunting or even just riding to one of the nearby villages to check on things – but it was better than being accosted by the prior who seemed in surprisingly good health considering his supposed ordeal at the hands of the outlaws. Of course, they'd sent men to recover the corpses of de Monte Martini's murdered entourage but the search party hadn't returned yet. If they came back with a dozen brutalised bodies things would be very bad for Robin and his men.

There was a gentle rap on the door which the sheriff recognised as his steward, William's and he called for the retainer to enter, hoping it wasn't bad news.

"My lord." William made a shallow bow as he stepped into the room. "Your presence is...*requested*, in the great hall. Prior de Monte Martini has some news, apparently."

De Faucumberg muttered an oath and dropped the documents he'd been working from. No doubt the prior had demanded rather than requested his presence and what choice did he have but to obey the summons? He could make the old pain in the arse wait of course but what would be the point? He'd have to make his way to the hall and find out what this was about eventually.

"Alright," he groused, getting slowly to his feet, limbs tight from sitting too long. "But don't be giving him any more of our good wine. He's had enough of it already – give him the cheap stuff. If the bastard wants better he can visit a tavern and buy it himself. Come on."

Pontefract Castle was just as grand as the one he'd left back in Nottingham and it took a while for them to traverse the stone staircases and draughty, high ceilinged corridors that led to the great hall. Time for the sheriff's mind to whirl through possible reasons for this summons.

Most likely the meeting was simply for the prior to reiterate his desire that the wolf's head – Hood – be brought to justice, but maybe there was some new development in the ridiculous saga.

William threw open the heavy oak door that led into a corner of the great hall and Sir Henry strode in without announcement or fanfare, heading directly for his chair which sat on the raised dais at the head of the room, ignoring de Monte Martini's greeting until he'd taken his seat.

"What's this all about?" he demanded without preamble. He might need to pander to the clergyman but he wasn't going to pretend he liked the tonsured old tit. "I'm a very busy man you know, I don't have time for frivolities."

"Frivolity? My entire party raped and slaughtered and you call it a 'frivolity', Sir Henry?"

The sheriff tried to protest but de Monte Martini carried on without pause.

"It seems one of your own men knows exactly where Robin Hood is hiding but, instead of informing us, actually rode to meet the wolf's head and *warned him he was to be arrested.* That is why their party hasn't returned here as expected."

The sheriff had to stop himself from glancing over instinctively at Thomas, who he'd seen in his usual place to the side of the dais. How the hell had the prior found out about this? And did he know it was the sheriff that sent the messenger to Robin with the warning?

"I know you couldn't possibly have known about, or been involved in this," de Monte Martini went on smoothly, his expression saying the exact opposite to his words, "but that's not important. What you have to do is, first, arrest that traitor there," he nodded in Thomas's direction, "and then send soldiers to the location I've marked on this map. Your men know how to read a map I trust? If not, I'll lead them myself, should someone be kind enough to help me mount a horse."

De Faucumberg raged inside but he was experienced enough in statecraft not to let it show on his face.

"I trust you have some evidence to back up your accusation of my guardsman, Father? The man has been a loyal servant to me for years and –"

"I have enough proof to satisfy me, Sir Henry," the prior nodded. "Another of your men – someone who was in Hood's own party until this morning, in fact – passed this information onto me. I can't tell you the man's name, of course, I agreed to keep his identity confidential in case he should suffer reprisals from friends of the outlaw. Trust me," he said, almost leering at the sheriff, "my accusation is sound. Your man there – Thomas is it? – is guilty of aiding and abetting a wanted criminal. I suggest you arrest him now, before he does any more damage to this investigation."

De Faucumberg sat there for a time, not sure what he should do. He'd told Thomas to ride out and warn Robin after all – the man had only been following orders. That whoreson he'd seen earlier, the guard who'd been out of uniform, it must have been him that had informed on Thomas. Why? It wasn't important right now, although the sheriff vowed to find out sooner rather than later.

He gestured to a pair of his soldiers who flanked the huge main double doorway into the hall. "Arrest him," he said, motioning towards Thomas. He looked directly at the messenger as the guards converged on him, trying somehow to silently tell the man not to worry, they'd sort this, one way or another.

Wordlessly, Thomas allowed himself to be grasped by the guards who disarmed him with apologetic looks then led him out of the room, towards the dungeon. Sir Henry turned his gaze back to the prior, nodding his head.

"That's the first of your suggestions done then. But your demand that I send men to that location on your map, well...You're asking me to send my men into a probable ambush. You know better than any how deadly Hood and his men are. They'll cut my soldiers to shreds as soon as they get close to his hiding place, assuming your information is accurate." He shrugged and made an exaggerated sad face. "On top of that, most of my garrison know the wolf's head and respect him. I doubt we'll be able to find anyone willing to lead this hunt with any enthusiasm, since my captain, Sir Roger, is already off on a similar errand."

The sheriff spread his hands and stretched out in the high-backed chair, pleased with himself, knowing his words were true.

"I'll do it."

Every eye in the great hall turned to the speaker – a slightly overweight, balding man of advancing years, wearing the livery of a sergeant.

De Faucumberg cursed inwardly, feeling as if the entire situation had run away from him and was no longer within his control.

The speaker was his own quartermaster, one of a handful of men he'd brought with him from Nottingham thanks to his efficiency as a storeman. What the hell was he doing here, in the great hall, instead of at the barracks?

"What was that?" De Monte Martini asked, a small smile playing on his lips as he turned to look at the volunteer. It was obvious the prior had expected this, although the sheriff couldn't explain how. Did the quartermaster have an issue with Robin or one of the other men in his group? If so, it was the first time de Faucumberg had heard about it.

The prior was a weasel, that much was certain. Somehow he'd managed to gather information on the sheriff's own men, and all while he was apparently recuperating from a near fatal encounter with a gang of brutal outlaws.

"I said, 'I'll do it,'" the quartermaster repeated. "Sam Longfellow, sergeant of the sheriff's garrison." He introduced himself, as if it was the first time he'd ever met de Monte Martini but de Faucumberg knew that must be a sham.

"There you go, Sir Henry," the prior beamed, clearly delighted to have won this battle of wits. "It seems we have someone to lead your men in the hunt for the depraved wolf's head."

De Faucumberg glared down at the quartermaster, gesturing the man to stand before him so he could see him better. He knew him of course, but not particularly well and, as he eyed him now it was plain the man spent most of his time in a storeroom rather than in combat or even training for combat. Longfellow was of average height and carried a roll of fat around his midriff. His eyes were hard and determined however, as if he'd waited all his life to be given a chance like this and meant to make the most of it.

The sheriff waved a hand, partially in agreement, partially in irritation. Fine – let the portly oaf lead a few men to find Hood. He was absolutely certain the legendary wolf's head would have no trouble evading the quartermaster, who was from Nottingham after all, or sticking an arrow through his eye if necessary.

"So be it," he growled, looking again to the prior. "The sergeant can take a dozen men –"

"Come now, sheriff. He'll need a larger force than that."

"Well it's all I can spare," de Faucumberg retorted. "In case you didn't know there's another gang of outlaws running wild in the county – I need men to look for them too, not to mention the captain of my guard has already gone off with many of my soldiers on your errand. So think yourself lucky I'm even giving you a dozen."

"No matter," the prior said, bowing his head apparently deferentially but that small, superior smile was still on his red face. "I'm sure it will be enough. They have no idea we know exactly where they are so it should be a simple enough matter, shouldn't it?"

De Faucumberg didn't answer the question. He got to his feet and, with a final contemptuous nod to the prior, left the hall, William-atte-Burn following faithfully at his heels.

As he strode back to his study the sheriff contemplated the recent turn of events. It was as bad as having Sir Guy of Gisbourne around, watching his every move. Well, Robin had dealt with Gisbourne, and no doubt he would deal with Prior John de Monte Martini as well.

Christ, if he doesn't, de Faucumberg vowed, *I'll shove the old bastard down a long flight of stairs myself.*

CHAPTER TWENTY-FIVE

Thomas allowed himself to be led away by the two guards – men he knew and had even shared a few drinks with on occasion if they happened to meet in the barracks or town when off-duty.

In truth, he was too stunned to do anything except walk numbly, meekly, from the room, flanked on either side by the other soldiers. Thankfully, they respected him enough not to try and restrain his arms or any other rough treatment that was routinely doled out to prisoners.

In fact, none of the trio said a word as they headed along the echoing corridor that led towards the prison beneath the castle. The guards were clearly embarrassed at having to detain their erstwhile colleague, and Thomas's mind was still whirling, as he wondered what would happen now.

Would he be left to rot in the prison, forgotten like so many others before him? Would the sheriff set him free and restore him to his duties once the prior left to go home to Lewes? Yes, he felt quite sure Sir Henry, honourable and fair as he always appeared, would let him go eventually, and the thought helped him relax, the knot in his stomach slowly dissipating as they walked.

And then he thought of Robin and his friends, hiding not far from there, oblivious to the fact that crawler Longfellow was going to attack them with a much larger force. If someone didn't warn Robin – again! – he would surely be cut down by the quartermaster's men. He glanced surreptitiously at his escorts, wondering which of them might carry the message in his stead but realised that would be a mistake.

He didn't know how either man felt about Hood and besides, could he ask the young men to put themselves in that position, with Prior de Monte Martini desperate to weed out what he saw as informers?

No, it was no use, there was only way to warn Robin.

Without giving himself time to think, he turned slightly to the side and threw a vicious punch that connected with the guard on the left's temple. It was a tremendous blow and sent the man clattering, dazed to the floor, his halberd falling on top of him as he went.

The second guard reacted quickly, but the halberd was a clumsy weapon, wholly unsuited for combat in such close quarters. He tried to bring the butt up, into Thomas's guts, but the sharp end of the long pole-arm smashed into the wall, spraying sparks, long before it came close to the messenger's body.

"I'm sorry," Thomas grunted through teeth gritted so tightly he wondered they didn't shatter under the pressure, and grabbed the unfortunate guard by the head, pulling him down while bringing his own leg up.

The man's cry broke off as he took the full force of Thomas's knee in the mouth. He wasn't unconscious though, so, despite his natural aversion to it, Thomas landed a punch on the side of the downed man's head, then another, before he rose up, panting, staring wide-eyed at the two incapacitated soldiers.

I hope I haven't injured them badly, he thought, but there was no time to waste worrying too much about their fate. If he didn't get the hell out of the castle right now his chance would be gone; and any other guards seeing what he'd done to their colleagues wouldn't look too kindly on him, even if he was one of the better liked of de Faucumberg's garrison.

He quickly sized up the situation, realising there wasn't time to find rope to bind the guards. Still panting from the fight, he began to run, heading back, the way they'd came, desperately praying no-one else would come out of the entrance to the great hall as he charged past, heading for the nearest way to the stables.

As he burst through the door into the courtyard it became apparent news hadn't yet filtered out from the hall of his own arrest and incarceration. A few workers – labourers mostly, tidying up the worst of the day's refuse after a number of food and drink deliveries had been made – glanced his way but, seeing his blue livery, turned back to their tasks. It didn't do to stare at soldiers; perfect recipe for a sore face or even a night in the gaol.

Still, Thomas knew running as if all the demons of hell were after him would attract attention from someone who might try to find out what was wrong, so, when he spotted another guard outside the stables he slowed his pace to a fast walk, which felt to him more like a crawl.

"Well met," the soldier smiled at him as he approached, and Thomas's heart sank again. It was young Andrew, a lad with Scottish parents and someone he really didn't want to have to assault if the sounds of pursuit reached the courtyard. And that was sure to happen within the next few heartbeats, as soon as one of the beaten guards regained their senses.

"Afternoon," Thomas grinned, doing his best to appear calm as he strode right past the guard, into the stables where he grabbed his saddle and tack and pulled the bolt that held his mount's stall shut. "What you up to today? I've just been given an urgent message to take to Nottingham. The sheriff's not a happy man – think that prior's causing him all sorts of trouble." He grinned, feeling like it must have looked more like a terrified grimace and, without stopping to putting the saddle properly on Ajax he jumped nimbly up, onto the palfrey's back and kicked his heels in, urging the beast into a walk towards the main gates.

Andrew's eyes narrowed in surprise as he took in the sight of the sheriff's messenger riding bareback, while holding the redundant saddle grasped between his legs and the horse's neck, and he ignored Thomas's question, dismissing it, no doubt, as meaningless small-talk.

"Are you not going to saddle that animal before you ride out?" he asked, his unlined face showing confusion although not hostility. Yet.

"Ah shit," Thomas muttered as, finally, cries of alarm filtered out from the doorway he'd just come through moments earlier.

Andrew's hand fell to his sword and he began to draw it, still hesitant, yet apparently beginning to realise he should do something, even if he didn't have a clue what.

"Wait," he shouted, just as Thomas's mount broke into a canter.

"Stop him!" It was the guard that had taken a knee to the face. Blood caked his nose and upper lip, but he seemed otherwise unhurt and Thomas sighed inwardly, as he glanced back and saw him, thankful he hadn't hurt the man badly.

"Stop him!" The cry was repeated, louder, more forcefully and the two guards manning the gate looked across, wondering what the noise was about. Thomas was well known to both of them and the sight of him riding towards the gates was a familiar one, so it took a few heartbeats before they understood what was happening.

"Close the fucking gates, close them now! Stop him escaping!"

The gate-men, at last, ran down the steps from their positions atop the ramparts and threw themselves at the big gates, shoving them slowly yet inexorably shut, as Thomas bore down upon them, his steed's hooves thundering on the hard earth like hammers.

Andrew had joined the chase by now too, sword fully drawn and Thomas knew he'd be lucky to survive this. The guard he'd assaulted would probably lay about him in sheer rage and Andrew and the gate-men would join in as the battle-fever and confusion overtook them.

The courtyard was filled with excited and angry voices now, as soldiers ran to cut off his escape and workers stopped what they were doing to watch the entertainment, some cheering Thomas's escape while others hoped the gates would shut. None of them had ever seen a horse running head-first into a gate before.

But Ajax was the fastest horse Thomas had ever ridden, and the most fearless too. Despite the danger, it allowed itself to be urged on at full tilt and, somehow, impossibly, they were through and out onto the main road!

The gates clattered shut behind them just a moment later, muffling the outraged, despairing cries and Thomas couldn't help laughing out loud, punching the air with his fist at their great escape.

He chanced a look back and saw the gates were already being dragged back open. Inside, for sure, soldiers were mounting the other horses in the stables and would soon be after him. He prayed they wouldn't follow until Longfellow and his whole force were ready. At least then Robin and his mates would have time to get their own horses and ride off with something of a head-start.

Another laugh tore from his throat as he pushed Ajax along the road towards the greenwood. He might be an outlaw himself now, but he'd never felt so alive!

* * *

"What's that?"

"What's what?" Stephen replied to Little John's rumbling question, eyeing the dry skin on the tip of his index finger before pulling a small dry piece off flicking it onto the grass.

"That. Listen."

They did, and Piers nodded. "I hear it now. Hooves. Someone's coming this way."

"Not again," Arthur muttered, getting to his feet reluctantly.

"Let's move," Robin ordered, his voice low but the command carrying easily over the sounds of sighing foliage.

The men flowed towards the road almost as one single body, their old training and previous time together lending them an intimate understanding of one another's movements and anticipation of Robin's desires in regards to their positioning.

Will, along with Stephen, Piers and Arthur, hid in the trees on the far side of the road, while Robin, John, Peter and James found places on the near side, stringing longbows or drawing swords, ready for who – or what – ever was charging towards them.

They didn't have to wait long for the rider to reveal himself – Thomas's voice filled the air as he approached, the alarmed tone reaching them long before the words resolved themselves into a meaningful message and Robin held his great warbow ready to loose should any threat appear at the back of the sheriff's messenger.

"Robin! John! If you're still here, show yourselves! You've been betrayed!"

Before he could thunder past on his impressive warhorse Robin and John raised their own voices and stood out in the road, waving at the oncoming rider.

Thomas spotted them and even at that distance the relief was plain on his face, but he barely slowed as he came on, his eyes almost as wide as his mount's.

"Get your horses," he shouted. "We have to move. One of the guards from your party came back to Pontefract a short time ago and told the prior you were here. They arrested me but I escaped. The entire garrison will be on their way; we have to flee, now!"

"Do as he says," Robin shouted, sprinting back in the direction of the clearing where they'd tethered their mounts, the men following close on his heels.

"What about the two prisoners?" James shouted, glancing back at Groves's men.

"Leave them," John ordered. "The sheriff's men will find them and know who they are. Justice will be served. Now, move it!"

Before long, all of the friends were leading the horses through the undergrowth, back to the main road, where they hastily mounted and looked to Thomas for guidance since he seemed to be the man that knew the most about their situation.

"Where to?" Stephen asked, simply.

"For now, anywhere," Thomas replied grimly, kicking his heels in and leading them at a canter towards the west.

"Ride for Wakefield," Robin commanded, to looks of surprise. "I know it's probably the first place they'll look for us, but trust me – we'll be safe."

They pushed the horses hard for a time, until they skirted Featherstone and at the fork Robin led them off the main road, onto the less used, less well maintained track to the north-west. It would take a little longer to reach Wakefield that way, but would keep them hidden from any pursuers. Robin knew it was too late in the day to reach his home village so, as soon as possible, they led their horses off the path and into the trees.

Exhausted, both from the ride and the fact night was beginning to fall, Robin and the others dismounted and began to set up camp with hardly a word passing between them. Despite their tiredness they went about their business efficiently and, before long bedrolls were sited under animal skin shelters, water had been collected from the nearby beck, and lots drawn for watches.

As the sun finally passed beneath the horizon and only a dim glow lit the camp, the men wondered what had happened in Pontefract Castle earlier that day.

"So why did one of the sheriff's soldiers betray our position to de Monte Martini?" Little John wondered, when Thomas had filled them in on what he knew of the day's events. "Not to mention Thomas's part in it, and de Faucumberg's too."

"Who knows," Robin shrugged. "Maybe the man owed money for gambling debts, or rent or something, and he hoped the prior would pay him for the information. It's not important now."

"Not important?" Will demanded, brow furrowed in consternation. "It's important to me when someone tries to have me killed! We should be finding out who the informant is and hang the scum from the nearest tree. Like we'd have done in the past."

"Maybe you're right," Robin conceded the point, not looking for another argument over morals and honour. "But we've got more to worry about right now than some faceless guardsman."

"What *are* we going to do?" Arthur wondered. "And, more to the point, what about my family down in Nottingham?"

Robin raised a hand reassuringly. "Have no fears for them, the sheriff wouldn't do anything to them, even if he thought we genuinely had turned feral and carried out the attack on de Monte Martini's party. No, they're safe and better off out of the way, trust me." He shook his head though, sipping at a cup of stream water – none of the men really felt like supping ale that night, not with the knowledge pursuers were after them. "As for what we're going to do? I have no idea. For now, we escape that fat quartermaster and let things settle down a bit. Then..."

"Then we need to do what we were supposed to be doing all along," John growled. "Find Groves's gang and put an end to them. If we can capture any of them alive, they can tell of their part in the crimes against the prior and we'll be free and clear."

Piers, James and Arthur all liked that plan and murmured their appreciation, but Will wasn't so keen.

"This is all down to that fucking churchman," he spat. "If what you say is true, the sheriff knows the charges against us are horse-shit – he's just declared us outlaws to appease the prior, right? So why don't we just ride to Pontefract and kill the bastard?"

"Kill de Monte Martini?" Peter Ordevill demanded. "Are you serious? We can't just walk into Pontefract Castle. Have you ever seen it? The place is a fortress!"

"So we camp outside on the road until he heads back to Lewes," Will retorted. "He won't stay up here for long, he's an old man and if the sheriff's not making him too welcome..."

Robin looked at Stephen. The Hospitaller didn't say much but he was shrewd and his time as sergeant-at-arms for their old friend Sir Richard-at-Lee had given him valuable experience.

"What d'you think, Stephen?"

The bluff Yorkshireman was picking idly at his fingertips but he glanced up and nodded towards Will.

"I like Scarlet's idea. God knows I've had enough of corrupt, self-serving churchmen. But –" he continued before Will's smile could grow too wide. "We don't have the luxury of time. We're not the fabled band of outlaws everyone knew and feared any more. Those days have passed and now we're just another group of men fallen foul of the law. Aye, our reputations might see us safe for a while, but there'll be plenty of hard men in the villages hereabouts that might want to try and collect any bounty they think's on our heads."

Robin blew out a long breath thoughtfully, glad he'd asked Stephen's advice; the man was more perceptive than people realised.

"So, although killing the prior might very well solve our problem," the Hospitaller went on, "I don't believe we have time to wait – we have to act fast. And that means finding the remnants of Groves's gang and destroying them, as John suggested."

There were a few, "aye"s and Robin smiled. "That's settled then? Will, are you happy to go along with that?"

Scarlet looked angry at losing the chance to hunt down their accuser but he brightened at last. "Aye, fair enough. I want revenge on those Groves almost as much as I want to choke the life from the prior."

"All right," their young leader stood up, unlacing his breeches and making his way behind a tree to empty his bladder, his voice carrying easily through the still evening air. "We'll head for Wakefield at first light then, and see about finding where Groves has gone to ground."

"Why Wakefield?" Arthur wondered. "Wouldn't we be better heading for somewhere less obvious? Somewhere none of us have ties to?"

Robin reappeared from the gloom, shaking his head. "As Stephen just said – there's going to be people all over the country who'll want to make a name for themselves by taking us down." He smiled and tapped the side of his nose with a wink. "Besides, the sheriff's men will never find us in Wakefield. You'll see what I mean on the morrow..."

* * *

Sergeant Samuel Longfellow, lately quartermaster of Pontefract Castle's barracks, now leader of a dozen men with no ties or loyalty to Robin Hood, sat atop his cantering horse as if he was the king himself. He'd waited all his life for an opportunity like this, and now it had fallen into his lap he meant to make the most of it.

Of course, he was no regular foot soldier – he was a sergeant, and he enjoyed the prestige that position brought. But he'd always felt he deserved something more; something that would allow him to make his mark on the world, not to mention earn a decent wage at the same time.

He'd been an only child whose father died when he was fourteen, but his uncle managed to secure him a place as a raw new recruit in Nottingham's garrison, where he'd served loyally for a few years. His mother had been inordinately proud of him when he won a promotion to sergeant and the position of quartermaster, but that had been fifteen years ago, when he'd just turned twenty. She was long in her grave now, and Sam had never managed to progress out of the stores he occupied almost every day, ordering boots or shields or docking soldiers' wages for not taking care of their kit.

When Sheriff de Faucumberg had moved north from Nottingham to Pontefract his captain told Sam he'd been hand-picked to make the move with them. At first he was cheered, and wondered if it would mean a new role but... although he'd never admit it to himself, he was far too comfortable as quartermaster to seek advancement. It could be a dangerous job, guardsman, and he liked a cosy storeroom when the days grew cold and winter winds howled about the castle, be it Nottingham or, more recently, Pontefract.

Still, that jumped up yeoman Robin Hood came from nothing – a wolf's head, for Christ's sake! – to the position of *de facto* bailiff. When the younger man had come swanning into Sam's barracks back in Nottingham, making demands and then actually assaulting him...it was too much. Sam had never been hit in all his adult life and it was indescribably humiliating to cower before the huge former outlaw, especially with that giant oaf John Little smirking down at him the whole time.

Now, Hood and his men rode ahead of them, judging by the tracks in the mud, surely aiming for Wakefield, and Sam Longfellow meant to kill the wolf's head, or at least see one of the soldiers the sheriff had granted him do it.

One way or another Hood would die – not be arrested, that was too dangerous –and Sam's name would be remembered for generations to come as the man that finally stopped the legendary outlaw who'd run riot over northern England for so many years.

It was early morning, not long after sunrise, and Longfellow had woken bright and eager, rousing his men with shouts and kicks any drill sergeant would have been proud of. He may not have boasted the experience, or physique, of a battle-hardened knight, but he had plenty of self-belief and arrogance.

It didn't take long for the party to splash some water on their faces from the skins in their horses' saddlebags, down a little ale with some bread or cheese then hastily mount up and resume the ride towards the little market town Robin Hood hailed from. They hadn't seen any sign of the fugitives since last night, when their trail had led off along a smaller track that was almost overgrown with lush summer foliage.

Longfellow and his scout – a grizzled old veteran of almost fifty years named Harry who knew the area well – both felt sure Wakefield was Hood's ultimate destination and decided to ignore the narrow trail that their quarry had taken, with its encroaching vegetation and treacherous footing. They guessed it would be quicker for them to take the left fork in the path, past Sharlston Common and head for the well-maintained main road that led straight to Wakefield over good ground.

Now, as the rising sun cast long shadows over the land it seemed a prudent choice. Wakefield was almost in sight, according to old Harry but, even better than that, they could see Hood and his men on the clear road ahead. The outlaws must have rejoined the main road to cross the River Calder and now the chase was truly on.

"Sam," one of the men near the front of the party shouted back over his shoulder. "We might catch them before they reach the village if –"

"You address me as 'sergeant'," the quartermaster retorted haughtily, although his voice carried away in the wind and he wasn't sure the impudent soldier heard him. He went on anyway. "Charge men, let's catch the bastards before they can lose themselves amongst the hovels in Wakefield! Remember, Hood and some of the other men in his gang are from around here so we may face some resistance."

The formation turned into a loose arrowhead shape, as the faster and more enthusiastic of the soldiers kicked their heels in and urged their mounts into an almost uncontrolled gallop. Sam found himself not quite at the back of the group and that suited him fine. He could direct his men better from there, he thought.

He was no coward – he still had brawny arms despite the paunch, and knew a bit about how to wield the sword at his waist – but the best leaders kept themselves back so they could direct their forces, didn't they? It was only sensible.

As they approached the village Longfellow tried to count the men they were pursuing. Eight, as far as he could tell, although the speed of his mount made it hard to be sure. He wasn't used to riding as fast as this, but he knew his force outnumbered the outlaws and that was all that really mattered. He could see Thomas, the sheriff's erstwhile messenger, riding in the ranks of the wolf's head's gang and he wondered what insanity had caused the man – a career soldier with years of dedicated service – to throw everything away, simply to help that arsehole Hood.

His thoughts were brought up short as it became clear his party would never catch up with the fleeing outlaws before they reached Wakefield.

What should he do? His lack of experience made him hesitate and the men he led, without a direct command from their leader, held back, allowing the outlaws to disappear into the village, behind low houses and winding, random streets.

"The church!" Longfellow cried out, staring ahead at the direction the fugitives had taken through the buildings with sudden understanding. "They must be heading there to seek Sanctuary. Aim for the steeple, and..." he drew his sword from its scabbard and brandished it in the air as heroically as possible, "grant them no quarter! These men are outlaws and –"

His noble speech went unheeded by the men he led, who, ignoring the villagers that milled about narrow streets, shouting angrily at them for riding like lunatics, spurred their horses through the streets towards St Mary's, eager for glory and renown.

Cursing at the fact his orders weren't being listened to, even if the outcome was ultimately the same, the quartermaster kicked his heels in and gripped his mount with thighs he knew would ache in the morning, unaccustomed as he was to riding like this.

"There, they've gone inside!" Harry shouted excitedly, as the lawmens' party bore down on the small church with its recent extension to the rear. The face of a giant, bearded man glaring out at them was momentarily visible, before he slammed the heavy door into place and Longfellow expected to hear the sound of a lock or bar being thrown into place.

Only the door hadn't shut properly – it had become lodged on something – a small stone or other piece of debris perhaps – and now whoever stood behind it slammed it again with a similar lack of success.

Longfellow saw his chance and spurred his horse towards the jammed doorway, throwing himself clumsily off the beast as he arrived, somehow managing to land on his feet.

A voice could be heard from inside.

"Move, John, get into the room there with the others, I'll get this."

Longfellow recognised Hood's voice and, sensing an opportunity, ran up to the door which opened wide.

The famous archer stretched down and brushed aside the little stone that lay there and then rose to slam the door shut at last.

With a grunt, Longfellow threw himself forward, the tip of his sword snaking inside. There was a cry of pain and dismay and then the door bounced off the steel blade, which the quartermaster drew back for another thrust, but he was too slow this time.

The heavy door was, at last, slammed shut with a great boom that shook its frame then there was the unmistakeable thud of a locking bar being thrown into position.

"Surround the place, lads," the sergeant shouted, inspecting his bloody sword with a grin on his face. "There's bound to be other ways out of the building and I don't want to lose them; not when we've got them cooped up nicely like this."

The soldiers did as they were told, dismounting and spacing themselves evenly around the building, weapons drawn, as Harry also climbed down from the saddle and warily approached his sergeant standing by the barred doorway.

"I got him," Longfellow grunted to the scout, a satisfied smile on his round face. "I don't know how badly, but I injured Hood. Look."

He showed the crimson on his sword to Harry, who mumbled, "Nicely done, Sam," then the quartermaster stepped back and took in the small church, admiring its pleasant lines and general state of good repair. The newer part to this side of the building was somewhat jarring to the eye – the stone being less worn and less discoloured than the original structure which, Longfellow surmised, must date from at least a century earlier, but, overall, it was a pleasant looking old edifice.

As they stood there, shouting could be heard from around the corner of the far wall. Angry shouting that was coming their way.

"Ready men," the sergeant warned, his voice wavering only slightly. "That could be them attacking from another direction."

It wasn't. The voices owners' came striding around the side of the church towards them and Longfellow allowed himself a tiny inward sigh of relief. It wasn't the outlaws, it was just a couple of clergymen, although the fury in their eyes shone like an oil lamp at midnight and even old Harry took a hasty step backwards as the churchmen came close.

"What's the meaning of this?" the biggest of the two demanded. "Armed soldiers seeking to enter our church by force? Have you no honour gentlemen?"

Longfellow squared his shoulders and glared indignantly at the speaker – a friar judging by his somewhat tatty grey cassock and tonsured head.

At that moment a group of hard-looking men turned up, led, shockingly, by a young woman with strawberry-blonde hair. They glared at the newcomers but the blue surcoats each of Longfellow's soldiers wore marked them clearly as the sheriff's men and the villagers held back without drawing their weapons.

"What's all this, Tuck?" the woman demanded, eyes never leaving Longfellow, hand resting threateningly on the pommel of the sword at her waist.

"We're pursuing a gang of vicious outlaws, girl," the quartermaster broke in angrily, feeling somewhat nervous under the woman's hard stare. "They've locked themselves inside this building and I mean to see them evicted and taken to Pontefract to face justice. So stand aside, the lot of you, before we start breaking heads!"

"Have you never heard of Sanctuary?" the second clergyman – a simple priest and far less intimidating than the friar – demanded from behind his friend.

"Aye, of course" Sam replied. "But I fear these men are so wicked even God wouldn't see them protected. They attacked one of your own – Prior John de Monte Martini of Lewes – killing and despoiling his entire party in mean and blasphemous ways!"

"Did they now?" the friar asked softly. "Well, be that as it may. It's not up to you, or I, to decide who deserves Sanctuary. Those men inside are under God Almighty's protection and there they shall remain, so I suggest you ride off back to the sheriff and report your failure."

"I'll do no such thing," Longfellow cried, his face turning scarlet at the friar's lack of respect. "I didn't come all this way to be turned back by a single door. If you won't show us another way into the building, I'll have the damn thing broken down. I have the sheriff's authority in this." He turned to one of the soldiers and pointed at him imperiously. "You – find the village blacksmith and requisition a sledgehammer. We'll take the door right off its bloody hinges if needs be."

It seemed fairly obvious where the smithy was and the guardsman, with a nod of assent towards his sergeant, hurried off towards the southern outskirts of the village where the sound of a hammer striking an anvil could be clearly heard.

The priest appeared to gain courage at this threat to his beloved church and he pushed round the friar to face up to the quartermaster.

"You'll regret this," he muttered. "Damaging the house of God? Defying the protection that He's granted to those inside?"

"Aye," the big friar agreed, his voice taking on a powerful tone that spoke of fire and brimstone and divine wrath. "May the Lord strike you down should you seek to enter this church without His blessing!"

The heavy portent in the friar's words made Longfellow nervous but he had no intention of giving up now, when Robin Hood himself was only a couple of inches out of his grasp. Surely God wouldn't protect such a notorious wolf's head, would he?

As they stood, at an impasse and glaring silently at one another, the soldier sent to fetch a sledgehammer reappeared and he wasn't alone, the blacksmith following at his back demanding to know what was going on. It seemed word had spread about the trouble at St Mary's, as everyone in the village began to congregate in the road. The sheriff's men fidgeted and fingered their swords nervously, not liking the angry atmosphere that seemed to pervade the entire crowd.

"Got it." The soldier held out the hammer to Longfellow, adding, as an afterthought, "Sergeant."

The quartermaster looked at the tool but didn't reach out a hand to take it. He was in charge after all; this wasn't a job for a leader.

"Break the door down then, man," he ordered, waving a hand towards the thick slab of oak and black-painted iron that separated them from the outlaws.

"Here, what's going on?"

The friar replied before Longfellow could even see the speaker.

"The sheriff's sent these men to hunt down Robin Hood who has, apparently murdered some people and sought refuge in our church, Patrick. The sergeant here wants to force his way inside and arrest them."

The man addressed as Patrick pushed his way through the ever growing crowd and stood beside the clergymen, his face every bit as indignant as the friar's, but the quartermaster had suffered enough now. He was the sheriff's representative and, as such, had the authority to do what he had to do to apprehend or kill the dangerous criminals inside St Mary's stone walls.

"Enough of this!" he shouted, grabbing the hammer from the guardsman. "Everyone step aside or you'll all be arrested for obstructing the king's justice." He glared around at the villagers who didn't seem to take his threat too seriously which only angered him further, and he swung the heavy hammer up onto his shoulder as he stepped towards the church door.

The locals muttered amongst themselves, but they enjoyed a decent relationship with Sir Henry de Faucumberg, particularly in recent years, and no-one wanted to ruin it by impeding his soldiers.

"This is ridiculous," Patrick scowled. "Robin is a lawman like you."

"*Was*, a lawman like me," the sergeant replied. "Now, he's nothing more than an outlaw. Now stand back. Men!" he shouted. "Prepare to move inside and take these bastards – dead or alive. I've already bloodied Hood, and the rest will face the same fate."

The locals reacted in various ways to that statement: some cried out in fear for Robin, while others laughed at the idea of this portly quartermaster besting Hood in battle. The young woman leading the armed men seemed to shrink though, which surprised Sam and lent him courage as he watched her turn to the burly friar with a stricken look on her lovely face.

With a great cry, Longfellow hefted the great hammer aloft and brought it down to batter against the door which shuddered and splintered but only a little.

"We have to stop them," the girl shouted, making to draw her sword, eyes blazing, but Tuck restrained her, whispering something into her ear which seemed to calm her, as he did so.

"I'm warning you," the friar shouted at Longfellow, still holding the furious young woman's arm and raising his head skyward as if invoking God's righteous wrath. "Enter this building by force and you'll pay the price."

As if in answer to the man's pronouncement, it began to rain. There was nothing as dramatic as the boom of thunder or a sheet of lightning, but the sky did grow gloomy and Longfellow felt the first droplets of drizzle land on his cheeks and forehead.

Falling to his knees, the friar began to recite some prayer in Latin, his voice a low, unnerving monotone. When the sound of the crowd faded and the voice of the priest joined in with the prayer Longfellow felt the hairs on the back of his neck rise. Even the young woman that had been ready to stab him mere moments ago stood placidly, watching the sky.

Sam smashed the hammer into the door again though, his forehead creased in determination.

The rain fell and the churchmen's prayer grew even more disturbing as the priest's voice rose slightly in pitch, away from the friar's, and the originally harmonious chant became dissonant and jarring.

It seemed to Longfellow that the only sounds in the entire world now were the rain, which had grown heavier, the hellish prayer, and his own laboured breathing as he battered the hammer's iron head against the door for a third time.

This time, though, he was rewarded with a splintering and the wood gave way around the lock.

Dropping the tool from his tired hands the sergeant stepped back a pace, wiped the rain from his eyes and sucked in lungfuls of air. The door had swung open of its own accord but the interior of the church was dark, and the opening gaped like a hideous mouth.

He shook his head at the absurd thought, realising the clergymens' sinister prayer and the gloomy atmosphere were combining to make him nervous.

"This is your final warning," the friar muttered as Longfellow stepped towards the door, sword back in his hand and the scout, Harry, at his side.

"Enter this place at your peril."

The door suddenly slammed shut against its frame with a bang and the quartermaster jumped involuntarily, but it must have only been the wind. The lock was useless now anyway and the door simply fell open again, but now the dingy interior looked even more intimidating.

Even if God wasn't about to strike him down for violating his Sanctuary, Hood and his men were inside and armed to the teeth.

The young woman who'd led the small war-band glowered at the sheriff's men, white faced and clearly on the brink of drawing her sword and unleashing the killing fury that blazed in her eyes. Longfellow knew she'd be more than a match for him if it came to that, but the friar held his palm up to her, smiled reassuringly, and it seemed enough to hold her in check.

Thank God.

"Come on you men," he shouted at his soldiers. "Do what you're paid for. Get in there and arrest the wolf's heads. Move it!" He gave old Harry a shove but the scout stumbled to a halt and simply stood, gazing wide-eyed in through the shattered doorway. The rest of the soldiers also refused to move at first but Longfellow screamed at them to obey his orders or face charges of insubordination and, eventually, they did as they were told and headed for the entrance.

"You'll pay for this," the friar told him softly, but he simply snarled in return and followed the soldiers.

As they funnelled slowly inside there was an enormous crash that seemed to reverberate throughout the entire structure. As one, the sheriff's men stopped in their tracks and turned to gape, wide-eyed at Longfellow.

"What the hell was that?" he shouted, spinning to gaze outside at the two watching clergymen, soaked in the rain.

"What was what?" the priest replied, brow furrowed in confusion.

"That banging sound," the sergeant shouted, turning to stare nervously back into the gloomy church.

Thunder rumbled overhead, culminating in a massive crack of lightning and at least one of the soldiers actually whimpered in fear. Longfellow glanced back again at the impassive churchmen then, squaring his shoulders and mumbling a prayer of his own to God, pushed past his soldiers, deep into the new section of the building.

It comprised a single, large room that, from the look of it, served as a private area of worship. In essence, it was a smaller version of the main church, with a few pews facing towards a small, sparsely furnished altar. In the left corner was a statue of the Virgin Mary cradling the infant Christ, while the right housed another female statue which Sam assumed must be the Magdalene.

But the room was empty. Hood and his men were nowhere to be seen.

"Where are they?" the quartermaster whispered, eyes drawn to the statue of Mary Magdalene which seemed to be glaring back at him judgementally.

"Where are they?" he repeated, almost hysterically. The room had only one other exit, through a door that led into the main, old building. But it was bolted from *this* side – the outlaws couldn't have possibly gone through that way.

"God has granted them Sanctuary," a voice said, close to his ear, and he jumped in fright, spinning to see the portly friar standing there. The man had somehow managed to sneak up on him without making a sound, like a wraith.

"And now," the friar continued, voice rising to a crescendo as his gaze moved from one soldier to the next, finally coming to rest on Longfellow himself. "I suggest you leave, before you feel the force of His righteous wrath!"

There was another almighty crack of lightning outside and that was it. The soldiers panicked and ran for the exit, not wanting to spend another moment in a church that had somehow swallowed up half-a-dozen outlaws without a trace.

Longfellow, feeling the hard stare of the friar on him, was loathe to scurry out like a frightened child; not without a parting word.

"I'll find Hood," he growled, pressing his face close to the tonsured clergyman's. "Sanctuary or no, I *will* bring him to justice. And if I find out you had anything to do with this…"

The friar stared back at him, totally unafraid, which angered the sergeant further, and he jerked his forehead forward, aiming for the man's nose.

Somehow, despite the dim interior of the church, the friar evaded the attempted head butt and before he knew what was happening, Sam found himself sprawling face-first on the hard stone floor, a horrendous pain in his right kidney.

The storm growled outside, blending in with the groan of agony that slipped from his mouth and he wondered what the hell had just happened. The fat friar couldn't possibly have moved that fast without some divine intervention.

"If you ever return here seeking to defile His hospitality again God will not be so merciful." The churchman hissed, glaring down at him with the murderous strawberry-blonde woman at his back, a terrible expression on her face. "Now – begone!"

Sam knew he was beaten. His men had fled and he'd been knocked to the ground by some invisible angelic force. How could he fight against God Himself?

Without another word, the lawman scrambled back to his feet and staggered out of the church. Whatever had happened here, his quarry was gone. He should have known the legendary wolf's head Robin Hood would have help from Above.

As he ran to catch up with the rest of the sheriff's men he failed to notice the short cudgel in the friar's hand, or the enormous grin that spread across the man's round face.

Another huge crack as lightning sheeted across the sky made him run even faster, oblivious to the incredulous stares of the villagers.

CHAPTER TWENTY-SIX

When Robin slammed the door on the pursuing soldier there had been a brief, welcome moment of respite as he and his men caught their breath in the cool church interior.

It didn't last long.

"Why the fuck are we running from those arseholes?" Will Scarlet demanded, puffing hard, and, in a moment of clarity, Robin was hit by the fact his friend was already well into middle-age. It made him feel old himself, despite his mere twenty-two years on God's Earth.

"What else can we do?" he replied. "We can't fight them."

"Why not?" Scarlet spread his arms wide and glared at his leader. "They might outnumber us but we'd still take them down easy enough."

"That's not what I mean. Me and John have probably played dice and drank and even been on jobs with some of those men. They're only following the sheriff's orders. I won't cut them down like deer, not if I can avoid it."

"Aye," John rumbled agreement, his beard and hair rendering him almost invisible in the gloom. "Besides, the sheriff's men aren't all unskilled, clumsy oafs. If we get into a pitched battle with them there's a good chance at least some of us will die."

Will snorted in disgust, then noticed Robin clutching his side and he squinted, trying to see what was wrong.

"What's up with you?" he demanded, coming across to stand next to his captain, a look of concern replacing the anger that had been displayed there for most of that day. "You been cut?"

"Aye," Robin admitted, glancing down himself at his side. He took his hand away and the sparse light made the fresh blood there glisten. "It's just a scratch but I'll need it dressed before long."

"And yet you won't let us just go outside and kill those bastards?" Will shook his head in disbelief. "Even though they tried to kill you. So what the hell *are* we going to do then? They won't just give up now that we're in here – they'll be hunting for some way to smash the door in as we speak. We'll have no choice but to fight them then."

"Aye, he's right," Stephen said, the white cross on his red Hospitaller surcoat plainly visible despite the paucity of light. "It's noble of you to avoid engaging them and all, but...when they come through that door I won't be hanging around." There was a soft hiss as he pulled his sword from its leather sheath. "The whoresons mean to put an end to us and I'll not stand here praying to God when I've got cold steel in my hand that can do its own bloody work."

The rest of the men murmured agreement but they couldn't see the small smile on Robin's face.

"All being well, none of us will need to strike a blow this day," he said, moving past them, further into the newly constructed section of the church which wasn't as dark, as the meagre daylight filtered through the narrow stained glass windows that depicted the Magdalene, Christ and some rapturous angels. He lifted a medium-sized candle from the altar and lit it from the sanctuary lamp that burned constantly to symbolize the presence of Christ.

The men followed him silently, and Tuck's irate voice carried through the thick door at their backs. The words weren't clear enough to make out but he was obviously haranguing some poor unfortunate.

"I think I'd rather be in here," Arthur said lightly, "than out there on the end of the old friar's tongue."

Robin handed his glowing candle to Piers, who was the closest to him, then headed past the small altar into the corner of the room, before he turned round and looked at the rest of the men, his right hand reaching up to grasp an iron candelabra set into the wall. The candles it held were dormant, but a flash of lightning lit up his face in a myriad of colours as it came through the multi-coloured panes of glass, revealing his gleeful smile which was like that of an expectant child at Yuletide.

"Look, Robin," Will muttered, turning to eye the door as if it might be broken down any moment,

"I don't know why you brought us here but we need to either get out through one of the other doors or make ready to fight." He glanced about the room, as if assessing its defensive qualities.

Robin pulled down hard on the candelabra he was holding.

"Like I said: no fighting."

Almost instantly there was a click from the centre of the chamber and the men nearest the source of the sound jumped back in surprise.

"What the fuck was that?" Peter Ordevill demanded, his voice low and tight.

"Watch your language," Robin chided, walking over confidently, bending down and...disappearing into thin air.

"Robin!" Scarlet shouted, charging forward, sword drawn, loyalty to his friend overcoming his fright. "What the hell?"

Beneath his feet, Robin smiled up at him.

"A secret chamber!" Piers burst out, his cultured voice brimming with excitement as he pushed past Will, almost extinguishing the candle in his hand as he hurried to look down into the floor at his grinning captain. "I've read stories about them, but never thought I'd see one for myself. This is great!"

"Did you know about this all along?" Scarlet demanded, glaring at Little John, who shrugged and smiled enigmatically but didn't reply as he jumped down into the hole beside Robin and reached up to take the candle from Piers.

"Come on, the lot of you," John commanded, as the sound of something striking the door reverberated around the room, mirroring the thunder that had started outside. "Get down here, before they break in and see us standing like cows ready for slaughter."

There was another booming thud and this time the head of a hammer was just visible as it tore through the thick wood of the door, and the men did as they were told, jumping down through the trapdoor into the newly revealed basement which they soon realised was much bigger than the small opening that Robin had disappeared into.

The guttering candle cast eerie shadows on the walls of the underground chamber, but every one of the men managed to fit inside before Robin leaned up, grasped a handle on the underside of the hinged flagstone and pulled it down over his head.

There was another click and, in the wan light, they could see there was no gap above.

"It's in," Robin muttered in relief, as if he'd been worried his clever device might not work properly. "Extinguish that candle, just in case the light can be seen from above."

Despite the fact they were underground the sounds of the storm outside and the thudding of the hammer on the door still reached them clearly as they huddled in their stygian hideaway.

"How did you know about this place?" Stephen's voice, bursting with curiosity, sounded harshly in the dead air of the secret chamber.

"Know about it?" Robin whispered in reply. "I paid to have this new section of the church built. Seemed a good idea to have the stonemasons put in this sanctuary, just in case I ever needed somewhere to hide. The floor is all heavy flagstones, apart from the trapdoor, which is the same stone but a much thinner, lighter design, supported by a timber frame and held shut by a lock. The candlestick has a wire running from it to the lock."

"So who's going to pull the candlestick back?" Will wondered. "We're all down here."

"No need. The lock has a spring mechanism so it slips back into place on its own, and we can open it from down here just by pressing on the wire."

The doorway above crashed in under the force of the hammer and the unmistakable sound of many booted feet filled the room directly over head. Confused – and clearly frightened – voices could be heard as the sheriff's guardsmen wondered where in God's name the outlaws had gone.

Another peal of thunder seemed to shake the very stones of the building and then...silence.

Robin nodded to himself in satisfaction. Tuck must have played his part perfectly, terrifying the soldiers so much that they believed God himself had literally spirited their quarry away.

And, given the fact a thunderstorm had blown up from nowhere, in the middle of a glorious summer's day, perhaps He had.

* * *

When the sheriff's men had gone – to where, Tuck wasn't sure, although he didn't expect them to return to Pontefract in disgrace just yet – those villagers curious enough to brave the storm crowded around St Mary's demanding to know what was happening. Where were the outlaws? Had they really been spirited away by God?

"I know no more than you," Father Myrc shouted in reply to the babble of questions. "But Robin himself paid for the extension to our church, from his own pocket. If God would grant Sanctuary to anyone here, it would be Robin Hood."

"Let us in," someone shouted, to a chorus of agreement.

Even the headman was caught up in the excitement. Had a miracle truly happened here in Wakefield today?

"Can we go inside?" he asked, his eyes moving between Father Myrc and Tuck with the expression of a dog begging for table scraps.

Tuck grinned. "Aye, Patrick. We should all go inside and witness God's work for ourselves. Follow me!"

The big friar led the way in through the recently smashed doorway, a smile of satisfaction playing around his lips. Robin's plan had worked perfectly – no-one, so far at least, suspected it was all an elaborate trick, the foundations of which had been laid, literally, when the church's new section was erected just months earlier. Only Tuck and Patrick knew about the hidden chamber beneath the great flagstones that the people all stood on.

Robin had kept the hideaway a secret, knowing it was safer for everyone. The fewer people that knew about it, the less chance there was of someone giving it away under duress. He'd told Tuck and the headman about it when the building work was completed and, although none of them expected there'd ever be any need to use it, they'd conspired to come up with the scenario that had just played out, almost exactly as planned.

The storm had been a quite incredible coincidence, coming at exactly the right time, Tuck mused, but it didn't surprise him that much. God had marked Robin Hood for great things, as as the Friar had already seen many times in recent years.

"Good God," Patrick Prudhomme muttered, wide eyes scanning the chamber's interior and Tuck nodded at the performance – the headman would have made a good mummer. "It's true. They've gone." He knelt, hands clasped before his breast, eyes raised aloft to the crucifix that hung from the wall high above.

The majority of the villagers that had followed them in – a good two dozen or more – dropped to their knees, mimicking the well-respected headman, sighs and even little laughs escaping their lips at the idea of Wakefield's legendary son and his friends being saved from death by God Himself. Truly, that young man had made life very interesting in the village since he'd come of age.

One or two, less credulous than the rest, peered around for signs of hidden exits, rapping the stone with the hilts of eating daggers in hopes of finding a false, hollow wall or stooping to inspect the floor for evidence of a trapdoor.

They didn't find anything and after a while left, shaking their heads and wondering what the hell had happened.

Tuck knew the hinged flagstone that swung up to allow access to the low basement was cunningly disguised but he also knew the gloomy interior of the church made it much harder to spot. If one knew where to look though, they might notice the lack of grout around that particular stone and perhaps realise the earthly nature of the outlaws' disappearance, so the friar sighed with relief when the less pious, more inquisitive members of the congregation filtered away, back into the still torrential rain outside.

The rest of the people inside the church were happy to accept the miracle though, and seemed like they might spend the rest of the day on their knees, offering prayers of thanks to God for delivering Robin and the rest from the wicked sheriff's guardsmen.

The plan had worked perfectly but there was still danger; that portly fellow who'd led the soldiers didn't look the type to give up easily. Tuck expected the sergeant would be back just as soon as he regained his courage and was able to cajole or threaten the rest of his troop into following him.

"What the hell happened here today?" Matilda whispered out of the corner of her mouth. "Where did Robin and the others go?"

Tuck winked at her but didn't reply.

"All right, everyone," the friar shouted, clapping his meaty hands loudly over the sound of muttered prayers. "There's nothing else to see and it's time you all returned to your work. You can come to Father Myrc's Mass tomorrow and give thanks properly then. Offerings too, will be gratefully received."

For once, no-one groaned at the transparent attempt to take money from them, so great was their astonishment at the miracle they'd witnessed that day. In reverential silence they walked, heads downcast, out of the church and back to their daily lives.

Tuck watched them leave then faced Matilda and lowered his voice. "You have to go too – we need to make this look as believable as possible. Trust me: Robin is safe. Come back when night falls and you can see for yourself."

"But –"

"Trust me," he hissed and it was enough, despite the questions burning within her. She knew Friar Tuck could be taken at his word

A small number of folk tarried, wanting to spend as much time as possible in the blessed room, and the friar – aided by Patrick Prudhomme – politely but firmly shooed them out into the rain, the headman following to make sure everyone left. When they'd all gone, Matilda included, Patrick stood beside Tuck and they shared a small smile.

Only Father Myrc remained inside the new wing of St Mary's, still kneeling, head bowed, facing the altar, and Tuck felt guilty at the sight of tears streaking the man's face. He truly believed God had blessed his parish that afternoon and the friar couldn't bring himself to tell the priest the truth of the situation.

"Come on," Tuck said softly, moving back inside and clasping Father Myrc's shoulder. "We need a drink after all that. Some of the good communion wine will help calm our nerves and we can work on a sermon together for tomorrow's Mass."

The priest looked up at him with an expression of such joy that he knew he could never let him find out about the hidden room. They left the chamber in silence together, through the bolted door that led to the main building.

Outside, the headman watched them go and slipped back inside, pulling the remains of the broken door over, shutting off most of the view to any prying eyes outside. Then he wedged a piece of smashed wood beneath it to stop any nosy villagers returning and wandering in.

The storm had slowly moved on into the east taking the worst of the rain with it, the thunder only a low occasional rumble and the sheeting lightning just a memory. Inside the church Patrick hissed, "You can come out, now," and there was a clicking sound.

Robin's face appeared in the trapdoor and Prudhomme grinned down at him.

"They believed it," the headman said to a nod of satisfaction from the wolf's head.

"Thank you, Patrick," Robin hissed sincerely. "You can get off now, if you like. Might be a good idea to get the carpenter to come and fit a new door as soon as possible, just in case anyone comes back and looks too closely at the floor. Oh, and can you ask Matilda to come and visit me here in a little while? Tuck told me she was worried but handled herself well. Best ask Will's girl, Beth, to come too."

He shook Patrick's hand gratefully, then unbolted the double doors that led into the main church building and stepped in, followed by his friends, who all grinned conspiratorially at the headman.

They'd escaped! Robin knew it had been worth asking the stonemasons not to fill in the new basement with rubble as they'd planned, and the money he'd paid them to fit the cleverly designed trapdoor had repaid itself in unspilled blood.

Well, perhaps not quite unspilled, he corrected himself, glancing down again at the crimson stain soaking his gambeson. He knew he should get that seen to as soon as possible.

* * *

"This is bollocks. I honestly thought you'd bring us riches and glory, even if we were outlaws." Mark shook his head in bemusement at Philip's leadership. His statement was accurate but he said it in front of all the men, knowing it would plant ever more seeds of doubt in their minds and, possibly, leave an opening for him to step into. If Groves wasn't going to make them rich, there wasn't much point in remaining part of his gang, not when the man was such an arsehole to him.

He looked at his old mate Ivo, hoping for some support, but the toothless bastard had looked disgusted with everything and everyone lately, and that expression remained on his seamed face as he picked dirt from his fingernails with a knife that was far too big for such a delicate job.

"What do you suggest?" Groves asked, voice low, almost earnest, as if he genuinely wanted Mark's opinion.

Mark knew better of course but he shrugged anyway, playing his part for the rest of the men's benefit rather than their leader.

"I don't know. Where are we?" He licked his finger and held it up theatrically, to feel which direction the slight breeze was coming from now that the storm which had utterly drenched them had moved away. An old, wise acquaintance had once told him you could tell where you were by the direction of the wind and, while he hadn't a clue what the man meant, he thought it would look impressive to pretend he did.

"About a four miles west of Mirfield," Groves replied with a hard stare, before Mark could go through his little routine any further.

"All right, we have a few choices then. Either we pick on one of the smaller villages – like Slaithwaite – knowing they'll not be able to fight us off, despite our depleted numbers." He returned Philip's stare, letting the horse's arse know he blamed him for their reduced force. "But Slaithwaite and those places are poor. Are we looking to steal a few loaves and a cask of ale? Or are we trying to make a bit more coin?"

"Get to the point," Eoin rumbled from his usual place at Groves's side.

"We're not all that far from Kirklees," Mark said, and left it at that.

He could see the men who'd gone to Kirklees just a few weeks earlier to kill the tanner thinking back, remembering what the place was like.

A few years ago the village was part of some Hospitaller's commandery, and the knight had overseen the place well, making it a prosperous settlement, with more wealth than most villages of its size. The Hospitaller was hanged for some reason though, and the king had replaced him with a faceless clerk, which meant the outlaws wouldn't have to face some grim crusader and his well-armed retinue if they chose to rob the place.

It would have been a fine target even without the priory situated not far from the main village.

"Kirklees Priory," one of the men, a fat middle-aged fellow with a shocking ginger beard, mused, "has nuns in it."

There were a few, excited shouts of "nuns!" at the fat man's pronouncement and he grinned, black teeth showing unpleasantly through the matted beard.

"Aye, nuns. I've seen 'em. The place is run by some tall bitch but there's a few tidy young girls cooped up like little birds in a cage."

The outlaws babbled amongst themselves, the ones who'd been to Kirklees before telling those who hadn't what it was like, enthusing about the prospect of defiling a pretty girl in a habit before stealing all the golden crucifixes and candelabras the priory certainly housed.

"Very well," Groves shouted, grinning and waving a hand with a flourish. "Kirklees it is. Sharpen your blades lads, and give your cocks a good clean. Nuns are a step above the usual whores you lot share a bed with."

There was a great deal of laughter and Mark felt a sense of satisfaction at his manipulation of the situation, knowing he'd have been ignored a mere week ago. The warm feeling left him though, and an icy chill ran down his spine as he caught Groves's eye, and saw the murderous gleam there.

He was playing with fire and he knew it couldn't go on for ever. The time when Mark would have to either sneak off in the night or kill Philip grew nearer with every passing day.

And Mark had no intention of running away.

CHAPTER TWENTY-SEVEN

"Bugger this!" Will Scarlet cursed, face the colour of his nickname, once the outlaws were safely gathered in the nave of St Mary's. The storm had cleared and it was dry outside but the interior of the old building remained gloomy and even somewhat chilly despite the season.

After the initial excitement of the day had passed and the village returned to its business, Friar Tuck, after spending some time in the manse chatting about the miraculous events with Father Myrc, left the awestruck priest with a skin of wine and returned to the church to find out what his friends planned next.

"Mind my language Tuck," Scarlet went on, "but I've served my time as a wolf's head and I'm done with this arsehole brother of Matt Groves. We've tried your hiding thing," he pointed at Robin, eyes almost glowing with anger in the gloom. "Now it's time we find Groves and his men and deal with their shit for good."

"Aye," Stephen said, and the rest of the men, Little John included, nodded and murmured their own agreement.

"You're right," Robin admitted. "The hard part will be finding the bastards and engaging them on ground of our own choosing."

"Well you can't hang around here," Tuck stated. "You'll be fine for tonight but the sheriff's men will be back tomorrow. I could see it in their captain's eyes. He's got it in for you Robin; you should be careful."

"Sergeant," Robin muttered in reply, to a confused look on the friar's round face. "Longfellow's no captain," he clarified. "Just a sergeant; and nothing more than a quartermaster at that. If he comes back, next time he might not escape without a broken face or worse."

They all gathered around Tuck and he smiled at them. "I'm so glad you managed to escape without bloodshed."

He stopped as he noticed Robin's grimace, then peered down at the big longbowman's side.

"You're wounded," he burst out, hurrying across to pull his young friend's hand away then, seeing the blood caking Robin's gambeson, his old battlefield instincts took over.

"One of you go to the vestry – it's over there – and bring me a piece of linen. Anything! There's plenty in there. Who's got a needle and thread?"

There was a moment where nothing happened as the men looked at one another in surprise, then Stephen headed towards the vestry, telling them he knew what to look for since he'd used it all himself many times over the years to help his injured comrades in arms.

Little John fished in his pockets and found his needle and some twine which he handed to the friar.

"Get that off," Tuck ordered, unbuckling Robin's light armour so, when Stephen returned the outlaw leader was naked from the waist up. His body was hard and lean, with toned muscles that rippled in the candlelight, but even his physique was no match for the sharpened steel that had pierced his side.

The injury wasn't life threatening, having missed all the major organs, but Tuck didn't want it becoming infected or opening even wider so he cleaned the wound with some communion wine, then he used the needle and thread to stitch it neatly shut and bound the whole thing with a long strip of linen which the Hospitaller had torn from an altar cloth.

"Your secret room came in handy, eh, Robin?" he said as he used his teeth to bite off the twine. "But now what? Where will you go? Do you think the sheriff will send more men after you? He has to know the charges against you are false." He brandished a fist vengefully. "Maybe I should have given Prior de Monte Martini more than just a bloody nose the last time we met. Ah," he sighed and bowed his tonsured head before looking up, skywards. "Forgive me Father, that is an uncharitable thought."

"This is all your fault right enough, you old sot," Will said, but his eyes sparkled playfully. He and Tuck had been through a lot together and formed a bond of friendship most men never experience. "If you'd killed him when you had the chance we wouldn't be in this position now."

"We'll spend the night here in the church," Robin said with a small smile as he watched his companions banter. "Then find somewhere to camp by the main road in the morning. Perhaps we can get some news about what's happening from travellers coming from Pontefract." He shrugged, clearly not holding out much hope of that but unable to formulate any better plan after such a long day. "If you could bring us a few supplies before we leave that would be good. Eggs, smoked meat, bread, that sort of thing."

"Ale," Arthur shouted. "Don't forget the ale."

"You want me to carry a cask of ale here?" Tuck demanded, one eyebrow raised in mock disgust. "Think again, lad. I might manage a sack of food, but you can find your own drink. Any ale I find will be going down here." He patted his paunch almost affectionately and Arthur laughed in defeat.

"Thank you, my friend." Robin came across and clasped the friar by the shoulders. "You played the part of the outraged, vengeful clergyman to perfection today. Without you, I'm sure Longfellow would have had his men tear this church apart stone by stone until they found us."

"You take care," Tuck replied, ignoring the complimentary words. "Be sure and set guards, even tonight with the stone walls to protect you. It's not just de Faucumberg's men that are after you, and we have no idea where Groves and his gang are hiding out."

"Have no fears for us. We know how to play this game better than any in England. You get back to Father Myrc and your communion wine and rest easy."

They clasped arms and then, waving cheerfully to them all, Tuck made his way out the front to return to the manse, James bolting the massive doors at his back, then the companions sat in thoughtful silence, exhaustion bearing heavily on all of them.

"He's a good man," Will said, after a time.

"Aye," Robin agreed, then his hand fell to his sword hilt instinctively as a sound from outside the rear door came to them.

The others grasped their own weapons and gathered around, ready to face whatever danger might appear from the darkening evening outside.

"It's just me."

The men sighed in relief as they recognised Patrick Prudhomme's voice.

"I've brought visitors."

* * *

There was a scream as the lad chosen to stand guard on the northern road into Kirklees spotted the outlaws, too late, and his cry was cut short by the blade that tore through his guts and out the other side.

Philip pulled it free, but plunged it in again, to end the boy's life and any chance he might alert the villagers with his sounds of dying.

"Nicely done," Ivo nodded approvingly and, again, Mark felt a little stab of dismay – jealousy even – that his long-time companion was so taken by Groves, despite the man's brutality leading them nowhere so far. Nowhere they couldn't have gone themselves at least.

What was it about the smiling lunatic that attracted hard men to him? Hard men who'd never needed or wanted a leader to tell them what to do before, yet even now, despite their lack of riches and ever-present threat of arrest or death, Groves seemed to have some sort of charisma that bewitched them all.

All except Mark, of course.

"Thank you," the outlaw captain smiled, acknowledging Ivo's praise. "You can do the next one if you like."

"Not if I get there first," one of the others hooted and Mark looked away in disgust. Unlike him, these men, even Ivo it seemed, weren't that bothered about making their fortune and heading off to somewhere they could live as free, wealthy men.

All they wanted to do was kill, and drink ale, and empty their balls into women, willing or otherwise. The thought brought him up short. Mark realised he was different to the others as he watched Philip, Eoin by his side like a faithful hound, striding along the main road as if they owned the place.

He enjoyed violence, it was true, but not in the way the likes of Groves did. A good fight was always the best way to work up an appetite, and if you could steal your target's purse and buy yourself a meal and a few mugs of ale, well, that was one of life's simple pleasures surely. Any man enjoyed that – it was just the way things were.

He began to move, hurrying to catch up, again feeling an irritation as Ivo didn't even notice he'd fallen behind.

Eoin was the exception, of course, he didn't enjoy hurting people so much, and surely had some aversion to seeing women raped, since Philip always sent him away when the wolf's heads were planning on enjoying some lass. It was a truly strange partnership between the smaller, vicious leader and the almost gentle giant.

Mark decided he'd see what the day brought them here in Kirklees before making up his mind what to do next. Perhaps he'd be better off just leaving and heading back to his old haunts outside Horbury. His plans, or hopes, to supplant Groves were plainly ludicrous – he wasn't popular enough with the others to carry it off. Even if their revered leader was killed by some frightened villager that day, their group would either select the docile Eoin as their new captain or, more likely, simply disband, returning to whatever holes they'd crawled from in the greenwood before Groves's brutality had rallied them to his cause.

There were cries of alarm now as more people saw them and, suddenly, from his left, Mark spotted movement in his peripheral vision. Instinctively, he pulled his sword free of its sheath and swung upwards, parrying a length of wood that had been destined to stave in the top of his skull.

It was one of those frightened villagers – a thin, middle-aged man, with brown hair flecked by grey. He stumbled as his blow was turned aside, gasping in fright, and Mark, blood really pumping now, forgot all about his earlier thoughts. With a vengeful grin he brought his blade around in a shallow arc, into the villager's neck, sending him stumbling sideways, a gaping red wound suggesting he'd be dead within moments as his his lifeblood pumped out onto the eager, dry ground.

"That was silly," he chided the dying man, stepping over him and wandering into the house he'd appeared from.

There was no-one inside and Mark moved slowly around the single-storey dwelling stuffing whatever valuables he could find into the sack he'd brought. A silver fork and spoon set and an engraved pewter mug were the best pieces there, so he went back out into the sun and, seeing the villager was now dead he rifled the corpse's pockets, happy to find a couple of coins.

Maybe their work today would be worthwhile after all – it had been a good idea of his to come to Kirklees. Perhaps they'd even try to break into the castle that once belonged to the Hospitaller knight; there was sure to be money and quality items for the taking there, assuming its current occupant didn't employ many guards, of course.

And then...the priory, and its pretty nuns.

He grinned wolfishly and, with a howl to match the expression, hurried along the road to catch up with the rest of the gang, never noticing the boy that watched him through a gap in a hedgerow.

* * *

For the third time that day, Robin heard almost the same worried cry.

"You're hurt!"

Matilda had come into the new wing of the church with a stony expression, wanting to make things hard for her estranged husband. The sight of him though – topless, with a bloody bandage around his torso – made her forget their recent squabbles and a hand flew to her mouth while her eyes met his fearfully.

Little Arthur, however, ran to his father with a huge smile and, oblivious to the bandage, buried his blonde head in Robin's side.

"Ow!"

The burly archer pulled back instinctively but a grin creased his face and he leaned down to lift the boy high in the air, spinning him around while his men scattered out of the way to avoid being hit by a tiny flying foot.

The squeal of delight made everyone there smile and Robin finally stopped whirling around and hugged Arthur in close, eyes shut, great arms squeezing gently yet so firmly it was as if he never wanted to let go.

Matilda came across and gazed at her husband. Her earlier concern had almost evaporated as Robin seemed to prove his wound was only a slight one after all with the wild spinning of their son.

He smiled at her though and the expression was infectious. She couldn't help returning it, despite herself.

"Da!"

Another diminutive figure appeared in the doorway beside Patrick and Scarlet's face lit up as his thirteen year-old daughter Beth charged into the room and mirrored Arthur's previous cuddle, hanging onto Will for dear life.

"Are you alright?" the girl demanded imperiously. "I heard you were an outlaw again. What were you thinking? We have a farm to look after."

Will looked down at her with an enormous smile on his face and a wistful look in his eye.

"You sound just like your ma," he said at last, before he led her to a corner of the nave where there was a low wooden bench. They sat beside one another and he tried to explain himself as if she were the parent and he a naughty child.

Will once had a wife and three children but hired thugs had murdered them all and Beth was the only survivor. For a long time Scarlet had believed she was dead too, and bitterness had threatened to consume him completely, until Robin had found her and reunited them five years ago.

Beth was the stars and moon to Will Scaflock. She was everything.

As the two families came together again the rest of the men made half-hearted excuses and went through the broken door into the night to allow them a little privacy. Some, like Little John and Arthur, had gloomy expressions as they went, wishing they too could see their wives and children, but they couldn't begrudge their friends this small measure of happiness in such an uncertain time.

"What's happening?" Matilda demanded when, at last, the men had gone and Robin ushered her and Arthur to another bench on the opposite side of the room from Will and Beth. She kept her voice low but her tone carried to every inch of the nave.

Robin replied in a low, dejected voice, almost as if he was about to burst into tears and Matilda's attitude softened noticeably as she grasped his hand and they began to speak. Much of their conversation could be overheard though and Will stood, gesturing to Beth, not liking what he was hearing.

"Come on, lass," he said loudly. "Let's go out for a walk and I can tell you what's been going on."

Beth threw him a pretty grin and they went out through the door, leaving Robin's family alone in the church.

When they'd gone, the big longbowman hugged his son again, loving the feel of the child in his arms as he and Matilda stared at one another.

"Well?" She finally broke the silence. "What are we going to do now?"

CHAPTER TWENTY-EIGHT

Once the village had settled down for the evening Robin and the men slipped away into the greenwood and found a suitable spot not far from the main road where they set up camp.

The place would have been useless in winter but the lush summer foliage meant they wouldn't be easily spotted by travellers and there was a small stream nearby where they could water their mounts, refill their own skins and rinse their faces when they awoke in the mornings. The vibrant green leaves of the beech and ash trees all around kept them sheltered from the bright summer sun too.

Of course, Robin hoped they wouldn't be there very long before some solution to the current mess presented itself. Still, it didn't hurt to prepare for the worst and the site they'd selected would be adequate for a week or so before they'd have to find somewhere more permanent.

Experience told him the men would soon grow bored of their life out in the greenwood. Hunting and fishing were fine pursuits, providing both entertainment and food, but they'd need more than that or tempers would fray and fights would break out over petty matters. Especially if some of them took to the ale as a way of offsetting the tedium.

So, seeing some of them had developed paunches, he and John set up archery targets and organised wrestling matches.

It was clear they'd all moved on in the years since Robin had led them previously. Little John, of course, was still used to being told what to do by his younger friend, but the likes of Will Scarlet and Peter Ordevill, both middle-aged men by now, didn't seem inclined to accept directions the way they used to. Which was perfectly understandable – they'd spent the past three years as free men, doing their own thing and answering to no-one. It was a lot to expect them simply to fall back into their roles as foot-soldiers as they'd once done.

The one that surprised him the most, though, was Arthur.

When they'd lived as outlaws before, Arthur had been barely out of his teenage years, with greasy brown hair and an easy, if toothless, grin. Now, he was a man nearing his mid-twenties, married, and a father to two children. He'd changed a lot in the past few years and now, although he wasn't disruptive, clearly resented where they'd ended up and wasn't as open to following orders or training with the others.

When Robin pointed all this out to John, the big man simply shrugged.

"It's only going to get worse the longer we're stuck out here. The lads have had their time out here and thought it was all done with when we were pardoned. They don't see themselves as wolf's heads any more, even if that's essentially what we all are for now. Our old hierarchy has dissolved. Arthur may be the most openly pissed off at present but the others will end up the same if we can't find a way out of this before much longer."

There didn't seem to be any way out of their situation for now, though, so Robin was pleased when most of the others joined in with the archery and wrestling fairly enthusiastically. They were forced to use muscles that hadn't been properly exercised in a long while but seemed to enjoy the opportunity to regain some of their old martial prowess.

Cleverly, Robin had kept Scarlet on side by drawing him aside the first day at the new camp and asking him, earnestly and truthfully, for his help leading the men. Specifically, he'd asked Will to reprise his former role as swordmaster, training the men in regimented exercises and organizing sparring matches.

Will, a farmer nowadays, raised a sceptical eyebrow at the idea but he'd agreed.

"I could do with brushing up on some of my old skills I suppose," he said, then smiled ruefully and squeezed one of his biceps. "Won't hurt to harden some of these ageing muscles either."

And so the sounds of swords – real, steel ones rather than the old wooden practise ones since they didn't have any with them – clashing together and the snap of bowstrings filled the air around their camp much as it once had years earlier.

"How come you don't have to do any of this shit?" Arthur groused, as he was paired off with Piers for another wrestling match.

Sweat dripped from his hair which didn't seem as greasy these days. Robin supposed his wife had made him wash it more often or maybe he'd just outgrown the condition.

In truth Robin *had* planned on joining in with the sparring – he simply hadn't got around to it that day as he and John had been setting up the archery targets and seeing to other things around camp. Still, he didn't need exercise half as much as the rest of the men, since he and his enormous right-hand man had continued to train with sword and bow and staff in the years since they'd been declared free. As bailiffs they'd not seen as much violence as they had as wolf's heads, but it made sense to remain fit and sharp since people didn't take too kindly to being put out of their homes over unpaid debts.

He didn't say any of that to Arthur though, as the man had presented him with the perfect opportunity to re-establish his claim to leadership of their group.

Robin wasn't their captain simply because he was a quick thinker, or charismatic, or skilled with words, although he was all of those things.

One reason he was the leader was because he was a better fighter than any of them.

Maybe it was time to remind them all of that fact.

"You think you can take me, Arthur?" he replied, eyes hard but a small smile playing on his lips to offset the tone of his words.

The other man looked a little taken aback at the challenge. That wasn't what he'd meant at all, he'd simply been irritated at having to sweat on such a hot day while Robin apparently took it easy. Still, he couldn't back down now, could he? Not in front of everyone. A steely expression came over his face as he remembered he wasn't a boy any more – he was a father, and could hold his own with any man in England.

"Aye," he nodded, trying to return Robin's smile but only managing a grimace. "Why not?" He spread his arms wide and made the age-old, universal gesture for, "come on then, if you think you're hard enough."

Excited looks passed between the rest of the men as they realised what was happening and caught the tense undercurrent in the air. They crowded round, forgetting their own training as they came to watch what was about to happen.

Arthur was a short man, more than a head smaller than Robin, but he was stocky, with strong limbs and an iron determination that had been such an asset to their gang in days gone by.

Could he beat their captain?

No-one offered odds and, without preamble, Robin squared up to his opponent and the match began.

Despite the size difference, they seemed evenly matched at first but it didn't last long.

Robin knew he needed to make a statement here, so, when they locked arms, straining against one another, he wasted no time in the usual staring-out contest that started such a fight. With lightning speed, he brought his hands inside Arthur's grip and broke it, knocking the other man's arms away, then he simply stepped past Arthur, set his foot, and used his shoulder to trip the smaller man.

"Wahey!" someone cheered and there were a few laughs but Arthur rolled and jumped back to his feet instantly. He was breathing harder than he should have been though and Robin could see his opponent really *did* need practise. He'd never have been winded at this stage of a wrestling match four years ago.

Without waiting for that "come on, then" gesture, Robin came forward again and, again, they grabbed hold of one another. This time Arthur was more careful, and also even more irritated, and he tried to spin around Robin so he could lock his arms around him and haul him down but, as he moved, Robin grabbed his hand and twisted. The move ended with Arthur's arm locked agonizingly behind his back.

Normally, Robin would have left it at that and let his opponent tap to concede but not this time.

Pulling up even further on his arm, he forced Arthur onto his knees on the grass and held him there for longer than was really needed.

He was sending a message though, wasn't he?

"Enough," Arthur shouted through gritted teeth, trying to offset his humiliation by laughing through the pain. "I yield. You win!"

Still Robin held him and turned to stare at the onlooking men. They looked back at him and he was sure they understood what was happening.

They remembered now why he was their leader. And they remembered not to fuck with him.

Allowing a grin to crease his handsome features, he released Arthur's arm and bent down to congratulate him on a hard-fought bout, even though everyone could see it had been anything but.

Arthur had the good grace to accept the comment though and, with that, it was over.

Robin knew the man wasn't the type to hold a grudge over the public defeat and he glanced back around at the rest, who were still watching the day's excitement.

"What are you lot gaping at?" he demanded, playfully now. "You've all gone soft. Get back to your training or Groves and the sheriff's men will squash you underfoot like a turd in Shitbrook Street."

They all moved off, chatting about Arthur's beating and John nodded in appreciation.

Before any more could be said the sound of running came to them.

"The road," Robin hissed, head tilted slightly as he tried to glean as much information as possible from what they were hearing. "Two runners I think, coming from west. Let's move."

Without so much as a mumble of discontent, the men followed his order, even Arthur who picked himself up from the ground and hobbled along at the back of the party, rubbing his bruised shoulder.

* * *

John Bushel was a hard worker. Everyone in Kirklees knew that, and they also knew how skilled he was as a carpenter so he was never short of work. As a result, he had a nice house with two storeys and the finest chicken coop in the whole village.

Life had been perfect, especially when his son, Ecbert, was born four years ago. But then, just last winter, his wife, Emily, was struck down by a fever from which she'd never recovered.

When she died their son became even more important than he already was to John. Little Ecbert was the thing that kept him going in the hard times, when Emily's face would appear in his mind's eye and grief would threaten to overwhelm him.

A man breaking down and crying in front of his fellow villagers? That wouldn't do at all – he'd be the talk of the place. So, unless he was in the privacy of his own home where he could let out his pain without fear, the carpenter would picture his son, smiling and playing, shouting "daddy!" whenever he felt that familiar hard lump in his throat.

As a result of all this, when Ecbert came running into their house that day, wide-eyed and breathless, John instantly rushed to him, dropping his hammer and forgetting the repair he was making to the wall.

"What is it my pet lamb?" he cooed, scooping the boy up and hugging him tightly. "Was someone mean to you?"

The child pressed his face into his father's shoulder and hugged him fiercely.

"Bad men. Bad men hurt David."

The words were muffled but John heard them well enough, and the boy's fear couldn't be clearer. It transmitted itself to him like a disease as he remembered the warnings Robin Hood had given them about the dangerous outlaws stalking the area.

Still holding his son close, he hurried back to the rotten wall joist he'd been replacing and leaned down to lift his hammer. All he cared about at that moment was defending Ecbert, no matter who had come to their village.

"What did you see?" he asked, voice soft and as reassuring as he could make it given his own anxiety. He knew the boy wasn't a liar; knew something terrible had happened in Kirklees.

Maybe still was happening.

"Scary man, daddy. Lots of them came along the road but one was behind the rest. David ran out of his house and tried to hit him with a stick but the bad man had a sword. There was a lot of blood, and David wasn't moving." He stopped and looked at his father with innocent curiosity. "Is David dead?"

John's heart was pounding by now and he tried desperately to clear his head. What should he do?

He should go and help the rest of the villagers fight off whoever was attacking Kirklees, of course. That was what he *should* do.

But his son – who appeared to have forgotten all earlier fears as he looked curiously at the blackened, mouldy wall stanchion his father had been removing – was the only thing that truly mattered to John Bushel.

They would have to look after themselves.

The sounds of fighting came to them then – men shouting, thuds as weapons connected, a scream of sheer horror – and Bushel made up his mind.

Still holding on for dear life to his four-year-old son, he put down his hammer, grabbed a sack and filled it with cheese and bread from the larder dug into a hole in the corner of the room.

"Can you hold this for me?"

Ecbert responded with an earnest smile, apparently recognising the seriousness of the situation, and pushed out a small hand to grasp the food.

John ran for the door, retrieving the hammer as he went, and peered cautiously outside along the road.

The sounds of fighting were done already. Now there was simply an eerie silence.

"Hold onto me tightly."

He was a fit, lean man of twenty-five and, moving from house to house so as not to be seen out in the open by their invaders, soon made it to the eastern edge of the village, away from where the sounds of fighting had emanated from, heaving a huge sigh of relief as they reached apparent safety.

"Wait, daddy!"

His son gripped him tightly and he stopped reluctantly to look at the child, a chill running down his back, sweat making the hammer he held feel like it would slip from his grasp if he was forced to use it to defend them.

"What is it?"

"If we're running away," Ecbert said, matter-of-factly, "we need to take Herny."

Another relieved gasp escaped Bushel's lips and he resumed his flight.

Herny was Ecbert's favourite toy – a wooden soldier John had carved for him. He had, in fact, carved a full set of the little military figurines for the boy but, for some reason, one stood out from the others. The child couldn't say "Henry" and so the soldier had been christened "Herny".

Another Herny could be carved, if need be. Another Ecbert couldn't.

"We'll be back for him, don't worry."

Knowing he couldn't carry the lad, who was large for his age, all the way to Dewsbury, he set him down and grasped his hand.

"Come on, son. We need to get away from those bad men and bring help." He started walking and his son dutifully followed, face earnest, as if they were going hunting elves or fairies.

Part of John Bushel felt shame at leaving his fellow villagers behind, to die at the hands of the animals that had come to their quiet village.

But another part – the greater part – didn't give a damn about the villagers as long as his little boy was safe. On foot, as they were, they'd get to Dewsbury in a couple of hours and aid would be sent.

What else could he do?

So they walked, or ran when John could manage it, and, for much of the time, he carried the boy who began to complain of sore legs and hunger just a mile into their journey.

"Shut up," Bushel groused, his fear making him irritable, and he cuddled the lad in close, cupping the back of his head in a calloused hand and stroking his hair to offset his harsh tone.

Before he could mumble an apology to Ecbert though, he drew up short and hefted his hammer. Or he tried to heft it, but his hand was slick with sweat and the heavy implement slipped from his grasp to land on the dusty road with a dull thud.

"Jesus and all his saints," the man breathed in disbelief, not even stooping to retrieve the hammer. "Is that you Stephen?"

A group of dangerous looking men stood on the road before them and the child turned to look at them, before his arms tightened convulsively around his father's neck and a sob of fear filled the air.

It was the one dressed in chain-mail that Bushel's eyes alighted on, though. The one with the white cross and red surcoat; the livery of a Hospitaller.

"Aye," the soldier replied, although nothing more was forthcoming and John realised the man had forgotten who he was; it had been a few years since Stephen had lived in Kirklees after all, and Bushel must look quite different to how he'd been back then.

"Praise be to God," the carpenter mumbled, grasping little Ecbert tightly and leaning down on the floor before his legs gave way at the sheer relief he felt at that moment. Of all the people to meet, surely the Hospitaller sergeant-at-arms was exactly who was needed right then.

"What's wrong with you, man?"

Bushel glanced up at the tall speaker and now recognised him, and some of the other hard men flanking him, too.

"Praise be to God," he repeated. "Robin Hood. You boys have to get to Kirklees, now, before those bastards kill everyone!"

CHAPTER TWENTY-NINE

It didn't take long for Robin to extract the carpenter's story from him and Stephen, who still didn't remember the man, swelled with righteous fury. He'd been told of the tanner Edmond's murder and this – another attack on the usually sleep little village – was too much for him to stand.

"They would never have dared strike at Kirklees if Sir Richard-at-Lee was still the preceptor there. We'd have ridden out and smashed the scum to bloody pieces." His voice shook as it often did when he spoke of his former master, only this time there was an added edge to it as he imagined the horrors Philip Groves and his men would be doling out to the innocent folk he once lived beside.

The men hastily mounted their horses which were tethered to trees and bushes just beside the road, and Robin pointed down at John Bushel.

"You head for Dewsbury with your boy. You'll find a small track if you look to the right of the road, just about half a mile along the way. It'll lead you there quicker, and out of sight of any more marauding outlaws. When you reach it, raise the alarm and tell them to send word to Pontefract."

Will Scarlet cried out in disbelief.

"You want to bring the sheriff along at our backs? When the man wants us arrested?"

"Go!" Robin nodded grimly to the carpenter from Kirklees and the man didn't need to be told again, as he led the boy by the hand along the road at a trot.

They kicked their horses into a gallop and, shouting to be heard over the wind whipping past, Robin addressed Scarlet.

"We can't afford to let Groves escape again; the sheriff will bring men enough that we'll be able to track the outlaws before they have a chance to get very far."

There was a reply from behind but it was unintelligible, and that was probably just as well. The important thing was all the men were with him and Kirklees was only a short ride away. This time, he prayed, let us catch this evil monster and we can all go back to our own lives…

He'd only just begun to brood on that life of his back in Wakefield with Matilda when they saw the smoke and, from the amount, knew it wasn't a normal cooking fire.

Kirklees was ablaze again, and this time it wasn't just the tannery on the outskirts of the village.

They thundered into the village like avenging knights but there was no-one to be seen. Only a couple of dogs mooched around, ears flattened against their skulls, watching the newcomers fearfully as they slunk between buildings looking for food.

"No..." Stephen moaned, and it was the first time Robin could ever remember hearing such an anguished sound come from the taciturn Hospitaller. "We're too late."

Will waved a hand dismissively and jumped down from his horse, running to grab a bucket from beside the well in the middle of the road.

"I don't see any corpses, do you?" he demanded, rhetorically, lowering the vessel into the water and dragging it back up, brimming over. "Most of the villagers will have run away and hidden in the forest. Groves and his men have probably moved on already."

He ran over to the flaming building – a weaver's shop from the looks of it – and threw the water onto it. The flames died momentarily in that one spot, but the rest of the conflagration soon had it burning again.

"Come on, give me a hand for fuck sake, before the whole place goes up!"

Some of the men moved to obey Scarlet but Robin shook his head. "No, leave it. We're not here to put out a fire. Groves is getting further away the longer we stay here; if we don't catch him he'll be free to pillage and burn more towns and villages. Come on, Will, get back on your horse and let's find the outlaws tracks before it's too late. And be careful – they may still be here."

So they moved on, deeper into the village, eyes searching for signs of violence and death. It didn't take long to find it.

"There," Little John cried, his great voice startling almost everyone and they looked at where he pointed.

A man lay on the street, face-down, the back of his head a bloody mess.

As they continued along the road there were more dead bodies and Robin hoped fervently that Will's earlier assertion was right, and the majority of the villagers had indeed escaped.

"Bastards. Bastards."

Robin glanced across at Stephen and, when he saw what the Hospitaller was looking at, he shared in the sergeant's outrage.

An elderly woman lay in the shadow of a low house, her face bruised and her skirts thrown up.

Robin looked away, not wanting to violate the dead woman any more than she'd already suffered, but Stephen suddenly let out a little choked cry and threw himself from his saddle.

"She moved," he said over his shoulder to the unspoken question. "She's alive!"

"Stay alert," Robin growled, wary of an attack. Caught in the open like this, they'd be an easy target if Groves and his men were still around.

Stephen gently pulled the defiled woman's skirts down to cover her modesty and did his best to speak softly, reassuringly. His gruff voice and grim demeanour weren't usually viewed as reassuring but Robin could see the lady's body relax as the Hospitaller spoke.

"Find me some water," Stephen demanded and Ordevill dismounted, heading into the house the woman lay outside. He returned moments later with a small wooden cup which he handed gingerly to the sergeant-at-arms so as not to spill any of the liquid.

"Here."

The woman opened her blood caked lips and sipped at the cup the Hospitaller proffered. A small sigh escaped her as the cool water caressed her throat, although most of it dribbled down her chin and inside her torn tunic.

"The men who did this to you," Stephen asked, keeping his voice low. "Where did they go?"

For a time she said nothing, just stared up at the sky as if her spirit may already have fled, and Robin, growing impatient at their delay was about to order the advance, but then she looked at the Hospitaller and croaked something none of the men could quite make out.

"Where?" Stephen asked again, the patient tone of his voice surprising Robin who'd never seen this side of his old friend before.

Again, her voice came out as little more than a gasp but this time the single word she uttered was unmistakable: "Priory."

Stephen's head whipped around to look at Robin and they shared the dreadful thought. Groves and his gang had done their bloody work in the village and now moved onto the nuns just a short way along the road in Kirklees Priory.

The women there didn't stand a chance, unless Robin's men could get there soon.

The order didn't need to be given – Stephen sat, left hand fidgeting for a few heartbeats, wondering what to do with the dishonoured woman, but she waved a hand feebly and blood leaked from the side of her mouth as she mumbled, "Go. Stop them before they..."

Her voice trailed off and the Hospitaller reluctantly got to his feet, his eyes never leaving the woman as he stepped to his horse and expertly pulled himself into the saddle.

"You men: hold!"

Every head turned at the voice which came to them from the road they'd just come along, and Will cursed as they saw who it belonged to: the quartermaster, Longfellow.

"Fuck!" Robin muttered, echoing Scarlet. "We don't have time for this bollocks."

"That carpenter must have run into them on his way to Dewsbury," Arthur surmised.

"What do we do?" John asked, pulling his longbow from its place in his saddle and hurriedly, yet nimbly, stringing it by pressing it down on the ground to provide enough slack for him to loop the hemp noose around the upper horn, his massive arms making the task look easy.

Robin sat for a few heartbeats, weighing their few options. Either they killed the sheriff's men or they tried to enlist them in the hunt for the *real* killers of Prior de Monte Martini's party.

Whatever he decided, it was imperative they were quick, or every nun in Kirklees would be dead by the time they reached the place.

He took in the men approaching their position and cursed inwardly. He didn't know a single one of them so there was little chance any of them might feel any sense of friendship towards him. No, they were here to do a job and, spurred on by the vindictive quartermaster, they would do their best to arrest or kill Robin's men.

Thomas edged his horse forward, to face the newcomers, and the sight of his own blue tabard which matched their own, made the oncoming riders slow. They might not know Robin as a friend, but most of them knew Thomas and liked the man.

"Sam," he shouted, raising a hand to further try and halt the riders advance. "We can deal with this later; right now Philip Groves and his gang are on their way to the priory." He paused, to let the full meaning of this words sink in, then, as he opened his mouth to continue, Hood rode past him at a canter to meet Longfellow at the apex of the oncoming formation.

"You can arrest me once this is finished," Robin shouted. "I won't even put up a fight. But we have to stop the outlaws and, with our forces combined, we have a much better chance."

Longfellow's soldiers had taken in the scenes of death and devastation as they'd rode through the village and, although they didn't know Hood personally, they all knew of his reputation as an honourable man.

His suggestion made sense to them.

All, except their sergeant.

Longfellow wasn't interested in the nuns of Kirklees Priory, or in teaming up with the man he'd been sent to bring to justice.

The quartermaster's sword was already in his hand as he and his men rode along the road. The rest of his party fell back, warily, at the sight of Hood's men with their own weapons at the ready, understanding they'd already be dead if the likes of Little John with his huge loaded longbow had desired it.

Only Robin held no weapon. He faced the charge of Sam Longfellow, making no attempt to draw his blade or move to the side; he simply stared at the portly quartermaster whose red face was set in a determined grimace as he brought his arm back for a killing blow and the glory of fulfilling his mission.

Will and John shared a look, wondering if they should shoot the charging sheriff's man, but their young leader's calm demeanour suggested he knew what he was doing.

Or did he? Had his recent troubles with Matilda ruined his appetite for life? He'd already been injured by Longfellow not long ago, an injury which would preclude his movement somewhat if he *was* going to make some inspired acrobatic leap out of the way...

To be honest, Robin wasn't really sure what he would do when Longfellow's attack came but he knew from bitter experience how hard it was to ride a horse and swing a sword with any accuracy at the same time. He was praying that the quartermaster, who spent almost his entire life stuck on a chair in Pontefract Castle, wasn't a skilled horseman.

It didn't seem like much of a gamble but there was always the chance Longfellow liked to ride as a hobby.

If he did, well... Robin would be dead within the next few moments.

The sheriff's men watched in fascination as their leader's mount pounded along the hard road, wondering what the hell would happen to them when the wolf's head was decapitated, as he surely would be. And yet, Hood's men, who sat astride their mounts, apparently as calm as if they were watching a sunset, lent the scene a weird, otherworldly quality.

Screaming a monosyllabic battle-cry that contained all the frustration and anger at his life's unfulfilled potential, sergeant Sam Longfellow reached the immobile Robin Hood and brought his longsword around hard enough to cleave a man's body right through.

* * *

Robin wasn't riding a trained, battle-hardened warhorse, but the beast knew enough to jink, unbidden, to the side as Longfellow swung his blade.

The man's cry of rage ended embarrassingly as his blow met fresh air and, unbalanced, he fell right off the side of his own horse and landed head-first with a dull thud on the ground, sword flying into a bush. His mount continued to run for a short distance and then stopped, glanced back it its downed rider, then began cropping the grass at its hooves.

Robin heaved a sigh of relief as his men – and some of the sheriff's too – burst into mocking laughter, relieved at their friend's escape and finding the sight of the ruddy-cheeked quartermaster rolling on the ground like a stranded turtle utterly hilarious. Some of the men actually had tears rolling down their cheeks and clutched at their sides as if they'd split.

At last, the man got back to his feet, rubbing his knee where he'd landed hard on it, a mask of sheer rage twisting his red face.

"What the fuck are you pricks laughing at?" he demanded, glaring at his men. "Attack them!"

He looked once more at Robin then stepped towards the bush that had claimed his sword, but the wolf's head was finished giving the sergeant chances.

Kicking his heels in, he spurred his horse into a canter, closing the distance between himself and Longfellow in an instant, and, as the man spun to see what was happening, Robin kicked him hard in the face.

Again, the quartermaster fell to the ground unceremoniously but this time Robin threw himself from the saddle and landed on top of him, ready to deliver another blow or two to end the fight and move on – at last – to the Priory.

The injury he'd suffered at Longfellow's hands the previous day suddenly sent a burning pain lancing through his side though, before he could land a single punch and the quartermaster, outraged and now frightened for his own life, began throwing his arms around, jerking like a landed fish.

It was an unorthodox fighting style, but it worked, as a couple of times his arms clattered into some part of Robin and, buoyed by the fact he was still alive, he rammed his fist up and was rewarded with a sharp pain as it hit something.

"Christ above," Will muttered as they watched the combatants go at it. "I think we've seen enough of this. If Robin won't at least injure that bastard he's going to end up dead, and we've got a building full of nuns to save."

John nodded, his bearded face tight with concern. Seeing his friend struggling with the sheriff's sergeant was unpleasant to watch. Why didn't Robin just break his arm or something?

Before anyone could move, though, it became clear that the outlaw had, at last, finally decided enough was enough. The wound in his side had re-opened and fresh red blood could be seen staining the already brown, pierced gambeson.

"Enough of this!" he roared, pressing a forearm onto his opponent's neck and pushing down with the whole weight of his body. The quartermaster continued to throw his arms and body around but the combatants were locked too closely together now and it did him no good.

The men looked on in silence as Sam's eyes bulged horribly, his face turned purple, and the fight went out of him along with the spark in his eyes.

"Enough. You'll kill him," Harry shouted half-heartedly, dutifully, knowing his sergeant had brought it on himself. "He's one of the sheriff's men, just like you."

The words penetrated Robin's murderous haze at last and he released the pressure on Longfellow's throat, flopping back onto the grass with a heavy gasp.

For a few breaths the victorious wolf's head lay there, staring up at the near-cloudless sky, the quartermaster's riderless horse chewing a long patch of grass the only sound, then he sat up without so much as a glance down at his opponent and walked slightly unsteadily back to his own mount, staring at Longfellow's soldiers.

"You men can either join us as we seek to stop the real outlaw gang, or you can fuck off back to Pontefract to tell Sir Henry what's been happening out here." He pressed a hand to his bloody side with a wince then grasped his horse's bridle. "Or you can fight us and die here and now. I'm done playing games with you."

As he hauled himself back into the saddle the sheriff's soldiers looked warily at the men facing them. Will, Little John, Arthur and James had dismounted and all held their longbows ready to shoot at the first sign of an attack. Still mounted were the rest of Hood's party, the Hospitaller sergeant at the forefront, sword in hand, looking like something from a heroic fireside tale.

Harry nodded and turned to face the others in the sheriff's group. "Go with Hood and help him stop whatever's happening at the priory." He jumped nimbly down onto the grass and walked across to the prone Longfellow. "I'll stay here and try to bring Sam around, if it's not too late."

He met Robin's eyes but there was no accusatory note in his look – the quartermaster had started the fight and been beaten fair and square. He was lucky the fabled longbowman hadn't just shot him down as soon as the chase had begun, especially after Sam had stuck him with his blade the other day.

"Good luck," the grizzled scout said, grudging respect in his voice as he leaned down to loosen Longfellow's light armour. "You'd best get moving or it'll be too late."

"You should have that wound re-stitched," Stephen said as John and the rest clambered back atop their mounts, but Robin shook his head.

"No time, come on."

The party, swelled to more than double its previous size now, moved off at a canter along the track towards Kirklees Priory and Stephen shook his head in frustration.

"Fine, but when we get there you better stay back, out of the way, or the next fight you get in might be your last."

CHAPTER THIRTY

The guards in the blue surcoats looked unimpressed and the one facing Patrick Prudhomme shook his head.

"I don't care what's happened – the sheriff is busy. You'll need to come back in the morning and try again."

"In the morning?" Wakefield's headman's voice rose to a shout but he, somehow, managed to hold himself in check despite his instinct being to grab the obtuse soldier by the throat and throttle some sense into him. He was used to people doing as he told them back at home, but here, in the big castle, he wielded no power at all.

"It'll be too bloody late by morning you arsehole; it's probably too late already. Kirklees was under attack this morning. Philip Groves and his gang will have moved onto the priory by now. Even if de Faucumberg sends men they'll probably be too late to save the nuns but you have to at least tell him."

The guards looked at one another and shrugged. They had their orders: Sir Henry wasn't to be disturbed for the rest of the day and he'd been in a foul mood ever since Prior de Monte Martini had arrived there days earlier so no-one wanted to brave his wrath.

Patrick couldn't believe he was being fobbed off and refused to accept the rejection. The messenger from Dewsbury had come to Wakefield with the news of the assault on Kirklees earlier in the day and Patrick told the man he'd deliver the news to Pontefract himself. After riding here so hard, he *would* be heard!

"Listen, Robin Hood is in Kirklees right now. Or at least he was when I left Wakefield to come here."

That got their attention. By now everyone in Pontefract knew about Hood's new status as an outlaw and both these guards were friends with Thomas who'd escaped from custody only to ride off to join the wolf's head company.

The sheriff would want to know about this. Wouldn't he?

"All right," the smaller, yet apparently senior, guard nodded. "Follow me." He threw a glance back at his companion as they entered the keep. "If this goes tits up, I'm blaming you."

"I gave orders not to be disturbed."

The sheriff looked fed-up rather than angry which the guard, Joseph, took as a good sign.

"I know, my lord, forgive me, but..." He gestured at the messenger from Wakefield who, irritated by the long delay in delivering his news, pushed past and hurried to stand in front of de Faucumberg's stained oak desk.

"Groves's men have attacked Kirklees. Robin's gone after them but you'll have to hurry and send men *now*. I've been on the road for hours and your guards," he glared at Joseph who returned the look stoically, "have held me up even longer."

Patrick was glad to see his words had the hoped-for effect, as the sheriff jumped to his feet instantly and focused his own angry look on Joseph.

"Send word to the stables, I want my horse saddled and ready to ride. And have the duty sergeant muster a dozen men if he can find them. We must go to Kirklees."

When Joseph hurried from the room to see to de Faucumberg's orders, the sheriff moved into the adjoining chamber and returned moments later, strapping his sword-belt around his waist, an old yet pristine suit of chain-mail over his shoulder.

"How do you know about Groves attacking Kirklees?" he asked, glancing at Patrick as he threw the light armour over his head and hurriedly buckled it on. "Is Robin alright? I didn't seriously expect any of my men to injure him or try to arrest him, I was just trying to placate that bastard prior..."

He broke off as one of the gambeson's buckles got caught in the outer layer of brown fabric and Patrick moved to help the sheriff undo it.

"A carpenter from Kirklees reached Dewsbury around midday with his little boy and told them of the attack." He tugged at the thread around the sheriff's buckle and was rewarded with a small snap. Then he pulled the straps tight and locked them in place with a satisfied nod before looking at Sir Henry's face again. "He said Robin and the boys rode straight to the village to help but he had no idea what might have happened after that. He also met your men on the road. That sergeant – Longfellow is it? – headed for Kirklees too. The messenger from Dewsbury came through Wakefield on his way here and I offered to bring his news to you since his horse was old and hardly up to that ride."

The sheriff cursed, loudly and imaginatively.

"According to barrack gossips, Longfellow is more interested in killing Hood to gain de Monte Martini's favour than capturing the *real* outlaws. Damn that prior and his ridiculous accusations. Come on. God knows what we'll find when we get to Kirklees."

De Faucumberg walked through the doorway and along the deserted corridor that led towards the stables on the southern side of the castle.

Patrick, hurrying to keep up with the grim-faced sheriff, shook his head in bewilderment.

"If you know Robin's innocent of the crimes he's accused of –"

"Politics," de Faucumberg snapped, with a glare over his shoulder at Wakefield's headman as their footsteps echoed along the stone passageway. "Surely you know how things work, Prudhomme?"

Patrick didn't, but he held his peace, not wanting to show his ignorance.

They emerged into a bustling courtyard and Sir Henry nodded in satisfaction. The guard, Joseph, had managed to get things moving as around a dozen of the garrison were preparing to ride out. The balding stable master strode across leading a great warhorse and nodded his head respectfully to de Faucumberg.

"Kirklees, sheriff?"

"Aye," de Faucumberg confirmed, placing his foot into his mount's stirrup and, with a grunt, climbed into the saddle. "Kirklees. We're probably going to be too late – God help them – but we'll ride hard and pray."

He looked at Patrick. "Are you coming with us?"

Prudhomme shook his head.

"My horse isn't up to another fast ride like that, my lord."

"Spend the night here then," de Faucumberg nodded graciously. "I'll have word –"

"No. Thank you, Sir Henry but I'll head back home. I want to be with my family and friends this night. Just in case Groves and his men, well...escape..."

De Faucumberg pursed his lips but clearly saw the sense in Prudhomme's words.

"Fair enough. You head for home, but I promise you, Patrick, I'll do all I can to make sure Groves is hunted down and Robin is safe."

Wakefield's headman smiled and gave a small wave in salute as the sheriff's party headed at a trot for the gatehouse and the road west.

"De Faucumberg! Wait. Wait I say!"

The sheriff turned in the saddle, his whispered curse somehow reverberating around the stone walls over the hollow clop of hooves, and he didn't even attempt to force a smile onto his face as Prior John de Monte Martini ran out of the castle towards them.

"Where..." The prior laid a hand on Sir Henry's horse's rump and bent double, gasping for air after his short run. "Where are you going?"

The sheriff kept his horse moving so the accursed prior would have to keep up and become even more breathless. *Maybe the vindictive old bastard will keel over and die if I tire him out enough*, he thought hopefully, but replied in an even voice.

"You seem to have recovered well from your injuries, Prior. I've just had word that your attackers are at work again in Kirklees, so we ride there now to stop them. We may be too late already though, so..." he leaned back, raising himself high in the saddle so he towered over de Monte Martini, "we must be off!"

"You'll damn well wait on me," the prior spat, lowering his eyebrows imperiously and turning to raise one of the stable boys' attention.

"No time!" de Faucumberg shouted, but de Monte Martini shot his hand up in the air then brought it down to point imperiously at the sheriff.

"Enough. You *shall* wait on me." He glared at the boy who'd run to him. "Saddle a horse for me, lad. And nothing too big," he added, as the stable-hand ran off to do as he was told.

De Faucumberg nudged his mount closer to the prior and the sheriff leaned down to address the clergyman in a low voice.

"This is no joke. The outlaws – the *real* outlaws, I mean – have attacked the nearby town of Kirklees. And by now they've probably already torn the place a new arsehole. Forgive my language," he muttered, insincerely as the prior glared up at him. "I don't have time to wait on you, or to look after you once we get there. Apparently Groves was planning to attack the priory and, if he does, the nuns there can pray all they like but it won't save them."

"And neither shall you save Robin Hood," the clergyman replied. "I know what you're doing; you hope to kill this other gang of criminals then blame all the crimes of England on them so Hood and his lot get another pardon."

The stable-boy appeared leading a pony which was smaller than the others the sheriff's men were mounted upon, but it was young and strong and would have no trouble keeping pace with them.

"Not this time," de Monte Martini finished, as the lad helped him climb into the saddle. "I'll be there to see you either arrest or execute Hood for his many crimes. The king wields little power in England now – his queen, Prince Edward, and their supporters will come from France soon enough, and you can trust me when I tell you they are friends of mine."

He left the sentence hanging in the air between them as he nudged his pony over to stand next to the sheriff's warhorse.

De Faucumberg curled his lip and glared at the prior but he didn't rise to the bait.

From the front of the party the sergeant looked back, confirmed everyone was ready to move, and shouted the advance.

As they walked their horses through the gates then kicked them into a canter along the main road to Kirklees, Sir Henry wondered if he could just skewer the damned prior when no-one was looking, but immediately offered a silent prayer of contrition for such a wicked thought about one of God's chosen.

He couldn't just kill the man, but *something* would have to be done if Robin and his friends were to be saved the hangman's noose.

* * *

"Mother Elizabeth! There's men at the door, and I don't think they're here to pray."

The young nun – no more than sixteen years old – had come barging right into the prioress's chamber with barely a knock on the door and stood in front of her now, chest heaving from her mad dash. The alarm was evident on her sweet, unlined face and it transmitted itself to Elizabeth de Stainton.

"Get a hold of yourself, Sister Jane," the prioress ordered, keeping her voice level so as not to add to the girl's consternation which could easily lead to an outbreak of mass hysteria.

It wouldn't be the first such occurrence and it was never pleasant dealing with the aftermath.

"Are the men inside?"

"No, Mother," the small nun replied, shaking her head vigorously. "I wouldn't open the door to them – one of them looked right in the viewing hole and his breath stank of ale or wine or something

– so they've started hammering on it. They're laughing and joking as if it's all a big game, but I don't know how long the door will stand up to them." She looked at the floor sorrowfully, as if the whole situation was her fault. "They're very big men. Hairy," she finished in a whisper.

The prioress stood, her tall frame seeming to fill the small chamber, and looked down at her young charge.

"Don't be silly, girl," she admonished. "That door has stood against marauding Vikings. It's almost as old – and as strong – as the stones the priory's built from. Come – let us see what these frightening men want with us. I'm sure they only seek meat or ale or a bed for the night."

"That's what I'm afraid of," the young nun mumbled to herself but the prioress pretended not to hear.

It didn't take long for the pair to reach the front door which, thankfully, still stood intact although an unshaven, rough-looking face peered through at them.

Leered through at them.

Some of the other nuns had begun to congregate around the door, talking in excited, nervous voices, but they hushed as they saw the prioress appear. Her commanding presence seemed to calm them but the man peering in the open viewing port whistled softly in appreciation and made an extremely crude comment to his unseen friends. Their laughter made Elizabeth de Stainton's blood run cold but she kept the fear from her face and strode confidently across to the locked door.

"What do you want?" she asked, as cordially as she could manage although nervousness made her voice harsher than she intended.

It hardly mattered to the men outside who laughed and hooted suggestively at her question.

"What do we want? What do we want?" the face at the door shouted gleefully.

"A good fucking!" another voice cried and was met with uproarious laughter..

The prioress turned to Sister Jane and fixed her with a stern glare.

"Run to the bell tower and ring it has hard as you can. Don't stop until your arms can't take it any more." She glanced around at the rest of the gathered nuns and selected one at random. "You go with her and help. We must try and raise the alarm so the men in Kirklees come to our aid."

She'd tried to pitch her voice low enough that the would-be invaders couldn't hear her but there was another raucous, sinister laugh from the other side of the door and the man pressed his face against the iron grille to glare in at the prioress.

"The men of Kirklees won't come to help you, Mother. They're all dead."

The prioress shuddered as the insane, sadistic laughter filled the air outside again and was soon joined by a rhythmic hammering as someone sought to kick the door down.

Some of the younger nuns began to sob in terror and even the older ones who'd seen things like this before looked nervous.

The priory had been besieged by drunk men in the past but this was different. These men were truly frightening.

Evil.

"Get a hold of yourselves," Mother Elizabeth growled. "Follow me."

The front door was sturdy – constructed from oak with massive iron hinges and a heavy ash locking bar which she made sure was firmly in place – but it wouldn't last forever, not once the outlaws started hacking at it with axes or found a fallen tree to use as a battering ram. So the prioress led them through the chapter house to the infirmary, sending them all up the stairs to the tower which adjoined it.

There was only one person – an elderly man from the nearby village of Slaithwaite – in a sick-bed, and the prioress ordered two of her larger nuns to help him hobble out into the stairwell where they would be safe behind another sturdy door.

For a time at least.

"Sisters Pauline and Marjorie – gather blankets from the beds. Sisters Elaine, Sarah and Letitia – collect food from the larder next to the infirmary. As much as you can carry, hurry now. Sisters

Bernadette and Erin – bring that barrel of water. There's a cart to help you in the corner there. Come on now, move! We have little time before those heathens break the door down."

She watched in satisfaction as the women followed her orders without question, their tasks seeming to offset the terror that threatened to overwhelm them all.

"The rest of you – what are you staring at?" she barked. "Why are you standing on the stairs, watching us? Get up there, now! Into the tower with you all. Take the food and blankets with you as you go. The water barrel can stay at the bottom; it's much too heavy to lift up there."

As the ladies worked the sound of thumping came to them. The outlaws must have found a log to use as a battering ram much quicker than the prioress expected. Clearly some of them had been off finding the thing while the man at the door distracted the nuns.

"Get in, quick!"

The women followed their superior's order, wide-eyed and fretful, but then angry as the prioress closed the door from the outside and locked them in.

"What are you doing, Mother?" An old matron she recognised as Sister Joanne, her voice muffled by the sturdy door, demanded. "Get in here with us or the heathen invaders will defile you!"

The prioress wanted to get in there with them, more than anything.

It would have been the sensible thing to do. The easy thing.

But she had to remain out here and at least *try* to stop these men from rampaging through the entire priory, doing whatever they would to the nuns in her care.

"Push as much stuff as you can against the door!" she shouted through to the women in the tower. "Hold them off as long as possible; someone will come to our aid when they hear the bells. God will make sure of it, have no fear sisters!"

She ran to the infirmary door and pushed it shut just as one of the marauding outlaws appeared in the adjoining brede house, a maniacal smile on his face and, more worryingly, a bloody knife in his hand.

"Come out you bitch," he cried but the prioress threw the bolt just as his body hammered into the wood. It held, but the metal was thin and bent slightly under his weight. Gasping a prayer she grabbed a wooden linen cabinet that stood beside the entrance and, gritting her teeth, managed to upend it so its heavy body blocked the door.

Exhausted now, mentally and physically, she sank down, her back against the fallen cabinet and barely registered the thuds from the outlaws' hammering as they tried to get in.

"Try as much as you like," she thought with a grim satisfaction. "But by the time you get past me and this door, then into that tower where the rest of my girls are hiding out, help will be here."

And then she realised she'd forgotten Sister Jane and her companion in the bell tower.

CHAPTER THIRTY-ONE

"The bell!" Robin shouted as they neared the priory and heard the doleful tolling roll out across the countryside. "If someone's trying to raise the alarm that means they're still alive. Come on, we're not too late!"

He kicked his heels in and the palfrey surged forward. Behind him, he could hear the pounding hooves of the rest of the men's horses and he gritted his teeth, praying to God that they'd be in time to stop Groves's men from abusing the innocent nuns of Kirklees.

The bell never ceased its urgent clang as they thundered through the old, ruined gateway and into the main courtyard, but it was apparent the marauding outlaws had gained entry, as the main door was smashed to firewood and a makeshift battering ram – an upended young beech tree with most of its branches still intact – lay discarded in the opening.

Robin thought about splitting his men – sending some to circle the perimeter and prevent any of Groves's men from escaping – but he discarded the idea. The outlaws probably had more men than they did and, truth be told, if they wanted to escape it would be better than allowing them to rape the nuns.

That bell, though...It continued to toll, sending its peal of alarm throughout the land, and it was obvious the outlaws would seek to silence it as soon as possible.

"John!" he shouted. "With me. We'll try and get into the bell tower before Groves's men smash their way in and deal with whoever's trying to raise the alarm. Will," he turned and placed a hand on Scarlet's arm.

"You're in charge. Lead the rest into the main building and do what you can to take down Groves's men."

He nodded to Stephen, who returned the gesture grimly, as he finished his orders.

A big carrion crow watched them from the top of a wall, cawing irritably every time the bell rang and the bird reminded Robin of the last maniac he'd faced – Gisbourne. The Raven. A shiver ran down his back and he turned away from the black crow, hoping it wasn't an ill omen.

"Don't take any chances, lads. They outnumber us. Just drive them off if you can, but take care of yourselves first. Remember what these men have done; they're not to be taken lightly."

"Where are you going?" Arthur demanded.

"The belfry. Whoever's ringing that bell will need our help," Robin shouted in reply as he led John away, to the back of the building, hoping they'd find an entrance to the tower there.

"Now – go!"

* * *

"What are we going to do, Sister Mary? That door won't last for much longer."

The young nun was terrified and it was plain in her voice, which was shrill and bordering on hysterical, as she looked, wide-eyed, at her companion.

"Eh? What will we do? In God's name, why won't you ever talk?"

Sister Jane ran across and grabbed her silent companion by the arms.

"What are we going to do, Mary? They'll be in here soon and they'll ravish us, and kill us! Speak, damn you! Please, speak!"

The girl let go of her stoic, silent companion and slumped down, her back against the far wall, tears filling her eyes.

Of all the women in Kirklees Priory only one – the Prioress – knew why Sister Mary hadn't spoken a word since she'd joined them ten years ago after some terrible incident in her home village of Holderness.

And yet, the tall woman was popular thanks to her patient, forgiving nature. The rare smile she would bestow on one of them was like the sun breaking through heavy grey storm clouds.

That smile was completely absent today though, replaced – to Sister Jane's surprise – by a stony determination. It was the look, the younger girl imagined, of a knight about to lead his men into battle.

Only they weren't knights. They were simply two nuns trapped in the bell tower of the priory; separated from their hideous doom by nothing more than an oak door and its rusty old lock which would surely give way any moment under the protracted kicking and hammering from the men outside.

There was a splintering sound as the wood at the bottom of the door suddenly cracked under the assault from outside, and Jane shrank back, whimpering.

Where were the other nuns? Why had they forsaken her and Mary?

Tears streamed down her face at the incomprehensible thought of some filthy, brutal wolf's head forcing himself inside her, then she watched in amazement as her mute compatriot lifted an old broom from a corner of the room, smashed the bristled head off, and then stood facing the doorway with the pole as if she was St George about to battle the dragon.

The door buckled under another kick from outside and gave way just beneath the lock.

They were doomed.

"In nomine Patris," Jane muttered, staring at the ruined door, dreading her fate. "Et filii et Spiritus Sancti..."

The door came crashing in, smashed to pieces, and there was a cheer of satisfaction from outside.

Please, Holy Father, the girl thought, *let me die quickly...*

CHAPTER THIRTY-TWO

The jowly outlaw walked slowly into the belfry. Warily, like a stalking cat, his eyes swept the room, passing over the two nuns who had, by now, ceased pulling on the bell ropes. A look of surprise registered on his face as he saw the taller one holding a broom handle, but he looked past her dismissively, searching for, presumably, someone who might pose a real danger to him and the grinning companion that followed him inside.

"Oh, yes," the first wolf's head nodded, satisfied that only the two girls were there. He undid the lace on his breeches slowly, licking his lips and staring at Sister Mary. "One each, eh? God...is... good!"

He strode forward, breeches flapping open around his fat, hairy belly, but the silent nun jabbed her broken pole at him and he had to dodge backwards to avoid being stabbed.

"That's enough you bitch," the man spat, his smile fading. "Give me that."

He stepped forward, faster than his girth suggested, and snatched the makeshift weapon from Sister Mary's hand, throwing it back towards the broken down door. "That's better. Now, come here my beauty, and show me what a nun's tits look like."

His companion laughed and stepped past him towards the cowering girl on the floor who tried to back away; as if she could somehow disappear *inside* the stone wall.

"They're both young and pretty," the portly one noted, as if he was weighing up a pair of fresh loaves on a baker's table. "It's a shame we're in a hurry – I'd have liked a go on yours as well as this big one."

Sister Mary launched herself through the air at him, a furious scream tearing from her throat – the first sound Sister Jane had ever heard the older nun make – but the man brought his fist up and hammered it against her cheek, sending her crashing to the ground, dazed. The second sound she'd made in ten years or more escaped her lips then, and it was a groan of despair.

"That's better. Now, this won't take long, or hurt all that much."

The wolf's head leaned down and ripped the nun's habit open, exposing her breasts. He eyed them hungrily and glanced at his comrade who was similarly poised over his own conquest. The second outlaw had gone even further, stripping the younger nun completely naked and now grasped his engorged member in his hand as he tried to press it inside the sobbing girl beneath him.

The fat outlaw felt himself become even more inflamed with lust at the sight and turned back to Sister Mary who stared up at him from dead, cold eyes, all the fight apparently gone from her.

He was more experienced at this than his friend and managed to thrust himself inside her at the first attempt and he groaned loudly with pleasure.

It didn't last long.

Sister Mary's eyes fixed on a point behind her rapist and she mouthed a single, shocked, word. "You."

A chill ran down the outlaw's back and the climax he was so close to completely disappeared as he realised someone the girl found even more frightening than him was in the room with them.

Pain exploded in the side of his head as a massive boot slammed into him and he fell to the side, cursing, his ear ringing horrendously.

Before he could move to defend himself the boot cannoned into his head again. And again. Then he felt a fist punching repeatedly into his kidneys and, dimly, despairingly, understood that fist contained a knife.

"Bastard. Won't be raping any more women you bastard."

Little John straightened up, panting from the climb up the stairs and the effort of killing the outlaw.

Robin had dealt with the other man in a similar fashion and his blood now covered the nude Sister Jane who was crying hysterically, curled into a ball in the corner, her eyes locked on the dead face of her rapist.

John looked around for something to cover the girl's shivering body but there was nothing in the belfry.

Robin tried to calm her with soothing words but she'd gone into shock and didn't even seem to register his presence as he gently placed her torn clothing across her in what was, ultimately, a futile gesture.

Little John shook his head sadly and looked down at the nun he'd saved, if a little too late.

"Are you alright, lass?" he asked, softly, but something in her eyes made him pause.

She was much more lucid than her crying companion as she stared at him, fear and something else in her eyes. Disbelief?

"It *is* you," she mumbled, her voice a barely audible croak.

"Do I know you, girl?" John said, feeling a strange sense of deja vu settling over him.

"You killed my da."

Again, the words were nothing more than a raspy croak and John had to stand for a moment, replaying them in his mind before he finally understood her.

Little John had killed lots of people in the years when he was a wolf's head. He had no idea who her father might have been.

He looked at her with a growing sensation of dread, taking in her luminous eyes, and his mind was suddenly thrown back to a night ten years ago, when something just like this scene had played out back in his home village of Holderness.

"The baker," he whispered, and a sensation – as if someone had thrown a cask of ice-water on him from above – swept across his body.

His legs seemed to turn to mush and he slowly lowered himself to the floor as images filled his head and a lump rose in his throat threatening to make him almost as hysterical as the brutalised young girl in the corner.

"John!"

Robin, terrified by his friend's behaviour, assuming the giant had been mortally wounded, ran to his side and grasped him by the shoulder.

Tears sprang to the big man's eyes as he continued to gaze at Sister Mary, her own eyes glistening in a similar fashion.

"What is it?" Robin demanded, completely lost by this turn of events.

"You're the baker's lass," John mumbled. "That night...that night is the reason why I had to become a wolf's head. The reason why I missed so much of my son's growing up..."

The sounds of fighting seemed to have stopped in the priory beneath them and Robin strained to listen, wondering what the hell was happening, yet he knew whatever was going on in his friend's head right now couldn't be disturbed.

He hoped Will and the lads could take care of themselves for a while longer.

"I didn't mean to kill your da," John said to the girl, a hard edge appearing in his voice as self-pity vied with his naturally soft, generous nature. "I just wanted to help you and your sisters before he burned your house down."

Robin suddenly realised who the nun was.

Her father – the baker in Holderness, and a violent drunk – had killed his wife one night, threatened to burn down the house with his three daughters inside and then been in the act of raping one of them when John had broken down the door and stopped him. In the fight, John accidentally killed the man and, thanks to the corrupt local magistrate who demanded a huge bribe to let him off with the crime, the giant had been forced into the greenwood where he'd joined Adam Bell's gang and become a wolf's head.

The nun was that child John had saved from her rapist father.

The big man had told Robin the story a few years ago and he recalled it now. The poor girl had apparently gone mad with that night's horror, become completely mute, and been sent off to live in a priory.

Kirklees Priory, evidently.

Now, more than a decade later, the two of them stood here, reunited, in almost exactly the same horrifying situation.

"I just wanted to help," John repeated, his voice filled with the pain of his ruined life and wasted years apart from his family.

For a time no-one said anything and Sister Jane's heart-rending cries had dropped to become a low sobbing, but Robin finally became impatient. His friends might be dead or dying in the building beneath – they had to go to them.

"Come on, John," he said, not unkindly but firmly. "We can deal with this later. For now we need to get back to Will and the others and somehow find a way into the main priory buildings, past Groves and his men."

Sister Mary tore her eyes away from her two-time saviour and looked at Robin. She got to her feet, pulling her habit back around herself almost as an afterthought and reached inside one of its folds, pulling out a large iron key.

"To the undercroft. Door at bottom of this tower," she told him, pressing it into his calloused hand. "Leads underneath the chapter house to the gyle house." She stopped and rubbed at her throat as if the effort of speaking after such a long time had worn it out.

"Thank you," Robin nodded, assuming the chapter house or gyle house was where they needed to go. "Will you and your friend be all right?" He gestured to Sister Jane who, so shocked was she to hear Mary speak, had ceased sobbing and now watched them from unblinking eyes.

The tall nun nodded and he turned away to head back to the stairwell.

Little John remained standing, looking at Sister Mary, emotions vying within him: Satisfaction that he'd twice saved this young woman from rapists; anger that his own pleasant life had been ruined because of her father's wickedness; sorrow that her life had similarly been irrevocably changed from its previous course; and fear. Fear that had stayed with him for the past eleven years, that Mary and her sisters hated and despised him for killing their father.

Some men wouldn't have given that a second thought but John had carried their supposed hatred of him for years, like a child who couldn't understand why a previously friendly dog suddenly turned on him. He might have been the hardest man Robin Hood had ever known, but in some ways Little John was also the softest.

"I only wanted to help you," he repeated, voice breaking, and angry tears spilled down his cheeks to be lost in his great beard.

He flinched in surprise when soft arms encircled him and the nun stretched up to speak into his ear.

"I know that now. Thank you."

The full horror of that fateful night, and all its terrible repercussions, seemed to wash over John with her forgiveness and a huge sob racked his body. The two of them embraced as if millstones had been, at long last, removed from around their necks.

For a long moment they stayed like that, then John, embarrassed, stood back, nodded to Sister Mary while wiping his nose and eyes on his sleeve, then he gritted his teeth and lifted his quarterstaff from the floor where he'd dropped it when attacking her rapist. A dagger had been much more useful than the unwieldy length of oak in such close quarters.

"Right," he growled, the fire of retribution blazing almost joyfully in his eyes as he spun to follow his captain. "Let's get into that chapter house and deal with the rest of these bastards!"

* * *

Will and the rest of the men were pinned down with no way to get inside the chapter house. The door was smashed in from the outlaws forced entrance, but any time Scarlet's men tried to storm the room they were forced back by arrows and crossbow bolts.

Making a charge would be suicide but even so, Will was tempted when he heard their despised quarry, Philip Groves, shouting out at them.

"You boys out there better get comfy," the voice sneered. "It seems the prioress was too brave and noble to follow the rest of the nuns inside the stairwell. She's stayed right out here to entertain us! Very thoughtful of her wouldn't you agree, Hood?"

"He doesn't realise Robin's gone to help whoever was ringing the bells," Arthur whispered.

"Nah, he doesn't," Will agreed. "But it hardly makes a difference to us."

Arthur's slightly smug smile dropped away when he recognised the truth in Scarlet's words. It didn't matter where Robin was – the simple fact was, they were stuck out there while the scum inside were free to violate the prioress in whatever way they liked.

And, knowing what those 'men' had done to Prior de Monte Martini's party, Arthur feared the nun would not have a pleasant time of it before she was put to the sword.

"What are we going to do?" Stephen demanded, as there was a strangled shriek from inside the great chamber. "We can't just stand here like statues while they take turns to defile her!"

The Hospitaller – a soldier of God after all – was outraged at the way Groves and his men treated members of the clergy. It seemed, somehow, worse than anything they'd done to common laypeople. The prioress was the Lord's representative on Earth, by Christ! Raping such a woman was surely the worst of sins.

Will didn't like it much more than Stephen but he shook his head, eyebrows lowered in consternation.

"Not much else we can do," he said.

Thomas looked thoughtfully at the scowling sergeant-at-arms.

"Unless we can find another way into that room," the sheriff's messenger mused."You any idea how they usually lay out a priory like this, Stephen? Is there a standard plan the builders follow? I mean, can you think of a side entrance we might look for?"

The Hospitaller shook his head.

"I have no idea about that. Every building the Church owns is different. Besides, we'd need a key to get through any other doors leading in there; the prioress will have made sure they were all locked and tossed the keys out the window or something so the outlaws couldn't find them."

It was hopeless.

"So what are we going to do," Arthur repeated Stephen's original question.

Every one of the men gathered outside the chapter house gritted their teeth and grasped their sword hilts grimly – impotently – as a scream reverberated around the stone walls, only to be cut-off by the sound of an open hand meeting flesh as, presumably, Groves or one of his followers slapped her into silence.

The quiet didn't last for very long though, as mere moments later the high-pitched sound of pained gasping could be heard, mingled with grunts and sniggering.

"I don't fucking know," Will shouted, partially from rage and partially to drown out the distressing sounds from within the chapter house. "Robin's the one that always comes up with some clever plan."

Arthur nodded; that was true.

So where the hell *was* their young leader?

* * *

Right at that moment, Robin and Little John were traversing the undercroft, but the going was slower than they expected.

The key Sister Mary had given them worked perfectly, granting them access through the thick door that stood at the very bottom of the belfry stairwell. But, once inside, they realised getting from one end of the building to the other wouldn't be as easy as they'd hoped.

For the undercroft was, naturally, pitch black.

Of course, both men had flint and steel in their packs but they were in a hurry. The scream from the prioress came through the wooden floorboards from above just as they entered the black room, and they didn't want to waste time attempting to make a small flame to light the torch that sat in a sconce right next to the door.

So they blustered into the undercroft like blind men, stumbling into barrels and crates, tripping over many of the unseen obstacles with hissed curses or whimpers of pain, gripping one another's sleeves, one or the other taking the lead as they groped their way towards the opposite end of the room.

"Where the fuck are Will and the rest of the boys?" John murmured, as more laughter and another outraged scream filtered through the floor to them. "Why haven't they finished those bastards? Gah!"

His questions were cut off as he smashed his shin against some low, angular box and Robin, who'd somehow avoided the obstacle, pulled his giant companion towards him – and the safe path – with an exasperated sigh.

"They must be pinned down or something, I don't know. Wait!"

They came to a stop as the sound of many booted feet clattered above them, leading in the same direction they themselves were moving.

For a few heartbeats they simply stood there, in the impenetrable darkness, listening and trying to understand what was happening in the chapter house above.

All seemed quiet, but then voices could be heard – happy voices, no doubt belonging to friends sharing some joke.

What in the name of God was happening in the chapter house?

Robin and John strained their senses, feeling like newborn babes trying to make sense of a new, unfamiliar world, and then an all too familiar sound returned.

A woman crying in despair and rage.

But now, at last, Robin, hand stretched out before him to feel for obstructions, found his fingers pressing against solid wood.

They'd finally reached the door on the opposite side of the undercroft.

Urgently, he used his left hand to feel around for the lock then, finding its smooth iron easily enough, pushed the key in and, as slowly as possible to avoid a loud click, turned it.

He pulled back on the door and squinted as daylight flooded his eyes from a window high above.

With a nod to John, Robin led them up the stairwell, nervously grasping the hilt of his long knife while John followed.

The giant sheathed his own bloodstained knife as they climbed though – he knew the chapter house would be a large room with high ceilings. Plenty of space to crack skulls with his beloved quarterstaff...

They reached the landing and Robin held up a hand, pressing his eye up to the keyhole on the door that separated them from their goal.

The prioress's sobs were barely audible now but at least one of the outlaws was still using her, probably with the rest standing around either watching, or satisfied and therefore bored with the show.

"Ready?" His voice was almost silent.

John nodded. By now, after so many years together, he hardly needed to hear Robin to understand what he was saying.

"Let's go then. Hopefully Will and the others will see us coming in and attack from the opposite side. Make as much noise as you can."

He used Sister Mary's master key to open the door and, with one last look at each other, the two friends charged inside.

Little John could make a *lot* of noise.

CHAPTER THIRTY-THREE

For the second time in under an hour, Robin found himself killing a rapist.

When the door to the chapter house opened he ran into the centre of the room without slowing and slammed his knife, point first, directly into the outlaw's temple with such force that the man's head flew sideways in a burst of crimson while his thrusting body remained where it was, entwined with Mother de Stainton. Their bodies shuddered sideways and the prioress screamed, long and loud at the new horror, her mind unable to properly take in what was happening.

Robin stared down in disgust and sorrow, mind reeling as he recognised the man he'd just executed. Martin Black, former landlord of the Boar's Head in Dewsbury.

Time seemed to stand still as he tried to take in everything that had happened since he and John evicted Martin what seemed like a lifetime ago. Had Robin been the catalyst for it all? Was everything his fault? What if he'd never thrown the little man out of his alehouse?

Little John's enormous staff had, by now, taken out the only other man in the room.

That second outlaw had spun at their approach, hand reaching for his sword, but before he could pull it halfway free from its sheath John's staff had almost torn through his belly, sending him flying backwards onto the floor. As he lay there, gasping in agony, eyes wide with terror, that same quarterstaff had slammed mercilessly down into his face again and again.

"All right, John. I think he's dead."

Will Scarlet strode across the room, grabbed hold of the giant's arm and they locked eyes for a long moment, until John relaxed and nodded.

The outlaw – his face a smashed, red mess – was most certainly dead.

"Where the fuck's the rest of them?" Robin demanded at last, kicking Martin's corpse off the prioress, too angry and confused to care about his language on consecrated ground.

"Don't know," Stephen replied as the rest of the men funnelled into the chapter house, warily looking around for threats which, apparently, weren't there any more. "Things went fairly quiet a little while ago."

"Aye," Arthur agreed. "Must have known they couldn't hold out here forever so they escaped." He nodded at a door in the eastern wall which lay slightly ajar. "The two you just killed must have been desperate to empty their balls. Unlucky for them."

"Ask her what's been happening," John suggested, quietly, nodding towards the red-faced prioress who had thankfully managed to pull her habit around herself and now sat back against the stone wall just like Sister Jane in the bell tower, watching them silently.

Her face was pale and Robin's killing fury went right out of him at the sight of her.

So much misery Groves and his men had inflicted on these innocent nuns today, not to mention the dead and violated back in Kirklees. It almost made him question his own faith.

Shaking his head to clear the blasphemous thoughts he knelt beside the prioress and spoke to her softly.

"Where are the rest of your nuns?" he asked.

For a moment she simply stared at him, lost in her own private hell and surprised by the question. Was this man more interested in bringing her aid than killing the outlaws?

"In the infirmary."

Her voice was like the wind on a barren, invader-salted field and it was truly horrible to hear.

Will strode across, boots thumping on the flagstones, and glanced at the blood-stain on his leader's gambeson.

"Look, we need to move *now* if we're to catch those bastards. They've already got a head start, presumably through that open door. Are you going to just stand here talking to the nun while they make good their escape?"

Robin's eyes flashed but before he could make a retort John's low voice broke in.

"He's got a point. We have enough men to finally make an end of them, if we move now. One of us can stay behind and take care of the prioress and the rest of the women."

"All right. Arthur, you wait –"

"Arthur?" Will demanded. "Arthur's not got a scratch on him."

"But there might still be some of Groves's men here," Robin replied reasonably. "I want to leave someone behind that I know I can trust to take care of the situation."

"So stay here yourself," Scarlet growled. "You're badly wounded, Robin. That needs stitched up before it splits wide open and you bleed out; you're in no state to go on with us."

His young captain peered at the red on his gambeson and seemed surprised by the size of the fresh stain. The battle fury had hidden the extent of his injury until now. Still, he shook his head and made to push past the men.

"No, Robin," Will grabbed him and glared into his eyes, but his voice became surprisingly earnest. Almost pleading. He leaned in close so the others wouldn't hear.

"Listen, I saw you talking with Matilda back in the church at Wakefield. I didn't hear what you were saying but I can guess. I know you've had enough of this life but...you're my friend. I won't let your death wish lead you to an early grave."

He grasped Robin by the arms and squeezed, hard. "You have a wife and a little boy that need you. You're not throwing your life away."

The room became as silent as a tomb and Robin gave Will a strange look.

"I don't have any wish to die," he said.

"So stay here and look after the women. John can wait with you and stitch that wound; the two of you will be enough to secure the place. Me and the lads will go after Groves and his men and bring the bastards to justice. Then, when all this is over – take your family and make a new life for yourselves in Scotland, away from all the bad memories of Much's death, and Allan, and everything else."

There was silence, as everyone waited to hear what would happen next.

Unexpectedly, the prioress's voice chimed in.

"You're injured, Robin – you should stay here as your friends say. I'll have my girls take care of your wounds."

Robin thought about it, then, with a groan, dipped his head and grasped it in bloodied hands as if he would collapse.

"See?" Will chided, grabbing him and supporting him until the dizziness passed. "She's right."

Truly, Robin had lost more blood than he realised and, now that the battle-lust had worn off he felt almost as weak as a baby.

"All right. Go, Will. Hunt Groves and his rapist mates down."

He clasped Scarlet's hand and they shared a smile. "Give them no quarter. Wipe every last one of them from God's Earth."

"We will," Stephen grunted, clapping Robin on the arm and heading for the open door on the opposite side of the room. "Come on, boys, let's get moving. Eyes open, stay alert!"

As the experienced Hospitaller took control of the situation, marshalling the men behind him and passing through the doorway with weapons ready for a possible attack, Will grinned and turned back to Little John.

"You take care of Robin. Make sure the nuns get that wound cleaned and bound up. I've lost enough friends over recent years. Besides, all the stories say Robin Hood's immortal and I don't want to put that particular legend to the test."

"Get on with you," John nodded. "I'll see he's patched up."

When the men had gone it was as if a hurricane had just swept through the place and left only debris, dead bodies, and a sorrowful atmosphere.

"How do we get into the infirmary then?" Robin finally asked the prioress, forcing a smile. "Let's get those women out of there."

The nun looked at him for a moment, a strange look on her tear-streaked face before, at last, she nodded to another doorway and replied in a dead, hollow voice.

"Through there. The key to the stairwell is on top of the door frame within."

Robin nodded, wondering at the woman's state of mind, then, with a glance towards John, walked across and opened the door as directed.

As he passed into the room some sixth sense – some tiny sound perhaps, or a change in the air around him – made him flinch and check his forward stride.

It wasn't enough to stop the tip of Philip Groves's sword tearing through his gambeson and deep into his body.

* * *

"That was Robin!"

Will Scarlet reined in his horse, oblivious to the rest of the men he commanded. The others continued riding along the obvious trail left by the outlaws which led to a path through the trees a short distance away.

Stephen noticed Scarlet falling back in the formation and, slowing his own mount, turned in the saddle to raise his palms, and an eyebrow, upwards in surprise.

But Will was already riding back, hard, towards the priory.

The Hospitaller hadn't heard the scream of anguish from the old building behind them so he'd no idea why Scarlet had just left their party to ride back the way they'd just come.

Stephen had his orders from Robin though, so, as always, he followed them, kicking his heels in and urging his horse into a gallop along the outlaws' path again.

Scarlet would always be a law unto himself.

* * *

Little John's reflexes were honed to a razor's edge and he'd started moving almost before Groves launched his attack on Robin. With an anguished cry the giant lunged into the room the nun had pointed them towards and thrust his staff towards the wolf's head, catching the man – the bastard! – flush on the back of the skull.

John knew better than to think that was the fight done though, and he whipped the long length of oak back, close into his body, and it was just as well he did as a man nearly as big as he was tried to slide the tip of a short sword into his guts.

He spun the staff round and caught the blade, knocking it sideways before it could do him any harm. If it had been held by most other men it would have gone flying onto the floor, but the huge outlaw that faced him – the one called Eoin surely, from the descriptions John had heard – held onto the hilt with gritted teeth.

The strike must have hurt though, as the outlaw stepped back and switched the sword to his left hand, shaking the right vigorously as if that would deaden the pain from Little John's powerful parry.

On the stone flagstones Robin held the wound in his back, the gambeson there torn completely away to reveal a wide crimson stain that had begun to spread down his breeches.

John's eyes moved on to take in Groves who was still stunned but attempting to get back to his feet.

Two against one would be bad odds.

Roaring like a caged bear, Little John thrust out at Eoin again, pushing the man back, then, without thinking, he jumped onto Groves's back.

The outlaw crumpled under John's terrific weight and, before he could even cry out, John stamped down viciously on the back of his head, smashing his face into the floor.

"No! You'll kill him!"

Eoin's anguished voice rang around the cramped chamber and John glared at him.

"Just like you've killed *my* friend Robin you bastards."

The huge outlaw might have been unskilled, but he made up for it in fury now as he came for John, swinging his short sword in cut after cut and thrust after wild thrust and the vastly more experienced lawman had to employ every skill and technique he'd learned over the years to block or dodge everything Eoin threw at him until, at last, an opening presented itself.

There was a crack of bones snapping as an upward parry saw John's staff strike brutally against his attacker's wrist, shattering it, and the sword fell to the ground with a ringing clank that seemed to echo forever around the stone walls.

Ignoring the roar of pain, Little John stepped back, transferring his weight to the rear foot, then, mindful of the close quarters, he swung his quarterstaff and exploded forward, putting all of his considerable power into the tip of the wood.

It met Eoin flush on the forehead and threw the big outlaw flying like a rag doll.

Again, using only half the length of the staff because of the cramped dimensions of the room, John brought it back and then slammed it around, sideways, in a low arc into the side of the fallen Eoin's head.

When blood appeared from the outlaw's ear a short time later John knew his opponent was dead, and he dropped to his knees next to Robin who was gasping and clutching at his new injury.

"Are you all right?" John demanded, battle fury making his voice more brittle than he intended but he was too frightened by his young friend's wounds to disguise it. "Don't move! I'll need to see to that before you spill your blood all over the place. Why the fuck did that nun –" he broke off as he began gently easing Robin's gambeson buckles apart.

"Why the fuck did you send us in here to an ambush, woman?" John finished with a roar once he'd finally prised open the last of the ruined light armour's fastenings. "We came here to help you!"

"I'm sorry!" the prioress shrieked from the adjoining room, tears streaking her face. "They said they'd hide outside until you were gone then smash the door down and rape all my girls. They..." Her voice dropped and she continued in an anguished whisper. "The things they said they would do. I couldn't bear it. And two of them had already taken their turn on me by then – I knew they would fulfil their wicked promises. God forgive me..."

"God might, but I damn well won't," John cried. "You've sentenced Robin to death."

He'd finally managed to peel back his friend's gambeson and the blood-soaked tunic beneath, and what he saw terrified him. The wound was wide and deep.

It had to be fatal.

Tears sprang to his eyes and he could feel his mouth filling with saliva but he tried to hide it from Robin; he didn't want the injured lawman to see him sobbing like a child.

On the floor behind them Philip Groves turned his head slowly and looked up at the kneeling giant.

The outlaw's face was blood-stained and his nose so badly broken that he was forced to breathe through bruised lips. He was dazed and close to unconsciousness, but still held his short sword tightly in his right hand.

Taking a deep breath, he softly lifted the blade from the floor and swept it back, eyes fixed on Little John's hamstring. He may not be strong enough to slice right through the enormous lawman's leg, but he'd at least maim the big whoreson for life.

He gritted his teeth and a fierce, insane grin twisted his face as he swung the razor-sharp sword as hard as he could.

* * *

The scream reverberated around the priory and Little John turned, shocked, to see what the hell had happened.

Behind him, Will Scarlet had parried Groves's sword with his own, stopping the weapon just before it reached John's tree-trunk leg and now Scarlet stared at the scene before him.

His young leader lay blood-drenched and apparently mortally wounded beside a tear-streaked John, while another massive outlaw was dead on the floor and Philip Groves wept in fury and frustration at Will's feet. Outside, the prioress's crazed wailing provided a hellish backdrop to the whole thing.

John and Will both moved at the same time to finish the outlaw captain but before they could do it another man burst into the room, puffing and breathless.

"Hold! Hold, I say!"

It was Prior John de Monte Martini with Sir Henry de Faucumberg and more soldiers at his back.

"That man deserves a trial," the clergyman gasped, his voice tired but still filled with the natural authority men born into great wealth always have. "Leave him."

The sheriff looked anguished, especially when he saw Robin terribly wounded on the ground, but he seemed incapable of over-riding the prior's orders.

Will hesitated, glaring at the newcomers, then down at Robin's pale grey features, then at Groves's horrifically bruised yet smiling face. He turned back to Little John and it was as if they shared the same thought without a word passing between them out loud.

De Monte Martini wanted Groves alive so he could use the outlaw to testify against Robin and the rest of them. To blame them for his party's massacre. Groves would walk free again.

Not this time.

Scarlet roared and thrust his sword into Groves's back as John repeated his stamp from earlier. There was a dull thud as the outlaw's skull hit the floor, then a heartbeat later another, and another, as both John and Will gave free reign to their fury and everyone else shrank back through the doorway into the chapter house at the terrifying display of unrestrained, explosive violence.

When it was over Philip Groves was unrecognisable. His head was nothing but pulp and his torso a wet, red mess.

John and Will stood breathlessly, staring down at their handiwork with blank expressions on their faces as if they didn't know what had just happened.

Prior de Monte Martini was ashen faced but somehow pulled himself together. He stepped back into the small chamber and pointed at Robin's two friends, looking sideways at the sheriff who'd reluctantly followed him in again.

"Arrest those men. What are you waiting for de Faucumberg? We just watched them murder a man before our eyes!"

The sheriff stood, mute and stunned, glancing back out at his guards. Some looked as if they might vomit while others were almost as pale as Robin who still lay unmoving on the floor between Little John and Will Scarlet.

Even those of the sheriff's guards who'd seen many battles before were shocked by Groves's brutal death.

"Are you listening to me?" de Monte Martini demanded, voice seeming to regain its usual strength and power to irritate. "I told you to arrest those murderers, De Faucumberg. Arrest them! And know something else." His voice dropped to a satisfied whisper and he locked eyes with the sheriff, a smug little smile tugging at one side of his mouth. "I sent letters to Archbishop Melton in York and Henry of Leicester, one of the queen's closest friends, apprising them of Hood's crimes. There will be no pardon for the wolf's head this time, no matter what happens. The man *will* hang."

The prior grinned at Sir Henry's stricken look then turned and shouted out through the doorway to the blue-liveried soldiers who were pretending not to listen to their superiors' argument.

"Enough of this talk. Get in here you fools and take these murderers into custody. If the sheriff won't do his job, I'll do it for him."

The guardsmen hesitated.

"When the Queen supplants that fool Edward I'll see you stripped of your office, de Faucumberg," the prior growled in satisfaction. "Stripped of your office, penniless, with your family destitute –"

"Oh shut up, you old windbag."

The sheriff slipped his hand into a pocket on the side of his right thigh and the dull gleam of a blade glinted before he plunged it into the prior's stomach, dragged it upwards brutally, and then shoved the stricken man onto the floor next to Eoin's great body. He quickly knelt and placed the bloody dagger by the dead outlaw.

There was another shocked silence then as the guardsmen came back into the room and tried to make sense of the scene before them.

"At last," de Faucumberg cried, throwing his hands in the air. "The giant wasn't dead – he sat up and stabbed Prior de Monte Martini in the guts. Help him!"

His soldiers rushed forward but the prior was already dead. One or two of the smarter ones glanced up at the sheriff but no one questioned his version of events.

"He's dead, my lord sheriff," one reported in the clipped, spare tones of a drill sergeant.

"Oh no, best take him away then and see his body is returned to Lewes where it belongs."

The men hesitated and de Faucumberg gestured at them to hurry up. When they – and the prior's corpse – had gone he turned back to look at Robin and his friends.

"Good on you. I've wanted to do that for years," Will Scarlet grinned, and de Faucumberg returned the expression although with a little less enthusiasm and a lot more nausea.

"How's Robin?" the sheriff said to John, retrieving his blade and wiping it on Eoin's sleeve before returning it to its sheath. "Why haven't you cleaned and stitched his wound yet?"

"Give me a fucking chance," Little John shouted. "Every time I try to deal with it someone else comes into the damn room and distracts me."

"What the hell happened here anyway?" Will asked. "I thought the prioress said the outlaws had all left?"

"She lied," John growled.

"So where are they?" The sheriff was confused himself.

"The ones that aren't dead are heading north," Will replied. "Stephen and the rest of the lads will catch up to them soon enough. I just hope they're not outnumbered."

"I have reinforcements right here. Lead them after your friends, man! Let's end this for good when we have the chance."

Will shook his head at the sheriff's order.

"No. I have to wait here with Robin. It was only a few years ago I was laid up here at death's door myself and Robin never gave up on me."

De Faucumberg grabbed Will by the arm, none too gently. "Listen to me man – there's nothing you can do here now. But your friends might end up cut to pieces by the remnants of Groves's little army. Only you know the route they've taken. I'll wait here with Robin and see he's taken care of. He's my friend too."

"He's right," John agreed. "You should lead the reinforcements after Stephen and the others. With that lot at your back the outlaws won't stand a chance."

Will looked down at Robin, an anguished look on his ruddy face, and it seemed like he'd refuse to leave his captain's side yet again. But, at last he breathed a heavy sigh and nodded.

"All right, but you make sure someone deals with that wound of his properly." He gestured to the sheriff's guardsmen and strode towards the door. "Follow me then you lot, and fucking hurry up!"

When they'd gone the place was almost eerily quiet. The prioress had finally stopped sobbing and Robin's breathing was shallow now, after its earlier harshness.

John left the room, leaving Sir Henry staring impotently at his fallen bailiff and the giant's low voice could be heard asking the prioress for medical supplies. The sounds of hurried searching – cupboard doors being torn open unceremoniously and their contents tossed aside – came through the open doorway until, at last, the big man returned with wine, a needle, some twine and a long bandage.

"Help me."

Sir Henry nodded and knelt on the other side of Robin's fallen body.

"What do you want me to do?"

"Couldn't find any water to clean it, so this stuff will have to do. I hope it doesn't make things worse."

John poured the wine onto both wounds liberally – the main, entry one at the front, and the one on Robin's back where the sword had come right through. Then he used an extra piece of balled-up bandage to wipe clean the areas on Robin's skin around the wounds. They still oozed fresh crimson though, which couldn't be a good sign. At least the one on the back wasn't as wide as the one on the front, which would require stitching if their friend was to have any chance of survival.

"Hold it shut for me," John said to the sheriff, nodding to Robin's injury as he tried, more than once, to thread the twine through the eye of the needle, his shaking fingers refusing to co-operate.

At last he managed it and slid the needle into his friend's skin. As he did so, Robin's eyes flickered and he looked up at them, silently. He never said a word as the wound was stitched shut but when John had finished and the sheriff wound a piece of clean linen around his torso the fallen bailiff opened his mouth and gestured weakly for John to lean down.

"Listen to me, my friend; my brother." The voice was dry and resigned and carried the heavy weight of a dozen deaths. "I'm done."

"No, you're not," John disagreed, forcing a smile, but his eyes were welling up again and his grimy, anguished face was a terrible sight. "We've sewn you back together."

Robin shook his head feebly. "I'm done. Tell Will and the others that I love them all."

Tears streamed down John's cheeks again to become lost in his great beard and he choked back a sob as the best friend he'd ever had grasped his arm and squeezed it reassuringly.

"Now, before it's too late, I'd ask you and Sir Henry to do me one last favour..."

* * *

Stephen had managed to follow the fleeing outlaws north, possibly towards Scholes, but their pursuit wasn't as fast as he'd have liked, as the trail was hard to follow. The hard summer ground meant footprints were few and far between while the thick foliage not only masked any passage through it but might also harbour an ambush.

Will Scarlet came riding up at the back of them, Strawberry's hooves pounding furiously and two dozen blue-liveried soldiers at his back. Clearly Will wasn't worrying about any ambush and, when Stephen turned to watch his approach the look on Scarlet's face made it clear an ambush would bring a welcome opportunity for him to deal out more violence.

"What's happening?" the Hospitaller demanded. Never before had he seen the former-mercenary with such a strange expression on his face.

"Groves and his right-hand man are dead."

The rest of the men cheered at the news, and the reinforcements, but Will's face remained grim as he reined his horse in beside Stephen and glanced around at the others.

"I think Robin's done for."

"What? No, he can't be!" James gaped in disbelief. "No one can best him."

Will nodded. "Maybe not, but Groves surprised him; ran his sword right through him from the looks of the wound. The second bad injury he's taken in a few days. But the worst thing was John's face." He broke off and looked at Arthur and Peter. "You've known Little John for years, as I have. You ever seen him in tears?"

The two former outlaws thought about it for a second then shrugged. The very idea of the friendly giant weeping seemed somehow obscene.

"Don't think so," Arthur muttered. "I expect it would take a lot to make him cry."

"Exactly," Will agreed.

Stephen's voice cut through the melancholy.

"We can find out how Robin is once we've dealt with Groves's gang. Come on."

Will sighed sadly, nodded once, then his usual confident demeanour returned and he scowled at the Hospitaller.

"Lead on then, man. Let's fucking end this."

* * *

When Philip decided to remain behind in the priory so he and Eoin could lay their trap for Robin he'd wondered who to place in charge of the rest of his gang. None of them were really leaders, apart from one: the little devil from Horbury: Mark.

"I know this is what you've wanted all along," Groves had smiled at the smaller man as they stood by the open door that led outside. "And, in truth, I'm sure you'll make a decent captain. Just remember, Eoin and I will rejoin you soon enough so don't get any ideas. Even your mate Ivo will support me if it comes to it, and the rest of the men don't trust you."

"Where should we go?" Ivo asked, eyes shifting nervously as he looked at the priory grounds, fearing Hood's men might realise they were escaping and come for them.

Groves shrugged. "I don't know the area as well as some of you. Mark? You've been a wolf's head around here for years. Where do you suggest leading the boys?"

Mark thought about it, trying to picture the local area in his head.

"Scholes," he said at last. "It's a small village about four miles north of here. There'll be no threat from the locals but we can get supplies and wait there until you and Eoin catch up to us. You know where it is?"

Philip shook his head and Eoin grunted which Mark took as another negative.

"Just head directly north from here. Pass right over the first main road you come to, then turn east at the next one. That will lead you straight to us."

"We'll be in the ale-house," Ivo said, flashing his toothless grin which contrasted so starkly with Mark's own stunning white teeth.

"I'm sure you will." Groves returned the smile and waved them off, like a mother shooing naughty children back out to play. "Go on then. We won't be long, assuming the prioress does as she's told."

Mark nodded and wished Philip luck although, inside, he was hoping Hood and his lawmen would kill the bastard.

The gang looked around warily, then, seeing no danger, sprinted off towards the trees, the small man from Horbury at their head.

Now, almost an hour later, Mark knew they'd almost reached Scholes but they could hear the sounds of pursuit and he wasn't sure what they should do.

Ivo glared at him and spread his arms wide.

"Well? You're our leader now," he spat. "What do we do? We can't hope to outrun the bastards, not when they're mounted and we're on foot. I'm exhausted already."

Mark continued to jog but he knew his old companion was right; they'd be caught soon enough.

He turned back and looked at the men he was leading. Not one of them would he call a friend – even Ivo had switched his allegiance to Groves now. What did he owe any of them?

Nothing.

He'd be as well making off on his own, into the trees. He knew the area better than any of them and he'd have a better chance of surviving if he was on his own, since Hood's men would chase the main body of outlaws rather than searching for one lone straggler.

"You're right," he replied to Ivo, pulling his sword free from its sheath. "Hold, lads. We need to make a stand and this is as good a place as any."

The men stopped, most of them breathing hard, tired from the day's exertions and their flight here. Another fight with a group of mounted lawmen was the last thing they wanted.

"You men with longbows," Mark shouted, pointing at the nearest archer. "String them up and hide in the brush there, either side of this clearing. As soon as Hood's men show themselves – skewer the bastards."

He swept up his sword and gestured with the point at the remaining outlaws. "Everyone else, take up position in those bushes there, directly facing the trail. When the riders appear our bowmen'll bring the foremost of them down and throw the rest into a panic. When that happens, we fucking wade into them, all right?"

There was a low, half-hearted murmur of agreement and Mark shook his head in disgust.

They stood little chance of surviving this. They might take some of the lawmen down but that didn't interest Mark; he wasn't in this simply to kill – he wanted wealth and status and freedom, just like Robin Hood had found.

He was very much like the fabled wolf's head-turned-lawman, he thought.

As his men faded back into the undergrowth he too pushed through a stand of blackthorn bushes and dropped to the ground, curling into a ball so only the most assiduous of searchers would find him. Of course, he wouldn't be able to join the rest of his men when they engaged Hood's soldiers but he'd decided to wait and see how the fight went before leaving his hiding place.

If the outlaws were winning he'd crawl out and take his place at Ivo's side, just like old times. If they were being butchered – as Mark expected – he'd simply remain where he was until it was all over and the lawmen fucked off back to Pontefract or Kirklees or wherever they were based.

He didn't feel guilty about leaving the others to deal with the fighting – he owed them nothing. Besides, the odds of them surviving against Hood's men were tiny and there was no reason for him to throw away his life for men loyal to Philip Groves.

Fuck them all.

Safe in his blackthorn cocoon he peered out as a knight – no, not a knight, a Hospitaller sergeant-at-arms – rode into the clearing, flanked by a stocky horseman with a murderous look on his ruddy face, and braced himself for the thud of arrows hammering into those grim outriders.

But there were no snapping bowstrings and the colour drained from Mark's face as he realised his longbowmen had deserted.

Ivo hadn't though. He didn't read the situation and, like a fool, blundered out, shouting a war cry, into the path of the horsemen who hadn't slowed their progress at all.

The Hospitaller's horse careered into the toothless wolf's head, almost a thousand pounds of muscle and steel smashing him onto the ground.

A few more of Mark's outlaws shuffled into view, swords and axes raised, but they were clearly nervous and disorganised.

The second rider had reined in his mount when he noticed Ivo attempting to engage them and he now turned and charged back, sword in hand, to help his companion.

More of Hood's men appeared. Only the most foolhardy or battle-fevered of the outlaws stood their ground but they were mercilessly dispatched within mere moments and Mark tried to squeeze his body into an even smaller ball, knowing he'd be shown no quarter should the lawmen find him.

He looked on as the Hospitaller slid down from his saddle and grasped Ivo by the shoulders with gauntleted fists, dragging the wolf's head upright.

"Where's the rest of your gang?"

Ivo's face was twisted in pain and it was clear he'd be no use to anyone now. The collision with the horse must have damaged him internally, Mark thought, with a pang. They'd been through a lot together over the years, even if they had drifted apart over recent months.

The Hospitaller brought up his knee and hammered it into Ivo's guts, furious at the lack of a response. Then he punched the outlaw brutally in the face and let him drop onto the ground to die.

That was it.

Philip Groves's gang was finished.

Mark felt an almost hysterical laugh building up inside him at the terrible reality of his situation and he struggled to force it down. He'd planned on leaving his men to fight without him, but almost all of them had run off into the greenwood, and now he was alone and surrounded by those merciless lawmen.

At least he had a good hiding place – the bastard's would never find him and night would fall soon. He'd slip off and make for Horbury. If there was a bright enough moon that night, and he could stay awake, he'd be there by morning. There were friends in Horbury that'd help him, for the right price.

"Come out, Mark."

The voice was startling close behind him and he jerked around, hand flailing for his sword, but a boot hit him on the nose.

It wasn't a very powerful kick, as the blackthorn bush made it hard for his attacker to get a clean shot, but it still hurt.

"Over here lads, I've found one of them!"

Again, the face looked in at him and Mark almost sobbed with rage.

It was Hood's man and Mark's one-time gang-member, James. Another man who'd followed him only to betray him! It was too much to bear.

Knowing he'd be hanged as soon as these bastards took him in, the prone wolf's head exploded forward, the tip of his sword aiming for James's face but his target, knowing how violent Mark could be, was prepared and dodged easily out of the way.

This time the boot made a clean contact with the side of his head and he dropped like a stone onto the forest floor, dazed.

"Good work," the Hospitaller said, striding over to join James and clapping the big longbowman on the back. "Tie the whoreson up and we'll take him back to the sheriff. Looks like his mates have all gone off and left him."

The lawmen's mocking laughter stung – it sounded like they all joined in – and Mark tried to spit on the sergeant-at-arms.

"You'll be sorry, arsehole. Philip and Eoin will be along to help me any moment now. You'd be as well letting me go."

Even as he blurted it out, he felt disgusted with himself, but the fear of being hanged terrified him and, if threatening these men with retribution at the hands of Barnsdale's most notorious outlaw would save him, Mark would try it.

But the mocking laughter sounded even louder as he was punched full in the face by James then unceremoniously thrown over the back of a horse and tied there for the return trip to the dungeon at Pontefract Castle.

* * *

Will took a deep breath and, followed closely by Stephen, pushed the door open and stepped back into Kirklees Priory, dreading what they might find there.

The nuns had been freed from their incarceration in the infirmary tower and now they moved about the place – busy but silent, like wraiths, shocked at the nightmare that had visited their quiet little corner of England that day.

Most kept their eyes lowered as they went about the business of putting the place back in some sort of order, but one, a thin woman with a kindly face, led them into the chapter house. The bodies of the men killed there earlier had been removed, presumably for burial or, perhaps, for public display somewhere to deter other would-be outlaws. Will guessed Philip Groves's body would suffer such a humiliating fate but his lip curled in an unsympathetic sneer at the idea.

Serve the bastard right.

"Where is he?" Stephen demanded, his rough local dialect sounding harshly in the quiet chamber.

The sheriff appeared from the side room where Robin had been so terribly wounded by the wolf's heads and strode across to them, his face drawn.

Grim.

"Where is he?" Will repeated the Hospitaller's question. "Is he..." His voice trailed off before he changed tack. "Is he all right?"

"I'll be honest with you," Sir Henry said, looking Scarlet in the eyes. "You saw his injuries. He lives yet, as far as I know, but he asked to be taken back to Wakefield to see his family one last time."

"Why didn't you get him into one of the beds here and have the nuns patch him up?" Stephen asked. "Surely that would have been more helpful than carting him along the road. The women here helped Will recover when he'd suffered a terrible injury. I'm sure they'd have aided Robin."

De Faucumberg sighed heavily. "There's no doubt of that, but it was his wish to go home and it seemed the right thing to do. John went with him, taking a couple of my men as an escort."

The three men stood in silence for a time, none of them wanting to put their fears into words in case they came true.

"What now then?" the Hospitaller finally growled. "We managed to capture one of the outlaws alive. The rest we killed."

Sir Henry smiled at the sergeant's directness.

"One alive, eh? That's good. The people will enjoy seeing him receive justice – we'll make an example of him. I expect you and your friends will want to go after Robin and John?"

"Aye," Will nodded.

"Off you go then. I'll see you are all paid handsomely for your work in tracking down Groves's gang. For now, though, I'll take the prisoner back to Pontefract with my guards along with Prior de Monte Martini's body."

"He's dead?" Stephen demanded, eyes growing wide. He hated the churchman almost as much as Robin did, since de Monte Martini had tried to ruin his master, the Hospitaller knight Sir Richard-at-Lee.

"Aye, he's dead," Will confirmed, raising an eyebrow in the sheriff's direction but remaining silent on the true manner of the prior's death. "Come on, we can celebrate that later. For now, we need to get to Wakefield. I want to see my daughter and check on Robin."

They made to leave the high-ceilinged room but, as they began to move, de Faucumberg grasped Scarlet by the arm firmly and they looked at each other again.

"Prepare yourselves for the worst. It may be the time has come for Robin to leave us."

Will stared back at him for a heartbeat then nodded.

"We'll pray for him on the road."

Just then the prioress walked in, spine straight, head held up as proudly as ever. Outwardly, she appeared to be no worse off for her terrible ordeal that day.

"Where are you going?" she demanded. "You can't ride – it will be dark soon."

Will scowled at her, angry at her part in his leader's condition, even if her actions were understandable.

"Go – bring the rest of your men inside," she ordered. "You can all spend the night here in the chapter house. I'll have meat and bread brought in for you from the stores."

"Ale too?" Stephen asked, like a small boy hoping for a strawberry tart.

"We don't have much ale," the prioress replied. "But I'm sure there's plenty to be had back in Kirklees if you want to send someone to fetch it."

"I'll go myself," the sergeant-at-arms declared, already heading out the door. "I'll take Arthur and Piers with me and send the rest of the men in."

"If any of the villagers are in need of succour, bring them back with you," the tall nun commanded. "No doubt the wolf's heads left a trail of violence before they reached here."

"Thank you," Sheriff de Faucumberg bowed his head to Mother de Stainton when Stephen had gone. "I am grateful for your hospitality. I'll have my men do their best to repair the damage the outlaws did to your doors since we'll be here for the rest of the day now."

The nun dipped her own head to the sheriff and made her way out of the room.

Will held his tongue. Berating the prioress wouldn't help Robin and she'd suffered enough for now anyway.

"You should rest," de Faucumberg said, clapping Scarlet on the shoulder. "Before you collapse from exhaustion."

"Nah, I'd only make myself insane thinking about how fucking horrible the world is. I'll go out and help your men find timber to repair those doors."

It was going to be a long night.

* * *

The journey to Wakefield took longer than usual. The horses were well rested after the previous day's exertions, but none of them – Will, Stephen, James, Arthur, Peter or Piers – really wanted to reach their leader's home village.

What awaited them there?

The weather didn't help matters either. The day had started dull and grey, with a heavy, funereal fog covering the land all around the priory. As the sun made its inexorable way higher into the sky it burned the mist away but heavy grey clouds took its place and, when they were still five miles from their destination the rain came. Just a mist at first, it soon turned to a torrential downpour that even the best quality cloak couldn't keep out.

Even that couldn't spur the party into a gallop, but, eventually, inexorably, the miles were eaten up by their mounts' hooves and Wakefield came into sight.

"Where will he be?" Arthur asked no-one in particular.

"At home, idiot," Will retorted. "Where else would he be?"

Arthur took the rebuke with a sheepish grimace.

"In the ale-house?" Peter suggested, but his attempt at levity fell flat and the grim silence settled back over the small group as they rode towards Robin and Matilda's modest home.

"We'll wait here," Stephen said, gesturing to Will. "You go in and find out how things stand."

Will nodded and slid from his saddle, handing Strawberry's reins to Arthur who looked more frightened than Scarlet could ever remember seeing him.

"Don't worry, lad. He'll be fine."

Arthur forced a smile onto his face and Will patted his leg reassuringly before turning and walking up to the Hood's front door.

He knocked, but there was no answer from within. He tried again with similar results so he turned back to the others, gave a small wave, and pushed open the door.

The interior of the house was gloomy and it took a moment for his eyes to adjust but when they did he saw the great figure of Little John, sitting on a stool and staring straight ahead. On the other side of the room sat Matilda, who looked at him as he entered but didn't say a word.

And then Will's eyes were drawn to the centre of the room and settled on what John was staring at.

The Hood's table, where they ate their meals, contained something other than bread and cheese that day.

Will gasped and threw out a hand to steady himself against a wall as he felt the strength leave his legs at the sight of the shrouded body in the centre of the room.

"No! Matilda…?"

His voice became a pleading sob and he somehow forced himself to walk to the young woman's side.

She looked up at him and their eyes met, then she rose to her feet and embraced him as he began to weep uncontrollably.

* * *

St Mary's was busier than anyone in Wakefield could ever remember. It seemed like the entire village – along with folk from most of the settlements roundabout, including Sheriff de Faucumberg – had come to say farewell to their famous son.

Robin Hood.

The young man that had punched a lecherous prior in the face and fled into the greenwood five years earlier was now a legend, as were his friends Little John, Will Scaflock and Friar Tuck.

It was the latter who presided over the funeral mass that day and he'd never felt so sad before.

The rest of Robin's old gang stood near the front of the church, heads bowed, while the villagers looked at them, awestruck, as if they were heroes. Which they were, of course, since they'd stopped Groves's gang, but none of them felt like it. Their leader was dead after all. What was there to be proud of?

The mass began, hymns were sung, Tuck spoke and then Will, Stephen, John, Arthur, Piers, James and Peter Ordevill filed slowly outside. They came back a short while later carrying the shrouded corpse on a bier.

Some of them cried openly and Tuck wanted nothing more than to run to them and hug them all, to share in their unhappiness, to remember Robin in the greenwood, not here, in death.

He remained at the dais though, as was his duty, as Robin was brought forward.

Arthur had to step outside he was sobbing so hard. Others, like Little John, hid their sorrow behind stony masks until the bier was set down in the church and Tuck continued the mass.

Matilda stood at the front, her eyes downcast as if frightened to look at the shrouded body before them. Little Arthur wore a bored expression, as though he had no idea what was going on. Robin's parents, along with his sister Marjorie, stared straight ahead, perhaps unable to take in what was happening.

Tuck spoke of Robin's bravery, his skill in combat, his leadership, and his good deeds as an outlaw. Mostly, though, he talked about their friendship and how much he'd miss him. He had to stop at one point, as a great lump seemed to fill his throat and his composure deserted him. He simply stared out at the congregation, silently, as the tears streamed down his round face. At last he apologised and was finally able to continue the ceremony.

And then they all filed outside and the shrouded body – now lifted into a plain casket – was lowered into the ground and covered with dark, rich earth, while those that knew him best wept and sought to comfort one another.

Robin Hood was dead.

* * *

"What will you do now then, Will?"

Scarlet sat for a time, holding his drink and staring at the wall in the ale-house as if he hadn't heard Stephen's question. Robin's funeral had been held the day before and the men had remained in Wakefield, none of them wishing to leave yet, knowing that once they did it meant the end of their camaraderie for ever.

So here they sat, in the gloom of the local alehouse, fire lit even in summertime since the trees grew so thickly around the place that it was forever shrouded in shadow.

"Go back to my farm, I suppose," Scarlet finally shrugged, his finger playing with a small dribble of ale on the polished table before he finally looked up. "What about you?"

The Hospitaller shrugged and looked down as if he wanted some spilled ale of his own to play with.

"I hear the Grand Master of my Order has recommended Thomas l'Archer be removed from his position as head of the English chapter since he's an old doddering bastard that's blown all the Order's money. When he's gone I'll seek re-entry into the Order. It's all I ever wanted."

Will grinned and turned his eyes to the stocky young man beside him.

"Arthur? What you got planned now?"

Arthur smiled and sipped his ale. "Bring my family home from Nottingham and make a go of the tavern I hope. The money the sheriff paid us for killing the outlaws will help me do the old place up a bit and maybe bring in some more business. What about you lads?"

Piers, Peter and James had all decided to take up the sheriff's generous offer of a place in his guard as sergeants, with good pay. Each of them hoped to gain promotions within a short span of time and Piers said as much.

"You going back to the priory in Lewes, Tuck?"

"No, Will," the friar shook his head. "I'm quite happy here. Wakefield is my home now and, with de Monte Martini dead, I'm a free man again."

They sipped their drinks for a while and the alehouse started to fill up as the local labourers finished their days toil and trooped in looking for bread and beer.

The men all knew King Edward was close to being deposed by his wife and her supporters and it gave them great hope for the future of England. Edward had been a decent man, as Little John and Robin had found when they met him what now seemed like a lifetime ago, but he'd been a poor king who'd let their country fall into turmoil.

Isabella's expected invasion would surely see her and Edward's son – also called Edward – on the throne, and a new, glorious era for all in England.

"John?" Arthur asked softly, peering up from his ale mug as the volume in the alehouse rose with the influx of cheery new patrons. "You staying on as a bailiff?"

"I've seen enough sadness and death," the giant replied, shaking his head firmly. "For now at least. I might go back to smithing. Or I might take my wife and son off to visit some foreign land since we have all this reward money from the sheriff!"

He drained his ale mug and hoisted it aloft to draw the landlord's attention, a great smile appearing on his bearded face as he turned back to the others.

"Let's just get drunk tonight, lads, and forget how shit the world is. It's been an honour to fight alongside you all."

Another round of drinks was placed before them by the pretty serving girl and the men lifted the foaming mugs solemnly.

"To Robin Hood," John cried with a twinkle in his eye. "He brought us together, made us wealthy, notorious and – most importantly – *free*. I'm proud to have known him as a friend."

The others cheered as one, long and loud, raising their mugs high in a heartfelt, hopeful salute that filled the small alehouse with its power.

"To Robin!"

EPILOGUE

Two weeks after Robin's funeral, Will Scarlet came into the village to buy some supplies. Already, even in such a short space of time, the stories around Hood's death had begun to circulate and grow; it wouldn't be long before the minstrels would make the death much more romantic than it had actually been. One conversation Will had overheard at the alehouse two nights earlier brought a rueful smile to his face – apparently, according to the old sot telling the tale, Robin, knowing he was dying in Kirklees Priory, had forced himself to his feet, grasped his longbow, and with one final incredible effort, loosed an arrow out of the window, ordering Little John to bury him wherever it landed.

When one of his audience challenged the story-teller, saying Robin had been buried in St Mary's just along the road, the man nodded and smiled. "Aye, that's how far Hood's arrow went. All the way here, from Kirklees!"

On his way home that night Will passed St Mary's and stopped for a moment to look in on Robin's grave. Someone had stuck an arrow in the fresh earth.

It seemed Robin Hood's legend was destined to grow and grow. No doubt people would still be telling tales about him twenty years from now.

Will had moved back into his farm with Beth since the funeral, using some of Sheriff de Faucumberg's reward money to hire the local carpenter who repaired that damned fence that kept falling down. He'd then settled into the same routine he and his daughter had kept before Groves's gang had shown up.

The rest of the men returned to their homes or, in Stephen's case, to London, where he hoped to find a Hospitaller knight sympathetic to his quest to be welcomed back into the Order.

Their going, in the wake of his young friend's death, left Scarlet feeling bereft and he'd found himself trying to spend as much time as possible with Beth to offset the loneliness. She wasn't a little girl any more though and he knew his constant hanging around was beginning to irritate her so that was why he'd rode the short distance to the centre of the village that morning.

Beth did her best but, in truth, their farm had been neglected in recent weeks. Still, the field of barley he'd planted was ripening nicely and he wanted to hire a few of the local labourers to help him harvest it and the alehouse was the best place to put the word out for that.

As he rode Strawberry along the main road Robin and Matilda's house came slowly into sight and he felt a pang of sorrow.

The door opened and he reined the palfrey in, not really sure if he wanted to meet the young widow. What would he say to her? It was embarrassing but such situations made him awkward and he just wanted to avoid a meeting like that, for a few more days at least when their shared pain wasn't quite as raw.

It was then he noticed the laden cart on the other side of the road, already hitched to a pair of horses. Henry Fletcher and his wife – Matilda's parents – stood there, solemn faced.

Matilda stepped out into the street leading little Arthur by the hand and walked to the cart, helping the boy up into the back, beside whatever was already loaded there under a canvas.

Will thought back to the day in St Mary's when they'd been forced to seek sanctuary there, and the half-overheard conversation between Matilda and Robin. They'd talked of family in Scotland and a desire to start a new life there.

He felt another twinge of sadness as he realised Robin's young family were leaving Wakefield and then his eyes narrowed. Had he imagined it? As Matilda walked towards her parents the robe she wore parted slightly and, for just a moment, Will had caught a glimpse of her belly.

Was she pregnant?

The robe fell back, covering the young woman again and Will's sorrow returned, stronger than ever.

Robin would have been a father again in a few short months, had he not been taken from them by Groves's blade.

The fletcher and his wife embraced their daughter quietly, then she climbed onto the cart and took a last, lingering look at her home. At last she cracked the reins and forced the horses into a walk.

Scarlet remained silent, feeling like he was somehow intruding on this sad scene, but his eyes followed the slow-moving cart as it rumbled along the road. There was no-one else around right now since everyone was at work so it didn't take long for Matilda and Arthur to pass the last house in the village and reach St Mary's.

Will bowed his head and sighed. It felt like this, more than anything else, marked the end of the fellowship Robin's friends had enjoyed. The last, final severing of all ties as everyone went their own separate way. He doubted he'd ever see some of them again.

Knowing it would do no good to let such gloomy thoughts take hold of him right then, he heaved a deep breath that brought his shoulders up and raised his head as Matilda's cart rolled past the recently-extended church.

Just then the sun broke through the clouds directly over the street, making him squint but...what was that?

A figure seemed to detach itself from the shadows cast by the great oak beside St Mary's and haul itself into the cart which never slowed and was soon swallowed up by the trees on the outskirts of the village.

Shocked, Will wondered if it had really happened. And then he wondered if he should kick his mount into a gallop and make sure Matilda was all right.

One thing stopped him though, and a wave of cold seemed to run up his arms and down the back of his neck as he pictured again little Arthur's expression when the shadowy figure had climbed into the cart next to him.

The boy's face had broken into a huge smile.

For a time Will sat there atop his palfrey, and then a grin slowly spread across his face too.

"Come on, Strawberry," he muttered, kicking his heels in, urging the beast into a walk. "Let's go and hire those labourers. It's going to be a good harvest this year."

THE END

Author's Note

This has been the hardest book I've written so far. I expected it to finish around the 90,000 word mark but it kept going, as if I didn't want it to end! The Forest Lord series has been more successful than I could ever have imagined so perhaps it's understandable that, as it neared a conclusion, it became harder to write.

But I got there at last and I hope you enjoyed it and found the ending satisfying. I originally planned to kill Robin outright but when it came to it I decided to leave it open-ended and let the reader decide for themselves how things might have gone.

I know there are probably quite a few historical inaccuracies in the novel but it was unavoidable at this stage of the series. I could do pretty much whatever I liked with guys like Sir Henry de Faucumberg and Prior de Monte Martini in the earlier books and it would still fit within the historical time-line, but now they're entrenched in the stories and I had to make things fit my own narrative. So de Monte Martini did NOT die violently at the sheriff's hands in real life but I felt it made the story more exciting. I'm also sure he was nothing like as horrible as I've portrayed him in the books, for which I apologise profusely. Artistic license and all that...

Thank you so much to everyone who has bought these books over the past three or four years. You have made a dream come true for me and not everyone gets the chance to say that in their life, do they? Yes, I still have a day job, but the Forest Lord books have sold enough copies that I'm about to reduce my hours at work and that will mean I have a full day extra every week just to write.

And I have lots to write yet! I've just finished a brand new short story starring Little John and Robin, and then I'll do a Will Scarlet novella to fill out the time it'll take me to research my next series.

Does the idea of a warrior druid in post-Roman Britain sound interesting? It certainly excites me! Battles, magick, and adventuring, all against the backdrop of these wonderful windswept isles – what's not to like? I can't wait to get started on it. If you're a friend of mine on Facebook (add me!) you'll have seen the photos I take when I'm out working around Loch Lomond and Loch Long etc. and that's the sort of places that will make an appearance in my new books. Instead of being tied to Yorkshire and Nottingham I'll be exploring the whole of Britain, in all its glory.

Please join me for it – it'll be great!

With very best wishes to you all,

Steven A. McKay,
Old Kilpatrick,
September 23, 2016

If you enjoyed *The Forest Lord Collection* **please** leave a review on Amazon or Goodreads or wherever you can. Good reviews are the lifeblood of self-published authors, so, if possible, take a few moments to let others know what you thought of the books.
Thank you!

If you'd like a FREE short story take a moment to sign up for my mailing list. VIP subscribers will get exclusive access to giveaways, competitions, info on new releases and other freebies.
Just click the link below to sign up. As a thank you, you will be sent my short story "The Rescue".

https://stevenamckay.wordpress.com/mailing-list/

Otherwise, to find out what's happening with the author and any forthcoming books, point your browser to:

www.facebook.com/RobinHoodNovel

http://stevenamckay.wordpress.com

And on Twitter, follow @SA_McKay

THANK YOU FOR READING!

OUT NOW

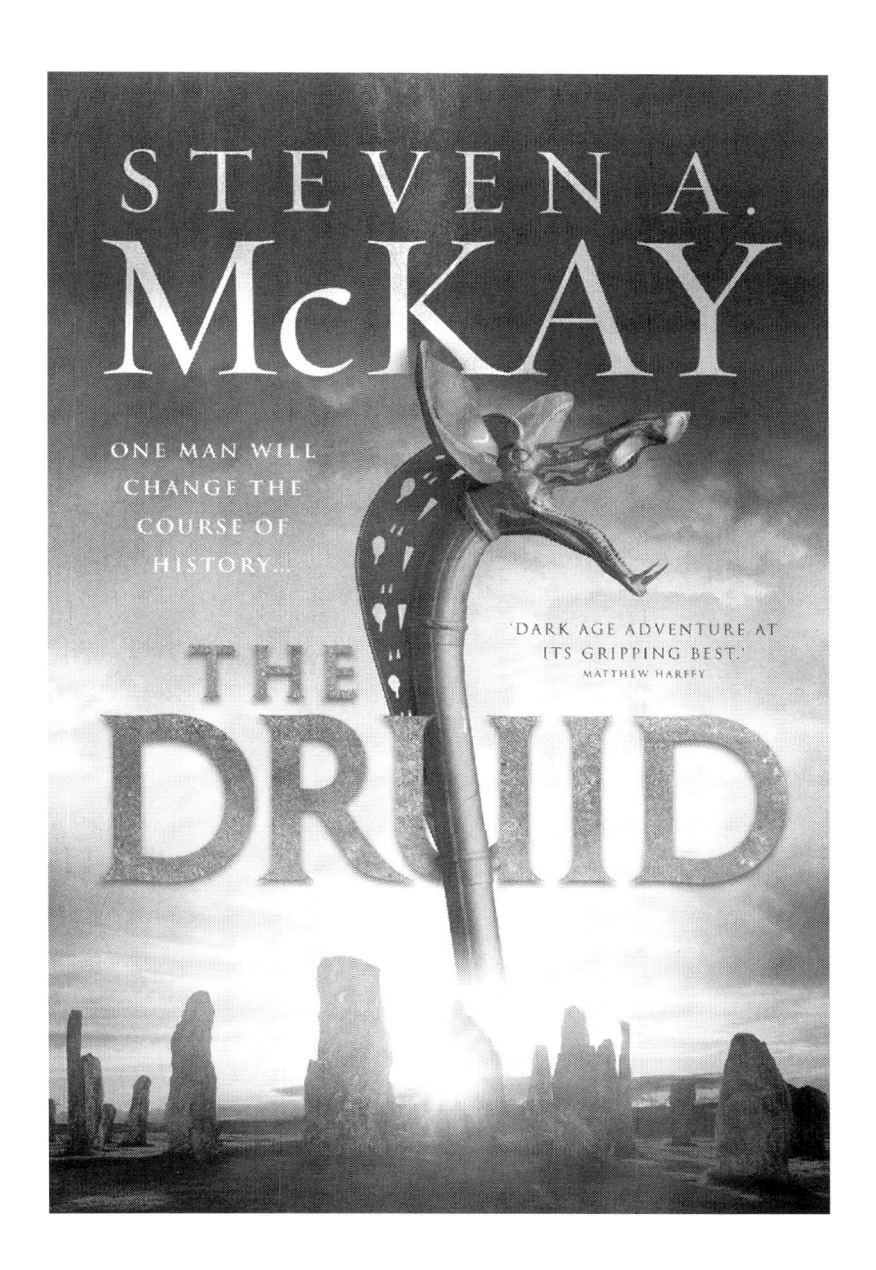

STEVEN A. McKAY

ONE MAN WILL
CHANGE THE
COURSE OF
HISTORY...

THE DRUID

'DARK AGE ADVENTURE AT ITS GRIPPING BEST.'
MATTHEW HARFFY

Printed in Great Britain
by Amazon